THE BEST OF
HAMMER AND BOLTER
VOLUME ONE

THREE MORE ELDAR riders were unseated by the sudden momentum of fully armoured Silver Skulls launching past them and grabbing them from the bikes. Without riders, the machines careened haphazardly. One struck the ground and exploded in a burst of whickering shrapnel. The others collided in mid-air and similarly detonated. More heat and smoke billowed out in plumes. The remaining two riders turned their bikes into the smog, leaving nothing but contrails in their wake. The warriors who had felled the eldar plummeted downwards with their victims, driving them to the floor with a satisfying crack of vertebrae.

More tales of adventure featuring characters from this volume

• HORUS HERESY •

AGE OF DARKNESS
Edited by Christian Dunn

• WARHAMMER 40,000 •

EISENHORN
(Contains the novels *Xenos, Malleus* and *Hereticus*)
Dan Abnett

THE GILDAR RIFT
Sarah Cawkwell

WRATH OF IRON
Chris Wraight

• WARHAMMER •

KNIGHTS OF BRETONNIA
Anthony Reynolds

KNIGHT OF THE BLAZING SUN
Josh Reynolds

SCHWARZHELM & HELBORG:
SWORDS OF THE EMPEROR
Chris Wraight

• TIME OF LEGENDS •

MALEKITH
Gav Thorpe

SHADOW KING
Gav Thorpe

CALEDOR
Gav Thorpe

DEAD WINTER
C.L. Werner

A BLACK LIBRARY ANTHOLOGY

THE BEST OF
HAMMER AND BOLTER
VOLUME ONE

Edited by Christian Dunn

BLACK LIBRARY

A Black Library Publication

All stories in this volume were originally published in the electronic magazine
Hammer and Bolter copyright © 2010-2011, Games Workshop Ltd.
All rights reserved.

This omnibus edition published in Great Britain in 2012 by
The Black Library,
Games Workshop Ltd.,
Willow Road,
Nottingham, NG7 2WS, UK.

10 9 8 7 6 5 4 3 2 1

Cover illustration by Clint Langley.

Internal illustrations by Jon Sullivan, Neil Roberts, Cheoljoo Lee,
Raymond Swanland, Winona Nelson and Stef Kopinski.

A CIP record for this book is available from the British Library.

UK ISBN13: 978 1 84970 177 8
US ISBN13: 978 1 84970 178 5

See the Black Library on the internet at

www.blacklibrary.com

Find out more about Games Workshop and
the worlds of Warhammer and Warhammer 40,000 at

www.games-workshop.com

Printed and bound by CPI Group (UK) Ltd, Croydon, CR0 4YY

CONTENTS

Introduction   7

Issue 1
The Strange Demise of Titus Endor – *Dan Abnett*   11
A Place of Quiet Assembly – *John Brunner*   33
Primary Instinct – *Sarah Cawkwell*   49
Questing Knight – *Anthony Reynolds*   77

Issue 2
The Dark Path – *Gav Thorpe*   141
Exhumed – *Steve Parker*   155
The Rat Catcher's Tale – *Richard Ford*   179

Issue 3
The Long Games at Carcharias – *Rob Sanders*   199
Virtue's Reward – *Darius Hinks*   233
Charandis – *Ben McCallum*   251

Issue 4
Waiting Death – *Steve Lyons*   273
The Barbed Wire Cat – *Robert Earl*   295
Hunted – *John French*   319

Issue 5

The Iron Within – *Rob Sanders*   337
Feast of Horrors – *Chris Wraight*   371
Action and Consequence – *Sarah Cawkwell*   385

Issue 6

Tower of Blood – *Tony Ballantyne*   409
The First Duty – *Josh Reynolds*   425
Grail Knight – *Anthony Reynolds*   445

Issue 7

Manbane – *Andy Hoare*   513
The Last Remembrancer – *John French*   529
Flesh – *Chris Wraight*   545

Issue 8

Cause and Effect – *Sarah Cawkwell*   583
Marshlight – *C. L. Werner*   605
Commander Shadow – *Braden Campbell*   629

Issue 9

The Arkunasha War – *Andy Chambers*   651
Sir Dagobert's Last Battle – *Jonathan Green*   671
Survivor – *Steve Parker*   701

Issue 10

The Last Charge – *Andy Hoare*   743
We Are One – *John French*   761
Mountain Eater – *Andy Smillie*   781

Issue 11

The Carrion Anthem – *David Annandale*   799
The Gods Demand – *Josh Reynolds*   817
Shadow Knight – *Aaron Dembski-Bowden*   839

Issue 12

Aenarion – *Gav Thorpe*   853
Bitter End – *Sarah Cawkwell*   875

INTRODUCTION

I HATE WRITING editorials.

It's not the actual act of committing words to the screen or the thought processes involved in trying to get something vaguely interesting onto the page, but rather no matter what I write, I'm delaying you from reading the fantastic stories contained within. As an editor, it's my job to bring these stories to your attention, be it brand-new talent pulled from the annual Black Library submissions window or a Black Library old-timer with a new take on an established army or Space Marine Chapter, but sticking a few hundred words of me telling you how good they are seems counterproductive when you could be *actually reading the stories*.

That's why the only issue of *Hammer and Bolter* we've (electronically) published to date to contain an editorial was the first issue (it would have been a little odd to just thrust a brand-new monthly anthology onto an unsuspecting world without even a wee bit of explanation, wouldn't it?) and, because of the age we live in, anything I can say in an editorial can just as easily be put across in a blog post, status update or even a 140 character tweet.

Just as social media is changing the way we lead our daily lives and communicate with each other, technology is also changing the way we consume the printed word, and the screen is rapidly encroaching on paper as the medium for reading fiction. No longer are publishers constrained by lengthy lead-times, prohibitive printing costs and complex distribution networks when they produce an issue of a magazine. The digital age has brought with it a cleaner, slicker process of spreading words to the masses, one that can produce a magazine such as *Hammer and Bolter* using only a single computer and disseminate it via the internet using the exact same machine.

But the eBook is no mere analogue for the dead tree format. eBooks are books plus one, the book evolved. No longer is the book just words on the page, it's also video, audio and hyperlinks and, thanks to the manufacturers of the eBook readers, it also has its own built-in dictionary. And as much as this is the best of *Hammer and Bolter*, it could never be the complete *Hammer and Bolter*, as mere ink and paper isn't capable of embedded audio. Not yet anyway.

Please don't get me wrong. Print is far from dead and it's not a case of which format is better but rather which format is better *for you*. But I will say this to all those who are sceptical of this brave new age of publishing: without the advent of the eBook and the opportunity for Black Library to once again produce a regular anthology you wouldn't be holding this book in your hands.

But no matter which format they're intended for, I still hate writing editorials.

Christian Dunn
Nottingham,
December 2011

HAMMER
AND BOLTER
ISSUE 1

THE STRANGE DEMISE OF
TITUS ENDOR

Dan Abnett

THE CITY WAS a hollow, failing place that was trying to turn its fortunes around, so it was apt that Titus Endor should wash up there. He'd long since lost the lustre that had made him one of the ordo's rising stars. Like a counterfeit coin, his value had been exposed as short weight. None of it had been his fault, just circumstances.

Titus Endor took another drink, and reflected that life could be worse.

IT HAD SEEMED to have been winter for two or three years. Snow fell all the time, but the city streets were so warm and busy, nothing lay for long. Slush filled the gutters, and the edges of the kerbs were crusted with polished deposits of old grey ice. Tiny snowflakes freighted the air, caught in the streetlights. They drifted like random thoughts, or disconnected clues.

THE CITY'S NAME was Marisberg. Or perhaps it was Chericoberg, or Zsammstadd? They were all alike, the brute towns clinging to the oily edge of Karoscura's western continent. The drifting clues had dragged him from one conurbation to the next, from one drab residentiary to another, and they all blurred into one: the same streets, the same sallow faces in the street lights, the same bars and dining halls, the same smell of wet rockcrete, the same snow. He walked alone, after hours, ate alone in eating rooms where the other tables were stacked with chairs, made calls and asked questions, and reviewed the notes he'd scribbled in his copy books.

There were a lot of copy books. He disliked data slates, and never threw his papers away. They formed the bulk of his luggage. He always made sure he had a spare crown or two to tip the next poor concierge confronted with the task of lugging his possessions from the street to a newly rented room.

Gonrad Maliko had been a professor of ethnic diversity at Sarum, specialising in taboos and stratified eating. Endor had a potted biography of him written out in one of the copy books. In another, a green-covered book marked 435, were the case notes of Maliko's crime, a shameless affront on Eustis Majoris involving eleven sub-adult males.

Endor had almost snared Maliko in the arctic city of Cazzad, but the timing had been out, and the tip-off too vague. None of it had been his fault, just circumstances.

Titus Endor had inherited the fondness for symphonic music from his first master, the late Hapshant. Hapshant had been a real character. Installed at a bar, in the late evening, a glass in his hand, Endor would riff tirelessly about Hapshant. 'Believe you me, a real character,' he would say to his conversation partner, usually the barman, or any solitary drinker with a spare seat beside him. 'Mad as a fiddle, in the end,' Endor always added, tapping his brow. 'Worms in the head, you see.'

Endor remembered the days, a long time ago, when he would patiently wind up the old voxcordian Hapshant took with him wherever he went, to play some old wax disc of crackling symphonic music to help his master think. Endor had been Hapshant's pupil, Hapshant's brightest pupil. As an interrogator, he had served Hapshant right up to the end of the great man's life. There had been two of them, actually, two interrogators, Titus and his friend Gregor. Tight, they'd been, best friends in service and out. Titus, though, had always been the one with a luminous future, because Gregor was too serious and charmless. They had both become inquisitors, and stayed friends. Until, that is, an unfortunate business some years before, a misunderstanding that Gregor had not seen fit to overlook. None of it had been Endor's fault, just circumstances.

His fondness for the classical repertoire had come from Hapshant. Attending the performances at Marisberg's Theatricala was therefore not a drudge for Titus Endor. He would arrive at the great, gilded palace, its high windows lit by a thousand yellow globes, brush the snow off his shoulders and take a drink in the bar before the start of the performance. The grandees would come and go, in their frock coats and silk scarves, their gowns and tires, and he'd watch them professionally. Sometimes his copy book would come out of his coat pocket, and he'd scribble a note or two.

The auditorium was painted crimson, with scarlet upholstery and gold woodwork. When the house lights came down, it was like being seated in the ventricle of a heart, a red cavity pumping with sound. He sat in the stalls, never in the same seat. His folded programme and his rented opera glasses lay in his lap.

Maliko's contact had the use of a private box, to the left of the stage. Endor watched it, night after night, seeing through his glasses the faint brass gleam of the inhabitant's own opera glasses in the dark balcony as they caught the stage light.

He identified the box: number 435. No matter how early he rose from his seat and went to the street door, he never managed to catch the occupants of 435 leaving the Theatricala. This rankled with him, though it was never his fault, just circumstances.

Liebstrum, his interrogator, had been missing for several days. Endor had sent Liebstrum to the palace of records in Zsammstadd to collate material on Maliko and his associates. The man was overdue, probably padding out his task so that he could waste time in the stews of Zsammstadd, on expenses. Endor had thought Liebstrum a promising candidate when he'd first met him, but lately he'd begun to fancy that Liebstrum was an idler, with no appetite for the hard work the ordo demanded. He wondered if he'd ever find himself signing the paperwork approving Liebstrum's advancement to full rosette. He doubted it.

The orchestra began the overture, a great swirl of busy strings and strident horns. Zoramer's *Oration*, one of Hapshant's favourite works. Endor settled back, and glanced from time to time at the private box, noting the occasional flash and glimmer of raised opera glasses, the only hint of habitation.

His head ached. The volume of the music didn't help. His head had ached a lot recently, and Endor put that down to the damnable climate he had been forced to endure in the prosecution of the Maliko case.

The stage was bathed in a limed light from directional lamps. As the red curtains spurred back, the dancers came out, performing in front of a hololithic drop of mountains and coppiced woods, in which dwelt a ruined temple or two, halcyon and timeless.

The woodwind section woke up with vigour, and the gauzy dancers swirled, soft and white as snowflakes. One took his attention immediately. Slender, she soared, faultless in her footwork, her arms expressive and immaculate. Her hair was drawn back tightly in a bun, and her face was as implacable as a death mask, powdered white like ivory, with cheek bones that aspired to the perfection of mathematical symmetry.

Endor moved his glasses away from her powerful, springing thighs, and watched the private box. Light on brass. Other eyes were watching her too.

AFTER THE PERFORMANCE, he took himself to a bar on Zeik Street, a bright, sparkling hall of mirrors and crystal chandeliers. It was bustling with patrons from the Theatricala.

'Your pleasure, master?' asked the uniformed barman.

'Grain joiliq, with shaved ice, and a sliver of citrus,' Endor requested. It had been his favourite tipple since the early days, since that place off Zansiple Street where he and Gregor had gone to wash away the day's efforts. The Thirsty Eagle. Yes, that was it, The Thirsty Eagle. Ah, how the memories eroded.

His drink arrived, served on a paper mat. The joiliq was substandard, and too warm. The ice had melted prematurely, and left the citrus wind adrift in a disappointing floe.

He drank it anyway and ordered another. His headache had eased.

The room was full of loud voices and busy discussion. He thought about calling Liebstrum, but didn't want to endure the impotence of another recorded message.

He ordered a third drink, and sat back on his stool to survey the room. Almost everyone was male, dressed in dapper evening wear. There was something rambunctious and fraternal about the gathering, like a coterie of men drawn together in some exclusive club. They roared at one another's jokes, and slapped one another's backs. The few women present were wives or courtesans, and acted like magnets, pulling crowds of attentive males in around them.

Karoscura needs women, he had noted in his copy book. He had under-lined it, and given the note two exclamation points. Like many colony worlds building their economies on mineral wealth, Karoscura had advertised for specialist workers, promising to pay travel costs and set up expenses, in order to attract a professional labour force. Men had flooded in from all parts of the sector, drawn by the attractive salary dividends. The womenfolk of Karoscura had been eclipsed. It was reck-oned that males now outnumbered females ten to one in the cities of the oily coast.

Endor missed female company. He'd never had any trouble in that department. In the past, his charisma, his looks and his professional status had all combined to win him the attention of any woman that took his eye. Karoscura was like a siege. There weren't enough supplies to go around.

HE WENT BACK to his lodgings. Liebstrum was not there, and hadn't called. It seemed to Endor that his piles of copy books had been dis-turbed, and rearranged. He started to sort through them. Had someone been in his room?

He woke late, bathed and shaved. He saw his reflection in the mirror. We all grow older, he told himself. His face seemed drawn and lined, and there was a sickly pallor to it. Too much winter light, Titus Endor told himself.

His hair had been grey for a while now. He tied it back, out of con-venience. There were distinguished scars on his face, the footnotes of a lifetime of battles. The biggest scar was on his leg, out of sight. Endor still wore the jagged saurapt tooth on a black cord around his neck. Gregor had dug it out of him, just after Endor had driven the beast off. Brontotaph, that had been the place, Brontotaph. How long ago now?

They'd been good friends, the best, close like brothers, until the unfortunate business some years before, a misunderstanding that Gregor had not seen fit to overlook. None of it had been Endor's fault, just circumstances.

It was sad. Endor missed his old friend. He wondered what had become of Gregor. Nothing much, he doubted, Gregor had never promised to anything.

Looking in the mirror, Endor toyed with the tooth. According to the lore on Brontotaph, he was damned. Even after death, a saurapt continued to stalk its prey, so the legend went, especially a prey item that had escaped or evaded its jaws. The spirit of the saurapt was out there, tracking him. One day it would find him at last, and strike, and balance the books.

Titus Endor laughed out loud. He saw himself laughing back at him. Plenty of ghosts stalked him, and a bestial reptilian predator was the least of them.

An inquisitor had to be rational about such things.

He wondered where Liebstrum was.

The tooth hung around his neck like a penance.

TITUS ENDOR PAID a man to let him into the Theatricala during the day. He prowled the upper galleries, looking for the door to box 435. There was no box 435. The gallery halls were dressed in red velvet carpet and scarlet wallpaper, like aortal tubes. The air smelled of stale lho-sticks. There was a 434 and a 436. His lingering fingers traced the soft red wall, hunting for a secret or concealed door.

LIEBSTRUM HAD NOT returned. Annoyed, his mood made worse by a nagging headache, Endor sent a damning report via courier to the ordos. In his lodgings, a glass of joiliq in his hand, he leafed back through his copy books, trying to build some kind of pattern.

435. Gonrad Maliko. The reflected flash of opera glasses in the shadows. The girl. The girl, the slender dancer.

HE THOUGHT ABOUT Gregor from time to time. Endor had always been the bright one, handsome, cunning, bound for glory. Gregor had been a dutiful type, a hard worker, stolid and solid.

'I wonder where you are now, my old friend?' Endor asked the empty room. 'I was always Hapshant's favourite, and look at the career I've built. What have you ever done?'

The unfortunate business still nagged at him. Endor had been put in a tough position, a damn tough position. Several of his prior cases had been placed in review. Details had been distorted and accusations trumped up, all of it so petty-minded and political. He'd had no choice, in the end. When the Ordo Malleus had suggested his transfer, he'd taken it. They'd told him Gregor had been up to no good, and that if Endor helped to set his old friend back on the straight and narrow, the case reviews would be dropped. Endor hadn't been spying. He had just been keeping an eye on his old friend. None of it had been his fault, just circumstances.

HE WENT TO the next show at the Theatricala, and then to a club, and then became mixed up in a group of Navy noncoms on shore leave. He'd followed them to the next bar, an off-street den, a dance parlour. There were women there, in an abundance at odds with the global statistics, women a man could dance with.

The dance was called the *zendov*, and it was as erotic as it was formal. The dance had evolved, Endor was told, because of the imbalance of men and women, a street dance of the lower classes originally popular in bordellos. Zendov allowed a man the opportunity of spending five or ten minutes with a woman, intimately. Zendov clubs were the most popular dives on Karoscura.

He took another few drinks, and then he saw her, the girl, the slender dancer. She was standing at the mirror-plated bar, smoking a lho-stick and contemplating her dance card. He hadn't recognised her at first, because she was wearing a leopardskin cloche and cape, and a gold dress, and had changed her makeup from the fierce white of the ballet. But her posture took his eye, the balance of her legs, the confidence in the set of her head, and he realised who he was looking at.

He introduced himself, and offered to buy her a drink. She regarded him distantly, and then asked his name. Her accent was thick.

'Titus,' he replied.

She marked it on her card. 'The fifth tune from now, Master Titus,' she said, adding, 'amasec on ice.' Then she walked away, and took the embrace of a noncom for the next dance.

He was perplexed, until he saw the way of it. Most of the women in the bar were dancers from the Theatricala. They supplemented their wages by partner-dancing at the zendov bars, efficiently exploiting Karoscura's paucity of female companionship. No wonder the clubs were popular. No wonder the clubs paid the girls well for after-hours dancing. They brought the men in, men so hungry for a five-minute intimacy with a woman while the music played, they'd stay all night, waiting their turn, and drink well in the meantime.

When his turn came, she found him at the bar.

'Master Titus?'

'What's your name?' he asked as she led him onto the dance floor.

She seemed surprised that he should care. 'Mira,' she replied.

The music began. Endor had watched the dancers closely, and had learned the steps. His mind worked that way. He took her in a close hold, and turned her about the floor, between other dancing couples. Glittering glow-globes rotated above them, casting down a blizzard of light like snowflakes.

She was close to him, taut, radiating heat. He felt how hard and sinewy her body was, how rigid. She was tiny, but all muscle. She smelled of cologne, but it did not mask the heat of her, or the residue of old ballet makeup, hastily removed, or the slight odour of sweat. She had come straight from the Theatricala, probably changing in a backroom in a hurry.

Sweat, hard limbs, the stale aroma of lho-sticks. He found it intoxicating. Pulled close to her, he noticed she had an old scar along the nape of her neck, just below the hairline.

The tune ended.

'Thank you, Mira,' he bowed. 'Your amasec awaits at the bar.'

'My card is full. I will come over later.'

He looked disappointed.

'Where did you learn to dance?' she asked.

'Tonight. Here.'

She scowled. 'I don't like liars. No one learns to zendov in an evening.'

'I'm not lying. I watched and learned.'

She narrowed her eyes. They were hard eyes, in a hard face. 'You're not very good,' she said, 'but you know the steps. Perfectly, in fact. You're too rigid, though. Your shoulders are too tight.'

He bowed again. 'I'll remember that. Perhaps you might educate me in the finer points of the dance?'

'Sorry, my card is full.'

'No room, not even at the end of the night?'

The music had begun again. A Navy officer was waiting for her, impatient anger in his face.

'Amasec,' she said. 'Perhaps, at the end of the night.'

IN THE ZENDOV clubs, the end of the night meant dawn. The queues of men danced the girls into exhaustion. Heading from the bar to find the washroom, Endor saw three or four shoeless girls in a back hall, smoking lho-sticks and dabbing at bleeding heels and swollen toes.

He went out into the snow, and searched for a public vox-station. He called Liebstrum's number, and got the message service.

'Where are you?' he shouted. 'Where are you?'

TWO GLASSES SAT on the bar. Joiliq in one, diluted with slowly melting ice, and amasec in the other. It was four-thirty.

'Master Titan?'

'Titus,' he corrected, looking around. What he saw made him forget the throbbing in his temples. 'My name is Titus.'

The girl nodded. 'Sorry. This for me?'

He smiled. She took up the amasec and sipped.

'A last dance, then, yes?' she asked.

'I've been waiting.'

There was a look in her eyes that told him how much she despised the men who waited to dance with her.

She led him to the floor. Her body was as hard as before, but now she was cold. There was no heat in her. The fragrance of lho-smoke and sweat had dulled into a thin, unhealthy smell.

'Loosen your shoulders,' she said, as the music began. 'Turn your head. No, too much. Turn it like this. And swing out. Yes. And back and back.'

'Am I getting it?' he asked. He felt like he was dancing with a corpse.

'Your footwork is fine. Excellent, actually. Your back is still a little stiff. Turn out, turn out, that's it.'

'You're a good teacher.'

'I do what I'm paid to do, sir.'

'You're tired.'

'Every day is a long day,' she whispered, her head against his chest. She looked up at him sharply. 'Please don't tell the bosses I said that. They'll dock my pay.'

'I won't,' he smiled, rotating her neatly. 'I know how long your day's been. I was at the Theatricala. You are a fine dancer.'

'This pays better than the classical shit,' she said. She stared up at him as they spun and readdressed. 'Have you been following me?'

'No,' he said. 'I just came here and saw you.'

'And learned the zendov.'

He chuckled. 'Something like that. Men must follow women all the time on this world. There are so few of you.'

'It does become a problem,' she admitted.

'So they follow you? Watch you?'

'I suppose they do,' said Mira.

'Who watches you?' he asked.

'You do,' she said, 'and everyone else.'

They swung and re-addressed, then promenaded again.

'How did you get the scar?' he asked.

She flinched. 'I hate it when men notice that.'

'I'm sorry.'

'It doesn't matter.'

'Will you tell me how you got it?'

'I got it years ago. That's all I want to say about it.'

He nodded, spinning her. 'I'm sorry I asked. We all have our scars.'

'Isn't that the truth?' she agreed.

The number ended. He stepped back and looked at her.

'Please, please don't ask me for another,' she said quietly.

'A last drink, then?'

'I'm dead on my feet, Master Titus.'

'Might I be first on your card tomorrow, then?'

'It doesn't work that way. Come along tomorrow, and we'll dance again.'

She walked away. The band was packing up. Endor went to the bar, where the barman was washing the last of the glasses.

'Grain joiliq, with shaved ice, and a sliver of citrus,' Endor requested.

The barman sighed, and fixed the drink. When Endor looked around, the girl had vanished.

IT WAS LIGHT when he got back to his residentiary. Snow was fluttering down out of a sky that was white and opaque. He tossed his copy book onto the desk, took off his jacket and fell down on his bed.

HE DREAMT OF Hapshant. There were worms coming out of his tear ducts. Endor tried to wipe them away. Gregor shouted at him, telling him he was a fool. Hapshant went into spasms, his heels kicking on the hardwood floor.

THE KNOCKING PERSISTED. It was suddenly late in the afternoon. Endor sat up, fully clothed. The knocking came again, not Hapshant's heels at all.

He went to the door and opened it.

Liebstrum stared at him.

'Why?' he asked.

'Well, hello to you too,' replied Endor.

Liebstrum pushed past him into the room. 'Throne of Terra, Titus. Why? Why do you keep doing this?'

'Doing what, exactly?'

'Calling me. Calling me with these messages and–'

'Where have you been?' Endor asked.

Liebstrum turned and looked at him. 'You've forgotten again, haven't you?'

'Forgotten what? Interrogator, I believe you have been singularly derelict in your duties these last few weeks. I'm afraid I've been forced to send a report of admonition to the ordos and–'

'Not again. Again with this,' Liebstrum sighed.

'Again with what, interrogator?'

Liebstrum pulled out his rosette. 'It's inquisitor, Titus. *Inquisitor.*'

'Since when?'

'Four years ago, on Hesperus. You elected me yourself. Don't you remember?'

Endor frowned. 'No, I don't.'

Liebstrum sat down on the bed. 'Throne, Titus, you have to stop doing this to me.'

'I don't follow.'

Liebstrum looked up at him sadly. 'What are you doing here?'

'Hunting Gonrad Maliko. You know that. Keep up.'

'We captured Gonrad Maliko five years ago. He's serving life in the penal colony on Izzakos. Don't you remember?'

Endor paused. He wandered over to his desk and poured the last dregs of a bottle of joiliq into a dirty glass. 'No, no, I don't remember that. Not at all.'

'Oh, Titus,' Liebstrum muttered.

'Maliko is loose. He's here, and he's loose. I have a lead, a girl in the Theatricala, and box 435–'

'Stop it! Stop it now!'

'Liebstrum?'

Liebstrum rose from the bed and approached Endor. 'Show me your rosette,' he said.

Endor took a swig of his drink and pulled his wallet out of his pocket.

'Look. Do you see, Titus?' Liebstrum asked, opening the leather wallet. 'There's no rosette in there. You were disavowed, three years ago. They took your warrant away. You're not an inquisitor any more.'

'Of course I am,' said Titus Endor, ignoring the bald patch in the wallet where his rosette had once been sewn in. 'I'm operating under Special Circumstances.'

Liebstrum shook his head sadly. 'Titus, I've tried to help you, Throne knows, but you've got to stop calling me. You've got to stop pretending.'

'Pretending? How dare you!'

Liebstrum walked towards the door. 'This is the last time I come running, you understand? The very last time.'

'No, I don't understand. I am affronted by your manner, interrogator. Maliko is still out there.'

Liebstrum turned to look back one last time. 'No, Titus, he isn't.'

ENDOR WENT TO the park in the last of the afternoon. Black trees and blacker ironwork benches stood up out of a skim of wet snow. He wondered how Maliko had got to Liebstrum. What did he have on him? He sat on a bench, and began to draft a report in his copy book, a report exposing Liebstrum's connections to the criminal, and recommending his immediate censure and suspension. But the bench was cold and damp, and it soaked his clothes and gave him a headache, so he walked to a local cafe and ordered a pot of chocolate and a thimble of amasec.

The light was going out of the sky. As the snow fell, it almost seemed as if the pale sky was shedding in little white flakes, leaving a dark undercoat behind.

ENDOR WENT BACK to the zendov club early, before the Theatricala turned out, and waited for the girl, but she never showed. He hung around until it was quite late, and then started asking questions. The other dancers, the girls, were reticent. They'd learned that you didn't give out personal details to men who loitered at the clubs.

Finally, Endor snagged a junior barman who, for rather too many crowns, said he was prepared to slip into the manager's office and take a look at the girl's contact address in the club ledger.

Endor met him out the back of the dance club just after one in the morning, and exchanged the cash for a slip of paper.

Mira Zaleed, 870 Arbogan.

He considered leaving it until the morning, but he was restless, so he bought a quart of amasec at a tavern on Oroshbyli Street, and rode the maglev to Corso Saint Helk in the north of the city. From the station, it was a long walk up the rockcrete walkways to the hab blocks: Solingen, Zarbos, Arbogan.

The stairwells were unlit, and choked with trash. A domestic quarrel was raging on the fifth floor, and the residents of other habs were yelling out protests at the noise. Just before he located 870, it occurred to him that 870 was twice 435.

Titus Endor stood in the gloomy hallway, listening to the racket of someone else's private life disintegrating, and wondered if the numbers were significant. Numbers could be dangerous. A life of study and an eventful career had shown him that. Certain numbers, usually abstract mathematical constructs, possessed power. He'd heard of several cases where cogitators had been corrupted by warped numbers, and he'd been party to another case, years ago, when some old fool had mistakenly believed he'd uncovered the Number of Ruin. He and Gregor had handled it, and it had come to nothing, but they'd taken it seriously. He couldn't remember the old fool's name now, some dusty scribe, but he remembered the case. They'd been interrogators then, him and Gregor, just starting out. They'd been friends.

An age ago, in another life.

His mind had wandered. He blinked, and wondered how long he had been standing in the dim passageway outside 870 Arbogan. The domestic had ended, and the night was still. From somewhere, he heard the frail sound of zendov music, playing on an old voxcordian.

He decided to steady his nerves with a sip of the quart of amasec, and discovered that the bottle was half-empty already.

He knocked on the door.

There was no answer. Someone in a neighbouring flat cried out, the half-awake mew of the nightmared.

He knocked again.

'Mira Zaleed?' he called.

The door was baffled shempwood in an iron frame, with double dead bolts and a triple-tumbler, Blaum et Cie safety lock. The lock had been retrofitted into the door, an expensive piece of kit for such a low-rent hab. He rummaged in his trouser pocket, and found his anykey. The slim blade extended from the grip, slipped into the lock and muttered as it explored the permutations.

He waited. One murmur more, and the anykey turned. The lock sprung with a clatter of rotating drums, and the deadbolts unlatched.

He put the anykey back in his pocket and pushed the door open with his toe.

'Mira?

The squalid apartment was cold and dark. The windows of the main room, overlooking the hab block's cinderblock courtyard, had been left open, and snow damp had blown in like wet breath. The drapes were lank and partly stiff with frost. He snapped on a pair of latex gloves and clicked the light switch. An overhead light bar woke up, lazy and slow. Frizzy purple mould had colonised the cups and plates left on the little dining table. A chair had been overturned on the bare floor. On the wall, faded picts of laughing friends and solemn family gatherings jostled with playbills and programmes from Theatricalas from a half-dozen worlds like Gudrun, Eustis Majoris, Brontotaph and Ligeria.

The bedroom was vacant. A single bed, crumpled with use, had been pushed against the wall, and yellow markings, made in chalk, had been scribed on the exposed floor space. The marks were arrows, circling and crossing, and numbers. 4, 3, 5 and then an 8, a 7, a 0. To the left, 87, the digits stacked as a column. 5, Endor thought, went into 435 87 times.

He stepped over the marks, and took out his little chrome picter. He took four or five shots of the markings.

He felt cold on his back, a shiver. In the little closet, packed tight, were dozens of dance costumes, all gauze and lace. They smelled, very faintly, of sweat and lho-smoke. He reached in and rifled through shoes and hats at the back of the closet space. His hand closed on something: a book.

He drew it out.

It was an unauthorised edition of *Stratified Eating Customs In The Halo Star Sub-Races*, by Soloman Tarsh. Tarsh was a pen name Maliko had used to publish his most scandalous theories. Endor smiled. Like the tumbling mechanism of a Blaum et Cie safety lock, things were falling into place. He bagged the book in a plastek evidence sheath, and put it in his pocket. Then, he rooted some more, and found a string of cultured pearls, a small jewellery box and a fetish made of bent wire and feathers.

He bagged them all.

The kitchen was a dank mess of grime and grease, stacked with culture-bearing crockery. He went to the bathroom.

Violent death marked the small, tiled room. Blood had extravagantly stippled the walls and dried into black scabs, and it had pooled in the enamel tub, separating into dark sediment and glassy surface plasma.

From the spray travel and the splash vectors, Endor approximated a frenzied attack, multiple stabs with a short, double-edged blade. There was no shower curtain, and the rings on the rail were broken and buckled. *The perp wrapped the body in the curtain*, he deduced.

'Are you dead, Mira?' he asked out loud. It was unlikely. The kill scene was a week old, and he'd danced with her just the night before.

'Who's in there?' a voice called. Endor stiffened.

'Come on out, unless it's you, Mira.'

The voice was sixty years old, and carrying twenty or thirty kilos too much weight. Endor unclipped his shoulder holster so his weapon was in grab range, and came out of the bathroom. A torch beam shone in his face.

'This had better be good,' said the sixty-year-old, overweight voice.

'Get the light out of my eyes, please,' said Endor.

The beam swung away, revealing a fat old man aiming a combat shotgun. The barrels of the weapon were pointing directly at Endor. The old man was wearing pyjama bottoms and unlaced, scuffed army boots. His belly stretched his stained vest. Old Guard insignia, the stitching worn, decorated his fatigue jacket.

'Who are you?' Endor asked.

'This says I get to ask the questions,' the old man replied, settling his shotgun. 'Who are you?'

'A friend of Mira's.'

The old man snorted. 'That's what they all say. They don't all get in, though.'

'She gave me a key.'

'Why would she do that?' the old man asked.

'We're friends,' said Endor.

'Round and round we go,' said the old man. 'Give me a good reason not to blast your lungs out through your spine.'

Endor nodded. 'I'm going to reach into my jacket, all right? I'm going to show you my credentials.'

'Slow as you like,' the old man replied.

Endor reached into his coat, forced himself to ignore the invitation of his gun, and flipped out his wallet.

'Titus Endor, Ordo Malleus. I'm an inquisitor operating under Special Circumstances.'

The old man's eyes widened. He lifted the shotgun away from Endor.

'I beg your forgiveness, sir!' he stammered.

Endor flipped the wallet away.

'It's no trouble. You are?'

'Nute Jerimo, from 868, just down the hall. I...' the old man cleared his throat, '... I'm kind of the unofficial super on this floor. The residents like me to keep an eye on things, keep the place safe, you understand?'

'You're ex-military?'

'Karoscura Seventh, and proud of it. Mustered out eighteen years ago.'

'You got a licence for that riot gun, Jerimo?' Endor asked.

The old man shrugged. 'It kind of followed me home from the wars, sir,' he replied.

'You keep the peace here, and watch over your neighbours. I'm not going to report you,' said Endor.

'Thank you, sir.'

'Tell me about Mira.'

Jerimo shook his head. 'Lovely girl, she is. A dancer. Moved in nine months back, keeps herself to herself. Always polite. Last spring, on my wife's birthday, she gave us tickets to a performance at the Theatricala. A present, you see? What a night! I'd never have been able to treat my wife so well, not on my pension.'

'She's a good girl.'

'She is that. Is she in trouble, sir? Is Mira in some sort of trouble?'

'That's what I'm trying to find out,' Endor replied. 'When did you last see her?'

The old man thought about that. 'A week ago, maybe nine days. It was early. She was just coming in when I was going out to tend the boiler. It won't fire the heating for this block unless someone cranks it, and so me, being me, goes downstairs and–'

'She was just coming in?'

'She always comes in late, sometimes with gentleman callers. Dawn or after.'

'That was the last time you saw her?'

'Yes, sir,' Jerimo replied.

'Go home, go to bed,' said Endor. 'I'll lock up here.'

The old man shuffled off, taking his shotgun with him.

Endor took a last look around the apartment and switched off the light.

He could smell Maliko.

BACK IN HIS room in the residentiary, in the small hours, Endor poured himself the last of the amasec. Sipping, he took the items he'd retrieved from Mira's hab and laid them out on his desk. The book, the fetish, the jewellery box, the pearls.

He unbagged the jewellery box and opened it with his anykey. The trays inside were dusty and empty. The only thing in it was a pendant, a gold chain fastened to a small, curved tooth. Titus Endor fingered the jagged tooth that hung around his neck.

Then he printed out the picts he'd taken of the markings on the floor, and studied them.

When he woke up, the prints were scattered across his chest.

* * *

HE HAD SLEPT badly. A recurring dream of death had stalked him. A supple ballet dancer with worms coming out of her eyes. A lizard carnivore, snuffling through the dark.

'Wake up,' he told himself.

He felt vile. He washed and dressed, and went to a dining house that was fifteen minutes away from the end of breakfast service. He ordered caffeine, poached eggs, black bread and a slice of the local sausage. He took the book out of his pocket and flipped through it as he waited for his order to arrive.

Stratified Eating Customs In The Halo Star Sub-Races, by Soloman Tarsh. It had been vanity-printed on low-quality paper. Someone had annotated the well-thumbed pages. Passages were underlined, and notes dotted the margins. Why would a dancer like Mira Zaleed own a copy of a specialist tract like this?

One section of the book had been especially heavily annotated. It was titled 'The Eaters and the Eaten' and it dealt with primitive customs relating to human communities and their local predators. Some hunter clans in the wilderness worlds of the Halo Stars ritually ate the flesh of apex predators in the belief that this would both proof them against predation and invest them with the traits of the killer creatures. On Salique, tribesmen drank the blood of local crocodilians so as to share their cunning. On Gudrun, in ages past, the powdered teeth and genitals of the giant carnodon were believed to imbue the ingester with feral potency. It was a recurring theme. Wherever man inhabited a world where he was in competition with a significant apex predator, rituals of devouring evolved. Eat what would otherwise eat you, and you would be magically protected. Hunt and consume what you fear will hunt and consume you, and you would be proofed against its fanged jaws.

This was nothing new to Titus Endor. His painful experiences on Brontotaph as an interrogator had taught him much about these curious beliefs. After his clash with the saurapt, an encounter he'd never care to repeat, the local tribes had treated him with the utmost respect. He had been 'in the jaws' and he had survived. This made him special in their eyes, as if some curious supernatural relationship had been forged between man and predator. They were bound together, both eaters, both eaten. The tribesmen had urged Endor to hunt down the saurapt, kill it and ingest its flesh, so as to become master of the compact.

Endor had laughed this off and refused. The old superstitions were ridiculous. 'But the saurapt will now stalk you forever,' the tribesmen had warned, 'to the end of your days, when it will claim you at last and finish its bite.'

Finish its bite. Quite a phrase. It had made Hapshant laugh. Endor had relished the notion of a predator's bite that took years, decades perhaps, to close entirely.

Many notes, most of them hard to decipher, appended the passages dealing with such traditions. Brontotaph was mentioned. Certain charms and prophylactic rituals were described, whereby sacrifices could be made to ward off the stalking killer. Fresh blood and surrogate victims could be offered up to stall the attentions of invisible beasts.

Endor wondered about the tooth he'd found in Mira Zaleed's jewellery box.

'Are you Endor?'

Titus looked up from his eggs. It took him a moment to recognise the barman from the zendov club.

'What can I do for you?' he asked.

'May I?' the barman asked, indicating the other chair.

'Please.'

The barman sat down. He was in casual clothes, a white shirt under a striped coat. Endor imagined the man's formal wear was being pressed somewhere in a backstreet laundry.

'Master Endor,' the barman began, 'Mira wants you to know that–'

Endor held up his fork. 'I don't talk to men unless I know their names. Especially over breakfast.'

The barman cleared his throat and looked uncomfortable. 'My name is Jeg Stannis, sir,' he said.

'And I'm Titus Endor. See, that wasn't so hard. You were saying?'

'Mira wants you to know that you can't follow her any more.'

'Does she?'

'You went to her hab last night.'

'Maybe I did.'

'She knows you were there.'

'And where is she?'

Stannis shrugged. 'She wants to stay well away from you. She asked me to come and deliver this message, as a favour to her.'

'I'll go where I like, Master Stannis.'

'The club has rules, sir,' Stannis said. 'The girls have to be protected from–'

'From what?'

'Predators,' said Stannis.

Endor bit the corner off a slice of black bread. 'I'm no predator, I assure you.'

'You went to her home, uninvited, and let yourself in.'

Endor sighed.

'The club has rules,' the barman repeated. 'Fraternisation with guests is strictly–'

'It happens all the time, Master Stannis,' said Endor. 'Please, we're both adults. Most of the dancers at your club are already supplementing their income from day jobs and Theatricala work. Let's not be naive. They add to their wages in other ways too. Women are a rare commodity on Karoscura.'

The barman's face darkened. 'Leave her alone.'

'Or what?' Endor smiled.

'Or things will go badly for you.'

Endor nodded. 'We'll see. Tell me this, Master Stannis…' He pulled a pict from his coat and set it on the white cloth. 'What does this mean?'

Stannis looked down at the print. It was a shot of the yellow chalk marks on the floor of Mira Zaleed's bedroom.

'They're practice marks,' he said. 'Dance steps. The girls often draw out the turns and steps.'

Endor picked up the print and looked at it. 'Are they really? I'm not convinced. The numbers–'

'Beat counts.'

'Who did she kill in her bathroom, Master Stannis?'

The barman got up. 'Kill? I think there must be something wrong with your head, mister. You leave her alone, you hear me?'

'I hear what you're saying,' Endor nodded.

AFTER BREAKFAST, ENDOR stopped at a street bar on Kalyope and took an amasec against the cold. Sleet was coming down, brittle and wet. He read some more of the book. Maliko, Throne damn him, had a way with words.

Endor looked up. Across the street, through the veil of sleet, he saw a man watching him, a tall, thin man, dressed in sober black, with a high black hat.

Endor looked away to pay the bill. When he got up, the thin man in the tall black hat had vanished.

'HOW MUCH?' ENDOR asked.

'Four crowns,' the adept replied.

'To turn it round by tonight?'

'Twenty crowns,' the adept replied.

Endor showed him his rosette, but the adept didn't seem all that impressed.

'Twenty crowns,' he repeated.

Endor paid him the money, and handed him Mira's tooth. 'Typed, by tonight, no excuses.'

The adept nodded.

Endor left the backstreet alchemist's, and trudged up into the cold. The sleet had stiffened into snow, and it was belting along the thoroughfare in waves. He pulled up the collar of his coat, and walked into it, head down.

HIS ROUTE TOOK him back past the Theatricala, unlit and drab in the daylight. He went in. Cleaners were mopping the marble floors, and turning out the waste bins.

'We're closed,' a man said, coming forwards to meet Endor. 'The box office opens at six.'

Endor looked the man up and down. 'My name is Endor, and I'm an inquisitor of the holy ordos,' he said. He didn't bother with his badge this time. It seemed to have lost its impact.

'My pardon, sir,' the man said.

'Do I know you?' asked Endor.

'I don't think so, sir.'

The man was tall and skinny. 'Do you own a very tall black hat?' Endor asked.

'No, I don't, sir.'

'You have a dancer here, by the name of Mira Zaleed. I would like to inspect her dressing room.'

'We don't do that, sir,' said the man.

'Oh, I'm sorry,' smiled Endor. 'I thought I'd explained that I was an inquisitor.'

'THIS IS WHERE they all change,' the man said. Endor stepped into the room and turned on the light. The man waited by the door.

The room was long and low, flanked with grubby mirrors. Piles of dirty laundry heaped the baskets behind the door. Floaty white dresses hung on a rail. On the work surfaces, pins and reels of thread and thimbles lay beside pots of greasepaint and waxy sticks of rouge and base white. The room stank of greasy makeup, sweat and smoke.

'Her station?' asked Endor.

'I have no idea, inquisitor,' the man said.

'None at all?'

'Maybe to the left there, third mirror along. It's very busy in here at night.'

Endor sat down in the seat indicated and looked at himself in the smeared mirror. He was overpowered by the smell of stale perfume. Spent lho-sticks choked a glass near his left hand. The words 'Good luck Mira XXX Lilo' were written in lip rouge in the lower right-hand corner of the mirror.

Endor opened the small drawer under the mirror. It was full of blood. He shut it again, hastily, trying not to slosh anything out onto his lap.

'Could I have a moment?' he asked.

'I'm not really allowed–' the man began.

'Inquisitor, inquisitor,' Endor snarled.

'I'll be outside,' the man said, and closed the door behind him.

Gently, Endor slid the drawer open again. It wasn't full of blood at all. It was full of dark rose petals. He laughed at himself. The rose petals were as black and red as the halls of the Theatricala. He dipped his hand in and slid it around. The petals were as soft and cold as snow flakes or random clues.

He took out the knife. It was double-sided and stained. He sniffed it. Blood. From the bathroom in 870 Arbogan, no doubt. He leant back into the seat, and took out the pict. Dance steps? Practice marks? Surely nothing so innocent.

Endor decided he had to get Liebstrum working on the Number of Ruin. He needed proper information. The Number of Ruin wasn't something one took lightly. There had been a case, years back, an old fool...

Endor wondered where Liebstrum was. He hadn't seen his interrogator in days.

He put his hand back into the petals and found a card, a business card. On one side, it read 'Cloten and Sons, Funerary Needs and Final Rituals'. There was a vox number and a street address.

On the other side, handwritten, was 'Master Titus, you need to conclude your business with these men. Order number 87.' 435, Endor thought, was divisible by 87 5 times.

'Hello?' Endor called out.

The man poked his head around the dressing room door. 'Sir?'

'What are the chances of a man getting a drink?' Endor asked.

CLOTEN AND SONS occupied a grim ouslite building at the end of Limnal Street. Polished long-bodied hearses sat in the snowy yard. A brass bell tinkled as Endor went in.

'Can I be of assistance to you, sir?' asked a young, pudgy man in mourning weeds.

'No, you can't,' Endor replied, 'but he can.' He pointed at the tall, slender man at the back of the musty little shop, a place of dark velvet drapes and samphorwood.

'Master Cloten?' the young man called. 'For you, sir.'

Master Cloten walked over the Endor. He was no longer wearing the tall back hat, but he was unmistakeable. His face was hard and pale and sinewy, the face a man wore when he had spent his life dealing with grief.

'How may I help you, sir?' he asked.

'Order number 87,' Endor replied.

The man went to his heavy ledger, and heaved it open, but Endor knew he already knew the details.

'Ah, indeed. Already fully paid. A nalwood coffin, and a confirmed site in the municipal yard. Headstone already inscribed. Eighteen paid mourners. We have two of our most saddest-faced boys ready, sir, a horse-drawn carriage. Full wreathes. Two hymns already chosen and applied. The choir of the Theatricala will attend and sing them. Well, everything looks in order.'

'Good,' said Endor, 'and it's all paid for?'

'Yes sir.'

'I saw you in the street this morning,' said Endor.

'Quite probably, sir,' the slender man agreed. 'Death visits all the time. It stalks us, so to say.'

'I've heard that,' Endor smiled.

'And it's never subtle,' the slender man said. 'It strikes where it wants. Such is the way of the cosmos.'

'Indeed. Well, the ceremony seems well catered, and I am thankful for that. I knew him well.' Endor looked at the slender man for a reaction. None came. 'A splendid send-off. These are the hymns?'

'They are.'

Endor studied the sheets. 'I had wanted to make a contribution towards costs,' he said. 'As I told you, I knew him well.'

'Mistress Zaleed has already paid for everything,' the slender man said.

'Has she? Has she?' Endor murmured. 'May I see the inscription?'

The slender man passed him a pict of the headstone.

'Such a lamentable loss,' the slender man said. 'To be killed by a monster like that. Throne, I didn't know there were any predators left on Karoscura, not like that. Imagine.'

'Indeed,' said Endor.

He looked at the pict. His own name was on the headstone.

THE BACKSTREET ALCHEMIST'S had shut up for the night. In the swirling snow, he hammered on the door until the adept unlocked it.

'Tonight!' Endor spat. 'Tonight, you said!'

'You're late,' the adept replied.

'Just tell me what you found,' Endor snapped. He felt peculiar, and in no mood for nonsense.

'I ground it down. It's a saurapt tooth, just as you thought, from Brontotaph.'

ENDOR JOINED THE queue at the doors of the Theatricala. The overture was pumping out already, the windows glowing with gold light.

'Anywhere in the circle,' he told the girl in the box office, pushing crowns at her as he waited for his ticket.

'Are you all right, sir?' she asked.

'I'm fine,' he replied.

He hired glasses, bought a programme and a glass of joiliq, and hurried to his seat.

The ruddy auditorium pulsed like a box of flesh, red and dark, pumping with movement. He took his seat after a few thank you's and excuse me's.

He swung his glasses up. Yes, there in 435, the glint of other opera glasses. I have you now, Maliko, he thought.

The overture ended. The curtains drew back and the dancers mounted the stage. There she was, perfect and poised. Where had she been hiding?

Endor's body started to twist and turn, dancing the zendov in his seat.

'Will you stop that?' complained the woman beside him.

'Sorry,' said Endor, sitting still and sipping his drink.

He looked up at the box, and saw the glint of brass and glass again. 435. 435.

Of course, there was no box 435.

Liebstrum sat down beside him.

'Ah, there you are,' Endor smiled. 'Just in time.'

Liebstrum looked at him strangely.

'I've been calling you, you know?' said Endor.

'I know,' Liebstrum sighed.

'Where have you been?'

'Busy. Look, sir–'

'Oh, hush! You can't talk through this. It's beautiful. Watch them dance. Watch her.'

'Sir, I... sir... the ordos sent me, sir,' said Liebstrum. 'I was concerned, sir. Your calls, and everything. I had them run some tests on your last routine clinical. They wanted you to know. I'm so sorry, I would never wish this on you, sir.'

'Wish what? For Throne's sake, watch her!' Endor craned forwards and looked through his opera glasses. They caught the light.

'Sir?'

'What?'

'Sir, the worms, sir, the cerebral worms. They think you may have been infected years ago, perhaps by Hapshant.'

'He was a real character.'

'Sir, your mind is being eaten up. Dementia, sir.'

'Don't be silly, Liebstrum. By the way, where the hell have you been?'

'Sir, I think it would be best if you came with me now. I have summoned doctors. They can make your last weeks comfortable.'

Endor lowered his opera glasses. 'Is this some kind of trick?' he asked.

'No, sir,' replied Liebstrum.

'Listen to me, Liebstrum, she's got me. It was very canny of her. There's a saurapt stalking her too.'

'A what, sir?'

'A saurapt. She fended it off, made the rituals. She transplanted her curse onto me, you see?'

'No, not really, sir.'

'Oh yes, you do!' cried Endor. He reached for his glass, but it was empty. 'I smelt the same, don't you see? I was *already* a target. She performed the rituals and switched her predator after me. I'm her blood sacrifice. I suppose it was easy, given that I'd already got the curse on me.'

'Sir, the doctors are waiting. They will look after you.'

* * *

'LIEBSTRUM? LIEBSTRUM?' ENDOR called. He dropped his opera glasses. Liebstrum had vanished. Below him, the performance was continuing. He was in a box. He turned around, and saw the number on the door.

435.

But there was no box 435.

He felt peculiar. His head ached worse than ever. He wanted a drink, something to dull the pain. Grain joiliq, with shaved ice, and a sliver of citrus. His hands were numb. Where was Liebstrum? Hadn't he just been talking to Liebstrum?

The performance ended with a flourish, and the Theatricala exploded with applause.

It was all over now. Endor smiled. He realised it wasn't his fault. Just circumstances.

Out of the red darkness behind him, something loomed and finished its bite.

A PLACE OF QUIET ASSEMBLY

John Brunner

'YOU'LL HAVE A comfortable trip,' the landlord of the coaching inn assured Henkin Warsch. 'There are only two other passengers booked for today's stage.'

Which sounded promising enough. However, before they were even out of sight of the inn Henkin was sincerely regretting the maggot that had made him turn aside from his intended route and visit a place he had last seen twenty years before. One of his fellow-travellers was tolerably presentable, albeit gloomy of mien – a young, bookish type in much-worn clothes, with a Sudenland cloak over all – and Henkin might have quite enjoyed chatting with him. But the third member of the party was a dwarf, reeking of ale and burdened with a monstrous axe, who thanks to his huge muscle-knotted arms took up far more room than might have been estimated from his stature. Worst of all, his crest of hair and multiple tattoos marked him out as a Slayer, self-condemned to seek out death in combat against Chaos – a most discomforting fellow-traveller!

If only I could pretend I don't speak Reikspiel, he thought.

The inn's bootboy, however, had put paid to any chance of that. While hoisting Henkin's travelling bag to the roof of the coach, he had announced for the world to hear, 'This here gentleman hails from Marienburg! I'll wager he can report much news to help you pass away the miles!'

Presumably he hoped the flattery would earn him an extra tip. It failed. Scowling, Henkin handed him the least coin in his pocket and scrambled aboard.

Whereupon the ordeal commenced.

It wasn't just that the road was hilly and potholed. He was expecting that. But somehow the dwarf – fortunately in a jovial mood – had taken it into his head that no one from the Wasteland had a proper sense of humour. Accordingly he launched into a string of what he thought of as hilarious jokes. They began as merely scatological; they degenerated to filthy; and at last became downright disgusting.

'...and there he was, over ears in the privy! Haw-haw!' Naturally, Henkin's disinclination to laugh served, in his view, to prove his original point. So he tried again, and again, and yet again. Mercifully, at long last he ran out of new – one should rather, Henkin thought, say ancient – stories to tell, and with a contemptuous scowl leaned back and shut his eyes, though keeping a firm grip on the haft of his axe. Within moments he began to snore.

At which point his companion murmured. 'I must apologise for my friend, mein herr. He has had – ah – a difficult life. Felix Jaeger, by the way, at your service.'

Reluctantly Henkin offered his own name.

'Well, at least the weather is fine,' the other went on after a pause. Glancing out of the window, he added, 'We must be approaching Hohlenkreis, I suppose'.

Against his will Henkin corrected him. 'No, we haven't passed Schatzenheim yet.'

'You know this part of the world?' Felix countered, his eyebrows ascending as though to join his hair.

Henkin, in his turn, started at the landscape. The road, cut from the hillside like a ledge, was barely wide enough for the coach. Here it wound between sullen grey rocks and patches of grassy earth. Higher up the slope were birches, beeches and alders, last outposts of the army of trees that occupied the valley they were leaving. Towards the crest of the pass they would cede place to spruce and larch. That was a haunt of wolves...

'There was a time,' Henkin said at length, 'when I knew this area better than my own home.'

'Really? How so?'

Henkin shrugged. 'I was sent to school near here. To be precise, at Schrammel Monastery.'

'That name sounds familiar...' Felix frowned with the effort of recollection, then brightened. 'Ah, of course! Schrammel is where we're due to be put up for the night. So we shall enjoy your company at the inn also?'

Henkin shook his head. 'No, by the time we arrive there should be an hour of daylight left. I'll walk on to the monastery – it isn't far – and invoke an ex-pupil's traditional right to a meal and a bed. Yesterday, on impulse, I decided that being so close I shouldn't miss the chance.'

'Hmm! Your teachers must have left quite an impression!'

'They did, they did indeed. Inasmuch as I've succeeded at all in life, I owe it to their influence. I don't mind admitting it now, but I was an unruly youth' – as he spoke, he thought how oddly the words must strike this stranger's ears, for today he was portly, well dressed and altogether respectable – 'to the point where our family priest feared there might be some spark of Chaos in my nature. It was his counsel that led to my being sent to a monastery run by followers of Solkan to continue my studies. At Schrammel I was rescued from danger that I didn't realise I was in. I often wish I'd been able to complete my education there.'

'You were withdrawn early?' Felix inquired.

Henkin spread his hands. 'My father died. I was called home to take over the family business. But – well, to be candid, I wasn't cut out for it. Last year I decided to sell up, even though I didn't get anything like a fair price.' An embarrassed cough. 'My wife had left me, you see... If only my teachers had had time to reform my character completely, cure me of my excessive capacity for boredom... At first I hated the place, I admit, because the regime was very strict. How I remember being roused in winter before dawn, having to break the ice in my washbowl before morning prayers! And the sound of a hundred empty bellies grumbling in the refectorium as they brought in the bread and milk – why, I can almost hear it now! As we boys used to say, it made nonsense of the monastery's watchword – "A Place of Quiet Assembly"!'

He gave a chuckle, and Felix politely echoed it. 'Of course, they had to be strict. Unvarying adherence to routine: that was their chief weapon against the threat of Chaos – that, and memorising. Memorising! Goodness yes! They stocked my head with lines I'll carry to my dying day. "Let loose the forces of disorder – I'll not quail! Against my steely heart Chaos will ne'er prevail!"'

'Why!' Felix exclaimed. 'That's from Tarradasch's *Barbenoire*, isn't it?'

Henkin smiled wryly. 'Yes indeed. They made me learn the whole thing, word-perfect, as a warning against arrogance. I forget what I'd done, but I'm sure I deserved it... I'm impressed that you recognise it, though. I thought Tarradasch was out of fashion.'

'Oh, I can claim nodding acquaintance with most of the great works of the past. To be candid, I have ambitions in that direction myself. Oddly enough, that's partly why I'm travelling in such – ah – unlikely company.'

'Really? Do explain!'

Felix obliged. After detailing the agreement whereby he was to immortalise his associate's valiant deeds in a poem, he described a few of the said deeds – thereby causing Henkin to cringe nervously away from the slumbering dwarf – and eventually turned to a general discussion of literature. Thus the time passed pleasantly enough until with a grating of iron-rimmed wheels on cobblestones the coach drew up outside Schrammel's only inn, the Mead and Mazer.

'I'd advise you,' Felix murmured, 'to get out first. Gotrek may resent being woken up... Will you return from the monastery to join us for the rest of the journey?'

'That's my intention, yes,' he said with a grimace. 'I shall be roused in plenty of time, I'm sure.'

'I look forward to seeing you then. Enjoy your – ah – sentimental visit.'

HAVING ARRANGED FOR his heavy luggage to be looked after at the inn, Henkin set off cheerfully enough with a satchel containing bare necessities. The weather at this hour was still clement, though ahead he could see wisps of drifting mist. He remembered how clammy it used to feel on his fair skin when he and other malefactors were sent on a punishment run. The prospect of being enshrouded in it dampened his spirits. Moreover the passage of time seemed to have made the path steeper than it used to be, and he often had to pause for breath.

Nonetheless, the sight of old landmarks encouraged him. Here, for example, was the gnarled stump of an oak which his school-friends had nicknamed the *Hexengalgen* – witches' gallows. Its crown was gone, felled no doubt in a winter gale, but there was no mistaking its rugose bark, patched now with fungi that he recognised as edible. Sight of them reminded him how hungry he was, hungry enough to be looking forward even to the meagre victuals on which the pupils at the monastery survived: coarse bread, watery bone-broth and a few sad vegetables. But the teachers ate the same, and they'd seemed hale enough.

Of course, he was accustomed to finer fare these days. He hoped his digestion would cope...

The way was definitely steeper than he had allowed for. The distance from the oak-stump to the next landmark – a moss-covered rock known as the Frozen Dwarf because it bore a faint resemblance to one of that quarrelsome and obnoxious race – seemed to have doubled. How different it had been when he was seventeen!

Nonetheless he plodded on, and the sun was still up when he breasted the final rise. Thence he could survey a peaceful view he once had hated, yet now had power to bring tears to his eyes.

Yes, it was unchanged. There were the buildings he recalled so clearly, ringed with a forbidding grey stone wall. Some were veiled by gathering mist, but he could identify them all. There was the dormitorium, with its infirmary wing that fronted on neat square plots planted with medicinal herbs as well as vegetables for the pot. The kitchen where the latter were cooked was a separate building, separate even from the refectorium, for its smoke and, in summer, the hordes of flies it attracted to the scent of meat, made it a noisome neighbour. Over there was the schola, which as well as study-rooms contained the library... He wondered who now had charge of the great iron keys that used to swing from the cord of

Frater Jurgen's brown robe, keys that granted access to the locked section where only the best and most pious students were admitted, there to confront revolting but accurate accounts of what evil the forces of Chaos had accomplished in the world. Jurgen, of course, must be long dead; he had been already stooped and greying in Henkin's day.

Then there were the byres, the stables, the sheds where wandering beggars were granted overnight shelter – and finally, drawing the eye as though by some trick of perspective every line of sight must climax with it, the temple, where worship was accorded to the God of Law and none other, the most dedicated and vindictive of Chaos's opponents. Unbidden, lines from a familiar hymn rose to Henkin's lips:

'Help us to serve thee, God of Right and Law! Whene'er we pray to Thee for recompense, Avenge our wrongs, O–'

That's odd! The name was on the tip of his tongue, yet he could not recall it. Surely it would come back if he recited the lines again? He did so, and there was still an infuriating blankness. Yet he'd known it when talking to Felix in the coach!

'Oh, that's absurd!' he crossly told the air. 'I must be getting senile before my time!'

Annoyed, he slung his satchel more comfortably and descended the path that led to the tall oak gate, surmounted by a little watchtower, which constituted the sole means of passage through the encircling wall. Darkness deepened around him at each step. On the hilltop the sun had not quite set, but before he reached the valley floor night had definitely fallen, and chilly shrouds of mist engulfed him even as he tugged the rusty bell-chain.

The dull clang was still resounding when there was a scraping noise from above – a wooden shutter being slid back in the watchtower – and a cracked voice demanded who was there.

Remarkable, he thought. That sounds exactly like Frater Knoblauch who kept the gate in my day! Oh, I suppose each gatekeeper must copy the mannerisms of his forerunner...

Stepping back, tilting his head, unable to make out a fact but discerning the glimmer of a lantern, he called out an answer.

'Henkin Warsch! I used to be a pupil here! I claim by right a meal and a bed!'

'Henkin Warsch!' the gatekeeper echoed in astonishment. 'Well, well! That's amazing! I'll unlock in a trice!'

And he was as good as his word, for the heavy panels swung wide before Henkin had drawn two more breaths. There in front of him, unmistakable in the faint yellow gleam of his lamp, was Frater Knoblauch in person, wheezing with the effort of hurrying down the narrow stairs.

'But – no, it can't be!' Henkin exclaimed. 'You can't possibly be Frater Knoblauch!'

'And why not?' the old man riposted.

'I thought… I mean, I left here twenty years ago!'

'So you expected me to be dead, is that it?' the other said caustically. 'Well, I suppose to a boy anyone over fifty seems an ancient. No, here I am, as hale and hearty as anyone may hope at my age. Our way of life is a healthy one, you know – we don't rot our bodies with drink or waste our vitality by wenching! Come in, come in so I can shut the gate. A bed you can certainly have, but if you want food you'll have to make haste. It's after sunset, you know, and we still keep the same hours.'

Henkin's stomach uttered a grumble at the prospect of going supperless to sleep, bringing back to mind the joke he had repeated to his travelling companion.

'But I don't think they'll have started yet,' Frater Knoblauch added reassuringly, and set off at a clumsy scuttle towards the refectorium.

He led Henkin through an entrance reserved for teaching staff, which as a boy he had been forbidden to use, and time rolled back as he found himself on the great dais where he had never before set foot save to sweep it free of crumbs, looking down on the dim-lit hall. There, just as in the old days, ninety or a hundred drawn, pale boys sat unspeakingly before bowls of stew and lumps of coarse black bread. Those whose turn it was to dish out this exiguous repast were returning tureens and ladles to shelves along the wall and darting back to their places on wooden benches the sight of which brought recollected aches to Henkin's buttocks.

'You're in luck,' Knoblauch murmured. 'Grace has not been spoken. Wait here. I'll inform the prior.'

Henkin followed Knoblauch with his gaze. Even if the gatekeeper was the same, the prior certainly couldn't be: Alberich had been over seventy. But it was the custom for the staff to eat with their cowls raised, to discourage even an exchange of glances that might infringe the spirit of the absolute rule against conversation at table, so the man's features were invisible. Listening to Knoblauch, he nodded gravely, indicated with a finger that the visitor was to be shown to a seat and food brought for him – in precisely the way Alberich would have.

No, that is impossible, he thought. He must simply have schooled himself into a perfect imitation of the former prior!

One of the senior boys was signalled and came at a fast walk, never of course a run. Having received instructions, he approached Henkin, looking dazed, as though he could not believe anyone would voluntarily return to this place once released. He ushered him to the last unoccupied chair at the high table, and delivered the same stew and bread as served all the company. Then he made for a lectern halfway along the left-hand wall, whereon reposed a large leather-bound book, and stood waiting, eyes on the prior.

Ah! It's all coming back, all coming back! During the main course there was always a reading, some kind of homily or moral tale! How I used to hate my turn for duty, not just because I read so badly but because it meant going hungry for still a while longer, until I was allowed to wolf down cold leftovers before rushing to catch up with the others...

The prior rose and spoke in a reedy but resonant voice, as much like Alberich's as were his movements – and, as Henkin now perceived, his stature, too: Alberich had been unusually tall. Instead of reciting the expected grace, however, he made an announcement.

'Fraters! Boys! Today we witness a singular event. We share our repast with a former pupil. Fleeing the hurly-burly of the world he has rejoined us in our place of quiet assembly. I bid you all to welcome Henkin Warsch.'

He turned his head towards Henkin, but the cowl so shadowed his fact that no expression was discernible. At a loss, Henkin did what he would have done at home: rose from his chair, bowed awkwardly first to the prior and then to the body of the hall, and resumed his seat.

Apparently nothing more was expected, for the prior proceeded to intone the grace. At once there was a susurrus of gulping and chewing and swallowing, as though the great room were full of ravenous hogs incapable of squealing. To his own surprise – for the stew looked and smelled even less appetising than he had expected – Henkin found himself tucking in just as eagerly. Bland and flavourless the food might be, not to mention half-cold, but it was filling, and his long trudge from Schrammel town had bequeathed him a ferocious appetite.

Having waited until the first frantic mouthfuls had been consumed, the boy at the lectern raised his voice. Henkin failed to catch his introductory words because he was chomping down on another hunk of bread–

And, speaking of missed words: that grace. It includes the name I couldn't remember just now: the name of – of...

He shook his head, confused. He hadn't heard it.

At least, however, it didn't matter that he had missed the title of the reading. He recognised the opening line, having heard it countless times, and read it too.

'The Hate Child,' he whispered soundlessly. 'Yes, of course.'

He composed himself to listen to the familiar tale, not certain whether he was actually hearing it, or whether it as well was emerging from memory.

'In the distant past, in a province of Bretonnia, there ruled a noble count named Benoist, surnamed Orguleux for his great vanity. It was his ambition to have his own way in all things, and for that he was a mighty man, of body large and of nature determined, rare were the times when he was disappointed. None, though, may stand against death, and it came to pass that his wife, whom after his fashion he may have loved, died in confinement with their first child, and the baby also shortly after.

'Distracted by fury and sorrow, he went forth among the villages and hamlets of that land, begging or stealing his food, sleeping in barns and ditches, until he looked to a passer's glance like a common vagrant.

'It so fell out one evening that he crossed a woman of surpassing fairness, feeding geese beside a river when the moons were full. Smitten by her countenance, he made himself known, saying, "I am Count Benoist, your lord and master. My wife is dead. It is you I choose to be my new consort, and to seal the bargain I shall take you now." Though he had seen himself reflected in the pools he drank from, and so knew that he was dirty and unkempt, he was used to his own way in everything.

'Now the beauteous woman, who was called Yvette, was versed in arcane lore. She understood he made no empty boast. Curtseying, she said, "My lord, this is an honour to me and my family. But you must not take me now. It is the Night of Savage Moons, a time when the forces of Chaos are drawn tidewise from the Northern Wastes, and warpstone dust, it's said, blows in the wind. Come for me tomorrow instead, and I shall willingly consent to be your bride."

'Enraged, Count Benoist threw her to the ground and used her as he would, despite her warnings. So cruelly did he whelm her that she fainted, and after he was done he slung her on his shoulder and bore her unaided to his castle, where he commanded servants to attend her.

'On the morrow when she woke, she said to him, "I keep my word. Summon priests that they may marry us." He did, for she was very beautiful. But he did not know she married him for punishment. Perhaps she too was unaware. It had happened on the Night of Savage Moons.

'In the fullness of time she bore a son and called him Estephe. He grew up tall and comely, a fit heir. But there was in him a certain moody wildness, so that now and then he and his youthful companions fell to riotous carousing, while at other times black misery held him in thrall and he would speak to none, but walked alone and muttered curses.

'It chanced that on the day he turned eighteen, by when he overtopped his father and was nimbler with a sword, he was in the grip of such despair. That day his mother told him how he had been got on her against her will. So presently he sought the count and ran him through, and on the battlements he played at kickball with his father's head, wherefore all held him for accursed, and rightly so.

'Thus may it be seen how we must always be on guard, for the subtlety of Chaos knows no bounds.'

The reader closed the book. The slowest eaters among the boys gobbled their last frantic scraps of food. All rose as the prior pronounced concluding grace – and once again Henkin missed being reminded of the name of the God of Law, for a frightening idea distracted him.

Why, he thought, there was something of that boy in me, and traces still remain! Thank goodness Father sent me here, for otherwise... I had just such bouts of depression, and I too ran amok and thought it funny to break windows or rob peasants on their way to market! Besides, my mother never welcomed her husband's physical attentions, which is why I was and am an only child... Was Estephe, too? The story doesn't say.

But there was no time to wonder. The boys were filing, quickly but silently, towards the dormitorium, bar those whose task it was to clear away the bowls and sweep up crumbs. He was expecting the prior and the rest of the staff to approach, ask questions, find out why he had decided to pay this visit, allow him to express the gratitude that had suddenly filled his heart as the moral of Count Benoist's fate sank home. But nothing of the sort happened. Nodding to him solemnly in turn, they too left the hall, and in a moment he found himself alone but for another of the older boys, this one carrying a candlestick, who confided in a whisper that he was to guide Henkin to his room. So at least he was permitted to sleep alone, instead of on one of a hundred hard platforms covered with bracken-filled bags by way of mattress, no pillow, and just a single threadbare blanket such as he had shivered under in the old days. However, the staff's quarters he was shown to were only marginally more luxurious...

He hadn't retired at such an early hour in years. At first he was sure he wouldn't be able to sleep. In a way he welcomed the prospect. As though some vestige of his youthful self had returned, he looked forward to brooding over his annoyance at this cold reception. Then, even as he closed the wooden shutters against the now-dense mist, he was overcome by a vast surge of weariness. Yawning so hard he felt his head might split, he tossed aside his boots and outer clothing, rinsed his mouth and splashed his face with water from a cracked ewer, blew out his candle and lay down. He was asleep before he could draw the blanket over him.

HE WOKE TO midnight darkness. But not silence. The stones enclosing him, the very air, were resonating, to the boom of a vast and brazen gong...

Even as he prepared to be angry at this premature arousal, a thrill of anticipation permeated his entire body. With it came a clear and penetrating thought, more naked feeling than mere words. Yet it might be glossed as:

I forgot this! Only now do I remember it! How could it have escaped my memory, this which offered compensation for the cold and hunger, this which made it worth my while to spend so many agonising months in quarters barely better than a prison? This is the summons to the Quiet Assembly!

He was on his feet, feverishly snatching at his boots and cloak, aware of stirrings beyond the walls on either side, in the dormitorium below, even above the roof where owls were circling, and doubtless bats, the soft pat of their wings adding to the wonderful reverberation of the gong. Fingers a-tangle with excitement, he finally contrived to tie his laces, and rushed to the landing.

He instantly checked his pace. Of course. It must be slow and solemn, like everything here. Recollection seized him as he saw the pupils emerging one by one onto the stairs ahead of him, moving as though they were still lost to sleep, but surely, and with implacable intent.

At their rear he fell in, and found as he would not have expected when he arrived, but now thought was perfectly natural, the prior himself standing beside an open door admitting curls of mist. Hood thrown back, he was flanked by two attendants handing lit torches to the boys. Still cowled, they bore remarkable likeness to Frater Jurgen the librarian, iron keys and all, and Frater Wildgans who had been Henkin's chief instructor. But he was of no mind to let such matters trouble him.

Yes: the prior was Alberich. And seemingly no older. And now confronting Henkin as he descended the last cold tread of the stone flight, and bowing to him. Bowing! Saying nothing – yet his action was more eloquent than words.

Henkin's heart began to pound in perfect unison with the gong, while his paces, and the pupils', likewise kept time to it. Conscious that this ceremony was the honour due him for his decision to return, he followed the triple line of torch-bearing boys. Jurgen (?) and Wildgans (?) fell in beside him, and the prior himself took up the rear.

They were, of course, being summoned to the temple.

Ah! This is how it was, he thought. This is the way we used to be brought face to face with the elemental essence of Law and Right! Not by dull rote learning, not by memorising moral tales and masterworks, not through obedience to the discipline impressed on us with bread and broth – and, occasionally, necessary stripes – but by being brought from slumber at the dead hour when the random fretful forces of the body are most sluggish, least subject to the whims and wilfulness of daylight, and shown the unbearable fact of the god whom otherwise we knew as nothing more than words...! This is what saved me, thanks to the selfless dedication of the teaching fraters. How could I never have thought of it from then till now? How could I have overlooked for twenty years this sensation of the marvellous, this drunken joy?

He felt himself swaying, so tremendous was the charge of expectation that imbued his being. No other prospect of high events had matched it: not his wedding, not the birth of his children, not his first coup in the trade he had inherited from his father, then in the others he had turned to as his early interest waned; nor this first (of many) undetected love-affairs – nor even the last which had been detected and cost him his marriage and his former livelihood. This had no parallel. This was what had made life here endurable, and now he was to experience it again.

He wanted to cry out in gratitude, although his tongue seemed tied,

exactly as it had been when he strove to recall that thought-to-be familiar hymn.

Ah, it didn't matter. Within the hour, within minutes perhaps, a name
would spring to his lips and set the seal on his destiny. He needed only
to utter it aloud, and he would be accepted, in some way he did not yet
comprehend, but he would. Oh yes: he would, when it was time.

Here at last was the entrance to the temple. Knoblauch stood on guard.
Passing him, the boys drew up in serried ranks to either side, facing a
high and distant idol. The torches they bore cast but wan illumination
on the rich hangings that lined the walls, for mist had gathered within
the temple, too, as though wafted indoors by the wings of the circling
bats and owls. The idol itself, so tall that its raised arms reached the roof,
was scarcely visible. It didn't matter, though. Henkin knew with comfortable assurance what god was honoured in this fane: the one whose
law upheld not only roof but sky, to whom he was already dedicated,
and who had drawn him hither after two decades.

Ah! How few among all humankind can boast they have held steadfast for so long to a pledge undertaken in youth!

Henkin started. He was curiously uncertain whether the thought had
sprung unbidden to his mind, or whether Prior Alberich had uttered
the words – which, oddly, had been followed by what sounded like
a chuckle. He made to ask, but was forestalled. Knoblauch swung the
heavy doors shut with a thud, and in the same instant the gong – which
had become almost deafening – ceased to boom.

Amid an air of total expectation, Henkin found himself advancing
along the central aisle of the temple, the boys on either side as still as
rocks, even when a splatter of wax dripped from a torch and landed
scalding on the back of a bare hand, staring with indescribable longing towards the mist-veiled idol. Henkin remembered that longing now,
how it ached, how it festered, how it could only be assuaged by such a
ceremony as was now in progress.

Yet there was no chanting of anthems, no procession of gorgeously
attired acolytes, no incense, no heaps of offerings, none of the trivia
to be found in almost any other temple. Of course not. This rite was
unique.

It was, after all, the Place of Quiet Assembly.

Of their own accord, his feet ceased to move. He stood before the
statue. If he glanced up, he would be able to recognise it, and the name
that hovered on his tongue would be spoken. The fruit of his education would ripen on the instant. He would become a perfect servant of
the god's cause – which, ever since his schooldays, had been what he
wanted most.

Wondering why he had not returned here long ago, to join Alberich
and Knoblauch, Jurgen and Wildgans and the rest, he glanced from side
to side seeking approval. He met an encouraging smile from the prior.

At least, he forced himself to believe it was a smile. It involved lips parted over a set of teeth remarkable for so elderly a man, and there was a glint of expectation in his eyes, so...

Deciding not to look too long, Henkin clung to the remnants of the delight he had felt on the way hither – now, for some strange reason, it had begun to dissipate – and boldly threw his head to stare directly at the image of the god.

And froze, caught between adoration and astonishment.

For those were not arms that reached to the roof. Arms there were, ending in monstrous hands, and legs with vast broad feet. Towering above them, though, sprouted by a hideous head, were – horns? No, tentacles! They flexed! And each one ended, as it curved towards him, in a gaping pseudopod-coronaed face...

It spoke – from which of its three mouths, Henkin could not tell. It said, in a voice like the grating of rocks against rocks when spring floods undermine a hillside and presage landslides in a valley:

'Speak my name. You only need to speak my name and life indefinite awaits you. Live forever!'

Almost, the name emerged. Yet, somewhere in the inmost depths of Henkin's awareness, something rebelled. Some part of him complained, its mental tone no better than peevish – like his mother's when his father had offended her by winning an argument – a sense , one might say, of obstinate conviction.

That's not the God of Law, he thought. It looks more like the one I've striven against throughout my life!

For what felt like half eternity, Henkin stood transfixed with puzzlement. He knew the name he was supposed to speak. He was quite unable to recall the other one. It followed, by the twisted logic that held him in its grip, that he should utter the one he could.

On the other hand, if he did, there was some kind of penalty... or something... or... Raising his hands to his temples, he swayed giddily, gathered his forces, licked his lips, prepared to make a once-and-for-all commitment–

And there came a thunderous crash at the oaken door, as of a monstrous axe shattering its timbers like the flimsy partitions of a peasant's cot.

Which turned out to be exactly what it was.

Slow, like a fly trapped by the resin that in a thousand years would be more profitably sold as amber for embalming it, Henkin turned. At the far end of the aisle something was moving so fast he could barely follow it. Also his ears were more assaulted than they had been by the gong.

The moving thing was the axe. He could not see its wielder. But it was the wielder he was hearing. He had been told, he had read, how terrible was the war-cry of a dwarf in berserk state. Not until it blasted back in echo from the arched roof of the temple was he able to believe its force. Gotrek's first victim, after the door, had been Frater Knoblauch, whose head, staring at his body on the stone flags, bore an expression suggesting it felt it should, but couldn't quite, recognise the nearby carcass.

At that sight the boys, screaming at the pitch of their lungs, broke and ran, trampling the fraters who tried to stop them, hurling their torches aside, headless of whether they landed at the foot of the hangings. Flames leapt up. Smoke mingled with the mist. Alberich and his companions, cowls thrown back, turned snarling to confront the intruder, Henkin for the moment forgotten.

'Hurry! Warsch, run! This way, you fool!'

Still bemused by the grip of enchantment, Henkin stared towards the speaker, waving frantically from near the door. He ventured muzzily, 'Is that you, Felix Jaeger?'

'Of course it's me!' Felix shouted. He had a sword in his hand, but such work was better left to his companion. 'This way! *Move!* Before Gotrek brings the roof down on our heads!'

Sluggishly, Henkin sought mute permission from the prior – he felt he had to. Or from Jurgen, or Wildgans. But the attention of all three was on the dwarf. Drawing themselves up within their cowled robes, they seemed tree-tall compared with him. Magical auras flashed as they mustered for a counterattack. 'Poor fool!' Henkin heard distinctly, in Alberich's voice. 'To think he imagines a mere axe can slay one who has lived a thousand years!'

They stretched out their arms. Horrors indescribable assembled at their conjunct fingertips.

Ignoring the other fraters and the fleeing boys, Gotrek ceased his bellowing. Poised on the balls of his feet, brandishing his axe, he looked far more terrifying than before: no longer dancing with the ecstasy of blood lust, but gathering himself into himself, eyes gleaming with mad joy... Shaking from head to toe, Henkin realised what he was watching: a Slayer on the brink of conviction that here might be the end of his quest.

As if to confirm it, the dwarf began to sing – not shout his war-cry, not utter threats, nor curses, but to chant in dwarfish. Surely, thought Henkin in wonder, it was the ballad of his family's deeds: that family who must all be dead, for else he'd not have taken to his lonely road.

Sneering contempt, Prior Alberich and his companions mustered all their magic force, prepared to cast–

And in exactly that brief moment when they had no power save what was being drawn into their spell, Gotrek hurled his axe.

He threw so hard it carried him with it, for he did not let go. Was it a throw or a leap? Or was it both? Dazed, Henkin could not decide. All he could tell was this: such was its violence, the flying blade *mowed* Alberich and his companions like corn beneath the harvest-scythe. The dwarf, who had spun clear around, landed on his feet before the idol. Panting, but still gasping out his song, he raised the blade anew, this time menacing the statue itself.

Where had the spell-power gone? Into the axe, Henkin abruptly realised. It must have! For what he had taken for arms upholding the temple roof – what turned out to be half-horn, half-tentacle – they were descending, their hideous fanged mouths like flesh-eroding lampreys closing on the stubby form of Gotrek. His singing, now the boys' screams had faded, was not the only noise to be heard. Suddenly there were menacing creaks and grinds as, its support removed, the building began to sag and sway...

'*Move*, you fool!' thundered Felix, seizing Henkin's arm, and dragged him away on quaking ground to the music of snapping timbers, tumbling stones and crackling flames, amid the destined downfall of Schrammel Monastery.

Abruptly it was bitterly cold, and they were very weak, and time seemed to grind to a stop.

Henkin wished the moving earth would do the same.

It was dawn. Dew-sodden, Henkin forced his eyes open and drank in the sights revealed by the returning sun. He saw mounds of rubble, the line of the fallen wall, smoke drifting from what had been the temple and now looked more like a tent propped up by broken poles – but no other movement save seekers of carrion come cautiously to glean the ruins. Plus a stir amid the smouldering wreckage, as though a trace of Chaos lurked there still, shifting and wriggling.

Of neither fraters nor pupils was there any sign.

Nor, come to that, of Gotrek.

Wrapped in his red wool cloak, Felix sat brooding on a nearby rock. Without preamble Henkin demanded, 'Where's the dwarf? He saved my life!'

Felix gave a dour shrug. 'It looks as though he's achieved his ambition. The temple collapsed with him inside. I only just dragged you out in time... Well, it's what he's always wanted. And I suppose I should be glad to be released from my pledge at last.'

'But how did it all happen?' Henkin sat up gingerly. 'Perhaps warpstone dust? In the air, the food, our very blood?'

'That, or some like manifestation. At any rate, for centuries this monastery has functioned as a tool for–'

'Tzeentch!' Henkin blurted. That was the word he had been tempted to utter, the name of the power his family's priest had feared already held him in his grip. And the name of the God of Right and Law came back to him, too.

Soberly, Felix nodded.

'Indeed. How better might the servants of the Changer of Ways disguise their work than by pretending to serve Solkan? It must have cost them dear to adopt such a static guise, but in the long term I suppose they felt it worth the effort to plant so many converts in staid, respectable families.'

Scrambling to his feet, Henkin said bitterly, 'If only my father and our priest could have known what a fate they were condemning me to! I did want to follow in my father's footsteps – I swear it! I wanted to build up our business, make it the wealthiest in Marienburg, and instead my life has been a *mess!* Here I am entering middle age without a wife, without a career, without anything my family hoped I would enjoy! And all because my father was duped into sending me here because I was so unruly and the monastery was called "A Place of Quiet Assembly"!'

'Quiet it wasn't!' roared a distant voice. 'Not last night, anyway!'

Startled, Felix and Henkin glanced around. Gotrek was emerging from the wrecked temple, axe over shoulder. He must, Henkin reasoned, have been the cause of what he'd mistaken for simple subsidence.

And the dwarf did not look pleased in the least.

Faintly Henkin caught a whisper from Felix: 'Oh, *no*…'

But there were things he still needed to know. Urgently he demanded, 'How did you find out? And why did you come after me? You too could have been ensnared!'

Resignedly, Felix explained.

'We discovered over dinner that everyone at the inn knew about the monastery – "the Monstery", as they call it. With that, we forgot all thought of food.'

'You mean the landlord could have warned me?' Rage boiled up in Henkin's throat.

'Sure he could! But he looked forward to inheriting your luggage.' Brushing dust from crest and eyebrows, the dwarf sat down beside Felix and inspected his axe, cursing under his breath.

'Why, the–'

'Save your breath,' Felix cut in. 'Gotrek made him a promise. He knows what's going to happen to him if when we get back he's so much as laid a finger on your belongings.'

'When…?' Henkin had to swallow hard. 'But, herr dwarf, were you expecting to return?'

Felix drew a hissing breath, as in alarm.

There was a long silence. Eventually Gotrek shrugged. In a tone so different from the one Henkin had heard during yesterday's coach-ride that it was hard to credit the same person was speaking, he said gruffly, 'Last night didn't pay off, but it was one of the likeliest chances to have come my way. For that, I'd even forgive someone who lacks a sense of humour! If I hadn't picked up such a charge of magic… In the upshot, though,' he said, glowering, 'all it's landed me with is another verse for Felix's poem and another doom cheated from me!' He lifted his axe as though to strike Henkin out of his way.

Henkin hesitated. Within him, he now knew, Tzeentch the Changer of Ways held sway but had not yet conquered. Very well! If Tzeentch's disciples could control their mutable nature long enough to delude the world into imagining they served the rigid Solkan, could he not govern himself at least for one brief moment, do and say the right and necessary thing? One did after all know a little about Slayers…

Resolved, he drew himself to his full height.

'Gotrek,' he said, daringly. 'I heard you sing as you confronted them!'

The huge-knuckled fists tightened on the axe; the muscles of the shoulders tensed; the glare intensified.

'Herr dwarf! I'm aware how rare a privilege that is! I'll treasure it!'

The massive hands relaxed, just a trifle.

'Of course, I shall never, so long as I live, mention the fact to another living soul! Not until your companion has completed his poem – the great work that will immortalise your deeds.'

From the corner of his eye Henkin noticed that Felix, visibly surprised, was nodding.

'I'm only sorry, *herr dwarf*, that my unworthy self could not after all be the means of your attaining your ambition!'

Had that gone too far? By now he was practically gabbling.

'If you'll accompany me back to the inn, although we must have missed the morning coach, I promise you we shall pass the time until the next most pleasantly, with abundance of food and ale at my expense, and you may tell me all the jokes you wish and I'll applaud the verses Felix makes about your deeds here today!'

For a moment Henkin imagined he might have won Gotrek over. But then the dwarf shrugged again, rising. Words could not portray the mask of misery he wore.

'What's the use? You humans care only about your own miserable lives. When Felix composes his account of what happened here, he'll miss the point, as usual… Ah, never mind. It was a good fight, at least. So I'll take you up on the ale. It does beat water. All right, let's get on back to Schrammel.'

Felix failed to suppress a groan.

But, since there was no better bargain to be had – and since last night not merely a life had been saved, but a soul – Henkin and he fell in behind the dwarf and duly trudged back to the Mead and Mazer.

PRIMARY INSTINCT

Sarah Cawkwell

Victory does not always rest with the big guns.
But if we rest in front of them, we shall be lost.

– Lord Commander Argentius,
Chapter Master, Silver Skulls

THE SOARING FORESTS of Ancerios III steamed gently in the relentless heat of the tropical sun. Condensation beaded and rose, shimmering in a constant haze from the emerald-green and deep mauve of the leaves. This was a cruel, merciless place where the sultry twin suns raised the surface temperature to inhospitable levels. The atmosphere was stifling and barely tolerable for human physiology.

However, the party making their way through the jungle were not fully human.

The dark Anceriosan jungle had more than just shape, it had oppressive, heavy form. There was an eerie silence, which might once have been broken by the chattering of primate-like creatures or the call of exotic birds. In this remote part of the jungle, there was no sign of the supposed native fauna. What plant life that did exist had long since evolved at a tangent, adapting necessarily to the living conditions. Everything that grew reached desperately upwards, yearning towards the suns. Perhaps there was a dearth of animal life, but these immense plants thrived and provided a home for a countless variety of insects.

There was a faint stirring of wind, a shift in the muggy air, and a cloud of insects lifted on the breeze. They twisted lazily, their varicoloured forms catching and reflecting what little smattering of dappled sunlight managed to penetrate this far down. They twirled with joyful abandon on the zephyr that held them in its gentle grasp, riding the updraft through to a clearing.

The cloud abruptly dissipated as a hand clad in a steel-grey gauntlet scythed neatly through it. Startled, the insects scattered as though some-one had thrown a frag grenade amongst them. The moment of confusion passed swiftly, and they gradually drifted back together in an almost pal-pably indignant clump. They lingered briefly, caught another thermal and were gone.

Sergeant Gileas Ur'ten, squad commander of the Silver Skulls Eighth Company Assault squad 'The Reckoners', swatted with a vague sense of irri-tation at the insects. They flew constantly into the breathing grille of his helmet and whilst the armour was advanced enough and sensibly designed in order not to allow them to get inside, the near-constant *pit-pit-pit* of the bugs flying against him was starting to become a nuisance.

He swore colourfully and hefted the weight of the combat knife in his hand. It had taken a great deal more work than anticipated to carve a path through to the clearing, and the blade was noticeably dulled by the experience.

Behind him, the other members of his squad were similarly survey-ing the damage to their weapons caused by the apparently innocent plant life. Gileas stretched out his shoulders, stiff from being hunched in the same position for so long, and spun on his heel to face his battle-brothers.

'As far as I can make out, the worst threats are these accursed insects,' he said in a sonorous rumble. His voice was deep and thickly accented. 'Not to mention these prevailing plant stalks and the weather.'

The Assault squad had discovered very quickly that the moisture in the air, coupled with spores from the vegetation that they had hacked down, was causing a variety of malfunctions within their jump packs. Like so much of the rediscovered technology that the Adeptus Astartes employed, the jump packs had once been things of beauty, things that offered great majesty and advantage to the Emperor's warriors. Now, however, they were starting to show signs of their age. Fortunately, the expert and occasionally lengthy ministrations of the Chapter's Tech-marines kept the machine-spirits satisfied and ensured that even if the devices were not always perfect, they were always functional.

Gileas sheathed his combat knife and reached up to snap open the catch that released his helmet. There was an audible *hiss* of escaping air as the seals unlocked. Removing the helmet, an untidy tumble of dark hair fell to his shoulders, framing a weather-tanned, handsome face that was devoid of the tattoos that covered the rest of his body beneath the armour. Like all of the Silver Skulls, Gileas took great pride in his hon-our markings. He had not yet earned the right to mark his face. It would not be long, it was strongly hinted, for the ambitious Gileas was reput-edly earmarked for promotion to captain. It was a rumour which had stemmed from his own squad and had been met with mixed reactions from others within the Chapter. Gileas repeatedly dismissed such talk as hearsay.

He cast dark, intelligent eyes cautiously around the clearing, clipping his helmet to his belt and loosening his chainsword in the scabbard worn down the line of his armoured thigh. The twisted, broken wreckage of what had once been a space-going vessel lay swaddled amidst fractured trees and branches. Whatever it was, it was mostly destroyed and it most certainly didn't look native to the surroundings. This was the first thing they had encountered in the jungle which was clearly not indigenous.

Reuben, his second-in-command, came up to Gileas's side and disengaged his own helmet. Unlike his wild-haired commanding officer, he wore his hair neat and closely cropped to his head. He considered the destroyed vessel, sifting through the catalogue of data in his mind. It was unlike anything he had ever seen before. Any markings on its surface were long gone with the ravages of time, and it was nearly impossible to filter out any sort of shape. Any form it may have once taken had been eradicated by the force of impact.

'It doesn't look like a wraithship, brother,' he said.

'No,' grunted Gileas in agreement. 'It certainly bears no resemblance to that thing we were pursuing.' He growled softly and ran a hand through his thick mane of hair. 'I suspect, brother, that our quarry got away from us in the webway. Unfortunate that they escaped the Emperor's justice. For now, at least.' His hand clenched briefly into a fist and he swore again. He considered the vessel for a few silent moments. Finally, he shook his head.

'This has been guesswork from the start,' he acknowledged with reluctance. 'We all knew that there was a risk we would end up chasing phantoms. Still...' He indicated the wreck. 'At least we have something to investigate. Perhaps this is what the eldar were seeking. There's no sign of them in the atmosphere. We may as well press our advantage.'

'You think we're ahead of them?'

'I would suggest that there's a good chance.' Gileas shrugged lightly. 'Or maybe we're behind them. They could already have been and gone. Who knows, with the vagaries of the warp? The *Silver Arrow's* Navigator hadn't unscrambled her head enough to get a fix on chronological data when we left. Either way, it's worth checking for any sign of passage. Any lead is a good lead. Even when it leads nowhere.'

'Is that you or Captain Kulle speaking?' Reuben smiled as he mentioned Gileas's long-dead mentor.

The sergeant did not reply. Instead, he grinned, exposing ritualistically sharpened canines that were a remnant of his childhood amongst the tribes of the southern steppes. 'It matters little. Whatever this thing is, it's been here for a long time. This surely can't be the ship we followed into the warp. It isn't one of ours and that's all we need to know. You are all fully aware of your orders, brothers. Assess, evaluate, exterminate. In that order.'

He squinted at the ship carefully. Like Reuben, he was unable to match it to anything in his memory. 'I feel that the last instruction might well be something of a formality though. I doubt that anything could have survived an impact like that.'

The ship was practically embedded in the planet's surface, much of its prow no longer visible, buried beneath a churned pile of dirt and tree roots. Hardy vegetation, some kind of lichen or moss, clung to the side of the vessel with grim determination.

The sergeant glanced sideways at the only member of the squad not clad head-to-foot in steel-grey armour and made a gesture with his hand, inviting him forwards.

Resplendent in the blue armour of a psychic battle-brother, Prognosticator Bhehan inclined his head in affirmation before reaching his hand into a pouch worn on his belt. He stepped forwards until he was beside the sergeant, hunkered down into a crouch and cast a handful of silver-carved rune stones to the ground. As Prognosticator, it was important for him to read the auguries, to commune with the will of the Emperor before the squad committed themselves. To a man, the Silver Skulls were deeply superstitious. It had been known for entire companies to refuse to go into battle if the auguries were poor. Even the Chapter Master, Lord Commander Argentius, had once refused to enter the fray on the advice of the *Vashiro*, the Chief Prognosticator.

This was more, so much more than ancient superstition. The Silver Skulls believed without question that the Emperor projected His will and His desire through His psychic children. These readings were no simple divinations of chance and happenstance. They were messages from the God-Emperor of Mankind, sent through the fathomless depths of space to His distant loyal servants.

The Silver Skulls, loyal to the core, never denied His will.

Prognosticators served a dual purpose in the Chapter. Where other ranks of Adeptus Astartes had Librarians and Chaplains, the Silver Skulls saw the universe in a different way. Those battle-brothers who underwent training at the hands of the Chief Prognosticator offered both psychic and spiritual guidance to their brethren. Their numbers were not great: Varsavia did not seem to produce many psykers. As a consequence, those who did ascend to the ranks of the Adeptus Astartes were both highly prized and revered amongst the Chapter.

Gileas knew that the squad were deeply honoured to have Bhehan assigned to them. He was young, certainly; but his powers, particularly those of foresight, were widely acknowledged as being amongst the most veracious and trustworthy in the entire Chapter.

'I'm feeling nothing from the wreck,' said Bhehan in his soft, whispering voice. The young Prognosticator hesitated and frowned at the runes, passing his hand across them once again. He considered for a moment or two, his posture stiff and unyielding. Finally, he relaxed. 'If it were a wraithship, if it were the one we were pursuing, its psychic field would still be active. This one is assuredly dead. Stone-cold dead.' He frowned, pausing just long enough for Gileas to quirk an eyebrow.

'Is that doubt I'm detecting there?' The Prognosticator looked up at Gileas, his unseen face, hidden as it was behind his helmet, giving nothing away. He glanced back down at the runes thoughtfully. The scratched designs on their surfaces were a great mystery to Gileas. However, the Prognosticators understood them, and that was all that mattered. An eminently pragmatic warrior, Gileas never let things he didn't understand worry him. He would never have vocalised the thought, but it was an approach he privately felt many others in the Chapter should adopt.

Bhehan shifted some of the runes with a practiced hand, turning some around, lining others up, making apparently random patterns on the ground with them. A pulsing red glow briefly animated the Space Marine's psychic hood as he brought his concentration to bear on the matter at hand.

Finally, after some consideration, he shook his head.

'An echo, perhaps,' he mused, 'nothing more, nothing less.' He nodded firmly, assertiveness colouring his tone. 'No, Brother-Sergeant Ur'ten,' he said, 'no doubt. The Fates suggest to me that there was perhaps something alive on board this ship when it crashed. Any sentience within its shell has long since passed on. Subsumed, perhaps, into the jungle. Eaten by predators, or simply died in the collision.'

He gathered up the runes, dropping them with quiet confidence back into his pouch, and stood up. 'The Fates,' he said, 'and the evidence lying around us.' He nodded once more and removed his helmet. The face beneath was surprisingly youthful, almost cherubic in appearance, and reflected Bhehan's relative inexperience. For all that, he was a field proven warrior of considerable ferocity. Combined with the powers of a Prognosticator, he was a formidable opponent, something the sergeant had already tested in the training cages.

Gileas nodded, satisfied with the outcome. 'Very well. Reuben, take Wulfric and Jalonis with you and search the perimeter for any sign of passage. All of this…' He swept his hand around the clearing to indicate the crash site. 'All of this may simply be an eldar ruse. I have no idea of the extent of their capabilities, but they are xenos and are not to be trusted. Not even in death. Tikaye, you and Bhehan are with me. Seeing as we're here anyway, let's get this ship and the surrounding area checked out. The sooner it's done, the sooner we can move on to the next location.' He grinned his wicked grin again and rattled his chainsword slightly.

The entire group moved onwards, aware of a shift in the weather. A storm front was rolling in. It told in the increased ozone in the air, the faint tingle of electricity that heralded thunder. Following his unit commander, Bhehan absently dipped a hand into the pouch at his side and randomly selected a rune. The tides of Fate were lapping against his psyche strongly, and the closer they got to the craft, the more intense that sensation became.

He briefly surfaced from his light trance to stare with greater intensity at the rune he had withdrawn and he stiffened, his eyes wide. He considered the stone in his hand again and tried to wind the rapidly unravelling thoughts in his mind back together. As though a physical action could somehow help him achieve this, he raised a hand and grabbed at his fair hair.

Noticing the sudden movement, Gileas moved to the Prognosticator's side immediately. 'Talk to me, brother. What do you see?'

A faint hint of wildness came into the psyker's eyes as he turned to look up at the sergeant. 'I see death,' he said, his voice notably more high-pitched than normal. 'I see death, I smell corruption, I taste blood, I feel the touch of damnation. Above all, above all, above all, I *hear* it. Don't you hear it? I hear it. The screams, brothers. The screaming. They will be devoured!'

He pulled wretchedly at his hair, releasing the rune which fell to the floor. A thin trail of drool appeared at the side of the psyker's mouth and he repeatedly drummed his fist against his temple. Gileas, despite the respect he had for the Prognosticator, reached out and caught his battle-brother's arm in his hand.

'Keep your focus, Brother-Prognosticator Bhehan,' he rebuked, his tone mild, but his manner stern. 'We need you.' He'd seen this before; seen psykers lose themselves to the Sight in this way. Disconcertingly, where Bhehan was concerned, the Sight had never been wrong.

It did not bode well.

'We are not welcome here,' the psyker said, his voice still edged with that same slightly unearthly, eerie, high-pitched tone. 'We are not welcome here and if we set one foot outside of the ship, it will spell our doom.'

'We *are* outside the ship…' Tikaye began. Gileas cast a brief, silencing glance in his direction. The young psyker was making little sense, but such were the ways of the Emperor and not for those not chosen to receive His grace to question. The sergeant patted Bhehan's shoulder gruffly and gave a grim nod. 'The faster this task is completed, the better. Double-time, brothers.'

He leaned down and picked up the rune that Bhehan had dropped, offering it back to the psyker without comment.

THE OTHER PARTY, led by Reuben, had skirted the perimeter of the clearing. At first there had been nothing to suggest anything untoward had occurred. Closer investigations by Wulfric, a fine tracker even by the Chapter's high standards, had eventually revealed recently trampled undergrowth.

Reuben took stock of what little intelligence they had gathered on this planet, far out on the Eastern Fringe of the galaxy. There had been suggestions of some native creatures, but as of yet, they had encountered none. Worthless and of little value, the planet had been passed over as unimportant and uninhabited with no obviously valuable resources or human life.

Just because there were no previous sightings of any of the indigenous life forms, of course, did not mean that there were none to actually *be* seen.

Reuben waved his bolter to indicate that Wulfric should lead on and the three Space Marines plunged back into the jungle, following what was a fairly obvious trail. They did not have to travel far before they located their quarry, a few feet ahead of them, in a natural glade formed by a break in the trees.

The creature seemed totally ignorant of their presence, affording them a brief opportunity to assess it. An overall shade of dark, almost midnight-blue, the alien was completely unfamiliar. Without any frame of visual reference, the thing could easily be one of the presumably indigenous life forms. Muted conversations amongst the group drew agreement.

A slight adjustment to his optical sensors allowed Reuben a closer inspection. The thing had neither fur, nor scales or even insectoid chitin covering its body. It was smooth and unblemished with the same pearlescent sheen to its form that the insects seemed to have. Its limbs were long and sinewy; the musculature of the legs suggesting to Reuben's understanding of xenobiology that it could very probably run and jump exceptionally well. The arms ended in oddly human-like five-fingered hands. Frankly, Reuben didn't care about its lineage or whether it had ever displayed any intelligence. In accordance with every belief he held, with every hypno-doctrination he had undergone, he found it utterly repulsive.

He reacted in accordance with those beliefs and teachings at the exact moment the alien turned its head in their direction, emitting a bone-chilling screech that tore through the jungle. It was so piercing as to be almost unbearable. Reuben's enhanced auditory senses protected him from the worst of it, but it was the sort of noise that he genuinely suspected could shatter crystal. Unearthly. Inhuman.

Alien.

Acting with the intrinsic response of a thousand or more engagements, Reuben flicked his bolter to semi-automatic and squeezed the trigger. Staccato fire roared as every projectile found its target. It was joined, seconds later, by the mimicking echo of the weapons in his fellow Space Marines' hands.

At full stretch, the xenos was easily the size of any of the Space Marines shooting at it. It showed no reaction to the wounds that were being ripped open in its body by the hail of bolter fire. It was locked in a berserk rage, uncaring and indifferent to the relentless attack. As the explosive bolts lacerated its body, dark fluid sprayed onto the leaves, onto the ground, onto the Silver Skulls.

Still it kept coming.

Reuben switched to fully-automatic and unloaded the remainder of the weapon's magazine. Wulfric and Jalonis followed his example. Eventually, mortally wounded and repelled by the continuous gunfire, the abomination emitted a strangled scream of outrage. It crumpled to the ground just short of their position, spasms wracking its hideous form, and then all movement ceased.

Smoke curled from the ends of three bolters and the moment was broken only by the crackle of the vox-bead in Reuben's ear.

'Report, Reuben.'

'Sergeant, we found something. Xenos life form. Dead now.'

Reuben could hear the scowl in his sergeant's voice. 'Remove its head to be sure it *is* dead, brother.' Reuben smiled. 'We're coming to your position. Hold there.'

'Yes, brother-sergeant.'

Not wishing to take any chances, Reuben swiftly reloaded his weapon and stepped forwards to examine the xenos. It had just taken delivery of a payload of several rounds of bolter fire and had resisted death for a preternaturally long time. As such, he was not prepared to trust to it being completely deceased. His misgivings proved unfounded.

Moving towards the alien, any doubt of its state was dismissed: thick, purple-hued blood oozed stickily from multiple wounds in its body, pooling in the dust of the forest floor, settling on the surface and refusing to soak into the ground. It was as though the planet itself, despite being parched, rejected the fluid. The pungent, acrid scent of its essential vitae was almost sweet, sickly and cloying in the thick, humid air around them. Wrinkling his nose slightly against its stench, Reuben moved closer.

Lying on the ground, the thing had attempted to curl into an animalistic, defensive position, but was now rapidly stiffening as rigor mortis took hold. Reuben could see its eyes, amethyst-purple, staring glassily up at him. Even in death, sheer hatred shone through. He felt sickened to the stomach at its effrontery to all that was right.

Just to be on the safe side, he placed the still-hot muzzle of his bolter against its head and fired a solitary shot at point-blank range into it. Grey matter and still more of the purplish blood burst forth like the contents of an over-ripe fruit.

Reuben crouched down and considered the xenos more carefully. The head was curiously elongated, with no visible ears. The purple eyes were over-large in a comparatively small face. A closer look, despite the odour that roiled up from it, suggested that they may well have been multi-faceted. The head was triangular, coming to a small point at the end of which were two slits that Reuben could only presume were nostrils.

Anatomically, even by xenos standards it seemed *wrong*. In a harsh environment like the jungle, any animal would need to adapt just in order to survive. This thing, however, seemed as though it was a vague idea of what was right rather than a practical evolution of the species. It was a complex chain of thought, and the more Reuben considered it, the more the explanation eluded him. It was as though the answer was there, but kept just out of his mental grasp.

For countless centuries, the Silver Skulls had claimed the heads of their victims as trophies of battle, carefully extracting the skulls and coating them in silver. Thus preserved, the heads of their enemies decorated the ships and vaults of the Chapter proudly. However, the longer Reuben stared at the dead alien, any urge he may have had to make a prize of it ebbed away. Forcing himself not to think on the matter any further, he turned back to the others.

Wulfric had resumed his search of the surrounding area and even now was gesturing. 'It wasn't alone. Look.' He indicated a series of tracks leading off in scattered directions, mostly deeper into the jungle.

Reuben gave a sudden, involuntary growl. It had taken three of them with bolters on fully-automatic to bring just one of these things to a halt, and even then he had half-suspected that if he hadn't blasted its brains out, it would have got back up again.

'Can you make out how many?'

'Difficult, brother.' Wulfric crouched down and examined the ground. 'There's a lot of scuffing, plus with our passage through, it's obscured the more obvious prints. Immediate thoughts are perhaps half a dozen, maybe more.' He looked up at Reuben expectantly, awaiting orders from the squad's second-in-command. 'Of course, that's just in the local area. Who knows how many more of those things are out there?'

'They probably hunt in packs.' Reuben fingered the hilt of his combat knife.

Unspoken, the thoughts passed between them. If one was that hard to put down, imagine what half a dozen of them or more would be like to keep at bay. Reuben made a decision and nodded firmly.

'Good work, Wulfric. See if you can determine any sort of theoretical routes that these things may have taken. Do a short-range perimeter check. Try to remain in visual range if you can. Report anything unusual.'

'Consider it done,' replied Wulfric, getting to his feet and reloading his bolter. Without a backwards glance, the Space Marine began to trace the footprints.

The snapping of undergrowth announced the impending arrival of the other three Space Marines. Straightening, Reuben turned to face his commanding officer. He punched his left fist to his right shoulder in the

Chapter's salute and Gileas returned the gesture.

All eyes were immediately drawn to the dead creature on the floor.

'Now that,' said Gileas after a few moments of assessing the look and, particularly, the stench of the alien, 'is unlike anything I have ever seen before. And to be blunt, I would be perfectly happy if I never see one again.'

Reuben dutifully reported the incident to his sergeant. 'Sorry to disappoint you, but Wulfric believes there could be anything up to a half-dozen other creatures similar to this one in the vicinity. I sent him to track them.'

Gileas frowned as he listened, his expression darkening thunderously. 'Any obvious weaknesses or vulnerable spots?'

'None that were obvious, no.'

Gileas glanced at Reuben. They had been brothers-in-arms for over one hundred years and were as close as brothers born. He had never once heard uncertainty in Reuben's tone and he didn't like what he heard now. He raised a hand to scratch at his jaw thoughtfully.

'These things are technically incidental to our mission,' he said coolly, 'but we should complete what we have started. It may retain some memory, some thought or knowledge about those we seek.' He turned to the Prognosticator, who was standing slightly apart from the others. 'Brother-Prognosticator, much as it pains me to ask you, would you divine what you can from this thing?'

'As you command.' Bhehan lowered his head in acquiescence and moved to kneel beside the dead alien. The sight of its bloodied and mangled body turned his stomach – not because of the gore, but because of its very inhuman nature. He took a few deep, steadying breaths and laid a hand on what remained of the creature's head.

'I sense nothing easily recognisable,' he said, after a time. He glanced up at Reuben. 'The damage to its cerebral cortex is too great. Virtually all of its residual psychic energies are gone.' His voice held the slightest hint of reproach.

Gileas glanced sideways at Reuben, who smiled a little ruefully. 'It was you who suggested I remove its head to be sure it was dead, Gil,' he said, the use of the diminutive form of his sergeant's name reflecting the close friendship the two shared. 'I merely used my initiative and modified your suggestion.'

The sergeant's lips twitched slightly, but he said nothing. Bhehan moved his hand to the other side of the being's head without much optimism.

A flash of something. Distant memories of hunting…

As swiftly as it had been there, the sensation dwindled and died. Instinctively, and with the training that had granted him the ability to understand such things, Bhehan knew all that was needed to be known.

'An animal,' said Bhehan. 'Nothing more. Separated from the pack.

Old, perhaps.' He shook his head and looked up at Gileas. 'I'm sorry, brother-sergeant. I cannot give you any more than that.'

'No matter, Prognosticator,' said Gileas, grimly. 'It was worth a try.' He surveyed the surrounding area a little more, looking vaguely disappointed. 'This is a waste of time and resources,' he said eventually. 'I propose that we regroup, head back the way we came, destroy the ship in case it is, or contains, what the eldar were seeking, and get back to the landing site. We'll have time to kill, but I'm sure I can think of something to keep us occupied.'

'Not another one of your impromptu training sessions, Gileas,' objected Reuben with good-natured humour. 'Don't you ever get tired of coming up with new and interesting ways to get us to fight each other?'

'No,' came the deadpan reply. 'Never.'

Bhehan allowed the Reckoners to discuss their next course of action amongst themselves, waiting for the inevitable request to see what the runes said. He kept his attention half on their conversation, but the other half was caught by something in the dirt beside the dead alien's head. From his kneeling position, he reached over and scooped it up in one blue-gauntleted hand.

Barely two inches across, the deep wine-red stone was attached to a sturdy length of vine: a crudely made necklace. Bhehan's brow furrowed slightly as he glanced again at the corpse. It had felt feral and not even remotely intelligent, but then most of its synapses had been shredded by Reuben's bolter. Putting a hand back against its head yielded nothing. He was feeling more psychic emanations from the trees themselves than from this once-living being. Of course, the charm may not have belonged to the animal; perhaps it had stolen it. It was impossible to know for sure without employing full regression techniques. For that option, however, the thing needed to be alive.

The young Prognosticator brought the stone closer to his face to study it more intently, and another flash of memory seared through his mind. This one, though, was not the primal force of nature that he had felt from the dead xenos. This was something else entirely. Sudden flashes emblazoned themselves across his mind. Shadowy images wavered in his mind's eye, images that were intangible and hard to make out.

A shape. Male? Maybe. Human? Definitely not. Eldar. It was eldar. Wearing the garments of those known as warlocks. It was screaming, cowering.

It was dying. It was being attacked. A huge shape loomed over it, blocking out the sunlight...

'Prognosticator!'

Gileas's sudden bark brought the psyker out of the trance that he had not even realised he'd fallen into. He stared at the sergeant, the brief look of displacement on his face swiftly replaced by customary attentiveness.

'My apologies, brother-sergeant,' he said, shaking his mind clear of the visions. He got to his feet and stood straight-backed and alert, the images in his mind already faded. 'Here, I found this. It might give us some clue to what happened here.' He proffered the stone and Gileas stared at it with obvious distrust before taking it. He held it up at arm's length and studied it as it spun, winking in the sunlight.

'I've seen something like this before,' he said thoughtfully. 'The eldar wear them. Something to do with their religion, isn't it?'

'In honesty, I'm not completely sure,' replied Bhehan. 'I haven't had an opportunity to study one this closely. We, I mean the Chapter's Prognosticators, have many theories...' Seeing that the sergeant wasn't even remotely interested in theories, the psyker tailed off and accepted the object back from Gileas, who seemed more than pleased to be rid of it.

'If this is an eldar item,' said Gileas, grimly, 'then it's not too much of a leap of faith to believe that they've been present, or *are* present, on this planet. Increases the odds of that wreck being eldar and also that this planet may well have been their ultimate destination.'

The others concurred. The sergeant nodded abruptly. 'Then we definitely return to the ship and we destroy the whole thing. We make damn sure that they find nothing when they get here. Are we in accord?'

He glanced around and all nodded agreement. They clasped their hands together, one atop the other. Gileas looked sideways at Bhehan who, surprised by this unspoken invitation into the brotherhood of the squad, laid his hand on the others.

'Brothers all,' said Gileas, and the squad responded in kind.

'Fetch Wulfric back,' commanded Gileas. Tikaye nodded and voxed through to his battle-brother.

There was no reply.

'Wulfric, report,' Tikaye said into the vox, even as they began heading in the direction he had taken, weapons at the ready.

THEY MOVED DEEPER still into the jungle.

It was rapidly becoming far more densely packed, the vibrant green of the trees and plants creating an arboreal tunnel through which the five giants marched. Despite the overriding concern at their companion's whereabouts, the Space Marines welcomed the moment's relief from the constant squinting brought about by standing in the direct sunlight. As they made their way with expediency through the trees, light filtered through to mottle the dirt and scrub of the forest floor. Parched dust marked their passage, rising up in clouds around their feet.

'Brother Wulfric, report.' Tikaye continually tried the vox, but there was still nothing. Bhehan extended the range of his psychic powers, reaching for Wulfric's awareness, and instead received something far worse. His nostrils flared as a familiar coppery scent assailed him, and he turned slightly to the west.

'It's this way,' he said, with confidence.

'You are sure, brother?'

'Aye, brother-sergeant.'

'Jalonis, lead the way. I will bring up the rear.' Gileas, with the practical and seemingly effortless ease that he did everything, organised the squad. They had travelled a little further into the trees when a crack as loud as a whip caused them all to whirl on the spot, weapons readied and primed. The first fall of raindrops announced that it was nothing more than the arrival of the tropical storm. The thunder that had barely been audible in the distance was now directly above them.

The vox in Gileas's ear crackled with static and he tapped at it irritably. These atmospherics caused such frustrating communication problems. It had never failed to amaze Gileas, a man raised as a savage in a tribe for whom the pinnacle of technological advancement was the longbow, that a race who could genetically engineer super-warriors still couldn't successfully produce robust communications.

More static flared, then Jalonis's voice broke through. It was a scattered message, breaking up as the Space Marine spoke, but Gileas had no trouble extrapolating its meaning.

'... Jal... found Wulfric... t's left... him anyway. Dead ah... maybe... dred yards or so.'

Gileas acknowledged tersely and increased his pace.

Another crack of thunder reverberated so loudly that Gileas swore he could feel his teeth rattle in his jaw. The light drizzle gave way rapidly to huge, fat drops of rain. The canopy of the trees did its best to repel them, but ultimately the persisting rain triumphed. The bare heads of the Silver Skulls were soaked swiftly. Gileas's hair, wild and untamed at the best of times, soon turned to unruly curls that clung tightly around his face and eyes. He put his helmet back on, not so much to keep his head dry, but more to reduce the risk of his vision being impaired by his own damp hair getting in the way.

The moment he put his helmet back on, he knew what he would find when he reached Jalonis. The information feed scrolling in front of his eyes told him everything that he needed to know. A sense of foreboding stole over him, and he murmured a prayer to the Emperor under his breath.

The precipitation did nothing to dispel the steaming heat of the forest, but merely landed on the dusty floor where it was immediately swallowed into the ground as though it had never been.

'Sergeant Ur'ten.'

Jalonis stood several yards ahead, a look of grim resignation on his face. 'You should come and see this. I'm afraid it's not pretty.'

Jalonis, a practical man by nature, had ever been the master of understatement. What Gileas witnessed as he looked down caused his choler to rise immediately. With the practice of decades, he carefully balanced his humours.

Wulfric's armour had been torn away and discarded, scattered around the warrior's corpse. The Space Marine's throat had been ripped apart with speed and ferocity, which had prevented him from alerting his battle-brothers or calling for aid.

The thorax had been slit from neck to groin, exposing his innards. In this heat, even with the steady downpour of rain, the stink of death was strong. The fused ribcage had been shattered, leaving Wulfric's vital organs clearly visible, slick with blood and mucus. Or at least, what remained of them.

Where Wulfric's primary and secondary hearts should have been was instead a huge cavity. Gileas stared for long moments, his conditioning and training assisting his deductive capability. Whatever had attacked Wulfric had gone for the throat first, rendering his dead brother mute. It had torn through his armour like it was shoddy fabric rather than ceramite and plasteel. The assailant, or more likely the assailants, had then proceeded to shred the skin like parchment and defile Wulfric's body.

The details were incidental. One of Gileas's brothers was dead. More than that, one of his closest brothers was dead. For that, there would be hell to pay.

'Take stock,' he said to Tikaye, who whilst not an Apothecary was the squad's primary field medic. 'I want to know what has been taken.' His voice was steady and controlled, but the rumble and pitch of the words hinted strongly at the anger bubbling just under the surface.

The stoic Tikaye moved to Wulfric and began to examine the body. He murmured litanies of death fervently under his breath as he did so.

'You understand, of course,' said Gileas, his voice low and menacing, 'this means someone... or *something* is going to regret crossing my path this day.'

The falling rain, evaporating in the intense heat, caused steam to rise in ethereal tendrils from the ground. It loaned even more of a macabre aspect to the scene, and the coils partially swathed Wulfric's body as they rose. It was a cheap mockery of the tradition of lighting memorial pyres on the Silver Skulls' burial world and it did little to ease their collective grief and rage.

Staring down at their fallen brother, each murmuring his own personal litany, the remaining Silver Skulls were fierce of countenance, ready for a fight in response to this atrocity.

'Several of his implants are gone,' came Tikaye's voice from the ground. There was barely masked outrage in his tone.

'Gone? What does *gone* mean?'

'Taken, brother-sergeant. The biscopea, Larraman's organ, the secondary and primary hearts, and from what I can make out, his progenoid is gone, too. I'd suggest that whoever or whatever did this knew what they wanted and took it. It's too clean to be an arbitrary or random coincidence.'

'You said they were animals, Prognosticator.' Gileas couldn't keep the accusation out of his tone. 'That conflicts directly with what Brother Tikaye suggests. One of you is wrong.' Bhehan shook his head.

'The creature we found *was* an animal,' he countered. 'That was before I found the stone, however. It's possible that it had been wearing it as some sort of decoration. I acknowledge that may potentially suggest intelligence. I–'

'I did not ask for excuses, neither did I ask for a lecture. The runes, Prognosticator.' Gileas's voice was barbed. The sergeant had a reputation amongst the Silver Skulls as a great warrior, a man who would charge headlong into the fray without hesitation and also as a man who did not suffer fools gladly, particularly when his wrath was tested. Da'chamoren, the name he had brought with him from his tribe, translated literally as 'Son of the Waxing Moon'. Gileas's power and resilience had always seemed to grow proportionately to his rising fury.

It was a fitting name.

'Yes, sir,' Bhehan replied, suitably chastened by the change in the sergeant's attitude. Without further comment, he commenced another Sighting. He felt a moment's uncertainty, but didn't dwell on it. At first, nothing came to him and he could not help but wonder if he was going to experience what his psychic brethren termed the 'Deep Dark', a moment of complete psychic blindness. Prognosticators considered this to be a sign that they had somehow fallen from the Emperor's grace. Bhehan had tasted the sensation once before and it had left a bitter flavour of ash in his mouth. He firmly set aside all thoughts of failure and closed his eyes. The Emperor was with them, he asserted firmly. Had He not already communicated His will through His loyal servant?

Reassured, his mental equilibrium ceased its churning and settled again. Bhehan allowed the reading of the runes to draw him. The stones served well as a focus for his powers, helping him to draw in all the psychic echoes that flitted around this charnel house like ghosts. Each Prognosticator found their own focus; some, like Bhehan, chose runes whilst others divined the Emperor's will through a tarot.

'The perpetrators of this butchery… I sense that they want something from us. To learn, perhaps? To understand how we are put together.' The Prognosticator's eyes were still closed, his voice barely more than a whisper. 'Why? If they were animals, they would have just torn the flesh from his bones. They have not. They have intelligence, yes, great intelligence… or at least… no. Not all of them. Just one, perhaps? A leader of sorts?' The questioning was entirely rhetorical and nobody answered or interrupted him during the stream of consciousness. The rain drummed on their armour, creating a background rhythm of its own.

Bhehan's hand closed around the eldar stone still in his hand. To his relief, a flood of warmth suffused him, a sensation he had long equated as the prelude to a vision. No Deep Dark for him, then. His powers were intact. The feeling of relief was quickly replaced by one of intense dislike as he sensed a new presence in his mind.

They know what you are because of us. Because of what we know. The gift unintentionally given.

The words were perfectly sharp and audible, but the image of the being who spoke them was not. Tall and willowy, the apparition shimmered before his closed eyelids like an imprint of the sun burned onto his retina.

They absorbed what we were, what we are. They seek to do the same to you through nothing more than a primitive urge to survive, to evolve. To change. Is this not the instinct that drives us all? Aspiration to greatness? A need to be better than we were?

Bhehan, made rational and steady through years of training, concentrated on the image.

You are eldar. He did not speak the words aloud. There was no need to.

I was eldar. Now I am nothing more than a ghost, a faint remnant of what once was.

I will not speak to you, xenos.

Such arrogance as this brought my own brothers and our glorious sister to their end. It will be your undoing, mon-keigh.

Bhehan sensed a great sigh, like the last exhalation of a dying man, and as rapidly as the spectre had materialised inside his mind, it was gone. With a sharp intake of breath, Bhehan's eyes snapped open.

'We should not linger,' he said, slightly unfocussed. 'We should take our brother and we should go.'

'Is this what the Fates suggest?'

'No,' said Bhehan, hesitating only momentarily. 'It is what *I* feel we should do.'

Gileas practically revered the majesty of the Prognosticators. Divine will or not, he would never question a Prognosticator's intuition. He nodded.

'The will of a Prognosticator and the will of the Fates are entwined as one. We will do as you say.'

Reuben stepped forwards. 'Perhaps…' he began. 'Perhaps we should not. Not yet.'

'Explain.' Gileas shot a glance at Reuben.

'We interrupted them. The aliens. We could lure them back out in the open.'

'Reuben, are you suggesting that we use our dead brother as *bait*?' Gileas didn't even bother keeping the disgust out of his tone. 'I can't believe you would even entertain such a thought.'

'Bait,' echoed Bhehan, his eyes widening. 'Bait. Yes, that's it. Bait!' He drew the force axe he wore across his back. 'That's exactly what he is.'

'Prognosticator? You surely aren't agreeing to this ridiculous scheme?'

'No! For *us*, sergeant. He's been left here to lure *us* out.'

Another echo of thunder rolled around the skies overhead in accompaniment to this grim pronouncement. The rain had slowed once again to a steady *drip-drip-drip*. It pooled briefly in the vast, scoop-like leaves of the trees and splashed to the ground, throwing up billows of dust before evaporating permanently.

None of the Reckoners other than Bhehan had psychic capability, but all of them could sense the sudden shift in the air, sense the threat hiding somewhere.

Just waiting.

'Keep your weapons primed,' snapped Gileas, his thumb hovering over the activation stud of his chainsword. 'Be ready for anything.'

'I sense three psychic patterns,' offered the Prognosticator, his hands tight around the hilt of the force axe. 'Different directions, all approaching.'

'Only three?' Gileas said. 'You are sure of this?'

'Yes.'

'Three of them, five of us. It will be a hard fight, my brothers, but we will prevail. We are the Silver Skulls.' Gileas's voice swelled with fierce pride. 'We *will* prevail.' Jalonis and Bhehan pulled their helmets back on at the sergeant's words.

With the squad at full battle readiness, Gileas turned his attentions to the reams of data which began scrolling in front of his eyes. He blink-clicked rapidly, filtering out anything not pertinent to the moment of battle, including the winking iconograph that had previously represented Wulfric's lifesigns. The brief glimpse of that particular image served as a visible reminder of the desire for requital, however, and fire-stoked battle lust raced through the sergeant's veins.

'They are coming,' Bhehan breathed through the vox.

Gileas made a point to double-check the functionality of his jump pack at the Prognosticator's warning. He diverted his attention to the relevant streams of data that fed the device's information into his power armour, and was satisfied to note that it was at approximately seventy per cent. Certainly not representative of its full, deadly performance, but good enough for a battle of this size. He ordered the rest of the squad to do the same. If these animals were seeking a fight, then the Reckoners would willingly deliver. They would deliver a fight and they would deliver what they gave best and what had earned them their name.

A reckoning.

For most Space Marines, engaging an enemy was all about honour to the Chapter, pride in the company or loyalty to the Imperium. Sometimes, like now, it was about righteous vengeance. Occasionally, it was simple self-defence. For Sergeant Gileas Ur'ten it was about all of these things. Above and beyond all else, however, it was the thrill that came with the anticipation of a fight. The burst of adrenaline and increased blood flow as his genetically enhanced body geared up to beget the hand of retribution that was the rightful role of all the Adeptus Astartes.

Another moment of silence followed and then a tumult of screaming voices rose as one. It preceded the charge of a slew of enemies from the undergrowth, each as massive as the one they had already encountered. Gileas thumbed the activation stud of his chainsword and it roared into deadly life, the weapon's fangs eager to feast.

The sudden appearance of so many of the xenos caused a moment's pandemonium, but that was all it was: a single moment during which the Assault squad formed a tight-knit, ceramite-clad wall of stoic defence. There was vengeance to be taken and they were ready to take it.

Each of the xenos radiated a palpable desire to kill. They walked upright, although with a certain stumbling gait that implied they may not always have done so. It seemed probable that their hind legs hadn't been used in this way for long. As though confirming these suspicions, three of them dropped to all fours.

As they prowled closer to the Space Marines, their movements became snake-like, a sinuous flow that allowed them to undulate across the uneven ground with hypnotic ease and disconcerting speed.

The skin of one creature's mouth drew back to reveal a double set of razor-sharp teeth. It didn't take much of a stretch of the imagination to work out how it was that the xenos had removed internal organs so swiftly and efficiently. Every single one of those teeth looked capable of tearing through flesh and muscle with ease. The attackers moved as a unit, almost as though they were as tightly trained and drilled as the Adeptus Astartes themselves.

A rapid headcount told the Silver Skulls that there were nine of them, and with determination every last one of the Assault squad entered the fray. Bhehan, his force axe at the ready in his right hand, raised the other, palm outstretched in front of him, ready to cast a psychic shield around his battle-brothers. The crystals in the psychic hood attached to the gorget of his armour began to pulsate as he channelled the deadly power of the warp, ready to unleash it at a moment's notice.

Gileas and Tikaye both charged the alien on the far right with their chainswords shrieking bloody murder. Jalonis and Reuben levelled their bolters and began firing.

Fury descended on the previously silent jungle. Orders were shouted, and the cries of alien life and the indignant, defensive answering retorts of the squad's weapons flooded the surrounding area in a cacophony of sound.

Gileas drove his chainsword deeper into the flesh of the alien he was fighting, putting all his strength into the blow. The thing lashed out at him, howling and chittering. Talons flashed like deadly knives before his helmet, but he ducked and weaved with easy agility, avoiding its blows. As far as he was concerned, as long as it remained affixed to the end of his chainsword, it was a suitable distance away from him and was dying at the same time. An additional bonus.

Reuben coaxed his weapon into life, discharging a hail of bolter shells at the onslaught. Beside him, Bhehan swept his hand forwards and round in a semi-circular arc, almost as though he were simply thrusting the xenos away from him. The one directly facing him stumbled backwards and howled its displeasure.

With a grunt of effort, Gileas yanked the chainsword out of the alien's flesh and swung it round, almost severing one of the wicked, scythe-like talons from its hand. He moved in harmony with the weapon as though it was merely an extension of his own body. Watching Gileas Ur'ten fight was aesthetically pleasing; even in the heavy power armour of the Adeptus Astartes he was agile, lithe and, more than that, he was a master at what he did. He enacted his deadly dance of death with practiced aplomb.

Tikaye, engaged as he was with his own opponent, did not immediately notice that another was prowling towards him. It reached out with a clawed hand and swept it towards the Space Marine. It caught him between his helmet and breast plate, and with a sudden display of strength sent him flying backwards. He landed heavily with an audible crunch of ceramite at Bhehan's feet. The Prognosticator, briefly distracted from gathering force for his next attack, glanced down at his battle-brother.

Within seconds, Tikaye was back on his feet, his weapon back in his hand, and he tore into the nearest enemy with a vengeance, letting his chainsword do the talking.

One of the three beasts that had been slithering towards the psyker leapt suddenly with a yowl of triumph. Instinctively, Bhehan trusted to the power of his force axe rather than his psychic ability and channelled his rage and righteousness into its exquisitely forged blade. The hidden runes carved deep into its metal heart kindled and throbbed with an otherworldly glow.

Years of training and dedication to the arts of war at the hands of the masters on Varsavia automatically took over and Bhehan planted his feet firmly on the ground, prepared for the moment of impact. The axe sang through the air towards its target, a low whine audibly marking its trajectory as it swept towards the enemy.

To his consternation, the force axe passed right through the alien's body. The unexpected follow-through of his own swing unbalanced him and he fell to one knee. He scrambled immediately back to his feet, ready to resume combat, only to realise that the thing was gone, utterly vanished before his very eyes. All that remained was a strange psychic residue, streamers of barely visible non-corporeal form that were consigned fleetingly to the air, and then to nothing more than memory.

'Something isn't right here,' he voxed, puzzlement implicit in every syllable.

'Really, Prognosticator? You think so?' The pithy reply from Gileas was harsher than perhaps it might otherwise have been, but given that the sergeant was locked in a bloody battle to the death with a creature seemingly quite capable of slicing through him like he was made of mud, it was understandable. 'Any chance that you'd care to elaborate on this outstanding leap of logic?'

Clenching his force axe with an iron grip, Bhehan whirled to intercept another xenos which was catapulting itself at him. He swung the weapon again and once more his blow met with no resistance.

He had sensed three minds. No more, no less. With the two illusory attackers dispelled, they were now facing seven.

'They are not all real, my brothers,' he stated urgently. 'Only three of them present a real threat.'

'They feel real to me,' responded Jalonis, who had just been viciously swept into the trunk of one of the vast trees. The armour plating across his back was cracked. His helmet flashed loss of integrity warnings at him and, ignoring them, he resumed his fighting. One of Reuben's arms hung limp at his side as his body worked swiftly to fix the damage that had been caused to it.

Gileas and Tikaye had fallen into battle harmony with each other and were battering determinedly at one of the enemy. As one, they both fired their jump packs, performing a vertical aerial leap that caused the xenos to snap its head up sharply, its eyes fixed on the now-airborne targets. The range of the jump packs was severely limited due to the tree cover, but they remained aloft, well out of its reach.

It dropped its long body low, coiling like a spring and readying itself to launch. Bhehan, thinking swiftly, took the opportunity to blast a psychic attack into the creature's mind.

It did not vanish.

'That one!' he shouted into the vox, gesticulating ferociously at the xenos and alerting his airborne brothers. 'That one, brother-sergeant! It's solid.'

The sergeant nodded brusquely. He had no desire to understand the whys or hows of the situation. Bhehan's words were little more than meaningless background noise to him at this moment. Only the solution was of importance at this stage. Only the battle mattered.

In full synchronicity, Gileas and Tikaye both bore their full weights downwards to land on the xenos beneath them. Close-quarters combat was one thing. During such a pitched battle, a being could fight back and stand a chance of being a danger. Being crushed beneath the full might of two power armour-clad Space Marines was something else entirely and not something so easily eluded.

The alien, anticipating its own demise, wailed in murderous rage for a few seconds before both Space Marines plummeted solidly onto it. Bones crunched and arterial blood spurted from puncture wounds caused by the creature's exoskeleton shredding through its flesh. Crude brutality, perhaps, but effective nonetheless.

Devoid of their source, two more of the psychic projections immediately melted into the ether. Gileas and Tikaye fired their jump packs again and blasted grimly towards the rest of the fray. Bhehan, witnessing the scene, paused momentarily as realisation bloomed.

It was suddenly so clear to the Prognosticator. So very, very simple.

'They are manipulating your minds! Brother-Sergeant Ur'ten, you must listen to me! They have extremely strong psychic capability. My mind should be awash with all these things, but it is not!' The Prognosticator bit down on the excitement and forced his mind to focus. He knew he was making little sense and that was no use to anybody.

He had removed two of the illusory aliens by passing his force axe through their psychically generated forms. With the death of one of the true alien forms, two more had dispersed.

From the nine who had attacked, the Silver Skulls now faced four. If Bhehan's theory proved correct, only two of them were real. Kill those, his theory suggested, and their intangible counterparts would vanish; eliminate the phantasms and only the real xenos would remain. It seemed that whatever trick they were playing with the squad's minds meant that they were unable to tell them apart. For them, the two decoy enemies were each as solid and real as the two who were weaving the illusion. They seemed immune to all but extrasensory attack. Only he could do anything about it.

His thought processes were lightning-fast and Bhehan began to gather his psychic might once more. The most decisive way he could think of to end this situation was to crush the opposing will of the xenos with a psychic flood of the Emperor's righteous fury. Whilst the melee had been tight and kept largely confined due to the jungle's enforced restrictions, it was still a reasonably large area. The desired result would be effective, but it would tax his constitution considerably.

It did not matter. His gift might temporarily be exhausted, but he was a fully trained battle-brother. He would never be totally defenceless. With an exultant cry, he flung both hands out in front of him. His voice carrying into the jungle with strident fervour, Bhehan called forth the powers of the warp.

With a fizzing crackle, a massive burst of energy lit his hood up in a flicker of blue sparks. The resultant shock wave not only targeted the xenos, but also caused the four battling Space Marines to pause briefly as their own minds were assailed from no longer one, but two directions. For them, a mental battle for supremacy took place as the will of the Prognosticator worked to force out the intruders.

Bhehan was trained, disciplined and strong. The aliens were clever, certainly, but they fought on instinct and did not truly know how to counter such a devastating blow to their defences. For a heartbeat,

Bhehan could feel his advantage slipping as the barb of the aliens' mental hooks worked in deeper. The silent struggle continued and then abruptly, he felt the fingers of deception release their hold and fall away.

Two of the attackers instantly disappeared. One screamed with fury and began to lope away into the undergrowth. Bhehan, staggering slightly from the sheer potency of his attack, automatically reached out for its mind. Instantly, he was filled with a sense of pain and, even better as far as he was concerned, of fear. It was injured, probably dying. It was unimportant. The final alien was also mortally wounded. It would be the work of but moments to end its foul existence.

'Good work, Bhehan,' said Gileas, his breathing heavy through the vox channel.

The remaining creature slunk around the Assault squad, fluidity implicit in its every movement. Before any of them could open fire or attack, the xenos reared back, a crest-like protrusion standing up on top of its head, and emitted a screech that was staggeringly high-pitched. Had the auto-senses in the warriors' helmets not instantly reacted, it would surely have ruptured eardrums. In the event, it achieved nothing.

The xenos clamped its jaws tightly shut and stared with renewed malevolence at its enemy as it realised the futility of its last defences. Without hesitation Gileas roared the final order, his voice like the crack of doom.

'Open fire! Suffer not the alien to live!'

With resounding cries that echoed those sentiments most emphatically, bolter fire razored through the air and tore into the alien's armour-hard exterior. Every last bolt was unloaded into it, spent shells rapidly littering the ground. Blood fountained out of the wounds in the xenos's body, the sheer force of it suggesting they had successfully hit something vital, and Gileas found renewed vigour in the scent of its imminent demise. A sudden, desperate desire to eliminate this foul abomination once and for all took hold.

With a roar of determination, he took out his bolt pistol and aimed it with deadly, pinpoint accuracy between the thing's eyes. Reuben discarded his spent weapon, taking his own pistol from its holster. Falling in beside his sergeant, he stepped forwards with him as they fired together.

Every bolt that burst against the alien's skull caused its head to snap back and drew further eardrum-splitting screeches.

Bhehan responded with a psychic blow, although due to his exhaustion, the effect was greatly diminished. Heedless of this fact, he focused all of his fury, sense of retribution and hatred and flung it towards the xenos with a practiced heft of his mental acuity. He was drained, but it provided a useful diversion. The enemy hesitated, crouching low, ready to spring at Reuben. It moved with uncanny alacrity, propelling itself with deadly grace for something that should surely have been dead by now towards the Space Marine, bearing him to the ground. It reared up, blood and saliva flying from its jaws as it prepared to strike.

'No!'

Bhehan brandished his force axe. He urged a ripple of power across its surface and bounded the short distance to his fallen brother. With an easy, accurate swing, he buried the axe deep in the alien's chest.

It stumbled back, licks of warp-lightning crackling across its carapace. It writhed on the ground in agony for a few moments and then was still.

A silence fell, disturbed only by the heavy breathing of everyone present.

Gileas lowered his pistol and nodded in grim satisfaction. 'It is done,' he said. 'Status report.'

Apart from several light wounds and Jalonis's fractured backplate, the squad had escaped almost completely unscathed from the encounter. Bhehan's weariness showed in the Prognosticator's posture and in his voice as he communicated via the vox, but he had expended a remarkable amount of energy in a very short space of time. The strength of will it must have taken for each of the xenos to maintain replicas had been quite the barrier for him to overcome. It gave him great satisfaction to acknowledge that not only had he overcome it but had also emerged triumphant.

'Are you well, Bhehan?' Gileas addressed the psyker directly, his tone brusque and formal. 'Do you require time to gather yourself?'

'No, brother! I do not "require time". I am tired, but I am not some weakling straight out of his chamber. I am fine.' The indignation in the young Prognosticator's voice put a smile on Gileas's face beneath the helmet. He may be young, but Bhehan already had the true fire of a Silver Skull with many more years of service behind him. The Emperor willing, the youth would undoubtedly go far.

'Puts you in mind of yourself, does he, brother?'

At his side, Reuben murmured the words softly enough for only the sergeant to hear. The squad commander's smile deepened.

'Just a little, aye.' Gileas leaned down slightly and wiped his bloodied chainsword on the ground. He stared up at the sky visible through the canopy. Daylight was beginning to give way to the navy-blue of what he had always known as the gloaming. The Thunderhawk would return just after dusk. For now, there was one thing only left to do.

'Brother-Prognosticator,' he said, turning to Bhehan. 'Would you do us the great honour of claiming the squad's trophy from this battle?'

Bhehan understood the largesse implicit in the gesture and was deeply flattered by the offer. He made the sign of the aquila and bowed his head in respect to the sergeant. He stepped up and raised his force axe above his head.

'The honour would be mine, brother-sergeant. In the name of the Silver Skulls, for the glory of Chapter Master Argentius and for the memory of our fallen Brother Wulfric, I claim your head as my prize. Let those who walk the halls of our forefathers gaze upon your countenance and give thanks for your end.' The axe flashed through the air and struck the neck of the dead xenos.

The moment the head and the body parted, there was a hazy shimmering and the unknown alien's body was replaced by something entirely more recognisable. Bhehan realised it first, but the others were not very far behind him.

'An illusion,' the Prognosticator breathed. 'It's woven a psychic disguise around itself!'

'No. No, that's impossible,' countered Jalonis, perturbation in his voice. 'That can't be correct. Kroot don't have psychic abilities.'

Indeed, the headless body on the ground was most definitely that of a kroot. It had the same wiry, sinewy build and avian-like features that matched every image that had ever been pict-flashed at them through doctrination tapes and training sessions. Yet despite its instantly familiar form, there were subtle differences. It varied from what was presumably the norm in a number of ways, not least of which was the most obvious which Jalonis had just voiced.

It was imbued with psychic powers. Unheard of, at least in the Silver Skulls' experience. Reports and research had never once suggested that the kroot, the fierce, mercenary warrior troops regularly employed by tau armies, were psychic. Moreover, this kroot wore no harness, carried no weapon. It was far more primitive than what they expected of such beings. An evolutionary throwback maybe, but one in possession of something perhaps far more deadly than a rifle or any other kind of physical weapon.

'A feral colony home world?' Jalonis made the suggestion first. 'A breed of kroot who have taken a different genetic path to their brethren?'

Gileas frowned. 'It is said that these things eat the flesh of their enemies, that they have the ability to assimilate their DNA. There have certainly been reports that this planet once sported animal life. It is surely not unreasonable to guess that the kroot have systematically destroyed whatever may have existed on this planet.'

He considered the dead beasts. 'These things, at least… the things that look like they did before we exposed the truth… are all we have encountered.' A thought occurred to the sergeant. 'When Reuben shot that other one in the head, it did not change its shape or form, did it?'

'The cerebral connection remained intact,' Bhehan commented absently. 'Brother Reuben obliterated its brain, yes. However, he didn't disconnect the spinal cord. Nerve impulses continued to flow after death. The mental disguise it wove remained stable until full brain death. We didn't stay there long enough to witness it change back.'

'Aye,' said Reuben, remembering the unnatural need to ignore the alien. Bhehan would have been better equipped to avoid that psychic shielding.

Something was niggling at the back of Bhehan's mind, but he couldn't quite put his finger on it. It danced tantalisingly outside his grasp and he reached out for it.

'Psychic kroot... This is a vital discovery for us. They cannot be suffered to live. This planet must be cleansed.' Tikaye offered up his opinion.

Gileas glanced up at Bhehan and remembered the deep red stone that he had found. 'Bhehan, you have a theory, I suspect. Tell me.'

Bhehan nodded slowly. 'There are, to the best of our knowledge, no psychic kroot. Not any that we've met before,' he hypothesised. 'However, what if it were to assimilate a psychic species? Say... the eldar?' He held up the red stone so that all the battle-brothers could see it. 'What would stop it from killing and eating one of the eldar? What would prevent it from the freedom to filter out the required genetic strands that would give it the most useful result?'

'Surely it must take several generations for a kroot to assimilate such powers?' The query came from Tikaye, and the others considered his words.

'We don't know what constitutes a kroot generation. We have no idea how old that ship is. We don't even know if it *is* an eldar ship. Perhaps it is a kroot vessel. Maybe they arrived before the eldar, maybe after.' Gileas's voice was grim. His patience was already strained to breaking point. 'It is without question, brothers, that both those xenos races have tainted this planet one way or the other. There are far too many unknown variables, and I have little interest in philosophical postulation about which came first.'

He put his chainsword back into its scabbard and reloaded the chamber of his pistol.

'Brother Bhehan,' he said, without another glance, 'collect the trophy. We will take Wulfric's body to the predetermined extraction coordinates and we will leave. This must be reported to Captain Meyoran. I do not presume to second-guess his actions on hearing the news, but I would not want to be on this planet when he found out.'

The Prognosticator tucked the eldar stone into the pouch with his runes and moved to the dead kroot. The very thought of such a being filled him with passionate hatred: a foul crossbreed of two xenos races with the most lethal features of both. It was an atrocity of the highest order, an abomination that had no right to exist. Yet here it was, albeit not for much longer once the Silver Skulls returned to the *Silver Arrow*.

The sudden truth of what the murderer had wanted with Wulfric's body hit the Prognosticator head-on. A kroot, with the psychic abilities and memories of an eldar, would have had some knowledge of Adeptus Astartes physiology, even if only as a basic, barely recalled memory. Imagine, then, a kroot, with the psychic abilities and memories of an eldar... and the strength and resilience of a Space Marine...

Bhehan straightened his shoulders and bent down to pick up the head of the kroot. Thanks to the Reckoners, such a thing would never come to pass.

What heat remained in the day began to sap steadily as the suns continued their slow descent towards the horizon. The air was thick with heat stored by the trees and the rocks. This, coupled with residual moisture from the rainstorm, left the air feeling thick and greasy.

The squad trampled through the trees for several more minutes, all senses on full alert. They had barely arrived at the extraction point when the general vox channel fizzed into life. The Thunderhawk would be in position in fifteen minutes.

Nocturnal life began to flood the jungle with a discordant symphony over which the approaching whine of the Thunderhawk could swiftly be heard. Once in situ, there was a hiss of servos and hydraulics and the front boarding ramp of the vessel opened, the light from within spilling out and bathing the jungle.

Gileas waited for the others to board before he joined them. He had always maintained that, as sergeant, it was his place to arrive first and leave last. He fired his jump pack, rose to the Thunderhawk and dropped to the floor with a clatter.

'All on board, Correlan. Give us a few moments to ensure that our fallen battle-brother is secure.'

'Understood. Good to have you back, sergeant.'

Gileas removed his helmet and ran his fingers through his hair. Already the words for his report to Captain Meyoran were forming clearly in his mind. They had been sent down to this planet for one thing and yet had found something entirely different and unexpected.

Bhehan remained standing at the edge of the landing ramp, staring down at the jungle. He reached into his pouch to draw a random rune and instead pulled out the eldar stone. Considering it thoughtfully, he indulged in a moment's wild curiosity as to what sort of portent the Emperor was sending him.

As his hand closed around it, he became aware of a strong push against the wards he had set in place, wards that had no doubt gone a long way towards allowing him to see through the kroot's duplicitous scheming. This mental touch was no wild and instinctual thing, though. This press against his defences was nearly as disciplined and practiced as his own. A sudden flicker of movement caught his eye.

At the jungle's edge, barely visible in the dusk and what remained of the light cast by the Thunderhawk, Bhehan saw it. A solitary figure. Tall, seemingly all whipcord muscle and sinew, the huge kroot stood boldly in direct sight of the Thunderhawk. To all intents and purposes it was little different to its kin, but it was not difficult to surmise that it was a more powerful or at least a more evolved strain of these twisted xenos. A cloak of stitched animal hide was slung around its shoulders and in one hand it held a crudely fashioned staff, from which hung feathers and trinkets of decoration. A number of stones also dangled from the staff, stones that looked remarkably like the very one in the psyker's hand.

He felt its vicious touch against his mind again and clamped the wards down tighter. The lesser kroot had been disorganised and fierce. This, though, was a calculated, scheming mind. This was a mind that would gladly extract the very soul of you and leave you to crumble to dust in its wake. It was barbed and brutal and uncannily self-aware.

The crystals on his psychic hood flickered, attracting the sergeant's attention.

'Brother-Prognosticator?' He moved to stand beside the younger warrior and his sharp eyes quickly made out what the psyker had seen.

'Throne of Terra!' he exclaimed and drew his pistol, ready to fire it at the alien. But by the time the weapon was out of its holster and in his hand, the kroot had gone, vanished into the jungle. Gileas lowered his weapon, his disappointment obvious.

Bhehan turned to the sergeant. His young face showed nothing of the vile revulsion he had felt at the kroot's mental challenge.

He felt one last, sickening touch on his mind and then the alpha, if indeed that had been what it was, let him go.

'This place needs to be purified,' said the psyker, fervently. 'To be cleansed of this filth.'

'It will be, brother,' acknowledged Gileas with absolute sincerity. As the gaping maw of the landing ramp finally sealed off the last sight of the Anceriosan jungle, he turned to Bhehan. 'It will be.'

WARHAMMER®

QUESTING KNIGHT

Anthony Reynolds

I

THE SILVER MOON of Mannslieb resembled a sickle blade hanging low in clear night sky. Patches of snow shone brightly beneath it, and while it was almost a month into spring, the wind whipping across the fields still held a touch of winter's bite. Hunched against the icy gale, two riders were making their weary progress along a muddy road, passing fields, abandoned hovels and isolated clumps of woodland.

They travelled in silence, one behind the other, offering no conversation. The only sound accompanying them was the steady clomping of hooves, the jingle of tack and the ghostly whispering of the wind.

The lead rider drew his travel-stained cloak tighter around his shoulders as the wind picked up. His features were completely hidden in the deep shadow of his hood, yet his eyes glinted in the moonlight. He rode a massive warhorse, over sixteen hands high at the shoulder, and had a large sword strapped across his back. In stark contrast to his companion, he rode in the languid manner of one who had spent most of his life in the saddle.

The second rider looked decidedly awkward, slumped in the saddle of a mange-ridden mule. The plodding beast was a picture of misery, head hanging almost to the ground as it trudged through the mud, laden with heavy packs and chests. This rider was shivering, for while he too wore a cloak, it was threadbare and moth-eaten. His head was nodding towards his chest. Losing the battle to keep his eyes open, he pitched sideways. He came awake with a muffled yelp, and after a brief, inelegant struggle, he hauled himself back upright.

'I will not wait for you if you fall off again, Chlod,' said the lead rider without turning. Chlod's hood had fallen back, exposing his brutish head. His hair was shaved short in a vain attempt to rid him of lice, and his eyes were piggish and uneven. He had only one ear, the other having been hacked off by a Norscan shaman years earlier, and his jutting jaw and heavy brow made him look like a simpleton. He glared at his master's back, and pulled a grotesque face.

'Make that face again, Chlod, and I will cut off your thumbs,' said his master.

'Sorry, my lord,' said Chlod, knowing that it was not some idle threat.

They continued along in silence once more. Chlod blinked the sleep out of his eyes and concentrated on his surroundings. He thought they looked vaguely familiar, but it was hard to say under the cover of darkness, and besides, it had been many years since last he had set foot in Bretonnia.

'Where are we, my lord?' he said at last.

'Home,' came the reply.

IT FELT STRANGE to say the word, thought Calard. *Home.*

Six long and difficult years had passed since he had left Castle Garamont. It felt like a lifetime. Six years ago he had taken up the grail quest, setting aside his lance and handing over the running of his castle and lands to his young cousin, Orlando, under the watchful eye of Baron Montcadas. Orlando had been just a boy when he had left, and by now he would be all but unrecognisable, on the cusp of becoming a man.

Calard had travelled the Old World and beyond seeking the Lady of the Lake, patron goddess of Bretonnia. Never in all that time had he spent more than a single night in one place, as per the decree of his oath, lest the Lady find him wanting.

Seeking the Lady's divine favour, he had bested creatures foul and murderous in the forests of the Empire, championed the oppressed in the burning lands of Araby far to the south, and battled alongside dwarf thanes against screaming hordes of greenskins far beneath the Worlds Edge Mountains. He had fought in a dozen duels of honour, one against a monstrous ogre tyrant. He had battled trolls upon the frozen oblast of Kislev, rescued a nobleman's daughter from sacrifice at the hands of a band of cultists beneath Altdorf, and emerged victorious from the famed Dance of Blades in the cutthroat city of Sartosa, off the coast of Estalia. Always, he chased the elusive presence of the goddess, yet always she led him further on. Now, she had brought him back to his homeland.

For months, Calard's dreams had been haunted by a recurring vision. Though he could not discern its full meaning, one thing was certain beyond any doubt; the goddess wished for him to return to Castle Garamont.

Calard reined his destrier in as he topped a tussocked rise. He drew his hood back. Gone was any hint of softness in his appearance, the years on the road having hardened his body and his mind. His eyes were dark and stern, and his cheeks rough with stubble. His hair was unwashed and hung past his shoulders, and his face was tanned. As alert and lean as a hunting wolf, he stared over the fields into the distance. His eyes narrowed.

'Master?' said Chlod, after a minute. 'What is it? I see nothing.'

'Exactly,' said Calard. 'Where are the lights of Castle Garamont? We should be able to see them on the horizon from here.'

The mighty fortress dominated the landscape for miles around, and its men-at-arms always kept its beacon fires burning through the hours of darkness. Nevertheless, the western horizon was ominously dark.

'Perhaps someone forgot to light them?' offered Chlod, but Calard shook his head.

'There is something wrong here,' he said, his eyes glinting fiercely in the moonlight. 'I'll move quicker alone. Follow after me, and keep to the road. Do not tarry.' Chlod nodded.

With a flick of the reins Calard urged his destrier into a canter and began riding towards the distant silhouette of Castle Garamont.

Mannslieb was just touching the horizon by the time he drew close. Dark and ominous, his family castle loomed above him. He circled around it in a wide arc, scouting for danger, but saw no sign of life other than a startled fox and a mated pair of ghost-owls hunting for prey. Calard's expression was grim. The scent of ash filled the air, and several of the castle's towers had collapsed. There were no sentries upon the walls, and no light in any of its windows. By all appearances, it was utterly abandoned, and had been left to ruin.

Nevertheless, Calard's experience had taught him to be cautious, and he completed his wide circuit around the castle before he began his approach from the south, angling towards Garamont's main gatehouse. Out of habit, he ensured that the wind was always in his face, so as to mask his scent from anything ahead.

The drawbridge was lowered and in a state of disrepair, and the rusted portcullis was up. Calard rode through the gatehouse into the courtyard beyond, staring around him at the ruin of his once great castle.

The keep was a burnt-out shell, its pale stone blackened with soot, and the wind howled mournfully through its empty halls. The stables were completely gone, with nothing but a few charred stumps and charcoal marking where they had stood. The north-east wall had partially col-lapsed, the debris scattered on the ground like grave markers.

Dismounting, Calard tied his warhorse to a fire-blackened post before climbing the stairs towards the keep. One of its doors was gone, while the other hung forlornly on one hinge, creaking in the breeze. Drawing his sword, he moved into the keep's dark interior.

He passed through its empty halls, his expression betraying none of his surging emotions. The inside of the keep was now open to the sky, the upper floors completely gone, and the stars were visible high overhead. A few thick supporting beams remained intact, but even these were charred and looked as though they might fall at any moment. The grand stone staircase that rose from the main entrance hall still stood, rendered pointless now that it climbed nowhere, and its steps were thick with ash.

Bones and scraps of armour protruded from the debris in one hall, and these Calard inspected carefully, turning them over in his hands in an attempt to discern what tragedy had befallen his home. Chipped bone showed evidence of heavy sword blows, and as he prowled deeper into the ruin, he found more evidence that a great battle had taken place here some years earlier.

Without conscious thought, Calard found himself in a small annex off the western wing, where the castle's shrine to the Lady was located. No divine power had protected it from the fire that had clearly ravaged the keep, and only a few jagged shards remained of its once beautiful stained-glass windows.

Something caught his eye, and Calard sheathed his sword and knelt before the fire-blackened altar. Half-buried amongst the rubble, a small statue of the Lady remained intact, lying on its side. It was covered in soot and chipped, but Calard picked it up and placed it reverently upon the altar. Closing his eyes, he began to pray.

There was noise outside and Calard was instantly on his feet, sword drawn. Moving silently and keeping to the shadows, he ghosted back through the ruined hall.

'Master?' called a voice.

'Silence, fool,' Calard hissed, stepping from the concealing darkness of the ruined keep.

'What happened here, master?' said Chlod. He half-climbed, half-fell from the saddle, and tied his mule to the post alongside Calard's steed.

Calard's eyes were locked on the ground at the peasant's feet.

'Stand still,' he ordered.

'What?' said Chlod, turning in Calard's direction.

'Be still! Stop moving,' said Calard, and the peasant froze. Calard moved forward, studying the ground intently. There were prints in the mud that he had not noticed earlier. 'Back away over there,' he said, gesturing.

'Shall I prepare you some food, master?' said Chlod, doing as he was bid.

'Fine, but no fire,' said Calard, not looking up. 'It would be seen for miles around.'

Careful not disturb the tracks, Calard crouched and studied them intently. They were difficult to read, for the prints were old and crossed over themselves time and again. Nevertheless, after several minutes Calard had identified the tracks of nine separate individuals and their steeds. He judged that they had made camp here a week ago, perhaps two.

His eyes narrowed when he came across one particularly clear hoof-print. The depth of the track indicated a horse heavily burdened, and the mark of its shoe was clear. In the centre of the imprint was the black-smith's mark. Calard recognised the heraldic device instantly.

'Sangasse,' Calard spat.

Standing, Calard marched towards his waiting warhorse, and called for Chlod to make ready to depart.

'Where do we go, master?' said the peasant as he hurriedly began packing up his pots.

'To visit an old neighbour,' said Calard, his voice filled with rage.

II

'MALORIC!'

The sky glowed with pre-dawn light. The peasants of Sangasse had been awake for hours, working the muddy fields. Many of them had halted their work as Calard had passed by, leaning on hoes and muttering under their breath. Calard had ignored them, his head held high and his face a grim mask.

Though they were neighbours, no knight of Garamont had set foot on Sangasse lands for over six generations without blood being spilt. The border between the two powerful noble families had long been disputed, changing hands countless times over the centuries. As Calard had ridden towards the border, his anger had deepened, for it was clear that the Sangasse family had claimed much of Garamont's land in his absence. By the time he arrived outside the gates of Castle Sangasse, a formidable bastion built atop a natural rocky bluff, his rage was incandescent.

'Maloric!' he bellowed again, wheeling his warhorse beneath him.

Nervous men-at-arms looked down from the castle walls at him. All of them were garbed in tabards bearing the heraldry of Maloric, the Earl of Sangasse. Maloric and Calard were of a similar age and had a long history of antagonism. Since childhood they had been raised to loathe one another, and even though they had fought side by side on dozens of occasions, even going so far as saving each other's lives on the field of battle, they could never be anything but rivals.

Chlod licked his lips. Hundreds of bowmen were stationed along the walls, and a pair of mighty trebuchets were positioned atop the gate-house. Scores of men-at-arms barred the way, shields locked together. Calard was undaunted, refusing to be intimidated by mere peasants.

'Show yourself, Maloric!' he shouted. 'Calard, Castellan of Garamont demands it!'

At last, a young knight appeared atop the gatehouse. His hair was dishevelled and he was still blinking the sleep out of his eyes. Calard did not recognise him.

'What is it you seek here, Garamont?' called the knight.

'Fetch your master, and be quick about it,' shouted Calard. 'I will not bandy words with you or any of Maloric's lackeys.'

Chlod winced as the knight's face reddened and several archers nocked arrows to strings.

'Speak to me in such a tone again, Garamont, and you will be cut down where you stand,' shouted back the knight. 'Speak your piece quickly, or take your leave!'

'I am a Questing Knight of the Lady,' shouted Calard. 'Any man who dares loose an arrow in my direction will be cursed by the goddess, as shall you if you give the order. Now be gone from my sight, I am done talking to you. I will speak to Maloric, and no one else. Fetch him from his bed if sleeping past dawn is his habit.'

His face flushed, the knight turned and disappeared from sight.

For long minutes, Calard and Chlod waited while men-at-arms and peasant bowmen shuffled their feet awkwardly. Chlod tried to shrink, making himself as inconspicuous as possible, while Calard paced back and forth before the gatehouse, his mount snorting and stamping its hooves in agitation.

Finally, the ranks of the men-at-arms in front parted, and an elderly knight appeared, his expression cold. This knight Calard recognised, though he could not recall his name. The knight bowed curtly, just low enough not to be openly discourteous.

'The Earl of Sangasse and his lady bid you welcome, Calard of Garamont,' said the knight. 'My lord is currently sitting for breakfast, and asks that you join him.'

Calard dismounted, and a peasant ran forwards to take his reins.

'Stay with the horses,' he said to Chlod, before turning back towards the knight of Sangasse.

'Lead on,' said Calard.

The knight nodded, and turned on his heel, leading the way into Castle Sangasse.

'CALARD, WHAT A pleasant surprise,' said Maloric with a sardonic half-smile. 'I thought you were dead.'

The earl was a lean man in his early thirties, handsome in an angular, sharp-featured way. His hair was pale and he sported a slender goatee beard. His clothes were finely made, and edged in silver. A long table laid with a spread fit for the king himself was before him. The rich aromas made Calard's stomach knot, and he began to salivate despite himself; it had been weeks since he had eaten a meal not prepared by his manservant Chlod, who was a poor cook at best.

'Sorry to disappoint, Maloric,' said Calard, dragging his gaze from the food on display.

The Earl of Sangasse did not rise from his high-backed seat – a subtle insult that Calard did not fail to notice – and he looked Calard up and down.

'My, my, you are quite a sight,' said Maloric. 'And what a stink! When was the last time you washed?'

'One does not have much time for such luxuries when embarked on the quest, Maloric.'

'Of course. I take it that you have still not yet been successful. It has been what, five years?'

'Six.'

'Six years,' said Maloric, taking a swig of wine. 'How time flies. Please, sit. No wait, I will send for a blanket. No offence, of course, but these chairs were imported from Cathay at not inconsiderable cost.'

'I will stand, thank you,' said Calard, coldly.

'As you wish,' said Maloric, shrugging. He gestured towards the food on the table. 'Eat. Drink. You look half-starved.'

'I did not come here to eat your food, nor to trade insults, Sangasse,' said Calard.

'Oh?' said Maloric. 'Then to what do I owe this unexpected pleasure?'

'I have returned home to find my castle in ruin,' said Calard, 'and to suffer the insult of seeing Sangasse peasants tilling Garamont land. I have seen no sign of even one of my vassal knights, nor my appointed heir Orlando or his guardian, Baron Montcadas. I come here to call you to account for these transgressions, Maloric, and I swear by all that I hold holy that if you have done harm to my household, I will kill you.'

Holding Calard's gaze, Maloric reached out and plucked a shelled quail's egg from a silver plate. He popped it between his teeth and washed it down with another swig from his ornate goblet.

'Are you done?' said Maloric, dabbing at his lips with a silk napkin.

'Long has Sangasse looked upon Garamont lands with envious eyes. I should have known that you would make a play for them in my absence,' said Calard. 'Did you murder Orlando with your own blade, Maloric, or did you have one of your knights do it for you?'

'I am no murderer of children, and I would be well within my rights to demand justice for such an insult, offered in my own hall no less. However, you are clearly aggrieved and not in full control of yourself. What god did your family offend, Calard, to see it suffer so? Truly your bloodline is cursed.'

'Do not speak of my family, Sangasse dog,' said Calard.

'I will forgive that this once, Garamont, for you speak in rashness and ignorance. But I warn you, do not fling your baseless insults and accusations in my direction again or I will not be so tolerant. I would not wish such a fate as your family has suffered on any noble son of Bastonne, even you, but my patience can be pushed only so far.'

'I saw men garbed in the regalia of Sangasse patrolling Garamont lands,' said Calard in an even voice, regathering some control of his temper. 'And I know that your men have camped in the ruin of my castle. What explanation do you offer for this?'

'I would not have an empty, unguarded land bordering my own,' said Maloric. 'Without a standing military force, Garamont would be a breeding ground for miscreants and outcasts, a haven for bandits and worse. I am merely ensuring the protection of my own lands by sending patrols into your homeland. I have annexed a portion of Garamont lands to pay for this additional militia, in lieu of recompense – for whom should I claim recompense *from*? As I said, I thought you dead.'

'And what of my nephew and heir, Orlando? What has become of him?'

Before Maloric could answer, a side door to the chamber opened and a lady swept into the room, trailed by handmaidens. Rose-scented perfume wafted into the room in her wake.

'You know my wife, Josephine,' said Maloric.

'Your wife?' said Calard in shock.

The last time he had seen the Lady Josephine had been in the halls of Garamont. She was Baron Montcadas's niece, and Calard had thought of her often during his long absence. On dark and lonely nights he had harboured romantic notions of marrying her on his return to Bretonnia, were she unwed. The old Baron Montcadas, who had always been more of a father than his own had ever been, had hoped to see the two of them wed years earlier, and had Calard not taken up the quest he believed they might have done. He had known her to be a warm-hearted and beautiful young woman, born of a wealthy and respectable noble family, and he had always found her company engaging.

'Calard, we thought you were dead!' said Josephine, rushing across to him. She hugged him tightly, tears in her gentle eyes.

'You married *Maloric*?' said Calard.

'He is a good man, Calard,' said Josephine, softly, 'and a dutiful father.'

'You... You have children?' said Calard, stepping awkwardly away from her embrace.

'You have been gone a long time, Calard,' she said. There were dirty smudges on her silk dress, and Calard was suddenly conscious of his travel-worn appearance.

'I'm sorry,' he said, but she waved away his apology.

'It is nothing.'

'Say you,' said Maloric, standing and moving to Josephine's side. 'I am the one who pays for these dresses. She has expensive taste,' he said to Calard as he embraced his wife.

Calard turned away, his mind reeling. He helped himself to a goblet of wine and downed it in one draught.

When he turned back around, his face was an unreadable mask.

'Have you heard from Bertelis?' asked Josephine.

'No,' said Calard. 'I hoped that you might have?'

Josephine shook her head sadly.

The last time Calard had seen his half-brother had been in Lyonesse, just months before he had taken up the quest, and he still carried the guilt over the last words they had exchanged. Calard had just witnessed the death of Elisabet, a noblewoman he had once loved. While he could see now that it had been an accident, at the time all he had seen was that she had died at his brother's hand. Blinded by grief, he had spoken angrily, and his words haunted him still, six years on.

'You are my brother no longer,' he had said. Calard had had many nights to regret those words, but he feared that he would never have the opportunity to atone for them. Bertelis and he had parted ways soon after.

'What happened to my home?' said Calard, dragging himself back to the present. 'Where is Orlando? Where is Montcadas?'

Fresh tears welled in Josephine's eyes and Maloric's expression darkened.

'I'm sorry, Calard,' Josephine said.

CALARD STARED AT the empty plate in front of him. Despite its quality and his hunger, the food had been like ash in his mouth.

'It was ablaze by the time my knights and I arrived,' said Maloric. 'There was nothing to be done. It burned solidly for two days, and it was a week before the embers cooled.'

'The goddess must have been looking over me,' said Josephine. 'Only my two handmaidens, a stableboy and I escaped.'

'How she didn't break a leg leaping from her window, I'll never know,' said Maloric.

'How could two knights have killed them all?' asked Calard. 'Fifteen of my vassal knights, as well as what, forty men-at-arms? Fifty? It is inconceivable. No two men could do that.'

'They were no men,' said Josephine. 'Of that I am certain. They were daemons in knights' bodies.'

'You saw them, you said?' said Calard.

'Only from afar. I was in my chambers preparing for bed when I heard them arrive at the castle gates. It was late. I heard the voices of your knights welcome these newcomers, as if they knew them. Their voices were raised, not in alarm but in surprise, joy even. At first I thought maybe it was you, Calard, returning home, but I was mistaken. The screams started soon after that.'

Calard leaned forward, focused completely on Josephine's words. Her face was pale and drawn, and her eyes misted over as she took herself back to that fateful night five years earlier.

'I know this is hard,' said Calard. Josephine composed herself before continuing.

'I left my room and was coming down the stairs. There were bodies everywhere. The screams were deafening. I could see one of them clearly through the open doors of the main hall. He – *it* – was covered in blood, from head to toe, and it moved faster than any man should. I ran to Orlando's room, but one of the monsters had already been there.' She sobbed, and took a moment to contain herself before continuing. 'He looked as though he was sleeping. His eyes were closed, but there was so much blood... The baron was there too. He died with a sword in his hand, blind as he was, the brave old fool. I ran to my room, and barricaded the door. I stayed there until I smelled smoke. The floor started to get hot. When the heat became unbearable I leapt from my window.'

'The knight you saw,' said Calard. 'Did you see his heraldry?'

'No,' said Josephine. 'But the devil was garbed in white.'

'Dressed in white...' breathed Calard. The vision that had been plaguing him for months sprang unbidden into his mind. The images were confusing, their meaning unclear, but he recalled again a shield of white lying discarded on the ground, splattered with blood. Bones and a skull, bleached white in the sun, were visible in the dead grass. A breeze picked up and black petals filled the air. Several flowers settled on the shield face, and only now did Calard recognise them for what they were.

'This knight. His shield bore a black fleur-de-lys, didn't it?'

'It is possible,' said Josephine, frowning, 'but I could not be sure.'

'I am certain,' said Calard. 'The Lady sent me a vision of black lilies falling upon a shield of white. She was telling me who did this.'

The lily was sacred to the Lady, and had been since the founding of Bretonnia. The tri-petalled symbol of the fleur-de-lys was a stylistic representation of the sacred flower, and while it had always been a sign of purity, the symbol had also been traditionally worn by the nobles of a house that was once proud and honourable, but had long fallen to darkness.

'The goddess has shown me who has brought this ruination on my house that I might seek vengeance,' said Calard, his eyes gleaming with conviction.

'If you say so,' said Maloric, putting his arm around his wife's shoulders.

'My path is clear,' said Calard, standing. 'I must leave.'

'Leave?' said Josephine, half-rising. 'What are you talking about?'

'If he wishes to chase foolish dreams, let him go,' said Maloric, placing a hand on his wife's arm.

'But go where?'

'The knight that you saw,' said Calard. 'I know who he is.'

'Who?' said Josephine.

'A black fleur-de-lys against a white field. That is the heraldry of Merovech of Arlons.'

'The knight that defeated your brother at the tournament in Lyonesse,' said Maloric. 'Am I right?'

'You are.'

'Arlons?' said Josephine. 'Where is that? I am not familiar with the name.'

'I am not surprised,' said Maloric, 'for it is a cursed place. It lies within the borders of Mousillon.'

'Mousillon,' breathed Josephine, her eyes widening in horror.

'And that is where I go,' said Calard.

III

MOUSILLON, REALM OF the Damned.

Chlod stared ahead with wide, unblinking eyes as the barge made steady progress across the black waters of the River Grismearie. His gaze was locked in the near distance, where a solid wall of fog rose up, linking the icy black water with the overcast sky, concealing the shores of Mousillon. The peasant shivered.

'It is like the edge of the world,' said Chlod. 'And we are sailing straight towards it.'

'Nonsense,' said Calard. 'It is fog, nothing more.'

He was turning a sword over in his hands, marvelling at its workmanship. The blade was flawless, gleaming silver and the pommel was beautifully crafted into the shape of a fleur-de-lys.

The Sword of Garamont was a priceless heirloom, and it had been in the family for generations. Said to have been blessed by the kiss of the Lady herself, Calard had presented it to his nephew Orlando when he had taken up his quest. He had feared it lost, stolen or destroyed when his castle was sacked, but such fears had been proven unfounded. Before he had left Sangasse three weeks earlier, Maloric had brought it to him, wrapped in velvet.

'My men found it in the ruins,' the Earl of Sangasse had said. 'I thought it best not to leave it for scavengers.'

Miraculously, perhaps protected by the Lady's blessing, the blade had survived the fire unscathed. Calard sheathed the sword, and buckled it around his waist.

They were approaching the midway point of the Grismarie, and the river's black water was flowing fast and deep beneath them. Squat guard towers could be seen along the river bank in the distance behind them, on the Bastonne side of the Grismarie. Similar towers were positioned all along the many hundreds of miles of Mousillon's borders. Funded by the king's coffers, these bastions had been erected almost five hundred years earlier, and they stood as silent sentinels, ever watchful for a threat from Mousillon. At the first sign of trouble, the massive pyres atop the towers would be lit, one after another, spreading the word faster than an eagle could fly.

Calard's horse whinnied and shuffled uneasily, hooves sounding sharply on the barge's deck. Standing, Calard moved back to where the destrier was tethered and spoke to her in soothing tones, stroking her neck. Five surly boatmen worked the barge in silence, but Calard ignored them. Having settled his warhorse, he made his way towards the bow, where Chlod sat clutching the gunwale. The barge rocked gently to and fro, and Calard, unused to being on the water, kept a solid grip on the railing as he moved to the front of the barge.

'No good will come of this,' said Chlod. The peasant was clearly terrified.

The fog loomed hundreds of feet above them, like the sheer walls of a castle marking the midway point across the Grismarie. The hunch-backed peasant closed his eyes and muttered a prayer as the barge entered the murk.

A chill descended on them, its touch wet and cloying, and visibility was suddenly reduced to less than a few feet. The mist seemed to swallow up all sound, making even the lapping of water upon the hull of the barge sound strangely distant. The fog seeped in under Calard's armour, making his skin wet and clammy, and he began to shiver.

Something ground against the underside of the barge, which began to rock back and forth alarmingly.

'What was that?' squeaked Chlod, eyes snapping open, fingernails digging into the wooden gunwale.

'Big fish,' said one of the grim-faced boatmen. Calard was unsure if the man was joking or not.

Within minutes, Calard was soaked to the skin, his hair clinging in long wet strands down his neck. The journey through the fog seemed to last an eternity. Strange noises echoed around them: creaks, groans and distant screams that Calard guessed were seabirds but sounded distinctly human. On more than one occasion he was convinced he heard whispering voices nearby, but saw nothing.

Chlod gave a yelp at one point, and Calard glared at him.

'I felt someone breathing on my neck,' said Chlod, his voice strained.

'You imagined it,' said Calard. 'Be silent.'

Calard was starting to doubt the boatmen's ability to guide the barge safely through the fog when the sound of gravel scraping against the hull signalled their arrival on the shores of Mousillon.

The riverbank appeared like a mirage through the fog as the barge came to a grinding halt in the shallows. The land was rendered in shades of grey and hidden in mist, but a narrow strip of black sand soon emerged forming a beach in front of them.

Clearly eager to be away, the boatmen unloaded the barge hastily. There was a brief struggle to get Chlod's mule off the deck. The obstinate beast was reluctant to step ashore, and the struggle only ended after Calard slapped it hard on the flank. His own steed was equally uneasy, but did as it was bid with less complaint, stepping off the front of the vessel and splashing into the shallow black water. Without a word of farewell, the boatmen poled the barge off the river bank and it was swallowed by the fog.

It was as dark as twilight, though it couldn't have been an hour past midday. Looking around them, it seemed to Calard as if all colour had been bleached from the land. The sun had been shining through the clouds on the other side of the river, but it was nowhere to be seen here. The grass and vegetation was shrivelled and dead. A lone tree stood nearby, its trunk twisted. A raven the size of a small dog perched on a leafless branch, watching them with its head cocked to one side. Calard saw movement in the corner of his eye, but whenever he turned to face it, it was gone.

'We're never leaving here alive,' said Chlod.

Somewhere in the mist, a wolf began to howl.

IV

SOMETHING WAS HUNTING them.

They had barely halted, riding westwards through lonely, wind-swept landscapes and muddy fields filled with rotting crops. They had passed through a number of isolated peasant hamlets, but seen only glimpses of the inhabitants peeking out at them through barred windows.

The haunted realm had at first seemed to exist in a permanent state of twilight, but the shadows deepened as that twilight gave way to night. With no visible moon or star in the sky overhead, the darkness was soon all-consuming. Only far beneath the Worlds Edge Mountains had Calard experienced such utter blackness. Lighting torches, they continued on through that first, nightmarish night.

The darkness was filled with the howling of wolves, the beat of heavy, leathery wings, and the rustle of unseen creatures in the undergrowth nearby. They dared not rest, and pushed on through the night. A multitude of eyes glinted in the torchlight, watching their progress. In a break in the ever-present fog, Calard glimpsed huge, black-furred wolves loping alongside the road, dogging their progress.

Wolves were not the only things stalking them. On more than one occasion Calard glimpsed hunched figures on the road behind them.

'They're back again,' said Chlod, his voice strained as he looked back along the road behind.

'They have been there for some time,' Calard replied.

'They are growing bolder.'

'We need to find shelter,' said Calard. 'We cannot travel on through another night without rest, not hounded by those... things.'

They continued on in silence as the shadows deepened around them. Abruptly, the muddy road turned and veered over a small creek, angling straight into the dark forest they had so far been skirting. The wood was shadowy and threatening, its trees bloated and misshapen. Their trunks were rotten and covered in lichen and fungus.

'Do we go in?' asked Chlod.

'It has to lead somewhere,' said Calard. 'And we have to keep moving.'

With a nudge, he urged his steed on. Its hooves sank into the marshy ground as it stepped down to the shallow creek. The water stank, and was covered in a film of scum. With a kick of encouragement, Calard's warhorse leapt forward, clearing the stream and climbing the bank on the other side.

Chlod's mule was incapable of such a leap and seemed reluctant to step into the foul waters. As Chlod kicked and swore at the stubborn beast, Calard's gaze was drawn upwards by the ugly cawing of carrion birds.

More than a dozen corpses were strung up in the trees overhead, hanging from ropes and gibbets. They spun gently as black birds tore strips of flesh from the bodies.

Movement in the trees dragged his attention down from the grisly sight. Shadows were detaching themselves from the surrounding darkness, edging towards them.

Calard reached over his back and drew his massive bastard sword from its sheath, holding it one-handed.

'Hurry up, peasant!' he hissed.

Perhaps catching a scent of the hunters on the breeze, the mule lurched forwards suddenly, almost throwing Chlod from its back, and the peasant lost his grip on the reins.

'Whoa!' shouted Chlod, clinging on desperately as the mule set off down the roadway, ears flat against its skull.

Calard's steed flared its nostrils and stamped its hooves, and he fought to keep it under control, guiding it skilfully with his knees as he took his sword in both hands. He heard something hiss nearby, the sound low and sibilant, and he kicked his steed into a canter. It needed no encouragement, and took after Chlod instantly.

Glancing back, Calard saw a pack of hunched creatures loping after them. He could not tell if they were human or beast, or some horrid blend of the two.

Something caught at his hair, scratching his neck, and Calard swung his sword with a cry. It was just a branch, and Calard swore, berating himself. Foul-smelling sap was dripping like blood from the tree, and it recoiled with a groan, twigs shivering.

'Lady above,' Calard breathed. The other trees seemed to lean in, branches reaching towards him. Ducking away from their snagging twigs, Calard urged his warhorse into a gallop.

Within a few heartbeats he had drawn alongside Chlod, still clinging vainly to his panicked mule, and he reached out and grabbed the beast's wildly swinging reins. Calard forced the animal to slow its wild gallop. Behind him, the road was clear again.

It was half an hour before they escaped the grotesque wood, and

Calard let out a breath that he didn't realise he had been holding. Up ahead he saw a small farmhouse. Turning up a muddy path, he led the way towards it.

There was no sign of life at the farm other than a starving three-legged goat tethered to a rotten stump. The pitiful animal's ribs were clearly visible beneath its stretched skin. It bleated frantically, pink tongue protruding as it strained on its chain.

Calard spied a small covered well, and slid from his saddle alongside it. He began drawing the bucket up from below, hauling it up on its thin rope. His horse was lathered in sweat, its mouth flecked with foam. Calard hoped the well-water was drinkable. He dragged the bucket over the lip of the well, and lifted it to his nose. Frowning, he brought it to his lips and took a swig. He spat it out instantly, coughing.

'Bad?' asked Chlod.

'Bad,' said Calard, throwing the bucket to the ground in disgust. It split like an overripe fruit, spilling its contents. His stomach churned as he saw bloated worms wriggling in the water.

A woman's cry sounded nearby, high-pitched and in pain, and it was joined by voices raised in anger or excitement. The sounds were coming from around the side of the farmstead's barn. Calard drew his sword and rode towards it.

A foetid stench assailed his nose as he approached the barn, something akin to rotting meat and excrement. Rounding the rotting structure, he saw a cluster of peasants gathered around a woman on the ground. They were beating her mercilessly with sticks, and Calard winced at the savagery of the attack. She screamed again, but was knocked back to the ground as she tried to rise. The peasants laughed cruelly, clearly enjoying their sport. Indignation and anger swelled in Calard, and with a yell, he kicked his steed forwards.

The peasants looked up in shock, then scattered. They took off over the fields, and Calard dragged on the reins, cutting short his pursuit.

'Cowards,' snarled Calard, shaking his head in disgust. He sheathed his sword and turned his attention to the woman.

She was sitting on the ground like a broken puppet, slumped forward over her splayed legs. Her hair was long and unkempt, hanging down over her face. Her thin shoulders heaved with each pained intake of breath.

'They are gone,' said Calard, stepping towards her. 'They will trouble you no more.'

Her tattered peasant garb was ripped at the shoulder, exposing skin that was purple with bruises and cuts. The girl made no move to cover herself, and Calard averted his eyes out of modesty.

'You are hurt,' he said, stepping close.

Her head snapped up and Calard caught a glimpse of bloodshot eyes staring out through the girl's tangle of matted hair. Thin lips drew back to expose filthy, jagged teeth, and as Calard recoiled in disgust she lashed out, seizing his forearm. Swearing, he tried to pull away, but the girl was surprisingly strong and held him in a vice-like grip.

With a feral hiss she slashed at him with her free hand, fingers curved like talons. Those fingers were long and bone-thin, their nails cracked and encrusted with filth. Instinctively, Calard turned his face away from the blow, a move that undoubtedly saved his eyes from being torn from their sockets. Still, he could not avoid the strike entirely, and her nails gouged four deep cuts across his cheek bone.

With a curse, Calard backhanded the feral peasant girl hard in the side of her head. She slammed heavily to the ground, losing her grip, and Calard backed away, blood dripping from the left side of his face.

Scrambling onto all fours, the girl glared up at him, pure hatred burning in her eyes. An animalistic growl rumbled from deep in her chest. Her teeth were bared and she began to crawl swiftly towards him, like a spider closing in on its prey.

Calard drew his bastard sword, and she hesitated. Sensing her indecision, he yelled loudly and took an aggressive step towards her.

With a hiss, the girl turned and fled. He watched her go, revulsion written on his face, but his head snapped around as he heard Chlod scream.

'Master!'

Moving quickly, Calard hauled himself into the saddle of his warhorse. Rounding the front of the barn, he saw his manservant pointing wildly.

There were dozens of loping figures approaching the farm from across the muddy fields. Calard could not be sure if they were the same ones that had been following them, but he thought it likely. He saw instantly that there were too many of them to fight, and while the notion of fleeing from them made his face burn with shame, he knew that it would not serve the Lady's purpose to die meaninglessly here.

'Forgive me, Lady,' he whispered. 'Peasant! We ride!'

Chlod's mule bucked suddenly as the wind shifted, bringing with it the scent of the approaching hunters. The hunchbacked peasant fell backwards into the mud, and the mule took off over the fields.

Calard swore, and made to go after the beast, but dragged himself back as more of the hunched figures appeared, rising from concealment. They leapt on the mule like a pack of wild dogs, and it screamed in terror as it was dragged to the ground. They were peasants, he saw now, undernourished and filthy, but some of them appeared so devolved and inbred as to be barely human at all.

His steed tensed beneath him, stamping its hooves and snorting in agitation.

The starving peasants were running towards them now, closing the distance quickly. Their faces were twisted in ravenous hunger.

'Keep back, or by the Lady's name I will not stay my blade!' roared Calard, holding his sword high. They came on undaunted, and he swore again.

Making his decision quickly, Calard rode forward and plucked Chlod from the ground by the scruff of his neck. He dumped him on the saddle behind him, and urged his destrier on.

If the warhorse was overburdened carrying two riders, it didn't show, and within heartbeats they were riding hard up the muddy roadway. The starving peasants ran after them, but they were easily outpaced. Only once the hellish farmstead was several miles behind them did Calard rein the destrier in, patting her neck appreciatively.

Darkness closed in, bringing all its claustrophobic terrors with it, and so their second night in Mousillon began.

V

IT WAS PITCH-BLACK as they approached the inn, yet it could only have been an hour after nightfall.

It was built like a fortress. It had few windows on its lowest level, and these were shuttered and barred. Fifteen-foot-high walls topped with spikes enclosed it completely. Braziers burned brightly in a vain attempt to keep the night at bay. A stout gatehouse was the only entrance to the compound, and to Calard's trained eye it looked able to withstand all but the most concerted siege.

As they rode into the light, Calard pulled his hood down over his face. They were spotted as they approached the inn's fortified gate, and sentries levelled heavy crossbows in their direction. Calard knew that his armour would provide scant protection at this distance, but if he felt any unease, he did not show it.

'Who goes there?' called out one of the guards.

'Travellers seeking a room,' replied Calard.

'The gates are sealed at nightfall, stranger,' came the reply. 'Move along.'

'What now?' said Chlod, eyeing the night with haunted eyes. Wolves howled in the distance and he shivered.

'I'll be damned if we're spending the night out here,' Calard said under his breath. 'We have coin, peasant,' he called out. 'We are not paupers.'

'How much?' called down the guard.

'Enough,' said Calard.

'Approach,' ordered the guard.

Calard nudged his warhorse forward, noting the deep scratches and gouges in the front of the gate. The sign swinging above the arched gateway proclaimed the inn to be called Morr's Rest. Below the sign was a carved icon of the god of death in his guise as the reaper. Unlike more formal representations, this carved wooden statuette clasped a foaming mug of ale in one skeletal hand, while in its other it held its more traditional sword. Calard frowned, uncomfortable at such disrespect, and he muttered a prayer of appeasement to the god of the underworld.

A hatch in the gate opened up, just large enough to show the pig-like face of a guard, who squinted at them through a latticework of bars.

'Show us the colour of your coin, stranger,' he said.

Calard edged his steed closer and slid from the saddle. He drew a copper piece from his coin pouch and held it out.

'You'll have to do better than that,' said the guard.

'This is more than you deserve,' said Calard. 'Take it and open the gate.'

'I don't think so,' said the porcine guard, grinning smugly. 'What else you got?'

Calard sighed.

'Fine,' he said, pulling a second pouch from beneath his travel worn tabard. This one was made of fine velvet, and the sentry's small eyes lit up.

'Closer,' Calard said in a conspiratorial whisper. 'I've only got the one, so it will only do for you, not the other guards.'

The man leaned in close, licking his lips. Calard's hand shot out, slipping through the bars to grab the guard by the throat.

'You should have taken the copper,' said Calard in a low voice.

The guard's eyes were bulging. Calard shifted his grip to the back of the man's neck and pulled him violently forwards, slamming his face against the bars. Before the guard could recover, Calard pressed the blade of a knife to his throat.

'I have a new proposition. Open the gate and you live to see another dawn.'

The man tried to speak, but Calard pushed the knife more forcefully into the rolls of fat beneath his chin, drawing blood.

'Nod your head if you agree,' he said, eyes cold and dispassionate. '*Gently*.'

The man's eyes were wide with fear, and he nodded his head slightly.

'Good,' said Calard.

'Open it up,' said the guard, his voice hoarse, and Calard heard the heavy bar being removed. He released the guard, his knife disappearing.

The gate swung wide.

'Try anything before I leave, and I'll gut you like the pig you are,' Calard hissed, leaning in close to the shaken guard as he walked through.

Calard caught a snatch of the conversation behind him as he led his steed into the walled inn's courtyard. He heard guards asking how much the gatekeeper had got. Calard glanced over his shoulder and caught the man's eye.

'Enough,' he heard him say, looking away quickly.

* * *

THE COMMON ROOM of Morr's Rest was crowded and filled with smoke, and even the aroma of cooking meat, sawdust and ale was unable to fully conceal the stink of humanity and vomit within. Conversation stopped and heads turned as Calard stepped through the door.

He drew his hood down lower over his face under the scrutiny and took in the layout of the place at a glance. He noted that the inn had holy sigils and loops of garlic hung above its entrances. The drinkers themselves were a surly lot, their expressions ranging from suspicion to outright hostility. He glared at those whose gaze lingered on him too long, and one by one they turned back to their drinks, muttering darkly, and the hubbub of conversation resumed.

A more disreputable crowd of people Calard had rarely encountered, and he wondered wryly if he would be better off facing the creatures of the night. The patrons of Morr's Rest scowled, bickered and spat as they gambled, drank and stuffed their faces with greasy stew and stale bread, laughing loudly at ribald jokes and groping the beleaguered serving girls as they squeezed from table to table. Calard kept one hand on the hilt of his sword as he pushed his way towards the bar, scanning for potential threats.

Most of the drinkers had the look of outlaws, brigands and vagabonds, though some of them might have been desperate merchants fallen on hard times or fleeing debtors. Nor were they all of low birth; many were knights, though few of them displayed their colours or heraldry. Most of these were outcasts and dispossessed nobles, Calard judged; knights who had fled to Mousillon in dishonour rather than face justice. Most were likely murderers, traitors and cowards, and Calard fought to keep the disdain off his face as he moved amongst them.

He bumped into one of these knights as he shouldered his way to the bar. The nobleman was tall, gaunt-featured and dressed in dark colours, and he had his hand on the hilt of his sword. He had a vicious scar across his throat, and his eyes were cold. Calard held the man's gaze for a moment, before pushing past him and signalling the squint-eyed innkeeper for service. An ogre stood nearby, easily nine feet tall, its brutal face a mess of scars. It had a bored expression on its face, and its arms, as thick as tree trunks, were folded across its massive chest.

'Keeps the rowdier ones in check,' said the innkeeper. He wore a heavily stained apron over his obese gut. 'What are you wanting?'

'A room,' said Calard, 'and feed for my horse.' He pushed a pair of coins across the bar and they disappeared in the blink of an eye.

'One of the girls will bring you food and drink,' said the innkeep, handing over a room key before turning to serve another patron. Calard grabbed the innkeeper by his arm and dragged him back.

'I'm looking for someone,' said Calard in low voice. 'A noble by the name of Merovech.'

The innkeeper pulled his arm away, scowling. 'You ain't from around here, are you?' he said.

'You know him?' said Calard.

The innkeeper nodded.

'Them's his knights back there,' he said, gesturing through the crowd. 'Bastards'll ruin me, drinking me dry and not paying a copper, but what can I do?'

Nodding his thanks, Calard found a secluded table in a dark corner and sat with his back against the wall. A bowl of gristly stew was brought to him along with a goblet of cheap wine, and he had some bread and water sent out to Chlod. He didn't touch his food, and made only a pretence of drinking his wine, eyes locked on the knights that the innkeeper had identified.

There were six of them, drinking heavily, and their table was piled high with empty dishes and goblets. Calard saw that one of their number was the cold-eyed knight he had bumped into at the bar, though he sat apart from the others, distancing himself from their drunken excesses. These other five were being loud, obnoxious and aggressive, shouting and pounding their goblets on the table as they watched a puppet show under way upon the small stage at the back of the inn.

Creepy-looking marionettes were re-enacting various events from history, and Calard's attention was drawn to the performance as something caught his eye. He saw a puppet knight dressed in a white tabard, and his eyes narrowed. The puppet's heraldry was unmistakable: a black fleur-de-lys on a white field. The knight's face was white, as was his hair, and he wore a crown of rulership upon his head.

'The duke invited all the nobles in Bretonnia to Mousillon, to celebrate his great victory!' screeched the voice of the story's narrator from behind the puppeteers' screen. 'The king himself came, and the Duke of Mousillon was proclaimed saviour of Bretonnia!'

A cheer erupted from the watching crowd as puppets representing the dukes of Bretonnia lifted the puppet of Duke Merovech high into the air.

'However, the king was jealous of our beloved duke's achievements,' continued the narrator, 'and he knew that Duke Merovech would make a far better king than himself. He began plotting our duke's downfall.'

The crowd booed as the puppet of the king, carved to look like a drunken buffoon, rubbed its hands together in an evil, conspiratorial manner. Calard frowned. He knew this tale, but its telling was unlike any he had heard before: its perspective was skewed, its heroes and villains flipped.

The true tale was from a dark period in the history of Bretonnia, hundreds of years earlier, and it told the story of the last Duke of Mousillon, who was, by all reports, a butcher and murderer, a drinker of blood and an eater of children. However, in the puppet show being performed here, the sadistic duke was portrayed as a living saint, while the king and his loyal dukes were little more than jealous inbreds, conspiring against him.

The crowd cheered as the Duke of Mousillon uncovered the conspiracy against him, and thumped their tables as the puppets of their duke and the king drew swords against one another. The marionettes duelled, the skilled puppeteers making them fight with surprising believability, and the inn resounded to the sound of swords clashing.

Cheers and laughter erupted as the king's head was lopped from its shoulders, and those in the front row were sprayed with pig's blood pumped up through the puppet's severed neck. The marionette of the Duke of Mousillon lifted up a tiny goblet to catch the rain of blood, which it then drank down in one gulp, which was met with further cheers.

The curtain fell, and the narrator continued.

'The traitor king was dead, but the jealous dukes turned against Mousillon.'

The curtain lifted again, showing the Duke of Mousillon and his knights battling against the other dukes.

'Led by the treacherous Duke of Lyonesse,' said the narrator, eliciting derisive hisses from the crowd, 'they besieged Mousillon. Yet even heavily outnumbered, our lord could not be bested, not with his five trusted lieutenants beside him. Finally, the Duke of Lyonesse resorted to treachery.'

Boos and hisses greeted the appearance of a cloaked and hooded marionette that reared up behind the Duke of Mousillon and stabbed him to death. The deed done, the puppet threw off its disguise, revealing its identity as none other than the Duke of Lyonesse. The lights dimmed and the curtain fell.

The crowd booed loudly, but they hushed as the curtain rose one more time. The stage was unlit and bare but for a puppet reclined in death, wrapped in a shroud.

'But before he died, our beloved duke swore an oath. He swore that he would return from beyond the grave and seek vengeance! He swore that Mousillon would be returned to its former glory, and that the rest of Bretonnia would pay for its betrayal!'

The death shroud was suddenly whisked away from the puppet-corpse and the figure of the Duke of Mousillon leapt up, a sword held in each hand.

'Long live Duke Merovech!' screeched the narrator, and the curtain fell for the last time.

Calard shook his head as the crowd cheered and banged their tables. His gaze settled on the knight that he had bumped into at the bar.

Perhaps sensing someone watching him, the knight looked up, but by the time he did, Calard had already gone.

* * *

VI

AN HOUR LATER, the knight made his way up the narrow staircase to his room. He unlocked the door, which opened with a drawn-out creak. It was dark within, and he cursed. He had left a lamp burning low on the table within, but a draught must have blown it out. Leaving the door ajar so that he could see by the light in the hallway, he moved towards the table.

The door clicked shut abruptly, and darkness swallowed him. He spun around on his heel, reaching for his blade. It was half-drawn when the tip of a sword touched his throat, and he froze.

'Sheathe it,' said a voice from the darkness. The gaunt-featured knight scowled but did as he was bid. The shutters of a lamp were opened, and the knight squinted against the glare.

'Sit,' said Calard. He forced the knight back with the point of his sword, making him sink into a moth-eaten chair. To his credit, the dishonoured knight showed no fear. 'Put your hands behind your head,' Calard said. The knight gave Calard a long look.

'You are making a mistake,' the knight said, placing his hands casually behind his head. His voice was coarse, little more than a growl. Calard lifted the man's chin with the point of his blade, exposing a jagged scar that reached across his throat from ear to ear.

'Nice scar,' said Calard.

'I'm alive,' growled the knight. 'The same cannot be said for the whoreson who gave it to me.'

'What is your name?'

'Raben,' said the knight. 'Who the hell are you?'

'You are going to answer a few questions for me, Raben.'

'You're the one with the sword.'

'You are one of Merovech's knights?'

'You already know the answer to that.'

'Where is he, then?'

'You honestly don't know?' said Raben.

'If I did, I wouldn't need you, outcast,' said Calard.

'Outcast, is it? Oh, that hurts,' said Raben.

'Where?' said Calard. A trickle of blood ran from Raben's throat.

'The ducal palace of Mousillon city,' he said in his gravelly voice. 'He does proclaim himself to be the long lost ruler of this realm, after all.'

'The mad duke was killed centuries years ago,' hissed Calard.

'Who am I to dispute his claim?' said Raben. 'I'm just an outcast.'

'Indeed.'

'Is that it?' said Raben. 'Are we done?'

Calard lowered his sword, and the dispossessed knight let down his hands. Without warning, Calard slammed the heavy pommel of his sword into the side of Raben's head. He fell sidewards from his chair and hit the floor, unconscious.

'We are done,' said Calard.

CHLOD AWOKE WITH a start, his heart pounding. It took him a moment to remember where he was: the stable of Morr's Rest. He lay there in the rotting hay, breathing hard. The sound came again – something like a heavy chunk of wood being dropped to the ground.

A shaft of torchlight seeped in from the courtyard outside through a knothole in the wall. Chlod squatted alongside it, squinting through the gap.

At first he saw nothing untoward. The courtyard of the inn was deserted. His eye swept the compound, and at last settled on the gatehouse. He frowned.

The shadows beneath the archway were dark, but even so he could see that the gate was open. The heavy locking bars were on the ground. Sealed, nothing short of a battering ram would be able to breach those gates, but they had been flung wide, an open invitation to the creatures beyond.

For a moment, Chlod half-considered a mad dash across the courtyard to lock the gates, for he knew well the horrors that lurked outside. However, he was no hero, and they would have been too heavy for him alone anyway. He stayed put, rooted in fear, staring at the gate in silent dread.

For long minutes he watched, barely daring to breathe. After what seemed an eternity, he saw a shadow appear, and the hairs on the back of his neck rose.

The dark shape hugged the ground, moving low. It paused at the edge of the torchlight, then edged forwards. Chlod saw a pallid face atop a scrawny, malnourished body. Bones were starkly visible beneath its skin. It sniffed the air like an animal, then hissed over its shoulder. Rising from the ground into a low crouch, the starving peasant padded warily into the courtyard of Morr's Rest, hands twitching.

A second peasant came through behind the first, a filthy bearded man carrying a rusted plough blade. More followed. Chlod's heart was hammering loudly in his chest, but he could not tear himself away from his spy-hole.

He froze as one of the peasants came within feet of him, separated only by the thin overlapping planks of the barn wall. This one was a foul creature, barely human at all. It came to a halt and cocked its head to one side, nostrils flaring. Chlod could make out the fine web of blue veins beneath its skin, and could smell its animal stink. It turned and stared straight at him. Chlod's heart skipped a beat as it saw him. It grinned, exposing stained, jagged teeth.

Chlod fell away from the wall with a gasp, scrambling backwards.

He heard footsteps inside the stable, and the horses and ponies began whinnying and kicking in their stalls. His master's warhorse was trembling, ears flat against its skull.

A scream close by made him jump. It was cut short, ending in the strangled gargle of someone dying.

Chlod's breathing was coming in frantic gasps, and his hands were shaking. Creeping forwards, he peered around the corner of the stall, looking out towards the entrance to the stables. He saw a handful of hunched peasants making their way up the aisle towards him. Their heads were low and swung from side to side, like dogs seeking a scent. He ducked back into the stall before he was seen.

'Ranald, protect me,' he said under his breath, invoking the trickster god of luck, benefactor of thieves, gamblers and ne'er-do-wells the Old World over. He turned around on the spot, undecided as to his best course of action. He considered hiding under the loose straw on the floor, but there wasn't enough to adequately conceal him, and the peasants would surely sniff him out. He thought about mounting his master's warhorse and riding free, but he doubted that he would have been able to haul himself up upon its back anyway, let alone ride it. And if he did somehow survive, his master would surely see him hang for sullying the noble beast.

He backed away into the far corner of the stall, edging past the powerful destrier. The horse's muscles were twitching; it knew that predators approached. The feral peasants would be only yards away now, and Chlod bit his lip, indecision paralysing him.

A shadow appeared in the open stall gate, and the warhorse shuffled uneasily, snorting. Without thinking, Chlod slapped the horse hard on the rump.

'Yah!' he shouted, and the warhorse reared, smashing the stall gate to splinters. It leapt forwards, hooves clattering loudly, and Chlod glimpsed several figures throwing themselves aside. The destrier slipped on the cobblestones and half-fell, before righting itself and bolting for the courtyard.

Grabbing his spiked club from his meagre pile of belongings, Chlod dropped to hands and knees and started crawling frantically under the barriers separating the stalls. As he scrabbled through the rotten straw and horse manure, he saw the slapping feet of the feral peasants running up the aisle.

He was almost trampled by an immense draught horse in one stall and barely avoided being kicked by a panicked pony in another. With a deep breath he hurled himself under the last barrier and scrambled to his feet, glancing behind him for signs of pursuit.

He nearly ran headlong into one of the peasants, who was crouched over the body of the stableboy. It was feeding, mouth caked with blood. Chlod could not halt his forward momentum, and bowled into the cannibalistic peasant. His knee cracked it in the face, and Chlod was sent sprawling on the ground at the stable's entrance.

In a heartbeat he was back on his feet and running. He risked a glance behind him and saw the peasant stagger to its feet. It leapt after him, hair streaming wildly as it bounded along on all fours. More of the cannibalistic inbreds were streaming through the open gates, and Chlod saw right away that he had no chance of escape there. He angled his awkward, limping run towards the inn itself, knowing that his best chance of survival now lay with Calard.

'Master!' he screamed as he ran. 'Master!'

At any moment he expected to be dragged down, but he made it across the courtyard and staggered up onto the inn's covered stoop, breathing hard. He was just feet from the door when a weight landed on his back, bearing him to the ground. The air exploded from his lungs and he lost his grip on his spiked maul, which clattered out of reach.

He was pinned to the ground, and though he fought like a wild animal, he could not dislodge the hissing peasant. Bony hands grasped his skull, and he felt nails biting deep into his scalp. He screamed wordlessly, neck muscles straining to resist as his head was lifted high, then slammed down with brutal force. White hot pain blossomed. Dazed, Chlod registered his head being lifted again. In moments, his skull would be pulverised, his brain matter splattered across the stoop.

Blinking heavily, unable to focus, he vaguely saw the door to the inn swing open before him. He saw a shadow emerge, and a flash of silver.

Calard took the peasant's head off with a double-handed sweep of his broadsword. The headless corpse slumped forwards over Chlod, blood pumping from its neck.

'Up!' shouted Calard, grabbing Chlod by back of his flea-ridden tunic and dragging him to his feet. His manservant's legs were unsteady, unable yet to support his weight, and he flopped back to the ground, struggling to focus. Blood was dripping from his forehead. Swearing, Calard adjusted his grip on his manservant, then hurled him bodily through the door of the inn. He kicked the club through after him, then spun back to face the courtyard as three rabid peasants hurled themselves at him.

He cut the first down with a heavy blow that shattered its ribcage, and sliced the second from groin to sternum with the return sweep. The third leapt on him, scratching and biting, but he threw it off, sending it crashing into the wall of the inn. It dropped to its knees, and before it could recover Calard stepped in close and brought the pommel of his sword down onto its head, killing it instantly.

Seeing dozens of the creatures swarming across the courtyard towards him, Calard stepped back inside the inn and slammed the door shut. He threw his weight against it.

'Chlod, the locks!'

A heavy impact struck the door, almost dislodging Calard. He gritted his teeth as his heels began sliding across the floor. The door was forced open a fraction, and claw-like hands reached around the edge.

Chlod picked up his spiked cudgel from the floor and bashed at the clutching hands, breaking bones and crushing fingers.

The door slammed shut and Chlod slid first the upper lock home, then the lower one. Breathing hard, Calard stepped away from the door, his sword levelled towards it. It shook violently, but held.

'What in Morr's name is going on?' came a slurred a voice. Calard looked over his shoulder to see one of Merovech's knights stumbling down the stairs, a drawn blade in his hands. He was clearly still the worse for wear from the night's drinking, and he was followed by several of his comrades, all in various stages of dishevelment. Other guests of the inn were emerging from their rooms, their faces drawn and pale.

'We are besieged,' said Calard.

The banging at the door subsided, and Calard edged towards it, listening intently.

'How did they get into the compound?' said one of the knights.

'Someone let them in, most likely,' said Calard, glancing around. 'The innkeeper would be my guess.'

'What?' said a voice. 'Why would you say that?'

'Do you see him here, or any of his staff?' said Calard, gesturing around him. 'They are probably all holed up in the gatehouse.'

'The bastard's sold us out to Mortis,' growled one of Merovech's knights. At mention of the name, Chlod whimpered.

Several of the other guests began to speak at once, their voices rising in panic.

'Quiet,' snapped Calard.

In the ensuing silence, they could all hear shuffling around the exterior of the inn. There were scuffling noises at the walls, and Calard looked up.

'They are going for the second floor windows,' shouted someone, and Calard quickly looked around him. There were over half a dozen armed men in the main room of the inn now.

'You three,' he said, jabbing a finger a cluster of men holding weapons. 'Get upstairs and barricade the windows.'

'I'll be damned if I take orders from–' snarled one of them, but Calard cut him off.

'Do it!' he thundered. The man looked like he was going to argue, but the others saw sense in Calard's words, and hurried up the stairs. Calard gestured towards other men with his sword. 'Get those tables on their sides to block the windows! You and you, help me slide this one in front of the door!'

Unseen by Calard, Raben staggered unsteadily down the stairs into the common room, one hand pressed to his temple. He had a sword in his hand, and his eyes burned with cold fury. He moved purposefully towards Calard as he heaved at a heavy oak table, positioning it to block the front door.

A shuttered window suddenly exploded inwards amid a shower of splinters, and feral peasants began clawing their way through, howling and braying like demented madmen. A table propped against another window was shoved aside, and more of the cannibalistic rabble began clambering inside.

'For the Lady!'

Calard leapt forwards and brought his sword down on the head of the first peasant to scramble through, cleaving its skull down to the teeth, spraying blood.

He smashed another peasant back with the pommel of his sword, but dozens more were straining to get in. He could hear banging from upstairs, but that was soon drowned out by shouting, the clash of weapons and the sickly sound of blades hacking into flesh and bone.

Hands clawed for him and he stepped swiftly away from the door, slashing with his sword. A clutch of fingers dropped to the floor, twitching.

Chlod backed off, looking around frantically for an escape route. He ran behind the bar and tugged at the cellar door, but he could not lift it.

The front door was ripped off its hinges and tossed aside suddenly, and a flood of peasants streamed in, scrambling over the table slid up against it. Some carried crude clubs and rusted farm implements, while others seemed intent on killing with nothing more than tooth and claw.

Chlod dropped to the floor and crawled under the bar, trying to make himself as inconspicuous as possible.

Calard found himself fighting side by side with Raben and two other men. Despite the knock Calard had given him, the outcast knight fought with poise and control. He was fast and deadly, his timing impeccable. Calard was careful not to turn his back on him.

The devolved peasants came on like a living tide, scrabbling over tables and sending chairs flying, forcing Calard and Raben back against the bar. For every one of their number that was cut down, two more squeezed through the windows and clambered through the gaping door.

The room was filled with their stink, a mixture of sweat, rotting meat and wet soil.

It was not long before they started to attack down the inn's stairs.

'They've taken the upper floor,' said Calard.

One of Raben's knights was knocked to the ground and brained with what looked like a human thigh-bone.

'This is hopeless,' growled Raben. 'There are too many of them!'

'I have no intention of dying here,' said Calard, kicking a twitching corpse off his blade. 'The Lady is with me.'

Raben ran another peasant through, then spat derisively. 'The Lady forsook this place long ago.'

One by one, the inn's defenders were dragged down, their heads smashed in with sticks and their throats ripped out with bloodstained teeth. The peasants descended on them like starved beasts, and screams rang out from those not yet dead when the cannibals began their gory feast.

'There must be another way out,' shouted Calard, now fighting back to back with Raben. The notion of fleeing from mere peasants wrenched at his sense of pride, but it would not serve the Lady's purpose if he died here.

Calard was wielding his bastard sword in one hand now, and had drawn the Sword of Garamont with his other.

A screeching, near-naked peasant leapt at Calard from atop the bar, its body scrawny and malnourished. Calard cut it down in midair, and it fell in a bloody heap to the floor. Calard glanced around him, getting a sense of their position within the common room.

'The kitchen,' he said, indicating towards it with a nod. 'That's our best chance. There must be a back door.'

Both Calard and Raben were splattered with blood, and while most of it was not their own, neither man was uninjured. Raben risked a quick glance back towards the kitchen. It was at least ten yards away, and they were now completely surrounded.

'We won't make it,' said Raben.

'Stay here and die then, damn you,' said Calard.

With a roar, he forced the enemy back, swinging his swords around in a pair of deadly arcs. Taking advantage of the space he had created, he leapt atop the bar and ran along its length towards the back of the inn. Peasants reached for him but his blades sliced out, keeping them at bay. He leapt off the far end, slamming a pair of enemies to the floor. He came to his feet in the kitchen doorway, blades at the ready. The kitchen was disgustingly dirty, and rats scuttled in the shadows, but it was free of foes. He spotted a door on the far wall.

Glancing back into the common room, he saw Chlod emerge from beneath the bar, scurrying under tables towards him.

'Quickly!' Calard shouted. Peasants were close behind his manservant, their red-rimmed eyes wide.

Raben was standing alone, surrounded. He turned on the spot, holding his sword at the ready as peasants closed in around him, too many to hold off alone. Briefly, Calard's gaze met Raben's across the room. He saw the outcast mouth a curse. The peasants attacked as one but Raben had pre-empted them and was already moving. He swayed aside from a vicious blow and launched a lightning counter that took off an arm at the elbow.

Calard shoved Chlod into the kitchen.

'Unlock the door!' he ordered. Calard stepped back to give himself more room to swing as the enemy came at him. The first through the doorway was hacked almost in two as he cleaved it from shoulderblade to armpit. He dragged his sword free and waited for the next to enter, but the peasants hung back, none willing to be his next victim. Glancing over his shoulder, he saw Chlod at the back door, and began to edge towards him. The peasants came after him, spreading out, but they were wary now of his blade. There was a commotion behind the peasants, and he caught a glimpse of Raben barging his way through the press of bodies.

'Wait,' he ordered Chlod as he heard the bolts of the back door sliding open.

The knight burst into the room, but the leg of a chair wielded as a club struck him, and he stumbled. Three peasants were on him in an instant. Without thought, Calard moved to his aid. He hacked into the bare back of one of the peasants crouched over the outcast, severing its spine. He kicked another away, sending it flying face-first into a bench top, bringing a pile of dirty pots down with a crash. He slashed at another, and it reeled backwards with a screech, blood spraying from its neck. The peasants had now circled around them, filling the kitchen.

Calard gripped Raben under the arm and helped him to his feet. Blood was dripping from bite wounds on his cheek and neck. The outcast knight had lost his grip on his sword, and drew a slender knife from his boot.

'You should have gone without me,' said Raben. 'I would have.'

'And that is the difference between your kind and mine,' said Calard.

The peasants came at them in a rush. Two died to Calard's bastard sword and another to Raben's stabbing knife before the two knights were overwhelmed.

Seeing his master disarmed and dragged to the ground, Chlod slid back the last bolt on the door in a rush and threw the door open. The cold night air washed in and without a backwards glance he bolted out into the darkness.

Before he had made two yards, a hand locked around his throat. His legs went out from under him, and he was hurled back into the kitchen. From the floor, he looked up to see a gaunt peasant appear in the doorway. His eyes widened as the figure came into the light.

'No, no, no, no, no,' said Chlod, scrambling backwards on his hands and knees.

The figure was covered in crude tattoos and wore a necklace of fingers around his scrawny neck. Splinters of bone had been pushed through the skin of his forearms. He looked down at Chlod and smiled, exposing stained teeth that had been filed to points.

'Hello, Chlod,' he said.

* * *

CALARD'S ARMS WERE wrenched behind his back and his wrists bound with tough, sinewy cord.

'Chlod,' he said. 'What in the Lady's name is going on?'

His manservant stood nearby, shivering, his eyes wide and staring. He avoided Calard's gaze as he too was bound.

'By all that is holy, I swear–' said Calard, but his words were cut short as a hastily tied noose was looped around his neck. A foot between his shoulder blades pinned him down as it was yanked taut, making him gasp for breath.

Alongside him, Raben was suffering similar treatment, held face down on the floor while he was trussed up like a prize hog.

The tattooed leader of the peasant rabble barked something indecipherable in a repulsive, guttural tongue and Calard and Raben were dragged to their feet. Another barked order and they were hauled out into the night. The tattooed peasant followed, holding Chlod tightly around the back of the neck.

'We've missed you, Chlod,' he hissed.

VII

FOR OVER THREE hours they were dragged through stinking marshes and haunted forests by the loping parade of filthy, cannibalistic peasants. Their captives were not the feral brood's only spoils; they had hastily ransacked the larder of Morr's Rest, filling sacks with cheese and bread, meat and wineskins. Corpses had been mutilated and dismembered, and several of the sacks were now soaked through with blood, stuffed with human body parts.

They kept off the roads, hauled along paths overgrown with thorn-bushes and rushes. Occasionally they were forced into the open, scurrying across muddy fields filled with rotten crops, watched over by the silhouettes of scarecrows. Sometimes they could see lights in the distance, but their captors seemed keen to avoid areas of habitation, and veered away from them.

They trudged knee-deep through vast tracts of swampland, beset by great clouds of stinging midges. They climbed from this stinking morass as the ground rose, and their pace picked up again as they ran through an abandoned village that had been left to rot. The peasants seemed more at ease here, speaking amongst themselves in their low, ugly tongue. Calard was poked and prodded by peasants whose eyes gleamed with hunger.

Feet slapped loudly on the roadway, which rose steadily, winding its way through the dead village. Soon they were in the countryside again, leaving the decrepit houses behind them, but their progress continued upwards, the muddy roadway clinging to the steep sides of a hill. A crumbling, six foot wall ran alongside the high side of the road.

They turned through a decaying stone gateway overrun with

thorn-bushes and ivy. An ancient gate hung on rusted hinges, and the procession of peasants passed through. Calard noted the hourglass carved atop the archway as he was bustled through beneath it.

'A Garden of Morr,' he said.

They rose above the cloying blanket of ever-present fog and Calard was afforded a clearer view of their surroundings. The graveyard reared up before them, clinging to a hilltop riddled with tombs and mausoleums. It was massive and sprawling, a veritable city of the dead; tens of thousands were likely buried here. The graves lowest on the hill were packed in tight and marked with cracked headstones and slabs worn smooth by the passage of time. Many had clearly been desecrated and dug up. Winged, skeletal statues being slowly strangled by ivy stood over some, while in other areas mass pit graves were commemorated with little more than crude epitaphs scratched into stone slabs. Large family mausoleums protruded from the hillside as they climbed higher, the richer tombs carved deep into the rock cliffs.

Black roses grew in abundance, their petals soft and velveteen, their deadly thorns curved and shining silver. They exuded a heady, sickly-sweet aroma.

Ravens perched in leafless, twisted trees clinging to the hillside, staring down at the procession passing below. Images of death were everywhere, from carved hourglasses and black roses on tombs and opulent facades to extravagant sculptures depicting the god of the underworld, Morr, in his various guises

The peasants became more animated, cavorting and leaping, grinning and guffawing. More of the depraved creatures joined their group, though Calard had no idea where they had appeared from. Within the tombs themselves, perhaps.

Feeling eyes upon him, he looked up to see a child clinging to the base of a cracked, moss-covered statue. The child – he could not tell if it was a boy or a girl – was clearly starving, little more than a skeleton encased in skin, its head too big for its frail body. It stared at him with red-rimmed eyes and its flesh was covered in open sores. Something about the child's intense gaze made his skin crawl. It hissed at him, baring small, pointed teeth.

Calard grimaced as his captors yanked at the noose around his neck, jerking him onward.

Ever higher they climbed, then down into the yawning mouth of one of the larger crypts. They passed under a lintel carved in the likeness of Morr, arms outspread as if in welcome. In was cold and dank in the low-ceilinged burial chamber, and it smelt of wet earth and things long dead. Roots hung through rough-hewn roof, like grasping, skeletal arms.

A massive sculptured sarcophagus dominated the tomb. The heavy lid, carved to represent a serenely posed knight with arms crossed over his chest, lay cracked and discarded on the floor.

'What is this?' said Calard through clenched teeth as he was dragged towards the casket.

'Get in,' hissed one of the peasants.

He strained against his captors, fighting against them as they tried to haul him towards the open casket. Had they dragged him all this way just to bury him alive? He was far bigger than any of them, and they struggled to make him move, but his face began to turn purple as the noose around his neck tightened.

'Enough,' hissed one of them, breaking the deadlock by kicking Calard hard in the small of his back. He staggered forwards into the casket, and looked down into it, gasping for breath.

Bones and rotting cloth had been pushed roughly aside, and he saw that a hole had been smashed in the bottom of the sarcophagus. He could feel a slight breeze coming up through the hole, bringing with it a foetid stench of decay.

One of the peasants crawled in, like a spider, and disappeared down the hole.

'Bring them,' came its voice, from the darkness.

'Lady, protect your servant,' breathed Calard.

THE ENTIRE HILL was riddled with tunnels, and they were dragged deep into the labyrinth. Chewed bones were strewn across the floor of these tunnels, and the way was lit by stinking candles burning in carved niches.

Faces crowded around to look upon these newcomers, from tiny children to ancient crones, and Calard realised that there must have been many hundreds of peasants eking out a horrid existence down here beneath the earth. What better place for them to call home than a graveyard, he thought darkly.

All of the inhabitants were starving. Their eyes were dull and lifeless, as if any hope that had ever dwelt there had long faded. Tiny, shrunken babes, too weak even to cry, were held to the bony chests of mothers unable to produce milk to feed them. Most of the peasants were stooped and hunched, their bodies and faces malformed and ugly from generations of inbreeding and malnutrition. Many were missing limbs, and more than a few bore evidence of leprosy and the wasting sickness. They were a pitiful bunch, and even Calard, who was generally inured to the fate of those of low birth, found himself disturbed. Hands covered in dirt reached for him as he was dragged deeper beneath the ground, touching his face and clothes in wonder.

The procession gathered a sizeable entourage as Calard, Raben and Chlod were led into the depths beneath the Garden of Morr. They crowded after the captives, straining to see. Every side-passage was filled with staring faces. Children ran behind them. As they descended further, the catacombs carved by the hands of men gave way to naturally formed caves, their walls slick with moisture.

At last they came to a rocky cavern at the dark heart of the hill. Hundreds of stubby candles lit the area with a flickering orange glow. It was cold and moist, and an acrid stink hung in the air. Looking up, Calard could see that the roof was a seething mass of furred shapes: bats.

Rock formations jutted up from the floor and hung from the ceiling. In places these had had come together, forming slick-sided columns. Drips fell from the ceiling like rain, causing ripples in milky pools of water that gathered in hollows.

Dozens of natural windows looked down into the chamber, each crowded with the graveyard's inhabitants, who bustled for the best vantages.

Calard and Raben were dragged towards a natural stone platform in the centre of the cavern. An empty throne was carved into the rock at the centre of this platform. Hundreds of human skulls were piled up around it.

Seated on the roughly hewn steps below the throne was a figure that Calard at first mistook for a dusty corpse.

Almost imperceptibly, the skeletal figure raised its head to regard their approach. Thick matted clumps of grey hair hung down over an overly long, ashen face. That face was ancient; so deep were its lines that they looked as though they had been carved with a chisel. Clouded eyes glinted in deep sockets.

Calard and Raben were forced to their knees. Their weapons were tossed to the floor nearby, and the clatter they made reverberated sharply off the cavern walls. Chlod tried to hang back, his head low, but he was shoved forwards to stand alongside his master.

'What have you been keeping from me, you little toad?' said Calard out of the corner of his mouth. It was the first chance that he had to speak to Chlod since their capture. The hunchbacked manservant made no answer.

'Quiet,' said a voice, and Calard was cuffed across the side of the head.

'How is it you are known here?' hissed Calard. 'Answer me!'

Still Chlod offered no explanation, and again Calard was struck, harder this time, knocking him to the ground.

A bone shard, as sharp as a dagger and three inches long, lay on the cavern floor just inches from his nose. He turned onto his side, wriggling, and as he was hauled back to his knees, he picked up the bone shard and secreted it in his clasped hands.

A hush descended over the cavern, broken only by the steady dripping of water. The figure on the steps regarded them in silence, his gaze inscrutable. Calard lifted his head high, eyes blazing.

'I demand that I be released,' he said in a low voice.

The grey man's eyes bored into Calard, but he remained silent.

'My purpose in this cursed land lies not with you, or your... people,' said Calard. 'Release me.'

The ashen-faced figure continued to regard him silently for a moment, then stood, his movements slow and deliberate. He looked as though he was unfolding as he rose to his feet, his limbs looking too long and too thin, like the legs on an insect. His matted hair hung past his thin waist. He wore a threadbare robe of faded majesty, something that might have been worn by a noble lord in a bygone era. Delicate, moth-eaten lace hung from the cuffs of his sleeves like dusty spider webs.

With regal grace he moved in front of the two kneeling knights and the quaking figure of Chlod.

His hands were long and slender, his fingers like ivory needles. He gestured for the two knights to rise, and they were hauled roughly to their feet. Calard stood with his head held high, refusing to be cowed before this pauper king and his tattered court.

The grey man was frail and corpse-thin, and his back was slightly stooped, yet even so he towered over Calard. He walked around the three of them, appraising them.

He came to a halt in front of Chlod. The hunch-backed manservant flinched as the grey man reached out towards him. Thin fingers lifted Chlod's chin until he was looking up into the ancient face. Tears ran down his face.

The skeletally gaunt figure began to laugh. The sound was deep and hollow.

'It has been a long time,' said the grey man, still chuckling. 'Welcome home, Chlod.'

'*Home*?' hissed Calard, glancing sidewards at his manservant. All colour had drained from Chlod's face.

'Allow me to introduce myself,' said the wasted old man, turning towards Calard. The ghost of a smile played at his ashen lips and the result was unsettling; he resembled nothing more than a grinning corpse.

'I,' said the deathly old man, 'am Grandfather Mortis.'

'Grandfather Mortis,' said Calard, dryly.

'The one and only,' said the old man, giving Calard a mocking bow.

'I am Calard of Garamont, a questing knight of Bastonne.'

'Engaged on the quest, is it?' said Mortis. 'And this?'

'Raben,' said the outcast knight.

'Just Raben?'

'Just Raben.'

'I see,' said Mortis. He looked at Raben for moment, then turned away. He stretched his skeletal arms theatrically wide, fingers unfurling. 'And these,' he said, 'these are my children. My loving, *trustworthy* children.' He looked pointedly at Chlod, who shrank under his gaze.

'Your children,' said Calard, 'are cannibalistic inbreds.'

'In lean times, needs must, and so forth and so on,' said Mortis with a shrug.

'To eat the flesh of one's fellow man is an abomination,' said Calard. 'These peasants would be better off dead.'

'Keep your moral outrage, it means nothing here,' said Mortis. 'My children *live*, and that is itself a triumph in this gods-forsaken land.'

'This is no life,' said Calard, looking around him. 'I'd sooner die that live like this.'

'That is a most interesting notion,' said Mortis. 'There's good meat on your bones.'

'Are you going to kill us?' said Chlod, tears still running down his face.

'Kill you?' said Mortis, reaching out a hand to stroke Chlod's face. 'These others, maybe. But you? Of course not, child! This is where you belong. All your sins will be forgiven, in time. You will be punished, of course, but you are home, and that is what matters.'

At the mention of punishment, Chlod paled. Turning from him, Mortis jabbed a finger towards Raben.

'This is one of the duke's knights,' he said. 'Why is it not dead?'

'This knight is under my protection,' said Calard. 'He is not to be harmed.'

'Is that so?' said Mortis. 'What are you doing here in Mousillon, Calard of Garamont? What brings you to our cursed realm?'

'The Lady herself has led me here.'

'Why?'

'What does it matter?' said Calard.

'Curiosity,' said Mortis. 'Indulge an old man.'

'I came to find someone,' said Calard. 'And when I do, I intend to kill him.'

Raben smirked at that.

'You came here to kill him?' he said. 'You are more of a fool than I thought! He cannot be killed, not by one such as you.'

'Any man can be killed,' said Calard.

'Merovech is no man,' said Raben.

'Man, fiend, devil; I care not,' said Calard. 'I *will* kill him.'

Mortis lashed out, grabbing Calard around the throat. His nails bit deep into his flesh, drawing blood.

'Merovech?' Mortis said, enunciating the name clearly so there could be no misunderstanding. 'You came here to kill Duke Merovech?'

Before anyone could react, Calard's hands were free, the tough cord falling away from his wrists. No one had noticed him cutting his bindings, and in the blink of an eye he had the razor-sharp bone shard he had retrieved from the ground pressed to Mortis's neck.

The old man released him, and held up both hands in a sign of submission. The cavern erupted in shouts and hisses. Hands tightened the noose around his neck, but Calard increased the pressure on the bone held to Mortis's throat.

'Call them off, or you die,' hissed Calard.

The old man made a sound like he was clearing his throat, and the peasants drew back, tense and uneasy.

'I am no friend of Duke Merovech's, Calard of Garamont,' said Mortis with a deathly grin. 'And the enemy of one's enemy is one's friend, no?'

'MEROVECH THE MAD,' said Mortis. 'The fool is obsessed with regaining Mousillon's lost prestige, and in doing so, eradicating all he sees as vermin. Namely my children and I. You don't mind if I sit?'

Calard had the Sword of Garamont in his hand, its point levelled at Mortis's skeletal chest. At Calard's order, Chlod had released Raben from his bonds, and retrieved their weapons. His shield and bastard sword were strapped to his back, and behind him stood Raben, blade drawn, eyeing the hostile peasants warily. Chlod stood nearby, wringing his hands.

Mortis lowered himself onto the stone steps below the throne with a sigh. At a guess, Calard judged the old man to be perhaps ninety years of age. Still, as frail as the old man appeared, Calard was not about to underestimate him. His mind was clearly still as sharp as a razor, and he had but to speak the word and the onlooking peasants would tear them limb from limb.

'Five years Merovech has waged war upon us. Always in that time, we have been protected by our lord,' said Mortis, gesturing towards the empty throne. 'But he is gone now, captured three nights past on the Shadow-Moors. Without him, we are lost.'

'The ancient one is gone?' gasped Chlod. Mortis nodded grimly.

'You would be doing me a great favour if you succeeded in slaying the duke,' said Mortis, his skeletal fingers drumming on the stone steps. 'Though it would not be easily achieved.'

'The Lady is with me,' said Calard grimly. 'The duke will die by my blade, you have my oath on it.'

'Let's just get out of here,' said Raben over his shoulder.

Mortis's fingers drummed upon the dusty stone surface of the steps.

'Leave that one with us,' he said, gesturing towards Raben, 'and you are free to leave.'

'Take me with you,' said Raben swiftly. 'I'll get you close to Merovech. You won't get within a hundred yards of him without me.'

Calard considered his decision.

'He comes with me,' he said finally.

'He is one of the duke's sworn knights,' said Mortis. 'You think you can trust his word?'

'Not for a moment,' said Calard. 'He is an outcast and has no honour, but he may prove useful.'

The sound of a bell tolling in the distance echoed down through the catacombs, and Mortis looked up.

The bats on the ceiling erupted into flight, the beat of their wings and their high-pitched cries deafening. They swirled around the cavern in a dense cloud, like a school of shoaling fish, then hurtled through an opening in the ceiling and were gone. The doleful bell continued to sound.

'What is it?' said Calard.

'A warning. They have come to end it,' said Mortis. The peasants all around began shouting and wailing, hissing and gnashing their teeth.

'I don't like this,' said Raben. 'We have to go!'

'Merovech marches against us,' said Mortis. 'The Warren is no longer a safe haven.'

'He is here?' said Calard, eyes lighting up. 'Merovech is here?'

'He would not sully his hands in person,' said Mortis, shaking his head.

'How can you be sure?' said Calard. 'This could end now.'

'He is not here,' said Raben, firmly. 'He waits at the palace. A victory banquet has been prepared to welcome back his captains in two nights' time.'

'And how would you know that?' said Calard.

'I was invited,' said Raben with a sardonic smile.

'Enough talk. We leave now,' said Mortis.

'We?' said Calard.

'I'll get you inside the city,' said Grandfather Mortis.

VIII

'GODS, HAVE YOU ever smelt anything fouler?' growled Raben. Calard had to admit that he hadn't. Even with a cloth anointed with perfumed oil tied around his mouth and nose, he could barely keep from gagging.

They were moving single file through a narrow sewer tunnel, choosing their steps carefully. Mortis's peasants led the way, picking the safest and most direct route. Every surface was slick with filth, from the curving walls to the narrow shelf beneath their boots. Beside them was a foetid flow, barely moving and stagnant. Pale things wriggled within, making Calard's stomach heave. They passed countless floating bodies, their flesh rotting and bloated.

The torches they carried filled the narrow tunnels with sickly black smoke. Spider webs crackled as they were consumed by flame, and rats the size of small dogs scurried into the darkness, where they stopped and stared back at these interlopers into their realm, eyes glittering like malignant red jewels.

They were beneath the walled city of Mousillon, drawing ever nearer their goal. It had taken them almost three days to get here. Calard longed to see daylight and be away from Mortis and his repulsive brood.

At sluice junctions, places where the water flowed more swiftly, they encountered peasants fishing out bodies and floating junk with long poles. They clasped their muddy hats in their hands and bowed their heads respectfully as Grandfather Mortis passed by.

'You were telling me of L'Anguille,' said Calard. Calard was certain that the rebel knight was omitting many facts, but even so, he painted a bleak picture of the events leading to his becoming an outcast.

Raben sighed. 'I slit the bastard's throat. His death was quicker than he deserved.'

'He was your liege lord, whom you were sworn to protect and serve,' said Calard. They turned a corner, and rats scurried away from their light.

'Earl Barahir was a debauched fiend and a murderer,' said Raben. 'He had no honour. He got what he deserved.'

Calard remained silent. In truth, he could not say that he would have done differently had he been in Raben's place.

'I was stripped of my land and titles and imprisoned. I did not resist, assured that my family would be spared if I gave myself in willingly. They were not,' said Raben, bitterly. 'My wife was flogged and forced into the fields with the twins. I was due to hang, but guilt over what I brought upon my wife and daughters consumed me. Bribing my gaoler, I escaped, but the pox had already done its work. Perhaps it was a blessing that they did not suffer long. My daughters would have been on the cusp of womanhood by now, had they lived.'

'I'm sorry,' said Calard.

In the gloom, he saw Raben shrug.

'And so you came to Mousillon?' prompted Calard.

'And so I came to Mousillon,' said Raben. 'I had nothing to live for, but not the courage to end it. I was hunted as an outlaw, but my pursuers dropped off once I came here. That was nine years ago.'

They continued along in silence for some time, until word was passed back along the line that they were nearing to their destination.

'Thank the Lady for small mercies,' said Calard. Raben scoffed at his piety, and Calard glared at him.

'What?' said Raben, looking back at Calard. 'Worship of the Lady is a sham. Just because one of our forefathers thought he saw some watery tart doesn't mean–'

The outcast knight's words were cut short as he slipped in an overflow of effluent. He would have fallen into the befouled waters had not Calard grabbed him under one arm and hauled him back, dumping him unceremoniously on the ground.

Even so, one of Raben's boots broke the surface of the stinking flow. In the blink of an eye, a decaying corpse floating face down nearby lurched at him. Worms writhed in its throat as its mouth gaped open, and fingers that had rotted down to the bone latched onto Raben's leg.

The outcast knight cried out in shock, kicking at the horrid dead thing. Calard's sword carved into its head with a wet, squelching sound and it slipped back into the mire, releasing its grip. Raben scrambled back away from the edge and hauled himself to his feet, clearly shaken.

'The dead do not rest easy in Mousillon,' said Grandfather Mortis with an evil grin, materialising like a wraith out of the gloom. 'Come. This is where we part ways.'

THE HEAVY SEWER grate was dragged aside, and Calard lifted himself up from the darkness, eyeing his surroundings. He was in a shadowy, refuse-strewn alley no more than three feet wide. Rats were feasting on the body of a dead cat nearby, and they hissed at him aggressively as he interrupted their meal. The smell was hardly any better here than it was down in the sewer, but at least he was no longer below ground.

Calard turned and helped Raben out, then looked back down into the darkness.

'Hurry, peasant,' he said. 'We have not got much time.'

Down at bottom of the rusted ladder, unseen by Calard, Grandfather Mortis had a tight hold of Chlod and was speaking to him in a low, threatening voice. The hunchbacked peasant's face was pale.

'Do this one thing and your past crimes will be forgotten,' hissed Mortis.

Chlod nodded vigorously, and Mortis released him. Straightening, he stepped backwards and was swallowed by the darkness.

'Do not fail me,' came his deep, hollow voice.

Shaking, Chlod climbed up towards street level. Calard grabbed him by the shirt front and lifted him up the last few feet.

Calard had not wished to take the peasant with him, but Mortis had been insistent.

'He is no longer yours to command,' the old man had said. 'He is mine, and mine alone, but he accompanies you to the palace.'

The idea of being abandoned beneath the city had not been an appealing one, for he doubted that he would have ever gotten out, and he had reluctantly agreed.

The sewer grate was dragged back into place, and Calard pulled his hood down low over his face.

'Let's end this,' he said.

NEVER HAD CALARD walked the streets of a city more wretched, threatening or foul.

Every building was dark and oppressive, and so twisted beyond its original construction that it looked as though it was contorted in silent agony. Timbers were warped and swollen with moisture, and brickwork was bulging and uneven. The foundations of some had sunk, while others had seemingly given up completely and collapsed in upon themselves.

The smell of rot was heavy in the air and mould covered every surface. A foetid yellow fog filled the streets, reducing visibility to little more than a dozen yards, deadening all sound. The ground was rutted and undulating, and refuse and filth was piled up high against the walls.

They were not alone in this city of the damned.

Everywhere they walked they saw hundreds of downtrodden, desperate people, filthy and dressed in rags. From shuttered windows and dark alleyways, the inhabitants of Mousillon watched their progress through the district of Old City. Lepers and crippled beggars clutched at them, holding out wooden bowls. Miserable, malformed street-sellers sat alongside carts filled with rotten produce, while others offered them such tempting treats as twitching toads on sticks and greasy bags of slugs.

Wasted children clutching butcher's knives ran by them, giggling as they chased a terrified, scabby dog. Muscled brutes wearing leather masks were throwing fresh corpses onto a wagon piled high with the dead. Whores with bruises and open sores on their faces called out to them from doorways. Sickly smoke rose from shadowy dens where a man could lose himself if he had the coin and inclination.

Footpads, pickpockets and bruisers lurked in the shadows, but Calard and his companions were left well alone. It seemed that Mortis was as good as his word. The cadaverous old bastard had told them that they would be untouched, claiming that his word was law in the poorer districts of Mousillon. Calard had thought this boast just to be bluster, but he saw now that he had been mistaken. He had had no doubt in his mind that their throats would have already been slit and their bodies dumped in a back alley without Mortis's patronage.

It took them the better part of an hour to wind their way through the slums. At last they came to a wide bridge lined with crumbling statues that crossed the River Grismearie. The smell of brine was strong, for the river opened up to the sea less than five miles to the west.

The river was wide and slow here, and it bisected the city, dividing it into two halves. To the south were the poorer and more populated districts, along with the sprawling docklands. On the north side was the old temple district, and beyond that, the ducal palace itself.

IT WAS SAID that Mousillon had once been the pride of Bretonnia, its most bustling, wealthy and beautiful city. It had been home to Landuin, the finest knight to have ever lived, and was said to have been a place of beauty, culture and learning. How things changed, thought Calard.

Thousands of downward-pointing spikes protruded from the high walls lining the river, set several feet above the high-tide mark. Similar spikes adorned the legs of the mile-long bridge itself. Calard frowned.

'They stop the city from being overrun,' said Raben. 'Look there.'

Following where the outcast pointed, Calard squinted through the gloom. A number of corpses were impaled on the rusting spikes. With a shudder, he saw that most of them were moving.

'Come,' said Raben. 'This is our gate.'

A fortified gate barred entry to the north side of the city, and as they walked towards it, Calard saw armoured figures waiting for them. If Raben was going to betray him, this was his moment.

'Just so we are clear, you're on your own once we're inside,' said Raben under his breath, as if on cue.

'Fine,' said Calard.

'And if by some miracle you succeed, I want full patronage. A title. And land. A castle by the sea would be nice.'

'What?' said Calard.

'A little something to ensure that I don't accidentally let the cat out of the bag,' said Raben.

'For a moment, I was starting to think you risked showing something approaching honour,' Calard snarled.

'No fear of that,' said Raben. Calard began to answer, but Raben interjected. 'Careful now, they're watching,' he said. 'You want to get near the duke, don't you? One word from me, and your quest is over.'

They drew closer to the checkpoint, and Calard saw that there were more than twenty soldiers stationed here, armed with crossbows and halberds. The gates were closed and barred.

'If we get through this, and you somehow prove to me that I would not regret it, I'll see you are rewarded,' said Calard. 'I will offer you no more than that, but you have my word.'

'Just keep silent then,' said Raben as they came to a halt in front of the gate. He flashed a sardonic smile at Calard. 'Trust me.'

'YOU I KNOW, sir, but who are these, then?' said the captain of the guard, eyeing Calard and Chlod suspiciously.

'My second-in-command,' said Raben, 'and my servant. Let us through, captain. I don't want to be any later than we already are.'

'What's his name?' said the captain, indicating Calard. 'I don't recognise him, and I've a gift for faces.'

Calard opened his mouth to speak, but Raben interceded.

'Valacar,' said Raben. 'His name is Valacar.'

'Why don't he speak for himself?' said the captain.

'He's mute,' said Raben in a deadpan voice, ignoring Calard's stare.

'He's not on my list,' said the captain. 'And neither is your servant. My orders are strict. Ain't no one not on my list getting through this gate.'

'Let me make this simple,' Raben said, reaching out to put his arm around the captain's shoulders. 'The Duke Merovech is a close personal friend of mine, and he is expecting us to be there tonight. We are already late as it is, and if we are any later, I will make certain that I inform the duke personally exactly who it was that detained us. It is Harol, isn't it? That is your name, if I am not mistaken?'

'You are not, sir,' said the captain, swallowing heavily.

'Are we done here, captain?' said Raben, slapping the man hard on the shoulder.

'We're done. I'll have a coach drop you at the palace right away, sir. Open them up!'

Raben released the captain, and gave Calard a wink as the gates yawned open.

'Oh, and sir?'

'Yes, captain?' said Raben.

'Enjoy the celebration.'

'Oh, we will,' said Raben with a smile.

IX

THE COACH ROLLED smoothly to a halt and its black lacquered doors swung open, seemingly of their own accord. A small set of steps unfolded with a clatter, and Calard and Raben stepped down from the plush, dark velvet interior.

Other coaches were lined up around the curve of the circular roadway inside the palace gates. Each was gleaming black, and on every door was emblazoned a black fleur-de-lys upon a white shield. Hunched coachmen sat up front of each, garbed in flowing black robes, their faces hidden by dark hoods. Six immense horses were harnessed to each coach, their coats the colour of the midnight sky, and immaculate feathered plumes the colour of congealed blood bobbed above their heads. Each horse stood unnaturally still, like statues.

Chlod had ridden up front with the driver, and he stood waiting for them, his face drained of colour and his eyes wide and unblinking.

Twelve-foot-high fences enclosed the palace, tipped with wickedly sharp silver points, each shaped as a fleur-de-lys. Calard noted that there was a heavy guard presence. They stood at regular intervals around the palace exterior, utterly motionless, their features hidden in fully enclosed black plate armour of ancient design.

Grandiose stairs of red-veined black marble swept up before them, and Calard's gaze rose towards the palace itself.

It was breathtaking in its scale and the sheer audacity of its darkly majestic design. It was oppressive and domineering, yet in places its architecture was as delicate as lace. Dozens of spires rose like needles above immense lead-plated domes, linked by a web of delicate buttresses. Hanging arches that seemed to defy all the laws of gravity stretched between knife-edged towers. Slender columns reared up to support heavy archways that concealed grand stained-glass windows in their shadows, the coloured glass glinting in the fractured moonlit straining to penetrate the clouds. Rainwater dripped from the gaping mouths of fanged gargoyles, and winged statues carved of black granite gazed down upon them in mute disdain.

Other late arrivals were hurrying past them up the steps. Flustered ladies garbed in velvet and adorned with precious jewels were being hastened towards the palace by knights wearing freshly laundered tabards over battered suits of armour.

Calard and Raben climbed briskly, their faces grim, while Chlod trotted along behind them in silence.

The entry hall of the palace was cavernous, the arched ceiling a hundred feet high. Statues of past dukes of Mousillon were arrayed on pedestals, each standing in heroic poses and dressed for war. Pre-eminent was a dramatic sculpture of Merovech himself, five times life size, carved from a block of faultless white marble. He stood gazing into the distance, hair flowing in a frozen wind, one foot upon the chest of a headless enemy. The expression he wore was one of noble arrogance.

Standing as still as any of the statues, dozens of guards stood arrayed around the grand foyer, blocking access to closed doors and sweeping staircases that rose up to higher levels. The doors to the west wing had been thrown wide, and it was through here that Calard and Raben marched, following the other late arrivals.

Oil paintings lined the hallway, some of them almost twenty feet in height. Their frames were opulent and heavy, though many were fading and crumbling. Gaunt, unfriendly faces stared down at them from dark and somewhat disturbing portraits. Eyes seemed to follow them as they hurried by.

Turning a corner, Calard instinctively reached for his sword as they were suddenly surrounded by a swarm of pale, aristocratic courtiers, richly dressed as if for a masquerade ball. The ladies wore extravagant ball gowns and seemed to barely touch the ground as they glided across the floor upon the arms of their partners, who were garbed in strange, archaic fashion. All wore bizarre, grotesque masks, complete with devilish horns, jagged teeth and long, pointed noses. An icy chill seemed to penetrate Calard's bones as the courtiers passed them in silence, and he released his grasp on his sword hilt.

They moved deeper into the palace and could soon hear the ring of clashing swords. The harsh sound echoed through the cold halls, and as it got steadily louder, they could also make out polite clapping and the dull murmur of conversation.

Rounding a final corner, they approached a large, domed chamber. Hundreds of knights were gathered within, clustered in small groups and drinking wine.

'Where is Chlod?' said Calard suddenly, coming to a halt as they approached the entrance to the large room. Raben looked behind them. The peasant was nowhere to be seen. The outcast shrugged.

The clash of swords echoed loudly, and there was an enthusiastic cheer.

'No matter,' said Calard, and they moved within, slipping effortlessly into the crowd.

The chamber was even larger than it had at first appeared, and Calard guessed that there must have been in the realms of three hundred nobles gathered within. Massive pillars propped up the exquisitely painted domed ceiling, and dozens of alcoves and side-chambers were set off the main expanse.

A raised dais was positioned against the western wall, dominating the room. The statues of five ancient warriors were seated in high-backed thrones there, covered in a thick layer of dust and cobwebs. They sat side by side beneath an immense window of stained glass that depicted them as they had been in life. The window was backlit with candles, and Calard frowned up at the scenes of depravity and wanton barbarism depicted there. They showed the warriors slaughtering men, women and children, cutting their hearts out and drinking their blood.

A covered altar lit with candles was positioned centrally upon the dais in front of the old statues. A large chalice of silver and ebony was housed within this tabernacle, its shape formed in the likeness of serpentine wyrms twisting around one another.

Raben took a delicate crystal glass of claret from a tray, smiling and nodding to those he knew. Calard scanned the room, his gaze darting from face to face.

'Take a drink,' said Raben under his breath. 'And try not to look quite so out of place.'

Calard saw the sense in Raben's words and made a conscious effort to relax. They slipped through the crowd, angling towards the raised dais, and he nodded to several knights who turned to coldly regard him. They nodded in return and turned away in disinterest.

They approached the centre of the room, where the revellers were gathered most tightly. A circle some thirty feet in diameter was sunk into the centre of the chamber, positioned directly below the domed ceiling. Three circles of steps descended down to this sunken floor, which was carved with intricate spiralling designs.

Two knights were duelling in this combat circle, while more gathered knights and their ladies watched on, politely clapping and cheering when either knight scored a palpable hit. Calard hardly glanced at the two combatants as he pushed through the crowd, his gaze locking on a figure on the opposite side of the circle.

Merovech stood engrossed in the contest, arms folded across his chest. A full head taller than any other knight in the room, he was armoured in archaic, fluted armour of such dark metal it was virtually black, its edges serrated. His face was handsome and cruel, and as white as the palest marble. He appeared not to have aged at all from the last time Calard had seen him, six years earlier. His pure white hair was long and straight, hanging halfway down his back.

'This is where I leave you,' said Raben under his breath. 'I wish you luck.'

Calard ignored him, completely focused on the duke. Raben backed away into the crowd, and was gone.

Moving slowly, like a man stalking a wolf, Calard closed the distance with his prey.

X

CHLOD RAN AROUND the corner, breathing hard, and leaned back against the wall. His heart was thumping loudly, and he closed his eyes for a moment, trying to control his breathing. From beneath his shirt he pulled a rat skull attached to a string. Lifting it to his lips, he kissed it, whispering a prayer to Ranald, before tucking it back into place.

Glancing back around the corner, Chlod saw a pair of guards marching down the hallway towards him, their movements unhurried and perfectly synchronous. Each held a large double-handed sword, and was armoured head to toe in black plate armour.

Cursing under his breath, Chlod broke into an awkward run, moving as quickly as his ragged breath and uneven legs would allow. He ducked into a side-passage, and loped through a storage room packed to the ceiling with dusty casks and wooden pallets.

He was five levels below the ground. The nobility clearly rarely came down this low in the palace, for the passages were narrow, cluttered and bereft of the opulent ornamentation of the upper levels. This was the domain of the duke's servants, though he had seen far fewer of them down here than he had imagined were needed to service the daily running of the palace.

Rounding a corner, he came upon the kitchens, which were utterly deserted. Rats and spiders scuttled across the floor, and everything was covered in a thick layer of dust. Chlod judged that no one had used them for decades. There were four kitchens all in all, connected by low arches, and there were enough ovens to feed an army.

Hearing the clomp of armoured feet behind him, Chlod bolted, running through the kitchens and passing through a host of empty walkthrough pantries.

A pair of closed double doors loomed ahead of him. A rotten chair and a desk were tucked into an alcove alongside them. A skeleton was slumped in the chair, a quill pen still clasped in its hand. Chlod could see what looked like a ledger upon on the sloped desk, its paper yellow with age. Neat handwriting could still be discerned on the pages. Evidently, this was the post of the larder-master, whose job it was to keep a tally of all goods taken in and out. Chlod had worked for a time in a middling-sized castle in Carcassonne, and he had made an art out of deceiving the larder-master there. It had been a good life, that, and he had not felt a moment's remorse when the man had been hanged for the irregularities in this ledger.

A dark shadow seemed to hover around the skeleton slumped in the larder-master's chair, and it coalesced into a roughly man-like shape as Chlod drew near. It solidified as he got closer, turning from an indistinguishable vague shape to that of a portly man with huge sideburns.

It opened its mouth to speak, but no words came out. It seemed angry, gesturing insistently at Chlod with its ghost quill, and it radiated a deadly chill. He had no wish to pass near this restless spirit, but he could already hear the sound of armoured boots closing in behind him.

Taking a deep breath, his blood running to ice in his veins, Chlod hurried to the double doors. The spirit became more agitated, shouting soundlessly at him and pointing at its ledger. The doors would not give, and he rattled them as he struggled to turn the rusted handles. He glanced over his shoulder and saw the two black-armoured guards marching towards him.

The shade of the larder-master was incandescent with rage, bellowing at him silently. It came out from behind its desk, separating completely from its skeleton, and hovered towards him. Chlod quaked, fighting with the double doors vigorously as panic set in.

The ghost reached for him. Chlod recoiled from its touch, but there was nowhere to go, and he was backed up against the closed doors. The shadowy form touched his face, and he screamed. It felt as though needles of ice were penetrating his skin, and the left side of his face went numb. He saw the ethereal shade of the larder-master smile.

The doors gave way behind him suddenly, ripping free of their hinges, and Chlod crashed through. Weevils and rot-worms writhed in the splintered chunks of rotten wood, and he scrambled backwards through the debris.

The shade stared down at him from the open doorway. Its image wavered, like a mirage, as the two black-armoured guards marched through it.

Chlod clambered to his feet and ran. He staggered through storerooms stacked with empty shelves and others hanging with meat hooks, until he came to the very back of the larder. Here, a heavy wooden crane was positioned above a large wooden trapdoor in the floor. A thick, corroded chain was spooled around the crane's mechanism, and a massive hook hung at head height from the end of its length. The underside of a further trapdoor was positioned directly overhead, leading to the upper levels of the palace.

It was through these trapdoors that the palace's stores were replenished. Branches of the Grismarie had been redirected beneath the palace in centuries past, and in times gone by, barges laden with produce were poled up the wide tunnels from upriver. Casks of wines, pallets stacked with meats and all manner of goods and foodstuffs from all across Bretonnia and beyond would have once been hauled directly into the palace from the canals below without the Mousillon nobility ever being forced to witness their arrival.

Chlod turned around on the spot, eyes darting around frantically for a way to release the trapdoor, before his eyes settled on a rusted lever set in the wall. A spider the size of his hand had constructed an intricate web between the lever and the stone wall, and it turned towards him, a myriad of eyes glinting in the darkness. He slapped it away, and took hold of the lever's handle.

The lever was ancient and rusted, and had clearly not been used for decades. It resisted him, and he closed his eyes as he strained to move it. He planted one foot against the wall and bent his back against it, groaning with the exertion. It did not budge.

The guards closed towards him unerringly, hefting their heavy swords. They were less than ten yards away.

'Come on!' shouted Chlod, tugging frantically on the lever.

With a horrendous screeching of metal, the lever gave way and Chlod fell to the ground. There was a grinding of gears and the two halves of the trapdoor swung downwards, like the floor beneath a hangman's noose. They struck the walls of the vertical shaft with a resounding boom, and at the same moment, the chain from the crane began to unspool. The heavy hook rocketed down into the darkness, and the sound of the chain unravelling was deafening.

A cloud of bats erupted from below, screeching and clawing. In their midst, eyes tinged red and their flesh covered in open sores and filth, the most devolved of Grandfather Mortis's children burst from the darkness. A narrow staircase descended around the edge of the vertical shaft leading down to the canal fifty feet below, and dozens of wild-eyed, emaciated figures appeared, crawling over each other in their haste.

One of them was cut almost in two by a black-armoured guard, the heavy blow splitting him diagonally from shoulder to hip. Then the two armoured figures disappeared beneath the feral tide, borne to the ground with a crash.

The chain had come to a shuddering halt, and after a pause, it began to reverse, hauled back up by toothed cogs and immense counter-weights hidden behind the stone wall.

Chlod lay still, breathing heavily, as he watched the demise of the two guards. Rocks pounded their helmets until the metal buckled inwards, and knives were slid between gaps in their plate. Finally, the two armoured figures were still. One of their visors had been wrenched completely out of shape and torn loose, and Chlod hurriedly looked away as he saw what was contained within. If ever the suit of armour had ever been worn by a living man, that time was long past.

The chain continued to recoil, clunking loudly as each link was reeled in. Finally, the massive hook reappeared. Four iron rings had been attached to it, each hooked into smaller chains that were orange with rust. A loading pallet was hauled into view, carrying the smiling figure of

Grandfather Mortis, who was standing with his arms raised above him like an ascendant god.

A cluster of filthy peasants manhandled the crane, swinging it away from the gaping trapdoor, and it settled to the floor with a final groan.

'Excellent, excellent,' said Mortis, stepping away from the platform and rubbing his skeletal hands together.

He moved towards Chlod, still lying against the wall, and lifted him gently to his feet. He stroked Chlod's cheek with the back of one grey, wrinkled hand. 'You have done well, my child,' he said. 'The sins of the past are forgiven.'

Grandfather Mortis continued to stroke Chlod's cheek for a moment, then he grabbed him tightly around the neck, his thumbs pressing hard into his throat. Chlod gaped like a landed fish, his eyes boggling.

'But don't even think about leaving us again,' said Mortis. 'You belong with us, and I will not tolerate any disobedience from you again.'

From somewhere distant, there came a ferocious roar, booming up through the lower levels of the palace. Mortis released Chlod, a look of rapture upon his face, and Calard's manservant fell to his knees, gasping for air.

'Harken, my children!' said Mortis, lifting a hand to his ear. 'Hear the call of our beloved lord!

XI

HIS FACE A mask of grim resolve, Calard slipped through the braying crowd. His gaze did not waver from Merovech. Calard was some ten people back from the edge of the fighting circle, and was making his way steadily through the press, closing the distance to the albino duke. His fist was clenched tightly around the hilt of the Sword of Garamont, sheathed at his hip.

There was a grunt of pain and a splash of blood in the fighting circle below, and the crowd roared its approval. Merovech alone made no reaction, his expression cold and detached. Calard ignored the glances he received from knights and ladies as he pushed his way through the onlookers, drawing ever nearer the butcher responsible for the sacking of Castle Garamont.

'Kill him!' shouted a woman wearing a spidery lace ruff around her slender neck. Her powdered cheeks were flushed and her pupils dilated. Her cry was echoed by dozens of others, all crying out for blood.

Calard was now directly behind Merovech, and he began to work his way forwards, shouldering through the crowd.

The duke stood alone, aloof and distant from all those gathered around him. No one came within arm's distance of his person, possibly out of respect, or perhaps more likely out of fear. Merovech was a motionless island amidst a braying sea of humanity, yet far from making him appear unthreatening or calm, his utter stillness was deeply unsettling.

It set him apart from those around him, perhaps even more so than his alabaster countenance, making him appear inhuman and alien.

Calard's gaze never wavered. Cold fury burned in his eyes. He was only yards away now, only seconds from attaining his vengeance. His whole being became utterly focused, his senses heightened to unsurpassed levels in anticipation of this final confrontation.

He could smell the sickly fragrance of the scented perfumes and oils worn by the courtiers, which did little to mask the excited sweat exuded by those watching the brutal contest below. He could taste the metallic tang of blood in the air. He could hear every grunt and grimace of the two duelling knights, the scrape of their boots upon the grooved floor of the killing circle, and the sharp *clang* of metal on metal. He could feel the reassuring weight of the Sword of Garamont beneath his grasp.

Calard stood directly behind the duke now. All he had to do was draw his blade and run the fiend through. No one, not Merovech nor any of his gathered knights would be able to stop him. He started drawing the Sword of Garamont before he regained control of himself.

Cutting an enemy down from behind, even a monster like Merovech, was an honourless, dog act, and one that would lessen him in his own eyes and the eyes of the Lady. And besides, Merovech was only one half of the murderous pair that had butchered his nephew and laid waste to his castle. Before Merovech died, he was honour bound to discover the identity of the second fiend, so that he too could be brought to justice.

The duel came to a sudden, brutal end. It was a shockingly one-sided affair, with one knight clearly toying with the other. Finally tiring of the game, he struck his opponent a vicious blow to the neck. The knight dropped to one knee, sword clattering from his grip.

Calard saw all this only dimly, the action taking place in his peripheral vision, his gaze still locked on Merovech.

The crowd hollered and stomped their feet, and Calard heard the fallen knight begging for mercy. The other knight turned his back on him, lifting his sword high into the air, accepting the roar of the crowd. The beaten warrior lowered his hand, and his head dropped in defeat. There was a lot of blood, but the wound was not fatal.

With inhuman speed and savagery, the victorious knight swung around suddenly, sword blade flashing. The defenceless knight was decapitated, and a fountain of blood erupted from the stump of his neck. The head bounced and rolled across the floor, coming to a halt against the lowest curved step of the killing circle. A surprised expression was etched upon its ashen face. For a second the headless corpse remained upright, blood spraying forth in rhythmic spurts, before it toppled forwards and was still. Blood continued to gush from the body, running into the spiralling grooves carved in the floor. The crowd cheered their approval.

The speed and savagery of the dishonourable blow dragged Calard's attention briefly away from his foe.

He looked upon the face of the duel's victor, and his blood ran cold. It was his brother, Bertelis.

XII

CALARD'S EYES WIDENED in horror.

Bertelis stood alone in the circle, splattered in blood. His face bore an unhealthy pallor, and a cruel half-smile ghosted across his blue-tinged lips. He dropped to his knees before Duke Merovech.

'For your honour, my lord,' said Bertelis in a voice that made the hairs on the back of Calard's neck stand on end. It was at once his brother's voice, and it wasn't, tinged with bitterness and cruelty.

Merovech laid his hand upon the back of Bertelis's head as if in some dark benediction. They held the pose for a moment, then Merovech spoke.

'Rise,' he said, his voice cold and dispassionate.

Calard was frozen in place, staring at his brother.

The duke loosened one of his exquisite, tight-fitting leather gloves and pulled it free, exposing a hand as pale as virgin snow. He drew a slender dagger from his hip and placed it across his naked hand. His fingers closed tightly around the blade, and with a smooth, slow movement, he slid the dagger free. His blood shone brightly upon the blade.

Sheathing the knife, Merovech clicked his fingers and a goblet of wine was handed to him. He lifted his pale hand above the goblet, still clenched in a fist, and let his blood drip steadily into the wine. When the flow ceased, he handed the goblet to Bertelis, who accepted it with a look of hunger.

'All of Mousillon salutes you, Bertelis, champion of champions,' said Merovech.

Bertelis lifted the goblet high, then threw his head back and gulped back its contents. He shuddered in rapture, his eyes half-closed as he lowered the drinking vessel from his lips.

Calard groaned in horror as he watched his brother drink the wine infused with blood, shocked to the core of his being. Bertelis wiped a ruby drip from the corner of his mouth, and Duke Merovech stepped down into the centre of the duelling ring. He moved with a lion's grace.

Bertelis had always been tall, standing half a head clear of Calard himself, but Merovech towered over him. He turned around on the spot, eyeing the gathered knights. His white features contrasted sharply with the black of his armour, and his red-tinged eyes glinted in the torch-light, like those of a wolf. All conversation had ceased in the chamber, and now all were gathered close in around the duelling pit to hear their master's words.

'Tonight is an auspicious night, my brothers,' said Merovech, his voice booming out to fill the expansive hall. He began to stalk around the perimeter of the circle, like a caged beast. 'Tonight is the dawning of a new era in Mousillon's history. Once, our realm was the most powerful in all Bretonnia. Now we have a chance to reclaim that glory, you and I.'

Calard found himself captivated by Merovech, unable to tear his eyes away from him.

'For seven hundred years I slumbered,' said Merovech. 'I awoke to find Mousillon a pale shadow of its glorious past, overrun with vermin, its lands annexed by its neighbours, its very name a byword for despair and failure. But now, I have returned. Now, Mousillon will rise again. And you, my brothers, will rise with it.'

Merovech had returned to the centre of the circle and now he stopped his restless pacing. Calard could feel the excitement building amongst the onlookers.

'Each of you has proven yourself worthy,' said Merovech, 'and so, I will grant you the greatest gift that you shall ever receive. Tonight, you become as gods among men, and together we shall take back what is rightfully ours. All of Bretonnia shall kneel before us, and the lands shall run red with blood.'

As if on cue, there came a grinding of gears and the turning of ancient mechanisms, and the domed ceiling overhead began to open, unfurling like the petals of a black rose under the midnight sky. The clouds were parting overhead, and the silver light of Mannslieb shone down into the expansive chamber. There were gasps from the crowd of onlookers, but it was not for this mechanical wonder, or the sight of the silver moon. No, those intakes of air were for the appearance of the second moon: Morrslieb, glowing malignant and green, that stared down at them like a baleful eye.

Merovech was standing with his arms raised to the heavens, bathing in Morrslieb's sinister emerald glow.

'It is time!' bellowed the duke. 'Bring forth the prisoner!'

BOUND IN HEAVY, ensorcelled chains and surrounded by armed guards, the prisoner was dragged up through the palace halls from the oubliette that had held it, far below. It bellowed its fury, the sound echoing deafeningly through the lower levels. Its massive body was a patchwork of burns, savage cuts and mottled bruises courtesy of the duke's finest torturers. More than a score of muscle-bound wardens hauled upon the thick chains, straining and heaving to keep the prisoner moving. They wore black leather hoods over their heads, and were accompanied by an entourage of palace guards, silent, long-dead warriors enclosed in black plate armour.

The ambush hit them hard and fast. The battle took place halfway up a wide marble staircase, with the attackers striking simultaneously from above and below. The fight was brutal and bloody, and over within thirty heartbeats. The prisoner itself tore apart half a dozen of its gaolers, ripping them limb from limb in a gory explosion of rage and savagery.

Grandfather Mortis approached the prisoner warily, hands raised, as one might approach a wounded bear. His eyes were full of pity as he looked upon his lord's tortured flesh.

Murmuring calming words, he laid a hand gently upon one of the prisoner's immensely muscled shoulders. Its heavy head came up sharply, snarling, and Mortis jerked back. Its snarl descended into a low, warning rumble deep in its chest, and Mortis placed his hand back upon its shoulder. This time it accepted his touch.

'It's over,' said Grandfather Mortis in a soothing voice. 'It's over.'

'No,' growled the prisoner, forming the words with some difficulty. Its mouth was built for tearing and ripping, not for speech. 'It is time for vengeance.'

CALARD SAW THE thrill of anticipation on Bertelis's ungodly pale face, mirroring the expression of every onlooker. His brother grinned, exposing needle-sharp canines.

'Blessed Lady of mercy,' Calard breathed.

As if hearing his words, Bertelis's head snapped around. For a second his eyes darted from face to face, searching for who had spoken, but then they settled on Calard. His grin widened, and he began to chuckle. With slow, unhurried movements he drew his sword and began walking towards Calard. The knights and ladies around the questing knight drew back away from him, leaving him isolated and exposed.

'Hello, Calard,' said Bertelis. 'What a pleasant surprise this is.'

'What has he done to you, my brother?' said Calard, standing alone.

'Nothing that I did not wish for,' said Bertelis with a grin, loosening the muscles of his neck and shoulders languorously, like a cat stretching. 'And it feels fantastic.'

'Finish it quickly,' hissed Merovech. 'The time of the conjunction draws near.'

'I've been looking forward to this for a long time, *brother*,' spat Bertelis, hefting his sword and moving purposefully across the killing circle.

Reluctantly, Calard drew the Sword of Garamont and stepped out to meet him. He swung his battered shield from his back and secured it on his left arm.

'It does not have to be like this, brother,' he said.

'Oh, it does,' said Bertelis. 'It truly does.'

BERTELIS ATTACKED WITH such savagery and speed that Calard was instantly fighting for his life, defending desperately as furious attack after attack rained down on him. It took all his concentration, skill and hard-earned experience just to survive the opening exchange, and such was the power and vitriol behind each blow that he was knocked physically backwards each time his sword met his brother's.

He was given no opportunity to even consider launching a counter-attack, and his left arm was numb from the jarring blows he took on his shield. He was doing all he could to evade Bertelis's furious assault, stepping off the line of attack and retreating hastily in an effort to put some distance between them. His brother came after him relentlessly, sword blade flashing as it sliced through the air again and again. Had any of those attacks struck home, they would have been fatal.

Calard knew that he was a vastly superior warrior now than he had been when he first took up the quest, six years earlier. The long years on the road had hardened him, body and soul, forging him anew and honing his killer instincts to a razor's edge. He was stronger, leaner and faster than he had been, and was confident enough in his own abilities to back himself against any man. Even so, he was struggling now with the pace of battle that Bertelis was setting, and struggling even more with his brother's unprecedented strength and fury.

Calard and Bertelis had trained together since childhood, and both had been schooled by Gunthar, the old weapon master of Garamont. Growing up, their duels had always been evenly matched, though it had been obvious that Bertelis was the more gifted of the two, a natural swordsman with the perfect blend of strength, balance, speed and instinct. He had always relied too heavily on his natural-born talents, however, and in his youth had been a lax student, earning many stern words from Gunthar. In contrast, Calard had worked hard at his swordsmanship, rising hours before the rest of the household to hone his technique and strengthen his body. It was only after Gunthar's death that Bertelis began taking his training more seriously, devoting himself to it with a focus bordering on obsession. Only then had he started to show his true potential.

It was clear now that Bertelis had eclipsed those expectations and taken them to a whole new level, reaching a plane that Calard had no hope of matching, and even less of competing with. Bertelis's skill was bordering the sublime, and Calard could think of few – perhaps only the Grail Knight Reolus, Lady rest his soul – that could have equalled it. The speed of his blade was incomparable, and Calard had rarely crossed blades with one who struck with such power. It was overwhelming how far Bertelis's blade skill had come in the last six years. Calard felt like a child facing a master.

A blow thundered into his shield, wrenching it out of shape, and he winced. He slashed a riposte towards his brother's neck, but it was batted aside with contemptuous ease. Bertelis grinned and stepped back, allowing Calard a moment to catch his breath. He realised that his brother was toying with him, just as he had his earlier opponent.

'You have grown soft,' said Bertelis.

'Turn from this path, Bertelis,' said Calard. 'It leads you only to damnation.'

'You drove me onto this path, brother,' snapped Bertelis. '*You* turned your back on *me*!'

'And I'm truly sorry,' said Calard. 'My words were spoken in haste. I was blinded by grief. I meant not what I said.'

'It is too late for apologies,' said Bertelis, and Calard knew he spoke the truth. There was a madness behind his eyes that Calard had never seen before, a simmering, insatiable rage that threatened to consume him. It was as if some wild beast had taken up residence in the flesh of his brother, directing his movements like a puppet.

'You are no longer the brother I knew and loved,' said Calard. His breath was ragged from the intensity of the fight, yet Bertelis appeared completely rested, barely having raised a sweat.

'No,' agreed Bertelis. 'I am something far greater.'

'Enough!' hissed Duke Merovech from the edge of the killing circle. 'Finish it, now!'

Calard's gaze darted between the fiend that was once his brother and the pale, immortal figure of Duke Merovech. Realisation dawned.

'It was you who sacked Garamont,' he said, looking back at Bertelis. 'It was you who killed Orlando and Montcadas, and butchered my knights.'

'I would have killed you too,' said Bertelis, 'had you been there. Now, the cycle will be complete, and every tie to my former life will at last be severed.'

'You are not even human,' said Calard. Bertelis smiled in response, exposing needle-sharp canines.

'My, you are quick, brother,' he said. The smile dropped from his face. 'And now, you die.'

For a moment the brothers regarded each other from opposite sides of the killing circle, before they began closing the distance, swords at the ready.

A deafening roar boomed through the cavernous chamber, echoing loudly and making the windows rattle in their frames. Calard could feel the reverberant sound in his bones. He looked up, the duel momentarily forgotten.

An arched balcony jutted out over the room, thirty feet overhead, and crouched upon its marble balustrade was a monster.

XIII

IT WAS HUGE, easily six times the bulk of a man, and it looked like some monstrous gargoyle come to life. It was hunched, and black matted fur covered its massive shoulders. Immense talons carved furrows in the marble as it tensed its huge arms, bulging with sinew and muscle. It howled at the heavens again, the sound deeply affecting on some primal level, before turning its baleful gaze down into the chamber below.

Its head was huge and wide, a hideous blend of man, bat and wolf. Its lips drew back to expose a terrifying array of fangs, and its snarl rumbled deep in its powerful chest. Its canines were heavily pronounced, and each was easily six inches in length. Its eyes were those of a predator, burning with fury and hunger, and they locked on the pale figure of Duke Merovech, far below.

The monster howled again, spittle flying from its maw, and it launched from its eyrie. Powerful leg muscles propelled it downwards at astonishing speed, and its huge taloned arms extended in front of it, veined membranes of skin unfurling from wrist to hip like vestigial wings.

It hurtled downwards, like a monstrous bird of prey dropping on its quarry, and shouts and screams erupted across the chamber. Calard heard the sound of weapons clashing along with cries of shock and pain, and through the dense crowd he spied the filth-encrusted forms of Grandfather Mortis's children, leaping and howling as they attacked. Like a frenzied pack, they descended on the crowded chamber, and chaos erupted.

Duke Merovech hurled himself to one side as the monster struck. It slammed down into the floor with titanic force, sending cracks shooting out across the surface of the marble from the impact. Merovech rolled neatly to his feet, a sword in each hand.

People were running across the killing circle in panic, separating Calard and Bertelis. He saw his brother fighting his way through the crowd towards him, his face a mask of fury. A knight slammed into Calard, knocking him back a step, and a heavy blow to his arm knocked the Sword of Garamont from his grasp. The ancient heirloom clattered to the ground and was kicked away, spinning just out of reach.

Calard swore and dived after it. Someone tripped over him and fell sprawling, and he grunted as he was kicked and trampled, but he ensured that he kept his eyes locked on the holy sword. He reached for it, and his fingers grazed its hilt tantalisingly, but then it was kicked away again, this time disappearing into the crowd. Glancing over his shoulder, he saw Bertelis storming towards him, hacking down knights, ladies and feral peasants alike, and he swore again.

Fighting back to his feet, he tore the shield from his arm and hurled it aside. He reached up over his back and yanked his hand-and-a-half sword from its scabbard as Bertelis drew close.

Had he been a fraction slower he would have been dead, and he only barely managed to block Bertelis's blow slicing in at his neck. He was knocked back a step and Bertelis came after him, getting inside the reach of his longer blade.

He was completely outclassed, and they both knew it. Confident that Calard could not match him, Bertelis was now fighting well within his own limits, and his form was slipping. Calard's anger swelled; he was determined to punish Bertelis for such arrogance, but knew he might only get one chance.

After a few more passes, Bertelis lunged. Calard sidestepped neatly, turning side-on to let Bertelis's momentum take him past him. His brother's blade slid by him, a hair's-breadth from his throat. With a grunt of exertion, he rammed his sword's heavy pommel into the side of Bertelis's head, putting his whole armoured weight behind it.

The move was expertly delivered, his timing perfect, and it should have caved Bertelis's skull in. His brother's head snapped back, but he did not fall. Calard used the moment to step back, adopting a ready stance with his blade held high, its point levelled at Bertelis.

A trickle of blood ran from Bertelis's temple, but he appeared otherwise unaffected by the blow. He reached up to the wound, and then licked the blood from his finger tips.

'For that, I'm going to make this really hurt,' said Bertelis.

Calard lunged at him and Bertelis danced out of the way. Calard turned, sweeping his blade overhead and bringing it crashing down in a heavy, diagonal strike. Bertelis parried it early and leapt in under the blade to grab Calard by the throat. He moved so fast, he was little more than a blur. His grip was like iron, and his snarling face was close. Up close, he looked barely human at all, his eyes glinting with fathomless hunger and madness, his skin almost translucent, and his expression twisted and bestial.

'Orlando's blood was so sweet, so innocent,' he hissed. 'It was like nectar on my lips, sweeter than the finest wine.'

Bertelis lifted Calard off his feet, holding him aloft with one hand before tossing him aside like a child. Calard slammed into one of Merovech's knights, bowling him over, and they fell in a tangled heap. Calard was up first, and as the knight grappled with him, he pummelled his elbow into the man's face, dropping him instantly.

Calard staggered to his feet, dragging his sword up. Bertelis's boot slammed down on it hard, snapping the blade halfway up its length, and Calard reeled back.

A knight lunged at him with a drawn sword, and Calard swayed to the side, avoiding the killing thrust. He stabbed the jagged end of his shattered sword into the man's face, and he fell away with a strangled cry. Another knight swung at him from behind, but Calard sidestepped neatly. Grabbing the man's arm as he came around, he pulled him off-balance, shoving him into Bertelis's path.

Without blinking, Bertelis ran the knight through, and the tip of Bertelis's blade burst from his back. He dragged his sword clear, and hurled the man aside.

Calard took a moment to survey his surroundings. The attack by Mortis's feral brood had taken the knights by surprise, but they were fighting back now, gathering into tight huddles to support each other, and both sides were taking heavy casualties. Bodies were strewn across the chamber floor, and more than a few of the hunched peasants had dropped to the ground to feed, unable to restrain their hunger amid the sight and smell of so much blood.

He saw Mortis standing alone, up on the balcony where the monster had appeared, watching the mayhem unfold.

The immense beast and Duke Merovech had taken their fight up onto the raised dais where the five statues sat enthroned, separating themselves from the chaotic melee below.

The creature was bleeding from a dozen wounds, but it did not appear to be slowing. Merovech danced and weaved like a dervish, ducking under blows that would have torn him in half, twin blades flashing. He moved with preternatural speed, but the monster he fought was almost as quick, despite its bulk. As he watched, he saw the beast catch Merovech a glancing blow that sent the duke skittering across the dais like a rag doll, crashing into the central altar holding the huge, dark chalice with bone-jarring force.

The beast roared in victory and leapt after him but Merovech recovered quickly, and rolled under the blade-like talons that hammered down towards him. As he came to his feet, both blades carved bloody furrows across the monster's chest, and it hissed in pain.

Using the immense beast's arm like a ladder, Merovech turned and leapt lightly up his enemy's body, spinning both swords around in his hands so that they were pointed downwards, like daggers. Kicking off the beast's chest, he turned in mid-air and plunged both swords into its neck.

The monster bellowed. Both swords were embedded to the hilt, and Calard could see their tips protruding from the back of its neck as it thrashed around in pain. It reached up and ripped both weapons free, hurling them away from it, and blood gushed from the wounds. Such a blow ought to have been fatal, but the beast merely shook its head and dropped to all fours, and began stalking towards the now unarmed Duke Merovech.

'Your master's going to die,' said Calard as Bertelis closed the distance between them.

'I think not,' said his brother. 'No devolved varghulf is a match for him.'

Bertelis lunged, feinting high and coming in low with a brutal attack intended to disembowel him. Calard saw it coming, and dropped his guard to block the vicious attack, but Bertelis had already shifted the angle of his attack once more.

Spinning on his heel, Bertelis turned quickly, his head whipping around and his body following. His sword slashed across Calard's shoulder, striking just under his pauldron. The blow hacked through his chainmail and padding, and bit deep into flesh before striking bone.

Before Calard could even cry out, Bertelis spun back around the way he had come and rammed his blade into Calard's body. The tip penetrated just inside his hip, slipping through the slender gap under his breastplate.

Calard gasped, and his shattered sword-blade dropped from his hands. He fell to one knee, and Bertelis loomed above him, his blade slick with blood.

'Goodbye, brother,' said Bertelis, drawing his sword back for the killing thrust.

A knight burst from the crowd nearby. He had a sword in each hand, and he shouted at the top of his lungs as he charged.

'Calard!' Raben cried, tossing one of the blades towards him.

Calard caught the sword, his fingers closing around the familiar hilt.

Raben swung a two-handed blow at Bertelis, who turned and blocked the attack with one of his own. Dropping to one knee, Bertelis slashed from right to left across Raben's stomach, carving through his chain hauberk and the muscle beneath, then rose and kicked the outcast away.

With a snarl, Bertelis rounded on Calard, but his eyes went wide as the Sword of Garamont impaled him.

Calard was on his feet now, and he grunted with effort as gave his sword another shove, ramming it up into Bertelis's body.

Blood gushed from the fatal wound, and Bertelis's face became increasingly gaunt, as if all the moisture in his body was being sucked out of him. His features became ever more skeletal and inhuman as his translucent flesh withered, his lips drawing back to expose his savage fangs. Calard stepped back, a look of disgust on his face, and slid his blade free.

The Sword of Garamont was glowing with an aura of white light, and Calard looked upon it in wonder. Bertelis's blood spattered off it, leaving the blade spotless. The shimmering radiance felt like sunlight on Calard's face, and despite the mayhem surrounding him, he felt a sense of calm and assurance envelop him.

Bertelis fell to his knees, blood pooling beneath him. His flesh continued to shrink upon his skull, until he looked barely human at all. His hands had withered to little more than talons, and their veins, purple and blue, stood out sharply. He glared up at Calard then. Hatred and fury burnt in his eyes, but also fear. He hissed like a cornered animal, teeth bared, as if he were devolving before Calard's eyes.

The luminosity of the sword in Calard's hands intensified, glowing hot and pure, and Bertelis's skin began to blacken and blister beneath its glare. He held his hands up, shielding his eyes, and they too began to burn. A pitiful wail emitted from his throat.

'Lady, give him peace,' murmured Calard, clasping his sword in both hands. Without pause, he stepped forwards and beheaded the creature that had once been Bertelis.

Raben was lying on the ground nearby, clutching at his stomach, and he smiled wryly as his gaze met Calard's.

'Thank you,' said Calard.

Raben grunted. 'That was your brother?' he said, indicating towards Bertelis's corpse with his chin.

'No,' said Calard. 'My brother died a long time ago.'

A roar of pain and fury dragged Calard's attention up towards the raised dais. The immense, loathsome beast that Bertelis had called a varghulf was down, blood pooling beneath it. Its flesh was slashed and torn, hanging from it in bloody tatters.

Duke Merovech stood before it, sword in hand. He too was injured. One of his pauldrons had been ripped away, exposing his shoulder, which was covered in blood. Four bloody rents were carved through his breastplate. Nevertheless, Duke Merovech stood victorious, and Calard shook his head in wonderment. Could nothing kill him?

The varghulf's powerful legs bunched for one final spring, but it was never given the chance. Duke Merovech hurled his sword aside and leapt towards his enemy with a blood-curdling battle cry, hands extended like claws. He grabbed the immense creature by the head, grappling with it, and with a roar of effort, he wrenched it upwards, exposing its neck.

Merovech's fangs flashed, and he tore into the varghulf's neck. The creature fought against him, but its strength was gone. For long moments Merovech drank, glutting himself before pulling away. His mouth and chin were caked in blood.

Duke Merovech dragged the immense weight of the varghulf across the dais floor, until he reached the altar. With one hand, he grabbed the chalice from altar's tabernacle. He glanced heavenward. The green moon of Morrslieb was eclipsing Mannslieb now, like a repulsive, burning pupil in a silver iris. Apparently satisfied, Merovech forced the varghulf's neck back, and lowered his mouth to its neck once more. This time he did not feed, but rather tore. He ripped open its throat, and the last of its blood began to gush forth.

GRANDFATHER MORTIS CLUTCHED unsteadily at the railing of the balcony as he watched his beloved lord and master slain. His children were being butchered down below, their will to fight evaporating as they too registered that their master was no more.

He staggered back, casting his eyes from the sickening sight of his master's body defiled. A took a deep, shuddering breath, and turned away.

A heavy spiked cudgel smashed one of his kneecaps to splinters, and he fell to the ground with a cry of pain and shock.

Chlod stood over him, and the old man gaped up at him.

'Fifteen years I was your slave, one of your cursed *children*,' said Chlod. 'I'll not be that again.'

The hunchbacked peasant spat in Mortis's face, making the old man flinch. That merely enraged Chlod more, and he slammed his spiked cudgel into Mortis's side. Ribs snapped like dry twigs.

'Fifteen years I stole and murdered for you, you old bastard,' said Chlod. 'Fifteen years you starved me. How many times did I feel the touch of your switch, hmm? How many bones did you break? How many scars did you leave?'

He made to strike Mortis again, and the old man recoiled, his face twisted in agony.

'Who has the power now?' said Chlod.

'I took you in, you wretched ingrate,' hissed Mortis between clenched teeth. 'I fed you! I clothed you! I! Without me you'd be dead! You'd be nothing! I made you what you are!'

'You did at that,' said Chlod. 'Do you like what you see?'

Chlod brought his spiked cudgel down again and again, and as loud as Mortis's screams were, no one came to his aid. He continued his brutal attack even after Mortis had ceased screaming, even after he was far beyond recognisable.

Finally, Chlod stopped his relentless assault. He was breathing heavily, and tears were running down his face. He was completely covered in blood, and chunks of skin and hair clung to the spikes of his club.

He spat down on the thing that had once been Grandfather Mortis, and then turned away.

CALARD KNELT BY Raben, and gently drew back the outcast's arm to see the extent of his injuries.

'How's it look?' said Raben. His face was pale.

'It's a scratch,' said Calard. 'You'll be whoring again in a week, mark my words.'

'Liar,' said Raben, with a sardonic smile.

'You'll survive,' said Calard, more seriously. 'Though you'll have one hell of a scar to match that one,' he said, indicating the jagged old wound that crossed Raben's throat.

'Ladies don't like a man that's too pretty,' said Raben.

'Well, you certainly aren't that,' said Calard, casting a wary eye around them.

There were few left standing, in truth. It seemed that both sides had practically annihilated the other, though from the looks of things, there were far more of Mortis's people dead than Merovech's.

Looking back up towards the dais, he saw that Merovech had filled the chalice with the varghulf's blood. Now he stood, letting the massive creature's head drop to the floor, dead. The vampire duke moved towards the first of the throned statues. He raised the chalice above its head, and tipped it slightly, allowing a trickle of frothing blood to drip onto the statue's head. Red rivulets ran down over its face, removing centuries of dust and grime. Calard's heart skipped a beat as the statue moved.

It turned its face up towards the stream of blood, its mouth opening wide, showing off impressively elongated canines. Its tongue lapped at the flow, and Calard saw its throat moving as it swallowed.

'That's not good,' said Raben.

Merovech righted the chalice, and the enthroned creature returned to its former position. The duke moved on to the next in line, but Calard's gaze was locked on the first. Its eyes snapped open, and it smiled.

Calard took a few steps towards the steps of the dais, knowing that he stood little chance against Merovech alone, even without with his newly awoken allies. Nevertheless, he had sworn an oath, and would see Merovech dead or die in the attempt.

'Calard,' called Raben, and he looked back. 'Don't throw your life away.'

'This is something I have to do,' Calard said. He swung back around. His step faltered as the holy light radiating from the Sword of Garamont dimmed, then died altogether. He halted, looking down at it.

What did it mean? Did the Lady disapprove of his actions? But how could she? Was it not she who had led him here?

Three of the 'statues' had come awake now, and were on their feet, blinking and stretching their necks like men awakening from a deep slumber. Each was as tall as Merovech himself, and all of them were garbed in similar, barbed armour.

Calard stood stock still, indecision plaguing him.

'Lady, give me a sign,' he whispered. 'Show me what it is you wish of me.'

A blinding flash exploded in Calard's mind, sending him crashing to his knees, his eyes tightly closed. He gasped at the searing pain in his temples, clutching his head in his hands.

A bewildering flash of images assailed him, overwhelming in their intensity and their power.

It was over in an instant, the pain gone as if it had never been, but the images were seared forever into his mind's eye.

'As you will it, Lady, so shall it be done,' he whispered.

'Calard?' called Raben, straining to see him.

'We have to go,' said Calard, turning his back on the dais, where all five of Merovech's vampiric lieutenants how now arisen.

Calard hurried to Raben's side.

'We have to go,' he said again.

'Sounds good to me,' said Raben.

'Put your arm around me,' said Calard, and then he lifted Raben to his feet. The outcast knight groaned in pain, but did not cry out. Together, they staggered across a floor littered with the dead, making their way towards the chamber's exit. The few of Merovech's knights that still stood paid them no heed, staring in wonder at the duke and his newly arisen entourage.

At the door of the chamber they paused, glancing back within.

The scene was one of utter devastation. Hundreds of bodies were sprawled across the marble floor. Many were not yet dead, and the ground rippled with movement. Their cries and moans were pitiful. Blood was splattered up the walls, and more than a few of the bodies had been partially devoured. The corpse of the monstrous varghulf lay motionless upon the dais. Merovech descended the stairs of the raised platform, flanked by the five lieutenants that had served him seven hundred years earlier.

The few living knights still standing in the room dropped to their knees before Merovech. The duke ignored them, walking past with barely a glance. His companions, however, circled them like wolves. As one, they closed in, and began to feed.

Merovech dropped to one knee alongside Bertelis's headless corpse, and Calard thought he saw something approaching sorrow ghost across the duke's features as he placed a hand upon his brother's chest. Then Merovech raised his head, looking down the length of the chamber directly at Calard. He stood, and began walking towards them.

'We have to leave,' said Raben.

Calard nodded, and supporting the outcast's weight, hurried from the room.

They almost collided with Chlod as he came bowling down a wide set of stairs. The peasant was covered from head to toe in blood.

No words were spoken, and after a brief pause, Chlod moved forward to help support Raben. The outcast threw his arm over his shoulder and the three of them began making their way from the palace of Mousillon.

'Gods, peasant,' said Calard. 'You stink.'

DRAINED OF BLOOD, the corpse was dropped unceremoniously to the ground. The vampire's flesh was flushed, and its mouth and chin was stained with congealing gore.

Nothing living moved within the great hall. Every corpse has been bled dry to satiate the thirst of the duke's newly risen lieutenants.

It would not be long now, Merovech knew.

Within the hour, the first of the drained knights stirred and rose unsteadily to its feet, staggering like a newborn colt. Darkness lingered in its eyes, and its lips curled back to reveal newly formed canines. More knights stirred as they awoke to darkness, and Merovech smiled.

'Welcome, brothers,' he said, spreading his arms wide. 'Welcome to damnation.'

HAMMER AND BOLTER

ISSUE 2

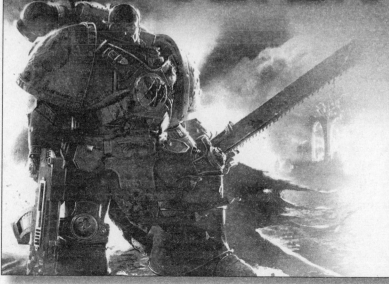

◄ TIME OF LEGENDS ►

THE DARK PATH

Gav Thorpe

Fields of golden crop bent gently in a magical breeze as the palace of Prince Thyriol floated across Saphery. A shimmering vision of white and silver towers and dove-wing buttresses, the citadel eased across the skies with the stately grace of a cloud. Slender minarets and spiralling steeples rose in circles surrounding a central gilded needle that glimmered with magic.

The farmers glanced up at the familiar beauty of the citadel and returned to their labours. If any of them wondered what events passed within the capital, none made mention of it to their companions. From the ground the floating citadel appeared as serene and ordered as ever, a reassuring vision to those that wondered when the war with the Naggarothi would come to their lands.

In truth, the palace was anything but peaceful.

Deep within the alabaster spires, Prince Thyriol strode to a wooden door at the end of a long corridor and tried to open it. The door was barred and magically locked. There were numerous counter-spells with which he could negotiate the obstacle, but he was in no mood for such things. Thyriol laid his hand upon the white-painted planks of the door and summoned the wind of fire. As his growing anger fanned the magic, the paint blistered and the planks charred under his touch. As Thyriol contemplated the treachery he had suffered, and his own blindness to it, the invisible flames burned faster and deeper than any natural fire. Within ten heartbeats the door collapsed into cinders and ash.

Revealed within was a coterie of elves. They looked up at their prince, startled and fearful. Bloody entrails were scattered on the bare stone floor, arranged in displeasing patterns that drew forth Dark Magic. They sat amidst a number of dire tomes bound with black leather and skin. Candles made of bubbling fat flickered dully on stands made from blackened iron. Sorcery seethed in the air, making Thyriol's gums itch and slicking his skin with its oily touch.

The missing mages were all here, forbidden runes painted upon their faces with blood, fetishes of bone and sinew dangling around their necks. Thyriol paid them no heed. All of his attention was fixed upon one elf, the only one who showed no sign of fear.

Words escaped Thyriol. The shame and sense of betrayal that filled Thyriol was beyond any means of expression, though some of it showed in the prince's face, twisted into a feral snarl even as tears of fire formed in his eyes.

FAERIE LIGHTS GLITTERED from extended fingertips and silver coronas shimmered around faces fixed in concentration as the young mages practised their spells. Visions of distant lands wavered in the air and golden clouds of protection wreathed around the robed figures. The air seemed to bubble with magical energy, the winds of magic made almost visible by the spells of the apprentices.

The students formed a semicircle around their tutors at the centre of a circular, domed hall – the Grand Chamber. The white wall was lined with alcoves containing sculptures of marble depicting the greatest mages of Ulthuan; some in studious repose, others in the flow of flamboyant conjurations, according to the tastes of successive generations of sculptors. All were austere, looking down with stern but not unkindly expressions on future generations. Their looks of strict expectation were repeated on the faces of Prince Thyriol and Menreir.

'You are speaking too fast,' Thyriol told Ellinithil, youngest of the would-be mages, barely two hundred years old. 'Let the spell form as words in your mind before you speak.'

Ellinithil nodded, brow furrowed. He started the conjuration again but stuttered the first few words.

'You are not concentrating,' Thyriol said softly, laying a reassuring hand on the young elf's shoulder. He raised his voice to address the whole class. 'Finish your incantations safely and then listen to me.'

The apprentices dissipated the magic they had been weaving; illusions vapourised into air, magical flames flickered and dimmed into darkness. As each finished, he or she turned to the prince. All were intent, but none more so that Anamedion, Thyriol's eldest grandson. Anamedion's eyes bore into his grandfather as if by his gaze alone he could prise free the secrets of magic locked inside Thyriol's mind.

'Celabreir,' said Thyriol, gesturing to one of the students to step forward. 'Conjure Emendeil's Flame for me.'

Celabreir glanced uncertainly at her fellow apprentices. The spell was one of the simplest to cast, often learnt in childhood even before any formal teaching had begun. With a shrug, the elf whispered three words of power and held up her right hand, fingers splayed. A flickering golden glow emanated from her fingertips, barely enough to light her slender face and brazen hair.

'Good,' said Thyriol. 'Now, end it and cast it again.'

Celabreir dispersed the magic energy with a flick of her wrist, her fingertips returning to normal. Just as she opened her mouth to begin the incantation again, Thyriol spoke.

'Do you breathe in or out when you cast a spell?' he asked.

A frown knotted Celabreir's brow for a moment. Distracted, she missed a syllable in the spell. Shaking her head, she tried again, but failed.

'What have you done to me, prince?' she asked plaintively. 'Is this some counter-spell you are using?'

Thyriol laughed gently, as did Menreir. Thyriol nodded for the other mage to explain the lesson and returned to his high-backed throne at the far end of the hall.

'You are thinking about how you breathe, aren't you?' said Menreir.

'I... Yes, I am, master,' said Celabreir, her shoulders slumping. 'I don't know whether I breathe in or out when I cast. I can't remember, but if I think about it I realise that I might be doing it differently because I am aware of it now.'

'And so you are no longer concentrating on your control of the magic,' said Menreir. 'A spell you could cast without effort you now find... problematic. Even the most basic spells are still fickle if you do not have total focus. The simplest distraction – an overheard whisper or a flicker of movement in the corner of the eye – can be the difference between success and failure. Knowing this, who can tell me why Ellinithil is having difficulty?'

'He is thinking about the words and not the spell,' said Anamedion, a hint of contempt in his voice. He made no attempt to hide his boredom. 'The more he worries about his pronunciation, the more distracted his inner voice.'

'That's right,' said Thyriol, quelling a stab of annoyance. Anamedion had not called Menreir 'master', a title to which he had had earned over many centuries, a sign of growing disrespect that Thyriol would have to address. 'Most of you already have the means to focus the power you need for some of the grandest enchantments ever devised by our people, but until you can cast them without effort or thought, that power is useless to you. Remember that the smallest magic can go a long way.'

'There is another way to overcome these difficulties,' said Anamedion, stepping forward. 'Why do you not teach us that?'

Thyriol regarded Anamedion for a moment, confused.

'Control is the only means to master true magic,' said the prince.

Anamedion shook his head, and half-turned, addressing the other students as much as his grandfather.

'There is a way to tap into magic, unfettered by incantation and ritual,' said Anamedion. 'Shaped by instinct and powered by raw magic, it is possible to cast the greatest spells of all.'

'You speak of sorcery,' said Menreir quickly, throwing a cautioning look at the apprentices. 'Sorcery brings only two things: madness and death. If you lack the will and application to be a mage, then you will certainly not live long as a sorcerer. If Ellinithil or Celabreir falter with pure magic, the spell simply fails. If one miscasts a sorcerous incantation, the magic does not return to the winds. It must find a place to live, in your body or your mind. Even when sorcery is used successfully, it leaves a taint, on the world and in the spirit. It corrupts one's thoughts and stains the winds of magic. Do not even consider using it.'

'Tell me from where you have heard such things,' said Thyriol. 'Who has put these thoughts in your mind?'

'Oh, here and there,' said Anamedion with a shrug and a slight smile. 'One hears about the druchii sorcerers quite often if one actually leaves the palace. I have heard that any sorcerer is a match for three Sapherian mages in power.'

'Then you have heard wrong,' said Thyriol patiently. 'The mastery of magic is not about power. Any fool can pick up a sword and hack at a lump of wood until he has kindling, but a true woodsman knows to use axe and hatchet and knife. Sorcery is a blunt instrument, capable only of destruction, not creation. Sorcery could not have built this citadel, nor could sorcery have enchanted our fields to be rich with grain. Sorcery burns and scars and leaves nothing behind.'

'And yet Anlec was built with sorcery,' countered Anamedion.

'Anlec is *sustained* by sorcery, but it was *built* by Caledor Dragontamer, who used only pure magic,' Thyriol replied angrily.

He shot glances at the others in the room, searching for some sign that they paid undue attention to Anamedion's arguments. There was rumour, whispered and incoherent, that some students, and even some mages, had begun to experiment with sorcery. It was so hard for Thyriol to tell. Dark Magic had been rising for decades, fuelled by the rituals and sacrifices of the Naggarothi and their cultist allies. It polluted the magical vortex of Ulthuan, twisting the Winds of Magic with its presence.

They had found druchii sorcerers hidden in the wilder parts of Saphery, in the foothills of the mountains, trying to teach their corrupted ways to the misguided. Some of the sorcerers had been slain, others had fled, forewarned of their discovery by fellow cultists. It was to protect the young from this corruption that Thyriol had brought the most talented Sapherians here, to learn from him and his most powerful mages. That Anamedion brought talk of sorcery into the capital was a grave concern. Saphethion, of all places, had to be free of the taint of Dark Magic, for the corruption of the power in the citadel could herald victory for the Naggarothi.

* * *

'*I am glad you have found us,*' *Anamedion said with no hint of regret or shame. 'I have longed to shed our secrecy, but the others insisted on this subterfuge.*'

The mention of the other mages broke Thyriol's focus and he took in the rest of the faces, settling on the blood-daubed features of Illeanith. This brought a fresh surge of anguish and he gave a choked gasp and lurched to one side, saved from falling only by the burnt frame of the doorway. He had been disappointed but not surprised by Anamedion's presence. Seeing Illeanith was one shock too many.

It was as if daggers had been plunged into Thyriol's heart and gut, a physical agony that writhed inside him, pulling away all sense and reason. The mages who had come with Thyriol began to shout and hurl accusations, but Thyriol heard nothing, just the arrhythmic thundering of his heart and a distant wailing in his head. Through a veil of tears and the waves of dismay welling up inside of him, Thyriol watched numbly as the sorcerers drew away from the door, adding their own voices to the cacophony.

'Everyone but Anamedion, leave me,' Thyriol commanded. 'Menreir, I will call for you when I am finished. We must discuss the latest messages from King Caledor.'

The mage and students bowed their acquiescence and left silently. Anamedion stood defiantly before the throne, arms crossed. Thyriol put aside his anger and looked at his grandson with sympathetic eyes.

'You are gifted, Anamedion,' said the prince. 'If you would but show a little more patience, there is no limit to what you might achieve in time.'

'What is it that you are afraid of?' countered Anamedion.

'I am afraid of damnation,' Thyriol replied earnestly, leaning forward. 'You have heard the myths of sorcery, while I have seen it first-hand. You think it is perhaps a quick way to achieve your goals, but you are wrong. The path is just as long for the sorcerer as it is for the mage. You think that Morathi and her ilk have not made terrible sacrifices, of their spirit and their bodies, to gain the power they have? You think that they simply wave a hand and destroy armies on a whim? No, they have not and do not. Terrible bargains they have made, bargains with powers we would all do better to avoid. Trust me, Anamedion, we call it Dark Magic for good reason.'

Anamedion still looked unconvinced, but he changed his approach.

'What good does it do us to spend a century learning spells when the druchii march against us now?' he said. 'King Caledor needs us with his armies, fighting the Naggarothi sorcerers. You speak of the future, but unless we act now, there may be no future. For seven years I have listened to the stories of horror, of war, engulfing Tiranoc and Chrace and Ellyrion. Cothique and Eataine are under attack. Must the fields of Saphery burn before you do something?'

Thyriol shook his head, fighting his frustration.

'I would no more send lambs to fight a lion than I would pit the skills of my students against Morathi's coven,' said the prince. 'There are but a dozen mages in all of Saphery that I would trust to fight the druchii in battle, myself included.'

'Then fight!' Anamedion demanded, pacing towards the throne, fists balled. 'Caledor begs for your aid and you are deaf to his requests. Why did you choose him as Phoenix King if you will not follow him?'

Thyriol glanced away for a moment, looking through the narrow arched windows that surrounded the hall. He did not see the greying autumn skies, his mind wandering to the ancient past. He saw a magic-blistered battlefield, where daemons rampaged and thousands of elves died screaming in agony. He saw the most powerful wizards of an age holding back the tides of Chaos while the Dragontamer conjured his vortex.

His memories shifted, to a time more recent but no less painful. His saw Naggarothi warriors, skin ruptured, hair flaming, falling from the battlements of Anlec while he soared overhead atop the back of a pegasus. Depraved cultists, dedicated to obscene sacrifice, wailed their curses even as lightning from Thyriol's staff crackled through their bodies.

War brought nothing but evil, even when fought for a just cause. Shaking his head to dismiss the waking nightmare, Thyriol returned his attention to Anamedion, his heart heavy.

'Your father thought the same, and now he is dead,' Thyriol said quietly.

'And your cowardice makes his sacrifice in vain,' Anamedion growled. 'Perhaps it is not Dark Magic that you fear, but death. Has your life lasted so long that you would protect it now at any cost?'

At this, Thyriol's frayed temper finally snapped.

'You accuse me of cowardice?' he said, stalking from his throne towards Anamedion, who stood his ground and returned the prince's glare. 'I fought beside Aenarion and the Dragontamer, and never once flinched from battle. Thirty years ago I fought beside Malekith when Anlec was retaken. You have never seen war, and know nothing of its nature, so do not accuse me of cowardice!'

'And you throw back at me accusations that I cannot counter,' Anamedion replied, fists clenching and unclenching with exasperation. 'You say I do not know war, yet condemn me to idle away my years in this place, closeted away from harm because you fear I will suffer the same fate as my father! Do you have so little confidence in me?'

'I do,' said Thyriol. 'You have your father's wilfulness and your mother's stubbornness. Why could you not be more like your younger brother, Elathrinil? He is studious and attentive... and obedient.'

'Elathrinil is diligent but dull,' replied Anamedion with a scornful laugh. 'Another century or two and he may make an adequate mage, but there is no greatness in him.'

'Do not crave greatness,' said Thyriol. 'Many have been dashed upon the cliffs of their own ambition. Do not repeat their mistakes.'

'So says the ruling prince of Saphery, friend of Aenarion, last surviving member of the First Council and greatest mage in Ulthuan,' said Anamedion. 'Maybe I have been wrong. It is not battle or death that you fear, it is me! You are jealous of my talent, fearful that your own reputation will be eclipsed by mine. Perhaps my star will rise higher than yours while you still cling to this world with the last strength in your fingers. You guard what you have gained and dare not risk anything. You profess wisdom and insight, but actually you are selfish and envious.'

'Get out!' roared Thyriol. Anamedion flinched as if struck. 'Get out of my sight! I will not have you in my presence again until you apologise for these lies. You have done nothing today but proven to me that you are unfit to rule Saphery. Think long and hard, Anamedion, about what you want. Do not tarnish me with your vain ambitions. Go!'

Anamedion hesitated, his face showing a moment of contrition, but it passed swiftly, replaced by a stare of keen loathing. With a wordless snarl, he turned his back on his grandfather and strode from the room.

Thyriol stumbled back to his throne and almost fell into it, drained by his outburst. He slumped there for a moment, thoughts reeling, ashamed of his own anger. Righteousness contended with guilt, neither winning a decisive victory. What if Anamedion was right? What if he really was jealous of the youth's prowess, knowing that his own existence was waning fast?

Closing his eyes, Thyriol whispered a few mantras of focus and dismissed his self-examination. The fault was not with the prince, but with his grandchild. For decades he had known that there was something amiss with Anamedion, but had turned a blind eye upon his deficiencies. Now that Thyriol had finally given open voice to his doubts, and Anamedion declared his own misgivings, perhaps the two of them could move on and resolve their differences.

With a sigh, Thyriol straightened himself and sat in the throne properly. Anamedion's small rebellion was a distraction, one that Thyriol could not deal with immediately. He had Caledor's messenger waiting, eager to return to the Phoenix King with Thyriol's answer. The world was being torn apart by war and bloodshed, and against that the petulant protests and naïve philosophies of a grandson seemed insignificant.

Thyriol twitched a finger and in the depths of the palace a silver bell rang to announce that the prince of Saphery wished to be attended.

Anamedion felt the other sorcerers opening the portal they had created for just this situation. The shadow at the back of their hiding place deepened, merging with the shadows of a cave some distance from the palace's current location. Something seethed in the shadow's depths, a formless bulk shifting its weight just outside of mortal comprehension.

Hadryana and Meledir lunged through the portal without word, fearful of Thyriol's wrath. They were soon followed by the other students and Alluthian, leaving only Illeanith and Anamedion.

'Come!' commanded his mother, grabbing him by the arm. Anamedion shook free her grasp and looked at his grandfather.

Thyriol was a broken creature. Anamedion saw an elf near the end of his years, frail and tired, his own misery seeping through every fibre of his being. There was no fight left in him.

'I am not ashamed,' said Anamedion. 'I am not afraid.'

'We must leave!' insisted Illeanith. Anamedion turned to her and pushed her towards the shadow-portal.

'Then go! I will send for you soon,' he said. 'This will not take long, mother.'

Illeanith hesitated for a moment, torn between love of her son and fear of her father. Fear won and she plunged through the tenebrous gateway, disappearing into the dark fog.

When Anamedion returned his attention to Thyriol, he saw that the prince had straightened and regained his composure. For a moment, doubt gnawed at Anamedion. Perhaps he had misjudged the situation. Thyriol's look changed from one of horror to one of pity and this threw fuel onto the fire of Anamedion's anger. His momentary fear evaporated like the illusion it was.

'I will prove how weak you have become,' said Anamedion.

'Surrender, or suffer the consequences,' growled Menreir, blue flames dancing from his eyes.

'Do not interfere!' Thyriol told his mages, waving them back. The pity drained from his face and was replaced by his usual calm expression. In a way, it was more chilling than the prince's anger. 'I will deal with this.'

Anamedion knew that he must strike first. He allowed the Dark Magic to coil up through his body, leeching its power from where it lurked within and around the Winds of Magic. He felt it crackling along his veins, quickening his heart, setting his mind afire. Uttering a curse of Ereth Khial, Anamedion threw forward his hand and a bolt of black lightning leapt from his fingertips.

A moment from striking Thyriol, the spell burst into a shower of golden dust that fluttered harmlessly to the bare stone floor.

Only now did Anamedion see the counterspells woven into his grandfather's robe. The sorcerer's cruel smile faded. The prince's body was steeped in magic, subtle and layered. Dark Magic pulsed once more, bolstering Anamedion's confidence. Thyriol's defences mattered not at all; the wardings were many but thin, easily penetrated by the power Anamedion could now wield.

THE VIEW WAS breathtaking from the wide balcony atop the Tower of Alin-Haith, the vast panorama of Ulthuan laid out around the four mages. To the south and north stretched the farms and gentle hills of Saphery, bathed in the afternoon sun. To the west glittered the Inner Sea, barely visible on the horizon. To the east the majestic peaks of the Anullii Mountains rose from beyond the horizon, grey and purple and tipped with white. Thyriol noted storm clouds gathering over the mountains to the north, sensing within them the Dark Magic that had gathered in the vortex over the past decades.

'I am going to tell Caledor that I will not open the Tor Anroc gateway,' the prince announced, not looking at his companions.

The three other wizards were Menreir, Alethin and Illeanith, the last being Thyriol's daughter, his only child. Thinking of her led the prince's thoughts back to Anamedion and he pushed them aside and turned to face the others.

'I cannot risk the druchii taking control of the gateway from the other end,' Thyriol explained.

The palace of Saphethion was more than a floating castle. It was able to drift effortlessly through the skies because the magic woven into its foundations placed it slightly apart from time and space. From the outside the palace appeared beautiful and serene, but within there existed a maze of halls and rooms, corridors and passages far larger than could be contained within normal walls. Some of those rooms were not even upon Saphethion itself, but lay in other cities: Lothern, Tor Yvresse, Montieth and others. Most importantly, one of the isle-spanning gateways led to Tor Anroc, currently occupied by the army of Nagarythe.

As soon as he had found out that the city had fallen into the hands of the druchii, Thyriol had closed the gate, putting its enchantments into stasis. Now the Phoenix King wanted Thyriol to reopen the gate so that he might send agents into Tor Anroc, perhaps even an army.

'Caledor's plan has much merit, father,' said Illeanith. 'Surprise would be total. It is unlikely that the druchii are even aware of the gateway's existence, for none of them have ever used it.'

'I wish to keep it that way,' said Thyriol. 'The wards upon the gate can resist the attentions of any normal druchii sorcerer, but I would rather not test their strength against the magic of Morathi. Even the knowledge that such gateways can exist would be dangerous, for I have no doubt that she would find some means to create her own. On a more mundane point, I cannot make the gate work only one way. Once it is open, the druchii can use it to enter Saphethion, and that puts us all at risk.'

'The Phoenix King will be disappointed, lord,' said Menreir.

'The Phoenix King will be angry,' Thyriol corrected him. 'Yet it is not the first time I have refused him.'

'I am not so sure that the druchii are still unaware of the gateways, prince,' said Alethin. 'There are few that can be trusted these days with any secret, and I am sure that there are Sapherians who once served in the palace now in the employ of the cults, or at least sympathetic to their cause. Even within the palace we have found texts smuggled in by agents of the druchii to sow confusion and recruit support.'

'That gives me even more reason to be cautious,' said Thyriol, leaning his back against the parapet. 'Tor Anroc is shrouded in shadow, protected from our augurs and divinations. Perhaps the druchii have discovered the gateway and guard it, or even now work to unravel its secrets. The moment it is opened, it will be like a white flare in the mind of Morathi – I cannot hide such magic from her scrying.'

'Forgive me, prince, but to what end do you tell us this?' said Menreir. 'If your mind is set, simply send the messenger back to Caledor. We are no council to give our approval.'

Thyriol was taken aback by the question, for the answer seemed plain enough to him.

'I had hoped that you might have some argument to change my mind,' he said. Sighing, he cast his gaze back towards the mountains and when he continued his voice was quiet, wistful. 'I have lived a long, long time. I have known the heights of happiness, and plunged into the depths of despair. Even when the daemons bayed at the walls of Anlec and the night lasted an eternity, I had hope. Now? Now I can see no hope, for there can be no victory when elves fight other elves. I wish an attack or a Tor Anroc, an assault on Anlec, could end this war, but there is no such simple ploy. Not armed force or great magic will end this conflict. We are at war with ourselves and the only peace that can last must come from within us.'

'Do not do this,' Thyriol warned.

'You are in no position to give me commands,' snapped Anamedion. A sword of black flame appeared in his fist and he leapt forwards to strike. Menreir stepped in the way, out of instinct to save the prince, and the ethereal blade passed through his chest. In moments the mage's body disintegrated into a falling cloud of grey ash.

Anamedion swung back-handed at Thyriol, but a shimmering shield of silver energy appeared on the mage's arm and the flaming blade evaporated into a wisp of smoke at its touch.

'You cannot control the power needed to defeat me,' Thyriol said. He was already breathing heavily, and Anamedion heard the words as nothing but an empty boast.

Dispelling the warding that surrounded the room, Anamedion reached out further into the winds of magic, drawing in more and more dark power. A black cloud enveloped him, swirling and churning with its own life, flashes and glitters in its depths. He urged the cloud forward and for a moment it engulfed Thyriol, cloying and choking.

A white light appeared at the cloud's centre and the magic boiled away, revealing Thyriol unharmed, glowing from within. Anamedion could see that his grandfather's pull on the winds of magic was becoming fitful and saw a chance to finish him off. Taking a deep breath Anamedion reached out as far as he could, a surge of sorcery pouring into his body and mind.

* * *

THYRIOL FELT A hand upon his back and turned his head to see Illeanith next to him.

'Anamedion told me that you have banished him from your presence,' she said. 'He is stubborn, but he is also brave and strong and willing to prove himself. Please end this dispute. Do not make me choose between my father and my son.'

'There are no words that will lift the veil of a mother's love for her son,' replied the prince.

'You think me blind to my son's faults?' snapped Illeanith, stepping back. 'Perhaps I see more than you think, prince. Other matters are always more important to you. For over a thousand years you have lived in the mystical realm; you no longer remember what it is to be flesh and blood. I think that a part of you was trapped with the other mages on the Isle of the Dead, a part of your spirit if not your body. Anamedion has not seen the things you have seen, and you make no attempt to show them to him. You think that you guard him against danger, but that is no way to prepare him for princehood. He must learn who he is, to know his own mind. He is not you, father, he is himself, and you must accept that.'

Illeanith glanced at the other two mages with an apologetic look and then disappeared down the steps from the balcony.

'I miss her, mother,' sighed Thyriol, leaning over the wall to peer down at the courtyard of the palace where armour-clad guards drilled in disciplined lines of silver and gold. 'She helped me remember how to stay in this world. Maybe it is time I moved on, let slip this fragile grip that I have kept these last hundred years. I wish I had died in peace, like Miranith. One should not be born in war and die in war...'

The other two mages remained silent as Thyriol's words drifted into a whisper, knowing that Thyriol was talking to himself, no longer aware of their presence. They exchanged a knowing, worried glance and followed Illeanith from the tower, each fearful of their prince's deterioration.

'Sorcery is not an end in itself, it is just a means,' said Anamedion. 'It need not be evil.'

'The means can corrupt the end,' replied Thyriol quietly, his hoarse whisper further proof of his infirmity. 'Just because we can do a thing, it is not right that we should do a thing.'

'Nonsense,' spat Anamedion, unleashing his next spell. Flames of purple and blue roared from his hands, lapping at Thyriol. The ancient mage writhed under its power, sparks of gold and green magic bursting from him as he deflected the worst of the spell, though it still brought him to one knee. 'You'll have to kill me to prove it!'

'I will not kill my own kin,' wheezed Thyriol.

'I will,' said Anamedion with a glint in his eye.

Anamedion could feel only Dark Magic in the chamber and knew that the prince's resistance was all but over. All he needed was another overwhelming attack and this would be finished. He would become prince of Saphery as was his right, and they would take the war to the Naggarothi.

Grasping the fetish at his throat, the rune-carved knuckle bones burning his palm, Anamedion incanted words of power, feasting on the sorcery that was now roiling within every part of his body. He visualised a monstrous dragon, drew it in the air with his mind's eye. He saw its ebon fangs and the black fire that flickered from its mouth. Thyriol attempted a dispel, directing what little remained of the winds of magic, trying to unpick the enchantment being woven by Anamedion.

Anamedion drew on more Dark Magic, swamping the counterspell with power. He focused all his thoughts on the spell, as Thyriol had once warned him he must. He had no time to appreciate the irony, all his mind was bent on the conjuration. He could see the shimmering scales and the veins on the membranes of the dragon's wings. The apparition started to form before Anamedion, growing more real with every passing heartbeat.

In a moment the dragon-spell would engulf Thyriol, crushing the last breath from his body.

THYRIOL WAITED PATIENTLY in the Hall of Stars, gazing up at the window at the centre of the hall's ceiling. It showed a starry sky, though outside the palace it was not yet noon. The scene was of the night when the hall had been built, the auspicious constellations and alignments captured for all eternity by magic. Thyriol had come here countless times to gaze at the beauty of the heavens and knew every sparkling star as well as he knew himself.

A delicate cough from the doorway attracted Thyriol's attention. Menreir stood just inside the hall, a cluster of fellow mages behind him and a worried-looking servant at his side.

'We cannot find Anamedion,' said Menreir. 'Also, Illeanith, Hadryana, Alluthian and Meledir are missing, along with half a dozen of the students.'

Thyriol took this news without comment. The prince closed his eyes and felt Saphethion around him. He knew every stone of the palace, the magic that seeped within the mortar, the flow of energy that bound every stone. The golden needle pulsed rhythmically at its centre and the winds of magic coiled and looped around the corridors and halls. He could feel every living creature too, each a distinctive eddy in the winds of magic. It would not take long to locate his grandson.

But it was not Anamedion that Thyriol found first. In a chamber beneath the Mausoleum of the Dawn, there was a strange whirl of mystical power. It flowed around the room and not through it, masking whatever was within: a warding spell, one that Thyriol had not conjured. It was subtle, just the slightest disturbance in the normal flow. Only Thyriol, who had created every spell and charm that sustained Saphethion, would have noticed the anomaly.

'Come with me,' he commanded the mages as he pushed through the group. He showed no outward sign of vexation, but Thyriol's stomach had lurched. Mages were free to use their magic in the palace, why would one seek to hide their conjurations? He suspected sorcery. Despite his reasons for being in the Hall of Stars, this was more pressing than his division with Anamedion. His grandson would have to wait a while longer for their reconciliation.

Thyriol whispered something, almost bent double, his eyes fixed on his grandson. Anamedion did not hear what the prince had said. Was it some final counterspell? Perhaps an admission of wrong? A plea for mercy?

For the moment Anamedion wondered what Thyriol had said, his mind strayed from the spell. The distraction lasted only a heartbeat but it was too late. The Dark Magic churning inside Anamedion slipped from his grasp. He struggled to control it, but it wriggled from his mind, coiling into his heart, flooding his lungs. Choking and gasping, Anamedion swayed as his veins crackled with power and his eyes melted. He tried to wail but only black flames erupted from his burning throat. The pain was unbearable, every part of his body and mind shrieked silently as the sorcery consumed him.

With a last spasm, Anamedion collapsed, his body shrivelling and blackening. With a dry thump, his corpse hit the ground, wisps of thick smoke issuing from his empty eye sockets.

THYRIOL KNELT DOWN beside the remains of his grandson. For the moment he felt nothing, but he knew he would grieve later. He would feel the guilt of what he had done, though it had been unavoidable. Thoughts of grief recalled the death of Menreir, his oldest friend. Thyriol had barely noticed his destruction, so engrossed had he been in his duel with Anamedion. Another link to the past taken away; another piece of the future destroyed.

'What did you whisper?' asked Urian, his eyes fixed upon the contorted remnants of Anamedion. 'Some dispel of your own creation?'

Thyriol shook his head sadly at the suggestion.

'I cast no spell,' he replied. 'I merely whispered the name of his grandmother. His lack of focus killed him.'

Thyriol stood and faced the mages clustered around the blackened doorway. His expression hardened.

'Anamedion was young, and stupid, and ignored my warnings,' said the prince. 'Illeanith and the other sorcerers will not be so easy to defeat. There will be more of them than we have seen. The war has finally come to Saphery.'

EXHUMED

Steve Parker

THE THUNDERHAWK GUNSHIP loomed out of the clouds like a monstrous bird of prey, wings spread, turbines growling, airbrakes flared to slow it for landing. It was black, its fuselage marked with three symbols: the Imperial aquila, noble and golden; the 'I' of the Emperor's holy Inquisition, a symbol even the righteous knew better than to greet gladly; and another symbol, a skull cast in silver with a gleaming red, cybernetic eye. Derlon Saezar didn't know that one, had never seen it before, but it sent a chill up his spine all the same. Whichever august Imperial body the symbol represented was obviously linked to the holy Inquisition. That couldn't be good news.

Eyes locked to his vid-monitor, Saezar watched tensely as the gunship banked hard towards the small landing facility he managed, its prow slicing through the veils of windblown dust like a knife through silk. There was a burst of static-riddled speech on his headset. In response, he tapped several codes into the console in front of him, keyed his microphone and said, 'Acknowledged, One-Seven-One. Clearance codes accepted. Proceed to Bay Four. This is an enclosed atmosphere facility. I'm uploading our safety and debarkation protocols to you now. Over.'

His fingers rippled over the console's runeboard, and the massive metal jaws of Bay Four began to grate open, ready to swallow the unwelcome black craft. Thick toxic air rushed in. Breathable air rushed out. The entire facility shuddered and groaned in complaint, as it always did when a spacecraft came or went. The Adeptus Mechanicus had built this facility, Orga Station, quickly and with the minimum systems and resources it would need to do its job. No more, no less. It was a rusting, dust-scoured place, squat and ugly on the outside, dank and gloomy within. Craft arrived, craft departed. Those coming in brought slaves, servitors, heavy machinery, fuel. Saezar didn't know what those leaving carried. The magos who had hired him had left him in no doubt that curiosity would lead to the termination of more than his contract. Saezar was smart enough to believe it. He and his staff kept their heads down and did their jobs. In another few years, the tech-priests would be done here. They had told him as much. He would go back to Jacero then, maybe buy a farm with the money he'd have saved, enjoy air that didn't kill you on the first lungful.

That thought called up a memory Saezar would have given a lot to erase. Three weeks ago, a malfunction in one of the Bay Two extractors left an entire work crew breathing this planet's lethal air. The bay's vid-picters had caught it all in fine detail, the way the technicians and slaves staggered in agony towards the emergency airlocks, clawing at their throats while blood streamed from their mouths, noses and eyes.

Twenty-three men dead. It had taken only seconds, but Saezar knew the sight would be with him for life. He shook himself, trying to cast the memory off.

The Thunderhawk had passed beyond the outer picters' field of view. Saezar switched to Bay Four's internal picters and saw the big black craft settle heavily on its landing stanchions. Thrusters cooled. Turbines whined down towards silence. The outer doors of the landing bay clanged shut. Saezar hit the winking green rune on the top right of his board and flooded the bay with the proper nitrogen-oxygen mix. When his screen showed everything was in the green, he addressed the pilot of the Thunderhawk again.

'Atmosphere restored, One-Seven-One. Bay Four secure. Free to debark.'

There was a brief grunt in answer. The Thunderhawk's front ramp lowered. Yellow light spilled out from inside, illuminating the black metal grille of the bay floor. Shadows appeared in that light – big shadows – and, after a moment, the figures that cast them began to descend the ramp. Saezar leaned forwards, face close to his screen.

'By the Throne,' he whispered to himself.

With his right hand, he manipulated one of the bay picters by remote, zooming in on the figure striding in front. It was massive, armoured in black ceramite, its face hidden beneath a cold, expressionless helm. On one great pauldron, the left, Saezar saw the same skull icon that graced the ship's prow. On the right, he saw another skull on a field of white, two black scythes crossed behind it. Here was yet another icon Saezar had never seen before, but he knew well enough the nature of the being that bore it. He had seen such beings rendered in paintings and stained glass, cut from marble or cast in precious metal. It was a figure of legend, and it was not alone. Behind it, four others, similarly armour-clad but each bearing different iconography on their right pauldrons, marched in formation.

Saezar's heart was in his throat. He tried to swallow, but his mouth was dry. He had never expected to see such beings with his own eyes. No one did. They were heroes from the stories his father had read to him, stories told to all children of the Imperium to give them hope, to help them sleep at night. Here they were in flesh and bone and metal.

Here! At Orga Station!

And there was a further incredible sight yet to come. Just as the five figures stepped onto the grille-work floor, something huge blotted out all the light from inside the craft. The Thunderhawk's ramp shook with thunderous steps. Something incredible emerged on two stocky, piston-like legs. It was vast and angular and impossibly powerful-looking, like a walking tank with fists instead of cannon.

It was a Dreadnought, and, even among such legends as these, it was in a class of its own.

Saezar felt a flood of conflicting emotion, equal parts joy and dread.

The Space Marines had come to Menatar, and where they went, death followed.

'MENATAR,' SAID THE tiny hunched figure, more to himself than to any of the black-armoured giants he shared the pressurised mag-rail carriage with. 'Second planet of the Ozyma-138 system, Hatha sub-sector, Ultima Segmentum. Solar orbital period, one-point-one-three Terran standard. Gravity, zero-point-eight-three Terran standard.' He looked up, his tiny black eyes meeting those of Siefer Zeed, the Raven Guard. 'The atmosphere is a thick nitrogen-sulphide/carbon-dioxide mix. Did you know that? Utterly deadly to the non-augmented. I doubt even you Space Marines could breathe it for long. Even our servitors wear air-tanks here.'

Zeed stared back indifferently at the little tech-priest. When he spoke, it was not in answer. His words were directed to his right, to his squad leader, Lyandro Karras, Codicier Librarian of the Death Spectres Chapter, known officially in Deathwatch circles as Talon Alpha. That wasn't what Zeed called him, though. 'Tell me again, Scholar, why we get all the worthless jobs.'

Karras didn't look up from the boltgun he was muttering litanies over. Times like these, the quiet times, were for meditation and proper observances, something the Raven Guard seemed wholly unable to grasp. Karras had spent six years as leader of this kill-team. Siefer Zeed, nicknamed Ghost for his alabaster skin, was as irreverent today as he had been when they'd first met. Perhaps he was even worse.

Karras finished murmuring his Litany of Flawless Operation and sighed. 'You know why, Ghost. If you didn't go out of your way to anger Sigma all the time, maybe those Scimitar bastards would be here instead of us.'

Talon Squad's handler, an inquisitor lord known only as Sigma, had come all too close to dismissing Zeed from active duty on several occasions, a terrible dishonour not just for the Deathwatch member in question, but for his entire Chapter. Zeed frequently tested the limits of Sigma's need-to-know policy, not to mention the inquisitor's patience. But the Raven Guard was a peerless killing machine at close range, and his skill with a pair of lightning claws, his signature weapon, had won the day so often that Karras and the others had stopped counting.

Another voice spoke up, a deep rumbling bass, its tones warm and rich. 'They're not all bad,' said Maximmion Voss of the Imperial Fists. 'Scimitar Squad, I mean.'

'Right,' said Zeed with good-natured sarcasm. 'It's not like you're biased, Omni. I mean, every Black Templar or Crimson Fist in the galaxy is a veritable saint.'

Voss grinned at that.

There was a hiss from the rear of the carriage where Ignatio Solarion and Darrion Rauth, Ultramarine and Exorcist respectively, sat in relative silence. The hiss had come from Solarion.

'Something you want to say, Prophet?' said Zeed with a challenging thrust of his chin.

Solarion scowled at him, displaying the full extent of his contempt for the Raven Guard. 'We are with company,' he said, indicating the little tech-priest who had fallen silent while the Deathwatch Space Marines talked. 'You would do well to remember that.'

Zeed threw Solarion a sneer then turned his eyes back to the tech-priest. The man had met them on the mag-rail platform at Orga Station, introducing himself as Magos Iapetus Borgovda, the most senior adept on the planet and a xeno-hierographologist specialising in the writings and history of the Exodites, offshoot cultures of the eldar race. They had lived here once, these Exodites, and had left many secrets buried deep in the drifting red sands. That went no way to explaining why a Deathwatch kill-team was needed, however, especially now. Menatar was a dead world. Its sun had become a red giant, a K-3 type star well on its way to final collapse. Before it died, however, it would burn off the last of Menatar's atmosphere, leaving little more than a ball of molten rock. Shortly after that, Menatar would cool and there would be no trace of anyone ever having set foot here at all. Such an end was many tens of thousands of years away, of course. Had the Exodite eldar abandoned this world early, knowing its eventual fate? Or had something else driven them off? Maybe the xeno-hierographologist would find the answers eventually, but that still didn't tell Zeed anything about why Sigma had sent some of his key assets here.

Magos Borgovda turned to his left and looked out the viewspex bubble at the front of the mag-rail carriage. A vast dead volcano dominated the skyline. The mag-rail car sped towards it so fast the red dunes and rocky spires on either side of the tracks went by in a blur. 'We are coming up on Typhonis Mons,' the magos wheezed. 'The noble Priesthood of Mars cut a tunnel straight through the side of the crater, you know. The journey will take another hour. No more than that. Without the tunnel...'

'Good,' said Zeed, running the fingers of one gauntleted hand through his long black hair. His eyes flicked to the blades of the lightning claws fixed to the magnetic couplings on his thigh-plates. Soon it would be time to don the weapons properly, fix his helmet to its seals, and step out onto solid ground. Omni was tuning the suspensors on his heavy bolter. Solarion was checking the bolt mechanism of his sniper rifle. Karras and Rauth had both finished their final checks already.

If there is nothing here to fight, why were we sent so heavily armed, Zeed asked himself?

He thought of the ill-tempered Dreadnought riding alone in the other carriage.

And why did we bring Chyron?

THE MAG-RAIL CAR slowed to a smooth halt beside a platform cluttered with crates bearing the cog-and-skull mark of the Adeptus Mechanicus. On either side of the platform, spreading out in well-ordered concentric rows, were scores of stocky pre-fabricated huts and storage units, their low roofs piled with ash and dust. Thick insulated cables snaked everywhere, linking heavy machinery to generators, supplying light, heat and atmospheric stability to the sleeping quarters and mess blocks. Here and there, cranes stood tall against the wind. Looming over everything were the sides of the crater, penning it all in, lending the place a strange quality, almost like being outdoors and yet indoors at the same time.

Borgovda was clearly expected. Dozens of acolytes, robed in the red of the Martian Priesthood and fitted with breathing apparatus, bowed low when he emerged from the carriage. Around them, straight-backed skitarii troopers stood to attention with las- and hellguns clutched diagonally across their chests.

Quietly, Voss muttered to Zeed, 'It seems our new acquaintance didn't lie about his status here. Perhaps you should have been more polite to him, paper-face.'

'I don't recall you offering any pleasantries, tree-trunk,' Zeed replied. He and Voss had been friends since the moment they met. It was a rapport that none of the other kill-team members shared, a fact that only served to further deepen the bond. Had anyone else called Zeed *paper-face*, he might well have eviscerated them on the spot. Likewise, few would have dared to call the squat, powerful Voss *tree-trunk*. Even fewer would have survived to tell of it. But, between the two of them, such names were taken as a mark of trust and friendship that was truly rare among the Deathwatch.

Magos Borgovda broke from greeting the rows of fawning acolytes and turned to his black-armoured escorts. When he spoke, it was directly to Karras, who had identified himself as team leader during introductions.

'Shall we proceed to the dig-site, Adeptus? Or do you wish to rest first?'

'Astartes need no rest,' answered Karras flatly.

It was a slight exaggeration, of course, and the twinkle in the xeno-hierographologist's eye suggested he knew as much, but he also knew that, by comparison to most humans, it was as good as true. Borgovda and his fellow servants of the Machine-God also required little rest.

'Very well,' said the magos. 'Let us go straight to the pit. My acolytes tell me we are ready to initiate the final stage of our operation. They await only my command.'

He dismissed all but a few of the acolytes, issuing commands to them in sharp bursts of machine-language, and turned east. Leaving the platform behind them, the Deathwatch followed. Karras walked beside the bent and robed figure, consciously slowing his steps to match the speed of the tech-priest. The others, including the massive, multi-tonne form of the Dreadnought, Chyron, fell into step behind them. Chyron's footfalls made the ground tremble as he brought up the rear.

Zeed cursed at having to walk so slowly. Why should one such as he, one who could move with inhuman speed, be forced to crawl at the little tech-priest's pace? He might reach the dig-site in a fraction of the time and never break sweat. How long would it take at the speed of this grinding, clicking, wheezing half-mechanical magos?

Eager for distraction, he turned his gaze to the inner slopes of the great crater in which the entire excavation site was located. This was Typhonis Mons, the largest volcano in the Ozyma-138 system. No wonder the Adeptus Mechanicus had tunnelled all those kilometres through the crater wall. To go up and over the towering ridgeline would have taken significantly more time and effort. Any road built to do so would have required more switchbacks than was reasonable. The caldera was close to two-and-a-half kilometres across, its jagged rim rising well over a kilometre on every side.

Looking more closely at the steep slopes all around him, Zeed saw that many bore signs of artifice. The signs were subtle, yes, perhaps eroded by time and wind, or by the changes in atmosphere that the expanding red giant had wrought, but they were there all the same. The Raven Guard's enhanced visor-optics, working in accord with his superior gene-boosted vision, showed him crumbled doorways and pillared galleries. Had he not known this world for an Exodite world, he might have passed these off as natural structures, for there was little angular about them. Angularity was something one saw everywhere in human construction, but far less so in the works of the hated, inexplicable eldar. Their structures, their craft, their weapons – each seemed almost grown rather than built, their forms fluid, gracefully organic. Like all righteous warriors of the Imperium, Zeed hated the eldar. They denied man's destiny as ruler of the stars. They stood in the way of expansion, of progress.

He had fought them many times. He had been there when eldar forces had contested human territory in the Adiccan Reach, launching blisteringly fast raids on worlds they had no right to claim. They were good foes to fight. He enjoyed the challenge of their speed, and they were not afraid to engage with him at close quarters, though they often retreated in the face of his might rather than die honourably.

Cowards.

Such a shame they had left this world so long ago. He would have enjoyed fighting them here.

In fact, he thought, flexing his claws in irritation, just about any fight would do.

SIX MASSIVE CRANES struggled in unison to raise their load from the circular black pit in the centre of the crater. The eldar had buried this thing deep – deep enough that no one should ever have disturbed it here. But Iapetus Borgovda had transcribed the records of that burial, records found on a damaged eldar craft that had been lost in the warp only to emerge centuries later on the fringe of the Imperium. He had been on his way to present his findings to the Genetor Biologis himself when a senior magos by the name of Serjus Altando had intercepted him and asked him to present his findings to the Ordo Xenos of the holy Inquisition first.

After that, Borgovda had never gotten around to presenting his work to his superiors on Mars. The mysterious inquisitor lord that Magos Altando served had guaranteed Borgovda all the resources he would need to make the discovery entirely his own. The credit, Altando promised, need not be shared with anyone else. Borgovda would be revered for his work. Perhaps, one day, he would even be granted genetor rank himself.

And so it was that mankind had come to Menatar and had begun to dig where no one was supposed to.

The fruits of that labour were finally close at hand. Borgovda's black eyes glittered like coals beneath the clear bubble of his breathing apparatus as he watched each of the six cranes reel in their thick polysteel cables. With tantalising slowness, something huge and ancient began to peek above the lip of the pit. A hundred skitarii troopers and gunservitors inched forwards, weapons raised. They had no idea what was emerging. Few did.

Borgovda knew. Magos Altando knew. Sigma knew. Of these three, however, only Borgovda was present in person. The others, he believed, were light years away. This was *his* prize alone, just as the inquisitor had promised. This was *his* operation. As more of the object cleared the lip of the pit, he stepped forwards himself. Behind him, the Space Marines of Talon Squad gripped their weapons and watched.

The object was almost entirely revealed now, a vast sarcophagus, oval in shape, twenty-three metres long on its vertical axis, sixteen metres on the horizontal. Every inch of its surface, a surface like nothing so much as polished bone, was intricately carved with Eldar script. By force of habit, the xeno-hierographologist began translating the symbols with part of his mind while the rest of it continued to marvel at the beauty of what he saw. Just what secrets would this object reveal? He and other Radicals like him believed mankind's salvation, its very future, lay not with the technological stagnation in which the race of men was currently mired, but with the act of understanding and embracing the technology of its alien enemies. And yet, so many fools scorned this patently obvious truth. Borgovda had known good colleagues, fine inquisitive magi like himself, who had been executed for their beliefs. Why did the Fabricator General not see it? Why did the mighty Lords of Terra not understand? Well, he would make them see. Sigma had promised him all the resources he would need to make the most of this discovery. The holy Inquisition was on his side. This time would be different.

The object, fully raised above the pit, hung there in all its ancient, inscrutable glory. Borgovda gave a muttered command into a vox-piece, and the cranes began a slow, synchronised turn.

Borgovda held his breath.

They moved the vast sarcophagus over solid ground and stopped.

'Yes,' said Borgovda over the link. 'That's it. Now lower it gently.'

The crane crews did as ordered. Millimetre by millimetre, the oval tomb descended.

Then it lurched.

One of the cranes gave a screech of metal. Its frame twisted sharply to the right, titanium struts crumpling like tin.

'What's going on?' demanded Borgovda.

From the corner of his vision, he noted the Deathwatch stepping forwards, cocking their weapons, and the Dreadnought eagerly flexing its great metal fists.

A panicked voice came back to him from the crane operator in the damaged machine. 'There's something moving inside that thing,' gasped the man. 'Something really heavy. Its centre of gravity is shifting all over the place!'

Borgovda's eyes narrowed as he scrutinised the hanging oval object. It was swinging on five taut cables now, while the sixth, that of the ruined crane, had gone slack. The object lurched again. The movement was clearly visible this time, obviously generated by massive internal force.

'Get it onto the ground,' Borgovda barked over the link, 'but carefully. Do not damage it.'

The cranes began spooling out more cable at his command, but the sarcophagus gave one final big lurch and crumpled two more of the sturdy machines. The other three cables tore free, and it fell to the ground with an impact that shook the closest slaves and acolytes from their feet.

Borgovda started towards the fallen sarcophagus, and knew that the Deathwatch were right behind him. Had the inquisitor known this might happen? Was that why he had sent his angels of death and destruction along?

Even at this distance, some one hundred and twenty metres away, even through all the dust and grit the impact had kicked up, Borgovda could see eldar sigils begin to glow red on the surface of the massive object. They blinked on and off like warning lights, and he realised that was exactly what they were. Despite all the irreconcilable differences between the humans and the aliens, this message, at least, mean the same.

Danger!

There was a sound like cracking wood, but so loud it was deafening.

Suddenly, one of the Deathwatch Space Marines roared in agony and collapsed to his knees, gauntlets pressed tight to the side of his helmet. Another Space Marine, the Imperial Fist, raced forwards to his fallen leader's side.

'What's the matter, Scholar? What's going on?'

The one called Karras spoke through his pain, but there was no mistaking the sound of it, the raw, nerve-searing agony in his words. 'A psychic beacon!' he growled through clenched teeth. 'A psychic beacon just went off. The magnitude–'

He howled as another wave of pain hit him, and the sound spoke of a suffering that Borgovda could hardly imagine.

Another of the kill-team members, this one with a pauldron boasting a daemon's-skull design, stepped forwards with boltgun raised and, incredibly, took aim at his leader's head.

The Raven Guard moved like lightning. Almost too fast to see, he was at this other's side, knocking the muzzle of the boltgun up and away with the back of his forearm. 'What the hell are you doing, Watcher?' Zeed snapped. 'Stand down!'

The Exorcist, Rauth, glared at Zeed through his helmet visor, but he turned his weapon away all the same. His finger, however, did not leave the trigger.

'Scholar,' said Voss. 'Can you fight it? Can you fight through it?'

The Death Spectre struggled to his feet, but his posture said he was hardly in any shape to fight if he had to. 'I've never felt anything like this!' he hissed. 'We have to knock it out. It's smothering my... gift.' He turned to Borgovda. 'What in the Emperor's name is going on here, magos?'

'Gift?' spat Rauth in an undertone.

Borgovda answered, turning his black eyes back to the object as he did. It was on its side about twenty metres from the edge of the pit, rocking violently as if something were alive inside it.

'The Exodites...' he said. 'They must have set up some kind of signal to alert them when someone... interfered. We've just set it off.'

'Interfered with what?' demanded Ignatio Solarion. The Ultramarine rounded on the tiny tech-priest. 'Answer me!'

There was another loud cracking sound. Borgovda looked beyond Solarion and saw the bone-like surface of the sarcophagus split violently. Pieces shattered and flew off. In the gaps they left, something huge and dark writhed and twisted, desperate to be free.

The magos was transfixed.

'I asked you a question!' Solarion barked, visibly fighting to restrain himself from striking the magos. 'What does the beacon alert them to?'

'To that,' said Borgovda, terrified and exhilarated all at once. 'To the release of... of whatever they buried here.'

'They left it alive?' said Voss, drawing abreast of Solarion and Borgovda, his heavy bolter raised and ready.

Suddenly, everything slotted into place. Borgovda had the full context of the eldar writing he had deciphered on the sarcophagus's surface, and, with that context, came a new understanding.

'They buried it,' he told Talon Squad, 'because they couldn't kill it!'

There was a shower of bony pieces as the creature finally broke free of the last of its tomb and stretched its massive serpentine body for all to see. It was as tall as a Warhound Titan, and, from the look of it, almost as well armoured. Complex mouthparts split open like the bony, razor-lined petals of some strange, lethal flower. Its bizarre jaws dripped with corrosive fluids. This beast, this nightmare leviathan pulled from the belly of the earth, shivered and threw back its gargantuan head.

A piercing shriek filled the poisonous air, so loud that some of the skitarii troopers closest to it fell down, choking on the deadly atmosphere. The creature's screech had shattered their visors.

'Well maybe *they* couldn't kill it,' growled Lyandro Karras, marching stoically forwards through waves of psychic pain. 'But *we* will! To battle, brothers, in the Emperor's name!'

SEARING LANCES OF las-fire erupted from all directions at once, centring on the massive worm-like creature that was, after so many long millennia, finally free. Normal men would have quailed in the face of such an overwhelming foe. What could such tiny things as humans do against something like this? But the skitarii troopers of the Adeptus Mechanicus had been rendered all but fearless, their survival instincts overridden by neural programming, augmentation and brain surgery. They did not flee as other men would have. They surrounded the beast, working as one to put as much firepower on it as possible.

A brave effort, but ultimately a wasted one. The creature's thick plates of alien chitin shrugged off their assault. All that concentrated firepower really achieved was to turn the beast's attention on its attackers. Though sightless in the conventional sense, it sensed everything. Rows of tiny cyst-like nodules running the length of its body detected changes in heat, air pressure and vibration to the most minute degree. It knew exactly where each of its attackers stood. Not only could it hear their beating hearts, it could feel them vibrating through the ground and the air. Nothing escaped its notice.

With incredible speed for a creature so vast, it whipped its heavy black tail forwards in an arc. The air around it whistled. Skitarii troopers were cut down like stalks of wheat, crushed by the dozen, their ribcages pulverised. Some were launched into the air, their bodies falling like mortar shells a second later, slamming down with fatal force onto the corrugated metal roofs of the nearby storage and accommodation huts.

Talon Squad was already racing forwards to join the fight. Chyron's awkward run caused crates to fall from their stacks. Adrenaline flooded the wretched remains of his organic body, a tiny remnant of the Space Marine he had once been, little more now than brain, organs and scraps of flesh held together, kept alive, by the systems of his massive armoured chassis.

'Death to all xenos!' he roared, following close behind the others.

At the head of the team, Karras ran with his bolter in hand. The creature was three hundred metres away, but he and his squadmates would close that gap all too quickly. What would they do then? How did one fight a monster like this?

There was a voice on the link. It was Voss.

'A trygon, Scholar? A mawloc?'

'No, Omni,' replied Karras. 'Same genus, I think, but something we haven't seen before.'

'Sigma knew,' said Zeed, breaking in on the link.

'Aye,' said Karras. 'Knew or suspected.'

'Karras,' said Solarion. 'I'm moving to high ground.'

'Go.'

SOLARION'S BOLT-RIFLE, A superbly-crafted weapon, its like unseen in the armouries of any Adeptus Astartes Chapter but the Deathwatch, was best employed from a distance. The Ultramarine broke away from the charge of the others. He sought out the tallest structure in the crater that he could reach quickly. His eyes found it almost immediately. It was behind him – the loading crane that served the mag-rail line. It was slightly shorter than the cranes that had been used to lift the entombed creature out of the pit, but each of those were far too close to the beast to be useful. This one would do well. He ran to the foot of the crane, to the stanchions that were steam-bolted to the ground, slung his rifle over his right pauldron, and began to climb.

The massive tyranid worm was scything its tail through more of the skitarii, and their numbers dropped to half. Bloody smears marked the open concrete. For all their fearlessness and tenacity, the Mechanicus troops hadn't even scratched the blasted thing. All they had managed was to put the beast in a killing frenzy at the cost of their own lives. Still they fought, still they poured blinding spears of fire on it, but to no avail. The beast flexed again, tail slashing forwards, and another dozen died, their bodies smashed to a red pulp.

'I hope you've got a plan, Scholar,' said Zeed as he ran beside his leader. 'Other than *kill the bastard*, I mean.'

'I can't channel psychic energy into Arquemann,' said Karras, thinking for a moment that his ancient force sword might be the only thing able to crack the brute's armoured hide. 'Not with that infernal beacon drowning me out. But if we can stop the beacon... If I can get close enough–'

He was cut off by a calm, cold and all-too-familiar voice on the link.

'Specimen Six is not to be killed under any circumstances, Alpha. I want the creature alive!'

'Sigma!' spat Karras. 'You can't seriously think... No! We're taking it down. We have to!'

Sigma broadcast his voice to the entire team.

'Listen to me, Talon Squad. That creature is to be taken alive at all costs. Restrain it and prepare it for transport. Brother Solarion has been equipped for the task already. Your job is to facilitate the success of his shot, then escort the tranquilised creature back to the *St. Nevarre.* Remember your oaths. Do as you are bid.'

It was Chyron, breaking his characteristic brooding silence, who spoke up first.

'This is an outrage, Sigma. It is a tyranid abomination and Chyron will kill it. We are Deathwatch. Killing things is what we do.'

'You will do as ordered, Lamenter. All of you will. Remember your oaths. Honour the treaties, or return to your brothers in disgrace.'

'I have no brothers left,' Chyron snarled, as if this freed him from the need to obey.

'Then you will return to nothing. The Inquisition has no need of those who cannot follow mission parameters. The Deathwatch even less so.'

Karras, getting close to the skitarii and the foe, felt his lip curl in anger. This was madness.

'Solarion,' he barked, 'how much did you know?'

'Some,' said the Ultramarine, a trace of something unpleasant in his voice. 'Not much.'

'And you didn't warn us, brother?' Karras demanded.

'Orders, Karras. Unlike some, I follow mine to the letter.'

Solarion had never been happy operating under the Death Spectre Librarian's command. Karras was from a Chapter of the Thirteenth Founding. To Solarion, that made him inferior. Only the Chapters of the First Founding were worthy of unconditional respect, and even some of those...

'Magos Altando issued me with special rounds,' Solarion went on. 'Neuro-toxics. I need a clear shot on a soft, fleshy area. Get me that opening, Karras, and Sigma will have what he wants.'

Karras swore under his helm. He had known all along that something was up. His psychic gift did not extend to prescience, but he had sensed something dark and ominous hanging over them from the start.

The tyranid worm was barely fifty metres away now, and it turned its plated head straight towards the charging Deathwatch Space Marines. It could hardly have missed the thundering footfalls of Chyron, who was another thirty metres behind Karras, unable to match the swift pace of his smaller, lighter squadmates.

'The plan, Karras!' said Zeed, voice high and anxious.

Karras had to think fast. The beast lowered its fore-sections and began slithering towards them, sensing these newcomers were a far greater threat than the remaining skitarii.

Karras skidded to an abrupt halt next to a skitarii sergeant and shouted at him, 'You! Get your forces out. Fall back towards the mag-rail station.'

'We fight,' insisted the skitarii. 'Magos Borgovda has not issued the command to retreat.'

Karras grabbed the man by the upper right arm and almost lifted him off his feet. 'This isn't fighting. This is dying. You will do as I say. The Deathwatch will take care of this. Do not get in our way.'

The sergeant's eyes were blank lifeless things, like those of a doll. Had the Adeptus Mechanicus surgically removed so much of the man's humanity? There was no fear there, certainly, but Karras sensed little else, either. Whether that was because of the surgeries or because the eldar beacon was still drowning him in wave after invisible wave of pounding psychic pressure, he could not say.

After a second, the skitarii sergeant gave a reluctant nod and sent a message over his vox-link. The skitarii began falling back, but they kept their futile fire up as they moved.

The rasping of the worm's armour plates against the rockcrete grew louder as it neared, and Karras turned again to face it. 'Get ready!' he told the others.

'What is your decision, Death Spectre?' Chyron rumbled. 'It is a xenos abomination. It must be killed, regardless of the inquisitor's command.'

Damn it, thought Karras. I know he's right, but I must honour the treaties, for the sake of the Chapter. We must give Solarion his window.

'Keep the beast occupied. Do as Sigma commands. If Solarion's shot fails...'

'It won't,' said Solarion over the link.

It had better not, thought Karras. Because, if it does, I'm not sure we *can* kill this thing.

* * *

SOLARION HAD REACHED the end of the crane's armature. The entire crater floor was spread out below him. He saw his fellow Talon members fan out to face the alien abomination. It reared up on its hind-sections again and screeched at them, thrashing the air with rows of tiny vestigial limbs. Voss opened up on it first, showering it with a hail of fire from his heavy bolter. Rauth and Karras followed suit while Zeed and Chyron tried to flank it and approach from the sides.

Solarion snorted.

It was obvious, to him at least, that the fiend didn't have any blind spots. It didn't have eyes!

So far as Solarion could tell from up here, the furious fusillade of bolter rounds rattling off the beast's hide was doing nothing at all, unable to penetrate the thick chitin plates.

I need exposed flesh, he told himself. I won't fire until I get it. One shot, one kill. Or, in this case, one paralysed xenos worm.

He locked himself into a stable position by pushing his boots into the corners created by the crane's metal frame. All around him, the winds of Menatar howled and tugged, trying to pull him into a deadly eighty-metre drop. The dust on those winds cut visibility by twenty per cent, but he knew he could pull off a perfect shot in far worse conditions than these.

Sniping from the top of the crane meant that he was forced to lie belly-down at a forty-five-degree angle, his bolt-rifle's stock braced against his shoulder, right visor-slit pressed close to the lens of his scope. After some adjustments, the writhing monstrosity came into sharp focus. Bursts of gunfire continued to ripple over its carapace. Its tail came down hard in a hammering vertical stroke that Rauth only managed to sidestep at the last possible second. The rockcrete where the Exorcist had been standing shattered and flew off in all directions.

Solarion pulled back the cocking lever of his weapon and slid one of Altando's neuro-toxic rounds into the chamber. Then he spoke over the comm-link.

'I'm in position, Karras. Ready to take the shot. Hurry up and get me that opening.'

'We're trying, Prophet!' Karras snapped back, using the nickname Zeed had coined for the Ultramarine.

Try harder, thought Solarion, but he didn't say it. There was a limit, he knew, to how far he could push Talon Alpha.

THREE GRENADES DETONATED, one after another, with ground-splintering cracks. The wind pulled the dust and debris aside. The creature reared up again, towering over the Space Marines, and they saw that it remained utterly undamaged, not even a scratch on it.

'Nothing!' cursed Rauth.

Karras swore. This was getting desperate. The monster was tireless, its speed undiminished, and nothing they did seemed to have the least effect. By contrast, its own blows were all too potent. It had already struck Voss aside. Luck had been with the Imperial Fist, however. The blow had been lateral, sending him twenty metres along the ground before slamming him into the side of a fuel silo. The strength of his ceramite armour had saved his life. Had the blow been vertical, it would have killed him on the spot.

Talon Squad hadn't survived the last six years of special operations to die here on Menatar. Karras wouldn't allow it. But the only weapon they had which might do anything to the monster was his force blade, Arquemann, and, with that accursed eldar beacon drowning out his gift, Karras couldn't charge it with the devastating psychic power it needed to do the job.

'Warp blast it!' he cursed over the link. 'Someone find the source of that psychic signal and knock it out!'

He couldn't pinpoint it himself. The psychic bursts were overwhelming, drowning out all but his own thoughts. He could no longer sense Zeed's spiritual essence, nor that of Voss, Chyron, or Solarion. As for Rauth, he had never been able to sense the Exorcist's soul. Even after serving together this long, he was no closer to discovering the reason for that. For all Karras knew, maybe the quiet, brooding warrior had no soul.

Zeed was doing his best to keep the tyranid's attention on himself. He was the fastest of all of them. If Karras hadn't known better, he might even have said Zeed was enjoying the deadly game. Again and again, that barbed black tail flashed at the Raven Guard, and, every time, found only empty air. Zeed kept himself a split second ahead. Whenever he was close enough, he lashed out with his lightning claws and raked the creature's sides. But, despite the blue sparks that flashed with every contact, he couldn't penetrate that incredible armour.

Karras locked his bolter to his thigh plate and drew Arquemann from its scabbard.

This is it, he thought. We have to close with it. Maybe Chyron can do something if he can get inside its guard. He's the only one who might just be strong enough.

'Engage at close quarters,' he told the others. 'We can't do anything from back here.'

It was all the direction Chyron needed. The Dreadnought loosed a battlecry and stormed forwards to attack with his two great power fists, the ground juddering under him as he charged.

By the Emperor's grace, thought Karras, following in the Dreadnought's thunderous wake, don't let this be the day we lose someone.

Talon Squad was *his* squad. Despite the infighting, the secrets, the mistrust and everything else, that still meant something.

* * *

SOLARION SAW THE rest of the kill-team race forwards to engage the beast at close quarters and did not envy them, but he had to admit a grudging pride in their bravery and honour. Such a charge looked like sure suicide. For any other squad, it might well have been. But for Talon Squad...

Concentrate, he told himself. The moment is at hand. Breathe slowly. He did.

His helmet filtered the air, removing the elements that might have killed him, elements that even the Adeptus Astartes implant known as the multi-lung would not have been able to handle. Still, the air tasted foul and burned in his nostrils and throat. A gust of wind buffeted him, throwing his aim off a few millimetres, forcing him to adjust again.

A voice shouted triumphantly on the link.

'I've found it, Scholar. I have the beacon!'

'Voss?' said Karras.

There was a muffled *crump*, the sound of a krak grenade. Solarion's eyes flicked from his scope to cloud of smoke about fifty metres to the creature's right. He saw Voss emerge from the smoke. Around him lay the rubble of the monster's smashed sarcophagus.

Karras gave a roar of triumph.

'It's... it's gone,' he said. 'It's lifted. I can feel it!'

So Karras would be able to wield his psychic abilities again. Would it make any difference, Solarion wondered?

It did, and that difference was immediate. Something began to glow down on the battlefield. Solarion turned his eyes towards it and saw Karras raise Arquemann in a two-handed grip. The monster must have sensed the sudden buildup of psychic charge, too. It thrashed its way towards the Librarian, eager to crush him under its powerful coils. Karras dashed in to meet the creature's huge body and plunged his blade into a crease where two sections of chitin plate met.

An ear-splitting alien scream tore through the air, echoing off the crater walls.

Karras twisted the blade hard and pulled it free, and its glowing length was followed by a thick gush of black ichor.

The creature writhed in pain, reared straight up and screeched again, its complex jaws open wide.

Just the opening Solarion was waiting for.

He squeezed the trigger of his rifle and felt it kick powerfully against his armoured shoulder.

A single white-hot round lanced out towards the tyranid worm.

There was a wet impact as the round struck home, embedding itself deep in the fleshy tissue of the beast's mouth.

'Direct hit!' Solarion reported.

'Good work,' said Karras on the link. 'Now what?'

It was Sigma's voice that answered. 'Fall back and wait. The toxin is fast-acting. In ten to fifteen seconds, Specimen Six will be completely paralysed.'

'You heard him, Talon Squad,' said Karras. 'Fall back. Let's go!'

Solarion placed one hand on the top of his rifle, muttered a prayer of thanks to the weapon's machine-spirit, and prepared to descend. As he looked out over the crater floor, however, he saw that one member of the kill-team wasn't retreating.

Karras had seen it, too.

'Chyron,' barked the team leader. 'What in Terra's name are you doing?

The Dreadnought was standing right in front of the beast, fending off blows from its tail and its jaws with his oversized fists.

'Stand down, Lamenter,' Sigma commanded.

If Chyron heard, he deigned not to answer. While there was still a fight to be had here, he wasn't going anywhere. It was the tyranids that had obliterated his Chapter. Hive Fleet Kraken had decimated them, leaving him with no brothers, no home to return to. But if Sigma and the others thought the Deathwatch was all Chyron had left, they were wrong. He had his rage, his fury, his unquenchable lust for dire and bloody vengeance.

The others should have known that. Sigma should have known.

Karras started back towards the Dreadnought, intent on finding some way to reach him. He would use his psyker gifts if he had to. Chyron could not hope to beat the thing alone.

But, as the seconds ticked off and the Dreadnought continued to fight, it became clear that something was wrong.

From his high vantage point, it was Solarion who voiced it first.

'It's not stopping,' he said over the link. 'Sigma, the damned thing isn't even slowing down. The neuro-toxin didn't work.'

'Impossible,' replied the voice of the inquisitor. 'Magos Altando had the serum tested on–'

'Twenty-five... no, thirty seconds. I tell you, it's not working.'

Sigma was silent for a brief moment, then he said, 'We need it alive.'

'Why?' demanded Zeed. The Raven Guard was crossing the concrete again, back towards the fight, following close behind Karras.

'You do not need to know,' said Sigma.

'The neuro-toxin doesn't work, Sigma,' Solarion repeated. 'If you have some other suggestion...'

Sigma clicked off.

I guess he doesn't, thought Solarion sourly.

'Solarion,' said Karras. 'Can you put another round in it?'

'Get it to open wide and you know I can. But it might not be a dosage issue.'

'I know,' said Karras, his anger and frustration telling in his voice. 'But it's all we've got. Be ready.'

* * *

CHYRON'S CHASSIS WAS scraped and dented. His foe's strength seemed boundless. Every time the barbed tail whipped forwards, Chyron swung his fists at it, but the beast was truly powerful and, when one blow connected squarely with the Dreadnought's thick glacis plate, he found himself staggering backwards despite his best efforts.

Karras was suddenly at his side.

'When I tell you to fall back, Dreadnought, you will do it,' growled the Librarian. 'I'm still Talon Alpha. Or does that mean nothing to you?'

Chyron steadied himself and started forwards again, saying, 'I honour your station, Death Spectre, and your command. But vengeance for my Chapter supersedes all. Sigma be damned, I *will* kill this thing!'

Karras hefted Arquemann and prepared to join Chyron's charge. 'Would you dishonour all of us with you?'

The beast swivelled its head towards them and readied to strike again.

'For the vengeance of my Chapter, no price is too high. I am sorry, Alpha, but that is how it must be.'

'Then the rest of Talon Squad stands with you,' said Karras. 'Let us hope we all live to regret it.'

Solarion managed to put two further toxic rounds into the creature's mouth in rapid succession, but it was futile. This hopeless battle was telling badly on the others now. Each slash of that deadly tail was avoided by a rapidly narrowing margin. Against a smaller and more numerous foe, the strength of the Space Marines would have seemed almost infinite, but this towering tyranid leviathan was far too powerful to engage with the weapons they had. They were losing this fight, and yet Chyron would not abandon it, and the others would not abandon him, despite the good sense that might be served in doing so.

Voss tried his best to keep the creature occupied at range, firing great torrents from his heavy bolter, even knowing that he could do little, if any, real damage. His fire, however, gave the others just enough openings to keep fighting. Still, even the heavy ammunition store on the Imperial Fist's back had its limits. Soon, the weapon's thick belt feed began whining as it tried to cycle non-existent rounds into the chamber.

'I'm out,' Voss told them. He started disconnecting the heavy weapon so that he might draw his combat blade and join the close-quarters melee.

It was at that precise moment, however, that Zeed, who had again been taunting the creature with his lightning claws, had his feet struck out from under him. He went down hard on his back, and the tyranid monstrosity launched itself straight towards him, massive mandibles spread wide.

For an instant, Zeed saw that huge red maw descending towards him. It looked like a tunnel of dark, wet flesh. Then a black shape blocked his view and he heard a mechanical grunt of strain.

'I'm more of a meal, beast,' growled Chyron.

The Dreadnought had put himself directly in front of Zeed at the last minute, gripping the tyranid's sharp mandibles in his unbreakable titanium grip. But the creature was impossibly heavy, and it pressed down on the Lamenter with all its weight.

The force pressing down on Chyron was impossible to fight, but he put everything he had into the effort. His squat, powerful legs began to buckle. A piston in his right leg snapped. His engine began to sputter and cough with the strain.

'Get out from under me, Raven Guard,' he barked. 'I can't hold it much longer!'

Zeed scrabbled backwards about two metres, then stopped.

No, he told himself. Not today. Not to a mindless beast like this.

'Corax protect me,' he muttered, then sprang to his feet and raced forwards, shouting, *'Victoris aut mortis!'*

Victory or death!

He slipped beneath the Dreadnought's right arm, bunched his legs beneath him and, with lightning claws extended out in front, dived directly into the beast's gaping throat.

'Ghost!' shouted Voss and Karras at the same time, but he was already gone from sight and there was no reply over the link.

Chyron wrestled on for another second. Then two. Then, suddenly, the monster began thrashing in great paroxysms of agony. It wrenched its mandibles from Chyron's grip and flew backwards, pounding its ringed segments against the concrete so hard that great fractures appeared in the ground.

The others moved quickly back to a safe distance and watched in stunned silence.

It took a long time to die.

WHEN THE BEAST was finally still, Voss sank to his knees.

'No,' he said, but he was so quiet that the others almost missed it.

Footsteps sounded on the stone behind them. It was Solarion. He stopped alongside Karras and Rauth.

'So much for taking it alive,' he said.

No one answered.

Karras couldn't believe it had finally happened. He had lost one. After all they had been through together, he had started to believe they might all return to their Chapters alive one day, to be welcomed as honoured heroes, with the sad exception of Chyron, of course.

Suddenly, however, that belief seemed embarrassingly naïve. If Zeed could die, all of them could. Even the very best of the best would met his match in the end. Statistically, most Deathwatch members never made it back to the fortress-monasteries of their originating Chapters. Today, Zeed had joined those fallen ranks.

It was Sigma, breaking in on the command channel, who shattered the grim silence.

'You have failed me, Talon Squad. It seems I greatly overestimated you.'

Karras hissed in quiet anger. 'Siefer Zeed is dead, inquisitor.'

'Then you, Alpha, have failed on two counts. The Chapter Master of the Raven Guard will be notified of Zeed's failure. Those of you who live will at least have a future chance to redeem yourselves. The Imperium has lost a great opportunity here. I have no more to say to you. Stand by for Magos Altando.'

'Altando?' said Karras. 'Why would–'

Sigma signed off before Karras could finish, his voice soon replaced by the buzzing mechanical tones of the old magos who served on his retinue.

'I am told that Specimen Six is dead,' he grated over the link. 'Most regrettable, but your chances of success were extremely slim from the beginning. I predicted failure at close to ninety-six point eight five per cent probability.'

'But Sigma deployed us anyway,' Karras seethed. 'Why am I not surprised?'

'All is not lost,' Altando continued, ignoring the Death Spectre's ire. 'There is much still to be learned from the carcass. Escort it back to Orga Station. I will arrive there to collect it shortly.'

'Wait,' snapped Karras. 'You wish this piece of tyranid filth loaded up and shipped back for extraction? Are you aware of its size?'

'Of course I am,' answered Altando. 'It is what the mag-rail line was built for. In fact, everything we did on Menatar from the very beginning – the construction, the excavation, the influx of Mechanicus personnel – all of it was to secure the specimen alive, still trapped inside its sarcophagus. Under the circumstances, we will make do with a dead one. You have given us no choice.'

The sound of approaching footsteps caught Karras's attention. He turned from the beast's slumped form and saw the xenohierographologist, Magos Borgovda, walking towards him with a phalanx of surviving skitarii troopers and robed Mechanicus acolytes.

Beneath the plex bubble of his helm, the little tech-priest's eyes were wide.

'You… you bested it. I would not have believed it possible. You have achieved what the Exodites could not.'

'Ghost bested it,' said Voss. 'This is his kill. His and Chyron's.'

If Chyron registered these words, he didn't show it. The ancient warrior stared fixedly at his fallen foe.

'Magos Borgovda,' said Karras heavily, 'are there men among your survivors who can work the cranes? This carcass is to be loaded onto a mag-rail car and taken to Orga Station.'

'Yes, indeed,' said Borgovda, his eyes taking in the sheer size of the creature. 'That part of our plans has not changed, at least.'

Karras turned in the direction of the mag-rail station and started walking. He knew he sounded tired and miserable when he said, 'Talon Squad, fall in.'

'Wait,' said Chyron. He limped forwards with a clashing and grinding of the gears in his right leg. 'I swear it, Alpha. The creature just moved. Perhaps it is not dead, after all.'

He clenched his fists as if in anticipation of crushing the last vestiges of life from it. But, as he stepped closer to the creature's slack mouth, there was a sudden outpouring of thick black gore, a great torrent of it. It splashed over his feet and washed across the dry rocky ground.

In that flood of gore was a bulky form, a form with great rounded pauldrons, sharp claws, and a distinctive, back-mounted generator. It lay unmoving in the tide of ichor.

'Ghost,' said Karras quietly. He had hoped never to see this, one under his command lying dead.

Then the figure stirred and groaned.

'If we ever fight a giant alien worm again,' said the croaking figure over the comm-link, 'some other bastard can jump down its throat. I've had my turn.'

Solarion gave a sharp laugh. Voss's reaction was immediate. He strode forwards and hauled his friend up, clapping him hard on the shoulders. 'Why would any of us bother when you're so good at it, paper-face?'

Karras could hear the relief in Voss's voice. He grinned under his helm. Maybe Talon Squad was blessed after all. Maybe they would live to return to their Chapters.

'I said fall in, Deathwatch,' he barked at them, then he turned and led them away.

ALTANDO'S LIFTER HAD already docked at Orga Station by the time the mag-rail cars brought Talon Squad, the dead beast and the Mechanicus survivors to the facility. Sigma himself was, as always, nowhere to be seen. That was standard practice for the inquisitor. Six years, and Karras had still never met his enigmatic handler. He doubted he ever would.

Derlon Saezar and the station staff had been warned to stay well away from the mag-rail platforms and loading bays and to turn off all internal vid-picters. Saezar was smarter than most people gave him credit for. He did exactly as he was told. No knowledge was worth the price of his life.

Magos Altando surveyed the tyranid's long body with an appraising lens before ordering it loaded onto the lifter, a task with which even his veritable army of servitor slaves had some trouble. Magos Borgovda was most eager to speak with him, but, for some reason, Altando acted as if the xeno-hierographologist barely existed. In the end, Borgovda became irate and insisted that the other magos answer his questions at once.

Why was he being told nothing? This was *his* discovery. Great promises had been made. He demanded the respect he was due.

It was at this point, with everyone gathered in Bay One, the only bay in the station large enough to offer a berth to Altando's lifter, that Sigma addressed Talon Squad over the comm-link command channel once again.

'No witnesses,' he said simply.

Karras was hardly surprised. Again, this was standard operating procedure, but that didn't mean the Death Spectre had to like it. It went against every bone in his body. Wasn't the whole point of the Deathwatch to protect mankind? They were alien-hunters. His weapons hadn't been crafted to take the lives of loyal Imperial citizens, no matter who gave the command.

'Clarify,' said Karras, feigning momentary confusion.

There was a crack of thunder, a single bolter shot. Magos Borgovda's head exploded in a red haze.

Darrion Rauth stood over the body, dark grey smoke rising from the muzzle of his bolter.

'Clear enough for you, Karras?' said the Exorcist.

Karras felt anger surging up inside him. He might even have lashed out at Rauth, might have grabbed him by the gorget, but the reaction of the surviving skitarii troopers put a stop to that. Responding to the cold-blooded slaughter of their leader, they raised their weapons and aimed straight at the Exorcist.

What followed was a one-sided massacre that made Karras sick to his stomach.

When it was over, Sigma had his wish.

There were no witnesses left to testify that anything at all had been dug up from the crater on Menatar. All that remained was the little spaceport station and its staff, waiting to be told that the excavation was over and that their time on this inhospitable world was finally at an end.

SAEZAR WATCHED THE big lifter take off first, and marvelled at it. Even on his slightly fuzzy vid-monitor screen, the craft was an awe-inspiring sight. It emerged from the doors of Bay One with so much thrust that he thought it might rip the whole station apart, but the facility's integrity held. There were no pressure leaks, no accidents.

The way that great ship hauled its heavy form up into the sky and off beyond the clouds thrilled him. Such power! It was a joy and an honour to see it. He wondered what it must be like to pilot such a ship.

Soon, the black Thunderhawk was also ready to leave. He granted the smaller, sleeker craft clearance and opened the doors of Bay Four once again. Good air out, bad air in. The Thunderhawk's thrusters powered up. It soon emerged into the light of the Menatarian day, angled its nose upwards, and began to pull away.

Watching it go, Saezar felt a sense of relief that surprised him. The Space Marines were leaving. He had expected to feel some kind of sadness, perhaps even regret at not getting to meet them in person. But he felt neither of those things. There was something terrible about them. He knew that now. It was something none of the bedtime stories had ever conveyed.

As he watched the Thunderhawk climb, Saezar reflected on it, and discovered that he knew what it was. The Adeptus Astartes, the Space Marines… they didn't radiate goodness or kindness like the stories pretended. They were not so much righteous and shining champions as they were dark avatars of destruction. Aye, he was glad to see the back of them. They were the living embodiment of death. He hoped he would never set eyes on such beings again. Was there any greater reminder that the galaxy was a terrible and deadly place?

'That's right,' he said quietly to the vid-image of the departing Thunderhawk. 'Fly away. We don't need angels of death here. Better you remain a legend only if the truth is so grim.'

And then he saw something that made him start forwards, eyes wide.

It was as if the great black bird of prey had heard his words. It veered sharply left, turning back towards the station.

Saezar stared at it, wordless, confused.

There was a burst of bright light from the battle-cannon on the craft's back. A cluster of dark, slim shapes burst forwards from the under-wing pylons, each trailing a bright ribbon of smoke.

Missiles!

'No!'

Saezar would have said more, would have cried out to the Emperor for salvation, but the roof of the operations centre was ripped apart in the blast. Even if the razor-sharp debris hadn't cut his body into a dozen wet red pieces, the rush of choking Menatarian air would have eaten him from the inside out.

'No witnesses,' Sigma had said.

Within minutes, Orga Station was obliterated, and then there were none.

DAYS PASSED.

The only things stirring within the crater were the skirts of dust kicked up by gusting winds. Ozyma-138 loomed vast and red in the sky above, continuing its work of slowly blasting away the planet's atmosphere. With the last of the humans gone, this truly was a dead place once again, and that was how the visitors, or rather returnees, found it.

There were three of them, and they had been called here by a powerful beacon that only psychically gifted individuals might detect. It was a beacon that had gone strangely silent shortly after it had been activated. The visitors had come to find out why.

They were far taller than the men of the Imperium, and their limbs were long and straight. The human race might have thought them elegant once, but all the killings these slender beings had perpetrated against mankind had put a permanent end to that. To the modern Imperium, they were simply xenos, to be hated and feared and destroyed like any other.

They descended the rocky sides of the crater in graceful silence, their booted feet causing only the slightest of rockslides. When they reached the bottom, they stepped onto the crater floor and marched together towards the centre where the mouth of the great pit gaped.

There was nothing hurried about their movements, and yet they covered the distance at an impressive speed.

The one who walked at the front of the trio was taller than the others, and not just by virtue of the high, jewel-encrusted crest on his helmet. He wore a rich cloak of strange shimmering material and carried a golden staff that shone with its own light.

The others were dressed in dark armour sculpted to emphasise the sweep of their long, lean muscles. They were armed with projectile weapons as white as bone. When the tall, cloaked figure stopped by the edge of the great pit, they stopped, too, and turned to either side, watchful, alert to any danger that might remain here.

The cloaked leader looked down into the pit for a moment, then moved off through the ruins of the excavation site, glancing at the crumpled metal huts and the rusting cranes as he passed them.

He stopped by a body on the ground, one of many. It was a pathetic, filthy mess of a thing, little more than rotting meat and broken bone wrapped in dust-caked cloth. It looked like it had been crushed by something. Pulverised. On the cloth was an icon – a skull set within a cog, equal parts black and white. For a moment, the tall figure looked down at it in silence, then he turned to the others and spoke, his voice filled with a boundless contempt that made even the swollen red sun seem to draw away.

'Mon-keigh,' he said, and the word was like a bitter poison on his tongue.

Mon-keigh.

WARHAMMER®

THE RAT CATCHER'S TAIL

Richard Ford

THE CANDLE HE kept by his bedside had long since burnt out and Hugo's room was bathed in blackness. The shutters over his windows kept out any encroaching moonlight, the double bolts serving to lock him fast within his mansion fortress.

He listened through the darkness, straining his ears for any sound. His eyes were wide as he peered over the top of his fine-stitched Estalian sheets, but could see nothing through the gloom.

There it was again, as it had come every night for the past week – the incessant scratching and pattering of tiny feet. Hugo could no longer deny the fact that it was slowly beginning to drive him insane. They were in the walls, under the floorboards, crawling across the attic, and Hugo was powerless to stop them. He had spent the past two days crawling around his own home with nothing but a sputtering candle for illumination, waiting behind half-closed doors for sound of the vermin's passing. When he heard it he would burst in, walking cane in hand, but the snuffling, chittering, furry beasts were nowhere in sight.

Would he have no peace?

Hugo Kressler was known throughout Talabheim as a well-respected, and very wealthy, merchant. His business had seen emperors come and go, had survived Chaos incursions and peasant uprisings.

When he had accrued enough wealth, Hugo had commissioned the building of the largest private property in the Manor District and on its completion he could not have been happier. It was a triumph of architecture, sporting wood panelling bought in from Ostland, lancet archways carved by dwarf masons, and boasting the latest security guaranteed by the Locksmith's Guild of Altdorf. Above all it satisfied Hugo's requirements for total privacy. For two years he had been ecstatically happy in his new abode, walking his hallways and admiring the works of art from Tilea and Bretonnia, sampling his vast wine cellar and counting his hard-earned coin.

Now all that was falling apart.

He had not slept for days and his usually voracious appetite had all but vanished. Hugo was now a wan shadow of his former self, a bag of saggy flesh with red-rimmed eyes that stared from beneath an unkempt mass of shaggy grey hair. It was like being a prisoner in his own home. He dare not leave for fear of what state his beloved mansion would be in when he returned. What would the pink-eyed beasts do to his belongings in his absence? The filth they would leave behind, the teeth marks... the droppings!

Wrenching back his sheets, Hugo leapt out of bed. He blindly felt around for his bedside candle and the single match he kept on the dresser in case he was caught short during the night. With the candle lit he strode across his bedroom, one hand shading the precious illumination. He opened the bedroom door and stepped out into the wide, panelled corridor.

All the while the noise from within the walls seemed to get louder, the rodents seeming to mock him, knowing they were winning, knowing that Hugo's wits would soon be frayed to nothing.

'I know you can hear me!' he screamed, his voice echoing along the pitch-black corridor. 'You won't win. Mark me! Do you know who you're dealing with? I'm Hugo Kressler, the most powerful merchant in Talabheim!'

As if in answer, the rats fell silent.

Hugo stood in the dark, watching... waiting.

Nothing.

With a sigh of relief he stumbled back to his bed, climbing within the fine, smooth sheets and pulling them up to his chin. Within seconds the gentle mercy of sleep overcame him.

Hugo was running.

He found it curious – normally when he ran in dreams it was as though he were wading through thick treacle, his legs sluggish and listless no matter how he willed them to move. Now however he was speeding along, scurrying even, moving with all the stealth and snap of a wild animal. At first this thrilled him, his heart pounding like a taxman at the door, but soon he realised the reason for his alacrity... he was being chased!

Something was after him, something big and mean and casting a long black shadow, and no matter how he tried to escape it he could not. He jinked left and right, over and under obstacles, but still he could not shake off his pursuer.

It was a losing battle, the hunter was gaining, Hugo could hear its pounding feet at his back, and the stink of its hot breath…

HE AWOKE, BREATHLESS and panting. His fine satin sheets were drenched, his silken nightgown clinging to his clammy flesh.

This would not stand – awake he was tormented by invaders in his home, asleep he was plagued by night terrors. He had to do something, had to rid himself of these torturous vermin.

Hugo leapt from his bed, flinging open his door and tramping through the corridors of his house, which were slowly brightening in the dawn light. In the porch he donned his boarskin greatcoat and the boots made especially for him from Arabyan horsehide, then ventured out into the chill morning air.

The streets of Talabheim were all but deserted this early in the day, particularly in the Manor District. It was inhabited by the city's great and good, and only their footmen and domestics would be out of bed at this ungodly hour. Consequently, when he stepped onto the Avenue of Heroes and headed west to his destination, Hugo had only an endless row of posturing statues to keep him company.

As he stamped through the streets they gradually became busier, and when he moved into the district known as Guildrow the bare cobbled road had become a hive of bustling activity. The Guildrow was a hub for Talabheim's industry, with blacksmiths and brewers, tinkers and tanners all going about their business. It was here that Hugo would find what he was looking for.

Eventually he located it and with renewed vigour Hugo marched to the front door of the trapmaker's shop. The lintel had been painted black, and written on it in faded white script was the legend: *Gerhardt Moller – Master of Traps, as appointed by Helmut Feuerbach, Elector Count of Talabecland*. This on its own filled Hugo with some relief as he rapped on the door. Moller would clearly have the answer to the twitching, scurrying, defecating problem that was assailing his home.

At first there was no answer, but after several successive, and steadily more frantic, knockings at the door it was hauled open. The man Hugo could only assume was the 'master' trapmaker stood staring from within the gloom, his hair dishevelled, his body encased in a tattered, furry robe of indeterminate origin.

'What?' said Moller gruffly, clearly none too impressed at being disturbed at this hour of the morning.

'I have a problem,' Hugo replied, a little more desperately than he had intended.

'Clearly,' said Moller, looking Hugo up and down. 'You'd best come in then.' He pushed open the door, allowing Hugo to step into the gloomy interior of the shop.

Once inside, his eyes slowly adjusted, revealing the dusty wares on sale. All manner of grim and dangerous-looking equipment lined the walls: spiked cages, leghold- and bear-traps, manacles of varying length and thickness, weighted nets and snares.

'What is it you're after, then?' asked Moller. 'Bear? Wolf? Boar? I'll assume it's game since you certainly don't look the bounty hunting type.'

'Erm, no,' Hugo replied. 'It's... well, it's, erm... rats!'

Moller narrowed his eyes, staring across the dark room with clear disdain. 'Rats?'

'Yes, I'm plagued by the filthy degenerate vermin. I need traps, and plenty of them.'

Moller shook his head, grumbling to himself as he entered a back room. Hugo could hear banging and clattering as the man searched through a mass of clutter until he eventually found what he was looking for. He returned with a small wooden box which he dropped on the shop counter with a disconsolate shrug. Peering in, Hugo could see a collection of jumbled garbage, some of it recognisable as trap components, but mostly it was a box full of broken wood and rusted metal hinges.

'Is that it?' Hugo said. 'On your door it says Master of Traps!'

Moller frowned, grasping the box. 'Now look here – I've crafted traps for elector counts in four provinces, hunters come to me from as far as Nordland. If you don't want–'

'No, no. I'll take it,' said Hugo in a panic, producing a purse from inside his coat. 'Here, for your trouble.' He placed four shiny gold crowns on the counter.

Moller seemed to instantly brighten, clapping his hand over the coins and sliding them into his meaty palm.

Hugo grabbed the box and was about to leave when Moller held up his hand.

'I've got something else that might help,' he said. 'If you're interested.'

Hugo nodded, unsure whether to trust the wry smile on Moller's face. The trapmaker disappeared into the back room once more, but this time there was no sound of clattering. What Hugo heard was far worse, as though Moller were wrestling with some kind of foul daemonic creature. He reappeared seconds later, holding a large object with a tattered piece of sacking draped over the top. Once he had slammed it down on the counter he jumped back, as though the object might explode in his face. Hugo could hear a frenzied gnashing and spluttering emanating from beneath the sack, and he too retreated to a safe distance.

'This,' said Moller, grasping the cloth between the fingers of his outstretched hand, 'is Gertrude!'

He whipped away the sack to reveal a cage beneath. Hugo couldn't tell what the sight within it filled him with more: fear or revulsion. Gertrude was the sorriest looking excuse for a cat he had ever seen – all gnashing teeth and mangy fur. She attacked the cage with a frenzy to rival any

Norscan, howling like a banshee all the while.

'Best ratter in the Taalbaston, although she does have some... issues. Yours for only five crowns.'

Hugo stared as the cat tried to chew her way out of the mesh cage, her chipped yellow teeth grinding against the metal.

'No thanks,' he replied. 'The traps will do for now.'

'Suit yourself,' said Moller. 'But if you change your mind, you can always come back.'

'Of course,' Hugo said, backing out into the street, and closing the shop door behind him. 'I'll be back – right after I've flashed my fruits at the Emperor's Parade.'

IT TOOK HIM hours to disentangle the mess of traps Moller had sold him. Some had broken hinges, some brittle bases, others were rusted beyond use, but eventually Hugo managed to salvage over a dozen usable rat traps.

After much planning, he located them strategically throughout his house then carefully baited each one with Grossreiche Blue – the most pungent cheese he owned. As he carefully secured the clasp on the last one, Hugo giggled at his visions of an unwary quarry wandering up, summoned by the tantalising aroma, only to have its neck snapped as it tried to take a bite.

Still chortling to himself, Hugo retreated to his bedchamber, snuffed out the candle and jumped into bed.

IN THE MORNING, Hugo was awoken to brilliant sunlight invading the slats in his Cathayan blinds. He could remember no nightmares; in fact his sleep had been so sound he couldn't remember dreaming at all.

With a spring in his step he crossed his room and flung open the door, eager to see the carnage his traps had wrought. He padded, barefoot, to the end of the corridor then gingerly peered around the corner. Hugo had never had the strongest of stomachs, and despite the inevitable joy he knew it would bring, he was still reluctant to view a splattered rat's corpse.

But there was nothing there – no trap, no Grossreiche Blue, and definitely no dead rat.

Hugo stared for several seconds. He was certain he had placed one of the traps right on that spot, but there was nothing. Scratching his head, he moved on to the next trap.

Perhaps he was mistaken, he thought as he moved through the house, perhaps his frenzied eagerness to eliminate the vermin had confused him and fuddled his mind. It was perfectly possible, he was under a lot of strain after all, but when he reached the location of the next trap he let out an audible yelp. That one had also disappeared!

With rising panic, Hugo rushed through the mansion, his feet slapping against the bare floorboards as he hurried to view each carefully-planned spot in which he had left his baited traps. Every one was missing, with not even a crumb of cheese left to mark where they had been.

His heart was beating now, slamming against his ribcage, the blood pumping audibly in his ears. The pressure in his head felt as though it would smash through his skull, releasing his frustration in a black gout of foetid steam.

'I know what you're up to!' Hugo screamed, his voice echoing through the chambers and corridors of his mansion. 'You're trying to send me mad! Well it won't work! Do you hear me? I'm Hugo Kressler, the greatest merchant of Talabheim, and I won't be beaten by scavenging pests!'

At that he raced down the stairs, this time not bothering to don his greatcoat or boots before hurrying into the morning air.

HUGO RETURNED TWO hours later. He tramped up the garden path bearing a heavy package, made all the more cumbersome by the gnashing, whining, spitting creature that was secreted within its wire mesh confines. On any other day his entrepreneurial nature would have compelled him to haggle with Moller over the price, but this was not a day for bartering – besides, five crowns had seemed like a bargain under the circumstances.

The front door slammed open as Hugo entered, a maniacal grin on his face.

'I'm back!' he screamed. 'And I've brought a friend with me!'

After placing the cage down in the centre of the reception hall he removed the sack that covered it, eager to release Gertrude on his unsuspecting houseguests. On seeing the raging whirlwind of fur and claws though, Hugo had second thoughts. Perhaps he should try and bond with Gertrude first, at least enough to stop her trying to claw his throat out.

He raced to the pantry, sniffing the pail of milk that sat within. It was a bit on the sour side, but he doubted Gertrude would notice – by the looks of her she'd not been offered anything this fresh for months.

Pouring some of the milk into a saucer he returned to the entrance hall and placed it in front of the cage.

'How about a little peace offering?' he said, sliding back the bolt.

In response, Gertrude calmed a little, seemingly mesmerised by the promise of milk.

Hugo swung the cage door open and backed away, leaving the saucer between him and the cat. She padded forwards with a sniff, then tentatively lapped up a mouthful. To Hugo's relief, his souring milk appeared to Gertrude's liking and she finished off the saucer with gusto, then sat back with a satisfied purr.

'There,' he said, taking a step forwards to pat her head. 'You're not all that bad after all, are you?'

His hand didn't reach within a foot of her before she screeched, clawing at him, yowling her hatred and attacking with unrestrained fury.

Hugo fled, sprinting up his staircase pursued by the angry cat all the way back to his bedchamber. He just managed to slam the door before Gertrude inflicted any further harm, and slid the bolt across just in case.

IT WAS SEVERAL hours before he mustered the courage to open his door, peering out into the dark corridor beyond. When he saw there was no wicked, hissing cat waiting for him, he let out a sigh of relief and stepped out into the passage.

His bare foot squelched down on something soft and unctuous. It oozed between his toes, unleashing the most horrendous odour Hugo had ever had the misfortune to experience.

He didn't have to look down to know that Gertrude had left him a gift reflecting just what she thought of him.

Well, she didn't have to like him, did she – she just had to do what he'd bought her for!

Hugo hopped to his nightstand, removed the doily that sat atop it and wiped the pungent cat crap from his foot, then went in search of Gertrude.

After checking the ground floor and finding no trace of the cat or her prey, Hugo moved to the first floor. As he reached the top landing he cringed as he saw fresh claw marks on his fine oak banister. He clenched his teeth against the fury, and moved towards the stair for the second floor, only to slip and stumble on a warm puddle of what could only be cat piss.

Hugo clenched his fists, moving to the foot of the stairwell and dragging his sodden foot along his embroidered Kislevite rug. It was then there pealed forth a horrendous sound the like of which he had never heard before. It was a tortured crowing, as though some wild animal were braying its last in agonising pain, and he was suddenly frozen to the spot by the sound.

Steeling himself, Hugo moved up the stairs onto the second-storey corridor. A number of doors led off into his various guestrooms and the sound seemed to be emanating from within one of them. It was louder now, and clearly coming from the first room on the right. Hugo grasped the door handle, girding his loins as he pushed open the door, squinting as he entered lest the sight be too much for his delicate sensibilities.

Gertrude let out another shattering howl, and Hugo's jaw dropped open at the sight. The cat lay in the middle of the room, her fur in tattered pieces, and clasped to her body, from the tip of her tail to the ends of her ears, were Hugo's missing rat traps.

What could have done this? What foul creature could overcome Gertrude so? What fiendish jester was taunting him in such a manner?

The answer was clear – these rats were revealing themselves as a force to be reckoned with!

186   *The Best of Hammer and Bolter: Volume One*

'Bastards!' Hugo cried. 'You may have won this battle, but the war isn't over yet!'

WITH GERTRUDE SAFELY de-trapped and placed in her cage, Hugo left his mansion once more. This time he had the wherewithal to dress himself, albeit shabbily, before he set out onto the darkening streets.

The Frog and Trumpet was one of the more upper-class drinking establishments of Talabheim, being situated in the affluent Manor District and with a clientele to match. Although Hugo received a curious look from the doorman as he walked in, his face was well-known enough to secure him entry despite his drab appearance.

Dergen Henschnapf was sitting in his usual spot by the fire, supping his schnapps and listening to the well-versed lute player secreted in one corner of the drinking house. When Hugo slumped into the grand leather chair opposite, Dergen peered curiously over his half-moon spectacles, barely recognising his old friend.

'I have a problem,' Hugo said, his eyes wide and desperate.

'Clearly,' Dergen replied.

'Why does everyone keep saying that? Anyway, you have to help me, I have nowhere else to turn.'

Dergen took another sip of schnapps before giving Hugo his *Do go on, I'm listening* look.

'I have rats. In my house. They're everywhere,' Hugo said before glancing around furtively, as though admitting he had rats in public might be more of a social *faux pas* than turning up at the Frog and Trumpet looking like a pauper's dog.

Dergen said nothing, merely altering his expression to *What would you like me to do about it.*

'You have connections,' said Hugo, growing ever more desperate, unable to keep his voice below a hoarse whisper. 'You move in those kind of circles.'

Dergen raised an eyebrow. 'What exactly are you suggesting?' he replied.

'Do I have to spell it out? You know people in the *extermination business.*'

Now it was Dergen's turn to glance furtively before sitting up and moving closer to Hugo.

'I have contacts, yes, but they're not skilled in exterminating the kind of vermin you're talking about.'

'You must know someone, Dergen. There must be something you can do, I'm at my wits end!'

Dergen reclined in his chair, deep in thought. Then he nodded, a sly smile crossing his lips. 'Actually I do know someone who may be able to help. Owes me a favour, and he's skilled in just this line of work.'

'Really?' Hugo's face brightened. 'You do?'

'Yes. You can find him in the Ten-Tailed Cat. Just ask for Boris, the barman will know who you mean.'

Hugo suddenly glared with indignation. 'You expect me to go to the Ten-Tailed Cat? I'm Hugo Kressler, the most powerful merchant–'

'–in all Talabheim. Yes, I've heard it before, Hugo, but I'm guessing the rats in your house don't care about that. And let's face it, you hardly look too powerful or merchant-like for the Ten-Tailed Cat right now, do you? In fact, dressed as you are I'm guessing you'll fit right in.'

Hugo glanced down at his apparel, then ran a trembling hand through his straw-like mop of hair.

'Well, I've been under a lot of stress,' he said.

'All the more reason for you to hurry along,' replied Dergen, waving Hugo towards the door.

Hugo could only nod, thanking his old friend and rushing from the Frog and Trumpet before anyone else could see him in such a dishevelled condition.

THE DOCKS STANK of rotting fish and ale, mixed in with the sickly-sweet aroma of cheap perfume wafting from a gaggle of preening harlots. None of them bothered to give Hugo a second glance as he made his way through the shadows towards the Ten-Tailed Cat.

A muted din of conversation emanated from the confines of the alehouse and, as Hugo approached, the door was suddenly flung open, allowing a drink-addled patron to stumble out into the night. The raucous interior was revealed in all its insalubrious glory; a heady mix of dirty laughter and thick pipe smoke.

Hugo hesitated at the threshold. What had he been reduced to? Sneaking through the dark of Talabheim's most woe begotten streets to mix with the patrons of the city's foulest dives. But he was here for a reason... a quest some might say. Even the heroes of legend had to reach their lowest ebb before rising to victory. This was merely another step on his path to defeating the enemy in his home.

Raising his chin, Hugo strode forwards, opening the door to the Ten-Tailed Cat and walking in as though he owned the place. Immediately, several sets of mean, hard-bitten eyes turned his way, and any confidence he may have summoned immediately vanished.

Dropping his head to avoid eye contact with anyone, Hugo made a dash for the bar. It turned into a weird kind of dance as he jinked and dodged to avoid touching any of the hulking, brutish patrons in his path, but eventually he made it in one piece. He squeezed between two grimy dockers and signalled the barman. Over the din of the alehouse he explained he was looking for Boris, and with a nonchalant nod of the head, the round-faced barman signalled towards a booth in one dank corner.

As Hugo approached he saw that Boris was a hulking figure, his head encased in a tight leather skullcap, his bare arms bulging with thick, corded muscle. He nursed a large pewter tankard into which he stared with a strange melancholy and, despite his rough exterior, Boris looked as out of place amongst the boisterous carousers of the Ten-Tailed Cat as Hugo felt.

'Erm, Boris?' Hugo asked as he reached the booth. The man seemed to brighten at Hugo's approach, nodding and offering the bench opposite. 'You've been recommended to me by Dergen Henschnapf as a man who might be able to eradicate a certain pest problem I currently have,' said Hugo, taking the proffered seat.

Boris frowned, suddenly deep in thought. 'Can't say as I recognise the name,' he replied in a rumbling voice. 'But my memory's not been all it was since I got retired from sewer duty.'

'Retired? Does that mean you're no longer in the business?'

'Depends what the problem is.'

Hugo glanced around, but it was clear the rest of the alehouse was too busy with its own revelry to care about his problems. 'I have... rats. In my house,' he whispered over the din.

'Have you tried traps?' asked Boris.

'Of course I've tried bloody traps,' Hugo snapped with immediate regret. 'I mean, yes. But these ones are clever, devious... cunning.'

Boris smiled knowingly. 'Ah. You'll be needing an expert then.'

Of course I will, that's why I'm in this stinking fleapit! was what Hugo wanted to say, but he merely nodded in reply, keeping his lip firmly buttoned.

'Well, you've come to the right man,' Boris continued. 'I'm the best rat catcher in the city. Let me know the address, I'll pick up some supplies and be right round.'

Hugo felt a sudden rush of elation. 'Excellent,' he replied.

He gave Boris the details of his mansion, along with easy instructions on how to find it, then stood to leave. Before he could escape the cloying confines of the Ten-Tailed Cat, though, he paused, curiosity getting the better of him.

'You say you were retired from sewer duty? What exactly happened?'

Boris smiled, gripping the leather skullcap and pulling it from his head to reveal a gristly stump where his right ear should have been. 'Big 'un took my ear off. Made a right bloody mess it did. Don't worry though, I took the bugger's own ear right back.' With that he reached into his hide jerkin and pulled out a chain, on the end of which dangled what was clearly the ear of a cow.

Hugo began to wonder whether this was a good idea – Boris was plainly unhinged, but then he guessed most rat catchers were.

'How come losing your ear meant you had to retire?' he asked, not really wanting to hear the answer.

'Oh, it's not because of this. Me ear wasn't all the big 'un took.' With that, Boris heaved himself out from behind the table, to reveal a chipped and weathered wooden leg, which he patted affectionately.

'A rat took your leg?' said Hugo in astonishment.

'Like I said; it was a big 'un.'

Hugo could only smile, staring down in bewilderment. A rat took his ear and his leg? The man was clearly out of his gourd. Was this the kind of person he wanted running riot through his house – his beautiful home? Some nutter with delusions of monstrous rats that could tear you limb from limb?

The answer was obvious.

'On second thoughts,' Hugo said, trying to smile through his discomfort. 'I've just remembered I may have double booked. Yes, that's right, I have someone else on the job, so there's really no need for you to trouble yourself. Anyway, must dash.'

With that he stumbled away from the booth, turning to push his way through the crowd, this time not caring who he nudged and shoved out of the way to escape the madhouse.

Once out in the street he breathed in the foetid air, sucking it into his lungs in relief.

The Ten-Tailed Cat indeed! What was Dergen thinking to recommend such a place, and such a man? Once this whole business was over, Hugo was sure he would be having stern words with his old friend regarding his recommendations, and with the sound of the bawdy house ringing in his ears he made his way back home.

That night, Hugo dreamed again.

He was running flat out, his tiny heart fluttering like a hummingbird's wing, his feet tapping against the hard ground in a staccato beat. The hunter was after him once more, pounding the earth in his wake, chasing him down, relentless and indomitable. Still Hugo dare not look back, dare not look upon the beast on his trail, so determined was he to avoid his fate.

But he could not.

No matter how fast or how far he ran it was still there, always there, breathing down his neck, slavering at the mouth in anticipation of the catch.

Hugo suddenly stumbled, losing his footing, falling, rolling. In an instant he was back on his feet, ready to move once more, but that single mistake was enough for the hunter to gain on its prey.

Strong hands, iron hard and huge, grasped him tight, digging their fingers into his flesh, lifting him, raising him towards that infernal maw...

HUGO SCREAMED HIMSELF awake, his eyes wide, staring into the blackness of his bedchamber. He panted in the dark, feeling every bit the helpless child. It was all he could do not to cry out for his mother. Once he realised he was alone, and there was no dark hellish beast after him, he let out a laboured sigh of relief. It was only then he realised he was sitting in a damp patch of his own urine.

With a low moan of resignation, Hugo donned his clothes, his boots and his greatcoat. It was a long walk back to the Ten-Tailed Cat, and he didn't want to catch his death in the night chill.

WHEN BORIS KNOCKED at the door of the mansion the next day, Hugo almost fell over himself in his eagerness to open it. The rat catcher stood there with a huge grin on his face, stinking of stale booze and pipe smoke.

'Come in,' said Hugo, stepping aside as Boris clunked forwards on his wooden leg. The sturdy appendage clacked against the polished wood floor of the entrance hall and Hugo winced at the prospect of having to call in the polishers to retouch and varnish it.

Boris gawped in astonishment at the interior of the opulent mansion, the grin never leaving his face. 'Nice place you've got,' he said.

Hugo didn't reply; he was too busy staring at the paraphernalia Boris was carrying. Some of it was clearly designed for a purpose – two cages, a snare and various traps dangled from the thick belt at Boris's waist – but there were other items that Hugo did not recognise.

'What's that?' he said, pointing at the wooden barrel under the crook of Boris's arm.

'Rat poison,' Boris replied. 'Got to be careful though, it's very potent.'

'And that?' Hugo pointed at the huge steel-headed maul strapped to the rat catcher's back.

'Oh, that's for the big 'uns I mentioned before. You can never be too careful in this game. Anyway, shall we get to it?' Without invitation Boris moved into the mansion, placing his cages down, securing his snares and traps, all the while sniffing the air and muttering to himself about 'infestations' and 'soon having this all sewn up'.

Hugo could only look on with trepidation as the gigantic rat catcher stomped through his beautiful house, exuding his unique aroma and making a mess of his floorboards.

'Right, all done,' Boris said finally. 'Just got to lay the poison and we're all finished. Of course, you might want to wait outside while I put it down, it doesn't half hum.'

'Are you sure this is strictly necessary?' Hugo said, looking around his home with growing concern.

'Course I am. Poison's the best way to flush 'em out. Then the fun starts.' Boris patted the head of his maul affectionately.

Hugo nodded uncertainly and made to leave, but he paused at the doorway, a portentous feeling of dread filling the pit of his stomach like corked wine. With one last glance around his magnificent entrance hall, he retreated to the safety of the garden.

Boris appeared some time later, trailing the contents of his barrel over the threshold of the doorway and out into the garden. Hugo could only look on in confusion. With the poison laid, Boris placed the barrel down on the lawn and turned, a self-satisfied smile on his broad features.

'Now the fun starts,' he said. 'Once we've flushed 'em out of course.'

The burly rat catcher took something from his pocket, and knelt down at the end of the trail of poison. Hugo heard a clinking sound as Boris ministered to the trail of powder on the ground.

The trail of black powder.

Hugo was suddenly gripped with a panic. He dashed forwards, about to ask what in the hells Boris was doing, when a flaring sound and the stink of phosphor suddenly struck the air.

'No!' was all he could manage to scream as Boris lit the powder trail with a strike of his flint. It ignited, sending a blazing spark along the garden path towards the house. Hugo chased it, vainly trying to catch the burning trail before it ran rampant through his house and set light to the floorboards, but he was not fast enough. Once in the hallway he saw that the powder trail ran of in several different directions – up the stairs, into the parlour, down into the cellar – setting the floor alight in a flickering trail as it went. Flames began to spread throughout the house, and Hugo ran forwards, stamping vainly at the blackening floorboards in an attempt to rescue his home.

Boris walked in after him, and Hugo glared up with unrestrained hatred. 'What have you done, you imbecile? You told me it was rat poison!'

'It is,' replied Boris, a hurt expression on his face. 'Rats can't stand it – they likes it even less when you set fire to it. It's the best thing for flushing them out – look!'

With that he pointed towards the cellar entrance as a horde of rats suddenly scurried out of the dank pit to safety.

Boris grinned, unslinging the maul from his back and rushing forwards with an expression of pure glee on his dumb features. The maul came down with an audible swipe, smashing one of the rats to sludge and knocking a huge hole in the floorboards.

'I told you it would work,' he yelled as he went about decimating the rat swarm, crushing them to a bloody pulp, along with the polished floor of the entrance hall.

More rats began to flood from various parts of the house, rushing down the stairs in a squeaking, scurrying mass in their eagerness to escape the flames. Boris was waiting, the delight he derived from his work seeming to increase with every sweeping blow of his maul.

Hugo couldn't just stand by and watch as his house was demolished. In a panic, he ran to the cupboard under the stairs, ignoring the swarm of rats that billowed from it, and grabbed a bucket. He rushed out into the garden, filling the bucket with pond water and a few unlucky fish, then rushed back inside to quench the flames that were threatening to set fire to his embroidered Bretonnian drapery.

The mansion's systematic destruction went on for almost an hour, with Boris stomping along the best he could on his wooden leg, swinging his maul with abandon at the fleeing rats, as Hugo gradually emptied his stagnant pond onto the spreading flames. In the end he managed to put out the fires before his house was completely gutted, but meanwhile Boris had managed to lay waste to almost every room. Smashed furniture and squashed rats littered every floor, and as Hugo surveyed the carnage a tear rolled down one cheek. Boris stood in the entrance hall, or what remained of it, gasping for air, a satisfied grin on his face.

'Well,' he said cheerily. 'This was a good start, don't you think?'

At first Hugo couldn't speak, so griefstricken was he over the destruction of his home and the precious contents within it. Artworks he had collected over decades had been smashed to shards and the fine décor was blackened by smoke and flame. As he looked at Boris with that idiot's grin on his face, his grief suddenly turned to anger.

'A good start?' he growled. 'A good bloody start? Are you insane, you brainless oaf? Look what you've done to my house! Get out! Get out now and take that thing with you!' Hugo pointed accusatorially at the huge maul in Boris's hand that had wreaked so much destruction in the house.

Boris could only look back with a hurt expression. 'I was only trying to help,' he said dejectedly, before turning and limping off into the evening air.

Hugo watched him go, making sure he was well off the boundary of his property before he slumped down on what remained of his grand staircase and wept.

The next day, Hugo Kressler found himself in Kreiger's Gunsmiths of Wehrmunchstrasse. He had at first intended to purchase a pistol, one of the finely crafted matchlocks that Herr Krieger was so famous for, but after browsing for several moments he espied something much more suitable. Hugo had never fired a blunderbuss before, nor a matchlock pistol for that matter, but he guessed the wide spread of its shot would make it much a more suitable firearm for a novice such as himself.

Once back home, he loaded the weapon, dressed himself in his finest regalia, or at least what he could salvage from his partially singed armoire, and sat on the edge of his bed.

At the time of purchasing it, Hugo hadn't quite decided whether he would use the weapon to defend himself from the remaining rats in his house, or if it was to blow his own head from his shoulders. Now it came down to it, he still couldn't make up his mind. He sat for almost an hour, glaring at the blunderbuss, cocked and ready for action by his side.

But Hugo knew deep down in his tiny withered heart that he couldn't do it. It would take a braver man than he to take his own life; he simply didn't have the courage for it. And so, saying a little prayer to thank Shallya for her mercy and guidance, he placed the blunderbuss by his bed, laid down still fully clothed, and cried himself to sleep.

* * *

AN EXPLOSION ROCKED Hugo's mansion to its very foundations and at first, as he awoke bleary-eyed and terrified, he thought his newly acquired blunderbuss had suddenly gone off of its own accord. He quickly realised something far more sinister was afoot, as the sound of falling masonry echoed from beyond the door of his bedchamber.

Hugo rose from his bed, having the wherewithal to grab the loaded blunderbuss before venturing out to investigate the calamity. He did not have to move very far along the corridor before he saw what the source of the noise was. A huge crater had suddenly appeared in the middle of the mansion. Two floors had collapsed into a deep hole which, from the look of the passages that led off from it, was some kind of mine shaft.

Possible causes for this started to swirl around Hugo's head. Had this been here all the time? Was it part of the ancient sewer system? Were dwarf prospectors digging beneath his house? Before he could begin to think of the litigious consequences for the guilty parties involved, something moved along the shadows of the corridor. As he stared, dumbfounded, a stooped and filthy figure slowly emerged from the dark and Hugo realised that those responsible for the crater were not dwarfs.

It was four feet tall with clawed hands and feet. Filthy robes covered it from the neck down and they stank of putrescence and muddy earth. But it was the face that most filled Hugo with terror – a rat's face, with red, baleful eyes and monstrous incisors that clacked together hungrily.

He didn't even think, raising the blunderbuss in his numb hands, and as the creature rushed towards him he pulled the trigger. The blunderbuss roared, bucking in his hands and knocking him flat on his backside. A spray of white-hot buckshot blasted from the barrel, destroying the creature's bestial face in a splatter of crimson gore.

Gingerly, Hugo pulled himself back to his feet, staring down at the filthy animal's corpse.

'Ha!' he bellowed. 'Not so clever now are you!'

As if in answer, something pulled itself from the pit in the centre of Hugo's mansion – something huge and hairy. Its muscles were thick, its flesh covered in a thick, shaggy down, its hands like clawed shovels, built for tunnelling through solid earth. It too bore the face of a rat, but this was no diminutive drone like the last; this was a beast, nine feet tall and monstrous to behold.

It glared at Hugo, anger burning in its tiny eyes, and as it approached Hugo noticed that one of its huge ears was missing. Despite the necessity for flight in this situation, Hugo found his feet simply would not move, and all he could do was stare as the creature approached, its foetid breath washing over him, inducing the need for him to vomit. He could only close his eyes, and await his inevitable fate.

'Oi!'

The deep cry echoed through the cavern that now made up most of Hugo's home. The massive rat creature craned its neck to see who dared to disturb its feasting. Hugo, too, glanced towards the entrance of the mansion to see a burly figure framed in the doorway.

'I told you there'd be big 'uns,' shouted Boris hefting his maul. 'Remember me?' he said cheerily. Then a sudden dark intent fell across his visage as he limped forwards on his wooden leg.

The monstrous fiend roared, and Hugo was all but forgotten as it leapt down from the balcony to land in front of the rat catcher. It swept its shovel-like hand toward Boris, but despite his peg leg he was nimble enough to avoid it, slamming his maul down on the creature's clawed foot. It roared in pain, hopping back as Boris advanced.

'I've been after you for ages,' he said, slamming the maul forwards again. There was an audible crack as the maul struck the creature's knee and it fell forwards, foundering in what remained of the entrance hall. Hugo could only watch agog as Boris set about the creature with gusto, smashing it with the hammer as it tried its best to avoid the solid blows that rained down, cracking its bones and smashing its limbs.

In the end it teetered at the edge of the huge crater, beaten and bloody, and with a final mighty swing Boris smashed it back into the black pit from whence it came.

Hugo's knees knocked together, his body wracked by a convulsive spasm, but he still managed to descend from the first floor, avoiding the crater that had opened in the middle of his house, to fall at the rat catcher's knees.

'Thank you, thank you, thank you,' was all he managed to say as he clung to Boris's wooden leg.

'All right fella,' Boris replied, clearly embarrassed. 'No need to make a scene.'

When Boris finally managed to extricate himself from Hugo's unrestrained display of gratitude he glanced down into the pit and frowned.

'Ah,' he said, pointing into the crater. 'There's your problem. Weirdstone!'

Hugo looked down, and running along the side of the shaft beneath his house was a seam of glittering black ore.

'That's most likely what they were after,' Boris continued. 'It draws 'em like flies to sh… well, you know what I mean? If you're planning on staying here, make sure you get that removed.'

'Yes, yes, I'll do that,' Hugo replied, still trying to take in what had just happened.

'Anyway, must be off. Lads'll never believe me down the Cat when I tell 'em what I've just done.'

With one last grin, Boris swung the maul over his shoulder, and sauntered out of the mansion, his wooden leg clicking against the ground as he went.

Hugo watched as he left, standing amidst the ruin of his house. 'Thank you,' was all he could think to say.

* * *

He was running, always running, in perpetual motion, legs pumping, breath coming in quick rasps. On it came in pursuit, on his heels, keeping pace, smelling his scent, dogging his trail.

This time he was slower, or was his pursuer just faster? Either way it caught him quickly, those iron hands grasping him in a solid embrace, squeezing the air from his lungs, raising him high.

He turned, looking at the hunter for the first time, seeing it glaring down at him with hate in its beady eyes, and he recognised that face, those bedraggled features. It was the face of Hugo Kressler.

In terror he squeaked, squirming for freedom, lashing his pink tail, twitching his whiskers…

HUGO'S EYES BLINKED open and he panted for breath. He was wrapped up in a tangle of sheets that held his arms and legs tight. With some difficulty he unravelled himself from the stark white bedding and sat up, breathing a sigh of relief.

All was well, he told himself, the rats were gone – there was nothing to fear.

He rose with a smile, suddenly remembering that it was to be a good day. He had commissioned Gepetto Montalban himself, the most famous architect in the province, to oversee the mansion's renovations. The Guild of Miners had sent a dozen men to remove the strange glittering ore from beneath the cellar, and he had even started to put weight back on.

A smile crossed Hugo's lips as he walked to the window, opening the shutters and looking out onto Talabheim. It wasn't the most aesthetic of cities, it was certainly no Praag or Luccini, but it was still *his* city.

Glancing down he noticed the small black statuette that sat at his bedside, the first new piece of art Hugo had commissioned. It was in the shape of a hammer, in honour of Boris, and was crafted from the glittering black ore that had run beneath his house. Yes, Boris had warned him about it, and he had heeded that warning and had the glittering ore removed – but what harm could one little statuette do?

Taking a deep breath he turned, ready to break his fast heartily and sate the ravenous appetite he had recently developed, when the statuette suddenly fell from the table. Hugo stared down at it curiously. He was two feet away, how had he managed to knock it from the nightstand?

Then he saw it, just from the corner of his eye, something behind him, something long and sinuous.

He turned, looking down to see with horror that it was protruding from beneath his nightgown, twisting and writhing of its own accord, an appendage that had seemingly grown overnight – a long pink rat's tail.

Hugo opened his mouth wide and squeaked in terror…

HAMMER
AND BOLTER

ISSUE 3

THE LONG GAMES AT CARCHARIAS

Rob Sanders

THE END BEGAN with the *Revenant Rex*.

An interstellar beast. Bad omen of omens. A wanderer: she was a regular visitor to this part of the segmentum. The hulk was a drifting gravity well of twisted rock and metal. Vessels from disparate and distant races nestled, broken-backed, amongst mineral deposits from beyond the galaxy's borders and ice frozen from before the beginning of time. A demented logic engine at the heart of the hulk – like a tormented dreamer – guided the nightmare path of the beast through the dark void of Imperial sectors, alien empires of the Eastern Fringe and the riftspace of erupting maelstroms. Then, as if suddenly awoken from a fevered sleep, the daemon cogitator would initiate the countdown sequence of an ancient and weary warp drive. The planet-killer would disappear with the expediency of an answered prayer, destined to drift up upon the shores of some other bedevilled sector, hundreds of light years away.

The *Revenant Rex* beat the Aurora Chapter at Schindelgheist, the Angels Eradicant over at Theta Reticuli and the White Scars at the Martyrpeake. Unfortunately the hulk was too colossal and the timeframes too erratic for the cleanse-and-burn efforts of the Adeptus Astartes to succeed: but Chapter pride and zealotry ensured their superhuman efforts regardless. The behemoth was infested with greenskins of the Iron Klaw Clan – that had spent the past millennia visiting hit-and-run mayhem on systems across the segmentum, with abandoned warbands colonising planetary badlands like a green, galactic plague. The Warfleet Ultima, where it could gather craft in sufficient time and numbers, had twice attempted to destroy the gargantuan hulk. The combined firepower of hundreds of Navy vessels had also failed to destroy the beast, simply serving to enhance its hideous melange further.

All these things and more had preyed upon Elias Artegall's conscience when the *Revenant Rex* tumbled into the Gilead Sector. Arch-Deacon Urbanto. Rear Admiral Darracq. Overlord Gordius. Zimner, the High Magos Retroenginericus. Grand Master Karmyne of the Angels Eradicant. Artegall had either received them or received astrotelepathic messages from them all.

'Chapter Master, the xenos threat cannot be tolerated...'

'The Mercantile Gilead have reported the loss of thirty bulk freighters...'

'Master Artegall, the greenskins are already out of control in the Despot Stars...'

'That vessel could harbour ancient technological secrets that could benefit the future of mankind...'

'You must avenge us, brother...'

The spirehalls of the Slaughterhorn had echoed with their demands and insistence. But to war was a Space Marine's prerogative. Did not Lord Guilliman state on the steps of the Plaza Ptolemy: 'There is but one of the Emperor's Angels for every world in the Imperium; but one drop of Adeptus Astartes blood for every Imperial citizen. Judge the necessity to spill such a precious commodity with care and if it must be spilt, spill it wisely, my battle-brothers.'

Unlike the Scars or the Auroras, Artegall's Crimson Consuls were not given to competitive rivalry. Artegall did not desire success because others had failed. Serving at the pleasure of the primarch was not a tournament spectacle and the *Revenant Rex* was not an opportunistic arena. In the end, Artegall let his battered copy of the Codex Astartes decide. In those much-thumbed pages lay the wisdom of greater men than he: as ever, Artegall put his trust in their skill and experience. He chose a passage that reflected his final judgement and included it in both his correspondence to his far-flung petitioners and his address to the Crimson Consuls, First Company on board the battle-barge *Incarnadine Ecliptic*.

'From Codicil CC-LXXX-IV.ii: The Coda of Balthus Dardanus, 17th Lord of Macragge – entitled Staunch Supremacies. "For our enemies will bring us to battle on the caprice of chance. The alien and the renegade are the vagaries of the galaxy incarnate. What can we truly know or would want to of their ways or motivations? They are to us as the rabid wolf at the closed door that knows not even its own mind. Be that door. Be the simplicity of the steadfast and unchanging: the barrier between what is known and the unknowable. Let the Imperium of Man realise its manifold destiny within while without its mindless foes dash themselves against the constancy of our adamantium. In such uniformity of practice and purpose lies the perpetuity of mankind." May Guilliman be with you.'

'And with you,' Captain Bolinvar and his crimson-clad First Company Terminator Marines had returned. But the primarch had not been with them and Bolinvar and one hundred veteran sons of Carcharias had been forsaken.

Artegall sat alone in his private Tactical Chancelorium, among the cold ivory of his throne. The Chancelorium formed the very pinnacle of the Slaughterhorn – the Crimson Consuls fortress-monastery – which in turn formed the spirepeak of Hive Niveous, the Carcharian capital city. The throne was constructed from the colossal bones of shaggy, shovel-tusk Stegodonts, hunted by Carcharian ancestors, out on the Dry-blind. Without his armour the Chapter Master felt small and vulnerable in the huge throne – a sensation usually alien to an Adeptus Astartes' very being. The chamber was comfortably gelid and Artegall sat in his woollen robes, elbow to knee and fist to chin, like some crumbling statue from Terran antiquity.

The Chancelorium began to rumble and this startled the troubled Chapter Master. The crimson-darkness swirl of the marble floor began to part in front of him and the trapdoor admitted a rising platform upon which juddered two Chapter serfs in their own zoster robes. They flanked a huge brass pict-caster that squatted dormant between them. The serfs were purebred Carcharians with their fat, projecting noses, wide nostrils and thick brows. These on top of stocky, muscular frames, barrel torsos and thick arms decorated with crude tattoos and scar-markings. Perfectly adapted for life in the frozen underhive.

'Where is your master, the Chamber Castellan?' Artegall demanded of the bondsmen. The first hailed his Chapter Master with a fist to the aquila represented on the Crimson Consuls crest of his robes.

'Returned presently from the underhive, my lord – at your request – with the Lord Apothecary,' the serf answered solemnly. The second activated the pict-caster, bringing forth the crystal screen's grainy picture.

'We have word from the Master of the Fleet, Master Artegall,' the serf informed him.

Standing before Artegall was an image of Hecton Lambert, Master of the Crimson Consuls fleet. The Space Marine commander was on the bridge of the strike cruiser *Anno Tenebris*, high above the gleaming, glacial world of Carcharias.

'Hecton, what news?' Artegall put to him without the usual formality of a greeting.

'My master: nothing but the gravest news,' the Crimson Consul told him. 'As you know, we have been out of contact with Captain Bolinvar and the *Incarnadine Ecliptic* for days. A brief flash on one of our scopes prompted me to despatch the frigate *Herald Angel* with orders to locate the *Ecliptic* and report back. Twelve hours into their search they intercepted the following pict-cast, which they transmitted to the *Anno Tenebris*, and which I now dutifully transmit to you. My lord, with this every man on board sends his deepest sympathies. May Guilliman be with you.'

'And with you,' Artegall mouthed absently, rising out of the throne. He took a disbelieving step towards the broad screen of the pict-caster. Brother Lambert disappeared and was replaced by a static-laced image, harsh light and excruciating noise. The vague outline of a Crimson Consuls Space Marine could be made out. There were sparks and fires in the background, as well as the silhouettes of injured Space Marines and Chapter serfs stumbling blind and injured through the smoke and bedlam. The warrior identified himself but his name and rank were garbled in the intruding static of the transmission.

'...this is the battle-barge *Incarnadine Ecliptic*, two days out of Morriga. I am now ranking battle-brother. We have sustained critical damage...' The screen erupted with light and interference.

Then: 'Captain Bolinvar went in with the first wave. Xenos resistance was heavy. Primitive booby traps. Explosives. Wall-to-wall green flesh and small arms. By the primarch, losses were minimal; my injuries, though, necessitated my return to the *Ecliptic*. The captain was brave and through the use of squad rotations, heavy flamers and teleporters our Consul Terminators managed to punch through to an enginarium with a power signature. We could all hear the countdown, even over the vox. Fearing that the *Revenant Rex* was about to make a warp jump I begged the captain to return. I begged him, but he transmitted that the only way to end the hulk and stop the madness was to sabotage the warp drive.'

Once again the lone Space Marine became enveloped in an ominous, growing brightness. 'His final transmission identified the warp engine as active but already sabotaged. He said the logic engine wasn't counting down to a jump... Then, the *Revenant Rex*, it – it just, exploded. The sentry ships were caught in the blast wave and the *Ecliptic* wrecked.'

A serf clutching some heinous wound to his face staggered into the reporting Space Marine. 'Go! To the pods,' he roared at him. Then he returned his attention to the transmission. 'We saw it all. Detonation of the warp engines must have caused some kind of immaterium anomaly. Moments after the hulk blew apart, fragments and debris from the explosion – including our sentry ships – were sucked back through a collapsing empyrean vortex before disappearing altogether. We managed to haul off but are losing power and have been caught in the gravitational pull of a nearby star. Techmarine Hereward has declared the battle-barge unsalvageable. With our orbit decaying I have ordered all surviving Adeptus Astartes and Chapter serfs to the saviour pods. Perhaps some may break free. I fear our chances are slim... May Guilliman be with us...'

As the screen glared with light from the damning star and clouded over with static, Artegall felt like he'd been speared through the gut. He could taste blood in his mouth: the copper tang of lives lost. One hundred Crimson Consuls. The Emperor's Angels under his command. The Chapter's best fighting supermen, gone with the irreplaceable seed of their genetic heritage. Thousands of years of combined battle experience lost to the Imperium. The Chapter's entire inheritance of Tactical Dreadnought Armour: every suit a priceless relic in its own right. The venerable *Ecliptic*. A veteran battle-barge of countless engagements and a piece of Caracharias among the stars. All gone. All claimed by the oblivion of the warp or cremated across the blazing surface of a nearby sun.

'You must avenge us, brother–'

Artegall reached back for his throne but missed and staggered. Someone caught him, slipping their shoulders underneath one of his huge arms. It was Baldwin. He'd been standing behind Artegall, soaking up the tragedy like his Chapter Master. The Space Marine's weight alone should have crushed the Chamber Castellan, but Baldwin was little more than a mind and a grafted, grizzled face on a robe-swathed brass chassis. The serf's hydraulics sighed as he took his master's bulk.

'My lord,' Baldwin began in his metallic burr.

'Baldwin, I lost them...' Artegall managed, his face a mask of stricken denial. With a clockwork clunk of gears and pistons the Chamber Castellan turned on the two serfs flanking the pict-caster.

'Begone!' he told them, his savage command echoing around the bronze walls of the Chancelorium. As the bondsmen thumped their fists into their aquilas and left, Baldwin helped his master to the cool bone of his throne. Artegall stared at the serf with unseeing eyes. They had been recruited together as savage underhivers and netted, kicking and pounding, from the fighting pits and tribal stomping grounds of the abhuman-haunted catacombs of Hive Niveous. But whereas Artegall had passed tissue compatibility and become a Neophyte, Baldwin had fallen at the first hurdle. Deemed unsuitable for surgical enhancement, the young hiver was inducted as a Chapter serf and had served the Crimson Consuls ever since. As personal servant, Baldwin had travelled the galaxy with his superhuman master.

As the decades passed, Artegall's engineered immortality and fighting prowess brought him promotion, while Baldwin's all-too-human body brought him the pain and limitation of old age. When Elias Artegall became the Crimson Consuls' Chapter Master, Baldwin wanted to serve on as his Chamber Castellan. As one century became the next, the underhiver exchanged his wasted frame for an engineered immortality of his own: the brass bulk of cylinders, hydraulics and exo-skeletal appendages that whirred and droned before the throne. Only the serf's kindly face and sharp mind remained.

Baldwin stood by as Artegall's body sagged against the cathedra arm and his face contorted with silent rage. It fell with futility before screwing up again with the bottomless fury only an Adeptus Astartes could feel for his foes and himself. Before him the Crimson Consul could see the faces of men with whom he'd served. Battle-brothers who had been his parrying arm when his own had been employed in death-dealing;

Space Marines who had shared with him the small eternities of deep space patrol and death-world ambush; friends and loyal brethren.

'I sent them,' he hissed through the perfection of his gritted teeth.

'It is as you said to them, my lord. As the Codex commanded.'

'Condemned them...'

'They were the door that kept the rabid wolf at bay. The adamantium upon which our enemies must be dashed.'

Artegall didn't seem to hear him: 'I walked them into a trap.'

'What is a space hulk if it not be such a thing? The sector is safe. The Imperium lives on. Such an honour is not without cost. Even Guilliman recognises that. Let me bring you the comfort of his words, my master. Let the primarch show us his way.'

Artegall nodded and Baldwin hydraulically stomped across the chamber to where a lectern waited on a gravitic base. The top of the lectern formed a crystal case that the Castellan opened, allowing the preservative poison of argon gas to escape. Inside, Artegall's tattered copy of the Codex Astartes lay open as it had done since the Chapter Master had selected his reading for the First Company's departure. Baldwin drifted the lectern across the crimson marble of the Chancelorium floor to the throne's side. Artegall was on his feet. Recovered. A Space Marine again. A Chapter Master with the weight of history and the burden of future expectation on his mighty shoulders.

'Baldwin,' he rumbled with a steely-eyed determination. 'Were your recruitment forays into the underhive with the Lord Apothecary fruitful?'

'I believe so, my lord.'

'Good. The Chapter will need Carcharias to offer up its finest flesh, on this dark day. You will need to organise further recruitment sweeps. Go deep. We need the finest savages the hive can offer. Inform Lord Fabian that I have authorised cultivation of our remaining seed. Tell him I need one hundred Crimson sons. Demi-gods all, to honour the sacrifice of their fallen brethren.'

'Yes, Chapter Master.'

'And Baldwin.'

'My master?'

'Send for the Reclusiarch.'

'High Chaplain Enobarbus is attached to the Tenth Company,' Baldwin informed Artegall with gentle, metallic inflection. 'On training manoeuvres in the Dry-blind.'

'I don't care if he's visiting Holy Terra. Get him here. Now. There are services to organise. Commemorations. Obsequies. The like this Chapter has never known. See to it.'

'Yes, my master,' Baldwin answered and left his lord to his feverish guilt and the cold words of Guilliman.

* * *

'BY NOW YOUR lids are probably frozen to your eyeballs,' growled High Chaplain Enobarbus over the vox-link. 'Your body no longer feels like your own.'

The Crimson Consuls Chaplain leant against the crumbling architecture of the Archaphrael Hive and drank in the spectacular bleakness of his home world. The Dry-blind extended forever in all directions: the white swirl, like a smazeous blanket of white, moulded from the ice pack. By day, with the planet's equally bleak stars turning their attentions on Carcharias, the dry ice that caked everything in a rime of frozen carbon dioxide bled a ghostly vapour. The Dry-blind, as it was called, hid the true lethality of the Carcharian surface, however. A maze of bottomless crevasses, fissures and fractures that riddled the ice beneath and could only be witnessed during the short, temperature-plummeting nights, when the nebulous thunderhead of dry ice sank and re-froze.

'Your fingers are back in your cells, because they sure as Balthus Dardanus aren't part of your hands any more. Hopes of pulling the trigger on your weapon are a distant memory,' the High Chaplain voxed across the open channel.

The Chaplain ran a gauntlet across the top of his head, clearing the settled frost from his tight dreadlocks and flicking the slush at the floor. With a ceramite knuckle, he rubbed at the socket of the eye he'd lost on New Davalos. Now stapled shut, a livid scar ran down one side of his brutal face, from the eyelid to his jaw, where tears constantly trickled in the cold air and froze to his face.

'Skin is raw: like radiation burns – agony both inside and out.'

From his position in the twisted, frost-shattered shell that had been the Archaphrael Hive, Enobarbus could hear fang-face shredders. He fancied he could even spot the telltale vapour wakes of the shredders' dorsal fins cutting through the Dry-blind. Archaphrael Hive made up a triumvirate of cities called the Pale Maidens that stood like ancient monuments to the fickle nature of Carcharian meteorology. A thousand years before the three cities had been devastated by a freak polar cyclone colloquially referred to as 'The Big One' by the hivers. Now the ghost hives were used by the Crimson Consuls as an impromptu training ground.

'And those are the benefits,' Enobarbus continued, the High Chaplain's oratory sailing out across the vox waves. 'It's the bits you can't feel that you should worry about. Limbs that died hours ago. Dead meat that you're dragging around. Organs choking on the slush you're barely beating around your numb bodies.'

He had brought the Tenth Company's second and seventh Scout sniper squads out to the Pale Maidens for stealth training and spiritual instruction. As a test of their worth and spirit, Enobarbus had had the Space Marine Scouts establish and hold ambush positions with their sniper rifles in the deep Carcharian freeze for three days. He had bombarded them endlessly with remembered readings from the Codex Astartes, faith instruction and training rhetoric across the open channels of the vox.

Behind him Scout-Sergeant Caradoc was adjusting his snow cloak over the giveaway crimson of his carapace armour plating and priming his shotgun. Enobarbus nodded and the Scout-sergeant melted into the misty, frost-shattered archways of the Archaphrael Hive.

While the Scouts held their agonising positions, caked and swathed in dry ice, Enobarbus and the Scout-sergeants had amused themselves by trapping fang-face shredders. Packs of the beasts roamed the Dry-blind, making the environment an ever more perilous prospect for travellers. The shredders had flat, shovel-shaped maws spilling over with needle-like fangs. They carried their bodies close to the ground and were flat but for the razored dorsal fin protruding from their knobbly spines. They used their long tails for balance and changing direction on the ice. Like their dorsals, the tails were the razor-edged whiplash that gave them their name. Their sharp bones were wrapped in an elastic skin-sheen that felt almost amphibious and gave the beasts the ability to slide downhill and toboggan their prey. Then they would turn their crystal-tip talons on their unfortunate victims: shredding grapnels that the creatures used to climb up and along the labyrinthine crevasses that fractured the ice shelf.

'This is nothing. Lips are sealed with rime. Thought is slow. It's painful. It's agony. Even listening to this feels like more than you can bear.'

Enobarbus pulled his own cape tight about his power armour. Like many of his calling the High Chaplain's plate was ancient and distinct, befitting an Adeptus Astartes of his status, experience and wisdom. Beyond the heraldry and honorifica decorating his midnight adamantium shell and the skullface helmet hanging from his belt, Enobarbus sported the trappings of his home world. The shredder-skin cape hung over his pack, with its razor dorsal and flaps that extended down his arms and terminated in the skinned creature's bestial claws: one decorating each of the High Chaplain's gauntlets.

'But bear it you must, you worthless souls. This is the moment your Emperor will need you. When you feel you have the least to give: that's when your primarch demands the most from you. When your battle-brother is under the knife or in another's sights – this is when you must be able to act,' the High Chaplain grizzled down the vox with gravity. Switching to a secure channel Enobarbus added, 'Sergeant Notus: now, if you will.'

Storeys and storeys below, down in the Dry-blind where Enobarbus and the Scout-sergeants had penned their captured prey, Notus would be waiting for the signal. A signal the Chaplain knew he'd received because of the high-pitched screeches of the released pack of shredders echoing up the shattered chambers and frost-bored ruins of the hive interior. The Codex Astartes taught of the nobility of aeon-honoured combat tactics and battle manoeuvres perfectly realised. It was Guilliman's way. The Rules of Engagement. The way in which Enobarbus was instructing his Scouts. But in their war games about the Pale Maidens, Enobarbus wasn't playing the role of the noble Space Marine. He was everything else the galaxy might throw at them: and the enemies of the Imperium did not play by the rules.

With the Scouts undoubtedly making excellent use of the hive's elevation and dilapidated exterior – as scores of previous Neophytes had – Enobarbus decided to engage them on multiple fronts at once. While the starving shredders clawed their way up through the ruined hive, intent on ripping the frozen Scouts to pieces, Scout-Sergeant Caradoc was working his way silently down through the derelict stairwells and halls of the hive interior with his shotgun. The High Chaplain decided to come at his Scouts from an entirely different angle.

Slipping his crozius arcanum – the High Chaplain's sacred staff of office – from his belt and extending the shredder talons on the backs of his gauntlets, Enobarbus swung out onto the crumbling hive wall exterior and began a perilous climb skywards. The shell of the hive wall had long been undermined by the daily freeze-thaw action of Caracharian night and day. Using the sharpened point of the aquila's wings at the end of his crozius like an ice pick and the crystal-tip claws of the shredder, the High Chaplain made swift work of the frozen cliff-face of the dilapidated hive.

'There is nothing convenient about your enemy's desires. He will come for you precisely in the moment you have set aside for some corporal indulgence,' Enobarbus told the Scouts, trying hard not to let his exertions betray him over the vox. 'Exhaustion, fear, pain, sickness, injury, necessities of the body and as an extension of your bodies, the necessities of your weapons. Keep your blade keen and your sidearm clean. Guilliman protect you on the reload: the most necessary of indulgences – a mechanical funeral rite.'

Heaving himself up through the shattered floor of a gargoyle-encrusted overhang, the High Chaplain drew his bolt pistol and crept through to a balcony. The tier-terrace was barely stable but commanded an excellent view: too much temptation for a sniper Scout. But as Enobarbus stalked out across the fragile space he found it deserted. The first time in years of such training exercises he'd discovered it as such.

The High Chaplain nodded to himself. Perhaps this cohort of Neophytes was better. Perhaps they were learning faster: soaking up the wisdom of Guilliman and growing into their role. Perhaps they were ready for their Black Carapace and hallowed suits of power armour. Emperor knows they were needed. Chapter Master Artegall had insisted that Enobarbus concentrate his efforts on the 10th Company. The Crimson Consuls had had their share of past tragedies.

The Chapter had inherited the terrible misfortune of a garrison rotation on the industrial world of Phaethon IV when the Celebrant Chapter
could not meet their commitments. Word was sent that the Celebrants
were required to remain on Nedicta Secundus and protect the priceless
holy relics of the cardinal world from the ravages of Hive Fleet Kraken
and its splintered tyranid forces. Phaethon IV, on the other hand, bordered the Despot Stars and had long been coveted by Dregz Wuzghal,
Arch-Mogul of Gunza Major. The Crimson Consuls fought bravely
on Phaethon IV, and would have halted the beginnings of Waaagh!
Wuzghal in its tracks: something stirred under the factories and power
plants of the planet, however. Something awoken by the nightly bombing raids of the Arch-Mogul's 'Green Wing'. Something twice as alien
as the degenerate greenskins: unfeeling, unbound and unstoppable. An
ancient enemy, long forgotten by the galaxy and entombed below the
assembly lines and Imperial manufacturing works of Phaethon, skeletal
nightmares of living silver: the necrons. Between greenskin death from
above and tomb warriors crawling out of their stasis chambers below,
the industrial worlders and their Crimson Consuls guardians hadn't
stood a chance and the Chapter lost two highly-decorated companies.
As far as Enobarbus knew, the necron and the Arch-Mogul fought for
Phaethon still.

The High Chaplain held his position. The still air seared the architecture around him with its caustic frigidity. Enobarbus closed his eyes and
allowed his ears to do the work. He filtered out the freeze-thaw expansion of the masonry under his boots, the spiritual hum of the sacred
armour about his body and the creak of his own aged bones. There it
was. The telltale scrape of movement, the tiniest displacement of weight
on the balcony expanse above. Backtracking, the High Chaplain found a
craterous hole in the ceiling. Hooking his crozius into the ruined stone
and corroded metal, the Crimson Consul heaved himself noiselessly up
through the floor of the level above.

Patient, like a rogue shredder on ambush in the Dry-blind – masked
by the mist and hidden in some ice floor fissure – Enobarbus advanced
with agonising care across the dilapidated balcony. There he was. One
of the Tenth Company Scouts. Flat to the steaming floor, form buried
in his snow cloak, helmet down at the scope of his sniper rifle: a position the Neophyte had undoubtedly held for days. The balcony was
an excellent spot. Despite some obstructive masonry, it commanded a
view of the Dry-blind with almost the same breathtaking grandeur of
the platform below. Without a sound, Enobarbus was above the sniper
Scout, the aquila-wing blade-edge of his crozius resting on the back of
the Scout's neck, between the helmet and the snow cloak.

'The cold is not the enemy,' the High Chaplain voxed across the open
channel. 'The enemy is not even the enemy. You are the enemy. Ultimately you will betray yourself.'

When the Scout didn't move, the Chaplain's lip curled with annoyance. He locked his suit vox-channels and hooked the Scout's shoulder with the wing-tip of the crozius.

'It's over, Consul,' Enobarbus told the prone form. 'The enemy has you.'

Flipping the Scout over, Enobarbus stood there in silent shock. Cloak, helmet and rifle were there but the Scout was not. Instead, the butchered body of a shredder lay beneath, with the hilt of a gladius buried in its fang-faced maw. Enobarbus shook his head. Anger turned to admiration. These Scouts would truly test him.

Enobarbus switched to the private channel he shared with Scout-Sergeant Notus to offer him brief congratulations on his Scouts and to direct him up into the ruined hive.

'What in Guilliman's name are–' Enobarbus heard upon the transferring frequency. Then the unmistakable *whoosh* of las-fire. The High Chaplain heard the Scout-sergeant roar defiance over the vox and looking out over the Dry-blind, Enobarbus saw the light show, diffused in the swirling miasma, like sheet lightning across a stormy sky. Something cold took hold of the High Chaplain's heart. Enobarbus had heard thousands of men die. Notus was dead.

Transferring channels, Enobarbus hissed, 'Override Obsidian: we are under attack. This is not a drill. Second and seventh, you are cleared to fire. Sergeant Caradoc, meet me at the–'

Shotgun blasts. Rapid and rushed. Caradoc pressed by multiple targets. The crash of the weapon bounced around the maze of masonry and worm-holed architecture.

'Somebody get me a visual,' the High Chaplain growled over the vox before slipping the crozius into his belt. Leading with his bolt pistol, Enobarbus raced for the fading echo of the sergeant's weapon. Short sprints punctuated with skips and drops through holes and stairwells.

'Caradoc, where are you?' Enobarbus voxed as he threaded his way through the crumbling hive. The shotgun fire had died away but the Scout-sergeant wasn't replying. 'Second squad, seventh squad, I want a visual on Sergeant Caradoc, now!'

But there was nothing: only an eerie static across the channel. Rotating through the frequencies, Enobarbus vaulted cracks and chasms and thundered across frost-hazed chambers.

'Ritter, Lennox, Beade...' the High Chaplain cycled but the channels were dead. Sliding down into a skid, the shredder-skin cape and the greave plates of his armour carrying him across the chamber floor, Enobarbus dropped down through a hole and landed in a crouch. His pistol was everywhere, pivoting around and taking in the chamber below. A shotgun lay spent and smoking nearby and a large body swung from a creaking strut in the exposed ceiling. Caradoc.

The Scout-sergeant was hanging from his own snow cloak, framed in a gaping hole in the exterior hive wall, swinging amongst the brilliance of the Dry-blind beyond. The cloak, wrapped around his neck as it was, had been tied off around the strut like a noose. This wouldn't have been enough to kill the Space Marine. The dozen gladius blades stabbed through his butchered body up to their hilts had done that. The sickening curiosity of such a vision would have been enough to stun most battle-brothers but Enobarbus took immediate comfort and instruction from his memorised Codex. There was protocol to follow. Counsel to heed.

Snatching his skull-face helmet from his belt, Enobarbus slapped it on and secured the seals. With pistol still outstretched in one gauntlet, the High Chaplain felt for the rosarius hanging around his neck. He would have activated the powerful force field generator but an enemy was already upon him. The haze of the chamber was suddenly whipped up in a rush of movement. Shredders. Lots of them. They came out of the floor. Out of the roof. Up the exterior wall, as the High Chaplain had. Snapping at him with crystal claws and maws of needle-tip teeth. Enobarbus felt their razored tails slash against his adamantium shell and the vice-like grip of their crushing, shovel-head jaws on his knees, his shoulder, at his elbows and on his helmet.

Bellowing shock and frustration, Enobarbus threw his arm around, dislodging two of the monsters. As they scrambled about on the floor, ready to pounce straight back at him, the High Chaplain ended them with his bolt pistol. Another death-dealer tore at him from behind and swallowed his pistol and gauntlet whole. Again, Enobarbus fired, his bolt-rounds riddling the creature from within. The thing died with ease but its dagger-fang jaws locked around his hand and weapon, refusing to release. The darkness of holes and fractured doorways continued to give birth to the Carcharian predators. They bounded at him with their merciless, ice-hook talons, vaulting off the walls, floor and ceiling, even off Caradoc's dangling corpse.

Snatching the crozius arcanum from his belt the High Chaplain thumbed the power weapon to life. Swinging it about him in cold fury, Enobarbus cleaved shredders in two, slicing the monsters through the head and chopping limbs and tails from the beasts.

The floor erupted in front of the Space Marine and a hideously emaciated shredder – big, even for its kind – came up through the frost-shattered masonry. It leapt at Enobarbus, jaws snapping shut around his neck and wicked talons hooking themselves around the edges of his chest plate. The force of the impact sent the High Chaplain flailing backwards, off balance and with shredders hanging from every appendage.

Enobarbus roared as his armoured form smashed through part of a ruined wall and out through the gap in the hive exterior. The Crimson Consul felt himself falling. Survival instinct causing his fist to open, allowing the crozius to be torn from him by a savage little shredder.

Snatching at the rapidly disappearing masonry, Enobarbus elongated his own shredder claw and buried the crystal-tip talon in the ancient rockcrete. The High Chaplain hung from two monstrous digits, shredders in turn hanging from his armour. With the dead-weight and locked jaw of the pistol-swallowing shredder on the other arm and the huge beast now hanging down his back from a jaw-hold on his neck, Enobarbus had little hope of improving his prospects. Below lay thousands of metres of open drop, a ragged cliff-face of hive masonry to bounce off and shredder-infested, bottomless chasms of ice waiting below the white blanket of the Dry-blind. Even the superhuman frame of the High Chaplain could not hope to survive such a fall.

Above the shrieking and gnawing of the beasts and his own exertions, Enobarbus heard the hammer of disciplined sniper fire. Shredder bodies cascaded over the edge past the High Chaplain, either blasted apart by the accurate las-fire or leaping wildly out of its path. Enobarbus looked up. The two talons from which he hung scraped through the rockcrete with every purchase-snapping swing of the monsters hanging from the Crimson Consul. There were figures looking down at him from the edge. Figures in helmets and crimson carapace, swathed in snow cloaks and clutching sniper rifles. On the level above was a further collection looking down at him and the same on the storey after that.

Enobarbus recognised the Scout standing above him.

'Beade...' the High Chaplain managed, but there was nothing in the blank stare or soulless eyes of the Neophyte to lead Enobarbus to believe that he was going to live. As the barrel of Beade's rifle came down in unison with his Space Marine Scout compatriots, the High Chaplain's thoughts raced through a lifetime of combat experience and the primarch's teaching. But Roboute Guilliman and his Codex had nothing for him and, with synchronous trigger-pulls that would have been worthy of a firing squad, High Chaplain Enobarbus's las-slashed corpse tumbled into the whiteness below.

The Oratorium was crowded with hulking forms, their shadows cutting through the hololithic graphics of the chamber. Each Crimson Consul was a sculpture in muscle, wrapped in zoster robes and the colour of their calling. Only the two Adeptus Astartes on the Oratorium door stood in full cream and crimson ceremonial armour, Sergeants Ravenscar and Bohemond watching silently over their brothers at the circular runeslab that dominated the chamber. The doors parted and Baldwin stomped in with the hiss of hydraulic urgency, accompanied by a serf attendant of his own. The supermen turned.

'The Reclusiarch has not returned as ordered, master,' Baldwin reported. 'Neither have two full Scout squads of the Tenth Company and their sergeants.'

'It's the time of year I tell you,' the Master of the Forge maintained through his conical faceplate. Without his armour and colossal servo-claw, Maximagne Ferro cut a very different figure. Ferro wheezed a further intake of breath through his grilles before insisting: 'Our relay stations on De Vere and Thusa Minor experience communication disruption from starquakes every year around the Antilochal Feast day.'

The Slaughterhorn's Master of Ordnance, Talbot Faulks, gave Artegall the intensity of his magnobionic eyes, their telescrew mountings whirring to projection. 'Elias. It's highly irregular: and you know it.'

'Perhaps the High Chaplain and his men have been beset by difficulties of a very natural kind,' Lord Apothecary Fabian suggested. 'Reports suggest carbonic cyclones sweeping in on the Pale Maidens from the east. They could just be waiting out the poor conditions.'

'Enjoying them, more like,' Chaplain Mercimund told the Apothecary. 'The Reclusiarch would loathe missing an opportunity to test his pupils to their limits. I remember once, out on the–'

'Forgive me, Brother-Chaplain. After the Chapter Master's recall?' the Master of Ordnance put to him. 'Not exactly in keeping with the Codex.'

'Brothers, please,' Artegall said, leaning thoughtfully against the runeslab on his fingertips. Hololithics danced across his grim face, glinting off the neat rows of service studs running above each eyebrow. He looked at Baldwin. 'Send the Tenth's Thunderhawks for them with two further squads for a search, if one is required.'

Baldwin nodded and despatched his attendant. 'Chaplain,' Artegall added, turning on Mercimund. 'If you would be so good as to start organising the commemorations, in the High Chaplain's absence.'

'It would be an honour, Chapter Master,' Mercimund acknowledged, thumping his fist into the Chapter signature on his robes earnestly before following the Chamber Castellan's serf out of the Oratorium. Baldwin remained.

'Yes?' Artegall asked.

Baldwin looked uncomfortably at Lord Fabian, prompting him to clear his throat. Artegall changed his focus to the Apothecary. 'Speak.'

'The recruitment party is long returned from the underhive. Your Chamber Castellan and I returned together – at your request – with the other party members and the potential aspirants. Since they were not requested, Navarre and his novice remained on some matter of significance: the Chief Librarian did not share it with me. I had the Chamber Castellan check with the Librarium...'

'They are as yet to return, Master Artegall,' Baldwin inserted.

'Communications?'

'We're having some difficulty reaching them,' Baldwin admitted.

Faulks's telescopic eyes retracted. 'Enobarbus, the *Crimson Tithe*, the Chief Librarian...'

'Communication difficulties, all caused by seasonal starquakes, I tell you,' Maximagne Ferro maintained, his conical faceplate swinging around to each of them with exasperation. 'The entire hive is probably experiencing the same.'

'And yet we can reach Lambert,' Faulks argued.

Artegall pursed his lips: 'I want confirmation of the nature of the communication difficulties,' he put to the Master of the Forge, prompting the Techmarine to nod slowly. 'How long have Captain Baptista and the *Crimson Tithe* been out of contact?'

'Six hours,' Faulks reported.

Artegall looked down at the runeslab. With the loss of the Chapter's only other battle-barge, Artegall wasn't comfortable with static from the *Crimson Tithe*.

'Where is she? Precisely.'

'Over the moon of *Rubessa*: quadrant four-gamma, equatorial west.'

Artegall fixed his Chamber Castellan with cold, certain eyes.

'Baldwin, arrange a pict-link with Master Lambert. I wish to speak with him again.'

'You're going to send Lambert over to investigate?' Faulks enquired.

'Calm yourself, brother,' Artegall instructed the Master of Ordnance. 'I'm sure it is as Ferro indicates. I'll have the Master of the Fleet take the *Anno Tenebris* to rendezvous with the battle-barge over *Rubessa*. There Lambert and Baptista can have their enginseers and the Sixth Reserve Company's Techmarines work on the problem from their end.'

Baldwin bowed his head. The sigh of hydraulics announced his intention to leave. 'Baldwin,' Artegall called, his eyes still on Faulks. 'On your way, return to the Librarium. Have our astropaths and Navarre's senior Epistolary attempt to reach the Chief Librarian and the *Crimson Tithe* by psychic means.'

'My lord,' Baldwin confirmed and left the Oratorium with the Master of the Forge.

'Elias,' Faulks insisted as he had done earlier. 'You must let me take the Slaughterhorn to Status Vermillion.'

'That seems unnecessary,' the Lord Apothecary shook his head.

'We have two of our most senior leaders unaccounted for and a Chapter battle-barge in a communications blackout,' Faulks listed with emphasis. 'All following the loss of one hundred of our most experienced and decorated battle-brothers? I believe that we must face the possibility that we are under some kind of attack.'

'Attack?' Fabian carped incredulously. 'From whom? Sector greenskins? Elias, you're not entertaining this?'

Artegall remained silent, his eyes following the path of hololithic representations tracking their way across the still air of the chamber.

'You have started preparing the Chapter's remaining gene-seed?' Artegall put to the Lord Apothecary.

'As you ordered, my master,' Fabian replied coolly. 'Further recruiting sweeps will need to be made. I know the loss of the First Company was a shock and this on top of the tragedies of Phaethon IV. But, this is our Chapter's entire stored genetic heritage we are talking about here. You have heard my entreaties for caution with this course of action.'

'Caution,' Artegall nodded.

'Elias,' Faulks pressed.

'As in all things,' Artegall put to his Master of Ordnance and the Apothecary, 'we shall be guided by Guilliman. The Codex advises caution in the face of the unknown – Codicil MX-VII-IX.i: The Wisdoms of Hera, "Gather your wits, as the traveller gauges the depth of the river crossing with the fallen branch, before wading into waters wary." Master Faulks, what would you advise?'

'I would order all Crimson Consuls to arms and armour,' the Master of Ordnance reeled off. 'Thunderhawks fuelled and prepped in the hangars. Penitorium secured. Vox-checks doubled and the defence lasers charged for ground to orbit assault. I would also recall Roderick and the Seventh Company from urban pacification and double the fortress-monastery garrison.'

'Anything else?'

'I would advise Master Lambert to move all Crimson Consuls vessels to a similarly high alert status.'

'That is a matter for Master of the Fleet. I will apprise him of your recommendations.'

'So?'

Artegall gave his grim consent, 'Slaughterhorn so ordered to Status Vermillion.'

'I CAN'T RAISE the Slaughterhorn,' Lexicanum Raughan Stellan complained to his Librarian Master.

'We are far below the hive, my novice,' the Chief Librarian replied, his power armour boots crunching through the darkness. 'There are a billion tonnes of plasteel and rockcrete between us and the spire monastery. You would expect even our equipment to have some problems negotiating that. Besides, it's the season for starquakes.'

'Still...' the Lexicanum mused.

The psykers had entered the catacombs: the lightless labyrinth of tunnels, cave systems and caverns that threaded their torturous way through the pulverised rock and rust of the original hive. Thousands of storeys had since been erected on top of the ancient structures, crushing them into the bottomless network of grottos from which the Crimson Consuls procured their most savage potential recruits. The sub-zero stillness was routinely shattered by murderous screams of tribal barbarism.

Far below the aristocratic indifference of the spire and the slavish poverty of the habs and industrial districts lay the gang savagery of the underhive. Collections of killers and their Carcharian kin, gathered for security or mass slaughter, blasting across the subterranean badlands for scraps and criminal honour. Below this kingdom of desperados and petty despots extended the catacombs, where tribes of barbaric brutes ruled almost as they had at the planet's feral dawn. Here, young Carcharian bodies were crafted by necessity: shaped by circumstance into small mountains of muscle and sinew. Minds were sharpened to keenness by animal instinct and souls remained empty and pure. Perfect for cult indoctrination and the teachings of Guilliman.

Navarre held up his force sword, Chrysaor, the unnatural blade bleeding immaterial illumination into the darkness. It was short, like the traditional gladius of his Chapter and its twin, Chrysaen, sat in the inverse criss-cross of scabbards that decorated the Chief Librarian's blue and gold chest plate. The denizens of the catacombs retreated into the alcoves and shadows at the abnormal glare of the blade and the towering presence of the armoured Adeptus Astartes.

'Stellan, keep up,' Navarre instructed. They had both been recruited from this tribal underworld – although hundreds of years apart. This familiarity should have filled the Carcharians with ease and acquaintance. Their instruction and training had realised in both supermen, however, an understanding of the untamed dangers of the place.

Not only would their kith and kin dash out their brains for the rich marrow in their bones, their degenerate brothers shared their dark kingdom with abhumans, mutants and wyrds, driven from the upper levels of the hive for the unsightly danger they posed. Navarre and Stellan had already despatched a shaggy, cyclopean monstrosity that had come at them on its knuckles with brute fury and bloodhunger.

Navarre and Stellan, however, were Adeptus Astartes: the Emperor's Angels of Death and demigods among men. They came with dangers of their own. This alone would be enough to ensure their survival in such a lethal place. The Crimson Consuls were also powerful psykers: wielders of powers unnatural and warp-tapped. Without the techno-spectacle of their arms, the magnificence of their blue and gold plating, their superhuman forms and murderous training, Navarre and Stellan would still be the deadliest presence in the catacombs for kilometres in any direction.

The tight tunnels opened out into a cavernous space. Lifting Chrysaor higher, the Chief Librarian allowed more of his potential to flood the unnatural blade of the weapon, throwing light up at the cave ceiling. Something colossal and twisted through with corrosion and stalactitular icicles formed the top of the cavern: some huge structure that had descended through the hive interior during some forgotten, cataclysmic collapse. Irregular columns of resistant-gauge rockcrete and strata structural supports held up the roof at precarious angles. This accidental architecture had allowed the abnormality of the open space to exist below and during the daily thaw had created, drop by drop, the frozen chemical lake that steamed beneath it.

A primitive walkway of scavenged plasteel, rock-ice and girders crossed the vast space and, as the Space Marines made their tentative crossing, Navarre's warplight spooked a flock of gliding netherworms. Uncoiling themselves from their icicle bases they flattened their bodies and slithered through the air, angling the drag of their serpentine descent down past the Space Marines and at the crags and ledges of the cavern where they would make a fresh ascent. As the flock of black worms spiralled by, one crossed Stellan's path. The novice struck out with his gauntlet in disgust but the thing latched onto him with its unparalleled prehensility. It weaved its way up through his armoured digits and corkscrewed up his thrashing arm at his helmetless face.

Light flashed before the Lexicanum's eyes. Just as the netherworm retracted its fleshy collar and prepared to sink its venomous beak hooks into the Space Marine's young face, Navarre clipped the horror in half with the blazing tip of Chrysaor. As the worm fell down the side of the walkway in two writhing pieces, Stellan mumbled his thanks.

'Why didn't you use your powers?' the Chief Librarian boomed around the cavern.

'It surprised me,' was all the Lexicanum could manage.

'You've been out of the depths mere moments and you've already forgotten its dangers,' Navarre remonstrated gently. 'What of the galaxy's dangers? There's a myriad of lethality waiting for you out there. Be mindful, my novice.'

'Yes, master.'

'Did it come to you again?' Navarre asked pointedly.

'Why do you ask, master?'

'You seem distracted: not yourself. Was your sleep disturbed?'

'Yes, master.'

'Your dreams?'

'Yes, master.'

'The empyreal realm seems a dark and distant place,' Navarre told his apprentice sagely. 'But it is everywhere. How do you think we can draw on it so? Its rawness feeds our power: the blessings our God-Emperor gave us and through which we give back in His name. We are not the only ones to draw from this wellspring of power and we need our faith and constant vigilance to shield us from the predations of these immaterial others.'

'Yes, master.'

'Behind a wall of mirrored-plas the warp hides, reflecting back to us our realities. In some places it's thick; in others a mere wafer of truth separates us from its unnatural influence. Your dreams are one such window: a place where one may submerge one's head in the Sea of Souls.'

'Yes, master.'

'Tell me, then.'

Stellan seemed uncomfortable, but as the two Space Marines continued their careful trudge across the cavern walkway, the novice unburdened himself.

'It called itself Ghidorquiel.'

'You conversed with this thing of confusion and darkness?'

'No, my master. It spoke only to me: in my cell.'

'You said you were dreaming,' Navarre reminded the novice.

'Of being awake,' Stellan informed him, 'in my cell. It spoke. What I took to be lips moved but the voice was in my head.'

'And what lies did this living lie tell you?'

'A host of obscenities, my lord,' Stellan confirmed. 'It spoke in languages unknown to me. Hissed and spat its impatience. It claimed my soul as its own. It said my weakness was the light in its darkness.'

'This disturbed you.'

'Of course,' the Lexicanum admitted. 'Its attentions disgust me. But this creature called out to me across the expanse of time and space. Am I marked? Am I afflicted?'

'No more than you ever were,' Navarre reassured the novice. 'Stellan, all those who bear the burden of powers manifest – the Emperor's sacred gift – of which he was gifted himself – dream themselves face to face with the daemonscape from time to time. Entities trawl the warp for souls to torment for their wretched entertainment. Our years of training and the mental fortitude that comes of being the Emperor's chosen protects us from their direct influence. The unbound, the warp-rampant and the witch are all easy prey for such beasts and through them the daemon worms its way into our world. Thank the primarch we need face such things for real with blessed infrequency.'

'Yes, my lord,' Stellan agreed.

'The warp sometimes calls to us: demands our attention. It's why we did not return to the Slaughterhorn with the others. Such a demand led me beyond the scope of the Lord Apothecary's recruitment party and down into the frozen bowels of Carcharias. Here.'

Reaching the other side of the cavern, Navarre and Stellan stood on the far end of the walkway, where it led back into the rock face of pulverised masonry. Over the top of the tunnel opening was a single phrase in slap-dash white paint. It was all glyph symbols and runic consonants of ancient Carcharian.

'It's recent,' Navarre said half to himself. Stellan simply stared at the oddness of the lettering. 'Yet its meaning is very old. A phrase that predates the hives, at least. It means, "From the single flake of snow – the avalanche".'

Venturing into the tunnel with force sword held high, Navarre was struck by the patterns on the walls. Graffiti was endemic to the underhive: it was not mere defacement or criminal damage. In the ganglands above it advertised the presence of dangerous individuals and marked the jealously guarded territories of House-sponsored outfits, organisations and posses. It covered every empty space: the walls, the floor and ceiling, and was simply part of the underworld's texture. Below that, the graffiti was no less pervasive or lacking in purpose. Tribal totems and primitive paintings performed much the same purpose for the barbarians of the catacombs. Handprints in blood; primordial representations of subterranean mega-vermin in campfire charcoal; symbolic warnings splashed across walls in the phosphorescent, radioactive chemicals that leaked down from the industrial sectors above. The Carcharian savages that haunted the catacombs had little use for words, yet this was all Navarre could see.

The Chief Librarian had been drawn to this place, deep under Hive Niveous, by the stink of psychic intrusion. Emanations. Something large and invasive: something that had wormed its way through the very core of the Carcharian capital. The ghostly glow of Chrysaor revealed it to Navarre in all its mesmerising glory. Graffiti upon graffiti, primitive paintings upon symbols upon markings upon blood splatter. Words. The same words, over and over again, in all orientations, spelt out in letters created in the layered spaces of the hive cacography. Repetitions that ran for kilometres through the arterial maze of tunnels. Like a chant or incantation in ancient Carcharian: they blazed with psychic significance to the Chief Librarian, where to the eyes of the ordinary and untouched, among the background scrawl of the hive underworld, they would not appear to be there at all.

'Stellan! You must see this,' Navarre murmured as he advanced down the winding passage. The Librarian continued: 'Psycho-sensitive words, spelt out on the walls, a conditioned instruction of some kind, imprinting itself on the minds of the underhivers. Stellan: we must get word back to the Slaughterhorn – to Fabian – to the Chapter Master. The recruits could be compromised...'

The Chief Librarian turned to find that his novice wasn't there. Marching back up the passage in the halo of his shimmering force weapon, Navarre found the Lexicanum still standing on the cavern walkway, staring up at the wall above the tunnel entrance with a terrible blankness. 'Stellan? Stellan, talk to me.'

At first Navarre thought that one of the deadly gliding worms had got him, infecting the young Space Marine with its toxin. The reality was much worse. Following the novice's line of sight, Navarre settled on the white painted scrawl above the tunnel. The ancient insistence, 'From the single flake of snow – the avalanche' in fresh paint. Looking back at the Lexicanum, Navarre came to realise that his own novice had succumbed to the psycho-sensitive indoctrination of his recruiting grounds. All the wordsmith had needed was to introduce his subjects to the trigger. A phrase they were unlikely to come across anywhere else. The timing intentional; the brainwashing complete.

Stellan dribbled. He tried to mumble the words on the wall. Then he tried to get his palsied mouth around his master's name. He failed. The young Space Marine's mind was no longer his own. He belonged to someone else: to the will of the wordsmith – whoever they were. And not only the novice: countless other recruits over the years, for whom indoctrination hid in the very fabric of their worlds and now in the backs of their afflicted minds. All ready to be activated at a single phrase.

Navarre readied himself. Opened his being to the warp's dark promise. Allowed its fire to burn within. Slipping Chrysaen from its chest scabbard, the Chief Librarian held both force blades out in front of him. Each master-crafted gladius smoked with immaterial vengeance.

For Stellan, the dangers were much more immediate than brainwashing. Stripped of his years of training and the mental fortitude that shielded a Librarian from the dangers of the warp, Stellan succumbed to the monster stalking his soul.

Something like shock took the Crimson Consul's face hostage. The novice looked like he had been seized from below. Somehow, horribly, he had. The Librarian's head suddenly disappeared down into the trunk of his blue and gold power armour. An oily, green ichor erupted from the neck of the suit.

'Ghidorquiel…' Navarre spat. The Chief Librarian thrust himself at the quivering suit of armour, spearing his Lexicanum through the chest with Chrysaor. The stink of warp-corruption poured from the adamantium shell and stung the psyker's nostrils. Spinning and kicking the body back along the treacherous walkway, Navarre's blades trailed ethereal afterglow as they arced and cleaved through the sacred suit.

Howling fury at the materialising beast within the armour, the Chief Librarian unleashed a blast wave of raw warp energy from his chest that lit up the cavern interior and hit the suit like the God-Emperor's own fist.

The suit tumbled backwards, wrenching and cracking along the walkway until it came to rest, a broken-backed heap. Even then, the armour continued to quiver and snap, rearranging the splintered ceramite plating and moulding itself into something new. On the walkway, Navarre came to behold an adamantium shell, like that of a mollusc, from which slithered an explosion of tentacles. Navarre ran full speed at the daemon while appendages shot for him like guided missiles. Twisting this way and that, but without sacrificing any of his rage-fuelled speed, the Chief Librarian slashed at the beast, his blinding blades shearing off tentacular length and the warp-dribbling tips of the monster feelers.

As the psyker closed with the daemon nautiloid, the warp beast shot its appendages into the fragile walkway's architecture. Hugging the snapping struts and supports to it, the creature demolished the structure beneath the Crimson Consul's feet.

Navarre plummeted through the cavern space before smashing down through the frozen surface of the chemical lake below. The industrial waste plunge immediately went to work on the blue and gold of the Librarian's armour and blistered the psyker's exposed and freezing flesh. Navarre's force blades glowed spectroscopic eeriness under the surface and it took precious moments for the Space Marine to orientate himself and kick for the surface. As his steaming head broke from the frozen acid depths of the lake, Navarre's burn-blurry eyes saw the rest of the walkway collapsing towards him. Ghidorquiel had reached for the cavern wall and, pulling with its unnatural might, had toppled the remainder of the structure.

Again Navarre was hammered to the darkness of the lake bottom, sinking wreckage raining all about the dazed psyker. Somewhere in the chaos Chrysaen slipped from Navarre's grip. Vaulting upwards, the Space Marine hit the thick ice of the lake surface further across. Clawing uselessly with his gauntlet, skin aflame and armour freezing up, Navarre stared through the ice and saw something slither overhead. Roaring pain and frustration into the chemical darkness, the Chief Librarian thrust Chrysaor through the frozen effluence. Warpflame bled from the blade and across the ice, rapidly melting the crust of the acid bath and allowing the Crimson Consul a moment to suck in a foetid breath and drag himself up the shoreline of shattered masonry.

Ghidorquiel was there, launching tentacles at the psyker. Hairless and with flesh melting from his skull the Librarian mindlessly slashed the appendages to pieces. All the Space Marine wanted was the daemon. The thing dragged its obscene adamantium shell sluggishly away from the lake and the enraged warrior. Navarre bounded up and off a heap of walkway wreckage, dodging the creature's remaining tentacles and landing on ceramite. Drawing on everything he had, the Chief Librarian became a conduit of the warp. The raw, scalding essence of immaterial energy poured from his being and down through the descending tip of his force sword. Chrysaor slammed through the twisted shell of Stellan's armour and buried itself in the daemon's core. Like a lightning rod, the gladius roasted the beast from the inside out.

Armour steamed. Tentacles dropped and trembled to stillness. The daemon caught light. Leaving the force blade in the monstrous body, Navarre stumbled down from the creature and crashed to the cavern floor himself. The psyker was spent in every way conceivable. He could do little more than lie there in his own palsy, staring at the daemon corpse lit by Chrysaor's still gleaming blade. The slack, horrible face of the creature had slipped down out of the malformed armour shell: the same horrific face that the novice Stellan had confronted in his dreams.

Looking up into the inky, cavern blackness, Navarre wrangled with the reality that somehow he had to get out of the catacombs and warn the Slaughterhorn of impending disaster. A slurp drew his face back to the creature; sickeningly it began to rumble with daemonic life and throttled laughter. Fresh tentacles erupted from its flaming sides and wrapped themselves around two of the crooked pillars of rockcrete and metal that were supporting the chamber ceiling and the underhive levels above.

All Navarre could do was watch the monster pull the columns towards its warp-scorched body and roar his frustration as the cavern ceiling quaked and thundered down towards him, with the weight of Hive Niveous behind it.

THE ORATORIUM SWARMED with armoured command staff and their attendants. Clarifications and communications shot back and forth across the chamber amongst a hololithic representation of the Slaughterhorn fortress-monastery that crackled disturbance every time an officer or Crimson Consuls serf walked through it.

'They discovered nothing, my lord,' Baldwin informed Artegall in mid-report. 'No High Chaplain; no Scout squads; nothing. They've scoured the Dry-blind around the Pale Maidens. They're requesting permission to bring the Thunderhawks back to base.'

'What about Chief Librarian Navarre?' Artegall called across the Oratorium.

'Nothing, sir,' Lord Apothecary Fabian confirmed. 'On the vox or from the Librarium.'

'Planetary defence force channels and on-scene Enforcers report seismic shift and hive tremors in the capital lower levels,' the Master of the Forge reported, his huge servo-claw swinging about over the heads of the gathering.

'What about the *Crimson Tithe*?'

'Patching you through to Master Lambert now,' Maximagne Ferro added, giving directions to a communications servitor. The hololithic representation of the Slaughterhorn disappeared and was replaced with the phantasmal static of a dead pict-feed that danced around the assembled Crimson Consuls.

'What the hell is happening up there, Maximagne?' Artegall demanded, but the Master of the Forge was working furiously on the servitor and the brass control station of the runeslab. The static disappeared before briefly being replaced by the Slaughterhorn and then a three-dimensional hololith of the Carcharian system. Artegall immediately picked out their system star and their icebound home world: numerous defence monitors and small frigates were stationed in high orbit. Circling Carcharias were the moons of De Vere, Thusa Major and Thusa Minor between which two strike cruisers sat at anchor. Most distant was *Rubessa*; the Oratorium could see the battle-barge *Crimson Tithe* beneath it. Approaching was Hecton Lambert's strike cruiser, *Anno Tenebris*. The hololithic image of the Adeptus Astartes strike cruiser suddenly crackled and then disappeared.

The Oratorium fell to a deathly silence.

'Master Maximagne…' Artegall began. The Master of the Forge had a vox-headset to one ear.

'Confirmed, my lord. The *Anno Tenebris* has been destroyed with all on board.' The silence prevailed. 'Sir, the *Crimson Tithe* fired upon her.'

The gathered Adeptus Astartes looked to their Chapter Master, who, like his compatriots, could not believe what he was hearing.

'Master Faulks,' Artegall began. 'It seems you were correct. We are under attack. Status report: fortress-monastery.'

'In lockdown as ordered, sir,' the Master of Ordnance reported with grim pride. 'All Crimson Consuls are prepped for combat. All sentry guns manned. Thunderhawks ready for launch on your order. Defence lasers powered to full.'

Captain Roderick presented himself to his Chapter Master: 'My lord, the Seventh Company has fortified the Slaughterhorn at the Master of Ordnance's instruction. Nothing will get through – you can be sure of that.'

'Sir,' Master Maximagne alerted the chamber: '*Crimson Tithe* is on the move, Carcharias bound, my lord.'

Artegall's lip curled into a snarl. 'Who the hell are they?' he muttered to himself. 'What about our remaining cruisers?'

Faulks stepped forwards indicating the cruisers at anchor between the hololithic moons of Thusa Major and Thusa Minor. 'At full alert as I advised. The *Caliburn* and *Honour of Hera* could plot an intercept course and attempt an ambush…'

'Out of the question,' Artegall stopped Faulks. 'Bring the strike cruisers in above the Slaughterhorn at low orbit. I want our defence lasers to have their backs.'

'Yes, my master,' Faulks obeyed.

'Baldwin…'

'Lord?'

'Ready my weapons and armour.'

The Chamber Castellan nodded slowly, 'It would be my honour, master.' The Crimson Consuls watched the serf exit, knowing what this meant. Artegall was already standing at the head of the runeslab in a functional suit of crimson and cream power armour and his mantle. He was asking for the hallowed suit of artificer armour and master-crafted bolter that resided in the Chapter Master's private armoury. The gleaming suit of crimson and gold upon which the honourable history of the Crimson Consuls Chapter was inscribed and inlaid in gemstone ripped from the frozen earth of Carcharias itself. The armour that past Masters had worn when leading the Chapter to war in its entirety: Aldebaran; the Fall of Volsungard; the Termagant Wars.

'Narke.'

'Master Artegall,' the Slaughterhorn's chief astropath replied from near the Oratorium doors.

'Have you been successful in contacting the Third, Fifth or Eighth Companies?'

'Captain Neath has not responded, lord,' the blind Narke reported, clutching his staff.

Artegall and Talbot Faulks exchanged grim glances. Neath and the Eighth Company were only two systems away hunting Black Legion Traitor Marine degenerates in the Sarcus Reaches.

'And Captain Borachio?'

Artegall had received monthly astrotelepathic reports from Captain Albrecht Borachio stationed in the Damocles Gulf. Borachio had overseen the Crimson Consuls contribution to the Damocles Crusade in the form of the Third and Fifth Companies and had present responsibility for bringing the Tau commander, O'Shovah, to battle in the Farsight Enclaves. Artegall and Borachio had served together in the same squad as battle-brothers and Borachio beyond Baldwin, was what the Chapter Master might have counted as the closest thing he had to a friend.

'Three days ago, my lord,' Narke returned. 'You returned in kind, Master Artegall.'

'Read back the message.'

The astropath's knuckles whitened around his staff as he recalled the message: '... encountered a convoy of heavy cruisers out of Fi'Rios – a lesser sept, the Xenobiologis assure me, attempting to contact Commander Farsight. We took a trailing vessel with little difficulty but at the loss of one Carcharian son: Crimson Consul Battle-Brother Theodoric of the First Squad: Fifth Company. I commend Brother Theodoric's service to you and recommend his name be added to the Shrine of Hera in the Company Chapel as a posthumous recipient of the Iron Laurel...'

'And the end?' Artegall pushed.

'An algebraic notation in three dimensions, my lord: Kn Ω iii – π iX (Z-) – ⊠ v.R (!?) 0-1.'

'Coordinates? Battle manoeuvres?' Talbot Faulks hypothesised.

'Regicide notations,' Artegall informed him, his mind elsewhere. For years, the Chapter Master and Albrecht Borachio had maintained a game of regicide across the stars, moves detailed back and forth with their astropathic communiqués. Each had a board and pieces upon which the same game had been played out; Artegall's was an ancient set carved from lacquered megafelis sabres on a burnished bronze board. Artegall moved the pieces in his mind, recalling the board as it was set up on a rostra by his throne in the Chancelorium. Borachio had beaten him: 'Blind Man's Mate...' the Chapter Master mouthed.

'Excuse me, my lord?' Narke asked.

'No disrespect intended,' Artegall told the astropath. 'It's a form of victory in regicide, so called because you do not see it coming.'

The corridor outside the Oratorium suddenly echoed with the sharp crack of bolter fire. Shocked glances between Artegall and his officers were swiftly replaced by the assumption of cover positions. The armoured forms took advantage of the runeslab and the walls either side of the Oratorium door.

'That's inside the perimeter,' Faulks called in disbelief, slapping on his helmet.

'Well inside,' Artegall agreed grimly. Many of the Space Marines had drawn either their bolt pistols or their gladius swords. Only Captain Roderick and the Oratorium sentry sergeants, Bohemond and Ravenscar, were equipped for full combat with bolters, spare ammunition and grenades.

With the muzzle of his squat Fornax-pattern bolt pistol resting on the slab, the Master of Ordnance brought up the hololithic representation of the Slaughterhorn once more. The fortress-monastery was a tessellation of flashing wings, towers, hangars and sections.

'Impossible...' Faulks mumbled.

'The fortress-monastery is completely compromised,' Master Maximagne informed the chamber, cycling through the vox-channels.

Bolt shells pounded the thick doors of the Oratorium. The Seventh Company captain held a gauntleted finger to the vox-bead in his ear.

'Roderick,' Artegall called. 'What's happening?'

'My men are being fired upon from the inside of the Slaughterhorn, my lord,' the captain reported bleakly. 'By fellow Space Marines – by Crimson Consuls, Master Artegall!'

'What has happened to us?' the Chapter Master bawled in dire amazement.

'Later, sir. We have to get you out of here,' Faulks insisted.

'What sections do we hold?' Artegall demanded.

'Elias, we have to go, now!'

'Master Faulks, what do we hold?'

'Sir, small groups of my men hold the Apothecarion and the northeast hangar,' Roderick reported. 'The Barbican, some Foundry sections and Cell Block Sigma.'

'The Apothecarion?' Fabian clarified.

'The gene-seed,' Artegall heard himself mutter.

'The Command Tower is clear,' Faulks announced, reading details off the hololith schematic of the monastery. Bolt-rounds tore through the metal of the Oratorium door and drummed into the runeslab column. The hololith promptly died. Ravenscar pushed Narke, the blind astropath, out of his way and poked the muzzle of his weapon through the rent in the door. He started plugging the corridor with ammunition-conserving boltfire.

'We must get the Chapter Master to the Tactical Chancelorium,' Faulks put to Roderick, Maximagne and the sentry sergeants.

'No,' Artegall barked back. 'We must take back the Slaughterhorn.'

'Which we can do best from your Tactical Chancelorium, my lord,'

Faulks insisted with strategic logic. 'From there we have our own vox-relays, tactical feeds and your private armoury: it's elevated for a Thunderhawk evacuation – it's simply the most secure location in the fortress-monastery,' Faulks told his master. 'The best place from which to coordinate and rally our forces.'

'When we determine who they are,' Fabian added miserably. Artegall and the Master of Ordnance stared at one another.

'Sir!' Ravenscar called from the door. 'Coming up on a reload.'

'Agreed,' Artegall told Faulks. 'Captain Roderick shall accompany Master Maximagne and Lord Fabian to secure the Apothecarion; the gene-seed must be saved. Serfs with your masters. Sergeants Ravenscar and Bohemond, escort the Master of Ordnance and myself to the Tactical Chancelorium. Narke, you will accompany us. All understood?'

'Yes, Chapter Master,' the chorus came back.

'Sergeant, on three,' Artegall instructed. 'One.' Bohemond nodded and primed a pair of grenades from his belt. 'Two.' Faulks took position by the door stud. 'Three'. Roderick nestled his bolter snug into his shoulder as Faulks activated the door mechanism.

As the door rolled open, Ravenscar pulled away and went about reloading his boltgun. Bohemond's grenades were then followed by replacement suppression fire from Captain Roderick's bolter.

The brief impression of crimson and cream armour working up the corridor was suddenly replaced with the thunder and flash of grenades. Roderick was swiftly joined by Bohemond and then Ravenscar, the three Space Marines maintaining a withering arc of fire. The command group filed out of the Oratorium with their Chapter serf attendants, the singular crash of their Fornax-pattern pistols joining in the cacophony.

With Roderick's precision fire leading the Lord Apothecary and the Master of the Forge down a side passage, Bohemond slammed his shoulder through a stairwell door to lead the other group up onto the next level. The Crimson Consuls soon fell into the surgical-style battle rotation so beloved of Guilliman: battle-brother covering battle-brother; arc-pivoting and rapid advance suppression fire. Ravenscar and Bohemond orchestrated the tactical dance from the front, with Artegall's pistol crashing support from behind and the Master of Ordnance covering the rear with his own, while half dragging the blind Narke behind him.

Advancing up through the stairwell, spiralling up through the storeys, the Space Marines walked up into a storm of iron: armoured, renegade Crimson Consuls funnelled their firepower down at them from a gauntlet above. Unclipping a grenade, Ravenscar tossed it to his brother-sergeant. Bohemond then held the explosive, counting away the precious seconds before launching the thing directly up through the space between the spiral stair rails. The grenade detonated above, silencing the gunfire. A cream and crimson body fell down past the group in a shower of grit. The sergeants didn't wait, however, bounding up the stairs and into the maelstrom above.

Dead Crimson Consuls lay mangled amongst the rail and rockcrete. One young Space Marine lay without his legs, his helmet half blasted from his face. As blood frothed between the Adeptus Astartes' gritted teeth the Space Marine stared at the passing group. For Artegall it was too much. Crimson Consuls spilling each other's sacred blood. Guilliman's dream in tatters. He seized the grievously wounded Space Marine by his shattered breastplate and shook him violently.

'What the hell are you doing, boy?' Artegall roared, but there was no time. Scouts in light carapace armour were spilling from a doorway above, bouncing down one storey to the next on their boot tips, bathing the landings with scattershot from their shotguns. Bolt-rounds sailed past Faulks from below, where renegade Crimson Consuls had followed in the footsteps of their escape. The shells thudded into the wall above the kneeling Artegall and punched through the stumbling astropath, causing the Master of Ordnance to abandon his handicap and force back their assailants with blasts from a recovered bolter.

'Through there!' Faulks bawled above the bolt chatter, indicating the nearest door on the stairwell. Again Bohemond led with his shoulder, blasting through the door into a dormitory hall. The space was plain and provided living quarters for some of the Slaughterhorn's Chapter serfs. Bright, white light was admitted from the icescape outside through towering arches of plain glass, each depicting a bleached scene from the Chapter's illustrious history, picked out in lead strips.

Ravenscar handed Artegall his bolter and took a blood-splattered replacement from the stairwell for himself.

'There's a bondsman's entrance to the Chancelorium through the dormitories,' Artegall pointed, priming the bolter. Their advance along the window-lined hall had already been ensured by the bolt-riddled door being blasted off its hinges behind them.

'Go!' Faulks roared. The four Space Marines stormed along the open space towards the far end of the hall. The searing light from the windows was suddenly eclipsed, causing the Astrartes to turn as they ran. Drifting up alongside the wall, directed in on their position by the renegade Space Marines, was the sinister outline of a Crimson Consuls Thunderhawk. As the monstrous aircraft hovered immediately outside, the heavy bolters adorning its carrier compartment unleashed their fury.

All the Space Marines could do was run as the great accomplishments of the Chapter shattered behind them. One by one the windows imploded with anti-personnel fire and fragmentation shells, the Thunderhawk gently gliding along the wall. The rampage caught up with Ravenscar who, lost in the maelstrom of smashed glass and lead, soaked up the heavy bolter's punishment and in turn became a metal storm of pulped flesh and fragmented armour. At the next window, Artegall felt the whoosh of the heavy bolter rounds streak across his back. Detonating about him like tiny frag grenades, the rounds shredded through his pack and tore up the ceramite plating of his armoured suit. Falling through the shrapnel hurricane, Artegall tumbled to the floor before hitting the far wall.

Gauntlets were suddenly all over him, hauling the Chapter Master in through an open security bulkhead, before slamming the door on the chaos beyond.

By comparison the command tower was silent. Artegall squinted, dazed, through the darkness of the Chancelorium dungeon-antechamber, his power armour steaming and slick with blood, lubricant and hydraulic fluid.

As Artegall came back to his senses, he realised that he'd never seen this part of his fortress-monastery before; traditionally it only admitted Chapter serfs. Getting unsteadily to his feet he joined his battle-brothers in stepping up on the crimson swirl of the marble trapdoor platform. With Sergeant Bohemond and Master Faulks flanking him, the Chapter Master activated the rising floor section and the three Crimson Consuls ascended up through the floor of Artegall's own Tactical Chancelorium.

'Chapter Master, I'll begin–'

Light and sound: simultaneous.

Bohemond and Faulks dropped as the backs of their heads came level with the yawning barrels of waiting bolters and their skulls were blasted through the front of their faceplates. Artegall span around but found that the bolters, all black paint and spiked barrels, were now pressed up against the crimson of his chest.

His assailants were Space Marines: Traitor Astartes. The galaxy's arch-traitors: the Warmaster's own – the Black Legion. Their cracked and filthy power armour was a dusty black, edged with gargoylesque details of dull bronze. Their helmets were barbed and leering and their torsos a tangle of chains and skulls. With the smoking muzzle of the first still resting against him, the second disarmed the grim Chapter Master, removing his bolter and slipping the bolt pistol and gladius from his belt. Weaponless, he was motioned round.

Before him stood two Black Legion officers. The senior was a wild-eyed captain with teeth filed to sharp points and a flea-infested wolf pelt hanging from his spiked armour. The other was an Apothecary whose once-white armour was now streaked with blood and rust and whose face was shrunken and soulless like a zombie.

'At least do me the honour of knowing who I am addressing, traitor filth,' the Chapter Master rumbled.

This, the Black Legion captain seemed to find amusing.

'This is Lord Vladivoss of the Black Legion and his Apothecary Szekle,' a voice bounced around the vaulted roof of the Chancelorium, but it came from neither Chaos Marine. The Black Legion Space Marines parted to reveal the voice's owner, sitting in Artegall's own bone command throne. His armour gleamed a sickening mazarine, embossed with the necks of green serpents that entwined his limbs and whose heads clustered on his chest plate in the fashion of a hydra. The unmistakable iconography of the Alpha Legion. The Space Marine sat thumbing casually through the pages of the Codex Astartes on the Chapter Master's lectern.

'I don't reason that there's any point in asking you that question, renegade,' Artegall snarled.

The copper-skinned giant pushed the anti-gravitic lectern to one side, stood and smiled: 'I am Alpharius.'

A grim chuckle surfaced in Artegall. He hawked and spat blood at the Alpha Legionnaire's feet.

'That's what I think of that, Alpha,' the Chapter Master told him. 'Come on, I want to congratulate you on your trademark planning and perfect execution: Alpharius is but a ghost. My Lord Guilliman ended the scourge – as I will end you, monster.'

The Legionnaire's smile never faltered, even in the face of Artegall's threats and insults. It grew as the Space Marine came to a private decision.

"I am Captain Quetzal Carthach, Crimson Consul,' the Alpha Legion Space Marine told him, 'and I have come to accept your unconditional surrender.'

'The only unconditional thing you'll get from me, Captain Carthach, is my unending revulsion and hatred.'

'You talk of ends, Chapter Master,' the Legionnaire said calmly. 'Has Guilliman blinded you so that you cannot see your own? The end of your Chapter. The end of your living custodianship, your shred of that sanctimonious bastard's seed. I wanted to come here and meet you. So you could go to your grave knowing that it was the Alpha Legion that had beaten you; the Alpha Legion who are eradicating Guilliman's legacy one thousand of his sons at a time; the Alpha Legion who are not only superior strategists but also superior Space Marines.'

Artegall's lips curled with cold fury.

'Never...'

'Perhaps, Chapter Master, you think there's a chance for your seed to survive: for future sons of Carcharias to avenge you?' The Alpha Legion giant sat back down in Artegall's throne. 'The Tenth was mine before you even recruited them – as was the Ninth Company before them: you must know that now. I lent you their minds but not their true allegiance: a simple phrase was all that was needed to bring them back to the Alpha Legion fold. The Second and Fourth were easy: that was a mere administrative error, holding the Celebrants over at Nedicta Secundus and drawing the Crimson Consuls to the waiting xenos deathtrap that was Phaethon IV.'

Artegall listened to the Alpha Legionnaire honour himself with the deaths of his Crimson Consul brothers. Listened, while the Black Legion Space Marine looked down the spiked muzzle of his bolter at the back of the Chapter Master's head.

'The Seventh fell fittingly at the hands of their brothers, foolishly defending your colourfully-named fortress-monastery from a threat that was within rather than without. The Eighth, well, Captain Vladivoss took care of those in the Sarcus Reaches – and now the good captain has earned his prize. Szekle,' the Alpha Legion Space Marine addressed the zombified Chaos Space Marine. 'The Apothecarion is now in our hands. You may help yourself to the Crimson Consuls' remaining stocks of gene-seed. Feel free to extract progenoids from loyalists who fought in our name. Fear not, they will not obstruct you. In fact, the completion of the procedure is their signal to turn their weapons on themselves. Captain Vladivoss, you may then return to Lord Abaddon with my respects and your prize – to help replenish the Black Legion's depleted numbers in the Eye of Terror.'

Vladivoss bowed, while Szekle fidgeted with dead-eyed anticipation.

'Oh, and captain,' Carthach instructed as Artegall was pushed forwards towards the throne, 'leave one Legionnaire, please.'

With Captain Vladivoss, his depraved Apothecary and their Chaos Space Marine sentry descending through the trapdoor on the marble platform with Bohemond and Faulks's bodies, Carthach came to regard the Chapter Master once again.

'The *Revenant Rex* was pure genius. That I even admit to myself. What I couldn't have hoped for was the deployment of your First Company Terminator veterans. That made matters considerably easier down the line. You should receive some credit for that, Chapter Master Artegall,' Carthach grinned nastily.

A rumble like distant thunder rolled through the floor beneath Artegall's feet. Carthach seemed suddenly excited. 'Do you know what that is?' he asked. The monster didn't wait for an answer. Instead he activated the controls in the bone armrest of Artegall's throne. The vaulted ceiling of the Tactical Chancelorium – which formed the pinnacle of the Command Tower – began to turn and unscrew, revealing a circular aperture in the roof that grew with the corkscrew motion of the Tower top.

The Alpha Legionnaire shook his head in what could have been mock disappointment.

'Missed it: that was your Slaughterhorn's defence lasers destroying the strike cruisers you ordered back under their protection. Poetic. Or perhaps just tactically predictable. Ah, now look at this.'

Carthach pointed at the sky and with the Chaos Space Marine's bolter muzzle still buried in the back of his skull, Artegall felt compelled to look up also. To savour the reassuring bleakness of his home world's sky for what might be the last time.

'There they are, see?'

Artegall watched a meteorite shower in the sky above: a lightshow of tiny flashes. 'I brought the *Crimson Tithe* back to finish off any remaining frigates or destroyers. Don't want surviving Crimson Consuls running to the Aurora Chapter with my strategies and secrets; the Auroras and their share of Guilliman's seed may be my next target. Anyway, the beautiful spectacle you see before you is no ordinary celestial phenomenon. This is the Crimson Consuls Sixth Company coming home, expelled from the *Crimson Tithe*'s airlocks and falling to Carcharias. The battle-barge I need – another gift for the Warmaster. It has the facilities on board to safely transport your seed to the Eye of Terror, where it is sorely needed for future Black Crusades. Who knows, perhaps one of your line will have the honour of being the first to bring the Warmaster's justice to Terra itself? In Black Legion armour and under a traitor's banner, of course.'

Artegall quaked silent rage, the Chapter Master's eyes dropping and fixing on a spot on the wall behind the throne.

'I know what you're thinking,' Carthach informed him. 'As I have all along, Crimson Consul. You're pinning your hopes on Captain Borachio. Stationed in the Damocles Gulf with the Third and Fifth Companies... Did you find my reports convincing?'

Artegall's eyes widened.

'Captain Borachio and his men have been dead for two years, Elias.'

Artegall shook his head.

'The Crimson Consuls are ended. I am Borachio,' the Alpha revealed, soaking up the Chapter Master's doom, 'and Carthach ... and Alpharius.' The captain bent down to execute the final, astrotelepathically communicated move on Artegall's beautifully carved Regicide board. Blind Man's Mate.

Artegall's legs faltered. As the Crimson Consul fell to his knees before Quetzal Carthach and the throne, Artegall mouthed a disbelieving, 'Why?'

'Because we play the Long Game, Elias...' the Alpha Legionnaire told him.

Artegall hoped that the Black Legion's attention span didn't extend half as far as their Alpha Legion compatriots. The Space Marine threw his head back, cutting his scalp against the bolter's muzzle. The weapon smacked the Chaos Space Marine in the throat – the Black Legion savage still staring up into the sky, watching the Crimson Consuls burn in the upper atmosphere.

Artegall surged away from the stunned Chaos Space Marine and directly at Carthach. The Alpha Legionnaire Marine snarled at the sudden, suicidal surprise of it all, snatching for his pistol.

Artegall awkwardly changed direction, throwing himself around the other side of the throne. The Black Legion Space Marine's bolter fire followed him, mauling the throne and driving the alarmed Carthach even further back. Artegall sprinted for the wall, stopping and feeling for the featureless trigger that activated the door of the Chapter Master's private armoury. As the Chaos Space Marine's bolter chewed up the Chancelorium wall, Artegall activated the trigger and slid the hidden door to one side. He felt hot agony as the Chaos Space Marine's bolter found its mark and two rounds crashed through his ruined armour.

Returned to his knees, the Chapter Master fell in through the darkness of the private armoury and slid the reinforced door shut from the inside. In the disappearing crack of light between the door and wall, Artegall caught sight of Quetzal Carthach's face once more dissolve into a wolfish grin.

Throwing himself across the darkness of the armoury floor, the felled Crimson Consul heaved himself arm over agonising arm through the presentation racks of artificer armour: racks from which serfs would ordinarily select the individual plates and adornments and dress the Chapter Master at his bequest. Artegall didn't have time for such extravagance. Crawling for the rear of the armoury, he searched for the only item that could bring him peace. The only item seemingly designed for the single purpose of ending Quetzal Carthach, the deadliest in the Chapter's long history of deadly enemies. Artegall's master-crafted boltgun.

Reaching for the exquisite weapon, its crimson-painted adamantium finished in gold and decorated with gemstones from Carcharias's rich depths, Artegall faltered. The bolt-rounds had done their worst and the Chapter Master's fingers failed to reach the boltgun in its cradle. Suddenly there was sound and movement in the darkness. The hydraulic sigh of bionic appendages thumping into the cold marble with every step.

'Baldwin!' Artegall cried out. 'My weapon, Baldwin… the boltgun.'

The Chamber Castellan slipped the beautiful bolter from its cradle and stomped around to his master. 'Thank the primarch you're here,' Artegall blurted.

In the oily blackness of the private armoury, the Chapter Master heard the thunk of the priming mechanism. Artegall tensed and then fell limp. He wasn't being handed the weapon: it was being pointed at him through the gloom. Whatever had possessed the minds of his Neophyte recruits in the Carcharian underhive had also had time to worm its way into the Chamber Castellan, whose responsibility it was to accompany the recruitment parties on their expeditions. Without the training or spiritual fortitude of the Adeptus Astartes, Baldwin's mind had been vulnerable. He had become a Regicide piece on a galactic board, making his small but significant move, guided by an unknown hand. Artegall was suddenly glad of the darkness. Glad that he couldn't see the mask of Baldwin's kindly face frozen in murderous blankness.

Closing his eyes, Elias Artegall, Chapter Master and last of the Crimson Consuls, wished the game to end.

VIRTUE'S REWARD

Darius Hinks

In the city of his sisters he will return to us on wings of fire.

– The Cantos of Maccadamnus.
Verse CXXVI

'WHAT WAS THAT?' said Frederick with a sniff, plucking a thick clot of blood from his nose.

'What?'

'I thought I heard something.'

He leant unsteadily on the shattered doorframe, still weak from the fight, and looked up and down the street. Like most of the city, it had seen better days. The colourful stalls of Hauptmarktstrasse's famous market were long gone. All that remained were a few pitiful-looking shreds of awning hanging from the blackened timbers.

'I can't hear nuthin',' Otto replied from within, straining and huffing as he tried to shift the corpse.

'Leave that for a minute, you idiot. I heard something.' He squinted, trying to see through the perpetual gloom, but his head was still spinning from the blow that had shattered his nasal bone and the darkness seemed sickeningly animated. 'Sigmar,' he muttered under his breath, 'Who am I kidding? If there is anything out there, I'd rather not know.' He lowered his lantern with a shudder. 'Probably nothing,' he called out, but the tremor in his voice betrayed him and, as he stepped back into the theatre, Otto eyed him suspiciously.

The impressive bulk of the creature still lay sprawled across the stage with a stream of blood flowing slowly from its monstrous head.

'Haven't you moved it yet?'

'Maybe if you helped,' gasped Otto as he attempted to turn the body over with a broken rafter.

Frederick ignored the request and shook his head slowly. 'Have you looked at the thing? Where else could spawn such a horror? Is it man… or beast?' He knelt to examine it closer. The massive, pockmarked body was vaguely human in shape, but the grotesque head was almost completely bovine. Gnarled horns twisted from beneath its matted scalp and where its feet should have been there were two huge, battered hooves. Frederick studied the body for a few moments in silence, then laughed suddenly, kicking a lifeless arm that jutted out from beneath it. 'Reinhard may have been a worthless layabout, but I've got to give him credit where it's due. I thought we'd met our match, but he showed it. That blow to the head must have killed it. What a catch!'

Otto turned and grasped him roughly by his jacket, his eyes feverish. 'If we don't go soon we'll be the catch.' He looked around at the ruined theatre. Rows of charred stalls and boxes reared up all around them, reaching out of the darkness like claws towards the vaulted ceiling of the amphitheatre. The heat of the cataclysm had warped the furniture into a tableau of sinister shapes and Otto had the unnerving feeling that not all of the seats were empty. 'We need to take what we came for and get out of here, before…' he paused to scratch nervously at his scalp, 'well, before anything happens.'

'All right, all right,' Frederick replied in a soothing voice, patting Otto gently on the shoulder, 'let's shift this brute then.' They grasped the monster by its broad shoulders. 'On the count of three: one, two, three.' There was an exhalation of stale breath as they rolled the beast off the flattened remains of their former partner.

'That,' said Frederick, stooping down beside the creature's face, 'is beautiful.'

Otto knelt down beside him with a sigh of pleasure and clapped his hands together like a child.

Hanging around the thing's neck was a stone – about the size of a plum, and glowing faintly with an inner fire. Frederick's eyes widened as he stretched a trembling hand out towards it. 'After weeks of crawling around this stinking nightmare of a city, we finally have it. A piece of weirdstone. Can you believe it Otto?' Then his hand froze, and his voice dropped to a whisper. 'You must have heard it that time,' he said, looking back towards the door.

Otto didn't reply, but nodded his head slowly, and as he followed Frederick out onto the street the colour was draining from his face.

'There,' Frederick said with a note of panic in his voice, 'what's that?' As they watched with growing horror, a shadow across the street elongated, split into three and moved slowly towards them.

They readied their weapons and Otto stepped nervously back towards the theatre. 'What is it?'

As the shadows moved nearer, they gradually solidified until the men saw that they were actually three hooded women – draped with chains and spikes – but women nonetheless. 'Thank Sigmar,' said Frederick, exhaling with relief and lowering his sword. He began to laugh. 'Now what have we found?'

'Absolution,' replied the woman nearest to him, and slammed a two-handed warhammer into his face.

Frederick's head snapped backwards with a click, and he dropped heavily to the ground.

Otto stood, frozen with shock, then howled with pain as a steel whip licked across his face. His eyes ran down his cheeks like tears and an agonising blackness engulfed him.

'I'll pray for you,' said a soft voice in his ear, as a quick blade at his throat finally released him from the City of the Damned.

'Gutless worms,' said novice sister Wolff, spitting on one of the dead mercenaries. 'I won't pray for them.'

Von Stahl looked over at the young girl. Beneath her hood, her pale aristocratic features could just be seen, and as she rifled through the corpse's pockets her face was twisted in a sneer of disdain.

'They barely seem worth the effort,' – Wolff gave up her search with a sigh – 'and they don't have so much as a speck of weirdstone on them.'

'You didn't seem to think them so gutless a minute ago,' said von Stahl quietly.

'What do you mean by that?' replied Wolff.

The third woman – novice sister Elsbeth Faust – stifled a laugh.

'Well, you seemed happy for me and Elsbeth to waste our energies on them, but I couldn't seem to spot you when the fighting started.'

'Fight? I'd hardly call that a fight.' Wolff's eyes were wide with emotion as she stepped towards von Stahl. 'If you want to waste yourself on such worthless prey as this' – she spat on the corpses again – 'then go ahead, but I haven't forgotten why we're here. There is the small matter of a trial to be considered.' Her face was now almost purple. 'Anyway, how dare you accuse me of cowardice? Remember your place, wastrel.'

Von Stahl winced at the nickname. Few dared to use it since she'd reached adulthood, but it still had the power to hurt. 'I'm not accusing you,' she snapped, wiping the mercenary's teeth from her warhammer, 'and I haven't forgotten the trial. Didn't you listen to their conversation? They've found something' – she gestured over towards the ruined grandeur of the theatre – 'over in the Magdeburg Playhouse.'

Stepping into the theatre was like stepping into a fractured mirror of the past. Broken marionettes lay scattered across the stage and faded, peeling faces smiled sadly down from the shattered balconies.

'I came here as a child,' said Elsbeth as they picked their way through the wreckage, 'to hear Giotto Vasari. It was beautiful. I remember–'

Von Stahl silenced her with a wave of the hand. They carried no torches and the darkness was almost complete, but she thought she could see movement on the stage. As they crept silently through the shadows, each taking a different path through the stalls, von Stahl noticed Wolff nervously lagging behind again and frowned. Is she ready for this, she wondered?

The dusty boards creaked loudly as they stepped out onto the stage, and von Stahl winced at the noise. Then she stooped to examine something. Sprawled before the broken footlights lay the corpse of a man. 'Look,' she said, 'he seems to have been crushed somehow.' Wolff and Faust crouched next to her. 'It's as though a great weight has fallen on him.' She prodded his chest with a grimace. 'His bones have been completely destroyed.'

'It's another Marienburger,' whispered Wolff, noting the man's flamboyant outfit. 'More gold than sense, the lot of 'em.'

Von Stahl raised her eyebrows.

'What?' replied Wolff, raising her voice a little and blushing again, 'a blood-tie to Lady Magritte doesn't lower me to the level of these dandies.'

Von Stahl ignored the petulant tone in her voice, and simply put a finger to her mouth. 'Look,' she whispered and gestured to the area of stage next to the body. 'Something was there. The dust has been disturbed. And all that blood didn't come from our friend here.'

With a growing sense of unease they rose to their feet – as they all saw a trail of blood that led towards the back of the stage. Wolff tightened her gromril armour and stepped closer to Elsbeth.

'What did the dandies find, I wonder?' said von Stahl, throwing back her hood and straining to see through the dark.

Wolff's voice sounded uneven as she pointed towards the curtains. 'Is that… what is that?' In front of the tattered velvet, there was an area of darkness even more intense than the surrounding gloom – a tower of shadow that seemed too solid to be a mere play of the light. For a few seconds no one spoke, as they tried to discern the outline of the large shape.

Slowly, as her eyes grew accustomed to the pitch dark, von Stahl made out a monstrous face, glowering down at them. 'Sigmar preserve us, it's–'

Before she could finish, the stage exploded as a huge beast stepped forward and ripped the floorboards from beneath their feet – hurling the three novices in different directions and sending von Stahl's hammer flying from her fingers.

Von Stahl landed heavily in the pit, momentarily winded and powerless as the creature lunged towards her. It was fifteen feet tall, covered with matted greasy fur and bore a look of such malevolence that she found it impossible to meet its blazing red eyes.

'Wolff,' she gasped, 'wait,' but the terrified girl didn't even look back as she fled from the building. Von Stahl's heart sank as she realised that she and Elsbeth would have to face the creature alone. She rolled to one side as a hoof the size of a small cart crashed down beside her.

Still incapable of breathing, she staggered away through the tiered stalls, trying to gain herself a few seconds to catch her breath.

To her surprise, the beast didn't follow, but instead gave out a deafening roar of frustration and grasped desperately at its throat. Elsbeth had climbed up the shreds of curtain and leapt down onto its back, from where she was now proceeding to throttle it with her steel whip.

As the monster careered back and forth, howling with rage at its inability to free itself from Elsbeth's grip, von Stahl searched desperately amongst the seats for her hammer. It was nowhere to be found and as Elsbeth's cries for assistance grew more desperate, she realised she would have to find another weapon. She grabbed an ornamental sword from the wall and tested its blade. She cursed – it was nothing but a rusty prop.

'Blessed Sigmar, help,' cried Elsbeth as the maddened beast span around the theatre, smashing furiously against the already unstable walls.

Von Stahl had no choice. She could hear the frame of the building groaning each time the beast slammed against it – the whole structure sounded like it was about to come down. Clutching the blunt weapon she rushed to help.

By the time she reached it, the creature was in such a frenzy of rage and asphyxiation that she was afraid she wouldn't be able to get its attention. Its bestial face had taken on a deep purple hue as Elsbeth's whip bit deeply into its thick neck. A mixture of spittle and blood ran freely from its gaping jaws. After being repeatedly slammed against the walls of the theatre, Elsbeth looked like a broken doll hanging from beneath the beast's filthy mane.

Von Stahl cried out to the monster from across the stage, waving her pitiful weapon defiantly at it. It whirled around and rooted her to the spot with a withering stare. With a bellow of rage, it threw its massive frame towards her and von Stahl screamed back in defiance and terror.

As she had hoped, it never reached her. In its anger, it overlooked the hole it had torn through the floorboards and crashed through the stage – skewering itself on the jagged planks with a thunderous howl.

An even greater fury now consumed it. It had sunk waist-deep into the floor and one of the planks was deeply embedded beneath its ribs, pinning it to the spot. However much it howled and thrashed about it couldn't free itself, and every twist increased the flow of blood from its torso.

Von Stahl dropped weakly to her knees and watched the monster's fury as it gradually ripped itself to pieces on the jagged planks. Soon, the whole stage was slick with blood and with each lunge its struggles grew weaker. Finally, with a gurgled bark of rage, it fell forward onto its chin and lay still.

Silence descended on the theatre, and for a few moments von Stahl lay motionless on the stage, her eyes closed. Then she sat bolt upright. 'Elsbeth,' she said in a hoarse voice. 'Are you there?'

'I think so,' came a weak reply from out of the darkness, 'although maybe not for much longer.'

Von Stahl climbed to her feet, and trod carefully up to the dead creature. Its chest was still, but just to be sure she took her blunt blade, and with all her strength, thrust it deep into the thing's throat. 'Nothing,' she whispered. 'Dead.' Only then, as she was about to walk away, did she notice the stone around its neck. 'Oh, Sigmar. Weirdstone... and the size of my fist.'

A weak cough reminded her of Elsbeth.

'We've done it,' she cried, rushing to her fellow novice. 'We've got a piece of the stone. One of us at least has passed the trial.'

'Not me,' said Elsbeth, grinning through bloody teeth. 'I think this is my last performance.'

Von Stahl saw with a jolt that the girl was dying. Her face was almost white from blood loss, and her body was as twisted and broken as the marionettes that lay around her.

'Elsbeth,' said von Stahl, taking her hand. She tried to think of something to say but the words caught in her throat, and she simply hung her head.

'You have a piece of the stone,' said Elsbeth, after a few moments, trying to smile through the pain. 'You've passed the test – they'll let you back into the abbey, and you'll be ordained as a fully-fledged sister. This is a good day, Virtue. You'll be a novice no more.'

For a few moments von Stahl was unable to speak. Her fellow sisters were her only family and to watch Elsbeth slipping away before her eyes was almost more than she could bear. 'I can't return without Wolff,' she said eventually, hardly aware of what she was saying but desperate to break the awful silence. 'I must try and find her. Maybe together we can find a second shard and both pass the trial.'

Elsbeth grabbed von Stahl firmly by the arms and pulled her close. 'Leave her,' she hissed. 'She's no good! Take the stone and return without her.'

'I can't.'

'You must!' Elsbeth groaned and dropped back to the floor. 'She should never have been inducted into the order. Matriarch Ebner was just too scared to offend Lady Magritte, otherwise Wolff wouldn't even be a novice.'

'But I can't just desert her. I can't just leave her out here – alone in the city.'

'Take the stone back to the abbey and leave her to her fate. It's all she deserves. Don't die a novice like me just to save her worthless hide.'

'But what of my vows – how can I just desert a fellow sister? I know what she is, but she's still a member of our order. I can't just–'

'She betrayed us! If she had stayed to fight–' Elsbeth's voice caught with emotion. 'Well… who knows, but she's not worth a single drop of your blood.' She dug her fingers deep into von Stahl's arm. 'Promise me you won't go after her.'

Von Stahl shook her head sadly, but could think of nothing else to say and a short while later, Elsbeth passed away. She prepared the body according to the rituals of her order and laid it out on a makeshift pyre of scenery and curtains. As flames lit up the stage of the Magdeburg Playhouse for the last time, she snapped the stone from around the creature's neck and dropped it carefully into a small pouch around her own neck. Then, with a final bow to the blazing pyre, she took Elsbeth's whip and slipped out into the darkness.

NOVICE SISTER WOLFF grimaced as she crept along the crumbling rooftops. However much she tried, it was impossible to ignore the thick, slightly sweet smell of death. She pulled her hood tighter around her face in an attempt to block out the stench, but Mordheim's acrid stink had a way of seeping into your skin. She paused, sensing movement in the streets below, and crouched low on the shattered lintel of a long gone window to listen. She picked out a sound, so faint that she thought she had imagined it, but gradually growing louder. It was a kind of undulating wail, drifting up towards her. Music maybe, she thought, or was it screaming? As the minutes passed, she realised that it wasn't one sound but many, emanating from several different directions. With growing horror, she realised that a symphony of howls and moans was floating towards her out of the dark. She shifted her position slightly and, using her steel whip as leverage, she leant out from the ruined window frame to peer down into the streets below.

The sight that greeted her turned her stomach. As a novice she had ventured into the city before, but only in the company of a matriarch, and never far from the safety of the sisters' fortress abbey. Until now, she had largely been spared the full horror of Mordheim's inhabitants, but here they were in all their awful glory. A tightly-packed crowd was shuffling towards her and to Wolff's amazement it seemed to be some kind of grotesque carnival. The light of hundreds of torches punctuated the narrow, winding streets, and a cacophony of drums, bells and whistles echoed discordantly across the plazas and gardens. 'What are they?' she whispered as her pulse quickened with fear. The figures marching towards her were torn from a lunatic's worst nightmare: she saw men whose faces were in their bellies; men with the bodies of animals; women with serpents for limbs; people whose pulsating viscera lay outside their skins; every possible perversion and permutation of human flesh was crawling and sliding slowly towards her. 'Blessed Sigmar, save me,' she said, feeling hot tears forming in her eyes. 'Save me from the damned.'

She climbed back through the broken window into the remains of a small chapel. 'What am I to do?' she said, collapsing to the floor and curling into a foetal position. 'How can I pass the trial now? Without a piece of weirdstone I can never become a sister,' – a sickening thrill of adrenaline rushed through her – 'and I can never return to the abbey.' Great sobs began to shake her body. 'Oh, why did von Stahl have to take us into that cursed theatre? She has killed me. She has killed us all.'

She might have lain there, weeping quietly, until the horde of lost souls finally discovered her, but to her dismay she realised that the approaching crowd was not her only problem. Sounds were coming from just below her, within the chapel.

She pressed her ear to the floor to listen. A pompous heavily-accented voice was talking: '–to the west?' it said. 'What do you expect to find that way? The rat-things came from the quayside, you oaf. Are you really so keen to be more intimately acquainted with them?'

'We need to go somewhere,' replied another voice. 'If we reach the river we might find a merchant's barge and head south – past the sisters' rock and out through the South Gate.'

'Ah, that delightful waterway, the Stir. What a haven of peace and tranquillity that will be. Maybe we could stop for lunch somewhere – perhaps with that wonderfully fragrant family we met in the cemetery, or those quaint creatures we discovered in the Executioner's Square. Remember, the ones who seemed so interested in our stone?'

At the word 'stone', Wolff's eyes widened.

'Listen,' cried the increasingly desperate voice. 'That mob will be here any minute.' Wolff realised that he was right, the hideous chorus was growing louder. It could only be a few streets away. 'If we don't move now, we're dead anyway. What choice do we have?'

A note of resignation now filled the first voice. 'What possessed me to follow you into this festering pit of a city?'

'But it was your idea, sire. I was just–'

There was a loud crack, followed by a whimper of pain. 'Now,' said the pompous voice, 'take me to this blessed river, and kindly refrain from speaking. If I could have even a few moments' respite from your whinging, I might even survive this absurd expedition.'

Wolff heard the sound of equipment being hastily packed and felt a sudden panic. Using all the skills she had developed during her training, she crawled silently across the chapel's dusty attic and peered carefully down through a hole in the floorboards.

Fortunately, the men had their backs to her. In fact, they were already climbing out through a crumbling window and down onto the street. As she watched them, Wolff could easily identify which figure belonged to which voice. One was a tall, distinguished-looking foreigner, wearing a suit of polished plate armour, a brightly-plumed helmet and a shield bearing a colourful chalice motif. How has he survived more than a day, she thought incredulously, in such a gaudy and noisy outfit?

The other figure seemed little more than a human carthorse. He was squat, ugly, dressed in filthy rags, and laden with dozens of bags and weapons – including, she noted with bemusement, a jousting lance.

As the men dropped from sight, Wolff lowered herself cautiously down into the room they had just vacated. She rushed to the broken window just in time to see the gaily-plumed knight and his servant disappear up an alleyway. She hopped out onto the street, and sped after them. That feathered ponce can't survive much longer dressed like that, she thought, and the fat one wouldn't put up much of a fight. If there was some way of separating the two, it would be a simple task to get the stone from the servant.

Images of a triumphant return to the abbey suddenly filled Wolff's thoughts. Then the sound of the approaching mob interrupted her thoughts and, with a nervous glance over her shoulder, she picked up her pace.

VIRTUE SPED THROUGH the dark narrow streets, all sense of caution abandoned as she raced across the gloomy squares and scrambled noisily over the crumbling ruins. The novice did not go unnoticed. As she passed beneath the crooked townhouses, indistinct figures peered down at her through filthy windows, while others shuffled awkwardly from doorways in slow pursuit.

'Where are you, girl?' she gasped, finally coming to a stop outside a large fenced garden. Her training had led her this far – a footprint here and a piece of robe there had been enough to signpost Wolff's route, but now she was at a loss. 'Where are you heading?' Shaking her head in frustration she began to clamber up the warped, rusted iron of the garden fence, in the hope a better vantage point might give her some clues.

She tried to clear her thoughts and imagine what her fellow novice might do. The girl's flight from the theatre had confirmed her cowardice: Elsbeth's accusations had all been true. So what would she do now? She'll head back to the monastery, decided Virtue, but which way? With a final heave, she swung her leg over the top of the fence and looked out across the wretched pall of the city. 'Why has she been heading west?' she asked, as though the ruins themselves might reply. 'Why head further into the merchants' quart...' She laughed grimly. Mordheim looked more shadow than fact, more like a ghost of a city than real bricks and mortar, but deep in the heart of its dark twisted spires and fallen masonry, she glimpsed light: the dull flickering of water, snaking south, back towards the Rock. Back towards home. 'Of course,' she breathed. 'She's headed for the Stir.'

THE CLANKING OF the knight's armour was almost as loud as his booming voice, and it was all too easy to follow the pair through the dark side streets of the merchants' quarter. In just a matter of minutes they had reached the river's edge. 'Ah, here we are… the Stir,' exclaimed the knight, picking his way carefully through the rubble. 'How picturesque.'

From her vantage point on the roof of an old tavern, Wolff could see the two men as they stepped out onto the quayside. The broad river that lay before them had once teemed with barges, laden with exotic goods from across the Old World, but now it was a pitiful sight. Most of the wharves had crumbled into the ink-black water, and the warehouses and taverns that lined the water's edge were all empty and dark – shadowy reminders of the city's former glory. Everything she knew about this foul expanse told her that it was not a place to loiter, and she fidgeted nervously as the knight stamped noisily up and down a wharf, complaining loudly to his servant.

'Fools,' she hissed, 'don't bring every fiend in the city down on your heads.' As she crept cautiously towards them however, Wolff realised she wasn't exactly sure what she did want them to do. Wasn't she hoping that they would call attention to themselves? If not, how could she get her hands on their stone? Did she dare to face them in open combat? For all his ridiculous posturing, she had a suspicion that the knight would be a fierce opponent. 'Curse you, von Stahl, for putting me in this position', she whispered. Still, at least she was alive – it seemed unlikely that her companions could have escaped from that horror in the Magdeburg Playhouse.

As these thoughts played through her head, she barely noticed that she had crept silently out onto the shadowy wharf, and was now only a few feet away from the two men. She stopped with a start, just short of the light of the servant's lamp.

'I think we could climb down to the boat,' she heard him say as he leant out over the water. 'There are still a few steps left intact.'

The knight dealt his servant a sharp clip to the ear that almost knocked him into the water. 'You think I'm crawling down there like some kind of navvy?' He hammered his fist noisily against the metal of his delicately engraved breastplate. 'This is no bathing suit, Diderot. If I fall into that filth I'll be picking trout out of my teeth for all eternity. Or whatever monster passes for trout in this city.'

'But, sire, I'll help you down. It's only a few steps and I'll–'

The knight dealt him another stinging blow to the ear. 'Stop speaking!'

The servant looked at his feet and waited in silence as the knight glowered down at his bald pate.

'Good,' said the knight after a few moments. 'Now let's get down into this dingy. Take my hand, oaf.'

The servant leapt to obey, and carefully began to lower the heavily-armoured knight off the edge of the rickety pier.

A broad smile spread across Wolff's face as she saw her chance.

Drawing a knife from within her robes, she stepped calmly towards the two struggling men.

'What are you doing?' cried the knight as his servant suddenly loosed his hand and sent him plummeting towards the water. Diderot's only reply was a dark bubble of blood that rose from his mouth as he fell backwards onto the wharf.

'Confound it all,' said the knight as he crashed through the surface of the Stir and sank like a stone towards the riverbed.

Diderot thrashed around on the rotten wood of the pier, trying to free Wolff's knife from his back. 'Witch,' he gasped, glaring up at her. 'You don't know what you've done! That was Ambrose of Mousillon!' To her amazement he began to crawl towards the edge of the pier, with the blade still embedded in his back. 'He'll be drowned. We must save him!'

'Why do you care?' she asked, laughing, 'I've just freed you from a tyrant, and you're cursing me. You should thank me.' She stooped down and yanked her knife from between his shoulder blades. He grew rigid with pain, and then flopped weakly onto the pier. 'Don't die,' she hissed, flipping him over onto his back. 'Tell me where the stone is.'

The man's eyes were already glazing over, but he managed to focus on her for a second. 'Stone?' he gurgled through a blood-filled mouth. 'What stone?'

'Don't play the fool. I've been following you. I know you have a stone – the one you almost lost in the Executioner's Square, remember?'

Recognition crossed his anguished face. 'Oh,' he muttered, 'that's what you want.'

'Yes, you moron, give me the stone!'

The man shook his head defiantly at her for a few seconds, then made a pitiful attempt to throw one of his bags off the pier. It landed just a couple of feet away and Wolff laughed again. She turned away from the dying man and picked it up. As Diderot continued to curse her, she plucked a stone from out of his bag. 'I've done it,' she said, holding up Diderot's lamp to examine her prize closer, 'I've got a piece of…' – she grimaced – 'What's this?' In the light of the lamp, she saw that the stone was a beautiful blood-red ruby. 'What's this?' she exclaimed again, grabbing the servant by his filthy jerkin, but he was dead and the face she was screaming into was already growing cold. She threw him back to the floor with a howl of frustration.

'MOVE, YOU IDIOT,' hissed von Stahl as she crept towards the water's edge. 'Don't just stand there, out in the open.'

She had begun to think her skills as a tracker had led her astray, but there was no mistaking the figure on the pier – it was Wolff. The young novice could clearly be seen ranting and shouting at a corpse. Von Stahl grimaced. With every cry and petulant stamp of the foot, Wolff was drawing unwanted attention to herself. The girl was obviously so consumed by rage that she hadn't noticed the vague, sinister shapes congregating at the foot of the pier.

'Sweet Sigmar, what are they?' whispered von Stahl as she slipped carefully out from a doorway. It was hard to see clearly in the dark, but whatever the creatures were, they had a lank, unwholesome appearance that chilled her blood. She remembered Elsbeth's last words and paused. Should I just leave? she wondered as she watched the figures crawl towards Wolff. No one would know, she thought, clutching the stone around her neck. I could just leave her and take the weirdstone back to the abbey. Relief washed over her as she turned and began to jog back towards the burnt-out warehouses. She betrayed me first, she thought, so why should I die for her?

A hideous scream echoed out across the river and brought her to a halt. She looked back to see that the creatures had now stepped out onto the pier and were forming a loose circle around Wolff, who, having finally seen them, was wailing with terror. Von Stahl made the sign of the hammer. She saw now that they were ratmen: foul oversized rodents, dripping with river slime and wielding long, jagged blades. As she looked on in horror, the largest stepped forward and clubbed the screaming Wolff to the ground with the back of his hand. Von Stahl gasped with revulsion as the creatures crowded hungrily around her fellow novice. With a rush of indignation, she realised that she couldn't leave anyone to such an awful fate. She began to run back towards the pier.

As she ran she called out to the ratmen, trying to gain Wolff a few seconds to escape. As one, they span towards her with their long yellow teeth bared. Their greasy snouts twitched as they sniffed new blood and several began skulking towards her.

Wolff had regained her senses though, and while their backs were turned, she smashed Diderot's lamp over the largest of the creatures and then leapt over the edge of the pier.

The lamp's oil exploded spectacularly over the rodent's greasy fur and by the time von Stahl had reached the foot of the pier the ratmen were screaming in dismay. The agonies of their leader distracted them completely and by the time they'd remembered von Stahl's presence, three of them had fallen to her steel whip.

The surviving creatures were in a frenzy of indecision, unsure whether to defend themselves against von Stahl, pursue Wolff or help their screaming leader. As they lurched around in confusion, von Stahl's steel whip continued to lash back and forth, knocking one of them to its knees and sending another two flying into the river.

A glimmer of hope rose in her mind. There were now only three of the creatures left standing – including the largest, who surely couldn't survive the flames much longer. Then, to her joy, the burning creature leapt from the pier, leaving her with only two remaining opponents.

She readied herself for their attacks, but the loss of their leader had unnerved them and as soon as von Stahl raised her whip for another blow, they turned tail and dived headlong into the river.

She stood for a few moments in dazed incomprehension. The whole fight had only lasted a few seconds and her adrenaline-charged body remained tensed for battle, waiting for another opponent, but none came.

Another scream echoed across the water.

Von Stahl looked over the edge of the pier. Down below, in a small boat, lay Wolff. Looming over her, still steaming and smouldering from the fire, was the largest of the ratmen. Large patches of its fur had been scorched away, and the thing was obviously dazed with pain, but its eyes still burned with bloodlust.

'Virtue,' called the novice, as she tried to fend off the hideous creature, 'for the love of Sigmar, help me.'

The rat pulled a long, ceremonial dagger from out of its robes and began lunging clumsily at Wolff as she wormed this way and that, trying to avoid the blows.

Even in its confused state, Wolff couldn't evade the creature for long in so small a space, so von Stahl took the only available option and leapt feet-first from the pier.

It was a drop of twelve feet or more and as she landed heavily in the boat, she cried out in pain and fell to her knees. Her left ankle had snapped like an old twig and her foot had folded back at an unnatural angle.

Her heroics were not completely wasted though. The impact of her landing had rocked the boat so violently that the creature fell sprawling onto its face. Simultaneously the two novices clambered onto its smouldering back and began to rain blows down upon it.

'Thank Sigmar,' gasped Wolff, as they pummelled the struggling beast. 'I thought you were dead.'

'Not yet,' replied von Stahl, trying to ignore the wrenching agony in her ankle, 'and we're halfway to passing the trial.'

Wolff paused, mid-punch. 'What do you mean?'

Von Stahl smiled and tapped the pouch at her throat. 'The thing in the theatre wore some interesting jewellery.'

Wolff remained frozen in shock as she tried to take on board the news. 'You mean you have–'

The creature suddenly rose to its feet and shrugged them off its back, as easily as if they were children.

Wolff shrieked with fear and began to clamber up the pier's rotten struts.

Von Stahl tried to follow, but white-hot pain ripped through her ankle and she fell to her knees once more. Then a terrible whistling noise exploded in her left ear and the world went black. When she came to, she was lying on her side with warm blood rushing from the side of her face where the beast had struck her. She looked up to see him raising his ornate dagger over her head.

With her last reserves of strength she rolled out of the way and the dagger plunged harmlessly into the keel of the boat. Then, holding back tears of pain, she clambered to her feet. As the creature struggled to retrieve his blade, she began to climb up the side of the pier.

'Quick,' gasped Wolff from above, reaching down to her. 'Give me your hand.'

With agonising slowness she climbed up the rotten pier. Then, just as she was about to grasp Wolff's hand, she felt a new pain explode in her leg. She looked down to see the foul creature leering with pleasure at the sight of his cruel blade embedded deeply in her calf. She gave an animal howl of pain.

'Reach for me,' cried Wolff desperately. 'You can still make it.'

Delirious with pain, von Stahl gave one last lunge for Wolff's hand and finally grasped it.

Wolff gave a powerful tug and dragged her up until she was almost at the top of the pier.

Virtue looked into Wolff's face and felt a tide of relief rushing over her. 'Wolff,' she said, 'you've saved us both.'

'Well,' said Wolff with a crooked smile as she plucked the small pouch from around von Stahl's neck and loosed her hand, 'maybe not both of us, wastrel.'

'What?' stammered von Stahl in confusion, but Wolff would say no more. She simply stood up, dusted herself down and ran back towards the quayside, leaving von Stahl clinging helplessly to the edge of the pier.

Pain and despair washed over her and with a sigh of misery she felt her fingers begin to slip from the damp wood.

COLD, HARD FINGERS pressed painfully into von Stahl's arms and she awoke.

'Virtue,' whispered a voice. 'It's time'.

She opened her eyes to see an old woman's careworn face leaning over her. She recognised the kind rheumy eyes and the steel-grey hair, but she couldn't place the woman.

'Who are you?' she asked croakily.

The old woman laughed gently, and stroked her hair. 'Who am I, she says! You know who I am, Virtue. Matriarch Margareta Ebner. I practically reared you, child.'

The name triggered a confused jumble of memories in von Stahl's drowsy mind. A kaleidoscope of violent images filtered through the remnants of her quickly fading dreams and the heavy scent of herbs that filled the room. She looked around in confusion and saw that she was lying in an infirmary. At the foot of the bed there was a small leaded window and beyond it a wide grassy cloister, filled with fountains and fishponds. Hooded figures could be seen, sat alone in quiet contemplation or talking in small groups. She could hardly believe her eyes. It was the Holy Convent. She was home.

'I was on a trial,' she said, frowning with concentration.

The Matriarch nodded encouragingly.

'The trial of Ordination. I had to find a piece of weirdstone to become a fully-fledged sister, or–'

'Or be banished from the order,' said the Matriarch, nodding.

Fear quickened von Stahl's pulse as she remembered how miserably she had failed. She saw Elsbeth's pitiful funeral pyre in the Magdeburg Playhouse. She saw Wolff's cruel mocking eyes as she stole the stone from around her neck and left her to die. Then, with a grimace, she remembered falling back into the boat, and struggling desperately with the rat-creature. She buried her face in her hands and groaned. 'How am I here? I failed the test. I have no weirdstone. How is that you have allowed me back into the abbey?'

The Matriarch was about to reply, but then paused, distracted by the sound of approaching footsteps. 'I think you have your first visitor,' she said.

The door flew open and, to von Stahl's horror, Wolff burst into the room. Disbelief drained the colour from both girl's faces and each was momentarily at a loss for words. Then, recovering her composure a little, Wolff flew to von Stahl's bedside, dropped to her knees and hugged her tightly. 'Oh, Virtue, can it be true? Have you really returned to us?'

Anger welled up in von Stahl, and she struggled to free herself from the girl's grip, but Wolff wouldn't let go. She spoke quickly. 'I thought you had perished at the hands of that foul creature in the theatre. I never dreamt you were still alive.'

Disgust and hatred filled von Stahl, but she couldn't manage to interrupt the girl's torrent of false concern.

'I have been distraught thinking of you and Elsbeth. If it were not for the comforting words of the High Matriarch, I believe I would have lost my mind with grief.'

At the words 'High Matriarch', Wolff looked meaningfully at von Stahl, and squeezed her a little tighter.

The message was clear, and von Stahl's heart sank. To receive words of comfort from the High Matriarch herself was a reminder of Wolff's honoured position within the order. As a blood relative of the sisters' most invaluable patron, Lady Magritte, Wolff had a special place in the High Matriarch's heart, and if a lowly foundling like von Stahl were to accuse her of treachery, the claims would be dismissed out-of-hand as madness... or heresy.

Realising the futility of her position, von Stahl gave Wolff no reply and simply slumped back weakly into her pillow.

Wolff's eyes lit up as she saw that she had been understood. Then, assuming once more an expression of concern, she turned to matriarch Ebner and said. 'But what of the trial? Without a piece of the weirdstone she has failed, and cannot be ordained.' With the ease of a practiced liar she squeezed a few tears from her eyes. 'Which must surely mean that she will be banished from the order and sent back,' she gulped, 'into the city.'

Von Stahl put a hand to her mouth to stifle a sob. Wolff was right. She had failed, and must now be banished, alone in the City of the Damned. The best she could hope for was a quick death at the hands of whichever of Mordheim's terrible inhabitants found her first.

'It seems so cruel,' said Wolff, forcing more tears from her eyes, 'that she has managed to return to us only to be sent away again,' she looked searchingly at Matriarch Ebner, 'but I presume there is no alternative?'

The old woman looked carefully at Wolff. There was something strange in the girl's manner, but she couldn't quite put her finger on it. 'Well,' she said, ignoring Wolff, and taking von Stahl's hand, 'it seems that Sigmar has his eye on you, Virtue. You must have fought bravely indeed. When Sister Schönau plucked you from the river, you were half-gutted. The boat you were drifting in was drenched with blood. Some was yours but luckily there was much more from whatever you had been fighting.'

As the Matriarch spoke, images of the fight returned to von Stahl. She remembered how her rage at Wolff's betrayal had given her renewed strength. She had fought furiously with the rat-creature as the small boat drifted slowly south down the Stir. With its blade stuck deep in her leg her opponent had found itself unarmed and after a merciless storm of blows from her steel whip, it had finally dived back into the river, leaving her weak and bleeding in the boat.

'I remember defeating that... that vermin, but then nothing.' She looked up desperately at the matriarch. 'And I have no stone. I have failed.'

The old woman rose from her chair, and fetched something from a small table beneath the window. She handed it to von Stahl with a smile. 'When sister Schönau pulled you from the boat, she had to remove this from your leg.'

Von Stahl looked at the long sacrificial knife. She remembered with a shudder the leer on the creature's face as it thrust the blade into her leg. Then, a dawning realisation washed over her and she smiled back at the matriarch.

'What is it?' demanded Wolff, snatching the blade from her. 'Just a knife? What's so special about that?'

Von Stahl continued to smile as she pointed towards a small dark stone embedded the blade's hilt. 'Weirdstone,' she said.

CHARANDIS

Ben McCallum

I

PREY, DRUNK AND foolish, blundered onward, oblivious and uncaring.

The scent stung his wet nostrils, sinking hooks into his brain, flaring his bloody instincts. He could taste the blood that ran in their veins even from this distance, a coppery tang that made his lolling tongue ache, and sang up the length of his killing fangs.

Each step he took betrayed a burning hunger that physically hurt. Claws that were too long slid in and out of his monstrous paws with a lethality he had forgotten how to control. They itched so incessantly, so furiously, with pain that echoed up limbs swollen by the anger that had plagued him for so long.

Thick ropes of sour drool swung from his open maw as he moved, his lethal bulk passing soundlessly through a woodland that had been blessed by rain only a few hours ago. Water was no longer a relief to him. Each raindrop that fell from the leaves of whispering trees sent spikes of migraine-fierce pain through his leonine skull. A pelt that was once the pearly white of pure moonlight felt heavy on his back, soaked with cold rainwater and caked with a thousand kinds of filth.

He quickened his pace, his loping gait lengthening into a staggering gallop. The prey-scent intensified, and his nose burned in sympathy. He was close enough to hear the breath in their lungs, and smell the stinging reek of alcohol sweating through their pores.

Other smells clung to them, too; scents he dimly remembered as city-smells, laden with the promise of glittering spear tips and baying horns.

251

There was a time when he would have shrunk from this scent in favour of softer, less dangerous prey. But now the anger wouldn't let him. The anger burned in his guts and banished his instincts, compelling him to drown his pain in the hot rush of the kill.

They were making noises, now. Elf-speech whispered under the trees, their voices softened by the wine that had compelled them to journey out here. The sound lanced into his mind, firing a predator-rage he once knew how to contain. This was wrong. This was not how he was supposed to hunt.

His quarry stopped, and the low murmur of their soft voices began to grow louder. This prey was not as lethal as the other elf-creatures that moved through the woods like ghosts, but he was not blind to the danger of the metal that gleamed in their slender hands.

Slowly, agonisingly, he prowled forward, even as the unkind rage knifed arcs of pain into his bleary eyes and screamed at him to lunge.

When the moment was right, it would be satisfied.

'A CHRACIAN MYTH,' Darath said through smiling lips, his thin arms spreading in an expansive gesture. 'That is all this is, my friends.'

He spoke the words in the sing-song accent of the Lothern aristocracy, his diction flawless. The bleariness of his dark eyes betrayed his drunkenness.

'Hundreds dead?' Nesselan slurred, announcing every glass of wine he had put away today. 'This is no myth, Darath. There is a terror loose.'

'There is no terror here in this Chracian wilderness,' Darath snapped, the wine fouling his temper. 'You are a fool to believe so. We are all fools for coming here, through the rain and the wind, hunting for a ghost that does not exist.'

Darath's sculpted cheekbones flushed red. Here, in these woods, even as the sun edged ever closer to the distant horizon, he wanted to strike Nesselan. The fool was bleeding the fun from this journey with every word that passed his lips. He had never met an elf so negative in all his days.

Thyran tried and failed to banish the tension with a false laugh.

'These woodsmen are not liars,' Nesselan said, crouching low and pressing his fingers to the damp earth, as if this somehow proved the truth of his words. 'Hundreds, this ghost of yours has claimed over the years. I swear to you, by Asuryan's blood, that this beast is real.'

Darath knew he believed those words. Only hours ago, as they strode into the woodland of mighty Chrace, they had been warned off the trail by unwashed, uncouth locals. A great beast, they claimed, was skulking beneath this canopy. Whole scores of men had fallen to its filthy claws. Armed men, too.

In Darath's most humble opinion, this tale was a mean-spirited jest by the lesser folk of this barbarian wilderness.

It simply would not do.

Thyran held a flask to his lips and drank deeply. The wine was perfection, if a little too sweet.

'Exaggeration, Nesselan, you silly man,' Thyran laughed, ever the voice of reason. 'Maybe it does skulk through these trees. This doesn't mean it has slain so many. This doesn't mean it can't die at the tips of our blades.'

Darath watched as Thyran's sword rasped from its sheath, feeling a jealous pang at the work of art in his fellow noble's hand.

'I have sparred with the very best Lothern has to offer,' he continued, brushing a strand of fair hair from his eyes, a smile tugging at the corners of his mouth. 'I promise you, we are in no danger here.'

Darath filled his lungs to speak, to curse them both for their foolish notions and their uncouth bravado. They were nobles, after all. Maybe the other two were minor nobles, of lesser houses, but the blood in their veins was of privileged stock. They were being ridiculous. They were above this.

But the words caught in his throat.

'What was that?' both Nesselan and Thyran said at once.

All of them had distinctly heard the loud, brittle *crack!* of a fallen branch being snapped in half. Darath's fingers, thin digits armoured in gold rings, wrapped around the handle of his sword. His tongue traced a nervous circuit around his lips.

'I told you this was no ghost,' Nesselan hissed, his eyes wide with fear.

'Be quiet!' Darath could feel how heavy his breath was, laden with alcohol fumes. They should not have taken the wine with them.

'Do not worry,' Thyran spoke, sounding infuriatingly composed. 'I think it was just–'

The sound that interrupted him was torn straight from a nightmare.

'Charandis,' Darath breathed, as the lion pounced.

A SMALL SOUND escaped the prey's trembling lips as he thundered from cover in a blur of dirty white fur and scything black talons.

He associated those three syllables with hunt-kill sensations: the pungent sting of urine in the air; the quickening percussion of a fluttering heartbeat; the cloying fear-musk screaming from their pores; the widening of their dark eyes as their gaze locks with his, a connection between predator and prey.

He would never know the significance of that frightened little noise. He would never know that the elf-creatures had characterised him as a soul-shaking rumble of deadly thunder, the booming echo of lightning lashing the wet ground.

To him, it was just a noise they made before they died.

His paw thundered like the hammer of a wrathful god into the first elf's fragile skull, pulping bone and flesh. The echo of its snapping neck jarred up through his front leg from claw to shoulder, throwing the elf ten yards.

His claws snagged on skin, stunting the creature's flight. It landed in a wet crunch of broken bones, twitching fitfully as it died.

His head swung to face his other prey, their harsh breathing and thundering hearts like a balm to the disease that was slowly killing him. His eyes were bleary red orbs, locking the two elf-creatures somewhere between fight and flight.

He opened his jaws and roared. A sound like a volcanic eruption tore from his chest. The fury of a predator king vomited forth in a deafening torrent through fangs that had snatched life from a hundred souls.

It was only natural that they fled.

The chase was brief and violent, and his instincts sang with exultant rightness. This was how things were supposed to be. This hunt was pure, lifting him from the ravages of sickness. Blood slicked his claws as he pounded across the wet soil, his breath rumbling like a summer thunderstorm in his chest.

He tasted elf blood before the creature even knew it was dead. His fangs crunched through ribs and pierced lung and heart in the time it took for them both to hit the ground. He lashed out with leonine claws at the body beneath him in afterthought, spattering blood against a tree, painting it in wet smears.

His limbs burned, though unlike the pain behind his eyes, this was wholly natural. Welcome, even. It was the ache of taut muscles and expended strength, the kind to be slept off with a full belly.

The third creature actually turned. A yard of shining metal sang from its sheath, making a series of panicked slashes. Maybe it actually thought it could survive. Maybe this display of desperate aggression was intended to scare him off.

It did not.

The elf was in two pieces in as many seconds. Both fell to the ground. Both bled crimson fountains into the soggy earth. One tried to crawl away, raking its fingers across the earth in an effort to escape.

Even as the creature burbled a garble of broken syllables, Charandis bellowed another peal of thunder to the skies.

Everything was as it should be. Everything was normal again.

II

'YOU SAID YOU were coming alone,' he says, as if I am not even here. His teeth flash milky yellow in the afternoon sun, his white lips pulling taut against a dozen scars. His tone is even, but he doesn't look happy. And those scars tell me that saying something... brash, would be unwise.

Very unwise.

'Is this a problem?' Alvantir's voice is confident, yet his hand strays to the oval birthmark blotching his cheek. I know these men make him nervous, and I don't blame him.

There are three of them, and underneath the swaying trees they look like kings. Their pointed helms rest in the crooks of their arms, glinting bright silver against the sunlight, each adorned with oval sapphires staring out like cyclopean eyes.

Their armour is... magnificent. I have never seen craftsmanship like this before; not even on the shoulders of strutting peacocks on the streets of Tor Achare. From steel cuirass to masterfully wrought sabatons, they radiate authority. They lean on their heirloom axes with a casual ease born of confidence; centuries-old weapons gripped by well-oiled gloves.

But it is what they wear upon their shoulders that sends my heart racing.

The dead faces of conquered lions glare at me from over their armoured spaulders. The pelts are draped like tattered banners over their armour, frayed in places like forgotten standards, ending in claws the length of my fingers. Their leonine faces snarl soundlessly, the empty sockets of their eyes still narrowed in silent fury.

It marks the greatest honour a Chracian can earn. It demonstrates the exultant heights to which a lowly woodsman like myself can rise.

I am... jealous.

I stand before the Phoenix King's chosen blades; his loyal shields against which a thousand foes have fallen. The eyes of the White Lions are upon me, and all I can think of is how jealous I am.

'You said you were coming alone,' the lead elf repeats, his thunderstorm-black eyes locked on Alvantir. The sound of creaking leather reaches my keen ears. I know this to be his grip tightening on the oak haft of his weapon.

My companion dips his head. I can feel his aching desire to be anywhere but here.

'I crave your pardon, kinsman,' he says evenly, sweeping a braid of autumn-brown hair behind his ear. 'He knows these woods unlike any other. Whatever you are looking for, he can find.'

He looks at me for the first time, and I see nothing but cold, pitiless scrutiny in those dark eyes. I fold my arms across my chest without thinking, shielding myself from his attention.

He nods, as if satisfied.

'I am familiar with your friend,' he says to me, directly. His voice is deep, worn raw and gravelly by distant battlefields. 'But not you. Tell me your name, and we can begin.'

I incline my head as I speak, but I do not break eye contact.

'My name is Korhil.'

THE SCENE BEFORE us is repugnant in a thousand ways.

Chrace's forests are famously beautiful, but equally dangerous. A woodsman does not roam beneath the evergreen canopy unprepared. This is why our axes know the kiss of a whetstone every day. This is why our tunics are oiled and treated every time we leave our homes. This is why our fathers spent endless years teaching us the manifold ways of surviving the forest. This is why we are Chrace's proud children.

I step over a severed hand bedecked in fabulously expensive rings, fighting the rising urge to empty my guts. Blood paints the boles of trees in dried smears, and innards festoon the forest floor like wreckage wreathed in swarms of black flies.

The first body lies by a mossy boulder. His features are... gone, but I know him to be a noble by the fine cut of his bloodstained clothes. His arms and legs are bent in ways that defy reason, and the blow that snapped his neck was close to taking the head from his shoulders.

The second body sprawls near the roots of a powerful tree. This one died as he fled, that much is obvious. His chest is crushed, his broken ribs jutting outward in angles that speak of unthinkable strength. Whatever killed him came back after it had finished, and vented its wrath on the ragged corpse. The coils of vital organs decorate the gnarled fingers of clawing roots.

The third is in two pieces, and the upper half tried to crawl away. His spine is a jutting cord of bone, black with dried blood and alive with a carpet of flies. His legs bear the ugly lacerations of scything claws and...

And I have to look away.

When outsiders speak of Chrace's wild and untamed beauty, this is what they mean. This is what they foolishly think they know. I have been a woodsman for a long time; long enough to know that I am the best at what I do. I have seen a wealth of unsettling scenes underneath this canopy; a menagerie of horrors that have actually made me want to run.

But this... this is something else.

Alvantir worries at the plain band of gold around his finger, a wedding ring he could barely afford. The look on his face tells me that his thoughts are awash with worry. He thinks of his stunningly beautiful young wife, and the son who he has tried to shield from the hardships of the forest.

But beneath these thoughts, I know he is also thinking the same thing as I.

There is something in the air; something that lingers between a taste and a smell. It settles on my tongue and gathers at the back of my throat; a copper tang that speaks of old blood, and a musty reek that whispers of burial grounds.

There are too many flies. The drone of the feasting insects is loud, aching my ears and building a pressure behind my eyes. This is unnatural.

Alvantir meets my gaze. Both of us know what did this.

'They were nobles,' the lead elf says, breaking the uneasy silence. He hefts an axe that is almost the mirror of my own over his armoured shoulder, the lines and angles of his face tightening. 'Lothern born and bred.'

'Why were they here?' I ask, with genuine curiosity. I know outsiders to be stupid at times, but this…

'An adventure in wild Chrace? I neither know nor care.' The words leave his lips laced with bitterness, biting like acid into the still air.

'And why are you here?'

He laughs, a series of hoarse barks that are anything but genuine. 'We are their shields against harm; their bulwark against danger. They were our charges.'

Realisation is a shard of ice knifing into my guts. This is why these men are so grim and unwelcoming. This is why they stare out at the forest with narrowed eyes.

'I am sorry,' I say, and not because Lothern lost three of its spoiled children this week.

'Charandis.' Alvantir blurts out the name because he can hold it in no longer. Four pairs of eyes turn to look at him. Only one grasps the meaning of what is said.

'What about Charandis?' This is asked by another White Lion, the one with a sickle-shaped scar blighting his cheek. He sounds as if he is stung by that name being spoken in the presence of such an atrocity.

Every woodsman knows Charandis. He is Thunder, the King of Prides, the Child of Kurnous, the Hunter under the Canopy. A thousand romanticised poems detail the tragic fall of his pride, the clack of his claws upon the rocky mountains, the grace of his every movement, the mercy in his killing blow…

'Charandis is no longer pure.' There is no regret in my tone. Not even slightly.

'A foul wind blew down from the Annulli Mountains last year,' Alvantir elaborates. He clutches a small wooden token around his neck, a mirror of the one he carved for his boy.

'You are saying the lion is tainted?' This, asked by the third White Lion, sallow-faced and hook-nosed.

'A child of Kurnous does not hunt like this. If this slaughter were pure, then why have only the flies come to feast?'

Silence. Droning.

'Then our path is set? Thunder dies by our hand tonight?' says Sickle-Scar.

'No.' My reply is coloured by my smile, brought unbidden to my lips at the look on Alvantir's face. 'Mine.'

'I WILL RESTORE your honour,' Korhil said, still with that smile creasing his slanted eyes. 'But more importantly, I will earn my own.'

Alvantir pinched the bridge of his nose, suppressing a heartfelt groan. The silence that met this *wondrous* announcement was filled by the frenzied buzzing of a thousand flies, ignorant of the staggering stupidity that just left Korhil's lips.

'You,' spoke the senior White Lion, 'are going to restore *my* honour.' His tone didn't make it a question.

Korhil unfolded his arms – noticeably big, eye-catchingly brawny – and laughed.

'This is no longer about you. I mean you no insult, kinsman, but you have failed today. We stand in the aftermath of an evil you were duty bound to prevent. I will right this wrong. I will kill Charandis. And I will walk with you to Lothern with his carcass slung over my shoulders.'

So this was it. The glory Korhil had been talking about for years. Korhil did not see a gaggle of bereaved lovers and mourning relatives in the clotting blood of these dead nobles. He did not see lives cut short and ambitions slashed by a sick beast.

This was about the glory.

Bringing him here was a bad idea.

To say the lead Lion looked stung was understating things. White-lipped, he stood speechless for several long moments, his gloves creaking as he tightened and relaxed his grip on his weapon.

Finally, 'You would stand in defiance of the Phoenix King.'

'I would.'

He sighed, a weary exhalation whispering through his teeth.

'Then go, Korhil. We will camp nearby for two days. That is how long I will grant you. That is how long I will wait before I come and destroy this beast myself.'

Alvantir cleared his throat.

'Come, Korhil. I will help you pick up the trail.'

A FOOL COULD find where Charandis's claws had touched bare earth.

Alvantir silences the question about to pass my lips with a withering glare, his brow creasing in ugly furrows.

'Fool.'

'I can track him easily–'

'You insulted Valeth.'

For this, I have no response. Valeth the Wyrmslayer. Valeth the Kinhammer. Valeth the Mighty. Why, I ask myself, do I live to regret insulting his honour?

This… puts things into perspective.

'You don't realise, do you? We stood under the gaze of Captain Ironglaive's second.' When I don't respond, he continues. 'The Phoenix King himself knows his name. This goes straight to the top. This is…' He gestures weakly. 'Big.'

I look at my closest friend walking next to me, our boots sinking into wet mud as we leave the White Lions and their charnel scene behind. He sees my perplexed smile.

'Why is this a bad thing, Alvantir?'

'Charandis will kill you.'

'No, he won't.'

'What if he does?'

I laugh, and he knows why. He should know better than to say 'what if' in my presence. A bad habit of his.

'Why does Ironglaive send his most esteemed warrior to Chrace, picking up after foolish nobles?'

Alvantir answers with a shrug of his narrow shoulders, ducking under an overhanging branch. 'It is a different game in Lothern, Korhil. It is political.'

'Nonsense is what it is. When I stand astride the White Lions, I will march to the defence of worthy charges. Generals, scholars, spellweavers; not spoiled children. Never spoiled children.'

'They march in regiments, fool. You go where they tell you.'

'But I'm about to kill Charandis. You think they would damn me to mundane duties like that?'

'Why don't you ask Valeth that question?'

I ignore this last remark, lowering my gaze to the ground, focusing on my task. The forest speaks to me in a voice I know well: a patchwork of muddy browns and vital greens, whispering morsels of secret knowledge.

My strength is my axe – it always has been. Tracking is Alvantir's expertise, but it takes no master to follow the trail Charandis has left behind him. Here, a faded print twice the size of my hand. There, a claw mark, scored into the jutting root of a tree. The clumsiness of the lion's passing is a testament to how sick the creature is. White lions move with a grace that matches their savagery. That is why the Chracian rite is such a hard test. Usually, finding them is hard enough.

Usually.

'I have come far enough.' Alvantir thumbs his wedding ring, giving me a look that I find hard to read. 'I am not going to convince you that this is folly.'

'No,' I agree. 'Because it is not.'

He sighs.

'I will go back to Valeth for my payment. Be swift. And don't die, fool.'

In the shadow of the forest, as the sun sets in crimson fire, we shake hands.

III

AT FIRST, HE could not move.

This was something new. This was a fresh affliction, added to the dozens that already blossomed in his blood and bred behind his eyes.

It was impossible. His bones were shafts of ice, his muscles frozen in painful stiffness. Breath vented between his locked jaws in volcanic hisses. Dreadful cold was beginning to settle on his guts. The thump of his heart was sluggish, beating without vigour, languishing beneath his ribs.

In the stillness of night, the lion whined.

Perception had steadily become harder to grasp as he awoke from slumber these last weeks. He always emerged from a realm of nightmares – where prey is predator – into a world of threats he couldn't see, and dangers he couldn't hear. Being aware of any difference between the two was difficult. So sometimes he would awake roaring, lashing out at shadows with extended claws and yellow fangs.

But not tonight.

Again, a whine escaped his jaws.

Maybe he would slip into prey-sleep. Maybe it would be for him that the ravens wheeled overhead. Maybe it would be his bones that the wolves gnawed upon.

But that didn't happen.

The prey-scent was faint, diluted by distance. It reached him as a weak spice, hanging loose in the air, drifting at the mercy of gentle breezes. It spoke of something far away, alert yet relaxed; wary, yet oblivious. He tasted flesh, wet and tender, torn from the bones of something taken by surprise. The promise of a successful kill raced through his mind.

Normality. Rightness. Relief.

With a snarl of effort, the lion moved.

It was slow, at first. He clawed trenches into the ground in an effort to crawl forward, his muscles burning red-hot under his skin. Agony came afresh with every beat of his heart, coursing fire through his veins, painting his vision in varying shades of murderous red.

But at least he wasn't cold any more.

At least he would hunt again.

The lion staggered shakily to its feet, no longer mewling meekly at imagined predators. His perception was sharpening again, throwing his world into blade-sharp clarity. His eyes rolled in their gummy sockets, identifying his surroundings. His nostrils flared, sucking in lungfuls of nectar-rich prey-scent.

It was… that way. Beyond the trees. Out of the forest.

He reeled at first, his gait drunken and clumsy. Twice, he stumbled, and both times he vented his aggression on thin air, lashing out at nothing.

He couldn't hear the soft thump of his shaky footfall as he moved. He couldn't even hear the blast of his breath, gusting in and out of his lungs. All he heard was a strange buzzing.

Like flies gathered on a carcass.

SHE FOUGHT A rising thrill of panic, straining to see out into the void-black darkness.

Nothing moved. There were no animals out here, tonight. The familiar rustle of fallen leaves as the nocturnal foragers came out to hunt was an absence she sorely wished wasn't there.

There wasn't even a breeze. Not even slightly. The treeline was a collection of pale silvers and dark greys, unmoving and soundless in the moonlight. It was an unreasonably close night. The air spoke of thunderstorms yet-to-be, which was hardly ideal, given the situation they found themselves in.

She clutched her boy closer to her waist.

'We are lost.' He stated this simple truth without a trace of fear, in a matter-of-fact voice that reminded her painfully of his father.

The father that should have been here. Now. At this very moment.

'Hush.'

The silence that met this gentle scold told her everything she didn't want to hear. The boy was young – an infant, even, but he was perceptive beyond his years. She knew that *he* knew she was scared. But then wasn't his father always saying she was so easy to read?

'Where is he?' This, not so blunt. A tremor of doubt crept into the boy's voice, making him sound like the child he pretended he wasn't. She squeezed his shoulder.

'I don't know, dearest. Just keep walking. Please.'

Their feet whispered over the rocky outcrop, their slow advance defined in the soft swish of a silk dress and the gentle creak of the boy's handmade shoes. The moonlight was dim and worthless, spilling weak silver light across shoulders of jutting rock, casting shadows that made leering faces of mundane features.

They stuck to the line of trees because it was a point of reference. Her instinct was to turn the other way, and be as far from the shadows under the canopy as possible – but that would make them more lost than they already were. She knew that they would find shelter if they walked for long enough, but walking in the dead of night, blind, unarmed, scared...

'He said we shouldn't leave the house,' the boy whispered. She heard his fingernails scrape along the wooden token that hung around his neck.

'I know he did. But if anyone can find us, it's your father. You know this.'

He was silent for several moments.

'What if he doesn't?' This question scared her, spoken from the lips of her own son.

'I said hush. He will. I promise you.' To her own ears – city ears, as her husband called them – these words sounded empty.

The need to blame someone for this nightmare was a tingling in her fingertips. Her husband, for not returning home tonight. Her, for leaving the house regardless of his absence. This Kurnous-damned wilderness, for its silent promises of danger.

He had enough money. This was what he had told her, yesterday. He had enough money to move them into the city, away from the pointless harshness of life out here. Years of guiding outsiders through the safe trails of Chrace had paid off.

One more errand. That was all he said it was. One more errand, for a wealthy outsider, and then they could leave.

But he had not come home tonight. Why did she leave? Why did she drag her child into this?

'There is something over there.' The boy pointed towards the trees.

She squinted until she saw. A gleam of something white moved on open ground, a ghost something big made small by distance.

It looked like it was... running. Bounding, on muscular legs. Straight for them.

'What is that?'

She clutched him tighter, her slender hands grabbing his shoulders white-knuckle tight.

In the dead silence, she thought she heard the droning of flies.

THE LION WAS galloping.

His claws sought purchase on rock that the great lion prides had claimed as their own for generations. He had run across this very same plateau years ago, before the world had become varying shades of danger and pain. The females of his pride had shed the blood of countless prey, hooved-creature and elf-creature alike, across this highland of rock and tall grass. The land was fat, nurturing his cubs into strong hunters, almost without exception.

Good land. Rich land.

His prey was no different now, even if he hunted for reasons other than hunger. A female, scared and alone with her cub, had spotted him. He didn't need to see this to know it was true. Prey-scents were rich in the air, the usual cocktail of fear-laced sweat and... something else. Something that stung his nostrils. A curious musk that females often had coating their skin. It would taste vile, but that was not what this was about.

They were running, and he savoured what all but one of his senses told him. He was still deafened by the constant dirge inside his head. He was denied the patter of running feet and the rapid gasp of filling lungs.

He quickened his pace, a bound lengthening into a sprint. Flecks of drool stood at the corners of his mouth, spraying behind him in sour ribbons as he began to close the distance.

He was probably close enough for them to smell him with their blunted and clumsy senses. The blood that caked his filthy hide was nearly four days old, the gory dappling blighting a mane that had once shone silver under the moonlight.

His moment came all too soon. The female looked over her shoulder as he leapt, his finger-sized claws flexing in predatory menace. Their eyes met before the kill came, as he widened his jaws and bared his leonine fangs.

With hunt-kill came blood.

And with blood, there came relief.

* * *

MY AXE IS in my hands.

The haft is two yards of Chracian oak, carved with a screed of flowing Asurii script. The names of my forefathers are tiny grooves against my fingers, reminding me of the weapon's legacy every time I shift my grip.

The head is a work of art that could shame princes. Subtly enchanted steel catches the dawn's first rays as I turn the weapon over; as light as a walking staff, and in the right hands, as deadly as dragonfire.

A weapon Vaul himself would be proud to wield.

A blade that could one day save the life of my king.

I bring the weapon to bear because there is something up ahead. The shapes that lie across the rocks tell an ugly story. I know a kill when I see one.

The flies alone are enough for me to be wary as I approach.

The woman's dress would be pretty if the body it clothed wasn't lying in a dozen pieces. Her hair is black. Her skin is pale, paler even than mine. There is literally nothing else I can see that identifies her, save for the ring that adorns a hand that would once have been long-fingered and slender.

I blink sweat from my eyes and turn to look at...

No.

Blood of Kurnous, no.

That is a child.

I cannot – will not – look at the ruins of what was once a mother and son. I have seen enough. My boots whisper over grey stone as I stalk around the edge of the killing, my jaw hardening, my eyes watchful for clues.

These bodies are hours old. They died in the hours before dawn. Why they were out here at night is anyone's guess, but the clues are arrayed before me. I see recent gouges in the earth where something huge propelled itself forward. I see a scattering of tracks that speak of a lethal sprint from the forest. I see bloody paw-prints leading a meandering, drunken path back to the line of trees.

Still new. Still fresh.

Charandis is scant hours ahead of me. I can waste no time.

A burial for the dead is not even an option. I will not touch what this tainted beast has defiled. I will not be surrounded by those fat-bellied flies. I will not draw another breath of this sickly air, blighting my lungs in the name of ceremony.

No, mother and child can lie here, in the first minutes of dawn's pale light. My quarry is too near. My glory is too close.

I break into a run, leaving the mounting drone of feasting flies behind me.

* * *

IV

THE LION WAS afraid.

He paced in wide circles, his fear manifesting in strangled whines coughed up from the back of his throat. The wind was back – the wind that had brought this sickness to him, blown down from the ephemeral peaks – but this time it was... everywhere.

Literally, everywhere.

On every moon-drenched leaf, on every fallen branch, even on the ground he walked upon, the wind had settled. It was a filmy substance, sticking to his claws; a slime that squelched between his toes and burned his skin like acid.

He could feel himself becoming sicker by the minute. His consciousness waxed and waned, coming and going like a red tide. He couldn't focus. The buzz of flies had become all-consuming.

He made a sound, something between a yelp and a roar.

He saw creatures watching him. Their eyes were the pale yellow of dying suns, leering from every shadow, bright with the promise of yet more pain, yet more agony... The predators from his dreams. They had come with hunt-kill on their minds.

His own eyes felt like they were aflame. They burned in their sockets, making the predators little more than phantoms, escaping his vision.

But he knew they were there. And he wouldn't let them drag him into prey-sleep. Ever.

TONIGHT IS A night of ill omens.

I have tracked him for a day. I have followed his trail without rest, tailing him deeper and deeper into the forest. My cloak is unrecognisable under the inch-thick layer of grime, earned from the tireless chase through mile after mile of endless nothing.

My braided hair falls about my face in dirty ribbons, sticking to my sweat-slick skin. My heels burn with hot blisters, and I bleed from a dozen minor cuts and scrapes on my cheeks and forearms.

That is not why my confidence has fled me. That is not why I am certain I am going to die tonight.

It shows through a crack in the clouds, staring blearily down at the world below. It colours everything in its own sickly shade of venom-green, staining the skies noxious.

Tonight, as I set my gaze upon the tainted lion I must kill, the Dread Moon waxes.

Fear is my guts turning to ice, and my skin crawling with each moment I linger out here, in the open. I should be indoors, hidden from the Dread Moon's baleful gaze. Not risking my life for a glory that could see me dead.

Charandis howls again, and I rise to my feet. I am being ridiculous. I have come this far. At this point, I would rather die than turn back.

My axe leaves its sling in a whisper of motion, its weight a balm to my sudden doubts. The subtle enchantments laced within the age-old steel shines bright in the insidious glow of the watchful eye above me.

I step from my hiding place, emerging from a thorny bush.

I am ready. Charandis must die.

As it moved from the shadows, the lion flinched.

He knew what it was. Pale-skinned and baleful-eyed, it stalked forward with something lethal clutched in its hands, hunched and feral. It flashed its leonine fangs in angry challenge, a territorial roar hammering from its throat.

Maybe it walked upright like an elf-creature. Maybe it clothed itself like an elf-creature.

But he knew that the pride leader of the dream-predators was coming for him.

The lion's reply was thunder of his own, a hoarse bellow torn from ravaged lungs. They stood at opposite ends of the clearing – aggressor and defender, challenger and challenged.

The lion wasted no time.

He charged.

My eyes widen as this... thing... comes for me.

I do not even recognise the beast as a lion. Haggard and sunken-eyed, it is wreathed in flies. Patches the colour of sour milk show through what little isn't a chittering, buzzing carpet.

Its mane hangs loose on its ravaged frame, sagging with each leaping bound. As it tries to barrel me to the ground, I leap sideways, moving fluidly into a painful roll over jutting stones.

Charandis moves fast. He is nearly on me by the time I have regained my footing, his stinking, foetid breath a hot blast in my face. My axe howls in a blistering arc, thumping into the lion's side.

I wait for the scream of anguish. I wait for him to back away from me, bleeding from his crushed ribcage, mewling in his last moments of defeat.

But none of these things happen.

My axe bounces from Charandis's hide as if it were made of rubber. This is unthinkable. I have felled trees with a single swipe of this weapon. That is their purpose. That is what they were made to do.

He does not bleed, nor does he back away.

Instead, he nearly kills me.

The lion's claws tasted the flesh of his tormentor in a flash of venomous fury.

Blood, salty and stinging, flecked the lion's face in spattering droplets. The dream-predator staggered backwards, clutching his ruined visage.

Three bloodied canyons ran from cheek to brow, raining waterfalls of crimson down the aggressor's front. The predator roared in anger, futilely lashing out again with the gleaming blade it held in its clawed hands. It was useless.

The lion was the dominant one here.

He went for the throat, even as it screamed a meaningless screed of guttural sounds.

EVEN AS I circle around Charandis's lethal bulk, I roar in pain. My vision is painted arterial red, my face a bleeding mess snagged by filthy talons. I will have these scars for the rest of my life, even if that life is measured in minutes or years. But at least he didn't take my eyes. At least I can still see.

We pace around each other like dominant males sizing each other up, gazes locked and teeth bared. My axe is useless, here. The taint must allow him to endure the blessings wrought into the steel of my blade.

He comes at me for a third time, his matted fur flashing acid-green under the fell light of the moon as he thumped forward. My life is saved by throwing up my hands, letting his claws scrawl against my axe's haft. Countless names of my bloodline vanish under his talons, buckling my knees with the force of impact.

As his sword-like talons lock with my weapon, he begins to push down.

I do not know how I manage to even begin resisting. Ropes of drool hang down in foul-smelling strands as I push back against the lion's strength, the muscles of my arms and legs burning with slowly faltering effort. He is slowly forcing me to the ground.

What I do next is out of desperation. I do not know what I am trying to achieve, but my life at this point can be measured in painful seconds.

I drop to my back.

My hands fasten around the small stone as if it were as precious as the Phoenix Crown itself. It leaves my fingers in a blur of motion, just as the lion sweeps down.

I hear the *thok* of impact, and close my eyes.

Death does not come.

THE LION COULD not breathe.

Something cold and hard lodged deep in his throat, filling his windpipe with a painful lump. It was as if a band of iron had been placed over his chest. His lungs could not move.

He could not even roar in pain.

His heart – wet and thumping – began to beat faster, soaking his blood in adrenaline. The fight was bleeding from him rapidly. He leapt away from the predator under his claws, trying to choke and gasp.

Soon he was writhing on the ground. His lungs were burning. The desperation to draw breath was a need that sang in his blood. He rolled over onto his back, writhing in fear.

He was not aware that the predator had gotten to its feet.

I TOSS MY axe aside. It has failed me here. My walk is a purposeful stride, my features bloodied and ruined. Charandis is on his back, like a dog rolling in mud, swiping gamely at imagined assailants. He makes no sound. He can't even choke. I bare teeth, wet with my own blood, in a triumphant smile.

But I am not finished yet.

My fingers are not slender, delicate things. When they wrap around Charandis's throat, they squeeze with vice-like strength. I climb atop this Chaos-maddened lion – thrashing and biting – and I throttle him in the light of the Dread Moon.

I know he would die if I just left him. He would choke to death on the stone I picked up in desperation, but that is not enough. That is not how I want this to end. A legend dies under my hands, caked in the filth of his own corruption. I will throttle the last vestiges of life from his ravaged body.

And I do.

THE LION WAS dying.

He did not feel sick. Not any more. There was still pain, settling on every bone, biting into every muscle, but this ache was an absence of affliction. It was… gone. Just like that. It vanished, as if it had sensed he would soon be gone, fleeing his body.

He was still going to die. He had stopped fighting his impending demise – that was pointless. He had been sick for too long to even think of surviving beyond these next minutes.

The predator was on him, and with the sudden passing of the sickness, he saw what was truly there. No fangs. No hunched shoulders, overgrown with a mane that had no place there. No claws. No bleak yellow eyes.

It was just an elf. Blunt, rugged features; maybe brawnier than most elf-creatures, but one of them all the same.

As prey-sleep took him, he still looked upon a predator.

V

VALETH SPAT THE pulpy remains of a bitter herb onto the fire.

Two days, he had said. Two days, and the White Lions would hunt the beast themselves. That was his promise to Korhil. That was the terms upon which he allowed the woodsman the honour of this hunt.

The Khaos Moon had set over the distant Annulli Mountains, the jutting peaks that knifed up from the faraway horizon. The sun took its place in a rising curtain of ruby fire, bathing the trees in warmth, banishing the moon's corrupting influence.

The woodsman had not returned, and that meant he was probably dead. Who knew what last night could have done to creature like Charandis?

No, he had said a prayer for him this morning. That would have to do.

Alvantir was twitchy, and had been this whole time. He kept on mentioning how he should get home to his wife, but Valeth bade him stay. The tracker was phenomenal, he had a nose like a wolf's, and eyes like a hawk's. He would be useful when it came to finding the beast.

Valeth rose to his feet, his shoulders unburdened by the weight of his trophy and armour. 'Get kitted up.' His voice was clipped and tightened by discipline. 'We move after we eat.'

His two companions murmured their assent, and went about their tasks silently. Only Alvantir didn't move.

'He might still come back,' he said, chewing at his fingernails. 'There is still a chance.'

Valeth hadn't the heart to tell him that his closest friend was probably lying in pieces. 'Maybe,' came his doubtful answer. 'Maybe.'

'Such little faith, kinsman.'

The voice was hoarse, gravelly and raw from a night without rest. It rumbled over the clearing, reaching their fire in a hoarse whisper. Four pairs of eyes widened in surprise.

The speaker looked as if he were dead. The bags under his eyes spoke of exhaustion and fatigue, and the clumsy stitching across his face did little to halt the blood that oozed from his ugly wounds. His teeth were a slash of white in a sea of grime; a smile that seemed out of place considering what the man had on his broad shoulders.

The head was… huge. Bigger than the rest of its kind, by far. Blood-caked dirty white fur in inch-thick blotches, most of it the lion's own; some of it the blood of its old victims. The mouth was still open, still roaring soundlessly. Its empty sockets glared with the anger that had sealed its demise, biting through the air with hot intensity.

'You…' Valeth began, uncomprehending.

'Yes,' Korhil replied. 'I did it.'

I BECAME USED to the smell on the journey. My nose is numb to the stench, now. It does not affect me.

I watch as it hits them, one by one, and my smile widens. I know I have stunned them. They look at me, slack-jawed and wide-eyed.

I do not blame them. They have just witnessed the birth of a legend.

'I did it,' I say again, savouring the way the words sound. 'I have passed the rite. I am a White Lion.'

Silence, again. As I walk forward, dry blood falls from my skin in crimson snowflakes.

'That is Charandis?' Alvantir asks, choking on his own words. This is the first time he has seen the beast.

I shrug my shoulders, feeling the heavy weight of my burden. The skull alone weighs as much as a child. 'Yes, my friend. This is Charandis.'

He laughs, cutting through his shock with surprised amusement. As he does so, he runs his fingers through his hair. The gleam of the ring adorning his hand catches the firelight. I begin to laugh, too, and–

The ring.

'Alvantir,' I say, my heart thumping. 'Let me see your hand.'

He obeys, still laughing, still hardly believing what I have achieved.

The ring is a band of plain gold, its plainness its true uniqueness. It is tradition for rings of betrothal to be gaudy and bejewelled. This is something Alvantir has never cared for.

Neither does his wife.

I step forward and snatch at the wooden disc he has hung around his neck. It, too, is simple – carved into a rough circle, engraved with the Asuuri rune for courage.

His boy has such a pendant, too.

'No…'

'Korhil? What?' He sees my fear. He sees the recognition in my eyes as I look at these very personal trinkets.

'Alvantir, I…' I cannot say it. I cannot say I am wearing the carcass of the beast that has killed my closest friend's only family.

But he is a smart man. He knows.

'No!' He shouts at first, railing at me. 'That is not true!'

'My friend, I am so sorry…'

But he is gone. He sprints into the woods, choking on his grief, following the trail I have left behind me.

The weight on my shoulders doubles.

My elation vanishes.

'Come, Korhil,' Valeth says, clueless as to what has just transpired, here. 'It is time for you to come with us.'

HAMMER AND BOLTER

ISSUE 4

WAITING DEATH

Steve Lyons

BOREALIS FOUR.

Can't say it was the most distinguished campaign of my career. A jungle planet orbiting a red giant on the inner rim of the Segmentum Tempestus. A hundred and ten degrees in the shade. Serpents lurking under every leaf, stinging insects as big as a man's fist. Even the flowers coughed out a nasty muscle-wasting virus. It was a damned disappointment, I can tell you. I had hoped for a challenge.

Never did find out if Borealis Four was worth saving. Could be that its crust was packed full of minerals and precious stones. Could be it was as dry as a corpse's throat. All that mattered back then was that, when the explorators set foot on this green new world, they had found a surprise waiting for them: a Chaos-worshipping cult, proud of the fact that the Dark Gods had begun to pervert their flesh and deform their bones.

And that's where I came in: Colonel 'Iron Hand' Straken – along with three regiments of the finest damned soldiers in the whole of the Imperium.

Catachan Jungle Fighters.

THE CULTISTS ON Borealis Four were one of the worst rabbles I had ever seen. Yet again they came bursting from the trees, howling at the top of their voices, throwing themselves at us with no care for their own lives. That was fine by me – we didn't care about their lives either.

'Well, don't just dance with those damned sissies, Graves – use your knife, man,' I shouted. 'And Barruga, you're as slow as a brainleaf plant.

273

You idle slugs, you gonna let this filth spew on the good name of the Catachan Second? I could whip this bunch with my one good arm if you sons-of-groxes weren't in my way. Thorn, stop flapping about like a damned newborn – you still got one damned hand, so pick up that lasgun! Kopachek, you got a clear shot with that flamer, what the hell are you waiting for? Emperor's teeth, do I have to do everything myself?'

We tore through that scum like blades through a reed bed. They were ill-disciplined, ill-equipped, didn't know what had hit them. They'd wasted their damned lives dancing around altars in dresses, waving stinking candles. Should have spent a few days on my world; they'd have learned how to fight like men.

I'd made a bet with my opposite number, Carraway of the Fourteenth, that we'd be done here in four months, tops. Two months in, it looked like I was going to collect on that bet. Until that one night.

That one night, when my platoon of some thirty hardened veterans – along with a certain General Farris – was cut off from our comrades, stranded in the darkest depths of the Borealis jungle. That night, when I faced one of the toughest, most desperate challenges of my life.

That night, when I had to fight my own damned men.

THE JUNGLE ON Borealis Four was nothing compared to Catachan, but the march was taking too damn long. Cutting a way through the high vegetation was slowing us up, and the men were tired. But sunset was coming soon, and things out here tended to get a whole lot worse after dark, so I decided to offer a few words of encouragement.

'Pick up the pace back there! What do you think this is, a newborn's trip to the mango swamps? Myers, put some muscle into those knife strokes. Levitski, Barruga, keep trying to kick some life into that damned vox-caster.'

Still the machine offered nothing but a metallic *thunk* and yet another blast of static.

'Emperor's teeth, it's come to something when you mommas' boys can't finish off a bunch of damned half-mutant freaks.' I shouted down the line. 'And in front of the general! Well, I don't care how long it takes, not one of you is slacking off for a single damn second till we're back behind our lines. I promised you today was gonna be a cakewalk, and the man who makes a liar out of old 'Iron Hand' Straken, I'll throttle with his own entrails. What…?'

I drew to a halt, and the march stopped all around me. The constant buzz of insects and howl of jungle creatures had suddenly been joined by another noise – the faint tinkling of wind chimes.

'What am I looking at here? Where the hell did this come from?' I asked.

Without warning, we had come to a clearing, at least half a kilometre wide. The jungle canopy opened right up, and I was dazzled by the final rays of the setting sun. The air was suddenly cool and fresh, scented with blossom. And, squinting against the light, I could make out dark, unnatural shapes: Buildings. Dark-timbered wooden huts.

My first thought was that we'd found an enemy bolthole. But these huts were sturdy and well-kept, arranged around a larger central hall. Our enemies could never have built anything so orderly. Besides, if the taint of the Ruinous Powers had been there, I'd have damn well smelled it.

Why, then, was my gut warning me of something rotten about this place? And why the hell didn't I listen to it?

As we stood gawping, a figure approached us from between the huts. A boy, barely into his teenage years – but, with the last of the blood-red light behind him, I couldn't make out much more than that. Of course, my men reacted as they had been trained to do, raising their lasguns and taking aim, but the boy didn't seem at all worried by the sight of thirty muzzles pointed at his heart.

He padded closer, as the sun disappeared and the clearing was washed in the faint blue light of a swollen moon. I could make out the boy's face now, round and gentle, his eyes bright and wide. His skin was sun-bronzed to perfection, and the moonlight made his bald head shine like a halo. He was wearing a simple white robe, ornamented by a garland of flowers.

'Welcome,' he offered.

The boy cocked his head a little, his full lips pursed as if he found the sight of thirty bloodied vets on his doorstep somehow amusing.

'Welcome to Safe Haven.' He continued. 'I am Kadence Moonglow – and all that my people have, we offer to share with you.'

'So you say, kid,' I spat back. 'But before we break out the damned peace pipe, I got a few questions for you.'

General Farris stepped forward with a diplomatic clearing of his throat. It was the first time I'd heard his voice all day.

'What Colonel Straken means to say is that we weren't aware of any settlement in this area.'

'And seeing as how, in two months here we haven't found a single life form that hasn't tried to eviscerate us–'

'I assure you that nobody in this village would wish harm to another being,' interrupted Kadence. 'We have learned to live in balance with even this harsh environment. As for your enemies... yes, they were a part of our commune once, but no longer. They have been cast out of this place.'

Sounded like bull to my ears. But General Farris motioned to the men to lower their guns – and, with a few uncertain glances at me, they obeyed.

Farris introduced himself, and the rest of us, to this Kadence Moonglow, and accepted his offer of hospitality.

'Now hold on a minute, sir.' I said. 'I told the men I'd get us back to the camp tonight. Nothing has changed. We can still–'

Farris shook his head firmly. 'The men are tired, Straken.'

'And some of them need proper medical attention. You think they've got a damned hospital tent set up here?'

Kadence interjected again. 'We will do what we can for your wounded. We have balms and tinctures, and most importantly our faith in the healing spirits.'

Yeah, I thought, *'cos a few herbal potions and a bit of wailing to the skies, that's gonna sew Trooper Thorn's damned hand right back on.* But Farris wouldn't be moved on the subject.

'We'll keep the men in better shape by letting them rest than by force-marching them overnight through that jungle.'

I wondered if he was really talking about the men, or about himself. Farris had taken a scratch in the fighting today. His left arm was held in a makeshift sling. He'd kept up with the rest of us so far, and hadn't whined about it – but I'd been watching him sweating and stumbling for a while now, waiting for him to drop.

Either way, I couldn't fault his logic – even if he hadn't been my superior officer. So, taking my silence as a sign of assent, the general asked Kadence to lead the way forward, and ordered my men to follow. I caught Thorn's eye as he passed me. He was still holding his bloodied hand to the stump of his left wrist.

'Never mind, kid.' I told him. 'That hand's looking a bit green now, anyway. Probably too late to save it. Have to make do with an augmetic. Hell, I once had my whole damned arm ripped off by a Miral land shark, you don't hear me grizzling about that. It's character forming.'

Walking into that village was like stepping onto a different world. The jungle suddenly seemed a long way away, and I was surprised to see children playing on the grass between the huts. Some of them stopped to stare at us as we passed. There was excitement and wonder in their wide eyes, but not a trace of fear, although we must have presented a terrifying sight in our jungle camouflage, laden down with weapons.

Farris dropped back, falling into step beside me.

'How do they survive?' he asked. 'They let their children play outdoors, for the Emperor's sake, just a few hundred metres from the monsters and the poison and the sickness out there.' He shuddered at the thought. 'We have to evacuate them, Straken. First thing in the morning. They aren't safe here.'

General Farris, you might have gathered by now, was not one of us. He hailed from Validius, a world so inbred that eighty per cent of its population belonged to the monarchy, and didn't they just love to let you know it. To be fair, Farris had posted himself to the front line this morning – he must have had some guts. Somehow, though, during the fighting, he'd been separated from his own regiment and ended up with ours. A scrawny, pasty-faced man, the general clearly wasn't used to jungle conditions. He had brightened up plenty now that we had found shelter.

Kadence led us into the spacious central hall. It was packed with more of his people, all dressed in white robes, talking and laughing and sharing out bowls of plump, ripe berries. They cleared spaces for us, on benches or on cushions, and handed us fruit, hunks of sweet-smelling bread and mugs of crystal clear water.

Farris was in his element, shaking the hand of anyone who looked like they might be important, thanking them for their kindness, promising to repay it. I was happy to leave all the jawing to him.

My men were approaching the villagers' gifts with caution. I'd have stuck my boot up the backsides of any of them who hadn't. As Catachans, though, we have good instincts about food and drink; wouldn't last too damned long otherwise. We were soon satisfied that no one was trying to poison us.

In fact, the fruits in particular were sweet and moist, quenching the flames in my throat. I couldn't help but wonder why I hadn't seen their like before on Borealis Four.

Soon, my men were mixing with the villagers as if they'd been friends all their lives. I listened in on their conversations, heard a lot of small talk about Catachan and life in the Imperial Guard, but not so much about our hosts. They were good at deflecting questions.

Then Farris introduced me to two village elders – white-haired, straight-backed and dignified but with the same glint of humour in their eyes that I'd seen in Kadence's – and it seemed he had pried some information out of them, at least.

'They've been telling me of their people's legends,' Farris began. 'They believe they came to this world in a "great sky chariot" a thousand generations ago.'

'The Stellar Exodus?'

I knew that some of the first colony ships had strayed beyond the Segmentum Solar, and so in those pre-warp days had become lost to history. It had even been suggested that one of those ships had seeded human life on Catachan.

'Their ancestors were born on Holy Terra. They're the Emperor's people, like us.' Farris said.

'It seems we have a great deal in common, and much to talk about on the morrow.' One of the elders spoke up. 'For now, you and your men must sleep. We can clear this meeting hall for you. I see you have bedrolls. We can fetch more cushions and pillows if you wish.'

'That would be more than acceptable.' Farris responded. 'Thank you.'

As Kadence and the elders left, I grumbled something about making the men soft. Farris let out a sigh. 'You know, your men don't all have your... advantages, shall we say. You can push them too hard.'

I didn't bother to answer that. No outsider could understand the bond between me and my men. They'd have crawled through a Catachan Devil's nest on their bare bellies if I'd asked them to. That much I knew.

'All right, you milksops, that's enough damned pampering for one day. Get out there, start laying traps around the village's perimeter. Go easy on the mines, we're running dry. I want toe-poppers, lashing branches, anything that'll kick up a damn good racket. Graves, put that cushion down! Hop to it, you slackers, or do I have to do everything myself? And once you're done, I want four volunteers to join me on first watch. McDougal, Vines, Kopachek, Greif, you'll do.'

IT DIDN'T TAKE me long to find a good sentry position, in an old tree right on the jungle line. Its star-shaped leaves gave off a eucalyptus reek that would mask my scent, and my camouflage would be more effective here than against the buildings behind me.

I lowered myself onto my stomach along a low, stout branch, and shouldered my plasma pistol.

I was almost invisible now. So long as I didn't move a muscle, or make a sound. But then, I had no reason to do either.

Something was wrong.

It was nothing I could see, nothing I could hear. But I knew there was something. Something out there, at the edge of my senses.

I held my breath, straining to catch the slightest sound. There was nothing. Just the night-time breeze. Without turning my head, I refocused my gaze, through my pistol's sights. I reexamined my surroundings through an infrared filter, but again there was nothing.

My damned comm-bead was still dead. I couldn't sub-vocalise a warning to the other four sentries, couldn't shout to them without giving myself away. It didn't matter, I told myself. They'd have sensed it, too.

For the next fifteen minutes, I stayed frozen in place – as did my unseen opponents. A waiting game. That suited me. I could wait all night.

Of course, I knew I wouldn't have to.

They made their move, at last. If I'd blinked, I'd have missed it. I knew then that these couldn't be the same cultists we'd been fighting these past months. They were too damned good.

But I was better.

There was a subtle shift in the texture of the darkness, the crunch of a leaf on the ground. I had already teased a frag grenade from my webbing and thumbed the time-delay to its shortest setting.

It plopped into the jungle grass just where the disturbance had been, and it lit up the night.

I had hoped to hear screaming, but instead I saw shadows streaming from the impact point, just an instant ahead of the earth-shattering blast. These were lumpen, gnarled shapes that could have belonged to nothing entirely human. I squeezed off ten shots, until my pistol was hot in my hands. I couldn't tell if I had struck true. The explosion had shot my night-vision to hell. I knew one thing, though. I had to move.

I rolled out of the tree, hitting the ground running beneath a barrage of las-fire from the jungle. Whoever – whatever – was out there, like the cultists, they had Imperial weaponry. At least I had made them reveal themselves.

I feigned a stumble, faltering for an instant, making myself a target. I was hoping to make the hostiles bold – and careless. A few steps forward, and they'd hit the tripwire that I knew was strung between us.

No such luck. I heard a soft thud at my heels, and I leapt for the cover of the line of huts ahead of me. The grenade that had just landed exploded, the blast wave hitting me in midair, engulfing me in a broiling heat but buoying my flight. I was propelled much further than my legs could have carried me. I landed hard, and instinctively rolled onto my augmetic shoulder, letting it take the brunt of the impact. I heard something break inside it, and a servo sputtered and whined, but I felt no loss of function as I pushed myself up and put a charred hut between myself and my attackers.

The sound of las-fire across the clearing told me that Kopachek had also engaged the enemy. I thought about going to his aid, but knew I had a line to hold.

I swapped my pistol for my trusty old shotgun: primitive, in some people's eyes, but reliable, and suited to firing from the hip. My eyes were readjusting to the dark, and I peered around the hut's side. The jungle was still again, silent. As if nothing had happened. But that silence was a lie.

The hostiles were still out there. Chastened, maybe; tonight, they had learned that Colonel 'Iron Hand' Straken was no pushover. They would be regrouping, redrawing their plans. But they hadn't retreated. I could still feel their presence, like a stench of old bones in the air.

They were waiting.

A second burst of gunfire took me by surprise. This one came not from one of the other sentry posts, but from the meeting hall at the village's centre. I hesitated for about half a second before I turned and pelted towards the sound. When I got there, the men were spilling out of the hall. They were still shrugging on jackets, tying bandanas, checking their weapons, but were already awake and alert to their surroundings, looking for a target. I grabbed the nearest of them – Levitski – and ordered him to replace me at the jungle's edge. I sent the next to relieve Kopachek – I wanted him back here with a situation report.

Trooper Graves was nursing a fresh wound. Snatching his hand from his temple, I saw the familiar red welt of a glancing las-beam hit.

'What the hell's been going on here?' I shouted.

I pushed my way into the hall, where I found the remains of my platoon in disarray – and two of them dead on the floor.

Standing over these two, with his laspistol drawn, was General Farris – and as he turned to me with a regretful slump of his shoulders, I realised what he must have done. He had shot them. A tense silence filled the hall before Farris leapt to defend his actions: 'I had no choice. They were lashing out, screaming, firing everywhere. This one, he came at me with his knife. He was saying crazy things, calling me a monster. I think... I think the cultists must have got to them.'

'No!' The protest came automatically to my lips. 'No damned way!'

It was one thing to see a comrade cut down in battle, dying for what he believed in. This... This was senseless. I felt cold inside. I felt numb. I felt angry.

I remembered how Myers had fought so well that morning, laughing as he'd sunk his knife arm up to the elbow in cultist guts. I remembered how Wallenski had been so proud, last week, when the men had honoured him with an earned name. 'Nails', they had called him.

'They were good men, *my* men. You had no right.'

Farris's eyes darkened.

'Do I have to remind you, colonel, that I am the ranking officer here? You weren't even present. You don't know what–'

'I knew them, *sir*. I know my men, and they were two of the best.'

A heavy silence had fallen upon the hall. All eyes were fixed upon the general and me. Still, my words provoked a ragged, defiant cheer from the dead men's comrades.

'Either one of those soldiers would have given his last damned drop of blood for the Emperor.' I continued. 'It must have been... They must have come down with some virus. A fever. It made them see things.'

'Whatever the cause of their behaviour, they were threatening us all. I had to act.'

'You didn't even know their damned names!'

And the silence returned, almost a physical force between us.

It was broken by a quiet voice. Kadence Moonglow had entered the hall, and walked right up to my shoulder without my being aware of him. That, as much as any of the night's events so far, disquieted me.

'The covenant has been broken,' the boy said.

'What the hell does that mean?' I rounded on him.

'Blood has been shed. Now, they will not rest until they have blood in return.'

'Who will not rest? The cultists?' Farris asked.

Kadence shook his head. 'The jungle has bred far worse than those misguided souls. There are monsters out there. Monsters that the eye cannot see, but whose presence is felt nonetheless.'

'Yeah, well, thanks for the warning,' I said, 'but those "monsters" of yours already tried to blow me into chunks.'

Kadence shot me a sharp look – and, for a moment, his calm facade slipped and I caught a glimpse of something darker beneath it.

'They would not have attacked you except in self-defence.'

Then, composing himself, he continued.

'We welcomed you into our village, our home, because we sensed that you were noble souls. We only prayed that, in return, you could leave your war at our doors.'

'I don't know if you're aware of this, kid, but your monsters have this village surrounded.' I replied.

'And now they are free to enter it as they please. By sunrise, all we have built here will be ashes. No one will survive.'

'In a grox's eye!' I spat. 'Those things out there, whatever they are – they aren't dealing with a bunch of tree-hugging pushovers any more. If they want this village, they'll have to go through us to get it.'

'Colonel Straken has a point.' Farris cut in. 'We will do everything in our power to protect you.'

'There are less than thirty of you. Their numbers are legion.'

'But we have the defensive advantage,' I said. 'My boys can keep those hostiles at bay till dawn, or I'll want to know the damned reason why.'

'And once the sun is up, we'll be able to lead you – all of you – to safety. We have an army, not twenty kilometres from here.' Farris said.

Kadence bowed his head.

'As you wish.'

THE NEXT HALF-HOUR was given over to frenetic activity.

I trebled the guard around the village, this time counting myself out of the assignments. I wanted to be free to go where I was needed. I sent Barruga and Stone around the huts, telling people to pack their things and move to the central hall. They would be safer there, harder to reach. General Farris stayed in the hall, too – his choice. Someone had to organise things in there, he claimed.

I debriefed Kopachek. His story was similar to my own – except that, in his case, the enemy had fired first. Like me, he hadn't managed to get a good look at them. I sent him, along with MacDougal, Vines and Greif, to grab an hour's sleep in one of the vacated huts. Farris had been right about one thing: my men were the toughest damned sons-of-groxes in the Imperium. Sometimes, it was easy to forget that they didn't all have chests full of replacement parts to keep them going.

I hadn't forgotten about Wallenski and Myers. There would be a reckoning for their deaths, and soon. Meantime, I had warned every man to keep an eye on his watch partner – and to call for a medic if he felt the jungle sweats coming on.

* * *

THE QUIET OF the night was broken only by the occasional squawking bird, and the deeper cries of much larger and much more dangerous jungle creatures. Trooper Thorn was sprawled on his stomach, alongside a small, square hut, his wiry body masked by the long grass. His lasgun barrel rested on a mound of dirt, waiting for a target. I hurried up to him, keeping my head down, and dropped to my haunches beside him. He gave me a situation report without my even asking.

'Nothing, sir. Not a sign of the hostiles. Perhaps you made them realise what they're facing, and–?'

'They're out there.' I interrupted. I had rarely been more sure of anything in my life.

'Do you think…? That boy, sir, what he said… was he right? Are we facing… monsters? Daemons, or…?'

'Trust me, kid, I've seen enough monsters in my lifetime, and nothing – not a damned one of them – would last two minutes in a scrap with a Catachan Devil, or make it through a patch of spikers alive. So, don't you dare start shaking in your boots just 'cos you've seen a few drops of blood today and heard some damned fairy tale.'

'No, sir. It's just that… Colonel Straken, sir, is something wrong? You… you're sweating.'

'What the hell are you talking about?' I asked.

'What… what did you say?' asked Thorn.

Suddenly he was clawing at the ground with the bandaged stump of his left arm, pushing himself away from me and to his feet. His eyes had widened with fear, and his voice was loud – too loud. He had blown our cover for sure.

'Trooper Thorn, to attention!' I snapped. 'You're behaving like a damned newborn yourself. Hell, I know you're not long out of nappies, but–'

'Take that back, sir. Take it back!'

'I beg your damned pardon, trooper?'

We were both standing now, and Thorn had managed to grab his lasgun and was pointing it shakily at my head. I had brought up my shotgun in return – an instinctive reaction - but the image of a comrade in its sights shocked me to my core.

I lowered my gun, brought up my hands.

'Listen, kid.' I said. 'You're not yourself. You're sick. Like Wallenski and Myers, they were sick. But you can fight it.'

'I don't want to believe… This is a test, right? Tell me it's a test. Don't make me–'

'Why do you think you're here? Do you think I make a habit outta taking every snot-nosed brat fresh out of training into my command platoon? "Barracuda" Creek back at the Tower reckons you're the next damned Sly Marbo. You gonna prove him wrong?'

'The fever!' he cried and, for a moment, I thought I'd got through to him.

'It must be the fever, making you say those things. Please, sir, just... drop your weapons. I don't want to have to shoot you – not you – but I swear in the Emperor's name, if I must–'

His sentence was broken by a barrage of las-fire, which provided just the distraction I needed. I tackled Thorn before he could say another word, and the lasgun fell from his grip as we hit the ground together. I'd saved his life, my instincts and a keen ear keeping me a half-second ahead of the fresh salvo of enemy fire that had just erupted from the jungle.

In return for that favour, Thorn was trying his damned best to kill me.

I had him pinned with my knee, keeping him from drawing his knife. But the fingers of Thorn's one hand were locked tight about my throat. He was stronger than he looked.

No match for my augmetic arm, of course. I fought out of his grip, breaking a few bones in the process. Thorn was screaming curses, thrashing about wildly as he tried to unseat me, foaming at the mouth. In the meantime, I knew the hostiles wouldn't exactly be sitting around making daisy chains. They couldn't have asked for a better distraction, or easier targets, than these two damned fools brawling in the open.

I had no choice but to finish this. Fast. I could already hear my men returning fire, and this one was going to get ugly, and quick.

I twisted my shotgun around, trying to jam the barrel up beneath Thorn's chin. I had no intention of shooting him, of course. If he'd been in his right mind, he'd have known that. Instead, he fought with all his strength to push the gun away from himself. I let him succeed, even as I blindsided him with my metal fist.

The punch knocked Thorn spark out, and left a dent in the side of his skull that would probably take a metal plate to straighten out. The way this kid was going today, he was liable to end up like me.

While we had been grappling, the hostiles had made their move.

They came running, screaming, firing out of the jungle, somehow managing to evade all of our traps. My men were shooting furiously at them, but Thorn's little turn had left a gaping hole in our defences – and the hostiles knew exactly where our blind spots were.

I was a damned sitting duck. I didn't know why I wasn't dead already – but, seeing as I wasn't, I figured I could spare another second to hoist the unconscious Thorn across my shoulders before I ran for cover. No one gets left behind if I can help it.

My men were closing with the invaders, yelling for the rest of the platoon to back them up. I deposited Thorn on the ground behind a hut. I didn't stop to check how he was. No time for that. I had a battle to get back to. I raced back to join my men, running at the hostiles with my shotgun blazing. Emperor's teeth, but they were ugly! It was all I could do not to puke at the sight of them.

They had been human once, that much I could tell. Cultists, no doubt, some of them still wearing the tatters of their black robes.

Kadence had been right about them. They were monsters, now, no two of them alike. Their flesh had run like wax, set in revolting shapes. Arms had been fused to torsos, fingers melted together, heads sunken into chests. Some of the monsters – the mutants – had sprouted new limbs, from their ribs, their spines, even out of their heads. Some of them had six eyes, four noses, or mouths in their bellies. They were bristling with clumps of short, black hair, with blisters and blood-red pustules.

And they outnumbered us about five to one. There was no way we were going to survive without some discipline, so I started spitting out orders.

'Barruga, aim for the slimy one's eyes. No, its other eyes! Emperor's teeth, this one has a face like a grox's back end, and it stinks as bad. Greif, wake the hell up, you'd have lost your damned head if I hadn't shot that one behind you. Move it, you slowpokes, I want you up close and personal, right in their damned faces. Marsh, stop holding that knife like you're eating your breakfast. It only takes one hand to hold in your guts, so keep the other one fighting. Kopachek, where's that damned flamer? I want the smell of burning mutants in my nostrils!'

One thing I have learned about mutants over the years: they might be strong – damned strong, some of them – but it's rare that they're fast. They're clumsy, unwieldy. Comes from fighting in bodies they hardly know. That, and having the brain power of a blood wasp on heat.

And, at first, it appeared that these mutants were no different.

I was right in the thick of them. It was safer that way. It made it impossible for their snipers, on the edge of the melee, to keep me in their sights, or to use their grenades without decimating their own ranks.

So, the mutants were swiping at me with poison-dipped claws, straining for my throat with misshapen fangs, and I can hardly deny it, this is one battered old warhorse who has started to slow down himself. I always figured that, what I've lost in speed, I make up for by having a tougher damned hide than most. Even so, in a fight like this one, I'd have expected a few cuts and bruises. Not this time, though. This time, it felt like I was charmed. Like those damned freaks couldn't lay a hand on me.

And yet…

And yet, somehow, my knife thrusts weren't hitting home either. The mutants were ducking and weaving like experts. And whenever I thought I had a clear shot at one, as I started to squeeze my trigger, my target was gone, spun away, and there were only comrades in my sights instead.

My men were faring no better than I was. They'd slashed at a few of those melted-wax faces, cracked a few twisted skulls, but no more than that. And they'd taken surprisingly few wounds in return, just a shallow cut here and there. It was almost like… like the mutants were playing with us.

Insulted, enraged, I lashed out with my feet and my elbows, widened the arc of my knife swipes, turned my shotgun around and used its butt as a cudgel, but nothing got through. So, I took a calculated risk. I did what every nerve in my body was screaming at me to do.

I leapt at the nearest mutant and I slashed its throat, my frustration bursting out in a cruel bark of laughter as its hot blood spattered my face. My first kill of the night. But to make that leap, I'd had to drop my guard, leave my right flank exposed.

I expected to feel a talon in my ribs, to die in agony, but no such blow came. My instincts had been right. The mutants weren't trying to kill us. It was worse than that.

'They want to take us alive!' I shouted. 'Well, they can't have met a Catachan Jungle Fighter before. Time to step up your game, you gold-brickers. Show these mutant scum that we don't lie down and roll over till we're damn well stone cold dead!'

With a roar of enthusiasm, the men followed my lead. They fought with abandon, not caring what risks they took with their own safety as long as they hurt the enemy.

The switch in tactics took the mutants by surprise. They were thrown off balance, reeling, falling like tenpins. I knew it couldn't last.

They must have identified me as the leader, because now they were swarming me, grasping at me with filthy hands. I landed a few good blows, but then strong arms encircled me from behind, and a cold, clammy tentacle seized my left wrist and twisted it almost to breaking point. My shotgun fell from my numbed fingers. My knife hand… that was stronger than my opponents had bargained for.

For a moment, it looked like the struggle – my augmetic arm against three of those freaks – could have gone either way. But then, a flailing limb – or a tail, I suspected – whipped my legs out from under me, something blunt and hard struck the back of my head, and I was toppling backwards.

And the first thing I realised, as I blinked away stars, as I fought to keep awake and on my knees at least, was that my blade – my Catachan Fang – had indeed been wrenched from my grip.

Someone was gonna pay for that!

The mutants were looming over me. Seven of them, I counted. Or maybe just six; I wasn't sure if one had two heads. They were shouting at me in a language I couldn't understand, but one that made my every nerve jangle like the strings of a grox-gut harp. I had no doubt that they were screaming blasphemy of the vilest kind, and all I longed to do was to shut them up, to stop those awful, hateful words escaping into the world.

The grenade felt cold in my hand, and reassuringly solid. It gave me strength, put me back in control. I knew it would rip my body apart. I knew that this time not even the most skilled surgeon would be able to stitch me back together. But a glorious death was far preferable to defeat. And a death that took six – or seven – of my enemies with me...

Then, just like that, the mutants were gone. Withdrawn. Swallowed up by the jungle once more, with hardly a ripple to mark their passing. The quiet rhythm of the jungle settled in again as I unsteadily picked myself up. I saw a number of my men doing the same, looking as confused as I felt.

'How many wounded?' I asked.

There were only a few, and nothing a can of synth-skin couldn't fix. It didn't make any sense. The mutants had been winning!

They had left a handful of misshapen bodies behind them. I glared down at one as if it could tell me in death the secrets it had kept in life. The mutant was lizard-like in appearance, a forked tongue lolling from its open mouth, a thorny tail tangled about its ankles. It hurt my eyes to look at it. I blinked and shifted my gaze along the grass until it found a more welcome sight.

I didn't dare believe it at first. My knife. My Catachan Fang. Half a metre of cold steel, its early gleam dulled through a lifetime of use but still the most precious thing in the damned world to me. An extension of myself, a part of my soul. And the mutants had left it, standing upright in the ground. Almost... respectfully.

I spent a long time kneeling beside that knife, looking at it, before I picked it up, wiped it down and returned it to its sheath.

I spent a long time thinking about what it might mean.

TWENTY MINUTES LATER and I was back in the central hall butting heads with Farris.

'We gotta ship out of here.' I told him. 'We can't wait till morning.'

General Farris shook his head.

'We've been through this before, Straken. I won't have us marching through that jungle at night.'

'The men can cope with the jungle.'

'Maybe they can, but the villagers...'

'If we stay here, and those mutants attack again, I can't guarantee we can hold them back. Our best hope is to take them by surprise, punch through their lines and keep on going.'

'With the hostiles at our heels?' he asked.

'We only have to reach base camp, then the odds'll be even.' I said. 'With a couple more platoons, we can turn back around and blast that damned Chaos scum to–'

'But the villagers, man! Some of them are old. There are children. They won't be able to keep pace with us.'

'So, we lose a few civilians. Better that than–'

'No,' he insisted. 'We stick to my original plan. You said yourself that there were no casualties of the first attack.'

'Because the mutants weren't trying. They thought they could take us alive. Now they know better.'

'If I didn't know *you* better, I'd be starting to wonder if you'd lost your nerve.'

And for the second time that night, I had to fight down the urge to punch this damned Validian upstart in his smug damned mouth. Through gritted teeth I said: 'You're asking me to sacrifice my men, my entire command platoon, for a lost cause.'

'You have your orders, Colonel Straken,' he said coldly.

ONE HOUR TILL dawn, and a forbidding bird call broke the morning silence. The cold crept into my old bones as I lay waiting, and I longed to feel the warmth of the sun – any sun – one final time.

In the jungle, nothing had stirred. Still, I was sure that the shadows had grown longer. And darker. A deep, unnatural darkness. The mutants – the monsters – were gathering their forces, increasing in number.

There were butterflies in my stomach. That wasn't like me. A Catachan's patience is his greatest strength. But tonight, it didn't feel that way. It felt like we were only postponing the inevitable.

My mind flashed back to my talk with Farris, and I felt my blood heating up at the memory. But I realised something now. The general had had a point. Not about my motives – 'Iron Hand' Straken is no damned coward. But I *had* been reluctant to face the mutants again. I still was.

I couldn't explain why. It was a churning in my gut. An itch in my brain. An instinct that there was something wrong here, something I'd missed. Thinking back, I realised that the itch had been there all night. Ever since I had first clapped eyes on this damned place.

So, what was I doing out here? Waiting for an attack that I couldn't defend against, waiting to die? I was following my orders. But the Emperor knows, I've defied enough fool-headed generals in my time. I'd have stuck my knife in Farris's damned heart and been glad to do it, if I'd thought it would save a single one of my men. The problem was, this time, I didn't know if it would. I didn't know what to do for the best.

Or maybe I did. Maybe, at some level, I had known all along.

Maybe I just had to listen to my gut.

I climbed to my feet, and I walked towards the jungle, grass rustling beneath my feet.

As I passed the outermost huts of the village, I could almost feel the sights of a hundred lasguns upon me. I was out in the open now, at the mercy of those guns – but not one of them fired. I stooped and laid my guns on the ground, then I shrugged off my backpack and webbing, and set them down too. Finally, I raised my hands to show that they were empty.

I almost choked on the words I had to say, the last words I had ever imagined would come from my throat. I didn't raise my voice; there was no need.

'My name is Colonel Straken, and on behalf of the Second Catachan regiment of the Imperial Guard – on behalf of the God-Emperor Himself – I offer you my unconditional surrender.'

It was a minute – a long, anxious minute – before anything happened.

Then, I heard a whisper of leaves to my left and a near-human shape detached itself from the foliage. It padded towards me, lasgun raised, and I felt my fists clenching involuntarily.

The mutant was beside me now. I recoiled from its rancid breath. It spoke to me, in the same unholy language as before, and I wanted with all my soul to lash out. I wanted to punch, to kick, to spit, to pull my knife and to carve my name in that abomination's chest.

Instead, I just watched as the mutant signalled to its comrades. One by one, they stepped out from the jungle behind it. Each was an abomination, and the sight of them gathered together just made the violent urge grow even stronger.

From behind me, a single lasgun shot rang out. A mutant fell to the floor, clutching its shoulder.

'Hold your damned fire! That's an order!' I cried. 'No one is to engage these… the hostiles. It's not us they want.'

The mutants had brought up their own guns, but now they lowered them again. I couldn't meet their eyes, any of them. I felt sick inside, and my flesh was crawling like I'd been dipped in fire ants.

And now the mutants where shambling past me, a score of them – two score, three – and into the village. Towards the meeting hall.

I saw MacDougal and Stone springing to their feet, getting out of the mutants' path, drawing their knives but resisting the urge to use them. I was grateful to them. They trusted me. Even though, for all they knew – for all any of my men knew, watching this scene from their vantage points – I must have gone out of my tiny mind. Maybe I had, too.

But, somehow, this felt good to me. It felt like the smart thing to do. For the first damned time in this forsaken night, something felt right. From behind me, I felt the familiar rush of heat and flame as the mutants' grenades blew the meeting hall apart.

The villagers must have heard them coming – but for most of them, there had been no time to escape. The survivors came charging out of the fire and the billowing smoke. I saw old men and young boys, their faces darkened and twisted by hatred and rage. It was hard to believe they were the same peaceful people whose food we had shared. The villagers moved towards the mutants with an angry roar, lasguns firing wildly as they sought to kill the intruders.

The mutants showed no mercy. Half the villagers were shot down before they could take two steps. The remainder closed with their attackers, but they were unskilled in combat, quickly shredded by mutant claws. Their screams filled the clearing, drowning out the sounds of las-fire and conflict. This was the last thing I wanted to see, but I forced myself to pick up my feet, to get closer. Because I *had* to see this. I had to know.

Even transfixed by the unfolding horror, my old battle instincts hadn't deserted me entirely. Someone was coming at me from behind. I sidestepped his charge, threw him over my shoulder. The figure regrouped quickly, scrambling back to his feet. I was horrified to see that it was General Farris. The left side of his face had been burned away. He must have been in incredible pain. He was cursing at me, calling me all the damned names he could think of, and his fury gave him a strength that I'd never have expected. I may have hesitated too, because he managed to plant his foot in my stomach and push me into the wall of a hut.

'This isn't what it looks like,' I forced out. The words sounded pathetic, even to me.

Farris was marching on me with his pistol levelled and eyes bulging white with fury.

'I knew it would come to this. I've been watching you, Straken. You're undisciplined, insubordinate. I put up with your backchat because this was your regiment. But I always knew you were one step from turning, from betraying us all. I should have put this bolt between your eyes hours ago.'

The fighting suddenly seemed very far away, and in that moment it was down to just me and him.

I could have taken him alive.

But a pair of lasgun beams struck Farris from behind, and he stiffened and gasped, then crumpled to the ground.

Emerging from the shadows, Trooper Vines crouched over the general's fallen body, and pronounced him dead.

'I had no choice,' Vines said dryly. 'He was lashing out, screaming. He was saying crazy things, calling you a monster.'

I remembered that Vines had been close to Wallenski. I acknowledged, and dismissed, his actions with a curt nod.

The fighting was almost over.

The villagers were struggling to the very end, but there were only a handful left standing. It would be – it had been – a bloody massacre. One for which I could take much of the credit. And in that moment, I was filled once more with a crippling self-doubt.

But only for that moment.

The meeting hall was still alight – and where the blaze flickered across the faces of the last few combatants, native and invader alike, a transformation was taking place. I blinked and I refocused, unsure at first if

I was imagining things. But I couldn't deny what I saw.

In the glow of those cleansing flames, the lies of the moonlight were dispelled at last, and the truth stood revealed.

IT WASN'T TILL some days later that I heard the other side of the story. Colonel Carraway came to see me in my hospital bed, where I'd just been patched up once again, and he told me how lucky I'd been.

The explorers, it seemed, had left a survey probe in Borealis Four's orbit – and the tech-priests at HQ had tapped into its scans of the planetary surface. The aim had been to produce a tactical map, locate a few cultist strongholds. Instead, they had discovered a whole damned settlement, where a moment before there had only been trees.

Carraway and I worked out that the village must have shown up on the scans about the same time my men and I found it. As if, by crossing its threshold, we had broken some kind of foul enchantment.

Anyway, the upshot was that Carraway needed someone to investigate – and, since half my regiment was already in that area searching for me and my platoon, they were quick to step forward.

Kawalski, one of my toughest, most experienced sergeants, led the recce. He found the village soon enough – but his first impressions of it were quite different from mine. In his report, he described tumbledown shacks standing on scorched earth, twisted trees bearing rotten fruit, and a putrid stink in the air that made him want to retch.

I don't know why Kawalski and his men saw the truth when I couldn't. Maybe Kadence's mind-screwing mumbo-jumbo could only affect so many of us at once. Maybe that was why it hadn't worked so well on Wallenski and Myers, or on Thorn. Or maybe that damned psyker meant for things to turn out just as they did, Catachan at war against Catachan.

Kawalski sent a pair of scouts along the village's perimeter. They returned with reports of booby traps, and sentries hiding in the trees. Even when some troopers exchanged fire with one sentry, they weren't able to identify him. I had just been a shadow to them.

It was only when Kawalski's men broke cover and attacked us that they saw who we were. That was why they had fought so defensively, trying not to hurt us, though we were trying to kill them. Kawalski himself took me down, with some help. He was trying to get through to me, but he couldn't seem to make me understand.

We thought we were fighting Chaos-infected mutants. Instead, we were the ones infected. I'll always be haunted by the fact that it was me who killed Trooper Weissmuller, and laughed as I ripped out his throat. Standing orders say that Kawalski should have shot me there and then.

But he had more faith in me than that.

* * *

IT WAS A damned relief to be back on my feet again, and to have my time on Borealis Four done with.

Or so I'd thought.

We were all sat around a warming fire, with the sights and sounds of the jungle around us. But this wasn't the familiar scenery of Catachan – this was still a world marked by Chaos, and the ruined village around us was just another reminder of that.

I was the only one who saw him.

I don't know what made me look, why I chose that moment to tear my eyes away from the dying fire. But there he was, standing in the shadow of a hut – a ramshackle, worm-eaten hut, I could now tell. After all that had happened, he appeared unscathed, his robe still pristine and white. Kadence Moonglow.

He was watching me.

Then he turned, and he slipped away – and I should have alerted my men, but this was between him and me now.

I followed him alone.

TROUBLE WAS, THE boy was faster than I expected. We were already a good way into the jungle when I caught up with him. Or rather, I should say, when he stopped and waited for me.

'Colonel Straken. I knew it would be you who came after me. Leading from the front. You always have to do everything yourself.'

I was in no mood for talking. My knife was already in my hand. I only wished I hadn't laid down my shotgun in the village.

I leapt at my mocking foe. And missed.

I hadn't seen him move. One second, Kadence had been in front of me, and now he was a few footsteps to the left. I almost lost my balance, having to grab hold of a creeper to steady myself. It was bristling with poisoned spines. If I'd gripped it with my good hand, instead of my augmetic one, I would have been on the fast track to a damned burial pit.

I tore the creeper from its aerial roots and snapped it like a whip, but again, my target wasn't quite where I'd thought him to be.

'Your men aren't here now, colonel,' he said. 'You were overconfident, strayed too far from them. They won't hear your cries.'

And suddenly he threw out his arms – and although he wasn't close enough to touch me, I felt as if I had been punched. The impossible blow staggered me, and Kadence was quick to press his advantage. More strikes followed – once, twice, three times to the head, once in the gut. I was flung backwards into a thorny bush, caught and held by its thin branches. A thousand tiny insects scuttled to gorge themselves on my blood.

'You wanna hear crying, kid?' I yelled, wrenching myself free from the clinging vegetation. 'How about you get the hell out of my head? Stop making me see things that aren't damn well there, and face me like a... like a... whatever the hell it is you are.'

Kadence just smiled. And he gestured again, and my left leg snapped. It was all I could do not to gasp with the pain, but I refused to give him that satisfaction. I just gritted my teeth, transferred my weight onto my right foot, and continued to advance on him.

'I didn't ask for this fight,' said Kadence. 'I was content with my tiny domain, and a handful of followers who would do anything for me. For centuries, we hid from the outside world. Until, by the whims of a cruel fortune, you came blundering into our safe haven.'

I thrust at him with my knife. I missed again, his dodge too quick to even register.

'Your followers were mutants. Perverted deviants. And you tricked me into eating with them. You made me think... You made me see my own men as...'

I roared in frustration, my rage getting the better of me. I was swinging wide now, hoping to nick my target wherever he might be. My blade whistled through the empty air, and he was suddenly behind me.

'I knew that, once you had found us, more of your kind would come.' he said. 'I could not cloud so many minds at once. I hoped it would be sufficient to make you few see my followers as friends, your comrades as the thing you most despise.'

'You didn't count on me.'

'No. No, I did not. But for all you have taken from me this night, Colonel Straken, you will pay with your life.'

He made an abrupt slashing motion with his hand, and my leg broke again. A flick of his fingers, and my left shoulder dislocated itself. Kadence extended his right arm, formed his fingers into a claw pattern and twisted his wrist, and something twisted inside of me.

I was buckling under the pain, straining to catch my breath, but determined to close the gap between me and my tormentor, even if I had to do it on my hands and knees.

'Think you can finish me?' I struggled out. 'Good... good luck, kid. Better monsters than you have... have...'

I felt my ribs crack, one by one. My augmetic arm popped and fizzed, and became a dead weight hanging from my shoulder. I was on the jungle floor, not sure how I had got there. There were tears in my eyes and blood in my throat. And as I looked up, trying to focus through a haze of black and red spots, I saw Kadence making a fist, and it felt as if he had reached right into my chest and was crushing my damned heart.

And that was when something miraculous happened.

I felt the warmth of the rising sun on my back, saw the first of its light piercing the jungle canopy above me. And where those red rays touched the slight form of my assailant, like the flames of the fire back in the village, they exposed his deceptions for what they were.

Kadence Moonglow – the boy in the white robe – faded from my sight. But a few steps behind him, exposed by the sunlight, was a twisted horror.

I couldn't see the whole shape of the monster. The parts still in shadow were invisible to me. But I could make out a rough purple hide, six limbs that could have been arms or legs, and a gaping, slavering maw that seemed to fill most of the monster's – the daemon's – huge head.

I could make out a single red eye, perched atop that great mouth. And it blinked at me as it realised that I was returning its glare.

As my Catachan Fang left my good hand.

As it flew on an unerring course towards that big, bright target.

It was the shot of a lifetime. My blade struck the dead centre of the daemon-thing's eye, piercing its shadow-black pupil. It buried itself up to the hilt. And the daemon that had been Kadence Moonglow gaped at me, for a second, with what I took to be an expression of surprise.

And then he exploded in a shower of purple ash.

I DON'T KNOW how many hours I lay there, face down in the jungle.

I couldn't lift my head, couldn't move my legs without my broken bones grinding against each other. My insides felt like jelly, and most of my augmetics had failed. I was dying.

And if I didn't go soon, I knew there were any number of predators gathering in the brush, ready and eager to help me on my way.

I wasn't worried. Far from it.

I knew that my men were nearby. I knew they would never stop searching for me. And I knew that, whatever it took, they would find me. They would carry me off to the surgeons, as they had done a hundred times before.

I could trust them.

And when I heard their distant footsteps, I was still able to force a smile.

WARHAMMER®

THE BARBED WIRE CAT

Robert Earl

IN THE DARKNESS, the thing called Skitteka sat and schemed and stroked his pet. A single lantern lit his stone-gnawed burrow. The guarded flame produced barely enough light to lend a twinkle to his beady eyes, although it was sufficient to set the blonde of his pet's hair aglow. Everything else was in shadow.

Skitteka hadn't had a pet before. Apart from anything else, not many humans could have borne his touch. Most would have cowered or flinched, or just broken and tried to run. But Adora was not most humans. She purred as he dragged his filthy claws through her hair, and pressed herself into his verminous caress with every semblance of pleasure.

'I wonder, little cat,' Skitteka said, 'how long I will have to wait to become chief overseer.'

Despite his bulk Skitteka's voice was a high-pitched shriek, like nails being drawn down a slate. Adora seemed not to mind. Quite the opposite, when she cocked her head to listen it was with a keen interest and that, at least, she didn't have to fake.

'The slaves all wonder the same, master,' she told him, her voice perfectly modulated to that sweet spot that lay just between terror and adulation; that sweet spot she'd spent so many hours practising. 'They see that you are the most powerful, and the most magnificent. And they fear that when you become chief overseer they will have to work harder.'

Skitteka hissed with pleasure, the twin chisels of his incisors gleaming in the scant light.

'They are right,' he boasted, his claws scratching deeper into her scalp to show his pleasure. 'That fool Evasqeek doesn't know how to handle humans. He should be removed. Replaced.'

The tremble in his paw belied the defiance in its voice and Adora felt a flash of frustration.

So she thought about her father. He had died when she had been a toddler. All she remembered about him was a kindly face, the smell of pipe smoke, and the one thing he had said which she had understood and remembered. *It's a poor craftsman*, he had told her three-year old self, *who blames his tools*. Perhaps he would be proud to know that, whatever else Adora had turned out to be, it was not a poor craftsman. Ignoring the tremble in Skitteka's paw she arched her back and hummed in a way that she knew pleased him.

When he had stopped trembling she said, 'Some of the slaves heard Evasqeek talking yesterday, master. He was in the main seam hiding behind his stormvermin.'

'Hiding, yes,' Skitteka said, finding reassurance in the description. 'And what did he say?'

'He said that he was tired of being frightened all of the time,' Adora decided. 'He said that it was too much and that he just wanted to go back to his burrow and sire lots of whelps.'

'He said that it was too much?' Skitteka asked, his voice as flat as a blade on a grindstone.

'That's what the slave who heard him told me,' Adora said, and wondered if she had gone too far.

She had.

'No,' Skitteka said. 'No, no, no. Evasqeek wouldn't tell his stormvermin that. They would kill him.'

'That slave must have got it wrong then,' Adora said, letting the blame slide from her with a practiced ease.

'Perhaps,' Skitteka said, grabbing a fistful of her hair and squeezing so that every root screamed out in pain. 'Or perhaps it's lying. Either way, it can't be trusted. Which one was it?'

Most humans would have hesitated. Even those whose decency had been outweighed by their terror would have struggled to fabricate a scapegoat without missing a beat. But Adora wasn't most humans.

'It was Jules,' she said, handing out the death sentence with an instinctive understanding of who was valuable to her and who was not.

'Jules,' Skitteka said, savouring the name of its next victim as much as it would any other tasty morsel. 'Jules. Very well, little cat. Send Jules to me. I will sharpen his ears for him.'

Adora pretended to share the amusement of the thing as he hissed, his murderous laughter as sibilant as an adder's.

'But first,' he said, throwing something splattering down onto the stone of the floor. 'Eat up, my little cat. I need healthy little helpers in this mine.'

The shapeless gobbet of flesh lay in the filth, glistening. Adora gave effusive thanks as she crawled forward to it. It was meat. That, she told herself, was all that it was. Meat. Down here you could either eat it or you could be it, but either way, meat was life. Adora gnawed off a chunk and swallowed. Then she went to find Jules.

SKITTEKA DIDN'T KILL Jules outright. Skitteka never killed anybody outright. Despite his stupidity and his clumsy bulk, the thing had a surgeon's skill and the wounds he inflicted, although always lethal, were seldom immediately so.

Adora found her scapegoat lying by the side of one of the access tunnels. He had been left there so that the other slaves could see him as they trudged down past the warped and trembling mine supports and into the cancerous glow of the main seam. His intestines had been wound out of him and tied into grotesque shapes. His limbs ended in cauterised stumps. He had been blinded. And worse.

The slaves bowed their heads in sympathy for the ruined man. Why not? Sympathy was easy. But none of them dared to brave the guards' whips by offering him comfort. None but Adora. She sat beside Jules and cradled him. He had been the one who had taught her how to make soap down here: how to mix charcoal and fat, combining dirt in order to achieve cleanliness.

He died in her arms. The last fading rhythms of his pulse disappeared within his wasted frame, pattering away in contrast to the strong beat that pounded within her own breast. He sobbed for his mother right until the end, but it wasn't his mother who comforted him during his last hours in this eternal night. It was Adora. When he was dead she kissed him, a final blessing, then left the cooling meat of his corpse and hurried along after the other slaves. As Skitteka's pet she had some privileges. She was left unshackled, loose and generally untouched. Even so, there were things down here with more authority than her patron, and their whips left scars.

She hurried down the claustrophobic squeeze of the narrow tunnel to rejoin her fellow slaves. Even the shortest of them walked with a permanent stoop, the ceiling of their captors' tunnels being too low for them. Their guards had no such problem. This subterranean world had been built around their rat-like forms, and they scuttled back and forth effortlessly, the razored tips of their whips hissing towards anybody who faltered or stumbled.

As the column entered the weird green glow of the mine proper, one of the slaves fell to his knees. There was a cacophony of shrieking voices, the busy whine of whips and then screaming. The man in front of Adora used the distraction to turn and whisper to her.

'Was he dead?' he asked, his voice thick with an Estalian accent. He was called Xavier, and of all the men down here Adora judged him to be the strongest. Although smaller than the northerners she was used to, he had a wiry strength that even this hellish captivity hadn't been able to sap. He had a hardness in his eyes too. It suggested that, even though he was defeated, he still had enough pride to dream of revenge.

Adora had high hopes for him. So much so that, after casting a quick glance around, she took the risk of whispering a reply.

'Yes,' she said. 'He's dead.'

'He's lucky.'

'Don't be a fool,' she told him.

The man looked at her. In the sickly green light it was impossible to make out his expression but Adora could see that it was either anger or amusement. As far as she was concerned, either would do.

'How long have you been down–' he began, but the sentence changed into a hiss of agony as a guard sliced him with a whip.

'No talking,' it squeaked, then chittered something unintelligible as it struck him again. The leather cut through rags and skin both, and his blood spattered onto the floor, black in the sickly light.

Then the column was moving again. The green glow of the wyrdstone grew brighter. Adora felt her skin crawl and her teeth ache as they reached the first deposit. Tools were handed out and she stumbled forward, eyes watering as she started to hack away at the stone in search of the wyrdstone fragments entombed within.

She studied her captors as she worked. As always happened in the presence of the wyrdstone, their demeanour had changed. They had not become calm so much as transfixed by the sickly green glow. They still watched the slaves, in as much as the slaves were revealing the accursed stuff, but mainly they watched each other. The pure black orbs of their eyes glittered with suspicion, and although their whips rested, their paws often strayed to the hilts of their poisoned blades.

Adora could recognise greed when she saw it. That was why today, as every day, she waited to see if an opportunity would present itself.

It did. One of the slaves hacked a lump of the wyrdstone loose, crying out in pain as it sprang away from the rock face with a sudden burst of painful light. The overseers clustered around the find, their scaly tails twitching with horrible excitement and their beady eyes blind to all else, and that was when Adora struck. In a single, fluid movement she grabbed the wyrdstone fragment she had been standing on and concealed it amongst the rags which bound her legs. She only touched it with her bare skin for a moment, but in that moment her bones ached and her muscles squirmed and she had to choke back the cry of horror which rose unbidden to her lips.

The pain faded slowly as she carried on working. She paid it no heed. However vile the wyrdstone was, it was valuable to them and so, she reasoned, it was valuable to her.

* * *

'HE'S COMING? HERE?' Evasqeek bared his incisors. The guards who were gathered in the chief overseer's burrow cowered at their master's agitation. Only the runner who had brought the tidings remained unmoved by his reaction.

'Yes, master,' said the runner, revelling in malicious pleasure at the fear it had brought. 'Chief Vass will visit the mine to see that all is well. He is concerned that production is down.'

Evasqeek lashed the ground with his tail, and his eyes rolled around in panic.

'The seam is running out,' he whined. 'There is less and less of the stone every day. It's not me, it's the deposit.'

Then he remembered who he was talking to. Vass was one thing, the vicious old fool, but this runner wasn't worthy of an excuse. Worthy of punishment, perhaps...

The runner, as though seeing the vengeful turn of the chief overseer's thoughts, interrupted them.

'My Lord Vass requests that I return with your estimate of the stone you will have when he arrives,' he said. In fact, Lord Vass had requested no such thing. It was just that the runner's whiskers were twitching with the knowledge that this chief overseer wanted a victim, and that it wasn't going to be him.

'Tell him forty ingots,' Evasqeek decided.

'Is that all?' The runner asked, pushing his luck.

'Maybe more,' Evasqeek said, suddenly aware of how dangerously frightened he had begun to smell in front of his stormvermin. 'Now go. I have work to do.'

'I know,' the runner said and, before Evasqeek's spite could overcome his caution, it turned and scuttled back out of the burrow.

'Go and fetch Skitteka,' Evasqeek said at length. 'He is the slave master, and the slaves produce the stone. So if we aren't producing enough, it's his fault.'

It was a reassuring thought and one that Evasqeek clung to as he worked out how best to shift the blame.

THE SLAVES HAD no idea how long their shifts lasted. There was no day down here, only an eternal night. The guards merely waited for the first of their charges to collapse before letting the rest of them return to their quarters. All but the one who had collapsed, of course. He'd be flayed alive, a miners' canary of human frailty who paid the ultimate price for everybody else's rest.

When that was done the survivors would drag themselves back to where they were quartered, gulp down a bowl of whatever vile broth their captors provided, and then clamber down into the lightless oubliette where they were kept. There were no other exits from the dungeon apart from the hole in the roof though which the ladder descended. The dank cavern stank of human misery and human waste, and if it hadn't been for the cracks in the rock the inmates would have drowned in the latter long ago.

Now, after gulping down a bowl of something greasy and congealed, Adora climbed down into this stinking pit. The rest of the slaves had already collapsed, allowing themselves to fall victim to terror and exhaustion. Adora felt a flicker of contempt for them as she forced herself to keep moving, keep thinking. Keep one step ahead.

The trapdoor banged closed above her and the darkness became complete. It was a heavy leaden thing, this darkness, as though it bore every ounce of the tons of rock that lay above. The weight crushed some of the slaves, and their howling and sobbing echoed against the damp stone walls. Others raised their voices in a ragged chorus of desperate prayer, the Sigmarite chants a feeble defiance against the all conquering night.

ADORA IGNORED THEM as she ignored the soft confusion of broken bodies beneath her feet. She was too intent on the cache she had hidden in one of the crevasses that lined the walls.

Over the past weeks she had amassed perhaps half a kilo of wyrdstone. The fragments produced a nerve shredding heat even through the rag bundle she had wrapped them in, and it was no coincidence that the ground beneath them was the only part of the cavern not tumbled with human bodies.

When she had made sure her poisonous treasure was secure she took a deep breath and finally allowed herself to think about sleep. Not here, though. Not by the wyrdstone.

She started picking her way back through the mass of bodies, ignoring the whimpers and cries of protest. Then from beneath her she heard one voice that was neither fearful nor hurt.

'I'll thank you not to stand on my hand,' it said, and Adora realised she had found the Estalian.

'Then I'll thank you to make room for a lady,' she said and, pausing only to knee somebody aside, slid down beside him.

'Feel free to take a seat,' he said, and when Adora heard the unmistakable tone of irony in his voice, her heart leapt. Irony. It was like the scent of clean air or a glimpse of blue sky, a thing that could only come from a place of freedom.

'My name is Adora,' she said, as though she had just handed him the keys to a kingdom.

'And my name is Xavier Esteban de Souza,' he replied, sounding as though she actually had.

'You haven't been down here long, have you?' she asked, and leaned into him with a total lack of self-consciousness. He was lean but not wasted, his slim frame corded with the tight muscles of a fencer, or perhaps an acrobat. She pressed against him, enjoying the warmth of his body against hers.

'Perhaps a month,' he said, carefully not moving away. 'Perhaps more. It's difficult to keep track.'

'Try,' Adora told him.

'Why bother?' he asked.

Adora didn't reply. Instead she slid her hand gently down his forearm, selected a hair, and pulled it out. He yelped with surprise as much as pain.

'If you and I are to be friends,' she told him, 'you are never to ask that question again. Never even to think it.'

He grunted, and she thought he understood. She hoped so. Nobody survived down here once they started to ask that question. Nobody.

'Where are you from?' she asked him, stroking the forearm from where she had plucked the hair.

'From Estalia,' he said simply. 'I am a swordsman, as was my father and his father before him.'

'Are you any good?' Adora asked, and she could tell by the way he sat a little straighter that he was.

'One of the best. When we are boys, the sons of our family train amongst pens full of the *toros negros*, the wild bulls from the mountains. They have horns blacker than this night and natures as fickle as any woman's.'

'As fickle as that?' Adora asked.

Xavier chuckled, and the sound was so alien in the darkness that a silence descended around them.

'Yes,' he said, 'as fickle as that. You can never tell when they will turn on you or your opponent. It gives those of us who survive eyes in the back of our heads.'

'If you have eyes in the back of your head,' Adora teased him, 'then how were you caught?'

'Sorcery,' Xavier replied simply. 'I was a guard on a caravan. One night there was an alarm and suddenly we were all choking. After that, I don't remember much. We were all split up, and then there were endless passages. Endless days.'

'There is no such thing as endless passages,' Adora told him with the cast iron assurance of a mother telling her child that monsters don't exist.

Xavier just shrugged.

'You're right, of course,' he shook himself. 'But endless or not I will escape through them. I just haven't found a way yet.'

'Maybe I can help with that,' Adora said. 'In the meantime let us remember why we should bother.'

She turned her head towards his and kissed him, and amongst the squalor, the madness and the fear, they reminded each other that it was worth staying alive.

* * *

UNCOUNTABLE HOURS LATER the trapdoor opened and the ladder descended into the pit. In the sudden flare of torchlight, Adora watched the struggling mass of slaves as they fought to climb it. They pushed and elbowed each other aside, their tiredness forgotten as they raised their voices and clenched their fists.

One man struck another with a crack of knuckles against bone. Another was pulled down and trampled by the men behind him. With a sudden shriek another gave in to panic and hurled himself towards the ladder, trying to swim through his fellows. He didn't get far.

'Why do they rush back to their labours?' Xavier asked Adora who stood up beside him. 'Are they mad?'

'No, just stupid,' she said. 'The overseers always beat the last couple of people to come out.'

'Maybe we should hurry too, then,' Xavier said, but Adora shook her head.

Even in this gloom he could see the way the light played in her hair, its lustre untarnished. She was beautiful, he decided. The only beautiful thing left in the world.

'Save your strength,' she said. 'There are always a few left stunned by the melee.'

Xavier frowned. 'What if there aren't?'

'Then we'll stun a couple,' Adora said and smiled, her teeth as white as a shark's in an ocean full of seals.

Xavier grunted and decided that she was joking. Soon the crowd cleared and she led him forward, pushing through the weaker of the slaves who remained below. If some of them flinched when they saw who was pushing them, Xavier didn't notice, or if he noticed, then he didn't think about it.

He let her climb the ladder first, admiring her form as she did so. Then he followed her up into the waiting torchlight. After the lightless hours spent in the pit he found that he was squinting, and he rubbed his watering eyes as the iron shackles which bound him to the chain gang were snapped around his ankle. When he looked up his breath caught in his throat.

Adora was not locked into the chain with the rest of them. Instead she was cowering beneath the touch of a monster. Like all of its verminous kind the thing had chisel teeth and a scaly lash of a tail. It had the beady black eyes too, glittering with malevolence and cunning, and an obscenely naked wrinkle of a snout. Unlike its fellows it was huge. Even with its stoop it was as tall as a man, and even wider across the shoulders.

But what choked Xavier with horror was not the thing's bulk but the way it was touching Adora, dragging its filthy claws through her hair with some grotesque parody of affection.

Before he knew what he was doing he was on the balls of his feet, weight balanced and shoulders loose. Had it not been for the shackle on his ankle he would have attacked, weapon or not, and that would have been the end of him. As it was, the dead weight of the steel and the deader weight of the slaves around him gave him pause, and in that moment Adora looked at him.

She winked, and for the first time he realised how blue her eyes were. As blue as the pure seas and clear skies that awaited them above. Then she tilted her head, gesturing him to leave her. It was a barely perceptible sign but he followed it as thoughtlessly as a bull followed the flicker of a red cape.

They would survive, he knew that now. They would survive together.

He let himself be led away with the slaves and didn't even look back as he heard the soothing sweetness of Adora's voice whispering in the distance.

AND ADORA NEEDED to be soothing. Once his underlings had scurried off, their whips dancing gleefully across the skin of their victims, Skitteka turned and lumbered off to the sanctuary of his burrow. It was only when safely ensconced behind the heavy iron doors that he turned to Adora and unburdened himself.

'Vass is coming,' he said simply. As he said the name his tail trembled and even Adora could smell the change in his odour. She said nothing. She didn't need to. Skitteka obviously needed to speak, and of all the creatures down here Adora was the only one it could trust.

'Evasqeek, Evasqeek, Evasqeek,' the thing gibbered, its voice a high pitched whine. 'He will betray me, the vile thing. He will use me to avoid paying for his own failings and make them mine instead. When Vass comes, Evasqeek will blame me for the slackening flow of the stone, the thrice-accursed liar.'

Skitteka clawed at her as he spoke, but she endured his painful caresses as uncomplainingly as ever. In truth she barely felt them, for as her verminous master spoke she saw the first cracks appearing in her confinement.

'Oh, Vass,' Skitteka moaned, his voice a terrified combination of horror and admiration. 'In Qaask he chained all the slave handlers together and let the slaves work them. None of them survived their own whips. Then there was Tsatsabad where they say he simply sealed the entire mine and flooded it with poisoned wind. Imagine how they must have scrabbled and fought as their lungs melted.'

Skitteka paused and licked the yellowed blades of his incisors with a long pink tongue.

'And in Isquvar he had the overseer sealed into a cauldron and then rendered down into slave gruel. They say he added one scrap of coal to the fire at a time so that it took an entire day for his victim to stop screaming. Mind you, he had been caught stealing warpstone.'

The cracks which Adora had seen appearing at her confinement blossomed into real possibilities. They were tenuous possibilities to be sure, but they were real enough to set the carefully nurtured embers of her hope ablaze. As Skitteka continued to speak her eyes burned blue in the darkness.

'Curse Evasqeek,' Skitteka continued, turning from admiration of Vass to shrill self-pity. 'He will give me to Vass and something horrible will happen.'

Adora felt a flash of contempt, and wondered how this weakling had become the master of the slaves. She supposed it was because of his muscle. It certainly couldn't have been his courage.

'My lord,' she said, her face lowered. 'If Evasqeek does betray you, I will be finished. Without you I am nothing.'

Skitteka struck her. It took her by complete surprise, and she was sent tumbling across the stone floor of the burrow. There was no pain, not yet, but there was numbness down one side of her body and a warm trickle of blood had already begun to flow.

'Ungrateful creature!' Skitteka shrieked as she staggered back to her feet. It had drawn its dagger, and although the metal was dull, the liquid that coated it glowed with a toxic intensity. 'How can you be so selfish?'

It lurched towards her, its monstrous bulk blotting out the light from the lantern, and Adora knew that in these nightmare depths, death was finally upon her. She didn't waste time worrying about it.

'Forgive me, my lord. I only meant that I would like your permission to kill Evasqeek.'

Skitteka stopped and staggered backwards as though he had been shot by a jezzail.

'Kill him?' he asked, a new hope in his voice. 'But how can a little cat like you kill Evasqeek?'

Adora looked at him, and for the first time since she had met the creature she made no effort to compose her features. No pretended humility marred the porcelain hardness of her features; no false fear widened her predatory gaze or trembled on the hungry perfection of her lips. No simulated respect bowed the straight perfection of her stance, nor did it smooth the arrogant composure with which she carried herself.

As she stood before him unmasked, Skitteka took another step back, and another. He felt as though he had bitten down into soft flesh to find a razor blade hidden within. Adora, seeing his beady eyes swivel uncertainly, lowered her head demurely.

'I will do it because I must. Without you I am nothing, my lord. Get me within striking distance of Evasqeek when Vass arrives and I will do for him.'

Skitteka hesitated, paralysed by hope. Then he sheathed his dagger, the blade hissing like a serpent as it disappeared, and slumped back into his chair.

'Maybe,' he murmured, scrabbling in his filthy robes for something. 'Maybe you will.'

THE FIRST HINT the slaves got of the impending visit was the sudden cessation of work. In the days preceding their lord's arrival Vass's servants insisted on checking every inch of the mine for traps, and while they did so the slaves were locked into their oubliette.

At first they wallowed in their idleness, savouring every moment of it as a starving man will savour every mouthful of a feast. But as time dragged on their permanent exhaustion was replaced by another torture. Forgotten in the blinding darkness, starvation started to take its toll.

It wasn't long before rumours of cannibalism began to circulate.

'I think it's time to escape,' Xavier said, whispering into Adora's ear so that they wouldn't be overheard. 'What do you think?'

Adora enjoyed the warmth of his breath on her neck. She had long since learned to use such scraps of pleasure to distract her from… well, from everything. She leaned closer to him before she replied.

'I think we should be patient,' she said and tried not to sound patronising. 'Even if you could climb up to the trap door, and even if you could get it open, what do you think would be waiting for you there?'

'Perhaps nothing. Perhaps we have been abandoned.'

'Do you really think so?' Adora asked.

'Well then, the vermin,' Xavier said carelessly. 'I'll have to kill them to get out eventually anyway.'

Adora smiled and sighed contentedly. Men were all fools, of course, so that was all right. What was important was that she had finally found one with the courage to be a leader. Like all shepherds she knew the value of a good sheepdog and she had truly found one in this tough little Estalian.

'It might be better to fight them when they aren't standing on top of a hole waiting for you,' she said, and felt him pull away.

'I do not appreciate being mocked,' he said, and Adora smiled again. Pride. Was there a better way to handle a man? Well, maybe one. She reached for him, but she was interrupted by the *clang* of metal and a shaft of light cutting down into the darkness. After the blind days she had spent down here the light seemed as solid as a stream of molten iron, and her eyes ached as she looked towards it.

When her tears cleared she could see the mass of slaves that huddled around her, hope and terror warring on their upturned faces. When one of the guards appeared in the trap door opening they froze like a field full of mice beneath the shadow of a hawk.

'Skitteka wants his pet,' the creature shrilled.

Adora got to her feet and walked towards the opening. The other slaves pulled away from her, all but Xavier. As she waited for the ladder to tumble down he appeared beside her, and his hand brushed against hers.

'I'm coming with you,' he said.

'You can't,' Adora told him, surprise lifting the perfect arcs of her eyebrows. 'You haven't been summoned.'

'They won't care,' Xavier said with a fatalistic confidence. 'And I need to see more of this place. Need to start finding weaknesses.'

'No,' Adora shook her head. 'No, it's not worth the risk.'

'I'm coming,' Xavier insisted.

'Don't come,' Adora said. 'It's better if—'

'Quick-quick!' the creature above shrieked, and Adora realised that the ladder had reached the ground while they had been arguing.

'Stay here,' she said, and started up it. When she reached the top she was not surprised to see Xavier clamber up behind her. She was sure that the verminous guards who awaited them would kick him back down, but they seemed hardly to notice.

It slowly dawned on Adora just how distracted they were. Their whiskers twitched at every draft of air and the scaly lengths of their tails coiled and uncoiled nervously. Once, there was a boom of some distant falling rock, and all the guards sprang into the air, their beady black eyes rolling in terror.

When they finally arrived at the entrance to Skitteka's personal burrow they hung back, chittering nervously.

'Go on!' the leader said, pushing Adora towards the iron door. She went, trying not to let her guards' terror infect her. Xavier followed closely and, as soon as she had gone through the iron door, she closed it behind her, pushing him against it.

'Wait here,' she hissed. 'Any further and we'll both be killed.'

To her relief he nodded, and she paused to give him the briefest of kisses before composing herself and padding down the corridor into Skitteka's chambers. As soon as she saw him she knew why his underlings had been so terrified. He had been gnawing on wyrdstone.

Adora felt something like despair as she looked at her chosen master. He wasn't aware of her or of anything else. His eyes were rolled so far back in his skull that she could see the whites, and pink foam bubbled down from his mouth.

She glanced down and saw the remains of one of Skitteka's underlings. Its carcass was torn and broken, and as she crept a little closer she could see that it had been partially eaten.

That was no problem. What would be a problem would be if the wyrdstone had brought on more than a fit of madness. She knew what it could do, had seen the half-glimpsed horrors that were occasionally driven screaming from the mine. The wyrdstone didn't just kill, it transformed.

She squinted into the gloom as she padded silently around Skitteka's paralytic form. As far as she could tell the body which sweated and wheezed beneath its filthy pelt was the same grotesque bulk as always.

'Is he dead?'

Adora spun around and glared at Xavier. After a quick glance back at Skitteka she paced angrily towards him.

'I told you to wait,' she hissed, but he didn't respond to her fury. Instead he just pushed past her.

At first she thought that he was making for the half-eaten corpse that lay crumpled on the floor but he hurried past it and into the shadows on the far side of the chamber. When he stood up she saw the glitter of a sword in his hand. He weighed it, looked at Skitteka and smiled.

'Vengeance comes to those who wait,' he said softly, and Adora saw that he was going to kill Skitteka. Skitteka the vicious. Skitteka the coward. Skitteka, the weak link upon which all of her plans for escape hung.

'No,' she said, starting forward to intercept him. 'No, leave him. We need him, can't you see that? We need him!'

But Xavier wasn't listening to her. His eyes were ablaze with a devouring hatred, and he was holding the blade with professional ease.

She knew that she wasn't strong enough to stop him. Knew that no words could quench the rage she saw in his eyes. Knew that even if she called for the vermin none of them would arrive in time to help.

So she reached up to her neck, untied the ragged shift and let it fall to the floor.

Xavier stopped, his mouth falling open. She looked like something from another world.

Of course she was scrawny. Scrawny enough that he could count her ribs. But she was still whole, her breasts and hips and thighs still curvy enough to catch the same torchlight which glowed within the golden mane of her hair. She was also incredibly, unbelievably, impossibly untarnished. No trace of disease marred the smooth silken perfection of her skin. Neither did any dirt.

Who was clean down here, he wondered? How was it possible?

But more than that, much more, was her fragility. Only things that haven't been broken yet can be fragile and he could see that Adora, alone amongst all of the slaves, hadn't been broken.

He tried to hold on to his outrage but then she was running one hand along the clenched line of his jaw and standing so close that he could smell soap. Soap!

'I don't understand,' he said. They were his last words. A sudden explosion of pain blossomed in his belly, and then thrust upwards into his liver.

'I'm sorry,' said Adora, and twisted the blade she had taken from him. If she had punctured his heart first it would have been easier, or at least cleaner. As it was his heart carried on beating as he died, pumping great gouts of blood from his desecrated body. It spattered on to her chilled skin with hideous warmth.

'I'm sorry.'

The look of confusion stayed on his face, pinned there by death, and he collapsed onto the floor next to the verminous corpse of Skitteka's half-eaten victim. Adora knelt down, twisted out the dagger, and slipped it into the stillness of his jugular just to make sure.

'I'm sorry,' she said, her face expressionless. Then she tore off the ragged remains of his shirt to wipe herself clean of his blood, and clean her dagger before slipping back into her clothes. Then, sitting on the cold stone floor, she put her head in her hands, and wept.

An hour later Skitteka regained consciousness. By then she was as composed as ever.

VASS HAD BEEN born last into a litter of thirteen. He had also been born the runt. Not many of his species could have survived such twin disadvantages but Vass did. He not only survived but thrived, doing so by the simple expedient of devouring his siblings. He started with the weakest, losing three of his milk teeth in the process, and finished with the strongest. That had been just as soon as he had learned to lift a rock above its sleeping head.

This was an exceptional beginning even for one of his species, and his dam was so distressed that she died soon after the last of her other offspring. It was not a sacrifice Vass had let go to waste. The rest of his life had been a continuation of that promising start. He joined his clan's warriors almost as soon as he was out of the burrow, and soon set about translating the fratricidal excesses of his whelphood into political progress.

Now, at the ripe old age of twelve, Vass had developed a reputation for savagery that made him the envy of his kin. It had preceded him into this miserable mine, a dread that was almost a physical thing. He could see it now in the crouching forms and twisting tails of the chiefs and leaders who abased themselves before him, grovelling in the dirt of what had once been their domain but which was now so effortlessly his.

He had gathered them in the audience chamber. His personal guards stood around the walls, magnificent in their arrogance and cruelty. They would satiate their bloodlust before the day was out, and anticipation of the joys to come set their eyes agleam in the darkness. Their presence did little to help Evasqeek's nerves.

Instead of executing the chief overseer immediately for his treacherous inefficiency, Vass had decided to let him talk first. Not that it was doing him any good.

'It was the cave-in, your worship.' Evasqeek chittered. He was grovelling so abjectly on the floor that the blades of his incisors tapped intermittently on the rock.

'The cave-in?' Vass asked, his beady eyes as hard as glass.

'Yes,' Evasqeek pleaded, and squeezed his paws together so tightly that he might have been holding a throat. 'Yes, the cave-in. We lost fifty slaves and a score of the best handlers.'

Vass shifted comfortably on the raised litter that dominated the room. As always on these occasions he was thoroughly enjoying himself.

'When was this cave-in?' he asked ingenuously, and was gratified to smell a fresh wave of terror emanating from his victim.

'A month ago, my liege,' the mine supervisor admitted and, realising that the excuse had been a mistake, suddenly changed tack. 'But the real problem is the indolence and treachery of slave master Skitteka. He is too soft on the slaves. He doesn't look after them either. They keep dying from the lightest of wounds.'

'I see,' Vass said. His spies and informers had already determined that the real reason for Evasqeek's failure was that his mine was almost exhausted. He would still need to make an example of somebody, of course, but it occurred to him that it wouldn't necessarily have to be Evasqeek himself.

'Yes, yes, yes,' Evasqeek jabbered. 'It's Skitteka's fault. He's lazy, too.'

'Then perhaps I should speak with this Skitteka,' Vass decided. He heard a whimper from amongst the assembled throng and saw an exceptionally bulky figure trying to press itself into the floor.

'You're Skitteka, I suppose?' Vass asked. But before the skaven could reply a voice rang out. A human voice.

All eyes turned to the slave who stood at the entrance of the audience chamber. Ordinarily the guards would have lashed the flesh from her bones for such an intrusion, but now they were too busy cowering themselves. The hungry eyes of Vass's guard had transformed them from predators into prey.

And so Adora padded unbidden into the audience chamber. Evasqeek watched her dumbly and felt vaguely grateful that at least attention had been turned away from him.

His relief was to be short lived.

'My Lord Evasqeek,' the slave said, her tone perfectly pitched into the place where hope and terror meet. 'We are sorry the tribute is late. Please forgive us. It was because we were locked up.'

So saying she fell to the floor besides Evasqeek, pressed her head down even lower than his, and slid a ragged bundle across to him. He reached out for it unthinkingly, and as the rags loosened he was bathed in the hypnotic green glow of wyrdstone.

It pulsed inches away from his snout, and he seemed to feel his blood boil and fizz. Desire and revulsion tore through his thoughts, and he hardly heard Vass when he spoke.

'I thought that wyrdstone was supposed to be handed directly to the clan's treasurer,' Vass said.

Evasqeek felt blood trickling from his snout. He licked his teeth and, eyes still on the pulsing light of the stone, said: 'What?'

'Why are the slaves delivering the stone directly to you?' Vass asked, his tone mild. It seemed that Evasqeek would provide him with his example after all. And why not? He would do as well as anyone. He suddenly had an idea of what that example would be, too.

'I don't know,' Evasqeek said vaguely, and managed to tear his eyes away from the fragments of stone. He looked up at Adora, and although he didn't recognise her, he did recognise Skitteka's marking on her.

'Wait,' he said, understanding dawning. 'Wait, this is a trick. Skitteka–'

But at Vass's signal the guards were already closing in. Evasqeek saw his doom waiting in the manacles they carried, and panic burst inside him. With a scream he launched himself towards the exit, clawing through his fellows as he tried to escape, but he had left it far, far too late. Within seconds he had been beaten down and chained up, transformed from the mine's master to its most miserable captive.

'It seems you have developed a taste for the stone,' Vass said, prowling towards him. 'But fear not. I have a mind to be merciful. I am going to feed you of much of it as you can take. And then,' he bent down to whisper into his captive's ear, 'I'm going to feed you some more.'

Evasqeek's last coherent thought as they pinned him to the floor was one of surprise. Who would have thought that the fat fool Skitteka had the wit to set him up like this? How could he have maintained such a facade of gluttonous incompetence whilst setting these wheels in motion?

He saw Vass stalking towards him, the bundle of stone held in his trembling paw. As soon as he realised what was going to happen he started shrieking, froth flecking his snout as he spasmed and writhed. The guards waited for their chance then slipped ligatures around his lower and upper jaws, pulling them open to reveal the thrashing pink of the tongue within.

'That's right,' Vass said softly. 'Open wide.'

And with that he started to feed Evasqeek. He pressed the stone down his throat one cancerous piece at a time. At first his victim hissed and rolled his eyes in terror. Then he started to shrill and his eyes bulged with a crazed joy. Eventually he started to change.

Fur sloughed away. Limbs withered. A second tail grew from the melting knots of his spine, a paw blossoming from the end of it. Eyes blinked open across his disintegrating form and the claws on his feet lengthened into talons.

Vass's guard worked to keep pace with the transformation. They tightened some chains, loosened others. The tail was bound with leather ligatures and the eyes blinded as soon as they opened. They worked fast, concentrating on the knots and chains and ligatures that bound the monster's form with the desperate skill of sailors adjust the rigging of a storm-tossed ship.

Even after Vass ran out of stone the transformation continued. It only slowed after the thing that had been Evasqeek was no longer recognisable. It bubbled and hissed and mewled within the mesh of its confinement, its image reflected in a hundred pairs of horrified eyes.

Alone in the chamber Adora regarded the horror before her with equanimity. Her eyes were as calm as a deep blue sea on a still summer's day, and a smile played around the perfect curve of her lips. There was a faint blush in the cream of her complexion too, just as much as there might be had she just returned from a vigorous horse ride on a warm afternoon.

Then she shook herself and, whilst her captors still gazed hypnotised at the horror that had once been their master, she slipped away as silently as a cat in twilight.

'YOU BRING ME much luck, little cat,' Skitteka mused and pawed idly at his pet. Although it had only been a few weeks since Vass had appointed him as mine overseer, he had already gained over twenty pounds in weight. Even the pads on his paws had fattened, and he had taken to slapping Adora to hear the sound echo in the great audience chamber.

His audience chamber.

'You are truly the only one deserving of this honour, lord,' Adora told him, and in a way it was true. With Evasqeek out of the way Skitteka was the only one with a vicious enough reputation to rule his subordinates. Since he had taken over, things had certainly run smoothly.

That was something that Adora knew that she had to change. So she said:

'My lord Skitteka, can I ask you a question?'

Skitteka slapped her playfully, the impact of his paw numbing her back. He was in a high good humour today.

'Of course you can,' he hissed. 'As long as it isn't a boring one.'

'Thank you, lord,' Adora said. 'I just wondered why you keep the thing that used to be Evasqeek locked in a cell?'

Skitteka hesitated and Adora waited for another blow, harder this time. Instead Skitteka answered her.

'Vass and I decided to keep him,' he said, by which he meant that Vass had told him what to do while he had grovelled miserably before him. 'It's a reminder of what happens to traitors and thieves.'

Skitteka took a pawful of her hair and twisted it for reassurance. Adora ignored the pain and risked another question.

'Very wise of you, my lord,' she said. 'But what does the thing eat?'

'Anything,' Skitteka said with a shiver. 'Anything at all. And it's always hungry. But enough about that. Tell me what you have learned in the past few days.'

'Three of the slaves are planning to break through their chains and escape,' she said, not because it was true but because it wasn't. The three she had in mind spent every night howling and sobbing and wailing with a misery close to madness. Adora knew that unless she removed them quickly, their despair would weaken others who might otherwise prove useful.

'Give their names to the guards when you get back,' Skitteka said.

'Yes, lord,' Adora said. 'There's also a rumour that an army of ghosts are gathering in some of the worked out tunnels.'

Skitteka hissed and twisted at her hair.

'Ghosts? What makes them say that?'

'Some of them have heard things. Seen things. It's probably nonsense, my lord, but that's what they say.'

Skitteka shifted, his whiskers twitching in thought. Adora pretended not to watch. She had almost invented something a bit more tangible for Skitteka to send his guards chasing after. Orcs perhaps, or some other monsters. But as always, it seemed, she had judged Skitteka's gnawing anxieties correctly.

'Something to investigate,' he mused, beady eyes darting around the empty spaces of the chamber. 'What else?'

'Nothing definite...' Adora began, then trailed off.

Skitteka, catching something in her tone, forgot about ghosts and fixed his attention on her.

'Tell me,' he said, and twisted one of her ears. Pain screamed as the flesh came close to tearing. Adora ignored the white-hot agony and spoke with a perfectly contrived hesitancy.

'The guard Tso-tso,' she began. 'Whenever I am near him, he and his friends stop talking. It is almost as though they are suspicious of me.'

Skitteka released her ear and chittered with agitation. Tso-tso! He should have known that he was a traitor. He was capable and respected by the others. He no doubt had his own designs on Skitteka's position. Well, he would see where those would get him.

'Very good,' he said, and absent-mindedly tossed a gobbet of meat onto the floor in front of Adora.

'Thank you, my lord,' she said and scuttled over to claim it. She ignored the rotten iron taste of the raw flesh just as studiously as she ignored the provenance of it. Her gag reflex almost betrayed her as the first torn-off morsel slithered down her gullet, but she massaged her oesophagus and thought about how close she was. How terrifyingly close.

'I HEARD IT took Tso-tso over three days to die,' one of the guards said to the other.

'Three days, yes,' his companion replied.

Their conversation died. Their tails writhed. Their nostrils wrinkled. Something banged against the iron-bound door behind them and they both leapt into the air. When they landed they turned towards the cell they were guarding. The iron held firm, and the heavy beams that held it shut remained intact. But was that a new crack in the timber?

'Our shift must be over by now,' one of the guards chittered. 'Must be, must be.'

'It's that cowardly scrunt Kai,' the other agreed, fear turning to hatred within the black orbs of his eyes. 'He's always late.'

Something heavy slid against the door. It seemed to bulge beneath the guards' terrified gaze, yet it still held firm. For now at least.

'Look,' said one. 'Why don't I go and get our relief? You can stay here while I'm gone.'

His companion didn't deign to reply. He merely hissed with annoyance. Their concentration was focused so intently on the door that they didn't hear the footsteps padding up behind them.

'Permission to speak, my lords,' a voice said. The guards shrieked as they spun around. When they saw that it was a slave their terror blossomed into rage, and they scrabbled for their whips.

'I have a message from Lord Skitteka,' Adora said. 'It is very urgent.'

'Speak then,' one said, paw still closed around the hilt of his whip. 'Speak, speak.'

'My lord Skitteka requests that you go to his audience chamber immediately.'

'What for?' the two guards said in perfect unison, their voices sharp with suspicion.

'He didn't tell me,' said Adora.

The guards exchanged a troubled glance.

'But who will guard–'

This time the sound that came from the cell was not an impact but a series of squelches, as though something was being dismembered. Something big.

'He wants both of us?' one of the guards asked hopefully.

'Yes, lord,' Adora said. 'And I am to wait here until you get back.'

The guards looked at her. If the thing escaped she wouldn't be anything more than a morsel for it. But so what? That was gloriously, wonderfully, tail-liftingly no longer their problem.

The two guards took a final look at the door then skittered off. Adora waited until they had disappeared around the corner before she turned to the door.

Three thick wooden beams had been slotted into holes cut into the stone on either side of the door. A lump of ancient iron and battered timber, it rested on crude iron hinges each as big as Adora's head. The hinges were rusty and the door was heavy, but it opened outwards so that was all right. The thing within would have no problem opening it. No problem at all.

As she tested the weight of the first of the beams that held the door closed, she heard something slither behind it. It would be waiting for her when she freed it, of that she was sure. Waiting hungrily.

'Good,' she told herself.

Adora wedged her shoulder beneath the beam and lifted it, freeing one end from the stone slot in which it had rested. Then she dropped it and sprang away as it thudded onto the floor. The noise echoed down the passageway. When the echoes had gone there was silence on the other side of the door.

Ignoring the twist in her stomach Adora removed the second beam, letting it tumble to the floor next to the first. When she stooped to remove the third an almost paralysing sense of reluctance came over her. She had seen the creation of the thing that had been Evasqeek, and beside it all the horrors down here paled into insignificance. There was wrongness to it, a terrible, life-hating wrongness.

'Good,' she repeated, lifting her chin and gazing defiantly into space. 'Then it will serve my purpose.'

Without giving herself any more time to think she wrestled the final bar free and stepped back from the door. It was as well that she did. No sooner had the last bar been lifted than the horror within hurled forward. Iron and wood shattered as it impacted on the stone wall and the thing which had been Evasqeek emerged.

Adora tried to scream, but her throat had locked tight. Her knees had locked tight too, and even though instinct screamed at her to run, run, *run damn it*, she remained frozen as the thing slithered and lurched towards her.

It had grown during the dark weeks of its captivity. Now it was three times the size of the creature it had once been, and a confusion of pseudopods and limbs grasped greedily at the world about it. The eyes that dotted its form like so many bullet holes swivelled towards Adora and then she was screaming, and she was running, and she had never been so terrified in her life.

The thing chased her and although that was what she had wanted all along she wasn't happy about that. Not any more, no, not one little bit. For the first time she understood how all of those that had died around her had been able to give up on life.

But she was still Adora. Even as panic gripped her she made sure that the thing remained behind her as she followed the route she had decided upon. This was her one chance to escape, her only chance. And, she decided, she would take it just as surely as a dropped cat will land on its feet.

The guards had just closed the hatch on the last of the slaves when Adora burst in on them. Although they were used to having Skitteka's pet sidling around they had never seen her like this, fleeing and terrified and suddenly dangerous looking.

'In the hole with you,' one of them said and pointed to the trap door that led down into the oubliette. He went to lift it and Adora had a terrible vision of what would happen to the trapped mass of humanity below if the thing behind her got down amongst them.

'Run,' she told him and hit him straight armed. He tumbled backwards, shrilling in outrage as he drew his weapon, but then the thing which had been pursuing Adora was upon them.

Their squeals echoed after her as she ran, adrenaline burning within her. After a while she slowed down and eventually forced herself to stop. The sound of the struggle behind her had already died away, and she had no doubt as to who had won. She rubbed the sweat from her face, ran her fingers through the slick of her hair, then circled back around to the oubliette.

The thing had already gone, searching for new victims. The remains of those it had left behind lay scattered around the chamber, torn and dismembered. Adora rolled a head away from the trap door, lifted it, and pushed down the ladder. A ring of terrified faces looked up at her, squinting in the light she had let into their darkness. She looked down upon them and smiled, the radiant expression framed by the golden halo of her hair.

'Glorious news,' she told them. 'Today the gods have given you the chance to take your vengeance.'

With that she threw the rat-featured head of the guard down in amongst them. They looked from Adora to the head and then back again. And then with a collective cry that sounded more like the roar of a wounded beast than anything human they swarmed up the ladder, made fearless by the miracle they had witnessed.

HAD SKITTEKA LED the battle against the thing which had been Evasqeek, it might have gone better. Without the confusion it might have been lured into a place where it could have been attacked from all sides at once, or where it could have been pushed down a mineshaft or crushed beneath falling stone.

But Skitteka hadn't led the battle against the horror. Instead he had driven his underlings towards it, hiding behind their desperate savagery until they had finally overwhelmed it. Their victory had come at a terrible cost. The remains of a score of guards had been smeared throughout the mine, and dozens of survivors lay shattered and broken amongst them.

Even then, had Skitteka led the battle against the slaves he might still have saved the mine. The humans were desperate but compared to the guards they were slow and clumsy, and their makeshift weapons were no match for the razored perfection of the guards' own poisoned blades.

But Skitteka hadn't led the battle against the slaves. Instead he had locked himself into his burrow, sweating and stinking and waiting for others to save him.

They hadn't.

And now he sat, terrified and alone. Although the mine still rang with the sounds of battle, he ignored them. Instead he had withdrawn into the paralysing cocoon of his own cowardice. He was only shaken from it when, heralded by the squeal of a guard who had chosen to skulk rather than flee, one of the slaves slipped into the room.

Skitteka hissed and scrabbled for the handle of his blade, but then the slave stepped into the pool of light and he recognised the blonde of her hair and the meek expression on her face.

'My lord,' Adora said, padding forwards. 'Thank the gods you are still alive. Can I wait with you until the fighting is over?'

Skitteka's fur bristled, and suspicion wrinkled his snout.

'Why aren't you with the other slaves, little cat?' he said, gesturing towards her with his sword. The murderous sliver of steel gleamed with the venom which coated it.

'They are mad, my lord,' Adora said as she closed the distance between them. 'They think that I am a traitor because of my loyalty to you.'

Skitteka started to speak, then jumped as the door crashed open behind her. The men who charged into the chamber were as filthy and starved as all the humans, but there was a terrifying lack of fear about them. Compared to that, their lack of shackles seemed almost secondary.

'Save me, lord!' Adora cried and rushed towards Skitteka, who had no intention of saving anybody but himself. He leapt out of his chair and turned to flee to another exit.

But Adora was even quicker than his panic.

As he turned his back on her she lunged forwards, slicing through first one of his hamstrings and then the other. He collapsed with a squeal and Adora reversed her grip. She punched the steel between his vertebrae with the thoughtless accuracy of a seamstress pushing thread through the eye of a needle.

Skitteka shrieked and spasmed on the cold floor. He tried to make his crippled body work. He failed.

'Stand back,' Adora barked at the men who were closing in on their crippled tormentor. They paused uncertainly, their picks and shovels raised for the killing blow. Adora turned on them, and when they saw the rage on her face they retreated.

'Go and finish off the others,' she told them as she closed in on Skitteka. 'This one is mine.'

His spine severed, he was thrashing his limbs as uselessly as a cockroach Adora had once seen nailed to the wall of an inn. She had been a serving girl at the time, and although she didn't know who had visited the cruelty upon the creature, she had never forgotten it. Between her duties she had watched it dying for almost a week, its struggles getting weaker and weaker. Eventually, when it could manage no more than the occasional twitch, its fellows had returned to devour it.

Unfortunately she didn't have the time to organise a similar fate for Skitteka.

Never mind. She would make do with what time she had.

'See this?' she told him, holding up the bloodied dagger. He rolled his eyes and hissed an entreaty.

'Please help me,' he said. 'I will give you clothes, lots of clothes. And meat! As much meat as you want.'

Adora felt her control tearing.

'What I want,' she said softly, 'is for you not to touch me anymore. Instead,' she lifted the dagger, 'I'm going to touch you.'

So she did.

It took a long, long time. When she had finished and the last of his screams had bled out she turned to find that some of the men had stayed to watch her. Their open mouths and wide eyes made them look like startled cattle.

'Go,' she said, and tried to ignore the horror on their faces as they fled from her.

SUNLIGHT PLAYED UPON the rippling surface of the stream. A breeze whispered soothingly through the branches of the trees. There was the smell of jasmine and fresh sap and something that might have been a distant ocean. Even the remains of the fire smelled clean, fresh ash and burned fish bones. Adora enjoyed the fragrances of freedom as she sat in the shade and waited for her rags to dry. She had washed them as thoroughly as she had washed herself and now she was working on her nails, cleaning beneath them with a gnawed twig.

She had left the other survivors as soon as they had emerged from the mine. They were too wild and starving to be of much further use, so she had abandoned them. That had been two days ago, and she was beginning to wonder if it had been a mistake. She had no idea where she was, and there might be anything in this forest.

She was so lost in thought that she didn't hear the hoofbeats until they were almost upon her. With a startled glance upwards she sprang to her feet and hurriedly pulled her damp slip over her nakedness. A moment later, an apparition of coloured silk and burnished steel emerged from the forest. It rode a towering warhorse and carried a lance that was twice as long as she was tall. Adora padded towards the knight.

'Excuse me, kind sir,' she said bowing her head so that her hair tumbled forward from her shoulders. 'I wonder if you might help me?'

The knight stopped and lifted his visor. His dark features were hard with arrogance but as he took a closer look at Adora the expression turned into something else.

'I would be honoured to, my lady,' he said and bowed towards her. 'But first we should leave this place. The enemy are not far behind. Would you ride with me?'

'I would be honoured, my lord,' Adora said as he swung her up into the saddle behind him and carried her, sweet and smooth and lethal, back into the world of men.

HUNTED

John French

THADDEUS BLINKED AND his world vanished in a scream. Blind darkness surrounded him, caged him in a dream of pain. Then light and sensations came in a burning rush: a white room, a wide face, eyes glowing red in the dark cave of a hood, the ground splitting with cracks of fire, the wetness of tears, anger like a red storm, a ringed hand, then darkness and silence.

He blinked again and was looking an enemy in the eyes. They were black eyes that glittered from a blunt hairless head, jagged patterns burned into the flesh. The man's body was a massive slab of hard muscle, covered in tarnished armour and stained ochre fatigues. His head was cocked as if Thaddeus had stopped speaking in the middle of a sentence and the man was waiting for it to finish. Rusted metal lined the walls around them, their surfaces scratched with evil runes and lit by the fever yellow light of a glow-globe. The air reeked of blood, sweat and raw meat. Every detail told Thaddeus that he stood in a lair of the enemy, and with an enemy in front of him.

A frown creased the man's face and his mouth began to move, forming a question. Thaddeus slammed a fist into his throat. The man gave a strangled cry, staggered, hit the grime-smeared metal wall behind him and exploded forward with a roar, trying to drive Thaddeus off his feet with raw strength. Thaddeus pivoted an instant before the charge struck, grabbed the man's head in both hands and felt his brute power slide past him as he twisted. With a loud snap, the man's body crashed onto the metal floor and was still.

Shaking with adrenaline, Thaddeus looked at the corpse at his feet. Sinuous tattooed patterns and eight-pointed brand scars covered the dead man's skin. He looked at his own hands. Tattoos spiralled around his fingers and palms; they were the marks of ruin and blasphemy, like those on the hands and arms of the man he had just killed. Thaddeus ran his hands over his body, feeling the scars on his scalp and face, the beaten metal of a breastplate and the saw-toothed blades at his waist. Panic surged through him and he fought to keep it down. Who was he? Inside his mind a locked door opened and memories returned: he was a servant of the Imperium, a warrior in a war of shadows and lies. The realisation was like the touch of a cool hand on his head: comforting, removing doubt. He knew where he was and what he had to do: he was in the heart of enemy territory and far from help. He had to reach a vox-caster, transmit an extraction location to Imperial forces and reach that location at any cost. Beyond this driving need there was something else, something always just beyond his grasp, always out of sight in the labyrinth of his mind.

'Lost in the land of the damned,' he muttered to himself and began to run. He passed through narrow tunnels, ducking into the shadows as figures passed him. He saw the scars patterning their skin, heard the cruel tongue in which they muttered to each other. The air pulsed to the hiss-thump of air processors shifting foetid air.

When he reached the communications room he slid a long, serrated knife from a sheath and banged on the door until it opened. A renegade trooper in dark fatigues looked out; a fabric mask covered his head, bloodshot eyes wide behind grimy glass eye-holes. Thaddeus could hear static and fragments of distorted noise spilling from the room. It was small and rank with the smell of sweat and ozone, consoles lined the walls, the light of readouts pulsing to the sounds from speaker grilles. There was a moment of stillness the length of a heartbeat.

Thaddeus's first movement was a backhanded cut with the knife that took the renegade in the throat, severing his neck to the spine. Warm red spray splashed his face. The man collapsed, blood bubbling dark on the floor. Thaddeus stepped forward with the momentum of the cut. Terror and fury flowed through him; he could feel its acid touch in his guts and a copper tang in his mouth. He was screaming. A spindle-limbed man with a face like a dried corpse stood, a laspistol in his hand. Thaddeus heard a crack and felt the shot burn across his temple. He stepped to the outside of the man's gun arm, reversed his knife and rammed it into the neck. The body jerked as the man died and Thaddeus yanked the blade out in a thick spray.

He stood in pooling blood, gasping air as the rage receded and fear returned. Lurching to the console he examined the equipment, frequencies and ciphers flashing through his mind. His hands moved over controls without guidance, sending the location of the Fallen Spire far out in the no-man's-land beyond the underground fortress in which he stood.

He picked up the renegade's laspistol and stripped power cells from the corpses. The jagged marks and eight-pointed stars cut into the men's skin made him retch. He thought of the killing rage that had surged through him; its touch had been alien, like someone touching the inside of his skin. It made him feel tainted, unclean, as if the marks on his skin were scars on his soul. He shook the thought off and pushed himself to his feet again. The one thing that was certain was that if he were to live, he had to reach the Fallen Spire. He stepped out of the chamber, pulled the hatch door shut and began to run.

FROM THE HIGHEST tower of the Imperial command fortress Colonel Augustine Tarl looked out on a ruined world. It was sunset, but the sky remained the dull tan of a soiled funeral shroud. From here he would have once looked across a string of hives, their sides rising liked armoured mountains into a cobalt sky. Seismic charges and plasma warheads had reduced those hives to a sea of torn metal and ash that extended to the horizon like a frozen sea; its wave crests ragged edges of metal, its troughs filled with spreading shadows. They were called the Murder Wastes; the vast no-man's-land in the war between the Imperium and the forces of Chaos on Hranx.

'Admiring the rewards of hubris, colonel?' Inquisitor Sargon said from behind Tarl who turned and snapped a sharp salute. Tarl was tall, with a broad face, bright blue eyes and a strong jaw. It was a face full of confidence, the type of face that inspired trust. Clad in the gloss-red armour of an Inquisitorial storm trooper he stayed at attention as the inquisitor advanced towards him.

'At ease, colonel,' said the inquisitor. He was shorter than Tarl, broad-shouldered with a big pockmarked face. Bronze plate armour glittered under a heavy robe of deep purple.

Tarl tried to adopt a casual stance as the inquisitor came to stand next to him; it was difficult to relax in the presence of this man who had the power to kill billions with a word.

'You summoned me, my lord,' said Tarl.

'Yes I did. I am giving you a mission that will be the most important of your service.' The inquisitor's voice was a bass rumble like the grating of stone. Tarl kept his face impassive but he felt a jolt of anticipation run through his gut. 'I am trusting in your nature and abilities. The Imperium is trusting in them too.'

'I understand, my lord,' said Tarl.

The inquisitor twitched his lips as if at a joke.

'Not yet, colonel, but you will.' The inquisitor leaned on the tower's parapet, his red bionic eyes staring out at the darkening world from within his deep hood. 'An hour ago we received a signal on a long unused frequency.' A hand, thick with rings, emerged from under the sleeve of the inquisitor's robe and handed a brass-framed data-slate to Tarl, who took in the information on its surface with a glance.

'A set of location coordinates in the Murder Wastes and a single word: Thaddeus?' Tarl looked up at the inquisitor.

'You are to take an assault carrier and go to that location. Take a hand-picked squad of storm troopers.' The inquisitor turned away from the parapet to look at Tarl. 'There you will find and retrieve a man in my service.'

Tarl looked back at the signal data displayed in glowing green symbols on the data-slate.

'These analysis readings indicate that the signal came out of the renegade's fortress zone; probably transmitted using enemy equipment.'

'Yes, the signal came from within the enemy stronghold.'

'It is not a trick, a lure?'

'No. It is victory.' The inquisitor smiled at the puzzled look on the colonel's face. 'How long have we been fighting here, Tarl?'

'At least a decade, my lord.'

'Too long, and we have paid too high a price.' The inquisitor gestured at the land below the fortress tower. Tarl knew what the gesture meant: he had been here when the Imperium had levelled the hives hoping to destroy the rebellion within. The Chaos renegades led by the Alpha Legion had been prepared, and had buried themselves beneath the ground in a subterranean fortress complex they called the Pit of the Hydra. There they survived and endured while the Imperium burnt its own flesh to try and kill a disease that had already spread. If Hranx did fall then the Alpha Legion would have secured a gateway for its corruption to spread into other sectors and kill other worlds. The Imperium was caught in a snare: unable to yield and unable to destroy its enemy.

'And this man will win the war, my lord?' asked Tarl.

'Our forces are infiltrated by Alpha Legion agents. They are serpents in our midst, killing us with a thousand bites. How many of our operations and offensives have been blown or crippled? And while they rob us of our strength, theirs grows.' The inquisitor turned and placed his hand on Tarl's shoulder and looked directly into his eyes. 'The man you are to retrieve is a servant of the Imperium who has infiltrated the renegades and remained hidden within them for several years.' Tarl allowed his shock to show on his face.

'How is that possible?'

'His personality and memories have been replaced with a constructed identity so that he is incapable of giving himself away.' The inquisitor let his hand drop, looked away from Tarl. 'He has believed that he is one of them. Under particular circumstances he is conditioned to shake off his false self and return to us.'

'What circumstances, my lord?' Tarl asked, though he thought he knew. The inquisitor smiled, revealing silver-inlaid teeth.

'He was conditioned to return to us once he had learned the identities of the agents the Alpha Legion have infiltrated into our forces,' he said.

NIGHT WAS FALLING when Thaddeus heard the howl of the hunters at his back. It rose in a harsh, high note gathering replies and echoes until it was a wailing chorus calling him to oblivion. He had known that his flight would not go undiscovered, and so once above ground he had run hard, knowing that every stride was a moment stolen from death. He knew the hunters were close; they had tasted his scent on the wind and they howled in anticipation of the kill.

The cries of his pursuers faded as Thaddeus scrambled up another slope of jagged rubble, his hands bloody from a thousand sharp edges. In the distance the Fallen Spire rose above the Murder Wastes like the broken tip of a god's spear thrust into the ground; a far away promise of safety. He slithered down a slope of ash into a wide valley, its bottom filled with debris and blade-like shadows; a hundred paces away a wide pool of liquid glittered like a dark mirror. A gust of dry wind brought a thick chemical stench to his nostrils from the pool's surface.

Thaddeus began to move across the floor of the valley, running from cover to cover, ash rising from his footsteps. A whisper-soft sound of movement reached his ears; he glanced behind and went very still. Long, lean shapes were slinking down the side of the valley where he had been. Each was humanoid but moved close to the ground on reverse jointed-legs and long arms, their muscles taut under pale skin. The hunters had found him. They were human mutants selectively altered by the renegades to hunt the Murder Wastes. They were blind and stalked by scent, tasting the air with long tongues. Thaddeus gripped the butt of his laspistol. He could count at least three of them and knew there were more. They would be fast. He watched one of them pause on a lip of rubble he had passed seconds before. The hunter crouched, its elongated head turning from side to side, its long tongue flicking between needle teeth.

He began to ease himself into cover, moving one limb at a time, blood hammering in his ears. Could they hear his heart beating, he wondered? He lifted his foot to step forward, and a stone shifted with a small noise; he froze. Another shape bounded onto a rise of rubble ten paces away. Thaddeus felt a drop of sweat run down his face. The hunter bounded towards him. Behind it the others snarled and followed. Thaddeus drew his laspistol and fired. The hunter jinked aside with unnatural speed and the bolt of energy fizzed into the air. He fired again, the shot kicking up a hot splash of melted dust where it hit the ground. He turned and ran, knowing that he could not escape. Even if he killed some of the hunters there were others and they had his scent.

The pool was in front of him, its surface black and still, its chemical stench thick in his throat. The hunters were blind and if his scent vanished, so did he. He dived in and felt the liquid darkness swallow him. It was silent under the surface of the pool, and he kept his mouth and eyes closed. He felt the acid burning his skin and pain began to spread from his chest. For a second he thought of letting the liquid wrap him in its corrosive embrace forever. He would not be losing much; he could remember almost nothing but a handful of hours filled with death and fear. There would be nothing in the future but more fear, more blood and the breath of enemies at his back. An image came to him of a world burning around him, and he knew he had seen it happen, had been there as the forces of ruin had destroyed something very dear to him. The loss and anger was like a raw wound in his soul from which snatches of memory poured: a hand on his shoulder, a bronze aquila ring, a face with red eyes. He was a warrior that walked amongst the enemy. It was his purpose; he was a servant of the Imperium.

Thaddeus kicked for the surface, bursting into the air with a suppressed gasp. He trod water, eyes sweeping the darkness, ears straining for any sound. There was no sign of the hunters. He swam to the pool's edge and pulled himself out, chemical sludge dripping from his body. The smell would hide his scent from the enemies, or so he hoped. He lay on his back for a moment, breathing hard, his eyes looking up towards where the Fallen Spire glinted against the dull black sky. With a grunt of effort he got to his feet and scrambled through the dark, pushing himself until he was in the shadow of the Fallen Spire but could go no further. Exhausted, he found the entrance of a wide pipe and dragged himself inside. Curled and shivering in the dark he fell into a sleep disturbed by dreams filled with burning worlds and a wide face with red eyes.

THE VALKYRIE SWEPT across the darkened plain towards the Fallen Spire. Its hunched fuselage and wings were a matt charcoal-grey broken by a night camouflage pattern of black lines sprayed in an irregular grid. Its cockpit and crew compartment were dark, all readouts and displays disabled, its pilot flying by night-vision and instinct. From its open side door Colonel Tarl watched the ground below, his own night-vision visor showing a rushing expanse of luminous green. From the crew compartment behind him Tarl could hear the low noises of the squad of storm troopers checking equipment and eating rations. Each would be wearing night-vision visors and passing the time with mundane routines to keep their minds focused. Even for men such as these, who were hardened by years of war, the time before an action was a battle against boredom and fear.

'Hungry, colonel?' came a voice from behind Tarl. It was Kulg, the squad sergeant, a smiling slab of a man who was one of Tarl's best.

Tarl turned and leaned back into the crew compartment; his night vision showing his storm troopers sitting on the flight benches, their black armour making them look like statues carved of obsidian. Each had a hellgun strapped tight across his chest and a bulky grav-chute on his back. Kulg was holding out a foil-wrapped bar in a gloved hand.

'Field rations?' Tarl took the bar and bit into it. The sergeant grinned. 'Thanks,' said Tarl making a face; the rations tasted vile. 'So kind of you to spare some for me.' The sergeant chuckled, his teeth gleaming in the green tint of the night-vision. Tarl grinned back. Kulg and his squad were cold killers to ordinary men, but Tarl had that combination of competence and good humour that made these men like and trust him. 'Now, if you happen to have a flask of hot caffeine, I might just forget about the taste of this.'

'Here, sir.' The sergeant smiled and handed Tarl a small metal flask.

'Thanks,' said Tarl sipping the hot liquid. Now was a good time to tell them, he thought. 'Listen up,' he said, raising his voice over the drone of the Valkyrie's engines. 'You know the brief: we drop using grav-chutes, form a perimeter, secure the target, and the Valkyrie pulls us out.' He waited for assenting nods. 'The target will look like one of the enemy, a renegade in every detail.' Tarl paused 'Securing him is of absolute importance.'

'We're clear on the plan, sir,' said Kulg.

'Don't forget that the Alpha Legion has used witches, flesh-changers, even turncoats before.' There was a scattering of nods; all of them had seen the tricks and lies used by of the servants the Dark Gods. 'Until we are sure it is him, assume nothing. Be ready to respond if it is a trap, and wait for my authentication of the target's identity.' He looked around at each of them. 'Understand?' Each gave a clipped 'Sir' in reply. Tarl nodded and turned back to looking out of the side hatch; the sky had begun to lighten. The pilot and weapons officer already had their special orders and would be ready if he needed them. He took a sip from the flask and thought of the man out there in the dark, running to him bearing the greatest of secrets.

THADDEUS WOKE TO the sound of whispers. He could not see the speakers and so lay still, and listened. Grey light seeped into the pipe mouth where he shivered in the dawn chill. His vision was restricted to a circular scoop of mud grey sky cut by the looming silhouette of the Fallen Spire. The whispering voices were coming closer; he could hear the soft brush of fabric against webbing, and the low clink of weapons. Whoever they were, they were moving with deliberate slowness: searching, hunting. He prayed that they would not check the pipe that hid him.

A boot crunched a pace away. Adrenaline began to seep into his cold muscles, the instincts of the cornered animal making his mouth dry and his gut twist. Keeping his breath slow, he began to move his hand towards his knife. Memories flicked through his awareness: a smiling face, a bright white room, a world dying around him. Then something else rose from the depths of his mind like a grinning skull pulled from a slaughter pit. Anger overwhelmed his thoughts; he was not prey to be run to ground and gutted; he was the predator. His hand closed around the handle of his knife, and a red cloud unfolded in his mind like blood pouring into water.

A figure blocked out the light at the pipe opening, a slouch-shouldered silhouette, the barrel of its lasgun pointed into the darkness. A cyclone of rage boiled through Thaddeus's mind and body, its surface alive with flashes of pain and black coils of hatred. He wanted blood; he wanted to feel the warm wash of it on his hands, and to see the life leave his kill's eyes. The figure was three paces away, its wide eyes blind to the death that waited in the darkness. Thaddeus's muscles coiled ready to spring forward in a killing leap.

There was a blurt of static from out of sight, and a muffled voice speaking clipped Imperial Gothic into a vox-caster. The figure in front of Thaddeus twitched at the sound, took a pace back into the light, and Thaddeus saw the glint of the grubby bronze aquila on the figure's helmet. He remembered a bronze aquila ring, and red eyes staring at him. The tide of anger receded leaving him shaking silently in the darkness. He was a servant of the Imperium, not a beast, but for a moment he had been someone else, someone monstrous. To infiltrate the renegades he had become one of them, and something of that other self remained inside him. He thought he could hear it whispering to him, telling him secrets. The damned still walk in me, he thought.

'Throne, no!' came a voice, loud enough for Thaddeus to hear.

'What is it, sarge?' asked the man Thaddeus could see. He looked young, his green fatigues smeared with ash, eyes shot red with days of fatigue and fear. This was a sweeping patrol, a small unit that probed deep into the Murder Wastes with nothing but their nerves and a lasgun to keep them alive.

Thaddeus thought of stepping out of his hiding place; he was a servant of the Imperium, so were they: they would help. But then what would they see step from the shadows? A man clad in barbed armour and dark cloth, dried blood on his hands, and a face twisted with evil runes. They would see an enemy, a predator like those that took their comrades and stalked their nightmares. They would see a renegade, and how could he persuade them that he was not?

'We pull out now,' said an unseen voice, its tone harsh. As it spoke, the ground began to shake.

'Wait, what...' asked another voice out of sight, trailing off as a sound like the beating of great drums became louder and louder.

'Run!' Thaddeus could hear more than fear now, he could hear terror. The air shook with a roar like rolling thunder. The man at the pipe mouth stared at the sky and fled. Thaddeus, scrambling to the end of the pipe, looked up and knew why. A wave of flames surged towards him, and above it the sky burned.

THE VALKYRIE SHUDDERED as black pillars of smoke rose into the air around it. Looking down from the side door of the assault carrier, Tarl could see a tide of fire roll across the Murder Wastes towards the Fallen Spire. There was a stink of burning oil on the furnace-hot air and the ground seemed to ripple under the impact of the artillery fire. The renegades had artillery buried underground that they hoisted up to hidden firing points along the edge of the Murder Wastes. There were hundreds of guns and they were all firing: a rhythmic chorus of war wiping the wastes clean of life. The Chaos forces were burning the land to kill one fleeing traitor. That, or they were driving their quarry into the jaws of the hunter, thought Tarl.

'Bring us in over the spire's tip,' shouted Tarl. The Fallen Spire loomed through a haze of dust and smoke. As tall as a Titan, it was a blackened spit of metal jutting out of the ground at an angle. At its tip there was a flattened point no more than twenty paces across. It had once been the peak of a now dead-hive that had fallen as it burned, embedding itself upright in the ruin below. It thrust above the vast tangle of wreckage like the tip of a sword from a dead man's back. It was the location the infiltrator, Thaddeus, had transmitted, the place from which the inquisitor had sent Tarl to collect him.

Tarl stood, gripping the rail that ran down the centre of the Valkyrie's crew compartment. He wore the red storm trooper carapace, a respirator mask hanging unfastened at his cheek. The squad were on their feet, their faces hidden by bug-eyed faceplates, their black armour glistening. A caress of static ran over Tarl's skin as he powered up his grav pack.

'Extraction point in twenty kilometres,' said the pilot. Tarl nodded to Sergeant Kulg.

'Form up,' shouted Kulg, and the storm troopers formed two lines facing the closed rear hatch, their shoulders touching, left hands gripping cleats in the ceiling. The sergeant gave Tarl a thumbs-up.

'Open rear hatch, and ready for drop,' said Tarl into his throat mic. The pilot gave a curt reply and the rear hatch split with the hiss of pistons, opening to show the land and sky racing to a vanishing point behind the Valkyrie.

'Jump on my command,' said Tarl, and fastened his respirator.

'Death and honour' shouted Kulg, and the squad echoed the words.

'For the Emperor,' said Tarl, but his words were lost in the roar of the wind.

THE FIRESTORM SURGED towards him and Thaddeus fled before it. White-hot sparks drifted down around him and sweat poured down his soot-smeared face. He did not know where the guardsmen were, his only instinct was to run, to reach safety. The fire tide surged on in a blazing wall that flowed over the rises and gulleys of rubble with a roar as it sucked in air. It was fifty paces behind him and he could feel the heat sear across his exposed skin. Above him the black speartip of the Fallen Spire thrust into the sky. It was so close that he could see the bent girders that jutted from its sides. Safety was so close, but the fire tide was at his heels.

He heard howls rise over the roar of the fire as the long, lean shapes of the hunters appeared out of the smoke-filled air, their pale bodies black against the flame, oblivious to the danger now that they had found their prey. There were dozens of them, their skin scorched and blistered but their fanged mouths wide with glee. He could not turn, could not fight, he could only run. His lungs felt as if they were on fire, his legs shot with pain. Then he was over the crest of an ash dune and the side of the Fallen Spire was in front of him. He gripped a jutting girder, swung up and began to climb without thinking, feet and hands scrabbling for purchase.

He was ten feet off the ground when the hunters crested the dune behind him. The first bounded to the base of the spire's side and leapt, springing up the tangle of projecting girders. With a snarl of triumph it was on him, talons raking his leg. Thaddeus screamed as pain ran up his body, but inside he felt a part of him bellow for blood. He kicked down with his other leg and felt bone crunch beneath his boot. The mutant fell, its limbs thrashing, its mouth snapping at the air. More were climbing, pulling themselves up with long arms, their claws screeching on the metal. He looked up at the spire's summit and took another grip. With a shriek of super-heated air the fire tide crested the dune and crashed into the base of the Fallen Spire. The hunters that had only just begun to climb were vapourised, others higher up screamed as the heat cooked their flesh and they fell into the inferno. Those above the tide of flame came up faster, their arms reaching for Thaddeus, tongues flicking at the blood dribbling from his leg.

With a grunt of pain Thaddeus gripped the girder above him with one hand and drew his laspistol with the other. Twisting to look down, he thumbed the safety off and pulled the trigger. Glowing bolts of energy plunged onto the hunters, burning through flesh and bone. Thaddeus kept the trigger squeezed until the clip was empty and the pistol was hot in his hand. He dropped the spent pistol and climbed, shutting out the numbness spreading from his shredded leg and the scrabbling noise of the surviving hunters climbing after him.

THE VALKYRIE TURNED hard, dropping in a controlled spiral towards the Fallen Spire. In the crew compartment the high pitched whine of grav-chutes cut through the bass rumble of the engines. A view of the spire's blunt summit, set above a surging ocean of flame, filled the open hatch.

'Jump!' shouted Tarl and the storm troopers leapt into the smoke-darkened air.

THADDEUS HEAVED HIMSELF onto the flat summit of the Fallen Spire. It was no more than twenty paces across, a sheer drop all around and the burning plateau below. He could hear shouted orders and see blurred images out of the corner of his eyes. Storm troopers in black armour were landing around him, tucking into tight rolls as they landed with the lightness of windblown seeds. They fanned out with mechanical precision and speed, scanning for targets. He tried to stand but his savaged leg gave way and he sprawled onto the rough metal, blood dripping from him in thick runnels. He rolled onto his stomach, the storm troopers ringing him; they had come for him, he had reached the extraction location, and the secrets he held would reach his master.

A tall man, the only one in red plate, crouched down by Thaddeus, his face hidden by a respirator, a bolt pistol held loose in his hand.

'Who are you?' said the red-armoured man.

'I am a servant of the Imperium. I am Thaddeus,' he said. The man leaned closer, unclipping the respirator to show a smooth, handsome face.

'Do you know who I am?' his voice was low. Thaddeus felt something whisper inside his head as a feeling like the pricking of needles ran over his skin. He could feel the red cloud of his other self within him thrashing as though it sensed and saw something he did not.

'Colonel Tarl, the Valkyrie's inbound. Is the target cleared for extraction?' shouted one of the storm troopers, and in that instant Thaddeus knew. *Tarl*. The name echoed in his mind. *Colonel Tarl*. Names, faces, details flickered past an inner eye, as secrets unlocked inside his skull. He knew this man, knew what monster lay beneath his unscarred skin. He saw the bolt pistol held casually at the man's side, a finger on the trigger, and the unscarred face. It was the face of an Alpha Legion infiltrator, an enemy of the Imperium. Tarl's eyes met his.

Tarl saw the recognition in Thaddeus's eyes and brought the bolt pistol up to fire. Thaddeus rammed his fist into Tarl's face with bone-splintering force. Teeth and blood arced up as Tarl's head snapped back. Thaddeus pushed away from the floor, raw anger blotting out pain and exhaustion.

'It's a trick,' shouted Tarl, through blood and ruined teeth.

Hellgun blasts sliced the air where Thaddeus had been. Inside his mind he could hear the beast within howling at the gates of his will, laughing; he was going to die at the hands of his own side because of a traitor. He spun looking for safety, but there was none, only death waiting in the hellguns' muzzles.

There was a howl and mutants were leaping onto the summit, their bare skin blistered from the fires below, and their mouths wide as they tore into the ring of storm troopers, clawing and biting. In an instant everything was confusion and bloodletting. A storm trooper fell to the ground, a mutant on top of him, its jaws fastened upon his neck. Glowing energy from a hellgun punched through a mutant in mid-leap, burning through its chest. The storm trooper that had fired shifted target and fired again, his shot hissing wide, and then a mutant had him in its clawed grasp. Gore sprayed across the platform. Thaddeus had his knife in his hand as a mutant came at him, its claws raking over his arms and face, the anticipation of the kill in its rank breath. He brought the tip of the blade up under its ribs and felt it die with a surge of delight.

A bolt round passed over Thaddeus's shoulder, hit the corpse of the mutant he had just killed, and exploded in a spray of flesh. Thaddeus reeled and stumbled as another explosive round passed over his head. Tarl stalked towards Thaddeus, uncaring of the slaughter around him, his pistol aimed, his face a mask of blood and triumph. Thaddeus stared back into the waiting blackness of the bolt pistol's iron mouth. Blood dripped from the tip of his knife and he felt the red cloud rise within him. He stopped resisting it and let it slide into his limbs and senses. Pain like a hot knife stabbed into his head, and images rushed through his mind: a wide smile, a hand, a white room. Then it was gone and the beast had him.

Thaddeus leapt towards Tarl, his knife held high, face locked into a snarl. Tarl's bolt pistol roared fire into empty air, as Thaddeus landed and cut down at Tarl's neck. It was a fast cut, but Tarl was faster, pivoting around the blow and hammering a kick into Thaddeus's chest. Bones cracked and Thaddeus stumbled, his lungs empty. Tarl brought the pistol up and Thaddeus sprung at the arm forcing it up as it fired. Hands locked around Tarl's bolt pistol, Thaddeus twisted with all his strength. Tarl's fingers snapped in the trigger guard and Thaddeus ripped the pistol free. Tarl stumbled near to the summit's edge, his splintered fingers clutched to his chest, his other hand gripping his throat mic. Thaddeus levelled the bolt pistol at Tarl and smiled.

'Now,' said Tarl.

With a roar of engines the Valkyrie rose up next to the platform. It was so close that Thaddeus could see the pilot's thumb poised over a firing stud. Multi-laser fire poured across the spire's summit, incinerating mutants and storm troopers alike. Thaddeus rolled as the surface of the summit melted around him. Tarl was on his feet as the Valkyrie slewed around, its side door open. He jumped, landing on the deck of the crew compartment with a clang. Thaddeus came up from his roll and sprinted towards the Valkyrie. He saw the pilot looking at him, shock on his face. He reached the edge and leapt, hitting the edge of the Valkyrie's side door, his legs swinging in space, his free hand scrabbling for a hold. Tarl came at him, kicking at his head as Thaddeus pulled himself into the vehicle. The kick sent Thaddeus lurching against the metal wall at the front of the compartment, and the bolt pistol slipped from his hand. Tarl was on him, hands locked around his throat. Thaddeus saw the bolt pistol sliding across the floor of the crew compartment towards the open hatch. The summit of the Fallen Spire loomed in the opening as the Valkyrie pitched and yawed. Thaddeus slammed his forehead into Tarl's face, ducked, grabbed the pistol and brought it up to fire. Tarl's good hand locked on Thaddeus's wrist, and the false colonel snarled with effort as he twisted the gun arm upwards. Thaddeus felt his strength breaking, the killing rage draining away. Thaddeus looked into Tarl's face and pulled the trigger.

The bolt round ripped through the roof of the crew compartment, hit the engine, and exploded. The Valkyrie began to spin, trailing debris and black smoke. Tarl fell back across the compartment as the floor tilted, fumbling to keep his grip on Thaddeus. The summit of the Fallen Spire spun into view beyond the open hatch as Thaddeus broke from Tarl's grip, scrambled to the hatch, and jumped. He hit the blood and fire-marked summit as the Valkyrie exploded in a black edged cloud, debris spilling down the spire in a cascade of flame.

THADDEUS OPENED HIS eyes and blinked at the bright light. He sat on a chair in a white room, his body covered in a loose smock. His wounds had been sealed and clean bandages covered burned skin and there was an empty chair opposite him. A door opened in the smooth white wall, and a man in deep purple robes over bronze battle plate stepped in.

'Good, you are with us again,' said the man, settling himself into the empty chair.

'Where am I?' asked Thaddeus.

'Don't you recognise it?' Thaddeus looked around. It was a bright white room. He snapped his eyes back to the man who sat opposite him. He saw the broad face and the red lenses of bionic eyes looking back at him.

'You are–'

'Yes,' said the inquisitor.

'I made it then,' breathed Thaddeus, relief washing through him.

'Yes, you did. Even if we had to dig you out of the debris. That leap onto the spire saved your life.' Thaddeus thought of the spinning Valkyrie, of the fireball and of falling, the summit of the spire coming up to meet him with a hard kiss.

'So...' began Thaddeus. Confusion was replacing relief; he had to give something to this man, something he could not remember.

'I have already obtained and acted upon the information you brought to me. I removed it from your mind while you were unconscious.' The inquisitor smiled but his flame red stare made it seem grotesque. 'And thank you for dealing with Colonel Tarl. I had my suspicions, and you provided not only the confirmation but the solution.'

'What?' Thaddeus frowned at the inquisitor.

'Ah yes, you don't remember that. Sorry, I had to be sure.'

'What are you talking about?'

The inquisitor just smiled. Thaddeus could feel anger building inside him. He could remember what he had done to survive, but he could not remember the exact reason why. 'Tell me.' He was nearly shouting, rising from his chair. Something was whispering on the edge of his thoughts, begging to be set free.

'Yes, the beast is close isn't it?' The inquisitor had not moved but Thaddeus could feel an atmosphere like a gathering storm pressing against his skin. He felt as if the inquisitor was looking into his skull. 'Can you feel it?' Thaddeus slumped back into his chair. He felt sick; it was still part of him, that shard of the renegade he had become to serve this inquisitor.

'Why is it–'

'Still part of you?'

'Yes.' Thaddeus watched as the inquisitor examined a ring-covered hand, watching the light play over metal and jewels.

'How much can you remember of your time before you infiltrated the renegades?'

'Not much,' replied Thaddeus. 'Snatches. I can remember a face, an aquila ring.' He looked up at the inquisitor. 'I saw a world destroyed once, it makes me–'

'Angry. Yes it would. It still makes me angry.'

'What?' Thaddeus looked at the inquisitor, his mouth open. The inquisitor let the hand he had been examining drop and looked straight into Thaddeus's eyes.

'Those snatches of memory are not yours. They are mine.' Thaddeus felt as if he was drowning in his own fragmented thoughts and memories. He tried to grab on to something that would make sense of what the inquisitor was saying.

'I…' Thaddeus began.

'They are selected instances in my life: things that drive me to do what I do; to hate the enemy, to be an inquisitor.' he was leaning forwards a look of pride on his face. 'That drive to serve is mine: your loyalty to the Imperium, all the imperatives that made you return to me are mine. They are all mine. I gave them to you. I put them into you.'

'But I am…' stammered Thaddeus, and inside he thought he could feel another self howl with mirth.

'Real renegades make the best infiltrators, Thaddeus.' The inquisitor's voice was low, the whisper of a priest speaking a secret in a dying man's ear. 'Why make a loyal Imperial servant believe they are a soldier of Chaos? Why? When I can take a soldier of Chaos and make them what I need?'

'I am not… I have never been…' said Thaddeus.

'No you have not. You are a renegade, Thaddeus. The beast caged inside you is not a remnant of a false life. It is you caged behind lies that I created.' The inquisitor stood up. Thaddeus watched him through tear-filled eyes as he reached out a hand. The ring-covered fingers were cool against his hairless scalp. He felt the air take on a charged lightning storm quality. The inquisitor, his master, looked down at Thaddeus and spoke in a voice that echoed inside his skull. 'You have served the Imperium many times, and you will serve again.' Darkness swallowed him with a scream.

THADDEUS WOKE AMONGST the dead. There was a knife in his hand and blood on its blade. He looked at the corpses around him, their dark robes woven with twisting runes. He looked at his own hands and saw the jagged scars and sinuous patterns marking his skin; he was alone amongst the damned. He remembered a white room, a man with a broad face and red eyes; he must return to his Imperial masters.

He began to run.

HAMMER
AND BOLTER

ISSUE 5

338
A rasping cough
rising and falling
Imperial A
watch
The Best of H

The Horus Heresy

THE IRON WITHIN

Rob Sanders

THE IRON WITHIN. The iron without. Iron everywhere. The galaxy laced with its cold promise. Did you know that Holy Terra is mostly iron? Our Olympian home world, also. Most habitable planets and moons are. The truth is we are an Imperium of iron. Dying stars burn hearts of iron; while the heavy metal cores of burgeoning worlds generate fields that shelter life – sometimes human life – from the razing glare of such stellar ancients.

Empires are measured in more than just conquered dirt. Every Iron Warrior knows this. They're measured in hearts that beat in common purpose, thundering in unison across the void: measured in the blood that spills from our Legiones Astartes bodies, red with iron and defiance. This is the iron within and we can taste its metallic tang when an enemy blade or bullet finds us wanting. Then the iron within becomes the iron without, as it did on what we only now understand to be the first day of the Great Siege of Lesser Damantyne…

THE WARSMITH STEPPED out onto the observation platform, each of his power-armoured footfalls an assault on the heavy grille. The Iron Warrior's ceramite shoulders were hunched with responsibility, as though the Space Marine carried much more than the deadweight of his Mark-III plate. He crossed the platform with the determination of a demigod, but the fashion in which his studded gauntlets seized the exterior rail betrayed a belief that he might not make the expanse at all. The juggernaut ground to an irresistible halt.

racked the depths of his armoured chest, his form
...g with the exertion of each tortured, uncertain breath.
...my sentries from the Ninth-Ward Angeloi Adamantiphracts
...d the Warsmith suffer, uncertain how to act. One even broke
...nks and approached, the flared muzzle of his heavy carbine lowered
and scalemail glove outstretched.

'My lord,' the masked soldier began, 'can I send for your Apothecary
or perhaps the Iron Palatine...'

Lord Barabas Dantioch stopped the Adamantiphract with an outstretched gauntlet of his own. As the Warsmith fought the coughing fit
and his convulsions, the armoured palm became a single finger.

Then, without even looking at the soldier, the huge Legiones Astartes
managed: 'As you were, wardsman.'

The soldier retreated and a light breeze rippled through the Iron
Warrior's tattered cloak, the material a shredded mosaic of black and
yellow chevrons. It whipped about the statuesque magnificence of
his power armour, the dull lustre of his Legion's plate pitted with
rust and premature age, lending the suit a sepia sheen. He wore no
helmet. Face and skull were enclosed in an iron mask, crafted by
the Warsmith himself. The faceplate was a work of brutal beauty,
an interpretation of the Legion's mark, the iron mask symbol that
adorned his shoulder. Lord Dantioch's mask was a hangdog leer of
leaden fortitude with a cage for a mouth and eyes of grim darkness.
It was whispered in the arcades and on the battlements that the Warsmith was wearing the mask – pulled glowing from the forge – as
he hammered it to shape around his shaven skull. He then plunged
head and iron into ice water, fixing the beaten metal in place forever
around his equally grim features.

Gripping the platform rail, Dantioch drew his eye-slits skywards
between his hunched, massive shoulders and drank in the insane genius
of his creation. The Schadenhold: an impregnable fortress of unique and
deadly design, named in honour of the misery that Dantioch and his
Iron Warriors might observe if ever an enemy force was foolish enough
to assault the stronghold. During the process of Compliance, as part
of the Emperor's strategy and holy decree, thousands of bastions and
citadels had been built on thousands of worlds, so that the architects of
the Great Crusade might watch over their conquered domain and the
new subjects of an ever expanding Imperium. Many of these galactic
redoubts, castles and forts had been designed and built by Dantioch's
Iron Warrior brothers: the IV Legion was peerless in the art of siege warfare, both as besiegers and the besieged. The galaxy had seen nothing
like the Schadenhold, however – of that Dantioch was sure.

Under his mask the Iron Warrior commander's pale lips mumbled
the Unbreakable Litany. 'Lord Emperor, make me an instrument of your
adamance. Where darkness is legion, bless our walls with cold disdain;

where foolish foes are frail, have our ranks advance; where there is mortal doubt, let resolution reign…'

The Warsmith had blessed the Schadenhold with every modern structural fortification: concentric hornworks; bunkers; murder zones; drum keeps; artillery emplacements and kill-towers. The fortress was a monstrous study in 30th Millennium siegecraft. For Dantioch, however, location was everything. Without the natural advantages of material, elevation and environment, all other architectural concerns were mere flourish. A stronghold built in a strategically weak location was certain to fall, as many of Dantioch's kindred in the other Legions had discovered during the early trials of Compliance. Even the Imperial Fists had had their failures.

Dantioch had hated Lesser Damantyne from the moment he had set foot on the dread rock and had felt instantly that the planet hated him also. It was as though the world did not want him there and that appealed to the Warsmith's tactical sensibilities: he could use Damantyne's environmental hostilities to his advantage. The small planetoid was situated in a crowded debris field of spinning rock, metal and ice that made it seem unfinished and hazardous from the start. The cruisers of the 51st Expedition that had brought the Warsmith and his Iron Warriors there had negotiated the field with difficulty. Although the planet had tolerable gravity and low-lying oxygen that made an outpost possible, the surface was a swirling hellstorm of hurricane winds, lashing lightning and highly corrosive, acid cloud cover. Nothing lived there: nothing could live on the surface. The acidic atmosphere ate armour and ordnance like a hungry beast, rapidly stripping it away layer by layer in an effort to dissolve the flesh and soft tissue of the Legiones Astartes beneath. Even the most heavily armoured could only expect to survive mere minutes on the surface.

This made vertical, high-speed insertions by Stormbird the sole way down and that was only if the pilot was skilful enough to punch through the blinding cloud cover and down into one of the narrow, bottomless sinkholes that punctuated the rocky surface. Through some natural perversity of Damantyne's early evolution, the planetary crust was riddled with air pockets, cavities and vast open spaces: a cavern system of staggering proportion and labyrinthine madness. Dantioch chose the very heart of this madness as the perfect location for his fortress, in a vaulted subterranean space so colossal it had its own primitive weather system.

'From iron cometh strength. From strength cometh will. From will cometh faith. From faith cometh honour. From honour cometh iron. This is the Unbreakable Litany. May it forever be so. Dominum imperator ac ferrum aeturnum.'

The Iron Warriors were not the first to have made Lesser Damantyne their home. Below the surface, the lithic world was rich with life which had evolved in the deep and the dark. The only real threat to the Emperor's chosen were the megacephalopods: monsters that stalked the caverns with their sinuous tentacles and could collapse their rubbery bulk through the most torturous of cave tunnels, creating new entrances with their titanium beaks. The Legiones Astartes first few years on Lesser Damantyne comprised a war of extermination on the xenos brutes, who seemed intent on tearing down any structures the IV Legion attempted to erect.

With the alien threat hunted to extinction, Dantioch began construction on his greatest work: the Schadenhold. While Iron Warriors had been battling chthonic monstrosities for planetary supremacy, Dantioch had had his Apothecaries and Adeptus Mechanicum advisors hard at work creating the muscle that would build his mega-fortress. Iron Warrior laboratories perfected genestock slave soldiers, colloquially known as the Sons of Dantioch. Although the Warsmith's face had been hidden for many years behind the iron of his impassive mask, it was plain to see on the gruesome hulks that had built the Schadenhold.

Taller and broader than a Space Marine, the genebreeds used the raw power of their monstrous bulk to mine, move and carve the stone from which the fortress was crafted. As well as physical prowess the slave soldiers had also inherited some of their gene-father's cold, technical skill and the Schadenhold was more than a hastily constructed rock edifice: it was an enormous example of strategic art and siegecraft. With the fortress complete, the Sons of Dantioch found new roles in the maintenance and basic operation of the citadel and as close-quarters shock troops for the concentric kill zones that layered the stronghold. It pleased the ailing Warsmith to be surrounded by brute examples of his own diminished youth and physical supremacy and, in turn, the slave soldiers honoured their gene-father with a simple, unshakable faith and loyalty: a fealty to the Emperor as father of the primarch and the primarch as father of their own.

'I never tire of looking at it,' a voice cut through the darkness behind. It was Zygmund Tarrasch, the Schadenhold's Iron Palatine. Dantioch grunted, bringing an end to his mumbled devotions. Perhaps the Adamantiphract had sent for him; or perhaps the Iron Palatine had news.

The Space Marine joined his Warsmith at the rail and peered up at the magnificence of the fortress above. Although Dantioch was Warsmith and ranking Legiones Astartes among the thirty-strong Iron Warrior garrison left behind by the 51st Expeditionary Fleet, his condition had forced him to devolve responsibility for the fortress and its day-to-day defence to another. He'd chosen Tarrasch as Iron Palatine because he was a Space Marine of character and imagination. The cold logic of the IV Legion had served the Iron Warriors well but, even among their number, there were those whose contribution to Compliance was more than just a conqueror's thirst – those who appreciated the beauty of human endeavour and achievement, not just the tactical satisfaction of victory and the hot delight of battle.

'Reminds me of the night sky,' Tarrasch told his Warsmith. The Iron Palatine nodded to himself. 'I miss the sky.'

Dantioch had never really thought of the Schadenhold in that way before. It was certainly a spectacle to behold and the final facet in the Warsmith's ingenious design, for the two Iron Warriors were standing on a circular observation platform, situated around the steeple-point of the tallest of the Schadenhold's citadel towers. Only, the tower did not point towards the sky or even at the cavern ceiling: it pointed down at the cavern floor.

The Schadenhold had been hewn out of a gigantic, conical rock formation protruding from the roof of the cave. Dantioch had immediately appreciated the rock feature's potential and committed his troops to the difficult and perilous task of carving out an inverse citadel. This hung upside-down, but all chambers, stairwells and interior architecture were oriented skywards. The communications spires and steeple-scanners at the very bottom of the fortress were hanging several thousand metres above a vast naturally-occurring lake of crude promethium, which bubbled up from the planet depths. At the very top of the stronghold were the dungeons and oubliettes, situated high in the cavern roof.

As Dantioch cast his weary eyes up the architecture, he came to appreciate the comparison the Iron Palatine was making. In the bleak darkness of the gargantuan cavern, the bright glare of the fortress searchlamps and soft pinpricks of illumination escaping the embrasure murder holes appeared like a constellation in a deep night sky. This was accentuated further by the phosphorescent patches of bacteria that feasted on the feldspar in the cavern roof and the dull glints reflecting off the shiny, pitch surface of oozing promethium below: each giving the appearance of ever more distant stars and galaxies.

'You have news?' Dantioch put to Tarrasch.

'Yes, Warsmith,' the Iron Palatine reported. The Space Marine was also in full armour and Legion colours, bar gauntlets and helmet, which he clutched in one arm. The vigilance (or paranoia, as some of the other Legions believed) of the Iron Warriors was well known and the Schadenhold and its garrison maintained a constant state of battle readiness. Tarrasch ran a hand across the top of his bald head. His dark eyes and flesh were the primarch's own, a blessing to his sons. As the Warsmith turned and the light of the observation platform penetrated the slits of his iron mask, Tarrasch caught a glimpse of sallow, bloodshot eyes and wrinkled skin, discoloured with age.

'And?'

'The flagship *Benthos* hails us, my lord.'

'So, the 51st Expedition returns,' Dantioch rasped. 'We've had them on our relay scopes for days. Why the slow approach? Why no contact?'

'They inform us that they've had difficulty traversing the debris field,' the Iron Palatine reported.

342   *The Best of Hammer and Bolter: Volume One*

'And they hail us only now?' Dantioch returned crabbily.

'The *Benthos* accidentally struck one of our orbital mines,' Tarrasch informed his master. Dantioch felt something like a smile curl behind the caged mouth of his faceplate.

'An ominous beginning to their visit,' the Warsmith said.

'They're holding station while they make repairs,' the Iron Palatine added. 'And they're requesting coordinates for a high speed insertion.'

'Who requests them?'

'Warsmith Krendl, my lord.'

'Warsmith Krendl?'

Tarrasch nodded: 'So it would appear.'

'So Idriss Krendl now commands the 14th Grand Company.'

'Even under your command,' Tarrasch said, 'he was little more than raw ambition in polished ceramite.'

'You might just get your night sky, my Iron Palatine.'

'You think we might be rejoining the Legion, sir?'

For the longest time, Dantioch did not speak – the Warsmith lost in memory and musing. 'I sincerely hope not,' the Warsmith replied.

The answer seemed to vex the Iron Palatine. Dantioch laid a gauntleted hand on Tarrasch's shoulder. 'Send the *Benthos* coordinates for the Orphic Gate and have two of our Stormbirds waiting near the surface to escort our guests in.'

'The Orphic Gate, sir? Surely the–'

'Let's treat the new Warsmith to some of the more dramatic depths and cave systems,' Dantioch said. 'A scenic route, if you will.'

'As you wish, my lord.'

'In the meantime have Chaplain Zhnev, Colonel Kruishank, Venerable Vastopol and the cleric visiting from Greater Damantyne meet us in the Grand Reclusiam: we shall receive our guests there and hear from Olympian lips what our brothers have been doing in our absence...'

THE GRAND RECLUSIAM rang with both the wretched coughing of the Warsmith and the hammer strokes of his Chaplain. The chamber could easily accommodate the thirty-Iron Warrior garrison of the Schadenhold and their cult ceremonies and rituals. In reality – with the fortress in a state of constant high alert – there were ordinarily never more than ten Legiones Astartes in attendance during any one watch.

Dantioch and his Chaplain had not allowed such a restriction to affect the design and impact of the chamber. The Iron Warriors on Lesser Damantyne were few in number but great of heart and they filled their chests with a soaring faith and loyalty to their Emperor. To this end the Grand Reclusiam was the largest chamber in the fortress, able in fact to serve the spiritual needs of ten times their number. From the vaulted stone ceiling hung a black forest of iron rods that dangled in the air above the centrum altar approach. These magnified the cult devotions, rogational and choral chanting of the small garrison to a booming majesty – all supported by the roar of the ceremonial forge at the elevated head of the chamber and the rhythmic strikes of hammer on iron against the anvil-altar.

The aisles on either side of the centrum consisted of a sculptured scene that ran the length of the Grand Reclusiam, rising with the flight of altar steps and terminating at the far wall. Towering above the chamber congregation, it depicted a crowded, uphill battle scene crafted from purest ferrum, with Iron Warrior heroes storming a barbaric enemy force that was holding the higher ground. The primitive giants were the titans and personifications of old: the bastions of myth and superstition, smashed upon the armour and IV Legion's virtues of technology and reason. As well as serving as an inspiring diorama, the sculpture created the illusion that the congregation was at the heart of the battle – and there was nowhere else Dantioch's men would rather be.

Beyond the sculpture on either side, the rocky walls of the chamber had been lined with polished iron sheeting, upon which engraved schematics and structural designs overlapped to create a fresco of the Emperor looking on proudly from the west and the Primarch Perturabo from the east.

'My lord, they approach,' Tarrasch announced and with difficulty the Warsmith came up off one devout knee. Shadows and the sound of self-important steps filled the Reclusiam's grand arch entrance. The Iron Palatine turned and stood by his Warsmith's side, while Colonel Kruishank of the Ninth-Ward Angeloi Adamantiphracts hovered nearby in full dress uniform. His reverential beatings complete, Chaplain Zhnev uncoupled the relic-hammer from a slender, bionic replacement for his right arm and shoulder. He handed the crozius arcanum attachment to a hulking genestock slave whose responsibility it was to keep the ceremonial forge roaring. Zhnev made his solemn way down the steps, nodding to the only member of the congregation who was not part of the Schadenhold garrison: a cleric dressed in outlandish, hooded robes of sapphire and gold.

'They come,' Zhnev murmured as the delegation marched into his Reclusiam and up the long approach to the altar steps.

Out front strode Idriss Krendl, the new Warsmith of the 14th Grand Company. The intensity of his Olympian glower was shattered by the scarring that cut up his face. Following, clad in the crimson robes of the Adeptus Mechanicum, was an adept, whose own face was lost to the darkness of his hood. A sickly yellow light emanated from three bionic oculars that rotated like the objective lenses of a microscope. Beside him was a Son of Horus. The eyes on his shoulderplate and chest were unmistakable and his fine armour was of the palest green, framed in a midnight trim. His unsmiling face was swarthy and heavy of brow, as though in constant deliberation. Flanking them, and marching in time, were Krendl's honour guard: a four-point escort of Legiones Astartes veterans in gleaming, grey Mark-IV Maximus suits lined in gold and gaudiness.

'Warsmith,' Krendl greeted his former master coolly, at the foot of the altar steps.

A moment passed under the engraved eyes of the Emperor.

'Krendl,' Dantioch replied.

The Iron Warrior pursed his mangled lips but let the failure to acknowledge his new rank pass. 'Greetings from the 51st Expedition. May I introduce Adept Grachuss and Captain Hasdrubal Serapis of the Sons of Horus.'

Dantioch failed to acknowledge them also. The Warsmith gave a short cough and waved a gauntlet nonchalantly behind him.

'You know my people,' Dantioch said. Then added, 'and yours.'

'Indeed,' Krendl said, raising a ragged eyebrow. 'We bring you new orders from your primarch and your Warmaster.'

'And what of the Emperor's orders? You bring nothing across the stars from him?' Dantioch asked.

Krendl stiffened, then seemed to relax. He gave Serapis a glance over his armoured shoulder but the captain's expression didn't change.

'It has long been the Emperor's wish that his favoured sons – under the supreme leadership of his most favoured, Horus Lupercal – guide the Great Crusade to its inevitable conclusion. Out here, amongst a cosmos conquered, the Warmaster's word is law. Dantioch, you know this.'

'Out here, in the darkness of the East, we hear disturbing rumours of this cosmos conquered and the dangers of the direction it is taking,' Dantioch hissed. 'Rector, come forth. You may speak.'

The cleric in sapphire and gold stepped forwards with apologetic hesitation. 'This man,' Dantioch explained, 'has come to us from Greater Damantyne with grave news.'

The priest, at once scrutinised by the supermen, retreated into the depths of his hood. He fumbled his first words, before gaining his confidence.

'My lords, I am your humble servant,' the rector began. 'This system is the terminus of a little-known trade route. Merchants and pirates, both alien and human, run wares between our hinterspace and the galactic core. In the last few months they have brought terrible news of consequence to the Emperor's Angels here on Lesser Damantyne. A civil war that burns across the Imperium, the loss of entire Legions of Space Marines and the unthinkable – a son of the Emperor slain! This tragic intelligence alone would have been enough to bring me here: the Space Marines of this rock have long been our friends and allies in the battle with the green invader. Then, a dread piece of cognisance came to my ears and made them bleed for my Iron Warrior overlords. Olympia – their home world – the victim of rebellion and retribution.

A planet razed to its rocky foundations; mountains aflame and a people enthralled. Olympia, I am heartbroken to report, is now no more than an underworld of chain and darkness, buried in rotten bodies and shame.'

'I have heard enough of this,' Serapis warned.

Krendl turned on the Warsmith. 'Your primarch–'

Dantioch cut him off. 'My primarch – I suspect – had a hand in these reported tragedies.'

'You waste our time, Dantioch,' Krendl said, his torn lips snarling around the hard consonants of the Warsmith's name. 'You and your men have been reassigned. Your custodianship here is ended. Your primarch and the Iron Warriors Legion fight for Horus Lupercal now and all available troops and resources – including those formally under your superintendence – are required for the Warmaster's march on ancient Terra.'

The Grand Reclusiam echoed with Krendl's fierce honesty. For a moment nobody spoke, the shock of hearing such bold heresy in a holy place overwhelming the chamber.

'End this madness!' Chaplain Zhnev implored from the steps, the forge light flashing off his sable-silver plate.

'Krendl, think about what you're doing,' Tarrasch added.

'I am Warsmith now, Captain Tarrasch!' Krendl exploded, 'whatever rank you might hold in this benighted place, you will honour me with my rightful title.'

'Honour what?' Dantioch said. 'The rewards of failure? You command simply because you lack the courage to be loyal.'

'Don't talk to me about failure and lack of courage, Dantioch. You excel in both,' Krendl spat. He bobbed his head at Serapis, the splinters of frag still embedded in his face-flesh glinting in the chamber light. 'That is how the great Barabas Dantioch came to be left guarding such a worthless deadrock. Lord Perturabo's favourite here came to lose Krak Fiorina, Stratopolae and the fortress world of Gholghis to the Vulpa Straits hrud migration.'

As Krendl growled his narrative, Dantioch remembered the last, dark days on Gholghis. The hrud xenos filth. The infestation of the unseen. The waiting and the dying, as Dantioch's garrison turned to dust and bones, their armour rusting, bolters jamming and fortress crumbling about them. Only then, after the intense entropic field created by the migratory hrud swarms had aged stone and flesh to ruin, did the rachidian beasts creep out of every nook and crevice to attack, stabbing and slicing with their venomous claws.

Most of all, Dantioch remembered waiting for the Stormbird to lift the survivors out of the remains of Gholghis: Sergeant Zolan, Vastopol the warrior-poet and Techmarine Tavarre. Zolan's hearts stopped beating aboard the Stormbird, minutes after extraction. Tavarre died of old age in the cruiser infirmary, just before reaching Lesser Damantyne. Vastopol and the Warsmith had considered themselves comparatively fortunate but both had been left crippled with their aged, superhuman bodies.

'He then thought it wise,' Krendl continued with acidic disdain, 'to question his primarch's prosecution of the hrud extermination campaign. No doubt as a way to excuse his loss of half a Grand Company, rather than laying the blame where it really belonged: the Emperor's bungled attempt at galactic conquest and his own failed part in that. The IV Legion spread out across the stars. A myriad of tiny garrisons holding a tattered Compliance together in the wake of a blind Crusade. Our once proud Iron Warriors, reduced to planetary turnkeys.'

'The primarch was wrong,' Dantioch said, shaking his iron mask. 'The extermination campaign prompted the migration rather than ending it. Perturabo claims the hrud cleansed from the galaxy but, if that is the case, what is quietly wiping out Compliance worlds on the Koranado Drift?'

The new Warsmith ignored him.

'You disappoint and disgust him,' Krendl told Dantioch. 'Your own primarch. Your weakness offends him. Your vulnerability is an affront to his genetic heritage. We all have scars but it is you he cannot bear to look upon. Is that why you adopted the mask?' Krendl smiled his derision. 'Pathetic. You're an insult to nature and the laws that govern the galaxy: the strong survive; the feeble die away. Why did you not crawl off and die, Dantioch? Why hang on, haunting the rest of us like a bad memory?'

'If I'm so objectionable, what is it that you and the primarch want with me?'

'Nothing, cripple. I doubt you would live long enough to reach the rendezvous. Perturabo demands his Iron Warriors – all his true sons – for the Warmaster's offensive. Horus will take us to the very walls of the Imperial Palace, where the Emperor's fanciful fortifications will be put to the test of our mettle and history will be made.'

'The Emperor has long grown distracted in his studies on ancient Terra,' Hasdrubal Serapis insisted with venom. 'The Imperium has no need of the councils, polity and bureaucracy he has created in his reclusion. We need leadership: a Great Crusade of meaning and purpose. The Emperor is no longer worthy to guide humanity in the next stage of its natural dominion over the galaxy. His son, Horus Lupercal, has proved himself worthy of the task.'

'Warsmith Krendl,' Zhnev said, blanking out the Son of Horus and taking several dangerous steps forwards. 'If you stand by and do nothing, while the Warmaster plots patricide and pours poison in his brother primarch's ears, then you too plot a patricide of your own. Perturabo is our primarch. We must make our noble lord see the error of his judgement – not reinforce it with our unquestioned compliance.'

'Lord Perturabo is your primarch, indeed. Is it so difficult to obey your primarch's order?' Serapis marvelled at the Iron Warriors. 'Or does mutinous Olympian blood still burn in your veins? Krendl, to have your home world rebel in your absence is embarrassment enough. I trust you will not allow the same to happen amongst members of your own Legion.'

'Save it, pontificator,' Krendl snapped at the Chaplain. 'I have heard the arguments. Soon the Legion will have little use for you and your kind.' The Warsmith turned on the silent, seething Dantioch. 'You will surrender command of this fortress and troops to me immediately.'

A moment of cool fury passed between the two Iron Warriors.

'And if I refuse?'

'Then you and your men will be treated as traitors to the primarch and his Warmaster,' Krendl promised.

'Like you and your Cthonian friend are to his majesty, the Emperor?'

'Your stronghold will be pounded to dust and traitors with it,' Krendl told him.

Dantioch turned and presented the grim iron of his masked face to Colonel Kruishank, Chaplain Zhnev and his Iron Palatine, Zygmund Tarrasch. Their faces were equally grim. Allowing his eyes to linger for a second on the visiting rector, Barabas Dantioch returned his gaze to his maniacal opposite. Krendl was flushed with fear and fire. Serapis merely watched: a distant observer – the puppet master with strings of his own. Adept Grachuss gurgled rhythmically and rotated his tri-ocular, the lens zeroing in on Dantioch. The Warsmith's honour guard stood as statues: their bolters ready; their barrels on the custodians of the Schadenhold.

'Vastopol,' Dantioch called. 'What do you think?'

A vox-roar boomed around the chamber, causing the iron rods suspended above the Reclusiam to tremble and dance. Something large and ungainly moved amongst the giant, iron sculptures of the aisle diorama. The most primitive of preservation instincts caused Krendl and his honour guard to spin around in shock. One of the sculptures had come to life. Seeming small in the choreographed throng of titan attackers, the assailant's bulk and breadth swiftly grew as it advanced and towered over the astounded Iron Warriors.

The Legiones Astartes were presented with one of their own. A Dreadnought. A brooding, metal monster, as broad as it was tall and squatset with chunky weaponry. The Venerable Vastopol: with his Warsmith, the last surviving Iron Warriors of the Gholghis fortress world. Wracked with horrendous injury and premature age, Dantioch had had the Space Marine entombed in Dreadnought armour, so that the warrior might continue to serve and keep the chronicles of the company alive. The war machine had been hastily sprayed black in order to blend in with the surrounding diorama and with movement the fresh paint left a black drizzle behind the beast.

As the wall of ceramite and adamantium came at them, Krendl's armed escorts tried to bring their bolters to bear. The Venerable Vastopol's gaping twin-autocannons were already loaded, primed and aimed right at them. The weapons crashed, chugging explosive fire at the two rearguard Space Marines and filling the chamber with the unbearable cacophony of battle. At such close range, the heavy weapon reduced the two Legiones Astartes to thrashing blurs of blood and shattered armour.

With more grace and coordination than would have been thought possible in the hulking machine, the charging Dreadnought turned and smashed a third Iron Warrior guard into the opposite aisle with a power claw-appendaged shoulder. The Space Marine's glorious Maximus suit crumpled and the Legiones Astartes within could be heard screaming as bones snapped and organs ruptured. With Krendl and Serapis backing for cover, silent pistols drawn, and the Mechanicum adept knocked to the Reclusiam floor, the Warsmith's remaining honour guard flung himself at the Dreadnought. Lifting his bolter above his head, the Iron Warrior blasted the Venerable Vastopol's armoured womb-tomb with firepower.

Sparks showered from the Dreadnought's adamantium shell. Vastopol gunned the chainfist bayonet that underslung his autocannons. Slashing at the Iron Warrior with the barbed nightmare, the war machine chewed up the Space Marine's weapon before opening up his armour from the jaw to the navel. With chest cavity and abdomen spilling their contents out through the ragged gash, the honour guard dropped to his knees and died. Having come away from the wall of sculpture, the Dreadnought had allowed the crushed Legiones Astartes he'd pinned to the merciless iron to thunk to the ground. Lifting a huge metal foot, Vastopol stamped down on the Iron Warrior's helmet, bespattering the polished stone with brain matter and putting the mauled Space Marine out of his howling misery.

As Dantioch came forwards, flanked by Tarrasch and Zhnev on one side and the rector and colonel on the other, Krendl and the Son of Horus retreated: the rage and horror evident on their contorted faces. Both Legiones Astartes officers were backing step by step towards the Grand Reclusiam entrance, their pistols aimed at the unarmed Warsmith and his heavily-armed Dreadnought. Krendl and Serapis were politicians, however, and knew that their best chance of escaping the fortress alive lay in their threats rather than their pistols.

The Venerable Vastopol plucked Grachuss from the floor with the chisel-point digits of his power claw, holding the Mechanicum adept by the temples and hooded crown like an infant's doll. The sickly yellow lens of the tech-priest's tri-ocular revolved in panic while his respiratory pipes bubbled furiously.

'I fear Warsmith Krendl brought you with instructions to catalogue our fortifications,' Dantioch addressed the suspended Grachuss, 'so that you might return with stories of our siege capability. A greater Warsmith than he would have done that himself, of course. Vastopol here was the chronicler for our company: he's not much of a talker now. Vastopol,' Dantioch called. 'How does Adept Grachuss's story end?'

The Dreadnought's power claw attachment began to revolve at the wrist, wrenching the tech-priest's hooded head clean from his spinning shoulders. His body struck the altar steps, a cocktail of blood and ichor pumping from the ragged neck stump.

'Insanity!' Krendl bawled at the advancing Dantioch. 'You're dead!' The threats had begun.

'Captain Krendl,' Dantioch hissed. 'This is an Iron Warrior stronghold. It does not, nor will it ever serve the renegade Warmaster. My garrison and I are loyal to the Emperor: we will not share in your damnation.' The cold pride that afflicted the Legion, as well as their iron father, glinted in Dantioch's cloudy eyes. 'It seems I have one last opportunity to prove my worthiness to the primarch. I will not fail him this time. The Schadenhold will never fall. Do you hear me, Idriss? This stronghold and the men that defend it will never be yours. The Iron Warriors on Lesser Damantyne fight for their Emperor and they fight for me. You will taste failure and it will be your turn to return to the primarch's wrath. Now run, you cur. Back to your renegade fleet and take this heretic dog with you.'

Stepping back through the archway of the Grand Reclusiam with a wary Serapis, the wide-eyed Krendl thrust his pistol behind him and then back at the Iron Warriors and their Dreadnought.

'All of this,' Krendl waved the muzzle of the bolt pistol around, 'dust in a day. You hear, Dantioch? Dust in a day!'

'I dare you to try,' Dantioch roared, but his challenge dissolved into raucous coughing. As the Warsmith fell to his armoured knees with wheezing exertion, Tarrasch grabbed Dantioch's arm. Patting the Iron Palatine's ceramite, the Warsmith caught his breath. Tarrasch let him go but the exhausted Iron Warrior commander remained kneeling and head bowed. Slowly he turned to the hooded rector.

'So,' the cleric said, 'you hear it for yourself: straight from traitor lips. Our brothers' hearts steeped in warped treason.' The rector reached inside the rich material of his robes. The soft whine of the displacer field – all but imperceptible before – died down through the frequencies, unmasking the priest and revealing his true dimensions. As the cleric lowered his hood the reality about the huge figure fell out of focus for a moment before reassuming a searing clarity.

Their minds unclouded, the Schadenholders beheld a brother Space Marine: his ornate plate of the deepest blue. He held a plumed helmet under one arm and an ornate gladius sat in a sheath across his thigh. His surcoat robes hung from the resplendent flourishes of his artificer armour, with battle honours and commendations dripping from his glorious plate. The symbol on his right shoulder identified him as an Ultramarine; the bejewelled Crux Aureas crafted into his left as Legionary Champion, Tetrarch of Ultramar and Honour Guard to Roboute Guilliman himself.

'You played your part well, Tetrarch Nicodemus. Are the Ultramarines usually given to such theatricality?' Dantioch asked.

'No, my lord. We are not,' the champion answered, his cropped hair and fair patrician looks the mark of Ultramar's warrior elite. 'But these are uncommon times and they call for tactics uncommon.'

'Let me be candid, Ultramarine. When you arrived on Lesser Damantyne with your slurs and distant intelligence, I almost had Vastopol blow you from the Schadenhold's battlements.' The Warsmith came up from his knees, once again with the help of Tarrasch. The Tetrarch shot him hard eyes: one of which was encircled by a neat tattoo of his Chapter symbol.

'It is not easy for an Iron Warrior to hear of his brothers' weakness,' Dantioch continued. 'In that, even Idriss Krendl and I agree. You slandered my father primarch and besmirched the IV Legion with accusations of rebellion, heresy and murder. We've allowed your insults to go unpunished; you've allowed us the luxury of hearing kindred treason first hand. Our accord is sealed in truth. What now would Roboute Guilliman have of us?'

Tauro Nicodemus looked about the gathering. Tarrasch and Zhnev's bleak pride matched their Warsmith's own; the Venerable Vastopol existed only to fight and Colonel Kruishank's default loyalty was plain to see on his face – allegiance to the Emperor offering him solace in the face of calamity.

'Nothing you haven't freely given already,' Nicodemus insisted. 'Deny the Warmaster resource and reinforcement. Hold your ground for as long as you can. The efforts of a faithful few could slow the traitor advance. Minutes. Days. Months. Anything, to give the Emperor time to fortify Terra for the coming storm and for my lord to cut through the confusion Horus has sown and prepare a loyalist response.'

'If we are to give ourselves for this, level Iron Warrior against Iron Warrior, then it would be good to know that Guilliman has a strategy,' said Dantioch.

'Yes, my lord. As always, Lord Guilliman has a plan,' the Ultramarine champion told him evenly.

As the congregation went to leave the blood-spattered Grand Reclusiam, Dantioch asked, 'Nicodemus?'

'Yes, Warsmith?'

'Why me?'

'Lord Guilliman knows of your art and expertise in the field of siegecraft. He suspects these skills will be sorely needed.'

'He could count on my skill but what of my loyalty?' Dantioch pressed.

'After all, my Legion has been found wanting in its faith.'

'You spoke candidly before, my lord. Might I be allowed to do the same?'

Dantioch nodded.

'The Warmaster could exploit the weakness of your primarch's pride,' the Tetrarch explained cautiously. 'Your history with Perturabo is no secret. Lord Guilliman feels he too can rely on this same weakness in you.'

Once again, the Warsmith nodded. To Nicodemus and to himself.

I WAS THERE. On that tiny world, in a forgotten system, in a distant corner of the galaxy: where a mighty blow was struck against the renegade Warmaster and his alliance of the lost and damned. There, on Lesser Damantyne. I was among the few, who stood against many. The brother who spilled his brothers' blood. The son who betrayed his wayward father's word. And that word was… heresy.

For a bloody day beyond an Ancient Terran year we fought. Olympians all. Iron Warriors answering the call of their primarch and Emperor. The cold eyes of both watching from afar. Judging. Expecting. Willing their Iron Warriors on like absentee gods drawn to mortal plight by the reek of battle: the unmistakable stench of blood and burning.

I was there when Warsmith Krendl visited upon us a swarm of Stormbirds. Disgorged from the fat cruiser *Benthos* and heavily-laden with troops and ordnance, the aircraft blotted out the stars and fell upon our world like a flock of winged thunderbolts. Blasting through the thick cloud of Damantyne's hostile surface, the Stormbirds would have rocketed through the cave systems and disgorged their own brand of horror on our readying position. Warsmith Dantioch had ordered the Orphic Gate collapsed mere hours before, however, and all the flock found there was rock and destruction, as, one after another, they struck the planet surface.

I was there when the mighty god-machines of the Legio Argentum, denied entrance to the gate also, had to stride through the acid hellstorms of Lesser Damantyne. Like blind, tormented behemoths they tumbled and crashed through the squalls and cyclones, their armoured shells rust-riddled and giant automotive systems eaten away. The infamous *Omnia Victrum*, the sunderer of a hundred worlds, was one of three flash-flayed war machines that managed to stumble to a sinkhole colossal enough to admit their dimensions. And there the screaming hordes that crewed the god-machines were confronted with the unfathomable labyrinth of the planet's gargantuan cave system and the reality that they might be lost for eternity in the deep and the dark.

I was there when Warsmith Dantioch ordered the giant ground-pumps to life and the lake of crude promethium burst its banks, flooding the floor of our huge cavern-home with a raging, black ichor. I watched as the Nadir-Maru Fourth Juntarians and more bombardment cannon than a man could count were drowned in a deluge of oil and death. I roared my dismay as columns of my traitor brethren marched on the pumps through the settling shallows, to sabotage the great machinery. I roared my delight when my Warsmith ordered the slick surface of the crude promethium ignited about them. A blaze so bright that it not only roasted the Iron Warriors within their plate but brought light to the cavern that the depths had never known.

I was on the Schadenhold's battlements as our own cannon and artillery placements reduced Warsmith Krendl's reserve Stormbirds to fireballs of wreckage. I saw the small armies they landed on our keeps and towers fall to their deaths like rain from our inverse architecture. I fought with the Sons of Dantioch – genebred hulks of monstrous proportion – as they tore Nadir-Maru Fourth Juntarians limb from limb in the kill zones and courtyards. I walked amongst Colonel Kruishank's Ninth-Ward Angeloi Adamantiphracts as their disciplined las-fire lit up the ramparts and cut their traitor opposites to smouldering shreds. I looked down on a fortress swamped in carnage, where you could not walk for bodies and could not breathe for the blood that lay hanging in the air like a murderous fog.

Finally, I fought in the tight corridors and dread architecture of the Warsmith's design. Took life on an obscene scale, face-to-face with my Iron Warrior brethren. Murdered in the Emperor's name and matched the cold certainty of my brothers' desire. Killed with the same chill logic and fire in my belly as my enemy had for me. Measured my might in the blood of traitors whose might should have measured my own. I was there. In the Schadenhold. On Lesser Damantyne. Where few stood against many and, amongst the fratricidal nightmare of battle, brothers bled and heresy found its form.

THE SCHADENHOLD SHOOK.

Dust rained from the low ceiling and grit danced on the dungeon floor. The subterranean blockhouse seared with gunfire. Its hoarse boom split the ear and the flash of hot muzzles dazzled the eye. Barabas Dantioch had supreme confidence in his nightmare stronghold's design. He'd told Idriss Krendl that the Schadenhold would never be his. Even at this stage – three hundred and sixty-six Ancient Terran days into the murderous siege – he could count on the fortress keeping his word. With traitor Titans and Mechanicum war machines haunting the caverns, swarms of Stormbirds strafing the citadel towers and enemy Legiones Astartes storming its helter-skelter battlements, he knew the brute logic of the Schadenhold's design and the rock from which that inexorability had been crafted would not let him down. Dantioch's tactical genius extended far beyond the unrelenting architecture of the stronghold exterior: any Warsmith worth their rocksalt, regardless of the boasts they might make, planned for the inevitability of failure. A life lived under siege had taught the Iron Warriors that enemies were not to be underestimated and that all fortresses fall – sooner or later. A Warsmith's gift was to make this eventuality as late as possible. The blockhouse was a perfect example of the principle in action.

Throughout the citadel, on every level and in every quarter, there was a blockhouse chamber. A fallback position for the Iron Warrior garrison within: each bolthole was equipped with its own secreted supplies of food, water and ammunition, as well as rudimentary medical and communications equipment. The chambers themselves were dens of devious geography, every one with its own unique design and layout. No lethal opportunity had been left unexploited and every fire arc and angle had been measured to perfection. In each the Warsmith had created a crenellated deathtrap of chokepoints, hide sites and killspots that doubled as training facilities for the Legiones Astartes warriors during the simpler, silent times of peace.

The blockhouses had not only provided Dantioch's hard-pressed garrison with respite and supplies but had also frustrated any hopes Warsmith Krendl might have had of a swift victory, once his invading force had breached the citadel's considerable exterior defences. Fighting inside the Schadenhold had been as bloody as the slaughter on the battlements beyond. The fortress stank of hot metal and swift death. Every wall was a bolt-hammered vista of splatter and gore, every chamber carpeted with armoured bodies.

Kneeling down on one rusted knee, Dantioch mused over a crumpled, blood-spotted pile of schematics. The Schadenhold diagrams covered the floor of the embrasure platform and were stained and scratched with ink, Dantioch's strategic annotations almost obscuring the detail of the stronghold's grand design. About the Warsmith, armoured feet shuffled and the air sang with the relentless crash of firing mechanisms. Nearby slumped an Angeloi Adamantiphract, breathing through a ragged hole in his chest, while another bled away his life as an Imperial Army chirurgeon fussed over his missing arm. The edges of the schemata vellum soaked up the growing pool, but the Warsmith – feathered quill to the mouth grate of his mask – was so involved in his three-dimensional visualisation of the two-dimensional prints, that he barely noticed.

'Have Squad Secundus fall back to the hold point on the floor above, they're about to be cut off,' Dantioch ordered.

While Adamantiphracts lanced the long corridor approach to the blockhouse with broad-beam las-fire from the flared barrels of their carbines, the ranking Angeloi Adamantiphract officer in the blockhouse – Lieutenant Cristofori – carried a useless, mangled arm in a sling and doubled as Dantioch's tactical and communications dispatch. Operating a small but robust vox-bank, set in the embrasure wall, Cristofori was the Warsmith's eyes and ears about the Schadenhold. While the lieutenant conveyed the order through a bulky vox-receiver, he filtered the flood of reports coming in from the vox-links of individual Iron Warriors and the comms stations of different blockhouses. Replacing the receiver, he put a finger to his headset and nodded.

'Sir, Nine-Thirteen reports enemy reinforcements on the hangar deck,' the lieutenant relayed.

'Legiones Astartes?' Dantioch asked. It would be hard to believe. If the bodies were anything to go by, Krendl must have committed a full demi-Grand Company by now. The Schadenhold was swarming with Perturabo's progeny.

'Imperial Army, my lord. Looks like foot contingents of the Bi-Nyssal Equerries.'

Dantioch allowed himself a hidden smile. New blood. It seemed that Krendl had been reinforced. This both pleased and vexed the Warsmith. Krendl had been sent to acquire reinforcements for the primarch and Horus Lupercal, not expend the Warmaster's valuable manpower. That would be embarrassing enough. The problem with reinforcement was that it meant that Krendl had been outfitted to see the siege through to the end. Horus could not allow word of Lesser Damantyne's resistance and the loyalty of the Iron Warriors to reach other Legions. The end was near.

'Nine-Thirteen have been forced back to the fuel depot. Awaiting orders,' Cristofori added.

Dantioch grunted. 'Tell the ranking wardsman that he has permission to use the Nine-Thirteen's remaining detonators on the promethium tanks.' The Warsmith slashed a cross through the Schadenhold's Storm-bird hangars on the floor schematic. 'We won't be needing them. Let's deny our enemy also. Nine-Thirteen can fall back by squads to this maintenance opening,' he continued, stabbing the quill point through the vellum. 'Then on to Sergeant Asquetal in the North-IV blockhouse.'

'Sir, also – blockhouses South-II and East-III report dwindling supplies of ammunition.'

'Collapse all of our people on levels two and three back to Colonel Kruishank's hold point in the Hub,' Dantioch grizzled above the gunfire.

'The colonel's dead, sir.'

'What?'

'Colonel Kruishank is dead, sir.'

'Then Captain Galliop, damn it! They still have some limited supplies.'

'Yes, my lord,' Cristofori said unfazed and began relating the Warsmith's orders.

This had been the order of things for as long as the Schadenholders could remember: battle coordinated a hair's-breadth under the fury of boltfire. Whereas the elevated embrasure was intended to provide space for such luxury, below on the chamber floor, Iron Warriors, Adaman-tiphracts and gene-stock ogres fought with adrenaline-fuelled frenzy.

Each knew that his life depended upon the relentless taking of others and nowhere was this more evident than at the gauntlet-entrance to the blockhouse. The walls about the opening had lost their angularity and harsh edges. The perpetual assault of bolt-rounds and las-fire had chewed up the stone and returned the entrance to the rocky, cavernous irregularity of the cave system beyond. From the ceiling rained the gore of those who had failed to breach the chamber; the floor underneath was a mound of gunfire-shredded bodies and trampled armour.

At the centre of the blockhouse stood the Venerable Vastopol. The Dreadnought was too large to take advantage of much of the architectural cover and instead had stood its ground like a machine possessed, hammering anything advancing with the glowing barrels of its raging autocannons. The war machine had borne the brunt of the blockhouse defence; however, the reinforced plate of its sarcophagus body was a sizzling, bolt-punctured mess. The monstrous machine stood in a pool of its own hydraulic fluid and showered sparks from one of its clunky legs. The muzzle of its lower cannon barrel had been shorn off and the mangled chainfist bayonet below hung in a serrated tangle. About the Dreadnought, firing from loopholes and crescent alcoves in merlon walls, were its superhuman kindred. Experts in the art of encumbrance, the Legiones Astartes prided themselves on their beleaguered worth: every defending Iron Warrior had to slay so many of his traitor brothers in order to satisfy the Warsmith's equations: algebraic notations calculated in time and blood.

'Missile launcher!' Tarrasch yelled from the chamber floor. As Legiones Astartes and Adamantiphracts retracted barrels and slammed their backs into protective scenery, the warhead rocketed up the passage and into the blockhouse. Striking a merlon wall the missile exploded, showering razor frag across the heads of hidden defenders.

Angeloi Adamantiphract marksmanship seared the length of the approach, hammering the plate of storming Iron Warriors and cutting up their Imperial Army opposites, las-fodder from the Expeditionary Fleet's Nadir-Maru 4th Juntarians. Those that made the gauntlet-entrance faced a storm of their own: disciplined, ammunition-conserving blasts from the barrels of garrison battle-brothers. Armoured Legiones Astartes besiegers who breached the chamber dived out of the path of withering autocannon fire and las-streams and peeled off left and right, desperate for cover. Their desire to establish a foothold in the blockhouse took them straight into the reach of the Iron Palatine and his assault troops.

The Sons of Dantioch, scarred genebred hulks, pumped to obscenity with hormones and fervent loyalty, came at the interlopers with the mammoth tools of their trade – diamantine-tip hammers, serrated shovels and clawpicks. If that wasn't enough of a nightmare for the blockhouse breachers, the Iron Palatine, Chaplain Zhnev and the Ultramarine Tauro Nicodemus were leading the charge.

An Iron Warrior invader broke from a cannon-mauled throng, a yellow and black-striped blur. With his Mark-IV plate alive with ricochets, the brute pushed himself away from one wall and then the other before tumbling into a messy roll. He was followed by two other traitors who blazed away with their bolters and a trail of opportunistic Nadir-Maru 4th Juntarians.

Genebred hulks descended upon the spearheading Space Marine, their picks and shovels sparking off his savaged ceramite. The second turned his wild bolter straight on Nicodemus, the azure glint of the Ultramarine's armour instantly attracting the warrior's attention. Zhnev wasted no time with the third, firing the pistons in his replacement shoulder. His hammer-fashioned crozius arcanum swung through the air in an unpredictable, pendula-jointed arc, crashing past the Iron Warrior's helmet. Cleaving through armour plating and bone where the Space Marine's neck met his shoulder, the Iron Warriors Chaplain fired his pistons again, swiftly retracting the sacred relic. Spinning with the pendula motion of the crozius, Zhnev howled his fury before striking the heretic's helmet from his body.

Tarrasch plugged the resulting bloodhaze with alternate rounds from each of his bolt pistols, cutting down the Nadir-Maru troopers streaming in through the gauntlet-entrance. Dark, shiny faces beneath extravagant turbans bared bleach-white teeth at the Iron Palatine. The former Iron Warrior captain barked directions to the Angeloi Adamantiphract warriors at the embrasure walls and the Sons of Dantioch below to bring down the Juntarians in their own inimical ways.

With an enemy Legiones Astartes pounding across the killing ground at him, Brother Nicodemus of Ultramar took several practice sweeps with the gleaming blade of his gladius. On his other arm he supported the weight of a huge storm shield. The shield was as tall as the Ultramarine – a sub-rectangular plate, the curved, semi-cylindrical surface of which crackled with a protective energy field. The champion clutched it to his side like an airlock bulkhead.

Dantioch's Iron Warriors were savage hand to hand fighters – equals of the unstoppable World Eaters or the Blood Angels' loyal fervour. The Iron Warriors were deadlier still when they were cornered: cold machines of dread and determination. None had the martial grace or unadulterated skill with a blade that Nicodemus exhibited. Nicodemus batted the Iron Warrior's bolter aside with the weight of the sizzling shield before shearing through the weapon with a murderous downwards cut of his gladius. Before the dazed Iron Warrior could snatch a hammer from his belt the Ultramarine had flashed the gladius back and forth across his opponent's armour. The blade sang through the Iron Warrior's chestplate and helmet, spraying the chamber with Olympian blood.

Nearby the Space Marine that had spearheaded the daring assault broke free of the geneslave mob. A chainaxe screamed from the scrum of hulking bodies. The Iron Warrior burst from the prison of muscular flesh, sweeping heads and elephantine limbs from the Sons of Danti-och in his path. Chaplain Zhnev's crozius sang through the air on its pendula attachment, smashing the motorised axehead into pieces. The Iron Warrior responded immediately by plunging his gauntlet into a holster and drawing a bolt pistol. Before he could end the Chaplain, Tarrasch hammered the heretic with a feverish hail of bolts from his own pistols. The angle was hastily improvised and no one round found its way through the Maximus suit plating. The onslaught had cut the Space Marine's escape dead, however, and the genestock hulks – hungry for a rematch – seized the Iron Warrior. One monster got a bulging arm around the Legiones Astartes' armoured neck while two others snatched an arm each. The ogres gave a brutal heave on the traitor's limbs and with a sickening crack and sudden release, the suit seals and the body within tore apart.

On the opposite side of the gauntlet-entrance the ogres' genestock brothers were murdering Nadir-Maru Juntarians with equal delight. As las-fusillades and dark faces parted, two more armoured figures were revealed. Their armour was busy with chevron designs and yellow strip-ing, and on their backs – either side of their suit packs – were a pair of brass promethium canisters. Stomping up through the Juntarians, the Iron Warriors presented their chunky nozzles, the scorched, dribbling muzzle of each weapon situated at the end of a long firepole.

Tarrasch turned to the blockhouse with just two words on his thin lips: 'Take cover!'

The blast wave from the erupting inferno knocked the Iron Palatine from his armoured feet. In the confines of the chamber, the heavy flam-ers did their worst. Everything became roasting heat and smoke, the ink-blot obscurity punctuated by blinding streams of pressurised prome-thium. As gouts of destruction felt their fiery way through the defensive architecture, sound and smell dominated. Above the boom of the Iron Warrior firepoles, the chatter of bolters could still be heard. Above this was the strangled shrieking of men aflame: Angeloi, genebreeds and Nadir-Maruvians all. Scorched within their suits, Iron Warriors stum-bled through the firestorm, searching for respite.

It could have been a bolt-round, fired blindly into the darkness and fury, or perhaps a stream from the flared muzzle of a lascarbine or laspistol. Most likely it was a blast from the Venerable Vastopol's raging autocannons, but something hit one of the brass fuel canisters. A suc-cession of explosions rippled through the thick smoke, knocking all that still lived in the chamber onto their backs. Flame rolled across ceiling and floor; through the tactical arrangement of the blockhouse; through the gauntlet entrance and down the crowded passage beyond.

Dantioch's gauntlet grabbed the top of the platform wall like a grap-nel. The Warsmith heaved himself to unsteady feet in the swirling smoke, stamping out the small fire that was his burning schematics. Cristofori was dead, as well as the injured Adamantiphract and his chirurgeon. As the smoke began to clear, Dantioch took in the blockhouse floor. There were bodies everywhere, both loyal and traitor: a carpet of scorched armour and charred flesh. Similar destruction extended up the passage to the gauntlet entrance. There was movement, however, and it wouldn't take their attackers long to organise an assault to capitalise on the inferno.

Leaning against the wall for support, the Warsmith came down the embrasure steps.

'Tarrasch!' Dantioch called. From the soot and smaze came sudden movement.

'Sir,' came the Iron Palatine's reply. The explosion had knocked the Iron Warrior senseless into a wall. His words were shaky but the Space Marine was alive.

'It's over. We are compromised. Enemy forces imminent. Get the living to their feet.'

'Yes, my lord.'

As Tarrasch stumbled through the carnage, searching for survivors, Dantioch ran his gauntlets along the wall. The Warsmith began to knock experimentally against the stone as he slouched along its expanse. Satisfied, the Warsmith stopped and turned on the hulking Dreadnought that still stood sentinel in the middle of the blockhouse, autocannons at the ready.

'Vastopol, are you still with us, my friend?' the Warsmith asked.

In answer the Dreadnought just burned. The explosions had done little to the machine but scorch its adamantium and set fire to the scrolls, banners and decorative flourishes that adorned the bulky form.

'Don't be like that,' Dantioch said. 'It's over. We could fight to the last man but what would that achieve?'

Still the Dreadnought stood immobile.

'This isn't Gholghis,' Dantioch told his battle-brother. 'It is the prerogative of the Warsmith when to war and when not to. We are beaten here. It is time to take the war elsewhere. Now get over here and help me; you may still have a story to tell.'

As the Venerable Vastopol dragged its mangled and sparking leg across the bodies of the blockhouse floor, Tarrasch worked his way through the dead and dying. The Angeloi were all dead, as were the remaining Sons of Dantioch. The raging inferno had done for both and only a handful of Legiones Astartes, protected from the worst of the explosion by their battle-plate, had survived the catastrophic accident.

'Enemy advancing!' Tarrasch called from the gauntlet entrance.

'Come on, come on!' Dantioch urged Space Marines emerging from the smoke and destruction.

Tauro Nicodemus was suddenly beside him: his immaculate armour soot-stained and blood-spattered.

'I thought this was the fallback position,' the Tetrarch said. The Ultramarine had accepted that he was to die there, taking as many traitor lives with him as he was able.

'Game's not over,' Dantioch said. 'Gather your weapons.'

'Where are we going?'

'Through this wall.'

Dantioch knocked on a section of the blockhouse wall. A deliberate, architectural weak point. 'Vastopol.'

The Dreadnought limped at the wall, crashing through the masonry with one of its chunky shoulders. Rock and dust fell about the war machine. Extracting itself from the ragged aperture, Vastopol stood back to admit the surviving Legiones Astartes: the Warsmith, the Iron Palatine, Brother-Sergeant Ingoldt, Brothers Toledo and Baubistra, the Ultramarine Nicodemus and Chaplain Zhnev. Beyond a broad set of steep, rocky stairs extended, running parallel with the wall and reaching up into the Schadenhold's cavernous ceiling foundations. With the Legiones Astartes striding up ahead, the Venerable Vastopol negotiated the steps with difficulty, its mangled leg a handicap on the shambling ascent.

The stairwell rumbled and shook.

'What was that?' Tarrasch called. For a moment nobody answered in the darkness. Then a quake rolled through the stone about them. The steps shook under their feet and fractures split the stairwell's rough roof and walls.

'It's the *Omnia Victrum*,' Dantioch said. 'Krendl finally has his Titans in position.' The Warsmith tried to picture the acid-scarred colossi outside, the remaining war machines of the Legio Argentum. The *Omnia Victrum* was an Imperator-class Titan. A mountain of rust-eaten armour, striding across the cavern like a vengeful god. At its sides it mounted weaponry of titanic proportion: monstrous instruments of destruction, capable of razing cities and felling enemy god-machines. Upon its hunched back sat a small city of its own: a Titanscape of corroded steeples, towers and platforms. A base of operations and a mobile barracks of waiting reinforcements.

'She's softening up the south face of the Schadenhold with her cannons and turbolasers before landing troops.' The Imperator was huge and certainly tall enough to stand beside and beneath the Iron Warrior citadel. It could disgorge a siege-ending horde of traitor Iron Warriors and reinforcement foot contingents of the Bi-Nyssal Equerries. As fresh blood rampaged through the south section of the Schadenhold, joining Krendl and his depleted forces in the north, loyalist Iron Warrior resistance would be overrun and crushed. Even Dantioch's ingenious blockhouse fallbacks would not be able to save the Schadenholders from the wall-to-wall carnage that was to come.

Tremors swept through the stairwell once more, knocking several

Space Marines from their footing. Dantioch fell into Tarrasch, who steadied his Warsmith, but most were staring at the ceiling. Rock and dust rained down on the Iron Warriors and the walls trembled.

'The passage is collapsing,' Nicodemus called, holding his storm shield above him.

'The structure will hold,' Dantioch assured them. They were in the cavern ceiling foundations of the Schadenhold. The *Omnia Victrum's* artillery assault was pummelling the citadel into submission, shaking the fortress to its rocky core. From the bottom of the stairwell came the fresh chatter of weaponry. Bolters and lascarbines, clutched by the traitor Legiones Astartes and Nadir-Maru Fourth Juntarians. The enemy that had flooded the empty blockhouse had followed them through the hole in the wall. Firepower came up the stairs at the loyalists with Krendl's besiegers climbing behind. 'Come on!' Dantioch shouted and continued his ascent.

'Warsmith,' he heard Tarrasch call and upon turning found his Iron Palatine skidding back down the steps towards the Venerable Vastopol. Although the south wall had held, it had partially collapsed, creating a bottleneck through which the Dreadnought's broad bulk could not pass. With his armoured shoulders askew but braced between the walls of the stairwell, the war machine was trapped: held fast by the rock and unable to find footing with his mangled leg.

Enemy fire hammered into the Dreadnought's armoured back. Brother-Sergeant Ingoldt and the Iron Palatine grabbed the war machine's limbs and heaved at the metal monster. With the intensity of firepower beyond growing and casting the Venerable Vastopol in silhouette, the Iron Warriors fought to free their comrade. The Dreadnought's vox-speakers trembled with the groans of the warrior inside, as the relentless streams of las-fire and bolt-rounds shredded Vastopol's rear plating.

Baubistra and Chaplain Zhnev ran down the steps at the war machine. Brother Baubistra leapt onto the front of the sarcophagus body section and clambered up the chunky weaponry. Between the top of the Dreadnought's mighty shoulders and the stairwell roof, Baubistra found a gap for his bolter and began answering back with ammo-conserving blasts. Zhnev came straight at Vastopol's midriff, slamming his battle-plate into the Dreadnought in the hope that his assault might dislodge the war machine. The Chaplain failed. The Venerable Vastopol had become the immovable object. Only the unstoppable force of Krendl's traitor troops would remove him and until then, the Iron Warrior Dreadnought became a wall of adamantium and ceramite dividing the two.

Tarrasch heard a familiar whine.

'Missile launcher!' he called.

A rocket slammed into the back of the Dreadnought, knocking Baubistra from his perch and drawing from the Venerable Vastopol a vox-roar of agony and anguish. Two more followed, ravaging the armoured shell of the beast. Vastopol's groans were constant now and the Iron Warrior's hulking, metal body was failing about him. Dantioch stomped down the steps towards the Dreadnought.

'Get him out,' the Warsmith ordered.

'He'll die,' Zhnev replied over the boom of battle beyond.

'Do it.'

Tarrasch looked to Dantioch and his Chaplain. Then up to Tauro Nicodemus, who was waiting further up the stairwell.

'My lord,' Tarrasch said, 'we need specialist tools and Magos Genetor Urqhart for such a procedure.'

Dantioch laid his gauntlets on the cold metal of the Venerable Vastopol's sarcophagus section. The Iron Warrior within continued to moan his agonies through the vox-speakers.

'Vastopol, listen to me,' the Warsmith said. 'We won't leave you, my friend. We need to get you out. Can you help us?'

The Dreadnought's power claw came up slowly between them. Askew as he was, the war machine still had use of the appendage, but little else. Bringing the clawtips together like a spike, the Dreadnought thrust the weapon through the armour plating of his sarcophagus. Magna-pistons and hydraulics shifted and locked in the appendage, opening the claw within. With a mighty heave the arm retracted. The Dreadnought's armoured body fought back, resisting the act of self-mutilation, but finally the plate tore away from the machine's pock-marked shell.

Amnio-sarcophagal fluid cascaded from the pod within, splashing the steps and nearby Space Marines. Power arced across the ruined section and the cavity steamed. The stench was overpowering. Small fires had broken out within, while lines and wires smoked and sparked. Interred, like an ancient foetus, lay what remained of the former Brother Vastopol. The warrior-poet was barely alive. His parchment skin was both wrinkled and pruned and his arms skeletal and wasted. He'd long lost his legs and his torso was a scrawny cage of bones, infested with life-support tubes and impulse plugs that ran lines between the aged Legiones Astartes and his metal womb-tomb.

'Get him out,' Dantioch ordered.

Chaplain Zhnev and Brother Toledo pulled the emaciated Iron Warrior from the sarcophagus, extracting tubes from between his withered lips and yellow teeth and unplugging the pilot from his mind-impulse interface with his shattered Dreadnought body. With his arms draped over ceramite shoulders, the two Iron Warriors carried Vastopol between them, his skullface and wet, threadbare scalp resting against the Chaplain's plate.

More missiles struck the barricade of the Dreadnought's evacuated shell and the Iron Warriors fled up the rocky stairwell. Despite being exhausted from the siege the Space Marines made swift progress, slowed only by the fragility of Vastopol's failing condition and the hacking cough that paralysed the Warsmith with infuriating regularity. At the top of the stairwell they encountered an iron hatch set in the passage roof. Making his feeble way up the final few steps, Dantioch ordered the hatch unlocked and the Iron Warriors through.

The chamber beyond was large and dark. The Warsmith pulled down on a robust handle set in the stone of the wall and lamps began to flicker on. The still air about the Legiones Astartes came to life with the rumble of powerful generators.

'Seal it,' Dantioch told Brother Baubistra, indicating the hatch. Striding across the chamber, Dantioch was followed by questions. The chamber was no blockhouse, although it did seem to house a small armoury of its own: bolters on racks, ammunition crates, grenades and several suits of Mark-III plate. The Warsmith ignored his brothers' enquiries and fell to work at a nearby runebank. 'Sergeant Ingoldt, Brother Toledo, please be so good as to clad the Venerable Vastopol in one of those suits of spare plate.'

'That won't save him,' Zhnev informed his Warsmith.

'Chaplain, please. While there's still time.'

'Warsmith, I must press you for an explanation,' Tauro Nicodemus said, after casting his eyes about the chamber. 'I thought we were falling back to a further hold point.'

'To what end, Ultramarine?' Dantioch put to him as his gauntlets glided over the glyphs and runes of the console. 'The Schadenhold is lost. Those loyalists remaining in the citadel will be overrun by Krendl's reinforcements and the *Omnia Victrum* will reduce the rest to rubble. This stronghold has bought the Emperor and Roboute Guilliman three hundred and sixty-six Ancient Terran days. Three hundred and sixty-six days bought with Olympian blood, so that they might formulate a response to the Heresy and better fortify the Imperial Palace – to buy a more favourable outcome than our own.'

'What is the plan, my lord?' Tarrasch said, his words giving shape to the thoughts of all in the chamber.

Dantioch looked about their cavernous surroundings.

'This is the last of the Schadenhold's secret strategies,' the Warsmith said. 'A final solution to any siege and an answer to any enemy that might push us this far.'

'You said the fortress was lost,' Nicodemus said.

'There are many moments in a battle, when we can exploit our enemy's weakness. We have, over the course of this siege, exploited nearly all of them. It is nothing less than irony that an enemy is at its very weakest mere moments before victory: when they are at their most stretched and committed in seeking such success. We are going to capitalise on that now.'

'How?' the champion pressed him.

'In a siege, finalities must come first. We must accept our eventual doom and prepare for its coming. This chamber was one of the first I had constructed when crafting the Schadenhold. It is situated in the cavern ceiling, right in the rocky foundations of the fortress. It houses two important pieces of equipment, linked by a common console: a trigger for both if you will. The first is a small teleportarium with the associated generators required to power such a piece of equipment. The second is a detonator: wired to explosives situated at key weak points in the citadel foundations. Gravity will do the rest.' Dantioch let the enormity of his plan sink in. 'Chaplain Zhnev, please begin the rites for teleportation. Our journey will be swift but our destination important.'

As the Chaplain approached the transference tablets of the teleporter beyond, Tarrasch helped Ingoldt and Toledo get the barely breathing Vastopol sealed in plate.

'Where is that destination?' Nicodemus asked the Warmith. The Ultramarine was unused to being kept in tactical darkness.

'The enemy has committed everything they have to taking this stronghold, undoubtedly leaving their own weak. We are going to teleport to the *Benthos* and take the bridge by surprise and by force. Brothers, time is upon us. Take your positions, please.'

As Tarrasch and the two Iron Warriors dragged the power armoured form of the Venerable Vastopol over to the transference tablets, Nicodemus hefted his storm shield up onto a shoulder mounting. The Ultramarine followed uncertainly.

With his helmet to the hatch, Baubistra said: 'I think they've broken through, Warsmith. The enemy are approaching.'

'Very good, Brother Baubistra: now join your brethren.'

As Baubistra strode by, Dantioch went through the motions of arming the explosives sunk deep in the ceiling rock of the Schadenhold's foundations. Then he opened channels on all floors and vox-hailers across the citadel.

'Idriss Krendl,' Dantioch hissed. 'Captain, this is your Warsmith. I know that you are there, somewhere in my fortress. I know you keep company with traitors and stand in the shadow of the Collegia Titanica's god-machines. Faced with such odds, I am speaking to you for the last time. And I say to you again that this fortress will not serve the interests of our unloving father or his renegade Warmaster. But, captain, I was wrong when I told you that the Schadenhold would never fall. Idriss, it will fall...'

With that the Warsmith locked off the channels and initiated the trigger for both teleporter and detonators. Taking his position amongst Nicodemus and the Iron Warriors on the transference tablets, Dantioch straightened his cloak. Sealing his mask, the Warsmith blinked about the darkness within and felt the unnatural pull of the warp on his armour. Somewhere in the distance he fancied he heard the first of the detonations: massive explosions, ripping through the strategic weaknesses of the fortress foundations. With his eyes closed and the horrors of teleportation about him, Dantioch imagined what he had always known he could never see.

The fall of the Schadenhold. Its literal fall from the ceiling of the cavern. Trillions of tonnes of rock and devious architecture falling to the rocky floor, taking with it the thousands of traitor Iron Warriors and Imperial soldiers that had secured the Schadenhold's defeat. The fortress's final defiance, issued in gravity, fire and stone: falling and crushing beneath it, in a behemothic mountain of blood and rubble, the mighty *Omnia Victrum* and the colossal god-machines of its undoing.

UNSEALING HIS MASK, Dantioch cast his eyes across the flight deck of the flagship *Benthos*. The deck was largely empty; most of the cruiser's Warhawks and Stormbirds had been involved in deployment and aerial attacks on the Schadenhold. The Stormbird around which the Iron Warriors had materialised was pale green and bore symbols and flourishes marking it out as belonging to the Sons of Horus – Hasdrubal Serapis's personal transport.

Tarrasch marched down the Stormbird's ramp carrying a teleport homer. Dantioch had ordered the device secretly planted on the vessel during their meeting with Krendl and the Sons of Horus captain in the Grand Reclusiam.

'How are we going to get to the bridge?' asked Chaplain Zhnev.

'With as little bloodshed as possible,' the Warsmith told him. 'This is the 51st Expedition's flagship. Iron Warriors are a common sight among its decks. Let us be that common sight.'

'What about him?' Tarrasch asked of Tauro Nicodemus. Despite the soot and gore, the brilliance of the Ultramarine's armour still shone through.

'The crew will not question a Legiones Astartes.'

Marching out purposefully across the flight deck, Dantioch was followed by his loyalist compatriots. The Space Marines fought their desire to hold their bolters at the ready, opting for more casual or ceremonial poses. Brother Toledo and Sergeant Ingoldt carried the limp plate of the Venerable Vastopol between them, lending the infiltrators even less the appearance of an attacking force.

There were virtually no Legiones Astartes left aboard the vessel, almost every Iron Warrior being committed to the depths of the planet below. Largely the Space Marines encountered regimental staff and the cruiser's multitudinous crew. Few among these mortals allowed their eyes to linger on the demigods – especially under Krendl's brutal regime – and their passage to the command deck was uneventful. Dantioch's strategy had been so bold and audaciously executed that none aboard the *Benthos*, even for a second, entertained thoughts that they were under attack.

Their silent, uneasy approach to the bridge was shattered by an unexpected klaxon. Bolters came up and the Iron Warriors fell immediately into defensive positions.

'As you were,' Dantioch instructed.

The loyalists could hear the thunder of power armoured boots on the deck ahead. 'We are not discovered. We are not under attack,' Dantioch said. Fighting natural inclination and the brute vulnerability of their situation, the Iron Warriors let their barrels drift back down to the deck. A small contingent of Krendl's Fourteenth Grand Company veterans marched across an intersection in the corridor ahead. As their footfalls faded, Dantioch turned to his own veterans. 'By now,' he told them, 'survivors on Lesser Damantyne will have reported the devastation below, the loss of Krendl, the Warmaster's forces and the *Omnia Victrum*. Whoever is in command will want visual confirmation of such an impossible report. Five fewer brother Legiones Astartes for us to deal with.'

Dantioch turned and marched with confidence up the steps to the bridge, flanked by Brother Baubistra and the Iron Palatine. As the Warsmith reached the top and looked down across the expansive bridge of the *Benthos* he fell into a coughing fit once more: a spasm of hacking convulsions that turned heads and drew attentions.

The bridge of the *Benthos* was a hive of activity, with petty officers and sickly servitors busy at work amongst the labyrinth of runebanks, cogitators and consoles that dominated the command deck. Two Maximus-plated Iron Warriors stood sentry on the bridge arch-egress and Lord Commander Warsang Gabroon of the Nadir-Maru 4th Juntarians stood at conference with turbaned officers of his tactical staff. The Lord Commander stood as Dantioch remembered him, unconsciously twirling the braids of his beard and launching stabbing glares of jaundiced incredulity and disappointment at his inferiors.

At the epicentre of the activity and the destination of all reports, data and information were three Sons of Horus: swarthy Cthonians with superior sneers and knitted brows of insidious cunning. Among their number was one who immediately recognised what all others aboard the *Benthos* had failed to: the threat before them. The enemy Warsmith, Barabas Dantioch.

Baubistra and Tarrasch barged onto the bridge, past their master. Putting the muzzles of their weapons to the temples of the traitor sentries they roared at their Olympian brothers to drop their weapons and fall to their knees. Abandoning their burden, Sergeant Ingoldt and Toledo came forwards with bolters raised and pointed at the Sons of Horus. The two traitors flanking Hasdrubal drew their bolt pistols and activity on the bridge slowed to a raucous stand-off. The traitor captain screamed his disbelief and insistence as Iron Warriors and Sons of Horus held each other in their sights. With the Chaplain kneeling beside the dying Vastopol and Dantioch clutching the archway in his coughing fit, it fell to Tauro Nicodemus to break the deadlock.

The Ultramarines champion strode forwards, the only thing moving on the stricken command deck. Undaunted, Nicodemus marched past an apoplectic Lord Commander Gabroon, who was screaming, 'No shooting on the bridge,' at the warring demigods. Hasdrubal Serapis's face screwed up with rage and confusion. The destruction on Lesser Damantyne and the appearance of Dantioch and his Iron Warriors on the bridge had been disturbing enough. Now one of Guilliman's sons stood before him: a mysterious Ultramarine who had involved himself in the Warmaster's business and no doubt had something to do with the Iron Warrior resistance on the planet below.

Hasdrubal backed towards one of the great lancet screens that towered above the bridge: the thick glass was the only thing separating the Space Marine captain from the hostile emptiness outside. His two sentinels held their ground, tracking the advancing Nicodemus with their bolt pistols. Hasdrubal looked at the Iron Warriors, with their weapons aimed up the bridge and at him in front of the huge window. Gabroon continued to screech his alarm. Hasdrubal nodded, confident that the Iron Warriors were not foolish enough to fire and blast out the viewport, dooming all on the bridge to a voidgrave.

'Kill that damned Ultramarine,' Hasdrubal seethed.

The Sons of Horus fired. Iron Warriors thrust their bolters forwards with an intention to respond in kind.

'Hold your fire!' Dantioch managed between torso-wracking convulsions. With his Iron Warriors facing the bridge lancet screens, he could not afford a stray shot to pierce the hull of the ship.

Nicodemus hefted the mighty storm shield from its shoulder mounting and brought it around just in time to soak up the first of the traitor Space Marine's bolt-rounds. As the shots hammered into the cerulean sheen of the plate, the Tetrarch thumbed the shield's protective field to life. The marksmanship of the Sons of Horus was a beauty to behold. Every bolt-round found its mark, and had Nicodemus not been advancing behind the storm shield he would have been run through by a relentless onslaught of armour-piercing shot.

Closing on the traitors, the pistols' effective range shortened and the storm shield's energy field was breached. One of the adamatium-core Space Marine killers passed through the armour plating and clipped the Ultramarine's shoulder. As Guilliman's champion continued to advance, Hasdrubal's features contorted further in fury and disbelief. The Sons of Horus ejected spent magazines from their sidearms before slamming home another and repeating the treatment. Nothing would stop Nicodemus, however.

As Hasdrubal's Space Marines emptied their weapons for the second time, Nicodemus took a round through the thigh, one in the chest and another in the shoulder. This time the adamantium slugs found their target and punctured holes through the shield and the Ultramarine's artificer armour. The energy field sizzled and spat to overload and all Nicodemus had was the bolt-punched plate between him and his enemies. Running the final stretch of command deck, the Ultramarines champion closed with the Sons of Horus.

Desperate now, the traitors went for their Cthonian blades. Nicodemus already had a gauntlet on his own gladius. His armoured palm was slippery with the blood that had run down his arm from the grievous wound in his shoulder. Spinning between the two Legiones Astartes, Nicodemus slammed the storm shield into the first. He felt the slash of the enemy blade on the battered plate and hammered the Son of Horus again. Extending his arm and moving the shield aside like an open door, the Ultramarine allowed the traitor a single, wild thrust. The sword stabbed through the open space between the champion's elbow and hip. Nicodemus swept down with the blade of the gladius, cutting through the Space Marine's armoured forearm. Gauntlet and blade clattered to the deck.

The Ultramarine pressed his advantage: one honour guard to another. He smacked the traitor senseless with the storm shield, the plate edge dashing his helmet this way and that. Dazed, the Son of Horus slipped in his own gore and hit the deck. Nicodemus buried the toe of one power armoured boot in the traitor's faceplate, rolling him over. Standing over his prone enemy, Nicodemus hovered the bottom edge of the rectangular shield over the Space Marine's throat. He looked to Hasdrubal and his one remaining sentinel, who stood defiantly between the Ultramarine and his master. Nicodemus brought down the weight of the storm shield with a sickening crack. The seal between helmet and suit cracked and the shield edge cut through the traitor's neck.

The Ultramarine's armoured chest heaved up and down with exertion as he took a moment to recover, before hoisting the mighty shield around and running straight at the Son of Horus sentinel. Again, Nicodemus felt the pointless slash of the lighter, Cthonian blade on the bolt-shot plate. This time the Ultramarine didn't stop. He rammed the Son of Horus straight into the thick glass lancet window. Crushed between the observation port and the Ultramarine, the traitor abandoned his weapon and tried to grab the edge of the shield with his ceramite fingertips. Nicodemus smashed him into the glass a second and third time. Finally, the Son of Horus managed to get a grip on the shield – his intention to push the plate aside and get his gauntlets around the Ultramarine's neck.

He never got the chance. Pulling back his gladius, Nicodemus rammed the point of the blade through the back of the storm shield and skewered the Space Marine beyond. There was a gasp. Light. Almost inaudible. Retracting the blade, Nicodemus stepped aside and allowed the shield and Son of Horus to smash to the bridge floor.

Hasdrubal had turned away. Like everyone else on the bridge, the captain had thought that the Ultramarine was going to put the Space

Marine straight through the window, crashing thick glass about them and inviting the void inside. The captain looked fearfully at Guilliman's champion. Nicodemus paced up and down in front of him with the gore-smeared gladius held in one gauntlet. He unclipped his helmet and slipped the plumed helm off the back of his head. Gone was the martial grace and patrician calm. Nicodemus spat blood at the deck. A bolt pistol shook in Hasdrubal's gauntlet. Iron Warriors surrounded them both, bolters gaping at the traitor.

'It's over,' Dantioch called, his grim insistence cutting through the cacophony of a bridge in uproar. Hasdrubal turned from the Ultramarine's fury to the cold, foreboding of Dantioch's iron mask. 'You lost,' the Warsmith informed his enemy.

Hasdrubal's bolt pistol tumbled from his ceramite fingers. As Toledo and Sergeant Ingoldt secured the prisoner, Nicodemus sheathed his gladius and limped back up the length of the bridge. Lord Commander Gabroon was still shrieking his protestations. The demigod silenced the officer with a slow finger to his lips.

Nicodemus joined Dantioch on the deck, next to the Venerable Vastopol. The Warsmith had ordered Tarrasch to take command of the bridge. Ingoldt and Toledo had been tasked with securing the traitor Hasdrubal Serapis and preparing him for interrogation. Chaplain Zhnev and Brother Baubistra were assigned to Warsang Gabroon, to ensure that the Lord Commander's remaining troops and the crew of the *Benthos* accepted the swift and relatively bloodless change of regime and the new orders that accompanied it.

Standing over the two survivors of the Gholghis fortress world, the Ultramarine asked: 'Is there anything I can do, Warsmith?'

Dantioch didn't look at the Tetrarch. The Warsmith's eyes were on the helmetless Vastopol. The ancient lay motionless in battle-plate on the deck, propped up against the wall. The Iron Warrior's grizzled and aged skull was criss-crossed with wisps of white hair and his face lined with premature centuries. Two milky orbs twitched and wandered between Dantioch, Nicodemus and the bridge.

'Our honoured brother is taking his leave,' Dantioch said. His words were hollow and shot through with loneliness and the simple sadness of loss. The Venerable Vastopol had not only survived the dreaded hrud on Gholghis. He'd resisted death's cold invitation and forged on through the agonies of age to be of use to his brothers once more. Untimely ripped from his metal womb, Vastopol had still clung to life. Until now.

'He was our chronicler,' Dantioch said, 'and carried with him our remembered triumphs. Once, on Gholghis, he told me that such stories of the past ground us in the challenge of the present, like a fortification or citadel built upon foundations of ancient rock. I have none of his skill – crafting in iron and stone what he would in words. I live to tell the tale, however, of the Iron Warriors' final victory: the last loyal triumph of the IVth Legion. He would want the story to go on. Alas, his story,' Dantioch said grimly, 'like that of our Legion, is at an end.'

'Warsmith,' Nicodemus began slowly, 'that need not be the case. I assured you once that my Lord Guilliman had a plan. You have executed your part of that plan flawlessly, Iron Warrior. Lord Guilliman still has need of such ingenuity and skill. The Imperium is frail, Dantioch. An Iron Warrior's eye could spot such weakness and the good grace of his hand might make it strong once again.'

'What more would you ask of me?' the Warsmith said.

'To stand shoulder to ceramite shoulder with my Lord Guilliman and help him fortify the Imperial Palace.'

'Fortify the Palace…' Dantioch repeated.

'Yes, Iron Warrior.'

'Perturabo will make us pay for such fantasies.'

'Perhaps,' Nicodemus said solemnly. 'But I believe the genius of your victory today lay in your acceptance that the Schadenhold – for all its indomitable art – would fall. Lord Guilliman shares your vision. Humanity's future lies in such contingency.' The Ultramarine let the enormity of the idea linger.

Dantioch didn't answer. Instead he watched the remaining vestiges of life leave the body of his friend and battle-brother. Vastopol's crusted eyes fluttered before rolling and gently closing, the dry whisper of a dying breath escaping the warrior-poet's lips.

As the Venerable Vastopol faded and left them, he heard Dantioch tell the Ultramarine: 'You talk of the arts of destruction. Perturabo's progeny are unrivalled in these arts: indomitable in battle and peerless in the science of siegecraft. Show me a palace and I'll show you how an Iron Warrior would take it. Then I'll show you how you would stop me. I don't know how long I am for this Imperium, but I promise you this: whatever iron is left within this aged plate, is yours…'

THE IRON WITHIN. The iron without. Iron everywhere. Empires rise and they fall. I have fought the ancient species of the galaxy and my Legiones Astartes brothers will fight on, meeting new threats in dangers as yet unrealised. We are an Imperium of iron and iron is forever. When our flesh is long forgotten, whether victim to the enemy within or the enemy without, iron will live on. Our hives will tumble and our mighty fleets decay. Long after our polished bones have faded to dust on a gentle breeze, our weapons and armour will remain. Remnants of a warlike race: the iron of loyalist and traitor both. In them our story will be told – a cautionary tale to those that follow. Iron cares not for faith or heresy. Iron is forever.

And as our battle-plate, our blades and bolters rot in the sand of some distant world, they will pit and tarnish. Their dull sheen will corrode and crumble. Grey will turn to brown and brown to red. In the quietly rusting scrap of our fallen empire, iron will return to its primordial state, perhaps to be used again by some other foolish race. And though the weakness of my flesh fails me, as the weakness of my brothers' flesh will ultimately fail them, our iron shall live on. For iron is eternal.

From iron cometh strength. From strength cometh will. From will cometh faith. From faith cometh honour. From honour cometh iron. This is the Unbreakable Litany. And may it forever be so.

WARHAMMER®

FEAST OF HORRORS

Chris Wraight

HELMUT DETLEF DREW his steed to a halt. The sun was low behind him. The shadows in the forest were long, and the tortured branches beckoned the onset of a bitter night. If he'd been alone, Detlef might have felt anxiety. The deep woods were no place for a young, inexperienced squire to be after dark.

But he wasn't alone. The figure next to him sat astride a massive warhorse. He was decked in full plate armour and carried a long, rune-carved sword. A thick beard spilled over his chest, falling over the Imperial crest embossed on the metal. His cloak hung down from gold-rimmed pauldrons and the open-faced helm was crowned with a laurel wreath. Only one man was permitted to don such ancient armour – the Emperor's Champion, Ludwig Schwarzhelm, dispenser of Imperial Law and wielder of the dread Sword of Justice.

By comparison, Detlef's titles – squire, errand runner, occasional herald – were pretty unimpressive. Still, just to serve under such a man was an honour almost beyond reckoning. Detlef was barely out of the village and less than two years' service into the Reikland halberdiers. In the months since joining Schwarzhelm he'd already seen things men twice his age would hardly dream of.

'That's it?' he said, pointing ahead.

'That's it,' replied Schwarzhelm. His voice was iron-hard, tinged with a faint Averland accent. Schwarzhelm spoke rarely. When he did, it was wise to take note.

The trees clustered near the road on either side of them, overhanging as close as they dared as if eager to snatch the unwary traveller and pull him into the dark heart of the forest. So it had been for the many days since they'd ridden from the battlefront in Ostland. The Forest of Shadows had been true to its name every step of the way.

A few yards ahead, the wood gave way to a clearing. In the failing light it looked drab and sodden, though the bastion rising from it was anything but. Here, miles from the nearest town and isolated within the cloying bosom of the forest, a sprawling manor house stood sentinel. The walls were built from stone framed with age-blackened oak. Elaborate gables decorated the steep-sided roofs rising sharply against the sky. The seal of Ostland, a bull's head, had been engraved ostentatiously over the vast main doorway, and statues in the shape of griffons, wyverns and other beasts stared out across the bleak vista. Warm firelight shone from the narrow mullioned windows and columns of thick smoke rose from the many chimneys.

'How should I address him?' asked Detlef, feeling his ignorance. The task of learning his duties had been steep, and Schwarzhelm was intolerant of mistakes.

'He's a baron. Use "my lord".'

Or, more completely, Baron Helvon Drakenmeister Egbert von Rauken, liege lord of an estate that covered hundreds of square miles. Detlef might once have found that intimidating, but after serving with Schwarzhelm, very little compared.

'I'll ride ahead to announce you.'

Schwarzhelm nodded. His grey eyes glittered, in his craggy, unsmiling face.

'You do that.'

THEIR ARRIVAL HAD been unexpected. Despite that, the baron's household managed to put on a good show. Servants preparing to turn in for the night were dragged from their chambers and put to work in the kitchens. The household was roused and told to put on its finery. By the time the sun had finally dipped below the western horizon, a banquet fit for their visitor had been thrown together. Detlef found the process intensely amusing. The combination of irritation and fear on the faces of the mansion staff was worth the long trek on its own.

Rauken's banqueting hall, like all the rooms in the house, was a study in baroque excess. The high-beamed roof was decorated with tasteless frescos of Imperial myths, all lit by an oversized fire roaring in the marble-framed hearth. The floor was also marble, black and white chequers like the nave of an Imperial chapel. The table looked as if it had been carved from a single slab of wood, even though it was over thirty feet long. Its surface had been polished to a glassy sheen, reflecting the light of the dozens of candelabras and sending it winking and flashing from the crystal goblets and silver plates.

The guests, a dozen of them, were no less opulent. All looked well-fed and comfortably padded. The ladies were decked in frocks of wildly varied shades, draped with tassels, bows and lines of pearls. Even at such short notice they'd managed to arrange their greying hair in heaps of tottering grandeur, laced with lines of gold wire and emerald studs. Their sagging faces were plastered with lead whitener, their lips and cheeks heavily rouged. Their male companions were also finely turned out, replete with sashes, medals, powdered wigs and jewel-encrusted codpieces. They strutted to their places, jowls wobbling with anticipation as the food arrived.

From his seat on the edge of the chamber, Detlef watched them intently, trying to pick out the ones Schwarzhelm had told him about. Most of the party were Rauken's blood-kin, but some of his more senior aides had been invited. Among them was Osbert Hulptraum, Rauken's personal physician, a fat waddling grey-faced man with a balding pate and bags under his eyes. Next to him sat Julius Adenauer, the chancellor, all thin lips, clawed fingers and sidelong glances. His scraggy beard looked wispy even in the low light, and he minced around like a parody of a woman.

At the head of the table sat Rauken himself. He was massively corpulent, red-cheeked, with a bulbous nose laced with broken veins. He'd chosen to cover himself in robes of velvet, not that they did much to hide his generous belly. As he beckoned the guests to take their seats, his many chins shivered like jelly.

'We are honoured,' he said, his voice surprisingly high. 'Truly honoured. It's not every day this house hosts one of the finest heroes of the Empire.'

A murmur of appreciation ran across the throng. Schwarzhelm, sitting at Rauken's right hand – the place of honour – remained impassive. He'd heard it all before. He'd exchanged his armour for simple robes in the red and white of the Imperial palace, but still looked by far the most regal presence in the room.

'So let us eat,' Rauken said, 'and celebrate this happy occasion.'

The guests needed no encouragement. Soon they were shovelling heaps of food on to their plates – lambs' livers, roast pigeon, jugged hare, moist sweetbreads, slabs of pheasant pie, slops of something dark brown with quail's eggs floating in it, pig's cheeks in jelly, all washed down with generous slugs of a dark red wine brought all the way, Detlef had learned, from the vines of the Duc d'Alembourg-Rauken in Guillet Marchand on the banks of the Brienne.

Like all the servants present, Detlef had been seated behind his master in case he was needed during the meal. His stomach growled as he watched the guests begin to cram the fine food into their mouths. At least his position let him hear the conversation.

'So to what do we owe this honour, my lord?' asked Rauken, munching delicately on a fig stuffed with mincemeat.

'The Emperor likes me to meet all his subjects,' said Schwarzhelm. He'd not touched the food, and had taken strips of dried meat from a pouch at his belt.

'Well then, I hope we've not been amiss with the tithes. Adenauer, are we up to date?'

'We are, my lord,' replied the chancellor, dabbing grease from his chin. 'The records are available for scrutiny.'

'Very good,' said Rauken, looking at Schwarzhelm nervously. 'You're not eating, my lord?'

'Not muck like this. I prefer my own.'

Schwarzhelm's flat refusal cut through the conversation like a blunt axe-blade. There was a nervous laugh from one of the women, soon cut off when she realised he wasn't joking.

Detlef smiled to himself. The dinner promised to be an amusing one. It was only then that he caught the eye of the serving girl sitting beside him. She was as fleshy and rosy-cheeked as the rest of them, but much younger. He found his eyes drawn to her chest, appealingly exposed by a low-cut, tight-laced bodice.

She smiled at him, and her eyes shone in the candlelight.

'Have you eaten?' she whispered.

'No,' he hissed back. 'I'm starving.'

'Come and find me when this is over. We'll see what we can do about that.'

Detlef grinned. This evening was getting better all the time.

BY MIDNIGHT, THE chairs had been kicked back and the guests had tottered back to their rooms, belching and wiping their mouths. Baron von Rauken had taken his leave last of all, having heroically demolished a four-tier suet pudding arranged in a pretty good approximation of the Grand Belltower in Talabheim.

Soon the room was empty apart from Schwarzhelm and Detlef. The candles had burned low and the polished tabletop was slick with grease. Detlef found himself gazing at the extensive remains on the salvers, his stomach rumbling.

'Avoid it,' said Schwarzhelm. 'This is no food for a soldier.'

'Yes, my lord,' said Detlef, privately hoping he'd go away so he could attack the pickled pig-shins.

'Get some sleep.'

'Yes, my lord.'

'After you've cleaned my armour.'

'Yes, my lord.'

Schwarzhelm looked at him carefully. As ever, his expression was inscrutable. It was like trying to read the granite cliffs of the Worlds Edge Mountains.

'Where are your quarters?'

'Above the kitchen.'

'Stay in them tonight. And keep your sword by your bed.'

Detlef felt a sudden qualm. 'Do you expect trouble?'

'I don't call on these fat wastrels for enjoyment,' Schwarzhelm said, not hiding the contempt in his voice. 'The Emperor's worried about this one.'

'Is he behind on his taxes?' asked Detlef.

'On the contrary. He's paid them all.'

Detlef shook his head. The ways of the aristocracy were a mystery to him.

'I'll keep an eye out, then.'

Schwarzhelm grunted in what might have been approval.

'Maybe I'll take one of these for later,' said the knight, pulling a juicy chunk of bull's stomach from the table. Without a further look at his squire, he stalked off to his room, slamming the door behind him.

Detlef waited for the heavy footfalls to recede, then started to help himself. Knowing what was to come, his stomach gurgled with anticipation.

'Take it easy,' Detlef said to himself. 'Just a few of the good bits to keep my strength up. Then I have an appointment to keep.'

AN HOUR LATER, and the house was still and silent. High up in the west tower, the physician Hulptraum paced up and down inside his bedchamber. He was still dressed in the black robes of his office. His bed was untouched, and a large goblet of wine stood drained on his desk. He looked agitated, and his fingers twitched. Next to the goblet was a long, curved dagger. It was hard to see the hilt in the meagre candlelight, but the blade had some script engraved on it. The language wasn't Reikspiel.

'Tonight,' he hissed. 'Of all nights...'

There was a knock at the door. Hulptraum started, his eyes bulging. 'Who is it?'

'Adenauer. Can I come in?'

Hulptraum put the knife into the top drawer of the desk and slid it shut. 'Of course.'

Adenauer entered, looking terrible. His skin, pale before, was now deathly white. His wispy beard seemed to have become little more than a curling fuzz and his eyes were rheumy and staring.

'Osbert, you've got to help me,' he said, through gritted teeth. One hand was clutching his distended stomach, the other was clasped against his temple.

'You're still here?' asked the physician, not obviously evincing sympathy.

'What do you mean? I'm ill, man. Surely you can see that?'

Hulptraum smiled coldly. 'I'm a doctor. And yes, you're ill. You should be down in the kitchen with the others.'

Adenauer looked bewildered. 'Can't you give me something? I... oh, gods below...'

He started to belch loudly. A thin line of sputum ran down his chin and his body bent double.

Hulptraum remained supremely indifferent. 'I don't have time for this, Julius. Nothing I could give you now would help. The fact is, this has been prepared for months. All for this night. This one night. The night *he* turned up.'

Adenauer was now on his knees. The sputum became a watery trail of blood. His stomach was writhing under his robes, as if an animal were trying to get out of it.

'Sigmar!' he cried, spasming in agony. 'Help me!'

Hulptraum crouched down beside him, ignoring the increasingly putrid stench coming from the chancellor. 'He can't help you now, old friend. You'd better get down to the kitchen. You'll find the others there too.'

Adenauer's eyes didn't look as if they were seeing very much. Sores had begun to pulse on his face, spreading with terrifying speed. His tongue flickered out, black as ink, leaving loops of saliva trailing down to his chest. He collapsed on the floor, clenched with pain.

Hulptraum got up and returned to the desk. He retrieved the dagger, ignoring the thrashing of the transforming chancellor.

'You will *not* prevent this,' he hissed, no longer talking to Adenauer. 'I don't care who you are. You will *not* prevent this.'

With that, he left the room, padding out into the corridor beyond. Behind him, Adenauer retched piteously. Caked lumps of bile slapped to the floor, steaming gently. He remained stricken for a few moments longer, heaving and weeping, streaming from every orifice.

Then something seemed to change. He lifted his thin face. It ran with mucus like tears. The eyes, or what was left of them, shone a pale marsh-gas green.

'The kitchen!' Adenauer gurgled, though the voice was more like that of an animal. It looked as if he'd finally understood something. 'The kitchen!'

Then he too was gone, dragging himself across the floor leaving a trail of slime behind him. The door closed, and the candle shuddered out.

No candles burned in Schwarzhelm's chamber. The shutters were locked tight and the darkness was absolute. Nothing moved. Deep down in the house, there was a distant creak, then silence again.

Heartbeats passed in the dark.

Slowly, silently, the door-handle began to turn. The door swung open on oiled hinges. It was just as dark outside as within. Something entered. Quietly, slowly, it made its way to the bed. A blade was raised over the mattress.

It hung there, invisible, unmoving, for a terrible moment.

Then it plunged down, once, twice, three times, stabbing into the soft flesh beneath. Still no noise. The knife was an artful weapon. It had killed many times before over many thousands of years and knew how to find the right spot.

Hulptraum stood, shaking, lost in the dark. He could feel the warm blood on the knife trickle over his fingers. It was done. Thank the Father, the feast was safe.

Moving carefully, he went over to a table on the far wall. He had to make sure.

He struck the flint and a flame sparked into life. He lit the candle's wick and light spread across his hand. The shaking was subsiding. He'd done it. He'd saved it all. He turned around.

Schwarzhelm smashed him hard in the face, snapping his neck and sending him spinning across the table and slamming against the wall. Hulptraum slid to the floor. Blood foamed from his open mouth, locked in a final expression of shock. The dagger clanged to the stone floor.

'Pathetic,' Schwarzhelm muttered.

He walked over to where he'd hung his sword. The bull's stomach was still leaking fluid across the bed. He took the holy blade and unsheathed it. Still dressed in his robes, he made for the door.

Rauken did have something to hide then. Time to uncover it.

DETLEF BELCHED LOUDLY. Perhaps he'd overindulged. Still, at least he'd taken the edge off his hunger. Now he had an appointment to attend to. A final look around his bedchamber revealed Schwarzhelm's armour lying in pieces in the corner, still mottled with grime from the journey. He could polish it all before dawn – the old curmudgeon wouldn't need the suit before then.

Then he caught sight of his short sword lying by the bed, just where Schwarzhelm had warned him to keep it. Perhaps he ought to take that with him. He still wasn't convinced there was anything much to worry about, but it might impress... what *was* her name? He'd have to remember before he found her. In his experience, women – even as willing and fruity as this one – liked to have the little things observed.

Gretta? Hildegard? Brunnhilde?

He grabbed the sword and crept out of the chamber. It would come back to him.

The corridor was drenched in shadow. It seemed almost preternaturally dark, as if the natural light had been sucked from the air and somehow disposed of. He held his candle ahead of him with one hand and kept a tight grip on the sword hilt with the other. There were no sounds, no signs of anyone else about. Now all he had to do was remember the way to her room.

Past the scullery and the game-hanging room, then down towards the kitchen. Should be easy enough.

Detlef shuffled along, feeling the old wooden floor flex under him. He passed a series of doors in the gloom, all closed. The house gently creaked and snapped around him. Dimly, he could hear the scratching of trees outside as the night winds ran through their emaciated branches.

At the end of the corridor, a staircase led directly downwards. From where he stood, it seemed like there was a little more light coming from the bottom of it. Detlef picked up the pace. Perhaps Gertrude had left a candle lit for him.

He reached the base of the stairs. Another corridor yawned away with fresh doors leading from it on either side. One of them was open. He thrust the candle through the doorframe. The light reflected from the corpses hanging there, eyes glinting like mirrors.

Pheasants, rabbits, hares, all strung out in bunches on iron hooks. The game-hanging room. He was close. Detlef pressed on, heading further down the corridor. There was a light at the end of it, leaking around the edges of a closed wooden door. Excitement began to build within him. Brigitta had been as good as her word.

He reached the door, making sure his sword was properly visible. All the nice girls liked a soldier. Then, with as much of a flourish as he could muster with both hands full, he pushed against the wood.

The door swung open easily. Marsh-green light flooded out from the space beyond, throwing Detlef's shadow back down the corridor. What lay beyond wasn't Gertrude, Brigitta or Brunnhilde.

Detlef found that, despite all his anticipation, he wasn't really disappointed. He was too busy screaming.

SCHWARZHELM HURRIED DOWN the corridors, lantern in hand. There was no one about on the upper levels. The whole place was deserted. That in itself was cause for worry. He'd slammed open a dozen doors, uncaring whom he disturbed, and the chambers had all been empty.

He barged into Detlef's room, keeping the light high. He saw his own armour, untouched, heaped in the corner. There was a tin plate on the bed with a few crumbs on it and nothing else. There was no sword, and no squire.

'Damned idiot,' he muttered, heading back out. At the end of the corridor, a staircase led down. Very faintly, he could see a greenish glow. His heart went cold. He drew his sword, and the steel hummed gently as it left the scabbard. The Sword of Justice was ancient, and the spirit of the weapon knew when it would taste battle. Schwarzhelm could feel it thirsting already. There were unholy things close by.

He broke into a run, thudding down the stairs and past the empty, gaping doorways. He saw the open portal at the end of the corridor, glowing a pale green like phosphor. Shapes loomed beyond, hazy in a mist of swirling, stinking vapour.

'Grace of Sigmar,' Schwarzhelm whispered, maintaining his stride and letting the lantern smash to the floor – it would be no further use.

He charged through the doorway. Green light was everywhere, a sickly, cloying illumination that seemed to writhe in the air of its own accord. The walls dripped with slops of bile-yellow sludge that ran into the mortar and slithered over the stones. The stench was astonishing – a mix of rotting flesh, vomit, dung, sewage and bilge-water. He felt spores latch on him as he plunged in, popping and splattering as his powerful limbs worked.

Once this must have been the bakery. There was something that might have been an oven, now lost under polyps of mouldy dough-like growths. There were flies everywhere, buzzing and swarming over the slime-soaked surfaces. They were vast, shiny horrors, less like insects and more like pustules with wings.

'Detlef!' roared Schwarzhelm trying to spot the exit through the swirling miasma.

His call was answered, but not by his squire. The guests from the meal dragged themselves towards him, hauling their burst stomachs behind them. What was left of their skin hung like rags from glistening sinew, flapping against the tendons and their crumbling, yellow teeth.

'Hail, Lord Schwarzhelm!' they mocked, reaching for him with pudgy, blotched fingers. 'Welcome to the Feast!'

Schwarzhelm ploughed straight into them, hacking and heaving with his blade. The steel sliced through the carrion-flesh, sending gobbets of viscera sailing through the foetid air. There were a dozen of them, just as before, and they dragged at his robes, hands clawing. He battered them aside, hammering with the edge of his sword before plunging the tip deep into their ragged innards. They were carved apart like mutton, feeling no pain, only clutching at him, scrabbling at his flesh, trying to latch their slack, dangling jaws on to his arm.

Schwarzhelm didn't have time for this. He kicked out at them, shaking one from his boot before crunching his foot through a sore-riddled scalp, crushing the skull like an egg. They kept coming even when their limbs had been severed and their spines cracked. Only decapitation seemed to finish them. Twelve times the Sword of Justice flashed in the gloom, and twelve times a severed head thumped against the stone and rolled through the glowing slurry of body parts.

He pushed the remaining skittering, twitching torsos aside and pressed on, racing through the bakery and into the corridor beyond. So this was the horror Rauken had been cradling.

The further he went, the worse it got. The walls of the corridor were covered in a flesh-coloured sheen, run through with pulsing arteries of black fluid. There were faces trapped within, raving with horror. Some had managed to claw a hand out, scrabbling against the suffocating film. Others hung still, the black fluid pumping into them, turning them into some fresh new recipe.

Schwarzhelm killed as many as he could, delivering mercy to those who still breathed and death to those who'd passed beyond humanity. The steel sliced through the tight-stretched hide, tearing the veils of flesh and spilling the noxious liquid across the floor. As he splashed through it, a thin screaming broke out from further ahead. He was coming to the heart of it.

The next room was vast and boiling hot, full of massive copper kettles and iron cauldrons, all simmering with foul soups and monstrous stews. Lumps of human gristle flopped from their sides, sliding to the gore-soaked floor and sizzling of their own accord. Thick-bodied, spiked-legged spiders scuttled through the mire, scampering between the bursting egg-sacs of flies and long, white-fleshed worms. Vials of translucent plasma bubbled furiously, spilling their contents over piled slabs of rancid, crawling meat. Everything was in motion, a grotesque parody of a wholesome kitchen.

At the centre was Rauken. His body had grown to obscene proportions, bursting from the clothes that once covered it. His flesh, glistening with sweat and patterned with veins, spilled out like a vast unlocked tumour. Dark shapes scurried about under the skin, and a long purple tongue lolled down to his flab-folded chest, draping ropes of lumpy saliva behind it. When he saw Schwarzhelm, he grinned, exposing rows of black, blunt teeth.

'Welcome, honoured guest!' he cried, voice thick with phlegm. 'A good night to visit us!'

Schwarzhelm said nothing. He tore into the monster, hacking at the yielding flesh. It carved away easily, exposing rotten innards infested with burrowing grubs. Rauken scarcely seemed to feel it. He opened his swollen jaws and launched a column of vomit straight at the warrior. Schwarzhelm ducked under the worst of it, the stomach acid eating through his robes and burning his flesh. He ploughed on, cleaving away the rolls of stinking flab, getting closer to the head with every stroke.

'You can't spoil this party!' raved the baron, gathering itself for another monstrous chunder. 'We've only just got started!'

More vomit exploded out. Schwarzhelm felt a sharp pain as the bile slammed into his chest, sheering the cloth away and burrowing into his skin. Flies blundered into his eyes, spiders ran across his arms, leeches crawled around his ankles. He was being dragged down into the filth.

With a massive effort, Schwarzhelm wrenched free of the clutching horrors and whirled his blade round in a back-handed arc. The steel severed Rauken's bloated head clean free, lopping it from the shoulders and sending it squelching and bouncing into a vat of steaming effluvium. The vast bag of flesh shuddered and subsided, leaking an acrid soup of blood and sputum. Ripples of fatty essence sagged, shrank and then lay still.

Schwarzhelm struggled free of it, slapping the creeping horrors from his limbs and tearing the vomit-drenched rags from his chest. There was a movement behind him and he span around, blade at the ready.

He turned it aside. It was Detlef.

The boy looked ready to die from fear. His face was as pale as milk and tears of horror ran down his cheeks.

'What *is* this?' he shrieked, eyes staring.

Schwarzhelm clamped a hand on his shoulder, holding him firmly in place.

'Be strong,' he commanded. 'Get out – the way up is clear. Summon help, then wait for me at the gates.'

'You're not coming with me?'

Schwarzhelm shook his head. 'I've only killed the diners,' he growled. 'I haven't yet found the cook.'

THE HAZE GREW thicker. It was like wading through a fog of green motes. Schwarzhelm went carefully, feeling the viscous floor suck at his boots. Beyond the kitchen there was a little door, half-hidden behind the collection of bubbling vats. The flies buzzed furiously, clustering at his eyes and mouth. He breathed through his nose and ploughed on.

The room opened out before him. It was small, maybe twenty feet square and low-ceilinged. Perhaps some storechamber in the past. Now the jars and earthenware pots overflowed with mould, the contents long given over to decay. The air was barely breathable, heavy with spores and damp. Strings of fungus ran like spiders' webs from floor to roof, some glowing with a faint phosphorescence, obscuring what was in the centre.

'You're not the one I was expecting,' came a woman's voice. Schwarzhelm sliced his way through the ropes of corruption, feeling the burn as they slithered down his exposed flesh. 'Where's the boy? His flesh was ripe for feeding up.'

The last of the strings fell away. In the centre of the floor squatted a horribly overweight woman. She was surrounded by rolls of flaking parchment, all covered in endless lists of ingredients. Sores clustered at her thick lips, weeping a constant stream of dirt-brown fluid. She was dressed in what had once been a tight-laced corset, but the fabric had burst and her distended body flopped across it. The skin was addled with plague. Some parts of her had been eaten away entirely, exposing slick white fat or wasted muscle. Others glowed an angry red, with shiny skin pulled tight over some raging infestation. Boils jostled for prominence with warts, virulent rashes encircled pulsing nodules ready to burst. Her exposed thighs were like long-rotten sides of pork, and her eyes were filmy and rimed with blood.

'He's gone,' said Schwarzhelm. 'I'm not so easily wooed.'

The woman laughed, and a thin gruel-like liquid cascaded down her multiple chins. 'A shame,' she gurgled. 'I don't think you've had many women in your life. Karl Franz's loyal monk, eh? That's not what they say about Helborg. Now *there's* a man I could cook for.'

Schwarzhelm remained unmoved. 'What are you?'

'Oh, just the kitchen maid. I get around. When I came here, the food was terrible. Now, as you can see, it's much improved.' She frowned. 'This was to have been our party night. I think you've rather spoiled it. How did you know?'

'I didn't,' said Schwarzhelm, preparing to strike. 'The Emperor's instincts are normally good.'

He charged towards her, swinging the sword in a glittering arc. The monstrous woman opened her jaws. They stretched open far beyond the tolerance of mortal tendons. Rows of needle-teeth glimmered, licked by a blood-red tongue covered in suckers. Her fingers reached up to block the swipe, nails long and curled.

Schwarzhelm worked quickly, drawing on his peerless skill with the blade. The fingernails flashed past him as he weaved past her defences, chunks of blubber carved off with precise, perfectly aimed stabs.

Her neck shot out, extending like a snake's. Her teeth snapped as she went for his jugular. He pulled back and she chomped off a mouthful of beard, spitting the hairs out in disgust. Then he was back in close, jabbing at her pendulous torso, trying to get the opening he needed.

They swung and parried, teeth and nails against the flickering steel of the Sword of Justice. The blade bit deep, throwing up fountains of pus and cloying, sticky essence. The woman struck back, raking her fingernails across Schwarzhelm's chest, digging the points into his flesh.

He roared with pain, spittle flying from his mouth. He tore away from her, blood pouring down his robes. The neck snapped out again, aiming for his eyes. He pulled away at the last moment, slipping in a puddle of slop at his feet and dropping one hand down.

'Ha!' she spat, and launched herself at him.

Schwarzhelm's instinct was to pull back, to scrabble away, anything to avoid being enveloped in that horrific tide of disease and putrescence.

But instinct could be trumped by experience. He had his opening. As fast as thought, he lunged forward under the shadow of the looming horror, pointing the Sword of Justice upwards and grasping the hilt with both hands. There was a sudden flash of realisation in her eyes, but the momentum was irresistible. The steel passed through her neck, driven deep through the morass of twisted tubes and nodules.

She screamed, teeth still snapping at Schwarzhelm's face, flailing as the rune-bound metal seared at her rancid innards.

This time Schwarzhelm didn't retreat. He kept his face near hers. He didn't smile even then, but a dark look of triumph lit in his eyes. He twisted the blade in deeper, feeling it do its work.

'Dinner's over,' he said.

DAWN BROKE, GREY and cold. His legs aching, his chest tight, Schwarzhelm pushed open the great doors to the castle, letting the dank air of the forest stream in. It was thick with the mulch of the woods, but compared to the filth of the kitchens below it was like a blast of fresh mountain breeze. He limped out, cradling his bleeding chest with his free hand. The cult had been purged. All were dead. All that remained was to burn the castle, and others would see to that. Once again he had done his duty. The law had been dispensed and the task was complete. Almost.

Just beyond the gates, a lone figure shivered, hunched on the ground and clutching his ankles. Schwarzhelm went over to him. Detlef didn't seem to hear him approach. His eyes were glassy and his lower lip trembled.

'Did you find anyone up here?' Schwarzhelm asked. Though it didn't come naturally, he tried to keep his voice gentle.

Detlef nodded. 'A boy from the village. He's gone to get the priest. There are men coming.'

The squire's voice shook as he spoke. He looked terrible. He had every right to. No mortal man should have had to witness such things.

'Good work, lad.'

Schwarzhelm looked down at his blade, still naked in his hands. Diseased viscera had lodged in the runes. It would take an age to purify.

He turned his gaze to Detlef. It was a pity. The boy was young. His appetites were hot, and he must have been hungry. There were so many excuses, even though he'd warned him not to eat the food. This final blow was the worst of them all. He'd shown promise. Schwarzhelm had liked him.

Detlef looked up, eyes imploring. Even now, the sores had started to emerge around his mouth.

'Is it over?' he asked piteously, the tears of horror still glistening on his cheek.

Schwarzhelm raised his blade, aiming carefully. It would at least be quick.

'Yes,' he said, grief heavy within him. 'Yes, it is.'

ACTION AND CONSEQUENCE

Sarah Cawkwell

Vincit Qui Patitur.

The words of the company motto were bold and confident, standing out in silver lettering on the midnight-black of the Eighth Company's war banner. *He conquers who endures.*

On board the strike cruiser *Silver Arrow*, the chapel was the same as many thousands of other such chapels scattered throughout the Space Marine ships of the Imperium. A quiet place of reflection, prayer and preparation, the battle-brothers of the Eighth Company all found their way here eventually prior to deployment. Some came, gave due deference to the statue of the God-Emperor and retreated.

Others lingered.

Within this cradle of ultimate faith, a warrior could assert his place in the universe. Within this sacred place, a warrior of the Imperium could come as close to knowing peace as he was ever likely to.

Gileas Ur'ten, a man rarely at peace, knelt at the front of the chapel. His dark hair fell forwards, framing his face as his head bowed in reverence. Softly, he recanted his own personal litanies of battle, paying particular care to those that honoured his forebears. Above his head, the company's war banner was displayed proudly, pinned wide to display all the names written on it in tiny, delicate filigree script. Battle-brothers would gladly sit for hours to add a name to the banner. It was always considered to be an honour, never a duty.

Hundreds, even thousands of names were represented on the banner: brothers-in-arms he had fought alongside in his one hundred and twenty years of service, and still more names there of those he had never met, but whose deeds were legendary. His eyes lifted briefly and rested on the name of Captain Andreas Kulle, his own mentor and the only man who had initially believed the savage little boy from the south had possessed the potential to succeed. Kulle had long passed to the arms of the Emperor. But his name lived on, and as long as the banner remained, that would never change.

Whoever was chosen to bear the standard into battle was greatly honoured. Gileas had carried the relic many times over the campaigns of the last five years. He had held on to it with grim tenacity against seemingly overwhelming odds, and had always returned it. He was a valiant, fearless warrior whose own deeds on the battlefield were earning him a reputation that many envied and others watched with cautious uncertainty.

Gileas Ur'ten's career had gone from strength to strength. The first recruit from the tribal people of Varsavia's southern continent to achieve a sergeant's rank, Gileas was stalwart and confident. He had led his squad for several years, and it was grudgingly acknowledged that they were amongst the best in the entire company. He was a charismatic man whose brothers followed him willingly and without question. Even the majority of his greatest antagonists had reluctantly accepted that his promotion to the rank of sergeant had been well earned.

And yet this was not a universal opinion. To others, Gileas was still considered a loose cannon, a Space Marine whose tempestuous nature and fiery spirit could not truly be trusted. A savage southerner whose instincts overruled his head on far too many occasions.

If Gileas was aware of the opinions of his brother Space Marines, he rarely – if ever – commented on them. He was, he had reasoned many years ago, who he was. He lived only to serve the Imperium and he would die in the line of duty. It was a reward he anticipated with the inherent pragmatism of all the Adeptus Astartes. He was loyal, honest and, as far as his superior officer was concerned, completely trustworthy. It was these qualities that had marked him out for the honour that had become his.

The death of Brother-Sergeant Oniker during the last campaign had left a void in the Eighth Company that many of the other company sergeants were eager to fill. The captain would need to nominate his chosen second-in-command, a role that Oniker had filled until his untimely death at the hands of the ork warboss Skullrencha. Each one of the sergeants had brought unique qualities to the table. The final decision, however, had gone to the company Prognosticator.

Shae Bast, Captain Meyoran's advisor, had cast the runes. For long hours he had communed with and channelled the Emperor's will. He had finally brought forth the Emperor's decision, knowing that there would be unrest in the wake of the announcement. The captain had been completely satisfied with the choice of Gileas Ur'ten, but there were plenty amongst the Eighth Company with whom the decision did not sit comfortably. Indeed, there were rumblings about what was considered an ill-omened choice from other companies throughout the Chapter.

Gileas knew it well. Despite his own misgivings and barely understood concerns, he bore it all without comment, other than to take up the mantle of his new role with the same enthusiasm with which he approached everything. He looked now at the statue of the Emperor which stared impassively ahead, its gaze as cool as the stone from which it was carved. The solidity and permanence of the Emperor's presence was a soothing balm to Gileas's troubled heart, and he took quiet strength from it.

'I am not disturbing you, I hope, brother-sergeant?' The voice came from behind him, low and rumbling. Gileas raised his head and turned to take in the sight of his captain filling the chapel's doorway.

'Not at all, brother-captain.' Gileas rocked back onto his bare heels. Whilst aboard the *Silver Arrow* and not in the training cages, most of the battle-brothers of the Eighth Company wore simple surplices and either soft leather sandals or chose to go barefoot. Gileas settled into a cross-legged sitting position and looked up expectantly.

With the quiet confidence that marked his every action, the captain strode into the chapel, crossing the short distance between the doors and the altar swiftly. Like most of the men under his command, Keile Meyoran was exceptionally huge – even for a genetically altered Space Marine. He kept his head and face shaved completely smooth, barring a long, thin-plaited black beard that served only to make him look even more aggressive. The years of honour tattoos that were painstakingly designed and worked into his face made him look at one and the same time both barbaric and mystical to those who did not understand the Silver Skulls' tradition of marking themselves in such a way. They recruited from worlds other than Varsavia, but all were introduced to the planet's tradition of tattooing on their induction into the Chapter.

Meyoran joined Gileas at the altar and looked up wordlessly at the statue of the Emperor. His lips moved in a silent prayer and he placed his right hand on the figure. Gileas watched his captain without comment until the older warrior turned to study him thoughtfully.

'Are your preparations complete, brother?'

'Aye, sir.' Gileas made a move to get to his feet, but Meyoran held up a hand, forestalling him.

'There is no need for me to interrupt you for long, Gileas. I merely wanted to bring you a message. Your presence is greatly desired in the strategium. We will translate in-system in less than four hours – and your experience in urban warfare will prove invaluable to us.' His lips curled upwards into a smile at the look on Gileas's face. 'Is this invitation such a surprise to you, brother?'

'Surprised? No, sir.' As the youngest sergeant in the company, he had rarely been invited to attend a war meeting in the strategium – and never a direct invitation from the company captain. 'Not surprised, merely… honoured.'

Gileas had never been a good liar, and given the way the tips of his ears turned slightly pink where they were visible beneath his unruly dark curls, it seemed that he was unlikely to start grasping the concept now. Meyoran's smile broadened and he reached down and clasped the younger warrior's shoulder.

'You will be fine, Gileas,' he said, quietly. 'I have every faith in your ability to put your personal stamp on this position. I know that you have misgivings. I know also that some have questioned your own suitability for this role. You have commanded – what is it? Twenty missions as sergeant?'

'Twenty-five, sir.' Such pride in his voice. Only twenty-five missions. Practically a novice.

Meyoran nodded. 'Twenty-five missions. *Successful* missions.' The flicker of a smile tweaked the captain's lips, then he resumed his serious expression. 'But Gileas, whatever your misgivings may be… when we deploy, there will be no opportunity to dwell on them. I need to know that your head is in the right place. I need to know that your heart and mind are focussed on the mission.'

'Of course, sir,' said Gileas, a faint tone of indignation coming into his voice. 'I am fully prepared and I will not let you down.' This time, he was not lying.

'No,' mused Meyoran, touching his hand to the statue of the Emperor once again. 'No, I don't believe you will, lad.'

It will be the actions of the rest of my company that worry me, he added silently.

LESS THAN FOUR hours later, Gileas found himself in an environment as far removed from the peace of the chapel as could possibly be imagined. The familiar, almost comforting roar of the retro-jets filled his aural senses as the drop-pod punched through the haze of cloud lying in a perpetual gloom over the planet. Pressed down hard in his seat by the harness, the sergeant put a hand to the hilt of his chainsword and cast a glance around the pod's interior.

His companions were all murmuring pre-battle litanies, apart from Theoderyk the Techmarine, whose voice soared loudly above the others. His litanies were fervently directed at the machine-spirits that guided them to their destination. Gileas allowed his own thoughts to stray to that particular outcome. There was a great battle to be had at the end of this drop and the thought of it filled his veins with fire.

He blink-clicked through final system checks, absorbing the vast quantities of scrolling information and runes that flashed before his eyes. His jump pack was functioning well and he had lovingly stripped and cleaned his weapons in the hours before they had deployed. He was as ready as he was likely to be.

The potential pressures of additional responsibility had not really bothered him. Like all the Silver Skulls, he was an enormously pragmatic man. He knew that he had the competence and the training to handle whatever these enemies could throw at him and he also knew that on the field of battle, the men under his command would obey his orders unquestioningly. Whatever his battle-brothers might have thought of him off the field of war was inconsequential.

Such confidence came easily. Certainty in those thoughts did not.

'Prepare for impact.' Theoderyk's voice crackled across the vox and Gileas, along with the others on board, murmured their acquiescence. The sergeant's hand closed still more tightly around the hilt of the chainsword and he offered up an impassioned prayer to the God-Emperor that this matter would be dealt with swiftly and without heavy losses. The Eighth Company was already low in numbers. It could not afford further deaths.

With enough force to completely flatten the remaining structures in this part of the already-devastated city, three drop-pods smashed into the landscape with deadly accuracy. Scant seconds later, the echo of release charges detonating resounded across the crater-pocked landscape, heralding the deployment of two dozen Silver Skulls. Each warrior was filled with righteous fury, ready to be unleashed against the xenos invaders who had made the fatal mistake of daring to set foot on Imperial soil, daring to commit the most heinous of transgressions.

Thumping the release button on his grav harness, Gileas was on his feet in seconds, sword in hand, ready for action. He gathered the others together and scanned the landing zone.

Gileas turned to the horizon, his auto-senses feeding critical information that might affect the performance of an Assault Marine's jump pack. Wind speed. Humidity. All of these details and more were fed directly into his neural sensors. The auspex in Theoderyk's hand picked up no life signs other than those of his fellow Space Marines – which was not what their intelligence had led them to believe.

'Sergeant Ur'ten, report.'

Captain Meyoran's voice came across the vox, announcing itself in Gileas's ear as he led his men clear of the landing site. Three Thunderhawk gunships screamed overhead, heading towards the smouldering hive ruins to the east. A fledgling world under the protection of the Silver Skulls, Cartan was still in the earliest stages of colonisation. And the planet was already under threat.

'Three pods down here, sir.' Gileas scanned them swiftly. All had opened, releasing their passengers, including Brother Diomedes, one of the Chapter's deeply venerated Dreadnoughts. The sight of the ancient lumbering towards him filled Gileas with even more fire than before. It would be a deep honour to serve alongside him.

'Diomedes?' Meyoran addressed the ancient directly.

'Deployed and at your command,' the Dreadnought responded, his voice mechanically altered by the body that housed one of the brightest and greatest warriors the Chapter had ever known.

'No enemy contact,' Gileas reported. 'Intelligence suggested that the xenos had a temporary base here. If they did...' He looked around him at the destruction caused by the arrival of three drop-pods. '...it was destroyed on our arrival.'

'They move swiftly, sergeant. Be on your guard. Rendezvous as soon as possible at the coordinates I'm transmitting.'

Gileas turned to Theoderyk, designated the squad's coordinator for the mission. The taciturn Techmarine, a silent yet dependable member of the company, gave an abrupt nod as he assimilated the stream of information. He pointed to the east. The servo-harness on his back hissed into life and the servo-arm ending in a plasma cutter came to the fore. With the harness, Theoderyk was easily half as big again as the giant Gileas. A huge, shaggy bear of a man, even without his Adeptus Astartes implants, Gileas would have been enormous.

Gileas surveyed the demolished remains of the outlying habs. Those who had worked here were undoubtedly long dead, or captured by the enemy. The burned-out husks of silos stood to one side of what had been a storage facility. The air, even filtered by their helmets, was rank with the scent of burning promethium and the chemical reek of weapons discharge. There had been fighting here recently.

Thoughtfully tapping the fingers of his free hand against the thigh of his power armour, Gileas turned to the Dreadnought standing motionless beside him.

'Ancient one,' he said, his voice filled with reverence.

'Brother-Sergeant Ur'ten,' the Dreadnought responded, the low rumble of his voice resonating deep in Gileas's chest. 'Your command?'

'The last communication from Sergeant Kyaerus was less than fifteen hours ago and this was his given location,' Gileas mused aloud. 'I find it hard to believe that he has strayed too far from this position. I know him too well.' The sergeant grinned. 'I suspect he will already have met up with the captain. Nonetheless, we will scout this immediate area for any signs of activity. You take the east side. Report back with anything that you find.'

'As you command,' the Dreadnought acknowledged. 'Thoroughness is essential. Wise words, Brother-Sergeant Ur'ten.' With his seal of approval thus stamped, Diomedes left with a growl of machinery, the ground shaking under his tread.

Gileas watched the Dreadnought leave, its armoured form testament to the highest honour any of them could hope for. To serve, even in death... that was the ideal.

'We missed whatever happened here, Gileas.' One of the Reckoners, Gileas's assault squad, marked by the red skull on his right pauldron, moved to stand beside him.

'Maybe. But there are xenos involved. They are therefore not to be trusted.' Gileas frowned beneath his helmet. 'Keep your wits about you and your thumb on that activation stud, Reuben.'

Gileas signalled to the group to move out, scanning the horizon as he did so. As of yet, Theoderyk had reported no activity on the auspex. But the speed and cunning of the enemy was about to be proven. Bare moments later, the whine of engines filled the air.

Half a dozen vehicles came tearing into view and recognition was instant. Eldar reaver jetbikes. Fast-moving and deadly, they were swift and sure in their attack. Wickedly edged blades caught the light of the weak sun and glinted the briefest warning, but not soon enough to prevent Brother Lemuel losing an arm. A razor-sharp blade tore through his armour with ease.

For the next few seconds, all that mattered to the Silver Skulls were sounds. The bizarre, alien whine of the jetbikes, the rotating scream of Diomedes's assault cannon as the Dreadnought pounded back to the scene and levelled the weapon at the enemy. There was the unified roar of chainswords thumbed into deadly life and the battle cries of the Silver Skulls as they launched themselves at their assailants.

'IT'S GOOD TO see you, Captain Meyoran.'

The voice belonged to Sergeant Kyaerus of the Tenth Company. Slender for a Space Marine, seeming more so against the oversized warriors of the Eighth Company, the Scout-sergeant's face, prematurely aged by the mass of burn scars that covered the whole left side, showed signs of early fatigue as he emerged from the cover of a half-destroyed building.

The captain considered the other warrior. 'It's good to be seen, sergeant.' A mirthless smile flickered across his face. 'Make your report.'

'Yes, sir.' Meyoran quietly approved of the sergeant's stoicism, even in the face of his current situation. He gestured to his men to maintain a perimeter and to keep a watchful eye out for anything that moved.

Kyaerus reattached his bolt pistol to the mag-clamp on his thigh, taking advantage of the arrival of backup in order to afford himself a little less vigilance. His augmetic left eye whirred softly as he spoke, constantly adjusting to every nuance on the face of the captain.

'In accordance with the Chapter Master's instructions, I travelled to the Cartan Hive to gather the first batch of aspirants and to receive reports from the Governor regarding the state of the mining operations.'

Cartan V was rich in mineral deposits, and it had been this more than anything else that had made it a desirable place for settlement. The Silver Skulls themselves had overseen the relocation of the beleaguered citizens of a largely destroyed hive world – on the agreement that they could return at any point in the future to acquire new recruits.

Kyaerus continued. 'During my conversations with the governor, we received a report. A group of engineers were planning a detonation in order to construct a new minehead. They uncovered something else.' Kyaerus's mutilated face contorted in barely concealed rage. It was a look that Meyoran had come to know all too well in recent years. 'And less than an hour after it was uncovered, the first attack was upon them.'

Meyoran scowled. 'Eldar.' A blunt statement of fact, not a question. The sheer depth of hatred in Kyaerus's face engendered by the captain's words spoke more than his reply did.

'Aye, sir. Obviously my squad and I took a stand with the local military force out at the blast site. We found out very quickly what it was that they had uncovered.' His hand clenched into a fist. 'Only uncovering it wasn't where they stopped. In their curiosity, they had raised it. The local militia were quickly depleted. They just weren't prepared to deal with an incursion of this scale. And the eldar sent through a massed force. They have made several raids on the garrison, as you see.' Kyaerus gestured around the ruined barracks before continuing.

'They hit hard and fast. They've practically destroyed the hive. A large percentage of the population have made their way to the sub-levels and are seeking sanctuary there. Those people the raiders *have* found...' He hesitated, made both angry and deeply regretful by the next bit of information.

'Prisoners.' The Adeptus Astartes standing just beside Meyoran, dressed in armour of cobalt-blue that marked him apart from most of the others, stepped forwards and spoke, filling in the pause. Prognosticator Bast's voice was whisper-soft, and whenever his eyes passed over anybody, they got the feeling that they were being scrutinised very closely. 'The xenos have rounded up living souls and have imprisoned them. Including our aspirants, yes, sergeant?'

Kyaerus nodded, his face darkening with anger. Meyoran felt a hollow form in the base of his stomach. For the Silver Skulls, recruits were a precious commodity. To lose a batch to the hands of the eldar...

'Your thoughts, Prognosticator?' Meyoran finally shifted his gaze from the sergeant to the psyker. The two men had served side by side for decades and he deferred without question to the other's judgement.

'The artefact was presumably a webway portal?' Bast directed the question at Kyaerus, who nodded. 'It would be a reasonable hypothesis to presume that raiders probably attacked this planet at some point in its past. Uncovering the portal may have alerted them to an opportunity to do so again.' The psyker shrugged his giant shoulders. 'None of us truly understand the heathen technology of the webway.'

The Prognosticator reached up to remove his own helmet. The face that emerged was so lost in tattoos and tribal markings that it was hard to make out any specific features. Dark hair worn in tight braids was shot through with silver, but beyond that, it was impossible to approximate the Prognosticator's age.

Cold eyes, so pale a shade of blue that they were almost entirely colourless, fixed on the sergeant, who held the gaze with cool confidence for a few moments before he wavered and looked away. A flicker of a smile played around the Prognosticator's face and he enjoyed the moment of startled uncertainty that he lifted from the sergeant's mind.

'Whereabouts is the portal?' Meyoran asked, snapping his helmet back on. 'If that is the heart of the enemy, then that is where we will strike.'

'To the south-west.'

The words came from the Prognosticator rather than the sergeant as Bast almost lazily took the answer from his mind. He was not a particularly cruel man, but he had always taken a cynical delight in reminding others of his psychic capabilities. He treated the sergeant to a slow smile before he hid his face once again behind the helmet. In the legends of Old Terra, Bast was the name the great people of Gypta had associated with cats – and Meyoran had always felt there was something faintly feline in Bast's methods. He liked to play with his enemies before killing them, too.

'The south-west,' Kyaerus acknowledged. He tapped a data-slate. 'All the coordinates and information I've gathered are there.'

'Good work. Then we move out.' Meyoran waved a hand and the Silver Skulls fell into practiced formation. Kyaerus also gestured, making signs with his fingers, and four hitherto unnoticed Scouts, young neophytes in carapace armour and armed with sniper rifles, appeared from various locations around the compound. Meyoran grinned his approval.

'You're training them well, sergeant. You will make a superb captain some day soon.' Next to him, Bast turned slightly, considering Meyoran's words.

Kyaerus inclined his head, accepting the compliment with a slight twist of his lips.

'Let's go and get our boys back.'

THE THUNDEROUS REPORT of the Dreadnought's assault cannon filled the air as Brother Diomedes fired on the attacking reavers. The long, lean armoured bikes moved utilising the anti-grav technology that belonged to their race. Each one was piloted by a single rider armed with pistols that they fired with unerring accuracy at the Silver Skulls. Viciously sharp blades lined the vehicles and it was one of these that had taken Brother Lemuel's arm from his body.

It took far more than losing a limb to stop a Space Marine though. His body was already working to close over the neat amputation. Lemuel had borne the worst of the pain with little more than a brief yell. He had lost his chainsword when the limb had been severed, but he merely levelled his bolt pistol and fired at the enemy instead.

Gileas blink-clicked through the runes scrolling in front of his eyes until it brought up Lemuel's data. His systems were coping with the injury well, but he was far from optimal. There were so many combat narcotics and analgesics now coursing round his veins that his reaction time was gravely compromised.

'Lemuel,' he voxed. 'Take a step back, brother. Leave this to us.'

'I can still fight, brother-sergeant.' Lemuel continued to fire on the bikes. which were presently turning for another attack. Diomedes paused briefly, scanning the half-dozen or so vehicles and determining vulnerable points. The massive assault cannon tracked the leading bike. Then the Dreadnought acted, concentrating his fire.

In a burst of blue flame, the bike detonated, throwing its eldar rider free and sending pieces of armour plate and blades in all directions. The burning xenos was thrown to the ground with an audible *crump*, the body twisted at an unnatural angle. The other bikes veered errati-cally, thrown off from their planned attack run by the sudden loss of the leader.

'Squad Ur'ten, on me.' Lemuel and his obstinate behaviour was not an issue. Lemuel was an Adeptus Astartes. He was bred and trained to purge the galaxy of all that was wrong, and to the Silver Skulls there was little that met the criteria so much as the eldar – particularly these pirates. Lemuel would either survive to fight another day with an augmetic limb, or he would die fighting in the Emperor's service. Either outcome was ultimately satisfactory.

With a single burst of his assault cannon, Diomedes had already coun-tered the surprise attack and Gileas would lead his squad as he led every mission he had commanded so far in his career. From the front.

The venerable ancient pounded forwards, his massive Dreadnought body shaking the ground under the Space Marines' feet and cracking the ferrocrete. At one time, this blistered area would have seen the comings and goings of Imperial vessels, bringing supplies to the planet for the building of the hive, delivering people and resources and shipping out whatever had been mined. Now it was a ruin, a place that seemed far older and scarred than something so new had any right to be.

'For the Emperor and Argentius!' the war machine bellowed in his thunderous voice. 'Do not suffer these abominations to live, brothers. We are Silver Skulls. We will prevail!'

'We will prevail,' the squad chorused, eager to engage the enemy.

For the tiniest fraction of time, a pause so brief that even Theoderyk could not have captured it on his exquisitely forged chronometer, there was silence. Anticipation. The calm before the storm.

And then the storm broke.

Complete pandemonium descended for several minutes. To the unfortunate xenos attackers, the rapid discipline and fearsome strength that their prey demonstrated meant that those few minutes seemed to stretch out beyond reason. Any advantage they may have had in altitude was reduced by the fact that they had underestimated the fighting prowess of nearly half an Assault company. Even as Gileas fired his jump pack into life, all around him other Silver Skulls were rising to meet their enemies in mid-air.

With Diomedes present, the cleansing of this filth was a matter of course for the Silver Skulls. They entered the fray with customary enthusiasm. Their reputation as a barbaric fighting force was not without reason. They were brutal, efficient warriors who were not adverse to using whatever tactics were necessary to win a fight. This was said of the entire Chapter, but bore particular relevance to the Eighth Company.

Three more eldar riders were unseated by the sudden momentum of fully armoured Silver Skulls launching past them and grabbing them from the bikes. Without riders, the machines careened haphazardly. One struck the ground and exploded in a burst of whickering shrapnel. The others collided in mid-air and similarly detonated. More heat and smoke billowed out in plumes. The remaining two riders turned their bikes into the smog, leaving nothing but contrails in their wake. The warriors who had felled the eldar plummeted downwards with their victims, driving them to the floor with a satisfying crack of vertebrae.

Gileas cast a brief glance at the rune on the bottom left of his display, blinking rapidly to cycle the lenses in his helmet, enabling him to see more effectively through the smoke. The fires from the destroyed jet-bikes raged on, continuing to spew ash and cinders into the air.

The cacophony of the past few minutes ebbed back to the soft thrum of chainswords on low power. There were still two reavers out there and the destruction of their compatriots meant that they were temporarily masked in the resultant smoke.

'Sergeant Ur'ten, report,' Meyoran voxed. Gileas glanced around. Of the twenty-four warriors who had exited the drop-pods, there were still twenty-two standing. One was dead, the other injured.

'Eldar raiders, sir,' he responded. 'On jetbikes. They struck without warning.'

'Dead?'

'Job almost complete, sir. Two left out there. I'm almost certain that–'

With a sudden, screaming whine, one of the remaining jetbikes burst out of the smoke, heading straight for Gileas's broad-shouldered back. Without so much as turning around, the Assault Marine thumbed his chainsword back into life, sidestepped lazily and brought his weapon around in a murderous arc. The serrated, whirring blade chewed through the pilot from just below its right ear, down through the thorax and severed the body diagonally. The head and left arm fell away in a shower of gore, leaving an out-of-control jetbike, a still-twitching eldar gripping the controls with a lifeless hand.

With a single burst from his cannon, Brother Diomedes finished it.

'Correction. One left, sir.'

Gileas's tone had not changed at all.

'Good work, sergeant. Transmitting coordinates. Sergeant Kyaerus has found us.' Gileas smiled. Not, he noted, the other way around. 'Meet us as soon as you can. Stay alert for that rogue rider. Try to get here in one piece.'

'Aye, captain.' Gileas grinned beneath his helmet. 'On our way.'

THEY ENCOUNTERED NOTHING as they traversed the largely obliterated compound. All the Silver Skulls remained alert, aware that there was a reaver close by. The intelligence that had been broadcast with the emergency transmission had suggested a reasonably sized force in-situ on this planet. It was the reason the decision had been taken to deploy a large proportion of the company.

During the meeting in the strategium, Gileas had queried the necessity for Captain Meyoran to come down to the surface at all. The captain had laughed dismissively, clasping Gileas's shoulder.

'Brother-Sergeant Ur'ten, I hope that you don't plan to let this promotion turn you into my keeper,' he had said. 'Prognosticator Bast has communed with the Emperor. It is His will that I lead this expedition. Besides, why should I let you have all the glory? You will take command in my place soon enough.' The words had sounded ominous; prophetic, even.

Gileas had begun to protest, which had earned an indulgent grin from the captain. 'I jest, brother,' he had said with a gruff laugh. 'By the Throne, Gileas, learn to be less literal.'

Bast, assigned directly from the psyker-led prognosticatum, had nodded solemnly. 'The omens are most auspicious for the battle to come, Brother-Sergeant Ur'ten,' he had pronounced in his soft whisper. 'It is vital that the captain is present.'

Unsettled by the Prognosticator's words without quite knowing why, Gileas had put his worries to the back of his mind and they had instead concentrated on the importance of eliminating the eldar forces.

Over the centuries the Silver Skulls had repeatedly encountered the eldar in their many and varied forms. Whilst the justifiable detestation of all alien races was the right of the Adeptus Astartes, the Silver Skulls reserved an especial hatred for the eldar. Many good battle-brothers had been lost at the Battle of Oram Pass. Many good battle-brothers who had yet to be replaced. The Chapter was dipping well below its normal numbers and the recruitment process was slow for many reasons.

As a result, the prospect of visiting righteous retribution on the eldar was one that Eighth Company relished with grim enthusiasm. Fifty warriors had been deployed, more than half the company's current complement.

By the time they reached the rendezvous point, Meyoran and his warriors were already gathered. Prognosticator Bast and the only other psychic battle-brother present stood to one side, conspicuous by the colour of their armour. The prognosticatum had suffered more losses at the hands of the eldar at Oram Pass than any other. For a Chapter whose home world was sparsely populated with psykers, it had been a harsh toll. The prognosticatum had more reason than most to hate the foul eldar pirates.

'You took your time,' greeted Meyoran, his tone light, but his voice slightly strained with the tension of what he had established of the situation thus far.

'Apologies, sir.' Gileas joined his captain and removed his helmet. 'Undisciplined xenos taking an attack of opportunity. We made short work of them thanks to Brother Diomedes.' The sergeant nodded reverently in the Dreadnought's direction.

'You know what it is that we face here, then?'

'Aye, sir.' Gileas's hand closed into a fist. 'Eldar raiders.'

'Mostly correct. Eldar raiders, yes. Eldar raiders with access to a webway portal.'

Gileas faltered only slightly. That changed things. With access to a portal, he knew well from experience that it would be impossible to plan any sort of attack based on numbers. More could arrive at any given moment. Their priority was clear. He nodded his understanding and Meyoran continued.

'I will lead the attack on the portal with the majority of our fighting force – and Diomedes,' he said. 'You will take the Reckoners and command the rescue mission.' He indicated a young Scout Gileas recognised. One of Kyaerus's squad, the callow youth was looking eager to get the battle under way. 'Tyr took the liberty of going ahead to assess the situation as best he could under the circumstances. The eldar have a considerable number of human captives, including our aspirants. As of a few minutes ago, they were in holding pens, presumably awaiting loading into one of their ships. Time is of the essence.'

Meyoran tweaked his long plaited beard. 'Priorities are to destroy the portal, eliminate the xenos threat and ensure as many citizens as possible survive the ordeal. This may present difficulties given that the raiders have arranged the cages around their central position. Those are our objectives. In that order.'

'Slaves?' Gileas was aware on an unconscious level that Meyoran was assessing his reaction to being denied the honour of leading the attack, and kept his face as neutral as he could. Despite his best efforts, disappointment stirred in the pit of his belly.

'Possibly.' Meyoran's tattooed face twisted into a scowl, the black ink contorting grotesquely. 'Or worse. Either way, expediency is critical.'

Gileas set his jaw angrily. 'So they are utilising human shields?'

'Aye. There may well be Imperial casualties during this operation,

Gileas, but do what you can to minimise risk.' Meyoran waited a moment as though expecting an argument. Gileas was far more suited to the task of taking the portal than he was of search and rescue, and they both knew it.

The serpent of rebellion that had woken at Meyoran's orders writhed in Gileas's stomach again, threatening to rise its hooded head and strike. But Gileas quelled it. He would question the captain's orders when they were back on the *Silver Arrow*, not whilst they were in the field. He knew he was being tested and he would be damned before he failed.

'As my captain orders,' he replied, snapping his helmet back on again. 'Reckoners, on me.'

Meyoran glanced at Bast as Gileas turned to walk away. The Prognosticator inclined his head almost graciously.

'Sergeant.' Meyoran called after Gileas's retreating back.

'Brother-captain?' Gileas turned slightly.

'Endure, brother.' There was a passion in Meyoran's voice that poked the seed of uncertainty that had been planted in Gileas's mind during the meeting in the strategium. His doubts and misgivings burst into bloom, and he almost turned to consider the captain fully. But there was no time to dwell on thoughts and feelings. He had promised Meyoran back in the chapel that he would maintain his focus. He had his orders and he would carry them out to the best of his ability.

THE ALIEN PORTAL rose up from the ground, a slim, tapering arc casting a faint rippling visual distortion in its curve. It looked frail, a thing that could be easily broken under the onslaught of the Silver Skulls, and yet they had fought enough eldar raiders to know that they were disasters just waiting to happen. At any given moment, more troops and vehicles could arrive without warning. Then their troubles would be multiplied exponentially.

A Raider, one of the transport ships that the pirates so favoured, hovered silently next to the portal. It was a massive thing, painted with incomprehensible symbols. An eldar pilot was seated at the rear of the vehicle, his long, thin alien face with delicately pointed ears clearly visible. He was looking out at the makeshift arena in the compound.

From the vantage point below the rising ridge that led to the blast site, Meyoran had already assessed the battleground. He had noted potential risk points and possible cover. The cages were pulled into a rough circle, a curtain of human flesh drawn between them and their prey.

Meyoran and his force would lead the battle inwards, away from the civilians. Diomedes had been charged with the destruction of the webway portal. By creating such a chaotic distraction, they might buy Gileas and his squad enough time to liberate the prisoners. Perhaps.

Turning his attention to the Raider, Meyoran reviewed the data the Chapter had assimilated over the years on eldar tech. He knew where the weak points were and exactly how he could destroy the vessel. It looked customised; an ornate throne had been pushed forwards to the front of the main deck, where what was presumably the leader of the mission sat, watching with undisguised delight over the chaos he had wrought.

The humans in the cages were sobbing pitifully, calling out for the Emperor's aid, or in the case of several burly young men, screaming promises of revenge. The recruits.

Occasionally, one of the warriors mingling around the makeshift arena would jab into the cages with cruel blades, or fire a shot from the weapons they carried. Elsewhere, the xenos were fighting one another. High-pitched cackles of delight filled the air.

The overseer shouted something in his harsh tongue and several of the raiders raced to a cage, pulling one of their captives into the middle of the circle. Even as Meyoran watched, the aliens began to torture their victim, slicing strips of skin from his face with wickedly curved knives. The man screamed in pain, but for every scream that bubbled from his lips, the more his captors screamed back – only their screams were of joy.

Closing his ears to the sound, Meyoran completed his scan of the area. A rough ring of scrap metal framed the entire scene, bedecked with spikes and broken plexglass. Some of the spikes were further decorated by the grisly addition of human heads. Some still wore their Cartan Militia helmets.

'Prognosticator?' The captain turned to the blue-clad battle-brother at his side. He and Shae Bast had worked together for so long that they knew one another's methods inside out. Alone, Bast was a dangerous opponent. Teamed with the brute force of a Space Marine Assault company, he was nigh-on unstoppable.

The Prognosticator's head snapped up and the sparks of psychic energy flowing steadily through the crystal mesh rising from his gorget began to pulse. He was gathering his powers. As soon as he gave the word, they would attack.

Meyoran's eyes flickered once again to the Raider. He had already established his own personal objective. The power fist at the end of his arm hummed softly. Beside him, Bast was motionless.

The hunger for action was like a living, breathing thing.

Finally, Bast's whispering voice transmitted across the vox to all the Silver Skulls who were coiled like springs ready for the attack.

'Commence,' was all he said and the steel-grey force washed over the ridge like a tide of doom, weapons at the ready, raging litanies of war and hatred.

Within seconds, the Silver Skulls were met by a forest of dancing xenos whose voices raised in harsh, ear-searing counterpoint to the Space Marines' battle roar. The eldar were all flashing blades, cruel edges and needle points. The howls and whoops of half-crazed joy accompanied their attack as their narcotic-soaked minds engaged instantly with the fight.

Even as he raised his crackling fist to smite them where they stood, Meyoran could not help but assess them. They were the complete antithesis of their Space Marine counterparts: a chaotic rabble with no style or structure to their methods. They would fall under the onslaught of the Adeptus Astartes, of that there was little doubt. It remained to be seen what the toll would be on the company.

Perched like grotesque gargoyles on broken spars, a number of bat-winged warriors unleashed bizarre alien weaponry. With brays of uncontrollable delight, they fired their weapons. Toxic crystalline shards scattered over the Space Marines, a glittering rain that broke over battle plate with the discordant sound of crashing chimes. The sound of sniper rifles joined in the jarring noises that echoed around the natural basin as Kyaerus's young Scouts took aim and fired on them.

Aboard the Raider, the overseer had got to his feet. Long, lean and with cruelty etched into his features, he pointed at the Prognosticator and shouted something to his warriors. Some of them broke away and concentrated their efforts on the encroaching psyker, the sound of laughter intensified to near-hysteria. Through it all, Bast continued to walk towards the centre of the compound, determination implicit in every step. His psychic hood crackled with barely contained power.

Meyoran fought with grim determination, pouring silent scorn on an enemy who were so keen to die. They practically threw themselves into the path of his fist, dying with gurgling ecstasy. Everything about these xenos offended and sickened him to the core. That fury channelled itself into every swing, and he broke bones and shattered skulls wherever he walked.

A group of eldar had turned their weapons on the prisoners in the pens and were preparing to open fire. The unfortunates within huddled into a corner of the cage, sobbing pitifully and waiting for the death that was sure to come. The lead eldar gestured with his rifle and barked an order.

Bare seconds later he was pulverised into the ground when Gileas Ur'ten dropped onto him from the sky. Meyoran felt a surge of something that may have been exhilaration, but could just as easily have been relief.

'Excellent timing, sergeant.'

Meyoran received little more than a grunt in response. Around the compound, the Reckoners were descending from the heavens, having used their jump packs to lend momentum to their attack.

In the heart of the battle, Bast stopped walking and stood, raising his helmeted head to meet the gaze of the overseer on the Raider. The eldar lifted his right hand and bellowed a command. Meyoran could hear the urgency in the tone, but it was too late. Far too late.

Dropping to a stoop, Bast laid his gauntleted hand on the ground and brought forth his power. At first nothing seemed to happen, but then there was the very faintest rumble. Bast's powers had always been elemental in nature and the seismic shock he brought forth from the willing earth was enough to knock many of his would-be attackers off their feet.

'Get those prisoners clear, sergeant,' Meyoran voxed urgently, his voice strangely distorted by the earth tremor. 'Use whatever means necessary.'

'Acknowledged, sir.'

The Reckoners had secured the area around the cages easily enough. The problem now would be holding them long enough for an evacuation. It didn't remain a problem for long, however, as Diomedes ploughed through the rocky ridge, effectively creating the perfect escape corridor. The Dreadnought continued towards the portal, scattering the foe before him.

'They're activating the portal, Gileas,' Meyoran advised. 'Get these people to safety. Diomedes, level that device now before they can retreat, or worse, reinforce their position.'

The massive war machine fired at the alien device without hesitation. The first stream of shells seemed to do little more than inflict surface damage. Delicate and fragile it may have looked – but it was a sturdy structure.

Everywhere was noise and carnage as the Reckoners fought for the liberation of the human prisoners. The eldar did everything they could to prevent their delicious prize being stolen from them, lashing themselves into a frenzy with archaic – but, as several battle-brothers discovered, deadly – gladiatorial weapons. Toxic shards rained on the humans as they fled. Many died, but the Reckoners did what they could to prevent too many losses. Even in the midst of battle, Meyoran quietly approved of the calm efficiency with which Gileas carried out his orders. Not for the first time, he felt pride in the younger warrior.

As the shimmering haze within the portal rippled unnaturally, a handful of eldar troops ran into it and vanished. The overseer called out something to his pilot in an urgent tone.

'They're retreating, Diomedes!' Meyoran bellowed in fury. He wasn't going to let the architect of this destruction get away if he could help it. The Dreadnought rumbled a reply and began another assault on the portal.

With a sudden scream of engines, the jetbike that had escaped from the earlier attack ripped into view, its mounted splinter rifle firing on prisoners and Silver Skulls alike. Distracted by the unexpected arrival, Meyoran turned his attention away from the overseer, just for a moment.

It was to prove to be the most costly moment of his life.

'Captain Meyoran!'

Several voices came across the vox almost simultaneously, cutting into and over each other urgently. Behind him, the leader had raised a weapon that looked for all the world like a barbed whip. With expert ease, the eldar flicked back his wrist almost lazily. A thin, snakelike tendril writhed towards Meyoran with preternatural speed, wrapping itself around his gorget. The eldar jerked the whip tightly, pulling the captain to the ground.

Searing pain came and went as Meyoran realised that the whip had sliced through his power armour at the neck seal. Felled by the blow, the warrior struggled to stand as the jetbike turned towards him, firing unceasingly, weapon mounts chattering. His power armour sparked, buckled and finally gave way under the onslaught. He fell back to the ground and almost immediately a ravening pack of eldar swarmed over him. Meyoran fought for all he was worth, but he was losing.

'Sergeant Ur'ten, get the prisoners clear. You have two minutes by my estimate.'

His voice felt strained and unnatural. Perhaps there had been some sort of xenos toxin contained in the weapons strike. Perhaps it was simply the fact that there were presently eldar warriors clinging to him like limpets. Death was imminent and he felt no regret. The omens had spoken of this. He would not defy fate.

That was not *his* destiny.

'Captain Meyoran, I'm heading your way. I will–'

'No, Gileas. There isn't time. We need to finish this. *You* need to finish this. You have to get the aspirants back.'

'I can stop them–'

'Follow your orders, Gileas Ur'ten.' Shae Bast's cold, impassive voice cut across the conversation.

'But–'

'Look to your duty, brother-sergeant!' It was Meyoran this time who snapped the order. 'I'm not finished yet. You must endure, brother.'

There was no reply.

Engines fired into life and the Raider began to move, heading towards the damaged portal into which the remaining eldar were racing headlong.

You *must* endure, Gileas Ur'ten, Meyoran willed silently.

With a roar that started deep down in his stomach, the mortally wounded captain rose to his feet, the eldar still clinging to him, hacking, slashing, firing. Several fell from his body as he stood, and they scuttled frantically into the portal.

He powered his jump pack into life and soared skywards, landing unsteadily on the Raider beside the overseer. The last of his strength was bolstered by the ceaseless flow of combat stimms around his system. Were he to remove his helmet, he suspected his eyes would be as wild and staring as those of the creature he now faced.

Having not anticipated this move, the alien screamed its defiance. The noise was curtailed as Meyoran reached out and crushed the fragile skull in one hand. He tossed the corpse over the side with casual contempt.

He raised his power fist and cast a glance around the compound. Gileas and the Reckoners were ensuring that the humans were clear. The other Silver Skulls were finishing off the remaining eldar and Diomedes was pouring fire onto the portal.

All was as it should be. The Silver Skulls were doing more than prevailing. They were *winning*. If this was to be the last thing he ever saw, then he would die with pride and honour.

Meyoran's helmeted gaze met that of the Prognosticator, who raised a hand in silent salute.

With every last ounce of strength left in his body, the captain thrust his armoured fist into the heart of the vehicle. The fragile engine housing splintered under the force of the impact, crushing power circuits and couplings just beneath the surface. The pilot lost all control as the fist's energy field flared, igniting the vessel from within. Simultaneously, Diomedes's persistence was rewarded as the ship reached the webway's active field.

Both the portal and the half of the Raider that had failed to translate to the webway detonated in a expanding ball of fire and debris. Gileas and the Reckoners had done their job; the civilian survivors, whilst thrown to the ground by the shockwave of the blast, were far enough away that the explosion itself did little more than singe an eyebrow or two.

The remaining threat was dealt with swiftly. The jetbike was ripped apart by Diomedes. The other aliens, who had descended into even more chaos at the loss of their leader, were dead in moments.

Dead.

Gileas reached up and snatched off his helmet, flinging it to one side. He would not accept the blinking rune that told him of Meyoran's demise. He *could* not.

'Prognosticator!' His voice bellowed across the smouldering battlefield. 'Prognosticator, I need to speak to you right now!'

'Gileas…' Reuben, Gileas's oldest friend and his brother-in-arms since the days they had been novitiates, laid a gauntlet on his sergeant's arm. He could feel Gileas's fury and grief. 'Now is not the time.'

The sergeant shook his arm free from Reuben's grip and turned furious hazel eyes on him. 'You are wrong, Reuben. Now *is* the time. There are rituals to observe. And, damn it, I will observe them. Prognosticator!'

'Sergeant Ur'ten.'

The Prognosticator's whispering voice came from behind him, channelled through the vox-bead in his ear.

'Confirm Meyoran's death.'

'You saw the explosion yourself, sergeant. Surely–'

'I said confirm his death.' Gileas took a step towards the psyker, who held his ground serenely.

'As you command, brother-sergeant.' The Prognosticator drew his concentration in once again. Gileas felt the brief touch of the psyker's mind on his own as Bast allowed his attention to drift around the battlefield.

'Nothing, brother-sergeant.' Bast's helmeted head lowered in respect and Gileas was temporarily thrown off his raging stride by the genuine sorrow he heard in the other's voice. 'The captain is gone.'

Gileas ran a hand across his stubble-shadowed jawline and stared at the Prognosticator. The words were there, but the meaning would not connect with his synapses. Bast took a step closer, leaning in to whisper so that only the stunned sergeant could hear him.

'Meyoran is gone, Gileas,' he said, quietly. 'Control your inner beast for once in your life and do your duty.'

Duty. There it was again. That word.

Born into a nomadic tribe which had struggled just to survive, reborn into a tribe of warriors upon whom the very fate of the Imperium depended, the word had always had a profound effect on Gileas. He was a Space Marine. He was a Silver Skull.

'Yes,' he said, his shoulders automatically straightening. 'Yes, of course.' Bast inclined his head and stepped back.

The battle was over. There was nothing more they could do here other than to recover the legacies of their fallen brothers and take back however many of the aspirants remained. The recovery of the hive would fall to the local troops and emergency aid would be sent in due course.

Gileas cast a glance at the smouldering portal. The eldar might return, but it would undoubtedly take time for them to assimilate any galactic coordinates they might have been able to glean from their brief time on Cartan.

'Silver Skulls,' Gileas said, over the vox, bending to retrieve his helmet. 'Withdraw.'

THE CHAPEL ABOARD the *Silver Arrow* once more wrapped Gileas in its cocoon of calm. This time, however, he was not hardening his core, grounding himself in battle doctrine and preparing for a fight. This time he was there for a different reason.

Keile Meyoran.

The captain's name had been painstakingly written letter by agonising letter onto the company's war banner, along with the names of other brothers who had fallen. As his position dictated, the job of adding Meyoran's name had been his right.

It was an honour, but one that he had not wanted ever to fulfil.

'He should not have died,' Gileas said softly to the Prognosticator who stood by his side, staring up at the banner. Out of his battle plate, the Prognosticator's years were more evident in the slight stoop of his shoulders, as though he held the weight of his centuries on them.

'It was his destiny. It was predetermined before we even left the ship.

For every action, Gileas Ur'ten, there has to be a consequence. By leaving the ship to come down to the surface with the company, Meyoran set an irreversible chain of events in motion.' The psyker's colourless eyes skimmed over the banner with cool detachment. 'It was the Emperor's will that he was lost today. He knew that and he accepted the omen gladly.'

Gileas angled his head abruptly in Bast's direction. The Prognosticator held a silver rune in the palm of his leathery-skinned hand. He turned it over and over almost idly, such a complacent gesture that Gileas felt his blood start to boil.

'He should *not* have died.' The sergeant spun on his heel and turned to face Bast fully. 'He could have been spared to fight another day. He should not have listened to you.'

Taller than the psyker by a considerable amount, the Space Marine towered threateningly. In any other circumstances, it would have been no question as to who would have the upper hand should things come to blows. But the power of the prognosticatum over the whole Chapter meant that nothing was ever so certain.

Gileas was well aware of the extent of Bast's powers. He had seen the Prognosticator crush dozens of warriors with a word. He had been indoctrinated over the decades to revere the Prognosticators of the Silver Skulls and to defer to their ultimate judgement. And yet right now, all he felt was anger. Anger at the power the Prognosticator wielded. Anger at the fact that Meyoran, a good warrior and a good soul, had been taken from them. Anger at something he could not put a name to.

An amused, almost indulgent smile twisted Bast's features. Involuntarily, Gileas's hands clenched into fists as he allowed his anger to be quenched in the physical face of his duty. He could not, in all good conscience however, allow the words to pass unsaid.

'Auspicious, you said. You said that the omens were auspicious for the battle down there. You knew, didn't you? You knew he would die if he went down there, and still you let him go?'

Bast nodded. 'Our lives are about adapting to circumstances. Change is a fundamental part of the life of a Space Marine, Gileas. This *had* to happen in order for future events to occur to the fullest benefit of the Chapter.'

'What events?'

Bast paused, and for a heartbeat Gileas sensed the psyker's touch on his mind. Then Bast's eyes left him and the older Space Marine pocketed the rune. 'It remains to be seen. For now, though, do not mourn Keile Meyoran too much. Remember him as we all will, but give thanks to the Emperor that his death was a glorious one. Put your energies into your own life instead. You endure, Gileas Ur'ten. Remember that.'

The Prognosticator bowed deeply and took his leave, his bare feet padding almost silently on the cold metal floor of the chapel. Gileas watched him go, pondering his words. His eyes lifted once again to the banner and were caught by the motto.

Vincit Qui Patitur.

He conquers who endures.

HAMMER AND BOLTER

ISSUE 6

TOWER OF BLOOD

Tony Ballantyne

THE CEILING WAS dripping blood.

It dripped on the bald head of Goedendag Morningstar, Adeptus Astartes of the Iron Knights Chapter, and the Space Marine made no move to wipe it away.

'How many floors lie above us?' he asked.

Though the Imperial Guard trooper was a big woman, she would still have been dwarfed by Goedendag even had he not been wearing his power armour.

'One hundred and forty-three floors,' she managed to say, awestruck by this post-human demigod. She straightened up, despite her exhaustion. 'Eight hundred and sixty-five lie below us. We met the horde in battle at the nine hundredth floor. They pushed us back to here. Many lives were lost in action, many more civilians were evacuated.'

'But not all,' said Ortrud. The Iron Knights had completed their survey of the eight hundred and fifty-sixth floor; now they clustered around their commander.

'Not all,' agreed the Guard, looking around the seven men now towering over her in their gunmetal and black armour, streaked red with dripping blood. Their unhelmed heads seemed so small, lost in the heart of the powerful machinery of their suits. 'By no means all. There are thousands still trapped above us, all at the mercy of the warp fiends.'

'The warp fiends do not understand the meaning of mercy,' said Fastlinger. 'Commander, may we now don our helmets?' He drew his hand across his face.

'No,' said Goedendag. 'We fight unhelmed. We do not want to lead civilians into areas where we are safe and they are not. What if we led them into a vacuum?' He noticed the way the Imperial Guardswoman was looking at him. 'Do you have a question?' he asked.

'I'm sorry,' she said. 'I was just wondering, why do you wear two morning stars on your back?'

Goedendag smiled.

'For weapons.'

'You seem different to other Space Marines.'

'Have you met many?' asked Fastlinger.

Goedendag flashed him a warning look. The Imperial Guard were an honoured force; they did not deserve to be ridiculed.

'The Iron Knights are siege specialists,' said Goedendag. 'The warp fiends have sealed off the top floors and surrounded this tower with a warp instability that is spreading across the sky, threatening the neighbouring hives. This siege needs to be broken *now*.'

The Guardswoman was torn between exhaustion and awe. Still, something caused her to speak.

'Are you going to wait for the Ordo Malleus?'

'The inquisition's daemonhunters are not here,' interrupted Telramund. 'Goedendag, I grow weary. Let us join the fight!'

'Peace, Telramund! This soldier stands alone in a room with seven Iron Knights in full armour–'

'Save for their helms,' muttered Fastlinger.

'If things had been otherwise, we would have found nought here but corpses. She is brave indeed.' Goedendag looked down at her.

'What's your name?'

'Kelra.'

'Then listen to me, Kelra. You and your troops have done well to hold back the daemons, but now it is our turn.'

He waved a hand around the floor. It was empty save for the four lift shafts that ran to the top of the hive building. All the internal walls, all the possessions of those who had once lived here were vaporised, smashed, shattered, destroyed by the weapons of the Imperial Guard as they had fought to hold their ground. The wide, low space was filled with darkness, the stench of battle, the drip of blood. Even the stairs had broken away. The stairs; the last route of escape for those lucky civilians who had not taken the lifts. The shafts still creaked with the agony of those caught within.

'Kelra, before we leave, you mentioned something about the origin of the warp rift?'

Kelra nodded, pleased to help.

'I have heard something. Escaping civilians have spoken about a Gutor Invareln who lived on the nine hundred and ninety-second floor. He was a bitter man, an outcast. He claimed he was a latent psyker, that he had been ignored by the Imperium. His neighbours laughed, they thought he was seeking attention. The children mocked him, asked him why he had not been taken to Terra, but Invareln would scowl in answer that he was deliberately forgotten.'

'He *was* a psyker,' said Franosch, concentrating. 'His mind is now possessed by a daemon. A greater daemon. He is the portal by which the lesser daemons are entering this world.'

Kelra's eyes widened as she looked to Franosch.

'He's a psyker too?' she asked.

'Gamma level at best,' answered Franosch. He turned to Goedendag. 'Commander, there are daemonettes above us. Many, many daemonettes.'

'Enough talk,' said Telramund. 'The instability is spreading.'

Goedendag looked up at the ceiling, watched the clotting drops forming stalactites.

'So much blood,' he said. 'Telramund is right. We move out. Draw your chainswords.'

Telramund was already holding his meltagun. 'This weapon will suit me fine, commander.'

'And what of the civilians who stand above us? No meltaguns, no flamers, no frag grenades…'

'How about missile launchers?' said Fastlinger, innocently.

'How about you take point, Fastlinger?' replied Goedendag. He noted the look of disappointment on Telramund's face. 'Telramund, you accompany him.'

Telramund smiled as he holstered his meltagun and drew his chainsword. An angry buzzing noise sounded as he set it in motion, a buzz that was immediately answered by Fastlinger's weapon.

The Iron Knights began to move apart, assuming combat positions.

'Gottfried. The battle cry.'

Gottfried looked down at the floor and clasped his hands together. In a low voice, he intoned the words: 'Strike, death, as silent as the swan.'

The rest of the group repeated the words.

Now the other chainswords powered up, the angry screeching made all the louder as it echoed from the low ceiling. Low ceilings, the better to cram in more humans, ready to work on this manufactory world.

The time for joking had passed, and Fastlinger looked to his comrades and saw they were all ready. He looked to Goedendag last. The commander nodded and Fastlinger raised his sword to the ceiling, the angry buzz rising to a scream as it cut through the thin metal. Immediately, there was a convulsive eruption of blood, dark blood rupturing through the widening crack. It spilled down over Fastlinger's cutting arm and shoulder, running down the blue gunmetal and black of his powered armour. He shifted his position and his feet slipped on the pools that congealed around his feet. Retractable spikes sprang forth from the soles of his power armour, holding him in place.

Kelra, the Imperial Guard trooper, backed away, dodging a second burst of blood as Telramund too began to cut into the ceiling. The tide of blood widened with the hole, and now smooth yellow shapes slipped through amongst the liquid. Rounded and polished, they splashed and knocked on the floor.

'That's a skull,' said Kelra. Still, she stood her ground, noted Goedendag. Not for nothing had the Imperial Guard gained the respect of humanity.

Goedendag gestured Franosch forward, and the psyker stood at the edge of the widening waterfall of blood.

'They know we're here,' he said. 'They are eager to meet us.'

'Who? The daemonettes?'

'Oh yes. They are filled with the bitter joy of battle, and yet… something is holding them back.'

'What?'

'I don't know. Something at the top of the tower.'

'Will this tide never end?' called Telramund impatiently. He was itching to fight.

'Surely this is more blood than all the humans of the hive would hold?' said Kelra.

'Some of it spills from the portal,' said Franosch.

'Enough of this,' said Goedendag. 'The gap is wide enough! Through it! Go!'

Fastlinger crouched and then jumped upwards on leg muscles massively expanded by the biscopea implanted in his chest. He soared through the gap above him in a spray of ruby, followed closely by Telramund.

Now Goedendag stepped forward. Despite the fact that he heard the buzzing of chainswords above him, the innate courtesy of the Iron Knights caused him to pause for a moment and turn to Kelra.

'Thank you for your help,' he said.

'I'll be waiting here for your return.'

Drips of blood bouncing from his bald head and matting his long white beard, Goedendag Morningstar jumped up into the space above.

He landed on the eight hundred and fifty-seventh floor, his balance thrown by the tide of blood swirling into the hole. Something white came flashing in at his side; something sharp was pricking towards his eye. He swung his chainsword, shearing through the crab claw of the daemonette who bore down upon him. The white skinned woman hissed at him, her rusty hair plastered by blood to her bare shoulders.

'*Goolvar h'nurrgh!*' she spat, and made to draw something from behind her back. It was a feint! As Goedendag brought his chainsword up to parry the attack, she kicked out at him, a three-toed foot tipped in razor-sharp claws scratching across the armour on his sword arm. Goedendag made to chop at her leg, but she gripped him with her foot and held on, twisting the chainsword upwards.

Now the daemonette smiled at him, her sweet, seductive body undulating as she brought the snake-fiend from behind her back. She hissed, and lashed the fiend forwards like a whip. Its eyes blazed, its mouth, surrounded by a ring of venom pierced needles, snapping towards Goedendag's face. His chainsword-wielding hand was trapped by the daemonette's foot.

The betcher's glands in Goedendag's mouth had been working overtime, and he spat corrosive acid into the eyes of the lashing snake-fiend. The creature screamed and drew back in pain. Goedendag flicked the chainsword to his left hand, then brought the weapon up as if to parry *quinte*, slicing through the snake-fiend's body. He carried on with the movement, circling down to cut through the daemonette's leg. She screamed and jumped forward, needle teeth moving within her mouth, but Goedendag's right hand now reached to his shoulder and took hold of one of the morning stars there. He brought the weapon forward in a circle, cracking it down on the daemonette's skull as, simultaneously, his sword thrust into her body.

She thrashed as she died, her bitter scream rippling the pools of blood gathered on the floor.

'You took your time on that one,' said Fastlinger, standing coolly nearby over the bodies of two more dead daemonettes. 'And we saved her especially for you, too.'

'You talk too much,' said Telramund, three daemonettes to his credit.

The other members of the squad were now entering the room, jumping up from below.

'One hundred and forty-two floors to go,' announced Ortrud, looking at the dead daemonettes.

'There are many more above us,' said Franosch, looking to the dripping ceiling, 'yet still they hold back.' He looked at Goedendag. 'Do you think they know it is us? Are they waiting for us?'

'Who cares?' said Telramund. 'We shall meet them soon enough.'

The daemonettes had been fought to a standstill here as they descended the tower from the warp portal. As they had fought, they had ripped apart the thin walls that partitioned the human apartments crowded into the hive block. The ceiling above had been punctured in many places, and Goedendag and the other Iron Knights could now look up through several floors.

Ortrud waded through ankle-deep blood, kicking aside yellow skulls, the flesh recently ripped from the bone.

'They sealed this floor to keep the blood in,' he said.

'There is blood still dripping down upon us,' said Telramund, ever impatient.

Franosch was frowning, straining to understand.

'They carry some of the living through the warp portal,' he says. 'I hear their screams. But the daemonettes grow bored. They torture and kill those who remain.'

'Then let us make speed to meet them,' said Telramund.

'Telramund speaks well,' said Goedendag. 'Franosch, I see the stairs resume undamaged on the next floor. Is it meet that we should take them?'

'For the moment.'

They advanced in turns, running in pairs up flights of stairs whilst those behind covered them. As they climbed through the floors, the damage inflicted by the holding action lessened. The internal walls of the hive tower reasserted themselves, and Goedendag and the rest began to make out the tiny apartment spaces in which the civilians had lived.

'What do they make here?' asked Gottfried.

'On Minea? Phosgene gas, mainly. They also export Banedox ore.'

'Look,' said Gottfried.

Goedendag looked to the floor. A child's toy lay there, a model Space Marine.

'There were children here,' said Fastlinger. He looked sick. Sometimes the jokes were not quite enough to shut out reality. 'What did they do with them?'

'Next floor up,' said Ortrud. 'You'll see.'

They climbed the stairs to the next level.

'Nine hundredth floor,' said Gottfried.

'They sealed the stairwell above,' said Telramund, looking up.

'Then we cut through with chainswords,' said Goedendag.

'We won't need chainswords,' replied Telramund bitterly.

Goedendag moved forward to get a better look. A patchwork had been stitched over the stairwell. Shapes of brown, pink and yellow. Blood seeped through the stitches.

'That's children's skin,' said Goedendag.

'That's daemonettes amusing themselves, killing time,' said Telramund.

'It's a warning line,' said Franosch. 'It will summon trouble.'

'Then I will invite trouble to join me,' said Goedendag, cutting through the patchwork of flesh with a knife. Blood spurted through, and amongst the curling currents and eddies slipped the writhing bodies of snake-fiends, pouring through the gaps, wriggling as they sought out their human prey. Chainswords buzzed into life once more, and the warriors began to swing at the prickling creatures.

'They cannot penetrate our armour!' shouted Fastlinger, cutting a snake-fiend in two in a spray of green ichor that steamed and sizzled on contact with the clotting blood.

'They're not trying to penetrate,' called Ortrud. 'They seek to entangle us.'

As he spoke, a bundle of snake-fiends whipped their way out of the bloody stream and corkscrewed their way towards Goedendag's sword arm, seeking to wrap it to his body. Goedendag feinted to the side and then brought his chainsword down on the mass of bodies, their scales dark and shining. The scream of the sword joined the splashing of blood and the hiss of ichor. Through the mass of moist movement he saw the white bodies of the daemonettes of Slaanesh dropping down to join the melee.

'Too much blood,' gasped Franosch, launching a *coulé* attack on a snake-fiend, grazing the chainsword down the side of its body before neatly flicking back to sever the head.

'Less technique, Franosch,' called Ortrud, 'More slashing!'

'There is too much blood,' repeated Franosch, stamping down on a bundle of snake-fiends with his spiked boots. 'Still it pours from the warp.'

''Ware the daemonettes!' called Gottfried, launching a *fleche* attack at the closest enemy. A white female staggered towards him, seemingly drunk on blood. Goedendag brought his chainsword up beneath Gottfried's strike, parrying it.

'Hold,' called Goedendag, seeing the look of betrayal in his comrade's eyes. 'She's human.'

The Space Marines halted as one, the mocking laughter of daemonettes filling their ears. They took a moment to discern the situation: the followers of Slaanesh stood at the far side of the wide room, bending, taunting, snapping their crab-like claws at the Space Marines. Now Goedendag's men realised just what the daemonettes had pushed towards them: human women, stripped naked and daubed with white paint, their hair tied up and stained with blood. Prisoners, sent forward to die on the Space Marine's blades, for was it not a fact that the followers of Slaanesh delighted in killing their opponents in the most vile and tormenting ways?

'More snake-fiends!' called Goedendag, as the writhing creatures rose out of the rising tide of blood, circlets of needle teeth glistening with poison, redoubling their attack, this time on the human women as well as the Space Marines themselves.

It was left to Gottfried and Hellstedt to dispatch the snake-fiends. Ortrud and Fastlinger launched themselves at the daemonettes screaming with insane laughter at the other side of the room. They waited a moment as the Space Marines advanced and then retreated at a sedate pace back up the stairs to the next level, wriggling their bodies in an alluring fashion as they did so, taunting their pursuers.

'Leave them,' called Goedendag. 'Look to the women first.' Reluctantly, Ortrud and Fastlinger returned to his side.

The unceasing flow of blood continued from above, though the tide was diminishing. It swirled in whirlpools around the stairwells leading further down the tower. Seven human women stood weakly, buffeted by the dying tide. And now Goedendag saw why they had remained silent throughout their torment: their mouths had been sewn shut with thick, red thread. He took a knife from his combat armour and cut through the thread sealing the first woman's mouth.

'There are more of them above,' she shouted, red thread piercing her lips in a grotesque moustache. 'Hundreds, thousands. They're waiting for you.'

'Peace,' said Goedendag Morningstar. 'We have the advantage.'

The woman's eyes widened.

'No! There are only seven of you. You have no advantage. They make ambushes, deadfalls.'

'Yes,' said Goedendag. 'But they must fight us one floor at a time.'

The other women now had their mouths cut free. Goedendag was impressed to see how they held themselves. Frightened, hurt, it was true, but they had not broken down. He remembered Kelra, the Imperial Guardswoman, and he realised that they bred them tough on Minea.

Franosch stepped forward.

'There is a warp portal near the top floor,' he said. 'Have you seen it?'

'No,' said the women in unison, but one of them stepped forward. She was rubbing white ichor from her body as she did so, exposing the dark skin underneath.

'I have not seen the warp portal, but I have heard from one who has. One who fled down the stairs while the lift shafts filled with fire. He told me there is a daemon up there, a greater daemon.'

'I knew it!' exclaimed Franosch.

'Yet why does it not attack?' said Ortrud. 'Why does its horde remain at the top of the tower?'

'They're waiting for something. It's part of the deal.'

'What deal?'

'Gutor Invareln,' said the woman. 'There was a phosgene leak, his body was badly scarred. He was a bitter enough man before his injuries, afterwards he blamed the world for his troubles. He turned upon all his fellow humans; he claimed he was a latent psyker and that he would have his revenge on us all.'

'Surely this would have brought the Inquisition down upon him,' called Franosch. 'Most latents try to avoid their attention.'

'None of us thought anything of his words. Gutor had always sought any attention to make himself seem more important. To him, even the inquisition would have been welcome.'

'You believe that Gutor made a deal with a daemon?' said Goedendag.

'Yes. He wanted to live to see the destruction of all those who lived around him. Only after that would he surrender to death and allow the portal to fully open! And after that...'

'After the portal is fully open there will be daemons enough for all of Minea,' said Franosch.

'Then we must hurry to make the greater daemon's acquaintance,' said Goedendag.

'Meltaguns?' said Fastlinger.

'What about the humans?' said Ortrud.

'Use them,' said one of the women. 'Better a quick death than what *they* plan.'

'Chainswords,' said Goedendag. 'Telramund. Less than one hundred floors to go. Move out!'

THEY SPLASHED UP the stairs of the tower. Globs of blood gathered in clumps on their boot spikes. They had to pause to shake them free.

The corridors they passed through were empty; they looked into empty rooms where humans had once lived and saw signs of fighting – overturned chairs, broken tables, even food scattered across the pooled blood on the floor – but of bodies, living or dead, there was no sign.

'Carried away,' said Franosch. 'Sport for now or later.'

They passed floor nine hundred and ten, then nine hundred and twenty.

'What's that?' asked Ortrud. The noise came again, a shrieking sound as of many voices crying in agony.

'It's coming from the elevator shaft,' said Goedendag.

The black metal wall of the elevator shafts was their only constant as they climbed, that and the never ending flow of blood. Each set of doors had buckled and melted shut. Once more, the metal of the shafts seemed to hum with an unearthly music.

'Like a trumpet call, blown from the warp,' said Ortrud, darkly.

'The bodies of those who fled,' said Franosch. 'Trapped, still living, in the shafts. Boiled in blood and feasted on by snake-fiends.'

On they climbed. On the nine hundred and twenty-seventh floor, the rooms were filled with human feet. On floor nine hundred and twenty-nine, glistening hearts lay in pools, still beating. They pumped blood from pool to pool, from room to room.

'This is sick even by Slaaneshi standards,' said Fastlinger. Goedendag said nothing.

Still they climbed.

Franosch concentrated.

'Next floor,' he said. 'Daemonettes. Hundreds of them. The humans lie beyond them. And then...'

He paused, pushing his meagre psychic ability to its limit.

'...and then nothing again. Nothing until the top of the building, and whatever awaits us there.'

'It's an invitation,' said Goedendag, calmly. 'Whatever is at the top is waiting for us. Waiting for me.'

The Space Marines looked at each other. Each felt the guilt of their Chapter, each felt the determination to atone for the sins of their fellow Iron Knights.

'Tell us what to do, Goedendag.'

Goedendag looked at his chainsword. His lyman's ear was attuned to the noises from above now, the pitiful cries of the tortured.

'We've climbed nine hundred and forty floors in search of a fight,' said Goedendag. 'Now we'll have one. I have a plan.' He smiled slowly. 'And Fastlinger, it's time for you to sheathe your chainsword for a while...'

THEY FIXED MELTA bombs to the ceiling, retreated to the floor below and waited for the explosion.

Ortrud was an expert at demolition. The bombs broke the ceiling and nothing more. Or rather, he broke more than the ceiling, for the ceiling was a floor as well, and as the ground beneath their birdlike feet gave way, the daemonettes of Slaanesh found themselves falling, falling down in a rain of blood, of thrashing limbs, of dust and screams and noise, falling towards floor nine hundred and forty, falling in a tangled mass. And erupting from the centre of this confusion came Goedendag and his Iron Knights.

Chainswords buzzed as they chopped at limbs and clove heads in two.

The daemonettes recovered quickly, righting themselves and lunging towards the Space Marines, slashing their crab-like claws and kicking with taloned feet. The Iron Knights formed a circle; seven chainswords thrust, cut and parried with elegant precision. More daemonettes dropped down from the floors above and Goedendag withdrew to the centre of the circle, the better to take on this new attack. One daemonette dropped headfirst towards him, one clawed arm stretched out, pointing at his face. He sidestepped, took her arm and rammed the claw straight down into the floor, piercing the metal there. He pushed her forward, breaking her arm, but at that moment a second daemonette fell on his back and he felt the eldritch power of her claw pierce the shell of his armour, the shrieking pain transmitted to his body through his black carapace. He reached for one of the two morning stars strapped to his back and pulled it free, the spiked head of the ball scraping across the face of the daemonette. Now he swung the ball around, as if to hit his own back. He heard the sickening crunch as her body was crushed between the ball of the morning star and the ceramite of his suit.

Still more daemonettes dropped into the room. The space was filled with white flesh, the slash of claws and the buzz and shriek of chainswords. Above him, Goedendag saw a space leading to the nine hundred and forty-second floor, two floors up.

'Telramund, you're in charge,' he called. Summoning all of his enhanced strength, he leapt upwards, catching hold of the bottom-most step.

A claw slashed down and he caught it, pulling the daemonette down to join her sisters below. Quickly, he scrambled up to the next floor.

Daemonettes crowded towards him. Goedendag took a last look at his fellows fighting below, and then he raised his chainsword and charged forward, cutting his way through to the stairs.

He fought his way upwards against the tide of daemonettes, against the tide of blood. All the while, he had the impression that they were playing with him, that they were allowing him to pass, allowing him to climb higher. The waves of daemonettes diminished, though one or two of them still launched themselves at his chainsword.

Now he passed through the floors where the humans lay prisoner. Some were bound, some crawled on their knees, lacking feet, some lay half eviscerated, their shouts of pain weak in their throats, their tormentors called away to fight the Iron Knights.

The humans called out to him for succour. Goedendag ignored them. He could better aid them by confronting whatever lay at the top of this tower.

He pounded on up the flights of stairs, his anger acting as a buffer, pushing away all those that came before him. Now the daemonettes hung back as he passed; now they stood and watched as he climbed, or they turned and headed downwards to the fray with the remaining Iron Knights.

Now he was certain something was waiting for him at the top of the tower. As he climbed higher, a feeling of anxiety prickled at his heels, and he began to understand the nature of what lay ahead.

THE SOUND OF fighting faded to leave an eerie emptiness, a weariness that weighed down on his very soul.

He reached the nine hundred and ninetieth floor, and glimpsed an open space above him.

On floor nine hundred and ninety-two, he stepped out into a vast cavern. The last eight floors had been removed to leave a huge space at the very top of the hive tower. A nascent warp portal hung in the middle of the space, silver and black roiling in a halo on the boundary between this reality and the dreadful void of the otherworld. Blood flowed through the warp portal in a thin stream, splashing onto the mound of dead bodies below that lay folded up to look like pebbles. A mound of pink and brown and yellow pebbles, bound in red cord. And there, standing at the summit, surrounded by the dark halo of the nascent warp, bathed in the blood that ran from it, a shape within a shape.

Goedendag climbed the pile of the dead, and finally he came face to face with Gutor Invareln, latent psyker, the cause of all the horror.

Around the human, Goedendag could see the outline of the creature that had possessed him. Huge and powerful, with a bovine face, one female breast and four arms. Two of them ended in human-like hands, two of them in crab-like claws.

A greater daemon of Slaanesh. A Keeper of Secrets.

The daemon had not achieved full corporeality; it seemed to be still existing in some halfway state as it entered this universe. The psyker was completely possessed, looking out from the translucent form of the demon that surrounded him, eyes vacant, an idiot grin on his face.

The daemon giggled at the sight of Goedendag.

'How appropriate,' said the daemon. 'For the Iron Knights have their secrets, do they not?'

'And you are a Keeper of Secrets,' replied Goedendag.

'What is your name?'

'Goedendag Morningstar.'

There was silence, broken only by the ever present dripping of blood.

'Don't you wish to know my name?' asked the daemon.

'No.'

A look of petulance crossed the daemon's face, like that of a small child denied a toy. It quickly passed.

'And yet I believe I do hold a secret you wish to know. Do you wish to know the location of your brethren?'

'I don't know what you're talking about.'

The daemon laughed.

'I *know* that you are lying. Everyone knows of the penitence of the Iron Knights. Few outside the order know the reason. I am one of them. I am a Keeper of Secrets, and I know the location of your traitor brethren. It lies beyond the portal, Goedendag Morningstar, but I think you know that already. Why else would you have come here?'

'To kill you, of course.'

The daemon looked beyond Goedendag's shoulder. Goedendag did not turn. He could hear the skittering, giggling sound made by the daemonettes who filed into the room behind him.

'My daughters are here. It would appear the comrades you left behind on the floor below have fallen, Goedendag Morningstar.'

'It is no disgrace to die in battle.'

'The traitors you seek thought otherwise, Goedendag Morningstar. They chose Chaos, Goedendag Morningstar. And you nearly chose the same!'

Goedendag said nothing, for to speak with a daemon was to be drawn into an argument with a daemon.

'I will take your silence as agreement.' The half seen features of the daemon looked down. Within its form, the psyker beamed with happy idiocy. 'There is no need for you to lie, Goedendag Morningstar. I can sense the shame within you. It is the only thing that you have that outshines the temptation you feel, for you are full of lust for the pleasures of life. The pleasures denied to a Space Marine.'

Still Goedendag was silent.

'And I should know. Isn't that what I am about? The Keeper of Secrets? What secrets could be greater than those *we do not want to know about ourselves*?'

'What secrets, indeed?' said Goedendag tightly.

'See? You speak! You should not be ashamed, Goedendag Morningstar. Your behaviour does not surprise me. Who is more zealous in following a path than one who has almost fallen from it? A man who was never tempted would not have half your ferocity. Look, it brought you to the top of this tower!'

'I came to destroy you.'

'So you say. Come, Goedendag Morningstar. Soon the portal will open fully. Why not pass beyond it? Join your dark brethren. Join the Iron Knights that you call traitors.'

'Enough talk, daemon. It is time to fight.'

The daemon laughed.

'Fight? It is all that you can do to stand, Goedendag Morningstar. Look at you. My very presence induces anguish and ecstasy within you.'

Goedendag looked down at the floor, focused on the corporeal feet of the psyker that stood within the outline of the daemon, and he tried to concentrate on the reality of the situation. In truth, he felt a savage joy within him that he usually knew best from battle, but this time it was mixed with something more innocent, something that rang with the purity of childhood, but a tainted purity, something polluted by blood and perverted in daemonic fashion. He felt the excitement that he had known when, as an aspirant, he had first begun the transition to Space Marine, when the gene-seed had been implanted and he had begun the long process of modification. Except now he felt something that he hadn't known at the time. A deep anguish, a total certainty that the procedure would fail, that his body would reject the process and he would be branded a failure, that he would let down those who had come to depend upon him.

'You're strong, daemon' admitted Goedendag. 'You are affecting even me.'

'This human is strong,' said the daemon, indicating the psyker within himself. 'Strong enough to offer himself in sacrifice in order to open the portal.'

'He was a weak man!' shouted Goedendag.

'He was a bitter man. Bitter that his powers were overlooked by the Imperium.'

'He should have been executed as a danger to all.' Goedendag felt his willpower draining away.

'Lucky for us that he was not. You know what price he asked in order to sacrifice himself to the portal? Only that he lived long enough to see us succeed. That was one bargain that we were happy to keep.'

Goedendag felt the chainsword getting heavier in his hands.

'You're getting weaker,' said the daemon, as the chainsword slipped though Goedendag's fingers and clattered to the floor.

'I can still fight.'

'I don't think so. And so, Goedendag, before you die, I have one final question to ask you. Goedendag means Morningstar, does it not?'

'It does. This is the last question you wish to ask me?'

'No, you interrupt me. Your name, therefore, is Morningstar Morningstar. Why is that?'

'Because of this,' said Goedendag. And he crossed his hands over his chest and, gripping the two morning star handles that were fastened on his back, he swung them up and around, through the translucent outline of the daemon and brought them together, crushing the psyker's head. There was a crunch of bone, grey matter exploding in a disk between the spikes of the two balls.

The daemon shrieked, and immediately Goedendag felt the sense of anguish and ecstasy decrease.

'The portal is closing,' said the daemon. 'But I will make my mark in this world first!'

Goedendag stooped and scooped the chainsword from the floor. The daemon saw what he was doing and laughed.

'That will not harm me in this form!'

'I am not aiming for you,' replied Goedendag coolly as he triggered the chainsword and used it to cut through the dead psyker's neck. 'Removing the head will speed the closing of the rift.' He straightened up and moved around so that his back was to the shrinking portal.

'And now,' he said. 'What will your daemonettes do? Will they attempt to pass me as they flee for the closing warp?'

The daemon laughed.

'One man against the force of the daemonettes? I only wish I could sustain corporeality enough to watch you die under their onslaught! As it is, I will take comfort in the fact the location of your Iron Brethren will remain my secret!'

'Daemon, when I have disposed of your daughters, I will come looking for you. You have my word on that.'

The daemon laughed louder.

'You say that when you fight only with a chainsword? And listen! My sisters approach now!'

It was true. Goedendag heard the skittering of claws on blood and iron.

'Only a chainsword, you say,' said Goedendag, smiling grimly. 'You forget my morning stars.'

'And will that be enough?' laughed the daemon.

'Let us see,' said Goedendag, and he triggered the chainsword. The angry buzzing was an invitation to the approaching daemons. He stepped forward and raised his sword.

Simultaneously, eight white-bodied daemons leapt at him, screaming in unison. They raised their crab-like claws and plunged towards Goedendag, teeth bared. Eight more leapt up behind them.

'Goodbye,' said the daemon, and Goedendag stepped forward to meet the lithe attackers. The first lunged forward with one snapping claw. Goedendag swung his chainsword in a tight circle that sliced through the claw and into the side of the daemonette that followed. A clawed foot lashed out and took hold of his armoured boot. Goedendag ignored it and slashed at another attacker.

'Come on!' he called. 'Come on, all of you!'

White bodies advanced on all sides. Claws, screaming, blood, ichor. Goedendag stood at the top of a mound of naked, bound bodies, bathed in blood, and he fought like a daemon himself. But there were too many of them. The sheer weight of numbers began to overwhelm him.

And then he heard a shout. There, in the distance, he saw Telramund, armour half broken, bathed in blood and ichor. And behind him, Fastlinger, and then Franosch.

The shout came again.

'The humans are clear.'

Tired though he was, Goedendag smiled.

'Now,' he said, holstering his chainsword. 'Now it is time for meltaguns!'

THE IRON KNIGHTS looked at the bodies of the fallen. Goedendag and Franosch watched the shrinking remnants of the closing portal.

'Anything?' asked Goedendag.

Franosch shook his head.

'Sorry. Nothing.' He wiped his forehead, removing a splash of blood. 'Did it occur to you that the daemon could be lying?'

Goedendag looked thoughtful.

'I don't think so,' he said. 'It knew too much.'

'Then the Iron Brethren exist somewhere in the warp. The story is true.'

'Perhaps...' He place a warning hand on Franosch's arm. Kelra, the Imperial Guardswoman, had entered the room.

'So, Goedendag,' she said, 'you succeeded. The tower is secure. The civilians are safe. Thank you.'

'We don't do this for gratitude,' said Goedendag. 'Don your helmets, brothers. It's time to leave.'

'But–' called Kelra.

'Thank you, sister,' said Goedendag. 'We'll see ourselves out.'

THE FIRST DUTY

Josh Reynolds

'WHAT IS THE first duty, young Goetz?'

'To go where we are needed, *hochmeister*,' Hector Goetz had said promptly. Goetz was a young man, tall and broad in all the right places with the pale, fair features of the Talabheim aristocracy. His hair was shorn close to the scalp, as was proper for one of his station, and his wrists and shoulders were thick with muscle. It had been only three short weeks since he'd won his spurs in his final test – a bloody melee with a band of orcs in the hills near Talabheim.

'And what is the second?'

'To do what must be done!' Goetz had replied, crashing a fist against the embossed twin-tailed comet on his brightly polished cuirass.

And the *hochmeister* had smiled sadly. Goetz hadn't realised why at the time.

Now, however, he was beginning to understand.

Armour the colour of brass reflected the light of the burning mill as the horse reared, steel-shod hooves lashing out to connect with brutish skulls. A man howled as a sword sheared through his raised arm, sending both his blade and the hand that wielded it flying off into the smoke. Another warrior staggered as the sword whipped around to chop through its shield and into the skull beyond.

Hector Goetz grunted and ripped his sword free with a surge of muscle as his horse spun, bugling a challenge to the stallion charging to meet them. Goetz, eyes narrowed within his helm, set his horse into motion to meet this newest threat. The rider, a pale-skinned, spade-bearded

425

brute, gave a guttural cry as he swung his heavy, chopping blade wildly.

Goetz twisted to the side as the horses crashed against one another and swung his shield between himself and his opponent's weapon. As the blade *chunked* into the surface of the shield, Goetz shifted, pushing the sword away and his opponent off balance. His own blade met the bared surface of the man's neck in a spray of blood. The head toppled, jaws still champing. Goetz grabbed the reins and turned the horse.

With a rending crash, the mill wheel collapsed into the Talabec, taking part of the mill with it. His attention diverted, the young knight barely managed to avoid the stroke of the axe that was aimed at his hip.

Goetz threw himself from his saddle, crashing to the ground with a clatter. Rolling to his feet, he stumbled back as the axe chopped towards him.

It was a crude thing, battered and beaten into a rough approximation of shape. Despite its crudity it was still dangerous and Goetz bent backwards as it looped past his visor. Its wielder wore the stink of death like a cloak, and his grunt of effort as he regained his balance was bestial.

He swung the axe up again and brought it crashing down on Goetz's shield. The ill-treated blade shivered and splintered, and Goetz swept it aside without thought as he drove his sword point-first into the man's belly. The man folded up over the blade and dropped, screaming.

Goetz wrenched his weapon free and stepped back, fighting a surge of nausea as his opponent thrashed on the ground.

'Sir Hector, look out!'

Goetz ducked as a hammer pummelled the air inches away from the back of his skull. He reversed his blade and stabbed it back into his attacker. The man wailed and slid off the blade as Goetz turned. Breathing shallowly, he looked around. 'Thank you, Captain Hoffman,' he said.

'Think nothing of it, Sir Hector.' Dressed in the crimson and gold finery of an officer in the Talabecland militia, now smudged and fouled with soot, Captain Hoffman leaned on his sword and spat. 'All dead, curse the luck.'

'All–' Goetz pushed up his visor and looked around. Bodies lay scattered everywhere around the burning mill. 'No! No!' he said. Then, more quietly, 'Too late.' He stabbed his sword into the dirt to clean it. 'Again, too late.' He looked at the other man. 'Call your men together, Captain Hoffman. We need to put this fire out and check for–'

'Let it burn,' a rough voice interjected. Goetz turned. A man clad in the tanned leathers and rough pelts of a forester gestured towards the fire with his bloodstained hatchet. 'Let it burn. There won't be any survivors and no sense wasting the effort. Not when we could be putting it to better uses.'

'You don't know that!' Hoffman snarled, wiping sweat and soot off of his brow. He looked at Goetz. 'Sir Hector, we have to at least try!'

Goetz hesitated but then regretfully shook his head as he looked at the crumbling mill. 'No. No, Lothar is correct. Let it burn out.' He spat, trying to clear his mouth of the taste of smoke. 'They're all dead.'

Just like last time. Just like every time. Every person they had come to save, every person in every isolated mill and farmstead between the river and Volgen. 'It was just wishful thinking, I suppose.'

He forced himself to breathe and planted his sword point first into the ground. Prayer wasn't something he was normally comfortable with, being from the aristocracy. He knelt and bowed his head, murmuring a swift prayer to Myrmidia, the patron-goddess of the Order of the Blazing Sun. It seemed fitting that he ask the Goddess of Battle to take in the souls of those slain in such a manner. Six times he had done such, and this time made him feel no better than the first.

If anything, he felt worse.

A shadow fell over him, and he broke off and looked up at Lothar. Yellow, square teeth surfaced in a mocking grin from beneath the man's thick beard. 'Begging your pardon, sir knight, but when you're finished, there's doings afoot.'

Goetz rose stiffly, armour creaking. 'What is it?' he said.

'Something you ought to see,' the forester said, crooking a finger. 'Since you're here and all and in charge, so you are.'

Goetz sheathed his sword with a touch more force than was necessary and, squashing the flare of indignation that the man's impertinent tone had brought up, followed him. The *hochmeister* had warned him that the foresters were an unruly lot, and impatient with rank.

Not at all like the stiffly formal militiamen that had accompanied Goetz from Volgen. Captain Hoffman was a stickler for the rules and formalities that he likely had little enough opportunity to use in a town like Volgen. Goetz joined Lothar and the captain in examining the body of one of the men he'd killed.

'First time we've been able to catch the devils at their work,' Hoffman said. 'Too bad we didn't get them alive.'

'They'll talk all the same,' Lothar said, dropping easily to his haunches. The contorted body was well-illuminated by the light of the flames. He wore cast-off leathers and rags of chainmail that had proven more decorative than protective in the end. Lothar grunted and used the blade of his hatchet to rip open the man's filthy tunic. He grimaced at what was revealed and made a sign in the air.

'Witch's mark,' he said, looking up at Goetz. 'Sure as I'm alive.'

'A tattoo,' Hoffman said, slapping his leather gloves into his palm. 'A bit of peasant crudity. It proves nothing.'

'It proves what we've been saying is all,' Lothar said, cramming his helmet back on his head. 'Even a lackwit townie like you should be able to see that. These men are devil-spawn!'

'Insulting a superior officer?' Hoffman said, his eyes narrowing. 'A man can get the lash for that.'

'True. But who would you get to wield it?' Lothar said, grinning in an unfriendly fashion. The two men had been at each other's throats since they'd set out from Volgen. The foresters were nominally under the command of the local militia commander, but in reality they were completely autonomous. They functioned as scouts most of the time, but rarely responded when the Imperial Levy was called, unless it was a case like this. Most local authorities turned a blind eye – the foresters were far too useful, given that Talabecland was mostly forest and hills.

Regardless, it was a constant point of friction with Hoffman. 'There's no need to bother Sir Hector with your suspicions,' Hoffman said harshly, his face pinched and disapproving. 'Get your men back here.'

'Why?' Lothar snorted.

'Why, to bury the dead of course!' Hoffman said incredulously.

'A waste of time. The rest of them can't have gone far! Not if these–' he waved a hand at the dead men, '–were still here!'

'Far enough,' Goetz murmured, glancing over his shoulder and casting a glare at the dark stretch of forest that loomed just beyond the wide trade-bridge that connected the mill to the far shore. Running beneath it, the River Talabec marked the boundary of Talabecland.

The others had followed his gaze. Lothar unconsciously made a gesture that Goetz recognised as the sign of Taal. Goetz frowned. While the Empire had a state religion, the old faiths lingered here on the fringes. Being himself a worshipper of one of those faiths, Goetz said nothing. Hoffman, however, had no such compunctions.

'Taalist filth,' the militia commander said when he caught sight of the forester's gesture.

'No, they're the filth,' Lothar said, jerking a thumb at the body.

'Trust one to know another,' Hoffman spat. 'For all I know, you're in with these–'

'Enough,' Goetz interjected sharply. He'd been playing mediator between the two since they'd left Volgen and it was beginning to grate on his nerves. 'Enough. Hoffman is correct. It is our duty to see to the bodies.'

Lothar snorted insolently. 'Begging your pardon then, sir knight, and I'll gather my men.' Without waiting for a reply, Lothar stumped off. Hoffman grunted.

'The impertinence of the man.' He looked at Goetz. 'Pardon my familiarity, sir knight, but that man is a–'

'Yes. But good at his job, I'm told,' Goetz said. 'And these are no ordinary brigands, captain.'

'The foresters see devils in every shadow,' Hoffman said dismissively. He turned away and began bellowing orders to his men.

'Maybe,' Goetz said. He reached up and touched the stylised twin-tailed comet on his breastplate, a gesture he'd found comfort in since his days as a novice in the Order.

In truth, Goetz didn't feel much different now, despite winning his spurs. He was a Knight according to the *hochmeister* and according to the Order's laws, but he didn't feel like one. Not truly, not in the way he'd hoped. He wasn't really sure what he'd expected – a new sense of competence, perhaps. Wisdom, maybe. Instead, things seemed even more complex than when he'd been a novice, and him no more able to figure out the what and the where of it all.

'We go where we are needed and do what must be done,' he said to himself as he knelt beside the body, examining the man and the mark that Lothar had been so interested in. The mark wasn't a tattoo, despite Hoffman's assertions to the contrary. Instead it was a gouge in the flesh. A brand, and a fairly recent one. Ragged scratches in the flesh that seemed to undulate as Goetz looked at them closely. He blinked and looked away, unable to fully grasp the shape of it.

A Chaos mark, sure enough. Though of what variety he could not say. Nor, in truth, did he wish to know. That it was what it was, was enough for him. It defined his enemy.

He turned and looked at the river again. On the other side of it was Middenland. And the Drakwald.

A slight shudder ran through him as he contemplated the dark trees. As a breeze caught the distant branches, they seemed to reach for him.

'Sir Knight!'

Goetz looked up as Lothar hurried forward. The forester waved a hand. 'Come! We found a survivor!'

Goetz sprang to his feet as quickly as his armour would allow and hurried after the forester. Excitement hummed through him. They had never found a survivor before. Indeed, this was the first time they had even come to grips with any of the foe.

Hoffman hurried after him, face drawn. 'An evening for firsts,' he murmured.

'My thoughts exactly, captain.'

The survivor proved to be a woman. Middle-aged, with wild hair and blank features. Her hands and feet were bloody and she was covered in newly-blossomed bruises and black filth. She sat hunched on the ground, hands dangling over her knees, body pressed up against the rough wood of the outhouse.

'My men found her inside,' Lothar said as Goetz and Hoffman came up. 'She was hiding in the jakes. She's a bit ripe.'

Goetz looked down at the woman. Her eyes were unfocused and staring at nothing in particular. A stab of pity cut through him and he dropped to one knee. Carefully, he reached for her. Her scream, when it came, was unexpected, and he nearly fell in surprise.

The scream faded into whimpers as she huddled away from him and pressed her face to the wood. Her bloody fingers clawed at the outhouse and Goetz lunged for her. 'Help me!' he snapped. 'Grab her arms!'

Lothar and Hoffman started forward, but the woman gave a sobbing howl and flung herself into Goetz's arms. He rocked back, eyes wide. She clung to him with terrified strength and he rose awkwardly, one arm around her.

'I – what do we–' Goetz began.

'Give her a smack,' Lothar said harshly. 'It's the only way we'll get anything worthwhile out of her.'

'She's been through a great deal,' Hoffman said. 'A sympathetic hand might do better than the rude shake a forester's woman gets.'

Lothar glared at the other man, but nodded stiffly. Hoffman crouched beside the woman and began to murmur to her, softly stroking her hair. Just as Lothar began to grumble impatiently, one of his men signalled him.

'Lothar! Tracks!' Lothar looked at Goetz, who looked at Hoffman.

'I'll take her,' Hoffman said softly. Goetz gratefully peeled the woman off and turned her towards the other man. Then he followed Lothar, who was already hurrying towards his men. The forester who'd called them, a young man with coiling scars on both cheeks, squatted and tapped his fingertips against the ash-coated grass. 'Hoofprints, looks like. And feet.'

'Not big enough for horses,' Lothar muttered, dropping to his haunches. 'And something else. Shoes.'

'Shoes?'

'Home-made. Too small for a man, likely a woman.' He traced a mark and looked up at Goetz. 'See?'

'Yes?' Goetz said, though he didn't really. 'Meaning?'

Lothar looked at the other forester, then back at Goetz. 'Means more survivors than just her,' he said, jerking his chin at Hoffman and the woman. He locked eyes with Goetz. 'Means we might also have been wrong before.'

'You mean survivors from the other attacks?'

'I mean that this might not have been a pillaging expedition,' Lothar said flatly, clutching his medallion. The other foresters murmured and Goetz swallowed. 'We have to follow them.'

He looked back at the woman, and then the body of the man he'd killed. 'They were looking for her, weren't they?' he said.

'Most likely. If she broke away…' Lothar tapped the ground with his fingers. 'These hoof-prints, though, are a puzzlement.'

'Scrub ponies perhaps,' Hoffman said, striding up. The militia commander sniffed. 'Hardly expect bandits to be riding warhorses, now can we?' He looked at Goetz. 'My men are making the woman comfortable. If we can get her back to Volgen, perhaps–'

'Not horses of any stripe, I don't think,' Lothar interrupted, rising. 'Wrong shape.'

'Oh? And you're an expert on horseflesh then? Stolen many, have we?' Hoffman said.

'Enough to know these aren't horse-tracks,' Lothar said, glaring at the other man. His gaze swivelled to Goetz.

'What are they?' the knight said.

'Beast-kin.'

Hoffman snorted. 'Preposterous. They've never come this far south.'

'The tracks go over the river. Our missing folk went with them.'

Goetz looked at the trees on the opposite bank. The Drakwald wasn't simply a collection of trees, like the Great Forest. It was home to nightmares: men with the heads of beasts, witches and heretics. A prickle of latent childhood fear caressed his spine and he brushed it aside. 'Then we will go after them.'

'Sir Hector, I must protest,' Hoffman said. 'We are a Talabecland Levy. We'll be out of our jurisdiction!'

'Only if they catch us,' Lothar said.

'And if they do, I'll make sure you're the first up the gallows-stairs,' Hoffman said. 'We should return to Garndorf or Werder and send an official inquiry. The Middenlanders have experience with this sort of thing.'

'Daemons, you mean,' Lothar said, snickering.

Hoffman whirled on him. 'No. Organised bandit activity,' he said through gritted teeth. He looked back at Goetz. 'My men are not equipped for–'

'They have supplies and weapons. Good enough, I should think,' Lothar said.

'For your illiterate band of half-savages, possibly. But my men are soldiers,' Hoffman shot back.

'Under my command,' Goetz said quietly. 'As are the foresters.' The two men fell silent, looking at him. It was a tense moment, and not the first such. He looked at Lothar. 'Can you catch them?'

Lothar spat. 'Yes.'

'Then we go. Lothar, find that trail. If these raiders have captives, they're likely moving slow. Meaning we can catch them. And when we do…' Goetz clenched a fist. 'Middenland be damned.'

Lothar gave a snarl and Hoffman banged a fist against his breastplate. As the dark of the night wore into the fiery orange of morning the party moved across the Talabec.

The bridge was old and sturdy. Dwarf-work, it was said, with vast blocks of smooth stone bestriding the waters. There were several like it, the length of the Talabec and on the Stir. Goetz had always admired them, admired the craftsmanship that went into them. Part of him wished that he could have built bridges instead of learning the art of the blade. He thought perhaps bridge builders had happier lives, on the whole.

The river was deceptively calm as it flowed beneath the bridge. Goetz knew that it could spring from docile placidity to roaring viciousness in moments. The Talabec brought trade, but it also brought death.

Most thought that was a fair swap. Goetz wasn't sure, but then he wasn't a merchant. His father was, and a fine one, but a trade in trade had never been Goetz's fate.

They left the bridge behind and moved slowly into the trees, on foot. Hoffman's troops, all thirty of them, formed into two ranks, halberdiers and crossbowmen clad in cuirasses and greaves that clanked and clattered softly as they marched in disciplined formation. Lothar's foresters ranged ahead, fifteen shadowy shapes threading through the close-set trees like ghosts.

The foresters were hard to figure out. Goetz knew that they weren't truly soldiers, being more in the manner of thief-takers or road-wardens. It made them hard to trust. There was no guarantee that they would stay in a fight, rather than simply fading away. And he was down two men, to boot.

They had sent the woman back to Werder, the closest town, along with two of Hoffman's men. She'd ridden off on Goetz's horse, something which had brought a pang to Goetz, and he briefly wished he'd kept his mount. The order normally fought mounted, but in situations like these Knights were expected to fight on foot so as to be more effective. Too, a lone man on a horse was easy to pick off. The flesh between Goetz's shoulder blades crawled at the thought.

He didn't fear death, as such. But he was afraid of dying badly. Of being unable to fight back against his death. Arrows were a bad way to die. Then, in his darker moments, he thought that perhaps there was no good way to die, regardless of what the Order taught.

The pace was slow, but steady. Occasionally one of the foresters would drift back to report, but not often. Goetz took the lead, mindful of the honour of the Order. The Drakwald didn't seem to care about either his honour or the men he was in charge of, however.

Overgrown roots rose like the humps of sea-serpents through the dark soil and the trees became bloated and massive the further away from the farm they drew. Unconsciously, the militia clustered together, their previously pristine order decaying into a stumbling mass of men. Nervous murmurs rippled through the ranks as the sunlight was strangled to the merest drizzle by the thick branches that spread overhead.

Hoffman stilled his men with a look. Goetz stopped and turned. The men were sweating and listless, as if the trees were sucking the life out of them. Some of that was exhaustion – the militia wasn't used to being pushed this hard, having mostly performed only garrison duties – the rest was what? Fear? Nervousness, maybe.

The Drakwald had a well-deserved reputation, even outside the borders of Middenland. It had inspired more than one nightmare in the children of Talabheim. Why should the children of Volgen, living far closer as they did, be any different? Birds croaked and cawed to each other in the trees, and several times Goetz had caught himself wondering whether or not those cries meant something other than the obvious. He forced himself to release the hilt of his sword as he caught the looks he was getting.

'No need to be nervous, Sir Hector,' Hoffman murmured.

Goetz glanced at him. 'Knights do not get nervous,' he said stiffly. 'We merely anticipate the worst.'

Hoffman smiled. 'You're a bit young to be a knight, if you'll pardon the familiarity.'

Goetz chuckled. 'My father saw to it that I started my training early. My brother… disappointed his expectations, and the honour of the family had to be considered.' Goetz fell silent, realising that he'd said more than he intended.

His brother Caspar had been pledged to the Order, but had refused the honour in the most vociferous terms possible. Caspar had been headstrong and single-minded, much like their father, and his obsessions had taken precedence over familial obligations.

'Goetz is not a common Talabecland name,' Hoffman said, changing the subject.

'My family came from Solland originally,' Goetz said, rubbing the comet on his cuirass. 'Before the – ah.' He made a gesture.

'Yes,' Hoffman said. Solland's sad fate was well known, and many great families of Talabecland, Ostermark and Wissenland could trace their origins to that doomed province, their ancestors having fled the orcish invasion that ravaged the province beyond recovery.

Mention of Solland brought Caspar to the forefront of Goetz's thoughts once more. Even as a child, his older brother had been obsessed with the history of Solland, even going so far as to joining a hare-brained expedition to find the lost Solland Crown, despite his father's protests. Caspar and his expedition had vanished in the maelstrom of the recent northern invasion. Goetz shook his head, banishing the dark thoughts.

'I wanted to be an artisan. Or a scribe,' Goetz said. Hoffman raised his eyebrows and Goetz nodded at the unspoken question. 'Oh yes. I excelled in the arts of engineering. My tutors saw a great future for me, and the Order's engineers agreed, though the exact nature of my future projects differed. Instead of bridges and walls, I'll now construct devices to demolish such structures.' The last bit was said sadly. Goetz shook himself. 'Funny how things work out, in the end.'

'Speaking of funny,' Hoffman said and leaned close. 'I haven't seen those damned foresters in awhile.'

'Then you weren't looking close enough,' Lothar grunted, slipping out from between the trees. He whipped off his helmet and ran a hand through his hair.

'Have you found the trail?' Goetz said, fighting to keep the eagerness out of his voice. 'Have you found them?'

'In and out,' Lothar said. 'Comes and goes. The forest – bah. They've got them some woodcraft, sure enough.'

'Better than yours?'

Lothar grinned. 'No one is better than us.'

'Then why haven't you found them yet?' Hoffman snapped. 'They can't have gone far, and we've been at this for hours! If anyone noticed us coming over the river–'

'Hunts like this can take days,' Lothar said mildly. His eyes hardened. 'And the more noise you make, the harder it is, so it is.'

'You're blaming me?' Hoffman said incredulously.

'I – hsst.' Lothar raised a hand. He cocked his head.

'What?' Goetz said, looking at Hoffman.

'Hear that?' Lothar said, turning. He made a sound like a bird call. It was answered from deeper within the trees. Goetz's nape prickled. He heard it now. It was a bone-deep sensation, echoing from everywhere and nowhere. He had felt it before, but dismissed it as the background noise of the forest, or perhaps the echo of the river.

'What is that?' Hoffman said.

'I don't know,' Lothar said. He looked at Goetz. 'We've been hearing it off and on since we came into the woods.' His face was grim.

'And you're just thinking now to inform us?' Hoffman spat. 'Have you been leading us in circles all of this time?' He swung an arm out. 'My men are exhausted. They've been marching all day!' Hoffman frowned. 'Or is that what you intended?'

'What are you accusing me of?' Lothar said, his eyes narrowing dangerously.

'I've heard the stories of what the Taalists got up to before the light of Sigmar was brought to these regions. Worse than the worshippers of the Wolf-God! Burn any men alive in wooden cages lately?' Hoffman said, fingering the pommel of his sword.

'No. Are you volunteering?' Lothar said, clutching his medallion.

'You'd like that, wouldn't you, you savage?' Hoffman said. 'I know what you foresters get up to, you know. You're half-bandit yourselves, helping yourself to the odd merchant's goods! Oh yes, I have those reports memorised!'

Goetz blinked and looked at Lothar. The forester shifted uncomfortably. Then, he lunged forward, stabbing a finger into Hoffman's polished breastplate. 'And if you tight-fisted city-rats bothered to pay us for spilling our blood to keep you safe–'

'Not doing a good job of that lately,' one of the nearby militiamen barked. A forester turned and drove a fist across the speaker's jaw, dropping him like a bag of rocks. Another trooper came to his comrade's aid and several foresters drifted out of the trees, faces set.

Hoffman's knuckles were white on his sword-hilt. 'Admit it! You've been leading us in circles! What is it? Trying to give your comrades time to get away?' he bellowed in his best parade-ground voice. 'I bet they didn't even come into the Drakwald! Just more stories, like your witch-marks and hoof-prints!' Behind him, crossbows were hastily readied by the militiamen as several foresters surreptitiously readied their bows.

'Comrades?' Lothar roared. 'You think we'd have any dealings with witches or beastmen?'

'You knew an awful lot about those marks–' Hoffman began. Lothar growled and snatched his hatchet out of his belt even as Hoffman made to pull his sword.

'Enough!' Goetz shouted, even as he silently winced at the way his voice cracked. He drew his sword and planted it in the ground, point-first. 'Enough.'

All eyes turned towards him. He took a breath and thought of building bridges, even if they were only metaphorical. 'We are all on the same side here. We are all servants of the Empire, all soldiers in the Emperor's service.' He let his gaze sweep across the gathered men. 'If any of you wish it to be otherwise, you may leave. Otherwise you will stop this foolishness.'

Lothar lowered his hatchet and stepped back. 'I'll not serve with this man. Not a moment longer,' he grunted, gesturing to Hoffman. 'We are loyal soldiers, but we cannot do our job with these plodders following us!'

'Perhaps there's another way of going about this,' Goetz said, raising a hand and stretching it between them before Hoffman could reply. 'We could set up a temporary camp and let your foresters find our opponents… drive them towards us perhaps? Or failing that, find them and report back to us?'

Lothar scrubbed his chin. 'Could work.'

Goetz nodded. 'We'll set up here then.' The forester grunted and then headed back into the woods without a backwards glance.

'Nicely done,' Hoffman said, after a moment.

'Yes,' Goetz said. He looked around at the trees, feeling slightly repulsed. He had never felt that way about a forest before. He was sweating beneath his armour, despite the oncoming chill of night. The sun was setting, and shadows were bunching thickly beneath the trees. 'Would you have killed him?' he said, after a moment.

'Better to ask him whether he would have killed me, I think,' Hoffman replied grudgingly. 'The foresters aren't to be trusted, Sir Hector. They are thieves, poachers and worse.'

'Then why sanction them?'

'Set a thief to catch a thief,' Hoffman said, shrugging. 'This wouldn't be the first time that a group of them has decided to go over the fence.' Around them, the militia began setting up a temporary camp, moving with practiced precision.

'You believe this is the case now?' Goetz said softly.

Hoffman looked at him. 'I know that Lothar and his men have never respected Imperial authority. And I know that Lothar himself used to rob coaches on the Emperor's Road.'

Goetz shook his head. 'I didn't know that.'

'There are a lot of things you don't know, sir,' Hoffman said, turning away. 'Get those defensive hedges up!' he shouted as two of his men unrolled a length of flat leather pierced with wooden stakes that pointed outward. The hedge hung at chest height around the circumference of the camp, and was nearly invisible to the eye of anyone creeping up on them. That was the thought anyway. Goetz examined the hedges with an engineer's eye, finding the design to be brutally simplistic. He had no doubts as to their effectiveness, however.

'Steichen! Get a fire going!' Hoffman continued, jabbing a finger at the man in question. He turned to Goetz. 'A few minutes, and we'll be ready for whatever troubles those damnable foresters are bringing down on our heads. Whenever they do so. If they do so.'

'Yes.' Goetz looked around. 'Perhaps you were right, Captain. Perhaps we shouldn't have attempted this.' He sighed. 'I'll be honest with you… I'm a bit new to this sort of thing.'

Hoffman smiled and his features softened. 'You're doing fine, Sir Hector. Even that ill-mannered brute Lothar believes so, I'd wager. And, if I might be frank, better a commander who fears he knows nothing than one who thinks he knows everything.' Hoffman sighed. 'Not what I would have picked for a first duty though, I must say.'

'We of the Order go where we are needed, Captain.'

'True enough, sir. True enough.' Hoffman sniffed. 'And now we're needed here.'

For a moment, Goetz wondered whether or not that was true. Then, he wondered whether that was what the future held for him now that he had won his spurs. Was this merely the first out of an unending series of duties, going from horror to horror, upholding the honour of the Order of the Blazing Sun until, at last, he met an enemy that he could not beat? He pushed aside that grim thought and tried to concentrate on his surroundings. 'Go where needed, do what must be done,' he said to himself.

The night wore on, and the sound seemed to grow with it, rising in tempo. Mixed in with the vast beat was the deep thudding of distant drums. Goetz paced the line like a tiger in a cage, his nerves screaming warnings that his brain fought to ignore. He heard the men on picket duty snap at one another in irritation, and Hoffman's mood grew fouler.

It was the drums that were doing it. Why hadn't Lothar returned yet? Surely it was easy enough to find where the noise was emanating from. Goetz busied himself with his sword, swiping a whetstone across the length of the blade.

As he honed the edge of his sword, he wondered why the men – no, the *creatures* – they were pursuing had even come into Talabecland. A matter of chance? Or something else?

What if Hoffman was right? The whetstone skittered to a stop. Goetz closed his eyes. What if the creatures had come because they were invited? Invited by the very men he had sent out to find them?

The scream, when it came, was brief. Goetz shot to his feet. A sentry staggered back into the defensive line, clutching at the thin shape that protruded from his throat. Before Goetz's horrified eyes, he collapsed over the line, gurgling.

A moment later, arrows cut the air with a steady *rattle-hiss*, piercing the gloom of the trees. Men fell screaming, and Goetz spun, his sword flashing as it split an arrow into splinters. Another struck his pauldron, rocking him.

'That devil Lothar has betrayed us!' Hoffman howled as men sprouted feathered shafts and died. Goetz swung around, trying to spot their attackers. It didn't make sense! Was Hoffman right?

A militiaman screamed as one of his fellows put a crossbow bolt into his back by accident. Halberds flashed as men turned on one another, trapped as they were by their own defensive perimeter. Goetz watched in shock as his men began to tear one another apart. Shaking himself, he turned, only to come face to face with a daemon's mask.

The soldier shrieked like a bird of prey and lunged for the knight, driving a dagger towards his face. Goetz reacted on instinct, swatting the blade aside with the flat of his sword and then slashing the edge across the man's belly as he stumbled, off-balance.

'No! Sigmar's Oath, no!' he said, as the militiaman fell, his shrieks becoming animal whines of pain. He writhed on the ground, trying to hold his belly together and spat vile oaths at Goetz, each one striking him like the blow of a hammer. Pale and shaken, he stumbled back, unable to look at the dying man.

'Traitors,' Goetz murmured. He had heard the stories and the whispered rumours, but he'd never expected to face it himself. Lothar had been right. He'd been right all along. Goetz looked for Hoffman. He had to get the men under control. To retreat. They could come back later, with more men. He caught sight of Hoffman, defending himself from a screaming militiaman. Goetz swung past him and drove his blade into the man's shoulder, dropping him.

'Hoffman! We need to–' he began. The sword danced across the buckles of his breastplate, scoring the armour and driving a spike of pain into his side. Goetz's arm swung down, trapping the blade. He jerked forward, ripping the weapon out of its owner's hands and turned, letting it fall. His eye widened. 'Captain?' he said.

Otto Hoffman didn't answer, instead lunging for the knight, his fist cracking against the latter's breastplate. Goetz staggered. Another blow caused him to stumble back. Hoffman snatched up his sword and then came again, lunging smoothly. Goetz parried the blow, stunned by the inhuman strength the militia commander displayed.

'Hoffman! Captain! What are you doing?'

'Fool,' Hoffman grunted, baring his teeth. 'You walked right into it, didn't you?'

Goetz didn't bother to reply. Instead he lashed out with a foot and kicked the man in the knee. Hoffman wobbled, and Goetz brought his sword down on the man's neck. Blood spurted, and Hoffman squealed. His sword licked out as he clamped a hand onto the gouting wound. Goetz jerked back as the sword-point carved a line across his throat-guard. The sword in the militia commander's hand darted out again and again, snake-swift. Goetz parried desperately as Hoffman shuffled in pursuit.

'Die,' Hoffman gurgled.

'You first,' someone called out. A bow string twanged and Hoffman froze as an arrow sprouted from between his eyes. He croaked, the sword falling from his fingers. Then he toppled. Goetz leaned on his sword, breathing heavily.

'Lothar?' he said, blinking sweat out of his eyes.

'I never liked him much,' the forester said, stalking out of the trees. 'Now I know why.' He paused to spit on Hoffman's body, then looked at Goetz. 'You fought well, sir knight.'

'What – what–'

'We ambushed the ambushers. Came up behind them and cut their throats,' Lothar said, jerking a thumb across his throat. He gestured to Hoffman. 'Didn't expect that, though.'

'Expect what?'

'This,' Lothar said, dropping to his haunches and grabbing Hoffman's head. He pulled the dead man's gorget aside and exposed the eerily familiar brand on his flesh. He bared his teeth in a vicious grin. 'It was a trap.'

'For who?' Goetz said.

'You. Us. Anybody.' Lothar let Hoffman's body flop back down and stood. 'Looks like about half of them were in on it with Hoffman. Likely intended to capture or kill the other half. And you.'

'Why?'

'Something's going on out here, in the deep woods. Hear the drums?'

'Yes,' Goetz said absently, staring down out the body.

'Happens sometimes, when the moons are up and fat. Drums deep in the trees, and hoofmarks in the loam.' Lothar spat. 'Didn't realise it until I saw them back at the mill. Only one reason the twisted folk take ours...'

'Sacrifices,' Goetz said. 'Sigmar's Hammer. He said something about a celebration.' He looked at Lothar. 'Where are they?'

'Waiting for these to join them,' Lothar said, kicking the body. 'And for them in the forest who set off the ambush.' He shook his head. 'Wondered why them in the city were slow about going for help.'

Goetz grimaced. 'They're in the town. A cult... Myrmidia preserve them.'

'Not many, likely. Volgen isn't that big. Those here in the forest worry me more,' the forester said. 'Those and them they took.' He looked at Goetz. 'What are your orders, sir knight?'

Goetz hesitated. Of the thirty men in the militia, only eight or so remained standing. And they looked as out of sorts as he felt. Confused, wounded and on the verge of running for safety. This wasn't their land, and the temptation to leave was likely great. He licked his lips. 'If we headed back,' he said, not quite asking.

'Then whatever them drums mean will be done and over, and them as sounding them will be gone.'

Goetz closed his eyes. The faces of the dead swam up out of his memories to meet him. He thought of the people they'd been unable to save, and the one they had, though likely too late for her own mind. His eyes opened. 'We go where we are needed and we do what we must.'

Lothar nodded brusquely. He shouted orders to his men as Goetz faced the remaining members of the militia. They watched him warily. 'You can't make us do this,' one said. 'You can't.'

'Twenty-four men stand better odds than sixteen,' Goetz said. He used his sword to prod a body. 'They led you into a slaughter. Would you have others suffer the same fate?' he said gently. He touched the comet on his cuirass. 'We go where we are needed,' he said, trying to capture the *hochmeister*'s cadence.

None of them looked at him. He sighed. 'I'm going. Come with us or not.' He started towards the foresters. He did not turn around when he heard the militiamen fall in behind him.

They moved swiftly through the forest, following the pounding sound. It rose and fell, and the ache in Goetz's head grew. It was spiritually painful, like a soreness in his soul. It pulsed like a blister or a bad tooth, growing worse the closer they got to wherever they were going.

He had fallen into a rhythm when Lothar suddenly broke it with a hard jerk on his arm. 'Stop!' the forester hissed. He made a sharp motion and the men sank to the ground. He pulled Goetz with him as he crawled forward through the heavy brush towards a strange, flickering brightness that seemed to seep between the trees.

Below them, at the bottom of a slope, beasts danced beneath the dark pines, pawing the soil around a crackling fire and braying out abominable hymns. Mingled amongst the brute forms of the beasts were the smaller shapes of men and women. All were naked, save for unpleasant sigils daubed onto their flesh by means of primitive dyes and paints.

The shriek of crude pipes slithered beneath the trees, their rhythms carrying the gathered throng into berserk ecstasy as the dance sped up.

The flames curled higher, turning an unhealthy hue, casting a weird light over the proceedings as man and beast engaged in unholy practices. As vile as it was, however, Goetz couldn't look away from the foul spectacle, no matter how much he might wish to.

What drew his eye, however, was something infinitely worse than the dancers. Something fouler even than the worst thing he could have expected.

'Taal,' Lothar whispered, his voice hoarse and his eyes wide. 'What is it?'

'Something that doesn't belong here,' Goetz said, running his fingers across the double-tailed comet embossed on his breastplate. And it was. A vast scar in the earth near the bonfire, it was like a scab of blackened dirt. Whatever it was, it had pushed aside trees and rocks in its haste to reach the surface and now it sat like a pustule ready to burst. There was a stink about it, worse than anything Goetz had smelled before, even in a greenskin camp. And from its pearly surface came the aching hum that had plagued them all since they'd entered the forest.

As he and the forester watched, a burly creature with a leprous stag's head shoved a squalling man into the milky surface of the foul bubble. He sank in with a shriek, his struggles seemingly pulling him deeper. A moan arose from the huddled group of victims, and snarling beastmen reached in among them to find the next sacrifice.

Lothar half-rose, a curse on his lips. Goetz grabbed his arm. 'No. Get your men into position.' Lothar stared at him incredulously. Goetz licked his lips and looked back at the fire. It seemed to play tricks on his eyes, showing him first this many gathered around it, then fewer. He tasted bile in the back of his throat. He spat and continued. 'There are too many of them. More than twice our number. Your foresters will soften them up. How quickly can your men get into position?' he asked.

'Quick enough,' Lothar said. He patted his bow. 'What will you do?'

'A quick charge might be enough to scatter them. At least long enough for us to save the prisoners.'

'If it's not?'

Goetz swallowed. 'Then run. As fast and as far as you can.'

Lothar nodded and clapped a hand to Goetz's shoulder. Then he crawled back towards his men. Goetz waited, listening to the dim crackle of the fire and trying to ignore the throb of the thing in the clearing. He did not look at it, or dwell upon it.

He knew little of the things of Chaos, but he knew enough. It would have to be fire. That was the only way to be sure.

Behind him, he heard the trill of a bird. Seconds later, the air was heavy with the hiss of arrows and crossbow bolts. Down below, things screamed in pain. With a shout, Goetz rose to his feet and charged down the slope.

He met a thin creature coming the opposite way, its goatish face twisted in an almost comic expression of shock. Goetz didn't stop, instead letting his sword take the thing in the neck. Its head flopped free as he landed in the clearing. For a moment, he stood alone as the shock of the sudden barrage of arrows wore off. From behind him, he heard a shout of 'Talabecland!' and then he heard nothing but the clash of steel.

The battle was a confused mess of darting shapes and screaming voices. Goetz blundered towards the fire, sweeping his sword out with instinctive skill. He lopped off an offending sword-hand and kicked something with too many limbs away. As screaming faces drew too close, the arrows of the foresters swept them aside.

Goetz ducked and grabbed up a burning brand from the bonfire and turned towards the pestilent mass. It had to be fire. He charged forward, swinging the brand in preparation to throw it.

Something struck him across the back, nearly knocking him into the fire and slapping the air from his lungs. Flat on his belly, Goetz tried to breathe. He coughed as a raw, animal scent invaded the confines of his helmet. His eyes opened, and he looked up into a face out of nightmare.

The beastman was an ugly thing, all muscle and fang and claw. Piece-meal armoured plates strung together with twine and less savoury things clung to its bulky frame, less protection than decoration. Stag-horns curled up from its flat skull and back in on themselves. Dark eyes glared balefully at him from beneath heavy brows, and snaggle teeth snapped together in a deer's mouth, its foul breath misting in the cold air as it grunted querulously. Using his sword as a crutch, Goetz levered himself to his knees and stifled a groan. His body felt like a bag of broken sticks.

He shook his head, trying to clear it. He could hear the gentle rumble of the river in the distance, somewhere past the crooked, close-set pines of the forest. The beastman pawed the ground and snorted. Some of them, it was said, could speak. This one showed no such inclination. Instead, it lunged clumsily, swinging its crude axe towards Goetz.

Still on one knee, Goetz guided the blow aside with a twist of his wrist, and countered with his own weak thrust. The beastman stumbled back with an annoyed bleat as his sword sliced a patch of rusty mail from its cuirass. It was larger than the others, larger than Goetz himself by more inches than he cared to consider. Its axe was so much hammered scrap, but no less dangerous for that. It was strong too. Muscles like smooth stones moved under its porous, hairy hide as it swung the blade up again and brought it down towards Goetz's head. He caught the blow on his sword and grunted at the weight. Equal parts adrenaline and terror helped him surge to his feet, shoving the creature back. Weapons locked, they strained against one another. Goetz blinked as the weird runes scratched into the creature's axe-blade seemed to squirm beneath his gaze. Its smell, like a slaughterhouse on a hot day, bit into his sinuses and made it hard to breath. Goetz kicked out, catching the creature's knee. It howled and staggered, and they broke apart.

Steady on his feet now, Goetz stepped back, raising his sword. The beastman clutched its weapon in both hands and gave a throaty snarl. Teeth bared, it bulled towards him. Despite his guard, the edge of the axe skidded across Goetz's breastplate, dislodging the ornaments of his order and the ribbons of purity he wore in order to announce his status as a novice of the Order of the Blazing Sun. Sparks flew as crude iron met Imperial steel, and Goetz found himself momentarily off balance. The beastman was quick to capitalise. It crashed against him, clawed hand scrabbling at his helm, trying to shove his head back to expose his throat even as it flailed at him awkwardly with its axe.

Smashing the hilt of his sword against its skull, Goetz thrust his forearm against its throat and forced the snapping jaws away from him. They fell, locked together, and rolled across the ground, struggling. Goetz lost hold of his sword, but managed to snatch his dagger from his belt. He drove it into the beastman's side, angling the blade up, aiming for the heart, his old fencing teacher's admonitions ringing in his mind. The beastman squealed in pain and clawed at him. He closed his eyes and forced the blade in deeper, ignoring the crunch of bone and the hot wet foulness that gushed suddenly over his gauntlet.

The creature's struggles grew weaker and weaker until they stopped completely. It expired with a whimper, its limbs flopping down with a relieving finality. Breathing heavily, Goetz pushed the dead weight off of himself and stared up at the stars dancing between the talon-like branches of the pines. The sky seemed to spin.

Grimacing, he climbed to his feet and snatched up his fallen brand. Staggering, he moved towards the mass, which seemed to quiver at his approach. The stink grew heavier, almost solid. He caught a glimpse of bones scattered around it, and in the light of the fire he though he saw something floating within. Something that turned in its bloated womb to look at him with eyes like open wounds.

Deep in the woods, something was being born. Something horrible and beautiful. A whisper of sound caressed his ears, and a lovely voice spoke to him, making promises and predictions. A sweet smell, like sugar on ice tickled his nose, and he hesitated.

What had he been doing? What–

'Sir knight!' Lothar roared, lunging past him with his hatchet. The forester struck the thing with the weapon and the hum screamed forth, bringing blood to Goetz's ears and nose and he bit into his tongue. Screams rose from behind him, but he ignored them, ignored Lothar, ignored it all and concentrated on shoving the burning brand into the sticky foulness. The flames caught quickly and he fell back, coughing as the hum rose to a shrill shrieking whine that seemed to shake the entire clearing.

The promises were gone, swept away by the begging, the pleading notes that sank insidiously into his brain. He slashed at the quivering burning mass with berserk abandon, ignoring the ichors that splashed him and ate into his armour. Ignoring the shrieks that tore at his soul.

The whine faded as he turned away and fell to his knees, leaning on his sword. Goetz looked tiredly at the surviving captives, who squatted in a huddle nearby. They all looked unharmed, save for exhaustion and fear.

'You're safe,' he croaked. 'We've come to take you home. Lothar, get–' He turned, spotting Lothar's body lying nearby, his sightless eyes locked on the stars above. Goetz paused, but only for a moment. He pushed himself to his feet and began to rasp orders to his surviving troops.

They would burn the dead. Better than interring them in the foul earth of this place. As he watched his men get to work, Goetz sat wearily on a charred stump. He finally understood why the *hochmeister* had smiled so sadly that day. There were some bridges that needed burning and some walls that needed shattering, but the cost of doing so was always going to be high.

'We go where we are needed. We do what must be done,' Goetz whispered, as he watched bodies get thrown on the pyre and thought of bridges, and the men who built them.

WARHAMMER®

GRAIL KNIGHT

Anthony Reynolds

I

TWILIGHT DEEPENED, SLOWLY giving way to dusk. As the sun slipped over the western horizon, its last rays reflected off Calard of Garamont's armour. Then it was gone, and darkness descended over the land.

The ground was rough and overgrown, and a creeping mist hung low over the land. Patches of snow resisted the encroachment of spring, yet blooming wildflowers spoke of its imminent arrival. There were no roads in this wilderness, and Calard's progress was slow. Ten miles behind him the rolling landscape gave way to the verdant pastures and farmlands of Quenelles, but here on the borders, the land was left untouched by human hand. The early ancestors of the Bretonnians had learnt that lesson well in centuries past.

Calard guided his armoured warhorse up a steep ridge, picking a path through the heather and scratching gorse. The sides dropped off sharply, and the sheer slopes were strewn with rocks before disappearing into mist.

His hair was long and unkempt and his cheeks unshaven, yet he radiated an undeniable nobility, and his battle-worn appearance demanded respect. His right hand rested on the pommel of the ornate sword at his hip, a priceless family heirloom said to have been blessed by the Lady herself. A second, much larger sword was strapped across his back. It was a practical blade, heavy and devoid of ornamentation, and was quite capable of cutting a man in half with a single blow.

At the peak of the hill, Calard reined in his dappled grey destrier, staring to the east. From his vantage atop the ridge, the land spread out before him like a map.

His gaze was drawn to the vast tract of primal forest dominating the view, now less than a mile distant. It extended before him like an endless dark ocean, its fathomless depths harbouring untold secrets and hidden dangers. Even this far off he could feel the power of the forest, a strange and ethereal miasma that made the hairs on the back of his neck stand on end.

This was the Forest of Loren, a place of nightmare and dream, magic and mystery.

Its densely wooded edge resembled the soaring wall of some grand arboreal fortress, extending north and south as far as the eye could see. No tree strayed beyond its stark border, not even the tiniest sapling, as if an invisible force held it at bay. He knew that eventually the forest gave way to the foothills of the Grey Mountains, but from here it looked as though it went on forever. Low cloud obscured the highest treetops, and the canopy disappeared into haze only a few miles in.

Impenetrable, dark and heady with ancient magic, the Forest of Loren had long resonated in the hearts and minds of every son and daughter of Bretonnia. From childhood they were raised on stories of the fabled realm, tales of capricious beings of inhuman beauty and trees that came to life, of mischievous trickster spirits and malicious forest creatures that ensnared the unwary. On any given night one could hear the stories of the fey being told in hushed tones across Bretonnia, from the campfires of the lowliest peasants, to the grand halls of the king himself.

Few dared breach the borders of the ancient forest, and of those that did, fewer still returned. Those that managed to find their way out were more often than not discovered wandering its edges come dawn, babbling incoherently, their sanity shredded.

Indeed, if even a fraction of the tales surrounding these wildwoods were true then it was a place to be approached only with great caution.

Nevertheless, Calard felt no fear, for it was the will of the Lady, the patron goddess of Bretonnia, that he was here.

The first stars were appearing, like tiny pinpricks in the roof of the world. Brightest of all was the evening star, hanging low in the eastern sky above the forest. Known as the Lady's Grace, it was the first star to appear and the last to depart come morning.

'As you lead me, Lady, so shall I follow.'

For a moment longer Calard lingered atop the rocky bluff, breathing in the full spectacle before him. He could see a slender pinnacle of stone on the threshold. The evening star blinked above it, like a beacon.

'Forward, Galibor,' he said, urging his steed with a gentle kick. He rode down the ridge, towards the guiding evening star and the looming Forest of Loren.

* * *

TWENTY FEET HIGH and carved with elegant, spiralling runes, the waystone marked the very edge of the forest. Ivy clung to its smooth surface, and Calard felt a strange tingling sensation on his skin in its presence.

Galibor stamped the ground, nostrils flaring. Calard could feel the warhorse's powerful muscles tensing, and he gripped the reins firmly.

Calard had ridden the destrier's grandsire, Gringolet, as a young knight errant, and so knew the horse's pedigree. The warhorse was feisty and bellicose in nature, and though she had only recently come into his possession, he had been assured that she was fearless in battle. He had no reason to doubt this, and knew that it was unusual for the destrier to display such unease as she now did.

'Be calm, brave one,' he said, stroking its neck.

The warhorse relaxed under his trained hands, though he could still feel her agitation. Indeed, he felt a measure of it himself.

As a boy, Calard had been taught never to stare directly at a deer or boar when hunting, for the animal would instinctively feel a hunter's gaze upon it. Calard felt that same odd sensation of being watched now, a crawling feeling in the back of his mind. He felt vulnerable, like prey locked in the sights of some unseen predator.

Tearing his gaze away from the waystone, he scanned the treeline. Shadows lurked within, but he could see no threat. Mist coiled from the gloom, insubstantial tendrils reaching out towards him. It wound around the legs of his destrier, which pawed the ground again, snorting.

'There's nothing there,' said Calard, as much to convince himself as his horse.

He dismounted, and took a few steps towards the waystone. Mighty oaks towered over him, their thick branches straining to breach whatever force held them at bay. It was cold in the shadow of the forest; an icy chill seemed to radiate up from the dark soil underfoot. A vague feeling of menace pulsed from within the forest depths, as if it resented his proximity to its border. Since he was a boy he had dreamed of the day when he would see the fabled realm, but standing now in its presence as night drew in, he wondered if his desire had been a foolish one.

The previous night he had been a guest in the halls of Lord Eldecar of Toucon, an elderly nobleman of Quenelles, and a feast had been laid on in his honour. His quest precluded him from lingering though, and the entire hall had fallen silent when Calard had spoken his intention.

'If I have caused offence, it was unintentional, and I apologise,' Calard had said, unsure if he had broken some local protocol.

Eldecar had waved away his apology, but his eyebrows were knotted in concern.

'No, of course not,' Eldecar had said, finally breaking the awkward silence, 'but you do know, sir knight, that it is the eve of the vernal tide?'

Calard had frowned and shrugged.

'You have not lived your life in the shadow of the forest, so can be forgiven for not understanding,' said Eldecar. 'Even in Bastonne, you must have heard tell of the wild hunt?'

'When the barriers to the otherworld fall, and the faerie court rides across the night sky? Surely that is merely superstition?'

Eldecar's expression remained grim.

'As old as I am, I would cut down any man that called me coward,' said Eldecar, 'and yet I would not dare venture out of doors after nightfall on the Spring Equinox. Nor would any sane man of Quenelles.'

'It is by the Lady's will that I must go,' said Calard. 'My faith shall be my shield against any fey witchery.'

'Then I shall pray for your soul, Calard of Garamont.'

The words came back to Calard now as he stood at the edge of the forest, and an involuntary shiver passed up his spine.

'Superstitions, nothing more.'

Walking towards the slender stone marker, he drew the Sword of Garamont. Reversing his grip on the ancient weapon, he plunged its blade into the moist earth. Dropping to one knee, he pressed his forehead against the fleur-de-lys hilt of his blessed sword.

'You have called, my Lady, and I have answered,' he said. 'Grant me the vision to know what it is you would have me do, and I shall gladly do it.'

Falling silent, Calard remained motionless, eyes closed in prayer. As his breathing evened out and deepened, he felt a profound sense of peace descend over him. All his concerns and doubts washed away.

It was not long before he felt a presence nearby. Opening his eyes, his saw a majestic stag at the very edge of the forest, watching him. It was huge, larger even than Galibor, and its branching antlers were easily ten feet from tip to tip. Its thick winter coat shone, ghost-like amidst the shadows of the forest.

Never had Calard seen such a regal creature, and he scarce dared to breathe, unsure if it was real or imagined.

With unhurried movements it walked into the forest. About ten paces in it stopped and turned to stare back at him. Its intent was clear; it wanted him to follow.

Was this the Lady's will, or some trick of the forest, attempting to lure him within its borders?

Not for the first time Calard felt the desire to ride from this place, to join the king and face the undead legions of Mousillon that were marching, even now, against his homeland. Surely that was where he belonged?

He shook his head to throw off these doubts. No, the Lady had brought him here for a reason, and he was honour bound to see that through to the end.

Rising, he sheathed his sword and took the reins of his steed. Galibor did not resist as he led her towards the edge of the forest, though he could feel her trembling. He paused at the tree-line. The stag continued to look back towards him, waiting.

'Blessed Lady, protect your servant,' he said, and entered the forest.

II

A SHIVER THAT had nothing to do with the cold passed through Calard as he crossed the threshold of Athel Loren. The air felt instantly different, clear and crisp like a mid-winter morning, and the temperature dropped markedly. The biting chill filled his lungs, bringing with it the rich scent of the forest – a heady mix of soil, rain, rotting leaves and other less identifiable but not unpleasant aromas. His breath fogged the air. A low mist coiled around the twisted roots of the trees.

Movement flickered on the periphery of Calard's vision, and unseen things rustled in the undergrowth. He heard fluttering and chattering in the boughs overhead, and a tumble of twigs, dead foliage and disturbed snow fell around him, but he was not quick enough to locate the source.

Massive oaks reared up, their trunks gnarled and old, their limbs heavy with lichen. Stars flickered in and out of view overhead, obscured by the criss-crossing canopy of skeletal branches. No new leaves or buds were in evidence; it seemed that winter still reigned here.

The forest was painted monochrome in the deepening twilight, as if all colour and life had been leeched away in the winter months. The leafless trees were the colour of unyielding stone, and the blanket of ferns were shining silver, as if their fronds had been dipped in molten metal. It was a coldly beautiful realm, ghostly and silent.

The white stag waited for him close by, half obscured by the low fog. It regarded him steadily, only turning and leading the way further into the forest once it was sure that Calard was following.

While the creature moved effortlessly through the woodland, Calard stumbled over rocks and roots, and twigs scratched at his face and caught in his hair. It was as if the forest were purposefully making his progress difficult, hindering his every step. Even as he discounted the notion as foolish, his foot caught between a tangle of roots that seemed to tighten around his leg like a trap. He fell to his knees with a curse. He thought he heard high-pitched, childish laughter from nearby, but it was gone in an instant, and might have been nothing more than a trick of the wind.

A glint of metal in the undergrowth caught his eye. Disentangling himself from the grasping roots, he parted the ferns for a clearer view.

A corpse lay encoiled beneath the roots of a broad oak. It appeared to be slowly dragging it down into the earth, as if swallowing it whole, yet even half-buried Calard saw enough to recognise a knight of Bretonnia.

The knight was long dead, his armour rusted and encrusted with dirt. There was not a skerrick of flesh left upon his skull, though tufts of matted reddish hair still clung to his scalp and chin.

A slender arrow protruded from his left eye-socket.

A hand on the hilt of his sword, Calard scanned the area for danger. Beams of silver moonlight speared down through the canopy, lending the forest a dream-like quality. Shadows danced around him and the trees creaked and strained like ships at sea, though there was no wind to stir their branches.

Briefly, he considered digging the corpse free in order to give it a proper burial, for no knight of Bretonnia deserved such ignominy in death. He discounted the notion with some reluctance – the roots of the tree were wrapped tight, and would not easily relinquish their prize. He spoke a brief prayer, willing the knight's spirit on to Morr's kingdom.

Looking back the way he had come, Calard expected to see the way-stone marking the forest's edge and the open land beyond. He had ventured no more than twenty yards into the woods, after all. The way behind him now looked as impenetrable as the way forward.

'What in the name of the Lady?'

He turned around on the spot, wondering if he had somehow lost his bearings. The forest stretched out in every direction, dark and claustrophobic. Its edge was nowhere to be seen. Calard's brow furrowed. He didn't recognise a single tree or rock that looked familiar, nothing providing any clue to the way back out.

The white stag too was gone. Forcing back his rising unease, Calard scoured the ground in a wide arc, but could not find its tracks. It had disappeared without a trace, as if it had been nothing but an apparition all along.

Recalling the tales that spoke of the forest luring the unwary within its boundaries, and the inevitably grim fate that awaited them, Calard cursed himself for a fool. He had been so certain that it was the Lady's will that he followed the noble creature, but now, alone and lost in the Forest of Loren as night descended, he was not so sure.

Calard turned back. Perhaps it was just some trick of the light, he thought, and he would stumble out of the forest any moment.

The woods became increasingly dense and oppressive the further he went, and within minutes he knew that this was not the way back. It was getting colder as well, the isolated patches of snow on the ground becoming an ever-thickening layer that crunched beneath his boots.

Turning back in the face of this unnatural winter, Calard retraced his steps, intending to return to the corpse of the knight and pick another direction.

Thankfully, the snowfall thinned as he backtracked. But there was still no sign he had passed this way before.

Calard was an accomplished tracker and huntsman, and had lived for long periods in the wilds of the Old World. He was self-reliant and comfortable in such situations, confident in his own abilities. But here in the shadowy realm of Athel Loren he felt like a child lost in the woods, vulnerable and unsure which way to turn. His usually faultless sense of direction had deserted him, but he trusted his instincts enough to know that this was not some failing on his part, but rather that something was actively working to disorient him. It was as if the forest itself were conspiring to confound his senses.

He clambered over a half-buried log, but the way in front was blocked by an impenetrable tangle of branches. He turned back, intending to take a different route.

Impossibly, the log he had just climbed over had disappeared. Even his footprints were gone – the snow behind him was pristine.

'This is madness.'

He heard a whisper of laughter behind him and turned quickly, searching. The forest was utterly still, giving nothing away.

Silence descended like a shroud, oppressive and all encompassing.

There was not a hint of movement in the undergrowth or in the canopy overhead, as if time itself was frozen. There was no breeze to cause even a ripple of movement or break the illusion. The air was charged with tension. It was the deceptive lull that came before a raging tempest was unleashed.

As silently as he was able, Calard drew his sword.

He forced himself to breathe evenly, emptying his mind of doubt and forcing the tension from his limbs. Whatever was coming would do so whether he wished it or not, and he would face it free of anxiety and hesitation.

Over the course of the last seven years he had battled hulking trolls in the blizzards of the northlands, and tracked and killed the dread Jabberslythe of Ostwald in the forests of the Empire. He had been hunted by pallid, blind ogre-kin through the labyrinths beneath the Mountains of Mourn and emerged triumphant, and had slain – several times – a monstrous wyvern that refused to stay dead. Most recently he had journeyed into the nightmare realm of Mousillon and fought the restless dead. He had faced his own brother, twisted into a hateful vampiric creature of the night, and had not faltered, delivering him into Morr's care.

And having quite literally travelled to hell and back – the burning heavens in the Realm of Chaos still haunted him – there were few things in the world that could truly unnerve him.

As he turned, his gaze swept across something that made the hairs on the back of his neck stand on end.

A motionless figure was watching him, bathed in moonlight.

It was a knight, encased in ornate plate mail of archaic design. Utterly motionless, it stood atop a rocky outcrop that rose above the ground-cover of snow and ferns. The towering figure was tinged the greenish-grey of weather-beaten rock, and Calard might have mistaken it for a statue but for the unnatural light of its eyes, burning coldly within the darkness of its helm.

Calard's heart began to pound.

It was the Green Knight.

III

CALARD STOOD FROZEN, his heart thumping.

The knight staring balefully down at him was a figure from myth and legend, and while it was the fervent hope of every boy and young knight of Bretonnia to face this supernatural avenger, few believed that they would ever be so blessed.

Calard had seen the Green Knight depicted a thousand times, in plays, illustrated manuscripts and stained glass, yet nothing could have prepared him for the reality.

Feared and revered in equal measure, some said that the Green Knight was the immortal spirit of Gilles the Uniter himself, founder of Bretonnia, and that he served the Lady even in death. Few claimed to have glimpsed the potent spectre, and those that did spoke little of their encounter.

It was said that the ancient being may appear to a questing knight nearing the conclusion of his ordeal, challenging him in order to test his resolve. Calard's mouth went dry as he dared to think that perhaps this was his time.

The Green Knight's gauntleted hands rested upon a broad-bladed sword – the Dolorous Blade – embedded in the earth before it. How many souls deemed unworthy had been cut down by that infamous weapon?

For years Calard had longed to face this potent being, but now that he did, he found himself transfixed, scarcely able to breathe. He felt a trembling thrill in his gut such as he had not experienced since he was a young knight errant. Sweat trickled down his back, despite the cold. His fingers tightened around the hilt of his sword, and he forced himself to take a slow breath.

All the while, the Green Knight remained motionless, eyes searing through Calard's soul, stripping him bare. Fog seeped up from the ground and billowed around the ethereal champion like a cloak.

In one smooth motion, the mythical figure drew its sword from the earth, and began to advance towards him.

Mist rolled out around the Green Knight, rushing towards Calard like a tide. It crashed over him in a soundless wave, and he was instantly chilled. Behind him, Galibor whinnied and reared, but Calard did not turn, unable to tear his gaze from the spectre bearing down on him.

Everything but this supernatural foe faded from view. The fog thickened, and the forest became vague and indistinct, then disappeared altogether. For a moment Calard heard haunting music, the refrain impossibly beautiful. He heard lyrical, inhuman voices rising in song, the sound so emotive and filled with longing that tears came unbidden to Calard's eyes.

Roiling eddies of vapour curled and billowed around him on a sudden breeze. The Green Knight advanced, wading through the suffocating mist towards Calard, yet as it thickened, the distance between them seemed to grow. Calard hastened his pace towards his opponent, but the fog closed in.

The otherworldly figure was becoming increasingly hard to discern. Its terrible eyes and burning blade were growing faint, like the lights of a ship pulling away from port in the dead of night.

'No,' said Calard, hastening his step as he felt his opportunity to face the potent spirit slipping away. 'No!'

Calard ran, straining to keep the Green Knight in view, but within heartbeats the spectre was gone, subsumed by the heavy fog. Calard was alone, adrift in a sea of nothingness.

He edged forwards, sword and shield at the ready, half expecting the Green Knight to loom up at any moment and cut him down. His steps were halting as he felt his way forward, wary of pitfalls and rocks.

The fog muffled all sound, but after a few moments, Calard realised that he *could* hear something: a dull roar, akin to rolling thunder or the pounding of waves on distant shores. It was impossible to gauge the direction that the sound came from, and with no point of reference, he quickly lost his bearings.

For long minutes Calard advanced blindly. The sound of rushing water echoed around him, and soft spray wet his cheeks. He was stepping through ankle-deep water. Tiny rapids swirled as it rushed over his boots.

He thought he saw something taking shape before him, a vague dancing light in the distance that might have been a lantern or torch. Again he heard that ethereal, haunting music. The light bobbed and weaved, mesmerising and strangely alluring, as if calling to him. Calard took an involuntary step towards it before he dragged himself back, recalling the tales of malevolent will-o-the-wisps leading unwary travellers to their doom.

No sooner had the thought registered than the dancing light disappeared. The fog began to retreat, rising like a curtain to reveal his surroundings.

Calard took a hasty step backwards as the forest took shape around him. He was standing on the edge of a cliff, hundreds of feet high. One more step forwards, and he would have walked out over the edge.

His senses reeled at the drop; he was looking down on the forest canopy below. It extended far into the distance, treetops glittering beneath the silver moon of Mannslieb.

Turning, he surveyed his surroundings. A second waterfall fell from above, crashing down over a sheer cliff face into a deep pool. The water's surface was turbulent, and shimmered like liquid metal. The roar of the falls was deafening, and spray filled the air, glistening like rippling veils of diamond dust. Galibor stood nearby, drinking from the pool.

Trudging through the shallow water, Calard climbed the banks of the pool and peered into the forest. He could see no more than ten yards; it was almost impenetrable.

The sky was clear, allowing Calard to regain his bearings. He shook his head in wonder. From what he could make out, he was many miles from the forest border, closer in fact to the Grey Mountains in the east than the western fringes of Loren. He was also many miles to the north of where he would have expected to be. Still, a day and a night of travel should see him to the northern edge of the forest.

He whistled, and Galibor's eyes swivelled. The warhorse looked at him.

'Come,' Calard said, and the warhorse cantered obediently through the shallow water to its master.

Calard took Galibor's reins, readying to enter the forest. He looked over his shoulder one last time, at the clouds of vapour coming off the waterfall.

Before he turned away, Calard saw something come over the falls. It disappeared from view a moment later, swallowed by the raging torrent, but for a brief few seconds he saw it clearly as it fell. It was a body, arms and legs flailing as it tumbled.

V

WITHOUT HESITATION, CALARD plunged into the icy pool. The body had disappeared beneath the thunderous white water, but he waded in deep, fighting the strong currents. He was not certain anyone could have survived that drop, and when they didn't surface, he began to fear they had become snagged by rocks or already been carried past him and over the second falls.

Calard ducked under the surface, but it was hard to see anything. As he came up, he glimpsed the body surging facedown towards the drop of the second falls. Risking being swept away himself, Calard launched himself towards it, and caught the figure under one arm.

For a moment he was locked in an impasse with the surging waters. He was unwilling to let go, yet unable to drag it to safety. Groaning with effort, he managed to pull it from the swift moving current and haul it into the shallows. By the time he got it to shore, his chest was heaving and he was soaked to the skin.

It was a man, clothed in little more than a loincloth of woven grass and twigs and a heavy cloak of tawny feathers. He was lean and slender, his limbs long and powerful. Broad antlers like those of a stag protruded from a helmet of dark leather, and hair the colour of sand hung past his waist, tied in intricate plaits and knots. Dozens of necklaces, torcs and bracelets encircled his neck and arms, and a huge hunting horn hung across his back. His pallid skin was covered in swirling tattoos and war paint. Lacerations criss-crossed his flesh, as if he had been whipped to the brink of death.

Calard rolled the figure over, shifting the massive hunting horn strapped across his back so he could lie flat. For a moment he stared at the man's pale face in shock and wonder. His features were angular and long, and tall, pointed ears poked through his tangle of hair. The face was handsome, in a fashion, yet unutterably inhuman.

Many in Bretonnia spoke openly of their disbelief in those known as the fey – the woodland elves said to dwell within the Forest of Loren – yet here before Calard's eyes was evidence of their existence.

Calard dropped to his knees and pressed one ear to the elf's chest. The heartbeat was weak and faltering. The elf's chest was not rising and falling. By holding his hand before his mouth he nose confirmed the elf was not breathing.

Gripping the slender figure's jaw in one hand, Calard leant down and breathed air into the elf's lungs.

After several breaths, the elf jolted convulsively. He coughed up a lungful of water, and his eyes flicked open. They were large and almond shaped, and the irises were golden.

'*Noth athel'marekh, taneth'url aran,*' said the elf, struggling and failing to rise. When he saw Calard, his eyes widened. He reached for a weapon, but the scabbard at his waist was empty.

'I mean you no harm,' said Calard, showing his palms.

The elf cocked his head to one side, studying the questing knight with narrowed eyes.

A piercing scream tore through the air, and Calard reached for his weapon. It was not human, nor was it the cry of any bird or beast. It was cruel, seething with malice, and the promise of pain.

The elf snarled, and using the water-slick rocks to help him, he dragged himself upright, gritting his teeth against the pain of his wounds. He couldn't stand unsupported, but he searched the forest edges. Calard was surprised the elf was even alive considering his wounds.

'*Drycha noth Kournos athos,*' said the elf, spitting the words out like a curse. His strength deserted him, and his eyes rolled backwards. Without a sound, he crumpled to the ground, unconscious.

Moving to him, Calard pressed his fingers to the elf's throat. The heartbeat was erratic, and the skin was an unhealthy shade of blue. If his wounds were not tended soon, and warmth restored to his body, then the elf would surely not see out the night.

Another horrid cry echoed through the trees. This scream was nearer, and though it was hard to gauge, Calard judged it to be perhaps half a league away. It was followed almost instantly by another scream, slightly further off, coming from yet a third direction. It was the sound of predators coordinating a hunt, in the manner of a wolf pack, though these were no wolves; this was something infinitely more dangerous. Another cry sounded, closer still, and Calard realised that he was already surrounded.

Calard lifted the elf onto his shoulder, surprised at how light he was. He draped him over the warhorse's saddle, and gripped Galibor by the bridle.

They needed shelter, and fast – somewhere to hide from whatever was hunting them, and a place where he could tend the elf's injuries. Keeping close to the sheer rock face, Calard guided his warhorse back into the forest, judging the best chance they had was to find a hollow or an overhang in the cliff wall. There were dozens of cracks in the cliff face, but few extended far, and none offered much in the way of protection from the biting wind or prying eyes.

Another scream sounded, louder than any so far. The hunters were closing in fast.

Calard spied one crack in the cliff wall that looked marginally wider than the others, and in growing desperation, he scrambled forward to investigate, guiding Galibor towards the narrow chasm. It was barely wide enough for the armoured warhorse, but he pressed on, praying to the Lady. Water dripped down the sheer sides of this natural ravine, and ferns clung to its sides.

The passage narrowed, and Calard feared that he would have to turn back. Galibor snorted in displeasure, but did not resist as Calard continued on. After twenty paces, the ravine became a tunnel, a narrow passage delving deeper into the rock.

Sliding back past Galibor, Calard used a fallen branch to cover their tracks, obscuring their prints in the snow as best he could before leading the way deeper into the dark.

The roar of the waterfall echoed up through the tunnel, becoming louder the further they went. While the first few steps were through near total darkness, the way ahead brightened steadily; clusters of glowing crystal clung to the rock walls, radiating a pale phosphorescent glow.

Calard paused beside one of these formations. It was a mass of dagger-like shards, many as long as his forearm. The blue-white illumination they emitted pulsed like a heart-beat. Peering closely, he saw tiny spider-like creatures patrolling the crystal formation, swarming industriously, like bees within a hive. Their bodies were pearlescent and chitinous, and they too pulsed with inner luminosity.

Moving on, the crystal formations became ever more complex and impressive, until the winding tunnel opened to a broad, light-filled cavern. It was like walking into a cathedral of glass.

Grand pillars of crystal rose from floor to ceiling, and huge formations hung down like delicate chandeliers, glimmering coldly.

A hushed roar echoed through the cavern, and Calard wandered through its halls, awestruck, leading Galibor and the unconscious elf. He came to a gaping aperture, like a vast arched window, though in place of glass was a shimmering veil of water. They were behind the waterfall.

Others had recently used this place as a campsite. In a hollow in the floor he found ashes and charcoal, and in a nook in the wall was a pile of dry tinder and wood. Several low shelves extended from the walls around this fire pit, and pallets of tightly bound leaves upon them indicated that they were used as bedding.

He had no way of knowing who used this place as a refuge, nor if they would return, but he cast away any concern and thanked the Lady for leading him here. Easing the unconscious elf from Galibor's saddle, he lowered him onto one of the pallets. His skin was cold and grey, and blood was leaking from his wounds. His heartbeat was fluttering and faint, and his breathing shallow. Knowing he needed warmth, Calard set to building a fire.

Within minutes he had a blaze roaring, and turned his attentions to the elf's injuries.

His tattooed flesh was covered in scratches and raking cuts. The majority of these wounds were focused on his upper body and torso. There were few marks upon his back, suggesting the elf had been facing his assailant. His hands and forearms were shredded, as though he had tried to ward off the attacks.

Dozens of hooked thorns, some several inches long, were embedded in his body. They leaked a pungent, sticky green sap.

Some of the lacerations were superficial – no doubt painful, but not life threatening – but many were deep enough for serious concern. Calard winced as he probed at one particularly vicious injury.

Broken ribs protruded like snapped twigs from a serrated gash in the elf's side, and blood was flowing steadily from it. Left untended, he would certainly bleed to death. But even if the flow was stemmed survival was not certain.

Of greatest concern was a noxious discolouration surrounding each laceration. It spread out beneath the skin like the roots of a tree. These malign, creeping tendrils were dark-green in colour; poisoned.

Without delay, Calard set to removing the barbs. He concentrated his efforts on the serious torso wound first, cleaning and stitching it up as best he could. In a small bowl he ground up a mixture of herbs that he'd collected on his travels, mixing it with the last remnants of honey from a clay jar he had procured in the Empire six months earlier. The herbs were medicinal in nature, and combined with honey would aid in preventing infection. Calard applied the sticky poultice to the elf's jagged wound. Cutting strips from a spare tunic, he bound it in place.

For an hour he ministered to the elf's wounds. His patient cried out in his restless slumber, but his words were indecipherable. Several times he awoke, but his eyes were glazed and unfocused, and he didn't register Calard's presence.

Still wearing his horned headdress, the elf projected a savage nobility even in unconsciousness. The inhuman cast to his features was emphasised by the cold light emitted by the walls, making his flesh appear luminous. It was impossible to guess his age – he might have twenty or two hundred and twenty – for the fey were thought to be long lived, perhaps even immortal. The span of their lives, so it was said, outstripped even those of dwarfen kind.

The cavern was warm now, the fire burning strong. Judging that he could do little more for the elf, Calard saw to his warhorse. He brushed her down and checked her legs and hooves for injury. Only when his steed was fed and watered did Calard allow himself to relax. He leaned his broadsword and shield against the wall and settled down upon one of the cave's pallets. The Sword of Garamont sat across his lap. Its familiar weight was comforting. He watched the waterfall as he ate a meal of salted beef, and his mind drifted.

It had been seven years since he had set aside his lance and taken up the quest. Swearing his vow before the goddess, he had relinquished all his material wealth and instated his young cousin Orlando as his regent under the trusted guidance of Baron Montcadas. With nothing in the world to his name but that which he wore or was carried by Chlod, his manservant, Calard had ridden from Castle Garamont determined to succeed in his quest or die in the attempt.

The years on the road had hardened him, like a sword tempered in the forge. Through all the trials and hardships set against him he had emerged triumphant, and with every passing month his mind, body and soul had been strengthened.

Now, he prayed, his journey was coming to an end.

The vision had struck with all the force of a thunderbolt, taking his breath away and dropping him to his knees in the midst of battle. It has lasted just seconds, but the blinding series of images had been forever seared in his mind. Even now, he could see it whenever he closed his eyes.

He could not yet fathom the vision's full meaning, but he had faith that all would become clear. The Lady had wished for him to follow the evening star into the east – and that had brought him here.

As loath as he had been to depart the cursed realm of Mousillon while the fiend Duke Merovech still walked, he could no more disobey the Lady's command than choose for his heart to stop beating. And while he knew that even now Merovech and his bloodsucking seneschals were marching against Bretonnia at the head of a vast undead army, he could not ride to join the knights of the king until he had done as the Lady bid him.

Two others had ridden with Calard from the cursed realm: Chlod, his hunchbacked manservant, and Raben, a dishonoured rogue of a knight embarked upon the difficult road to redemption. Pursued by the nightmarish hounds of Duke Merovech, the three had fled Mousillon.

Knowing that haste was of the highest priority and that the path he now travelled was his alone, Calard had bid his companions farewell at Mousillon's border and ridden hard into the east.

Chlod he had foresworn into Raben's service, and the pair had ridden north into Lyonesse to raise the alarm. They had each seen the threat that Merovech posed, having glimpsed in the distance the army he had raised – literally – as they had fled the city. Thousands upon thousands of long dead warriors stood in serried ranks on the blasted fields to the north of Mousillon.

Calard's gaze settled on the ashen-faced elf lying before the fire.

The Lady had led him here to save this warrior, of that he was certain. But why? Whatever the reason, he prayed that the elf would live to see the dawn. His fate was in the hands of the gods now.

The noise of the waterfall was soothing, and lulled by the sound of rushing water and the play of firelight on the crystal walls, Calard drifted into a fugue-like half-sleep. He imagined he saw slender women in the waterfall, staring in at him from the rushing waters, their naked flesh the colour of the ocean. He heard them singing, filling the crystal sanctuary with their hypnotic song.

The fire was low when he jolted awake.

The elf stood before him, holding Calard's broadsword in a two-handed grip, the tip levelled at his throat. His golden eyes were unblinking.

The Sword of Garamont was still sheathed across Calard's lap. With some effort he restrained himself from drawing it. He could see by the elf's balanced stance that he was a warrior; he would be run through before he had the Sword of Garamont even half drawn.

Making no sudden or threatening moves, Calard lifted the sheathed sword from his lap and placed it beside him, flat on the pallet. He leant back against the stone wall and placed his hands behind his head.

'Well?' he said, his gaze steady. 'What now?'

The elf's eyes narrowed.

'*Aleth kegh-mon aeleth'os tark'a Loec-noth,*' said the elf. The cadence of his speech was lyrical, each unfamiliar word precisely enunciated and tinged with hostility.

'If you were going to kill me, you would have done it by now.'

Calard could see that the elf was weak, though he was trying his best to conceal it. His limbs were lathered in sweat, and blood was leaking from several of his bindings.

The Bretonnian bastard sword was heavy, and Calard could see that the elf was straining to keep it aloft. It looked overly large and crude in his hands, which were surely used to more elegant weapons.

'There is a poison in your flesh,' said Calard. 'You need healing. What was it that caused your injuries?'

'*Dae'eth Shael-Mara, noth,*' spat the elf.

'You don't understand me, do you?' said Calard.

'*Kaelan noth kegh-mon,*' spat the elf.

They stared at each other for a time, neither willing to make a move. Calard shivered. The fire had reduced itself to embers, and the cavern was cold. Moving slowly, he reached for more wood.

The elf hissed through his teeth and tensed, the tip of the sword hovering like the barbed tail of a scorpion, ready to strike.

Moving cautiously, Calard lifted a chunk of wood from the pile and tossed it onto the embers. Tongues of flame rose almost instantly, licking at the dry, crackling timber.

Leaning forward, he poked at the fire, and a flurry of glowing cinders drifted into the air, dancing and crackling. Over the glow of the flames, he saw the elf sway as he fought to stay conscious. The tip of the sword wavered and dipped.

Seeing his opening, Calard flicked a scoop of embers up at the elf. In the same movement he sprang to his feet and leapt the fire pit, intending to slam the elf from his feet with his shoulder before he had a chance to strike.

Even in his weakened state the elf was far quicker than Calard had anticipated. Before he had cleared the fire pit the elf had already spun out of the way, sidestepping the tumble of glowing coals and bringing the heavy bastard sword around in a lethal arc that sliced for Calard's neck. The blow was not a casual one; it was a killing stroke.

Calard threw himself to the side, and the blade hissed past, missing him by inches. Still turning, the elf launched himself into the air like a dancer, using his momentum to bring the bastard sword around for a second strike. The elf moved with exquisite balance, and Calard felt clumsy and heavy as he reeled back, trying to put some distance between them.

He cursed himself for misjudging the situation; he had been sure that he could disarm the elf without any harm coming to either of them.

The elf landed in a low crouch. His breathing was laboured, and a growing red stain could be seen on the bindings around his chest. The wound in his side had reopened.

The elf's strength was fading. His golden eyes were clouded and his legs shook. Determined to end things quickly, before the elf regathered himself, Calard surged forward. But the elf was not done yet, and he swung at the questing knight as he came at him.

The elf's speed was not what it had been at the start of the fight, and Calard caught the blade against the inside of his left vambrace, and while it cut deep, shearing through plate metal and the chainmail links beneath, it barely scratched his forearm. He grappled with the slender elf, and the two of them fought for control of the bastard sword.

The elf was Calard's equal in height, yet was far slighter of frame. There was a wiry strength in the elf's limbs, though, that defied his fragile appearance, and for a moment the pair were locked together, eye to eye.

Calard slammed his forehead into his opponent's face, breaking the stalemate. The elf's legs buckled, and the heavy bastard sword fell from his grasp with a clatter. Calard kicked it aside and muscled the elf to the ground, pinning him face down with a knee in the small of his back. The elf struggled against him, then went limp.

Calard lifted him from the ground and put him on one of the low palettes. The elf's breathing was shallow, his heartbeat arrythmic. Calard loosened the blood-soaked bindings. The deep wound had reopened, and Calard worked to staunch the flow. There was little that he could do to halt the spread of the insidious poison, however, and he was shocked to see that the sickness had already advanced in the last hour. The veinlike tendrils under the skin were now creeping towards the elf's heart.

Calard swore. Without a healer, the elf would die, but he felt certain that he would never find his way back here if he left to search for help.

Calard's eye fell upon the curved hunting-horn that he'd removed from around the elf's shoulders. If the elf had friends nearby, they might be able to help. Calard took up the horn and moved towards the passage leading back out to the forest.

A faltering voice gave him pause.

'No,' said the elf. 'You will draw the *Shael-Mara* to us.'

'You speak Breton?' said Calard.

'Some.'

'How did you come to learn it?'

'One of... your people dwelled... for a time within the Halls of... Anaereth... my home.'

'How long ago was that?' said Calard in wonder. The elf spoke an archaic form of his language that had not been used in hundreds of years.

'Many seasons.'

'My name is Calard of Garamont, My quest for the Lady's chalice brought me here, to your forested realm. It was she who led me to you.'

'Then you are a fool,' said the elf. 'The forest... will claim you. You'll not... see your lands again.'

'Are you a seer?'

The wounded fey warrior glared at him, golden eyes blazing.

'I do not... need to be a seer... to know the fate that awaits you.'

'What is your name, elf?'

'I am *Cythaeros Mithra'kinn'daek* of the *Shenti'ae Arahain* kindred,' said the elf.

'The Lady led me to your side, *Cythaeros*,' said Calard, forming the elf's name with some difficulty. 'It was by her will that you were saved.'

The elven warrior was about to speak, but was interrupted by a fit of coughing. Blood flecked his lips when it had passed.

'You said I would draw something to us if I used this horn,' said Calard, handing the curved instrument to the elf. 'What is out there? What manner of creature is hunting you?'

'The *Shael-Mara*,' said Cythaeros, taking the hunting horn and clutching it to his chest like a talisman. 'Handmaidens of Winter. They will... be searching.'

'Handmaidens of Winter?'

'Betrayers... Pawns of the branchwraith, *Drycha*.'

Calard's frowned, and he was about to voice his questions when he saw that Cythaeros had slipped into unconsciousness. He settled down next to him, wondering what the best course of action was.

With a gasp, the elf awoke again. He sat upright, grabbing Calard's arm, his eyes shining with fever.

'The compact... must be met. The King... in-the-Wood must rise.'

'Lie back,' said Calard. 'Your wounds.'

'No,' said Cythaeros, his voice a hoarse whisper, but he sunk back onto the pallet, his strength waning. His eyes began to close.

Calard could see he was fading fast. He leant in close, taking hold of the elf by his shoulders.

'There is a poison in you that is beyond my abilities to halt,' said Calard. 'You are in need of healing. Where are your people?'

'The forest,' breathed Cythaeros. 'Take me... into... the forest.'

VI

SNOW CRUNCHED UNDERFOOT as Calard delved deeper into Athel Loren. He eyed his surroundings with both wariness and wonder, one hand resting upon the pommel of the Sword of Garamont. Cythaeros was slumped unconscious astride his armoured warhorse. Calard had tied him into the saddle to ensure that he did not slip sidewards, but he glanced back regularly to ensure he was still in place.

The elf's condition was steadily worsening. It was still some hours before dawn, and Calard was unsure that he would ever regain consciousness. He needed help soon if he stood any chance of living.

Only hours ago, the forest had seemed impenetrable, dark and full of claustrophobic menace; now it was bright, and filled with space and air. Where before the forest had appeared to resent Calard's presence, turning him around and hindering him at every step, now it opened up before him, as if hurrying him on. Though he did not know where he was going, he took this as a good sign.

As he walked, Calard's gaze constantly drifted upwards. Immense trees rose all around him, soaring impossibly high, their silver-barked trunks glistening. Their scale was breathtaking, and he doubted their like existed anywhere in the world but here. Never would he have believed that any tree could grow so tall or straight; each must have been easily five-hundred feet tall. They were like vast pillars holding up the ceiling of the world.

The quality of the light was magical, with moonlight lancing down through the canopy above. Pristine, untouched snow glittered like crystal.

In the hours since leaving the safety of the cave, Calard had neither seen nor heard any sign of pursuit. Still, he remained alert, knowing that danger was assuredly all around, even if he could not perceive it.

Despite the unnatural winter, Calard glimpsed an abundance of life within the forest. He guessed it had been here before, but only now was he seeing it – or being *allowed* to see it.

Owls swooped through the trees, and rabbits and mink padded across the snow, oblivious to the danger above. He heard a lone fox barking in the distance, and glimpsed a pair of hawks roosting in the branches overheard. He saw a herd of deer grazing far away, though none of them came close to matching the sheer magnificence of the white hart that had led Calard into the forest. From afar, he saw the shuffling form of a great bear woken early from its winter slumber.

Once, Calard caught a glimpse of a huge white cat stalking through the trees some way off. Its body was sleek and powerful, and its ears were sharp and pointed like knives. It turned to regard him, violet eyes flashing in the moonlight, before melting with unhurried grace into the forest like a phantom.

All of those creatures were similar to ones Calard had seen outside the forest, yet there was something about them that was strange, an other worldly quality that set them apart.

Other creatures were less familiar.

A host of glowing sprites had descended around him at one point. From a distance they looked like fireflies, but as they came close, he had seen that they were something altogether different.

Each was a tiny being of light, perfectly formed and held aloft by diaphanous, gossamer wings. They were curious of him, darting in close to look at him, then speeding away again when he turned towards them. They were irritating, however, tying knots in his hair and pulling Gali-bor's ears, all the while filling the air with their high-pitched giggles. Calard had swatted at them as they flitted around him.

Most of them had soon grown bored and departed, but one of the tiny spirits stayed with him. He had given up trying to drive it off. At first it had darted frenetically, sticking out its tongue as he waved it away, but it appeared content now to sit on his shoulder, chattering away in its shrill, indecipherable voice.

Even the tiny sprite had finally fallen silent, however, and a reverential hush descended upon the forest. It began to snow. Each heavy flake fell in slow motion, descending with tranquil grace. The crunching of snow and the jangle of tack were the only sounds.

The attack came without warning.

Calard glanced back over his shoulder to ensure Cythaeros was still in the saddle, and a slender loop of rope slipped over his head. Before he had a chance to react, the rope was yanked tight around his neck and he was hauled into the air, legs kicking uselessly beneath him.

Struggling for breath, Calard clutched at the constricting noose, trying fruitlessly to get his fingers beneath the rope and ease its tension. It was crushing his windpipe, and his vision began to waver. The glowing sprite that had attached itself to him was flying frantically around him, tears of light falling down its cheeks.

As he spun helplessly ten feet above the ground, Calard saw shadowy figures in the branches of the trees. Their faces were hidden beneath deep hoods, and each levelled a nocked bow.

White spots were appearing before Calard's eyes, and he fumbled for his knife. The glowing sprite's tiny hands guided him, and his fingers finally closed around the hilt. He drew it quickly and slashed through the choking rope.

Hitting the ground hard, Calard ripped off the noose, gasping. He staggered to his feet and drew the Sword of Garamont. A dozen figures armed with bows had risen from concealment beneath the snow around him. The sprite hovered at his shoulder, spitting and glaring at these newcomers. Glancing up, Calard saw that easily the same number as were on the ground were crouched in the branches overhead, arrows trained upon him.

'Wood elves,' said Calard.

THE FEY BEINGS were slender and tall, clad in heavy cloaks the colour of winter. Most had their faces covered, leaving only their almond-shaped eyes exposed, glittering beneath their shadowed hoods. Their expressions gave away nothing.

One of them dropped from the branches overhead, landing lightly. The wood elf pushed the hood back from his face, revealing a strong, masculine profile, and ashen skin. He wore a curving black half-mask, and delicate tattoos in dark green were stencilled across his flesh.

His hair was gleaming black and tied in a series of braids. He moved with the supple grace of a dancer, and barely left an impression in the snow as he strode towards Calard. He halted ten paces away, and while his bow was lowered, he kept an arrow nocked to the string. His eyes were like chips of ice. Calard was in no doubt that the elf would kill him at the slightest provocation.

With slow and deliberate motions, Calard sheathed the Sword of Garamont.

'I found one of your people – Cythaeros,' Calard said, gesturing towards the unconscious elf. 'He is hurt. I have done what I can for him, but he needs a healer.'

The elf barked an order but did not take his eyes off Calard. One of the hooded sentinels stepped forwards, easing the tension from its bow-string, and moved to the side of the Bretonnian warhorse. The elf was a woman, though she was garbed identically to her companions. She spoke softly under her breath, and placed a gentle hand upon Galibor's nose. The proud warhorse accepted her touch, nuzzling into it.

The elven warrior-woman glanced in Calard's direction. He saw disdain in her eyes, before she turned her attention towards the uncon-scious figure of Cythaeros slumped in Galibor's saddle.

The leader of the elves spoke, his tone questioning. Calard saw the female warrior's eyes widen as she lifted the wounded elf's chin and looked upon his face.

She looked sharply at Calard.

'*Doth kail'enaeth,*' she said in a sharp voice. '*Cythaeros Mithra'kinn'daek, Kournos-dae!*'

Several of the elves began to speak at once, but they were silenced by the one Calard took to be their leader.

'*Kaela'Anara, vish'nu,*' he said.

The air shimmered and, as if a veil were parting, the white hart that had led Calard into the forest stepped into the moonlight, seemingly from nowhere.

'Not a delusion of the mind, then,' breathed Calard.

The proud creature walked towards him with unhurried majesty. Its broad rack of antlers gleamed. A rider sat astride the stag's shoulders, a lady bedecked in a gown of overlapping gossamer layers, each so deli-cate that they appeared to float in the air.

A veil concealed her face, held in place by a circlet of ivy around her brow. A gentle aura surrounded the lady.

Cythaeros was lowered from Galibor's saddle by a pair of elves. Calard made to help them, but the leader of the elves hissed between his teeth, raising his bow, and Calard froze.

The veiled lady slipped from the back of her mount. Although he could not see her eyes, hidden as they were, he could feel her gaze upon him, making his skin prickle. She was a sorceress then, Calard surmised; he had felt the strange, creeping sensation before.

Cythaeros was carried towards the white stag, which lowered itself in the snow to receive him. It had no bridle, reins or saddle and knelt of its own volition. The unconscious elf was placed over its broad back, leaning forward into its thick mane, and the veiled lady climbed behind him, putting her arms around his waist.

Calard's gaze returned to the leader of the elves, and he realised that he now stood alone. Those elves that had been nearest to him had rejoined their brethren. They now encircled him, silent, their expressions cold. Hooded and cloaked, the elves all looked as one: grim and unforgiving.

'If I have broken any law through my intrusion into your realm, then I apologise,' said Calard.

The elves were silent, staring with unblinking eyes.

'You have your man back,' said Calard, gesturing towards Cythaeros. 'My task here is done. I ask that I be allowed to leave safely, so I can join my kin in fighting the darkness assailing my lands.'

Still the elves made no response.

'It doesn't have to be this way,' said Calard, grasping the hilt of his sword.

The elven leader raised his powerful, recurved bow and drew back the string, arrow levelled at Calard's chest. At this range, it would drive straight through his breastplate.

'It is not the will of the Lady that I die here,' Calard said.

The elven warleader's eyes narrowed, but he did not loose his arrow.

Confronted with the prospect of being ignobly cut down by a coward's weapon, Calard felt nothing but calm. It was as though a blindfold had been lifted from his eyes, a weight removed from his soul.

'Lady of mercy,' he whispered, 'show me the path, and I shall walk it.'

A single black feather drifted into view, falling slowly between the elven leader and Calard, like a tainted snowflake.

The ugly cawing of crows sounded nearby, shattering the silence. The tiny sprite at Calard's shoulder gave out a shriek, and blinked out of existence. Further off, Calard heard an inhuman scream, infused with bitterness and savagery.

As if that hateful cry were its cue, an icy wind howled through the forest. Branches whipped back and forth in the wake of the sudden tempest, and Calard's tattered cloak rippled out behind him. Something was coming, and he readied his blade, his eyes slits against the gale.

The Handmaidens of Winter had found them.

VII

RIDING ON THE wind of the storm, crows erupted from the forest depths. Calard heard them long before he saw them, moving fast and flying in a dense black cloud. They dipped and dived through the branches, moving at tremendous speed, coming straight for the elves and Calard.

'*Shael-Mara!*' shouted the elven warleader, arrow still pointing at Calard. Without warning, he loosed.

Calard did not flinch, even as the arrow came towards him. It hissed by his ear, missing him by less than an inch, and he heard it thud home somewhere behind him, accompanied by a feral howl of pain and anger.

Glancing over his shoulder, Calard saw a figure pinned to a tree some thirty feet away. It was thrashing like some deranged marionette as it sought to free itself. It screeched horribly, sounding more like some monstrous bird of prey than anything even vaguely elven or human.

Seeing that the elves were ignoring him completely, Calard drew the Sword of Garamont and swung the battered shield off his back. It was painted red and blue with a resplendent silver dragon rampant emblazoned upon its face, but that paint was now faded and scratched, the bare metal underneath shining through. It was heavily battle-worn, covered in dents, evidence of the countless battles he had survived. As the flock of birds hurled themselves towards him, their cries deafening, he secured the shield on his left arm and readied himself for their onslaught.

They were big, more the size of ravens than crows, yet sleeker than any Calard had seen before. Their bodies appeared elongated for speed and manoeuvrability, perfectly adapted to a life beneath the forest canopy. They were not at all slowed by the dense foliage, spinning and weaving through the skeletal branches with enviable grace and swiftness. Their black feathers had a blue sheen to them, he saw now, and their beaks and talons gleamed like daggers. A dozen were felled by arrows, but the rest came on, screaming and cawing.

Seeing that they were not swerving from their course, Calard ducked behind his shield, protecting his eyes. The flock broke upon him like the tide, flowing either side of him. He was momentarily blinded, surrounded by their blurred, black-feathered shapes. He felt several impacts upon his armour, as if he were being pelted with rocks, and he wondered if what he felt were stabbing beaks, or claws. There was a sharp pain in the side of his neck and the birds were past him. They reformed into a single mass, wheeling to make another pass.

Calard dislodged a tiny splinter that had been embedded in his neck. 'What in the name of the Lady?' he said, examining it between his fingers.

It was less than an inch in length, and as thin a blade of grass. It looked like a tiny sliver of slate, but its tip was barbed like a hunting spear, albeit on a miniscule scale. A bead of blood dripped from the tip.

The flock of crows came at him again, filling the air with ugly cries and the flapping of wings. It was all but impossible to focus on any of the darting birds, so swiftly did they move, but Calard caught a momentary glimpse of a tiny figure that blinked into existence, perched on the neck of one of the crows as it hurtled by.

He saw it only briefly, but in that moment he discerned savage glowing eyes glaring out of a pinched face the size of Calard's thumbnail. Its features were pointed and as black as coal. It wore a red cap, and it snarled at him, exposing a plethora of tiny fangs. It hurled a tiny barbed dart towards his eyes before blinking out of sight, disappearing completely. It was only reflex that saved Calard from being blinded; the dart hit him on the cheek as he jerked away.

He lashed out, striking air. The birds darted around the weapon like smoke.

He brushed the dart from his cheek and plucked out another that had struck him in the chin. More were stuck in his cloak and between the links in his chainmail hauberk.

The wounds weren't deep, but they were already beginning to throb. Calard's vision swam, and he staggered.

Poisoned.

The birds came at him again. This time the flock did not pass over, but instead swirled around him in a blinding whirlwind, a cyclone of feathers and stabbing beaks. In his peripheral vision, Calard saw dozens of tiny red-capped imps, their faces twisted in savage glee as they attacked him with poisoned shot. Most of the barrage pinged off his armour, but other darts stabbed into the exposed flesh of his neck and face.

From out of nowhere, the tiny glowing sprite that had adopted Calard blinked back into existence, darting forward to rip one of the red-caps from its mount. The two diminutive nature-spirits tumbled through the air, fighting tooth and nail.

Calard lashed out around him, feeling fragile bodies break against his shield, wings and slender bones snap like dry twigs. More were cut down by his blade, leaving a flutter of blood-specked feathers in its wake.

The veiled lady appeared unaffected by the mayhem erupting around her, an oasis of calm in the maelstrom. Elves were falling in around her, forming a bodyguard to protect her and the unconscious elven warrior from harm.

Galibor reared, hooves flailing as the crows whirled around her. Calard fought his way through the swirling cloud of feathers to grab the warhorse's reins. The steed's eyes were wide in fear, but she calmed under Calard's firm hold.

An elf fell from above and hit the ground hard nearby. Calard saw the elf's face was peppered with tiny barbed darts. He was already convulsing as the poison spread though his veins.

More arrows skewered several of the hateful carrion birds and the flock splintered. Calard swatted at them as they hurtled by him. Darts bounced off his armour, but then the birds were gone, disappearing into the forest. The tiny glowing sprite returned to him victorious. One of its wings was tattered, but it smiled and puffed out its chest.

Calard's lips and fingertips felt numb, and his throat was so dry that it was hard to swallow. The colours of the forest seemed too bright, and the trees rippled and wavered like reflections in a lake's surface disturbed by a hurled rock. Blinking, his vision began to return to normal – thankfully, his armour had protected him from the worst of the arboreal barrage.

Inhuman screams erupted around the glade, dangerously close. The elves were scanning the area, bow-strings taut, still ignoring Calard. Evidently, the crows were only the vanguard of whatever was now closing in.

Snow was falling more heavily now, making it difficult to see. Stalking figures lurked at the edge of the questing knight's vision, but he could make out little of their appearance except their outline, and even that was vague and shifting.

Galibor whinnied, and Calard held her reins tightly.

Snow fell silently as they waited for the attack to come. When it finally did, it was shocking in its speed and ferocity.

Figures darted forwards and were met with a veritable storm of arrows, hissing like angry wasps as they sliced between the trees. Dozens of figures rushed from the shadows. They moved with preternatural speed, snarling and hissing like wildcats.

Calard was about to haul himself into Galibor's saddle when he felt an icy breath on the back of his neck, and he spun around, sword raised to strike.

Like a wood-carving come spontaneously to life, a nymph was emerging from the trunk of the tree directly behind him. Struck by her naked beauty, Calard's jaw dropped, and he held his blow.

The creature's skin was the silver-grey of the tree's bark. Her features were fine and perfectly formed, with high cheek-bones, youthful, full lips and wide-spaced eyes that remained closed as if in slumber. Silken hair filled with leaves and ivy fell around her shoulders as she pulled herself free and stepped out onto the snow.

Calard stared open-mouthed at this captivating nature spirit, but as its eyes flicked open, the spell of its allure was broken.

Its elongated orbs were black and filled with cruelty. As its lascivious lips parted, beetles, worms, centipedes and other nameless crawling things writhed forth.

Calard recoiled, and a sudden change came upon the nymph. Youthful features melted away, bark-like skin shrivelling and peeling back to expose a face of nightmare. Flakes of bark clung to its hollow cheeks, and its hair became a tangle of dead sticks and dry leaves. Swirling patterns were carved in its wooden flesh.

Slender elven limbs became twisted and gnarled, and its delicate hands elongated, distending into sharp, branch-like talons. Its back became hunched and stick-like ribs protruded from its emaciated, bark-flesh.

The creature resembled some ancient, spiteful crone of thorn and briar, as if the worst aspects of the winter forest had come to life and been granted physical form.

The entire transformation took place in the blink of an eye, and with a piercing scream the hellish dryad lunged at Calard, talons extended.

Calard lurched backwards, swinging his sword for its neck. The hideous creature came straight at him, raising one arm to deflect the blow. It was like striking a hunk of wood, and Calard's blade stuck fast.

The creature's features melted back to those of a beautiful maiden, and it licked its lips before shifting back to its horrific war-aspect. It slashed Calard's face, and while he turned away from the blow, avoiding the worst of it, its twig-like claws sliced across his left cheek.

The wound was stinging, but Calard ignored it and planted one boot in the hollow of the dryad's chest, shoving it back as he yanked his blade free. He felt dry stick-ribs snapping beneath his boot, and his sword came loose. Foul-smelling sap dripped from the blade. The creature recovered quickly and leapt at him again, seeking to drive its branch-like talons through his face.

An arrow struck it as it came at him, knocking the dryad out of the air. It tumbled in the snow, screeching as it sought to dislodge the shaft embedded deep in its head. Stepping in close, Calard brought his sword blade crashing down upon its crown, and its skull came apart like a sodden log filled with worm-rot, splattering woodchips and crawling things.

The dryad collapsed in upon itself, reduced to a stinking pile of rotting timber, sticks and mouldering leaf-mulch. Calard stepped away, covering his nose and mouth with the back of his hand.

Dozens of the feral dryads were among the elves now, darting forward to impale them upon branch-limbs and tear them apart. Elves screamed, and blood showered the snow.

Arrows sliced through the gloom, launched at a prodigious rate, and Calard saw scores of dryads scythed down. Still more of the vile nymphs were appearing, stepping out of the trees, their beauteous, temptress forms becoming twisted and vile as soon as they manifested fully.

The fight was equally as savage in the forest vaults as on the ground. Dryads were leaping from tree to tree, chasing elves that were running along the branches, loosing arrows as they went.

Sensing movement behind him, Calard turned. A hissing dryad was reaching for him, whipping vine-like tendrils around his sword arm.

With his free hand, Calard drew his broadsword from his back and brought it slicing around towards the side of the creature's head. It caught the blow mid-strike. Calard's muscles strained, but the dryad was stronger, forcing his arm painfully backwards. It drew him in towards it, and the tangle of roots that were its hair reached towards him, like leeches questing for blood.

He tried to fight it, but the horrid crone of winter was too powerful for him, and he was dragged into its embrace. Its mouth opened, exposing a feral array of predator's teeth and writhing bugs, and the stink of rotting wood-mulch and worms filled his nostrils.

The dryad jerked, and an arrowhead burst from its chest. The tip of the arrow was just inches from Calard's own chest. The dryad, refusing to give up its grip on him even in death, dragged him towards it.

Another arrow struck the dryad, this time in the back of its head. It collapsed, reduced to a lifeless husk that Calard kicked away in disgust.

The warleader of the elves stood behind it, lowering his bow, and

Calard gave him a nod of thanks. The warrior turned away to rejoin the fight, barking orders to his warriors.

Dozens of dryads had been cut down, yet still more were emerging from the shadows, bursting from the trees. Reading the battlefield, Calard could see that this was not a fight that could be won.

The elves were pulling back, smoothly loosing arrows as they retreated. Those overhead vaulted from branch to branch, moving almost as fast as those below, raining shafts down upon the baleful creatures.

Calard ran to Galibor's side, and hauled himself into the saddle. He could see the white stag galloping through the deep snow, surrounded by an escort of winter-clad elves.

Urging Galibor into a gallop, Calard set off in pursuit. Trees streaked by, and glancing sidewards he saw the forms of winter dryads matching his speed, leaping and bounding like horrid puppets of wood come to life.

The warhorse pounded through the snow, relishing the sudden release of energy. Calard tensed his muscles and leant forward in the saddle as Galibor leapt a fallen log. The sense of speed was exhilarating. He was amazed at how swift the elves were – he was having difficulty keeping pace with them, and they were travelling on foot. They darted through the trees like shadows.

He saw the elven warleader throw a glance in his direction. The grim warrior mouthed what might have been a curse.

Calard couldn't suppress a wild grin. With a shout of encouragement, Calard urged Galibor on.

VIII

THE RIDE THROUGH the forest was like a dream. Calard urged Galibor between the towering silver-barked trees for hours, ducking low-hanging branches and leaning forward in the saddle as the mighty warhorse leapt fallen logs, red and blue caparison rippling.

With cloaks billowing out behind them, the elves incredibly kept pace with them. For the time being they appeared to tolerate Calard, though they did not even so much as acknowledge his presence.

The white hart was tireless and swift, galloping ever onward, leading a twisting and turning path through the forest. Huge firs gave way to glades of leafless birchwood and yew, which in turn gave way to wintery oaks and ash.

They passed crumbling ruins overrun with ferns and twisted roots, and Calard marvelled at a pale stone tower that rose like a needle, disappearing into the canopy. They passed through a grand archway created by two enormous trees whose trunks had came together and entwined around each other, like lovers. At one point Calard glimpsed a wide and fast-flowing river, half-hidden by banks of weeping willow, but the stag's path veered away from this, turning what might have been north,

472   *The Best of Hammer and Bolter: Volume One*

or south; Calard's sense of direction was completely befuddled.

On the occasions when the canopy opened up, he glimpsed the constellations overhead, but far from allowing him to regain his bearings, he became ever more confused. At some points, it seemed as though the silver moon Mannslieb was higher in the sky than it had been previously, as if they were going backwards in time, and at other times he could not even recognise the flickering celestial formations. For one who prided himself on his knowledge of the astral bodies of the heavens, and had navigated his way across the Old World by their guiding light, Calard found this perhaps more disturbing than any of the other wonders he had seen that night.

Through water-slick ravines and narrow canyons they travelled, always at speed, as if the dryad hunters were still snapping at their heels, though Calard had seen no sign of them for many hours. The screams of the Handmaidens of Winter could be heard on occasion, echoing in the distance.

They passed an immense green-grey statue of a bare-chested elf – easily a hundred feet tall – with cloven hooves and the horns of a stag jutting from its brow. It was carved from a rocky spur jutting up beside an icy spring, and covered in ivy and lichen. Calard saw each of the elven warriors avert their eyes as they passed by, making a gesture of warding, or perhaps of respect.

Thousands of glowing sprites joined them for a time, emerging from the boles of trees and from beneath fern-fronds. The tiny pixie that had attached itself to Calard hovered at his shoulder, tattered wings a blur of movement. She was garbed in glowing plate armour in mimicry of Calard's own, and she wore a serious expression upon her tiny, pinched face. She clutched a miniscule lance under one arm, a ribbon-like pennant fluttering from its tip, and on her left arm carried a shield with the device of a man spewing forth a torrent of leaves and ivy from his mouth.

Finally, the white stag eased its relentless pace and drew to a halt in a protected glade along the banks of a frozen river. The elves spread out, many of them ghosting back into the trees. Others took up positions nearby, leaping lightly atop snow-covered boulders where they crouched, bows in hands, watchful for danger. As soon as they were still they became virtually invisible; even those in the open were almost impossible to see once their cloaks were drawn around their shoulders and their hoods lowered.

The white stag knelt in the snow, allowing the veiled lady to slip from its shoulders. Cythaeros was eased off its back by the leader of the elven warparty and laid gently upon the leader's cloak, which he had spread out upon the ground in the lee of a stand of rocks. The wounded elf still wore his antlered headdress.

Calard reined in Galibor, and slipped from the saddle. He moved towards the elven leader, who was kneeling beside Cythaeros, inspecting his wounds.

'How is he?' he said as he approached.

His words were ignored, but Calard could see that the green-black tendrils beneath the unconscious warrior's skin had spread. His eyes were sunken and surrounded by dark rings. He still clutched his large, curved hunting horn to his chest, even in unconsciousness.

For a moment Calard was unsure if the elf was still breathing, and he feared that the frantic ride had killed him. Then he saw the faintest of breaths misting the air around the elf's nose. For now at least, the elf lived.

'I will pray for him,' said Calard. The elven warleader grunted in what might have been acquiescence, and Calard moved around to stand at the feet of the injured warrior.

He drew the Sword of Garamont and reversed his grip on the hilt before driving its point into the snow and kneeling before it. Ignoring the pixie kneeling in the snow alongside him, mimicking his every move, he closed his eyes.

Lost in prayer, he did not hear the veiled lady approach.

'He is the Morning Star,' she said in fluent Breton, interrupting his communion.

Her voice was strange, like three voices overlapping and speaking as one, yet he recognised it – it was the voice that had spoken in his mind just before he had seen the Green Knight.

Calard kissed the fleur-de-lys crossbar of his sword, and pushed himself back to his feet.

The veiled lady stood nearby, looking down upon the unconscious elf. Of the elven warleader, there was no sign. The white hart and Galibor stood together, drinking melt-water from the lake.

'The Lady of the Lake would not have brought me to him if he were not important,' said Calard, sheathing his blade.

'We are all of us important,' said the lady in her trinity of voices. 'And yet as insignificant as leaves on the wind.'

'I don't understand,' said Calard, to which the lady merely shrugged.

'Those creatures,' he went on, seeing that she was not going to offer any further explanation, 'what were they?'

'The *Shael-Mara*,' said the veiled lady. 'Handmaidens of Winter. Dryads. They are furies, as twisted and bitter as their mistress.'

'Are they... daemons?' said Calard, realising only now that the sky was brightening. Dawn was close at hand.

'In a sense,' said the lady. 'They are of the forest. They *are* the forest.'

'But the fey and the forest, are they not bound to each other? Why would the forest seek to harm its elven protectors?'

The veiled lady laughed at that, the sound strange and unearthly.

'Have you never thought that perhaps it is not the elves that protect the forest from intruders, but rather that they protect intruders *from* the forest?'

'Is that true?'

'Yes. And no.'

Calard shook his head in exasperation.

'He is dying, isn't he?' he said, looking down at Cythaeros, whom the lady had called the Morning Star.

'He is.'

'Is it not in your power to save him, lady?'

'Perhaps,' she said, 'but I cannot.'

'Why? You said he was important.'

'He is of the highest importance, but it is not allowed,' said the veiled lady.

'And what of me?' said Calard.

'You will do what is right for you to do.'

'And that is?'

'The path you walk is yours to choose freely.'

'My place is in Bretonnia,' said Calard.

'A great darkness has risen. It threatens to engulf your homeland in eternal twilight,' said the lady. 'I see a black grail, overflowing with blood.'

'Merovech,' said Calard.

'The same,' said the lady. 'His legions are on the march.'

'Have you the gift of far-sight, lady? Can you see how far from Couronne Merovech is?'

'He is close,' whispered the lady. 'He will cross the Sannez within days.'

'How can that be?' said Calard in shock. 'It would take him months to march through Lyonesse and L'Anguille!'

'Time flows differently within the bounds of Athel Loren,' said the lady. 'It is like the river that you call the Upper Grismerie, and the *Asrai* call *Frostwater* – in places it runs swift and deep, while in other places it slows and pools, barely moving at all. Months have passed in the realms beyond the forest's borders since you stepped foot within its bounds, Calard of Garamont.'

'Months?' said Calard. 'My place is alongside the armies of the king! I must be away!'

One of the elves standing sentinel cried a warning.

'They come,' said the veiled lady.

The forest seethed with movement in every direction. They were surrounded.

The warleader was shouting orders, and the elves formed a pocket of resistance upon the banks of the frozen river, facing outwards. He ushered the veiled lady into the protective cordon, and she remounted the proud white stag. Calard too slipped through the semi-circular arc of elves, who were preparing themselves for a final, last stand. They knelt in the snow, arranging their arrows point first in the ground within easy reach, and readied their bows.

The sky was growing brighter. Dawn was less than an hour away.

Forest spirits in all manner of forms were emerging from the forest on all sides, and the ground resounded to the rhythmic step of immense, as yet unseen, creatures of wood and branch drew near.

Mounting Galibor, Calard turned the warhorse and moved into the wood elf battleline, ready to do his part in the coming battle.

'No,' said the ebony-haired elven warleader, his face stern.

'I would fight alongside you and your kin, elf,' said Calard.

'No,' repeated the elf, shaking his head. 'You are needed elsewhere.'

'What are you talking about?'

'The King-in-the-Wood must be reborn come the first rays of dawn, lest the compact be broken,' said the veiled lady. 'We must away.'

'How?'

'Over the ice,' she said.

Calard turned in the saddle to look across the frozen river.

'Then we all go,' he said. 'I will not flee like some craven coward while others fight my battles for me.'

'No,' snapped the elven warleader, his eyes hard. 'It will not hold the weight of us all. Go!'

The white hart was already stepping out onto the frozen lake. The ice groaned beneath its hooves, and cracks began to appear.

'This is madness,' said Calard.

The creatures of the dark forest were starting their advance now, and the elves began to launch their first arrows high into the air. Each warrior had loosed three arrows before the first had even struck home, all with unerring accuracy.

'Head towards the rising sun,' said the pale warleader. 'The Oak of Ages is near. Now go!'

Calard glanced along the line of elves. Each of them knew that they would die here, yet they remained stoic and calm, showing no fear. Cold and defiant, their leader flicked his braided black hair over his shoulder, and turned his gaze towards Calard.

'Go, *kegh-mon*,' he said. 'May Kournos guide you.'

'Fight well,' said Calard, before turning Galibor towards the ice. The white hart was standing twenty feet out on the ice, waiting for him.

'Go!' snapped the elven leader, 'Now!'

Calard nodded, and guided Galibor onto the ice. It shifted beneath Galibor's armoured weight, and Calard swore. The mighty warhorse resisted him, trying to step back onto solid land. With a firm hand, Calard urged Galibor forward, stepping out fully onto the ice, praying that it would hold.

The ice groaned, and he saw deep arcing cracks spreading across its surface. Swearing again, he kicked Galibor forward, racing the reaching cracks. The white hart began to gallop towards the centre of the frozen river, and Calard guided Galibor to follow.

He saw the huge, curved hunting horn drop from Cythaeros's lifeless fingers, falling onto the ice, unnoticed by the veiled lady. Calard made to ride on, then swore to himself and hauled on his reins, dragging Galibor to a halt.

The sounds of the battle echoed out across the lake but the shore was hidden in mist. Deep cracks in the ice were reaching towards him, as if in pursuit.

Calard slid from the saddle and dropped to the ice, which groaned alarmingly beneath him. Spider-web cracks were already appearing beneath his heels. Stooping, he picked up the hunting horn and swung back into the saddle as larger cracks began to appear.

With a yell, he kicked Galibor forward, even as the ice began to break up behind him. He raced to catch up with the white stag, the biting wind making his face sting.

The sounds of the battle echoed out across the lake behind them. Calard turned to look back, but the shore was hidden in mist.

The sky ahead of them was steadily lightening with the dawn, and the pair turned their steeds towards the rising sun.

Without knowing exactly why, compelled by some sudden, wild instinct, Calard drew in a deep breath and raised Cythaeros's curved hunting horn to his lips.

A deafening blast issued forth, the note deeply resonant and sonorous. The sound boomed out across the lake of ice like a shockwave, before bouncing back moments later, reverberating off the distant tree-line and cliffs. Calard's ears were still ringing when he heard an answering horn in the distance.

Cythaeros stirred, raising his head briefly, golden eyes blinking. He mouthed a few words of elvish, before he slumped forward one more, unconscious.

'The Wild Riders come,' said the veiled lady.

'Wild Riders?' said Calard.

'The Untamed,' said the veiled lady. 'The Pyremasters. The Hounds of Kournos.'

'Are they friend or foe?' said Calard, and even though the wind whipped his words away from him, he was confident that she heard him.

'Neither, and both. They are dangerous, but they will see us safely on our path.'

'Where? What path?'

'The Oak of Ages.'

* * *

IX

RACING THE RISING sun, Calard leant over the neck of his powerful war-horse, urging her on. She was tired, but galloped hard through the wilderness alongside the majestic white stag.

It had grown steadily colder the nearer they came to the Oak of Ages. Frost had formed upon Calard's eyebrows and unkempt beard, and he pulled his cloak around his shoulders, shivering. He kicked the ice off his stirrups, and brushed snow from his shoulders.

He could sense that this was an old part of the forest, and he suspected that it had been here long before the birth of the Bretonni, perhaps even before the elves.

Oaks large enough to hold small villages aloft within their branches rose above them, their gnarled limbs thick and heavy.

An icy mist hugged the ground, despite the imminent daylight.

Calard could not have said when the Wild Riders arrived. One moment they had been alone, the next they were surrounded by a great ethereal host of savage, unearthly warriors. It was as if they had materialised from within the mist itself, like wraiths or vengeful phantoms. At first Calard was unsure if they were truly beings of flesh and blood, or merely echoes of warriors long dead. Certainly they were more forest spirit than elf.

Tall and proud, they rode snorting steeds as ferocious and untamed as themselves. Naked from the waist up but for sweeping fur cloaks, they appeared oblivious to the cold. Their torsos and arms were covered in intricate tattoos and war-paint that baffled the eye. The painted designs were in flux, shifting and writhing across their flesh, forming ever more complex patterns and swirling knot-work.

Their flesh was tinged green, and their eyes blazed with fey light and callous savagery. Curving horns like those of young bucks protruded from their temples, revealing their animalistic nature, and they bared their teeth at Calard like wolves. Their mane-like hair was braided and long, filled with sticks and ivy and bones.

They carried spears and swords bound in runes and blood, and scorned the use of saddles and bridles. Skulls and severed heads hung from their belts, and bones and teeth were strung upon necklaces of sinew.

They radiated a ghostly inner light, as if moonlight were trapped within their flesh, and they exuded an untamed fury that threatened to be unleashed at any moment.

In some ways, the power emanating from the otherworldy beings was similar to that he had felt in the presence of the grail knight Reolus, though this power was far less refined, wilder and less predictable, and certainly more dangerous.

As if hearing his thoughts, one of the Wild Riders turned and grinned savagely at Calard, white fire flaring in his predatory eyes. He saw the warrior's muscles twitch, as if he were restraining the urge to lash out.

The tattoos upon the warrior's chest and arms writhed like constricting serpents.

Transfixed by the gaze of the savage rider, Calard found his heart beating faster, and his breath quickening. Images of blood and destruction filled his mind, and he felt a sudden urge to howl at the moon and let his baser instincts overwhelm him.

He wanted to run with the wolves, to join the hunt and hear the plaintive cry of the quarry as it was run down. He wanted to experience the joy that came as the prey was caught and torn apart in a glorious frenzy. He wanted to rip and rend at flesh. He wanted to taste hot blood in his mouth.

Calard blinked and turned away, severing eye contact with the grinning, fierce warrior. Breathing hard, he mouthed a prayer to the Lady and clutched at the fleur-de-lys pendant around his neck. The barbarous creature laughed at his resistance to its savage nature.

Others had joined their ride towards the Oak of Ages. Painted warriors with their hair stiffened into garish spikes ran alongside them, throwing themselves into acrobatic leaps and somersaults to the frenzied beat of drums, and immense warhawks the size of draught horses corkscrewed and dove through the branches overhead. Incredibly, elves were crouched upon the shoulders of these great hunting birds, and Calard marvelled at their preternatural skill and balance to stay mounted as their feathered steeds spiralled through the canopy.

Cloaked archers darted through the shadows, and ranks of elves bedecked in curving, leaf-shaped armour and carrying slender, twin-bladed spears jogged through the snow.

Calard could not guess how many warriors had joined them. For all he knew, the entire forest was marching with them.

If Calard had felt in awe of the Forest of Loren beforehand, that paled in comparison to what he felt as they drew near their final destination. His breath caught in his throat. Surely few men of human birth had ever set eyes upon what he did now.

It was tree of such scale that if defied belief. Every oak, ash and fir he had seen thus far was dwarfed by this arboreal titan, and he was left in no doubt that this was the Oak of Ages, their destination and goal.

A thousand men could have stretched out their arms around the bole of the ancient tree without ever touching fingertips, and he felt certain that had it been somehow transported to the very centre of Couronne its branches would spread from one side of the city to the other. It was larger than any castle in the known world and as high as a mountain, its upper reaches lost in the clouds. Even its lowest branches soared above every other tree in the area, casting them in shadow. Snow was heaped upon its bare branches, and ice encased its ancient gnarled trunk. Slender waystones carved with elegant runes that glowed with fey green light surrounded the immense oak.

Without any doubt, Calard knew that he stood in the presence of one of the oldest and largest living things in the world, and he felt humbled. The air was freezing here, and Calard realised that this was the source of the unnatural winter that had engulfed the forest.

The white hart came to a halt, and Calard and the savage Wild Riders fell in behind it. An expectant hush descended.

A mighty arch was set into the bole of the gargantuan grandfather oak, a shadowed gateway large enough for fifty knights to ride through side by side with room to spare. Icicles hung from the arch like the teeth of a dragon, ready to clamp down on any who dared pass beneath. Mist rolled out from this darkened entrance into the tree's secret depths.

Calard felt a strange tingling sensation across his flesh as he gazed upon the yawning archway. It prickled at his skin, and he tasted an acidic, metallic tang upon his tongue.

'Sorcery,' he muttered, drawing his sword.

The Wild Riders evidently felt these magicks at work as well, for they snarled and bared their teeth, brandishing weapons. Their horses stamped their hooves and tossed their heads in agitation, manes thrashing from side to side.

The knotted bark and gnarled wood of the Oak of Ages began to shift and warp, frozen branches contorting and twisting as if the tree were in silent agony. Ice cracked and fell from its flanks in great sheets, and snow tumbled from immense branches. An angry murmur rippled through the elven ranks.

The ground trembled, and roots as thick as tree-trunks burst from the ground in front of the white stag, throwing up a wave of snow and sodden earth, forcing it back. The roots of the Oak of Ages rose into the air, coiling and twining together into one thick, rope like stem. It climbed twenty, thirty, forty feet straight upwards, and its tip bulged like a rapidly growing rosebud the size of a small house. The petals of this bulging bud curled back, revealing a single figure. Icy fog spilled around it, falling towards the ground like a waterfall. It was a creature at once alluringly feminine and horrifying in aspect.

'*Drycha,*' spat one of the Wild Riders, and the name was repeated a hundred times around the glade, spoken with hatred and venom.

An ancient creature of malice and bile, she nevertheless had the body of a goddess. Her naked flesh was silvery-green and thick hair of tangled roots and dead leaves coiled down her back, writhing like a nest of vipers. Her slender arms became elongated branches at the elbows, and her hands were blade-like talons, each the length of a short sword.

Her inhuman features were exquisitely beautiful, yet disturbing. Her eyes were large and sharply elongated, and they shone with green light and murder.

The roots of the Oak of Ages coiled around her legs, twisting around her calves and thighs, encircling her slender waist. The roots retracted, and Drycha was lowered to the ground. She came to rest before the arched entrance into the frozen heart of the Oak of Ages, and the roots disappeared beneath the earth.

She regarded the white stag and the warriors arrayed against her with undisguised disdain. Her luscious green-tinged lips curled in a sneer.

'Begone, elven fools,' the malicious forest spirit hissed, the words spiralling around in Calard's mind. 'Athel Loren no longer welcomes your presence.'

Her whispering, insidious voice made a chill ripple down Calard's spine. It was the sibilant voice of a serpent, filled with bitterness and poison. Her words were spoken in the lilting, musical tongue of the elves, yet he found he could understand them.

'The King-in-the-Wood is ash and dust, and his consort-queen lies sleeping, locked in winter's embrace,' continued Drycha. 'Too long have those of elvenkind kept the forest imprisoned, and it rages to be free. Come the first rays of dawn, it will be.'

Calard could feel the mounting fury of the Wild Riders, a rising anger that threatened to erupt at any moment.

Alone, the veiled lady seemed unaffected. She slid from the back of the majestic white hart, and began to walk out to meet Drycha. The malign forest spirit regarded her with hatred, her talons flexing and her tangle of hair writhing.

'Stand aside, Drycha of the deep forest,' said the veiled lady, coming to a halt twenty feet away from the branchwraith. 'The Equerries of Kurnous have come, as they have on the eve of the vernal equinox since the Winter of Woe, so long past. They bring with them He-Who-Would-Be-King, the Morning Star, and you have no right to bar their progress. There is still time for the offering to be made, and for the forest to be appeased.'

'You are not of this place, mortal being,' hissed Drycha. 'You have no authority here, no right to speak or act. Dawn approaches. The offering is too late.'

As she spoke, Drycha began to walk backwards, hips swaying. She allowed her war-aspect to come upon her, and her face twisted into that of a murderous hag, her features becoming cracked and wooden and sharp, matching the vile darkness of her soul.

She stepped back into the shadow of the archway of the Oak of Ages, her glowing green eyes shining in the gloom.

'The dawn rises, red and bloody, and the compact remains unfulfilled,' Drycha hissed. 'The time of the Asrai is over.'

She raised her hands into the air, and an icy tempest billowed around her. She stretched her splayed talons towards the elves, and a storm of ice and frost blasted across the glade to engulf the veiled lady and the elven war-host arrayed behind her. Calard cried out as the veiled lady disappeared in the tempest. The temperature plummeted, and he was forced to shield his face as the howling blizzard crashed over him.

Elves were sent sprawling, their cries ripped away by the gale and their faces sliced by ice. Horses reared in panic and many lost their footing as the tornado raged around them, blinding and deafening.

As abruptly as it had come, the wind died away, and Calard saw the veiled lady still standing, untouched in the centre of the glade. Of Drycha, there was no sign, but he became aware of thousands of pairs of eyes twinkling in the shadow behind the Oak of Ages.

The darkened forest came alive, rippling with movement. A host from the deepest wildwoods came forth, a bewildering array of creatures united by hatred.

Flocks of crows took roost within the branches of the Oak of Ages, cawing and bickering, the red-caps perched upon their feathered backs waving tiny spears and bows.

Dryads emerged from the gloom to take up position before the great tree, their claws twitching in eagerness, eyes flashing. Some were ready for war, their features twisted into horrific masks of dead wood and briar, while others appeared as elven nymphs, their skin tinged green, their bodies youthful and deceiving.

Behind them came behemoths of wood and bracken, hulking monsters infused with the life-force of malevolent forest spirits. Some resembled uprooted husks of dead trees, while others appeared as little more than sodden piles of rotting wood and fallen branches crudely pulled together to form a vaguely humanoid form. Most were more than eight feet tall, while some were closer to twenty. Ivy and lichen clung to them, and many had ferns and brightly coloured fungus growing from their hunched backs. Crude parodies of men, they lumbered forward to smash and destroy, driven on by Drycha's hatred.

Clouds of shimmering sprites flitted between the boughs, hissing and spitting as they brandished tiny weapons, glittering wings beating fast. Others rode owls, weasels or large, powdery-winged moths while some merely swarmed across the snow, leaping and cavorting between the legs of their larger kin. Glowing will-o'-the-wisps bobbed and weaved through the air, and tiny beings that seemed to be made of nothing more than leaf and thorn stomped forward, black eyes glittering with the promise of violence. Spider-like beasts of bramble and sticks crept through the branches overhead, sap-like venom dripping from clicking mandibles. White-furred wolves slunk through the shadows, snarling and baring their teeth.

The sheer range of wildwood creatures that surrounded the Oak of Ages was staggering. Calard even glimpsed a small band of elves among the dark forest's ranks, outcasts who had blackened their faces with soot and bore twisted spider-web tattoos upon their flesh.

Towering over them all strode a creature fifty feet tall, an ancient and twisted oak come to life, its gnarled hide blackened by fire. Roots burrowed into the earth as each immense leg came crashing down into the snow, making the ground shudder and shake, and huge branch-arms capable of pounding a castle to dust swung heavily at its sides. Clusters of vindictive spites hid within the knots and hollows that pocked its charred bark-flesh, and a gaping maw filled with splinter-like teeth opened halfway up the monster's trunk. Above this vicious mouth, a pair of tiny, deep set eyes blinked.

'Ancient Coeddil walks among us, freed from the glamourweave's prison,' came Drycha's voice, hissing forth from within the Oak of Ages. 'Know fear, petty lordling mortals; the time of reckoning is come.'

With a booming roar, the gigantic tree-lord, Coeddil, thrust its arms into the ground. The earth shivered and bulged, as if things were burrowing beneath it, shooting towards Calard and the elven host. A heartbeat later, and a forest of roots burst up through the snow. They whipped around the legs of elves and horses alike, gripping tight and pulling them down.

They clutched at the white stag, reaching up to ensnare the kingly beast and its riders. White light flared and the clawing tendrils turned to ash, falling harmlessly to the ground.

Others were not so protected, and there were shouts of pain and fear as elves were yanked down by the clutching vines. Calard saw a dozen Wild Riders fall as their steeds were dragged to the ground, whinnying in panic. They fell hard, and were instantly covered by a tangle of roots that wrapped around arms, bodies and necks. The savage warriors strained against the living bindings, but could do little as they were dragged to their graves beneath the icy soil.

Galibor reared to avoid a cluster of worm-like tendrils that burst up through the snow beneath her, and Calard slashed at them as they coiled upwards, reaching blindly.

'Ride!' shouted the veiled lady.

Dozens of hunting horns echoed across the glade, and the elves surged forward to meet the dark host of forest spirits in battle, whooping and howling as they charged. Arrows darkened the sky, which was now the subtle grey-blue of pre-dawn, and formations of warhawk riders screamed down through the canopy from above, the huge hunting birds tucking their wings in tight. Painted elven warriors cart-wheeled forwards, their dance of blades both elegant and deadly, and fur-cloaked elves ran to join the fray, spinning their double-bladed staff-spears deftly.

The white stag galloped forward, surrounded by wild riders, and Calard felt himself pulled along with them. The veiled lady turned, and he felt her eyes boring into him, even though her face was obscured by her veil.

The branchwraith Drycha must be expelled from the Oak of Ages before the king-to-be can be reborn, she said, her strange triad of voices speaking in his mind. *Yet such is the geas that Drycha has woven upon the oak that no forest born creature nor one of elven blood can enter.*

'This is my task,' said Calard. 'This is why the Lady brought me here.'

Perhaps, brother.

Calard's eyes widened.

'Anara?'

'Ride, Calard!' cried the veiled lady, his twin sister, and the white stag leapt forwards.

The battle was savage, each side fighting with fury and passion.

Dryads cut down elves and impaled them upon their blade-like limbs, while others were ripped apart by towering monsters of the forest. Slender warriors were pounded into the ground by heavy wooden arms and set upon by swarms of dark faeries, wings fluttering and knives glittering. Ancient Coeddil sent elves flying with each sweep of his massive arms, and he dragged dozens more to their deaths, his clawing roots reaching up beneath them to ensnare them.

Through the confusion, the unearthly Wild Riders cleared a path for Calard and the white stag, selling their lives dearly. They were only fifty yards from the immense tree when Calard spurred Galibor on, breaking free of the entourage of savage warriors, riding hard for the shadowy archway.

Dryads screamed their fury and leapt into his path, their raking talons slashing at him, but he cut them down and was past them, galloping on.

He kicked Galibor into a leap, and they sailed through the huge archway. A wave of vertigo assailed him, and he felt his skin tingle strangely.

Then he was falling, surrounded by blinding, icy mist, and then... nothing.

X

WITH A GASP, Calard awoke.

He lay upon a plush four-poster bed and could hear birds singing their morning chorus outside. Sunlight streamed through arched windows, and the scent of spring wafted through the high-ceilinged bed chamber borne on a warm breeze.

He swung his legs from the bed and looked around in confusion. An open chest at the foot of his bed was overflowing with clothes – *his* clothes – and a half-eaten meal of quail and duck lay on silver platters on a side-table. His armour hung from a wooden stand in one corner of the room, and his sword leant against the unlit fireplace.

He was within his bed chamber in Garamont. He was home.

Strange, half-remembered images flickered through his mind. He saw a forest filled with malign spirits, and trees that walked like men. He saw one of the fey folk, with slanted golden eyes and pointed ears, and he shivered, remembering an unnatural winter that had blanketed the land in snow.

His dreams were fading fast, dissipating like lake mist under a rising sun. He knew there was something important he had to do, something important that he had to remember, but he could not recall what it was.

With a sigh, he pushed himself to his feet and padded towards his washbasin. The familiar sounds of the castle reached his ears. He could hear peasants in the fields, and the clatter of pots and pans from the kitchens downstairs. He heard weapons clashing and a yeoman bellowing orders as he put his men-at-arms through their training drills, and he could hear the rhythmic *clang* of a blacksmith's hammer upon an anvil. He heard a dog barking, and from somewhere, he heard a washer woman singing tunelessly as she went about her chores.

Calard filled the basin with a jug of water and splashed cold water across his face. He looked at himself in the mirror. His face was smooth and youthful.

The door burst open, and he turned to see his brother Bertelis stagger into the room. He threw himself down upon Calard's bed, groaning theatrically.

'I'll never drink again,' said Bertelis. 'What a night!'

Calard grinned.

'My head feels like it is going to explode,' said Bertelis. 'Make it stop!'

'I had the strangest dreams,' said Calard, turning back to his wash basin and staring into the mirror. His reflection seemed almost like a stranger...

'Oh?' said Bertelis. 'Did you dream you could beat me at the joust? Because that *would* be strange.'

'No,' said Calard. 'I was embarked on the quest. My clothes were torn and covered in dirt, and my armour battered and worn. I had a beard, and my hair was long and streaked with grey. I was tired. So tired.'

Bertelis snorted.

'You have such boring fantasies, my brother,' he said. 'Now *mine*, on the other hand...'

'I came home after many years of questing, but Garamont was in ruin,' said Calard. 'And Elisabet was dead. You killed her, my brother. It was an accident, but I was angry and grief-stricken. A distance grew between us, and you left. I had not seen you for many years.'

'Enough, Calard,' said Bertelis, sitting up. 'As you can see, Garamont is as intact as it ever was. I am here, and Elisabet is alive and well. The wedding is next week, after all.'

'The wedding?' said Calard.

Bertelis laughed.

'Your wedding, yes, you dolt,' he said. 'Don't tell me you forgot.'

'No, of course not,' said Calard.

'Forget the dream. This is all that is real,' said Bertelis, gesturing around the room. 'This is all that you need.'

'I... I think I went to Mousillon, in my nightmare,' said Calard. 'Yes, it is coming back to me now.'

'Ranald's balls, man! It was a dream, nothing more. Forget it!'

Calard could not understand why his brother was getting so angry, but he gave it little thought. He shivered, casting his mind back, struggling to latch onto the elusive memories. It had all been so *real*.

'Merovech,' he whispered. 'Duke Merovech the Mad. He had returned. He had raised an army of the living dead, and was preparing to launch an attack against the king. A great battle was coming. I wanted to fight, but something called me away – a vision, I think. It led me far away, to the haunted forest of Loren...'

'Enough!' snapped Bertelis. 'I don't want to hear it, brother.'

'You were there in Mousillon, brother,' said Calard, frowning as he remembered. 'You were there, but you were not yourself. You were... You were–'

'I was *what*, brother?' said Bertelis, his voice hostile and cold.

'Dead,' said Calard, flatly.

'Yes, dead,' said Bertelis. 'You killed me, remember?'

He was suddenly standing close behind Calard, though he made no reflection in the mirror. The hair on the back of Calard's neck stood on end. This wasn't his brother at all, Calard realised.

'You cast me aside, brother,' said Bertelis. 'You cast me aside to assuage your own guilt. You drove me to into Merovech's arms. It was *your* fault. And then you killed me. Now it is *your* time to die.'

Calard had a blade in his hands, and he spun around as the thing masquerading as his brother attacked.

He saw a horrific snarling face that seemed to be carved from wood coming at him, and the scent of rotting leaves filled his nose. Blade-like talons lashed for his face, but he fended them off with the Sword of Garamont, which blazed with white light.

He felt the blade bite deep into woody flesh, and the creature screeched. Claws raked across his face. He was knocked flying by the strength behind the blow and hit the ground hard. For a moment he thought he felt snow beneath his hands. Blood was running down his cheek, but he pushed himself back to his feet, bringing his blade around to defend himself.

His attacker was gone, and a cold wind was blowing through the blackened ruins of Castle Garamont.

'What in the name of the Lady?' he whispered, turning around on the spot.

He stood within his old bed chamber, but its walls had crumbled. The sky was dark overhead.

A movement behind him made his spin. A figure came forward from the shadows, and Calard's eyes widened in horror.

'No,' he said.

The figure glided into the moonlight, looking up at him with plead-ing, sorrowful eyes.

It was Elisabet, the young noblewoman whom he had given his heart to so long ago, and who had betrayed him. Her face was pale, and she was dressed in a flowing mortuary shroud that billowed around her. She reached for him, silently imploring for forgiveness.

'You're dead,' said Calard, backing away.

She nodded sadly, and blood began to flow down the side of her head, gushing from the wound in her temple, where her skull had cracked. He remembered the horrible sound as she hit the cold marble steps of Lyonesse. The blood began to soak her flowing gown, making it cling to her body. Tears ran down her face.

'I'm sorry,' said Calard as he backed away further, only stopping when he was pressed up against the fire-blackened wall.

'I'm sorry,' he said again as she drifted towards him. Her feet were hovering an inch above the ground. In trembling hands, he lifted the Sword of Garamont before him.

'Her death is on your conscience,' said a hollow, familiar voice.

'Father?' said Calard, looking around.

His surroundings had shifted again, and he found himself standing within the crypt below his family castle. Garbed in the deathly robes, his father stood motionless, staring at him with cold, dead eyes. His skin was grey.

'That poor, restless spirit wanders lost in the between worlds because of you,' said the former castellan of Garamont, Calard's father.

'She was poisoning you, father,' said Calard.

'Not a bad likeness,' said Lutheure, glancing down at the carved stone sarcophagus that held his own remains. The marble top had been crafted to look as Lutheure had in his prime, strong and proud, arms crossed upon his broad, armoured chest. 'She did what she thought was the best thing for her, and for you. She didn't deserve the cruelty that befell her.'

'It was not my fault, father,' said Calard.

'You are no son of mine,' said Lutheure. 'Not anymore. I had but one son I could be proud of, and you destroyed him. Had I not been so weak, I would have strangled you at birth, you and that witch of a sister. I should have seen your mother burn in the cleansing flames. Her tainted bloodline has destroyed Garamont.'

'No,' said Calard.

'If you had any courage yourself, you would have taken your own life,' said Lutheure. 'But in your craven cowardice, you could not even do that.'

'Father, please,' said Calard.

Again, his surroundings shifted. He stood outside the ruin of Castle Garamont, only now the shades of a hundred knights and peasants stood amongst the devastation, staring at him forlornly. They were as insubstantial as mist, and their eyes were filled with accusation.

'They all died because of you,' came his father's voice. 'If you had been here, doing your duty, they would yet live.'

'I was embarked upon the quest,' said Calard weakly.

'You swore an oath to protect them. Your place was here.'

Two figures pressed through the crowd of restless spirits, and Calard felt his heart wrench.

A slender adolescent, little more than a boy, led a barrel-chested bear of a man towards him. The youngster had wavy, shoulder-length hair and was garbed in the rich clothes of a nobleman. His face was honest and open, and he had a smattering of freckles across his nose and cheeks. The older man had a thick beard that was running to grey, and wore a scarf tied over his eyes.

The boy was Calard's heir, his nephew Orlando, whom he had named castellan of Garamont when he had set aside his duties to take up the quest. He had been a child when last he had seen him. The older figure was Baron Montcadas, who had pledged to look after Orlando while Calard was away. Both had been slain in one bloody night, a night that had seen Castle Garamont razed to the ground.

'You never came back,' said Orlando. His voice was empty, as if all his youthful joy and mirth had been sucked out of him. 'You should have been here.'

'I'm so sorry,' said Calard. 'I never meant for any of this to happen.'

'Your empty platitudes don't count for anything here, lad,' said Montcadas in his rumbling voice. 'This boy was an innocent. His blood stains your hands.'

Calard clenched his eyes shut, despairing, feeling the weight of guilt pressing down upon him. When he opened his eyes, his surroundings were once again altered.

He stood within a chirurgeon's tent, surrounded by the dead and dying. Laid out upon a table before him was the corpse of a grey-haired knight. His armour was rent in dozens of places, and tattered chainmail hung where it had been sundered. Broken spear-tips protruded from his body, and an axe was still embedded deep in the flesh above his hip.

'Gunthar,' said Calard, staring down at the body of his old weapon master and friend.

Gunthar had been more of a father to him than Lutheure ever had. The guilt of Gunthar's death still plagued him.

Foolishly, Calard had become embroiled in a challenge with Maloric of Sangasse when he had been just a young knight errant. Maloric had appointed a champion, as was his right – Ganelon, a murderous knight that had never been bested. Calard knew that he could never win, but Gunthar had stepped in as his own champion, and though he had slain Ganelon, he had been fatally wounded in the process.

Gunthar's lifeless head rolled to the side and his eyes flickered open.

'I died that you might live, Calard,' he said, 'but you have brought nothing but dishonour upon your household.'

Tears of shame rose to Calard's eyes.

'I'm sorry,' he said.

He stood on an island, surrounded by fog. He could hear the roar of the ocean, crashing against the rocks just off the coast. The pebbled beach was strewn with corpses of knights and savage Norscans.

Amidst the devastation walked a single figure; a knight, tall and proud, striding towards Calard. A regal blue cloaked whipped behind him, and his blue tabard was edged in silver. His armour was ornate, and he wore a tall unicorn-crested helm, surrounded by candles. None of them were lit.

'Reolus,' he said.

'He was the best of men, the most chivalrous and noble of paladins,' said a voice behind him. He didn't need to turn to see who it was that was speaking; he recognised his sister Anara's voice. 'He was my lover and companion, and he died needlessly.'

'He died an honourable death,' said Calard, eyes locked on the silent figure of the grail knight making his steady progress towards him.

'There is nothing honourable about death,' said Anara. 'We are born alone and we die alone. Death cares not whether we are good and noble and just in our brief time upon this world, nor if we are murdering savages. We are all just dirt in the ground in the end. You say he died a noble death. It means nothing. He is still dead, and the world is the poorer for it. His death was meaningless. It changed nothing.'

'He did not believe that.'

Reolus came to a halt before Calard, who dropped to one knee, bowing his head.

The ocean boomed, and sea birds screamed.

'He died because of *you*, my brother,' said Anara.

'No,' said Calard, shaking his head.

'Think of it, brother. There would have been no war with the Norscans had you died in place of Gunthar, on the fields of Bordeleaux, as things should have played out. It should have been you who fell beneath Ganelon's blade. Elisabet would have ceased poisoning our father – he would have lived to see grandsons taught under Gunthar's tutorage. Action and consequence.'

'Grandsons?' said Calard.

'Bertelis's children,' said Anara. 'They would have grown up to be strong and proud, with none of our mother's taint in their blood.'

'You could not know any of this would come to pass,' said Calard.

'I am a prophetess of the Lady, my brother. I speak the truth. Had you died in Gunthar's place, Garamont would have flourished. The Lady Elisabet would have had no reason to seek out the witch-crone Haegtesse. She would have mourned your death, but lived a happy, fulfilled life.

She would have grown old gracefully and passed away peacefully in her sleep, without regrets. Without her, the Norscan warlord Styrbjorn would never have come to our shores. He and his kinsmen would have perished in a meaningless feud with a neighbouring tribe, and his name would have been forgotten.'

'Stop,' said Calard. 'Please stop.'

Anara ignored him, stepping in close to continue her tirade.

'No daemon-child would have been spawned in Elisabet's womb. There would have been no war fought in Lyonesse to save her. Tens of thousands of lives would have been spared. That unborn child meant everything to the Norscan warlord – when you stole Elisabet from him, he would have torn the world apart to get her back. And in a noble attempt to save further bloodshed, my Reolus accepted the Skaeling's challenge – and paid the ultimate price.'

Calard was shaking his head, trying to blot out his sister's voice.

'Action and consequence, my brother,' said Anara. 'He died because of you. They all died because of you.'

Calard found himself upon a windswept plain beneath a featureless heaven, utterly devoid of colour. The dead stood in serried ranks as far as the eye could see, motionless. They were all there: his father, Elisabet, Gunthar, Reolus, Orlando, Montcadas, and tens of thousands of others. They stood in silence, staring, and the weight of accusation crushed down upon him. Bertelis stood nearest of all. Calard could not look him in the eye.

'It should have been you,' they said as one.

Without knowing how, Calard found himself holding the Sword of Garamont reversed in his hands, its point touching his throat. Tears were running freely down his cheeks. All he had to do was press forward, and all this pain, all this misery would end. A moment of pain, and then... nothing. All his guilt would be washed away, like a leaf on a stream...

'Do it, my brother,' urged Bertelis.

'Prove that you are indeed my son,' said Lutheure. 'Finish it now!'

'Do it!' brayed a thousand deafening voices.

Calard tensed, closing his eyes as he prepared to end his own life.

'Lady of mercy, forgive me,' he breathed. 'I have failed you.'

An unpleasant, cloying scent gave him pause. An earthy smell of rotting woodwork and leaf-mulch filled his nostrils, confusing him for a moment.

'Do it!' screamed the army of the dead, but Calard ignored them as his memories flooded back and the illusions woven by the branchwraith Drycha began to unravel around him.

He remembered that it was the Lady that had led him to the Forest of Loren, and that is was by her divine will that he was here at this place, at this moment in time.

Calard's eyes flicked open and he surged to his feet. The Sword of

Garamont burst into white flame, and he heard Drycha scream in frustration.

The illusion of the endless plain of the underworld shattered like crystal beneath a hammer, and the frozen heart of the Oak of Ages was revealed.

It was unlike anything Calard could have imagined. He stood within a vast, subterranean hall, a magical, frozen realm that stretched in all directions. Spheres of light bobbed gently through the air, radiating a diffuse glow akin to predawn. The earthen roof curved far overhead, and the vast roots of the Oak of Ages hung down low, entwined together to form pillars that came down to the ground. Other roots wove down the sloping, distant walls, forming archways leading off into other halls, deep beneath the forest.

The strange realm was like a small version of the world above. The crust of snow crunched beneath Calard's boots as he turned, gazing around in wonder. Gently sloping hills rose to meet the walls on every side, forming a natural valley in the centre of the otherworldy hall. A wide, frozen lake spread out in this depression, its surface mirror-like and gleaming, and in its centre rose a small island.

Calard found himself drawn towards the lake. Sheathing the Sword of Garamont, he began to walk, trudging through the powdery snow. His eyes were locked on the island. It was lightly wooded, its trees leafless and barren, and a winding path led to a low rocky headland jutting out from the ice.

The snow was knee-deep, but Calard picked up his pace, urged on by some ethereal impulse. He hurried down the powdery slope, passing through icy woods. The land levelled out as he came to the lake's edge, and without delay he stepped out upon its frozen surface.

The air was cold and crisp and still as he reached the island. He climbed a twisting path through ice-shawled trees, and passed through a stone archway carved with ivy and spiralling runes. He walked slowly out onto the low rocky headland, the highest point on the little island.

A circular dais was situated there, and it was to this that Calard was drawn. He hardly dared breathe as he approached. An elegantly designed stone plinth was carved into the dais, and lying upon it was a goddess.

Tall and slender, and so coldly beautiful that it made Calard's heart ache, the elven goddess slumbered. She might have been carved from marble, so perfect was her countenance and so porcelain-pale was her skin. Her hair was the deep blue-black of a midnight sky, matching her dress that spilt down the sides of the altar on which she lay and spread out over the dais. Frozen leaves encircled her slender waist and brow, and tendrils of ivy wound around her flawless, alabaster arms. Frost glittered upon her cheeks, and ice-crystals had formed upon her eye-lashes.

She was a vision of ethereal perfection, a frozen deity locked in the deathly sleep of winter.

Calard felt the presence of Drycha before he saw her. She ghosted up behind him, materialising like vapour. He tensed, grip tightening around the Sword of Garamont, and turned to face her.

He saw her talons hastily retract, and she came towards him wearing her most appealing form. Her emerald eyes were unblinking. She passed through the archway, moving with unhurried, feline grace, slender fingers trailing across the carved stone.

She was naked. All that protected her modesty was the serpentine flow of her hair, wrapping around her willowy form. Filled with twigs and ivy, her hair was like a living mass, caressing her body. Her feet were bare yet she walked through the snow as if untouched by the cold.

Calard felt no lust or desire stir within him as he watched the otherworldy creature approach. She was physical perfection beyond any earthly being, but nevertheless, he remained unaffected. He knew what vileness lurked beneath her veneer of beauty and grace.

'You should not be here, mortal,' said Drycha. Her voice was throaty and seductive. 'This is a sacred place.'

'You are the source of this unnatural winter,' said Calard. 'Can you keep spring at bay forever? Will your goddess not be displeased with you for having imprisoned her so?'

'She is no goddess. And with the compact sundered, she will be no faerie queen, either. You are not of the forest, and have no understanding of what you speak,' said Drycha, stalking closer, eyes glittering. Her hair began to writhe.

'I know enough to know that your heart is rotten,' said Calard.

'I walked this earth long before the birth of your short-lived race,' snarled Drycha, her full lips curling. 'And I shall walk it still when you and all your wretched kind are but a forgotten memory.'

'Perhaps,' said Calard.

'I remember the arrival of the elves, long before they became the *asrai*,' continued Drycha. 'I watched as they first ventured into the green. They were so full of fear. I laughed as their blood was spilt upon the forest floor. I screamed my fury when our fate became entwined with theirs. It was a mistake, but their time among us has come to an end.'

Drycha paced back and forth before Calard, and her voice grew bitter. Her fingers elongated into thorny claws, and her hair whipped around her.

'It was foolishness to have ever granted them the aegis of the forest. It was wrong to have put such faith in them. What could they offer us? We did not need their protection; they needed *ours*. We did not fear the bearded mountainfolk and their axes, nor the savage greenskins and their fire – it was the elves who needed *us*.'

Calard watched Drycha warily, his hand still clasped around the hilt of his sword. He had witnessed the speed and agility of Drycha's handmaidens, and knew that she could turn on him in an instant. He would not be taken unawares.

'They were ever weak-willed beings, filled with slyness and tricks. It was wrong to have trusted them as we did. They ingratiated themselves with us, taking from us what knowledge could be gleaned, giving back little. They stole our magicks and our secrets. They caged us, fencing us in with their wicked stones. The forest rages to be free,' said Drycha, 'and with the foolish compact between elf and forest finally annulled it shall be unleashed, and the world shall tremble.'

Drycha ceased her pacing. She stared at Calard with unmasked venom, her hands clenching.

'Leave this place, mortal,' said Drycha, her voice filled with ice. 'You are not welcome here. This is none of your concern.'

'No,' said Calard. 'It is by the Lady's will that I am here, and I shall not fail her.'

'I know all your hopes and desires, mortal,' said Drycha. 'Nothing is hidden from me. I can give you what it is you want. I can guide you along the darkling paths that wend and twine. You can stand alongside your kinsmen to face the darkness that threatens, even now.'

'No,' said Calard.

'Would you like to see the battle for your homeland? It is already underway. Why are you here, when that is where you ought to be? Is that not part of your duty? Is that not part of your sworn oath? "To defend the honour and life of the king, above your own"?'

'Get out of my head,' said Calard.

'The dead surround the stone prison you call Couronne, even now. The battle has been raging for many hours – its outcome hangs in the balance.'

'Silence, witch,' said Calard.

'I do not lie, Calard of Garamont,' hissed Drycha. 'The battle is close to lost.'

'I do not believe you,' he said.

'Look there,' said Drycha, pointing.

'I see nothing,' said Calard.

'Look again, Calard of Garamont.'

A wave of vertigo passed over him, but soon he realised that he *could* see something. The carved stone archway was dark now. He ought to have been able to see the trees and snow through it, but as he blinked he saw that it led into a shadowy tunnel. Torches burst into life, lighting the way. The passageway stretched on and on, and at its end he could just make out...

'Couronne!'

He could see the towering outer walls of Bretonnia's capital, pennants fluttering in a wind Calard could not feel. Stormy skies roiled above the white towers and battlements, and lightning flashed. Tens of thousands of warriors were embroiled in desperate battle, and Calard's eyes widened. Scores of trebuchets were firing from atop Couronne's walls, hurling great chunks of masonry into the endless horde, and the sky was dark with arrows. Thousand-strong formations of knights sallied forth in glorious charges, only to be surrounded and dragged down by the endless ranks of the dead.

Calard's breath caught in his throat. He was witnessing the death of his nation.

'How...?' he gasped.

'You know in your heart that what you see is true,' said Drycha, and he did, though he railed against it. 'Go. Join your people. Die with them. That is your wish, is it not?'

'What difference could I make?' said Calard, despairing. 'What effect could I alone have on the battle's outcome?'

'Go or stay, the choice is yours.'

The tunnel stretched out before him, and he thought he could hear the sound of the distant battle. That was where he ought to be, fighting and dying in the defence of his king. That was his duty.

It was with considerable reluctance that he turned away.

'No,' he said. 'My place is here.'

'Then you are a fool,' said Drycha. 'I'll flay the skin from your bones and feed your entrails to the *ban-sidhe*. An eternity of torment awaits you.'

'You are a pitiful creature,' Calard said. 'You are nothing but a slave to malice and resentment, consumed with bitterness and poison. Your heart is rotten. You bring nothing but shame to this ancient and magical forest. You failed to destroy me with your lies and your illusions. Your threats mean nothing to me. You fear me, or why would you bother with temptations? You fear me, and you know that my path is true.'

Drycha's alluring beauty sloughed away, replaced with a mask of vileness and fury. Her cracked, wooden lips slid back to reveal green needle-like teeth and oily black gums, and her slender, nubile body became a wasted cadaver of wood and thorn. She leapt at him, fingers fusing into points, and drew her branch-like arms back to impale him.

Calard had drawn the Sword of Garmont as soon as the change had come upon her. The light of the Lady filled him, guiding his arm and eliminating all doubt.

He stepped in to meet her as she hurtled through the air towards him, and taking hold of his sword in both hands, he thrust it up into her body, skewering her upon its flaming blade. The blow stopped her momentum dead, and she hung there transfixed, her face inches from his own. Black, sap-like ichor slid down over the hilt of his sword.

'It is over,' said Calard.

'Only for you,' hissed the branchwraith, breathing the stink of worm-wood and rot into his face.

Calard looked down, frowning. Both of the branchwraith's thorn-ridged arms had punched through his breastplate.

Drycha's blade-edged arms had driven straight through him, and three feet of their lengths protruded from his back. He felt no pain, but blood was flowing freely from the twin wounds in his chest. It looked incredibly bright and vibrant as it ran down his armoured body and legs.

For a moment the two were locked together – Drycha impaled and held aloft by Calard's sword, and he run through by her. Then she slid her arms free, gnarled talons becoming slender elven hands, thorned bark becoming smooth skin. Her slender arms were coated in gore, from fingertip to elbow, and Calard gasped as they were extracted from his body. Blood gushed from his wounds in a torrent, and choking red foam rose in his throat.

The white flame of his sword flickered and died as he relinquished his grasp upon the grip, and Drycha fell. She dropped to her knees in the snow, now wearing her elven form. Calard's blade was still embedded to the hilt in her belly, and she seized it in both hands, attempting to pull it free. Still, even through her pain, she smiled cruelly at Calard, enjoying his suffering.

Calard staggered, his lifeblood rushing from his body. His wounds were mortal. He tried to speak but blood filled his throat, making his words incomprehensible. Dimly, he registered that Drycha had become as insubstantial as mist, her eyes glittering as she faded away, leaving the Sword of Garamont lying on the ground. He tried to move to towards it, but reeled, stumbling and falling in the snow. He hauled himself back to his feet, determined to retrieve the blade, but staggered over the edge of the low headland. Turning as he fell, he reached forlornly towards the sleeping goddess.

Cold air rushed by him. He hit the ice hard and lay there on his back, blood pooling beneath him.

He knew he had to get up, but he felt so tired. It was all he could do to keep his eyes open. He lay there on the ice, his lifeblood forming an ever-widening circle around him. He didn't feel cold, and while dimly he knew that was a bad sign, he could not muster the energy to rise.

Calard turned his head, struggling to maintain consciousness.

He could see the plinth on which the goddess slept, and a ghost of a smile touched his blue lips. He blinked, seeing a second figure standing beside her, but he was having trouble focusing and could not make it out. It wasn't Drycha, for she was gone. He had banished her from this realm. It looked as though the second figure had horns. No, he realised a moment later, it was a helmet. *Cythaeros.*

He saw the elven warrior kneel down besides the sleeping goddess, kissing her ice-cold lips.

A sudden transformation came upon Calard's surroundings. The unnatural winter broke, and spring began to flourish. Grass-shoots and saplings pressed up through the rapidly diminishing crust of snow, and buds sprouted and unfurled upon the branches of the trees. Bluebells burst into spontaneous colour, and butterflies filled the air. The ice beneath Calard melted, and he plunged into the lake below.

The weight of his armour dragged him down, and he had not the strength to fight his descent. He felt no fear or regret as he watched the sparkling light of the surface receding above him. Ribbon-like strands of weed waved serenely around him, and the light began to fade. He felt utterly at peace as he settled gently to the bottom of the lake.

A thin trail of bubbles trickled from his mouth, then stopped.

XI

COOL HANDS WERE upon him, and he felt himself rising up through the water. He didn't want to wake; he wanted to stay in the silence at the bottom of the lake.

He tried to struggle, but there was no strength in his limbs, and despite his efforts, the gentle hands dragged him up to the surface.

Calard was on his hands and knees, coughing up lungfuls of water. He sucked in deep breaths, and slowly regained his senses. Two savage holes were punched through his breastplate, but the flesh beneath was unscathed, even unscarred.

He rose to his feet. He was on the banks of the lake, within a small glade overrun with bluebells, surrounded by mist.

The Green Knight loomed out of the dense fog. The immortal spirit's eyes flared, and its huge blade sang through the air as it sliced towards him.

Had that mighty sword struck it would have cloven him in two. Calard jumped back to avoid the blow, narrowly avoiding being cut down.

He reached for the Sword of Garamont but found the scabbard at his waist empty. The Green Knight swung again, and Calard hurled himself to the side to avoid being decapitated.

Reaching over his back, Calard drew his heavy bastard sword. The Green Knight came at him again, and he readied to block the fey spirit's next attack. Calard held the blade in two hands, yet even so he was brought to his knees by the force of the blow. Desperately, he regained his footing and brought his blade around to block yet another attack, this one coming around at him in a lethal arc, striking at his mid-section.

The blow shuddered up his arms, and he was knocked back two steps. The Green Knight came on relentlessly, allowing no time to recover. There was no subtlety or guile to the unearthly warrior's assault. He came on without pause and without remorse, delivering a tireless barrage of attacks. Each blow was delivered with staggering power, and any one of them would have felled Calard had it landed.

The fey knight stood over a head taller than Calard, and each strike sent him reeling. His hands were numb from the jarring blows, and he had no time to even consider launching a riposte.

The roiling mist continued to build. All that existed was the two of them. Nothing else mattered.

Calard frantically backtracked, using all his skill and battle-honed instincts to stay alive for another few seconds. His arms were tiring, the bastard sword in his hands a leaden weight. By contrast, the Green Knight was indefatigable.

Finally, Calard found an opening. He deflected a heavy overhead blow, letting his foe's dimly green-glowing blade slide down the length of his sword before whipping it around to parry a low attack. Sidestepping neatly, Calard spun around the immortal spirit's next blow and slammed his bastard sword into his neck, putting his whole body weight behind the strike.

His blade landed between archaic plate armour, sliding between helmet and gorget and cutting through the links of chainmail beneath – but it sank no further. It was as if the immortal spirit's flesh were made of iron, and the force of the blow rang up both of Calard's arms.

The Green Knight backhanded Calard across the jaw and he hit the ground hard, spitting blood. Scrambling, he threw himself aside to avoid the Dolorous Blade as it came again. The weapon embedded itself in the ground, and Calard staggered upright.

His arms were aching, and he backed off, panic clawing its way into his heart. He had put everything he had behind that blow, and its timing was perfect. Had he struck any mortal foe, their head would have sailed into the air, hacked clean from their shoulders, but onwards the Green Knight came, unharmed.

Clearing his mind, Calard pushed his fear aside and invoked the name of his goddess. Pale fire flickered along the edge of his bastard sword, and he felt fresh vigour infuse his limbs.

With a cry, Calard threw himself at the unyielding knight, thrusting and slashing. He feinted high and came in low, swinging his heavy sword around in murderous arcs. Every blow was met by the Dolorous Blade, and sparks flew as enchanted metal came together again and again.

Calard and the Green Knight battled toe-to-toe, trading blows, neither giving ground. Infused with the holy light of the Lady, Calard was able to match the fury and power of his foe, and for a time it seemed that the battle might rage on forever, a never-ending duel within the mists. Time lost all meaning. All that existed was the contest. Neither warrior was able to overcome the other, and their blades were a blur as they cut and thrust.

No end was in sight, but understanding came upon Calard in a rush.

'This is not a test of prowess,' he said under his breath, shaking his head that he had not realised it earlier.

He parried an attack slicing in towards his neck and reversed the grip on his blade suddenly, holding it like dagger in both hands, blade pointed downwards. With a sudden thrust, he drove it into the earth, and knelt on one knee. He lowered his head, exposing the back of his neck, and closed his eyes. He felt the Green Knight step in close, raising his sword for the fatal blow.

'I offer my life to the service of the Lady,' said Calard.

The Dolorous Blade came slicing down upon his neck... and stopped. The sword's edge was cold against his skin. Then it was whisked away, and the Green Knight stepped aside.

Opening his eyes, Calard saw the mists part before him, opening up a passage through the fog. A beauteous figure rose from waters of the lake, wreathed in light and garlanded with ivy and lilies. No ripple marred the lake's surface as she emerged. Her hair was long and the colour of sunlight, so bright that it made tears run unashamedly down Calard's cheeks. No power in the world could have made him turn away from this holy vision.

The Lady of the Lake floated towards Calard, her bare feet inches above the surface of the water. White lilies fell like rain from her hair, tumbling down to float upon the surface of the lake behind her. She was garbed in layers of flowing gossamer, and she smiled as she came towards him, holding aloft a chalice overflowing with water.

The goddess drifted near to the lake's edge, scant yards from where Calard knelt and wept. Her eyes sparkled like autumn leaves, filled with gold and amber and bronze, and she held the grail out towards him. Like sunlight in liquid form, water spilled from the holy chalice.

Barely daring to breathe, Calard rose to his feet and stepped into the shallows to meet his goddess. Light spilled from every pore of her being, warming his face, and with faltering hands, he reached out and took the chalice.

It was heavy, and he felt a strange tingle run up his arms. Looking down into the magical grail's fathomless depths he saw silent images of his past and future mirrored there, playing out before him. He drew the chalice up towards his lips, but he hesitated for a moment before drinking.

It was said that only those pure of heart and devoid of any hint of taint upon their soul could drink from the Lady's grail and live.

Drawing in a deep and shuddering breath, Calard lifted the golden chalice to his lips and drank.

XII

THE BATTLE BEYOND the Oak of Ages had been fierce and brutal. Sunlight revealed the corpses of elves scattered around the glade. Their blood was soaking into the sacred soil now that the snows had melted. The dead were being gathered up by their kinsmen, laid upon shields and biers of woven branches and carried away into the forest.

Mouldering piles of sticks and leaves marked where Drycha's hand-maidens had fallen. No one moved to disperse them. Clusters of rotting logs, bones and deadwood were all that remained of the tree-kin that had marched to battle, abandoned by their animating spirits as soon as the unnatural winter had broken. A handful of larger shapes were scattered around the glade – leafless dead trees that had a short time before been guided by malign intent, smashing aside elves and horses with every sweep of their wooden branches. Now they were hollow and motionless, empty husks that would soon collapse in upon themselves and be forgotten.

The vicious carrion birds, winter wolves and other rancorous creatures that had emerged from the wildwoods to join the slaughter had been scattered, slinking back into the darker reaches of the forest to lick their wounds.

Hunting horns echoed in the distance as the Wild Riders pursued the last remnants of Drycha's host, hounding them back into the shadows, slaughtering any too slow to outpace them.

Colour had returned to Athel Loren, and the forest was flourishing with new life. Birds and butterflies filled the branches, and an abundance of flowers burst open, turning their faces towards the rising sun. Ivy-vines crept up the trunks of trees like serpents, growing rapidly. Ferns blanketed the ground, their fronds waving gently in the spring breeze.

New leaves had sprouted from the fingers of the mighty Oak of Ages, and it stretched its branches upwards, reaching towards the sun. Squirrels bounded along its limbs, and swarms of sprites and pixies spiralled through its branches. Great eagles screeched a greeting to the spring from their eyries in the oak's upper reaches, and flights of warhawks wheeled above the canopy, elven riders perfectly balanced upon their shoulders. Dozens of their kind had been slain in the battle, and they bore their dead off towards the distant mountains, clutched in their mighty talons.

The majestic white stag had fallen too, pierced by the blade-arms of a dozen dryads. The Lady Anara, her veil now removed from his face, knelt upon the forest floor just beyond the immense arched entrance to the Oak of Ages, cradling the mighty beast's head in her lap.

She looked up as a shadow fell upon her. Tears were running down her heart-shaped face.

'Hello, sister,' said Calard, looking down upon her as he emerged from the Oak of Ages.

His eyes flickered with holy witchfire, and he was surrounded by a vague halo of light, as if the early morning sunlight were drawn to him. He stood taller than he had before, and the faint lines around his eyes had been smoothed away. The effect did not look young so much as ageless, and his eyes spoke of things unknown to mortal men.

'The Lady's light burns strong within you, my brother,' said Anara. 'You have drunk from the grail.'

'I have,' said Calard, nodding. 'We are both eternal servants of the Lady now. Our lives are no longer our own.'

'Father would have been proud.'

'He would,' agreed Calard, a hint of a smile touching his lips.

A hush descended upon the clearing. Every elf dropped to their knees as one, bowing their heads in honour and reverence.

Calard turned and sank to one knee, bowing his head down low.

'Rise, Calard of Garamont,' said a gentle, musical voice.

Calard lifted his gaze and looked upon the two godly beings emerging from the Oak of Ages.

They walked together, glowing with fey light. The one who had spoken was the goddess that been sleeping upon the stone dais, though her icy countenance was now filled with the warmth of spring, and her midnight-black hair was now golden, like honey or sunlight. Inhumanly slender, she moved with effortless grace and poise, radiating calm and serenity.

She stood several heads taller than Calard, yet her features were fine and beauteous, and she wore a regal tiara of silver and ivy, a large green stone glistening at its centre. A tall staff of pale wood was held in her right hand, and she walked with her left arm resting upon that of her companion, her consort-king.

He was a towering figure of grace and elemental power, striding bare-chested at his queen's side. He stood almost twelve feet tall, and his flesh was the green of new forest growth. His skin was inscribed with swirling patterns, and his legs were furred, his feet hooved. A huge rack of antlers rose from his temples. A hunting spear of gigantic proportions was clasped in his hand, thumping the ground with each step, and a large curved hunting horn that Calard recognised instantly hung over his back. He glared across the forest glade, his eyes filled with fury and rage.

'My Lady Ariel,' said Anara. 'My Lord Orion.'

In every way, the pair were each other's opposite. Where Ariel reflected tranquillity and peace, everything about Orion spoke of violence and aggression.

'Athel Loren owes you a debt of gratitude,' said Ariel, addressing Calard directly. 'Ancient Coeddil has been banished back to the darkness of the eastern fold, and winter has given way to spring. Balance has been restored.'

Calard bowed low.

Orion stepped away from Ariel's side then, and he strode towards Calard, his eyes filled with untamed fury. He stalked around the newly risen grail knight, staring fiercely down upon him.

'I remember you,' said Orion. His voice was deep and powerful, resounding with authority and magic.

Calard looked into the face of the vengeful god and saw something familiar there.

'Cythaeros?' he said.

Orion tilted his head to one side, eyes narrowing.

'The one who bore that name is gone,' said Orion, 'yet something of him remains within me. His memories and thoughts linger on.'

Orion's gold-flecked eyes were untamed and dangerous, and for a moment it seemed he might lash out, but the moment passed and the living god turned away, stalking back to rejoin his queen.

'Is there any boon that we may offer by way of thanks for your service?' said Ariel.

'I ask for nothing but the wisdom of your counsel, lady of the forest,' said Calard, his voice unwavering despite the unblinking stare of Orion upon him. 'Drycha spoke of a great darkness besieging my homeland. She said that the battle for Couronne was already underway, and that the blood of my king had been spilled. I fear there was no falsity in her words, yet I would know the truth.'

'Drycha spoke the truth, Calard of Garamont,' said Ariel. 'The battle balances on a knife's edge.'

Calard nodded his thanks, though his expression darkened.

Orion gestured, and Calard's warhorse, Galibor, was brought forward by an elven attendant. The loyal steed nuzzled at him, and he stroked her nose, still frowning as he thought of the battle underway at Couronne, many weeks ride away.

Another elf came forth, holding in his arms a lance wrapped in rich cloth.

'You asked for no boon, yet I would not have you leave our realm empty-handed,' said Ariel.

Calard took the proffered lance in both hands, marvelling at the artistry of its design. It was crafted from pale wood inlaid in silver, and its curving vamplate guard had been carved in the likeness of a dragon's head. He felt potent magicks stir within it as he held it, and he marvelled at its lightness and strength.

'Her name is *Elith-Anar* – the Dawn Spirit,' said Ariel. 'She was brought to the forest long ago, from distant Ulthuan. She will serve you well, Calard of Garamont.'

'Lady of the forest, this is too much,' said Calard.

'Take it, with thanks,' said Ariel, smiling. She turned her gaze towards Anara, still seated upon the ground, cradling the noble head of the slain white stag. 'You have made your decision, cousin of the forest?'

'I have,' said Anara.

'You are not coming back, are you?' said Calard. Anara shook her head.

'My place is here, now,' she said. 'There is nothing for me beyond the forest any longer.'

Ariel turned towards her consort-king, laying a slender hand upon his heavily muscled, green-tinged arm.

'It is time, my love,' she said, and Orion nodded, his eyes blazing with witch-light.

He dragged free his large, curling hunting horn, and lifted it high into the air. As if with an afterthought, he glanced down at Calard, pausing before he sounded the mighty horn.

'Will you ride with me, Calard of Garamont?' he said. 'Will you join the Wild Hunt?'

'I will, my lord,' said Calard.

Orion gave him a savage grin, and lifted the horn to his lips.

XIII

BOOMING THUNDER ROLLED across the heavens like the war-drums of the gods, and wind and rain lashed the battlefield. Jagged spears of lightning struck down through the roiling clouds, and with each blinding flash, the full extent of the desperate battle raging before Couronne's mighty walls was revealed.

The plains before Couronne were choked with the living dead, their endless ranks extending as far as the eye could see. The mass charnel graves of Mousillon had been emptied, the corpses of those slain by plague, pestilence and war exhumed and raised to cursed unlife. They shambled forward in endless ranks, impelled by the will of their vampiric master to rend and maim. Many were nothing more than skeletons clad in the tattered remains of tabards and scraps of rusted armour, while others, the more recently deceased, were walking cadavers, their flesh rotting and pallid. Some clutched the swords and spears they had borne in life but others carried no weapons at all, slaughtering the living with nothing more than filth-encrusted nails and rotten teeth.

Great clouds of arrows were launched from thousands of bowmen positioned along the battlements, but they made no visible dent in the endless horde. Mighty trebuchets hurled huge chunks of masonry high into the air, spinning end over end through the driving rain before smashing down into the foe, crushing hundreds as they bounced through the densely packed ranks. They marched on through the quagmire of mud and blood, knowing nothing of panic or fear.

Ten thousand men-at-arms bearing the king's colours were locked in desperate battle before the gates of Couronne, and the screams of the dying and horrible wet sound of blades hacking into flesh rose to those stationed along the city's walls. Yeoman wardens and foot-knights bellowed their commands, desperately trying to maintain order as the terrifying horde came at them again and again, clambering over the bodies of the fallen.

The two armies had been locked in brutal conflict for nearly six hours, and the Bretonnians were close to breaking. Exhaustion and the horror of their undead foe was taking its toll, and the resolve of even the staunchest warriors was beginning to crack.

Trumpets sounded as dozens of lance formations of knights that had gathered from all over Bretonnia charged yet again into the enemy ranks. Young Knights Errant rode at the fore, still hungering for glory, desperate to prove themselves. They carved through the undead, scything down hundreds with lance and sword, while countless more were crushed beneath the flashing hooves of their heavy warhorses.

The knights kicked their steeds on, desperate to maintain their momentum. To become bogged down in combat was death; with their impetus lost, the brave knights would become quickly surrounded and overwhelmed. One by one, the knightly formations faltered, ground down by the sheer number of foes pressing in against them. They laid about them, shattering skulls and chopping at reaching hands, yet were being dragged from their saddles and set upon by the ravening hordes. Their steeds screamed in fear as they too were pulled down into the mud, disappearing beneath the tumble of undead bodies clamouring to feast on living flesh.

Above the battling armies, great swarms of bats wheeled and dived through the lashing rain and clouds of arrows. They descended on the living, latching onto any exposed flesh to feed, biting and clawing. Some of these creatures were immense, bearing fully barded warhorses to the ground before wrapping leathery wings around their prey and draining them of blood.

At the centre of the fighting, Duke Merovech of Mousillon and his elite cadre of vampire knights, his seneschals, carved a swathe through the Bretonnian lines, butchering everyone that stood against them. Mounted on black warhorses with eyes that glowed like coals, they thundered forwards, smashing knights from their saddles, cutting down Bretonnia's finest with contemptuous ease. More knights pressed in to halt their rampage, but all fell before their murderous wrath.

Faster and stronger than any mortal man, these vampire knights fought with callous ferocity. Their eyes were red-rimmed and savage, their slitted pupils dilating as their bloodlust surged. They struck with such force that shields shattered beneath their axes and blades. Their lances punched straight through armoured breastplates, lifting warriors from the saddle and tossing them aside like children.

Merovech fought like a daemon, lips pulled back to expose his elongated canines. Blood splattered across his snow-white face as he hacked a questing knight's head from his shoulders and thundered on, driving his heavily armoured nightmare towards the immense gates of Couronne. He slashed left and right, killing with every stroke.

The centre of the Bretonnian battle-line was buckling inward, threatening to break at any moment. Desperate to hold the line, reserve companies of knights charged forward to bolster the defences, but the line continued to strain.

A shadow descended from above, and King Louen Leoncoeur joined the fray.

Mounted on ferocious hippogryph, the king landed amongst the vampire knights, smashing several aside with the force of his impact, stopping their momentum dead. One of the deathly pale knights was impaled upon his glittering lance, and two more were killed in the blink of an eye, ripped savagely apart by his beast. Gore stained the hippogryph's six-inch claws and dripped from the curved tip of its beak. It screeched a deafening challenge, talons clawing up the ground. The king hurled his lance aside and drew his ancestral sword, its blade shining like the sun.

A dozen knights each mounted upon the back of a snorting royal pegasus landed with their king, flailing hooves and well-aimed lance strikes smashing more of the enemy warriors from their saddles. One of them unfurled the king's standard, and a cheer rose from the Bretonnian ranks as the king's resplendent heraldry was revealed.

Leoncoeur slew the first of the dark knights that came at him, taking its attack upon his sacred lion shield and driving his blade through the vampire's chest. He swayed back in the saddle to avoid the thrust of another foe, and his lightning riposte took the undead knight in the face.

Leaping forward, the king's hippogryph bore another vampire knight to the ground, pinning it down beneath its eagle-taloned fore-limbs, claws biting deep into plate armour. The hippogryph tore the vampire's throat open, spraying blood and almost decapitating the undead creature.

With a deft twist of his sword, the king turned aside a serrated blade thrusting towards his heart. The vampire's fangs were bared, its eyes little more than glittering points. It hissed and recoiled from the blinding light of the king's sword, its face blistering as if in direct sunlight. Leoncoeur's blade struck down onto the vampire's head, carving through its helm and skull. With a twist, he freed his weapon and cast his fiery gaze around him, seeking the next foe.

A lance thrust into the chest of the king's hippogryph, the blow delivered with such power and force that it drove up through armour and muscle, pushing deep into the mighty creature's body, seeking its heart.

Every soldier stationed upon the walls of Couronne watched as with a final, piercing cry the king's royal hippogryph fell, collapsing in a heap upon the muddy plains. The rain continued to pelt down, and lightning flashed, throwing the terrible figure of Merovech into stark relief as he loomed over the king from the saddle of his nightmarish steed. Leoncoeur was pinned beneath the bulk of his slain mount, and he was unable to rise. He glared up at the vampire lord, mouthing a curse. The vampire duke smiled, exposing his elongated fangs. He swung himself from the saddle of his infernal steed, and drew a massive serrated sword, stepping forward to deliver the killing blow.

'The king! The king!' roared the royal battle-standard bearer, and knights surged forward to protect their liege-lord. They were met with the fury of Merovech and his warriors, and a desperate melee erupted. Dozens of loyal knights pushed forward, interposing themselves before their king and the murderous vampire knights, selling their lives dearly.

Merovech began to laugh as he killed, the hideous sound booming out across the battlefield.

The outcome of the battle balanced on a knife's edge. Merovech hacked down the knights standing between him and the king. He slammed his mighty sword into the standard bearer's neck, the blade biting through armour, bone and flesh, and the king's banner fell.

Knights and men-at-arms all the way along the battlefront saw that resplendent tapestry fall, and their resolve shattered.

It began as a trickle, one man-at-arms turning to flee from the overwhelming horde, but soon became an uncontrollable torrent. The panic was infectious, and soon thousands of peasant soldiers were turning and fleeing back towards the gates of Couronne, trampling each other in their haste to escape, ignoring the barking orders of nobles and yeomen to hold. The rout became unstoppable, gaining numbers with every passing second. It surged blindly, and the undead poured over their lines.

'The king lives!' roared a dark-featured knight, lifting the royal banner from the ground, but only those nearby heard his cry. His voice was lost in the tumult of panicked voices, and word of the king's fall continued to spread.

Trumpets sounded the retreat, and the Bretonnian army turned to quit the field, Merovech's sinister laugh echoing over the battlefield.

A resounding clarion horn sounded suddenly, echoing across the heavens, drowning out even the rumble of thunder and the terrible clashing of weapons. It was the sound of the hunt, and it came from the east, behind the undead army. Those soldiers upon the battlements turned their gaze, while those on the ground paused in their flight, necks craning to see what was happening.

Against the horizon the storm clouds broke, and sunlight speared down through the gap. The deafening hunting horn sounded again, and an army emerged from the woodlands behind the forces of Mousillon. With a mighty horned figure leading the charge, this newly arrived army streamed from the tree-line and surged down the hillside to smash into the enemy's rear.

A murmur rippled across the Bretonnian ranks.

'The fey,' said voices filled with awe. 'The fey have come to aid us!'

ORION LED THE charge, the deafening resonance of his hunting horn still echoing across the heavens. The mighty horned god of the hunt bounded down the hill towards the army of the dead, as fast as the swiftest elven steed, launching arrows from an immense bow as he ran. Each shaft was the length of a man and struck with titanic force, skewering half a dozen of the living dead with every shot.

Calard stormed down the hill alongside the living god, white fire flickering up the length of his magical elven lance, *Elith-Anar*. His heart was filled with rage as he saw the vast undead army besieging Couronne, and his eyes blazed with holy fire. He kicked his noble steed Galibor on to match the speed of the furious god of the woods, lowering his lance as he neared the enemy battle line.

The wild hunt thundered forward in the wake of their enraged king. All manner of creature, elf and forest spirit had been caught up in the rampaging hunt, unable to resist the bestial call of their lord. All were filled with Orion's insatiable bloodlust.

Painted in swirling warpaint, unearthly Wild Riders howled at the heavens as they galloped hard, leaning eagerly forward over the necks of their elven steeds, faerie-fire blazing in their eyes. Vengeful dryads wearing their war-aspect darted forwards, snarling and spitting, their limbs elongated into killing spikes and barbed talons. Lumbering tree-kin made the ground shake as they pounded forwards, emerging from the forest, their deep reverberating hoots akin to brazen war-horns.

Wolves, stags, boars and wildcats had all responded to the king-in-the-wood's clarion call, and they flowed behind him, gathering pace and numbers, driven mad by the enraged king's fury. Clouds of black-feathered crows, eagles and owls flew at his shoulder, wickedly sharp beaks and talons ready to rip and gouge.

Elves borne upon the backs of horses and warhawks streamed from the woods, spear-tips glittering. Others ran forward on foot, launching arrows as they came, their faces masks of animalistic fury.

Amongst the panoply flew vast clouds of spites, some riding upon the shoulders of birds or beasts, others flying through the air, borne aloft upon flickering, crystalline wings. Garbed in shining armour and with a tiny lance clasped under its arm, one diminutive sprite flew at Calard's shoulder, adding her own high-pitched war-cry to the din of roars and shouts.

Even the branchwraith Drycha had joined the hunt, focussing all her malice now upon the legions of the undead.

The hunt slammed into the rear of the undead legions, Orion scattering the walking dead before him. The forest lord did not slow his pace, thundering through the undead ranks, smashing dozens into the air with each sweep of his mighty barbed hunting spear. Calard galloped hard at his side, the enemy falling in droves beneath the thrust of his lance and the cut of his sword. Others were brutally knocked aside by Galibor's armoured bulk, or crushed beneath the warhorse's hooves.

The Wild Hunt charged into the enemy with untamed savagery, an unstoppable tide that swept through the army before them. On they rode, butchering and slaughtering, driving a wedge deep into the heart of Mousillon's ranks.

Skeletal men-at-arms clutching rusted polearms were smashed aside, their bones shattered, their skulls trampled into the mud. Fighting side-by-side, elves and dryads and wolves and sprites ploughed through the enemy, cutting, hacking, biting and clawing, leaving the wreckage of their fury in their wake.

Calard fought like the holy paladin of the Lady that he was, flames coruscating from his sword, his eyes flaring with fey light. He alone remained unaffected by the fury infusing the others that rode with Orion, yet he was no less dangerous for that. His every blow brought ruin upon the enemies of Bretonnia. He could feel the power of the grail pounding through his veins.

The enemy fell before him like wheat beneath a scythe. He foresaw the strike of every spear and rusted sword moments before it happened, and he turned them aside effortlessly, countering with devastating blows that splintered bones and shattered blades.

He saw the battle standard of the king through the press of battle, and his eyes narrowed. Sensing his intent, Orion glanced in his direction. His face was a mask of bestial savagery, yet there was nobility there. He nodded his horned head towards Calard in acknowledgement, and for a moment, he saw the young elven warrior, Cythaeros, in the living god's features. Calard bowed his head to the forest king, then, guiding Galibor with his knees, he veered away from the ride of the Wild Hunt, angling towards the king's banner.

He saw Merovech then, looming over the stricken figure of the king, and with a shout, he urged his warhorse into one last burst of speed. The undead fell before him as he galloped towards his reviled foe. He was a shining light spearing through the darkness and the driving rain.

'Merovech!' roared Calard, his voice suffused with the power of the Lady.

Unholy seneschals moved to interpose themselves between him and their dark lord. Their eyes were filled with hatred, but there was fear there too – the shining light of the goddess Calard exuded was anathema to these creatures of the night, and it caused them pain even to look upon him.

GARBED IN ARCHAIC armour of ancient design, each was a mighty warrior and dark champion in their own right, but even so, they could not hope to slow Calard's furious charge. He plunged the elven lance *Elith-Anar* through the chest of one, skewering its blackened heart and hurling the blood-sucking fiend from its saddle. His sword flashed, and a dragon-helmed head flew into the air, mouth locked in a silent scream.

'Merovech!' he bellowed again, and another dark knight fell beneath his blade. He batted aside a vicious swinging broadsword, and his lightning riposte stabbed deep into the face of a further seneschal, the white flame flickering up the Sword of Garamont's blade making the devil's flesh blacken and blister.

The fell duke of Mousillon swung towards him, turning away from the fallen Bretonnian king, still trapped under the weight of his steed.

His face was the white of untouched snow, his expression arrogant and dismissive. His hair too was like alabaster, hanging down his black-armoured back. He held his jagged sword loosely. The blade would have taken a strong man to lift it two-handed, yet the undead warrior drew a second sword as Calard bore down on him, twirling the twin-blades.

Calard had seen the vampire lord fight; he knew of his ungodly speed, and the brutal power that was contained within him.

'Lady guide my blow,' he breathed, readying his lance.

Time seemed to slow.

Galloping at full speed, Calard saw every detail of his foe in the moment before they clashed. He saw the aristocratic disdain in Merovech's eyes, eyes that gleamed like a wolf's, reflecting back at Calard the holy light that surrounded him. He saw the dimly glowing runes along the length of the vampire's swords, and he saw each individual raindrop coming down, splashing off his enemy's fluted black armour.

He saw the king looking up at him, and he saw Raben, the disenfranchised knight that he had fought alongside in cursed Mousillon, holding the king's banner high. Even more of a surprise, he saw his erstwhile manservant, the hunchbacked wretch Chlod, in the thick of the fighting, battling fiercely at Raben's side with his heavy, nail-studded club.

Calard rose in the saddle to deliver the strike. *Elith-Anar* speared towards the vampire's chest, but with preternatural speed, one of Merovech's blades swung up to deflect it with an elegant circular parry. With the smallest twist of the wrist, Calard caused the tip of his elven lance to roll around the vampire's blade, avoiding the deflection. Merovech's other blade came up, but in a display of skill and speed that surpassed even the vampire lord's abilities, Calard again rolled his wrist, and the flaming tip of *Elith Anar* flicked around his second blade.

The lancetip took Merovech in the throat, punching out the back of his neck in an explosion of dark blood. Calard released his grip on the lance and continued on past the vampire as it fell to its knees.

Hauling on the reins, Calard brought Galibor back around sharply. Dark blood pooled beneath the vampire, and his eyes registered the creature's shock. He tried to speak, but nothing emerged from his mouth but a splatter of blood. Calard swung from the saddle of his warhorse, and stormed towards the Duke of Mousillon, the Sword of Garamont blazing in his hand.

The vampire tore the lance from its throat and rose to meet him. Merovech had lost one of his swords; the other one he gripped in both hands. He hissed, and hurled himself at Calard.

The Sword of Garamont came up, smashing Merovech's blade aside. Calard's allowed his momentum to carry him around, so that he had his back turned to his enemy. With a movement so fast it was little more than a blur, he spun his sword around so that he was holding it in a downward, dagger-like grip, left hand resting upon the pommel. He surged backwards, driving his sword into Merovech's chest.

The blade slid deep, only halting when the hilt was pressed against the vampire's breastplate.

'It is over,' breathed Calard.

The vampire's mouth opened wide in final, soundless scream. His flesh began to wither and blacken, like parchment beneath a candle-flame.

Calard wrenched his sword free, and the creature that had been Merovech fell to the ground, collapsing to grave-dust. The entire army of the dead dropped, the dark magic binding and animating them dissipating. The rain ceased, and a howling wind began to clear the sky.

Knights leapt forward to aid the king, while others, bloodied and battle-weary, gazed around them blankly, not yet comprehending that the battle was over. Chlod was staring at Calard in slack-jawed astonishment.

'You took your time,' said Raben with a wry smile.

Freed at last from the weight of his slain hippogryph mount, King Louen Leoncoeur was helped to his feet, and Calard dropped to his knees, a move that was mirrored by every warrior on the field. Chlod was still staring open mouthed at Calard, and had to be dragged to his knees.

'Rise,' said the king, and Calard lifted his head. Leoncoeur nodded, and he stood.

'What is your name?' said the king.

'Calard of Garamont,' he answered, holding his head high. 'Grail Knight of Bretonnia.'

EPILOGUE

A LONE KNIGHT knelt in prayer upon the rocky beach as thousands of Norse longships ploughed towards the shore. An icy gale was blowing down from the Chaos, filling the vessels' sails, driving these barbaric warriors of the Dark Gods towards the Bretonnian coastline.

One of the ships, larger than the rest and its sail painted with ruinous sigils, pulled ahead of the pack, its dark iron ram slicing through the waves as it drove onwards. Heavily armoured huskarls hauled on the longship's oars, to the beat of a brazen war drum.

The longship rose upon the crest of a wave, but the steersman knew his trade, and the vessel was kept straight, hurtling towards the beach. Even as it ground ashore, driving a furrow through the black stones of the beach, the lone knight did not rise from his prayer. Nor did he so much as lift his head as the horn-helmed huskarls dragged the longship up the beach.

A huge fire-blackened throne was set into the stern of the longship, and from it rose a giant of a man, silver-haired and fork-bearded. He was the warlord Styrbjorn, High Jarl of the Skaelings, and while he looked perhaps sixty, he was in truth far, far older. Nevertheless, his arms were still strong and thick, and his battle-fury as potent as ever. Twin axes were strapped across his back, and he nodded as he saw the lone knight awaiting him upon the beach, as if he had expected him.

Only when this towering warrior approached did the knight rise to his feet.

An old hunched shaman cloaked in matted fur stood at the Norscan's side. He spat on the ground at the Bretonnian knight's feet.

'It is good that you are here,' said High Jarl Styrbjorn, his words translated by his shaman, who spoke Breton in a thick but recognisable accent.

'I said that I would be waiting,' said Calard of Garamont, his eyes shining with the light of the Lady, 'and I am not a man who breaks his word.'

For more than fifty years Calard had fought the enemies of Bretonnia as a Grail Knight, and his deeds and exploits were renowned across the lands. Nevertheless, his face was as unlined as it had been since the day he had supped from the grail, and there was no hint of silver in his hair.

Over the past half a decade he had seen sights that few men ever dreamed of, and had mourned the death of many brave and honourable men.

He thought of his old friends often, though they had long since passed over into Morr's eternal realm: Raben, who had risen to become a respected nobleman before he had disappeared seeking the grail in the arid sands of Nehekhara; the Empire nobleman, Dieter Weschler, who had married his Bretonnian mistress in something of a scandal and gone on to become an extremely wealthy and powerful political attaché in the king's court; and even his lowly manservant Chlod, who had risen far beyond anyone's expectations.

The High Jarl's gaze wandered past Calard, surveying the vast Bretonnian army that waited on the grasslands beyond the beach. Thousands of knights and peasant men-at-arms were gathered there, watching and waiting, just as behind the jarl waited his own army, blooded in decades of brutal warfare.

The icy wind continued to howl from the north, and thunder rumbled. Lightning flashed. It was a good omen.

'The eyes of my gods are upon us,' said High Jarl Styrbjorn.

'And the goddess of this land is with me,' said Calard. 'Let us finish this, Norscan.'

'As you wish,' said Styrbjorn. He turned and waved one of his men forwards.

Calard watched the warrior approach, his expression grim. He was not as large as some of the Norscan huskarls, but he was no less impressive for that. His skin had a strange coppery sheen to it, and his eyes were disconcerting, black with silver irises. He stared at Calard unblinkingly.

Calard could feel the daemon writhing within this warrior's flesh, but more disturbing still was the fact that he could see the features of

Elisabet, the woman he had once loved, reflected in the creature's face.

This was the offspring of Styrbjorn and Elisabet, the daemon-child for which so many had died.

'Fight well, my son,' said Styrbjorn, stepping aside.

The daemon came towards Calard, unsheathing the massive double-handed cleaver from a scabbard strapped across his back. Dark flames rippled along the length of the blade.

Calard drew the Sword of Garamont and stepped out to meet him, his own sword wreathed in pale fire.

'Lady guide my blade,' murmured Calard.

Thunder rumbled across the heavens, and under the watchful gaze of the Bretonnian and Norse armies, the two champions of the gods came together.

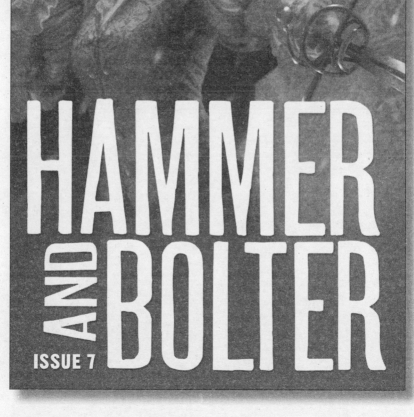

HAMMER AND BOLTER

ISSUE 7

WARHAMMER®

MANBANE

Andy Hoare

STINKING COLD MUD gushed into Duerr's mouth as he crashed to the root-choked ground, his ankle turning on a twisted stump. He coughed, spewed the bulk of the vile liquid from his mouth and blew through his nose to clear his nostrils. Gasping, Duerr cursed, invoking dread spirits only one of his calling could name. Duerr was a wizard, a student of the amethyst arts, what some might in their ignorance call a necromancer. Right now, stumbling through the night-shrouded depths of the Drak-wald Deeps, he felt he was closer than ever to joining those spirits he had so foolishly named but a moment before.

Up! Gritting his teeth Duerr hauled himself erect, his grasping hands finding purchase on the clammy trunk of a thoroughly rotten tree. He cast around to regain his bearings, then looked directly up into the sickly green orb of Morrslieb. The Dark Moon was high overhead and, as such, little use as a navigational aid. But Duerr was gifted of the arcane sight, perceiving the questing tendrils of raw Chaos that seethed around it like a slithering halo of snakes. Breathing deeply, he turned west, knowing that his one, precarious hope of survival lay in reaching one of the scattered settlements along the Altdorf-Middenheim road before his pursuers overtook him.

As if to underscore his predicament and drive him onwards, the dark woods suddenly echoed to a coarse, braying war cry. Duerr cursed once more, feeling his guts turn to ice as they threatened to void themselves there and then. The sound was unmistakably that of the savage beast-men, the Children of Old Night, of Chaos itself. Beasts that walked and

513

talked like men, or men that fought and rutted like beasts, the nature of the vile creatures that haunted the deep woods of the Old World mattered not. The only thing Duerr cared for was that his pursuers were closing on him, the scent of man-flesh and mortal fear sending them into an animal frenzy.

Another cry split the cold night air, and Duerr was spurred to movement. He pushed through the undergrowth in search of the path he had lost what seemed an age ago. The way ahead was even denser than the path he had already travelled, the trees more twisted and gnarled and the bracken ever more thick and treacherous. Thorns caught on his trailing robes, the deep purple fabric he had paid so much for soon tattered and stained with patches of crimson blood. His breath came in ragged gasps as he stumbled ever on, his arms flailing blindly before him to ward away branches that stabbed for his eyes from the darkness.

Another cry, far closer than the last. Duerr hurtled through the undergrowth, barely keeping his footing as he imagined hot, stinking breath on the back of his neck and razor-sharp, jagged fangs sinking into his flesh. A heavy thud sounded from somewhere behind, as if a body ten times his own mass had shouldered into, and through, the rotten tree he had just skirted. Heavy footfalls thudded hollowly across the moss-carpeted ground, but Duerr knew they were no normal feet. These were cloven hooves, trampling the undergrowth to pulp with their passage.

A hideous screech sounded from somewhere off to Duerr's left, and he knew that some smaller, faster variety of beastman was attempting to outflank him or to herd him into a trap. Desperation welled inside him and his vision closed down to a tunnel. His every footfall seemed like it would be his last, for now the woods behind were filling with the cacophony of uncounted braying creatures. His imagination populated his wake with fanged, tentacled horrors slithering and stampeding through the undergrowth, every one of them intent upon dragging him to the ground and plunging their teeth into his belly to haul out his guts and suck them dry before his dying eyes. And worst of all, the small part of him that had not yet surrendered to terror knew such visions were, if anything, but the least part of the horrible truth.

Now shadows darted amongst the trees to left and right, little more than darker patches against the black woodland backdrop. Upright creatures, agile and sinuous upon reverse-jointed legs dashed from tree to tree. The nearest beast-thing was little more than a loping silhouette, but Duerr could see it was carrying a short, crude bow in a one of its clawed hands and an arrow in the other. The thing halted, setting arrow to cord and aiming directly at Duerr.

A guttural, incomprehensible, sound escaped Duerr's throat as he flung himself to the ground at the exact moment the arrow sliced the air where his head had been. He rolled as he struck the ground, his hands sinking into the foetid mud almost up to his elbows. Gritting his teeth,

Duerr rolled over onto his back, kicking against the leaf-strewn ground as he backed away from his pursuers.

In an instant, they appeared. Though little more than shadows, the green light of Morrslieb glinting dully from rusted metal cleavers and ragged mail, the beastmen were mighty brutes, a head taller than most human warriors. Duerr was not a large man, and they towered over him as he desperately backed further away, his mind almost shot.

The nearest slowed as it approached, its every movement imbued with savage, raw, animal power. It cast its head, shaped not unlike that of an ox, left and right and huffed, its foul breath billowing in the cold air. Other shapes lurked in the undergrowth behind, but backed away, evidently warned off by this mighty creature of muscle and horn.

Silence hung heavy in the damp air, disturbed only by the ragged gasps of Duerr's breathing and the slow, steady tread of the beast as it approached. Duerr felt a damp tree trunk at his back, and he knew that he was cornered. He knew that he was about to die.

The thing turned its silhouetted head to look down at the form before it, and Duerr saw that one of its four curved horns was broken, snapped off at the tip in some challenge or fight for dominance. The beast halted not ten yards from Duerr's supine form, and the breath caught in the wizard's throat.

'Morr deliver my soul–' Duerr began. Something sharp and fast zipped through the air, cutting a stinging furrow across Duerr's cheek. He caught movement in the undergrowth to his left, and saw there the kneeling form of the creature that had shot at him moments earlier. Already, it was notching another arrow, which this time must surely strike home and bury itself in Duerr's flesh. In a flash, part of him recognised such a death as vastly preferable to what he could expect at the beast-leader's hands...

But the twisted wretch of a creature never loosed its third arrow, for the leader took a deep breath that seemed almost to draw the canopy down towards it, then unleashed such a dirge of a war cry that Duerr was forced back against the rotting tree. As the breath was forced from his lungs he screwed his eyes tight shut against a sudden gale that stank of mould and the earth between dead roots. Mindless with terror and deafened to all but the pounding of his own heart, Duerr scrambled around the trunk he was backed against. He stumbled against a looped root, lost his grip and struck his head against the hollow tree, the sudden impact bringing him somewhat back to his senses, though terror still threatened to overwhelm him. He looked desperately around and saw that a wide, open space lay behind the tree, though he had no time to gaze into the inky darkness.

The bellowing of the beast-leader had continued all the while, a steady drone of animal fury, but now it cut out with shocking abruptness. The damp air was silent once more, and Duerr could not help but peek cautiously around the tree trunk, holding his breath so as not to be betrayed by his own fear.

The smaller creature cringed at the leader's feet with its forehead, studded with two nub-like horns, pressed firmly into the soft ground in abject supplication. The leader reared above its underling, each half of the broken shortbow held in a clenched fist. Duerr's eyes widened in horror as the leader slowly raised a cloven foot over the smaller creature's head, the whipcord muscles of its leg tensed in readiness.

With a start, Duerr realised that he had a chance of escape, and he turned his head from the grisly scene to the open space at his back. At that very instant, he heard the leader's hoof come down with a wet thud, and he knew that the smaller beastman had received the ultimate punishment for the crime of interjecting in its lord's kill.

That very thought spurred Duerr to push himself from the tree trunk and power forwards blindly into the darkness. The instant he was moving he heard the unmistakable sound of the beastmen pursuing. He turned his head as he ran, glimpsing the brute rounding the tree, following after him. His attention elsewhere than on the ground he was crossing, Duerr lost his footing on the wet soil, his momentum propelling him forward several more steps before he slammed painfully down, the breath driven from his lungs by the force of the impact.

Duerr lay stunned for a moment, his face in the mud, knowing that he would be fortunate indeed to die as the twisted underling who had shot at him had. In what he assumed would be his final moments, Duerr found some peace.

After what felt like an age, death was yet to come. Duerr opened his eyes, not having realised that they were shut. He blinked and strained his ears, but all he heard was the sound of the forest: the swaying of branches in a light wind and the creaking of ancient bowers. He glanced around but saw no sign of any murderous beast-thing nearby. Blinking more rapidly, he dared look up then rolled onto his side and looked about.

Duerr was lying in an expanse of rough ground, a glade or clearing of some sort, though he could not tell if it was natural or manmade. As his eyes adjusted, he saw that the treeline a scant twenty yards before him was lined with beastmen, dozens of heavily muscled, horned, beast-headed abominations, all stood in silence with dark eyes glowering straight at him. The stillness was quite shocking in the aftermath of the desperate pursuit through the forest, and more disquieting still because at any moment the beasts could simply stride forward and tear Duerr limb from limb. Why, Duerr thought as his mind struggled to take in the scene, did they not simply do so?

'They fear this place,' a dry, death-rattle voice sounded from somewhere behind Duerr. That voice injected ice water directly into his veins, yet the effect upon the beastmen was greater still. They visibly shrank back from it like cringing animals, cornered and desperate for an escape route.

'And most of all,' the unseen speaker continued, 'they fear *me*.'

At that, the assembled beastmen backed away from the shadowed tree line, slowly at first, as if retreating from a foe that might lash out at any moment. Then they were gone, melting into the undergrowth silently without disturbing so much as a leaf. Duerr watched for long minutes, unwilling to trust that his would-be murderers were gone. He studied the shadows beneath the canopy and then turned slowly to locate the source of his deliverance.

The centre of the wide clearing was dominated by a tower: circular and tall, crooked and ramshackle. Its blocks were rough-hewn and irregular, black and glistening damply in the wan light of the Dark Moon. Ivy crept upwards, the leaves shimmering with silvered spider's webs and wet moss clothed vast swathes of the surface. As Duerr's glance climbed upwards, he saw dark, slit-like windows, their stone frames engraved with ancient devices rarely seen in the architecture of the Empire. At the summit, he could just make out an open-topped, crenulated turret set apart from the main structure, seeming like it must surely fall away and topple to the ground far below.

'You'd better come in,' the dry voice crackled from the base of the tower. Duerr looked to a dark portal set in its base and the door – heavy oak, iron-reinforced – swung partly inwards. 'Before they return.'

Galvanised to sudden motion by the thought of the beastmen reappearing from the trees, Duerr climbed shakily to his feet and stumbled towards the doorway. Glancing over his shoulder one last time, he passed through, the door swinging on screeching hinges and slamming shut behind him, plunging him into darkness far deeper than the moon-lit night outside.

ONLY AS DUERR had begun the ascent up the winding spiral stairs within the tower had he realised just how bone weary he truly was. The events of the last few hours had blurred into a terrible, confused melange of desperation and panic, which he was unable to string together into a coherent chain of events. How long ago had it been since the sun had set? How long since the beastmen had discovered him wandering lost through the haunted glades of the Drakwald Deeps?

As he climbed the stairs, one leaden step at a time, he gave up trying to make sense of any of it. He looked around as he climbed the narrow flight, which turned every few steps so that he became increasingly dizzy the higher he climbed. The stairs were so narrow and steep that he could set his hands upon them without bending over, which was fortunate because he was so tired he was almost reduced to climbing up on hands and knees.

At length, Duerr came upon a landing. It was dark, but the wan, sickly light of Morrslieb spilled in through an ached window, lending a half-light glow to the numerous objects strewn all about. As his eyes slowly adjusted to the gloom, Duerr saw that the walls were hung with all manner of artefacts, from blades of truly ancient pattern to shields the likes of which he had only seen in the most esoteric tomes of the Colleges of Magic. Fragments of armour were set in nooks, each coated in a layer of dust that had clearly not been disturbed in decades, perhaps even centuries. One floor to ceiling nook contained row upon row of glass containers, ranging from tiny phials to huge bell jars, the shoulders draped in the grey dust of ages and the contents dark and obscured.

A coldness settled upon Duerr's soul as his eyes grew more used to the gloomy interior and he took in the collection of objects arranged about the landing. As a student of Amethyst magic – the realms of the spirit, of dark dreams and of death, Duerr was well used to dabbling in matters most would find more than a little unsettling. But there was something else here, something old, something…

'Welcome…' the same parchment-dry voice that Duerr had heard earlier intoned. He cast about the dark landing, but saw nothing more alive than the spiders that haunted the dusty webs strewn across every surface. His breath quickening, Duerr prepared to answer, but was interrupted before a word had left his lips. 'The uppermost chamber, boy,' the voice said, a note of impatience evident. 'Don't keep me waiting.'

'Sit,' the old man ordered as Duerr came finally to the topmost chamber in the tower, excepting a small turret which he saw was accessible from a low side door. 'Rest.'

Duerr stepped over the threshold into a circular chamber that occupied the entire storey, finally coming face to face with the man who had apparently saved him from the beastmen. The chamber was lit by flickering blue and green flames dancing in archaic wall sconces, and it took Duerr's eyes long moments to locate the speaker.

To describe the man as old would be a drastic understatement. The crooked, black-robed individual before him was truly ancient. His robes were ragged, but had clearly been made of the very finest material, for they were patterned in intricate runes and sigils in thread of gold and silver. The ancient's hands were as twisted and gnarled as the trees outside, his wrists and fingers decorated with bands and jewels that whispered to Duerr of dusty tombs and long-dead cities.

Duerr looked into the ancient's face and his heart froze, just for an instant. For a moment, he had thought he was looking at a dry, wind-blasted skull, the mouth set in a rictus grin, the eyes hollow pits of darkness. Then the effect passed as the green and blue light flickering from the wall sconces changed its rhythm. Life, of a sort, glinted from the depths of the eye-sockets and the raw bone of the skull revealed itself to be covered with a paper-thin layer of dry, liver-spotted skin. Still,

Duerr thought as he steadied himself upon the high back of a nearby chair, there was scant muscle and flesh between skin and bone, the sharp edges of the skull threatening to tear through the thin covering.

'Please,' the ancient insisted, a wizened arm gesturing to the chair Duerr was leaning against. Duerr looked down at the dusty, black velvet padding, before his mind caught up with him. He nodded, gathering his wits, and seated himself.

'Well then,' the ancient said. 'So long has it been since I had a visitor pay me court. Your name, sir?'

Duerr opened his mouth to speak, then caught himself, his throat so dry he thought he might gag. It was the dust in the air, he realised, and the residue of mud and fear left over from his flight through the Drakwald. He coughed, and tried to speak.

'Where are my manners?' said the ancient, a dry chuckle sounding from somewhere inside his robes. 'Where indeed?' he continued as he shuffled across the faded, yet still ornate, Arabyan carpet. At length, he reached a cabinet seemingly carved of ivory and opened its doors, the creaking of the dry hinges shockingly loud in the confines of the chamber. The ancient muttered and chuckled as he withdrew a pair of crystal goblets and a decanter filled with liquid so dark it appeared black in the flickering illumination cast by the sconces. As the old man shuffled back the way he had come, Duerr risked a furtive glance about the chamber.

If the landing lower down the tower had been cluttered, this place was overrun with artefacts. Every square foot of the wall was occupied, most of it by curved shelves housing volume after volume of ancient tomes. He squinted as he sought to read the text inset in gold at the spines, then his breath caught in his throat and his eyes widened in disbelief. Mroggdok K'Thing's *Testimony*! He could scarcely believe that such a priceless work might be secreted away in the tower of some mad old wizard in the depths of the Drakwald. He scanned the spines of the next few volumes, his disbelief growing all the while. There were several volumes of Drivot's *Diatribes*, copies of which he had glimpsed once in the Colleges of Magic, but never been allowed to read. Next was a tattered, rat-chewed copy of Trakall's *Paradox*, a tome he knew by its fell reputation, but was unaware that any copy existed within the borders of the Empire.

'Trakall…' the old man sneered as he leaned over Duerr, a goblet of dark liquor proffered before him. The sudden speech made Duerr start and he felt suddenly guilty for his curiosity, as if he were a student again, caught rifling in the ingredients store.

'Bah!' the ancient continued, waving a hooked, claw-like hand in dismissal. 'Trakall was a hack,' he said as he backed away and eased himself down into a chair across from Duerr's. 'And he cheated at cards.'

Duerr realised that his throat was still painfully dry, and raised the goblet to his lips. A sharp tang rose from its contents, making his eyes water. He hesitated, yet did not want to appear ungracious to his rescuer.

'It's just Solland brandy,' the old man said, taking a sip from his own glass and grinning wryly. 'With a dash of black-eyed jenny,' he added. 'You've had a shock, by the looks of it.'

Duerr nodded as he sniffed the concoction gingerly. Black-eyed jenny was an archaic name for a rare variety of herb he knew to grow about the southern marches of the Midden Moors. It was not unrelated to the reason he had come to the Drakwald Deeps himself. He took a sip, the effect of the herb all but instantaneous. His mind cleared as the preparation worked its way through his system, while the brandy relaxed him, the chamber seeming to come into focus all around him.

'Back from the dead, eh?' the old man said, settling into his high-backed chair. 'What's your name, boy?'

'Benedi...' Duerr started, before taking a second draft on the dark liquor, his throat not quite wetted. 'Benedikt, sir. Benedikt Duerr.'

The ancient grinned, his features assuming the death mask rictus once more, if only for a second, before he replied, 'Welcome then, Benedikt Duerr. I am called Koth, Sidon Amen-Koth to be precise. I welcome you to my home, and to the Drakwald.'

Not quite sure how to take the welcome, Duerr decided he owed the old man some form of explanation for his presence. 'Sir,' he started. 'I came for the–'

'You came for the manbane,' the ancient interrupted. 'That much is quite clear, eh?'

'It is, sir?' Duerr stammered, his mind racing. How could this Koth have known his reason for coming to the Drakwald Deeps?

Koth grinned once more, the light in his eyes dwindling to a speck as the shadows closed in. 'You are not the first, young man. And I have no doubt you will not be the last.'

Duerr blinked and took another sip of the Solland brandy to steady his nerves. 'How could you–'

'How could I know?' Koth interjected once again. 'What else would one of our calling be seeking on the verges of the Midden Moors? You sought the manbane herb, to distil its blood, brew its essence and gain its power over dreams... and nightmares. Did you not?'

Duerr steadied the crystal goblet on the worn arm of the chair, and nodded. 'You are correct, sir. I needed the manbane to progress in my studies.'

'To attain the charter?' said Koth, grinning. 'To gain permission to practice your arts?'

'My master requires this of me, sir,' Duerr admitted, a feeling of dejection stealing over him. 'Or else I cannot attend to the funerary rites.'

'Hmm,' Koth nodded. 'And who is this mentor to whom you are apprenticed?'

'My master?' Duerr replied. 'My master is Lord Mhalkon, Adept of the Seventh Circle, he...'

'Hmpff!' Koth snorted, his grin twisting into a grimace. 'Seventh Circle, indeed. Lord Mhalkon, you say?'

'Yes, sir. Are you acquainted with my master?'

'Acquainted?' Koth answered. 'Never heard of him. Should I have?'

'Well, yes,' Duerr stammered. 'He is plenipotentiary-designate of the Cult of Morr, ambassador to the court of–'

Koth raised a wizened hand, affording Duerr a view of his curled and cracked nails. 'Young man,' he said, his voice low and dangerous. 'Do not be so quick to name our true lord and master.'

'Ours?' Duerr replied, realisation dawning. 'Then you serve M…' he caught himself. 'You serve those who wear the shroud?'

'I serve no man, young sir,' Koth replied. 'But to answer your question, in a manner of speaking, yes, I *serve*, though I have scant dealings with those mumbling fools in Lucinni.'

Duerr knew that Koth was referring to the convocation of the priests of Morr, the god of death, sleep and dreams, which gathered once every decade in the city-state of Lucinni, far to the south. The Cult of Morr was a loose affiliation of priests and wizards and followed precious little dogma, with no established church as such. That meant that each practitioner was apt to conduct themselves as they themselves saw fit, and some did so in widely divergent ways.

'If I might ask,' Duerr dared venture. 'How do you serve?'

Koth did not answer straight away, but looked about the chamber, his eyes, mere pinpricks of reflected light in the shadowy pits of their sockets, seeming to look beyond his mundane surroundings. His gaze swept over shelf after shelf of arcane tomes and dusty relics, over locked chests and baroque book stands, until, finally, it settled back on Duerr.

The ancient sighed, the sound redolent of stale air stirring within a tomb opened for the first time in centuries. 'I serve the past. I serve that which has gone before. Most of all, I *remember*. That is how I serve.'

Duerr nodded and swallowed hard. 'How long, sir?' he asked. 'How long have you served? How long have you *remembered*?'

The flickering of the wall-mounted sconces seemed to slow to a gentle pulse as Koth's gaze settled upon Duerr, the air thickening as if reality itself were leaning in closer to hear the ancient's reply. 'I have always served, Benedikt Duerr. And I always shall.'

'Sadly,' the old man continued. 'So too must you.'

Duerr's blood turned cold as he met Koth's gaze. 'Really, sir,' he started. 'I must return–'

'You cannot,' Koth replied.

'Sir, I–'

The ancient leaned forward, his death mask visage all Duerr could perceive as the shadows seemed to close in. 'Hush, Benedikt Duerr,' Koth whispered. 'This is no doing of mine, and I bear you no ill will.'

'Then what, sir?' said Duerr. 'What holds me here?'

Koth inclined his head towards the nearest window and, after a moment, Duerr broke his gaze and looked out. All he saw was the dark forest, the twisted boughs questing upwards towards the gibbous moon. Then a deep, coarse braying filled the night, and Duerr understood.

'The beasts?' he said.

'Aye. The Children of Old Night. How they hate this place.'

Duerr stopped himself from asking why the beastmen might hate the tower of this ancient wizard. His studies and the arcane knowledge he was party to came to him and he had no need to ask. 'They know this place is not subject to the laws of nature, the laws by which they themselves live and die. They know that *you* are not subject to such laws. Am I correct, sir?'

'Very good, young man,' said Koth. 'Very good. This… Mhalkon, is it? Yes, he has taught you something at least.'

Duerr glanced around the chamber once more, seeing as if for the first time just how *old* its contents truly were. How long had Koth dwelt here, coveting priceless relics of ages long gone, while the surrounding forests seethed with beastmen?

'There must be a way out,' said Duerr. 'Surely you have the power.'

'I may well have the power, Benedikt,' Koth replied. 'But I have no desire to leave.'

'They protect you?' Duerr asked. 'They keep the world at bay. They keep the past locked in.'

Koth chuckled, the sound like an ancient coffin lid sliding from its resting place. 'They do.'

'They keep all of your… artefacts, your tomes, your relics, safe.'

Koth nodded, though he did not reply.

'You have such power here,' said Duerr, aware that Koth was studying him, his skull-like head cocked at a slight angle. He looked towards the ancient volumes arrayed on the shelves. 'You have knowledge. If I could harness but a portion of that, I could win past them, and escape.'

Koth remained silent for another minute, though to Duerr it felt like ten times as long. The flickering of the sconces had slowed right down to a rolling rhythm, disturbingly synchronised with Duerr's own heartbeat. The longer Koth remained silent, the more resolved Duerr became. He was certain of it – Koth must surely have some weapon, some rune-bound blade that would turn the beastmen aside and secure his escape!

'I have no such talisman, boy,' said Koth at length. 'I am no Alaric to craft weapons that hack and hew.'

Without Duerr realising Koth had moved, the old man was across the chamber and standing beside a shelf piled high with dusty artefacts. 'What use to me Elbereth's Leash or the Mirrors of Mergith? I have no need for Urn Guards or the Cat of Calisthenes, Niobe's Torch or Rathnugg's Boots. Not that they did Rathnugg any good…'

'But you know spells,' Duerr insisted, knowing he was correct. 'You have power. This very *place* has power. I can feel it!'

Koth fixed Duerr with his pit-eyed gaze once more, regarding the young wizard with something akin to curious amusement. Duerr felt powers moving, energies aligning, and dead things stirring in cold, damp earth. He knew with terrible certainty that here before him was perhaps the most puissant master of the old ways of *shyish*, the Wind of Death, in all the land. That such a being dwelt within the very boundaries of the Empire, albeit deep within the Drakwald Deeps, was astonishing. He felt the draw of temptation, a small part of him begging leave to remain and to learn the secret arts and become master of nightmare and death. But a greater part of Duerr longed to escape this place and the perils pressing in on it from the forests all about. The sensation of dead things stirring grew ever more powerful, until he could feel movement beneath his feet though he stood upon stone flags. His nostrils filled with the musty stink of worm-chewed earth, his mouth with the copper tang of a mourning coin placed beneath his tongue in the funerary rites...

'Enough!' Koth ordered, and the power receded, the stink of rotten earth fled, and the slithering of dead things faded away. The copper tang lingered in his mouth as Koth rounded upon him.

'You are correct,' the ancient sighed. 'I cannot keep you here. But I would not see you consumed by things you have no knowledge of.'

'You will help me?' Duerr pressed. 'You will lend me your power?'

'I will lend you my *knowledge*, Benedikt,' Koth replied, holding up a gnarled claw to forestall interruption. 'Though be warned. You may not thank me, even should you escape.'

Now the blue-green illumination cast by the archaic sconces was all but frozen.

'I understand,' replied Duerr, though both men knew full well that he did not.

ONE MONTH LATER, Duerr stood high atop the tower of Koth, looking down from the highest turret upon the wind-lashed, night-shrouded Drakwald. Such knowledge infused his mind and his soul, such power was his to command, that he knew he would soon be gone from this place. He would be free of the beastmen, free to return to the Colleges of Magic. He would show his master and his peers that he was worthy, more than worthy, to serve Morr. Perhaps he would return to Koth's tower, and treat with him as an equal one day.

'I am ready, master,' Duerr announced, feeling a cold wind stir his robes. The gale was not entirely natural, the tang of dark magic underlying it.

'You know you cannot return,' the voice of the old man came from behind Duerr. 'Should you even escape.'

'I know,' Duerr lied as the wind increased. 'I am ready,' he repeated.

'Upon your own soul then,' said Koth as he proffered Duerr a rolled up, ribbon-bound scroll. 'Begin.'

Duerr took the scroll and broke the black wax seal, the discarded ribbon snatched away upon the wind to flutter to the dark clearing far below. He grinned as his eyes scanned the first lines of the spidery text written countless centuries earlier. Here was the last piece of the puzzle, the completion of the knowledge Koth had instilled upon him this last month. With it, he would turn the beasts to his service and escape this ancient trap.

Unfurling the scroll fully and holding it out before him, Duerr located the archaic sigil which he must enunciate in order to turn the beasts to his service. The night gale increased still further, and now it was clear that the Wind of *shyish* was building to a storm, an invisible vortex of magical energies forming overhead. The sigil glowed blackly upon the ancient parchment, tendrils of ebon power questing outwards as if to draw Duerr's soul inwards to embrace it…

'Speak the word and be done!' Koth shouted over the now howling winds. 'Before it is too late!'

Fully appreciating Koth's warning, Duerr took a deep breath and braced himself, the wind seeming to pause in its surging for that instant.

Then he spoke the ancient word of power.

The word had not been spoken in millennia, not by mortal lips at least. Only one schooled in the funerary rites could form it and not be blasted to crematory ashes or withered to a husk. It was a word that few ever spoke this side of the grave. The Wind of *shyish* whipped to a howling gale, buffeting Duerr and forcing him to set his feet wide lest he be snatched from the turret and tossed to the storm. The trees all about the clearing thrashed and dry leaves were whipped upwards. In an instant, the night was turned to a howling storm.

The feeling of power that Duerr had experienced a month before returned, only this time it was a thousand times more potent, and a thousand times more than that. He was the master of death and of dreams, the bearer of the forbidden key that would unlock the portal between this world and the next. The air about him transmuted into the cold earth of the grave and the air that filled his lungs was scented with the heady, cloying cocktail of incense masking decay.

The word resounded through the thrashing woods and Duerr knew it had been heeded. Soon, he would be master of life and death – his own life and the death of others. The beasts would turn pale and do his bidding, and he would be free.

'It begins!' Duerr heard Koth bellow into the wind, his voice tinged with terror.

A wet rending split the earth, and Duerr looked downwards into the clearing. The ground appeared to be boiling, as if the roots of the trees all about were stirring in hideous motion. His eyes widened in horror as he saw what he took for a root appear in the cracked earth, questing upwards with a jagged motion. But it was no root. It was nothing natural at all. It was an arm, or the skeletal remains of one, and it was dragging itself clear of the unmarked grave that must surely have held it fast for centuries.

In moments, the arm was clear and the body itself was visible, as were dozens more as they rose with jerking motions from the cold ground. Skeletons, the bones stained almost black by the raw earth, pulled themselves erect all about the clearing, and only then did Duerr see what he had wrought.

'Beasts...' he stammered. 'Beasts from the earth...'

'Yes, young Benedikt,' Koth whispered from behind Duerr, his dry voice somehow carrying over the howling wind and speaking directly into the wizard's mind. 'And they are yours to command as you will. Now you have the power to escape this place.

'Now you may leave.'

DUERR STEPPED THROUGH the portal at the base of the tower, out into the night and the clearing beyond. He trod cautiously, despite the knowledge that the army of dead things arrayed about was his to command. He felt as though he were walking the hunting ground of the most voracious of predators and knew that, in many ways, he was. Steeling himself, he walked through the tattered ranks, studying the rotting things he had brought into being.

The beasts were dark skeletons, rags of flesh and fabric caught amongst ribs and joints. Insects scuttled about disturbed nests while squirming worms fell to the churned ground. They stood upon cloven bone feet and clutched rusted cleavers and rotten shields in their dead grips. Their skulls were the sharp-snouted forms of cattle, though their teeth, where these had survived, were long and wickedly sharp. A pair of horns framed each skull; some curled tightly, others straight and proud. The eyes were empty sockets, but Duerr could perceive the faint spark of animal cognition deep within.

As he walked through the ranks of dead beasts, the sound of creaking bone and rustling dried flesh all about, he saw that one amongst their number was far larger than its fellows. Cautiously, he approached the mighty beast, looking up into its bovine-formed skull and perceiving in its empty eye sockets a vestige of raw, animal power. Echoes of the creature's death reverberated about the night, faded visions of blasphemy and desecration imprinting themselves over Duerr's vision. This beast lord had led its war herd against the hated tower and its fearful denizen, seeking to cast it down once and for all so that no stone was left standing upon another. The creature had failed; it and all of its herd had perished in the clearing. Yet, centuries later, its hatred remained, pure and distilled to the essence that still imbued it with fearful power.

At once quelled by the might of the undead beast lord before him and almost drunk with the fact that it was his to command, Duerr spoke the word of command. 'March!'

At first, nothing stirred but the wind. Then the wet creak of movement filled the clearing about the tower of Koth, and the army of long-dead beasts set out. Slow and unsteady at first, the dead things followed Duerr's order and were soon marching slowly and irregularly through the undergrowth beneath the dense canopy. Duerr hesitated at the treeline and looked over his shoulder towards the tower. There at its peak was Koth, looking down from the turret. He could not see the old man's expression for he was silhouetted against the green orb of Morrslieb. Then Koth was gone, the tower fading to the ramshackle aspect that Duerr had found it in weeks before. He turned, and followed his army into the black depths of the forest.

He did not get far.

Mere yards beyond the tree line, Duerr came upon the rearmost ranks of the war herd, stood still and silent. The air beneath the black canopy was still, the sounds of the wind muffled and distant. Duerr felt waves of animal threat spilling off of the dead things all about him and knew that death *beyond* death waited to be unleashed. He edged forward through the silent ranks until he saw the back of the undead beast lord before him.

Duerr saw then why his army had halted. The path ahead was blocked. A single massive beastman stood waiting, its every muscle bunched and tensed in readiness. Though the beast was wreathed in shadow, Duerr could see clearly the form of its four horns, one of which was broken off at the tip. It was the leader of the war herd that had pursued him through the Drakwald long weeks before, returned for its meat. Likely it had never left, but skulked out of sight in the dark, dank forests, biding its time for the trapped prey to emerge.

Though all but rooted to the ground with horror, Duerr knew what he must do. After all, this was the reason he had imbibed the ancient wisdom Koth had taught him, and why he had spoken that dread word of power from beyond the grave; to command this army of dead things to deliver him through the perils of the Drakwald that he might gain his freedom and escape alive.

'Kill it!' Duerr ordered the beast lord of his undead herd, his heart swelling with the desire to avenge himself. 'Stamp it into the ground! Grind it beneath your hooves!'

Grinning savagely, Duerr waited with bittersweet anticipation for his order to be obeyed. But it was not.

The two beast lords, one towering and skeletal, the other shorter of stature but very much alive, squared off against one another. The war herd of the living beast lord loomed from the shadows behind, but did not approach or attempt to intervene. Instead, the two armies backed off, making a space for their leader to face one another.

'What...?' Duerr stammered, before the truth of what he was witnessing dawned. He spun suddenly about to face the ranks of undead beasts behind him. 'Kill them! Just kill them!' he bellowed.

But none heeded Duerr's orders. Instead, the two beast lords began to circle one another in the space cleared for them by the herds. The living one huffed and snorted as its hooves stamped upon the rotten ground. The dead one moved with an oddly disjointed gait, patches of rusted mail rattling against dry, black bones. Though the shadowed pits of its eye sockets were empty, Duerr's wizard's sight perceived the dark unlife glinting deep within, responding to, and glorying in, this challenge.

Duerr backed away, his gaze fixed upon the sight unfolding before him. The instant his back pressed up against a rotten tree trunk, the living beast lord bellowed deafeningly loudly and launched itself at its rival. The other moved sideways and raised its shield, but the wood splintered under the attacker's two-handed cleaver. Splinters as deadly as crossbow bolts showered outwards, but the dead lord recovered, discarding the remnants and diving forward. The living beast lord's momentum carried it forward as its opponent stepped aside and both turned as one, their positions traded.

The beast that was living flesh snorted loudly, its breath so hot that it steamed from its flared nostrils like sulphurous smoke. The other redoubled its grip on its weapon, a sword of ancient fabrication clearly not made by the hand of his race or any other that Duerr knew of. Once more, the two circled the open ground, Duerr pressing himself against the tree all the while as the living beast lord's great, rippling back hove near.

'Morr…' Duerr breathed, desperately seeking to harness something of the power he had felt at the moment he had brought his army of dead things into existence. But he knew in that moment that the god of death and of dreams would not aid him; that this thing he had done was nothing of Morr's work. Morr was the god of rest, of eternal slumber and of oracles. This night, Duerr had blasphemed in the worst possible manner. Better that he died, he realised as the living beast lord stepped backwards towards him.

'Morr!' Duerr bellowed, his mind all but shattered with grief and horror. 'Morr, forgive–'

But he never completed his prayer, for the beast lord turned and bellowed its savage war cry directly into Duerr's face. Noise, and the creature's vile breath, forced him back hard against the tree trunk, knocking his head and causing his vision to blur. As he slid to the ground, he saw the beast turn in time to block a downwards blow from the undead lord and strike a savage counterblow in return.

The beast lord's two-handed cleaver struck the undead thing through the middle. Had the target had guts, they would have spilled across the clearing, but instead, the blade severed the exposed spine and brought the two halves of the unliving beast crashing to the ground. Its lower half came to rest amongst its followers, while the upper lay clawing the ground at the victor's feet.

The beast lord bellowed such a roar of triumph that the trees bowed and the canopy thrashed as if the storm that had whipped the forest when Duerr called forth the undead beast herd was returned. The sound left Duerr stunned and half-deafened, his balance shot and his vision all but gone. As he slumped to the ground, he saw the victor raise its cloven hoof high above the dead-thing's bovine skull head, and bring it crashing down with such force that the land itself cried out in pain.

The skull splintered into a thousand fragments and the undead beast lord was slain a second time. Slumping to the ground, Duerr rolled over onto his side in time to see the dead beastmen prostrate themselves before the victor.

The challenge was won; dominance was established; the herd was one and the rival beast lord was slain.

But Duerr knew that one more matter needed to be decided: his own fate. He felt his end drawing near, even as the heavy, cloven tread of the beastmen approached.

Imagining the beast lord's hoof raised above his head, poised to end his existence, he looked away across the ground. His blurred gaze settled upon a nearby object, a black-stemmed plant mere feet from his head, trampled into the ground. It was manbane, the very herb that he had so foolishly ventured into the Drakwald to obtain, so many weeks before.

He screwed his eyes tight shut as the beastmen gathered all about him. He waited for the inevitable, yet the killing blow never came. Instead of a cloven hoof slamming down upon his head, a stream of near-boiling acrid liquid struck him hard. Another joined it, then a third. One after another, the beastmen of the Drakwald demonstrated their disgust for this human, whose life was so meaningless to them that they would not even deign to snuff it out.

And high atop the Tower of Koth, the ancient necromancer returned to his studies of texts not read by mortal eyes for uncounted millennia, content to ignore the passage of the ages and the folly of man, until the end of time itself.

The Horus Heresy

THE LAST REMEMBRANCER

John French

In an age of darkness the truth must die.

– Words of a forgotten scholar
of ancient Terra

THEY MURDERED THE intruder ship on the edge of the Solar System. It spun through space, a kilometre-long barb of crenellated metal, trailing the burning vapours of its death like the tatters of a shroud. Like lions running down a crippled prey two golden-hulled strike vessels bracketed the dying ship. Each was a blunt slab of burnished armour thrust through space on cones of star-hot fire. They carried weapons that could level cities and held companies of the finest warriors. Their purpose was to kill any enemy who dared to enter the realm they guarded.

This star system was the seat of the Emperor of Mankind, the heart of an Imperium betrayed by its brightest son. There could be no mercy in this place. The ship had appeared without warning and without the correct identification signals. Its only future was to die in sight of the sun that had lit the birth of humanity.

Explosions flared across the intruder ship's hull, its skin splitting with ragged wounds that spilled dying crew and molten metal into the void. The two hunters silenced their guns and spat boarding torpedoes into the intruder's flanks. The first armoured dart punctured the ship's command decks, its assault ramps exploding open and disgorging amber-yellow armoured warriors in a roar of fire.

Each boarding torpedo carried twenty Imperial Fists of the Legiones Astartes: genetically enhanced warriors clad in powered armour who knew no fear or pity. Their enemy bore marks of loyalty to Horus, the Emperor's son who had turned on his father and thrust the Imperium into civil war. Red eyes with slit pupils, snarling beast heads and jagged eight-pointed stars covered the hull of the ship and the flesh of its crew. The air had a greasy quality, a meat stink that penetrated the Imperial Fists' sealed armour as they shot and hacked deeper into the ship. Blood dripped from their amber-yellow armour and tatters of flesh hung from their chainblades. There were thousands of crew on the ship: dreg ratings, servitors, command crew, technicians and armsmen. There were only a hundred Imperial Fists facing them but there would be no survivors.

Twenty-two minutes after boarding the ship the Imperial Fists found the sealed doors. They were over three times the height of a man and as wide as a battle tank. They did not know what was inside but that did not matter. Anything kept so safe must have been of great value to the enemy. Four melta charges later, a glowing hole had been bored through two metres of metal. The breach still glowing cherry-red, the first Imperial Fist moved through, bolt pistol raised, tracking for targets.

The space beyond was a bare chamber, tall and wide enough to take half a dozen Land Raiders side by side. The air was still, untouched by the rank haze that filled the rest of the ship, as if it had been kept separate and isolated. There were no jagged stars scratched into the metal of the floor, no red eyes set into the walls. At first it seemed empty, and then they saw the figure at the centre of the room. They advanced, red target runes in their helmet displays pulsing over the hunched man in grey. He sat on the floor, the discarded remains of food and crumpled parchment scattered around him. Thick chains led from bolts in the deck to shackles around his thin ankles. On his lap was a pile of yellow parchment. His hand held a crude quill made from a spar of metal; its tip was black.

The sergeant of the Imperial Fist boarding squad walked to within a blade swing of the man. More warriors spread out into the echoing chamber, weapons pointing in at him.

'Who are you?' asked the sergeant, his voice growling from his helmet's speaker grille.

'I am the last remembrancer,' said the man.

THE NAMELESS FORTRESS hid from the sun on the dark side of Titan, as if turning its face from the light. A kilometre-wide disk of stone and armour, it hung in the void above the yellow moon. Reflected light from the bloated sphere of Saturn caught in the tops of its weapon towers, spilling jagged shadows across its surface. It had been a defence station, part of the network that protected the approaches to Terra. Now the treachery of Horus had given it a new purpose. Here in isolated cells suspected traitors and turncoats were kept and bled of their secrets. Thousands of gaolers kept its inmates alive until they were of no further use: until the questioners were finished with them. There were countless questions that demanded an answer and its cells were never empty.

Rogal Dorn would be the first primarch to set foot in the nameless fortress. It was not an honour he relished.

'Vile,' said Dorn, watching as the void fortress grew nearer on a viewscreen. He sat on a metal flight bench, the knuckles of his armoured gauntlet beneath his chin. The inside compartment of the Stormbird attack craft was dark, the light from the viewscreen casting the primarch's face in corpse-cold light. Dark eyes set above sharp cheekbones, a nose that cut down in line with the slope of the forehead, a down-turned mouth framed by a strong jaw. It was a face of perfection set in anger and carved from stone.

'It is unpleasant, but it is necessary, my lord,' said a voice from the darkness behind Dorn. It was a low, deep voice, weighted with age. The primarch did not turn to look at the person who spoke, a grey presence standing on the edge of the light. There were just the two of them alone in the crew compartment. Rogal Dorn commanded the defence of Terra and millions of troops but came to this place with only one companion.

'*Necessary*. I have heard that often recently,' growled Dorn, not looking away from the waiting fortress.

Behind Dorn the shadowed figure shifted forwards. Cold electric light fell across a face crossed by lines of age and scars of time. Like the primarch, the figure wore armour, light catching its edges but hiding its colours in shadow.

'The enemy is inside us, lord. It does not only march against us on the battlefield, it walks amongst us,' said the old warrior.

'Trust is to be feared in this war then, captain?' asked Dorn, his voice like the growl of distant thunder.

'I speak the truth as I see it,' said the old warrior.

'Tell me, if it had not been my Imperial Fists that found him would I have known that Solomon Voss had been brought here?' He turned away from the screen and looked at the old warrior with eyes that had vanished into pits of shadow. 'What would have happened to him?'

The flickering blue light of the viewscreen spilled over the old warrior. Grey armour, without mark or rank, the hilt of a double-handed sword visible from where it projected above his shoulders. The light glittered across the ghost of a sigil on the grey of his shoulder guard.

'The same as must happen now: the truth must be found and after that whatever the truth demands must be done,' said the old warrior. He could feel the primarch's emotions radiating out from him, the violence chained behind a facade of stone.

'I have seen my brothers burn worlds we created together, sent my sons against my brothers' sons. I have unmade the heart of my father's empire and clad it in iron. You think I wish to avoid the realities that face us?'

The old warrior waited a heartbeat before replying. 'Yet you come here, my lord. You come to see a man who, in all likelihood, has been corrupted by Horus and the powers that cradle him.' Rogal Dorn did not move but the old warrior could feel the danger in that stillness like a lion poised for the kill.

'Have a care,' said Dorn, in a whisper like a sword sliding from a scabbard.

'Trust is a weakness in our armour, lord,' said the warrior, looking directly at the primarch. Dorn stepped forwards, his eyes deliberately tracing the bare grey surfaces of armour that should have displayed Legion heraldry.

'A strange sentiment from you, Iacton Qruze,' said Dorn.

The old warrior nodded slowly, remembering the ideals and broken oaths that had brought him to this point in time. He had once been a captain in the Luna Wolves Legion, the Legion of Horus. He was almost the last of his kind, and he had nothing left but his oath to serve the Emperor, and the Emperor alone.

'I have seen the price of blind trust, my lord. Trust must be proved.'

'And because of that we must throw the ideals of the Imperium to the flames?' said Dorn, leaning close to Qruze. Such focus from a primarch would have forced most mortals to their knees. Qruze held Dorn's gaze without faltering. He knew his role in this. He had made an oath of moment that he would stand watch over Rogal Dorn's judgement. His duty was to balance that judgement with questions.

'You have intervened, and so the judgement on this man is yours. He lives at your word,' said Qruze.

'What if he is innocent?' snapped Dorn. Qruze gave a weary smile.

'That proves nothing, my lord. If he is a threat he must be destroyed.'

'Is that what you are here to do?' said Dorn, nodding at the hilt of the sword on Qruze's back. 'To play judge, jury and executioner?'

'I am here to help you in your judgement. I do this for the Sigillite. This is his domain and I am his hand in this.'

An expression that might have been distaste ghosted across Dorn's face as he turned his back on Qruze.

On the viewscreen the side of the nameless fortress filled the screen; a toothed set of doors opening to greet them like a waiting mouth. Qruze could see a vast loading bay beyond lit by bright light. Hundreds of troops in gloss-red armour and silver-visored helmets waited in ranks, filling the docking bay floor. These were the gaolers of the nameless fortress. They never showed their faces and had no names, each was simply a number. Amongst them the hunched figures of the questioners stood in loose clusters, their faces hidden by hoods, fingers augmented with needles and blades protruding from the sleeves of their red robes.

The Stormbird settled on the deck with a purr of an anti-gravity field. Ice beaded its sleek body and wings as the warm air met void-cold metal. With a pneumatic hiss the ramp opened beneath the Stormbird's nose and Rogal Dorn walked into the stark light. He shone, the light reflecting from the burnished gold of his armour, glittering from rubies clutched in the claws of silver eagles. A black cloak lined in red and edged in ivory fell from his shoulders. As one every person in the docking bay knelt, the deck ringing with the impact of a thousand knees. Rogal Dorn strode through the kneeling ranks without a glance. Behind him Iacton Qruze followed in his ghost-grey armour, like a shadow in the sun's wake.

At the end of the ranks of crimson guards, three figures knelt and waited. Each wore armour the same gloss-red as the kneeling guards, their bowed heads encased by masks of tarnished silver. These were the key keepers of the nameless fortress. Qruze was one of the few people to have ever seen their faces.

'*Ave Praetorian*,' called one of the bowed figures in a booming electronic voice. With one voice every kneeling human echoed the call. The primarch spoke over the fading echoes.

'Take me to the remembrancer Solomon Voss.'

THE MAN WAS writing when the cell door opened. The light from the glow-globe above him created a murky yellow halo that cast all but the makeshift desk and the man into shadow. Thin shoulders hunched over a sheet of parchment, a quill in a thin hand scratching out black words. He did not look up.

Rogal Dorn stepped into the cell. He had removed his armour and wore a black tabard held around the waist with a belt of gold braid. Even without his battle-plate he seemed to strain the dark metal walls of the cell with his presence. Qruze followed, still in his grey armour.

'Solomon Voss,' said Dorn in a soft tone.

The man looked up at them. He had a flat, handsome face, the skin smooth and lined only around the eyes. His steel-grey hair was pulled back into a ponytail that hung over the rough fabric covering his back. In the presence of a primarch many people would struggle to speak. The man nodded and gave a tired smile.

'Hello, old friend,' said Voss. 'I knew someone would come.' His eyes flicked to Qruze. 'Not alone though, I see.' Qruze felt the disdain in the words but held his face impassive. Voss starred at him. 'I know your face from somewhere.'

Qruze did not reply. He knew who the man was, of course. Solomon Voss: author of *The Edge of Illumination*, witness to the first conquests of the Great Crusade, according to many the finest wordsmith of the age. Qruze had met Voss once, long ago in a different age. So much had left its mark on Qruze since then that he was surprised his old face triggered even the weakest memory in this man.

Voss nodded at the bare grey of Qruze's armour. 'The colours and markings of a Legion were always a mark of pride. So what does unmarked grey imply? Shame, perhaps?' Qruze kept his face emotionless. Such a remark would once have angered him. Now there was no false pride for it to cut. He had passed far beyond his lost life as a Son of Horus or Luna Wolf.

Dorn looked at Qruze, his face unreadable but his voice firm.

'He is here to observe, that is all.'

'The silent hand of judgement,' said Voss, nodding and turning back to the sheet of parchment. The quill began to scratch again. Dorn pulled a metal-framed chair close to the desk and sat, the chair creaking under his weight.

'I am your judge, remembrancer,' said Dorn in a low voice tinged with a tone that Qruze could not place.

Voss did not reply but completed a line of lettering. He made a low half-whistling noise as he paused over a word. Qruze thought he could see feelings play over the remembrancer's face, a twinge of apprehension and defiance. Then, with a flourish, the quill completed a line and Voss placed it on the desk. He nodded at the drying words and smiled.

'Done. In all honesty I think it is my best work. I flatter myself that you would not find its equal amongst the works of the ancients.' He turned to look at Dorn. 'Of course, no one will ever read it.'

Dorn gave a half-smile as if he had not heard the last remark and nodded at the pile of parchment on the desk.

'They let you have parchment and quill, then?'

'Yes,' sighed Voss. 'I wish I could say it was kind of them, but I rather think that they hope to scour it for secrets afterwards. They can't quite believe I am telling the truth, you see, but they also can't stop hoping that I am. The information on your brother, you see. I can feel their hunger for it.' Qruze saw the slightest tightening in Dorn's face at the mention of his brother.

'You have been questioned?' asked Dorn.

'Yes. But the heavy stuff has not started. Not yet.' Voss gave a humourless laugh. 'But I have a feeling that it was not far off. Until they stopped asking questions and just left me here.' Voss raised an eyebrow. 'That was your doing?'

'I was not going to let the great Solomon Voss disappear into an interrogation cell,' said Dorn.

'I am flattered, but there are many more prisoners here, thousands I think.' Voss was looking around at the metal walls of his cell as if he could see through them. 'I can hear the screams sometimes. I think they want us to hear them. They probably think it makes us easier to question.' Voss's voice trailed away.

This man is broken, thought Qruze. Something within him has died and left only a half life.

Dorn leaned towards Voss.

'You were more than a remembrancer,' said Dorn. 'Remember?'

'I was something once,' he nodded still starring into the darkness. 'Once. Back before Ullanor, when there were no remembrancers, when they were just an idea.' Voss shook his head and looked down at the parchment in front of him. 'It was quite an idea.'

Dorn nodded and Qruze saw the ghost of a smile on the primarch's normally grim face.

'Your idea, Solomon. A thousand artists sent out to reflect the truth of the Great Crusade. An idea worthy of the Imperium.'

Voss gave a weak smile. 'Flattery again, Rogal Dorn. Not *completely* my idea, as you must remember.' Dorn nodded and Qruze heard a note of passion in Voss's voice. 'I was just a wordsmith tolerated amongst the powerful because I could turn their deeds into words that could spread like fire.' Voss's eyes shone as if reflecting the light of bright memories. 'Not like the iterators, not like Sindermann and the rest of his manipulating ilk. The Imperial truth did not need manipulation. It needed reflecting out into the Imperium through words, and images and sounds.' He broke off and looked at the black ink stains on his thin fingers. 'At least, I thought so then.'

'You were right,' said Dorn and Qruze saw the conviction flow into the primarch's face. 'I remember the manuscripts you presented to the Emperor at Zuritz. Written by you and illuminated by Askarid Sha. They were beautiful and true.' Dorn was nodding slowly, as if trying to tease a response from Voss who was still looking at his hands. 'The petition to create an order of artists to "witness, record and reflect the light of truth spread by the Great Crusade". An order of people to be the Imperium's memory of its foundation: that was what you argued was needed. And you were right.'

Voss nodded slowly, then he looked up and there was a hollow look in his eyes. It was the look of someone thinking about what they had lost, thought Qruze. He knew. He had worn it himself in many dark hours in recent years.

'Yes, fine times,' said Voss. 'When the Council of Terra ratified the creation of the Order of Remembrancers, for a moment I thought I knew what you and your brothers must have felt, seeing your sons bringing illumination to the galaxy.' He gave a dismissive snort. 'But you are not here to flatter, Rogal Dorn, you are here to judge.'

'You vanished,' said Dorn in the same soft tone he had begun with. 'In the moments after the betrayal you vanished. Where have you been?' Voss did not answer for a second.

'I have been telling the truth since your sons took me from that ship,' he said, and looked at Qruze. 'I am sure it is in their mission accounts.'

Qruze stayed silent. He knew what Voss had said to the Imperial Fists that found him, what he had been saying to his interrogators ever since. He knew, and Rogal Dorn would know, but the primarch said nothing. The silence waited until Voss looked at Dorn and said what the primarch had been waiting for.

'I have been with the Warmaster.'

* * *

IACTON QRUZE KEPT his distance as the primarch watched the stars turn above him. They were in an observation cupola, a blister of crystal glass on the upper surface of the nameless fortress. Above them Saturn hung, its bands of muddy colour reminding Qruze of fat running through meat. Dorn had cut short the questioning of Solomon Voss, saying that he would return soon. He had said to Qruze that he needed to think. So they had come here to think beneath the light of the stars and the eye of Saturn. Qruze thought that Dorn had hoped that Voss would deny his earlier claim, that he would find a reason to set him free.

'He is as I remember him,' said Dorn suddenly, still gazing out at the scatter of stars. 'Older, worn, but still the same. No sign of corruption to my eyes.'

I must do my duty, thought Qruze. Even though it is like stabbing a blade into an unhealed wound. He took a deep breath before speaking.

'No, my lord. But perhaps you see what you want to see.' The primarch did not move but Qruze sensed the shift in atmosphere, a charge of danger in the cold air.

'You presume much, Iacton Qruze,' said the primarch in a low growl.

Qruze took a careful step closer to Dorn and spoke in a level voice. 'I presume nothing. I have nothing but one unbroken oath. That oath means I must say these things.' The primarch turned and straightened so that Qruze had to look up into his face. 'Even to you, lord.'

'You have more to say?' growled Dorn.

'Yes. I must remind you that the enemy is subtle and has many weapons. We can protect against them only with suspicion. Solomon Voss might be as you remember him. Perhaps he is the same man. Perhaps.' Qruze let the word hang in the air. 'But perhaps is not enough.'

'Do you believe his claim? That he was with Horus all this time?'

'I believe the facts. Voss has been amongst the enemy, whether willingly or as a captive. He was on a ship enslaved to Horus that bore the marks of the enemy. The rest could be...'

'A story.' Dorn was nodding, a grim expression on his face. 'He was the greatest teller of stories that I have ever known. There are billions in the Imperium that only know of our deeds by the words he wrote. You think that he is spinning a tale now?'

Qruze shook his head. 'I do not know, lord. I am not here to judge, I am here to question.'

'Then do your duty and question.'

Qruze took a breath and began to count off points, raising a finger for each one. 'Why did he go to Horus if he is not a traitor? Horus slaughtered the rest of the remembrancers when he purged the Legions. Why would he keep one of them alive?' When Dorn did not interrupt Qruze continued. 'And an enemy ship, with a single man held safe within it, does not drift into the Solar System alone.' He paused for a second, thinking of the thing that worried him most. Dorn was still looking at him, silently absorbing Qruze's words. 'It was not accident. He was returned to us.'

Dorn nodded, forming Qruze's worry into a question. 'And if he was, why?'

'WHY DID YOU go to Horus?' asked Rogal Dorn.

They were back in the cell. Solomon Voss sat by his desk with Rogal Dorn opposite him and Qruze standing by the door. Voss took a sip of spiced tea from a battered metal cup. He had asked for it and Dorn had assented. The remembrancer swallowed slowly and licked his lips before beginning.

'I was on Hattusa, with the 817th fleet, when I heard that Horus had rebelled against the Emperor. I could not believe it at first. I tried to think of reasons why, to put it into some form of context, to make some sense of it. I could not. But when I realised that I could not make sense of it I knew what I needed to do. I needed to see the truth with my own eyes. I would witness it and I would make sense of what I saw. Then I would put it into words so that others could share my understanding.'

Dorn frowned. 'You doubted that Horus was a traitor?'

'No. But I was a remembrancer, the greatest remembrancer. It was our duty to make sense of great events in art. I knew that others would doubt or would not believe that the brightest son of the Imperium could turn against it. If it was true I wanted that truth shouted from the works of as many remembrancers as possible.'

Qruze saw the passion and fire flash through Voss's face. For a moment the tiredness was gone and the man's conviction shone from him.

'You take much on yourself. To make sense of something that is senseless,' said Dorn.

'Remembrancers made what happened in the Great Crusade real. Without us who would remember any of it?'

Dorn shook his head gently. 'A war between the Legions is not a place for artists.'

'And the other types of wars we had been recording, were they more suitable? When all that had been built by you, by us, had been plunged into doubt, where else should I have been? I was a remembrancer; it was my duty to witness this war.' Voss put his cup of spiced tea down on his desk.

'I had started to make plans to get to Isstvan V by calling in favours and contacts.' Voss's mouth twisted as if chewing bitter words. 'Then the Edict of Dissolution came through. The remembrancers were no more, by the order of the Council of Terra. We were to be removed and dissolved back into mundane society. Those already amongst the war fleets were no longer to be allowed to record events.'

Qruze could feel the bitterness in the man's words. In the wake of the news of Horus's betrayal many things had changed in the Imperium.

One of these changes had been the removal of official backing for the remembrancers. With a stroke of a pen the remembrancers had been no more.

Better that than what could have become of them, thought Qruze. The image of men and woman dying under the guns of his former brothers flicked across his mind. An age ago, but no time at all, he thought. He blinked and the cell snapped back into sharp reality.

'But you did not obey,' said Dorn.

'I was angry,' spat Voss. 'I was the father of the Order of Remembrancers. I had witnessed the centuries of the Great Crusade since it began on Terra. I had looked on demigods and the scattering of blood amongst the stars that has been the birth of the Imperium.' He raised his hand as if gesturing to stars and planets above them. 'I made those events real to minds that will never see them. I bound them in words so that those wars will echo into the future. In millennia to come there will be children who listen, or read, and will feel the weight of these times in my words.' He snorted. 'We remembrancers served illumination and truth, not the whim of a council of bureaucrats.' Voss shook his head, his lip curled for a moment and then he blinked.

'Askarid was with me,' he said quietly. 'She said that it was an impossible idea, dangerous and driven by ego. A pilgrimage of hubris, she called it.' He smiled and closed his eyes for a moment, floating in lost happiness.

Qruze knew the name Askarid Sha, illuminator and calligraphist. She had lettered Voss's work into scrolls and tomes as beautiful as his words.

'Your collaborator?' asked Qruze, the question slipping out of his lips. Dorn shot him a hard look.

'Yes, she was my collaborator, in every sense.' Voss sighed and looked at the dregs of tea in his cup. 'We argued, for days,' he said quietly. 'We argued until it was clear that I was not going to change my mind. I knew it was possible to get to Isstvan V. I had contacts throughout the fleets, on both sides of the war. I knew I could do it.'

Voss paused, staring into space as if someone stood there looking back at him from a lost past. Dorn said nothing, but waited. After a few moments Voss spoke, a catch in his voice.

'Askarid came with me, even though I think she feared how it would end.'

'And how did it end?' asked Dorn. Voss looked back at the primarch, his eyes still wide with memory.

'Isn't that what you are here to decide, Rogal Dorn?'

'He was right, about the Edict of Dissolution,' said Dorn. Voss had asked to sleep and Dorn had permitted it. He and Qruze had returned to the dome of crystal beneath the starfield. Qruze could feel the leaden mood of the primarch as he stood looking at the stars.

'The end of the remembrancers?' said Qruze, raising an eyebrow and looking up at Dorn. 'You think that they should be allowed to wander through this war? Recording our shame in paintings and songs?' There was a pause. Qruze expected another growl of rebuke but Dorn showed no emotion other than in the slow breath exhaling from his nose.

'I had my doubts when the Council ratified the edict,' said Dorn. 'The position as presented at the time was perfectly logical. We are at war with ourselves; we do not know how far the treachery of my brother spreads. This is not a time to allow a menagerie of artists to walk freely amongst our forces. This is not a war to be reflected in poetry. I understand that...'

'But beyond logic, you had doubts,' said Qruze. He felt that he suddenly understood why Rogal Dorn, Praetorian of Terra, had come to see an old remembrancer in a prison cell.

'Not doubts, sorrow.' Dorn turned, pointing out at the stars beyond the crystal glass. 'We went out into those stars to wage war for a future of enlightenment. We took the best artists with us so that they could reflect that truth. Now our battles go unremembered and unrecorded. What does that tell us?' Dorn let his hand fall.

'It is a practicality of the situation we face. The survival of the truth that we fought for makes demands that must be met,' said Qruze.

'Demands that must be wrapped in silence and shadow? Deeds done that must remain unremembered and unjudged?' Dorn began to walk away from the glass, his steps raising dust from the floor.

'Survival or obliteration: that will be history's judgement on us,' said the grey warrior.

Dorn turned to stare at Qruze, the ghost of anger on his face. 'And the only way is for the Imperium to become a cruel machine of iron, and blood?' said the primarch in a hard-edged whisper.

'The future will have a price,' said Qruze, not moving from the viewport. Dorn was silent. For an instant Qruze thought he saw a flicker of despair in the primarch's eyes. Behind him the planets of the Solar System glittered as cold points of light beyond the towers of the nameless fortress.

'What will we become, Iacton Qruze? What will the future allow us to be?' said Dorn, and walked away without looking back.

'WHEN WE REACHED Isstvan V the massacre was complete,' continued Voss. 'I never got the chance to see the surface, but the void around it sparkled with debris. I watched it drift past the viewport of my stateroom, fragments still cooling, fires feeding on oxygen trapped in wrecks.'

Dorn nodded, his face unreadable as he listened to the remembrancer's story. Something had changed in the primarch after they returned from the observation deck. It was as if he had begun to wall something up inside him. It reminded Qruze of the gates of a citadel grinding shut before the advance of an enemy. If Voss noticed he did not show it.

'They came for us, the Sons of Horus. It was not until I saw them that I began to think that I had misunderstood this civil war.' Voss glanced at Qruze and the old warrior felt an ice-cold touch in his guts. 'Metal, sea-green metal, edged with bronze and covered with red slit eyes. Some had dried blood flaking from their armour. There were heads hanging on chains and by bunches of hair. They reeked of iron and blood. They said to come with them. Only one person asked why. I wish I could remember her name, but at the time I just wanted her to be quiet. One of them walked over to her and pulled her arms from her body, and left her screaming on the floor. We went with them after that.' Voss paused, his eyes unfocused, as if seeing the woman die again in her own blood.

Qruze found his hands had clenched, angry questions surging through his mind. Which one had it been? Which one of his former brothers had done that deed? One that he knew? One he had liked? He thought of the moment when he had learnt the truth about the men he had called brothers. The past can still wound us, he thought. He let out a quiet breath, releasing the pain. He must listen. For now, that was what he was here to do.

'There were many remembrancers with you?' asked Dorn.

'Yes,' said Voss with a shiver. 'I had persuaded a number of others to come with me. Other remembrancers who agreed we had a duty to show the truth of this darkening age. Twenty-one came with me. There were others too, taken from the ships of the Legions who had only just showed their allegiance.' Voss licked his lips, his eyes wandering again.

'What happened to them?' said Dorn.

'We were taken to the audience chamber on the *Vengeful Spirit*. I had seen it once before, a long time before.' Voss made a small shake of his head. 'It was not the same place. The viewport still looked out on the stars like a vast eye and the walls still tapered to darkness above. But things hung from the ceiling on chains, dried mutilated things, that I did not want to look at. Ragged banners, splattered with dark stains, covered the metal walls. It was hot, like the inside of a cave beside a fire pit. The air stank of hot metal and raw meat. I could see the Sons of Horus standing at the edge of the room, still, waiting. And at the centre of it all was Horus.

'I think I still thought I would see the pearl-white armour, the ivory cloak and the face of a friend. I looked at him and he was looking at me, right at me. I wanted to run, but I could not, I could not move to breathe. I could only stare back at that face framed by armour the colour of an ocean storm. He pointed at me, and said "All but that one." His sons did the rest.

'Three seconds of thunder and blood. When it was quiet I was on the deck on my hands and knees. Blood was pooling around my fingers. There was just blood and pulped meat all around me. The only thing I could think of was that Askarid had been stood beside me. I felt her hand around mine just before the shooting started.' Voss closed his eyes, his hands held together in his lap.

Qruze found that he could not look away from those ink-stained hands, the skin wrinkled, the fingers gripped together as if clutching a memory.

'But he kept you alive,' said Dorn, his voice as flat and hard as a hammer falling on stone.

Voss looked up, his eyes meeting the primarch's. 'Oh yes. Horus spared me. He walked to stand above me; I could feel his presence, that chained ferocity, like a furnace's heat. "Look at me," he said and I did. He smiled. "I remember you, Solomon Voss," he said. "I have cleansed my fleets of your kind: all but you. You I will keep. No one will harm you. You will see everything." He laughed. "You will be a remembrancer," he said.'

'And what did you do?' asked Dorn.

'I did the only thing I could. I was a remembrancer. I watched every bloody moment, heard the words of hate, smelled the stink of death and folly. I think for a time I went mad,' Voss chuckled. 'But then I realised what the truth of this age is. I found the truth I had come to see.'

'What truth is that, remembrancer?' said Dorn, and Qruze could hear the danger in the words like an edge on a blade.

Voss gave a small laugh, as if at a child's foolish question. 'That the future is dead, Rogal Dorn. It is ashes running through our hands.'

Dorn was on his feet before Qruze could blink. Rage radiated from him like the heat of a fire. Qruze had to steady himself as Dorn's emotion filled the room like an expanding thundercloud.

'You lie,' roared the primarch in a voice that had cowed armies.

Qruze waited for the blow to land, for the remembrancer to be nothing more than bloody flesh on the floor. No blow came. Voss shook his head. Qruze wondered at what the man must have seen to make this primarch's rage blow over him as if it were a gust of wind.

'I have seen what your brother has become,' said Voss, carefully measuring his words. 'I have looked your enemy in the eye. I know what must happen.'

'Horus will be defeated,' spat Dorn.

'Yes. Yes, perhaps he will, but I still speak the truth. It is not Horus that will destroy the future of the Imperium. It is you, Rogal Dorn. You and those that stand with you.' Voss nodded to Qruze.

Dorn leant down so that he was looking the man in the eye.

'We will rebuild the Imperium when this war is done.'

'From what, Rogal Dorn? From what?' sneered Voss, and Qruze saw the words hit Dorn like a blow. 'The weapons of this age of darkness are silence and secrets. The enlightenment of Imperial truth, those were the ideals you fought for. But you cannot trust any more, and without trust those ideals will die, old friend.'

'Why do you say this?' hissed Dorn.

'I say it because I am a remembrancer. I reflect the truth of the times. The truth is not something this new age wants to hear.'

'I do not fear the truth.'

'Then let my words,' Voss tapped his parchment, 'be heard by all. I have written it here, everything I saw, every dark and bloody moment.'

Qruze thought of the words of Solomon Voss spreading through the Imperium, carried by the authority of their author and the power of their message. It would be like poison spreading through the soul of those resisting Horus.

'You lie,' said Dorn carefully, as if the words were a shield.

'We sit in a secret fortress built on suspicion, with a sword over my head, and you say I lie?' Voss gave a humourless laugh.

Dorn let out a long breath and turned away from the remembrancer. 'I say that you have condemned yourself.' Dorn moved towards the door.

Qruze made to follow but Voss spoke from behind them.

'I think I understand now. Why your brother kept me and then let me fall into your hands.' Dorn turned from the open cell door. Voss looked back at him, a weary smile on his face. 'He knew that his brother would want to save me as a relic of the past. And he knew that I would never be allowed free after what I had seen.' Voss nodded, the smile gone from his face. 'He wanted you to feel the ideals of the past dying in your hands. He wanted you to look it in the eye as you killed it. He wanted you to realise that you two are much alike, still, Rogal Dorn.'

'BRING ME MY armour,' said Rogal Dorn, and red-robed serfs scuttled from the darkness. Each bore a section of gold battle-plate. Some pieces were so large and heavy that several had to carry them.

Dorn and Qruze stood once more in the observation dome. The only light in the wide, circular chamber was from the starfield above. Rogal Dorn had not spoken since he had left Voss in his cell, and Qruze had for once not dared to speak. Voss's words had shaken Qruze. No mad ranting or proclamation of Horus's greatness. No, this was worse. The remembrancer's words had spread through him like ice forming in water. Qruze had fought it, contained it within the walls of his will, but it still clawed at his mind. What if Voss had spoken the truth? He wondered if it was a poison strong enough to burn the mind of a primarch.

Dorn had stood looking out at the stars for over an hour before he had asked for his armour. The serfs would normally have armoured Dorn, cladding him in his battle-plate piece by piece. This time he armoured himself, pulling a hard skin of adamantium over his flesh, framing his stone-set face in gold: a war god rebuilding himself with his own hands.

Qruze thought that the primarch looked like a man preparing for his last battle.

'He has been twisted, my lord,' said Qruze softly and the primarch paused, his bare right hand about to slot into a gauntlet worked in silver with eagle feathers. 'Horus sent him here to wound and weaken you. He said as much himself. He speaks lies.'

'Lies?' said the primarch.

Qruze steeled himself and asked the question he had feared to ask since they had left Voss's cell. 'You fear that he is right? That the ideals of truth and illumination are dead?' said Qruze, an edge of urgency to his voice.

As soon as he spoke he did not want to know the answer. Dorn put his hand into the gauntlet, the seals snapping shut around the wrist. He flexed his metal-sheathed hand and looked at Qruze. There was a coldness in his eyes that made Qruze remember moonlight glinting from wolves' eyes in the darkness of lost winter nights.

'No, Iacton Qruze,' said Dorn. 'I fear that they never existed at all.'

THE DOOR TO the cell opened, spilling the shadows of Rogal Dorn and Iacton Qruze across the floor. Solomon Voss sat at his desk facing the door as if waiting for them, his last manuscript on the desk at his side. Rogal Dorn stepped in, the low light catching the edges of his armour. He looked, thought Qruze, like a walking statue of burnished metal. There were no sounds other than the steps of the primarch and the hum of the glow-globes.

Qruze pulled the door shut behind them and moved to the side. Reaching behind his shoulder he gripped the hilt of the sword sheathed at his back. The blade slid out of its scabbard with a whisper sound of steel. Forged by the finest warsmiths at the command of Malcador the Sigillite, Regent of Terra, its double-edged blade was as tall as a mortal man. Its silvered surface was etched with screaming faces wreathed by serpents and weeping blood. It bore the name *Tisiphone*, in memory of a forgotten force of vengeance. Qruze rested the blade point down, his hands gripping the hilt level with his face.

Voss looked up at the armoured figure of Rogal Dorn and nodded.

'I am ready,' said Voss and stood up, straightening his robe over his thin body, running a hand over his grey hair. He looked at Qruze. 'Is this your moment, grey watcher? That sword has waited for me.'

'No,' came the voice of Dorn. 'I will be your executioner.' He turned to Qruze and held out his hand. 'Your sword, Iacton Qruze.'

Qruze looked into the face of the primarch. There was pain in Dorn's eyes, unendurable pain locked behind walls of stone and iron, glimpsed for an instant through a crack.

Qruze bowed his head so that he did not need to look at Dorn's face, and held the sword out hilt first. Dorn took the sword with one hand, its size and weight seeming to shrink as he took it. He brought it up between him and Solomon Voss. The sword's power field activated with a crackle of bound lightning. The twitching glow of the blade cast the faces of both man and primarch in death-pale light and folds of shadow.

'Good luck, old friend,' said Solomon Voss, and did not look away as the blade fell.

Rogal Dorn stood for a moment, the blood pooling at his feet, the cell silent and still around him. He stepped towards the man's makeshift desk where the heap of parchment lay neatly stacked. With a flick, the power wreathing the blade vanished. Slowly, as if goading a poisonous serpent, Dorn turned the page with the tip of the deactivated blade. He scanned one line of text. *I have seen the future and it is dead*, it read.

He let the blade drop to the floor with a *clang* and walked to the cell door. As it opened he looked back at Qruze and pointed at the parchment and at the corpse on the floor.

'Burn it,' said Rogal Dorn. 'Burn it all.'

FLESH

Chris Wraight

Fifty years ago, they took my left hand.

I watched, conscious, heavy-headed with stimms and pain suppressants. I watched the knives go in, peeling back the skin, picking apart muscle and sinew.

They had trouble with the bones. I had changed by then and the ossmodula had turned my skeleton as hard as plasteel. They used a circular saw with glittering blades to cut through the radius and ulna. I can still hear its screaming whine.

They were simply following protocol. Indeed, they were further along the path than I was and there was something to be learned from the way they operated.

I kept it together. I am told that not everyone does.

It took three weeks for the new mechanism to bed down. The flesh chafed for a long time after that, red-raw against the metal of the implant.

I would wake and see it, an alien presence, bursting from the puffed and swollen stump of my left arm. I flexed iron fingers and watched micropistons and balance-nodes slide smoothly past one another. It looked delicate, though I knew it was stronger than the original had been.

Stronger, and better. Morvox spent a long time with me, explaining the benefits. He cast the issue in terms of pragmatism, of efficiency margins. Even back then I knew there was more to it than that.

This was an aesthetic matter. A matter of form. We were changing ourselves to comply with the dictates of taste.

Do not mistake this for regret. I do not regret what has been done to me. I cannot regret, not in any true sense.

545

My iron hand functions competently. It serves, just as I serve. It is an imple-ment, just as I am an implement. No praise can be higher.

But my old flesh, the part of me that was immolated in the rite, overseen by those machine faces down in the forges, I do not forget it.

I will, one day. Like Morvox, I will not remember anything but the aesthetic imperative.

Not yet. For now, I still feel it.

I

FROM THE TALEX to Majoris, then over to the spine shafts and the turbo-climbers. Levels swept by, all black, mottled with grime. Out of Station Lyris, and things got cleaner. Then up past the Ecclesiast Cordex, taking grav-bundles staffed by greyshirts, and into the Administratum quarter. That looked a lot like real grass on the lawns, baking under hololamps, before up again, through Securum and the plexiglass domes of the Excelsion.

Then things were really sparkling. Gleaming ceramics, floor-to-ceiling glass panels. You could forget the rest of the hive, the kilometres of squalid, close-pressed humanity, rammed into the angles between spires and manufactoria.

Right at the top, right where the tip of Ghorgonspire pierced the heavy orange fug of the sky, it felt like you'd never need a gland-deep dermo-scrub again. You could imagine that everything on Helaj V was pristine and smooth as a Celestine's conscience.

Raef Khamed, being a man of the world, was not prone to think that. He stalked up to Governor Tralmo's offices, still in his Jenummari fatigues, still stinking from what had happened in 45/331/aX and from the journey up. His lasgun banged against his right thigh, loose in its waist-slung holster. It needed a recharge. He needed a recharge. He'd emptied himself out on those bastards, and they just kept coming.

The two greyshirts flanking the doors saw him coming and snapped their heels.

'Jen,' they said in rough unison, making the aquila.

'She's in there?' asked Khamed, pushing the door open.

'She is,' came a voice from inside the chamber. 'Shut the doors behind you.'

He went in, and did as he was told.

Khamed stood in a large circular chamber. The floor was veined stone, grey and pink. False windows lined the walls, looking out on to false meadows and false skies. A bonestone statue of Sanguinius Redemptor stood by the walls, pious and gloomy.

There was a desk at the far end, but it was empty. Set off to one side, three low couches had been set around a curved table.

In one of the couches sat Governor Planetary Anatova Tralmo, tight-skinned from a century of rejuvenat and with oil-shimmer hair. Next to her was Astropath Majoris Eridh, milk-eyed and staring.

'How goes it?' Tralmo asked as Khamed sat down. She winced a little as his grimy fatigues marked the cream surface of the couch.

'Awful,' said Khamed, not noticing. 'Bloody awful. I'm not even going to try to describe what I saw this time.'

The Governor nodded sympathetically.

'Then you'll like this, I hope. Eridh?'

'A response,' said the astropath, looking at Khamed in that eerie, sightless way of his. 'Two cycles back, just deciphered and verified.'

Khamed's weary face lit up. He'd begun to doubt there'd be one.

'Throne,' he said, letting his relief show. The time for bravado was long gone. 'At last. Regiment?'

'It's not a Guard signal, Jenummari.'

'Then what? Who?'

Eridh handed him a data-slate with a summary of the transmission, elucidated into verbose Helaj vernac.

Khamed looked at it, and his muscles tensed. He read it again, just to be sure. He discovered he was holding the slate rather too tightly.

If he'd been less tired, he might have hidden his response better. As it was, when he looked up, he knew he'd given everything away. For the first time, he noticed the air of tight expectation on Tralmo's face.

Khamed had always liked her. Tralmo was tough. She didn't shake easily and had been good during the difficulties.

Just then, she looked like she was going to throw up.

'How long have we got?' he asked, conscious of the sudden hoarseness in his voice.

'Less than a standard Terran,' replied Tralmo. 'I want you to meet them, Raef. It's protocol. We should keep this military to military.'

Khamed swallowed. He was still holding the slate too tightly.

'Got you.'

Bitch.

THE DOCKING BAY doors were a metre thick. They dragged open, grinding along rust-weakened rails. Outside, the platform was open to the elements. On Helaj, the elements were always hateful.

Tracer lights winked in the orange gale. Further out, deeper into the sub-zero atmospheric bilge, more lights whirled. The storm roared, just as it always did, grumbling away like a maddened giant turning in its sleep.

There was another roar over the platform, closer to hand than the storm, and it came from the blurred outline of a ship. The thing was a brute, far larger than the shuttles that normally touched down at the spire summit.

Khamed couldn't make much out through the muck – his visor was already clouding up – but the engine backwash was huge. As he'd watched it come down on the local augurs he'd seen rows of squat gun barrels along its flanks, gigantic thruster housings and glimpses of a single infamous insignia.

That hadn't made him feel well. He was on edge. His hands were sweaty even in the thick gloves of his environment suit. His heart hadn't stopped thumping.

His men, twelve lostari lined up behind him, weren't any better. They stared into the raging clouds ahead, their weapons clutched tight, held diagonally across their body armour.

We're all soiling ourselves. Throne of Earth, trooper – get a handle on this.

The roar transmuted into a booming thunderclap, and the ship pulled away, back into the raging cloudscape. Its dark outline faded quickly, though the noise of those engines lingered for much longer.

New shapes emerged from the smog-filth, resolving into clarity like a carcharex out of the acid sea.

Five of them.

The Imperial Guard garrison in Ghorgonspire was over a hundred thousand strong. They'd made no progress against the incursion for six local lunars, which converted into a lot longer if you went with Terran.

Five of them. *Five.*

'Formal,' hissed Khamed over the vox.

His men snapped their ankles together and stared rigidly ahead.

The quintet approached. Khamed swallowed, and looked up.

Their armour was night-black and plainer than he'd expected. There were white markings on the shoulder-guards, but the finish was matt. Blunt, uncomplicated.

There was no getting away from the size of them. He'd been warned what to expect from Namogh, who'd witnessed a squad of Argent Sabres twenty years ago while on an exchange placement off-world.

'You never get used to it,' he'd said, his ugly face thoroughly disapproving. 'You think, *that's a machine. It has to be.* But in there, there's a man. And then it moves, all that plate, tonnes and tonnes of it, and you know it can move quicker than you can, it can kill you quicker than you can blink, and then you think: I was right the first time. It is a machine, a nightmare machine, and if we need to make a thing like this to keep us alive, then the universe is a scary place.'

Their armour hummed. It was barely audible over the roar of the storm, but you knew it was there. Just like the ship Khamed had seen, the power stored up in those black shells was obvious. They didn't need to hide it. They didn't want to hide it. They strode – *strutted* – up to him, every movement soaked in menace and confidence and contempt.

Khamed bowed.

'Welcome to Helaj V, lords,' he said, and was disgusted to hear how his voice carried a tremor even over the tinny transmission of his helm vox. 'We're grateful to have you.'

'I think that unlikely,' came the response. It was machine-clipped. 'But here we are. I am Iron Father Naim Morvox of the Iron Hands. Brief me as we descend, then the cleansing will begin.'

'THEY COME UP from the underhive. We isolate the spearheads and respond with contagion-pattern suppression.'

Khamed had to trot beside the stalking figure of Morvox as he tried to explain the situation. The Iron Hands Space Marine made no effort to slow down and kept up a punishing, metronomic stride. Behind him, the other four giants matched pace. Their heavy treads clunked on the polished surface of the transit corridor. Khamed's own men trailed in their wake.

'With little success,' observed Morvox. His voice. It was a strangely muted sound to come out of such a monstrous mouthpiece. Like all the Iron Hands squad, Morvox kept his helm on. The faceplate was a blank, dark mask.

'We've succeeded in keeping them from the upper hive,' replied Khamed, knowing how weak that sounded.

Morvox was approaching the honour guard: fifty lostari in greyshirt trim, ranked on either side of the corridor, guns hoisted.

'But you have not eliminated the source.'

'Not yet, no.'

From somewhere, Khamed heard Namogh's voice call the troops to attention, and their ankles slammed together. It wasn't done smoothly. The men were nervous.

'I need access to your hive schematics,' said Morvox, ignoring the troops and carrying on down the corridor. 'When did it happen?'

'8.2 Standard Terran lunars ago,' replied Khamed, shrugging an apology as he sailed past Namogh's position. His deputy looked even more irritated than usual. 'Insurgents control fifty-five per cent, all lower hive. We have no access to the levels below the base forge.'

'And I'll need full asset inventory. All troops are under my command. What is your name?'

Only now. Now you ask.

'Raef Khamed, Jenum–'

'You will remain with me. We will commence assault as soon as I have the data. Your men will be mobilised by then and I will order their deployment.'

'Very good. The men stand read–'

'Warn them they will need to be.'

They passed from the long corridor, through a pair of slide doors and into an octagonal command node. The walls were lined with picts. There were cogitator banks along the near flank, attended to by servitors bearing the cog-skull of the Mechanicus. Hololiths shimmered over projection pillars showing various cross-sections of the Ghorgonspire.

Morvox stopped walking. He said nothing, but his squad immediately fanned out and began to assimilate information from the picts. One of them pushed a servitor aside and extruded a dataclaw from a compartment in his gauntlet. None of them spoke out loud, though Khamed guessed that there was plenty of chat over closed channels.

'Leave us now,' ordered Morvox.

Khamed hesitated for a moment. Only minutes had passed since the docking bay doors had opened. This was all happening very quickly and he'd expected... well, he didn't know what he'd expected.

'Your will, lord,' he said, bowing.

He withdrew from the command node and blast doors slid closed behind him. He turned, and saw Namogh waiting for him.

'So?' the deputy asked. Orfen Namogh looked out of place in ceremonial armour, and it fitted him badly. Then again, the deputy only looked comfortable with dirt smeared on his face and a lasgun stock wedged against his shoulder.

'We asked for help,' said Khamed. He suddenly felt weary. He hadn't slept for twenty hours. 'We got it. Get everything together – we're going in again and they're in charge now.'

It took longer than he expected. The Iron Hands didn't emerge from the command node for over seven hours, during which time Khamed snatched some sleep, reviewed tactical readouts from the containment operation, and shared a meal of dried multimeat and tarec with Namogh.

'We're going to have to work with them, Orfen,' said Khamed, chewing through the gristle methodically.

'No,' said Namogh bluntly. 'No, we're not. You don't work with them. They order you into shitholes. You go down them. That's the way it works.'

'Fine. But stow your attitude. I don't want it getting down to the grunts.'

Namogh laughed, and took a swig of tarec. He had flecks of meat all over his big, yellow teeth.

'Don't worry. They're all crapping themselves already. And I haven't said a thing.'

A bead on Khamed's starched collar blinked red. Despite himself, he felt his stomach lurch.

'What are we afraid of?' he muttered, getting up and retrieving his helmet.

'You heard of Contqual?' asked Namogh, wiping his mouth and following Khamed out of the hab. 'You heard what they did there?'

Khamed brushed his uniform down and put his helmet on, twisting the seal as he walked.

'You shouldn't believe what you read, Orfen,' he said. 'There's a lot of crap on the grids.'

'One in three. That's how many they killed. Punitive measures, they called them. And those poor bastards were on our side.'

Khamed opened the blast doors from the officers' quarters and strode out into the antechamber of the command node. He kept his shoulders back, head straight. The little things were important.

'Like I said. There's a lot of crap out there.'

He opened the doors. Morvox was waiting on the far side of them, vast and mordant.

'We have what we need,' said the Iron Father. 'Now we go in.'

Out of the Excelsion, moving at a clip, and into the long bunkers of Securum, lit by gloomy strip-lumens. Administratum was amusing, with scholiasts looking terrified at the sight of the black giants striding through the lexchambers. Then down into the vaults of the Cordex. Some of the priests had tried to perform some kind of benediction on the Space Marines there, but had been simply brushed aside, just like everyone else.

After that, the dirt got bad. The air got hot. The floor got sticky, and the aircon wheezed like a phenexodrol junkie. There were men waiting at Station Lyris, arranged in ranks of a hundred. They looked pretty good, kitted out in full staff grey and assault armour. There wasn't much blood to be seen. The floors must have been swabbed.

'Will you address them?' asked Khamed, not really knowing whether that would be good or bad for morale.

'No,' said Morvox, and kept moving.

He never stopped moving. He just kept going.

Then you think: I was right the first time. It is a machine, a nightmare machine.

It was the implacability that was so unsettling. They looked almost invulnerable, to be sure, and their armour-hum was eerily threatening. But it was the sense you got, the sense that they would just keep on going, that got to you.

A mortal would know when to quit, even a dogged one like Namogh. They wouldn't. Ever.

'How do you want the Lostari deployed?'

'You have orders on the tac. For now, just try to keep up.'

Then down again, past the station bulwarks and along service runners towards the core hab clusters. The light got worse. The shafts got smaller and less well repaired. Loops of cables hung down from the roof, and moisture pooled in dark corners. Defective lumens guttered behind panels of iron mesh.

They were getting to the heart of it. Half a kilometre down in Ghorgonspire was like being a long way underground. The nearest patch of sky was buried under a lot of rockcrete. The air that coughed through the circulation systems was humid and smelled of human excreta. Major power grids had gone down early on in the difficulties, and battlefield gen-units struggled to keep the lumens in operation.

Khamed switched on vision-aug in his helmet. The men in his lead unit, twenty of them, did the same. They were all practically running in the wake of the Iron Hands, none of whom had broken their striding rhythm.

'This is Node 4R,' announced Morvox, coming up to a massive, closed siege gate at the end of the corridor. On either side of it, teams of greyshirt sentries waited warily, weapons hoisted. 'We will cleanse it. Consolidate in our wake. Are you prepared?'

Khamed was already out of breath. He shot a quick glance back down the crowded corridor. His lead unit was in readiness. Behind it, stretched out in the gloom of the long tunnel, were more squads coming into position. He could see some of them ramming energy packs into their lasguns and strapping helmets securely. They were as prepared as they would ever be.

'On your command,' he said, nodding to Morvox.

'We do not need your fire support. Do not join the assault. Secure the ground we clear. You will be given new orders on completion.'

Something was exchanged over a private channel, and the Space Marines unlocked their sidearms. Four of them, Morvox included, carried huge, boxy guns with blunt barrels and a chunky protruding magazine. They looked more like grenade launchers than regular firearms.

The fifth hoisted a truly massive weapon – an artillery piece with a core housing the size of a man's torso. It took both hands to hold it and there was a grip over the main carriage. A loop of ammunition hung underneath, stiff and chain-linked.

That wasn't all. They had blades. Some of them were like the short stabbing swords Khamed's own men used, albeit twice as big. Others weren't. Two of the giants carried massive rotary saws in their free hands, each one shaped like a gigantic broadsword.

Those weapons were ludicrous. Outsized, industrial-scale killing implements, dreamed up by some crazed enginseer and borne by super-humans. Khamed knew that he would have barely been able to lift one of those guns, and yet they hefted them lightly, one-handed.

He swallowed dryly. He also knew what was on the other side of the barrier.

'Open the gate,' he voxed.

And so the doors opened, grinding against metal, punishing old and arthritic gears, gradually exposing the chamber beyond and framing a window on to a nightmare.

II

LAND ENGINE. LONG for its class – a kilometre from sensorium fronds at the head to waste grinders at the arse. Vast, swaying, crowned with parapets of dusty smog that rolled down the side armour. Faint yellow lights studded weathered plate, tiny in the howling storm.

It rocked against the wind. Gigantic suspension coils flexed with the movement, supporting the thousands of tonnes of superstructure and its long, long train of drive mechanics, processing tracks, forges, crew habs and weapon banks.

All the time, the engines growled. On and on. They never stopped.

It was making good speed: 0.3 kilometres an hour, Medusan measures. The drives were operating noisily, making the floors tremble and shaking the black dust from the intakes.

Outside, it was blowing a gale, thick and black and grimy. There were voices on the wind, wailing.

On Medusa, it was always blowing a gale, thick and black and grimy. On Medusa, there were always voices on the wind.

Ahead of the Land Engine, the plain stretched away in a morass of cracks and sharp-stepped rock. On the far horizon, red lightning jumped down from the smogline.

Haak Rejn sat back in his metal lattice chair and rubbed his eyes. He felt the metal of his right optical implant snag on his skin.

There were picts around him in the sensorium chamber – a narrow control unit perched right out at the fore-left corner of the lead crawler unit. The screens were close-packed and flickering orange. Runes burned dimly, summarising feedback from the *Mordecai*'s seven thousand augur pinpoints. His implant helped him make sense of them.

It also gave him headaches. The implant burned the whole time, dull and hot. The damn thing was like a chunk of molten metal in his skull. But he didn't complain. It had never occurred to him to complain. Neither had it occurred to him to complain when they'd flank-wired him into the lattice chair, nor when the flesh of his thighs had withered away to straws from lack of movement, nor when he'd found he could no longer sleep except after a double shot of dousers and a course of binreflex exercises.

Very few people on Medusa saw the point in complaining. It wasn't that kind of place.

Something flickered on one of the picts. Rejn blinked blearily and reached over to it. He turned the gain up and calibrated his implant with it.

'Throne,' he swore, and ramped up the feed. 'Traak, you getting that?'

A thousand metres away, on the far side of the *Mordecai*'s lead unit, a commlink crackled into life.

'Yeah.' Traak's voice was sluggish, like he'd been trying to snatch a nap. 'I know what I'd like to think. Put a crawler down?'

'Good. I'm on it.'

Rejn's right hand, the one that could still move, worked the input vectors. His left, the one that terminated in a bunch of steel cables, twitched as his neural link communicated with the *Mordecai*'s Soul. It took a few moments for the protocols to clear.

Acknowledgement came back over the grid. From somewhere a long way down, he heard metal grind back against metal. There was a shuddering movement, and then a heavy crash. He switched to another pict, one that watched the port flank of the Land Engine's lead unit.

A hatch had opened near the base of the unit between two tread housings. A ramp extended from it, gouging a slow furrow in the rock below as it made contact.

A four-tracked crawler rolled down. Its angular, ugly frame rocked as it hit the plain. Exhaust columns belched black soot, and then it was off, lurching across the uneven surface.

Rejn switched to the crawler feed. Static rushed across the pict before clarifying. He saw the shape of a man resolve out of the blinding duststorm. The figure was still on his feet, leaning into the wind, limping badly. His ragged clothing was covered in plains-dust, making him look like so much charred meat.

The crawler reached his position and ground to a halt. The man staggered up to the back of it and hauled himself in. The crawler swung round and headed back to the ramp.

Rejn switched to an interior cam. The man was slumped in the corner of the crawler's load bay.

'Life signs,' ordered Rejn.

A series of indicators ran down his nearside pict. All low, all borderline viable.

Tough bastard. He'd make it, if they got him up to the medicae in time. Rejn punched the order into the grid and heard the click as the Soul registered.

'Any markings?' asked Traak, no doubt looking at the same feed.

'Not yet,' said Rejn, zooming in and scanning across the dirt-streaked face. Whatever the man had been doing, it had nearly killed him. Half his storm armour had been ripped away. 'He's not one of ours.'

'Can you patch an ident?'

'Yeah, just give me a second, dammit.'

Rejn watched as the crawler came back onboard. He ran a request and got clearance for a deep scan. The augurs calibrated, and a line of laser red ran down the man's body in a long sweep. The temple-stud got picked up and a fresh burst of data loaded on to the grid. Rejn looked at it carefully.

'Anything?'

Traak was getting annoying.

'Nothing to get excited about,' replied Rejn, preparing to shunt the data up to medicae and close the crawler hatch. 'Gramen clan, long way from home. Manus only knows what he's doing out here.'

'And a name?'

'Morvox. Doesn't mean much to me. You? Naim Kadaan Morvox.'

* * *

LAND ENGINE. SMALLER than the *Mordecai* but taller and more heavily armoured. It had no clan markings on the hull and its flanks were black. No lights blinked across the carapace, and the steep sided flanks were free of ore intake ramps.

As it inched its way across the desolate plain, the storm hammered uselessly against it. It didn't sway.

Deep within the core, far into the sarcophagus of metal and rockcrete and machinery, there was a half-lit chamber, perfectly square. The floor was black stone. The walls were lined with an organic mass of piping. The roof was vaulted, crowned with an iron boss and studded with weak downlights.

A man knelt in the centre of the chamber. He was naked, and the light glistened from the sweat on his skin. His shaven head was lowered in submission. Around him were robed figures, tall and broad-shouldered. They wore metal masks.

The grind of engines made the walls tremble.

One of the robed figures stepped out. He looked down at the kneeling figure for a long time, saying nothing.

When he spoke at last, the voice did not match his huge frame. It was thin and flat, as if run through overzealous audio filters.

'Of all the aspirants from Gramen, only you survived the trial of the plains. What lesson is there in this?'

The kneeling figure neither responded nor moved.

'Well?'

'I do not know, lord.'

'There is no lesson. You are not chosen. You are not unique. Some years, none come back. Some years, many do.'

The kneeling figure kept his head down. His muscles trembled slightly from holding position. His physique was impressive – tight, lean flesh over a tall frame. There were many scars on that flesh. Fresh wounds too.

'You may prosper in the trials to come. You may die from them. In all this, do not look for fate. Do not look for significance. There is only what functions and what does not.'

'Yes, lord.'

The robed giant withdrew a long steel blade. It was not a fighting blade – too clean, too fragile. It had a look of a surgical instrument, albeit one with a ceremonial purpose.

'You will learn this. You will learn that the path of your life is not unique. It has purpose only as part of a whole. You are an element within a system. You are a piece within a mechanism.'

The blade came closer. The kneeling man extended his left arm, holding it rigid before him, fist clenched. His head stayed bowed.

'As time passes, you will see the truth of this. You will wish to discard those things that remind you of how you are now. You will forget that you were the only survivor of the trial. You will only remember the trial

556   *The Best of Hammer and Bolter: Volume One*

itself. You will remember the process. You will be the process.'

The giant kneeled in front of the naked man, and placed the blade against the flesh of the forearm, halfway between wrist and elbow. The cutting edge rested on the sweat-sheened skin.

'This is the first mark of that process. Do you wish it to continue?'

The question was incongruous. The journey had already been started, and there were no choices left. Perhaps the question was a hangover from some older rite, a rite where personal determination had mattered more than it did now.

'I wish it,' came the response.

The blade pressed into the skin, carving deep. It slid to the right, leaving a clean cut in the muscle before slipping out. The man emitted the faintest intake of breath at the pain. Blood welled up quickly, thick and hot.

He was still mortal. His control was not yet perfect.

The giant stood up, letting the blood run down the blade, and withdrew.

'That is the mark,' he said. 'That is where the greater cut will be made.'

The blade passed from view.

'Rise, Aspirant Morvox. You are no longer what you were. From this point on, you will be a battle-brother of the Iron Hands Clan Raukaan, or you will be nothing.'

III

THE SIEGE GATES opened.

They exposed a long, wide hall beyond. It was almost totally dark, lit only by flares of orange gas from a broken supply conduit. The ceiling was lost in a writhing morass of gloomy mechanics. Bracing pillars, heavy columns of black iron, studded the rust-streaked floor.

They came out of the shadows, as if released by some soundless command. Dozens of them, bloated and chattering. Some hauled their distended stomachs along the ground, leaving trails of glittering pus in their wake. Others were emaciated, nothing more than sacks of leathery skin and splintered bone. Some of the bodies had fused together, creating sickening amalgams of men with multiple limbs, suppurating flesh and weeping organs hanging in chains. Some had talons, or bone outgrowths, or dull black teeth, or wickedly spiked spine ridges.

Only the eyes were the same on all of them. They glowed in the dark, lime green and as bright as stars. No pupils studded those eyes, just blank screens of eerie witchlight. As the gates opened to the full, the eyes narrowed. Faces, marked with fangs and hanging jaws and long lines of clumsy sutures, contorted into a mix of hatred and joy.

They scuttled into combat like spiders. They wanted it. What debased existence they possessed hungered for it in a way that they would hunger for nothing else ever again.

Khamed, still in the relative safety of the corridor outside the hall, watched them come, a weary sickness in his stomach. He'd been fighting those monsters for months. Every week, he'd fallen back a little further. Every week, a few dozen more of his men hadn't got back to the rally points in time.

And back then he'd always known that the next time he saw them the shambling horde would have more tattered grey uniforms hanging from hunched shoulders, and there would be more remnants of faces he recognised.

He gripped his sidearm with sweaty hands, keeping it in position, ready to go in again when the order came.

Then the Iron Hands got to work.

They didn't move fast. Khamed had heard that the Emperor's Angels could fight like daemons, hacking and whirling and tearing their foe apart in an orgy of destruction. These ones didn't. They walked out calmly, spreading out in front of the siege gates, opening fire from their massive weapons in long, perfectly controlled torrents.

Khamed just watched. The more he watched, the more he appreciated the truth of the legends he'd heard. For the first time in months, he dared to hope that the Spire would be saved. It was then that he realised just how strange that emotion – hope – had become to him.

The giants' firearms were neither las-tech nor solid ammunition. Khamed realised what they were as soon as the first volley went off. The Iron Hands used explosive charges, primed to ignite on impact. The noise of their discharge was phenomenal. They maintained a withering wall of fire, tearing apart the oncoming ranks of walking dead in an orgy of slime and fluid. The muzzle flashes lit up the hall in a riot of sharp electric light, exposing the tortured faces of their victims in brief, snatched freeze-frames.

The heavy weapon that one giant carried two-handed thundered like nothing Khamed had heard before. Its operator, placed right in the centre of the squad formation, wielded it calmly, drawing the devastating column of destruction across the enemy in a slow, deliberate sweep.

The enemy were not just killed. They were obliterated, blasted apart, torn into tatters of flapping skin and powdered bone. Bitter experience had taught Khamed that you couldn't down them with a flesh wound – you had to take them out with a headshot or knock their torsos into pulp. That wasn't a concern for the giants. They walked into the hall, methodically firing the whole time, laying down a maelstrom of destruction, not letting a single mutant get out of the path of their awesome, silent vengeance.

Then, suddenly, the deluge stopped. The echo of the massed volley died away. The hall sunk back into gloom. The Iron Hands remained poised to fire, their weapons held ready. They had advanced halfway across the space. Everything in front of them had been killed.

Khamed stayed where he was for a moment, ears ringing, stunned by what he had just witnessed. Then, cursing himself, he remembered his orders.

'Follow them in,' he snapped over the comm to his men. 'And look like you know what you're doing.'

He stepped over the threshold, sweeping his lasgun warily up and around. His boot nearly slipped and he looked down. The floor was covered in a thick carpet of bubbling sludge. It was moving. Some of it was bloody; some looked like sewage. An eyeball, swollen and yellow, floated past him, carried down into foaming drainage ducts by the current.

They'd been rendered down into soup. Flesh soup.

Ahead of him, the Iron Hands were calmly reloading. One of them took out what looked like a handheld sensor and tapped on it with a blunt armoured finger.

'Raef Khamed,' said Morvox. There was no inflexion there, nothing to indicate the extreme violence the giant had just unleashed. 'The area is cleansed. We will progress to Nodes 34, 45, 47 and then assess. Immolate this chamber and secure it. Deployment patterns are on the tac.'

'As you command, lord,' said Khamed, his voice sounding very quiet after the wall of noise.

The Iron Hands hadn't waited for the acknowledgement. They pressed on, heading deeper into the dark reaches of the lower hive. Already, from far below, sounds of scratching and screaming were massing.

Namogh's voice crackled over the comm.

'You need backup, Jen?' he asked. His voice sounded worried. 'We've got a lot of static at your position.'

'No,' said Khamed, knowing that he sounded distracted and not really caring. 'No, maintain your position. I think we're good. Throne, I actually think we're good.'

IT GOT HARDER. The lower levels had been dens of disease and corruption for years, and the mutants had had time to turn it into a paradise of pustulation.

The walls were alive with curtains of viscous slime. Growths burst out of air-con ducts, corpulent and luminous. Quasi-human mutants shambled up from the depths, heedless of their losses, jaws wide and ringed with filed-down teeth. They screamed like mockeries of children, stretching warped vocal cords beyond their tolerances. Khamed saw one grotesque long-necked mutant scream itself to a standstill, its throat overflowing with a bubbling cocktail of phlegm and clots. Morvox aimed a single shot and the creature's head exploded in a shower of sticky, whirling gobbets, silencing the shrill chorus from its owner.

As they descended, the layout of the tunnels changed. Ceilings closed in and walls narrowed. The slurry of excreta was ankle-deep at the best of times, knee-deep at the worst. There was no reliable light – just the sweeping lumen beams from helmets, exposing the breadth of the horror in fragmentary pools of surgical illumination.

Every mutant coming for them had once been a human inhabitant of the hive. Every contorted face had once run the full gamut of human laughs and tears. They had been technicians, lectors, machine operators, arbitrators.

No one knew exactly when it had started. The first signs had been small ones – increased workload at the medicae stations, reports of infection in the scholae, power-loss in the deep hive and rioting across the semi-policed hinterlands running out to the ore-plains.

The authorities hadn't been slow to act. Tralmo was sharp, and had never been negligent. There had been quarantines, shipments of antibiotics, blockades of crime-controlled sectors and curfews across the Ghorgonspire.

But by the time the 1324th Lostari 'Greyshirt' Imperial Guard had been mobilised to restore order, it was already out of hand. The situation had changed from a public health problem to a fight for survival, and so it had stayed for months.

They never got to the bottom of what had caused it. The originator was, presumably, buried far down in the depths, squatting in the dark places under Ghorgonspire that had long been lost to the contagion. The Holy Emperor alone knew what was down there, pumping bile and energy into the ruined bodies of those it had corrupted.

Such speculation was useless. The Iron Hands moved with purpose. They punched through the ragged columns of mutants like a blade through rusty armour, tearing and burning and hacking and blasting. They never sped up, never slowed down. Step by step, metre by metre, they reclaimed lost ground, operating like silent golems of myth.

In their wake came the mortal troops, reinvigorated by the example they had in front of them. Exhausted Lostari found the will to take the fight to the mutants. Volleys of lasfire suddenly found their marks more often. Objectives were isolated, taken and consolidated. With the indomitable example of the Space Marines in front of them, the 1324th Lostari of Helaj V stood up, and found they were stronger than their desperation had made them believe.

They descended from level to level in orderly bursts of activity, clearing out connecting chambers of filth and pressing on into the tunnels beyond. Flamers came next, boiling off the stinking layers of slime and acid and charring the metal beneath. Obscene sigils were scored from the walls. Power was restored. The mark of the Imperium was reinstated.

At the forefront, as ever, were the Iron Hands, the Emperor's holy Angels of Death.

And as they killed in those terrible, industrial quantities, never had a moniker seemed so apt.

* * *

THE EYES CAME out of the darkness as if swimming up from the frigid abyss. They swarmed, flocking at the invaders, locked into snarls and yells of utter mindless hatred. As they neared, limbs became visible. Limbs with hooks run through them, or stitches running down them, or iron pins shoved up under the necrotic skin and bulging like parasites.

Khamed shrugged off his tiredness and shouldered his lasgun. He moved smoothly, aping the frictionless methods of the Iron Hands who fought ahead of him, and drew a bead on the lead mutant.

He fired, and his las-beam cracked off, impacting between a pair of staring green eyes and cracking the skull into hemispheres.

Another kill.

And then he was moving again, marshalling his squad and pushing them forward. He swept his muzzle round, looking for mutants crawling across the roof or punching their way through sewer outlets.

They were deep down and the air was hot and seamy. No light existed save for the mess of helmet lumen beams, and every trooper was now on full infrared. The chamber was just like a hundred they'd already cleansed – close, claustrophobic, stuffed with a crawling mass of suppurating terror.

It had ceased to matter. Khamed had begun to forget his life had ever involved anything different. The undead poured towards him, snapping fangs and loping on all fours into contact. He reacted passionlessly, efficiently, optimising his shots and taking time over the targeting. He could rely on the Iron Hands to take out the mass of them – he was there to mop up the stragglers and the outriders.

He swung round just as three skinny mutants, their bulbous heads bobbing on scrawny necks, bolted from cover and out toward the leftmost Space Marine of the Iron Hands squad. Each one was carrying heavy projectile weapons and let off a flurry of lead as they splashed through the ankle-deep lake of effluvium.

Khamed got his aim and fired, missing the lead mutant by a finger's width. In the time it took him to curse, wipe his eyes and re-aim, it was over.

The Iron Hand didn't seem to move fast. He seemed to move with the same unearthly, ponderous manner as his brothers. But, somehow, he got his weapon up and fired off a round before the mutants had taken another step. The bolt crashed through the neck of the first, tearing the muscles open and leaving the head lolling on stretched sinews like an amulet. It exploded in the chest of the second, blowing open a ravaged ribcage into splayed splinters.

Then the sword, the mad sword with its insane rotary blades, swept round in a heavy lash, whipping out sticky fluid from previous kills. The surviving mutant tried to dart under it, aiming to get close enough to use a rusty killing blade it held in its left hand.

The Iron Hand adjusted the weapon's descent and the sword whirred into the mutant's leading shoulder. It burrowed down, carving its way through diseased muscle bunches and flinging out gouts of boiling, frothing blood. The mutant screamed for a fraction of a second, locked in agony as the juddering blades ate through its bony frame and minced what was left of it into a marrow-flecked broth of body fluids.

The Space Marine hauled the sword free, breaking the ruined body of his prey into two pieces as it was withdrawn. Then he turned, implacable as ever, and kept on fighting.

He'd never said a word. He'd not changed a thing. No hurry, no fuss.

Nightmare machines.

Khamed laughed.

The Jenummari laughed as he brought his own weapon round and splashed through the filth, looking for new targets. It was a laugh of disbelief, a laugh of wonder that killers of such intensity existed in the universe. It was a laugh of fear, and of relief that they were on his side. He had last laughed six months ago, and the noise of it was unfamiliar in his parched throat.

'Keep up, you dogs!' he snapped over the comm.

He wasn't scared anymore. His body pumped with adrenaline. He was beginning to enjoy himself.

That, of course, was his first mistake.

IT WAS FAST as well as strong. Its hide was pale brown, like old leather. It had four heavy arms, perhaps grafted on to the torso by some demented chirurgeon. Its face was long, stretched by weights nailed to its distended chin. The skin of its cheeks was ripped and weeping and its clustered eyes bled witchlight.

As it crashed through the slurry, it howled like a dog. Its hands clenched pairs of gouges, each dripping with virulent, glistening fluid. Long, lank hair flailed around it as it came, and trails of livid saliva hung down from a bloodstained jaw.

It veered sharply, crashing its way through a knot of its own warped kin. They were crushed underfoot as it came, trampled into the mix of blood and mucus that bubbled underfoot.

For once, the Space Marines missed the main target. They were all occupied, pinning back the tide of raging, screaming fury that hammered against them. Their guns slammed back into their armoured fists, spitting the surge of reactive rounds that cracked and boomed into the oncoming wall of corrupted flesh.

Khamed saw the mutant come in his direction, and the laughter died in his mouth. One of his men got a shot, and a las-beam whipped across it.

It didn't drop. It launched itself into the close-packed press of Lostari, limbs whirling, roaring a strangled cry of ecstasy and fury.

Khamed tried to swivel round to get an angle, but slipped. He crashed back to the ground, bracing himself with his free arm, only to see three of his men taken out by the mutant. It went for their throats, biting through the neck armour and shaking their limp corpses. Las-beams seared into it, ripping away whole strips of skin, but that didn't slow it down much. It rampaged through the knot of men, shrugging off anything that hit it, scattering the survivors. Then it turned and saw Khamed.

It smiled.

The mutant leapt at him, all four arms extended. Khamed fired again, hitting it once in its massive chest. Then he was scrabbling back through the scummy fluid, desperately trying to clear some distance.

The mutant stumbled from the las-impact, then regained its feet. It lurched down and grabbed Khamed's trailing boot. Khamed felt the vice close around his ankle and thrashed to escape, kicking wildly.

He stood no chance. The mutant pulled him back savagely, gurgling, readying its blades for the plunge that would rip his stomach open. Khamed was wrenched back, dragged through the liquid and along the chamber floor. Frothy slime splashed across his helmet, running across the visor and clouding it in a film of brown.

Khamed fired again, blindly, and heard the snap of the las-beam as it shot harmlessly into the roof. Then the gun was knocked from his grasp. He tensed for the bite of the gouges, knowing that they would plunge low, right into his gut.

Then something huge exploded above him, throwing the slime up in waves. The grip on his ankle released. Khamed pulled himself out of the grime and shook the screen of filth from his visor.

The mutant was gone. Its lifeless body was crumpled up against the metal wall, pumping black blood solidly. In front of Khamed loomed an Iron Hand, filling his field of vision, vast, black and indomitable.

'Can you fight?' came the voice from behind the visor.

It wasn't Morvox. The tone wasn't as metallic, not as heavily filtered. It almost sounded human, albeit far more daunting and resonant than any human Khamed had ever encountered.

'Yes,' he said, shaking himself down and bending to retrieve his lasgun. 'Yes, I can.'

'Then do so,' replied the Space Marine, turning away from him and striding back to the main fighting. The chamber was still full of the sounds of combat. Fresh Lostari were piling in to replace those felled by the mutant, but there was no sign yet of the horde of bloated horrors relinquishing the chamber. The clamour of bolter detonations, howls and screams just kept on going.

Khamed watched the Iron Hand go, his heart thumping hard. He realised his hands were shaking, and clenched his fists to stop it.

Then do so.

He hefted his lasgun again, checking to see if the fluids had interfered with the mechanism. The simple things helped.

'Very well,' he muttered, still trembling. He braced himself and looked for a target. 'I will.'

THE NOISE OF the assault died away. The Iron Hands began to move on, wading their way toward a long access shaft. They maintained the same pace as before, never speeding up, never slowing down.

The same punishing pace wasn't possible for the mortal troops. They needed rotations, rest periods, resupply and medicae treatment. After hours of fighting, almost without respite, Khamed's turn had finally come.

Namogh's force-signal flashed across his helmet display, indicating that he was moving into position to relieve him. Khamed turned to the Space Marine who had rescued him, still the closest to hand of the quintet. For some reason, it felt more natural to address that one than Morvox, who in any case had already stalked off into the dark ahead.

'My deputy will provide fire support beyond this node,' Khamed announced. His voice gave away his extreme fatigue. The adrenaline from the last encounter had drained away, leaving him feeling empty. 'This detachment needs to rotate.'

The Space Marine turned to face him. His facemask was streaked with blood and bile, making him look even more grotesque than normal. There was a pause, possibly due to some internal comms between the squad.

'We will maintain the assault,' the Iron Hand replied. 'Order relief forces to follow us down when they get here.'

The Space Marine turned to move off, then stopped. He looked Khamed up and down.

'How long have you been on your feet?'

'Fifteen hours, lord. The same as you.'

The Space Marine nodded slowly.

'Fifteen hours.' There was a strange noise from the vox grille. On a human, it might have been a laugh – a strange, attenuated snort. From one of the giants, Khamed wasn't willing to assume anything.

'We forget where we come from, sometimes,' said the Iron Hand. The tone of voice was almost reflective. 'You fought well, human. Tell the others they fought well.'

Khamed didn't reply at once, stunned by the unexpected compliment. Then suddenly, from nowhere, encouraged by the unlikely candour from the Angel of Death, he dared to ask for more.

'I will, lord,' he said. 'But I have no name to give them.'

Again, the noise. Perhaps irritation. Perhaps amusement. Perhaps warning.

'Ralech,' came the reply, before the Space Marine strode off to join his brother warriors. 'Ralech Grond, Clan Raukaan, Medusa. Tell them that.'

* * *

'HE SAID THAT?'

Khamed nodded between gulps of stimm-laced water. He was enjoying Namogh's expression – a cross between disbelief, horror and disapproval.

'I don't believe it.'

Khamed put the canteen down. He was sitting on an old iron crate, shoulders hunched and head low. He could already feel oncoming sleep crowding out his thoughts. The chamber was full of men, exhausted ones from his command being replaced with fresher ones under Namogh's.

'He was almost… normal.'

'Crap.'

'I'm telling you.'

Khamed watched the survivors of his platoon limp back up toward the transit shafts at the rear end of the chamber. Their armour was caked in filth and blood. Some couldn't walk unaided and hung like sides of meat from the shoulders of their comrades. He'd be joining them soon.

'I think they change,' said Khamed thoughtfully. 'The leader – Morvox – he's further down the road than the others. They forget.'

Namogh spat into the floor-slurry, and the spittle spun gently away toward the drain meshing.

'You've taken a hit, Jen,' he said, shaking his head. 'They don't feel nothing. They'd throw us into the grinder without a blink.'

'I'm not sure.'

'They ain't human.'

'Not now, no.'

'We're *nothing* to them. Just spare parts.'

Khamed looked up at his deputy. Namogh was as adamant as ever. His ugly face was twisted with distaste. There was anger there, to be sure, but also fear. Khamed couldn't blame him for that. The Iron Hands scared everyone, even the mutants.

'I don't want to believe that, Orfen,' said Khamed quietly. 'They are sons of the Emperor, just as we are. We fight together.'

'Crap. You're delusional.'

'But what changes them?' asked Khamed, ignoring Namogh. He remembered the way Grond's voice had sounded. 'Why do they change? I'd like to know that.'

IV

THE KNIFE WENT in, moving across the flesh of the arm, tracing a thin line of blood.

Morvox watched it. He had an almost uncontrollable urge to seize the nearest medicae servitor by its desiccated throat and slam it against the walls of the apothecarion.

That had been predicted. He fought the urge down. The hormones in his body, the ones introduced during the changes, made him belligerent in the face of injury.

The servitors carried on, heedless of the turmoil in their patient. They moved on tank tracks around the metal chair Morvox had been clamped into. Their faces were shiny curves of steel, dotted with sensoria. Their limbs were entirely augmetic and terminated in a dozen different surgical devices. They chattered to one another in a basic form of binaric. It was a soft, low clicking backdrop to their grisly work.

The skin was peeled back, exposing raw muscle. The ligatures below the bicep tensed. The knives went in again, parting the muscle mass.

Morvox watched it happen. He watched the rotary saw whine through the bone. It had only just finished growing into its new, improved form. Amputating it seemed wasteful.

They broke the bones. He watched his hand fall away, clutched in the claws of a metal servitor. He watched the blood run out of the wrist, steaming as it cooled in its steel bowl. He watched sutures run across his severed forearm, rebinding the muscles and stabilising them. He watched the drills go in and the pre-augmetic bindings lock on to his broken bones.

There was hours of work to come. Rods would be implanted, running nearly up to his elbow. Braces would encircle the pronator, studding through the skin of his forearm. Neural relays would be dropped into place, and nerve-sockets, and tendon housings. And then, finally, they would drill in the new hand, the mark of his Chapter, the sign of fealty to the primarch and to the ideals of Medusa.

He would watch it all. The procedure was the mark of passage, the signal of his transition from mortal to superhuman. When it was complete, it would make him stronger. He knew this. It was fact, as revealed by Iron Father Arven Rauth, and so could not be doubted.

But, even though he knew it to be true, even as he watched the rods go in, bisecting the muscles that had kept him alive out on the ash plains, he did not yet believe it.

One day, like the Iron Father who had retrieved him from the trials, Morvox would not remember anything but the aesthetic imperative, the desire to purge the machine of the flesh that impeded it. One day, Morvox would no doubt pass on the ways of Manus to another, believing it with both hearts, no longer regretting the loss of a part of himself.

But not yet.

For now, he still felt it.

THERE WERE MORE trials. Long years as a neophyte, learning the ways of the Adeptus Astartes. A hundred worlds, all different, all the same.

He saw them first as a Scout, learning to use his enhanced body without the full protection of power armour. He enjoyed feeling his augmented muscles flex. He revelled in the strength of his new sinews.

He could run for hours without fatigue, or lay in wait for days without the need for sustenance. He was a miracle, a scion of demigods.

The disquiet grew slowly. He noticed during an engagement with the greenskin how quickly his iron hand functioned, how elegantly it curled into a punching fist, how efficiently it was able to turn the cutting blade. He moved his close combat weapon to his left hand after that, trusting in its ability more than the natural flesh of the right.

It was after the Valan Campaign when he was elevated into the ranks of the Clan proper. His carapace protection was returned to the foundry and, for the first time, he was bolted into the hallowed shell of power armour. He remembered the cool touch of the interface nodes against his carapace, how the ceramite skin worked in such perfect conjunction with his own.

He remembered the first time the helm was lowered over his face, sealing him off from the universe in a cocoon of dense protection. He remembered how it made him feel. He flexed the gauntlets, watching the ceramic plates move over one another, watching the artificial perfection of the curves.

'What do you feel?' came a familiar voice.

Morvox looked at Rauth. His vision was mediated by the datastream of the helm's lensfeed.

There were a number of answers to the question. He felt powerful. More powerful than he had ever been. He felt honoured, and unworthy, and impatient for the next engagement. He felt all of these things.

'I feel…' he began, looking for the right words.

The Iron Father waited patiently, locked behind his own mask.

'I feel… imperfect,' said Morvox, landing at last on what he wanted to say. He looked down at his left hand and his emotions clarified. 'I feel flawed.'

Rauth nodded.

'Good,' he said.

MEDUSA WAS A planet of scarcity, of wastes, of darkness. Mars was a planet of wonder, of abundance, of dull red light that bled from a horizon of a million foundries.

The translation took several months, during which time Morvox trained incessantly. He read the rites of the Machine over in his mind until the words cycled in his sleep, burning themselves on to his unconscious mind like a brand. He learned the lore given him by the Iron Father perfectly, making full use of the eidetic function he'd possessed since his mind had been transformed. By the time he'd arrived, he felt almost prepared for what awaited him. All that remained was anticipation.

As the drop-ship fell steadily through the thin atmosphere, Morvox watched the landscape resolve into detail beneath him. Every metre of surface was covered in an industrial landscape of dark iron, belching red smoke from soaring towers. Structures ran up against each other like jostling herd beasts, massive and obscure. He could see transit tubes run across the face of gigantic factories like arteries on a flayed corpse.

The drop-ship flew low on its approach vector. It passed huge trenches, alive with glittering light, glowing at their bases from the magma that pooled there. There were clusters of cyclopean refineries, dark and shrouded in boiling walls of smog. Huge areas looked semi-derelict. Fields of tarnished steel ran away toward the horizon, marked by trenches and studded with arcane citadels. There were cages, each the size of a hive spire, within which vast war machines – superheavy vehicles, Titans, even starships – were being slowly assembled.

As the drop-ship slowed its descent ready to be received by its iron docking cradle, Morvox had a final glimpse of the Martian landscape at close quarters. Every surface was covered in a layer of red dust. The metal beneath was near black with age and corrosion. Nothing living was visible. Everything was ostentatiously artificial.

Morvox thought it was beautiful.

The vessel came to rest, and the airlock doors hissed open. Beyond them was a cavernous hall lit by long red strips of subdued neon. The air was dry and tanged with rust. The sound of hammering echoed up from deep vaults.

A single figure waited for him. It was human – of a sort. Deep green robes covered what looked like a skeleton of plasteel. No face was visible under the cowl, just a long iron snout from which wheezing breath issued.

Morvox's helm feed added extra information. He knew that the figure's rank was Magos, and that her name had been Severina Mavola on accession to the priesthood in 421.M38. He knew that her body was now 67 per cent augmetic and that she hadn't communicated verbally for nearly a century.

He also knew that she had once written poetry in the manner of Hervel Jho, but doubted that she retained the capacity. Service to the Machine-God demanded nothing less than full commitment.

+Naim Morvox,+ she canted in Martian-accented binaric. +Be welcome to Mars. I trust your journey was efficient.+

Few non-Mechanicus personnel could communicate directly with a Magos when they chose to speak natively, instead relying on intermediaries or translating cogitators.

The Iron Hands however, as in so many other ways, were different.

+Most efficient, Magos,+ he replied. +I am eager to learn.+

Mavola motioned for him to join her.

+You wish to become Iron Father,+ she said, walking with him into the colossal hall. Her gait was smooth, giving no trace of the artificial nature of her musculature. +You know the process will be arduous.+

+If it were not, it would not be worth aspiring to.+

+You will be on Mars for ten years. In those years, many of your battle-brothers will lose their lives. When you return, Medusa will be a changed place.+

+I know this.+

The Magos stopped walking. Behind her, a vast caldera boiled with molten metal. Servitors, some as large as Sentinel walkers, laboriously tilted it over, ready for the casts below to be filled.

+We will show you mysteries that we show no other Chapter of the Adeptus Astartes. We extend this privilege in honour of Manus. Know now that the value of the instruction is almost without price.+

Morvox looked at her carefully.

+Almost?+

Mavola didn't elaborate. She turned on her heel, and resumed her fluid walk across the hall.

+Come now,+ she said. +To the forges.+

When he returned to Medusa, almost eleven years after he'd left, it was as the Magos had warned him. Clan Raukaan had experienced a decade of near-constant action, and many faces he'd known well had been gathered into the Emperor's Rest. Iron Father Arven Rauth was now Clan Commander.

To replace losses in the ranks, new aspirants had been inducted from across the planet throughout the decade. Morvox was escorted to his appointment with Rauth by one of them, a raw recruit named Ralech Grond. The youth still had his natural hand intact and almost no sign of augmetics. Morvox couldn't decide whether he envied that or not.

Once Grond had left them, Morvox and Rauth stood alone in the inner sanctum of the Land Engine *Diomedes*. Both wore their armour, though the commander's skull was bare, revealing a pattern of steel markings across the synthetic skin like a circuit board.

'The training was successful?' he asked.

'As I judge it, lord. The Mechanicus reports are on the grid.'

'Much modification?'

Morvox raised his right arm. The ceramite of his vambrace slid back, exposing a deep well within. It looked like the entire forearm had been hollowed out and lined with nanotronics. Rauth examined it carefully.

'Unusual,' he said. 'What purpose did they have in this?'

Morvox withdrew the arm. As he did so, the covering clicked shut. From the outside, there was no indication that his right limb was anything other than normal.

'They did not tell me.'

'Nothing at all?'

'No. I assume it will become apparent.'

Rauth nodded.

'They do nothing randomly. Anything else?'

'No. I am ready to serve. It has been too long since I wielded weapons on the field. I'm eager to employ my new aptitudes.'

'You are not Iron Father yet,' warned Rauth.

'I know. On the day I left Mars, I asked for the Magos's prediction of when that day would come. She gave me a definite answer.'

Rauth's eyebrow raised. It was a curiously human gesture on a generally expressionless face.

'She told me I had incurred a debt on Mars,' said Morvox. 'They do not give up their secrets for free. A time will come when that debt must repaid. Only then will I earn the rank – at least in their eyes.'

'Presumptive of them. What kind of debt?'

Morvox looked down at his hands. Both were metal now, as was much of the rest of his limb structure. That ongoing augmentation would only accelerate now. He was beginning to forget his life out on the plains, back when he'd been nothing more than human muscle and blood. All that remained was the process, the long march to perfection, just as he'd been warned.

'I do not know,' he said.

V

TIME WAS MEASURED by chrono in the lower hive. There was no daylight to announce the dawn and no nightfall to bring the days to a close – just the endless cycle of artificial light, delivered via grimy lumens and flickering pict screens.

Except that these were all smashed now. In their absence, the deep dark was oppressive and eternal. The troops measured time in shifts, in hours-long assaults on the enemy. Only the chronos, ticking away like heartbeats in the dark, recorded the time they'd been down there.

Four days, Helaj-medium, before they encountered the beast. Four days of back-breaking slog and grind. More men died during those four days than had died in the last month of attritional defence.

The assault was driven by the Iron Hands and there was no respite. They fought their way down the transit shafts, clearing them with flamers before sending grenades down into the squealing hordes. Then the boltguns would open fire, tearing the corroded flesh of the mutant into scraps and strips of bloody pulp. The Iron Hands waded through seas of grasping hands, carving through them with the chainswords. They went in close, using those massive armoured gauntlets to choke the half-life from their prey. They stayed long, using ranged fire to blow out kneecaps or crack open skulls. Whatever the tactic, the result was the same.

In their wake came the Lostari, the ragged, exhausted mortal defenders of Helaj, mopping up in the aftermath and killing whatever got around the spearhead. The rotations began to blur and timekeeping slipped, but they kept stumbling onward, deeper and deeper, down toward the heart of the sickness.

Khamed was rarely away from the heart of the action, despite the need for down-periods. The more he fought, the more he watched the Space Marines fight, the more he hated to be away from the front. He could see why myths built up around such warriors. For the first time, the panegyrics on the grid seemed less than ludicrous. All the fear, the terrible fear that he'd suffered since learning that it was to be the Iron Hands responsible for the purging of Ghorgonspire, had gone. It was replaced by a wary awe.

Sure, they looked grim and sounded worse. They fought without pause or pity, but those were the qualities demanded by the task. They spoke rarely and had little patience for mortal weakness, but Khamed couldn't blame them for that. If he'd been in their position, he'd have felt the same way.

He managed to stay close to Grond. They exchanged few words during the engagements – just enough to keep the linked forces in coordination. Morvox seemed to have delegated responsibility for mortal-liaison to the lower-ranked Space Marine, which suited Khamed fine. Though Grond's huge presence could never have been mistaken for merely human, at least he sounded slightly like one.

Perhaps that was an illusion. Perhaps what lay under that facemask was nothing but gears and diodes.

But Khamed didn't believe that. Not entirely.

THE PURGING OF a narrow hab-block had been completed and the flames were dying down. The empty doorways of the hab-units gaped like maws. As Khamed and Grond strode toward the far end of the main access corridor, their boots crunched through a floor of powdered bone.

'My deputy still resents your presence here,' Khamed said.

Grond didn't reply. His armour was covered in a thick layer of filth. In proper light, it would have been a dirty brown.

'He's heard… stories,' continued Khamed, knowing he was pushing his luck. 'He mentioned Contqual.'

Did the Space Marine break stride, just a fraction, then? Maybe not. Hard to tell.

'He said you killed one in three. After the fighting was over. Is that true?'

Grond kept walking for a while, then stopped. His massive armoured head turned slowly.

'Suppose it were true,' said Grond. 'Would you disapprove, human?'

Khamed looked up at the facemask, guessing he'd pushed things too far.

'I wasn't there.'

'No. You weren't. You are here. Do not concern yourself with other worlds. They are the Emperor's concern, and ours.'

The tone was cold. Khamed instantly regretted his question. He felt ashamed and foolish.

'I'm sorr–'

Grond held his hand up. For a moment, Khamed thought the gesture was something to do with him. Then he realised the Iron Hand was listening to something on his internal comm.

'Prepare your men,' ordered Grond, resuming his stride toward the hab-block access corridor.

Khamed scurried to catch up with the Space Marine.

'What is it?'

'Objective. Morvox has found it.'

TWO LEVELS DOWN, and the air was hot and wet. Rebreathers wheezed against the filmy low-oxygen mix, struggling as particulates clogged the intakes. Slime was everywhere, coating the walls completely and obscuring whatever patterns had once been on the metal. The surface shone pale green where the lumen beams swept across the viscous matter, studded with bleeding sores.

They had to fight all the way down. Mutants had clustered tightly in the narrow access routes, and fought with a redoubled fervour. They hurled themselves on the blades of the Iron Hands, perhaps hoping to bring them down through weight of numbers.

The Space Marines maintained the pace as they always did, striding calmly into the onslaught, firing without pause. Bolters blazed, ripping holes in the torrent of diseased bodies. Screams echoed down the long corridors, throaty and gargled with phlegm. Khamed's men came in their wake, backing up the main advance and picking out anything that somehow escaped the rage of bolter rounds.

Smaller mutant breeds scampered and darted through the hail of fire, eyes alive with feral hatred and teeth bared. Khamed saw one spring from the bile-cloaked shadows and launch itself at one of his men. He took the shot and watched it slam into the far wall. There was a sickening squelch as the diminutive body plunged into the mucus layer and slid down into the bubbling miasma below.

Khamed tried not to notice the residual pigtails clinging to the otherwise clean-plucked skull, nor the tattered remnants of its dress flap weakly before it was swallowed by the filth.

They kept going. Step by step, they carved their way through the mob. And then, finally, they reached the heart of it.

A huge chamber opened up before them. Khamed knew what it was from the schematics – an old Mechanicus bunker, long disused even when the hive had been functioning normally. It was down in the heart of the underhive, one of the many forgotten relics of a distant past. Once, perhaps, there had been tech-priests there, doing whatever it was they did in their strange sanctums of industry.

Now it had all been changed. The high roof throbbed with pulsating veins of lurid bile-fluid. The expansive hexagonal floorspace swam with lapping slurry. Lines of what looked like saliva hung down in loops and the air drifted with tiny spinning spores.

Ranks of mutants splashed towards them, all distorted into lumpen, bloated bags of stretched-tight skin. They staggered into combat carrying rusted shards of metal or looted lasguns, howling in a mix of lust and agony, stumbling over one another in their haste to reach their foes.

But that wasn't what held Khamed's gaze.

'Hold your nerve!' he roared over the comm.

Around him, his men lined up and picked their targets. Las-fire cracked across the chamber, prompting fresh screams and gurgling cries.

The mutants began to tumble into the slime as they were felled. But they weren't the primary target any more. They were so much chaff, so much fodder. The real reason they were there reared up behind them.

It was massive. It filled the far end of the chamber and its vast, blubbery body ran up against the walls. The skin was translucent. Growths were visible beneath it, pulsing in sacs of pus. It was shaped like some obscene grub, warped and malformed into a veritable mountain of trembling, glistening flesh.

A face, sore-encrusted and sloppily fat, perched atop slick folds of blubber. It was still vaguely human, though its features were distorted horribly – a single eye stared out from a muscle-white face, red-rimmed and weeping. The mouth opened far wider than it should have done, exposing concentric rings of teeth and a huge, lashing tongue.

Many limbs extended from the mass of that expanded torso, some shaped into tentacles with grasping suckers, others twisted into claws. As the Iron Hands advanced towards it, the limbs lashed out, grappling for purchase.

It stank. Even through his helmet's filters, Khamed nearly choked on the stench. With his eyes streaming, he did his best to direct his troops. The creature screamed like its progeny, though the sound was even more disturbing – high and unearthly in a bizarre mockery of a woman's voice.

Khamed saw Grond go in, flanked by his battle-brothers. There was no hesitation. The Iron Hands plunged in close, firing the whole time from their bolters, stabbing holes in the vast flank of the obese monster. The translucent skin shook and burst as the bolts went off. Yellow liquid shot out from the wounds, thick and steaming. It cascaded down the black armour of the Space Marines, washing off the patina of days like a deluge of acid.

'Follow them in!' bellowed Khamed, feeling his heart beating like a drum.

He was scared. He could feel his muscles tensing up, locked into stiffness. Panic welled up in his gullet, and he fought to keep it down. The monster in front of him radiated such a wave of sickness that it nearly dragged him down into it.

He gritted his teeth, knowing his men would all be feeling the same.

This was what the Iron Hands had come to show them. The horror could be fought.

'For the Emperor!' he cried, swinging his lasgun round and cracking off another beam. It hit an oncoming mutant in the face and ripped its cheek away, exposing rotten sinews and bone. 'Fight, you dogs! Fight!'

The Iron Hands had closed in by then, and the swords came out. The blades shone in the darkness, lit up by disruptor fields. For the first time, the Space Marines' movements broke from uniformity. They span on their ankles, shifting to evade the lash of the tentacles, before chopping through the curtains of flab. They remained silent, working with cool expertise, moving their limbs with exactitude.

The beast was the first opponent capable of truly contesting their will. It raged against them, flailing and whipping. One of the Space Marines was slammed back on to its back by a lightning jab from the claws. It crashed to the floor, rolling across the slime before coming to a halt. The mutants were on it in a second, hacking and chopping.

The Iron Hand powered back to its feet, scattering the corrupted bodies around it as it rose. The bolter juddered as it was drawn around in a tight arc, blasting the mutants to slivers. Then he charged back into contact with the beast, just as silent as before, just as implacable. By then two more of the Iron Hands had been forced on to the defensive, rocked by the furious response from the bloated horror before them.

Khamed advanced cautiously, maintaining a steady rate of fire. His entire platoon was in the chamber, and the flicker of their las-beams lit the walls up. For the first time, it felt like his contribution might make a difference. The horde of lesser mutants began to thin out, exposing the monster at their heart.

'Aim for… that!' he roared, striding through the clinging fluid and feeling it slop over the lip of his boots.

The thicket of las-beams concentrated, cracking against the beast's hide and puncturing the wobbling epidermis. It wailed under the barrage. The las-beams alone would have done little to trouble it, but combined with the fury of the Iron Hands bolter fire and bladework, they had an effect.

The downed Space Marines cut themselves free. One of them – Morvox, perhaps – fought his way up to the folds of neck-flesh, slicing and plunging with his crackling energy weapon. Another took the killing claws off the end of a tentacle with a savage swipe from his sword.

Slowly, purposefully, they were killing it. Barbs snapped out, wrapping around necks and limbs, but they were snapped off. Bile streamed from the beast's mouth, acidic and searing. It splattered against the hard armour and cascaded to the floor in fizzing lumps. The heavy bolter kept up its drumming, thunderous roar, punctuated by staccato bursts from the sidearms.

The residual mob of lesser mutants was beginning to lose cohesion. They blundered around, no longer advancing with any purpose.

'Pick your targets!' shouted Khamed. 'Headshots! Maintain barrage on the beast! Do not give–'

Then it happened. The skirts of flesh shrunk back, withdrawing into a shivering kernel. The screaming reached a fresh crescendo of hate-laced desperation. The beast thrashed around in its death-agony, jaws splayed and bleeding, tentacles writhing. It bled from a thousand wounds, each of them pouring with jelly-like tumours. The bolts kept punching into it. The blades kept biting, crackling with disruptor energy.

Its face went white. Its eye stared wildly, straining from the single socket. Veins stood out from the white skin in a lattice of purple, throbbing and tight with incipient destruction.

For a second longer, it still burned in agony.

Just a second.

Then it exploded. The beast blew itself apart, rocking the structure above and around it to the core. A tide of rubbery flesh rolled out like a breaking wave, surging across the chamber and rushing up the walls. Greasy, fist-sized hunks of gristle peppered the chamber. Flaps of skin sailed into the air, trailing long lines of sputoid blood and plasma. Semi-formed organs sailed high, falling apart in mid-air and breaking into slabs of quivering muscle.

Khamed was knocked from his feet by the storm, just like the rest of his men. He crashed on his back, felled by a rain of slapping body parts. He hit the filth hard and body-hot fluid ran through the chinks in his armour.

Repelled, he staggered back to his feet, shaking himself down. He wiped his visor and dirty streaks of red ran across it.

Ahead of him was a crater of gelatinous meat, laced with sticky globules of nerve-endings and lymph-nodes. It shivered as the fluid cascaded over it, running over the floor and swaying with the current.

And amid the ruin of the beast, the five Iron Hands stood. Their armour dripped with sludge. Their guns were silent. For the first time in days, the howls of the mutants were gone. The only sound was the echo of the explosion and the slap and gurgle of the gore-tide as it ran against the walls.

Khamed watched them, feeling the weakness in his overtired limbs.

'Throne,' he whispered, hardly daring to believe it. 'Throne of Earth.'

KHAMED LOOKED AROUND him. His men – those that had survived – were dead on their feet. All were exhausted. A few had collapsed into the foul water and stayed there. Despite that, despite everything, most of the rest carried themselves with more pride that at any time over the past six months. They knew what they'd achieved.

Khamed let a smile crease across his grimy face.

'Namogh,' he voxed, hoisting his lasgun over his shoulder. 'Get your grunts down here.'

'Progress?' came the reply. He sounded worried.

'Pretty good. Fast as you can.'

Khamed killed the link and limped over to where the Iron Hands were congregating. All five of them were still standing in the centre of the beast's gigantic cadaver. Four of them, Grond included, were calming reloading their weapons. The fifth, Morvox by the look of his armour, had waded deeper into the slough of burned flesh and was rummaging around in the heap of entrails and fluid.

'You have our thanks, lord,' said Khamed, coming up to Grond and smiling broadly. 'We could not have done this without you.'

Grond didn't turn to face him. He was looking intently at Morvox. They all were. Intrigued, Khamed followed their gaze.

After some more searching, the sergeant seemed to find what he was looking for. He straightened up, clutching something in his left hand.

It was a tube, formed from dark metal. Khamed couldn't make much out in the dim light – it was less than twenty centimetres long, blunt and rounded at the ends. There were markings on it, but nothing he could make out clearly.

Morvox turned back and strode toward them. As he did so, the armour of his right forearm opened. The vambrace panel came apart in two halves, exposing an empty space where the limb should have been. Morvox stowed the tube inside the receptacle and closed the shell of ceramite over it again.

Khamed frowned. For some reason, he felt suddenly worried. There had been no mention, at any time, of a mission to retrieve an object from the underhive.

'What is this, Grond?' he asked.

The Iron Hand didn't reply. Morvox spoke instead.

'Our task is complete, mortal,' came the metallic voice, as eerily thin as ever. 'Our ship has been summoned from orbit. The cleansing is over.'

For a moment, Khamed didn't believe what he was hearing. He stumbled over his response.

'But, with respect, lord–' he began. As the words left his mouth, his earlier euphoria was replaced with a cold dread. 'There are hundreds of mutants left alive. We have cleansed less than half of what we came for. There may be more such beasts. We need you.'

Morvox's dark facemask loomed over him. Khamed suddenly realised that the other Iron Hands were all facing him. They said nothing. They were like images in a cathedral, cold and dead.

'You make demands on us now, human?' Morvox asked. There was no emotion in the question, but somehow it conveyed a sense of absolute, utter menace.

Khamed swallowed, and felt his fists clench uselessly. He felt ridiculous, like a child stealing in on some adult affair and demanding attention. Stubbornly, from somewhere, he found the will to protest.

'No demands,' he said, disgusted at how timorous his voice sounded. 'But, lord, we cannot defeat the enemy that still remains. You cannot leave us now.'

'You speak as if your battle here is the only concern we have. You know nothing of the war that burns across the galaxy. You know nothing of the demands on us. If you wish to be worthy of preservation, then guard this ground. The Emperor protects those who resist.'

Then Morvox pushed past him and began to stalk back the way he'd come, back through the thousands of shafts and chambers and up into the inhabited zones. One by one, his squad turned to follow him.

Khamed watched them go in desperation. He knew, just as they surely did, that for them to leave now was little short of murder. The mutants would rally. Mortal troops alone were no match for the horrors that still squatted in the underhive – something that had been proved time and again over the past six months.

'Grond!' he cried, reaching out to clutch at the Iron Hand who had saved his life. 'You cannot mean this! The Spire can be cleansed! Do not leave us. Mercy of the Emperor, do not leave us!'

Grond looked at him just once. Khamed stared up into the softly reflective surface of the helm's lenses. He realised then that he had no idea what kind of creature existed behind that mask. No idea at all.

'Can you fight?' asked the Space Marine.

The question needed no answer. Khamed knew what the responses were. Perhaps Grond had tried to warn him of this the first time he'd asked it. The Iron Hands only cared about strength.

Namogh had been right. Old, cynical Namogh.

Khamed hung his head, and let his hand slip from the Space Marine's arm. He could already hear scrabbling from the levels below. The mutants were stirring again.

Grond strode off to join his battle brothers, not giving Khamed another glance. All five of them walked past the Lostari in the chamber, ignoring the looks of disbelief from the human troops. Their heavy footfalls gradually receded as they passed through the connecting chambers and headed on up.

Khamed only raised his head when Namogh's squad burst into the chamber.

'What the hell's going on?' demanded the deputy. 'We just marched past your beloved Space Marines, and they're all going the wrong–'

He stopped short. Perhaps something in Khamed's empty expression told him all he needed to know.

'We're on our own,' said Khamed, and his voice was hollow.

For a moment, Namogh was lost for words. He looked at Khamed, then back at where the Iron Hands had gone, then back at Khamed.

'Those... bastards,' he spat. 'Those damned... bastards.'

The troops in the chamber, all of whom had heard the exchanges with Morvox, began to disintegrate. Some collapsed, empty-eyed and limp. Others started weeping. None of them ran. They knew there was nowhere to go.

Namogh managed to get a lid on his fury, and fixed Khamed with an urgent glare. His indignation made him speak too fast.

'What are we going to do, Jen?' he blurted. 'What are we going to tell Tralmo? What the hell am I going to tell my men? Holy Terra, what are they thinking, running out now? Why the hell come here, if they didn't intend to finish this thing off? What're we going to do?'

Khamed only half listened. He had no answers. He could hear the first screams of fury and lust from the tunnels below. The mutants were coming already. Soon they would be in the chamber, rushing through the slime, eyes shining with hatred.

Khamed felt a deep, horrifying weariness suffuse his limbs. His whole body ached. He'd pushed himself to the limit, and there was nothing left to give.

We're nothing to them. Just spare parts.

'Gather your men,' he said, unhoisting his lasgun and checking the charge. 'We'll make a stand three levels up. Call in the reserves – if we can get the siege doors closed, we might hold some ground for a while.'

Namogh looked at him as if he were mad.

'You think we'll hold them? You really think we stand any kind of chance? What's different this time?'

Khamed shook his head grimly.

'Nothing's different, Orfen,' he said. 'Nothing. Except, perhaps, for one thing.'

He looked away, past the stinking morass of the beast's carcass and down the tunnels beyond. He could feel the tide of unreasoning madness building down there. He knew it would not respect defiance. It respected nothing. It would just keep on coming.

Can you fight?

'I now know how the universe operates, my friend,' he said bleakly. 'For a while, I had dared to hope otherwise. I believed that this place might have some significance for them. That we might.'

He laughed bitterly.

'Better to die knowing the truth, do you not think?'

VI

THE PROBE MADE a 98-per cent efficient descent from orbital platform 785699 to the receiving station in sector 56-788-DE of Forge 34 Xanthe manufactorium-schola-astartes. The statistics were logged on the grid and interpreted by the usual team of lexmechanics, after which three anomalies were corrected and allowed for, resulting in a two percentage point increment, to the satisfaction of all involved.

From the docking claw, the contents of the probe were conveyed by servitor nineteen levels down, past the major foundry zones and into the dense ganglia of shrines known colloquially in the sector as 1EF54A.

The cargo was transferred to tech-Priests after a soak-test for data contagion and wrapped in three layers of soft dust-repelling cloth. The mark of the Machine-God had been embroidered on the material in gold thread.

Thus clad, it went through six further pairs of hands, only two of which had any organic flesh left on the bones. More tests were performed, and ledgers filled out, and records made for the core lists.

Then, finally, the cargo reached its destination. It came to rest on an obsidian tabletop in a room lit by dark red tubes. For a long time, it lay there alone, untroubled and untouched.

Several local days later, Magos Technicus Yi-Me, once called Severina Mavola, entered the chamber and carefully unwrapped it. A tube lay at the centre of the cloth, its glossy surface reflecting the light of the lumens.

Yi-Me studied it for a long time. She use her basic optical replacements, as well as seventeen additional sensors built into her plasteel cranium.

Deep within her, in a part of her body that had remained relatively unchanged throughout all the years of biosurgery, a sensation of deep pleasure blossomed. If she'd still had lips, she would have smiled.

The artefact was powerful. Powerful, if the initial readings were confirmed, beyond even her expectations. It would certainly suffice for the task she had in mind, and perhaps for many more in the years ahead. Lucky, that it had been discovered. Lucky, also, that it had proved possible to retrieve.

She bowed her head, silently acknowledging the service rendered by the one who had once been her pupil.

+Debt paid,+ she canted, knowing he couldn't hear her, but enjoying the irony of addressing him nonetheless. Such tropes were a staple of the Jho school, something she still appreciated. +Naim Morvox, Iron Father: debt is paid in full.+

A hundred worlds. All different, all the same.

As I bring the light of the Emperor to each of them, knowing that every foe I face could be the one that ends me, a single encounter remains prominent in my thoughts.

Helaj V, the Ghorgonspire. I remember the mortal there, the one named Raef Khamed. Even in sleep, sometimes, I see his face.

He expected much of us, once he had forgotten to fear. We could never match that expectation, not if we had eternity to accomplish the task and infinite resources to bring to bear.

Even so, I left the planet troubled. I never discussed it with Morvox. He would not have tolerated dispute from me, and that was before he was Iron

Father. It seemed to me that our task was not finished, even though the objective was secured and our goals satisfied.

I remember how the mortals fought. I remember how they rose up when we were with them. Back in the warp, where dreams are ever vivid, I heard them plead for us to return. Or perhaps I heard their screams.

We never went back. I do not know what fate befell them. Maybe they prevailed. Maybe they were lost.

For many years, that troubled me.

Now, it does not. I understand what Morvox was doing. He had been purged of sentiment by then, just as I will be. He saw the greater pattern, and followed it. Such is the galaxy we inhabit. Resolve will preserve us; sentiment will see the light of humanity extinguished.

And so we allow ourselves to become this thing. We allow ourselves to become the machine. We are the result of a necessity, of the process.

The alternative is weakness.

I see this now. I see the truth of what I have been told by Morvox. Perhaps Helaj was the last time that I doubted. I am stronger now. I feel the imperfection within me, and long to purge it. In time, Emperor willing, I will go to Mars and learn the mysteries, just as he did.

Not yet. For now, there is too much of my old self, my old corruption. The flesh remains, impeding the progress of the machine.

I still feel the ghost of my old hand, the one they took away to mark my ascension into Raukaan. Far less, it is true, but I feel it nonetheless.

I wish never to feel it again. I wish to forget the face of Raef Khamed, to forget that there is hope and disappointment in the universe.

This is my task, the reason for my existence, and nothing else will suffice. I will work at it. I will persevere. I will purge the weakness of the flesh.

I will be Ralech Grond, Iron Hand, or I will be nothing.

HAMMER AND BOLTER

ISSUE 8

CAUSE AND EFFECT

Sarah Cawkwell

THE WHISPER OF the Emperor's voice was his constant companion. But Vashiro, Chief Prognosticator of the Silver Skulls Chapter of Space Marines, could only properly discern His glorious truth by channelling the psychic connection into something more tactile.

Whenever he cast the sacred runes, or turned over the fading cards of his centuries-old Imperial Tarot deck, he reached through the immaterium and sought the Emperor's guidance as an infant reaches out to a parent. The use of the objects was a means to channel and focus that guidance. There was also an element of mystery attached which induced respect from all who witnessed a Prognostication.

When a metaphysical link was finally forged, when any of the psykers of the Chapter connected with their ultimate father, the shrouded futures of the Silver Skulls were unveiled and their paths paved with solid decision. The Emperor's psychic children simply took His words and will and divined their purpose.

At times, the obscurity of the visions meant that their meanings were difficult to extrapolate. When this happened, a great burden fell on the shoulders of the divining Prognosticator who frequently had to make a call to arms that could see squads, or even entire companies, devastated on the field of battle.

No matter how contrary or controversial, the decision of a Prognosticator was never questioned – except by another, more senior member of the Prognosticatum. Their word was never disputed. Their orders were obeyed without hesitation. They were revered above all other battle-brothers. They were few in number yet their power, both on the field of battle and politically, was immense.

A former Lord Commander Argentius had once refused to deploy when his psychic adviser had expressed doubt. It had proved a shrewd move when the presumed-dormant volcano on the planet burst into terrible life. As the violent eruption incinerated all in its path, it became obvious that it would have swept the Space Marines away in its pyroclastic flow as well. Prognostication was a great gift that, despite the risk, had the potential to save many lives.

But amongst these gifts, all these glimpses of what the future held, the psykers of the Silver Skulls Chapter all fervently hoped they would avoid one thing.

The Deep Dark afflicted all the psychic battle-brothers at least once in their service. An anxious time when the Emperor turned His face away from a beloved child. To each Prognosticator, this was translated as something different – but most agreed that it signalled the Emperor's great displeasure. It was a terrible, mentally devastating experience for a psyker; somewhere between crushing disappointment at being denied guidance and a selfish, desperate desire for approval from their master.

And from time to time there were visions like the one Vashiro had now. One that repeated itself over and over. Easy enough to understand, harder to truly translate into an appropriate course of action.

A shattered silver skull.

The Fortress Monastery of the Silver Skulls
Argent Mons, Varsavia

FOR COUNTLESS CENTURIES, the Silver Skulls had recruited from a number of worlds but all their warriors had been trained here on the far-flung world of Varsavia. A visiting dignitary from Terra many centuries ago had acknowledged that the monastery's design would have impressed the Primarch Rogal Dorn himself. It was highly defensible and nigh on impenetrable to the outside world.

The home of the Chapter was carved out of the rock of the Argent Mons, the highest peak of a vast mountain range in the far north of the planet. The veins of unmined silver that threaded through the rock had birthed not only the mountain's name, but also the name of the Chapter who called it home.

Apart from the serf quarters, only the chapel and the docking bays were above ground level. The chapel was a vast, cavernous chamber, large enough to contain several companies at the same time with room to spare. The rays of the weak sun bled through the beautifully worked stained glass and at the right time of day dappled the stone floor in a myriad of glorious colours where it filtered through the stylised image of the first Lord Argentius. It was a place of considerable peace and reflection, a contrast to the ever-bustling embarkation decks and docking bays. Everything else within the monastery was to be found deep in the bowels of the mountain range.

Argent Mons was difficult to reach and this was as much by design as coincidental geography. Novitiates were brought to the monastery largely by incoming vessels that approached from the west side of the mountain range, directly into the spaceport. Some youths, more tenacious and stubborn than many others, had been known to scale the mountain range itself in adolescent determination to follow a dream. This was rare, of course, for such a journey was fraught with perils. But there were battle-brothers serving the Chapter even now who had taken that very path.

Vashiro knew that they would have to discuss one such individual today and it made him uneasy for many reasons.

As was the case with Argentius, 'Vashiro' was a hereditary name and in old Varsavian translated literally as 'The One Who Sees'. It had passed down from the first Chief Prognosticator to each successor since the founding of the Chapter. The current incumbent had answered to the name for nigh on five hundred years.

He considered the Chapter Master, head bowed over the massive ledger before him. Vashiro's early confidence in him had been well founded. It had been the Chief Prognosticator's careful manipulation of the Chapter's various personalities – like pieces in a great game – that had ensured the former First Captain had risen to the position without contest.

Argentius's skill for strategy and planning had been second to none. As a leader, he was inspiring, intelligent, honest, even charming. As Chapter Master, he commanded unswerving loyalty and dedication from those who served him. He was an Emperor's Angel to the core, as fierce as he was valiant.

But then, the Silver Skulls were a loyal breed. Brutal, valiant warriors with a propensity for intense close-quarters combat, the Chapter was relentless in battle. Since the time of the Second Founding, the Silver Skulls had been an active force in the galaxy. Yet in more recent years the light of their star had begun to fade.

Increasing losses at the hands of the enemies of the Imperium meant that their numbers were gradually dwindling. Recently, there had been an unexpected surge in the intake of new warriors and it seemed that things were finally regaining some sort of equilibrium. Vashiro had once again dared to believe that all hope was not lost.

And yet...

The recalled memory of the vision clung to his thoughts with grim determination. A shattered silver skull. There was very little that could be clearer to interpret.

'Is the tithe set for despatch?'

Pulled from his reverie, Vashiro looked up at the Chapter Master's words and nodded sombrely. Argentius sat opposite him, a golden goblet of fine Varsavian wine in his hand. Even like this, out of his battle plate and dressed in a simple white robe, he was like a young golden-haired god. Swooping coils of spiral-inspired honour tattoos followed the lines of his face and accentuated the fierce set of his jaw and glint of danger in his deeply set hazel eyes. A prime example of the Adeptus Astartes, Argentius could have walked from the legends of old straight into their fortress-monastery.

'Yes, my Lord. The gene-seed tithe has been tallied and is now read-ied for its journey to Terra. We are also sending four new promising Techmarines to Mars.' This was news in itself; battle-brothers who displayed an affinity with the machine-spirits were almost as rare as Prognosticators.

'Was it as bad as we anticipated?' There was a brief heartbeat before Vashiro responded.

'The gene-seed tithe is, as we predicted, significantly reduced in number.'

The Chapter Master pursed his lips briefly and continued, consulting the vast ledger before him. 'The powers that be on Terra will hopefully remain content that our Chapter thrives. And the God-Emperor willing, it will be so.' He swirled the wine around in the goblet, considering its crimson depths thoughtfully.

'We are the Silver Skulls,' said Vashiro, watching the Chapter Master's obvious consternation. 'We will prevail.' The words were automatic, but heartfelt nonetheless.

'Aye.' Argentius lifted the goblet to his lips and downed the contents in a single pull, setting the vessel to one side. A silent serf stepped forward from the shadows and took the goblet away. He received no thanks. He did not expect them.

'And what of…' Vashiro moved to the next item, consulting his own data-slate. A ghost of a smile drifted across his face. 'Eighth Company?'

'Ah, yes. *That* matter.' Argentius mirrored Vashiro's smile with one of his own. 'Captain Meyoran, may the ancestors protect his soul, certainly recommended him highly enough in the past. Gileas's combat record speaks for itself. He is the most appropriate choice to take command. Young perhaps, but our best option.'

News of Keile Meyoran's recent death at the hands of eldar raiders had made its way back via astropathic telecommunication to Varsavia. Another unfortunate loss, but the story of his sacrifice had joined the annals of legend and was already being recited in the training halls. Keile Meyoran's legacy would live on.

'Gileas Ur'ten. Andreas Kulle's prodigy. Ah, now. Would that Kulle were still here to see how Gileas has risen above and beyond the foolish prejudices of his youth.' The Chapter Master paused and reached up to stroke his jaw thoughtfully.

'But?' Vashiro had no difficulty sensing the hesitation and gently teased it from his commander. Even one of the younger Prognosticators, without the years of practice, without the personal familiarity with the mighty warrior, could have sensed the inner turmoil. Not so many could have extracted the heart of the Lord Commander's worries so easily.

Another smile, this time slightly abashed and rueful. 'You know me too well, Aerus.'

'Of course.' Entirely comfortable with Argentius's use of his birth name, Vashiro inclined his head respectfully. 'It is, without wishing to offend, my job.' Argentius laughed warmly and slapped his hand on the vast desk in approval. Eventually the laughter died away. Watching the serious mien return was like seeing a cloud pass over the face of the sun.

'Gileas is a fine warrior,' he said, considering the data-slate carefully. 'That is without question. He is a good, honest man and such a promotion would lead Eighth Company to great things.' Argentius took a deep breath.

'Unfortunately, it seems that there are those amongst us who do not think a man of his...' The Chapter Master hesitated to use the word that had been bandied around, disliking its connotations immensely.

'Heritage, my Lord?' Vashiro offered the word softly.

Not much better, Argentius thought, but certainly something of an improvement on 'breeding'. The word had smacked too much of animal husbandry, a very carefully contrived and almost certainly intentional insult to Gileas Ur'ten's birth amongst the more savage and poorly educated tribes of Varsavia's far southern continent.

'Heritage. Background. Whatever it is, there has *never* been a south-born in the position of company Captain,' said Argentius. 'It would be an unprecedented move. Some say it would be dangerous to allow – how was it Brother Djul phrased the problem? "It would be dangerous to allow a borderline savage to wield that much control over a company of Adeptus Astartes."' Argentius's lip curled slightly. 'I do not truly understand these comments. Such old, petty distrusts. Are we not yet ready to move beyond, Vashiro?'

'Old wounds run the deepest, my Lord. Brother Djul is set in his ways, perhaps more so than others.' Djul was a Chapter champion, one of the Talriktug, First Company. Without psychic power, he was not one of the most elite, the Prognosticars.

Djul was well known for his piety, his zealous nature and his complete and utter dislike of change.

'Objectively,' Vashiro continued, 'the reason that none born in the south have ascended the ranks is well-known.'

'They burn brightly and they die fast.' Argentius sighed and got to his feet, moving to the stone terrace that overlooked the training quadrant. He felt surest when he stood here, when the cages rang out with the sounds of sparring and training or when companies drilled there. The clash of sword on sword, the ordered shouts and noisy, easy banter that drifted up to his chamber were somehow soothing; a reassurance that despite their continued hardships and challenges, the Silver Skulls *would* prevail.

'Gileas's temper is almost as famous as his prowess in battle,' the Lord Commander acknowledged reluctantly. 'I have received assurances however that he has gained much mastery of it in recent years. The fact that he is still living is testament to that truth.'

'I understand your dilemma, my Lord,' said Vashiro, coming to stand behind him. 'Promotion would surely inflame those who do not approve. And yet there are those who may resent the decision *not* to promote him.' The Prognosticator spread his hands wide. 'Your choice will upset one group or the other.'

'The future of our Chapter hinges on many things, Vashiro. The decision to promote a stalwart, honest warrior should not be one of them. And yet even I, not blessed with the Emperor's sight, can feel the importance of this choice. I fear that if I make the wrong decision, our Chapter will feel the consequences.'

At Argentius's words, Vashiro's vision swam back into sharp focus and all too clearly, he understood the full scope of the Emperor's subtlety.

A shattered silver skull.

Vashiro's head reeled. Steadying himself against the wall of Argentius's chamber, he employed his many years of training and calmed his churning psyche. Gradually, he got the flashing parade of images under his control and brought his considerable ability to bear.

Fumbling at the pouch he wore at his waist, he withdrew a handful of runes. Stumbling just ever so slightly, he moved back to the Chapter Master's massive desk.

'Aerus?' The Chapter Master turned away from the training quadrant and fixed his companion with a concerned look. Vashiro held up a hand for silence and scattered the runes on the desk, closing his eyes and murmuring the litany of guidance.

'The people of the south are barbaric, my Lord,' he mumbled. 'Gileas Ur'ten epitomises that barbarism every time he enters battle. He is a tame savage, yes. But he is a savage nonetheless. There are those who cannot see past that to the warrior beneath.' He drew in his psychic strength and prepared to receive the Emperor's will.

The runes tumbled from his hand with a clatter, their lovingly polished silver surfaces falling where they would. Each silver-coated rune was hand-carved from a splinter of skull bone, which had once nestled within the cranium of the first Lord Commander Argentius. The first Chapter Master's skull had been bequeathed to the Prognosticatum thousands of years ago. The runes were one of the Chapter's most valued treasures and only Vashiro, or his elected lieutenant, had the right to cast with them.

Unleashing his psychic potential, he opened his mind to the Emperor's will and opened his eyes to the future.

Genara
Orbiting Virilian Tertius

IT HAD BEEN a long, hard campaign and it wasn't over yet.

Since the death of Captain Meyoran, Eighth Company had been engaged in hunting down and battling eldar forces. Following the loss of their leader, the Assault Company had followed the trail the insane raiders had left, systematically cleansing neighbouring systems of their presence.

Eighth Company had paid a heavy price to reach this point, but they had finally found the main base of operations. This battle would see an end to xenos activity in this sector for the foreseeable future.

Barely large enough to even be considered a moon, let alone a planet, the misshapen lump of rock that passed for a satellite orbited the larger, densely populated hive-world of Virilian Tertius. The eldar had been planning from this vantage point, plotting attacks against the human populace on the various inhabited worlds in the Virilian system. They planned to strike, to abduct humans for slaves and torture – and to take the mineral spoils of the worlds for themselves.

During the course of the campaign, the eldar had snuffed out a good number of Silver Skulls lives, not least of which had been their own Captain. But sheer, bloody determination and well-coordinated strikes had seen the balance start to tip. The enemy forces they faced had been increasingly unprepared for such an intense counter-strike from the Adeptus Astartes. Unlike the Emperor's finest, the xenos had not been equipped for a lengthy campaign. Their weapons and ammunition supplies were running short – and the systematic destruction of their webway portals had limited their access to extra supplies. Their time now was counted in hours.

The Space Marines had only needed to wait for the right moment to take the enemy by their exposed jugular and tear out their throat. And now that the eldar had been weakened exponentially, that moment had arrived.

'DEPLOYMENT IN TEN minutes, sergeant.'

There was a barely responsive grunt from Gileas Ur'ten, who was presently absorbed in battle preparations, his eyes intent on the physical rituals necessary to arrange his equipment. His dark face wore an almost pained expression that barely concealed the battle lust pounding through his veins.

This was it. This was the moment he would carry out his promise to avenge Keile Meyoran's death.

He slammed a fresh magazine into his bolt pistol, then attached it to the magnetic holster on his thigh. He straightened up and looked around the interior of the Thunderhawk. Filled with almost all the remaining Space Marines of Eighth Company, every single one of them was looking to *him* for instruction. Just as they had done since Meyoran's death.

Gileas had meditated for long periods on his personal concerns regarding the fact that he had ended up in unofficial command of the Eighth. They were concerns that he did not share with anybody else and if it fazed him right now, he certainly did not let it show. He let his eyes roam over each of the assembled warriors – *his* warriors – in turn, assessing, judging, unconsciously encouraging.

'As planned, the Reckoners – led by myself – will form the core of the initial strike unit.' His voice was thickly accented in comparison to the majority of the fighting force, but his tone was calm and measured. 'We will occupy their remaining ground forces in close combat. That way, we can draw them out into the open. At that point, we strike.'

He grinned wickedly, his sharpened canines glinting dangerously. 'I cannot stress this point enough, my brothers. This is our last chance. This will be a *vital* strike. The xenos have gotten used to us advancing as a unit. Skirmish attacks such as we are throwing at them today will catch them unawares. Techmarine Kuruk will coordinate from above and feed reconnaissance data to us on the ground.'

He cast dark eyes around the interior of the gunship once again. Its occupants were all locked into their restraint thrones – bar himself and the other four warriors who were preparing to drop. 'We will end this today. We will quell the xenos threat and we will ensure the continued safety and compliance of the Virilian system. The Imperial citizens on that world down there will continue their contented, safe existence without ever once knowing what their fate may have been. We are the Emperor's own. We will execute His will. We will prevail!'

A roar of approval sounded from the Silver Skulls at this pronouncement, the acoustics of the ship's interior boosting and distorting their deep voices unnaturally as they echoed the sergeant's sentiment. The sound was a vocal call to arms and sent a thrill of impending battle fury coursing through them. The eagerness to fight was fierce and infectious.

Now fully prepared for the battle ahead, Gileas pulled on his helmet. The armour locked into the helmet's catches with the familiar, calming *hiss* of servos. The locks snapped closed, and he twisted his head this way and that to ensure the seals were secure. The systems check flickered in front of his eyes. His internal life support systems interfaced with the helmet and made a number of subtle, but vital adjustments. The familiar scent of recycled air and his own blood fired him still further. Runes flickered into being one after the other.

Data scrolled in front of his eyes and he bypassed his own readings until he located the runes that represented the status of his four squad members. All were presently displaying full health and their armour was at optimal functionality. The jump packs, while less satisfying, were as good as they could expect them to be after months of battle. Since Theoderyk's death during the last battle, they had only one remaining Techmarine. Kuruk had done what he could to appease the increasingly erratic temper of the machine spirits. It would have to be enough.

They were ready. They were Space Marines. They were *always* ready.

Space Marines in assault squads had always led with the simple promise of 'death from the skies'. To drop five of them into the depths of the enemy from a passing Thunderhawk was merely adding literal weight to that concept. The idea amused Gileas and inside his helmet, he grinned slightly manically.

His chainsword, lovingly maintained, was already held tightly in his gauntleted fist. Too many of his battle-brothers had fallen to the weapons of the eldar. Today, *Eclipse* would help him even that score. He brought the hilt of the blade up to his helmet and rested his head against it, murmuring a battle litany under his breath.

Eclipse had served the Silver Skulls even before it had become Gileas's. It had belonged to his former commanding officer, Andreas Kulle, who had bequeathed it to his protégé with his dying breath. Before Kulle, it had belonged, so it was said, to a former Lord Argentius. It was a jealously coveted weapon and Gileas knew well the honour of being its bearer.

No other blade in the company's armoury was as carefully cleaned and treated as *Eclipse*. Its owner was fiercely protective and proud of it and when he was not exercising it in war or in the training cages, he would maintain it; oiling, greasing and polishing it until it gleamed as brightly as the skull runes cast by Vashiro. In Gileas's hands it ceased to be a deadly inanimate object, still and silent, something as feral as its wielder, threatening teeth and death. Once it was in the Space Marine's hand, it became a living extension of Gileas; a shining silver serpent of whining doom. He connected, so he claimed, with the weapon's machine spirit the moment he thumbed it into life. The machine-spirit responded to his litanies every time and the two certainly seemed to share a harmonious co-existence.

It was thirsty. *Eclipse* was desperate to drink the blood of the eldar – and he would grant it that need imminently.

Absently, he allowed his hand to rest against the flat of the blade as though he were appeasing the spirit within. Inactive, the chainsword did not move beneath his touch, but he fancied that he felt the thrill of its quiescent power nonetheless.

'Soon,' he promised. 'Soon.' He resumed his quiet battle prayers.

The Thunderhawk banked slightly with a grating whine of its port engines and Gileas steadied himself, distantly irked at the interruption. The gunship steadied itself once again and levelled out for its approach to target.

'One minute to deployment.' Kuruk's voice sounded in his ear and the sergeant nodded his understanding. He concluded his prayer and put a hand to the newest purity seal affixed to the pauldron of his battle plate.

The oath, written in flowing script, had been witnessed earlier that day and the ink was hardly dry on the parchment. He had spoken the words with dedicated conviction. *On the witness of Eclipse, in the eyes of my brothers, this ends today. Death to the eldar. Vengeance for Keile Meyoran.*

'Four... three... two... one... Reckoners, deploy.'

Gileas's squad launched themselves without a second's further hesitation from the rear ramp of the Thunderhawk, plummeting like deadly silver meteorites to the ground below. The gunship continued on its way, presenting a useful temporary distraction to the assembled pocket of eldar raiders who stared up at it, firing heavy weapons in an effort to bring it down.

Unfortunately for them, all that came down were five argent-clad angels of retribution.

There was no wind on this virtually airless rock, but the gentlest of breezes nonetheless seemed to pre-empt the murderous descent of the Silver Skulls. They streaked into view, the roar of the jump packs heralding their enemy's doom.

As one, the closely packed knot of xenos turned, the movements synchronising perfectly with the five bodies thudding to the rock's surface. A vast cloud of amethyst-coloured dust billowed up, obscuring them from sight. The dust blossomed quickly from the point of impact, swirling wildly like a harbinger of doom. Eventually, however, the purple curtain began to dissipate and the scene resolved.

Having landed slightly to the fore of his squad, in a shallow crater formed by the solid blow of his own ceramite and plasteel body striking down, Gileas raised his head slowly and stared with unemotional detachment at the hated enemy. His huge Adeptus Astartes body was stooped in a deadly crouch and his fist was planted down before him on the ground. He was like some kind of primal animal, coiled and ready to spring at his prey. The eldar weapons temporarily ceased firing as they rapidly assessed this new, unexpected threat. Swift orders were barked. But not swift enough.

This time there was no humour in the smile that quirked Gileas's lips beneath the mask of his helmet. The glowing red lenses met the direct gaze of one of the eldar and the accumulated centuries of hatred for that race of xenos and all their foul kind fuelled him. The lenses stained his vision as red as the blood he planned to exact from the enemy. The desperate hunger that had burgeoned on board the Thunderhawk, the desire to purge the enemy, bloomed fully in his body. Responding almost instantly, his power armour channelled a fresh infusion of combat stimms into his system.

I am the arm of retribution, he thought. *In my hand, the weapon of the Emperor's divine justice. In my heart, the Emperor's light. Through me, may the Emperor's wrath know no bounds until the enemy are annihilated. Through me, may these filthy creatures know what it means to cross the Silver Skulls.*

Almost lazily, he thumbed the activation stud on *Eclipse*. It growled menacingly into life, responding to his touch on the throttle as efficiently as it had done the day it had first left the armoury.

I am Gileas Ur'ten of the Silver Skulls.

The chainsword's throaty roar ebbed down to a belligerent purr.

I am your doom.

'Reckoners,' he broadcast on the squad vox, as calmly as though he were taking a head count. 'Attack.'

Gunning their jump packs back into life, the squad leapt with deadly accuracy into the midst of the enemy, the orchestrated sound signalling that the end was more than nigh for the eldar.

Eclipse sang its song of visceral fury as it tore into the alien warriors and Gileas felt his heart soar alongside its melody. The foul xenos helmets wavered and blurred in his sight and become nothing more than targets. He roared his defiance and anger at their pathetic resistance and drew on the strength of his unshakable beliefs to deliver them to their end.

The fortress-monastery of the Silver Skulls
Argent Mons, Varsavia

'THERE HAS TO be a decision, Vashiro!'

Argentius slammed his bunched fist into the formerly flawless marble surface of his desk. It cracked beneath the power of his rage with a loud noise that sent the many chapter serfs scattering in terrified alarm at their master's rage.

'I understand your anger at this, my lord, but the Emperor's will remains unclear.' Vashiro kept his tone calm and his expression neutral. In a deep state of meditation, he had cast the runes over and over and every time they had given him the same response.

Uncertainty. Doubt.

And more. Something far, far worse. Something that many of the Silver Skulls were ill-equipped to deal with. It was a harshly honest realisation, but Vashiro knew it was truth.

Change.

'Cast the runes again.'

'I have already communed with the Emperor no less than a dozen times, my lord. There is no easy answer to this conundrum.'

'Why must it be a conundrum?'

Abrupt, almost shocked silence followed Argentius's moment of fury and the bellowed words. For a heartbeat, even the noise in the training quadrant stilled. Argentius sat down heavily on his seat, which creaked alarmingly under the Chapter Master's considerable weight.

'My apologies, my friend.'

'Not needed, my lord.' Vashiro remained standing. 'You must understand my position on this. I have been granted a vision. Should I interpret the Emperor's will incorrectly, then any damage done to the Chapter may be irreversible. I need to take my time. I beg leave to arrange a meeting of the Prognosticatum.'

Argentius considered Vashiro's weathered, nut-brown face for a long while. How the man could remain so calm in the face of what – to him at least – was the most tiresome of situations defied all logic.

'We are outdated,' he observed, bitterness in his voice as he looked at his adviser. 'I have felt it for a long time, but this is... beyond all I have ever known. I ask merely for the Emperor's blessing in rewarding a good, loyal warrior. In return, all I get is procrastination and endless requests for old men to sit around in a darkened, incense-filled room and talk about "the conundrum".'

Argentius hesitated. He knew he was bordering on insulting the psyker with his words, but Vashiro's face remained impassively neutral.

'You are angry, my lord, so I will let the insult go this time.' Vashiro gave Argentius a look that he recognised all too well. The Chapter Master shifted uncomfortably, feeling like a chastised child. 'The Prognosticatum will discuss the matter and we will find your solution. Trust to us.'

Argentius did not reply. As a former First Captain, he had once sat as a member of the Prognosticatum. He knew exactly what it entailed. Vashiro continued.

'Were it any warrior but Gileas Ur'ten, I believe the decision would be much easier. But he is volatile. He is unpredictable.'

'Does that not describe our Chapter's very core ethic?' There was unmistakable pride in Argentius's tone.

'The Silver Skulls pride themselves on their ferocity, of course. And Gileas is a sword of the Chapter, most certainly. But a sword that is not tempered, is not controlled... that, my Lord, is a sword that can cut both ways.'

'He is a superlative warrior. His eye for detail is outstanding. He is brave, noble, honourable and fearless. Damn it, Aerus, he has the potential to be a Chapter *hero*.'

'If notoriety equates to heroism, then he has that honour already.'

Argentius fell silent once again.

'Then by your leave...?' Vashiro had already turned to walk out of the Chapter Master's chambers and Argentius let him go, too angry to continue the argument. He would have to apologise for his words later.

Formed at the time of the Second Founding, the Silver Skulls earliest history was shrouded in mystery. The Chapter's records were amongst those lost long ago. The identity of their founding Chapter was unknown, but they had never let their lost parentage deter them in their steadfast loyalty.

Electing to settle on Varsavia, the Silver Skulls had initially adhered carefully to the Codex Astartes. Over time, however, they had begun to adopt aspects of native traditions. Their numbers were largely made up of the planet's tribal warriors, all of whom had brought something different with them. The one thing, however, that each tribe had had in common had been the shamanistic 'wise men' who led them. Apart from a few charlatans, most of these men had been psykers who latterly formed the core of the Prognosticatum. Few in number, but remarkably powerful, they were highly revered both by the humans of Varsavia and by the Adeptus Astartes of the Silver Skulls.

Inspired and guided by such spiritual leaders, the Chapter rarely – if ever – questioned what they were told. Only those with the strongest personalities dared to insult a Prognosticator. They had more power than the Chapter Master himself.

Far more power, Argentius thought as he rose from his seat. *Too* much power.

The time was ripe for a review of their practises. He knew that it had to be so and yet the genes and indoctrination of thousands of years dammed the flow of desire for that change.

Argentius knew that there would be questions soon, when the Administratum received a gene-seed tithe that was markedly smaller than it had been. Questions regarding their practises would be raised, practices which Argentius well knew that others in the Imperium of Man would consider barbaric. Questions that raised issues previous Chapter Masters had never had to address. It had been many years since the last tithe request, a generation at least. Much had changed.

If he could not answer these questions satisfactorily, he knew what the outcome would be. The great fighting force of the Silver Skulls would be disbanded, broken apart and the warriors incorporated into other Chapters to make up their numbers.

Perhaps this was the root of the vision the Vashiro had seen. Perhaps it was this that represented the shattering of the Chapter.

Argentius could not bring himself to believe it would come to a sundering. They were the Silver Skulls. For many thousands of years they had shone as a bright star in the blackness of space.

They would prevail.

They *must* prevail.

Genara
Orbiting Virilian Tertius

THE INITIAL STRIKE was swift and brutal. The five warriors of Gileas's Reckoners squad barrelled into their enemy with furious passion. Chainswords and bolt pistols met with little resistance from the beleaguered enemy and they were mown down in the onslaught. The Reckoners destroyed the eldar warriors in a matter of minutes.

'Talk to me, Kuruk,' Gileas voxed to the Techmarine who was coordinating the data their scout passes had received. Three Thunderhawks, including the one they had recently dropped from, were in low orbit ready for the final attack run. 'Tell me where we need to be.'

'Due east, sir.'

Gileas still couldn't get used to the respect that had come with his unofficial command. He had known Kuruk for many years and considered him one of his closest friends. Hearing the word 'sir' from him felt strange.

He signalled to his squad to move to the east and they obeyed immediately, stepping on the bodies of the dead and dying eldar as they left. One reached up with a long-fingered hand as though it was trying to reach out to those who had just felled it, but the Silver Skulls ignored the grasping, dying xenos.

'For too long these bastards have raided our recruiting worlds,' Gileas said across the company vox channel. 'For too long they have stolen our most precious of commodities. They have stolen our future, brothers. Young men of this system who might otherwise one day have received the honour of ascension. They are the cause of much of our Chapter's hardship – and today we draw the line.'

They marched relentlessly on towards the final conflict.

'You all know the problems we face. Our numbers are low. Our resources begin to deplete. And yet, we are the Silver Skulls. We continue, against all the odds, to prevail. And the Emperor is with us today. He watches over us as we make this stand against our ancient enemy. Their effect on us will lessen eventually. I say the time has come to tip those odds in our favour. What say you, Eighth Company? Are you with me, brothers?'

Scattered cheers and roars of solidarity came across the vox, filling Gileas's heart with the pride of his brotherhood and great strength of purpose. There was also a certain element of relief that his motivational words had been so well received.

Reuben, by his side as he had been for so many years now, caught his elbow and nodded to a rising hill. Gileas switched back to his squad vox channel.

'Our quarry lies beyond that ridge,' he said to his squad, looking from face to face. They all wore the same helmets, but even if they hadn't been identifiable by the markings on their armour, he could tell each one apart with the practise of years. The way Jalonis stood with his head cocked slightly to one side. The way Tikaye held his chainsword over his shoulder. Each one had unique mannerisms that made them who they were, that marked them as individuals in a world where conformity was the norm.

'We will lead the final assault. We strike – the rest of the company deploys and the Thunderhawks support us from above.'

He put his hand out. Reuben was first to lay his own gauntlet over his sergeant's.

'Brothers all,' he said.

'Brothers all,' the others chorused.

'Incoming recon data, Sergeant Ur'ten.' Kuruk's voice cut across the moment and Gileas nodded, blink-clicking his acceptance of the incoming intelligence. New runes streamed across his vision and his enhanced senses took everything in with barely a glance. The battle ahead would be prolonged, but the eldar they had fought during this campaign so far had demonstrated little martial prowess and even less intelligence. They had once had superior numbers, but Eighth Company's diligence in picking them off gradually had levelled the playing field exponentially. Had they the wits, they would already have fled back to the darkness from whence they had spawned.

'Then we end this.'

With a roar of fury, the Reckoners fired their jump packs into life and bounded skywards. They were over the ridge in seconds, beginning their descent into the midst of the remaining enemy.

There was no webway portal here. There had been, about two days ago, but a successful bombing raid had put paid to any thoughts the eldar may have had about leaving the planet that way. They were isolated from their people and the webway and were at the Silver Skulls mercy.

Not that the Silver Skulls planned to show any.

'For Argentius and the Emperor!'

The battle cry was sounded and the Reckoners dived towards the foe, ready to obliterate them from the face of this rock.

'Kuruk, deploy the company!'

'On the way, sir.'

Gileas gave no further orders. He was engaged almost instantly by two splinter-rifle wielding eldar who opened fire on him. The weapon discharges barely had strength enough for him to even feel any sort of kinetic force against his armour and he turned to the two warriors, *Eclipse* screaming its hunger once again.

He tore through them with ease, blood splattering the weapon and his battle plate, dismembered body parts flying. For good measure, he removed their heads. There would be many skulls to collect later; trophies that would mark Eighth Company's prowess. *Eclipse* sang its approval as it ground through their spinal cords.

The five-man squad was soon surrounded by a veritable sea of xenos, but they did not concern themselves with the fact they were presently outnumbered. Indeed, within minutes, the thunderous roar of the deploying Thunderhawk's engines was heard. All around the small, natural crater where the eldar had begun their operations, Silver Skulls dropped from the skies to deliver the Emperor's judgement.

Gileas watched the sight, a swell of pride causing a brief halt in his ceaseless attack. These were his brothers. This was what he had been reborn to. This, he thought with a soaring sense of righteousness, was who he was.

Bhehan, a young Prognosticator who had only recently formally been recognised by the Prognosticatum, was fighting alongside a different squad. He had fought with the Reckoners out on Ancerios III, when they had encountered the horror of psychic kroot. He had fought many more battles since then and as his blue-clad form strode through the enemy, scything them down with powerful swings of his crackling force axe, his confidence was almost palpable. His hand came up and swept outwards, unleashing his psychic attacks with disconcerting ease. Even in the short time since he had fought alongside the Reckoners, Bhehan's power had grown.

Everywhere Gileas looked, he could see signs of their impending victory. Brother Diomedes was on standby, the venerable Dreadnought brought to wakeful readiness and ready to deploy at a single word – but for now at least, the assault squads were holding their ground. The ancient could rest a while longer.

The brief interlude over, the sergeant subtly adjusted the grip on his chainsword and ploughed back into the fray. He swung the weapon with casual ease, its teeth chewing into any obstacles it met.

To his right, he became aware of Tikaye facing down an onslaught of no less than six eldar. He had no doubts at all that his squad brother would have any difficulty in dealing with the threat but fired his jump pack into life. He bounded skyward and made the leap that closed the distance between himself and Tikaye.

'I am more than capable of handling this situation, Gileas.' Tikaye's voice over the vox sounded faintly irked. 'There are more than enough of the enemy to keep you busy.'

'Surely the Emperor smiles upon he who shares, brother?'

Although he could not see Tikaye's face behind the steel-grey helm, he knew the other man shared the same grin he was wearing right now. Fighting side by side, the two warriors ripped the eldar apart in moments.

The last one standing flung himself wildly onto the point of his chainsword, inching his way towards Gileas, its pointed helm leering. Drawing back his fist, the Space Marine punched the xenos in the face. The thing's helmet shattered under the impact and it was knocked to the ground. Within moments, the alien asphyxiated; its physiology unable to survive in the thin air.

With a roar, the two Space Marines took to the skies once again, ready to complete their mission.

* * *

Chamber of Elucidation
Argent Mons
Varsavia

'You are sure?'

The question was directed to Vashiro by First Captain Kerelan. A veteran of many battles, Kerelan's face was marked by only a single tattoo. Worked in molten silver that had been mixed with the tattooist's ink, the insignia of the chapter – the stylised skull – was etched onto his face in a full skeletal mask. It had been an unusual choice of design. Its effect was nonetheless quite considerable and achieved its goal of marking him as a Silver Skull and, perhaps more importantly, it instilled fear in his enemies. Many a foe had seen that grinning, shimmering death mask encroach on their vision right before he despatched them.

'I am sure, captain. The Emperor's will in this matter is unclear.' Vashiro looked around the assemblage. Formed of nine senior Prognosticators and the First Captain, the Prognosticatum's Council of Elucidation was one of many such councils formed within the Silver Skulls to deal with issues of varying triviality. It was a place of wisdom and knowledge.

Right now, it was also a place of great anger and tension.

'The Chapter Master cannot possibly see this as anything other than an omen against recruiting Ur'ten to the position.' Kerelan stood forward from his designated spot and took a place at the table. Formed from black granite, the world map of Varsavia was reproduced below him, picked out in glittering crystalline shards. Kerelan's hands rested over the Sea of Sorrows, the land-locked ocean that separated the north continent from the south.

He leaned forward and spoke earnestly, the archaic words coming with difficulty to lips that were far more used to dealing with battle orders than they were with politics. He detested this part of his role. It was only because tradition dictated that the Chapter Master must not be allowed to sit on an advisory council that he had to attend these things at all. The burning incense filled the air with its sickly, cloying scent and made him feel more uncomfortable than he was already.

'The First Captain decrees that due to the lack of an apparent outcome, the Prognosticatum should refrain from taking this matter any further. The First Captain therefore moves that the matter should go to a vote.'

'The First Captain's comment is noted,' returned Vashiro gravely. Then he sighed a little and relaxed the formality. 'You know our creed, Kerelan. In matters of promotion, the Emperor's will is the deciding factor.'

'And yet you tell me that the Emperor's will is unclear.' Kerelan's tone was challenging, but not hostile.

Vashiro inclined his head. 'This is true. It is impossible for me to fully explain the methods we employ in these divinations, but there is a certain… obfuscation surrounding our young sergeant. It is as though the empyrean itself holds its breath waiting for him to make a decision, or a choice that will affect the outcome of this communication with the Emperor.'

'Gileas Ur'ten is not that important.' Kerelan sneered slightly, the skull mask taking on a ferocious aspect.

'With all due respect, First Captain, you are wrong. All denizens of the Imperium are important. Their decisions, no matter how small, cause ripples in the patterns of fate.'

Chastised, but not allowing it to show, Kerelan stepped back.

Vashiro shifted his gaze to one of the other psykers, who stepped forward to the table. Kerelan recognised Brother Andus.

His voice, when he spoke, was filled with reverential respect. 'Vashiro, of all of us, you are the most gifted with the ability to feel the shape of times yet to come. If your sight is unclear, the First Captain is right.' Andus bowed to Kerelan and continued. 'Yet I cannot, in good faith, agree to let this go to a vote. Not yet.'

Kerelan opened his mouth to comment, but Andus continued. 'I put to the First Captain that the decision is still in the hands of Vashiro. He must divine the Emperor's word here, in the presence of his peers and equals. I do this not out of disrespect, you understand, Vashiro?'

Vashiro nodded again. 'I see nothing but sense in your words, Andus. I know what you are thinking. If indeed the matter will not be settled by Gileas's actions, then it is likely that the Deep Dark is upon me. Perhaps I have displeased the Emperor in some way and he will not show me the answer until I have atoned.' Vashiro sighed, suddenly looking to Kerelan every bit as old as he was rumoured to be.

'My strength is yours, brother.' Andus laid his hand on the table, palm down. 'My strength is yours. Draw on my abilities to strengthen your own.'

One by one, the other Prognosticators stepped forward and rested their hands alongside his. Kerelan stepped back, sensing that his presence at this point was some kind of intrusion.

Vashiro, who seemed to have forgotten the First Captain's presence entirely, allowed his eyes to roam over his brother Prognosticators.

'So be it,' he said and brought forth the soft, black velvet pouch that contained his divining runes. 'I am the instrument of the Emperor's will. Through me, may He show us the way forward in this matter.'

Kerelan watched impassively as Vashiro cast the runes across the map of Varsavia. As one, the Prognosticators leaned forward. The ghost of a smile flickered across Vashiro's face.

'Well, now,' he said. 'Something has changed. A decision has been reached.'

* * *

Genara.
Orbiting Virilian Tertius

'WE ARE VICTORIOUS.'

The scene was a charnel house. Dead and dying eldar lay where they had fallen in the wake of Eighth Company's passage. Sightless eyes stared up at the amethyst skies.

'We are victorious.' Gileas repeated the words. Yes, they were victorious, but there had been a cost. The death of more of his men was an inevitability that they had all faced when they had deployed. But the losses weighed heavily on his broad shoulders.

Amethyst dust, thrown up from the violent skirmish, was still settling and the glittering motes shone as they settled on the sergeant's armour, subtly altering the hue from silver to mauve. Absently, he brushed the dust away. Around him, his brother Space Marines were collecting the bodies of the fallen, taking heads for skull trophies and piling them up in one place. They would be incinerated on the sergeant's say-so.

Despite the thin atmosphere, Gileas reached up and removed his helmet, shaking out his hair and inhaling the coppery tang of death. He had fulfilled the oath he had taken that morning. Keile Meyoran's death was avenged and the eldar were scrubbed from this system. The future recruitment of Silver Skulls from this system was, for now at least, secured.

As Eighth Company worked, so did Gileas. Without the company Apothecary present, the job of recovering the gene-seed from the five fallen battle-brothers fell to the commanding officer. It was an unpleasant job, not from a clinically detached viewpoint, but more from the fact he had to transcend the grief he felt for each of his dead brothers in order to carry out the procedure.

He recovered four of the five pairs of progenoids. Silas was appallingly injured, his body burned and destroyed in the wake of the explosion that had destroyed his jump pack, him, and four of the enemy simultaneously. His death touched Gileas the most. Silas, like him, was an Adeptus Astartes whose life had begun in the far south. He had shown great promise. Now his star was no longer in the ascendant, but was forever snuffed out.

'You fought well, my brother,' Gileas said softly, getting slowly to his feet. 'The Emperor protects your soul now.' He felt a particular sting at the loss of Silas. Whilst there was solidarity and deep friendship amongst the Eighth Company as a whole, Gileas found natural affinity with those who had grown up, like him, in the lethal surrounds of the Ka'hun Mao, what he now knew as the Southern Wastes; those who had fought from childhood just for the right to survive in the face of threats from neighbouring cannibalistic tribes or the countless predators and who prowled across the great plains.

A flash of recollection flickered and died. His childhood memories were mostly lost to the indoctrination and reprogramming he had received on his initiation into the Silver Skulls, but they were there, somewhere.

Shaking himself back to awareness, he gave the precious containers holding the progenoids to one of the other Space Marines and stretched out an ache in his shoulders. His gauntlets were smeared with the blood of the fallen Silver Skulls. But through the pervading mist of grief that he would save for later, something else crept from the shadows. A sense of certainty. The knowledge that he had made the right decisions here today. A sense that he was more than capable of assuming the mantle of leadership.

A change in attitude that would radiate unconsciously across the starry blackness that separated Gileas Ur'ten from Varsavia.

He moved to stand with his brothers and stared impassively at the pile of xenos. He spat on the ground, then turned.

'Burn them,' he said.

Promethium snaked out from the flamers in the hands of his battle-brothers onto the pile of dead aliens. From the weak cries that could be heard, it was evident that not all of them were quite dead. No matter, Gileas thought. Their existence would be ended swiftly enough.

The fire burned brightly and swiftly, eating up the meagre oxygen that fed it. The stench of charred flesh was stronger even than that of the spilled blood, but Gileas did not replace his helmet. He could survive in this weak atmosphere for a considerable length of time. He would watch this near-ritualistic burning of their fallen enemy with his own eyes.

The moment was only slightly marred by Kuruk's voice intruding across the vox.

'Sergeant Ur'ten?'

'What is it, Kuruk?'

'I have been contacted by the Astropath Primaris on board the *Silver Arrow*. There has been a communication from Varsavia. From the Lord Commander himself.' Kuruk's voice was filled with the reverence due the Chapter Master. Gileas nodded. He had been expecting this, but now that the moment had arrived, words failed him.

Sensing his brother's moment of discomfort, Reuben spoke up for him in order to fill the silence.

'What is the message, Kuruk?'

'Come home.'

There was a pause as Gileas assimilated this. He waited patiently for the rest of the message. When Kuruk said nothing else, he finally found his voice.

'Is that it?'

'That's the essence of it, sir. Brother-Sergeant Gileas Ur'ten; Greetings from Lord Commander Argentius. My apologies, brother, but I must ask you to end your campaign and bring Eighth Company back to Varsavia. Come home, Gileas.'

Gileas and Reuben exchanged glances. The Chapter Master was recalling Eighth Company to their home world, a place that Gileas had not seen for countless decades. A thrill of anticipation ran through him; an eagerness to see the fortress-monastery once more, the chance to look out over the peaks of the highest mountain ranges at the snowy landscape of his birth.

Gileas took several deep breaths and stooped to retrieve the head of the eldar leader he had taken as his trophy. He cast a final glance at the funeral pyre and began to walk way.

'Then let us not keep the Lord Commander waiting,' he said to his men. 'We are going home.'

MARSHLIGHT

C. L. Werner

'THICK AS A patroon's purse strings!'

Gustav Mertens wasn't sure which member of the *Aemilia*'s crew uttered the oath, but it was certainly an appropriate one. The sailor had never seen a fog so heavy as the one which now surrounded the three-masted barque, and he had travelled the River Reik long enough to have seen more than his share of ugly weather. He'd been in Altdorf on nights when the mist rising from the river looked solid enough to cut with a knife and had almost drowned downriver of Carroburg when the fog had been so impenetrable that his ship snuck up on a flat-bottomed barge and sent both it and herself to the bottom.

This fog, however, was different. For all the levity of the unknown crewman's outburst, the sailors were far from at their ease. There was an eerie, menacing quality in the air, a sense of wrongness that made the hair on Gustav's neck prickle. He could hear the anxiety in the voices of Captain Piedersen and his officers as they snapped orders at the crew.

Most of the sailors were old hands who had made the voyage between Altdorf and Marienburg many times before. They didn't need their officers to remind them of the danger the fog presented. The grey veil couldn't have set upon them at a worse time, when the broad Reik slithered its way into the morass cartographers had condemned and cursed, branding it simply 'the Wasteland'. The swampy maze of moors and fens stretched clear to the coast, surrounding the great port city of Marienburg on three sides. The muddy, treacherous ground would seep and slop its way into the Reik, choking the great river with mud and forcing the tight-fisted burghers of Marienburg to send barges out to dredge the river every fortnight to keep the Reik navigable.

The periodic dredging wasn't always enough, and ships always had to be wary of new mud flats and sand bars when they sailed into the Wasteland. Normally, a sharp-eyed lookout could spot such obstructions well in advance, but in the fog, a ship went blind. It was for this reason that Captain Piedersen had all hands at the rail, probing the river with iron-capped poles, seeking any warning that the *Aemilia* was entering shallow water.

Perhaps if there had been a lookout in the crow's nest, there would have been more warning. As it stood, Gustav only became aware of the ship's peril was when the sailor beside him suddenly stopped probing the river bottom. The man stood slack-jawed, staring out into the fog. Gustav's first instinct was to growl at his comrade, to get the man back to work before one of the officers came by with the lash.

However, there was a look of such fright on the sailor's face that Gustav couldn't help but follow the direction of the man's staring eyes. Gustav saw at once what had caused the other man's alarm. It was impossible to miss the flickering green glow shining behind the fog. Swamp gas and will-o-the-wisps were a common enough sight for any Wastelander, yet these lights were different. Gustav had never seen their like before. There were over a dozen of them, lurching and weaving through the fog, and each of the green orbs seemed to possess a certain uniformity of shape and size.

The sailor beside Gustav suddenly dropped his pole and dropped to his knees. His leathery hands curled awkwardly together, making the sign of Manann. The whispers of a prayer, half sea shanty and half orison, scraped past the sailor's wizened lips.

Gustav felt his body grow cold as he heard his comrade's prayer. Other voices were raised now, shouting warning to the rest of the crew. The green lights had been spotted by others. Men dropped their poles, replacing them with axes and belaying pins. The mates vanished into the forecastle, reappearing with half a dozen crossbows cradled in their arms. Captain Piedersen brandished his sword, bellowing commands to his crew, enjoining them to repel boarders.

River pirates. That was the first thought that raced through Gustav's mind as he drew the long knife from his boot and glared down at the approaching lights. Pirates and wreckers were a common hazard on this stretch of the Reik, though it would be a bold or desperate brigand who would ply his trade in such hideous conditions. They had chosen poor prey. Captain Piedersen's first ship had sailed the Sea of Claws, transporting goods between Marienburg and Erengrad. He was a man used to fending off the attentions of Norscan longships and had never gotten out of the habit of ensuring his crews were armed to the teeth. Any pirates who marked one of Piedersen's ships for plunder soon regretted it.

Even as such thoughts occurred to Gustav, he felt his stomach tighten and a cold chill run down his back. The more he watched the green lights, the less he felt they were anything made by man. Old stories, half-remembered myths from his childhood, rose up unbidden. The frantic prayers of the man kneeling on the deck beside him only added to Gustav's mounting fear. In his mind, he hoped it was only wreckers or pirates who menaced the ship.

The mates were still distributing the crossbows when the attack began. The only warning was a low 'thump' from somewhere out in the fog. A moment later, the sound of shattering glass sounded from the forecastle. Gustav turned away from the rail, following the direction of the noise. He saw a greenish haze settling across the top of the wheel-house. Captain Piedersen and a pair of sailors collapsed in the midst of the cloud, coughing and grasping at their throats. Blood bubbled from their mouths and oozed from noses, eyes and ears. Before anyone could move to help them, the three men gasped their last.

More thumps sounded from the fog. The crackle of breaking glass rose from every quarter of the deck now. Aware that the green haze brought death, the sailors screamed and howled in terror, scrambling to and fro in their desperate efforts to avoid destruction. There was no escape, however, for as soon as the men reached a clear part of the ship a glass globe would come hurtling down and shatter against the deck. The deathly cloud would rise from the broken fragments, destroying all who inhaled its lethal fumes.

Fear kept Gustav frozen in place beside the rail. It kept him from join-ing the mad, hopeless dash across the decks. It was fear which again saved him when the half-crazed sailor beside him suddenly lunged to his feet. Screaming at the top of his lungs, the sailor hurled himself over the rail. The man's flailing arms smashed into Gustav, knocking him over the side to join his comrade's plunge into the murky river.

The cold water revived Gustav's wits, if not his courage. After fight-ing his way to the surface, he was careful to keep quiet. He could hear his crazed companion sputtering and coughing, thrashing about in the water as he struggled to reach the marshy shore. Gustav felt a pang of guilt as he decided against trying to restrain his shipmate. There was nothing he could do. The sailor was making too much noise. Pirates or ghosts, whatever was out there in the fog had heard the commotion. Try-ing to help him now would only cause Gustav to share the wretch's fate.

Treading water with as much silence as he could manage, Gustav found it easy to follow his crazed comrade's progress. By now there were no more screams rising from the decks of the *Aemilia*; the barque was as silent as a grave. Only the sailor's gibbering moans broke the quiet. He could hear the man swimming towards the marsh. Following the sound, he could also see a half-dozen of the green lights moving to converge upon the sailor.

Soon, the lights closed upon the moans and all was silent in the fog.

It was some little time before Gustav became aware of soft, furtive sounds rising from the river. Straining his eyes, he watched as more of the green lights bobbed into view. He could tell from the way they rolled and shivered that the lights were floating across the river, drawing near to the *Aemilia*.

Gustav ducked his body into the river, keeping only his eyes and nose above the cold water. Steadily the lights came nearer.

Then Gustav saw a dark shape loom out from the fog. It was a long, narrow skiff of the sort used by the Wastelanders to navigate their swampy home. Gustav had seen the same sort of boat thousands of times, had even owned one himself before forsaking the marsh for the river. Yet the very ordinariness of the skiff only magnified the horror he felt when he saw the creatures paddling it towards the *Aemilia*, for they were anything but ordinary.

Things ripped from nightmare and the darkest imaginings of childhood, the fiends leered out of the fog and mist. There were at least a dozen of the things on the skiff. Each was roughly the size of a man, with a semblance of the human shape about it, but there was little real similarity. The things had great, bloated bodies, warty and shapeless after the fashion of a toad. Their hands were flabby claws, their skin was green and slimy with an oily sheen about it. A long, whip-like tail coiled behind their bodies and lashing about with serpentine undulations.

The faces of the fiends were the most ghastly. They stretched away from the skull in long floppy beaks with no suggestion of lips or chin. Two enormous flaring nostrils rose above the beak, glistening with a moist blackness against the slimy green skin. Above the nostrils rose the most hideous aspect of the creatures, the crowning horror of their inhuman physiognomy. A single great glaring eye, blazing with eerie green fire. The source of the sinister lights Gustav had seen glowing inside the fog.

All the old stories of marsh daemons came back to Gustav as he watched in mounting terror while the grotesque monsters assaulted the *Aemilia*. The creatures drew long hooks and stout cords from the bottom of the skiff, swinging the grapples until they caught upon the ship's rail. Then, with scuttling, skittering movements that belied their grotesque bulks, the monsters swarmed up the cables and boarded the ship.

Teeth chattering, his body numb with a cold that had nothing to do with the river, Gustav waited until the last of the marsh daemons left the skiff before daring to move. Praying the monsters would be occupied with whatever hellish purpose moved them, Gustav started to swim for shore.

He was the sole survivor. It was his duty to get back to Marienburg and tell the *Aemilia*'s owners what had befallen their ship.

Even if no one would believe him when he told them marsh daemons had emerged from the fog to claim the souls of the *Aemilia*'s crew.

'MAD AS A marsh hare.'

That was the decision voiced by Doctor Anton Kettmann as the physician turned his back on the dingy little cell. It was a decision that brought a frown to the white-robed women standing in the narrow brick hallway. The oldest of them, a silver pendant in the shape of a dove adorning her neck, shook her head and gave the physician a stern look.

'There is always hope if you have faith in the goddess,' she reproached the doctor.

Kettmann dropped his instruments into his satchel and tied the bag close. 'Tell me, Sister Agatha, what kind of faith do you think that mad thing in there has?' He jabbed his thumb back towards the door of the cell. 'He's been screaming about swamp devils for three days. The least Shallya could do is shut him up.'

'That may be, but given that this is a hospice of Shallya, I advise you to apologise for your impious remarks.' The threat came not from Sister Agatha or any of the other priestesses, but from a tall, grim-faced man dressed in light armour and with the band of a riverwarden tied around his arm. As a concession to the goddess of peace and mercy, the scabbard at his side was empty, the sword checked in the weaponhouse outside the temple grounds, but even without a sword, he looked ready for violence.

'Please, Master Visscher, let there be no bloodshed,' implored Sister Agatha, imposing herself between the riverwarden and the doctor. Kettmann hastily donned his hat and scrambled off down the hall before waiting to see if his antagonist would circle around the priestess.

'You should listen to Sister Agatha.' The advice came from a thin, wiry middle-aged man, his hair swept back in a widow's peak, his prominent cheekbones and deep set eyes giving his face an almost cadaverous quality. A fine black cloak trimmed with martin hung from his shoulders, a black-work doublet and matching long breeches and fustian gloves about his slender hands. His appearance was one of refinement and elegance beside the rough crudity of the riverwarden. Yet there was something about Hein van Seeckt that suggested an air of menace more potent than all of Tjarda Visscher's swords and armour.

'That man in there is the only witness that has turned up!' Visscher snarled. 'Ten ships lost in the marsh and this madman is the only survivor!'

Seeckt closed his eyes and nodded. It was true what the riverwarden said. Ten ships had been lost over the past three months. Lost with all hands. It had been something of a miracle that this lone survivor had been found, rescued from the Wasteland by a frogcatcher who, by some whim of the gods, both knew how to read and had seen the reward posters offering five guilders for any information about the fate of the *Aemilia*.

Yes, Seeckt could understand the riverwarden's frustration that this miracle might prove worthless. The loss of the ships, at first just a minor inconvenience, had escalated to the level of international incident, straining relations between the breakaway Free City of Marienburg and the Empire they had once been a part of. As the situation grew more tense, as the threat of war became more real with each vanished ship, the burghers of Marienburg increased their demands on the riverwardens.

Find out what was going on and put a stop to it, or find themselves languishing on Rijker's Island. That had been the decision of the burghers. And, as the most esteemed and decorated officer among the riverwardens, Captain Visscher had been given the unenviable duty of accomplishing the seemingly impossible.

'Gustav Mertens will tell us exactly what we want to know,' Seeckt stated.

Anger drained from Visscher's eyes, replaced with confusion. Though he didn't want to admit it, he was well aware that his witness was a babbling lunatic. 'He's out of his mind! How can he tell us anything?'

Seeckt smoothed his expensive doublet and glanced at the brick walls around him. 'In here, he can't tell us anything,' he said. 'That's why we're taking him with us.'

'You cannot!' protested Sister Agatha. 'This man has been entrusted into the care of Shallya's mercy!'

Seeckt fixed the outraged priestess with a withering stare. 'I am an agent of the Freeholders themselves,' he told her, his voice dripping with the arrogance of authority. 'If I say Gustav Mertens leaves with me, then he leaves with me.' His voice became an audible sneer as he saw Sister Agatha's jaw clench. 'Consider how much your charitable efforts would be diminished if the burghers ceased to donate to your cause. Ask yourself which is more important: helping the many, or sacrificing them for a single man? Shallya is a merciful goddess, but I believe she is also a practical one.'

Seeckt stalked past the silent priestess. 'Visscher, bring Mertens with you. I want to sail before nightfall.'

THE SHAKERLO SAILED upriver after taking on cargo in Carroburg. There was a palpable feeling of fear hovering about the decks of the ship. Ten other vessels had made the same voyage only to vanish in the marshes. That thought was foremost in the minds of the crew.

It was also foremost in the minds of her passengers. Seeckt and Visscher paced the decks like two hunters scenting prey. Gustav Mertens simply huddled next to the mainmast, gibbering and drooling, his madness doing little to quieten the fears of the crew.

The riverwarden fingered the strange mask Seeckt had given him, a curious contraption of waxed leather that extended outward into a slender, birdlike bill. It reminded Visscher of old woodcuts he'd once seen showing Westerland during the Black Death, gangs of plague doctors fleecing the sick and the dying. For the life of him, he couldn't understand why Seeckt had distributed these weird masks to every man aboard the *Shakerlo* or why he had ordered everyone to keep the masks with them at all times. Indeed, three crewmen had been discharged and put ashore at the little fishing village of Mierdorf for violating the agent's orders.

Everything about the voyage was strange. It made sense to Visscher that they would engage extra crew in case they ran into trouble and had to make a fight of things, but Seeckt had taken his preparedness to the next level, hiring the services of a dozen Carroburg swordsmen and a scruffy mob of Tilean crossbows. It seemed a colossal waste of gold should their journey back to Marienburg prove uneventful.

Visscher had a suspicion that Seeckt knew more about the vanished ships than he admitted. The agent was just a bit too certain they would encounter trouble. His assurance had to stem from something more substantial than Gustav's deranged mutterings. There was something, some link between the missing ships that the riverwardens had missed, a connection between them which Seeckt had uncovered and which the agent had ensured the *Shakerlo* would share. When he challenged the agent about his suspicions, however, the only reply Visscher got was a wry smile and a warning not to meddle in the affairs of the burghers.

The tension became a palpable thing when the grassy banks of the Upper Reik gave way to the muck and mire of the Wasteland. The crew murmured uneasily among themselves as fog began to settle across the river, forming a grey veil across the horizon. Prayers to Manann, Handrich and even Sigmar became common as the sailors watched their vessel draw ever closer to the fog.

Seeckt held a speedy conference with the *Shakerlo*'s captain and officers. When he dismissed them, the men circled among their crew, making sure that each man was armed and had his weird mask ready. Seeckt watched the officers go about their errand, then turned and made his way to where Visscher stood just below the forecastle.

'Have your mask ready,' the agent hissed. 'I think you will need it before much longer.'

Visscher removed the ugly mask from where he had tied it to his belt-sash. He grimaced at the long, beaked face and the dull, glassy eyes. 'You're more superstitious than any seaman if you think this will ward off marsh bogies,' the riverwarden grumbled.

'Humour me,' Seeckt said, his voice thin and mirthless.

Visscher glowered at him, his pride bristling at the agent's condescending manner. 'You really think we're going to run into trouble?'

'I'm counting on it,' Seeckt said. 'I've done everything to ensure this ship matches the *Aemilia* in every way. What happened to her should happen to us.'

'Now you can predict the ways of marsh daemons!' Visscher scoffed.

Seeckt fixed the riverwarden with a cold gaze. He didn't deign to respond to Visscher's baiting, but instead jerked a thumb towards the mainmast. 'Keep close to Mertens,' he ordered. 'Watch his every move. If he does anything unusual, don't wait but shout the alarm at once.' Seeckt prodded Visscher's chest with the tip of his finger. 'At once. You understand?'

'Your madman is chained,' Visscher snarled. 'He's not going to cause any trouble, however agitated he gets.'

'I'm not worried about him,' Seeckt said. 'I'm worried about what might upset him.'

As though responding to Seeckt's words, Gustav began thrashing about in his chains, an incoherent stream of moans and shrieks rising from his ashen face. The crew turned with undisguised horror as the madman's wails became more crazed with each passing breath. A few of the sailors closed their hands about their knives, fear goading them to advance upon the chained lunatic.

Visscher moved to stop the frightened sailors. He had no affection for Gustav, only the sort of pitying contempt a man might show a feral dog, but the riverwarden was not about to stand idly by while the helpless lunatic was slaughtered. His stern eyes glared at each of the seamen.

'I've had it with that madman's screams!' a broken-nosed sailor growled. He fingered the fat-bladed knife in his hand and glared back at Visscher. 'Get out of our way!'

With one smooth motion, Visscher drew the sword sheathed at his side. The blade licked out in a blinding flash of steel, whistling past the broken nose. A bead of blood dribbled from the tiny cut left by the riverwarden's steel.

'Make me move,' Visscher said. 'But make your peace with the gods first.'

The sailors looked anxiously at each other, glancing at the short knives in their hands and the long sword in the riverwarden's. They knew Visscher's threat wasn't an idle one. Their numbers might prevail against Visscher's sword, but not before the blade had claimed a few of them. Frightened as they were, none of the seamen wanted to be the first to die.

Oblivious to the drama playing out only a few feet away, Gustav's entire body contorted against the deck as the madman's lungs gave voice to a howl of pure terror. The sound reminded the sailor's of their own fears.

'Keep that mongrel quiet!' one of the sailors demanded. 'Shut him up, or we will!' The outburst brought angry mutters from the other seamen, pouring back into their veins the murderous determination Visscher had hoped to quell.

'You have more important things to worry about,' Seeckt's calm tones intruded upon the scene. The agent stood beside the rail, gesturing with his gloved hand at the roiling fog which now surrounded the ship. Every man gasped in fright as he saw the weird green lights flashing through the mist, bobbing and weaving across the marsh. Whispers of daemons and spectres passed among the crew.

A final shriek rose from Gustav, accompanied by the sound of snapping chains. Laughing maniacally, the lunatic lunged across the deck, his broken chains dangling from wrists and ankles. Visscher tried to intercept the madman, but the cunning of insanity gripped Gustav's crazed mind. Whirling about when he saw the riverwarden, Gustav dived for the portside rail. He leaped onto the rail, perched upon it for a moment, insane laughter shuddering through his body. Then, the moment passed and the madman lost his balance. He hurtled overboard, vanishing into the grey fog with a splash and the rattle of his broken chains.

Visscher reached the rail just after Gustav's fell. The riverwarden's eyes scoured the fog, trying to find any trace of the madman. Having taken it upon himself to protect Gustav from the sailors, he felt a sense of guilt that he had failed to protect the lunatic from his own madness.

Visscher was still staring into the fog when he felt Seeckt's gloved hand close about his shoulder. The agent's face was hidden behind the weird leather mask, his eyes just visible behind the tinted lenses. Seeckt pointed to the riverwarden's own mask, motioning for Visscher to put it on. 'Like I told them,' the agent said, his voice distorted and muffled by the mask, 'we have bigger problems to worry about.'

The riverwarden glanced across the *Shakerlo*'s deck. The crew and officers had donned their own masks and were huddled close against the sides, watching the green lights moving through the fog. Every man clutched a weapon in his hand, his body tensed for action. There were no more frightened whispers. The dread clinging to every man's heart had silenced talk of daemons and ghosts.

'Keep a careful watch,' Seeckt told Visscher. 'The attack will come soon. When it does, drop to the deck and play dead. You'll know when to stop playing.'

Visscher gripped Seeckt's arm. 'Attacked? By who?'

A sardonic chuckle rose from Seeckt's mask. 'Marsh daemons, of course.' He turned away, pacing across to the forecastle to issue final orders to the captain.

Visscher wondered what Seeckt's plans were. Again, the riverwarden felt suspicion twisting his gut. Seeckt had been just a bit too assured that the ship would be attacked, yet even at this late hour he preferred to play coy regarding the nature of the menace threatening them. And what possible sense could there be in playing dead when these unknown enemies attacked?

Visscher set aside his questions when he heard something crash against the deck not three feet from where he stood. Through the lenses of his mask, he could see little fragments of what looked like glass scattered about the deck, a mist of vapour rising from the shards. He turned his head as he heard the sound of more glass breaking somewhere towards the stern. Again, he could see shards and smoky vapour.

The riverwarden couldn't begin to guess the kind of weapon that had been set loose against the *Shakerlo*, but he knew enough to recognise it as a weapon. Clearly, Seeckt had anticipated just this sort of thing, issuing the weird masks to protect the crew from the undoubtedly poisonous vapour. Recognising that much of the agent's plan, Visscher thought he could guess the rest. Slowly, he dropped to the deck, stretching himself out in what he hoped was a convincingly dead attitude. He kept his hand closed about the hilt of his sword.

Once their attackers were satisfied their poison had done its work, they would board the ship in search of plunder. But this time the murderous pirates would be due for a surprise. Any fear of ghosts and spectres was gone now. Only something mortal would hurl glass globes filled with poison gas to kill an enemy. There was nothing supernatural about the fiends who had been preying upon the river trade.

Visscher was quite eager now to meet Seeckt's marsh daemons.

Lying upon the deck, Visscher trained his senses upon the sounds around him. He could hear the creaking of the *Shakerlo* as she drifted through the water. He could hear the crackle of glass breaking as more globes crashed down upon the ship. Slowly these sounds abated, replaced by the splash of oars cutting water. Boats, many of them from the sound, were closing upon the *Shakerlo*. Visscher felt the tremor of the boats as they bumped against the ship's hull. He smiled as he heard the scratch of grapples being thrown over the ship's rail.

The scratch of the grapples was soon followed by the sound of feet scrabbling against the hull, the mutter of muffled voices whispering to each other. There was an unpleasant quality about those voices, unpleasant enough to make the riverwarden's skin crawl. Despite the risk, he had to see what sort of men these pirates were. Visscher rolled his head against his arm, turning his eyes towards starboard.

What he saw brought every childhood story of fog devils and marsh daemons roaring back through his mind. The things crawling over the rail weren't men at all, but were creatures straight out of hag-haunted nightmare! The flabby green skin, the single glowing eye, the floppy snout dripping down from the bloated face... how many times had he heard the old folk of the Wasteland warn against these horrors, these malignant denizens of mist and shadow!

The daemons dropped down onto the deck, their cyclopean eyes shining across the ship as they looked over the *Shakerlo*. Smothered laughter wheezed from their grotesque faces, laughter that made Gustav's ravings seem beatific. More and more of the monsters climbed the rails until there were nearly two-score of the fiends prowling about the deck. Visscher could see the amphibian horrors shuffling towards the forecastle, their flabby paws closing about ugly bludgeons and rusty swords.

As the daemons approached the forecastle, they passed Seeckt's prone body. The cyclopean monsters paid the seemingly dead agent scant notice. It was the last mistake they would ever make.

Seeckt's lean body jolted upwards, a dagger clenched in each of his gloved hands. He drove one of the blades into the slimy throat of one of the daemons, slashing the other across the belly of its nearest comrade. Both of the monsters reeled back, black blood jetting from their wounds. The daemon with the transfixed throat crumpled without a sound, crashing to the deck, its body twitching, long tail drumming against the planks. The other daemon gave voice to a shriek and fell to its knees, its flabby claws pawing at its ghastly injury.

Seeckt threw the bloodied dagger full into the face of a third daemon, piercing one of its black nostrils. The fiend dropped to the deck, dead even before Seeckt drew his sword and slashed it across the monster's neck.

The *Shakerlo*'s crew lunged into action at that moment. Seeckt had told them to wait for the right moment – the moment when the enemy was aboard and battle was joined. The sailors, emboldened by Seeckt's violent display, attacked the fiends with a ferocity born of shame and outrage. To a man they had really believed these creatures to be some supernatural horror of the swamp. But Seeckt had shown them that these were no daemons, only mortal beasts that could bleed and die.

Visscher sprang onto his feet, tackling the monster closest to him. The cyclopean beast crashed onto its back, kicking and flailing at the riverwarden. The thing's slimy skin made it as slippery as an eel, but Visscher clung to its shoulder and drove the point of his sword full into the creature's glowing eye. The eye exploded in a burst of gas and glass, glowing vapour sizzling across the monster's slimy face.

The riverwarden stared in amazement at burning wreckage of the fiend's head. His wonder increased when the creature's struggles became even more intense and its flabby paw slammed into his face, jolting him backwards. The creature kicked at him with both legs, driving him away, but before it escaped completely, Visscher saw beady eyes glaring at him from the black depths of the fiend's nostrils.

As soon as it was clear of the riverwarden, the monster lifted its claws to its face and tore its own head off. The ruined, smoking husk of the cyclopean daemon fell to the deck. In its place, rising from the slimy shoulders, was an even more hideous countenance: the snarling muzzle of an enormous rat!

Visscher stared at the transformed monster, shocked, gripped with disbelief. The marsh daemons had faded back into the land of legend, but in their stead had come a creature just as fantastic, the verminous underfolk!

The ratman snapped its long fangs at the stupefied riverwarden, then lunged at him. Before the creature's fangs could sink themselves into Visscher's throat, a sword flashed between monster and prey. The slimy flesh of the monster was split open, exposing the furry body hidden inside. Black blood bubbled from a mortal wound and the ratman crashed to the deck, coughing and spitting as it tried to crawl away.

Seeckt stabbed the point of his bloodied blade into the ratman's neck, then wiped the sword clean with a scrap of sailcloth. The agent turned away from the dead monster, directing a reproving look at Visscher.

'Don't worry about what they are,' he told the riverwarden. 'Just kill them.'

THE BATTLE WAS swift and brutal. By its finish, no less than thirty of the ratmen were dead, strewn about the decks in their ghoulish disguises. Four of the ship's crew had fallen to the monsters. Surprise had thrown the ratmen into complete confusion, but Visscher thought the gods deserved some credit for delivering such a lop-sided victory.

The ship's crew kept to the forecastle, watching the fog for any sign of more enemies. They hadn't been pleased with Seeckt's insistence that the bodies of the monsters be left on deck and even less happy with his demand that the *Shakerlo* remain at anchor. Only the threat of the burghers kept the men from throwing Seeckt and the monsters overboard. Seamen all, they knew how far the enmity of the burghers could reach.

Visscher descended from the forecastle. There were enough eyes watching the fog. He was more interested in watching what Seeckt was doing. The agent was prowling among the dead ratmen, giving each a cursory examination before moving on to the next. There was something methodical about the way Seeckt was operating, and Visscher wanted to know the purpose behind it all.

'They're not beastmen, are they?' Visscher challenged Seeckt.

The agent looked up from one of the bodies, a cold smile on his gaunt face. 'Are you calling me a liar?'

Visscher nodded his head and gestured with his thumb at the forecastle. 'They don't believe you either. We've all heard the stories. These things are underfolk.'

'And does it make you happy to know the skaven exist?' Seeckt's voice dropped into a bitter chuckle. 'Better to hold onto whatever lies you are told. You'll sleep better.' He stooped down over another of the ratmen, pulling away one of the flabby paws and exposing a furry hand.

'They died easy enough,' Visscher said, shrugging his shoulders. 'If men knew how easily these things died…'

Seeckt reached down and lifted a fold of the slimy green costume the skaven wore. 'They were lumbered down by their vestments,' Seeckt explained. 'Unencumbered, a skaven is faster than any man. By the time you can think to stick your sword in its heart, it has its claws in your belly.'

'Then why did they take such a risk? Why make themselves vulnerable just to make us think marsh daemons were taking the ships?'

Seeckt tugged at the slimy skin, opening it along one of its seams. Visscher could see now that the flabby flesh was a sort of coat, with matching gloves, boots and pants. 'Protection,' the agent stated. 'Not against us, because we should have already been dead, but against the poison gas they were using.' He stared out at the fog. 'Somewhere out on the marsh, if we cared to look, I think we might find some sort of mortar or catapult.'

'The glass globes!' Visscher exclaimed.

Seeckt pointed to one of the spots where a globe had crashed. The planking was burned and pitted where the glass had shattered. 'Without our masks, we should have all been dead before they came near the ship.' Seeckt stood suddenly, marching across the deck to one of the dead ratmen. He reached down and pulled the cyclopean head from the skaven's shoulders. 'Here is your marsh daemon,' he said. 'Nothing but a mask to protect them from their own gas. The glowing eye nothing more than a lantern to help them see their way through the fog. With their snouts locked away inside their masks, they'd be unable to pick their way by scent, so they'd need to keep their vision keen.'

'But they look just like the old stories,' Visscher objected. 'The ones about the marsh daemons.'

Seeckt turned away, pacing to the rear of the body. Using one of his daggers, he cut away at the flabby tail, revealing it to be a leathery sheath covering a long naked tail. 'I grant that to be more than coincidence,' he said. Reaching to his belt, Seeckt withdrew a little bottle. 'Their leader must know quite a bit about men, enough to exploit the old legends to conceal his raiders. Just in case somebody like Gustav got away.' Casually, the agent opened the bottle, upending it and spilling it across the exposed tail.

'Clumsy!' Seeckt cursed. 'I'll have to go down to my cabin and get more.' Rising, the agent motioned Visscher to follow him. When the riverwarden was close enough, he whispered to him, 'Keep watching our "dead" friend over there. Don't stop him, just watch.'

In a louder voice, Seeckt called out to the crew, telling them that he was done with the bodies. He advised soaking them in lamp oil and burning them on shore.

No sooner were the words out of Seeckt's mouth than the ratman he had been examining leaped to its feet and scurried across the deck. Like the *Shakerlo*'s crew, the skaven had been playing dead, biding its time until the opportune time to escape. Seeckt's decision to burn the dead monsters instead of simply casting them overboard had forced the ratman into action. Before any of the crew could do more than curse at it, the skaven was across the deck and leaping over the side.

Visscher rushed after it, feeling stupid for letting the creature escape, whatever Seeckt's orders had been. The agent was more pragmatic. Calmly, he pointed to a glowing line of splotches that stained the deck.

'I'm afraid our friend has some paint on his tail,' Seeckt announced. 'It should be easy for me to follow him back to his lair.'

'You mean easy for us,' Visscher corrected him. 'It's the job of the river-wardens to put an end to this piracy, whoever or whatever is behind it.'

Seeckt stared hard at Visscher. 'This won't be like rousting ship wreckers or bullying smugglers.'

'I'm going to see this through,' Visscher said, his tone brooking no objection.

Seeckt relented with a sigh. 'On your head then,' he said. Turning, he called out to the captain. 'Keep the *Shakerlo* here until the fog burns off. If we're not back by then, I leave you to your own judgement.'

So saying, the two men lowered themselves over the side. On the marshy shore, a little trail of glowing splotches beckoned them.

To THE TWO men, the trail seemed almost without end. The little splotches of glowing paint meandered through the muck and mire of the marshes. Fog clung to the soggy earth, the grey mists so thick that Visscher thought they would need a knife to cut their way through. Sucking mud and black pools of stagnant water threatened them on every side, waiting to punish the men for the slightest misstep and drag them down into a nameless grave.

Quicksand and deadfalls weren't the only fears preying upon Visscher's mind. All the haunts and bogies of his childhood were lurking beyond the grey veil, the drowned corpses that lived again, the wailing swamp witches who could suck out a man's soul with a kiss, the cyclopean marsh daemons who carried their victims into the mist – never to be seen again.

To these, Visscher now added another fairytale horror, a horror all the more terrible for its awful reality. The skaven, the underfolk of nursery rhyme and nightmare. Seeckt hoped to follow the ratman he had marked back to the thing's lair, but how many more of the verminous creatures might even now be prowling the marsh looking for them?

The riverwarden tightened his hold upon his sword. He envied Seeckt's cool implacable self-assurance. The agent hurried through the marsh, leaping from one splotch of paint to the next, never hesitating, never questioning. He was like a hound chasing down game, his mind utterly fixated upon the hunt.

Visscher hoped that Seeckt's confidence was justified.

'There,' the agent suddenly hissed, his voice low and cautious. He pointed a gloved finger at a great jumble of mossy stones. The broken megaliths might once have formed some mighty castle or temple, but if they had, it had been long before the advent of man. There was a sense of hoary antiquity about the eroded, crumbling plinths that evoked a feeling of disquiet, an impression that the eye gazed upon something lost which had been better to remain forgotten.

'Just the sort of place for monsters, is it not?' Seeckt asked, indicating the line of glowing splotches. The trail led into the jumble of rocks, vanishing beneath one of the windswept stones.

'If that's their lair, we should go back and get help,' Visscher suggested, fighting down the urge to simply turn and run. 'There's no telling how many of the vermin are down there.'

'That is why we need to see for ourselves,' Seeckt said. 'We need to know how many of them there are. There could be more than the *Shakerlo* can handle.'

It was sound reasoning, but that didn't make it any easier for Visscher to accept. He hesitated when Seeckt began stealing towards the mound of stones, tempted to leave the arrogant envoy to his fate. Then he closed his eyes and saw again the loathsome creatures they had battled on the *Shakerlo*. Grimly, the riverwarden trotted after Seeckt. No man could abandon another to such vile monsters and still call himself a man.

'The swamp stink should help mask our scent,' Seeckt advised Visscher as they approached the stones. 'The fog will hide us from their eyes, but be careful about making any noise. The ears of a skaven are much sharper than ours.'

Staring down into the black gap beneath the stone, Visscher wasn't reassured by Seeckt's warning. The hole drove under the megalith at a slant, making the prospect of crawling down into it even more repugnant. A menagerie of odours drifted up from the cavity, a mixture of fur and filth, old bones and rotten meat and another, still more noxious smell that made Visscher's nose burn. He reached down for his mask, intending to replace it over his face and block out the smell.

It was at that moment that the attack came. The attention of both men fixed upon the hole, Visscher further discomfited as he fumbled with his mask, the ambush caught them at their most unguarded. A dozen furry shapes sprang at them from the fog, leaping down from the mossy stones, pouncing from covered pits, scurrying from behind jumbles of rock. The two men were smashed to the muddy ground beneath a fury of snapping fangs and flashing claws. Scrawny paws ripped the swords from their hands, one of the monsters chittering with sadistic humour as it pulled the mask from Visscher's grip. The ratman capered about proudly with his prize, then darted down into the hole when a larger skaven moved to take it from him.

The big skaven snarled in frustration, his black fur bristling as he glared after the vanished thief. He gnashed his fangs, then gestured at the two humans pinned to the ground. A stream of sharp squeaks and hisses rushed past the ratman's fangs, the spit-speak language of the underfolk. Sullenly, the other ratmen responded to the black-fur's commands. Visscher and Seeckt were roughly forced to their feet, prodded and kicked until they preceded their inhuman captors into the slimy murk beneath the toppled megalith.

HOW LONG THE two men spent in the winding network of muddy tunnels and passageways, neither of them could say. At every step, the slanted floor seemed to drop away, causing them to stumble and slip in the slime that coated the floor. Their difficulties brought chitters of malignant mirth from their captors, who only kicked and clawed them with increased brutality each time the men fell.

There was no sense of organisation or pattern to the tunnels. Occasionally a weird green lantern would appear, bolted to the stone ceiling overhead. The sickly green light did little to illuminate the darkness, but seemed to give the skaven a measure of comfort whenever they drew close. Visscher was reminded of the glowing lamps the *Shakerlo*'s attackers had worn and which he had mistaken for the eye of a marsh daemon. Recalling the caustic aftermath of breaking one of the lamps, Visscher wondered if the lanterns might not lend themselves to similar purpose.

After what seemed an eternity to the two men, the maze of winding tunnels opened into a vast hall-like cavern. Dozens of green lanterns illuminated the hall, casting weird shadows across the heaps of mud and splintered rock strewn about. Crates and boxes were piled throughout the chamber, the plunder from the ships the ratmen had been hijacking.

To one side of the cavern, where the stone ceiling was at its lowest, a jumble of rock was flanked by a nest of tattered flags and filthy banners, each of them bearing a three-clawed symbol picked out in yellow thread.

While there were skaven scurrying throughout the cavern, the largest congregation of them was around the pile of rock. The creatures sported a wild disarray of garments, from slick coveralls such as a smith might wear to spiked suits of armour. Several of the ratmen wore the same leathery green vestments as the *Shakerlo*'s attackers. A few of the monsters had massive harnesses strapped to their backs, an array of weird and menacing devices curling outward from the boxy frames.

All of the skaven faced towards a miserable figure who stood alone at the base of the rock pile. The protective green cloak and gauntlets had been stripped from the wretched ratman, but the phosphorescent paint clinging to its tail left no doubt as to its identity. The skaven's naked body was torn and mangled, its fur bloodied from dozens of cuts and bites. It grovelled before the rock pile, pressing its snout into the mud and whining in a continuous stream of squeaks.

The monster perched atop the rock pile glowered down at the wretch, unmoved by its pleas. Taller than the other skaven, his lean body was cloaked in a flowing robe of yellow silk, its edges marked with black symbols that seemed to squirm and writhe as the eye fell upon them. A belt of skin circled the skaven's waist, a motley array of strange implements hanging from the many hooks fixed to the belt. Dark grey fur, mottled with specks of brown, clothed the creature's body, fading into pure white at his throat. The eyes that glared down at the snivelling wretch lent a final aspect of horror to the skaven's countenance, for they were of a weird, almost spectral green, gleaming with the pitiless malignance of an inhuman intelligence.

'Gnawlitch Shun!' The frightened whisper escaped Seeckt's lips, giving name to the horror lording over this nest of monsters. The agent's outburst brought angry squeaks from their captors, the black-furred bully raking his claws across Seeckt's cheek. The ratman laughed as he licked the human's blood from his paw.

Visscher's mind raced. How was it possible that Seeckt knew this monster by sight? Exactly how much did the agent know about these underfolk?

There was no time for questions. A commotion had erupted at the base of the rock pile. Even as the ratkin with the painted tail was being dragged away, a spindly crook-backed skaven scurried out from the pack. He chittered happily at his enthroned lord, brandishing Visscher's stolen mask with the flourish of a conquering hero.

Gnawlitch Shun silenced the capering ratman's antics with an angry snarl. He raised his head, his nose twitching as he sniffed the air. The merciless green eyes turned, glaring directly at the mouth of the tunnel, fixing on the two human prisoners. The mask was proof that the men knew something about what the skaven had been doing and had come prepared.

'So-so, no one followed your tail-trail,' Gnawlitch Shun snarled in Reikspiel. His eyes still fixed upon the two humans, the ratman lifted his hand and snapped his claws.

A heavily-built skaven, his brown fur singed and scarred, lumbered out from among the pack. His bulk was curled under a massive metal drum, his face locked inside a bronze helmet. A monstrous, nozzle-like device was strapped about his left arm, a riot of wires and hoses streaming away to converge upon the tank tied to the ratkin's back. The skaven turned a dial set into the side of the contraption, causing it to shudder into life with a grinding growl and a spurt of smoke.

The other skaven backed away as the menacing war-rat answered his master's call. The captive ratman was unceremoniously shoved forwards into the space before the rock pile. For an instant, the unfortunate creature was frozen with uncertainty and terror. His head snapped from side to side in a frantic effort to find the safest route of retreat. On all fronts a mass of snarling skaven stood against his escape. Too craven to leap into any danger, the ratman remained gripped by indecision.

The war-rat pointed his left arm at the doomed skaven. Pulling back on a lever, he loosed the awful power of his weapon. Steam vented from the nozzle, sickly green light erupting from the barrel of the cannon and sizzling across the space between killer and victim. The wretch shrieked as the fur was flayed from his battered body, the murderous green light searing through skin and flesh, annihilating almost instantaneously everything down to the very bone. It was a smouldering skeleton that crashed to the ground, its feet and hands and painted tail rendered still more hideous for their wholesome state. When death had struck, those parts had been outside the disintegrating green light.

'Let that illustrate – Gnawlitch Shun is master of death,' the robed warlock hissed at the humans. He pointed a long claw at the two men. 'You will die-suffer when it amuses me and curse the ingenuity that led you here.'

Visscher felt his veins turn to ice as the skaven lord uttered his threat. The horrible way in which this monster had disposed of one of his own followers was a graphic demonstration of the fiend's merciless mind. How much worse would the ratman treat with captives of another race?

Seeckt fell onto his knees in an attitude of terror and submission. The skaven around the two men laughed at his grovelling, snickering among themselves. The black-furred brute swatted the back of Seeckt's head with his paw, glaring at him with undisguised contempt.

Doomed as they certainly were, Visscher felt a surge of fury rush through him. They were going to die, but at least they could die on their feet like men, not snivelling in the muck at the feet of vermin! The river-warden surged forwards, seizing the black-fur by the shoulder, spinning the skaven around and smashing his fist into the creature's nose. The black-fur yelped in pain, doubling over as he clapped both paws against his snout, leaving himself defenceless against the boot Visscher drove into the monster's groin.

The moment his tormentor yelped in pain, Seeckt was on his feet, his voice lifted in a fierce shout. 'Gnawlitch Shun!' the agent yelled at the fiend on the rocks. 'The Seerlord sends you the Twelfth Atonement!'

Seeckt's balled fist flashed forwards, flinging something at the rock pile. Gnawlitch Shun's tall frame wilted into a cowering ball, his arms raised protectively across his face. It took the warlock a moment to recover from the surprise of Seeckt's sudden attack, and another to appreciate that whatever havoc the human had intended, the Grand Warlock of Clan Skryre was unharmed.

Gnawlitch Shun jabbed his claw at his attacker. 'Kill the man-things!' he raged, sending the skaven gathered about the cavern scurrying towards the tunnel. The skaven around Visscher and Seeckt drew their blades, eager to carry out their master's command. 'Kill the traitor-meat!' Gnawlitch Shun's voice screeched.

In his fury, the Grand Warlock continued to shriek in Reikspiel rather than the squeak-spit of the skaven tongue, but the meaning of 'traitor-meat' wasn't lost upon the ratmen surrounding Visscher and Seeckt. The agent had brought some weapon into the cavern in an attempt to kill the warlock. That was only possible if his captors had allowed it. To the skaven mind, every mistake was evidence of treacherous plotting and scheming.

The marked skaven squealed in fright and began scurrying down the tunnel, fleeing for their lives back into the maze of slimy passages. Visscher stared after them for a moment, before Seeckt grabbed his shoulder and urged him to follow the retreating ratmen.

'Run!' the agent ordered. 'If we follow them we might have a chance of reaching the surface!'

As though to emphasise Seeckt's words, a motley barrage of missiles crashed around the two men – bullets fired from long muskets by wiry ratmen, bolts of electricity thrown from the weird armatures of the warlock-engineers, sheets of green flame billowing from the mouths of ghoulish fire-projectors. A squeal of mortal agony rang out as the two men made their dash down the tunnel. Visscher looked back to see the black-furred skaven he had struck being disintegrated by the green ray. The bronze-helmeted war-rat glared after the two men, scurrying in pursuit with hideous speed.

VISSCHER WAS THANKFUL for the darkness of the tunnels, feeling a sense of security in the all-encompassing blackness. Away from the lights of Gnawlitch Shun's cavern, the riverwarden felt there was a real chance they might escape the inhuman monsters chasing them. Without realising it, he allowed his pace to slacken.

'Keep running,' Seeckt snapped at Visscher. 'Just because they can't see us doesn't mean they can't find us! I told you, a skaven follows his nose more than his eyes. They'll have no problem following our scent down here!'

The reminder made Visscher's stomach turn. Suddenly, the dark didn't feel so safe. He clenched his fists in impotent fury. His occupation was one that fitted him to the role of hunter, tracking down smugglers and pirates. Playing the part of the hunted was new to Visscher, a novelty he found himself ill-equipped to accept.

'Back there,' the riverwarden said as he hurried to keep pace with Seeckt. 'I... I really thought you'd given up.'

'I needed to gull them into letting down their guard,' Seeckt replied. 'Our only chance to get out of there was to wrongfoot them. Your attack on old black-fur was a perfect distraction.'

Visscher's brow knitted with a question that had been nagging him. 'Just what was that you told their leader? And what was it you threw at him?'

Seeckt's sly smile was lost in the darkness. 'I threatened him by invoking the name of one of the underfolk's high priests.' The agent laughed. 'Then I threw a rock at him!'

Visscher joined in the agent's laughter, taking strength from the simple trick Seeckt had played upon the monstrous skaven leader. Their mirth faded after a moment, smothered by the damp darkness all about them. 'Do you think we really have a chance?' the riverwarden asked.

'No,' Seeckt admitted. 'But if they don't pick up our scent, we might give them a good chase. Come on.'

The two men groped their way through the gloom, following the slimy walls of the passageway with their hands. Furtive sounds, the scurry of normal rats, the creeping hop of toads and lizards, brought sweat dripping from their brows despite the clammy chill of the tunnel. A few times they heard the spit-squeak of skaven voices in the distance. Once, Visscher was certain, he heard a plaintive cry which sounded uncannily human. It reminded him somehow of the crazed babble of Gustav Mertens.

When the green glow of a lantern appeared at the far end of the passage the men groaned in relief, a relief that they felt down to their very toes. They did not think of the sickly hue of the glow or the unpleasant vapours billowing from the lamp. After the unremitting darkness, it was enough that there was light. Without thought or fear, the two fugitives rushed headlong down the tunnel.

They were only a few yards from the lantern when they discovered their mistake. The skaven hadn't been chasing them – they'd been waiting for them! By some infernal means, the ratkin had figured out which tunnel the humans were in and decided to lie in wait for them at the other end.

There were half a dozen of the monsters, their beady eyes gleaming in the ugly light. Foremost among them was the hideous war-rat with the bronze helmet and the warp-ray lashed to his arm. Spotting the two men, the war-rat snarled an order to his comrades, waving them forwards to seize the fugitives.

Visscher felt his stomach turn. He had seen for himself the speed these creatures could muster when they weren't burdened with respirators and protective coverings. There was no chance at all they could outrun the unleashed rat pack.

Deliverance came from the most unexpected source. As the ratkin surged forwards to capture the men, the war-rat stepped back towards the wall. He lifted the nozzle of his weapon and drew back the lever. A blazing ribbon of green energy surged from the projector, striking down the other skaven with murderous precision. The partially disintegrated bodies crashed to the slimy floor, the dying shrieks of the ratmen echoing from the walls.

The fratricidal war-rat released the lever, cutting off the killing warp-ray once the last of his comrades was destroyed. A chitter of malicious laughter rattled through the bronze mask. The war-rat had been happy to let other skaven share the hunt, but he wasn't going to let any of them share the rewards of victory.

The war-rat gestured with his weapon, motioning the two men to come towards him. 'Gnawlitch Shun like live-take,' the skaven's shrill voice assured them.

Seeckt glared back at the gloating vermin. 'Your master's plans are ruined,' he told the war-rat. 'Run while you still have the chance.'

Again, the war-rat's laughter wheezed through his metal mask. 'Funny-squeak!' the skaven hissed. 'All man-things die-suffer now!'

The war-rat raised his warp-ray projector, his paw reaching to the lever. Before he could unleash the disintegrating green light, however, something went flying past his face. The war-rat ducked aside, but the projectile wasn't aimed at him. Its target was behind the skaven, bolted to the ceiling. The glass face of the lantern exploded as the missile struck it, spattering the ceiling with phosphorescent dust and unleashing a cloud of sizzling vapour that crashed down about the war-rat.

Shrill squeals of pain shuddered from the war-rat's mask as the corrosive gas settled upon him. The ratman pawed frantically at his smouldering body, trying to smother the chemical fires burning his body. On his back, the engine of the warp-ray projector was likewise suffering from the caustic gas, but without the panicked paws of a skaven to diffuse the destruction. The corroded engine began to sputter and spark, then exploded in a burst of emerald light.

The war-rat was hurled down the tunnel at the two men. He landed in a mangled heap, his back evaporated by the unleashed malignance of his own weapon. Seeckt stared at the dead ratman, blinking in disbelief. Visscher strode over and kicked the vermin's armoured head.

'That worked pretty well,' the riverwarden quipped.

'What did?' Seeckt asked.

Visscher pointed at the shattered lantern. 'I threw a rock.'

Seeckt shook his head, his face going white. 'That lamp was fuelled with warpstone! You might have brought the entire tunnel down about our heads!'

Visscher shrugged, trying to hide the alarm Seeckt's words caused him. 'It looked like the eye-lamp the raiders wore,' he explained. 'I smashed one of those on the *Shakerlo*. I thought the lantern would do the same.' He gestured to the mangled body at his feet. 'Lucky for us it did.'

'Lucky indeed,' Seeckt said under his breath. The agent stooped, pulling a femur from one of the skaven skeletons on the floor. Raising it overhead, he scraped some of the glowing dust onto it. The result was too feeble to properly be called a torch, but at least it provided some illumination. Visscher followed his example and was soon similarly equipped. 'Hold it away from your body,' Seeckt warned. 'This stuff is toxic even to them,' he said, nodding at the dead skaven. 'Pray we don't need to use them very long.'

* * *

BACK IN THE maze of tunnels, the two men resumed their search for a way back to the surface. The eerie sounds of the slimy corridors became incessant and a foul reek, like the musk of a snake pit, began to fill the air. Slopping, glottal noises slithered through the passageways, bearing with them a nameless sensation that made skin crawl and blood curdle. Twice, Visscher stopped dead in his tracks, certain that he'd heard a human cry mixed amid the weird sounds of swamp and mire.

'I could swear I heard Mertens,' Visscher told Seeckt.

The agent stopped, cocking his head to one side, straining to pick out the noise from the cloying darkness. 'If he didn't drown, the skaven might have captured him,' Seeckt mused. He grimaced and directed a hard stare at Visscher. 'Even if they have, there's nothing we can do for the poor madman.'

'It makes me sick to leave any man in the hands of such monsters,' Visscher shuddered.

'We have to save our own skins,' Seeckt told him. 'Get back to the *Shakerlo*… and let them know about Gnawlitch Shun.'

Visscher bowed to the sense of Seeckt's decision, even as he felt his heart blacken with guilt. There was little enough hope of their own escape, they'd throw the small chance they had away if they lingered trying to find Gustav. He could only pray to Manann that the lunatic's death would be quick.

The two men resumed their prowl through the muddy darkness. The musky stink in the air grew more intense, almost bringing tears to their eyes. Despite the discomfort, Visscher was grateful for the foul smell. With that filth choking the air, there was no way the skaven would be able to track them by scent. It was a small enough advantage, but one that gave the riverwarden some hope.

That hope withered as the two men turned a corner and found themselves looking down into a vast cavern lit by glowing green lanterns and littered with crates. They had no problem recognising the skaven lair. All their wandering through the maze of tunnels had done was to bring them back to the place they started.

Visscher clenched his fist in impotent rage, despair clutching at his very soul. Their bold escape had come to nothing!

It was Seeckt who pointed out the change that had come across the cavern. A grey mist hovered above the floor, almost concealing the furry bodies strewn about the slimy stones. There were hundreds of dead skaven littering the cavern. Visscher thought at first the mist might be some of their poison gas, that some accident had struck and annihilated the scheming rodents. Then, through a gap in the mist, he was able to get a good look at the dead ratmen. The bodies were viciously mutilated, hacked and torn in an abominable manner. What had happened here had been no accident, but a massacre.

'They're all dead,' Visscher whispered. 'How?'

Seeckt shook his head, unable to conceive an answer. He turned his gaze across the cavern, then froze. He grabbed Visscher's shoulder, turning the him so he faced the far end of the chamber.

On the ground, mutilated as badly as any of the ratkin, was the body of Gustav Mertens. But it wasn't the lunatic's corpse that arrested the attention of the men. It was the thing walking off into the darkness, vanishing into a mist-choked passageway. Taller than skaven or man, its body covered in slimy green skin, its beaked head twisted into a fanged snout and great baleful eye. A single eye, shining with malefic intelligence, exuding the immortal hate of an eldritch race.

'When Gnawlitch Shun chose a legend to hide his raiders,' Seeckt whispered, 'he should have made sure the legend wasn't real.'

IT TOOK MORE courage than either of the men thought he possessed to descend into the mist-choked cavern, but necessity forced them to climb down from their perch and brave their fears. They tried not to look too closely at the dead skaven as they picked their way across the devastated lair.

Visscher, however, could not quite constrain his curiosity on one point. As the two men passed one of the boxes the ratmen had stolen from the missing ships, he stopped to open it. The riverwarden almost gagged at what he saw. The boxes were filled with wood shavings, but buried amongst the material were grotesque objects about the size of a human hand. They were squishy yet covered in a leathery skein that made them rough and resilient. In shape… there was a horrible resemblance to a human infant.

Visscher turned away from the box in disgust. Seeckt glowered at him.

'You shouldn't have done that,' the agent told him.

'Handrich's Purse!' Visscher exclaimed. 'What are they?'

Seeckt's eyes grew cold. The agent paced through the mist. 'They're skaven pups, or at least they were. They were killed at birth and then injected with certain chemicals. The brood-mothers, the creatures that birth all skaven, will eat a dead or weak pup so they can produce more milk for their healthy whelps.'

Visscher shook his head, sickened by the image Seeckt's words evoked. 'Someone hopes to… to poison…'

'The chemicals in these bodies would react with the brood-mother,' Seeckt explained. 'They'd make her produce a stronger litter. Black furred skaven, strong warrior-types. Clan Scuten needs warriors. Clan Moulder agreed to help them get them, but Gnawlitch Shun decided to intercept the shipments.'

The riverwarden gawped as he heard Seeckt speak. 'How… how do you…'

'How do I know all this?' Seeckt frowned and there was a trace of sadness in his eyes. 'The burghers pay me well for my services, but the skaven pay me better.' Before Visscher could react, Seeckt sprang at him. While the riverwarden had been busy with the box, Seeckt had recovered a sword from one of the dead ratmen. The skaven blade slashed across Visscher's neck. Taken by surprise, the man could only stare in uncomprehending horror as his life gushed across the slimy floor.

Seeckt turned away from the murdered man. It sat ill with him to kill a man who had saved his life, but he knew the riverwarden had to die. If not here, then when they returned to the *Shakerlo*. By now the skaven hidden in the ship's hold would have finished off the crew and cleaned up the bodies of Gnawlitch Shun's pirates. It would have been inconvenient to have Visscher tagging along when Seeckt went back to meet his employers. It was better this way.

Casting a last anxious look towards the tunnel he had seen the marsh daemon exit, Hein van Seeckt hurried towards the rock pile where Gnawlitch Shun had lorded over his minions. It was too much to hope that the Grand Warlock had shared the fate of the other skaven. A moment's inspection proved Seeckt's suspicions. The skaven overlord had built his perch so close to the roof of the cavern so that he could be close to a hidden bolthole.

Seeckt felt a certain irony employing his enemy's escape route. He was certain that little detail would bring an amused titter from Seerlord Tisqueek when he reported to him.

One day, the teeming hordes of skavendom would sweep away the Empire. When that happened, Seeckt intended to have enough gold to live quite handsomely someplace far away.

COMMANDER SHADOW

Braden Campbell

I AM A warrior of the fire caste. I have seen the carnage of battle before, wherever the Greater Good has struggled to overcome the dark barbarity so prevalent across the galaxy. Death and destruction are distasteful, yes, but I now know the deeper truth. They are an inevitable by-product of our people's civilising mission. *They cannot be avoided, and thus must be embraced.* That is a lesson not found in the curricula of the military colleges on Bork'an. That is something only my time here as Overseer of Cytheria could teach me.

The battle of Herzen Ridge is where it began. My enlightenment, that is, not our conflict with the gue'la rebels. That, as you well know, is a struggle that has dragged on for quite some time. We made great strides initially. By the third day of our occupation, we had destroyed an entire armoured regiment of the planet's primary defence force, the warriors of the 'Ka'Tashun Sept'. Yet, despite the fact that they had been decisively beaten in honourable combat, they refused to acquiesce. Remnants of their units retreated into the jungles and continued to engage us in a most uncivilised manner. They abandoned whatever standard military uniforms they might have once worn, making them visually indistinguishable from the gue'la citizenry who had submitted to our authority. They would remain hidden instead of openly presenting themselves, and would only attack vulnerable targets. So underhanded were their methods, so ignoble, that there existed no word in our language to describe it. My attaché, Por'el Tan'bay, eventually taught me the gue'la term for such violent opposition: 'insurgency.'

What kind of a people would consider this an acceptable methodology? That's the question I should have been asking myself all along; because the answer, when arrived at, would have clearly showed me the form my response should have taken. Instead, I dawdled. I tried to negotiate with them. I appealed to their reason. I hoped against hope that they would eventually come to their senses and see the futility of resistance. Then, I was called out to Marae'Taa Gorge.

For fear of Ka'Tashun snipers, I travelled via modified Piranha. The normally open top of the skimmer was now covered by a thick, windowless canopy. Even the cockpit was completely sealed. My pilot navigated with the aid of vidscreens and cameras mounted on the hull. Thus, I was unable to see anything of the surrounding countryside as I drew close to the site, but I could imagine the scenery blurring past. We were far beyond the plains by now, heading into the jungle highland with its dark red foliage, raging rivers, and jagged, broken topography. To one side of me was the mag-lev line; the track, when completed, would link Cytheria's two largest colony sites together with high-speed monorails.

Infrastructure. That's what the Tau Empire brings. When I first arrived here, the gue'la lived in a shameful state with their machinery in disrepair and their urban centres nothing but crumbling ruins. They believed this to be quite acceptable, for they had never known otherwise. I began to change all that. Before long, Cytheria had clean water to drink and fresh food to eat. Ample power ran to structurally sound buildings. Still, the Ka'Tashun called us oppressors. They were doing so even as I travelled to the gorge. All morning, the airwaves had been filled with their pirate signal, claiming responsibility for the attack on the railhead.

'The enemy is reeling,' a voice proclaimed through the static. 'Today, we have struck a decisive blow for freedom, and in the days and weeks to come, we will do it again and again. We will not rest until the xenos have been eradicated. Take heart citizens, for the Emperor is on our side. His wrath is coming, and will soon deliver us from the oppression of the tau!'

No one had yet been able to discern the source of these transmissions. It was maddening.

The vehicle slowed, and the canopy opened. As I climbed out of the piranha's rear compartment, I was immediately met by Tan'bay; typical of him to have arrived on the scene before me. I first met him the day the annexation of Cytheria began and had found him to be the epitome of the water caste ever since. He was always prepared with whatever pertinent information I might need, even before I myself realised that I required it. His demeanour was one of unchanging calm. He seemed never to show worry or doubt. When he spoke, his sentences flowed unceasingly, free from any pauses or interruptions of thought.

Tan'bay's hands were folded inside the voluminous sleeves of his robe as he bowed in deference. In the sky, an orange sun beat down, but his enormously brimmed hat kept his placid face in shadow. True to his years of training in the fields of diplomacy and interspecies negotiation, he constantly referred to himself using majestic, plural pronouns. One could actually hear the capitalisation in his voice. It was as if, when he spoke, he did so on behalf of the entire Tau race.

'The Shas'o honours us with his presence,' he lilted. 'May it please him to hear our initial assessment of the events preceding his arrival?'

Tan'bay was standing so close that I couldn't see past him. 'What is it?' I asked gruffly. I couldn't recall the last time I'd had more than a few hours of sleep. 'What's happened?'

'Our people have suffered yet another attack at the hands of the renegade gue'la of the Ka'Tashun Sept,' he said. 'A small contingent of fire warriors, assigned to guard the site, have fallen in battle, and will be remembered with all due honour for their valiant defence. The greater number of casualties consists of members of the earth caste; engineers and technicians involved in the building of the mag-lev bridge, which, to my lasting sadness, I must report has been effectively destroyed.'

I pushed past him then, and he dutifully melted off to one side. Marae'Taa Gorge, for those of you unfamiliar with Cytheria, is part of a massive chasm that bisects most of the continent. A river, which to my knowledge has never been named, rushes along the bottom. On average, the distance between the canyon walls is quite wide but in this one particular place, they are narrow. It was, therefore, a natural place to construct a crossing for the mag-lev system. I had seen the architectural designs months before. I am no expert, but I thought them to be quite aesthetically pleasing. The Fio'o in charge of the project was smiling as he described it, but I doubted he would be doing so now. The completed portion of the bridge had been firebombed; hit repeatedly with rockets and shaped explosive charges. Where once there had been graceful, white curves and support pillars, there was now only a twisted, blackened thing; a metal skeleton that sent plumes of acrid smoke up into the air even as the superstructure bowed down towards the river.

Then I saw the bodies. The rapid response team was reverently arranging them into two groups, earth caste on one side and fire warriors on the other. Within these, the fallen were being further organised into rows and columns from those with the highest rank and station to the lowest. Later, in accordance with caste traditions as old as the Greater Good itself, the workers would be buried and the soldiers would be cremated. The order and civility of it all should have given me some sense of peace, but it did not. The sheer number of the dead overrode such feelings.

'Four hundred and seventy-seven killed,' Tan'bay said gently. 'None wounded.'

I turned to face him. 'You mean there are no survivors? Not one?'

The man's face was impassive. 'It is half the reason we requested the Shas'o come in person.'

I blinked in the intensifying noon-day sun. 'What's the other half?'

SEVERAL BUILDINGS WERE still standing intact near the destroyed bridge. Tan'bay led me into one that, until recently, had been a facility for repairing heavy lifting equipment. It was now a makeshift field command. As we entered, several fire warriors of middling rank stopped their busy activities to bow. I was taken into a small office that contained two chairs set before a large vidscreen. On a nearby table lay a collection of metal tubes in varying sizes. As I seated myself, Tan'bay closed the door and dimmed the lights. He pulled a data crystal from some hidden pocket and, after inserting it into the machine, poured himself soundlessly into the chair next to mine.

The scenes that flicked past me were memory captures retrieved from damaged or destroyed security drones. They must have been stationed not only on the bridge itself but all around the compound, for the perspective was constantly changing. Through their electronic eyes, I watched with growing horror as the Ka'Tashuns launched their early morning assault.

No one saw the first barrage coming, but it was certainly audible. There was a series of muffled booms, followed by a high-pitched whistling. Many of the earth caste looked around in puzzlement, or turned to ask one another if they had heard the same thing. Then the first of the missiles slammed into the bridge's support pillars. The structure shook and, as the workers began to flee, part of the deck twisted to one side. With a terrible, shearing sound, the entire thing sagged downwards. Those who had been trying to escape clawed frantically for handholds, but there were few to be found. Their eyes were wide as they fell off the bridge, tumbling down, down into the gorge to smash apart on the jagged rocks or drown in the churning water.

The element of surprise was now spent. Unlike the workers, our fire warriors were calm, disciplined. Within seconds they had formed into cohesive squads, and began to shoot back. Their pulse rifles tore the tree line to shreds with crackling beams of energy. Even the drones were firing now, following their programming and networking themselves into squadrons. Despite all this outpouring of fire, it was impossible to tell if any of the Ka'Tashuns were actually being hit, ensconced as they were in the jungle foliage. The quiet, ordered peace of the morning was now filled with the cacophony of battle.

There were small explosions all around. The ground was being cratered by some type of shell or heavy canister. Then two things happened. The workers began to clutch their necks and collapse on the ground and the heads of the fire warriors began to snap back sharply as, one after the other, they fell down dead. A fine, red smoke began to drift across the scene. At first, I didn't understand what I was seeing. The fire warriors were being specifically targeted by long-range snipers; that much was obvious. But given the speed with which they were being cut down, the number of enemy marksmen hiding out there must have been great. The workers and engineers who had collapsed were now clawing the air, seemingly oblivious to everything else around them. Their eyes were bulging and their faces began to turn a deep purple. Suddenly, one of them shuddered so violently that I could hear his spine break. Something exploded from his mouth and nose. His body shook, and he was still. The same thing was happening to all of them now. Every tau not wearing a suit of environmental battle armour was likewise dying in a suffocating, epileptic fit. The red smoke thickened as it drifted across the scene.

I looked over at Tan'bay. 'Some kind of chemical agent?'

Tan'bay rolled one hand over in the air, a gesture he did often as if he were casting something away. 'The Ka'Tashun Sept is widely known to employ hyperlethal poisons.'

'Their snipers, yes' I replied sternly. I had studied the Ka'Tashun's methods and tactics down to the most minute of details. 'But never like this. This is being delivered in shell casings. That implies portable mortars or shoulder-mounted launchers.'

The vidscreen was a panorama of death now. Hundreds of earth caste lay twisted and broken on the ground. Red foam filled their every orifice. My fellow warriors were also gone. Only the drones remained, but they were being quickly dispatched by volleys of lasers. Those that did not explode outright, wobbled as their flight systems failed. When they crashed, they recorded a world turned at odd angles, where the land and sky were reversed or completely knocked askew.

'And in such a volume,' I continued. 'How could they produce so many toxins with their limited resources?'

'We believe the compound to be organic in nature,' Tan'bay said. 'I regret to inform the Shas'o, it is also most abundant in the deep jungle areas of this world to which our foe has now retreated.'

With that, he rose and went to the table. He picked up one of the grey metal tubes and handed it to me. It was sealed at one end and had a diameter large enough to accommodate my forearm. A fine, red, powdery residue clung to the interior. I wiped some off with my finger and immediately felt a stab of burning pain.

'These are sporepod blooms,' I said with realisation. The interior of Cytheria's major landmass was a steaming, foetid rainforest so thick as to be nearly impassable. It was home to all manner of biting, poisonous things, but few as bad as the hata'le bush. The fruit of this leafy, burgundy-coloured plant was a hollow pod about the size of a clenched fist. The slightest amount of pressure would cause it to spew forth its spores in a misty cloud. They were harmful to both tau and gue'la alike, burning any exposed skin they might land on, and causing haemorrhaging if ingested.

'Indeed they are,' Tan'bay replied.

'They can be dangerous, but not deadly. Certainly not like this.' I gestured towards the vidscreen where the slaughter continued to play itself out.

Tan'bay's voice was clinically calm. 'It appears that the Ka'Tashuns have somehow managed to amplify the plant's natural toxicity. The modified blooms are taken into the mucous membranes of the respiratory tract, where they begin to reproduce almost instantly. The victims not only bleed internally and go into toxic shock, but end up asphyxiating themselves as a hata'la bush literally takes root in their chest and nasal cavities. The sponge-like growth you see coming out of the victims' mouths are actually their lungs being forced outwards by the expanding plant.'

'How?' I asked. 'How could they have done this?'

'To that, Shas'o, We regretfully have no answer. Yet one thing is certain. What you now face is a weapon that works on two levels. The first as seen demonstrated here, but secondly, and of perhaps a more pressing concern, is the fear that it will generate; fear among our populace, both tau and acculturated gue'la. Fear leads to distrust, distrust to disharmony, and that, as the Shas'o well knows, is anathema to the Greater Good.'

'Using fear as a weapon,' I mused. The Ka'Tashun barbarity was physically sickening. I rose quickly, and turned to leave. Then I heard a voice speaking in the harsh language of the enemy.

'Sir, this one's still running.'

My head snapped back towards the vidscreen. One of the drones, whose camera eye was still functioning, had been lifted from where it had crashed. The image jostled for a moment, then came to rest on a gue'la's face. His skin was painted thick with mud and some kind of red camouflage. His mouth and jaw were covered by a stubbly, animalistic growth of fur. His brow was dark and heavy, and his eyes blazed with a white-hot hatred.

'Shas'o Rra?' he sneered. 'Can you hear me?'

I knew at once who it was by the insulting name he used. Only one person on Cytheria had ever called me that. Ezra Mihalik, the self-proclaimed leader of the Ka'Tashun Sept.

'Of course you can,' Ezra continued. 'That diplomat of yours will drag you out here in the name of procedure. And what's more, someone of your education, you'll want to see this first-hand.'

Off-camera, there was the sound of laughing.

'I'll be brief. This attack was a test and, I think, a pretty effective one. You and all your forces have eight days to leave Cytheria. If you don't, my men will release these spores into each and every population centre on the planet. And don't think I won't actually do it because my fellow humans would also be killed. You should know that, as far as I'm concerned, anyone who isn't helping to resist you is collaborating with you, and they deserve what they get.

'Eight days, Shas'o Rra, or watch your people die.' He looked away and nodded. The drone dropped back to the ground. From its new vantage point, I watched as several sets of boots walked away.

Tan'bay said nothing. Perhaps he was giving me time to think. Or perhaps there was simply nothing more to be said. I had one week to break the resistance. One week to somehow find Ezra Milhalik, and stop him. *I'll show you*, I remember thinking. *I am no 'Commander Shadow'.*

EZRA MIHALIK HAD come up with his insulting name for me during our first and only negotiations. This was perhaps a month prior to the attack on the railhead. I was still suffering under the delusion that he was a logical being. So I sent out word that I would meet with Mihalik and try to put an end to the Cytherian conflict. A short time later, my offer was accepted. Two heavily muscled Ka'Tashun soldiers arrived at the gates of my compound. They were shirtless, dressed in heavy boots and camouflage-patterned pants. Each of them wore a bright red cloth tied around their heads. They were armed only with knives. One of them carried some kind of large communications device strapped to his back. They told the guards that they were envoys from the Ka'Tashun Sept come to see me, but were otherwise stoic and silent.

Once they had been disarmed and scanned, they were brought into a spacious meeting room where Tan'bay and I were already waiting. They placed the bulky device on the table in front of me, switched it on, and then stepped back with their hands clasped behind their backs. A voice began to emanate from a tiny speaker in the machine. It spoke in the choppy, harsh language of the gue'la. Fortunately, I spoke it too.

'Are we good? Can you hear me?' it said.

'Yes,' I replied, 'I can hear you. To whom am I speaking?'

'Why, this is Ezra Mihalik, commander of the fifty-sixth Ka'Tashun Company. I also speak for the few remaining members of two other Ka'Tashun companies, the twenty-sixth and fifty-first.'

'I see. I take it then that you have chosen not to meet with us in person.'

'You're very perceptive,' the voice replied.

I looked at the two Ka'Tashuns. Their faces were impassive, but behind their eyes, they were smiling.

Tan'bay leaned forwards and launched into his carefully prepared opening. 'Commander, this is Por'el Tan'bay speaking on behalf of the Tau Empire, and may we begin by saying how pleased we are that you have agreed to negotiate with us, no matter the forum. If our two peoples can learn to live together in peace, then the benefits for both sides will, without doubt, be enormous.'

'Emperor wept,' Mihalik groaned. 'Are you the guy in charge?'

'If you are asking as to whether or not we are directly responsible for Cytheria's pacification and regime change, then, no. If, however–'

'Fine' Mihalik interrupted. 'Then let me talk to the one who is.'

I sat forward in my chair and addressed the transmitter. 'I am the person in command of our military forces.'

'Ah, good.' There was a creaking in the background as Mihalik leaned back into whatever he was sitting on. 'What do I call you?'

'I have not yet chosen a name,' I said slowly. 'You may address me by my rank: Shas'o.'

Mihalik chuckled softly. 'You… you have not yet chosen a name?' he parroted. 'What the hell does that mean?'

Tan'bay answered him with a lesson in protocol. 'Personal names should only be used between family members and close friends. At all other times, it is proper to address others according to their station in life. The only exception would be for those who have earned the right to embellish their title with simple descriptors, certain achievements, or places of importance.'

'And you haven't any of those, is that it?' Mihalik asked me.

I was anxious to move past such a personal subject. 'I am a commander of the fire caste. Thus, you will address me as Shas'o.'

'You said that means 'commander', right?'

'Correct.' I had the growing suspicion that the voice on the other end of the radio had no intention of negotiating for peace. 'Let us begin by–'

'Just commander,' Mihalik mused. 'Nothing else. Because you haven't chosen the name yet. Or because you haven't earned it?'

I took a moment to consider my reply. Before I could say anything more however, Mihalik spoke again. His voice was low and direct.

'They put you in charge of a whole planet, so this can't be your first time out.'

I cleared my throat. 'It is not. I have survived four trials by fire.'

'But there was nothing in those four that stood out enough for you to add them to your name, huh? And if 'trial by fire' is Tau for 'tour of duty', then how did you earn your rank with so little experience?'

'Commander Mihalik,' I began.

'Oh, you can call me Ezra. I have a name.'

'Ezra, then. If you must know, I was given the rank of Shas'o when I graduated from the most prestigious military training centre in all the Empire. I may have only completed four trials, but I have studied the art of war for half my life. It would be a mistake for you to underestimate me.' I smiled then, confident that the weight of my credentials would put this backwater rebel leader in his place.

'So,' Mihalik said after a pause, 'you read about war in a bunch of books, and now you think you have what it takes to actually conduct one. You're the shadow of a commander. You've got no substance. Hey, diplomat, how do you say 'shadow' in Tau?'

If Tan'bay was as outraged as I was he didn't show it. 'Rra,' he replied helpfully.

'Then that's what I'll call you: Shas'o Rra,' he said, once again speaking to me. 'What do you think of that?'

'I don't care for it,' I said between clenched teeth. 'May we return to the subject of negotiating a ceasefire?'

For a long moment the only sound coming from the machine was background static. The silence stretched out so long in fact, that I thought the transmission had somehow been cut off. I was about to ask Mihalik if he was still there when he spoke up.

'No,' he said flatly.

'No what?' I asked, puzzled.

'No, we can't discuss a ceasefire. You see, Shas'o Rra, you and I are a little bit alike. I've spent half my life studying war too. Only I didn't do it in some nice, clean school. I did it in swamps, and jungles, and burning cities. I learned about wars by actually being in them.

'So, in the interests of... diplomacy, I'll give you a choice. You can either pack up all your men, all your little drones and all your fancy war machines and go back to wherever it is you come from, or you can stay here and try to take me on. You haven't got what it takes to beat me, I know that now, but I promise you'll get a *real* education while you try.'

'I have two of your men here, Ezra,' I warned him.

'Yeah, good men. They volunteered for this mission. You know, what you should do is torture them for information and then kill them. But I figure you'll just set them free. They're unarmed, they haven't done you any harm, and it would be the civil thing to do. But maybe you'll prove me wrong. Either way, they're prepared.' With that, he signed off. 'See you around, Shas'o Rra.'

I released his men.

It didn't take long to discover where the Ka'Tashun were hiding. Their radio broadcast was easy to trace. At first, I thought this was strange. The enemy were very adept at relocating themselves and their dwindling supplies of weapons and equipment. Every time that our forces would locate and destroy one of their hiding spots, they would simply reappear days later in a new one. Only after I had met with Kor'el Che'rod did I understand.

Like all members of the air caste, everything about Che'rod was long and thin. A flex-screen map was spread out on my desk and he pointed to a highlighted area with a finger that was twice the length of mine. 'Here,' he said. His voice was a throaty whisper. 'Herzon Ridge.'

I leaned in to get a closer look. Che'rod was pointing to a plateau in the deepest heart of the jungle. It appeared to be completely inaccessible.

'You're certain?' I asked.

His face contorted slightly. 'There is no doubt, Shas'o. My pilots are most skilled. This is the location that you seek.'

I blanched. Of course he was certain. Kor'el Che'rod was not only a decorated veteran with far more trials to his name than I, but he was also many years my senior. How dare I question the validity of his actions like that? The lack of sleep was beginning to affect my judgment.

Tan'bay, seated in a corner, immediately came to my rescue. 'We are certain the Shas'o meant no disrespect,' he said. 'However, the stakes in this particular instance are so high that there cannot be the slightest doubt. We are certain the Kor'el would agree?'

Che'rod's eyes flicked from Tan'bay, to myself, and back again. 'Indeed,' he breathed. He squared his narrow shoulders and continued. 'The renegade gue'la are broadcasting their propaganda across half the planet, utilising a transmitter far more powerful than any they have in the past. It was quite easy to triangulate its source. The location was then visually identified using orbital satellite imagery, and double-checked by multiple overhead flybys with Barracuda-class fighters.'

Che'rod tapped the screen, zooming in on the ridge. A few outlines of buildings could be glimpsed through the otherwise unbroken canopy of red leaves. 'According to records, these structures are a botanical research station, constructed by the gue'la and dating back several centuries.'

'A botanical research station,' Tan'bay murmured. 'That would explain how the Ka'Tashun are able to produce so many altered sporepod blooms.'

'Our sensor sweeps indicate the presence of between sixty and seventy personnel. There is no evidence of any vehicles or anti-air defences.' His report concluded, Che'rod clasped his hands behind his back and waited.

'This is most excellent, Kor'el,' I said, beaming. That arrogant fool, Mihalik, had let his pride cloud his actions. His braggart radio messages would be his undoing. Things were finally about to turn around on this accursed planet. 'It would appear Herzon Ridge is where control of Cytheria will be secured once and for all, and the honour falls to you and your men. You may begin bombing at once.'

I could see it now. Plasma torpedoes would fall from the sky like a cleansing rain, and the cyclonic winds generated by the exploding cores would sweep the Ka'Tashun's ashes away. It would be quick and painless. A far better end than they deserved. *Who's the shadow of a commander now, Mihalik?* I thought.

Kor'el Che'rod was frowning. 'With all due respect, Shas'o, given the apparent nature of the gue'la bio-weapon, that would be most unadvisable.'

I narrowed my eyes at him, but a moment later understood. Of course.

Whatever spores weren't consumed in the initial explosions would be carried up into the atmosphere by the shockwaves. The prevailing winds would then spread them across half of Cytheria. No wonder then that Mihalik was unabashedly transmitting his location. He knew quite well that I daren't vaporise his stronghold from the air.

'Again, he mocks me.'

'Shas'o?' Che'rod asked, and I realised that I had been thinking out loud.

I cleared my throat to compose myself, and then nodded towards the door. 'I understand, Kor'el,' I said. 'You have executed your duties in this matter with honour and efficiency. Take my thanks to your men.'

Che'rod bowed his head, and left. I stared down at the map until my eyes were burning. The ridge couldn't be attacked from the air, which left a ground assault as the only option. However, the jungle was far too thick for sufficient numbers of battle suits to operate in, and any fire warriors sent in on foot would simply end up as fodder for Ka'Tashun traps and ambushes. My enemy seemed untouchable. Perhaps Mihalik had been right after all. All my years of study on Bork'an had failed to prepare me for this type of scenario.

'There is a gue'la expression,' Tan'bay said softly after some moments, 'that the Shas'o might be wise to meditate on. "One cannot fight fire with fire".'

I scowled at him. 'That only proves what a backward people they are. Fire is the element of war. Soldiers should always be pitted against other soldiers. Anything else would be uncivilised.'

'Then the Shas'o would agree the axiom is incorrect; that in effect, the only way to fight fire is with fire? That like should be met with like?'

'I would,' I snapped without consideration.

Tan'bay pressed his fingers together, and lifted his head to gaze up at the ceiling. At the time, I took it to be a pose of contemplation. Now I suspect that he was intentionally avoiding eye contact. He inhaled deeply and said, 'We are an enlightened people. The methods of fighting as have been displayed by our enemies on this planet are simply not in our nature, and that is well. However, there exist within the Empire certain other species who, owing mostly to cultural retardation, are not so civil. We have seen them in combat. They can be… quite effective. '

Outside, the sun was setting. The room began to darken.

'Where was this?'

'Along the eastern edge of the Empire. In our youth, we undertook a prolonged tour of the worlds beyond the Perdus Rift.'

There was a silence between us. Tan'bay waited. He was an advisor, not a military commander. His job was to offer avenues of action, to open doors. Whether or not I followed or stepped through was left entirely up to me.

'Where is the closest War Sphere?' I said at last.

'As it so happens, there is one in-system.'

'Contact it.'

Tan'bay's robes rustled as he stood. He bowed his head and spread his arms wide. 'It is an honour to serve the Shas'o,' he said.

When he was gone, I moved to the window and stared out across the grounds. Dark clouds were gathering across a violet sky. Out in the jungle, Ezra Mihalik was sitting atop Herzon Ridge, smugly thinking that he had beaten me. He was positive that I lacked the bloodlust required to shift him, and he was right. Such a thing was beyond a tau such as myself. Not so for the kroot.

During my officer's training on Bork'an, I studied all of the tau's various alien allies. The kroot were even taller than the air caste, but not at all fragile. Their limbs were taut with ropey muscles. Their skin was greasy leather. Their heads were crowned with quills and their faces dominated by a massive, serrated beak. They had a knack for picking up new languages and when they slept, they did so lightly, crouched together in large groups. They were also ferocious cannibals. They believed that by eating the remains of their fallen enemies, they could gain their strengths. This may have been more than primitive superstition, in fact. Scientists within the Empire were of the opinion that something in the kroot genetic structure did indeed cause them to take on the characteristics of whatever they ate. Despite decades of trying, no one had been able to break them of this particularly barbaric trait. Still, they were so adept in certain areas that commanders across the Empire were willing to turn a blind eye to it. Their home world, Pech, was covered in vast coniferous forests, and thus, they were renowned for their ability to move through even the thickest cover at great speed and in absolute silence.

They were exactly what I needed with which to fight the Ka'Tashuns. Fire with fire.

I PLANNED TO lead them myself. Allies though they may be, a people as primitive and uncivilised as the kroot must still be supervised. More importantly though, I was now determined to kill Ezra Mihalik personally. He would not be captured or subdued. Nor was he going to die in an honourable or gentlemanly way. I was going to shoot him into pieces and leave him in the jungle as fodder for the beasts. It was what he deserved.

For the next three days, I met with earth caste engineers and modified a stealth battle suit specifically for my needs. It was nearly completed when Tan'bay appeared to tell me that the kroot had arrived. Dawn was still hours away and the sky was pouring rain. I walked out of the mechanical bay to appraise them. There were forty in all. They stood barefoot in the mud, naked, save for a few scraps of leather armour. Their skin, the grungy brown colour of dead leaves, was exuding a greasy substance that made the rainwater bead and run off. They stank of dirt and sweat, salty and earthy. In their taloned hands they each clutched a long-barrelled rifle made of wood and tarnished metal. Some of these were adorned with clusters of feathers or glass beads strung on pieces of copper wire. Every one of them was capped with a primitive bayonet. Several canvas packs lay scattered about them. Off to one side, a pack of roughly two dozen kroot hounds snorted about in the sopping ground and nipped at one another viciously.

Tan'bay gestured, and one particular kroot stepped forward. He wore a string of half-chewed bones around his waist, and had applied some kind of white makeup underneath his left eye. Otherwise, he would have been completely indistinguishable from the rest. They all look alike to me.

'Shas'o,' Tan'bay announced loudly, 'may it please you to meet Shaper Awl.' I nodded slightly

Awl made a clicking noise from somewhere in the back of his throat. 'We have sworn to fight for the tau.' The pitch and tone of his voice was disturbingly melodic, like birdsong echoing up from the bottom of a well. 'Their enemies are our enemies. Lead on. We will follow.'

'I take it you have been briefed on the nature of this mission?' I asked him. 'You know our objective?'

Awl had no lips with which to smile. Instead he opened up his beak, and clacked his thick tongue against the roof of his mouth. 'You shall have your prize,' he said slyly. He whistled sharply to the other kroot, and they began to gather what meagre supplies they had. As they did so, Tan'bay moved to my side.

'Good fortune to you, Shas'o. We will take our leave now, and hope to see you again upon your safe return.'

'Wish you were coming along?' I asked, raising an eyebrow.

'The Shas'o has no need of us,' Tan'bay replied. He looked at the kroot, then turned back to me. His face had a gravity to it that I had never seen before. 'There will be no diplomacy where he now goes.'

A pair of drop-ships waited on the nearby landing field. By the time I had encased myself into the stealth suit, the kroot had already clambered aboard. I joined them, sealed the ramp behind me, and signalled for the pilots to take off. Within minutes, we were airborne, speeding over the plains towards the jungle lowlands. I spent the time in silence, checking and rechecking my suit's systems. I synchronised its inbuilt positional relay to the satellites above, and studied our insertion route on my heads-up display. I ran a test on the integrated shield generator. Finally, I familiarised myself with the automatic stimulant injector, an experimental piece of technology that would flood my bloodstream with painkillers should I become wounded. The kroot, on the other hand, jabbered incessantly in their squawking, clicking, chirping native language. They made barking sounds that I assumed were laughter.

Awl haphazardly poured some kind of thin oil all over his rifle, then produced a leather rag and began to work it into all the mechanical housings. He seemed to take no notice of how the others behaved until we were very near the landing zone.

The lights in the troop compartment changed from white to yellow, and we began our descent. Awl barked for his troops to get ready, and they immediately fell silent. The aft ramp opened, and within a minute, we were out. The engines flared as the drop-ships rocketed away. I watched them vanish up into the heavy clouds above. When I turned back, the kroot were already moving swiftly into the thickening under-brush. I activated my suit's adaptive camouflage and followed. It was not always easy. The kroot preferred to climb up into the trees and swing from limb to limb. The hounds kept pace on the ground. They raced from one trunk to another, constantly snorting and sniffing the air.

The rain had let up, but very little light managed to filter through the foliage above. I walked along the forest floor surrounded by a deep gloom. I saw increasing numbers of hata'le bushes, all of them picked clean of their sporepods. Hours later, as I pushed my way through a thorny shrub twice my height, I stopped to find Awl crouched on the ground ahead. His head was cocked to one side. All about him, kroot were clinging to the sides of the trees. The second he saw me, his clenched fist snapped up, and I froze. Without saying a word, he gingerly brushed at the ground before him. Buried just below the surface there was some kind of explosive device.

Awl spoke to his warriors in a rapid string of squeaks, and they van-ished back up into the trees. He turned to me. 'Plasma mine,' he said quietly. 'Short proximity sensor.' Then, with a single bound, he too leapt back up into the jungle above. I carefully manoeuvred around the trap, all the while amazed how Awl had known it was there. I double-checked my scanners, but there were no telltales. Whatever materials the Ka'Tashuns had used to make their landmines, they did not register.

The afternoon was growing late and the rain had begun again when we arrived at Herzon Ridge. I cautiously moved forward and joined Awl, who was lying prone beneath a bushy shrub. I saw no sign of the other kroot, but knew that they couldn't be far off. Awl pointed to his eyes, then flicked a talon forwards. Ahead of us was a rough clearing with three sizable buildings. The first was low to the ground and rectangular-shaped. It had a single large door set into one face, and only the thinnest of slots for windows. A tall, metal tower adorned with dishes was affixed to its otherwise flat roof. The second structure was an enormous glass-enclosed dome filled with plants and greenery; a multitude of cylindrical storage tanks that ran along one side of it. The third building, set apart from the other two, was actually more of a raised, flat area. It was octagonal in shape, and stood atop four squat pillars. Armoured walls hung from every side, but these look rusted and long since used.

'Landing platform,' I whispered to Awl.

He nodded, and pointed to the thickly shadowed area underneath it. 'There are gue'la under there. Thirty or so by the smell. They must not like the rain.'

Switching my optics into the infrared, the enemy platoon sprang to life. The Ka'Tashuns, for reasons I had never been able to fathom, eschewed environmental combat armour. Their multiple areas of exposed skin therefore lit up my display in brilliant hues as they radiated their body heat. Oddly, when I looked back at the kroot shaper, he was nearly the same colour as the surrounding jungle. The disgusting grease that his skin exuded was apparently some natural adaptation for stealth.

'More over there,' I said, indicating the area between the glass dome and the building with the radio tower. Another thirty men milled about. Underneath waterproofed tarps, I noted the telltale shapes of two huge machine guns; blocky things that fired kinetic bolts the size of my fist. 'I think they're expecting us.'

Awl grunted. 'We must strike quickly, and close the distance. We will stand little chance against their heavy guns. What is the Shas'o's command?'

'We'll divide in two. Take half your fighters and circle around to the left. Eliminate that unit near the glass dome. I'll go with the others and clear out the area beneath the landing field. Then, we converge on the final building.'

Without another word, Awl slithered backwards and vanished into the undergrowth. I made my way as close to the elevated pad as I dared, and found twenty kroot waiting for me. A dozen hounds lay in the mud, panting softly. I was about to ask how it was they kept the beasts so controlled and quiet, when the jungle around me exploded.

I had no idea how the Ka'Tashuns knew that we were about to strike, but it didn't matter. They opened up on us with everything they had. A mortar shell sailed up into the trees above me, and detonated. Huge shards of wood rained down. Lasers tore into the underbrush all around me, striking several of the kroot warriors. Their death screams were ear-piercing. A second shell of some kind landed directly amidst the hounds. The explosion lifted half of them high into the air and smashed them against the trees.

'Go! Go!' I shouted, but all the kroot still able to do so were already charging towards the Ka'Tashuns. I stood and ran into the clearing. I now saw that there were four groups sheltering underneath the landing platform. One of these contained a heavy weapon, and the kroot made straight for it. They leapt up into the air with their rifles clutched two-handed above their heads. Then they crashed down, caving in skulls and shattering limbs as they swung their weighted guns every which way. The remaining three Ka'Tashun squads backed up a few steps and prepped their rifles. I recognised the strategy. They weren't going to rush in and try to help their comrades. Instead, they were going to let them die, sacrificing one small unit so that the rest could gun the kroot down in a massive, point-blank volley.

The stealth suit's robotic exoskeleton amplified my every movement, and with a single bound, I had flanked them. The barrels of my burst cannon became a blur as I opened fire. Pulse blasts ricocheted off the nearest support column, and several of the Ka'Tashuns, forgetting about the kroot for a moment, ducked low. They searched about frantically, but my adaptive camouflage made me appear as little more than a moving blur, a ghost, a piece of the jungle come to life.

I am a shadow, I thought.

The kroot had finished slaughtering the heavy gun crew, and were moving towards a fresh target. More than a dozen Ka'Tashuns fired into them with their primitive laser weapons and sniper rifles. It had little effect. The kroot were like a wave of violence now, surging forwards and smashing into the foe. I continued to provide covering fire for them, but the truth was that they were doing fine without me. I gunned down the two gue'la closest to me and moved to yet another position.

There was one Ka'Tashun there that I took to be an officer of some kind. He wore a crimson rag tied over his hair, and his arms were covered with scars and tattoos. His sidearm was also larger and heavier than any of the weapons carried by the others. He levelled it and let loose with a bolt of plasma. It bounced harmlessly off of my shield generator, splashing across the surface of my battle suit in brilliant blue droplets. His face registered a look of stunned disbelief that was almost amusing. I let the burst cannon roar and he flew apart into gristly chunks.

For a moment, I stopped moving and drank in my surroundings. Lightning lit the clouds in ripples of purple. There were corpses everywhere. Many of the trees, I noted, were on fire, despite the pouring rain. Nearby, a pair of hounds were gnawing on a fallen Ka'Tashun. He was screaming obscenities and stabbing at them with his combat knife. They severed one of his arms and pulled off his face and he finally shut up. I watched several kroot use their rifles to sweep another man's legs out from under him. Then they beat him relentlessly, breaking his limbs and pulverising his ribcage. Across the clearing, there was an orange flash as one of the few remaining rebels used his flamer. Several hounds caught fire. They ran around in circles as they burned to death, barking and whining. I saw Awl, in retribution, kick the man in the head with such force that it nearly flew off. Less than a quarter of his kroot were still alive, but those that were had formed a ring around the final Ka'Tashun.

For a moment, I thought it must be Ezra Mihalik, cornered at last, and my pulse raced. As I ran closer though, I saw that it wasn't. He was just another officer, dressed similarly to the one I had blown apart a moment ago. He had a crimson head wrap and heavily tattooed arms. He held a sword in one hand that crackled and glowed, and in the other he had a pistol. His face was a portrait of defiance: his eyes narrowed and his teeth bared. He was a cornered animal. The last three hounds were circling around him, growling and snapping as they looked for an opening. It never occurred to me to put a stop to such cruelty. The kroot were delighted to see this sport, and I left them to it. I had prey of my own to find.

There was no movement in the glass dome. That left the flat roofed building as Mihalik's only possible remaining location. The solitary door did not appear so thick or armoured that I couldn't break it down, but I knew better. It would be trapped somehow, or would have half a dozen heavily armed men waiting just behind it. I followed the example of the kroot and simply avoided it altogether. I squatted down, then kicked out hard. The stealth suit's augmented legs and thrust assist boosters sent me rocketing upwards. As I descended, I pulled my legs in tight, and fired my burst cannon at the building's roof. When I landed, I again kicked out, crashing through the roof and landing in a crouch.

I sprayed the room. The pulse blasts sparked and snapped as they impacted on tables and chairs, blew through computer screens, shattered glass and overturned wooden supply crates. The ammo counter on my heads up display rolled backwards at a furious pace. Finally, I stopped. There was no one here. I was surrounded by all manner of destroyed electrical and scientific equipment, but a quick sensor check revealed it to be devoid of life. I briefly considered the possibility that the entire building was a trap of some kind; that it was about to explode and release the sporepod blooms across Cytheria. Then the audio pickups built into the suit registered something below me.

I saw now that there was a stairwell in one corner of the room. I moved to it and peered cautiously over the railing. Metal steps vanished down into a basement level. I amplified the background noise and heard the distinct sound of running feet. *Of course*, I thought as I descended after them, *attack and run. That's what you do, Ezra. No glorious last stands. No honourable self slaughter. Just run and live to fight another day. But not this time.*

At the bottom of the stairs was a long hallway roughly hewn into the bedrock. Multiple doorways branched off to the left and right. I followed the sounds, passing unoccupied rooms filled with beds, and a sizable eating area where food still steamed on plates. There was an open doorway at the end of the passage. I moved towards it and was met with a volley of laser fire. Most of it was safely absorbed with the additional armour plating I had specifically installed into the battlesuit, but as I barrelled into the next room, I felt a white-hot stab of pain in my left shoulder. Alarms lit up inside my face plate, informing me that my suit had been breached. Not a second later, there was a soothing, hissing sound as painkillers were automatically injected into my bloodstream, and topical medicines were applied to the wound.

I had charged into a generator room. Four huge, blocky fusion reactors provided cover for Mihalik's small cadre of veteran bodyguards. There was a heavy-looking blast door set into the back wall. There was a control panel beside it, at which Mihalik was frantically working. I raised my burst cannon, but before I could shoot, his men had rushed me. Three of them tackled me around the waist, hoping to knock me down. I leaned in to their charge and braced my legs against the doorway so as to remain upright. The fourth man activated a long melee weapon with jagged, metal teeth that blurred into motion. He drove it down across my helmet. My face was stung from a hundred shallow cuts as my faceplate shattered, but again, the suit's medical systems made even this pain a distant and irrelevant thing.

I cleared the chainsword out of the way with my burst cannon, then punched its wielder in the face with all the strength I could muster. His nose exploded with a spray of blood and a snapping of cartilage, and he stumbled back. To his fellows, I delivered a flurry of elbow strikes and low kicks until they too had been distanced from me. Before they could recover themselves, I shot them dead.

Mihalik froze in place. He had a pistol holstered on his hip, and a ridiculously oversized mechanical glove on one hand. The heavy door was open now. Beyond it, I could make out a vertical tunnel and a ladder. A warm breeze blew into the room.

His eyes flashed. 'Well,' he said slowly. 'I guess you don't plan to let me escape. Are you here to respectfully demand my surrender, then?'

I levelled my weapon at him.

'Oh,' he nodded. 'OK then.'

Mihalik dashed forwards with a speed of which I would not have thought him capable. He held one arm rigid across his body like a shield, while his other, the one bearing the robotic fist, wound up to deliver a crushing blow. Had the thing not been so heavy and cumbersome, he might well have killed me. However, its awkwardness worked to my benefit. I grasped his shirt and used his own momentum to throw him to the floor. He landed with a heavy thud, and tried to swing his armoured fist into my thigh. I stomped down, pinning it, and with a burst from my cannon, blew off his forearm. The mechanical hand skittered across the room.

The stump below his elbow fountained blood. He began gasping for breath, but I was taking no chances. With two powerful kicks, I broke both of his legs. Then, still holding him by his shirt, I began to drag him along the corridor and back up the stairs.

'Wha… what are you… what are you doing?' he sputtered.

'I promised myself that I would leave you to the beasts.' I said flatly.

Outside, it was still raining. The kroot were making a meal out of the dead Ka'Tashuns, tearing off pieces of them and shoving the meat, raw and dripping, into their beaks. When I emerged from the building, they rose to their feet.

I threw Mihalik down into the mud. Awl approached. He clacked his beak the way another creature might salivate before an especially delicious meal. The other kroot began to gather around. The rebel leader's eyes grew wide as he realised how it was about to end.

'Shas'o Rra,' he panted. 'I guess… I was wrong to… to call you that.'

'No,' I responded. 'As it happens, you weren't.'

I did not turn away as they ate him. Nor did I try to mentally block out his agonising screams. I simply stood there. I felt neither remorse, nor disgust, nor pity. I didn't even feel a sense of satisfaction or poetic justice. I felt nothing. I was totally and absolutely cold inside. I embraced it then, the name the gue'la gave me. Mihalik had called me the shadow of a commander. He meant it as an insult, but I no longer saw it that way. I would be Shas'o Alo'rra – Commander Cold Shadow – and wherever the enemies of the tau are hiding, I would be there… intangible… unfeeling.

There were other, smaller groups of Ka'tashun yet to be dealt with. So in the days that followed, I ordered that the remaining kroot, who had been in orbit until then, land on the surface of Cytheria. I unleashed them into the wilderness and gave them free reign to seek out and eliminate whatever resistance they found. For a time, it worked wonderfully. Their savagery was more than a match for the rebels, and their bellies grew fat with the flesh of the enemy. Cytheria became largely pacified. Recently however, I have received a number of disturbing reports. The kroot increasingly refuse to obey the orders of their tau superiors and have taken to wearing red scarves around their foreheads. They speak in the gue'la language when they think no one is listening. Perhaps worst of all, in my subsequent conversations with Shaper Awl, he has begun calling me Shas'o Rra.

HAMMER
AND BOLTER

ISSUE 9

THE ARKUNASHA WAR

Andy Chambers

CYMBALS AND DRUMS sounded tinny and distant in the thin, cold air as they welcomed him to the new world. Looking down from the top of the ramp, the shuttle's only passenger seemed surprised to find any kind of welcoming committee, even as small and dispirited as this one, awaiting him. High overhead, twin suns lit the scene with a fierce glare but little warmth; what little heat there was to be had was being ripped away by a chilling breeze filled with fine, irritating dust. Gentle ripples of rust-red sand marked the edge of the landing pad and marched off towards the foreshortened horizon with monotonous discipline. A small collection of domes, blocks and stubby towers in the mid-distance constituted the apparent entirety of Arkunasha's one and only colony, the handful of off-white shapes looking lonely and isolated on the too-wide canvas of an empty world.

The newcomer was tall and broad-shouldered, and showed scarification, unusual in a society with the capacity to heal any such blemish at will. A warrior, clearly, past his first flush of youth but still vital. There was a penetrating look to his dark eyes as he squinted through the glare and stinging dust at the welcoming party, wishing he had accepted a filter plug for his nasal slit when the shuttle pilot had offered him one. He beheld the tall, serene-looking profile of the colony leader and the squat shape of the chief engineer among a handful of others at the bottom of the ramp. One of the cymbal players, a wiry-looking fellow with blue facial markings, broke away from the small crowd and hurried upwards.

'Please to be meeting with the exalted prince, great warrior, I, unworthy associate, will conduct you hence if willing?'

'Of course, I...' But the low-ranking associate was already backing away and gesturing as if to draw the warrior forward on invisible strings. The bemused warrior followed him, his armoured toe-hooves clacking down the ramp and onto the first true ground he'd touched in weeks of travel.

'To make introductions,' the associate said, gesturing to the broad-shouldered warrior and the colony leader in turn. 'This great warrior is Shas'o Vior'la Kais Mont'yr. This exalted prince is Aun'o 'l'au Vasoy Ty'asla.'

The warrior knelt before the stately Aun'o and bowed his head before rising and addressing him.

'Aun'o, I am flattered that you came to meet me but I would not have discomforted you so.'

The Aun'o's face was thin and high boned, virtually a T-shape with a narrow slit of a mouth at the bottom that radiated faint but constant disapproval. The Aun'o's mark of celestial devotion gleamed from the top of his nasal slit like a third eye. When he spoke his voice seemed dull and flat, a disinterested burr.

'Nonsense, Shas'o, it was only seeming for me to be present in order to make acquaintance and welcome you to Arkunasha at the first moment of your arrival.'

The associate cleared his throat and rattled his cymbals quietly before speaking again.

'Also, great and exalted ones, here is honoured trustee Fio'ui Ke'lshan.' The portly engineer nodded stiffly to the warrior, who saluted him in return.

'We shall have much to discuss, Fio'ui,' the warrior said politely, 'and I hope we can work closely together for the protection of the colony.'

The flat-faced engineer gave a non-committal grunt at the prospect, eliciting the shadow of a frown on the warrior's face. The associate smoothly broke into the moment of silence that followed.

'Please to be moving to the concourse area where refreshments are now being served.' Taking their cue the drums and cymbals rattled again as the water caste members began leading the way towards a torus-shaped structure nearby. The warrior refused to be immediately drawn after them, addressing a question to the associate.

'And where are the warriors I am to command? I am surprised to find that they have left greetings, welcome as they are, to others, while absenting themselves.'

The Aun'o answered directly, cutting across the associate's platitudes even as they began.

'The Shas'la are sulking in their barracks after being refused permission to bring weapons along to a greeting. They declared that they would rather go naked than suffer the shame of being disarmed at the first encounter with their Shas'o! This, on a world completely empty of any other living beings save for ourselves. Just whom do they propose to shoot, I wonder?' The Aun'o tittered briefly at the thought, before subsiding into an indulgent clucking. The frown returned to the Shas'o's face and remained there.

'WHAT'S THAT SUPPOSED to be?'

'It's a world, boss, the mekboss wants to go there.'

Ork Warboss Gorbag Gitbiter leaned forward, peering down at the wiry little gretchin before his throne. The gretchin quaked, the big shard of glass in its hands quivering and making the dirty yellow-brown ball on its surface bounce around uncertainly.

'The mekboss, eh?' Gorbag rumbled with a voice like stones tumbling down a shaft. 'Well, I'm the warboss and *I* say where we go!'

The gretchin rocked back on its heels at the blast of sound and spittle flying from the impressively tusked jaws of the hulking warboss. It desperately wanted to chuck away the viewing glass and run off behind a console or into a duct, but it was smart enough not to try. The complex symbiotic relationship between the warlike orks and their smaller, weaker gretchin cousins has long depended on the quick wits and diplomacy of the latter. Thousands of years of genetic heritage conspired to keep the gretchin's mind focused enough to squeal out the words that might save it.

'The mekboss said the ships are gonna break if we don't go!'

The warboss paused at that. Glaring red eyes pierced the quivering gretchin with new interest.

'What... did you just say?'

The gretchin's healthy green pallor had gained a distinctly whitish cast, the world in the viewing glass oscillated tightly back and forth in its grip.

'The mekboss said to tell you we got too many holes. Some are so big the boys are falling out and all the... the breathy stuff is leakin' out.'

Gorbag thrust his mighty jaw out truculently. 'Breathy stuff? You mean the air, you stupid little grot?'

'Yes boss!'

'So we're gonna be stuck there?' Gorbag's three-metre tall form seemed to sag at the prospect. No more reaving across the stars for him and his bloodthirsty crew of freebooters; they would be stuck on one stinking planet with no way off it and nothing to fight but each other.

'No, boss! The mekboss says there's metal on this world. We can fix all the holes an' keep goin'!'

Gorbag seemed to swell up visibly at the prospect. He grabbed the viewing glass from the gretchin with a gnarled claw as big as its torso and glared at it with a rapacious gleam in his eyes. The gretchin failed to relinquish its grip quickly enough and ended up dangling from Gor-bag's fist by one arm.

'Anything to kill?' Gorbag demanded.

'No boss,' the grot squeaked apologetically, 'leastways nothing good.'

THE SHAS'O FOUND the warriors beneath his command awaiting him at their barracks, just as the Aun'o had said. The warriors stood in ranks inside the quadrangle formed between their quarters, garages and armoury. Each was in full armour, the jointed plates giving them an insectile quality in the harsh glare of the twin suns. They held their pulse rifles upright before them, long-barrelled firing chambers point-ing rigidly at the skies. Small mounds of windblown dust reaching up to their ankles showed they had been silently awaiting him for quite some time. The Shas'o dropped his single carry bag with an audible clank before blowing out his cheeks in a long-suffering sigh.

'And just what is the meaning of this?' he shouted in a parade ground bark very different to the tone he had used with the Aun'o and Fio'ui. A fire warrior with the stripes of a Shas'ui took a step forward and replied.

'It is my responsibility, Shas'o,' the Shas'ui said, their voice made slightly distorted by the audio pickup of their enclosed helmet. 'Any punishment due is mine alone.'

A murmur of discontent rippled out behind the Shas'ui as they spoke and the forest of pulse rifles swayed slightly in response. The Shas'o raised a hand to silence it.

'I am led to understand you all refused to leave your barracks unarmed? On the idea that it would shame you in my eyes not to greet me as warriors?'

'The Aun'o believes that with no enemies present our weapons are only a danger to ourselves and others, Shas'o' The Shas'ui replied cau-tiously. 'The exalted one believes us too ill-trained and unreliable to bear arms.'

'ENOUGH! PUT DOWN your weapons at once!' The Shas'o barked. As one, the assembled fire warriors placed their rifles on the ground. 'Now take off your armour. You heard me, every piece!'

The Shas'o watched while the warriors more hesitantly unclipped shoulder guards and breastplates, thigh pieces and curved helmets. The Shas'ui proved to be an attractive female with a fine scalp-lock, the oth-ers lost their uniformity and were revealed as a selection of males and females of a young age, few probably even close to their first trial by fire. The variety of their physiognomy showed that they hailed from a variety of different septs. There were some dark faces from Vior'la that were eye-ing him with approval, a gaggle of pallid D'yanoi that look confused, several Sa'ceans that obeyed quickly and efficiently without hesitation.

Finally, each warrior's weapon and armour sat beside them in the dirt and they stood shivering in only their undersuits. The Shas'o walked over to the Shas'ui's neat little pile of equipment and kicked it over.

'These... objects do not make you a warrior!' he shouted into her face. He stalked to another pile and scattered it, catching the owner's look of horror as their cherished pulse rifle clattered to the ground. He laughed, a short, harsh sound within the confines of the quad, and pushed another warrior in the chest causing them to stagger back a pace.

'The will... the ability to fight, to be a warrior, does not reside in your weapons, nor is it inside your armour unless you bring it there yourself! The warrior begins within, a warrior is one who still fights with whatever they have and with nothing at all if they must!'

The Shas'o had their complete attention now, every eye was on him and he saw the unconscious flaring of nasal slits in approval on many faces. He bent down and drew two fighting sticks from his carry bag, ironwood rods as long and as thick as his forearm. He tossed one into the dust before the fire warriors and hefted the other in his fist.

'Now... who among you is enough of a warrior to fight me for the right to put your armour back on?'

Two days later, a Devilfish personnel carrier skimmed over low dunes with all the smooth agility of its namesake, its graceful lines speeding across the sands. Inside, the Shas'o watched the external monitors with interest, noting the tall double plume of dust snaking in their wake that would be visible for miles. He bore the pain of his bruises stoically, as did the five other fire warriors beside him in the passenger compartment.

He'd beaten all of them, one on one, even though it had taken all night and most of the next day. The smarter ones had waited until he was tired before taking their chances, managing to get a few telling strikes on him. Afterwards, the Shas'o had fought them in pairs and groups to allow them a little revenge. Not bad, but some of them really were ill-trained and all of them were very inexperienced. More importantly, they were now thinking of themselves as warriors again, instead of scolded children. He turned to the Shas'ui, raising his voice above the whine of the Devilfish's ducted turbines.

'No other living things on the entire planet?'

'Nothing at all, not a plant, not an animal'. The Shas'ui's responses were clipped and coolly professional but the Shas'o could tell that she was barely holding her excitement in check. The Aun'o, in his ineffable wisdom, had virtually confined the fire warriors to their barracks for fear of accidents or unnecessary wear and tear on their equipment. The current reconnaissance run into the desert would be their first training hunt in months.

'But our colony here is purported to extend over three-quarters of the planet's surface,' the Shas'o prodded.

'That is something of an exaggeration, Shas'o, the main colony is here in the Argap highlands. The Fio have indeed established many other facilities but they are all small, highly automated and widely dispersed.'

'Their purpose?'

'Metal extraction and purifcation. The sands we are traversing bear huge quantities of metallic oxides mixed with silica and carbon. The Fio believe them to be the detritus of a civilisation that once covered this world.'

The Shas'o blinked with surprise. 'My briefing material said nothing about this, perhaps you jest with me, Shas'ui?'

The Shas'ui gestured at the red dunes sliding past on the monitors, 'No, Shas'o, I do not jest. The sands you see out there really are composed of rust. The Fio don't know whether the gue'la or or'es'la lived here, certainly it was a long time ago.' She paused. 'Permission to ask a question, Shas'o?'

'Granted; I value obedience, but ignorance is a weapon placed in our enemy's hands. What is it?'

'Your name - Shas'o Vior'la Kais Mont'yr. You've earned two adjuncts to your name already; you have seen battle and been named as skilful by your fellow warriors. You must have passed at least three trials by fire to achieve the rank of Shas'o…'

'I'm sure you have a question in there somewhere, Shas'ui. What's troubling you?'

'It's just… why would the Shas'ar'tol send someone like you to a place like this? Surely you would do more good in an active conflict region than being crèche supervisor in some forgotten outpost.'

'I go where the Greater Good commands, like any diligent student of the Tau'va,' the Shas'o replied. 'If my seniors at high command believe I can have the most effect here, then that becomes my singular purpose and I give no thought to potential glories lost elsewhere.'

The Shas'ui looked at him in frank disbelief, and seemed to be trying to deduce just who he had offended and how. She opened her mouth to ask another, probably even more impertinent, question when the Devilfish lurched suddenly, banking sharply to one side. The fire warriors were thrown against their restraining harnesses with a chorus of suppressed groans. On the monitors, the Shas'o caught a glimpse of a yawning darkness amid the dunes that rapidly vanished down one side of the personnel carrier.

'Canyon,' the Shas'ui explained. 'Natural erosion cuts channels into the desert, they–'

'I know; that part was in the briefing materials. It also means we've arrived at our destination. Prepare to disembark.'

The sand-laden winds had ground the exposed rim of the canyon to a pitted smoothness. Across the gap, the far cliff was marked with uneven bands of strata made up of a fantastic array of reds, browns and blacks.

Thirty metres below, on the canyon floor, spires and mushrooms of basalt protruded from a bed of rust-coloured sand. Behind the Shas'o, three Devilfish carriers lifted off in unison and turned their elegantly curved prows back towards base. Three bemused squads of fire warriors were left standing in the thick cloud of dust kicked up by their departing personnel carriers. They looked questioningly at the Shas'o. He opened a common frequency to address them all.

'Until now, you've only thought about these canyons as obstacles to be crossed,' the Shas'o told them. 'We're here to learn that they can be your best ally or your worst enemy. In this hunt, you must simply return to the colony without being tagged. The Devilfish will be patrolling the desert; hostile pathfinders and gun drones are in the canyons. Question one, which way do you go?'

'Through the canyons, Shas'o,' the Shas'ui responded promptly.

'Very good,' nodded the Shas'o. 'Now tell me why.'

'The Devilfish would easily detect us and tag us in the open.'

'You discount the threat of pathfinders and gun drones?'

'No, but the pathfinders will require support to stop us and the Devilfish will be highly restricted if they enter the canyons. The gun drones can be outsmarted or outfought one-on-one as necessary.'

'I concur with your theories, Shas'ui. Now let's go and put them to the test. Pay close attention because we will be performing another hunt out here tomorrow, with battlesuits.'

PULSE BLASTS CRISS-CROSSED the canyon in a flickering web of light. Every nook and cranny seemed to birth and receive its own false lightning faster than the eye could follow. After a week of successive hunts in the desert, the fire warriors were improving, the Shas'o noted with approval. The blue 'prey' cadre in this hunt had turned on their pursuers and caught them with a classic *mont'ka*, a killing blow. The strung-out red cadre suddenly found their lead elements caught in a canyon too narrow to redeploy in. In thirty more seconds the surrounded warriors would be cut down and the red cadre would become prey.

Shas'o and his team leapt from the canyon lip eighty metres above, the flat plates of their crisis battlesuits gleaming in the bright suns. Blue-white stabs of flame from their shoulder-packs steadied their fall as the canyon floor rushed up to greet them. At the last second, their jetpacks kicked in and robbed them of their momentum, their duralloy leg-claws crunching into the sands in unison. The three-metre tall armoured suits raised arm-mounted weapon pods and rapid bursts of plasma rifle fire ripped into the firefight from a new angle.

The blue cadre ambushers were caught between the crisis suits and the red cadre survivors. Decisive action could still have saved them; enough were combat effective that a concerted attack on either the battlesuits or the reds might have still carried the fight. But the blue cadre's cohesion had disintegrated when the crisis team landed. They panicked and fought their own immediate battles without regard to what was happening behind them. In a few seconds, the moment had passed and the red cadre carried the blue's position. The blue's hasty ambush became their last stand.

'You cheated!' the Shas'ui was standing before the Shas'o's suit, glaring defiantly up into the monitor lenses that peppered its head. The Shas'ui's own light armour was discoloured where simulated plasma fire had killed her in the fight.

'I'm sorry, Shas'ui, in what way did I cheat?' The voice came from the battlesuit's external speakers, somewhere in its midriff.

'You said that you would observe and take no part in the action!'

'I did, but sometimes in combat you will also find things to be different to what you anticipated.' The suit's speaker made the statement flat and unaffected, yet it ended the Shas'ui's tirade as if she had been struck.

'I apologise, Shas'o; I did not mean to impugn your teaching.'

The heavily-armoured suit raised one weapon-mounted arm in a curiously lifelike gesture of conciliation. 'No, it is I that should apologise, Shas'ui. The reds were fairly caught, and credit is due to you for that. I felt there was no further lesson left to be learned there. However, there was still a lesson for you to learn. Can you tell me what it was?'

'No rearguard,' the Shas'ui said bitterly. 'When I was sure we'd caught them, I didn't detail anyone to watch our back.'

The Shas'o broadcast his findings on the hunt to all of the fire warriors present, reds and blues alike.

'You have fought well, but with mistakes on both sides. Overlooking that a force of which you are unaware might come against you during an engagement is an easy mistake to make, just as easy as rushing headlong after a fleeing enemy and suffering a reverse. Natural eagerness to turn every weapon on the acquired target can obscure the need for a rearguard, or a reserve, to cover the eventuality that all does not proceed as hoped for. Learn from this.'

The Shas'ui was studying the patina of simulated pulse rifle hits on the commander's suit. 'Are those mine?' she eventually asked when the Shas'o's wisdom had been dispensed.

'Indeed they are; some nice grouping, Shas'ui.'

'I'll get you next time.'

It took two more weeks of training hunts before the Fio'ui took exception to the additional maintenance burden the fire warriors were incurring. As the Shas'o returned to the barracks after dusk, he sighted the Fio'ui's dumpy form waiting patiently beside the gate post like some carved heathen icon.

They had been using battlesuits again that day, and the Shas'o's was close to the limits of its endurance. The suit's armoured casing was streaked with smears of dust and its clogged servos whined plaintively with every step. They'd found that the crisis battlesuits were excellent for supporting the troopers in the close confines of the canyons, far more practical than the larger Devilfish or Hammerhead support vehicles. The only downside was the battlesuit's limited endurance, which meant they would need to cache extra power cells to operate in areas remote from the colony.

The Shas'o's mind was filled with plans as he approached, but the sight of the Fio'ui gave him pause. He halted the crisis suit and opened its chest cavity so that he could dismount and meet the Fio'ui face-to-face. One of the earth caste would never be intimidated by a piece of machinery, however martial its function, but it never hurt to show some politeness to another caste. The Fio'ui was of the Kel'shan sept, and so apt to be stubborn and mistrustful of outsiders at the best of times.

'Greetings Fio'ui,' the Shas'o began. 'You come without the Por'la at your side. Am I to understand that this is a social visit with no call for negotiation?'

'You understand wrongly,' the Fio'ui grumbled. 'I have come to inform you that your... outings must stop. There is serious work to be done and my apprentices are being distracted by your indulgence.'

'Training is no indulgence, Fio'ui, if my warriors are to retain any value as a fighting force. Just as your own apprentices would not expect a mechanism to function if it was left unattended, I cannot expect my warriors to fight if they never lift a weapon.'

The Fio'ui thrust his jaw out truculently and began again. 'It must stop. The Aun'o demands maximum output.' Having evoked the name of the Aun'o, the engineer closed his mouth and moved to leave, as if no more need be said.

'Wait, Fio'ui,' the Shas'o said. 'Even absent the Por'la can we not come to compromise?'

The Fio'ui seemed a little shocked by the concept, but he paused to listen. Encouraged by his own boldness, the Shas'o pressed his point further.

'I have many pairs of idle hands on Arkunasha colony, not to mention numerous drones without true purpose. Teach my fire warriors how to perform their own maintenance schedules and I will have them assist in monitoring the extraction and purification facilities across the planet. You would exceed your estimated output in no time.'

The Fio'ui's heavy brow furrowed uncertainly as he wrapped his mind around the unfamiliar concept. His voice was still gruff but there was a gleam of hope in his eye. 'The Shas'la would refuse,' he muttered 'you of the fire caste have always believed manual labour beneath you.'

'Bold words,' Shas'o smiled, 'some fire warriors would demand satisfaction for their bruised honour on hearing them. I am not so ignorant and I'm ready to shoulder my burdens alongside my brothers and sisters. The Shas'la will obey my commands, and they are just as eager to be of more value to this colony. Only caste barriers prevent their willing contribution to it.'

'Very well, Shas'o, I shall consider your unorthodox proposal and discuss with my own kind. I... thank you for your time.'

The Shas'o watched the chief engineer shuffle away through dim pools of illumination cast by the colony lights. He smiled to himself. Another opponent laid low by a surprise attack. After a time he went inside to prepare briefings for the next training hunt.

FIRE AND IRON thundered out of the void with twisting, belching black trails chasing at its back. One, two, then three fiery meteors were vomited from the sullen skies, the clouds peeling back in ragged tatters where the smoking lances pierced them from above. Distance made the churning smoke and fire trails seem absurdly slow-moving as their burning tips crawled across the sky.

The Shas'o watched the apocalyptic sight through the screens of the colony information center. A crisp line of characters at the bottom of the image announced that it was being relayed from a metal extraction and purification facility somewhere on the far side of the planet.

'Still no word from the *Vior'la Gal'leath M'shan*?' he asked.

The Fio'La technicians hunched their shoulders helplessly. The only ship within communication range of Arkunasha colony had dropped off the grid hours before. All their attemptss to raise it had met with stubborn silence. The Fio'ui was clinging tenaciously to the idea of a meteor storm being responsible for the break in communications. He gestured sharply at the screens.

'Meteors, see?' the engineer grunted. 'They're starting to break up.'

A handful of smoking coals were indeed dropping away from churning masses and curving downward at a steeper trajectory. The Shas'o shook his head as most of the smaller smoke trails corkscrewed and levelled out just before they hit the ground. One came rocketing straight towards the extraction facility, creating a momentary impression of something big and close before the image disintegrated into static.

'Facility 7352 is no longer transmitting, Fio'ui,' one of the Fio'la called apologetically.

'Because those are Ore's'la ships and attack craft, not meteors,' the Shas'o said quietly. 'Fio'ui, I need you to tell your people to prepare for evacuation–'

'You will do nothing of the kind, Fio'ui,' the Aun'o's voice rang out in the quiet information centre as he swept in through the outer doors. 'There is no call for such precipitous action at this time.'

The Aun'o stood at the entry surrounded by a small coterie of nervous-looking water caste members. His expression was that of a tutor finding his students engaged in some distasteful, and probably illegal, activity.

'My apologies, Aun'o,' the Shas'o replied somewhat tautly, 'but the protection of this colony is my responsibility and I must advise immediate evacuation.'

'Because a handful of pirates have landed on the far side of the planet? Something of an overreaction on your part. Understandable, I suppose – this must be very exciting for you.'

'Apologies again, Aun'o, but this is no mere handful of pirates. Or'es'la ships of that size carry tens of thousands of their warrior caste. I have insufficient forces to defeat them all when they locate the colony. We must remain mobile to stay ahead of the invaders until reinforcements can arrive.'

'Don't you mean *if* they locate the colony, Shas'o?'

'I mean what I say. It will only be a matter of time before the Or'es'la locate more of the extraction facilities, and believe me they will trace them back to us. They will travel any distance to find battle, Aun'o; we must not be here when they arrive.'

ABOARD THE LEAD ork cruiser, warboss Gorbag Gitbiter gripped the arms of his command throne and laughed uproariously at the sight of orks and grots being hurled around the ship's bridge. Smoke and blasts of flame accompanied their thunderous progress through the skies. The vibrations running through the ship felt like a thousand jackhammers were being jammed against its patchwork armour plating.

Gorbag mashed random buttons on the arm of his throne until a frightened-sounding grot voice squeaked from a speaker grill in response.

'Tell the flyboys it's time to drop and give 'em a boot up the arse from me,' Gorbag growled happily. With nothing to kill on this planet, the landing was going to be the most fun part and he was going to squeeze out every bit of it. Distant clunks reverberated through the hull as landers and flyers dropped away from the giant ship with all the aplomb of baby chicks falling out of a large, ugly nest.

A chaotic selection of viewscreens flickered into life around the bridge, half exploding in showers of sparks before immediately going dead. Of the remainder, some showed only static, but others showed the juddering, leaping views from the noses of the ork flyers. Boring-looking sand dunes and rocks bounced around on the working screens for a few seconds before one was lit by the stabbing flames of nose guns firing. Gorbag's attention snapped to the screen and his impressively-tusked jaws champed convulsively. A little sprawl of silvery towers and pipes in the desert was disappearing in a storm of explosions. Gorbag cuffed a nearby gretchin excitedly and sent him flying.

'Something to kill!' Gorbag roared, jabbing one clawed finger at the flickering image 'Get us down there! *Now*!'

THE DESERT HORIZON that had once been so crisp and clear was smudged with plumes smoke. The Or'es'la had been busy destroying every

extraction facility they could find in this part of the world, apparently
racing one another for the joys of reaching them first and destroying
the handful of drones defending them. The Shas'o glanced out to his
flank, where two Hammerheads were churning through the dust, their
dart-like hulls completely dwarfed by the long railguns they carried in
their turrets. He looked down into the canyon lying diagonally before
him, where fire warriors advanced through rocks and took up positions.

It had taken almost a week of strenuous argument to persuade the
Aun'o to allow the fire warriors out of the colony at all. Eventually the
Aun'o had conceded that at least tracking the invader's progress was
necessary, and some reconnaissance might be in order. If the Aun'o
had paid attention to the forces the Shas'o had chosen to take on his
'reconnaissance' mission, he might have questioned his intentions
more thoroughly. He had brought almost a full cadre; half a dozen fire
warrior squads in Devilfish carriers, pathfinders, two crisis teams and a
squadron of Hammerhead tanks as a 'covering force'. Even so they were
horribly outnumbered by the or'es'la in this region.

Flickers of light at the horizon caught the Shas'o's attention. He
increased the optical gain on his battlesuit's sensors in time to see several disc-shaped drones fly into view. Brightly glowing tracers chased
them, kicking up spurts in the dust as the drones bobbed and weaved
frantically to avoid them. A second later, the first of their pursuers leapt
over the horizon on a belching tail of smoke, a crude looking or'es'la
flyer with its nose aflame with twinkling gun flashes. The Shas'o's crisis
suit immediately registered two high-energy discharges to his flank as
the Hammerheads fired their railguns in unison. The flyer disintegrated
into an expanding cloud of flaming debris an instant later. The rain of
hot shrapnel was still falling as the horizon darkened with the arrival of
the main enemy force.

The dark silhouettes of what seemed like hundreds of vehicles came
streaming into view, a mobile mass of churning dust and metal. The
two Hammerheads turned tail and fled, in accordance with their orders,
turning their long railguns rearwards to menace their still distant pursuers. As the enemy drew closer, they became distinguishable as a column
of tanks, bikes, guns and trucks mixed together without any apparent
formation. They came on with the subtlety of a battering ram, completely intent on the vanishing Hammerheads and unaware of the fire
warriors lurking on their flank.

Invisible markerlight beams fired by the pathfinders reached out to the
onrushing horde to guide in a salvo of seeker missiles. The seekers were a
precious commodity, one-shot self-guided weapons being launched from
a trio of Devilfish hidden further down the canyon. The slender missiles
flashed unerringly into their designated targets, ripping ragged holes in
the column wherever they struck. The or'es'la dissolved into a chaotic
mess of vehicles, charging in every direction, careening into each other,

crashing into rocks and toppling down soft dunes. The rapidly-thinning horde spilled within pulse rifle range and the fire warriors' bright volleys crashed out to immolate individual vehicles in dirty orange explosions. Submunitions from the disappearing Hammerheads blossomed over the scene almost as an afterthought, shredding the exposed or'es'la gunners and drivers in a storm of hyper-velocity shrapnel.

The remaining vehicles turned for the horizon and sped away as fast as their tracks and wheels would carry them, leaving perhaps half of their number as twisted wrecks on the desert dunes. The Shas'o was tempted to lead his crisis teams into the field of burning wreckage to chase down the survivors to truly seal the victory. There would be no quarter asked or given by the or'es'la, and any that escaped now would fight again with renewed ferocity in their next battle. He checked his impulse and signalled the fire warriors to begin withdrawing to the waiting Devilfish. More smudges were appearing on the horizon all the time, showing that more or'es'la were converging on this position. It was time to leave and set another ambush elsewhere.

THE LINK TO Arkunasha colony was weak and uncertain, jumping and sliding as the signal bounced off the ionosphere. Even so, the Aun'o's disapproval communicated itself readily through the tiny screen in the Shas'o's battlesuit as he trudged through a shadowed canyon along with the rest of his weary cadre. Night was falling, the time when the or'es'la stopped moving and the Shas'o's dwindling force could quietly shift between sectors. Endless days and nights of ambushes and running fights had taken their toll on the Shas'o's endurance, and his patience.

'I understand your concerns, Aun'o,' he said tiredly. 'However, it is necessary for me to remain in action. As I explained before, should the or'es'la reach the colony, they will destroy it and kill everyone there. I can only ensure your protection by engaging the enemy–'

'You overrate your personal importance,' the Aun'o chided, 'even if what you say is true – which, frankly, I doubt – your Shas'ui can command in your absence, is that not a keystone of your warrior philosophy?'

'Leaving an inexperienced Shas'ui in command at this juncture would amount to a gross dereliction of duty on my part. My presence at the colony is completely unnecessary and would jeopardise my warriors.'

The tiny image bobbed and darted silently for a moment and the Shas'o feared the Aun'o was going to give him a direct order to return. The other tau's high-boned face turned away for a moment as someone spoke to him from off-screen. After several moments the Aun'o turned back with a pallid look on his face.

'A courier has arrived from the Shas'ar'tol... they say no reinforcements are available at this time. Limited evacuation may be possible later, but for now Arkunasha colony is exhorted to resist to its last breath, for the Greater Good.'

'For the Greater Good,' Shas'o agreed. He waited for the Aun'o to say something else but the silence stretched on until he spoke again.

'Aun'o, you must board that courier and leave the colony at once. I will accept no argument about this and, if necessary, I will return and put you on the ship myself. Your protection is my first responsibility and the dangers will only increase from now on. Leave now while you still can. I must attend to my warriors.' The tiny head on the screen nodded abruptly in response and the image vanished.

The Shas'o looked at the lines of fire warriors winding along the canyon on foot and felt an invisible burden lift from his soul. With the Aun'o gone, he would have a free hand at last, no more negotiating and explaining every action. He turned his mind to current dispositions. The surviving Devilfish were out some distance away, scouting for the enemy, and the Hammerheads were perched somewhere above on the dunes, keeping a watch for flyers. Their attrition so far had been light, but maintaining supplies of ammunition and energy cells was a constant concern. The supply cache they were approaching was one of the last that had been placed before the invasion and the only one close to what now amounted to the front lines. Risk of interception and limited resources meant most of the newer caches were only a day or two's travel from the colony. Too close, but they had been left with little choice.

One of the fire warriors left the line and picked their way to where the crisis suits were labouring along the soft sand of the canyon floor to conserve their energy. It was the Shas'ui, her armour flecked and chipped where she had been caught in an or'es'la shell burst that morning. The monocular eye-piece of her helmet gazed up at the Shas'o's monitor head in mute question until he opened a channel to her.

'Word has arrived from the Shas'ar'tol that there are to be no reinforcements,' the Shas'o told her simply. 'We must fight on with what we have.'

'Not long ago I would have said that was impossible, but these past weeks you've led the or'es'la around by their noses so well that I can't see why we can't do it forever.'

'Supplies, mostly, and the or'es'la will learn to be less cooperative over ti–'

An urgent communications request from the pathfinders was winking in the corner of one of the crisis suit's screens. The Shas'o accepted it and was treated to a grainy view of the desert above. His stomach turned over at the sight and his exhaustion vanished. An array of dark brown shapes were moving through the gathering gloom, the sullen flames gouting from their exhaust stacks briefly illuminating their rusting armour and the swarming or'es'la warriors clinging to every vehicle.

'Course?' the Shas'o snapped.

'Closing on our position. They haven't sighted us yet.'

'Pull back into the canyon and let them pass, we can't–'

'Second group sighted, Shas'o!' The view spun to show another distant column converging on the opposite side of the canyon. 'The first group are halting now, it looks as if they're stopping for the night.'

'Plant five photon grenades on maximum delay and pull back immediately.'

'Acknowledged, Shas'o.' He closed the link and addressed the Shas'ui on a direct channel.

'Pass the word, Shas'ui, I want the supplies recovered and brought back down the canyon as quietly as possible, no one is to engage the or'es'la.'

'Shas'o?'

'I have something much better in mind for them.'

The Shas'o triggered his jet pack and bounded away down the canyon in a series of low, swinging leaps to stay below its rim. He reached the retreating pathfinders and had them markerlight the position of their photon grenades up above. He turned and leapt for the opposite lip, using his remaining reserves of energy lavishly to thrust himself over the edge. Dark shadows blotted the frozen waves of dunes to either side of the canyon and were made hard-edged by guttering oil-fires lit by the or'es'la.

The Shas'o levelled his plasma rifle and let rip at the closest targets. They were beyond effective range, but he loosed off several incandescent bolts into the gloom before jumping back down into the canyon. A moment later, the photon grenades detonated, their stark white flashes burning away the night vision of anyone looking for the source of the incoming fire. Fat red tracers buzzed across the canyon in both directions, followed by the distinctive crack-swish sound of larger projectiles.

The crisis suit's energy reserves were into the orange, but the Shas'o leapt a short distance further along the canyon before mounting the opposite side and firing again. That provoked another wild burst of fire from the or'es'la, and in the brief moment he was above the lip of the canyon he glimpsed the insane crossfire already occurring between the two camps. He dropped to the canyon floor and left the or'es'la to their sport; with any luck they would keep shooting at each other all night.

'O'SHOVAH?' THE SHAS'UI'S voice was unsteady, the pain of her shattered body edging the word.

Shovah meant 'farsight'. The fire warriors had taken to calling him that during the desert campaign. O'Shovah, Commander Farsight, just a jocular nickname at first but it had grown into a watchword, almost a prayer. Farsight will see us through, Commander Farsight will outwit the or'es'la once again, they can never catch Farsight.

It seemed like a bitter reprimand now, trapped for weeks in the Argap highlands with no room to manoeuvre and endless hordes of foes surrounding them. Every day was another day of grinding siege, insane assaults, and casualties on both sides. The or'es'la died by the dozen for every fire warrior they dragged down, but each loss was keenly felt by the small band of defenders.

Now the Shas'ui was among the fallen, another casualty ticked off the shrinking roster of colony defenders. She had been caught in an or'es'la rocket attack while dragging an injured comrade clear, her limbs shattered and torso pierced by randomly flying metal. It all seemed so senseless.

'Rest easy, Shas'ui,' he said. 'Another shuttle got through. You're going to be evacuated.'

'No!' The Shas'ui lurched on her narrow cot, trying to rise 'I will stay and fight!'

'You will heal and fight another day,' the Shas'o, O'Shovah as he was coming to think of himself, said coldly. 'Your injuries would impede you in battle to the point of uselessness.'

The Shas'ui sank back, too weak to protest further, her eyes searching O'Shovah's face. 'Why don't they evacuate all of us? Why are we still here?'

O'Shovah had no answer. The Aun'o was gone, the colony ruined and most of its population killed or fled. There was no reason to stay but the Shas'ar'tol insisted that they hold on. Reinforcements were trickling in, but they were barely enough to keep pace with the attrition incurred by the siege. No counter-offensive was possible, only endless positional warfare through the peaks and passes of the highlands.

'I don't know, Shas'ui,' he confessed. 'We must place our trust in the greater good.'

SHELLS SCREAMED DOWN in ragged salvos, pulverising rock and throwing up towering clouds of dust at the edge of the colony. They were concentrating on the dugouts around the skeletal remnants of the workshops. Their howling mingled with the first explosions, and soon the fire warriors could hear nothing but the crash of explosions and the whickering of shrapnel.

In recent weeks the or'es'la had fallen into a pattern of hoarding up their ammo and loosing it all off before an assault. In terms of inflicting casualties, it was actually less effective than their old method of firing short, unexpected bombardments whenever a crate of shells was brought up, but it was a lot more unnerving. It meant the or'es'la were coming again.

O'Shovah crouched in his crisis suit inside a shelter he'd helped the Fio to dig for him at the head of a feature they'd dubbed the slipway. It was an erosion-cut channel leading down from Arkunasha colony to a nearby valley in the highlands. Windblown sand and dust from the plateau poured continuously down the slipway like a slow motion avalanche confined by high rock walls on both sides. The or'es'la had fixated on the area as the widest point of approach and it was already littered with half-buried wrecks left by their previous attempts to storm it.

O'Shovah crouched in his hole, feeling the bedrock tremble as shells burst nearby. He found that he trembled with it. The bombardment seemed endless, maddening. Shells of all calibres poured down and were joined by the howl of rockets just as it seemed it could get no worse. Red flames spurted up on all sides and flashes filled the air. The world seemed engulfed by roaring giants on every side.

Suddenly, the or'es'la barrage dribbled away to nothing, a few paltry shells whistling down as the towering smoke clouds began to drift away in the wind. Then he heard the roar of many engines and the rumbling sound of tracks. O'Shovah emerged from his shelter, far enough to see down the slipway, as around him, surviving fire warriors looked cautiously out from their own redoubts and bunkers. Perhaps four teams remained, holding onto a precarious horseshoe of positions at the top of the slope, with barely one team in reserve. Ugly or'es'la battle-tanks were crawling to the base of the slipway, five steel giants with groups of smaller vehicles ranged to their left and right. Behind them, another wave of at least twenty vehicles was coming into view, labouring hard in the soft sand.

O'Shovah was speechless. The enemy had never before attacked in such strength. A wave of improvised seeker drone-missiles flew past, plummeting into the approaching behemoths. Two of the leading vehicles crumpled in flames and were soon joined by others as two Hammerhead tanks began firing from the heights. The air was split by harsh flames as the duel was played out, the or'es'la firing at the blue-white flashes of the Hammerhead's railguns. The first enemy tank was hit and burst into flames. A second, immobilised with track damage, continued to fire until it was hit beneath a turret by a railgun round. The shot tore the turret from the vehicle in a spray of sparks. Flames shot into the air, enveloping the crew as they tried to escape.

A call came in. 'Infantry climbing the slipway, O'Shovah!'

From among the tanks appeared or'es'la warriors in blood-red armour. They were running up the slipway and making better progress than the slithering wave of vehicles. At an order from O'Shovah, precision pulse rifle fire swept across them, temporarily clearing the slope of running shapes. The Hammerheads were now firing in salvos. A dozen burning enemy vehicles lay scattered in the sand as testimony to their handiwork. The leading vehicles had climbed as far as a chain of tethered charges hidden in the slipway. Three were disabled with shattered tracks and the rest swung away to one side in apparent confusion. The second wave of vehicles began to climb the slope. Three took direct hits from the Hammerheads and blew apart, but the rest kept churning upwards towards the workshops with single-minded determination.

O'Shovah emerged from his shelter and signalled his surviving bodyguard to follow as he moved behind the protective glacis to reach the dugouts at the workshops. They loped along behind roughly-piled foam-metal blocks, already half buried by the sliding sand. Shells fired by the or'es'la hammered into the area. Red and yellow tracers from their secondary armaments buzzed around the fire warrior positions. A quick glance at his lateral monitors showed O'Shovah more vehicles climbing up on his right as he approached, while his two bodyguards loomed reassuringly in his rear view. O'Shovah leapt over the top of the glacis. Tracers streaked past him as he broke cover. He zig-zagged the battlesuit with surprising dexterity for such a cumbersome device, spotted a large, half-collapsed crater just below him and took cover in it. A moment later, his bodyguards were also in position above and below him on the slope.

Ahead of them, an or'es'la assault group was breaching the top of the slipway, moments away from overrunning the position. O'Shovah locked on to a vehicle and its surrounding infantry, punching a plasma bolt into the former and allowing a salvo of smart missiles to pick off the latter. More plasma bolts and fusion blasts from his bodyguards ripped into the flanked or'es'la. Almost simultaneously, a burst of heavy calibre slugs stitched across the upper torso of O'Shovah's armour, pitching him out of the crater and sprawling him full-length in the sand. His systems displays were alight with warning indicators as he struggled to stand. His bodyguards moved to protect him. One was blown almost in half by a stray shell, his crisis armour bursting open like rotten fruit.

The shattered remnants of the assault group were running towards them with a truly enormous or'es'la in the lead. Darkness was sliding across the battlefield behind the charging alien like the shadow of death. O'Shovah sighted manually on the bestial-looking warrior and punched a plasma bolt into its torso. To his dismay the creature's armour shrugged off the strike and it continued to surge forward with its hugely tusked jaws roaring thunderously. O'Shovah tried to fire his rifle again but found it inoperative. He tried to operate his jetpack and found that inoperative too. The or'es'la continued to charge forward, only metres away now.

A blaze of energy engulfed the or'es'la from above, brilliant white beams dancing from one figure to the next, leaving burning torches in their wake. Gazing up, O'Shovah laughed as he saw wide delta shapes blotting out the suns. The familiar silhouettes of Manta missile destroyers hovered above like guardian angels, finally enough of them to evacuate the whole colony.

THE AUN REFUSED his requests for an audience immediately after evacuation. It was just as well; he'd been furious when he first saw the tau war fleet in orbit. That anger had cooled and hardened in the intervening time. He had visited the Shas'ui and seen her adapting to her newly-grown prosthetics day by day. He had seen the other survivors of Arkunasha colony and mourned their dead with them. When the Aun finally sent for him he came calmly enough.

There was a triumvirate aboard the *Vior'la Gal'leath M'shan* comprising Aun'o T'au Vasoy Ty'asla and two other Aun, a male and a female, that O'Shovah did not recognise. They did not introduce themselves, nor speak at all when O'Shovah was conveyed to their veiled, opalescent sanctum. Instead Aun'o Vasoy smiled fondly at O'Shovah as he entered and bid his accompanying water caste associates to leave them. Only when they were alone did the female speak.

'You have done well, Shas'o. You bring credit to your caste and your sept. We understand that you are distressed by the casualties incurred under your command.'

She paused as O'Shovah shook his head.

'Casualties are a fact of war,' he replied. 'I am distressed by being starved of reinforcements that evidently exist and the unnecessary hardships thereby inflicted on my command.'

The unidentified male Aun spoke, 'Surely it is not your place to question the strategies of the Shas'ar'tol?'

'It is my place to question poor strategy whenever I see it, and this strategy did not originate from my honoured colleagues at the Shas'ar'tol.' He paused to pull a flimsy sheaf of message transcripts from inside his tunic. 'I checked.'

Aun'o Vasoy replied. 'Your success in small unit engagements with the or'es'la has enabled the build up of large reserves. When the campaign to retake Arkunasha begins, it will be undertaken with overwhelming strength.'

'In other words, you decided to throw away lives now for an easier victory later.'

'As is our remit, for the Greater Good.'

There was an awkward moment of silence as O'Shovah failed to respond. Aun'o Vasoy seemed genuinely puzzled.

'Shas'o, you act as if the war was lost, when your actions have virtually assured victory.'

O'Shovah dashed the transcript on the floor in sudden fury. 'Because I was not told!'

The Aun drew back from his anger, their eyes becoming hooded. O'Shovah breathed deeply, mastering himself before speaking again.

'You allowed me and my cadres to fight in the belief that no help was coming while you sat in orbit doing nothing. With sufficient forces, I could have ensured that the or'es'la never even reached the colony!'

'Possibly,' Aun'o Vasoy admitted. 'Yet your situation spurred you to the highest efforts. As you said yourself, casualties are a fact of war. Yet you minimised your own and maximised those incurred by the enemy. Is that not victory?'

'Of a sort,' O'Shovah admitted bitterly. 'And yet superior attrition seems to be the lowest form of success to my eyes.'

'Come now, you must lay aside your grief for your lost warriors,' Aun'o Vasoy said reasonably. 'You have the gratitude of the tau empire and the approbation of your fellow caste members. I understand that they have even gifted you a new name in celebration of your success.'

The warrior's face had become an immobile mask. He revealed nothing of his inner feelings when he responded finally.

'Indeed, they have dubbed me O'Shovah – Commander Farsight – for my alleged ability to see into the future, and I have pledged to them that in future times the tau empire will remember my name.'

WARHAMMER®

SIR DAGOBERT'S
LAST BATTLE

Jonathan Green

I

THE FIRST TO die had been Argulf's youngest.

The child had been making daisy chains in the high pasture when the first of the greenskins emerged from the forest, gibbering and hooting with savage delight. The girl, barely four summers old, panicked and froze, howling for her mother as the cleaver-wielding greenskin cut her down.

Reynard had witnessed the child's savage murder with his own eyes, his face slack with shock, his voice stolen from him in the same moment that the girl's life was taken. But that abrupt act of unthinking brutality had only been the precursor to the slaughter that was to come.

The goblins poured from the forest in a tumbling tide of bone-knotted loincloths, flint-tipped spears, feathered headdresses and moss-coloured flesh. Despite their number, they were little more than a disorganised rabble. There were a few desultory arrows fired towards the village, but there was no cohesion to their attack.

Reynard had fought for his feudal overlords in the armies of Gisoreux as a young man, when a proliferation of orcs had bled into the lands of Ombreux from the Pale Sisters to the north-east and laid waste to the fiefdom for miles about. And he would fight again now, despite having given up the life of a man-at-arms years ago, to protect his home and his loved ones.

Snatching up his pitchfork from beside the back door of his cottage, he ran to meet the goblins' insane charge. The stringy specimens he had encountered when still a young man had at least demonstrated some rudimentary discipline, even if it had been forced upon them by their larger cousins. But the shambling mob he was facing now had lost all semblance of order. Some squabbled with their own kin and they were not above trampling each other underfoot as they poured down the wind-swept escarpment from the forest's edge. Their chaotic charge made it look more like they were fleeing from something rather than hurrying to attack the village huddled in the valley below.

But what they lacked in organisation, they more than made up for in numbers. Only now they were one down, a squirming, mewling goblin skewered on the end of his improvised weapon. Bracing a booted foot against the creature's chest, Reynard twisted sharply, the action accompanied by a grisly sucking sound. The squealing goblin fell silent and stopped struggling as the peasant pulled the pitchfork free of its filthy carcass.

The horde had fallen upon Layon just as locusts had fallen upon the wheat crop three years before. The village had only just recovered from that disaster and now there was a host of greenskins at their door. The rampaging horrors trampled the corn that had been less than a week from the sickle and scythe, slaughtering the livestock that had been intended to feed the villagers during the bitter months of winter.

Reynard blinked in the face of the smoke drifting across the village, seeking the source of the echoing hoof beats.

A shadow fell across the village as light bled from the sky. 'Reynard!'

The scream snapped his attention back to the immediacy of the battle. It was his wife, Fleur. She stood at the threshold of their home, frying pan in hand, as a scrawny creature – no taller than a child of eight – bounded towards her, naked except for a strip of rabbit fur tied at its waist with grassy twine. It carried a rough axe in its bony fist, what looked like a large tooth set within it to create a serrated cutting edge.

As the greenskin lunged at his wife, Reynard sprang, thrusting the butt of his pitchfork forwards, using it as he would a quarterstaff. The hard wood connected with the base of the goblin's skull, knocking the creature sprawling to the ground. Reynard followed up with a second sharp blow to its skull, smiling grimly as he heard the sharp crack of bone fracturing.

Things were at their darkest now – the firmament the colour of pewter, the coming storm casting its pall across the face of the sun – as the greenskins rallied in the face of the villagers' desperate defence. Men and women, as well as the young, the elderly and infirm, had all been forced into the fight, using anything that came to hand to help them save their homes from the tumbling tumult of shrieking greenskins, whether it was an axe from the woodpile or an iron poker from the hearth.

The goblins were everywhere now, or so it seemed, swarming along alleyways, over the churned mud of the village square and around the flower-bedecked roadside shrine to the Lady.

A shrill whinny carried to Reynard's ears over the tumult of battle – the shrieking of goblins, shouted oaths to the Lady and the clash of billhook on axe – as if it rode upon a wave of power that deadened all sound before it. He turned, and his heart lifted.

On the ridge of the escarpment beyond the village, dark silhouettes against the beaten metal sky, was another ragtag band. Swords held aloft, they only numbered ten in all. But at their midst, sat astride a barded warhorse, was the unmistakable form of a noble paladin, the crest atop the warrior's helm clear for all to see, even in the failing light that came before the storm.

For this was not just any knight. Their saviour was a chosen champion of the Lady of the Lake, one upon whom the holiest of honours had been bestowed. A grail knight.

THE SILENT RANKS of the knight's entourage watched as the massacre continued unabated. Just as Reynard was expecting the knight to issue his challenge, the men dropped to their knees, bowing their heads in prayer. The knight's tabard rippled in the breeze that heralded the oncoming storm.

Reynard caught sight of a green blur from the corner of his eye and turned his attention from the silent men-at-arms back to the melee consuming Layon. He spun on his heel, sweeping the blunt end of his pitchfork before him, feeling the vibrations of the goblin's bone-cleaver vibrating through his arms as the two weapons made contact.

Knowing that a chosen champion of the Lady had come to their aid filled him with renewed strength. It felt as if the very life blood of Bretonnia was flowing through his veins.

Sliding the improvised weapon through his hands, grasping the shaft closer to the prongs, he swung the longer end round sharply. The goblin's blade slipped from the smooth wood, the creature stumbling forwards on its spindly legs and into the path of the whirling tip. The end of the weapon caught the goblin in the throat, the force of the contact throwing it onto its back in the battle-churned mud of the village square.

With a cry of 'For the Lady!' the fighting unit lined up along the spur of high ground moved as one, pelting down the steep slope of the escarpment. Swords raised, shields hanging loosely at their sides, they hurled themselves pell-mell towards the battle while the grail knight watched from his position at the crest of the hill.

Finally, with a harsh neigh from his steed, the paladin charged down the slope, a morning star swinging from the end of his outstretched arm.

Reynard turned from the charging battle line, feeling hope and pride swell within him. There was fire in his heart, in every fibre of his being. The end of the pitchfork sticky with goblin blood, the retired man-at-arms headed back into the fray, a cry of 'For Layon and the Lady!' on his lips.

* * *

THE BELLOWED ENTREATY to the Lady, that she might bestow her blessings upon the faithful, became an incoherent roar in the throat of the battle pilgrim known simply as Arnaud. With his blessed blade raised high, he had been the first to break from his position on the ridge. It was he who led the charge, a battle-cry of zealous fury on his lips.

The blade he held so tightly in his right hand, knuckles white around the worn leather bound about its grip, was scarred and pitted with the patina of age. Its edge was no longer as keen as it might have been had it enjoyed the kiss of the whetstone a little more often. The man's tunic was torn and patched, the rough fabric still bearing burn marks in places. The hair on his head was an unruly mess, his balding scalp forming a natural tonsure, such as those favoured by the faithful, while thick greying stubble coated his jowly cheeks like a rash. The end of his nose was swollen and purple with broken blood vessels.

But for all he lacked in attractiveness he was thickset and still strong. Every drunken brawl that had left him with a broken nose, or missing another tooth, had also honed his skills, teaching him to fight dirty. And there was no doubting his faith in the Lady, or the high regard in which he held his master, the thrice-blessed Sir Dagobert.

No individual among their number was greater than any other, for all commoners were equal in the sight of the Lady. They were simple folk who had given up their former lives, turning their backs on the lot that accident of birth had handed them, that they might have the honour of serving the noble paladin who had been chosen by the Lady, whose personal crusade it was to rid Her fair land of the greenskin, the rat-kin and the beast-spawn. There was no one among their number who held dominion over any other, for all were as maggots compared to the shining example set by the grail knight.

But there was one among their number, nonetheless, to whom the others looked for guidance and approval, whose strength of heart and absolute conviction in his faith in the knight and the Lady was an example to them all. That one was Arnaud.

Battle-cry still on his lips, the brawny pilgrim crashed into the goblin throng like a ship's keel ploughing through foaming waves. His notched blade descended as he brought the pommel down on the head of a greenskin. Still running, he levelled his sword and thrust forwards, putting all his weight and momentum behind it.

The weapon's tip pierced the spine of a stringy creature which died with a squeal as Arnaud barrelled into it, its skull crushed beneath his heavy hobnail boots. Then he was piling into the next, hacking at its legs, his weapon breaking the creature's kneecaps and then stopping, its dull edge failing to sever the bone and gristle completely.

The rest of Arnaud's brethren had joined the fray now with bludgeoning swipes of axe and mace, their weapons relics of other campaigns the grail knight had prosecuted against all that was unholy and an affront to the sanctity of fair Bretonnia.

'Praise be to the Lady!' a rangy, gaunt-faced pilgrim cried with evangelical glee, his eyes rolling into his head as the rapture took him, sinking a woodsman's axe, hung with pewter charms, into the head of another of the goblins. The man had to put both hands on its haft to pull it out again. 'Praise be!' he cried again, tears running down his grime-smeared cheeks as the axe came free at last.

The press of goblins and desperate villagers soon brought the pilgrims' eager charge to a halt. Surrounded by capering greenskins, Arnaud set about himself with renewed zeal. Every kick, every punch, every bludgeoning swipe he made with his shield, every headbutt, every barrelling body blow, every hack and slash of his blade was accompanied by an angry grunt or a bellow of pious rage.

He lashed out with his sword wildly, the flat of the blade smacking another of the greenskins on the head. He followed this up with a punch to the beast's face on the return stroke, the weapon's crossguard gouging out an eye.

Feeling teeth puncture the flesh of his calf he gave a cry of pain and annoyance. Dropping his shield, he grabbed hold of the wriggling green thing responsible, lifting it clear of the ground, kicking and snarling, before running it through with his blade. The blade came out again with a wet sucking sound, smeared with gore and what passed for blood among the greenskins. Dropping the limp body he met the charge of another of the vile creatures with a kick to the stomach that left it doubled up and in prime position to receive the kick to the face that followed.

As the goblin dropped to the ground gasping for breath, Arnaud recovered his shield from the quagmire at his feet and brought its tip down across the back of the creature's scrawny neck, almost slicing its head clean off.

Shield in place upon his arm once more, his blade ready to meet the next ill-considered charge, Arnaud braced himself, catching his breath for a moment, surveying the pockets of fighting that filled the village.

'For Sir Dagobert and for the Lady!' he shouted as he barged his way past startled combatants, making for the centre of the village where the fighting was at its most desperate and most savage.

THE SICKLE REYNARD had snatched from where it hung on a peg in the cowshed slipped from his hand as the goblin toppled backwards, the curved blade having carved through the creature's shoulder and into its neck. Returning his pitchfork to a two-handed grip, Reynard stepped out of the barn, leaving the distressed cattle anxiously lowing behind him, readying himself to meet the next charge. But none came.

Reynard looked across the village at greenskins faltering before the pilgrims' relentless retribution, those that could still walk turning tail and running for the sheltering shadows of the forest once more. His heart rose. The greenskins were in retreat. The goblins had been routed. 'Thank the Lady,' he gasped, the adulation escaping his lips as barely more than a whisper.

He could hear other cries of joy, supplications to the Lady and even cheers rising from the beleaguered defenders. The battle-hardened pilgrims, who had come to their aid when everything seemed at its blackest, dealt with the last of the greenskins that hadn't had the sense to flee while flight was still an option.

A few of the grizzled pilgrims looked ready to pursue the fleeing goblins until one of their number – a brawny, barrel-chested brute of a man, his nose broken in several places and purple from too much ale – shouted for them to hold.

Reynard looked at the man. Who was he to command his fellow pilgrims before the Lady's champion had even spoken? But then Reynard had not heard the knight issue one command since arriving at Layon. In fact, he could not even be certain that any battle-cry had issued from the noble paladin during the battle.

Head bowed low, keeping his eyes firmly on the ground, Reynard approached the pilgrim throng. The other villagers held back, happy to let Reynard take the lead. As a retired man-at-arms and former aide to the seneschal of the lord of Ombreux himself, Reynard had seen far more of the world than many of the inhabitants of Layon, the majority of whom had never travelled beyond the perimeter of the valley. He also had a better understanding of how to speak to nobility.

Nonetheless his heart was racing now, and not just from the exertions of battle. To speak out of turn to a knight was to risk the paladin's ire at best. At worst, it could result in him having his head cleaved from his shoulders by the Lady's champion.

'My lord,' he stumbled, anxiety getting the better of him as he neared the pack of panting men, catching a glimpse of the fire that had yet to leave their battle-ready bodies. Taking a deep breath in an attempt to quell his nerves he tried again. 'Most honoured lord, a thousand thanks. If you hadn't happened by, it's likely the greenskins would have done for us all. If there's anything we can do for you–'

'Sir Dagobert needs nothing you could offer him.'

Reynard started. He was sure it was the brawny battle pilgrim who had spoken out of turn again. Other gasps of shock came from those villagers assembled behind him. He was not the only one to have noticed the affront, and yet none of the pilgrim's fellows saw fit to comment.

'Sir Dagobert seeks only to serve the Lady.'

How could the knight allow this disgrace to continue?

Unable to help himself now, a melange of anger, fear and disbelief welling up inside him, Reynard slowly raised his head. And, for the first time since he had been aware of the knight's presence, he saw things as they really were.

He took in the chainmail shirt and faded tabard hanging loose about the knight's frame, and the morning star hanging limply from the knight's still outstretched arm. He saw the sheared-off lance gripped forever in his other hand. He saw the horse's battered barding, rusting at the rivet-joints, and the yellow gleam of bone beneath. He saw the votive trinkets draped across the knight's shield and became aware of the four men who acted as the knight's pall-bearers. And finally his eyes met the empty gaze of the skull locked within the knight's helm.

Reynard felt disappointment pour into him, filling the aching void that the aftermath of the battle had left. Their saviour was dead and had been so for a very long time.

'Sir Dagobert does not require anything of you,' the burly pilgrim said, a cruel sneer making him appear even uglier. 'But we do.'

'MORE ALE,' THE pilgrims' leader shouted from his place at the makeshift table – two apple barrels, a barn door and a couple of benches from the village shrine – upending the empty flagon clenched in his callused fist as if to emphasise the point.

Reynard motioned for Melisande to hurry up with the two earthenware jugs she was filling from the barrel at the back of the house. She nodded, wiping away the tears she shed for her younger brother – fallen during the initial greenskin assault – with the corner of her beer-stained apron, before hurrying to obey as quickly as she could, encumbered as she was by two heavy pitchers.

It seemed that half of those villagers who had made it through the goblin attack were now preoccupied with tending to the pilgrims' needs. And those needs were surprisingly considerable for men who had supposedly given up all worldly cares when they had chosen to follow the grail knight in service to the Lady.

The holy reliquae the pilgrims carried into battle, that acted as both standard and inspiration to the rabble, had been set down before the village shrine and a number of the village children were preparing garlands of meadow flowers with which to adorn it.

Curiously, with the routing of the goblins and the arrival of Sir Dagobert's entourage, the wind had changed and the coming storm had passed them by.

Reynard stared at the reliquae. It was effectively a portable altar. Had the passing of the storm been a coincidence, or was there more to it than that?

Before the girl could reach the pilgrims' table, Reynard intercepted her, taking the foaming jugs and dismissing her with a nod. Melisande gave him a grateful smile before running home, the tears for her dead brother coming anew.

'So, brother,' Reynard said as he began to refill the pilgrims' cups, 'to what do we owe the good fortune of your arrival? What brings you to Layon?'

'Not us, peasant, but Sir Dagobert, the thrice-blessed,' the pilgrim's leader corrected him. 'His quest takes him where the Lady of the Lake wills. We merely follow.'

Reynard glanced at the relics resting before the shrine. He could see quite clearly now that the saint's bones had been mounted on a scarecrow frame of bound sticks, as had the bleached bones of his former steed. The numerous votive medallions had been tied on with ribbons, along with entreaties to the Lady scrawled on strips of parchment.

'So what was it that brought Sir Dagobert–'

'The thrice-blessed,' the pilgrim added helpfully, the ugly, gap-toothed grin back on his face.

'The thrice-blessed,' Reynard echoed. 'What was it that brought him here, at the hour of our need?'

'I have already answered your question.' The pilgrim fixed him with beady black eyes. 'The Lady guides him. It was the Lady that sent him here now, when Sir Dagobert was most needed. Just as it was the Lady that sent him to join Duke Theobald's campaign to purge the lands north of here of the greenskin menace.

'But now we eat, for killing greenskins builds up an appetite like nothing else. And then maybe some women, that we might quench the fires of our ardour in their embraces.'

The succulent smells of the suckling pig that was being roasted in honour of their guests carried to Reynard on the breeze, making his mouth water and his stomach grumble, realising how hungry he was after his own exertions to repel the goblins. He nodded to the armoured skeleton atop its hobby horse steed. 'And will Sir Dagobert be joining the feast?'

The knight's spokesman could not hold back his guffaw of derisive laughter at that, and it was soon taken up by several of his fellows seated at the table. 'Don't be foolish, peasant!' he snorted. 'Sir Dagobert is fasting.'

II

IT WAS COLD inside the chapel, colder that the misty autumnal day beyond its walls, but the knight cared not.

'That which is sacrosanct I shall preserve. That which is sublime I will protect.'

The words spilled from his lips in what was little more than a whisper. The sound of the water escaping the mouth of the stone lion above the font was a soothing counterpoint to the knight's vow.

'That which threatens I will destroy, for my holy wrath will know no bounds. That which is sacrosanct–'

Hearing the chapel door groan behind him the old man faltered, but only for a moment. The only indication that he was irritated by the interruption was a tightening of his jaw.

'That which is sacrosanct I shall preserve.'

First there had been the squeaking of hinges, now came the sound of clumsy footsteps and a rough cough as the intruder cleared his throat. The peasant would have to wait; the old knight was at prayer.

'That which is sublime I will protect. That which threatens I will destroy, for my holy wrath will know no bounds.'

Only then, with his pledge complete, did the knight open rheumy eyes, blinking against the rainbow of sunlight that fell through the small stained glass window above the font. The painted panes were an inspiration to him, depicting the moment the Goddess had appeared to Dagobert and offered him the Grail, that he might drink of the restorative waters of the spring and be healed of the mortal wound he had suffered in battle with the dragon Crystophrax, the monstrous wyrm that had razed the Castle Perillus to the ground and made its lair within the ruins.

Putting his weight on the pommel of his sword he eased himself up from his genuflection, old joints and weary muscles protesting as he did so, a twinge in his back making him catch his breath.

The grimace of rheumatic pain on his face became a twisted scowl of annoyance. He did not need to lay eyes upon the one who had disturbed his vigil to know who it was. When he turned he would see the one who, for no obvious reason, had taken it upon himself to speak for the rest of the oafish rabble that dogged his every move, following wherever he led, although he had never asked them to and would have preferred to have been left alone.

But the pilgrims' adoration was just another duty that fell to a knight who had been blessed by the Lady, and in the old knight's opinion there was no duty more onerous. But bear it he did, for the sake of the Lady.

The Lady called men from all ranks of society to fight for Her – to defend Her fair fields and meadows, woodlands and babbling streams – and so the old knight tolerated them too. But of all the oafish rabble, the one he found hardest to abide was their pompous, self-appointed leader.

'My lord,' the ugly, gap-toothed oaf began. 'Much as it grieves me to disturb you whilst you are at your vigil–'

'What is it?' the old knight snapped. He was too old and life was too short for him to have to put up with another obsequious monologue from this jackanapes.

The man blinked in surprise. He appeared almost affronted. His mouth gaped open, affording the knight an unpleasant view of his appalling teeth. A moment later the pilgrim recovered himself.

'My lord, I thought you should know…' He broke off again, suddenly hesitant.

'Come on, man! What news could be so important that you broke my vigil to impart it?'

To his credit, the man remained firm in the face of the old knight's simmering anger.

'There is talk of ratmen in the region, the Lady curse them!'

'Rumours of ratmen? You disturbed my vigil to tell me this?'

'There is talk down in the village at the bottom of the valley, my lord. Word is that the vermin have crawled from their holes once more and are spreading like a plague across Vienelles, blighting crops and slaughtering livestock as they come.'

'You do not need to tell me the ways of the rat-kin,' the old knight muttered. 'And where did you hear these rumours?' he growled. 'At the bottom of a keg of beer, I'll warrant. By the Lady, I can smell it on your breath from here!'

'Are you saying you don't believe me?' the peasant railed.

The guardian of the grail shrine pulled himself up to his full height. He still cut an imposing figure in his chainmail and tabard, despite his age. His muscles were taut, his body made strong through a life of service to the Lady, and not one driven by the appetites of lesser men like the one before him now. He took a step forward and as he came between the pilgrim and the stained glass window, he was surrounded by a nimbus of radiant light.

'You forget yourself. You forget your place!'

The vassal bowed low, though he didn't once avert his beady stare from his master.

'No, my lord, never,' the pilgrim protested. 'It's just that a band of refugees arrived in Baudin last night. They had fled in advance of the horde reaching their doors. They said that Castain has already fallen.'

'I see,' the knight said levelly, 'and what would you have me do?'

'Lead us to war against the rat-things,' the pilgrim faltered, the look in his eyes making it clear that he wasn't sure if he was being tested.

The knight said nothing.

'Meet the abominations in righteous battle and soak Bretonnian soil with their vital juices.'

Still the knight made no comment.

'It is an affront to allow these *vermin–*' He spat the word, saliva flapping from his lips as he did so. '–to despoil the Lady's fair lands a moment longer.'

'You doubt my sworn duty to the Lady?' the old knight queried, taking another step closer to the pilgrim, raising the tip of his sword to point at the man's chest as he did so.

The other took a step back. 'No, my lord, I…' For once, the babbling wretch was lost for words, instead dropping to his knees before the knight, casting his eyes at the floor. 'I beg your forgiveness if I said anything that might have offended you,' he spluttered as he found his tongue again.

The knight stopped in front of him. 'And I grant it,' the knight growled, suggesting that it was not given willingly.

'My first duty is to the Lady,' the knight intoned, as if reciting another prayer. 'My second is to this holy place that I raised from the stones of fallen Castle Perillus with my bare hands.' At this declaration the old knight's voice began to crack, not with age but with raw emotion.

'I swore to protect this holy place and I have not forgotten the vow I made in all the years since the Lady deigned to appear to me...' The knight broke off, no longer able to speak.

He took a deep breath, his left hand bunching into a fist as he fought to compose himself.

'...since She appeared to me here. This is hallowed ground and I will defend it until the Lady sees fit either to release me from my solemn duty or send me a vision that she wishes me to fight upon another field.

'My third duty is to the people of these lands.'

He turned back to the gurgling font, the water droplets cascading from the font head into the catch bowl below, glittering like rubies, emeralds and sapphires in the light of the stained glass window.

'So, until the Lady wills it otherwise, I shall remain here and defend this shrine with my life's blood.'

An unaccustomed smile split his dry lips as he knelt once more before the shrine's simple altar, the silvered fleur-de-lys that stood upon it having once adorned the lance that now stood propped in the corner, before he earned the right to bear the image of the grail itself upon his coat-of-arms.

'After all, if she needs me, she knows where to find these old bones.'

'Yes, Sir Dagobert,' the vassal said getting to his feet and bowing once again as he left the shrine.

III

'DO YOU REMEMBER that time Sir Dagobert – thrice-blessed be he – purged that nest of corpse-eating ghouls in La Fontaine?' Arnaud demanded, his beery tones rising above the slurred conversations of his brother pilgrims.

The hubbub of other voices dropped to a murmur.

'Aye, Brother Arnaud,' said the gangly pilgrim whose name was Ambrose. The man had even less hair and fewer teeth that the brawny former blacksmith. 'That was a great day indeed, praise be.'

'And do you recall the expression on the baron's face when he discovered his own father was one of them?' Arnaud gave a bark of laughter.

The pilgrims were virtually alone at their makeshift table now, with only a pair of desultory maidens still waiting on them. The day was drawing on and the villagers had left them to their feast, having no stomach for food themselves, and taking the opportunity to tend to those who had been injured during their encounter with the goblins, and to take care of the dead.

Bonfires had been raised at the edge of the village, those who had fought greenskins and their kind before knowing from bitter experience that their corpses should be burnt, lest their pernicious spores settle in a dark, damp hollow and give rise to another harvest of death.

One of the girls was tying a strip of cloth from the hem of her skirt around Groffe's arm. Odo was muttering something through a mouthful of pork fat to Jules, who was slumped across the barn door-table, looking like he had already passed out. None of them were paying Arnaud much attention.

'Eh? Do you remember?' Arnaud laughed, louder this time.

'We remember,' Brother Hugo replied with less enthusiasm.

'I remember the time that wyvern almost did for us in the Pale Sisters,' Waleran muttered.

'And what about the time Sir Dagobert led us to the Sisterhood of Saint Salome?' Arnaud went on, ignoring Waleran's doom and gloom recollections. Arnaud was never one to tire of the sound of his own voice. 'I'd never seen so much sin in one place.'

'Yes, plenty to go around,' Groffe chuckled crudely, putting an arm around his nurse's waist and spinning her unceremoniously onto his lap. The girl gave a half-hearted squeal of protest, and when Groffe pulled her chin round to plant a beery kiss on her pretty mouth, she kicked him in the shins and pulled herself of his lecherous grasp.

At this, Arnaud burst out laughing again, spiteful mirth shaking his corpulent frame.

There was little left of the suckling pig now other than bones and grease. Tearing off a hunk of gritty bread from a hard end of loaf, Arnaud used it to mop up the congealing pork fat and stuffed the whole lot into his mouth.

'So where do you think Sir Dagobert will lead us next?' one of the others asked, indicating the garland-decked reliquae outside the shrine with a casual wave of a gnawed rib bone.

'Where the Lady wills, Brother Gervase. Where the Lady wills,' Arnaud replied, a thoughtful look on his face.

'Praise be!' piped up Brother Ambrose.

'But not for a while, I think,' Arnaud added, his gaze roving from the food on the table and the drink in his hand to the rolling hips of Groffe's failed conquest. 'No, not yet. I think Sir Dagobert – thrice-blessed be his name – likes it here.'

REYNARD MISSED THE boy's cries at first, what with all the noise coming from the pilgrim's table.

It was Fleur, who was fetching water from the well to wash the bodies of the dead in preparation for their journey into Morr's kingdom, who heard the child first.

Hearing her call his name, Reynard ducked under the lintel and into the street. Fleur pointed.

The boy was pelting across the field, the forest that bounded its edge spread out across the horizon, an impenetrable darkness lurking between the trees. Dusk had already fallen within that primal woodland.

It was Tomas, the woodcutter's son. As he came closer, not slacking off the pace for a moment, Reynard understood the look of blanching fear on his face. 'Greenskins!'

'More of them,' Reynard muttered under his breath. He turned to his wife. 'Get the children back inside and warn the others.'

He was running too now, joining the other men who had heard the boy's fearful warning, gathering up what weapons they had and what could be turned to the defence of the village.

'What was that?' the leader of the pilgrim band demanded, rising unsteadily to his feet and moving to join Reynard at the periphery of the village.

'There's more coming,' Reynard informed the pilgrim dejectedly, the fight all but gone out of him already.

'More you say?' the pilgrim railed. 'More of the heathen abominations?'

The pilgrim turned, shouting to his brothers who were already rising from their seats at the makeshift table.

'To arms!' he shouted. 'To arms! Ready yourselves, brothers! The bastards are coming back for another taste of our lord's fiery zeal, and we wouldn't want to disappoint them now, would we?'

'Praise be!' his gangly companion declared, leaping for the sword he had left propped beside a barrel.

Others moved to raise the reliquae upon their shoulders, ready to carry the dead knight into battle once more.

IV

DAGOBERT SLOWLY OPENED his eyes. His eyelids were sticky with rheum. Something had brushed his cheek, something as light and as soft as goose down. He looked down at the inlaid marble tiles of the sanctuary floor.

There it was: a tiny thing, nothing really, just a single curled white petal.

He blinked himself alert, startled by the presence of the flower. He inhaled sharply as he caught his breath in surprise–

–and suddenly the chapel was filled with the heady scent of apple blossom, petals falling like snowflakes all around him – on his head, his outstretched arms, his open palms – as moisture filmed his old eyes.

He peered beyond the drifting petals to the stained glass window above the altar. A blaze of light shone through the painted panes as the first rays of morning touched the shrine. The image of the Lady realised in glass and mineral pigments was shining like silver moonlight, her hair like spun gold ablaze with holy light, her eyes sparkling like stars in the night sky.

And at the edge of hearing he caught the lilting melody of angel voices singing.

As he stared at this radiant image of beauty divine, he fancied the Lady turned to him, reaching out to him from the glass. But it was no longer the grail she was holding in her lily-white hands, but his blessed blade.

He reached for the sword with shaking hands, clutching at the blade with trembling fingers, the tears coursing down his cheeks. But the blade dissolved like mist at his touch and he stumbled forwards, putting out a hand to stop himself from falling.

And there was his sword before him, the polished metal alive with myriad rainbow colours, light picking out the letters inscribed upon it. The letters that spelt out the blessed blade's name: *Deliverer*.

Sword in hand once more, Dagobert rose stiffly to his feet.

The door to the chapel burst open and a panting pilgrim entered the shrine at a run. He skidded to a halt on the stone flagged floor, struggling to catch his breath. Before he could open his mouth to speak, Dagobert fixed the man with his sapphire stare, silencing him.

'It is time,' the knight said. 'The Lady calls.'

THEY CAME TO him then, the penitent, the faithful, those who had given up everything to follow him, that they might receive the blessing of the Lady and, in return, purge the land of all unholy things that would despoil its sacred groves, its fertile fields, its abundant pastures and clean wells.

As the words of the grail vow spilled from his lips in a ceaseless declaration of honour and duty and love, the pilgrims helped him don his armour, and hand him his holy weapons of war.

And so, when all was ready at last, Dagobert stepped through the chapel door and out into the world once more.

There stood his charger, Silvermane, eighteen hands high, the magnificent white warhorse also ready for battle. His steed's barding draped with the knight's personal colours, the horse was champing at the bit, impatient to be about the business of killing vermin.

Stepping up into the stirrups, the old knight swung himself up into the saddle with the grace and ease of a man half his age.

The mists crept through the knots of grey trees, their roots worming between the tumbled stones of the tower that had once stood at this spot.

'The rat-kin are that way?' Dagobert asked, taking his lance from a retainer and pointing through the cloying fog towards the spot where the village of Baudin nestled at the foot of the valley.

'Yes, my lord,' the gap-toothed pilgrim confirmed, making a respectful bow.

'Then to battle,' the old knight said.

* * *

'THAT WHICH IS sublime I will protect!' Sir Dagobert bellowed, his declaration of duty a furious battle-cry. Silvermane whinnied, the stallion bringing its hooves crashing down on the armoured head of another of the black-furred vermin. The blow from the mighty warhorse caved in the mutant's bladed helm and splintered its skull. The ratman gave a brief tortured squeak which abruptly cut off as soupy brain matter bubbled from its ears.

'That which threatens I will destroy!'

As the horse wheeled and turned, Dagobert swung the morning star clutched tight in his right hand again, deft flicks of the wrist sending the spiked metal ball whirling in a killing arc. Silvermane pounded towards the scrabbling rat bodies, the air thick with the reek of the musk they involuntarily sprayed in fear as the pack broke. But they couldn't outrun Silvermane.

The morning star found its target, smacking into the back of another rat skull as the snivelling creature bounded from the knight's charge at a hunched run, practically moving on all fours. The blow sent the thing flailing into the dirt, to be trampled by the rest of the pack, their only concern saving their own flea-ridden hides as they poured over one another in a rippling torrent of greasy fur and scabrous flesh.

Yeomen fought side by side with Dagobert's followers, fending off the serrated blades of the vermin-kin, matching them in ferocity if not in number, and they were slowly gaining the upper hand. Bowmen stuck the ratmen with arrow after arrow.

Bodies lay all around him, the corpses of downtrodden peasants as well as the carcasses of the rat-kin.

Out of the corner of his eye he saw a yeoman, clad in hauberk and helm, pulled from his horse by myriad clawing hands. The weight of the man's armour only made the task easier for the rat-things. The yeoman's mount screamed as the vermin tore its belly open, ripping out the animal's entrails with chisel-sharp incisors.

Dagobert heard arrows zipping overhead and saw the trails of smoke and flame arcing through the clammy air. These were followed by more shrill squeals and enraged hisses of pain as the brazier-lit barbs penetrated armour and cauterised the flesh of the rat-things encased within.

Pulling hard on the reins, Dagobert brought Silvermane round again, the warhorse crushing another pair of fleeing ratmen under its hooves, breaking backs and splintering skulls.

As the vermin parted before the unstoppable charge of the Lady's champion and his powerful steed, something monstrous lifted its malformed head from where it had been busy gnawing at the carcass of another horse, the purple-grey ropes of equine intestines hanging from between its oversized yellow jaws. The sheer size of the monster gave Dagobert, veteran of a hundred battles, reason to pause, but only for the briefest second.

686 *The Best of Hammer and Bolter: Volume One*

A sound that might have been a deep-throated squeak, but which sounded more like a wolfish bark, escaped the monster's jaws as it snapped at the air with tusk-like incisors, catching the paladin's scent on the breeze. It was to one of the rat-kin as an ogre would be to a man. Its mere presence dominated the battlefield. As broad across its abnormally muscled shoulders as it was tall, its rodent head was disproportionately small, making the wobbling throat sac stitched beneath its chin seem even more grotesquely distended. Its hide was patchy and scabbed, and between clumps of mangy, matted fur the knight could make out the criss-crossing scars of clumsy stitching. In other places the unholy, claw-scratch ideograms that passed for script among the under-dwellers had been branded into its taut flesh.

It came at them at a loping run, clearing a path through the scrabbling throng of men and rats, claws like scythe-blades gutting and dismembering any and all that got in its way.

As Silvermane closed with the rat ogre, Dagobert thrust the grip of his morning star under the rim of his saddle and pulled the huge warhorse round sharply, spurring his steed away from the massively-muscled abomination.

Several villagers watched in bewildered fear, believing that the knight was quitting the field. But Dagobert had no intention of running away. He just needed the right tool to take the monster down.

Running down more of the rat-things that suddenly found themselves frantically fleeing towards the charging knight, Dagobert reached the spot where he had thrust his lance into the ground before he had engaged with the enemy, in case he should he need it later in the battle.

He needed it now.

As Silvermane drew alongside the waiting lance, Dagobert grabbed hold and pulled it from the soft loam. Silvermane whinnied. The knight could sense the warhorse's excitement as he turned it back towards the bounding rat ogre.

'That which threatens, I will destroy!' the grail knight bellowed, his pious battle-cry matching the ferocity of the guttural roar that escaped the monster's throat at his challenge.

Positioning the lance against his side, he lowered its tip, aiming it directly at the monster's chest.

'For my holy wrath will know no bounds!' he declared, his strident voice ringing out across the battlefield, filling the muster of Bretonnia with the resolve they needed to keep fighting.

Silvermane galloped past battling pilgrims, struggling peasant villagers and desperate, cornered ratmen. And then suddenly there were less than five horse lengths left between the knight and his quarry.

Dagobert's grip on the lance tightened, the tip barely wavering from its target as the horse thundered over broken bodies, discarded weapons and shattered, unnatural war machines in its urgency to engage with the foe. He saw too late that the brute beast was swinging its huge paw-hands together, intending to deliver a double-fisted sideways swipe as Silvermane closed.

The rat ogre was more intelligent than Dagobert had first thought, choosing to strike the knight's steed rather than the warrior himself.

The savage blow smashed the lance out of the way, splintering its smoothed ash tip even as the devastating punch connected with Silvermane's caparisoned head, ramming foot-long splinters through the animal's throat and into its eye.

Dagobert heard the sharp crack of bone over the screams of the rat-things, the clamour of battle, and the barking of the rat ogre.

The horse's forelegs gave way, Dagobert instinctively leaning back in the saddle as his steed ploughed into the ground. But it was no good. The horse's back end came tumbling over its head, such had been the force of its charge, and Dagobert was sent sprawling in the stinking mire of blood and mud.

Finding himself with a face full of the befouled soup, Dagobert felt the dead weight of Silvermane's body fall across his legs, pushing him still deeper into the sucking morass.

Dagobert knew there wasn't a moment to lose. The adrenaline rush of battle lending him the strength he needed, he pulled himself out from under his dead steed, using the broken haft of the shattered lance still in his hand to push himself to his feet.

He glanced back at the motionless corpse of the horse. Any one of the half a dozen dagger-sized splinters now sticking out of its head would have killed the warhorse had the rat ogre's blow not already broken the poor beast's neck.

Dagobert could tell that the beast was almost on him again by smell alone. Its foul stink was a noxious combination of foetid animal musk and the putrid reek of a septic war wound.

Barely on his feet, the old knight took a stumbling step forwards, his feet slipping in the liquid slurry, twisting his body around as he did so, the lance still in his hand. At the same moment the rat ogre pounced, as if Dagobert were the mouse and the monster the hunting feline.

The squealing roar that issued from the rat ogre's swollen throat sac as the broken spear of the lance pierced its sutured flesh was an appalling sound, but it could only mean one thing.

The creature arched its knotted back, its claws ripping the armour from the knight's body where they caught, the guttural scream showing no sign of abating as the creature writhed and jerked on the end of the ruined lance.

Bracing the end of the lance against his foot, Dagobert put all his weight and power against the planed ash, pushing it further inside the monster's cavernous chest. His own roar of rage escaped teeth gritted against the effort.

Thick black blood gouted from the wound as the broken shaft ruptured the monster's enlarged heart. Its death throes pulled the shattered
lance from the knight's grasp as a primal rage and insatiable appetite for
slaughter kept it fighting to the last.

But the Lady had decreed that the beast must die. Unsheathing his
sword, he felt its divine power coursing through him. With an incoherent cry of rage on his lips he swung the keen edge at the struggling
rat ogre. The sword took the monster's ill-proportioned head from its
shoulders with one clean cut.

The creature's hulking body slumped to the ground, thick black blood
pumping from the stump of its neck, and was still at last.

Dagobert turned from the massive corpse, but he was not done yet.
The unit of black-furred ratmen were almost upon him. Hefting his
holy sword in both hands, he laid about him with the mighty weapon,
prayers to the Lady accompanying every grievous wound he laid against
the enemy. The vermin-kin's defence could not stand in the face of his
holy wrath.

As the last of the verminous bodyguards fell, a host of squealing rat-
slaves parted, and there before the old knight crouched the warlord of
the pack. It was clad in armour, like the grail knight. But where Dagobert
cared for his plate mail, keeping it in immaculate condition so that it
might serve him as well in battle as he served the Lady in all things,
the rat-thing's armour was scarred and pitted with some unknown,
green-black deposit. Where Dagobert wore a fine helm upon his head,
a sculpted chalice rising from its crown and the polished metal glinting
silver where it was caught by the sun, the ratman had a crudely hammered helm topped with a crest of cruel blades.

'For the Lady!' the knight cried, raising the blessed blade *Deliverer* in
his hands once more, putting the aches and pains from his mind with a
prayer to the divine damsel.

Meeting his challenge, the verminous warlord gave a furious hiss, foul
spittle spraying from its elongated snout. Slabs of muscle rippled and
bunched under its scabrous hide as it took up what looked like a halberd looted from another battlefield. The tempered steel of the once
finely-wrought weapon was blackened and corroded, despoiled by the
runes scratched into it, and it pulsed with a sick green light. Totems of
rats' skulls and human hands had been bound to the haft with knotted
leather cords.

'That which is sacrosanct, I shall preserve. That which is sublime, I
will protect. That which threatens, I will destroy, for my holy wrath will
know no bounds!'

The grail vow swelling to become a bellow of holy rage, Dagobert
charged.

* * *

V

AT LEAST LAYON was ready for the goblins this time.

The first greenskin attack had found the men grown complacent after twelve summers of peace, with nothing to threaten the tranquillity of the valley beyond the occasional beastman incursion. But the goblins' initial chaotic assault had left the survivors suspecting that they had not yet seen the last of the forest dwelling primitives.

And so when young Tomas passed on his dire warning, the villagers and the grail knight's retinue set about preparing the defence of the village. Sharpened stakes were raised and thrust into the ground in a ragged line between the village boundary and the perimeter of the forest, forming a barrier of adze-sharpened points with which to greet the enemy.

With the non-combatants safe behind this defensive rampart and a line of bowmen protecting them, Reynard and the rest of the fighting men took up what weapons and shields they had – treasured family heirlooms and swords their ancestors had brought back from the crusades in Araby – and marched out across the field to deal with the greenskin threat once and for all.

The bones of Sir Dagobert went before them, the last rays of the sun, the colour of embers in the hearth, catching the myriad votive tokens – silvered fleur-de-lys and gem-encrusted medallions – and setting them blazing as if aflame.

When they were halfway across the field, the men-at-arms came to a halt as one man, as the hollow echoes of falling timber and the splitting of sundered saplings reached their ears. The sounds were coming from the shadowed gloom of the forest where night had already fallen.

The reverberating beat of a drum boomed from beneath the trees. It was echoed by the hammering of Reynard's heart as the stressed organ beat its own tattoo of nervous anticipation inside his chest.

Giving voice to a multitude of shrieking cries, the goblins burst from the treeline. Clad in loincloths, bedecked with feathered headdresses and waving crude spears, the scraggy greenskins bounded across the field, whooping in delight.

'For the Lady!' the pilgrim leader yelled, his fellows adjusting the position of the reliquae poles resting upon their shoulders. Sir Dagobert's devotees picked up the pace as they commenced their charge across the field.

WITH THE NEAR-NAKED greenskins bounding towards them, leering faces and wiry bodies daubed with warpaint, Arnaud spied something approaching through the forest: a vast shadow still hidden by the trees.

It demanded his whole attention and he took his eyes off the goblins, staring at the unsettling shape picking its way between the crowding crooked trunks.

'By the Lady...' he heard Groffe gasp behind him, as the goblins' monstrous ally hauled its grotesque, quivering bulk through the natural archway formed by a pair of ancient oaks.

Sir Dagobert and his entourage stumbled to a halt. The sense-numbing effects of the ale evaporated like alcohol fumes in an instant, leaving Arnaud with a queasy feeling in his belly.

REYNARD HAD NEVER seen anything so huge that hadn't been a building or part of the landscape. The thing didn't just look like a spider, it looked like it should be the primogenitor of arachnids everywhere. Glutted on blood-rich offerings, grown fat from decades as a prime predator, it now pulled its incredible bulk from the forest on eight chitinous limbs, each as long and as thick as a tree trunk.

As it emerged from the shadows, its carapace assumed a toxic yellow hue, a multitude of shining black eyes, like spheres of obsidian, reflecting the last light of the day. As big as a hill, capable of taking an ox between its crushing jaws as a normal spider might a fly, across its back had been lashed a sturdy platform of broken branches and filthy webs, which teemed with more of the deranged greenskins.

It was all Reynard could do not to soil himself. His worst fears regarding the fate of Forwin the woodcutter were confirmed when he caught sight of the bound body dangling from a gossamer rope as thick as an arm. The silk-bound parcel jerked with every movement the spider made as if it were a broken marionette.

He had heard tales told about such things before – fireside tales of the mythical arachnarok that he had listened to intently at his grandmother's knee, savouring every gruesome detail – but he had never actually believed such a thing could be real.

Now that his childhood nightmare had taken on an unnatural life of its own, Reynard dearly wished that it had stayed in the realm of myth. Worse yet, there could be more of the horrors waiting beyond the treeline in the primeval darkness of the ancient forest.

ARNAUD CURSED. DOUBT had no place in the soul of one of the faithful. To have doubt was to have lost faith, and he who lost faith did not deserve the blessing of the Lady of the Lake. Sir Dagobert would never have faltered in the face of a fight, and neither would he now.

As the immense spider emerged from the forest, its myriad legs moving with a jerky peristaltic motion, the pilgrim saw great rents in the softer flesh of its under parts, arrows sticking from its bony shell, cracks in its carapace where lumps of masonry fired by a field trebuchet had found their target and claw marks made by some great beast, congealing with the foul purple ichor that passed for the spider's blood.

The abomination was injured, a victim of Duke Theobald's purge, the same campaign that Sir Dagobert and his faithful had been a part of, the aftermath of which had led them to Layon in pursuit of the routed greenskins. But the spider was not dead yet. It still moved with a predator's gait and its gigantic mandibles worked ceaselessly, droplets of some deadly toxin dripping to the ground to form steaming puddles.

It was not dead yet, but it was dying, and it would be a worthy adversary for Sir Dagobert.

'Destroy that which threatens,' Arnaud announced, his voice as clear as his purpose. He raised the worn blade in his hand, what might have been incised script blazing in the light of the setting sun.

Hefting the reliquae upon their shoulders, the pilgrims resumed their bold march towards the monster.

Beneath its chainmail hood, the burnished skull of Sir Dagobert – polished to a lustrous sheen like mother-of-pearl – shone gold.

VI

DAGOBERT TWISTED AS the rat deflected his blade with a sharp swipe of its own weapon, the halberd scraping along *Deliverer's* keen edge. Foul sparks were thrown from the corroded metal and the rat used its momentum to carry it forward under the old knight's guard.

Turning his sword to deflect his enemy's attack, Dagobert brought the blade down swiftly, parrying the thrusting halberd. The warlord hissed again and rolled away from the paladin, throwing itself onto the ground and twisting its spine so that it was able to catch the bloodied blade against the haft of its weapon.

Dagobert spun round, raising an iron-shod foot, ready to bring it down on the rat-thing's skull. Moving with deceptive speed, especially considering it was clad in armour, the rat scrabbled out of his way. It was on its clawed inhuman feet again in a second, back hunched, chittering in a horrible high-pitched unvoice, holding the halberd with both hands, as if it were a quarterstaff.

His vow on his lips, gauntleted hands tight about the grip of his sword, the knight thrust the weapon's lethal point towards the pack-leader as the ratman angled its own hooking blade to parry the blow.

Dagobert rained blows upon the horror while the rat-thing tried every underhand tactic at its disposal to best the knight's skill with a sword.

To the pilgrims who fought with him, Sir Dagobert was a living saint, an inspiration to them all, a paradigm of what a life dedicated to the Lady could achieve. Every blow he laid against the warlord's battered armour gave them the courage they needed to push the chittering horde back still further. For every one of the faithful that fell to a poison-coated blade, five of the mangy vermin paid with their miserable lives as the pilgrims exacted their revenge.

But with his battle rage as hot as dragon's breath, Dagobert's attention was fully focused on the twisting, perfidious thing before him.

Where the knight was honourable, the rat-thing was conniving and treacherous, prepared to try any devious trick to gain the advantage. Where the knight was bound by oaths of duty to the Lady, the rat-spawn was motivated by nothing but its own loathsome self-serving nature. Where Dagobert's sword was straight and true, the rat's halberd was serrated and fashioned with snagging hooks. And every time the two blades connected, Dagobert's weapon threw virulent green sparks from the rune-etched halberd.

A bone-numbing, wearying pain was creeping up Dagobert's arms, but despite his failing strength, his faith in the Lady remained steadfast. And faith was the greatest weapon of all against such a foul and unholy enemy.

The warlord made a sudden lunge for the knight, ducking in under the smooth arc described by his sweeping blade. Contrary to expectations of age, Dagobert managed to jerk his torso round so that the warlord's blade scraped along the mail protecting his stomach, splitting the links of chain and sending more of the poisonous green sparks flying from the sundered steel rings.

The rat gave a squeal of enraged frustration as its lunge carried it forwards, exposing it to Dagobert's counter-attack.

'That which is sacrosanct, I shall preserve!' the old knight declared, with a bellow of vindication. Reaching the end of his sweeping swing and twisting his arm at the elbow, he turned *Deliverer* deftly in his grasp. The tempered steel sang as he brought it down towards the rat-thing's exposed neck.

'That which is sublime, I will protect!'

But the rat proved just as fast as the knight, and even more agile. It twisted its back, bringing its defiled weapon to bear once more, braced before it in both paws.

Dagobert would not be denied.

'That which threatens, I will destroy,' he chanted as he brought the blade down, muscles in his arm on fire as his faith in the Lady granted him all the strength he needed. 'That which threatens, I will destroy!'

The worn shaft of the halberd splintered beneath the blessed blade's keen edge, the gleaming steel catching the light for a moment as the sun burnt through the cloying mists at last. Just for a moment it seemed as if *Deliverer* burst into flame. The tip of the blade connected with the creature's breast, parting the exposed flesh between neck and sternum.

'For my holy wrath will know no bounds!'

Dagobert's declaration of faith rang out across the battlefield for all to hear. The vermin-kin squealed in fear. The knight's faithful followers rallied, driving home their advantage as the rat-things fled the battlefield, making their own evangelical calls to the Lady, routing the enemy with vigour.

Dagobert forced the tip of the blade home, ramming it through the throat of the struggling thing, skewering the rat to the ground with his holy sword. The warlord's shrieking screams dissolved into choked gurgles.

A sudden spear of pain burned in the knight's side.

Dagobert gasped, staggering back from the stricken ratman, releasing his hold on his sword that still pinned the treacherous creature to the ground. And then he saw the tip of the halberd clasped in its left hand, the dizzying symbols pulsing with sick green light. The knight's blood smoked as it ran down over the rune-etched blade.

Even with the tainted blade removed, the acid agony remained. The burning pain was joined by a pernicious cold that radiated from the point where the halberd had pierced his side with a creeping malignity.

He could feel his legs giving way under him. His stumbling steps carried him down the rugged hillside towards the babbling waters of a stream that ran pink with the blood of the men and vermin that had met their end upon its banks.

His vision greying, Dagobert made for the brook, his mouth suddenly dry, wanting nothing more than to sup of the waters that tumbled from the same holy spring that filled the font in the Lady's chapel. The Lady had chosen him to be Her champion and she gave succour to those who needed it and peace to those that had earned it.

Reaching the stream, he gave in at last to the numbness spreading throughout his body. He fell to the ground, feeling the damp earth beneath him as the soil of Bretonnia welcomed him with its soft embrace.

As he attempted to draw the waters of the stream to his mouth with one quivering cupped hand, the words of the vow he had first taken as a youth – so many years ago now – tumbled unbidden from his parched lips.

'When the clarion call is sounded, I will ride out and fight for liege and Lady. While I draw breath, the lands bequeathed unto me will remain untainted by evil. Honour is all.'

And so the last thing on his lips when oblivion took him was the first vow he had taken on setting out upon the path to honour and glory in the Lady's name.

VII

THE MONSTER'S BILE-YELLOW shell was thicker that a knight's plate armour. The creature must have survived for centuries within the lightless depths of some primeval forest, having nothing to fear from man or greenskin, growing fat on the flesh of forest goblins and the offerings they made.

Thorn-like protuberances studded the spider's carapace, forming symmetrical patterns across its back. Some of these spines had grown to enormous proportions, becoming great spears of bone-like chitin that thrust forward over its head, protecting it from attack as sharpened stakes did the ranks of Bretonnian bowmen.

694   *The Best of Hammer and Bolter: Volume One*

Buoyed by absolute faith in the divine blessing the bones of Sir Dagobert conferred upon them, Arnaud led his brother pilgrims across the field, despite the fact that the men of Layon's charge had already faltered with the monstrous spider's emergence from the forest.

Bellowing in triumph before they had even engaged the enemy – so sure was he of their forthcoming victory over the greenskins and their monstrous mount – Arnaud led Savaric, Aluard, Fulk and Elias as they bore the reliquae at the head of the pilgrims' zealous charge.

The spider moved with stilted steps, the gargantuan arachnid favouring its right side and yet still covering as great a distance with one rocking stride as the bier bearers did running at full pelt.

But the pilgrims' charge did not falter, even as the gibbering greenskins hanging from the web-strung platform rained crude arrows down upon their heads. Brother Hugo fell with a bolt through his thigh but the holy warrior continued on.

Brother Aluard stumbled and went down, a lucky goblin arrow piercing his eye. For a moment, the reliquae bearers – robbed of one of their number – stumbled too. Jules stepped up to take Aluard's place and the pilgrims surged on across the field.

Through the encroaching gloom and the haze of battle-lust, Arnaud saw again the spears and lances protruding from blackened rifts in the spider's side, the hafts of the buried weapons clattering together with every stalking step the monster took. He saw that one monstrous eye was gone, ichor oozing from the savage wound the monster had been dealt.

And yet, despite having suffered injuries that would have levelled an entire regiment of men-at-arms, the spider was still standing. More than that, it was still striding towards Layon. But the knowledge that it was hurt made one thing perfectly clear to Arnaud. If the monster could be injured, then it could be killed.

'In the name of Sir Dagobert! For the Lady! And for fair Bretonnia!' Arnaud bellowed as the pilgrims closed with the horror. '*Attack!*'

Sir Dagobert met the monstrous beast in battle.

A spearing tarsus came down among the pilgrim mob, running Brother Luc through from shoulder to groin and lifting him clear of the ground, screaming in agony. Another spider claw came down almost on top of the reliquae itself, missing Sir Dagobert's bones but snagging a piece of Silvermane's caparison and tearing it free.

Despite the best efforts of the spider and its frenzied passengers, the pilgrims found themselves directly beneath the monster's furiously working jaws. Strings of corrosive venom drooled from fangs the size of ploughshares, burning smoking holes in the crumbling raiment of the knight's tabard where they touched.

In no more time than it took Arnaud to blink in startled surprise, the spider struck.

Moving far more quickly than should have been possible for something so vast, the monster's discoloured fangs snapped closed about the body of the knight. The crushing bite punctured steel plate and splintered bone as if Sir Dagobert was nothing more than a scarecrow of sticks and straw. The idiot beast delivered a great jolt of poison through its fangs deadly enough to drop a giant, pumping the relic-knight's remains full of venom that corroded the smooth surface of his polished armour and dissolved the links of his chainmail.

Rising up on its hindquarters, the spider tore the reliquae apart, sending tatters of cloth, broken bones and pieces of armour raining down about the pilgrims.

With Sir Dagobert occupying the beast, his faithful followers made the most of the distraction and, out of range of the shrieking goblins, ran for cover beneath the bloated arachnid.

Caught within the cage of the spider's legs, Arnaud froze. The beast's underbelly seemed to pulse with disgusting peristaltic ripples, as if something was moving beneath the white puckered flesh.

Myriad tiny spiderlings swarmed over its leathery hide to drop down onto the pilgrims crouched beneath their monstrous brood-mother. They scampered across the ground around the spider as well, scuttling up the legs of the unwary, squirming inside jerkins and into hose, delivering crippling bites and making the men cry out in pain and horrified surprise.

'Come, brothers, do not fail Sir Dagobert now when his work here is almost done!' Arnaud shouted, tightening his grip around his blade. 'Stand firm and let not your sword-arms fail the Lady and Her champion!' With that, he thrust his own blessed blade high above his head.

It pierced the pulsating sac of the spider's abdomen and he pushed it home with both hands, feeling internal organs rupture as he forced its tip deeper into the monster's belly. Following their leader's example, the faithful hacked, pierced and bludgeoned the spider's soft flesh.

The spider made a sound like a high-pitched hissing scream and the pilgrims redoubled their efforts, chanting prayers that called down the Lady's divine retribution about the unholy monster.

Viscous fluid poured from the beast's wounds, drenching the pilgrims in a stinking torrent, but still they did not relent. The men hacked and slashed, opening up even more grievous wounds in the monster's abdomen. Brother Baldric lost his dagger inside the beast as the slime-slicked weapon slipped from his grasp. Reaching for the broken end of a splintered lance still hanging from the spider's side, he rammed the weapon further inside the beast, screaming with the fury of a zealot.

The gargantuan spider spasmed with every sword thrust, every axe that cleaved its flesh drawing from it more hissing screams. The creature twisted, trying to catch its tormentors in its terrible jaws, throwing screaming goblins from the howdah as it did so. But the pilgrims were sheltered beneath its belly and with every blow they dealt the beast, its strength ebbed, making it harder for the gigantic spider to keep out of reach of their vengeful blades.

Soon, the spider was possessed by the paroxysm of its death-throes, the forest goblins howling in terror, unable to believe that their god had been bested.

Sir Dagobert's followers had at last finished what the muster of Duke Theobald had begun.

VIII

DAGOBERT SLOWLY OPENED his eyes. Flickering shadows resolved into jostling figures and, as his sluggish senses finally caught up, he realised that someone was tugging at his body.

He could feel his slack limbs being pulled this way and that, but felt like he barely had the strength to breathe, let alone resist the attentions of the looters.

He could hear the babbling of a brook close by and smell the mingled scents of blood and fire on the air. Realisation came to him at last as he remembered where he was and what had happened.

He could still feel the burning pain of the death wound the warlord had delivered with its cursed halberd. And yet he was not dead and the hole in his side burned less than it had. Even the numbness was beginning to pass. He would yet live to fight another day.

He had lain dying of his wounds in the sacred stream, as if age itself had finally caught up with him, but the waters of the Lady's blessed well had saved him, washing the poison from that last grievous wound, and setting him on the road to recovery. With rest and time, and the ministrations of a grail damsel, he would recover, and even return to protect the Lady's shrine. But there was another obstacle he would have to overcome first.

Dagobert understood what was happening to him now. With the ratmen routed, his idiot followers – clearly believing him to be dead already – had returned to claim what relics and other trinkets they could from his body, whether it be a piece of his armour or some token of the Lady that he carried about him.

'I'm not dead,' he tried to say, defiant to the last, but all that escaped his parched lips was a hoarse whisper. Swallowing hard, trying to draw saliva to his mouth, he tried again. 'I'm not dead.'

A dark shadow passed across the canvas of the featureless white sky and resolved into the lumpen features of the pestering pilgrim. What was his name? Dagobert seemed to recall that the man had been a blacksmith before joining the knight's entourage. He was staring at the knight, an imbecilic grin splitting his ugly face. Arnaud, that was his name.

'Arnaud, help me,' Dagobert commanded, but his voice that was still little more than a cracked whisper. It was certainly unlikely that any of the other pilgrims had heard him. 'I'm not dead.'

Arnaud knelt down beside him and whispered in his ear. 'I know, my lord.'

For the briefest moment, hope filled the grail knight's world. But only for a moment.

'And I know, too, that you will live forever,' the pilgrim went on, his voice acquiring a disconcerting quality. A distant look glazed his eyes, as if the pilgrim could see a secret future the old knight could not. 'You will be an inspiration to all who follow you – to the downtrodden, to those in peril or in fear for their lives – a champion to the threatened and the oppressed. And you shall serve the Lady until the coming of the end times.'

Dagobert suddenly felt a great weight pushing down upon his ribcage, making it even harder for him to breathe. He fought against the pressure, struggling to even lift his head to see, blinking to clear his greying vision.

The pilgrim was sitting on his chest, examining the blessed blade that was now in his hands, turning *Deliverer* over and over as if scrutinising its craftsmanship in minute detail.

'But I'm not dead!' Dagobert spluttered, gasping for breath.

Arnaud leant over and whispered in the knight's ear again. 'You are the thrice-blessed; blessed by the Lady when you took up the mantle of a knight, blessed by Her when you drank from Her holy cup, and she blesses you again now with the honour of serving her forevermore.

'You are a living saint, an inspiration to us all,' the pilgrim went on. 'But saints are only ever really appreciated when they're dead.'

Dagobert wanted to thrash and kick and fight against the dying of the light, as he felt the pressure building behind his eyes and his vision began to fade. But he didn't even have the strength to lift his arms.

Arnaud didn't meet his gaze again. Holding the knight's sword in his right hand, the thug reached over and, without looking, put a firm hand on Dagobert's brow, forcing his head under the churning current of the holy stream.

Every fibre of his being fought against the pilgrim's unyielding grasp, but the warlord's toxic blade, having failed to kill him, had nonetheless robbed him of strength.

The pressure increased and deep inside himself, for the first time in a long time, Dagobert began to panic. The very waters that had saved his life twice now threatened to take it from him.

He could hold his breath no longer. He opened his mouth to cry out in rage at the pilgrim, to give a shout that the whole world might hear and realise he was not done yet. But rather than a wrathful roar, his final breath burst from his lungs in a torrent of furious bubbles.

As his greying vision gave way to the blackness of oblivion, Dagobert saw white flowers falling through the dark. The scent of apple blossom was in his nose and he heard the Lady calling to him across the gulf of eternity, guiding him to his long-deserved rest.

* * *

IX

THE SPIDER WAS dead and the goblins gone, having fled back into the forest in shrieking fear after witnessing the agonising death-throes of their forest god. And yet that night only the snores of the grail knight's entourage disturbed the darkness. No one else in Layon slept a wink.

With the rising of the sun came the thankless task of disposing of the dead. The howdah mounted atop the monster's carapace was loaded with the greenskin dead and set alight, the flammable webs soon catching and the fire spreading until it became a great conflagration that reduced spider, goblins and all to nothing but ash.

As far as Arnaud was concerned, only one task remained: recruiting others to the pilgrims' cause. There were those in the village who heeded the call of his rabble-rousing, men who had lost everything in the goblins' attack other than their pitiful lives. With nothing left to live for, and nothing to keep them in Layon, they readily rallied to the pilgrims' totem. With freshly tonsured scalps, they joined Arnaud and the others in reconstructing Sir Dagobert's remains from what was left of the grail knight's bones after the spider's desecration of the holy reliquae, making up any missing parts with what they could scavenge from the village shrine, their own family heirlooms and even the charcoal-black bones left after the funeral pyres had burned down.

'We cannot tempt you to stay?' Reynard asked as the battle pilgrims did what they could to reassemble the bones of the grail knight and his steed, shoring up the reliquae with copious sticks and borrowed twine.

'Do not seek to tempt me, peasant!' Arnaud said, glaring furiously at Reynard. The reek of alcohol was still strong on his breath. 'But you could lend us a few more of those apples and a couple of flagons of ale to see us on our way.'

'So where will you go now?' Reynard asked, once the requested victuals had been scraped together from what was left of the village reserve stores.

Eleven of the original fourteen battle pilgrims remained, but another eight had joined their number since the battle with the spider. As four of them raised the rickety reliquae upon their shoulders once more – Brother Gervase taking up the dead horse's hooves once more and giving an equine whinny – Arnaud looked back towards the ridge, from where Sir Dagobert's hunting party has first set eyes on the village of Layon only the day before.

'Sir Dagobert's quest is done,' he said, Reynard uncertain as to whether the man was gazing into the distance or into the future. 'He desires only to be laid to rest within the shrine that he raised himself from the razed ruins of the Castle Perillus.'

'Then I bid Sir Dagobert–'

'The thrice-blessed,' the other interrupted.

'–and you and your fellow brethren, farewell.'

Ignoring the hand Reynard offered him, Arnaud pointed towards the horizon with his cleaned blade once more and Reynard noticed for the first time how letters etched into the surface of the blade reflected the sun, spelling out a name.

Deliverer.

'In the name of the Lady of the Lake we march for Holy Well!' Arnaud declared, taking the first step on the path that would lead the pilgrims back up the escarpment to the ridge above.

Reynard watched until the pilgrims were no more than dark silhouettes against the skyline. Turning his back on the brooding hills, Reynard suddenly stopped and sniffed, catching the smell of something familiar, and yet out of season, on the breeze.

It was the subtle scent of apple blossom.

SURVIVOR

Steve Parker

BAS WAS UP and running full tilt before he even knew why. Part of his brain reacted the moment the cry went out, then his legs were moving, pounding the dusty alleyways as he flew from his pursuers.

The first rule was simple: *don't be seen.* He'd broken it only a few times since the monsters had come, and never by choice. This time, as before, it wasn't through clumsiness. It wasn't carelessness. It was just raw bad luck, plain and simple. He had taken all the usual precautions. He'd stuck to the shadows. He'd moved low and fast. He'd been patient and silent and constantly aware. But the monsters chasing him now, yapping and chittering joyously at the prospect of spilling his blood, had come from below. They had emerged from a sewer grate just a few metres behind him and the day's quest for clean water was suddenly forgotten in favour of a far more pressing need.

Bullets smacked into the alley walls on either side of him as he fled, blowing out little clouds of dust and stone chips. Some came near to ending his life, their passage close enough to whip at his filth-caked hair. That lent him an extra burst of speed, extra adrenaline to further numb the agony of his aching joints and muscles.

Up ahead, he saw the twisted remains of a fire escape and bolted towards it. The rooftops – those were his domain. In the months since *their* coming, he had spent hours laying boards and planks between what was left of the town's roofs. Up there, he moved where he pleased and saw all. He had the advantage. The big ones never went up there, and the smaller ones didn't know the terrain like he did. The rooftops were his – control your environment and you would always be one step ahead.

The crooked metal stairs shook and groaned as he thundered up them, heart hammering in his ears, skull pounding with accelerated blood flow. He chanced a look down and saw his pursuers, four scrawny green figures with red eyes and needle teeth. They reached the bottom of the fire escape and leapt onto it, clambering up after him.

Bas kept on and made the roof in a few more seconds. For the briefest moment, he took stock of where he was. Here in the town's south-west quarter, he had a few established hiding places, two of which were close by. But he couldn't risk leading his enemies to one of his sanctuaries. He had to put some distance between them first. He could go north across the makeshift bridges he had laid weeks ago, or he could head east where the gaps between the tenements were narrow enough to leap.

North, then. The monsters behind him could leap as far as he could. East was a bad gamble.

He sped on across the roof, avoiding the gaps where alien artillery shells had bitten great gaping holes. He was at the far side when the first of the wiry green killers topped the fire escape and resumed shooting wildly at him. The others appeared beside it and, seeing that their guns were missing the mark, they rushed towards him.

Eyes front, Bas told himself as he took his first hurried step out onto the twin planks. Don't look down.

The gap between the buildings was five metres wide. As he neared the middle, the wood sagged under him, but he knew it would hold. He had tested the strength of the wood before he laid it.

A couple of bullets sang past his ears. He half-ran the last few steps across and leapt the final one. Behind him, his pursuers were halfway across the previous rooftop.

Bas turned to face them. There wasn't time to pull the planks in like he wanted to, not with his enemies wielding those scrappy, fat barrelled pistols. Instead, he kicked out at the planks and watched them tumble end-over-end to the dark alley below.

His pursuers howled and spat in rage and opened fire. One, perhaps more reckless than the others, or perhaps with a greater bloodlust, refused to be beaten. The creature took a run up to the edge of the roof and leapt out into space. Bas was already sprinting towards the next rooftop. He didn't see the creature plunge to its death, but he heard the chilling scream. Soon, he had left his hunters far behind, their alien cries of frustration and outrage ringing in his ears.

HE WAS DYING.

Maybe. Probably. He couldn't be sure. Bas was only ten years old, and all the dying he had seen so far in this short life had been the violent, messy kind – and all of that in the last few months.

This was different. This was a loosening of his back teeth. This was a burning in his gut on those increasingly rare occasions when he ate something solid. This was blood in his phlegm when he spat and in his stool when he made his toilet. Pounding headaches came and went, like the sharp cramps that sometimes wracked his weakening muscles.

After his flight across the rooftops, all these symptoms came on him at once. He fought them off until he reached relative safety. Then he lay down, and the pain rolled over him like a landslide.

Had he known any better, he would have recognised the signs of dehydration and malnourishment. As his scavenged supplies dwindled, he was forced to spread them ever thinner. But Bas didn't know. He could only guess.

How long had he lived like this now? Was it months? It felt like months. What date was it? He couldn't be sure of anything. Time passed for him not in hours and minutes, but in periods of hiding and running, of light, tormented sleep and the daily business of surviving on a knife edge. He felt like the last rodent in a tower of ravenous felines.

If the green horrors ever caught him, his end would come quickly enough. It would be painful and horrific, but it would be short. Shorter than disease or hunger, anyway. He wondered if a slow, quiet death was any better. Something instinctual made him back away from that train of thought before he formed an answer. For now, he was alive, and here, in one of his many boltholes, he was safe.

He chided himself. No, not safe. Not truly. He was never that.

He heard the old man's voice in his head, berating him from memory, as sharp and harsh as a rifle's report.

Safety is an illusion, boy. Never forget that.

Aye, an illusion. How could Bas forget? The words had been beaten into him until he learned to sleep only lightly and wake to a readiness any frontline Guardsman would have envied. While living with the old man, if he wasn't up and at attention three seconds after first call, that heavy cane would whistle through the air and wake him up the hard way. Now, if a blow ever caught him in his sleep, it wouldn't be for the sake of a lesson. It would be the bite of a greenskin blade, and his sleep would be the eternal sleep of the dead.

His traps and snares, he knew, wouldn't protect him forever. One day, maybe soon, one of the savages would get all the way in. Not one of the tusked giants. Bas was careful to bed down only in small, tight spaces where they couldn't go. But the scrawny, hook-nosed ones could slip into all the places he could, and they were wicked, murderous things, gleeful in their bloodletting. He trusted his defences only as much as he trusted himself, so he was diligent to a fault. He triple-checked every last point of entry before he ever allowed his eyes to close. Simple though they were, his traps had already saved him a dozen times over. The old sod had drilled him relentlessly, and Bas had despised him for it. But those lessons, hard-learned and hated, were the thin line between life and death now, the reason one last ten-year-old boy survived in the remnants of this rotting town where eighteen thousand Imperial citizens had died screaming, crying out to the Emperor for salvation.

Bas *lived*, and that in itself was spit in the eye of the greenskin nightmare.

He had never thanked the old man. There had been a moment, back when they had parted company for good, in which Bas had almost said the words, but the memories of all the fractured bones and cuts and bruises were still too sharp back then. They had stilled his tongue. The moment had passed, never to come again, and the old man was surely dead. For what it was worth, Bas hoped the old bastard's soul would take some satisfaction in his grandson's survival.

Time to rest now. He needed it more than ever. It was blackest night outside. The wind screamed in the shell-holes that pocked the walls of this four-storey tenement. A hard cold rain beat on the remains of the crumbling roof and the cracked skylight above.

Good, thought Bas. The greenskins wouldn't be abroad tonight. They kept to their cookfires when it rained this hard.

At the thought of cookfires, his stomach growled a protest at long hours of emptiness, but he couldn't afford to eat again today. Tomorrow, he'd have something from one of the tins, processed grox meat perhaps. He needed protein badly.

Hidden deep at the back of a cramped metal air-vent, the boy drew a filthy, ragged sheet up over his head, closed his eyes, and let a fragile, temporary peace embrace him.

WHEN BAS WAS just seven years old, his parents died and what he was told of it was a lie. Two officers brought the news. His father's majordomo, Geddian Arnaust, asked for details, at which point the officers exchanged uncomfortable looks. The taller of the two said something about a bombing at the planetary governor's summer mansion – an attack by elements of an anti-Imperial cult. But Bas knew half-truth when he heard it. Whatever had really happened, the grim, darkly-uniformed duo in the mansion's foyer would say no more about it. Bas never found out the real story.

What they did say, however, was that, on behalf of the Imperium of Man and the Almighty God-Emperor Himself, the noble Administratum was taking full possession of the Vaarden estate and all assets attached to it. War raged across the segmentum. Money was needed for the raising of new troops. Imperial Law was clear on the matter. The mansion staff would be kept on, the tall officer assured Arnaust. The new tenant – an Administratum man, cousin of the planetary governor, no less – would engage their services.

'What will happen to the young master?' Arnaust had asked with only the mildest concern, less for the boy than for the simple practicality of dispensing with an unwanted duty. He had never held any particular affection for his master's son.

'Maternal grandfather,' said the officer on the left. 'His last living relative, according to records. Out east, by New Caedon Hive. The boy will be sent there.'

'There's a cargo train taking slaves that way this afternoon,' said the taller. 'It's a twenty-hour trip. No stops.'

Arnaust nodded and asked how soon the boy might embark.

'We're to take him to Hevas Terminal as soon as he's ready,' said the shorter officer. 'He can bring one bag, enough for a change of clothes. Whatever else he needs, the grandfather will have to provide.'

It was as simple as that. One moment, Bas had been the son of a wealthy investor with mining concerns on a dozen mineral-rich moons, the next he was a seven-year-old orphan stuffed into the smallest, filthiest compartment of a rusting train car with nothing but a tide of cream-coloured lice for company and a bag of clothes for a pillow.

At least he wasn't put with the others. Among the slaves all chained together in the larger compartments, there were several hunched, scowling men who had eyed him in the strangest manner as he'd walked up the carriage ramp. Their predatory stares, unreadable to one so naive, had nevertheless chilled Bas to the marrow.

Father and mother gone, and him suddenly wrenched from the security and stability of the wealth and comfort they had provided! Curled up in his grimy, closet-sized space, Bas had wept without pause, his body trembling with sobs, until exhaustion finally took over. Asleep at last, he didn't feel the lice crawling over his arms and legs to feed. When he awoke much later, he was covered in raw, itching bumps. He took vengeance then, the first he had ever known, and crushed all the blood-fat lice he could find. It took only moments, but the satisfaction of killing them for their transgressions lasted well beyond the act itself. When the pleasure of revenge finally subsided, he curled up into a ball and wept once more.

A SCREAM RIPPED Bas from a dream immediately forgotten, and he came awake at once, throwing off his filthy sheet and rolling to a crouch. His hand went to the hilt of the knife roped around his waist. It sounded again. Not human. Close by.

The traps in the hall! One of the snares!

Bas scrambled to the opening of the air-vent. There, he paused for a dozen thunderous heartbeats while he scanned the room below him.

No movement. They hadn't gotten this far in, thank the Throne.

He jumped down. Crouching low, he scooted towards the door in the far wall. Beyond the grimy windows to his left, the sky was a dull, murky green. Morning. The sun would rise soon, not that it would be visible.

The rain had ceased, but the clouds hung thick and heavy and low.

Bas stopped by the room's only door just long enough to deactivate the hinged spike trap above it. He stretched up on tiptoes to fix the simple safety lock in place. Then, cautiously, quietly, he opened the door and peered through, eyes wide against the liquid darkness of the hallway beyond.

A mewling sound guided his gaze towards the intruder. There, barely visible among the mounds of fallen concrete and shattered glass that littered the floor, was one of *them*, distinguishable from the rubble only by the sound it made and the panicked scrabbling of its long-fingered hands as it struggled with the wire that bit into its flesh.

Bas could smell its blood on the dusty air – salty and metallic like human blood, but with strong overtones of something else, something like mould.

He checked for any sign of movement in the shadows beyond the intruder. If the creature wasn't alone, he would have to flee. There could be no fighting toe-to-toe. Much as he valued the little sanctuary he had worked so hard to create here, he wasn't fool enough to die for it. He had abandoned other boltholes for less.

Though Bas matched most of the *hook-noses* in size, they had the physical edge. The hideous creatures were far stronger than they looked. Their long powerful hands and razor-lined mouths made them deadly. Even one so hopelessly entangled in his sharp wire snares could still do him lethal damage if he got careless.

But Bas hadn't lived this long by being careless.

The old man's voice rose again in his mind.

No slips, boy. A survivor minds his details. Always.

Satisfied that the monster was alone, Bas acted quickly. He dashed from the doorway, low and silent as ever, and closed on his scrabbling prey. Before the alien knew it had company, Bas was on it, stamping viciously down on its face. Bones snapped. Teeth broke. The vile, misshapen head hammered again and again against the stone floor. With the creature stunned, Bas straddled it, drew his knife and pressed the long blade up under the creature's breastbone. He threw his whole weight behind the thrust, leaning into it with both hands. The creature's body heaved under him. It began flailing and bucking wildly, but Bas held on, gripping its skinny torso between his knees. Then, with his knife buried up to the hilt, Bas began to lever the blade roughly back and forward, cleaving the creature's heart in two.

A wheezing gasp. A wet gurgle. A last violent tremor, and the creature went limp.

Bas rolled off the body, leaving the knife buried in his foe. Withdrawing it now would only mean spillage and he wanted to avoid that as much as he could. Lying in the gloom, catching his breath, he watched his hands for the moment they would stop shaking.

Don't be afraid, he told himself. This is nothing new. We've done this before.

That gravelly voice rasped again from the past.

Adrenaline is your ally, boy. Don't mistake it for fear. They're not the same thing.

The shaking subsided far faster than when he'd made his first kill, but Bas knew from experience that the hard work would start in earnest now. He had a body to deal with. If the other savages smelled blood – and they always did – they would come. He had to move the corpse.

Hissing a curse, he kicked out at the thing's ugly, dead face.

Being abroad in daylight was a constant gamble, much more so with a burden like this one, but he knew he could still save this precious bolthole from discovery if he moved fast. The more time he gave the greenskins to rouse, the more danger he'd be in.

With a grunt, he forced his aching, exhausted body to its feet and set about his grisly business.

THE CARGO TRAIN ground to a slow halt at noon on the day after its journey had begun. The iron walls of Bas's tiny cabin shuddered so much as the brakes were applied that Bas was sure the train would come apart. Instead, after what seemed an eternity, the screeching of metal against metal ended and the vehicle gave one final lurch.

Bas, unprepared for this, cried out as he was flung against the wall, bumping his head. He sat rubbing his injury, fighting to hold back tears.

A scruffy teenaged boy in the orange overalls of a loader came looking for him a few minutes after the massive vehicle's engines had powered down.

'Arco Station,' he rasped around the thick brown lho-stick he was smoking. 'It's yer stop, grub. Up an' out.'

Bas stood shakily and lifted his bag, then followed the young loader and his trail of choking yellow smoke to the nearest exit ramp. As they walked, he asked meekly, 'Why did you call me *grub*?'

Bas wasn't offended per se. He was unused to insult, sheltered as his life had been until now. He was simply confused. No one had ever called him names before. He had always been *the young master*.

The loader snorted. Over his left shoulder, he said, 'Lookit yerself, grub. Small an' pale an' fat. Soft an' squirmy. You got rich written all over you. I 'eard about you. Serves you right, the likes o' you. Serves you right, all what happened.'

Bas didn't understand that. He wasn't rich. That was his father. He hadn't done anything wrong. Suddenly, he felt fresh tears rising and a tightness in his throat. This boy hated him, he realised. Why? What had he done? Before he could ask, they reached the train car's portside personnel ramp. The loader stepped aside and shoved Bas forward. The light outside was blinding in contrast to the dank interior of the huge train. Bas felt the harsh radiance stabbing at his eyes. The sun was glaring, the sky a blue so intense it seemed to throb.

As his eyes adjusted, he squinted down the long ramp, taking in the rockcrete expanse of the loading platform. Beyond it, shimmering in the heat haze way off to the north, stood the shining steel towers of a great city.

New Caedon Hive.

His new home, surely, for one of the Civitas officers had mentioned the place by name. From here, it looked glorious. He had read all about the great hive cities of the Imperium in one of his father's databooks. Their streets teemed with all manner of people, living and working together in unity to fuel the glorious machine that was the Imperium of Man. He felt a momentary thrill despite his fears. What would it be like to live in such a place, so different from the quiet isolation of the estate? What grand role would he come to play there?

Already, indentured workers and mindless servitors were unloading crates from the other cars on to the sun-baked surface of the platform. Armed men, their faces hidden beneath black visors, pushed and kicked the newly arrived slaves into orderly lines. Someone Bas couldn't see beyond the rows of slaves was barking out a list of rules which, if broken, would apparently be met with the direst physical punishment.

'Go on, then,' spat the loader from behind Bas. 'Get on about yer business, grub. Someone's waiting for you, they are.'

Bas scanned the platform again. He had never met his maternal grandfather. His mother, distant at the best of times, had never once mentioned the man. Bas could see no one who stood out from those he had already noted.

A hand on his back started him down the ramp, forcing that first step. Numbly, he let his legs carry him further, step after step, clutching his bag tight, eyes still searching for his grandfather with a growing sense of panic and confusion.

'Emprah 'elp you, grub. Thassa mean-lookin' bastard you got waiting for you.'

Bas turned, but the loader was already tramping back into the carriage's shadowy interior. Returning his gaze to the platform, he saw it at last, a single figure marked out because it wasn't moving, wasn't hefting crates or bags or boxes or bundles. It was a man, and he stood in the shadow of a rusting green cargo container, his back resting against its pitted surface.

Bas couldn't see him well, not cloaked in such thick, black shadow, but his skin turned to gooseflesh all the same. The cold hand of dread gripped his heart. He slowed. He wanted to turn back, but to what? To a dark metal cabin crawling with lice? He kept moving.

When his feet touched level ground, he gave a start and looked down, surprised that he had descended the whole ramp. There was nothing else to do now. He had to keep on. His numb legs drove him reluctantly towards the green container. When he was five metres from it, a voice as rough as grinding rocks said, 'Took your blasted time, boy. What are you, soft in the head as well as the body?'

There was no introduction beyond this, no courtesies.

'Don't fall behind,' said the man as he pushed himself upright from the side of the container. 'And don't speak.'

As the man stepped into the glaring sunshine, Bas saw him properly for the first time and failed to stifle a whimper. A sudden hot wetness spread from his crotch, soaking his trousers. The old man turned at the lack of following footsteps. He took in the pathetic sight, a scowl of disgust twisting his awful features.

'Blasted Throne,' he hissed. 'If you've got any of my blood in you, it's not much!'

Bas stared back, frozen in place, lip quivering, hands trembling. This man *couldn't* be his mother's sire. There had to be some mistake. His mother had been beautiful and refined. Cold, if he were being honest, but nonetheless a woman he had loved and admired above all others. He searched the stranger in front of him for any sign of his mother's bloodline.

If it was there at all, it was buried deep beneath leathery skin and scar tissue.

The man before him was old, over seventy standard years if he was a day, but impressively muscled for his age. He carried barely an ounce of fat. Veins stood out on his hard shoulders and arms and snaked up his neck to the temples on either side of his shaved head. He wore a beard of middle length, untidy and uneven, and some kind of silver chain with two small metal plates hanging from it. His clothes were olive-green, both the sweat-stained vest and the tattered old pants, and his boots, which could hardly be called black anymore, were scuffed and covered with dirt.

The worst thing about the old man by far, however – the thing that held the boy's eyes for the longest time – was the huge crater of missing flesh where his right cheek should rightly have been. It was monstrous. The tissue that remained was so thin Bas could make out individual teeth clenched in anger beneath it.

The old man noted where the boy's eyes had settled.

'Think I'm a horror, boy?' he said. 'One day, I'll tell you about horrors.'

At this, a strange, faraway look came over him. In that instant, the old man seemed suddenly human, almost vulnerable somehow, a man with his own very real fears. But it was just a moment. It passed, and the hard, cold glare of contempt returned as fierce as before.

'The sun will dry your trousers,' said the old man as he turned away, 'but not your shame, if you've any left.' He started walking again, off towards the south-western edge of the platform where another broad ramp descended to ground level. It was now that Bas noticed the pronounced limp in the old man's right leg and the muffled sound of grinding metal that came from it with every step.

'Keep up, boy,' the old man shouted back. 'Keep up or I'll leave you here, Emperor damn you.'

Bas hurried after him and was just close enough to hear him mumble, 'I'm all you've got, you poor little bastard. Throne help the both of us.'

THE ALIEN'S BODY was heavy despite its size, and Bas laboured hard as he carried it across the roofs to a place he felt was far enough from any of his boltholes. He was glad for the clouds now. The assault of a blazing sun would have made the task that much harder. It might even have finished him off.

Dizziness threatened to topple him twice as he crossed his plank-bridges, but both times he managed to recover, just. There hadn't been time to eat. Once the body had cooled and the blood inside had congealed, he had withdrawn his knife from the beast's chest and stuffed the wound with rags. There was almost no spillage at all. He had bound the wrists and ankles with lengths of wire, to make carrying it more manageable, and had wrapped it in an old curtain he had torn from a third-floor window. Even so, as careful as he was, every moment he remained with the corpse was a moment closer to death. Hunger raged like a fire in the pit of his empty stomach and his legs and shoulders burned with lactic acid. As soon as he was done dumping the body, he promised himself, he would eat a whole can of something. Part of him balked at the thought of such excess. Eating well now meant running out of food that much sooner. But it couldn't be helped. He had felt it yesterday running for his life. He felt it now. He was getting weaker, putting himself at a disadvantage, and he had to sustain himself. One day soon, he would no longer be able to dump the ones he killed. He would be forced to cook their flesh and eat it just to survive. He knew it would come to that. It was inevitable. He'd have cooked and eaten sewer rats first, but they seemed to have disappeared, perhaps eaten by the strange ovoid carnivores the invaders had brought with them. Bas didn't care about taste, but he suspected alien flesh, cooked or otherwise, would fatally poison him. No matter what he did, one way or another, they would kill him in the end.

But not today. Not while he still had power enough to defy them.

Up ahead he could see the shattered chimney pots of the last standing tenement on the town's southern edge. There, on that rooftop, he would leave the body. The smell of its decay wouldn't reach the ground. The winds from the wastelands would carry it off.

He left the carcass near the centre of the roof, burying it in rubble so that any hook-noses that *did* come up here wouldn't see anything to get curious about. At least, not from a distance.

With his labours done, Bas was about to turn back and retrace his steps when he heard a great rumble from the plains south of the town. He flattened himself and crawled to the rooftop's edge. A vast cloud of dust had risen up, at least a mile wide. At first he thought it was a sandstorm, but it was closing on Three Rivers and the wind was blowing *against* it.

Insistent as it was, Bas forgot his hunger then. This was something new, something unexpected. He had to stay and watch. He had to know what it was and how it would affect his survival. A spark of hope almost lit in his heart. Could it be humans? Could it be Imperial forces come to take back the town? Throne above, let it be so.

But it was just a spark. The darkness inside him swallowed it quickly. He had lived too many days and nights without succour to believe things would change now. For all he knew, he was the last living human on Taos III. Given the unstoppable strength and violent nature of the alien invaders, that didn't seem unlikely at all.

Thus, he wasn't disappointed so much as unsurprised when the cloud of dust turned out to be a massive greenskin convoy. The air filled with engine noise that would have rivalled a summer thunderstorm. Vehicles of every possible description raced across the plains towards the town. There were hundreds of them, with wheels and treads in every possible configuration. Bas's eyes could hardly take them all in, such was the variety of strange shapes. Monstrous weapons sprouted at all angles from heavily plated turrets. Radiator grilles and glacis plates had been modified to look like grotesque faces. Gaudy banners of red and yellow snapped in the windblown dust, painted with crude skulls and axes rendered with childish simplicity.

There was nothing childlike about the riders, though. They were hulking brutes, all green muscle, yellow tusks and thick metal armour. They revelled in the noise of their machines, raising their bestial voices to roar along with them. They cavorted on the backs of bastardised trucks and troop transports. Those that fell off were crushed to red smears beneath the wheels and treads of the vehicles behind, drawing cackles of laughter from all that noticed.

They were terrible to behold and Bas felt his bladder clench. If they had come to stay, to reinforce the greenskins that already controlled Three Rivers, his time was surely up. The odds of evading numbers like these were slim at best. He still had to scavenge for old cans of food each day, still had to fill his water-bottles from any source he could find. He still had to venture out from the safety of his boltholes. When he did, he would face a town swarming with savage nightmares. Why had they come? What had driven them here?

It was then, as this question formed in his mind, and as the first of the vehicles roared along the street below him into the town proper, shaking the foundations of the building atop which he rested, that he saw them:

Humans!

At first, he couldn't believe his eyes. He stopped breathing and his heart beat a frantic tattoo on his ribs. He wasn't the last after all. He wasn't alone on this world. There were dozens of them, chained and caged in the back of slaver trucks. Bas ignored the warbikes and heavy armour that rumbled past now. He had eyes only for the cages.

They looked a weak lot, these people. Beaten down, tortured. It wasn't a criticism. Bas pitied them. He knew what they must have endured. He alone had lived to witness the deaths of the people of Three Rivers. So many deaths. He had seen what the invaders were capable of. Theirs was a brutality wholly reflected in their terrible appearance.

The slaves in the cages wore soiled rags or nothing at all, men and women both. At one time, Bas might have been curious to look on the women, naked as they were. What ten-year old boy wouldn't be? Not so now. Not like this. Now, he noticed only the wasted muscles, the clotted blood on their faces and scalps, the ribs that protruded from their bruised torsos.

Most of them looked dead already, like they had given up. Perhaps they didn't have it in them to end their own lives, but from the looks of them, they would welcome the end when it came.

They are not like me, Bas found himself thinking. *They are not survivors. And there are no children.*

In that last regard, he was wrong. A moment later, as the last slaver truck passed beneath Bas's rooftop perch and off up the street towards the town centre, he looked at the rear wall of its cage and saw a boy roughly his own age and height. A boy! Unlike the others, the child was standing upright gripping the bars of the cage, his knuckles white.

There was fire in his eyes. Even from this distance, Bas saw it, felt it. Defiance and the will to live burned bright in this one.

A brother, thought Bas. A friend. And suddenly he knew that his months of loneliness and torment had had a purpose after all, a purpose beyond just spitting in the red eye of the foe. He had survived to see this day. He had survived to find this boy, and he would rescue him so that he would never be alone again. Together, they could bring meaning to each other's lives. They could look out for each other, depend on each other. Between them, the burden of caution could be shared. Life would be better. Bas was certain of it.

His grandfather's voice snapped at him from the past.

Weigh everything against your survival. Live to fight. Don't throw everything away on lost causes.

No, Bas argued back. I can't go on alone. I will save him for my own sake.

If the old man had been alive, he'd have beaten Bas black and blue for that. Not out of anger – never that – but because each man gets only one life, and some mistakes, once made, cannot be undone.

The streets were still trembling with the roar and passage of the convoy as Bas got to his feet. He suppressed his hunger once again and followed the slaver trucks towards the town centre. There, he would stay low, observe, and draw his plans.

IT QUICKLY BECAME clear, as his grandfather drove them away from Arco Station, that Bas was not to live in the great hive-city to the north as he had imagined. The road they followed ran south and the rail terminal's blocky buildings soon fell away behind them, obscured by dust, heat haze and distance. The land on either side of the wide, empty road was flat and largely dry, populated by little else but hardy grasses and shrubs and the tall, strange cattle which plucked at them. Bas was too scared to ask his grandfather where they were going, or anything else for that matter. The old man smelled of sweat, earth and strong alcohol, and he drove his rickety autocar with his jaw clenched, neither looking at nor speaking to his terrified young charge.

After two or three hours in the vehicle's hot, stuffy interior, Bas saw a town materialise from the wavering line of the horizon. As the old man drove nearer, Bas became depressingly certain that this was his new home. The buildings at the settlement's north edge were lop-sided, patchwork affairs with rusting, corrugated walls. It was the first slum-housing Bas had ever seen. Beyond them, the structures got taller and more dense, though little more appealing. An oily pall hung over everything. Towering smoke stacks belched thick, dirty smoke into the sky. As they drove deeper into the town, Bas peered through the windows at the scowling, hard-eyed people on the streets. Tenements dominated. The inky alleys between them spilled tides of refuse onto the main thoroughfares.

Who would live like this? Bas asked himself. Who would stay here?

For the second time that day, he felt the desperate urge to turn around, to run to anywhere but here. But there was simply nowhere to go. He was a seven-year old boy, alone in the Imperium but for the man next to him, linked by blood and nothing else.

'Welcome to Three Rivers,' grunted his grandfather.

Bas didn't feel welcome at all.

Ironically, Three Rivers boasted only one. The other two rivers had dried up as the result of a Munitorum hydropower project some two hundred kilometres to the west, and the town, once prosperous, had gone into economic collapse. The agriculture on which it depended struggled to survive. The workhouses began to fill with children whose parents could no longer sustain them. Many turned to alcohol, others to crime. The streets became unsafe, and not just at night.

In this environment, a man like Bas's grandfather, former Imperial Guard, hardened and honed by decades of war, found work where others could not, despite his age. As Bas would later learn from snippets of hushed conversation on the streets, the old man worked as an occasional *fixer*, solving problems with violence for those willing to pay the right price. The local public house also paid him to keep troublemakers out, though, if word was to be believed, he caused at least as much trouble as he solved. But on that first night, Bas knew none of this. All he knew was that his former life was over and he had been cast into absolute darkness, a living hell. He had no idea then of just how bad things would get.

The old man's home was a dingy basement at the bottom of a black tenement in which every window was shielded by wire mesh. The steps down to its entrance were slick with urine and wet garbage. The smell made Bas feel sick for at least the first week. It was better inside, but not by much. A single glowglobe did its best to light a room with no natural illumination whatsoever.

Bas was shown where he would sleep – an old mattress stuffed into a corner near a heater that, in the three years he would live there, would never once be switched on. He was shown the tiny kitchen and told that, in return for food and lodgings, he would be expected to prepare meals for both of them, among a score of other chores. Bas couldn't even imagine where to start with cooking. His father had employed two private chefs back on the estate. He had never once thought about the effort that went into preparing food.

The lavatory was another shock – little more than a thirty-centimetre hole in the tiled floor with a water pump above it that had to be worked by hand. A steel basin could be filled for washing one's body, but the water was always ice cold. That first day, Bas held his waste in for hours rather than use that horrid little room, until finally, he thought he would burst. Necessity took him beyond his initial reluctance. He adapted.

They had dinner together an hour after arriving, if it could even be called dinner. His grandfather made that meal. It was a tasteless stew of tinned grox meat and potatoes and, though it smelled awful, Bas was desperately hungry by then and cleared his bowl. His grandfather nodded approvingly, though the hard look never left his eyes. When they had finished, the old man ordered Bas to clear the table. Another first. And so it went, day after day, until Bas learned how to do all the things that were expected of him. When he made mistakes or dared complain, he was punished – a hand as fast as a striking snake would flash out and clip him on the ear. Weeping brought him no sympathy, only contempt.

As hours became days, and days became weeks, Bas discovered he was learning something else he had never known.

He learned to hate.

SALVATION SQUARE HADN'T seen this much noise since its construction. Maybe not even then. The ruined buildings shuddered with the ruckus of the greenskin horde and the throaty rumbling of their war engines.

Bas crouched low behind the only intact statue left on the black-tiled roof of the Imperial church that dominated the square's west side. The sky above was clearing of clouds, beams of bright sunlight slicing through like a hundred burning swords.

He had arrived in time to see the slaver trucks emptied and their occupants whipped and kicked towards the broken double-doors of the Administratum building, carrying barrels and sacks. The boy from the last truck had trudged in line with the others, keeping his head down, never meeting the glare of the living nightmares that herded him, but Bas could still feel the boy's defiant hate radiating from him until he moved out of sight.

The greenskin newcomers began mixing with those that already occupied the town, sizing them up, eyeing their buggies and bikes and tanks. A few fights broke out, bringing hoots of laughter and encouragement that rose to compete with the rumble and stutter of their machines. Losers were butchered without mercy or remorse, to the delight of both groups. Despite the appeal of these fights, however, the alien crowds parted fast when a great red truck roared into the square, cutting down a dozen greenskins with the jagged blades fixed to its radiator grille. There it halted, the arms and legs of the slain sticking out from beneath its dirty red chassis.

From the back of this truck leapt a group of bellowing brutes, each bigger than the last. They glared at all those around them in unspoken challenge, but none dared answer. Their size and bearing made the others step back, creating a circle of open space around the truck. From the vehicle's rear, their leader stepped down. Bas was sure the statue to which he clung trembled as the huge creature's iron boots added fresh cracks to the square's ruined paving.

There could be no doubt that this was an ork of particular status. Size aside, his armour was bright with fresh paint and bore more iconography than any of the others. A pole jutted from the iron plate on his back, rising two metres above his head, seeming to give him even more height than his already daunting three metres. It was strung with helmets and human skulls, some still carrying dry, desiccated flesh. A banner with two crossed hatchets painted in red hung from it, rippling in the warm breeze.

The warboss stomped forwards to the centre of the square where the fountain of St. Ethiope had once stood, roaring and bellowing in what passed for its brutish language. Bas glanced across at the dome of the administratum complex. It had taken a lot of damage in the greenskin invasion. Most of its cobalt-blue tiles had been blasted off, revealing the fractured bare stone beneath. Great gaps had been blown in its surface, making it look like the detritus of a massive cracked egg from which some unimaginable animal had already emerged.

Bas had to see inside. He had to find the boy. He had to find a way to save him.

With a veritable army of orks filling the streets below, he knew he had never been at greater risk than he was now. It was broad daylight. If he moved, one of the beasts might spot him, and it would take only one to alert the others. More than ever, he felt himself balanced on a knife's edge. But there was no way he could turn back now. His mind was filled with thoughts of companionship. For the first time since he had emerged from hiding into a town held by horrors from another world, he knew purpose and, more importantly, and perhaps more dangerously, he remembered what it was to hope.

He needed to wait. He needed the horde below to become preoccupied with something.

He didn't have to wait long.

From the doorway of the Administratum building, the previously entrenched greenskin leader emerged, roaring and swiping at his subordinates to get them out of his way. In his own right, he was a monster of terrifying proportions, but to Bas's eye, the newcomer looked bigger and better armoured.

The two bosses locked eyes, both refusing to look down in submission. The horde parted between them, sensing the violence that was about to erupt. The newcomer threw his head back and gave a battle cry, a deafening, blood-freezing challenge. The other howled and foamed with rage, hefted a double-handed chainaxe over his head, and raced down the steps to meet his rival. The greenskin mob roared with delight and bloodlust.

Bas had his opening.

He didn't hesitate. Crouching low, he slid away from the statue and set off for the gaping wound in the side of the dome, moving roof to roof, careful to keep his distance from the edges lest his silhouette give him away.

He needn't have worried. Every beady red eye in the area was locked on the battle between the greenskin leaders.

AT THE END of his first week in Three Rivers, Bas's grandfather enrolled him in a small scholam owned and operated by the Ecclesiarchy, and the nightmare Bas was living became much, much worse. The other boys who attended were merciless from the start. Bas was a stranger, a newcomer, the easiest and most natural of targets. Furthermore, he had gotten this far in life without ever needing to defend himself, either verbally or physically, and they could smell his weakness like a pack of wild canids might smell a wounded beast. It drew them down on him from the first day.

The leader of the pack – the tallest, strongest and most vindictive – was called Kraevin and, at first, he feigned friendship.

'What's your name, then?' he asked Bas in the minutes before the day's long hours of work, prayer and study began.

Other boys drifting through the wrought iron gates noticed the newcomer and gathered round.

Bas was suddenly uncomfortable with all the attention. It didn't feel very benign.

'I'm Bas,' he answered meekly.

Kraevin laughed at that. 'Bas the bastard!' he told the others.

'Bas the maggot,' said another.

'Bas the cave toad!'

The boys laughed. Kraevin folded his arms and squinted down at Bas. 'I've seen you on Lymman Street. You're livin' with Old Ironfoot?'

Bas gaped at the other boy, confused. He didn't know who 'Ironfoot' was. His grandfather insisted on being called 'Sarge', never grandfather or any variation thereof. Bas had heard others call him *the* Sarge when they spoke *of* him, rather than *to* him. Then it dawned on him and he nodded.

Kraevin grinned. 'You like that? You know, because of his leg.'

He started walking around Bas with an exaggerated limp, making sounds like a machine. The other boys broke into fits of laughter.

Bas didn't. He had never asked the Sarge about his leg. He didn't dare. He knew it caused the old man frequent pain. He had seen that pain scored deep in his face often enough. He knew, too, that the leg made a grinding noise on some days and not on others, though there seemed no particular pattern to it. It didn't sound anything like the noise Kraevin was making, but that didn't seem to stop the boys enjoying the joke.

Kraevin stopped in front of Bas. 'So, what are you to him, eh? You his new boyfriend?'

Again, great fits of laughter from all sides.

'I… I'm his grandson,' Bas stuttered. It suddenly dawned on him that every moment spent talking to this boy was a moment spent digging a deeper hole for himself. He needed an escape… and he got it, for all the good it did.

A bronze bell rang out and a portly, stern-looking man with thick spectacles and a hooded robe of rough brown canvas appeared at the broad double doors of the main building. He bellowed at them to get inside.

'We'll talk later, maggot,' said Kraevin as he turned and led the rest of the boys in.

Bas barely made it back to the Sarge's home that evening. He had stopped screaming by then, but the tears continued to stream down his cheeks. His clothes had been cut with knives. His lip was ragged and bloody. One eye was so swollen he couldn't see out of it, and two of his fingers would no longer flex.

The Sarge was waiting for him at the rickety dining table in the centre of the room, bandages and salves already laid out.

'How many hits did you land?' he asked simply.

Bas couldn't speak for sobbing.

'I said how many hits,' the old man snapped.

'None,' Bas wailed. 'None, alright? I couldn't do anything!'

The old man cursed angrily, then gestured to the empty chair opposite him at the table. 'Sit down. Let's see if I can't patch you up.'

For half an hour, the Sarge tended his injured grandson. He was not gentle. He didn't even try to be. Bas cried out in pain a dozen times or more. But, rough as he was, the old man was good with bandages, splints and a needle and thread.

When he was done, he stood up to put away the medical kit. Looking down at Bas, he said, 'You're going back tomorrow. They won't touch you again until you're healed.'

Bas shook his head. 'I don't want to go back. Don't make me go. I'd rather die!'

The Sarge launched himself forward, getting right in Bas's face.

'Never say that!' he hissed. 'Don't you ever back down! Don't you ever let them win! Do you hear me, boy?'

Bas was frozen in absolute terror, certain the old man was about to rip him apart, such was the vehemence in his voice and on that terrible face.

His grandfather stood up straight again.

'The hard lessons are the ones that count,' he said in more subdued tones. 'You understand? Hard lessons make hard people.'

He turned and walked to a cupboard on the left to put the kit away.

'When you get sick of being an easy target, you let me know, boy. I mean it.'

He threw on a heavy groxskin coat and made for the door.

'Rest,' he said as he opened it. 'I have to go to work.'

The door slammed behind him.

Bas rested, but he could not sleep. His wounds throbbed, but that was not the worst of it.

Abject fear had settled over him like a wet shroud, clinging to him, smothering him.

Closing his eyes brought back stark memories of fists and feet pummelling him, of the wicked, joyous laughter that had mocked his cries for mercy.

No, there would be no sleep for him that night, nor for many others to come.

BAS FOUND THE human slaves already locked in a broad cage of black iron, the bars of which were crudely cast and cruelly barbed. As before, all but one of the slaves – and Bas judged there were over twenty of them – sat or lay like lifeless dolls. There was no talking between them, no sobbing or whimpering. They had no tears left. Bas wondered how long they had endured. As long as he had? Longer?

He saw the boy standing at the bars, hands clenched tight around them. What was he thinking? Did he always stand like this? Did he ever sleep?

The interior of the building had once been a grand place, even in the years of the town's decline. Now, though, each corner of the great lobby was heaped with mountains of ork excrement and rotting bodies. The walls were splattered with warlike icons in the same childishly simple style as the greenskin vehicles and banners. The air in here was foul, almost overpowering, even for Bas. Part of his success in remaining undetected for so long had depended on rubbing dried greenskin faeces onto his skin. At first, he had gagged so much he thought he might die. But after that first time, he had adjusted quickly, and the regrettable practice had masked his human scent well. Had it not, he would have been found and slaughtered long ago. Even so, the miasma of filth and decay in the wide lobby was sickening.

Much of the marble cladding which had graced the interior walls here had shattered and fallen to the floor, revealing rough brick and, in many places, twisted steel bars, making a descent fast and easy. Bas did a last visual scan to make sure all the greenskins were outside watching the fight, then dropped quickly to the lobby floor. The falls of his bare feet were silent as he moved around the west wall and closed on the black iron cage. None of the human captives saw or heard him until he was almost standing right in front of the boy. Even then, it seemed that they were too exhausted to register his presence. The boy continued staring straight ahead, eyes still intense, unblinking, and Bas felt a moment of panic. Perhaps the boy was brain-addled.

He took an instant to study him at close range. Like the others, he was skinny to the point of ill health, clearly malnourished, and bore the marks of cuts and bruises that had not healed properly. In the centre of his forehead was a black tattoo about three centimetres across. Bas noted it, but he had never seen its like before. He had no idea what it meant – a single stylised eye set within a triangle. Bas looked down at the boy's arms and noticed another tattoo on the inside right forearm. It was a bar-code with numbers beneath it. The greenskins had not done this to him. It was far too cleanly rendered for that. Bas couldn't imagine what these tattoos meant, and right here, right now, he didn't care.

He reached out and touched the boy's left hand where it gripped the bar.

Human contact must have pierced the veil over the boy's senses, because he gave a start and his eyes locked with Bas's for the first time.

Joy exploded in Bas's heart. Human contact! A connection! He hadn't dared hope to experience it ever again, and yet here it was. Damn the bars that stood between them. He might have embraced the boy otherwise for all the joy he felt at that moment.

He opened his mouth and tried to greet the boy, but the sound that emerged was a dry croak. Had he forgotten how to speak already? With concerted effort, he tried again, shaping his lips to form a word so simple and yet so difficult after his long months alone.

'Hello,' he grated, then said it again, his second attempt much better.

The boy blinked in surprise and whipped his hands from the bars. He retreated a step into the cage.

Bas couldn't understand this reaction. Had he done something wrong?

In his head, words formed, and he knew they were not his own. They had a strange quality to them, a sort of accent he did not recognise.

Who are you?

Bas shook his head, unsure of what was happening.

Seeing his confusion, the tattooed boy gingerly returned to the bars.

Who are you? the voice asked again.

'Is that you?' Bas returned hoarsely. 'It that you in my head?'

The boy opened his mouth and pointed inside. Most of his teeth were gone. Those that remained where little more than sharp, broken stubs. But this was not the reason the boy couldn't vocalise. Where his tongue should have been, only a dark nub of flesh remained. His tongue had been cut from his mouth.

Sounds of movement came suddenly from either side of the boy. Bas looked left and right and saw that the other captives had roused at last. Barging each other aside, they surged to the walls of the cage, shoving the tattooed, tongueless boy backwards in order to get closer to Bas.

Bas stepped away immediately, warily. He didn't like the look in their eyes. Such desperation. He felt the sudden burden of their hopes and expectations before anyone gave voice to them.

It was an ugly, shabby, middle-aged woman who did so first. 'Get us out, child! Free us, quickly!'

Others echoed her urgently. 'Open the cage, lad! Save us!'

Bas looked for the cage door and found it easily enough. It was to his right, locked and chained with links as thick as his wrist.

A tall, thin man with deeply sunken eyes and cheeks hissed at the others. 'Shut up, damn you. They'll hear!'

When he was ignored, he struck the loudest of the prisoners in the jaw, and Bas saw her sink to the cage floor. Another quickly took her place, stepping on the shoulder and arm of the first in her need to get closer to her potential saviour. Bas shrank further from them all. This was not right. He did not want to be responsible for these people. He just needed the boy.

Despite the logic in the words of the gaunt man, the others would not be quiet. They thrust their hands out between the bars, tearing their weak, papery skin on the iron barbs. Pools of blood began forming on the tiled floor, filling cracks there. Bas took another step back, searching the crowd in front of him for sign of the tattooed boy, but he had been pushed entirely from view.

'Don't you leave us, son,' begged a bald man, his right arm docked at the elbow.

'Emperor curse you if you leave us,' screeched a filthy woman with only a dark scab where her nose should have been. 'He will, boy. He'll curse you if you don't save us.'

Had the monsters outside not been making such a din of their own, they would surely have heard this commotion. Bas knew he had to go. He couldn't stay here. But it was hard to leave the boy. How could he open the cage? He had no way of cutting through that chain. Had he found this boy only to be frustrated by his inability to save him? Was the universe truly so cruel?

A mighty roar sounded from Salvation Square, so loud it drowned out even the wailing humans. The fight between the warbosses was over. The entertainment had ended. Three Bridges belonged either to the new leader or the old, it didn't matter to Bas. What mattered was that, any second now, massive green bodies would pour into the building through the shattered oak doors.

Go, said the tattooed boy's projected voice. *You have to go now.*

Bas still couldn't see him, but he called out; 'I'll come back for you!'

Don't, replied the boy. *Don't come back. You cannot help us. Just run.*

Bas scrambled back up the lobby wall like a spider. At the top, crouching on the lip of the great jagged wound in the dome, he paused and turned to look down at the cage one more time. The prisoners were still reaching out towards him despite being twenty metres away. They were still calling to him, howling at him.

Bas frowned.

'There's nowhere to run to,' Bas said quietly, wondering if the boy would pick up his thoughts. 'I only have you. I have to come back.'

Jabbering greenskins poured into the building then, laughing and grunting and snorting like wild boar.

Bas slid from view and made for the nearest of his boltholes to prepare for his return tonight. He didn't know how he would set the boy free, but something told him he would find a way. It was all that mattered to him now.

THERE ARE TWO ways to deal with fear, as Bas found out in his first few months in Three Rivers. You can let it corrode you, eat away at your freedom and sanity like a cancer, or you can fight it head on, maybe even overcome it. He didn't have much choice in the approach he was to take. His grandfather had already decided for him.

Kraevin and his gang of scum did indeed wait until Bas recovered before they brutalised him again. When it came, it was as vicious as the first time. They kicked him repeatedly, savagely, as he lay curled into a ball on the ground, and Bas thought they might never stop. Maybe they would kill him. Part of him wished they would. At least it would be an end.

When no more kicks came, it felt like a blessing from the God-Emperor Himself. He opened his eyes to see the gang strolling off down the street, the boys laughing and punching each other playfully on the arm. Two local women walked past and looked down at Bas where he bled on the pavement, but they didn't stop. There was no sign of pity in their eyes. They looked at him in passing as they might notice a dead rat on their path.

The next passer-by did stop, however. Bas didn't know him. He was a big fat man with skull and sword tattoos on both forearms. 'Having a bad day, son?' he asked as he helped Bas to his feet. 'Let's get you home, eh? The Sarge will fix you up.'

Bas hobbled along at the man's side, doing a fair job of stifling his sobs for once.

'D… do you know the Sarge?' he stammered.

The man laughed. 'You could say that,' he replied. 'I employ him.'

Bas looked up at him.

'I'm Sheriddan,' said the fat man. 'I own the public house on Megrum Street. You know, where your grandfather works at night.'

It turned out that Sheriddan liked to talk. In the twenty-two minutes Bas spent with him that day, he learned more about his grandfather than he had in the weeks since he had come to this accursed place. And what he learned, he could never have guessed.

According to Sheriddan, the sour old bastard was an Imperial hero.

AS HE HAD promised himself, Bas ate a full can of processed grox meat, knowing he would need the strength and energy it would give him. Sitting in the bolthole closest to Salvation Square, he thought hard about how he would get the boy out of the cage. One of the orks had to be carrying a key. Which one? How would Bas get it?

He thought, too, about what to do once the cage door was open. The others… he couldn't look after them. They'd have to fend for themselves. They were adults. They couldn't expect him to take the burden of their lives onto his shoulders. Such a thing was well beyond his power. It was too much to ask of him. They'd have to make their own way. He would lead the boy out at speed, climbing up to the rooftops before the orks realised what was going on. Together, they could return to this bolthole without drawing attention.

Bas looked at the few cans of food remaining in the metal box at his feet. There were no labels on them, but he didn't suppose it mattered. Like himself, the tattooed boy would be glad of whatever food he could get. Together, they would eat well in celebration of their new friendship. Tomorrow, they could search out new supplies as a team.

With these thoughts buoying his spirit, Bas bedded down and tried to sleep, knowing he would need to be well rested for the dangers of the night ahead.

* * *

DARKNESS FELL FAST in Three Rivers, and this night the sky was clear and bright. Overhead, the planet's three small moons glowed like spotlit pearls. The stars shone in all their glory. Had Bas deigned to look up, he might have noticed some of them moving inexplicably northwards, but he did not. His eyes were fixed on the scene below.

In the ruined plaza, ork cookfires burned by the dozen, surrounded by massive bodies turned orange by the flames. The majority of the brutes were drinking some kind of stinking, fermented liquid from barrels they had unloaded from their trucks. Others ripped hunks of roasted meat from bodies that turned on their spits. Bas didn't know what kind of meat the greenskins were cooking, but he could hear the fat pop and sizzle as the baking skin cracked and burned. Others still were barking at each other in their coarse tongue. Fights broke out sporadically, each ending in a fatality as the stronger hacked or bludgeoned the weaker to death.

Bas's stomach groaned, demanding he act on the savoury smell that wafted up towards his perch, but he ignored it. He needed all his focus, all his attention, to recognise the moment he could slip back inside the dome of the Administratum building.

It seemed that a great many hours passed as he hunched there atop the ruins of the old church once more, clinging to the statue that broke up his silhouette. In fact, only two hours had gone by when, with their fill of meat and drink and fighting, most of the orks settled down to sleep. Their communal snoring soon rivalled the noise of their engines from earlier in the day.

It was time to move.

With all his concentration centred on avoiding detection, Bas made his way across his plank-bridges and soon reached the gaping crack in the dome. There, pressing himself close to the exposed stone, he peered inside and scanned the hallway below.

There were fires in here, too, though smaller than the ones outside. Around them slept the biggest of the greenskins, those with the heaviest armour, the largest weapons, the most decoration. There were a few hook-noses, too, sleeping in groups near the fly-covered dung piles. They had not been allowed to bed down near the fires of their giant masters.

Bas watched and waited and decided that the orks within were as sound asleep as those without. He steeled himself for what had to be done, then stepped out from behind the cover of the dome and began his descent. The stars cast his shadow on the tile floor below, but nothing stirred, nothing noticed.

With all the stealth he could muster, Bas descended, his toes and fingers seeking and finding the same holds he had used earlier in the day. But while the daytime descent had taken only moments, this one took minutes. There was too much at stake to rush, and nothing to be gained.

Finally, his bare feet reached the cold tiles and he turned from the wall. He realised that, even had he slipped and made a noise, none of the orks would likely have heard him. Up close, their snoring was preposterously loud. Good. That would work in his favour.

Bas avoided looking directly at any of the fires. His eyes had adjusted well to the shadows over the last few hours of patient observation. He didn't want to lose that. He had to be able to see into the dark places, for the cage with the human prisoners was flush against the far wall and the marble staircase next to it cast a black cloak over it.

He moved, keeping to pools of deep shadow wherever he could, at the same time careful to steer clear of the huddled hook-noses. Had he not masked his scent with ork filth so often and so diligently, their sensitive noses might well have detected him. But they did not awaken. Bas reached the cage and stood exactly where he had earlier that day.

Gentler sounds of sleep issued from behind the black iron bars.

Good, thought Bas. Most of them are sleeping, too.

He hoped they would stay that way. But where was the boy?

A figure moved to the cage wall. Bas squinted, and was relieved to see the boy standing there before him. Bas smiled and nodded by way of greeting.

The boy did not smile back.

I told you not to come back. Don't take this risk. Escape with your life.

Bas shook his head and spoke in low tones, unsure if the boy could read thoughts as well as he transmitted his own. 'How do I open the door? How do I unlock this thing?'

He pointed to the heavy chain and crude cast-iron padlock where they lay at the foot of the cage door. The chain's coils wrapped around the bars twice.

I ask you one more time, said the boy. *Will you not leave me and save yourself?*

'No!' hissed Bas. 'I will not go on alone. I'm sick of it. Don't you understand?'

The boy's voice was silent in Bas's mind for a while. Then, it said, *There is a key. The head slaver wears it on his belt, tied to it by a piece of thick rope. If you can cut the rope and get the key without waking him...*

'Which one is he?' Bas whispered.

He lies by the fire closest to your left. His right ear is missing.

Bas stalked off towards the fire, still careful to avoid looking directly at its heart. There were seven orks around it and, as Bas drew close to them – closer than he had ever physically been to one of the tusked giants before – the sheer size of them truly dawned on him for the first time. He had always known they were huge, these savage horrors. But it was only this close, their wide, powerful backs heaving with each breath, that he realised how small and how fragile he truly was. There was nothing he could do against even one of them. If everything went wrong here tonight, he knew it would be the end.

Bas quickly found the slave master and moved around him to find the monster's key.

The slaver's barrel chest expanded like some huge bellows each time he took a deep, rumbling breath and, when he exhaled, strands of thick saliva quivered on his long, curving tusks. The smell of his breath in Bas's face was foul, like a carcass rotting in the sun.

Against his better judgement, Bas moved between the slave master and the fire. It was the only way to reach the key on the beast's belt. But, as his shadow passed over the closed eyes of the monster, its huge shoulders twitched.

It stopped snoring.

Bas's adrenaline, already high, rocketed. He stood rooted to the spot, his hands and knees shaking. If the beast came awake now, he didn't know what he would do. He simply stood there, and the seconds seemed to stretch out like hours.

But seconds they were, and only a few, before the monster settled again and began to snore even louder than before. Bas's relief was palpable, but he didn't want to be near the damned thing any longer than necessary, so he crouched down by the monster's thickly-muscled belly and, with slow precision, drew his grandfather's knife from the sheath at his waist.

The rope was thick and the key itself was heavy, but the Sarge's old knife was razor-sharp. It had never lost its edge, despite all the use it had seen. It parted the rope fibres with ease. Bas lifted the key, resheathed the knife and made his way back over to the barbed cage.

'I have it,' he whispered as he crouched down by the massive padlock.

'It turns clockwise,' said a voice from the deep shadows within the cage.

Bas looked up with a start and saw the tall, gaunt man from before standing in front of him on the other side of the cage door.

'I'll help you, son,' said the man, lowering himself into a crouch. 'You turn the key. I'll keep the chain and lock from rattling.'

Bas looked for the boy he had come to save and saw him come to crouch silently by the gaunt man's side.

'You'll need both hands to turn it,' said the man.

Bas fitted the head of the key into the hole and tried to turn it until his fingers hurt.

Nothing.

An act of no effort whatsoever for the aliens was near impossible for Bas. The torque in his wrists just wasn't enough.

'Here,' said the man, handing Bas a smelly rag that had once been clothing. 'Wrap this around the handle and try again.'

Bas did. With his teeth gritted and the effort raising the veins on his arms and neck, he wrestled with the lock. There was a screech of metal. The lock slid open. Bas turned, certain that he had achieved this feat only to bring death on himself. Every sound seemed so much louder when stealth was paramount. He scanned the hall behind him, not daring to breathe. He sensed the tension on the other side of the cage, too. The orks, however, slumbered on. Perhaps there was little to fear after all. Perhaps the beasts slept so soundly he could have run through here clapping and yelling and not have roused a single one.

Overconfidence kills more men that bullets do, snapped the remembered voice of his grandfather. *Stay grounded!*

'This will be tricky,' said the man in the cage. 'Lift the lock away from the chains and put it to the side. I'll try to uncoil this thing without too much racket.'

That made sense to Bas. The chain looked particularly heavy, and so it was. In the end, it took all three of them – the gaunt man, Bas and the tattooed boy together – to remove it quietly. Remove it they did, but before the gaunt man could try to open the door, Bas raised a hand. 'Wait,' he whispered. 'We should spit on the hinges.'

The man cocked an eyebrow, his face just visible in the gloom. 'Good thinking, boy.'

Bas was surprised by the compliment. His grandfather would never have handed one out so easily.

Regardless of how good the idea was, it proved difficult for the man and the tattooed boy to generate enough saliva for the task. Too long without adequate food and water had made their throats itchy, their mouths bone dry. After a few failed attempts, however, the man had an idea. Instructing the tattooed boy to do the same, he put a corner of his ragged clothing in his mouth and began to chew it.

Soon enough, the door's two large iron hinges gleamed wetly with fresh lubrication. Awakened by the sound of spitting, other prisoners rose and shuffled forward to see what was going on. That made Bas uncomfortable. He was sure they would give him away and bring the whole rescue down about his head. He was wrong. They had learned early in their captivity not to awaken their captors if they didn't want to be tortured and beaten, or worse.

'Stay quiet, everyone,' the gaunt man told them. 'The lad has freed us, but getting out will be no easy matter. You must stay quiet. Exercise patience or we'll all die here tonight.'

'We're with you, Klein,' whispered someone at the back. Others nodded assent.

Assured of their compliance, the gaunt man, Klein, turned back to the cage door and gently eased it open. The hinges grated in complaint, but only a little. At last, the cage stood open.

Bas stepped back.

Klein put a hand on the tattooed boy's shoulder and ushered him through first. He stopped just in front of Bas, who couldn't prevent himself from reaching out and embracing the boy.

'I told you I'd get you out,' Bas whispered, then stepped back, abruptly self-conscious.

Klein led the others out now, until they stood together outside the cage, a silent, terrified gaggle of wretches, all looking at Bas expectantly.

'What's your plan for getting us away from here, son?' Klein asked now. 'How will you get us to safety?'

Bas almost blurted, 'I only came for him,' but he stopped himself. Looking at these people, each hanging on to life and hope by the thinnest of threads, he knew he couldn't just turn his back on them. He had come into their lives, a light in the dark, and he could no more extinguish it now than he could abandon the boy who would give new meaning to his survival.

He turned and pointed to the broad crack in the dome up above. The closest of Taos III's moons, Amaral, was just peaking from the eastern edge of the gap, casting its silver light down into the hall, revealing just how many of the huge greenskin brutes lay sleeping there.

Bas's gut clenched. It could still go so wrong. One slip would bring slaughter down on them, and yet he was so close, so close to getting himself and the tattooed boy away from here.

Klein followed Bas's finger, his eyes roving from the gap in the dome, down the rough wall to the cold marble floor. He frowned, perhaps doubtful that some of his group would manage the climb. Nevertheless, he nodded and told Bas, 'Lead us out, son. We will follow.'

Thus, with the utmost care, the group picked its way between the ork fires, freezing in terror every time one of the beasts shifted or grunted loudly in its sleep. Crossing the hall seemed to Bas to take forever. This was foolish. Even if these people did get out, how slowly would they have to cross the bridges he had laid between the rooftops? It would take forever for them to...

To get where? Where was he going to lead them?

He couldn't take them to any of his boltholes. Those had been chosen for the difficulty of their access, for their small size. They were meant to be inconspicuous, but there was nothing inconspicuous about a group of clumsy adults struggling to pack their bodies into such a tiny space. And the smell of these people! They smelled so human. Bas hadn't realised until now, standing there among them, just how strong people smelled. The greenskins would track them like hounds when they awoke. No doubt these people thought Bas smelled foul, standing there with dried ork faeces rubbed into his skin, clothes and hair. But they would learn to do the same or they would die.

At the wall, the group huddled together and Klein spoke to them again.

'The boy will go first,' he said. 'All of you, watch him carefully. Watch how he ascends and try to remember the handholds he uses. We have to do this quickly, but not so quick as to cause any mishaps. Syrric,' he

said, addressing the tattooed boy, 'you will go second. Once you and –
I'm sorry, son, I don't know your name.'

'Bas,' said Bas.

Klein put a fatherly hand on Bas's head. 'Bas. And now we know the
name of our saviour.' He smiled, and Bas saw that he, too, had had his
teeth broken, no doubt by a blow from one of the greenskins. 'Bas, when
you reach the top, you and Syrric will help the rest climb up, okay?'

For an instant, Bas imagined just taking Syrric and running. The duo
would have far better odds alone. But no sooner had the thought come
to him than he felt the beginnings of a sickening guilt. What would his
grandfather have done? There had been no lessons about this. No tests.
How he wished there had been. Had the Sarge ever made such a decision? Had Bas's education simply never gotten that far?

What should I do, grandfather? Bas silently asked the old man in his
memories.

No sharp voice rose from the past to answer him.

He looked over at Syrric, and the boy nodded back at him in support.

'Right,' whispered the Klein. 'Up you go, son. Show us the way.'

Bas started climbing, not looking down, letting his hands and feet find
the holds he knew were there. He scaled the wall without noise or incident and, at the top, turned to find Syrric only a few metres below him.
As the boy neared the top of the wall where the dome opened to the air,
Bas reached down and helped him up.

Below, Klein was helping the first of the adults, a woman with short
hair, to begin her climb.

How frail they all looked. How shaky. Could they really manage it?

Bas heard a shout in his head.

No! Dara, no!

It was Syrric. He had seen or sensed something about to happen. From
the desperate tone of his thoughts, Bas knew it was bad.

Surging from the back of the group, a woman began shouldering others roughly out of her way, screeching hysterically, 'I have to get out! I
have to get out of here! Me first! Let me up first!'

Her mad cries echoed in the great hall, bouncing from the domed ceiling back down to the ears of the sleeping greenskins. With grunts and
snarls, they started to wake.

Klein tried to stop her as she surged forward, but panic had given her
strength and he reeled backwards as she barged him aside. Then, from the
bottom, she reached up and tore the short-haired woman from the wall,
flinging her backwards to land with a sickening crack on the marble floor.

The short-haired woman didn't rise. Her eyes didn't open.

Bas saw the orks rising now, vast furious shapes given a doubly hellish appearance by the light of their fires. The first to stand scanned the
hall for the source of the noise that had awoken it. Baleful red eyes soon
picked out the pitiful human escapees.

Roars filled the air. Blades were drawn. Guns were raised.

Bas loosed a string of curses. There on the lip of the crack in the dome, he and Syrric could see it all play out below them. It would have been wise to flee then, and deep down, Bas knew that. But there was something about the inevitable horror to come that kept him there, kept him watching. He had to bear witness to this.

Was this his fault? Were they all to die so he could assuage his loneliness?

Dara scrabbled at the wall, desperately trying to ascend at speed, ignorant of the imminent slaughter her foolishness had initiated. Though she hadn't been composed enough to map Bas's path in her head, she made progress by virtue of the frantic nature with which she attacked the task.

She was halfway up when the others began to scream. The first orks had reached them. Heavy blades rose and fell, hacking their victims to quivering pieces. Fountains of blood, black in the moonlight, geysered into the air, drenching the greenskins' leering faces. Deep, booming cries of savage joy sounded from a dozen tusk-filled maws. Bestial laughter ricocheted from the walls.

Bas saw Klein looking straight up at him, the last of the escapees still standing, hemmed in on all sides, nowhere to run. The orks closed on him, red eyes mad with the joy of killing. Klein didn't scream like the others. He seemed resigned to his fate. Bas saw him mouth some words, but he never knew what they were. They might have been *good luck*. They might have been something else.

A dozen ork blades fell at once. Wet pieces hit the floor. Klein was gone.

Outside Government Hall, the commotion spread to the rest of the horde. Those asleep in Salvation Square came awake, confused at first, then eager to join whatever fracas was taking place within the building. They began streaming inside, fighting with each other to be first. Perhaps they could smell human blood. It was thick and salty on the air. Bas could smell it, too.

Dara was almost at the gap in the dome now, still scrabbling manically for every protruding stone or steel bar that might get her closer to freedom. She was within reach. Bas looked down at her. He could have reached out then, could have gripped her arms and helped her up the last metre, but he hesitated. This madwoman had sealed the fate of the others. She had killed them as surely as the orks had. If he tried to bring her with him, she would get him killed, too. He was sure of it, and the darkest part of him considered kicking her from the wall to plunge backwards, joining those she had condemned. It would be justice, he thought. A fitting revenge for the others.

But he didn't kick her. Instead, without conscious decision, he found himself reaching out for her, committed to helping her up.

Even as he did, he became aware of a strange whistling noise in the sky.

He didn't have time to wonder what it was. The stone beneath him bucked violently and he grabbed at the wall for support. There was a blinding flash of light that turned the world red behind his eyelids. Blazing heat flooded over him, burning away his filth-caked hair.

Dara's scream filled his ears, merging now with more strange sounds from the sky. Bas opened his eyes in time to watch her plunge towards the bellowing greenskins below. He didn't see her hacked to pieces. Syrric grabbed his shoulder and spun him around.

Look at the square, he told Bas.

From the stone ledge around the dome, the two boys could see everything. The night had been turned to sudden day by great pillars of fire that burst upwards. Buildings on all sides, half-shattered in the original invasion, were toppled now as massive artillery shells slammed into them, blowing chunks of stone and cement out in great flaming clouds.

Bas watched with wide eyes. Again and again, high-explosive death fell screaming from the sky.

The orks were arming themselves and racing for their machines. Bas saw half a dozen armoured fuel trucks blown apart like cheap toys when a shell struck the ground between them. Burning, screaming greenskins scattered in every direction, their arms pinwheeling as the flames gorged on their flesh.

The whistling stopped to be replaced by a roar of turbine engines. Black shapes ripped through the sky above Bas's head, fast and low. They were too fast to see properly, but the stutter and flare of their guns tore up the square, churning ork bodies into chunks of wet meat. Greenskin vehicles returned fire, filling the air with a fusillade of solid slugs and bright las-blasts. Missiles screamed into the air on smoky trails as the aliens brought their vehicle-mounted launchers to bear. One of the black shapes in the sky was struck hard in the tail and began a mad spiral towards the ground. It struck an old municipal building not two hundred metres from Bas and Syrric. Both the building and the aircraft tumbled into the square in a cloud of smoke, flame and spinning shrapnel.

Bas grabbed Syrric's hand. 'We have to go!' he yelled over the noise.

He didn't wait for an answer. He pulled Syrric to the planks connecting the dome of their perch to the nearest roof and they crossed quickly, Bas first, then Syrric. Screeches from behind made Bas turn. Some of the hook-noses had scaled the wall inside the dome. They spotted the boys and gave chase, firing their oversized pistols as they came.

As soon as Syrric was over the first gap, Bas kicked the planks away. Then, grabbing Syrric's hand again, he ran.

Anti-aircraft fire poured into the sky, lighting their way across the rooftops. The shadowy shapes assaulting the orks from above were forced to pull out. Moments after they did, the artillery strikes started again. Bas was halfway across one of his makeshift bridges when a shell plunged into the building he was crossing towards. It punched through the tenement roof and a number of upper floors before it exploded somewhere deep within the structure. Bas watched in horror as the building in front of him began to disintegrate, turning to little more than loose stone. He turned and leapt back towards the edge of the roof where Syrric stared in horror, just as the planks beneath his feet fell away.

His fingers missed the lip of the roof. He felt his dizzying plunge begin. But small hands reached for him just as he fell, gripping his wrists and hauling him in towards the building. Bas struck the stone wall hard, winding himself, but the small hands didn't let go. He looked up and saw Syrric stretching over the edge, face twisted in pain, grunting and sweating with the effort of keeping Bas from plummeting to his death.

Bas scrabbled for a foothold and found a thin ledge, not enough to support his full weight, but enough to take some of the strain off Syrric.

Can you climb up?

Bas stretched and gripped the lip of the roof. Then, with Syrric pulling, he heaved himself up and rolled over the edge. There, with death averted once more, he lay panting, adrenaline racing through his veins. Syrric crouched over him.

We can't stay up here. Isn't there some other way?

The ground shook. More explosions rocked the town, striking just to the north of their position. Bas didn't have time to wait for the shaking to stop. As soon as he had his breath, he got up.

'The greenskins will be everywhere at ground level,' he said miserably, but, looking at the empty space where the next building had been only moments ago, he knew that staying high would be just as dangerous. Besides, that building had been the only one linked to this. It looked like there was little choice. If they couldn't travel *above* ground, and they couldn't travel *on* the ground...

'There's one more way,' said Bas. 'Let's go.'

BAS BEGAN TRAINING under his grandfather after the fourth time Kraevin's gang beat him up. It was the worst beating yet. One of the smaller boys – an ugly, rat-faced lad called Sarkam – had actually stabbed Bas in the belly with a box-cutter. It was the sight of so much blood that brought the beating to an early end this time. Instead of strolling off in casual satisfaction, Kraevin and his gang ran, knowing this level of violence would mean serious trouble for them if they were caught.

Bas staggered home, both hands pressed to his abdomen, drawing sharp looks from everyone he passed. A rough-looking woman in a filthy apron called out, 'You need help, boy?'

Bas ignored her and kept on. He knew the Sarge would be waiting at the table with the medical kit laid out. He had warned Bas that the other boys might attack him today. He had just about healed from the last beating, after all.

But this time was different, in more ways than one.

Bas wasn't crying.

More important than that, he had actually fought back.

True, his unpractised attempts to retaliate had met with dismal failure, but they had caught the other boys off guard. For the first time, Bas saw an instant of doubt in their eyes. They knew fear, too, he realised. They loved to dish out pain, but they didn't want any coming their way.

That was when he knew his grandfather was the answer.

This time, while the old man stitched the wound in Bas's belly, Bas glared at him.

'Something you want to say to me, boy?' said the Sarge.

Bas's words came out as a growl that surprised even him.

'I know who you are,' he told the old man. 'I know what you did, how you fought. Sherridan told me. He called you an Imperial hero!'

A sudden scowl twisted those terrifying features. 'You think Imperial heroes live like this, you fool?' the Sarge snapped back. He gestured at the dank, water-stained walls of their home. 'Sherridan had no business saying anything. I'll bet he didn't tell you I was stripped of my medals. I'll bet he didn't mention that I was dishonourably discharged after forty bloody lashes! Sherridan sees what he wants to see. You hear me?'

'I don't care about that,' Bas shot back. He would not be denied. Not this time. 'You could teach me. You could help me, make me stronger. Make it so I could kill them if I wanted to.'

His grandfather held his gaze. For what seemed an eternity, neither blinked.

'I can teach you,' the old man said at last with a solemn nod. 'But it'll hurt more than everything you've endured so far. And there's no going back once we start, so you'd better be damned sure.'

'It will be worth it,' hissed Bas, 'to smash those bastards even just once.'

The old man's eyes bored into his. Again, he nodded. 'We'll begin when you're able,' he told Bas.

And so they did.

It started simply enough. Bas drilled footwork for hours around the old dead tree at the back of the tenement. Slowly, the number of push-ups, chin-ups and sit-ups he could do increased from single digits to double. Within a month and a half, the old man had him into triple digits. Then they began training with weights, anything they could find, whether it be rocks or old tyres or bags of cement.

Bas learned to wield sticks, knives, broken bottles, anything that could be used as a weapon. He became lean and hard like the grox meat they ate at every meal. He became faster, stronger, better than he had ever believed possible, and every bit of it was bought with sweat and blood, but never tears.

Tears were forbidden.

His grandfather was a brutal, relentless instructor. Every day was harder, more painful, more severe than the last. But Bas endured, his hatred burning within him, spurring him on. It wasn't just hatred for Kraevin and his schoolhouse thugs. It was hatred against all the wrongs he had known. Even as his grandfather forged him into something new, something tough and independent, Bas learned a fresher, deeper hate for the old man. His mistakes, fewer and fewer as time went by, were exploited with merciless brutality, until Bas wondered who was worse: Kraevin, or the Sarge himself.

It hardly mattered. He saw the results. And others saw them, too.

Kraevin's gang spent less time taunting him as the days passed. Sometimes, he saw them glancing nervously in his direction from the corner of his eye. He recognised that doubt he had seen before. The weeks since they had attacked him stretched into months. Bas started to wonder if they had given up for good.

Then, as he was walking home three days before Emperor's Day, Kraevin and his gang ambushed him from an alley and dragged him in.

Bas lashed out immediately without pausing for thought and smashed one boy's nose to a pulp.

The boy yowled and broke from the fight, hands held up to his crimson-smeared face.

Kraevin shouted something and the whole gang backed off, forming a semicircle around their target. Bas watched as they all drew knives. If they expected him to piss his pants, however, they were gravely mistaken.

'Let's have it!' Bas hissed at them. 'All of you!'

Reaching into the waistband of his trousers, he pulled his own blade free.

The Sarge didn't know about this. Bas hadn't told him he was now carrying a weapon. He had found it on the tenement stairwell one morning, a small kitchen knife stained with a stranger's blood. After washing it and sharpening it while the Sarge was at work, Bas had started to carry it with him. Now he was glad of that. It was his equaliser, though the odds he faced here were still far from equal.

Kraevin didn't look so smug right then, but he motioned and the boys lunged in.

Bas read their movements, just as the old man had taught him. The closest boy was going for a thrust to his midsection. Bas slipped it. His hand flashed out and cut the tendons in the boy's wrist.

Screaming filled the alley and the boy dropped to his knees, clutching his bleeding arm.

Bas kicked him hard in the face. 'Come on, bastards!' he roared at the others. Again, he kicked the wounded boy.

This display was unlike anything the others were prepared for. They didn't want any of it.

The gang broke, boys bolting from the alley in both directions, knives abandoned, thrown to the ground. Only Kraevin remained. He had never run from anything. If he ran now, he'd be giving up all his status, all his power, and he knew it. Even so, Bas could see it in his eyes: the terroriser had become the terrified.

Bas rounded on him, knife up, stance loose, light on his feet.

'Bas the bastard,' said Bas, mimicking Kraevin's voice. 'You've no idea how right you were, you piece of filth.'

He closed in, angling himself for a lightning slash to the other boy's face. Something in Kraevin snapped. He dropped his knife and backed up against the alley wall, hands raised in desperate placation.

'Bas, please,' he begged. 'It wasn't me. It was never me. Honestly.'

Bas drew closer, ready to deliver a flurry of nasty cuts.

'He said never to tell you,' cried Kraevin. 'Said he'd see us right for money and lho-sticks. I swear it!'

'Groxshit!' snarled Bas. 'Who? Who said that?'

He didn't believe Kraevin for a moment. The boy was just buying time, spinning desperate lies.

'The Sarge,' Kraevin gasped. 'Old Ironfoot. He came to us after the first time we beat you. Honest, I thought he was going to murder us, but he didn't. He said he wanted us to keep on you, keep beating you down. Told us to wait until you were healed each time.'

Bas halted his advance. That couldn't be true. No.

But... could it? Was the old man that twisted? Why would he do such a thing?

'Talk,' he ordered Kraevin, urging him on with a mock thrust of his knife.

'Th... that's it,' stammered the boy. 'Two days ago, he found us and told us to ambush you. Said to use knives this time. I told him he was crazy. No way. But he tripled the money he was offering. My old man's got lung-rot. Can't work no more. I need the money, Bas. I didn't want to, but I had to. But it's over now, okay? Throne above, it's over.'

Bas thought about that for a second, then he rammed his right boot up between Kraevin's legs. As the bully doubled over, Bas kicked him again, a blistering shot straight to the jaw. Teeth and blood flew from Kraevin's mouth. He dropped to the ground, unconscious.

Bas sheathed his little knife in his waistband and looked down at the boy who had taught him the meaning of fear.

'Yes,' he told the crumpled figure, 'it *is* over.'

AT HOME, HE found the Sarge at the back of the tenement, leaning against the old dead tree, smoking a lho-stick in the sunlight.

'No medical kit this time?' Bas asked as he stopped a few metres from the old man.

The Sarge grinned at him. 'Knew you wouldn't need it.'

'You paid them to do it, didn't you?' said Bas.

The old man exhaled a thick cloud of yellow smoke.

'You've done well,' he told his grandson. It was all the confirmation needed.

Bas said nothing. He felt numb.

'Stay grounded, boy,' rumbled the Sarge. 'Stay focused. We're just getting started, you and I. You think you've bested your daemons, and maybe you have, for now. But there are worse things than childhood bullies out there. Never forget the fear and anger that brought you this far.'

Bas didn't answer. He stared at the dirt between his feet, feeling utterly hollow, consumed by a raw emptiness he hadn't known was possible.

'There's more to learn, boy,' the Sarge told him. 'We're not done here. Remember the chubby runt you used to be. Think of how you've changed, what you've achieved. I gave you that. Keep training, boy. Keep learning. Don't stop now. As much as you hate me, you know I'm right. Let's see how far you can take it.'

The old man paused, his brows drawing down, and added in a voice suddenly harsh and hateful, 'If you want to stop, you know where the damned door is. I won't give bed and board to an Emperor-damned quitter.'

Bas looked at his hands. They were clenched into fists. His forearms rippled with taut muscle. He wanted to lash out at the Sarge, to bloody him, maybe even kill him for what he'd done. But, for all he'd changed, all he'd learned, his hands were still a child's hands. He was still only seven years old, and he had nowhere else to go. Besting other boys was one thing, but the old man was right about greater foes. Bas had seen big, barrel-chested men from the refineries beating their wives and children in the street. No one ever stopped them. No one dared, despite how sick it made them to turn away. Bas always wished he was big enough and tough enough to intervene. The impotence inherent in his age and stature angered him. More than any daydreams of dispensing justice, however, he knew that training had brought focus and purpose to his life. His new-found strength, speed and skill had burned away that clinging shroud of fear he'd lived with for so long. Every technique he mastered brought him a fresh confidence his former weakness had always denied. He saw it, saw that he needed to keep growing, keep developing, to master every skill the old man offered and more. No. He didn't just need it. He *wanted* it. Right then and there, it was *all* he wanted.

There was nothing else.

He locked eyes with his grandfather, his gaze boring into him with cold fire.

'All right,' he spat. 'Show me. Teach me. I want all of it.'

A grin twisted the Sarge's scarred face. 'Good,' he said. 'Good.'

He ground his lho-stick out in the dirt at the base of the tree.

'Go change your clothes and warm up. We'll work on nerve destructions today.'

* * *

TWO AND A half years later, in the shadow of that same dead tree, a slightly taller, harder Bas – now ten years old – was working through a series of double-knife patterns while his grandfather barked out orders from a wooden bench on the right.

The sun was high and bright, baking the dusty earth under Bas's feet.

'Work the left blade harder!' the Sarge snapped. 'Watch your timing. Don't make me come over there!'

A deep rumble sounded over the tenement rooftops, throaty and rhythmic. It must have meant something to the old man, because the Sarge stood bolt upright and stared up at the azure sky, muscles tensed, veins throbbing in his neck.

Bas, surprised by the intensity of the old man's reaction, stopped mid-pattern and followed the Sarge's gaze.

Seven black shapes crossed directly overhead.

'Marauder bombers,' said the old man. 'And a Lightning escort out of Red Sands. Something's wrong.'

Despite their altitude, the noise of the aircraft engines made the air vibrate. Bas had never seen craft like these before. They had the air of huge predatory birds about them. They had barely disappeared below the line of tenement roofs on the far side before another similar formation appeared, then another and another.

The old man cursed.

'It was just a matter of time,' he said to himself. 'This planet was always going to get hit sooner or later.'

He limped past Bas, iron leg grinding, heading towards the tenement's back door. But he stopped halfway and turned.

'They'll be coming for me,' he said, and there was something in his eye Bas had never seen before. It was the closest thing to fondness the old man had ever managed, though it still fell far short. 'They always call on the veterans first,' he told Bas. 'No one ever truly retires from the Guard. I've done the best I could with you, boy. You hate me, and that's only proper, but I did what I had to do. The Imperium is not what you think. I've seen it, by the Throne. Terrors by the billion, all clamouring to slaughter or enslave us. And now it looks like they're here. Only the strongest survive, boy. And you're my blood, mark you. My last living blood! I've done my best to make sure you're one of the survivors.'

He paused to look up as more bombers crossed the sky.

'Come on inside,' he told Bas. 'There's something I want to give you before I go. May it serve you well in what's to come.'

They went inside.

A few days later, just as the old man had predicted, the Imperium came to call on him, and he answered.

It was the last time Bas ever saw him.

* * *

THE SHELLING FROM the sky had opened great craters in the streets below. Through choking clouds of smoke and dust, over hills of flaming debris, the boys searched for a way into the sewers. Many of the massive holes were filled with rubble and alien bodies, but Bas quickly found one which offered access to the dark, round tunnels that laced the town's foundations. He had mostly avoided these tunnels during his time alone. Those times he had come down here looking for sources of potable water, he had encountered bands of scavenging hook-noses. Each time, he had barely escaped with his life.

There didn't seem to be any of the disgusting creatures here now, however. In the utter darkness, he and Syrric held hands tightly, using their free hands to guide themselves along the tunnel walls. They couldn't see a damned thing. Bas had no idea how or when they would find a way out, but he couldn't let that stop him. The tunnel ceiling rumbled with the sound of war machines on the move and explosive detonations. If he and Syrric were to survive the journey to one of his boltholes, they would have to travel down here in the dark.

As they moved, Bas became sharply aware of the comfort he was drawing from Syrric's hand. He wondered if that made him weak. His grandfather had used that word like a curse, as if weakness was the worst thing in the universe, and perhaps it was. Bas hadn't lived this long by being weak. He knew that. But he wasn't so sure it was weak to want the company of your own kind. Syrric's presence made him feel stronger. His body seemed to ache less. The other boy was following his lead, depending on him. Here was the sense of purpose Bas had so desperately missed. Alone, his survival had been nothing more than an act of waiting, waiting for a time in which he'd find something to live for, to fight for. Now he had it: someone to share the darkness with, to watch his back. He had gotten Syrric out, just as he had intended. Despite the deaths of the others, it still felt like the greatest victory of his young life, better even than beating Kraevin.

Kraevin!

Bas hadn't thought of the former bully in quite a while. What kind of death had he suffered the day the orks came? Had he been hacked to pieces like Klein and the prisoners? Had he been shot? Eaten?

As Bas was wondering this, he spotted light up ahead.

'There,' he whispered, and together he and Syrric made for the distant glow.

It was moonlight, and it poured through a gap in the tunnel ceiling. An explosive shell had caused the rockcrete road above to collapse, forming a steep ramp. The boys waited and listened until Bas decided that the sound of alien battle cries and gunfire was far enough away that they could risk the surface again. He and Syrric scrambled up the slope to stand on a street shrouded in thick grey smoke.

Which way? Syrric asked.

Bas wasn't sure. He had to have a bolthole somewhere near here, but with all the smoke, he couldn't find a landmark to navigate by. It seemed prudent to move in the opposite direction from the noise of battle.

'Let's keep on this way,' said Bas, 'at least for now.' But, just as they started walking, a hoarse shout sounded from up ahead.

'Contact front!'

The veils of smoke were suddenly pierced by a score of blinding, pencil thin beams, all aimed straight at the two boys.

'Down!' yelled Bas.

He and Syrric dropped to the ground hard and stayed there while the las-beams carved the air just above their heads. The barrage lasted a second before a different voice, sharp with authority, called out, 'Cease fire!'

That voice made Bas shiver. It sounded so much like the Sarge. Could it be the old man? Had he survived? Had he come back for his grandson after all this time?

Shadowy shapes emerged from the smoke. Human shapes.

Nervously, Bas got to his knees. He was still holding Syrric's hand. Looking down, he tugged the other boy's arm. 'They're human!'

Syrric didn't move.

Bas tugged again. 'Syrric, get up. Come on.'

Then he saw it. Syrric was leaking thick fluid onto the surface of the road. Arterial blood.

Bas felt cold panic race through his veins, spinning him, sickening him. His stomach lurched. He squeezed Syrric's hand, but it was limp. There was no pressure in the boy's grip. There was no reassuring voice in Bas's head. There was only emptiness, an aching gap where, moments before, the joy of companionship had filled him.

Bas stood frozen. His mind reeled, unable to accept what his senses told him.

Boots ground to a halt on the rockcrete a metre away.

'Children!' growled a man's voice. 'Two boys. Looks like we hit one o' them.'

A black boot extended, slid under Syrric's right shoulder, and turned him over.

Bas saw Syrric's lifeless eyes staring at the sky, that defiant glimmer gone forever.

'Aye,' continued the rough voice. 'We hit one all right. Fatality.' The trooper must have seen the tattoo on Syrric's head, because he added, 'He was a witch, though,' and he snorted like there was something humorous about it.

Bas sprung. Before he realised what he'd done, his grandfather's knife was buried in the belly of the trooper standing over him.

'You killed him,' Bas screamed into the man's shocked face. 'He was mine, you bastard! He was my friend and you killed him!'

Bas yanked his knife out of the trooper's belly and was about to stab again when something hit him in the side of the head. He saw the stars wheeling above him and collapsed, landing on Syrric's cooling body.

'Little bastard stabbed me!' snarled the wounded trooper as he fell back onto his arse, hands pressed tight to his wound to stem the flow of blood.

'Medic,' said the commanding voice from before. 'Man down, here.'

A shadow cast by the bright moonlight fell over Bas, and he looked up into a pair of twinkling black eyes. 'Tough one, aren't you?' said the figure.

Bas's heart sank. It wasn't his grandfather. Of course it wasn't. The Sarge was surely dead. Bas had never really believed otherwise. But this man was cast from the same steel. He had the same aura, as hard, as cold. Razor-sharp like a living blade. He wore a black greatcoat and a peaked cap, and on that peak, a golden skull with eagle's wings gleamed. A gloved hand extended towards Bas.

Bas looked at it.

'Up,' the man ordered.

Bas found himself obeying automatically. The hand was strong. As soon as he took it, it hauled him to his feet. The man looked down at him and sniffed the air.

'Ork shit,' he said. 'So you're smart as well as tough.'

Other figures wearing combat helmets and carapace armour came to stand beside the tall, greatcoated man. They looked at Bas with a mix of anger, curiosity and surprise. Their wounded comrade was already being attended by another soldier with a white field-kit.

'Gentlemen,' said the tall man. 'Unexpected as it may be, we have a survivor here. Child or not, I'll need to debrief him. You, however, will press on into the town as planned. Sergeant Hemlund, keep channel six open. I'll want regular updates.'

'You'll have 'em, commissar,' grunted a particularly broad-shouldered trooper.

Bas didn't know what a commissar was, but he guessed that it was a military rank. The soldiers fanned out, leaving him and the tall man standing beside Syrric's body.

'Regrettable,' said the man, gesturing at the dead boy. 'Psyker or not. Were you two alone here? Any other survivors?'

Bas didn't know what a psyker was. He said nothing. The commissar took silence as an affirmation.

'What's your name?'

Bas found it hard to talk. His throat hurt so much from fighting back his sorrow. With an effort, he managed to croak, 'Bas.'

The commissar raised an eyebrow, unsure he had heard correctly. 'Bas?'

'Short for Sebastian... sir,' Bas added. He almost gave his family name then – Vaarden, his father's name – but something made him stop. He looked down at the blood-slick knife in his right hand. His grandfather's knife. The old man's name was acid-etched on the blade, and he knew at that moment that it was right. It *felt* right. The old man had made him everything he was, and he would carry that name for the rest of his life.

'Sebastian Yarrick,' he said.

The commissar nodded.

'Well, Yarrick. Let's get you back to base. We have a lot to cover, you and I.'

He turned and began walking back down the street the way he had come, boots clicking sharply on the cobbles, knowing the boy would follow. In the other direction, fresh sounds of battle echoed from the dark tenement walls.

Bas sheathed the knife, bent over Syrric's body and closed the boy's eyelids.

He whispered a promise in the dead boy's ear, a promise he would spend his whole life trying to keep.

Then, solemnly, he rose and followed the commissar, taking his first steps on a path that would one day become legend.

HAMMER AND BOLTER

ISSUE 10

◄ TIME OF LEGENDS ►

THE LAST CHARGE

Andy Hoare

At the close of the first millennium after the unification of fair Bretonnia, in the year the men of the Empire measure 1974, the coastal regions of the Old World and far beyond were laid waste by a fell scion of Naggaroth, the beastlord named Rakarth. How many thousands were slain by his monstrous hosts is not written, for few who witnessed his attacks lived to tell the tale. Port after port, city after city was crushed beneath the clawed feet of the vile abominations the Beastlord herded into battle, those not devoured by his war hydras and black dragons enslaved and dragged screaming back to the Land of Chill.

Rakarth's age of destruction culminated in an unprecedented attack upon the fair land of Bretonnia, beloved by the Lady and defended by the stoutest of hearts. Heed the tale of the city of Brionne, beloved of Duke Corentin...

THE CITY OF Brionne slumbered fitfully beneath a night sky that seethed with ghostly luminescence. On nights such as these, so the Daughters of the Grail warned, the wastes far to the north of Bretonnia howled with the raw power of forbidden sorceries. The lights, so they said, meant that killers were abroad, men and other, darker creatures, roaming far and wide in search of slaughter.

The people of Brionne knew not to look upwards at the boiling energies, nor to meet the gaze of the eyes that glowered from the actinic depths. They knew from the stories told to them as children not to heed the lies uttered by the unreal lips that formed in the roiling, lambent clouds of balefire. Far better, the people of Brionne knew, to lock the bedchamber doors, shutter the windows, snuff out the candles and take what mortal comfort they could beneath the sheets. And well they might, for none could know for sure if the world would still be standing when dawn came.

But one man refused to take to his bed. Corentin, celebrated, among other titles, as the Paladin of Maelys, the Marcher-Lord of the Silver Plain, Defender of Fort Adeline, Champion of Gaelle's Virtue and Duke of Brionne, refused to be cowed by what he regarded as nothing more than an unusual storm. Even as violet-hued illumination flickered and pulsed outside his castle walls, Corentin stalked the dusty, candle-lit passages, long past the hour when any servant or courtier would be about to attend him. Wearing but his breeches and his sword belt, Corentin approached the inner sanctum of his castle, the Grail Shrine deep within its stone heart. Pausing to appreciate the solidity of the centuries-old oak doors, he set a hand upon each handle, bowed his head, and entered.

The Shrine was filled with golden light, cast by filigreed lanterns that had never been allowed to burn out since the city of Brionne had been founded. In the lantern light, Corentin saw the familiar scenes carved in stone across every surface. Miniature architecture, impossible to render in true scale, reared overhead, populating the Shrine with fantastically intricate tabernacle palaces. Tomb chests lined the walls, topped by stone effigies of long-dead knights in saintly repose, every one of them kin to the duke.

Corentin drew to a halt before the altar, upon which was mounted a golden cup with deep, twinkling rubies mounted on its flanks. The vessel glowed with a light that was nothing to do with the lanterns all about, for it shone from within the very metal of this holy relic of times long gone. Even after so many years in service to Bretonnia, Duke Corentin was humbled before the symbol of all that he and his fellow knights fought for. It was not *the* Grail, of course, but *a* grail, one of many sacred embodiments of the land and the people who dwelled within its borders.

The duke drew his gleaming sword and grunted as he went down upon one knee before the altar, the sword set before him point down. He was a powerfully built man, but he was far from young. In his youth he had been lithe and agile, in his majority as solid as an ox. Now, his muscle was softening and his former vigour deserting him a little more each day. But still he refused to cower like lesser men, regardless of what powers might be abroad this strange night.

When finally he was down, his good knee pressed hard into the cold flagstone of the chapel floor, Corentin looked upwards towards the grail. How many times had he done so, he pondered? How many battles had he begun by entreating the Lady of the Lake for victory? Dozens, he mused. Scores. Perhaps even hundreds. Truth be told, the battles Corentin had fought had started to blur into one another, as if his whole life had been but one long, bloody war against the innumerable enemies of Bretonnia. He supposed it had been, but he knew it must soon come to an end.

'Not yet,' Corentin said, his voice low and gruff, and somehow out of place in the sanctity of the Grail Shrine. The lanterns cast dancing light across the intricate architecture, the stone effigy of one of his ancestors seeming almost to stir as brilliance and shadow shifted across its surface. 'Let not the glory of service be done yet…'

The lanterns flickered once more, and the duke felt the air stir about him. It was as if a gust from the chill night had found its way through the winding passages, through the heavy oak doors, and into this most holy sanctum at the heart of his castle.

A heavy sense of foreboding settled over Corentin's heart. The duke feared no enemy, whether man, beast or abomination, for he had faced all in battle and cut them down with equal contempt. Rather, he knew dread, the notion that soon he might be forced by the advance of years to put up his lance once and for all, and to surrender himself to infirmity or senility. Anger waxed inside him as that thought took hold, and he grit his teeth in denial.

'No,' he growled, his voice too loud for his surroundings. 'I implore you…'

The light upon the altar redoubled, and through eyes misted with tears, Duke Corentin watched in stunned awe as the grail flared into pure, white illumination. Faith and adoration swelled within his chest as he knew that the Lady heeded his words and that, in some manner, she was here with him now, inside the chapel.

Knowing that the Lady of the Lake would hear him, Duke Corentin spoke aloud his heart's most secret desire.

'Lady,' he implored, his head filling with visions of past battles. 'Grant me one last, glorious moment. One last foe to banish in your name. One last battle to fight before the night draws in and claims me.'

The lanterns flickered once again, and the chapel grew chill. The cold seeped through the very stones, and into Corentin's body.

'Grant me an enemy to face,' he pleaded, the clamour of battle audible, if faint, over the crackle of the candles burning in the lanterns.

Screwing his eyes shut as he bowed his head in abject supplication to the Lady, Duke Corentin felt the air stir at his back and he knew without doubt that another had entered the Shrine. A scent met his nostrils, a rich and intoxicating mix of heady perfume and untouched skin.

'My lord,' a sweet, lyrical voice sounded from behind him. 'Do not ask this.'

A stab of anger flared in the duke's heart, but it was dulled by the presence at his back. He lifted his head and opened his eyes, immediately averting his face from the blazing white light streaming from the altar.

'Who…?' he stammered, scarcely daring to dream that he might be in the presence of…

'I am not her, my lord,' the voice said, and Corentin detected a familiar accent, if one made lilting by an alien manner. 'Please,' she insisted. 'Face me, my lord.'

The duke did as he was bid, rising on legs made unsteady by more than just age. Before him stood a woman, or a girl, he could not tell which for her features were truly ageless. Quite beyond that, her face was all but impossible to fully perceive, as if its details would be forgotten seconds after looking away, and so he dared not risk doing so. He recognised her as a damsel, a Daughter of the Grail, one of the blessed handmaidens of the Lady of the Lake, and as such a prophetess, miracle wielder and holy woman beyond compare. To the people of Bretonnia, such women – for no male ever returned having been called to serve the Lady – were but a step away from their patron deity, and their words were those of the Lady herself.

'Then who?' the duke stammered, unable to comprehend how this stranger had walked into the Shrine at the heart of his castle. 'Who are…'

'I come in answer to your prayer,' the damsel said, starting towards the altar. As she walked, the long, girded white shift that was all she wore ghosted behind her as a gossamer mist evaporating in the morning sun. He averted his eyes as her soft form was silhouetted through material made transparent by the silver glare. At the altar, she turned to look back upon him.

But the gaze that shone from her ageless eyes was ill-matched with the gentleness of her body. Of a sudden, those eyes were fathomless and dreadful, regarding Duke Corentin as a god standing in judgement over a mortal soul.

'You would answer my prayer?' he said, scarcely able to believe that it could be true. 'You would grant me one last glory before I die?'

The damsel did not answer straight away, but turned her face towards the shining grail, her long, dark hair stirring as if caught in a gentle breeze. Her eyes stared unblinking at the shining grail, before she turned to regard him once more.

'I come not to grant your heart's desire,' she stated. 'But I would warn you of the consequences of what you crave so.'

'Consequences, my lady?' the duke replied. 'I care not for consequences. I have fought every foe this cruel world has set before me,' he continued. 'I have defeated them all. What warning have you for me?'

The ghost of a smile touched the damsel's delicate lips, and she regarded the proud duke as if he were some boastful, callow youth bragging of the glory he would win upon the field of battle. Her eyes softened, and in an instant the dreadful power that had shone from them was gone, replaced by mortal, and very human, sorrow.

'I can offer you no counsel, my lord,' she said. 'For the Lady knows that you, above all others, are truly wise in matters of war and state. But any man would be wiser still to know what not to ask.'

Frustrated, the duke replied, 'Mock me not, my lady, for I am not one for riddles like those who treat with the fey. Am I to have that which I so desire?'

The damsel sighed, and replied, 'Would you have your prayer answered, my lord, even if it spelled your doom?'

'I would.'

'Then you shall have it. You shall have that which you most desire.'

THAT NIGHT, DUKE Corentin dreamed such dreams as no man could imagine. He relived every one of the battles he had fought over a lifetime of war. For a while, he was back at the Deliverance of Quenelles, following Master Joffre on that first, mad charge into the greenskin horde. Then he was bearing the standard at the Siege of Trantio, then cutting down the traitors as they turned against the River Tarano, the crossing suddenly impossible thanks to the blessings of the Lady. Then it was Castle Darkheart, the sight of the dead rising before the king's lines striking dread into his old heart just as it had three decades earlier. Deep in the Irrana Mountains, Duke Corentin had saved Carcassonne from the largest skaven swarm witnessed in living memory, though the lord of that dukedom had uttered scarcely a word of thanks.

For what seemed like hours, the battles flashed and boiled through feverish dreams, most blurring together, others standing out above the rest. The Battle of the Lagoon of Tears; the Siege of the ruined fortress of Vorag; the ill-fated Errantry War that scoured the Plain of Bones but in the process lost the king's war banner. Battles against every foe known to man, and some of which man had no knowledge, came to him. Barbarous greenskins, cruel dark elves, the savage and blasphemous men of the north, the pernicious mercenary-princes of Tilea and the petty barons of the Border Princes. All of these foes and more he had faced upon the field of battle, and whatever foul magics or cunning stratagems they had employed, Corentin knew that every one of them could bleed, and therefore die. And all the while, the blessed presence of the Lady of the Lake stood by, just beyond perception, watching over the bold deeds performed in her name and that of her land and all its people.

THE DUKE AWOKE with a start, the silken sheets damp and cold with sweat. His bedchamber was dark, the candles long burned down, but the wan light of dawn edged the heavy shutters on the lancet windows. The clamour of war still echoing in his ears as the dreams receded, Corentin rose from his bed and crossed to the windows. Opening the shutters, he looked out across the city of Brionne, his heart filled with the foreshadowing of something dreadful.

The morning sun was barely over the horizon, and its golden rays turned the pale sandstone of the city's soaring spires into shining needles made of glowing precious metal. From his window, the duke looked down upon the densely clustered rooftops, punctuated by dozens upon dozens of the impossibly delicate spires, the sharp conical roof of each one adorned with long pennants that fluttered in the morning breeze blowing in from the Great Ocean. Corentin's gaze followed the towers as they marched towards the distant city walls, a sea mist making the most distant ghostly pale in the morning air. Beyond the high walls, the sea was barely visible at all, and the horizon all but invisible.

A flash of nightmare strobed across the duke's mind, a spectre from the dreams that had haunted him throughout the night. He heard once more the distant roar of some mighty wyrm-lord from the dawn of time, and pictured its writhing form skewered upon his blessed lance. The roar grew louder, resounding not from the mists of time and nightmare, he realised, but from those creeping in from the Great Ocean. His breath catching in his throat and his blood freezing in his veins, the duke realised that the fog was not the remnants of the night-time sea mist, yet to burn off in the morning sun. It was, in fact, a fresh mist, its tendrils creeping in from the ocean, writhing and questing like the tentacles of some vast, sea-spawned kraken...

'To arms!' Duke Corentin bellowed from his bedchamber window as he leaned outwards over his castle. 'Muster the household!' he shouted into the marshalling yard below as the low droning of some ancient horror blared from the creeping fog. 'Call out the militia!'

'War is come!' he bellowed, his blood pumping with a heady cocktail of battle-lust and horror. Let them come, he prayed as he turned at the sound of his attendants entering the bedchamber. Whoever they may be, let them come, and know the cold taste of Bretonnian steel.

'THE ELVES OF Naggaroth,' said Duke Corentin's chancellor as the two men stood atop the walls of Brionne, the city's army mustered at the ramparts. The duke was resplendent in his ornate battle armour, its every plate burnished to a silvered finish and adorned with golden grail and fleur-de-lys icons. Nearby attendants bore his helm, his lance and his shield, while a groom in the yard below struggled to control his mighty steed.

The duke did not need telling just who this foe was or where they had come from. He had faced them many times and knew well their cruel ways. Indeed, the fine lattice of scars etched into the flesh of his belly told of the cruelties the dark elves, as they were known, were wont to inflict upon those they captured in battle. Those who had tortured Corentin in the aftermath of the Battle of the Deeping Moon had paid gravely for their sins, the duke turning the tables upon them having escaped captivity and returned with a vengeful army.

The enemy had come from the sea, stalking from the creeping ocean mists to surround the walled city of Brionne. That mist lingered still, and the dark form of a Black Ark loomed in the distance like an iceberg made of solid rock or a mountainous island thrown up by the sea overnight. From the cavernous sea-docks of the vast city-ship, hundreds of landing vessels had delivered thousands upon thousands of dark elves to the shore, the black-clad warriors forming into regiments and taking position on the plains surrounding the city. For miles all about, the lands were covered with the serrated forms of the dark elf cohorts, vile banners snapping in the breeze and shrill horns blaring.

But the ranks of warriors were just one part of the host and, though the most numerous, far from the most terrible. Corsairs, kraken-skin cloaks lending them the aspect of devils from the deep marched beside grim executioners, their faces covered and their cruel glaives poised to enact the most wanton of mutilations. Witch elves capered, their bare flesh smeared with the blood of the victims sacrificed to their blasphemous gods, that victory might be theirs. Formations of riders moved in around the flanks to cut off any hope that the city might get a messenger out, some upon night-coloured steeds, others riding the reptilian cold ones, their vile stink carried on the wind for miles.

Yet still, it was not even these terrible foes that the duke looked to as he regarded the army that had voyaged from the Land of Chill to lay siege to his fair city. Rather, it was the mighty beasts that towered over the ranks that drew his eye and filled his old, warrior's heart with awe. Never before had Duke Corentin seen such a number or range of abominations, even when facing the twisted hordes of the northmen. War hydras stamped and snorted as bold handlers struggled to keep each of the many-headed beasts' fanged maws from attacking nearby warriors or one another. A constant plume of black smoke boiled upwards from the beasts, each of their heads belching great gouts of flame as their necks twisted and darted to and fro. The beasts' hide was as grey as stone, and the duke knew from bitter experience that it was every bit as hard and cold. Scanning the horde grimly, he attempted to estimate the numbers of such beasts the dark elves were herding into battle against his city. He lost count after three dozen, the ranks of the beasts swelled by fresh arrivals before he could gain their measure.

A shrill cry, akin to the call of some vile carrion bird, split the air, and the duke's lip curled in disgust as he located its source. The smoke-wreathed sky overhead was slowly filling with darting shapes which might at first be easily mistaken for vultures drawn to the plain by the promise of freshly-slain carcasses to pick clean in the aftermath of battle. But as they dived and wheeled, it became clear that these were no natural creatures, nor even birds or any other beast. They were harpies, creatures of which the cautionary tales of the Bretonnian knighthood had much to say. Though curved and comely from a distance, the harpies were far removed from the feminine form they wore. Each was a creature as debased as vermin, incapable of any thoughts or deeds other than the most animalistic. They cared only for the tearing of raw flesh between needle-sharp teeth, and were said to be the servants of some vile dark elf god no virtuous knight would demean himself to name.

With a motion like a shoal of darting fish spooked by the approach of a far larger predator, the harpies scattered across the sky and were gone. From banks of mist, made grey by the smoke belching from the gullets of the hydras, came a sinuous black form upon pinions as dark as night. Duke Corentin's heart thundered as he took in a sight he had not seen in decades. It was a dragon, one of the ebon-scaled wyrms which it was said that the most cruel-hearted and despicable of dark elf lords could command to bear them into battle. Clearly such a tale held something of the truth, for a figure was visible mounted upon the black dragon's back, a banner snapping in the cold wind behind.

A ripple of fear swept up and down the defenders manning the mighty walls of Brionne, and Duke Corentin tore his eyes from the sight of the ebon beast wheeling through the clouds and looked down upon his men. The ramparts of the rearing curtain walls curved about the extent of the city, towers topped with mighty war machines punctuating them at regular intervals. The ramparts were manned by hundreds upon hundreds of warriors, the squires of the household and the men of the city militia. The former were semi-professional soldiers, trained and drilled to defend their fair nation against foes such as these and equipped with padded armour, shields and a variety of weapons from longbows to billhooks. The latter were only called to fight when dire circumstances allowed no alternative, for they were in the main peasants and villeins who would only fight when cornered by the enemy or forced to do so by the sergeants. The peasants bore what weapons they themselves could muster, those from the fields about Brionne armed with scythes and staffs, those from the city with iron or wooden tools and cudgels.

'Hold,' Duke Corentin ordered, his powerful voice clearly audible to hundreds of his troops. Men turned their faces from the limitless horde of malice sweeping steadily across the plains and the nightmare creatures swooping high overhead to regard their lord and master. The duke looked at the faces of those nearest to him, and it struck him then that he knew not one of the men looking back at him. In years long gone, he had taken pride in knowing the sergeants and captains under his command. The faces of the best of those men flashed through his memory before, sadness welling inside, he recalled how each had fallen in battle. So many brave, virtuous warriors had died at his command, he reflected, and here were more on the cusp of doing so. Forcing the ghosts of long lost companions-in-arms from his mind, Duke Corentin addressed his army from his vantage point high atop the wall tower.

'Men of Bretonnia!' he shouted, the assembled ranks falling to respectful silence as he spoke. 'Our fair city of Brionne is this day threatened by the most despicable of enemies. But shall we submit?'

Turning his head towards the enemy, Duke Corentin hawked, and spat a great gobbet of spittle over the ramparts towards the enemy. The nearest ranks erupted in approbation, cheering their liege's gesture of defiance. Soon, the rallying cry was taken up by those too far along the wall to have witnessed the gesture, and then by every warrior upon the ramparts of Brionne.

None saw that the cold breeze blowing in off of the sea had whipped up moments after the duke had spat into it, and blown the gobbet straight back into his face.

THE DARK ELF army continued to deploy upon the plains surrounding Brionne, and by early evening the noose was fully tightened. Numerous messengers had been dispatched to carry word of the invasion, but none who remained had any way of knowing if they had broken through the enemy lines. Duke Corentin had seen, many years ago, dark elf scouts and assassins, and so he doubted that any man could have stolen through if such creatures were abroad. Nonetheless, he offered pious entreaties to the Lady of the Lake that word might somehow reach the dukedom's outlying towns and castles, and an army might be gathered to drive the vile dark elves back into the sea.

As the sky darkened, with the approach of night as much as the smoke of numerous burned offerings sent up by the enemy's sorceresses, a dread silence descended upon attacker and defender alike. All throughout the afternoon, the duke's knights had marshalled behind the city's main gates, ready to sally forth against the foe when Corentin judged the moment right. These brave men had barely been able to contain their eagerness to charge through the gates and smite the enemy to ruin. Yet now, even they fell quiet and sullen. Standing upon his tower, looking down at the vast army spread out across the plain between the city and the sea, Duke Corentin felt it too.

The skies darkened still further as clouds the colour of livid bruises boiled in from the horizon. The black dragon appeared once more, diving from the heart of those clouds to swoop in towards the walls, the multitude of war hydras far below roaring as it passed over them. Where before, the appearance of the dragon had caused a murmur of fear to spread along the walls, now Duke Corentin heard terrified outbursts, even sobbing from the ranks. Though the sergeants bellowed for silence and order, the fact was unmistakable. The winged, stygian fiend was death and doom embodied, and men withered before it.

Yet the duke knew differently. Decades of experience had taught him that such beasts were only tamed, or dominated, by some manner of being an order of magnitude stronger, in will if not in muscle. He knew that, as fearful as the ebon wyrm undoubtedly was, the figure upon its back must be far more terrible to command such a creature.

As if to confirm his thoughts, the dragon swept in closer still, until it was close enough for the defenders to see its rider clearly. Mounted in a saddle lined with human skin, the duke and his men saw a warrior-lord clad from head to toe in jet-black armour worked into the most cruelly delicate forms by the hand of a master far superior to any mortal artificer. The dark elf lord's tall helm covered his features, but none could miss the light shining from the eyes like coals in the night. In one hand, the lord bore a long, coiling whip, which snaked and writhed as if possessed of some terrible inner vitality, while in his other hand he bore a shield adorned with the fell runes of forbidden magics.

In an instant, the dragon was soaring over the city's walls, though it made no assault upon the defenders. The peasants of the militia cried out in terror, and many dropped to their knees and covered their heads as if doing so would save them from the beast's scrutiny. A handful threw themselves from the ramparts in terror, the fortunate tumbling down flights of stone steps to the landings below, the unfortunate meeting the ground in the courtyard with a sickening crunch.

Duke Corentin refused to show even the slightest degree of fear as the huge beast soared overhead, the lung-searing, eye-watering reek of venomous gases thick in its wake. Instead, he stood tall, meeting the coal-eyed lord's gaze, an example to every man who looked on.

Within seconds, the dragon had passed overhead and was banking over the city, turning high above the rooftops and spires with a dreadful, stately elegance upon wings that spanned fifty feet or more. With a burst of black gas from flaring nostrils, the beast completed its turn and the air was filled with the sharp crack of the rider's long whip.

Extending its powerful hind legs and spreading wicked talons as long as a man's arm, the dragon swooped down upon one of the nearest of the spires rearing high above the city's rooftops. The spire was needle-thin and over two hundred feet tall. Its pinnacle was a tiled roof, and numerous small turrets extended from its flanks, pennants bearing the black axe on white field heraldry of the duke's line waving proudly. The beast descended upon the roof, hind legs first, its frontal claws closing around the finial in an impact that sent roof tiles plummeting to the ground below and the turrets to quake as if they too would fall away. A second great moan of despair went up from the assembled defenders and townspeople in the streets below could be seen fleeing as shattered slate and detached masonry rained down upon them.

Lowering its glowering head upon its sinuous neck, the black dragon shifted its weight and settled onto its perch. The dark elf lord seated upon his saddle regarded the defenders of Brionne with palpable disdain, his balefire gaze sweeping the ranks before settling upon the duke.

For long moments, the only sound was that of the sergeants bullying their men to order, and then that too faded. To the duke, it was as if he and this vile intruder into his realm were the only two warriors present, his vision narrowing as he met the smouldering eyes of the dark elf lord. The Bretonnians followed a particular form in matters of conducting a siege, a form that Corentin had never strayed from, and never would. That form required that the invader name his terms and that the defender heard them before hostilities were joined. For a moment, the duke wondered if the dark elf would observe such traditions, if he had even heard of them, before the enemy lord spoke.

'Heed my words, human,' the dark elf lord spoke, his voice like burning coals stirred in a grate. 'For you are not worthy to hear them twice.'

The duke bit back an angry rejoinder, determined to observe the proper form despite his foe's taunting. His only response was a grinding of his teeth and a narrowing of his eyes.

'I am Rakarth,' the dark elf announced, his hateful voice boastful and haughty, 'Called *Beastlord*.' Though tempted to quash his enemy's pride by claiming never to have heard the name, Duke Corentin bit his tongue. Quite aside from the dishonourable nature of such a reply, it would have been a lie. He knew the name of the Beastlord Rakarth well, as did all of those who dwelled along the coasts of the Old World. How could they not, for this fell being was said to have laid waste to countless towns and ports, from Norsca in the far north to the Bay of Corsairs in the south. Not for nothing was he called 'Beastlord', as the horde of roaring, smoke-spouting abominations below testified. It was said of Rakarth that in his dungeons he held at least one example of every predatory beast that ever lived, and his ceaseless crossbreeding had led to some of the very worst crimes against nature ever seen.

And it seemed that Duke Corentin was not the only man present to recognise the name of this foe. A wave of despair swept through the defenders, countless men dropping to their knees even as the sergeants set about such cowards with cudgels and whips in an effort to get them back on their feet. Through the corner of his eye, the duke detected movement in the courtyard far below, and knew that the warhorses of his knights, the best trained mounts in all the land, if not the world, were barely holding at bay. Such was the terror this being and his fell mount radiated in palpable waves.

'You shall render unto me one in five of your people,' the Beastlord continued. 'In equal number male and female, and of fighting age and fitness. This you shall do by sunrise tomorrow, or face the wrath of the host of Naggaroth!'

'What say you, human?' asked the dark elf.

Duke Corentin folded his arms across his broad chest, and angled his head to fix the enemy lord with a gaze of utter disgust. His armour rang as he moved, and he longed to draw his mighty sword and engage this arrogant monster in honourable combat. Yet he could not, at least not yet. His gorge rose as he considered the insult implicit in such a demand, but he fought to control himself, keeping his voice level when he eventually answered.

'I say,' he replied, projecting in voice with such force that hundreds, perhaps thousands of his warriors would hear it and take heart. 'Leave my lands now, elf, while still you are able.'

The black dragon shifted its weight upon the spire's pinnacle as if it perceived the insult to its master, displacing yet more roof tiles and stones. The defenders upon the walls remained silent, thousands of them steeling their hearts and daring to look upon the enemy lord to hear his reply.

That reply was many moments in coming, the silence stretching out for what felt like ten times as long. Duke Corentin fought the ever-growing urge to draw his blade and to order every war machine in the city to open fire upon the beast, yet he fought it down with a nigh superhuman effort.

Finally, the dark elf lord spoke. 'Then *all* shall die.'

With that, the lord cracked his long, steel whip against the flanks of his mount, drawing a roar from the dragon, which vented roiling clouds of noxious gas into the air through its flaring nostrils. The beast spread its wings to their fullest stretch and flexed its hind legs, bracing to propel itself high into the air. Almost as if in slow motion, the ebon wyrm beat its wings while pushing back and up with its hugely muscled legs. The two hundred foot tower upon which the beast had perched finally gave way, the peaked conical roof shattering into a thousand roof tiles and the entire top half of the spire seemed to bend as a branch in the wind. As the dragon lifted off, the destruction worked its way down the spire, sandstone blocks working their way loose in a rapidly growing cascade. Moments later, the tower collapsed, slowly at first but with mounting speed as gravity asserted itself. At the last, the tower fell across three streets far below, obliterating a score of townhouses in a single instant and sending up a dense cloud of billowing grey dust.

One last battle, Duke Corentin said to himself. One last foe to defeat...

As the sun set on what many feared would be the first day of a months-long siege of the fair city of Brionne, the duke began planning the defence. The manning of the walls was the first priority, and Corentin ensured that the most experienced companies of his household's squires were stationed at vital points, bolstering positions manned by the less experienced, poorly disciplined peasant militias. There were a thousand details of logistics to attend to, for the numerous war machines mounted upon the wall towers required constant manning, maintenance and supply. The thousands of archers upon the ramparts would have to be rotated in their duty, and the braziers from which they would light their flaming arrows kept burning. All of this the duke oversaw despite the cold bitterness threatening to consume him, for, ultimately, there was little glory in any of it. Ultimately, it was not the work of a knight of Bretonnia.

'My lord,' said Corentin's chancellor from behind him as he stood upon the highest tower on the wall, looking west across the night-shrouded enemy camp. 'Will you not take wine?'

Corentin lingered a moment, the plains before him seething with enemy activity. Numerous sounds of unspecified and unidentifiable cruelty drifted up from the enemy camp, mingled with the ever-present baying of all manner of monstrous beasts. Hundreds of campfires dotted the land as the far as the eye could see, forming a nigh-continuous ring of fire all about the city, orange cinders drifting upwards on the riotous thermals. At least, the duke hoped they were campfires. He knew from first hand experience that many were likely to be braziers, the searing coals within used to heat the very cruellest implements of torture.

'No, Erwen,' the duke replied. 'I must offer prayer to our lady. Leave me.'

When Erwen did not leave as he was bid, Duke Corentin turned to regard his chief counsellor. For an instant, he failed to recognise the individual stood before him, a part of him expecting to see old Winoc. Then he shook his head as memory reasserted itself. Winoc had fallen at the height of the War of the Giant's Skull, an ogre's cleaver having taken both of his legs in a single swing.

'My lord?' said Erwin, concern writ large across his patrician features.

'Speak your mind plainly, man,' Duke Corentin demanded, reaching out a hand to steady himself against the crenellated rampart. By the Lady, he was tired.

'My lord,' the chancellor began uncertainly, before ploughing on. 'You must rest, we feel–'

'Who?' Corentin demanded, drawing himself to his full height despite the weight of the full plate armour he had worn all day. 'Who says what of me? Speak!'

'Your knights, sir,' Erwin continued, 'Your companions, your guardians and your peers. All feel that–'

'My peers?' the duke raged, one hand gripping the pommel of his sword. 'I have no peers! All of them have fallen, all of them have given their lives in service to the land and to the Lady!'

'Yes, my lord,' the chancellor said, his arms held out in placation. 'But you must rest, for tomorrow…' He let the sentence trail away.

'Tomorrow?' said Duke Corentin, knowing now what he must do. Pushing the chancellor away, he spun to face the west and the enemy encamped on the plain before his beloved city. With a ringing of steel, he drew his sword and brandished it before him, before turning it point down with a single motion, and setting it to rest tip-first upon the stone floor. Bracing himself upon his weapon, the duke went down upon one knee as he had the night before in the Grail Chapel, and he bowed his head in prayer.

'Go,' the duke ordered through gritted teeth. 'I order you… go.'

* * *

SIX HOURS LATER, the sun was rising and Duke Corentin's armour glistened with dew. Slowly, he became aware that he had been locked in prayer throughout the long, cold hours of the night, and that the city was stirring all about him. Opening gummy eyes, he realised that so too was the camp before the city walls, thousands of cruel invaders busying themselves with preparations for the inevitable battle.

Grunting, the duke braced himself against his sword, and pulled himself upright. Pain shot through his every joint and he staggered to bring himself to his full height. Attendants, who had been lurking out of his field of vision, rushed to him. He thrust out his free arm to push them away.

'Back!' he barked, consumed with anger and frustration. 'I have a battle to win... Erwen?'

'My lord?' his chancellor said as he appeared nearby, bent almost double in genuflection.

'Order my war steed made ready!' the duke bellowed, flashes of long gone battles strobing across his mind's eye once again. 'Gather the knights and prepare to open the gates!'

'My lord, I cannot...' Erwen started, before stuttering to a halt, his eyes impossibly wide in his hawkish face. The duke regarded his chancellor with confusion for a moment, before turning as he followed the man's gaze. High above the invaders' camp, the black dragon soared directly towards the tower on which the duke and his attendants stood.

With an incoherent roar of denial and pain, the duke drew his mighty sword, its blade flashing in the morning sun. Bracing his legs wide, he raised the sword that had served him so well over so many campaigns, and waited as the dark elf lord approached.

The sound of the oncoming black dragon was as a storm descending from an otherwise clear sky, the beating of its wings a savage, deafening roar. Erwen and the other attendants were buffeted to the stone floor as the huge beast passed directly overhead, but Duke Corentin strained every sinew in his body to remain upright. He yielded to no man, and especially not to an elf.

'Then this is your answer, old man?' the dark elf called out as his mount banked over the wall and began a majestic return to the invaders' lines. 'This is the fate you choose?'

'Aye, vile one!' Duke Corentin bellowed in answer. 'This is my answer!'

With a final expulsion of reeking, poisonous gases from its nostrils, the black dragon was away, and every war machine in range opened fire upon it. The chances of even the best crewed trebuchet striking a flying target, least of all one moving rapidly in the opposite direction, was remote at best, but one huge stone projectile did sail dangerously close to the dragon, causing a roar of approval to sound from the massed ranks of defenders upon the city walls. But the cheer was short lived, for even as the black dragon receded into the distance, the countless war hydras upon the plain started forward, the ground actually trembling so heavy and concentrated was their tread.

'Get every company to the walls,' the duke barked to an attendant, and the man departed at speed to pass the order on. In moments, the thousands of warriors defending the ramparts were being reinforced by streams of additional defenders pouring up the stone steps. 'Attendants,' he shouted. 'Where is my steed?'

Now the walls themselves trembled to the approach of the massed hydras, yet the duke cared more for the readiness of his own mount. Losing patience, he made for the top of the flight of steps that led down the tower and into the courtyard far below where his knights had marshalled, but was interrupted as Sir Peirrick, the greatest knight of his household, emerged.

'My lord,' the knight greeted the duke as he bowed his head and struck a mailed fist across his armoured chest in respectful greeting. 'I am told–'

'Peirrick,' said Corentin. 'Good. Is my steed ready? Are the knights marshalled?'

'No, my duke,' the knight set his bearded face in a grim mask, his intense eyes betraying his concern.

'Then see to it, man!' the duke bellowed, flinging an arm wide in a gesture that took in the vast monstrous horde stampeding across the plain towards the wall. 'We have but minutes, and I would sally forth before it is too late!'

His face betraying his utter horror, Sir Peirrick stood resolute as his liege made to push past him towards the stairs. 'No, my lord,' he said with conviction. 'Your knights shall do as you bid, but you shall not lead them.'

The duke recoiled as if the knight had struck him across the face. Draining of colour, he fought for words to express his outrage.

'Let others shoulder this burden,' the knight pleaded, though his mind was clearly decided. 'Your place is here, my lord, commanding the defence of your city.'

'My place is leading the charge against the horde of filth even now bearing down upon my realm!' Duke Corentin thundered. 'And yours is upon one knee, or else following my banner!'

'No, my duke,' Sir Peirrick said coldly, barring the way. 'We shall not allow you to take to the field this day, nor any other henceforth, though every one of us would willingly give his life upon your word.'

The duke bit back a cry of anguish, and looked past the knight to his chief advisor who waited off to one side. Erwen nodded sadly, and it was clear that he felt compelled to agree with Peirrick. The thunder of the approaching host of hydras grew ever louder, so that the duke barely heard his own reply.

'Then go,' he bellowed over the roaring of dozens of monsters. 'Lady deliver us all.'

* * *

The Best of Hammer and Bolter: Volume One

THE CHARGE OF the knights of Brionne was a feat of epic glory. Hundreds of mounted warriors formed up into squadrons and streamed through the gates and sally ports of the city walls, fluttering pennants and proud banners boldly displaying the heraldry of countless knightly households. Their armour gleamed in the rising sun and their lances were as densely formed as an impenetrable forest. Those lances lowered as the squadrons spread out, forming a thunderous wave of steel and colour as it raced headlong towards the onrushing dark elf beasts.

Seeing this new enemy, the beast handlers cracked their whips and drove their charges forward in a frenzy of bestial savagery. Locking eyes upon their foe, the countless beasts roared in challenge, the air filling with deafening screeches and cries. The hydras vented thick clouds of noxious fumes and the morning light was tainted with a creeping, stinking fog that threatened to strike man and horse down before battle was even joined.

Yet still, the two waves came on. The knights drove through the billowing clouds of poison, and truly the blessing of the Lady was upon them, for not one fell to its effects. The hydras redoubled their charge in response, and seconds later, the two forces slammed into one another.

At the very point of impact, steel-tipped lances drove into stone-hard flesh, even the hides of the monstrous creatures unable to withstand weapons anointed in the holy waters of the font of the Lady. Black blood arced into the air and spattered across shields and armour as beasts fell, yet moments later, the true battle began.

Those beasts not slain outright fought back with snapping maws atop writhing, serpentine necks. Each creature bore five such necks and five sets of ferocious jaws, and only upon the decapitation of the fifth were they finally slain. Bold knights were cut in two by heads that darted in from all quarters, or torn apart as rival heads affixed to the same body fought jealously over the kill. Lances cast aside, the knights hacked and stabbed with blessed swords, and soon the fight was a desperate struggle for life and death.

From his vantage point atop his tower, Duke Corentin raged. His heart ached to be down there, upon the field of battle, leading his brave knights against the countless beasts that assailed his city. Yet, he could see what most down there could not, and he knew deep within his soul that Sir Peirrick had been correct. The knights were being slaughtered, their numbers simply too few to repel the monstrous host. With a pang of sadness, he saw that Peirrick had known this all along, and in his love for his duke had saved him from a fate he was simply too aged and too tired to repel.

Yet, Duke Corentin fumed, what right had the young knight to determine the fate of his master? Why should he not meet his end in one final, hopeless charge against such a foe?

Because he had a city to defend, he knew. Thousands of warriors and many times more defenceless innocents relied upon him, for no other would deliver them from the invading host that was even now charging en masse towards the city walls.

The air filled with the blaring horns and shrill, cruel war cries of the foe as the war hydras cut down the last of the bravest knights Duke Corentin had ever had the honour to see in battle. The beasts surged onwards, crushing the remains of the knights into the churned plain, the bright colours of their banners and shields smeared with mud and gore, and the once gleaming steel of their armour and swords dulled with filth. Roaring their foul victory cries, the beasts came on, closing on the walls even as the hosts of dark elves behind them began their march.

Nothing would stop the beasts, Duke Corentin knew as they reached the walls. Claws and teeth ground into the fair masonry, hauling down brickwork set there centuries before. The tower upon which the duke and his attendants stood shook violently, and the defenders upon the walls fought to keep their footing as more and more of the huge creatures clawed their way upwards, great chunks of stone discarded in their wake. Flaming arrows arced downwards like screaming comets, burying themselves in beast flesh and causing the hydras to screech in deafening pain, yet still the enemy came on.

A wave of panic passed up and down the wall as a sickening impact caused great cracks to spread throughout its fabric. A beast so large that it carried a howdah bristling with spears upon its back had joined the fray, stampeding its way through the press of monstrous bodies to slam headlong into the walls. Even as the defenders concentrated their flaming arrows upon this new, terrible enemy, the hydra dug its claws into the crumbling wall and began to haul itself upwards.

Only the insane could stand in the face of such a monster. Even as it climbed, it gouted great clouds of black gas up towards the ramparts. Men fell, their skin blistered and their eyes bulging, as five heads reared above the ramparts upon writhing necks. Each darted and snapped, and with every attack a man was snatched from his place at the wall, tossed into the air and swallowed whole by a gaping maw. That was all the remaining defenders could take, and those on the neighbouring sections broke in terror, fleeing from the inevitable.

In an instant, the defending army broke. Men flooded from the walls down flights of steps so choked with bodies that dozens fell screaming to their deaths below. With a sound like a mountain collapsing, an entire section of the walls crumbled, the towers on either side toppling downwards and slaying hundreds in the process. Through the billowing mushroom cloud over the huge breach, the black dragon of the Beastlord Rakarth soared, the beat of the massive wings parting the rising dust so that Duke Corentin could see his foe clearly. As the first of the war hydras pressed in through what the duke knew was only the first breach in his fair city's walls, the host of dark elves pressed in behind, and soon the cruel enemy was spilling forth into the rubble-strewn courtyard and streets beyond.

'Attendants,' the duke ordered, his voice grim and resolute. 'Arm me.'

None could argue, for there was clearly nothing to be gained from doing so. With silent reverence, the duke's attendants presented him with his lance, set his shield upon one arm and his helmet upon his head. Though the panoply of war had never felt so heavy, Duke Corentin bore the weight as he bore his duty to the land and the Lady. He descended the stairwell of the tower and emerged into the courtyard before the city's main gates. The area was strewn with rubble cast from the walls above, and cowards were fleeing in all directions, except towards the foe. Screams rent the air, those of the monsters now rampaging through his city, and those of the first of his people to be overtaken by the cruel dark elves. Even now, as he pulled himself up into the saddle of his war horse, his beloved subjects were being dragged screaming back to the Black Ark waiting out in the sea. He cast the tragedy from his mind as he set his steed in motion, the gates parting before him though he could not see who did so.

As the portal yawned open, blinding light spilled through, so white and so pure that the duke knew it was natural. Time slowed to a leaden crawl as his steed passed through the gate, its speed building as it bore him onwards. There beyond the gate was the enemy, the dark elf host laying siege to Brionne, the greenskin horde at Quenelle, the heretics at Trantio, the unquiet dead at Castle Darkheart, the stinking swarm of skaven spewing through the pass in the Irrana Mountains...

One last enemy, the duke's heart sang. One last battle. One last, glorious charge before death finally claimed him.

WE ARE ONE

John French

Victory and defeat are a matter of definition.

– from the *Axioms of War*,
Tactica Imperialis

I HAVE GROWN tired in this war. It has eaten me, consuming everything I might have done or been. I have chased my enemy across the stars and through the decades of my failing life. We are one, the enemy and I, the hunter and the hunted. The end is close now. My enemy will die, and at that moment I will become something less, a shadow fading in the brightness of the past. This is the price of victory.

My fist hits the iron door with a crack of thunder. The impact shatters the emerald scales of the hydra that rears across their width. Inside my Terminator armour, enfolded in adamantium and ceramite, I feel the blow jolt through my thin flesh. Lightning crackles around my fist as I pull it back, the armour giving me strength. I bring my fist down and the metre-thick doors fall in a shower of splintered metal. I walk through their shattered remains, my feet crushing the scattered ruby eyes of the hydra to red dust on the stone floor.

The light glints from my armour, staining its pearl-white surface with fire and glinting from eagle feathers and laurels. The chamber beyond the doors is silent and creeps with shifting shadows. Burning torches flicker from brackets on jade pillars, the domed ceiling above coiling with smoke. Targeting runes and threat augurs swarm across my vision, sniffing for threats, finding only one. The shackled power in my fist twitches like a thunderbolt grasped in a god's hand.

He sits at the centre of the chamber on a throne of beaten copper. Void-blue armour mottled with the ghost pattern of scales, swathed in spilling cloaks of shimmering silk, face hidden behind the blank face plate and glowing green eyes of a horned helm. He sits still, one hand resting on the pommel of a silver-bladed sword, head turning slowly to follow me as I advance.

'Phocron of the Alpha Legion,' I shout, my voice echoing through the shadow-filled silence. 'I call you to justice at the hands of the Imperium you betrayed.' The formulaic phrase of accusation fades to silence as Phocron stands, his sword in his hand. This will be no simple duel. To fight the Alpha Legion is to fight on a shifting layer of deception and trickery, where every weakness can hide strength and every apparent advantage may be revealed as a trap. Lies are their weapons and they are their masters. I am old, but time has armoured me against those weapons.

He moves and cuts, his blow so quick and sudden that I have no chance to dodge. I raise my fist, feeling the armour synchronise with the movements of my aging muscles, and meet the first strike of this last battle in a blaze of light.

Ninety-eight years ago – The Year of the Ephisian Atrocity

KNOWLEDGE CAN MAKE you blind, some say, but ignorance is simply an invitation to be deceived. I can still see the times when I knew little of the Alpha Legion beside a few dry facts and half-understood fears. I look back at those times and I shudder at what was to come.

The death of my ignorance began on the mustering fields of Ephisia.

Millions of troops stood on the dust plains in the shadow of soot-covered hives, rank upon rank of men and women in uniforms from dozens of worlds. Battle tanks and ground transporters coughed exhaust fumes into the cold air. Munitorum officers moved through the throng shouting orders above the noise, their breath forming brief white clouds. Above it all transport barges hung in the clear sky, their void-pitted hulls glinting in the sunlight, waiting to swallow the gathering mass of human flesh and war machines. It was the mustering of an army to break the cluster of renegade worlds that had declared their secession from the Imperium. It was a gathering of might intended to break that act of folly into splinters and return a dozen worlds to the domain of the God-Emperor. That was the intention, though perhaps ours was the folly.

'Move!' I bellowed as I charged through the crowd, shoving aside men and women in newly issued battle gear. Helena came with me, pushing people aside with her will. Grunts and oaths followed us, dying to silence as they saw the tri-barred 'I' engraved on my breast plate and the hissing muzzle of the inferno pistol in my hand. My storm cloak flapped behind me as I ran, the burnished iron of my segmented armour bright under the sun. Anyone looking at me knew that they were looking at an inquisitor, the left hand of the God Emperor, who had the power to judge and execute any beneath the Golden Throne. The crowd parted before me like cattle scattering in front of a wolf.

'There,' shouted Helena from two feet to my left. I twisted my head to see the dun-colour of our quarry's uniform vanish into a knot of troops. She was already moving before I had changed direction, confused-looking troops twitching out of her path as she ran through the parting crowd. I could feel the back eddies of the telepathic bow wave that she projected in front of her as she ran, hard muscles flowing under flexing armour plates, dark hair spilling behind.

I saw our quarry a second after Helena. A thin man in the ill-fitting dun uniform of an Ephisian trooper, his skin pale from bad nutrition and lack of daylight. He looked like so many of the rest gathered on that day, another coin of flesh for the Imperium to spend. But this man was no raw recruit for the Imperial Guard; he was an agent of rebellion sent to seed destruction at this gathering. We had been tracking him for days, knowing that there were others and that our only chance to stop them all was to let one run until he led us to the others. That had been the plan, my plan. But there was no more time. Whatever atrocity they intended was so close I could feel the cold fear of it in my guts.

'Take him down,' I shouted. Helena was raising her needle pistol when the man jerked to one side with the agility of a predator. He rolled and came up into a shooting crouch, lasgun at his shoulder. Helena dived to the ground as the lasgun spat a burst of energy in a wide arc around where she had been. People dropped in the crowd around us, shouts of pain spreading like a tide. Dead and dying troops lay on the ground around us while their comrades formed a blind herd without direction or order.

Our man was already up and moving, weaving amongst the panicked troops, using the tide of confusion he had created as cover. I felt a twinge of admiration at the man's ingenuity. He was good, I had to give him that: determined, ruthless and well trained.

I came level with Helena as she pulled herself off the ground.

'Wait,' she said. 'We will not outrun him. I will handle this, master.' She bit off the last word. I looked at her. She had a face that was too thin and pale to be pretty, and a Scholastica Psykana brand surrounded her left eye with a blunt letter 'I' and a halo of wings. She gave me a humourless smile. Helena was my interrogator, my apprentice in the duties of the Inquisition. We did not like each other. In fact, I was sure she hated me on some level. But she was a fine interrogator and a devoted servant of the Imperium. She was also a pysker, and a lethally powerful one at that.

I nodded in reply. She looked away, closing her eyes, and I felt the air around us take on a heavy burnt sugar texture as she drew power to her. Our quarry had already vanished into the shifting forest of human bodies around us. Hundreds of troops jostled like frightened cattle and I heard officers shouting for order and situation reports in the distance. There was a frozen moment, a sliver of time that for an instant was quiet and still. I saw a young trooper no more than a pace from me, his face frozen in puzzlement, his tan-coloured uniform still creased from storage. I whispered a prayer for forgiveness in that moment.

An invisible shock wave tore out from Helena, ripping bodies from the ground and tossing them into the air like debris in a cyclone's path. Bodies fell, broken, screaming as the telekinetic storm followed our quarry. It reached him, fifty paces from us, and flicked him off his feet. He hit the ground with a crack of bones. When I got to him he was sucking air in wet gasps, mashed fingers scrabbling at the lasgun just beyond his reach. I raised my inferno pistol and burned his reaching hand to a charred and blistered stump.

I did not bother to ask him how many other saboteurs were hidden in the mustering, or what their target was. I knew he would not give me an answer. It did not matter. He would give me the answers anyway.

'Take it from him.' I flicked my pistol at the broken man on the ground. 'We need to know how many of them there are and what targets they are intending to bomb.' Helena took a deep breath, closing her eyes for a second before looking down at the man who twitched and gurgled at our feet. He went still and I could feel the cold witch-touch on my skin. Helena's eyes were closed but as I looked at her she spoke.

'I have him, but...' her voice quivered and I saw she was trembling 'There is something wrong.'

'Get the information,' I snarled. 'We are running out of time. How many have infiltrated the muster? Where are the bombs?'

'They–' she began but was cut off by a laugh that bubbled up from the man on the ground. I looked down. He was staring back at me with corpse-white eyes. In that moment I knew I had made a mistake. We are cautioned that assumptions are worse than ignorance, and looking at the man I knew that my assumptions would see me dead. This was no saboteur ring bent on a mundane atrocity. This was something more, something far more. Cold fear ran through me.

'We are many, inquisitor,' he said, his voice a racking gurgle of blood and shattered ribs. Beside me Helena began to spasm, blood running from her mouth and eyes. Her mouth was working, try to form words.

'Witches. They are witches...' she gasped, her hand reached to grip my arm, as the psychic storm built around us. 'I can feel their minds. There are more, many more.' I could feel a greasy charge lick my skin, a stink of burnt blood on the air. The broken man laughed again, his skin crawling with lurid warp light.

'We are many,' he screamed, and he was still screaming as I vaporised his head. The sound did not end, but filled my head, getting louder and louder. I looked up from the dead man and saw the extent of my mistake.

Across the plane, figures rose into the air on pillars of ghost light, their limbs pinned to the air, arcs of lightning whipping from one to another, connecting them in a growing web. Dark clouds the colour of bile and dried blood spilled into the sky. Across the mustering fields, hundreds of thousands fell to their knees, moaning, clawing at their skin, blood dribbling from their eyes. Some, with stronger will, had been able to arm their weapons and fire at the witch chorus. Some found their mark and sent pyskers to their death. But there were many, and the witch storm rose in power with every heartbeat. I could feel the unclean power crawling over me like insects and the witches' voices pulling my thoughts apart. All I could hold on to was anger, anger that I had failed, that an enemy had fooled me. And all the while their voices grew louder and louder, spiralling around each other as a single word emerged from the telepathic cacophony.

Phocron.

Dozens of minds screamed the name and the storm broke in an inferno that washed across the mustering fields. It turned flesh to ash and scattered it on a superheated wind. Hundreds of thousands died in a single instant, an army to conquer worlds reduced to twisted metal and dust. I watched the fire come for me, and felt something enfold me like a cloak of ice. I realised that Helena still gripped my arm as I fell into darkness.

I woke on a plane covered in ashes. Helena was next to me, her exposed skin burnt and blistered, her breathing so shallow I thought she was dead until I saw her eyes twitch open. The energy needed to shield me still lingered on my skin as a cold shroud. I know now that she had saved us both, but at a price. The power she had channelled to shield us had almost burnt her psychic talent out. She lived, but she was a shadow of what she had been and never became an inquisitor. Amongst an overwhelming tragedy, her sacrifice still lives in my memory like the ghost touch of a lost life.

All around us there was nothing but an echoing desolation beneath a bruised sky. It was quiet, but in my head the name that had created this atrocity echoed in my mind.

Eighty-four years ago

WE CAME OUT of the iron-grey sky on streaks of blood-red fire. Staccato lines of flak and the bright blooms of defence lasers rose from the fallen city like the claws of a dying god raking the sky. Landing craft and assault carriers were punched from the air. Burning wreckage fell in oily cascades of smoke amongst the cities glittering domes and spires. The air rang with shells fired from orbit and the howl of attack craft engines. The wrath and might of the Imperium fell on the city, and it screamed as it burned.

In the gloom of my Valkyrie's crew compartment, we felt the ferocity of the invasion as shuddering blows that shook the frame around us. It was close inside the assault carrier, the air tinted red by the compartment's tactical lights and spiced with the smell of sweat. Even in such a confined space, my storm trooper detail kept its distance, even if that distance was only centimetres. I knew each of them by name, had fought beside all of them and personally selected them as my guard during this invasion. We had bled and struggled side by side, but I stood apart from them. To feel the power of the Emperor in your hand is to know what it is to be alone. It is a fact that I had long ago accepted.

'Lord?' The voice was raised against the thunder sound of the battle outside. I looked up from the holographic map to see Sergeant Dreag looking down at me, his face framed by oil-black armour. 'Theatre command wishes to know where you intend to make your landing.' I smiled, letting careless humour wash over my face.

'Do they indeed?' I asked. Dreag grinned back at me.

'Yes, lord. They say it is so that they can coordinate to properly support your operations.' I nodded, pursing my lips in mock consideration. I am not given to humour, but to lead people to death, you must wear many masks. Something exploded close by and the Valkyrie bucked. I felt my back pressed against the hard metal of the flight bench as the pilot banked hard.

'Little late in the day for a coordinated strike, don't you think Draeg?' I gave a small shake of my head. 'Tell them I will update them shortly.'

'Yes, lord,' nodded Draeg. 'And our actual target?' I looked back to the holo-display, coloured runes winking in clusters over a plan view of the city, shifting with objectives and tactical intelligence. The city was called Hespacia, a glittering jewel that had fallen to greed and lies and pulled the rest of its planet with it. The ruling guilds had overturned Imperial rule and given their souls, and those of their people, to the Dark Gods. This, though, was not why I had come to see it fall beneath the hammer of Imperial retribution. I had come not because of Hespacia's heresy but because of the cause.

'The Onyx Palace,' I handed the sergeant my holoslate. 'Assault position marked.' I watched the thinnest cloud of fear pass over the sergeant's blunt features. We were heading into the heart of the corruption, and we were doing it alone, without support.

'Very good, my lord,' said Draeg and began to bark a briefing to the other storm troopers. I checked my own weapons: a blunt-nosed plasma pistol holstered on the thigh of my burnished battle plate, and an eagle headed hammer that lay across my knees.

The Valkyrie bucked again, shaking to invisible blows. We were close. I did not need to see the tactical data to know it; I could feel it in the shuddering metal around me. In the decade after the burning of the Ephisian mustering I had changed much and learnt more. Suspicion is the armour of the Inquisition, and I had learnt its value in the preceding years. Rebellion had spread, pulling a dozen worlds into heresy and corruption, and with it had come a name, a name I already knew: Phocron.

Arch-heretic and puppet master of betrayal, his agents and traitors spread through our own forces like a contagion. Even with the might of crusade at our backs, we bought every victory with blood. Ambushes, sabotage and assassination ate our strength even as we advanced step by bleeding step. So I came to this damned city to cut off the rebellion's head, I came to kill the enemy I had never seen. I came to kill Phocron.

The side doors of the Valkyrie peeled back, and the burnt stink and howl of battle flooded over us. Beneath us, burning buildings flicked past, so close that I could see the pattern work on the blue-green tiles that covered so many of their domed roofs. In the streets, figures moved from cover to cover, the sound of their small battles lost amongst the roar as fire fell from the sky in an unending rain.

Above the burning city sat a tiered mountain of pale stone the colour of dirty ice. A series of ascending domes and balconies, it glowed under the luminous haze of void shields that flickered and sparked with the impact of munitions and energy blasts. This was the Onyx Palace, seat of governorship on this world and the heart of its betrayal. Phocron was there and the Onyx Palace was his bastion. The layered shields sheltered him from the bombardment, but they would not deny us.

The Valkyrie hit the void shield envelope, sparks arcing across its fuselage and an electric tang filling the air. The tiered balconies of the palace rose before us, studded with dark weapon turrets that spat glowing lines of fire. We banked and tipped, rounds hammering into the armoured airframe. The engines howled as they thrust us towards the palace summit. Others came behind us, delta-shaped wings of Vulture gunships and more assault craft. The air shuddered with the rolling scream of launching rockets and the bellow of explosions. Domes and statue-lined bridges flicked past. I could see figures, some crouched behind sandbags, others already running from the explosions that walked up the flank of the palace in our wake.

We crested the highest dome and I saw Phocron for the first time, a figure in dark armour with a single black clad companion, and a cluster of cowering figures in billowing silk robes. He stood close to the edge of the balcony as if he had been watching the ruin that he had forced the Imperium to bring to this world.

The Valkyrie pivoted, its engines screaming as it skimmed the stone slabs of the platform. My storm troopers were already dropping out of the door, hitting the ground one after another. Draeg gave me a grin, hurled himself out, and then it was me tumbling the few metres to hit the tiled platform. The world spun for a second and I was up on my feet, training and instincts doing the work of thought. My armour responded to my movements, thrusting me forward faster than muscle. Behind me, more storm troopers spilled onto the platform.

The robed figures clustered around Phocron died, the hellgun blasts burning through their silk finery. A few ran, swathes of coloured fabric spilling behind them, bare feet slapping on the marble. Phocron stood impassively, his hands empty, the sword at his waist undrawn. Behind him, a figure in a black storm coat and silver domino mask stood equally unmoved. I fired, plasma hissing from my pistol. Others were firing too. Bolts of energy converged on the two figures, but splashed against a shimmering dome of energy.

Draeg and his squad were in front of me, sprinting towards Phocron and his aide.

'Try and keep up in that armour, lord.' I heard the sergeant's grin over the vox. I spat back a very unlordly oath.

As the first shots hit Phocron's energy field, Draeg drew his sword. Lightning sheathed it with a crackle.

'Close assault, get inside the shield dome,' the sergeant spat over the vox. The hammer in my hand sprung to life, its generator making it vibrate with straining power. Draeg was the first through the shield dome, raising his sword for a backhanded cut, muscles ready to unfold the momentum of his charge into an armour cracking blow. Phocron moved at the last instant before the blow struck.

I have fought a lifetime of wars and met many enemies blade to blade. I have studied the business of killing, the workmanlike cut, the parry and riposte of a duel, the nicety of a perfectly timed blow. I have watched men kill each other in countless ways. The art of death holds no mystery to me. Yet I swear I never saw death dealt with more malign genius than at that moment.

Phocron's sword was in his hand. It was a long, its double edged blade damasked in a scale pattern. A saurian head snarled from its crossguard. It met Draeg's sword in a thunder crack of converging power fields. Draeg was fast, and conditioned from years of war to react to such a counter, but in this moment those instincts killed him. He shifted his weight to let the Space Marine's blow flow past and open his enemy to another cut. He did not expect Phocron to drop his sword.

With no resistance, Draeg's sword sliced down and cut air. Phocron turned around the sergeant's sword, so close their armour brushed. The gauntleted hand slammed into Draeg's armour at the throat. I saw the sergeant's head snap back, his body rag-loose as he fell to the ground.

The rest of Draeg's squad had not been far behind him and they opened up as they came through the shield dome. Phocron was already moving towards them at a flat run. The first died as he squeezed the trigger. Phocron's hand closed over the hellgun, crushing the storm trooper's fingers into the trigger guard. The man screamed. Phocron pivoted, the gun still spewing a stitched line of energy. The hellgun's fire hit the next two storm troopers at point-blank range, burning through flesh and armour. With swift delicacy, the Space Marine looped an arm around the screaming man and gripped the webbing belt of grenades across his chest.

I was a pace from the edge of the shield dome when I realised what was about to happen. Phocron turned and threw the screaming man at the rest of the storm trooper squad. The force of the throw broke the man's back with a sharp crack. I could see the pins of the grenades glinting in Phocron's fingers. The dead man hit the platform in front of his comrades and exploded.

The blast sheared through the rest of the squad in an expanding sphere of shrapnel. Fragments of metal, flesh and bone pattered off my armour. I could see Phocron and his storm coated henchman through the pall of smoke and dust. They were running.

'Target is moving,' I shouted across the vox. 'Close and eliminate.'

I fired, plasma burning ionised trails through the dust cloud. I ran after the two figures. Behind me, the rest of the strike force advanced. I reached the edge of the dust cloud. The fleeing pair were at the edge of the platform. Behind them, the city burned. They turned and looked back at the force running past the bloody remains of Draeg and his squad. They ran without looking at Phocron's sword, left forgotten on the ground.

The plasma charge concealed in the blade detonated, unfolding into a glowing sphere of sun-hot energy. I felt the heat through the skin of my armour as the blast tossed me into the air and slammed me into the paving. Warning chimes sounded in my ears as the armour systems sensed damage. Something wet moved in my chest as I sucked in a breath and found I was alive. For a few seconds, I could see nothing. I tried to raise my head and found that my vision was smeared with blood. I blinked until I could see. Bright light shone from behind me where the sphere of plasma still burned. Phocron stood, his blue armour black in the glare of the plasma bloom.

I pulled myself to my feet with a flare of pain and a grind of servos from inside my armour. My hammer was gone, scattered across the platform by the explosion. Two storm troopers that had been close beside me began to haul themselves up. Phocron shot them before they could stand, the guttural bark of the bolt pistol almost lost in the sound of the battle raging in the city. I was standing, my plasma pistol whining in my hand as it focused its power. The muzzle of Phocron's pistol pointed directly at me, a dark circle ready to breathe fire.

A Valkyrie crested the edge of the platform with a wash of downdraft. Its hull was painted in the storm grey of Battlefleet Hecuba. I could see the worn kill marks and unit tags under the cockpit. For an instant, I expected it to open up with its chin weapon, for it to rake Phocron and his companion with fire. Then it spun, drifting down until its open side doors were level with the platform. A crewman in an Imperial Navy uniform reached down to help the storm coated figure into the side door. Phocron vaulted after and the Valkyrie swooped away. I fancied that the Alpha Legionary was looking at me with his emerald eyes until the craft was lost amongst the hundreds of aircraft that swarmed above the dying city.

I breathed, letting pain and frustrated anger spill out. Something did not fit. It had seemed as if Phocron had anticipated our attack, waiting for it to come so that he could slaughter us. No, it was not just a slaughter. It was a demonstration of superiority. *I can defeat you in a thousand ways, I can kill you as I choose*, it had said. Then this sudden retreat, it did not fit. His forces were being overwhelmed, the city filling with thousands of Imperial troops, but then why not withdraw as soon as this became clear. Unless...

I suddenly felt cold, as if ice had formed inside my armour. I thumbed my vox-link, breaking through clearance ciphers until the voice of the invasion's commanding officer spoke into my ear. General Berrikade had a thick voice that spoke of his ample waist and heavy jowls. He was no fool though.

'Lord inquisitor,' he said, his voice chopped by static.

'General, all troops are to be withdrawn from the city immediately.' There was a pause, and I could imagine Berrikade staring at the vox-speaker in the strategium aboard an orbiting battleship.

'Lord,' he began speaking carefully. 'If I may ask...' He never finished because at that moment Phocron answered the unspoken question. At the same instant, the city's plasma reactors, promethium stores and chemical refineries exploded.

Across the city, glowing clouds rose into the sky, their tops broadening and flattening as they met the upper air currents. The shockwaves broke buildings into razor fragments and clouds of dust. An instant later, concentric waves of fire and burning gas swept through the streets. The sound and shockwave reached me a second later, flipping me through the air with a bellow of noise. I must have hit the ground, but I never felt it. The blast wave had already pulled me down into darkness.

Later, while I healed, I was told that tens of thousands of Imperial troops had been killed, hundreds of thousands more renegades and millions of civilians had burnt to nothing or crushed under rubble. The rebellion died, but the Imperium had taken a great wound and nothing was left but charred ruins. But the Onyx Palace had survived. Its plasma reactors had not been overloaded, and that had saved my life. When I was told this my first thought was that Phocron had wanted someone to survive to witness him rip another bloody chunk from the flesh of the Imperium. Then I thought again of the dark mouth of Phocron's bolt pistol and the death that he had withheld. No, I thought, he did not want just anyone to witness his victory: he had chosen *me* to witness it. To this day I do not know why.

* * *

A year ago

THE SHIP DRIFTED closer. Through the polished crystal of the viewport, I could see its crippled engines bleed glowing vapour into the vacuum. It was a small ship, barely large enough to be warp capable, and typical of the cutters used by traders and smugglers who existed on the fringes of the Imperium. The ship I stood on was massive by comparison, layered with armour and weapon bastions. It was a predator leviathan closing on a minnow. The *Unbreakable Might* was an Armageddon-class battlecruiser and mounted enough firepower to break other warships into glowing debris. Against the nameless clipper, it had barely needed to use a fraction of its might. A single precise lance strike had burnt the smaller ship's plasma engines to ruin and left it to coast on unpowered.

I turned from the view with a clicking purr of augmetics. My eyes focused on Admiral Velkarrin from beneath the cowl of my crimson robe. He was rake-thin, the metal flexes of command augmentation hanging from his grey-skinned skull in a tangled spill down the back of his gold-frogged uniform.

'Launch a boarding party, admiral,' I said. Velkarrin pursed his colourless lips but nodded.

'As you wish, my lord.' He turned to give an order to a hovering officer.

'And, admiral...' He turned back. 'They are to observe maximum caution.'

'Yes, my lord,' he gave a short bow. I could tell he resented my commandeering his command and his fleet. Hunting smuggler vessels and pirates while war washed across star systems must have galled him. Part of me was faintly amused by watching his pride war with fear of the Inquisition. The rest of me cared nothing for what he felt.

'I will meet the boarding team personally upon their return.' Velkarrin gave another curt bow in acknowledgement and stalked away, hissing orders at subordinates.

I turned back to watch our latest prey draw closer, my eyes whirring as they focused. They had rebuilt me after Hespacia. My eyes and face were gone, replaced by blue-lensed augmetics and a mask of twisted scar tissue fused onto a ceramic woven skull. My left leg and a portion of my torso had been so mangled that they had been replaced. Ceramite plating, organ grafting and a leg of brass mechanics meant that I still lived and walked, even if it was with a bent back and stutter of gears and pistons. For a while after the disaster of the Hespacia attack, I thought of my injuries as a penance for my lack of foresight, a price for ignorance written forever into my body.

Since that lesson I had done much to address my failing. The war against the rebel worlds had grown many times over, sucking in armies and resources from across many star systems. The Imperium was no longer fighting a war of containment but a crusade of retribution. Under my authority, and that of the Adeptus Terra, it was named the Ephisian

Persecution. I had watched our forces struggle for decades as more and more worlds had fallen to rebellion and the influence of the Dark Gods. It was a war we were losing because we were fighting an enemy for whom lies were both a weapon and a shield. Understanding that enemy had been my work in the decades since Hespacia burned.

I had expended great energy in tracking down information on the Alpha Legion. From the sealed reports of Inquisitor Girreaux to half-understood accounts from the dawn of the Imperium, I had reviewed them all. I knew my enemy. I knew their nature, their preferred forms of warfare, and their weaknesses. Sometimes, I thought I knew them better than I knew myself.

Their symbol was the hydra, a many-headed beast from legends born in mankind's earliest days. It was both a mark of their warrior brother-hood and a statement of methodology. To fight the Alpha Legion is to fight a many-headed beast that will twist in your grasp. As soon as you think you have a part pinned, another unseen part will strike. When you cut off one head, two grow to replace it. They weave secrets and lies about themselves, hoping to baffle and confuse their enemies. Subter-fuge, espionage, ambush and the untameable tangle of guerrilla warfare were their specialities. These specialities they wielded through networks of corrupted followers, infiltrators, spies and, on occasion, their own martial skill. They were wrapped in the corruption of Chaos, steeped in betrayal and bitterness since their primarch and Legion betrayed man-kind ten millennia before.

The enemy I faced now was a single scion of that heretic brood, but no less formidable for that. Phocron was a name that now ran through the Ephisian Persecution like a coiling serpent. I knew that even before we knew his name he had seeded a dozen worlds with insurgent ideologies and built up control over witch cults and heretic sects. Now he moved from warzone to warzone, plunging worlds into rebellion, corrupting our forces and punishing the Imperium for every victory. The Ephisian Atrocity and the Burning of Hespacia were just two amongst the subtle and devastating attacks he had made on the Imperium. Through his coiling dance of destruction, he had stayed out of my grasp, a shadow opponent locked in a dual with me across dozens of worlds.

Beyond the reflective layer of armaglass a shuttle boosted towards the crippled ship on trails of orange flame. Rather than follow Phocron's trail I had decided to attack him where he was most vulnerable, his mobility. He had no fleet of warships, he did not take planets by orbital invasion or the threat of bombardment. He took worlds from within, moving from one to another unseen. As far as I could tell he had no war-ships under his control. That implied that he moved using pirate and smuggler craft: small ships that could pass unnoticed and unremarked through the wild borderland of the subsector. A scattered task force of Imperial ships had tracked and boarded nineteen vessels so far with no result. The ship I watched would be the twentieth.

Two hours later, I stood amidst the promethium stink and the semi-ordered chaos of one of the *Unbreakable Might*'s main landing bays. Bright light flooded the cathedral-like space, gleaming off the hulls of lighters, shuttles and landing craft. Figures moved over them, working on the mechanical guts exposed under servicing plates.

I stood with Velkarrin and a guard of twenty armsmen, their bronzed void armour reflecting the bright light. The admiral stood a few paces away, consulting with two of his attending officers. The away team had reported that the vessel appeared to be nothing but a smuggler, crewed by deserters and outlanders. They had found a cargo of illegal ore destined for some pirate haven out in the Halo Margins. The lexmechanic who had accompanied them had drained the smuggler ship's data reservoirs for later analysis. As on the nineteen previous occasions no connection with Phocron or his shadow network existed. Still, I wanted to meet the boarding party on their return to search their accounts for details that they might have failed to report. Once that was done, the smuggler ship would be blasted into molten slag.

The armoured shuttle glided into the dock, its passive antigravity field filling the air with an ionised tang. It settled onto the deck with a hiss of hydraulics and a creak of ice-cold metal. The shuttle was a blunt block of grey armour the size of a mass ground hauler, its surface pitted and scored by atmospheric translation. Blast shields covered the armaglass of the cockpit. I heard the echoes of vox-chatter between the pilots and the deck crew as they moved in to attach power lines and data cables. The ramp under the chin of the shuttle hinged open, revealing a dark space inside. Velkarrin and the armsmen looked towards it, expecting the boarding team to appear from the gloom.

Something was wrong. I reached for the plasma pistol at my waist, my hand closing on the worn metal of the grip at the same moment that the docking bay went dark. Complete blackness enfolded us. For an instant, there was silence, and then voices rose in confusion. The pistol was in my hand, its charge coils glowing as it built power with a piercing whine. In the direction of the shuttle, two eyes glowed suddenly green. There was a motorised growl as a chain weapon gunned to life and then the shooting started. Our armsmen guard opened up, shotgun muzzles flaring as they fired into the dark. The noise was like a ragged, rolling bellow. In the jagged light of muzzle flare I saw my enemy standing on the ramp of the shuttle. His armour was dark, mottled by patterns of scales. In one hand he held a toothed axe, in the other a bolt pistol. He stood still for an instant as the shot rattled from his warplate, looking at us with glowing green eyes. Behind him stood a figure in a silver mask and storm coat. In that brief moment I thought that the empty eyes in the silver face were looking into mine.

The armsmen had closed ranks around Velkarrin and I, forming a deep circle of bronze armour. I aimed and fired, but Phocron was already gone, moving through muzzle flash, a whirlwind of slaughter caught through blinked instants.

He hit the first armsmen with a downwards blow. I heard the scream of motorised teeth meeting metal and flesh.

He was two strides nearer, an arc of dismembered dead at his feet. I heard a yelp of fear close by, recognising the admiral's voice by its tone.

The bolt pistol flared and roared, three armsmen dying in an oily flash of light. He was three strides away. There was a smell of offal and meat in my nose. Beside me, I heard Velkarrin turn to run and thud to the deck as his feet slipped on something slick and soft. The plasma pistol whined in my hand.

I raised my pistol, lightning dancing across its charge coils. Phocron was above me, chain axe raised, scale-patterned armour glistering with blood. He brought the axe down in a diagonal cut. I pulled the trigger and plasma flared from the barrel of my pistol.

I missed, but the shot saved my life. Jerking aside to avoid my shot, Phocron missed his target. The teeth of the chain axe met my gun arm just below the elbow, the back swing slicing through Velkarrin as he tried to stand.

The lights came on as shock hit me. Blood was spilling from the chewed stump of my arm. I staggered a step and my legs gave way, collapsing to the floor in a clicking whir of gears. People moved, shouting. I was aware of a lot of weapons surrounding me very quickly.

I looked around, trying to focus through a pale fog that seemed to be floating across my vision. Blood glistened under the bright light. The ramp of the shuttle was still open. Later, I would find out that none of its crew or the boarding party had returned from the smuggler ship, the voices in the vox-chatter and reports had been perfect mimicry. Of Phocron and the man in the silver mask, there was no sign.

One month ago

THE WAR COUNCIL overseeing the Ephisian Persecution gathered on board the *Unbreakable Might.* Generals, war savants, vice-admirals, magos, bishops militant, palatines, commissar lords and captains of the Adeptus Astartes: all came to my call. The strategium of the battlecruiser was a two hundred paces-wide circular chamber of raked seats carved from granite. I waited at the centre, under the eyes of the gathering worthies, and watched.

They came in small groups, looking for faces they knew, judging where it was their right to sit, who they had to avoid and who they had to greet. It was like watching the shifting gears of Imperial politics and power play out in miniature. There a Sparcin war chief in burnished half plate and white fur cloak, trailed by a clutch of tactical advisors. Here a psykana lord, a withered white face within a hood of cables, sat next to a spindle limbed woman in carmine robes, the cog-skull of the Adeptus Mechanicus etched on the brass of her domino mask. Servo skulls moved above the assembling throng, scanning, recording, sniffing the air for threats and spreading incense in thick breaths.

Amongst the crowd I saw some of my own kind, inquisitors or their representatives, moving amongst the rest like imperious masters, or remaining still and silent on the edges. I had invited none of them but they came anyway, my reputation enough to bring them. Some even called me 'lord inquisitor'. Rank within the Inquisition is a complex matter. No formal structure exists amongst this shadow hand of the Imperium that answers to none but the will of the Emperor. Lordship is a matter of respect, a title of acknowledgement granted by peers to one who has earned it by the power of their deeds. My war against Phocron had pulled respect and renown to me like a flame gathers insects. As the greatest masters of war in this volume of space gathered at my call, I could see why some might call me lord.

I sat on a high-backed chair at the centre of the chamber. A symbolic hammer rested beneath my left hand, my right on the black iron of the chair's arm, fingers of polished chrome clicking softly on the dark metal. It had been a year since I had lost my right arm in the ambush that had killed Admiral Velkarrin and nearly claimed my life. The bionic replacement still ached with phantom pain.

In that year, I had not been idle. Following his attempt on my life, Phocron had simply vanished. No trace of him could be found on the ship or on the smuggler vessel. This, and the sudden loss of light at the moment of attack, could only mean that his network of traitors extended deeper and higher in our forces than I had considered possible. Trusted acolytes and agents of my own had gone to work, and now I gathered together the leaders of the Persecution to share what I had found. A few knew what was about to happen, most did not.

I watched as black-visored troopers sealed the doors to the chamber and waited for the grumble of conversation to fade. When it had, I stood.

'There is much to speak of,' I said, my voice carrying up the tiered seats. I saw some shift at the lack of formal greeting or acknowledgement of the honour and position of those gathered here. I let myself smile at the thought. 'But first there is a matter that must be dealt with.' I gave a slight nod as if to emphasise the point, and those waiting for that signal acted as one.

Even though I was prepared for it, the psychic shockwave made me stagger. On the tiered seats, a dozen figures convulsed as the telepathic and telekinetic power enfolded them in a vice-like grip. I felt an oily static charge play over my skin. There was a sound like wind rustling through high grass. The needle slivers hit the convulsing men and women, and one by one they went still as the sedatives overrode nerve impulses. There was an instant of shocked silence.

'Do not move,' I shouted as the black-visored troopers moved through the crowd. They clustered around each of the stricken figures. Null collars and monowire bindings slipped over necks and limbs and the bound figures were dragged across the stone floor like sacks of grain. The shock in the rest of the crowd was palpable; they had just seen a dozen of their senior peers, men and women of power and distinction, overcome and dragged away. You could almost feel the thought forming in all their minds: *traitors in our midst.* The pale faced psykana lord nodded to me and I favoured him with a low bow of thanks. A murmur of anger and fear began to build in the chamber.

'Our enemy is among us.' I raised my hammer up and brought its adamantine head down on the granite floor. Silence gathered in the wake of the fading hammer blow. 'It walks amongst us, wearing faces of loyalty.' My voice was soft but it carried in the still air. 'Our enemy has used our strength against us, directed us into traps, mired us in blood and shackled our strength with lies. A year ago, on this ship, that enemy came close to ending my life with his own hand. That such a thing was possible is a testament to his ability and audacity.' I paused, looking around at the faces watching me, waiting to see what would come next. 'But I survived, and in that attempt he exposed the extent of the treachery within our forces.' I pointed to the dozen spaces on the tiered seats. 'Today I have removed the heads of the hydra from among us.' I paused as murmurs ran through the audience.

The traitors had been difficult to find without arousing their suspicion. It had been delicate work to find them, and more delicate still to prepare to remove them in a single instant. The twelve taken in the chamber had been the most senior, the most highly placed of Phocron's agents and puppets. Some, no doubt, had not known what end they served, others, I was sure, were willing traitors. There had been generals amongst them, senior Munitorum staff, an astropath, a confessor and even an interrogator. At the moment they had been taken, parallel operations had gone into action throughout the Persecution's forces, cutting the corruption out from among us. Most of the infiltrators would be killed, but many would be taken and broken until their secrets flowed from them like blood from a vein.

'The enemy has blinded us and led us by the hand like children. But at this moment he has also handed us weapons with which to destroy him. Knowledge is our weapon, and from the traitors that walked among us we will gain knowledge.' I stood and picked the hammer up, its head at my feet, the pommel resting under my hands. 'And with that knowledge, this Persecution will cut the ground from under the feet of our enemy. We will wound and hound him until he crawls to his last refuge. And when he is crippled and bleeding, I shall take the last head of this hydra.'

* * *

Twelve hours ago

A HUNDRED WARSHIPS came to bear witness to our victory. They ringed the jagged space fortress, their guns flaring as they hammered it with fire. The *Hydra's Eye* turned in its orbit around the dead world like a prize fighter too dazed to avoid the blows mashing his face to bloody pulp and splintered bone.

In the end, it had been the words of a traitor that had betrayed Phocron's refuge. One of those taken from the strategium of the *Unbreakable Might* had known of another agent in naval command. That agent had been taken in turn, and his secrets ripped from his mind by a psyker. That information had been added to fragments gleaned from others, winding together to make a thread that had led to the system of dead planets in which the *Hydra's Eye* hid. That it was the current refuge for Phocron was implied and confirmed by many sources once we knew where to look. Once I had the location of Phocron's base, I ordered an immediate attack.

The *Hydra's Eye* was truly vast, an irregular star of fused void debris over fifteen kilometres across at its widest point. Its hull was a patchwork skin of metal that wept glowing fluid as macro shells and lance strikes reduced its defences to molten slag. There had been enemy ships clustering around the irregular mass of the space fortress like lesser fish beside a deep sea leviathan. Most had been pirate vessels, wolf packs of small lightly-armed craft. All died within minutes, their deaths scattering light across the jagged bulk of the *Hydra's Eye*. Our guns went silent as a cloud of assault boats and attack craft swarmed towards the wounded fortress. I had not watched as Phocron's last means of escape died in fire. This was the end of my war and I was ready to strike its last blow myself. When the first wave of attack craft swarmed towards the space fortress I was there, my old body wrapped in armour forged by the finest artisans of Mars.

An animal is at its most dangerous when wounded and cornered. Phocron's followers did not fail to hammer this lesson home. The forces on the *Hydra's Eye* were a mixture of piratical scum and renegades inducted into Phocron's inner circle. They spent their lives without thought, their only care being to make us pay many times over for each of them that we killed. I could see Phocron's vile genius in their every tactic. Some hid in ceiling ducting or side passages, waiting for our forces to pass before attacking from behind. Others pulled guardsmen quietly into the dark, strangling them before taking their uniforms and equipment. Dressed as friends, the renegades would join our forces, waiting until the most advantageous moment to turn on the men beside them. The structure of the fortress itself spoke of a twisted foresight. Dead ends and hidden passages riddled the structure. Passages and junctions seemed to split and channel us, portioning our forces so that they became divided. We had bodies enough to choke every passage. We would win, that was without doubt, but every inch cost blood. Those bloody steps had led me here to this chamber and this final battle.

Yes, every step had cost blood; every step for a hundred years, from the mustering fields of Ephisia, through the burning of Hespacia to here where I will face my enemy for the last time. I am alone, the rest of the Imperial force lost behind me in the bloody tangle of the *Hydra's Eye*. So I will face my enemy alone, but perhaps that is as it should be.

PHOCRON MOVES AND cuts, his blow so quick and sudden that I have no chance to dodge. I raise my arm, feeling the armour synchronise with the movements of my aging muscles. My fist meets his strike in a blaze of light. For a second, it is his strength against mine, the energies of weapons grinding against each other. I am looking into his face, so close that I can see the pattern of finer and finer scales on his face plate. The deadlock lasts an eye blink. I fire my storm bolter a fraction of a second before he moves. The burst hits him in the chest at point-blank range and spins him onto the floor with the sound of cracking ceramite. I spray his struggling form with explosive rounds as he tries to rise.

I take a step closer – a mistake. He is on his feet faster than I can blink, spinning past me. The tip of his sword glides over my left elbow as he moves. The power field sheathing my fist vanishes, the power feeds severed with surgical care. I turn to follow him. His sword flicks out again, low and snake-strike fast. The tip stabs through the back of my left knee. Pain shoots up my leg an instant before it collapses under me. Tiles shatter under the impact. He is gone, moving into blind space behind me. I try to twist around, my targeting systems searching. He is going to kill me, one cut at a time. Despite the pain, I smile to myself. The Alpha Legion do not simply kill, they bleed you one bite at a time until you have no doubt of their superiority. But that pride is their weakness.

A cut splits the elbow of my right arm. I do not even see where it comes from. Blood is running down my alabaster-white armour and dribbling across the crushed tiles. My right arm is hanging loose at my side, but I hold onto my storm bolter through the pain.

He walks into my view. There is a casual slowness to his movements. He has stripped me of my strength, crippled me and now he wants to look into my eyes as he kills me. He stops two paces from me and looks down at me with green eyes. The tip of the blade rises level with my eye. His weight shifts as he prepares to ram the sword into my eye. This is the death stroke, and it is the chance I have been waiting for.

I bring my left arm around in a swing that hits him behind the right knee. The fist has no power field, but it is still a gauntlet of armour propelled by a layer of artificial muscles. It hits with a dry crack of fractured armour and bone.

Phocron falls, the hand gripping the knife splayed out to the side. I pull myself to my feet, gripping my storm bolter with the last of my strength. It does not take much. All I need to do is squeeze the trigger. Fired at point-blank range, the explosive rounds shred his arm. Before he can react, I move and squeeze the remainder of the storm bolter's clip into his left arm.

He flounders in a pool of blood and armour fragments. I put my knee on his chest and grip the horns of his helmet with my left fist. Seals squeal and snap as I wrench the helmet from his head. For an instant, I expect to see the face of a monster, a monster that created me, that drove me to become what I am. But the face under the helm is that of a Space Marine, unscarred, dark eyes looking up at me from sharp features. He has a small tattoo of an eagle under his left eye, the ink faded to a dull green.

I reach up and take my own helmet off. The air smells of weapons fire and blood.

'Phocron,' I say. 'For your crimes and heresies against the Imperium of mankind, I sentence you to death.'

He smiles.

'Yes, you have won. Phocron will die this day.' There is movement of the edge of my sight.

I look up. There are figures watching me from the edges of the room. They wear blue armour, some blank and unadorned, some etched with serpentine symbols, others hung with sigils of false gods. They look at me with green glowing eyes. Amongst them is a normal-sized man wrapped in a storm cloak, his face hidden by a silver mask. The image of a figure in a mask stood against the burning backdrop of Hespacia, and caught in muzzle flash on the *Unbreakable Might* flicks through my memory.

The man steps forward. His right hand is augmetic and holds a slender-barrelled needle pistol. There is a clicking purr of gears and pneumatics as the masked man walks towards me. I start to rise. The masked man reaches up with his left hand and pulls the silver mask away. I look at him.

He has my face.

THE NEEDLE DART hits the inquisitor in his left eye and the toxin kills him before he can gasp. He collapses slowly, the bulk of his armour hitting the tiled floor with a crash.

We move quickly. We have only a few moments to secure our objective, and we can make no mistakes. The inquisitor's armour is stripped from his body, piece by piece, the injuries he sustained noted as they are revealed. As the dead man is peeled from the armour I remove my own gear and equipment, stripping down until there are two near identical men, one dead and bleeding on the floor, the other standing while his half-brothers finish their work. My augmetics and every detail of my re-sculpted flesh match the man who lies dead on the floor. Years of subtle flesh craft and conditioning mean that my voice is his voice, my every habit and movement are his. There is only the matter of the wounds that were carefully inflicted to injure, but not kill. I do not cry out as my Legion brothers cut me, though the pain is nothing less than it was for him, the dead man whose face I wear. The wounds are the last details, and as the blood-slick Terminator armour covers my skin, all differences between the dead inquisitor and I end. We are one, he and I.

They take the inquisitor's body away. It will burn in a plasma furnace to erase the last trace of this victory. For it is a victory. They take away our crippled brother who was the last to play the role of Phocron. A corpse is brought to take his place, its blue armour chewed by bolter rounds and crumpled by the blows of a power fist. A horned helmet hides his face and a shimmering cloak hangs from his shoulders. This corpse is the final proof that the Imperium will require to believe they have won this day: Phocron, dead, killed by his nemesis. Killed by me. The Imperium will see this day as their victory, but it is a lie.

Phocron never existed, his name and legend only extant in the mind of the Imperium and the obsession of the man whose place I take. Phocron existed only to create this last meeting. Many of the Legion were Phocron, playing the role to create a legend that was a lie. I will walk from this chamber in victory and my legend will grow, my influence and power will spread further. Decades of cultivation and provocation have led to this one moment of transformation, the moment we give the Imperium a victory and transform it into a lie. This is our truth, the core of our soul, the essence of our craft. We are warriors unbound by the constraints of truth, assumption, or dogma. We are the reflection in the eternal mirror of war, ever changing, unfixed, and invincible. We serve lies and are their masters. We are their slaves and they are our weapons, weapons which can defeat any foe, break any fortress, and grant one warrior victory against ten thousand. I am the one who stands against many. I am Alpha Legion, and we are one.

WARHAMMER®

MOUNTAIN EATER

Andy Smillie

THE BEAST EMERGED into the light and screamed. It was an ugly thing, a creature meant for dark places, for the deep earth, not the radiance of the sun. It screwed its eyes shut, smothering them with malformed claws and fracturing a bone in its left cheek in a vain attempt to kill the pain. Still the world was too bright. Cowed, it stumbled back into the caves where it had spent its miserable life. The soothing darkness returned and it uncovered its face. Crouching, it watched the wind whip icy wash past the threshold of the cave. The baleful sun reflected off the white landscape.

The beast turned its back on the outside and looked down at the mangled ogre carcasses strewn around the cavern. Licking its lips, it remembered raking open their bloated bellies, exposing the juicy innards within. It ripped a piece of cloth off the leg of the nearest corpse and tied the blood-soaked rag tightly around its head. In utter darkness the beast settled.

With the absence of pain, the flesh hunger returned. Its heart beat faster as the beast remembered the carnage, its flesh sickly wet, rimed in the ogre's blood, the sour tang of gnoblar flesh wedged between its teeth. Its mouth twisted into a horrible parody of a smile. The worthless creature was little more than a morsel. Biting through its tiny ribcage was easy. Its head had cracked like an egg in the beast's mouth, hot juices flooding its palate.

The wind growled into the cave, disturbing the beast's remembrance. It carried the same message, the one it had whispered to the gorger for

781

days. Somewhere, up in the mountain where the ice was thick, there was more meat, more blood.

It needed only to climb.

DARHUR CUPPED A hand over his brow, squinting as he tried to see the cave mouth. Fierce crosswinds blustered around him, tossing a deluge of gritty snow into his face. He snarled. The hunter could just make out an entrance, a dark spot at the foot of the mountain. Darhur gauged the distance. It was maybe a few hundred paces away.

'Snikkit...' Darhur growled at an ageing gnoblar struggling through the snow in the hunter's wake. The diminutive creature immediately shrank further into the bear pelt heaped around his tiny shoulders. The ogre snarled. 'Take a look.'

Snikkit opened his mouth to protest, when a muscled feline beast idled up beside him and silently bared its massive incisors.

For a sabretusk, Golg's persuasive powers were surprisingly restrained.

'Yes boss, right away boss.' Snikkit held up his hands in a vain effort to ward off Darhur's beast, a mixture of cold and fear turning his green skin grey.

'And take those other two with you,' Darhur gestured to Brija and Najkit. He hadn't survived his years in exile by being reckless. Gnoblars were little good if you couldn't use them as bait. Watching the three ease their way towards the cavern, Darhur ran his leathern hand through Golg's coat. 'Don't you worry. You can eat 'em later.'

NAJKIT KEPT HIS distance from the other gnoblars. If there *was* a gorger in the cave, he wasn't getting eaten by it. Well, at least not before that idiot Brija. Najkit shook his head as Brija shuffled past him, mumbling gibberish as he tried to lick the snow off his knife.

Snikkit dug his hands into his pockets. Shiny things were hidden within that not even Darhur knew about. They were secrets, precious loot for Snikkit, and Snikkit alone. A pity they couldn't carry a fire or a broth-filled cauldron. His stomach rumbled, reminding him he was hungry. Then he shivered. It was freezing too. He hated the mountains, and had been perfectly happy hunting idiot humans in the lowlands. Darhur must have angered the Great Maw when he killed Skarg Backbreaker and earned banishment from the tribe. Tyrant Grut Face Eater favoured his Ironguts above all, save his own bloated gut. Famously, the Tyrant had proclaimed that he would only eat one of his precious bodyguard if the cooking pots were empty and all else had been consumed. Snikkit cursed his luck, regretting the decision to throw in his lot with the hunter. A butcher's pot would have been preferable to this slow freezing death. It irked him to be punished for Darhur's pride. The wind rumbled around in the cave mouth and coughed back out, arresting Snikkit's wallowing. Fishing his best shrapnel from his pocket, he loaded his favourite sling and approached the entrance. He shuffled inside, flanked by Brija and Najkit, eyes struggling to adjust after the glaring white of the outside.

'Watcha sees?' Najkit whispered.

'Nuffin' yet.' Snikkit kept his eyes fixed on the gloom in front of him. Slowly, the features of the cave resolved through the darkness. Stalagmites colonised the ceiling, several larger ones protruding like talons above his head. The cavern walls were pitted and irregular, as though hewn from the rock of the mountain by giant fists. Snikkit trembled as he thought about the mighty storm giants that once roamed these benighted crags. He took a cautious few steps forwards... the gnoblar let out a grunt of pain as his head struck the ground.

He'd slipped on something.

'You alive?' Not waiting for a reply, Najkit threw his knife in Snikkit's direction.

'Wotch it!' The grubby blade missed Snikkit's scalp by inches and clattered next to him. 'Sumthin' on the floor.' He sat up, rubbing his head and a small cut above his eye, which had already frozen closed. Snikkit ran his palm over the ground where he'd lost his footing. Peering through the darkness, he saw why. He followed the glint of the blood-ice to a pile of mangled bodies. He was already getting to his feet, backing away from the slaughter.

Ogres. Dead ogres. Lots of them.

'We shud get da boss.' Snikkit turned to Brija. He had no desire to be back out in the wind and urged the idiot to go instead. 'I keep watch.'

Brija though, took no notice, engrossed in trying to prise a knife off his tongue.

Snikkit hoped he'd cut it off, at least then they'd have something to eat.

'I go.' Najkit was a particularly selfish creature, not given to helping anything or anyone but himself. Survival dictated leaving the warmth of the cave, one that a gorger had only recently made into its lair. Even if the monster was gone, there were bound to be more of them lurking somewhere nearby drawn to the smell of blood, and Najkit wasn't about to be next on the menu.

THE TORCH FLICKERED in the darkness, casting strange shadows on the walls. Monstrous shapes appeared in the half light: the mastodon of Kruk's Peak, Gutslaab the slave giant and the winged fiend of Harrowing Crags. Darhur had killed them all and devoured their strength. He held the torch aloft, relishing the warmth of its flames as he followed Najkit further into the cavern.

'Hurry up,' Darhur snarled, kicking Najkit in the back to make his point, 'or it's somethin' sharper than my boot next time.'

Najkit muttered a curse under his breath, thinking about all the soft places he could stab Darhur with his knife when next the ogre hunter slept, and headed to where he'd left Snikkit and Brija. Unless, he thought, the gorger had returned and…

Najkit smiled. If the beast was feasting, Darhur could sneak up and kill it. He could rummage through what was left, the sinew and the grease, for Snikkit's lovely coat. Just imagining this grim turn of events made Najkit feel warmer. But then again, what if…

Picking up the pace, the gnoblar drew his knife and prayed the others were already food.

'Boss, boss. Over 'ere,' Snikkit waved Darhur over and let out a sigh of relief. The ogre was a welcome sight. Snikkit was mostly sure that whatever dangers lurked in the mountains, Darhur would kill them before they could eat him.

Darhur ignored the creature and swung the torch low over three ogre corpses. The bodies were dumped one on top of the other, the way Darhur discarded the legs of cave pheasant when he'd picked clean the meat. They'd been dead a good while but the cold had slowed decomposition. A deep incision to their abdomens had killed them. Darhur bared his teeth in anger. The beast had savaged then bled them – they had all died in pain. The bodies were top-heavy, their guts and thighs devoid of meat while the tougher gristle around their shoulders and arms had been left almost untouched. A blood trail ran further back into the cavern. There was no spatter on the walls and none of the damage to the stalagmites above that he'd have expected from a fight. The ogres hadn't died here.

The hunter turned over the remains with his foot, stopping when he saw a cracked gut plate. It was badly mangled and studded with claw and teeth marks but the glyph was unmistakable – Wallcrusher Tribe. Darhur shivered, though not from cold, only too aware that he'd suffer the same fate should he fail to slay the beast. Grut Face Eater had no sympathy for weaklings who let a dirty gorger eat them. He'd sent Darhur after the gorger because it'd eaten something else, something that did matter. Darhur sifted more carefully through the viscera and was rewarded with a small fragment of green rock. It belonged to Grut's personal gnoblar, Sneejit. The tyrant thought it turned Sneejit into some sort of lucky charm. Darhur thought it made the irritating little creature more so. He was almost sorry he was going to have to kill this beast.

'Golg.' Darhur bent down and picked up a handful of ragged cloth, holding it out for the sabretusk.

Golg padded over to the hunter. Burying its snout in the bloodied rags, it took a long sniff, filling its nostrils with the stench of sweat, piss and blood. Its heart quickened at the familiar scents. Sneering as it caught the faintest tang of unwashed gnoblar, Golg turned to Snikkit and growled.

'Eh, boss…' Panicked, Snikkit hid behind Brija. The idiot gnoblar was blissfully unaware of the drooling sabretusk, fretting at his flayed tongue. Excising the knife had cost him at least one layer of flesh.

'Not now.' Darhur cuffed Golg on the back of the head. Stooping, he pulled a large bone from the half-eaten feast. The hunter turned the femur over in his hand. It had been picked clean, scoured by a tongue so coarse that it had been left unnaturally smooth. Darhur grunted and tossed the bone to Golg. Catching it in his powerful jaws, the sabretusk devoured it, crunching and swallowing without pause.

Darhur snarled. His muscles bunched in anticipation of the fight to come. 'Find the gorger.'

WEAKNESS WAS NOT something Darhur was accustomed too. But this was a foe he could neither crush with a hammer nor skewer with a spear. It was the mountain. It was the earth, and the peaks of endless ice. He braced himself against a large boulder, drawing reassurance from its solidity. This high up, the air was whisker thin. Every breath came quick and shallow, his lungs struggling to feed oxygen to his massive frame. Darhur regarded the mountain. It soared past the limits of his vision, stabbing into the lifeless grey of the sky and disappearing into ugly cloud. He hoped the gorger hadn't climbed much farther. Darhur had crested Gut Spire, the highest peak roamed by none but the thickest skinned mammoths. Not even the cantankerous mountain carrion circled overhead, their nests confined to lower aeries. Darhur wondered what could have driven the beast onwards into the unknown mists. Even layered in thick hides and pelts, the hunter's skin was cracked and raw. A dozen times during the ascent, he'd been forced to stop and beat blood back into his aching muscles. He was amazed that the naked gorger, wiry and without a hardy gut, had not simply died from exposure. Truly, it was a resilient beast and worthy of his hammer. Golg growled from up ahead, urging his master to continue.

Darhur summoned the strength to bark at his companion, 'Take us the right way this time.'

More than once he'd followed the sabretusk to a dead end, the gorger's trail suddenly swallowed up by the wind and snow. The beast was seemingly a wraith, a figment of Darhur's fevered imagination given form and allowed to wander the frozen passes of the desolate upper peaks. Even doubling back, they'd found it almost impossible to get their bearings again, as though the mountain itself was trying to waylay them. Passages that had been open were suddenly closed, crags had become denser and caves disappeared only to reemerge elsewhere.

Darhur knew such things were impossible. Mountains were like the ogre tribes, permanent and unchanging except in the face of cast-iron might. The hunter crushed his suspicions, disregarding them as inane fantasies of his cold-numbed mind. Pulling the pelt tighter around his shoulders, he pushed his feet onwards through the thickening snow. The wind picked up, its blustering howl joined by the faint rumble of thunder from farther up the mountain. Darhur could barely see the ground beneath him anymore. One wrong step and he'd plummet over the edge into ignominious death and oblivion. A jag of lightning tore across the sky, opening a great wound that speared freezing hail down onto the hunter. Chunks of ice the size of fists battered his weary body.

'Maw!' Darhur cried out in defiance. A shard bit into his arm as he tried to shield his face from the sudden storm. Another cut his forehead, but the blood was like ice. It hammered into his broad back. It slashed his cheek and he roared, but the elements could not be silenced by his anger. It was as if the very mountain wanted to deny him his prey.

Numb with fatigue, Darhur's legs gave out. Crawling on all fours, he eked out a few more feet before grinding to a halt. His resolve broken, the hunter lay in the snow, letting the relentless storm batter him. Slowly, he was swathed in a film of white, invisible against the winter landscape. He should have been angry, furious that he would die in frozen shame, but the fire in his belly had cooled with the long climb. The mountain had defeated him after all.

PAIN STABBED THROUGH Darhur's shoulder, stirring him from his sorrow. Then he was moving, jerking over the rough ground. Something was dragging him. The hunter's instincts kicked in in an instant, his mind conjuring images of the fell beast that sought to haul him to its lair and make a meal of his flesh. Fumbling for his hammer, Darhur struggled to see beyond the snow that cascaded over his face. Straining, he glimpsed Golg. The sabretusk's jaws were clamped around his shoulder. Wincing, Darhur swung his arm up and slapped an open palm against the sabretusk's head. Growling, the beast let him go. The hunter got to his feet, swearing that he would wring the upstart feline's neck. Withdrawing, Golg dropped onto his rear legs and waited until the ogre was almost within arm's reach before skulking behind a bowed rock that concealed the path ahead. Darhur growled in annoyance, rolled his shoulder loose and strode after the impudent beast.

The hunter emerged onto a ledge that had been obscured from view. Thrashing winds tested his balance as he advanced to find Golg waiting for him in the lee of a cave. He let out a rasping laugh as he staggered into the cavern and slumped to the floor. Pulling his legs in against his chest, the hunter fought to rid the chill from his bones, massaging blood back into his arms. Golg dropped down next to him, bowing his head. Darhur considered striking the beast for its insolence but instead moved closer to the sabretusk, eager to share the heat from its pelt. The three gnoblars shivered in moments later, stood almost shoulder to shoulder in a huddle. Darhur snorted. He'd forgotten about them.

'Make sure there's nothin' back there,' Darhur snapped, the layer of frost riming his eyelids hindering his ability to see in the gloom of the cave.

Snikkit took a few cautious steps towards the back of the cavern, silently wondering how long it'd be before Darhur or Golg got hungry enough to eat him. Brija was beside him, muttering nonsense between chatters of his gnarled teeth.

'I's watch front,' Najkit took a swig from his flask and sat down opposite Golg. He wanted to keep the sabretusk where he could see it.

Snikkit muttered a curse and turned his attention to the cave. He wasn't afraid, just desperate to do as he was told and then get some sleep away from Brija. The ceiling was irregular, sloping down and then suddenly reaching up into the mountain. The ground was wet where the freezing cataracts from above had pooled. Snikkit sniffed the air – it was fresher than the choking grit of the blizzard, and there was something else...

"Ere, 'ere,' Brija had wandered ahead and was pointing at what looked to Snikkit like a pile of rocks.

On closer inspection, the rocks turned out to be bones. Snikkit kicked a few of them, the way he'd seen Darhur kick a body to see if it was still breathing. 'Ain't nuffin' but bones 'ere boss,' he called to Darhur, 'Sum animal musta crawled in an' died.'

The hunter was only half listening, his exhausted body beginning to slip into the great sleep, his mind already dreaming.

In his delirium, Darhur saw Skarg, laughing as Golg lost an eye to the irongut's upstart gnoblar. He relived the moment that his hammer had crashed through Skarg's gutplate to pulverise his organs, his ironshod boot trampling the irongut's head into the ice fields.

The hunter's frostbitten lips twisted themselves into a grin.

Darhur's joy was short lived, Tyrant Face Eater's words of admonishment rising in his mind like a dark cloud. Thoughts of home filled the hunter's head. He watched himself stand by his tribe's roasting fires, the smell of fresh human wafting from the butcher's pot, the cooking flames reflecting off the butcher's outsized cleaver–

A shadow fell across Darhur's face. His eyes opened to a hulking figure. It filled the mouth of the cave, a sliver of hardened ice in each clawed hand. Instinctively, Darhur drew his knife, its sickle blade deflecting a downwards blow meant to sever his head. Before the attacker could strike again, Golg sprang into its chest, knocking it backwards. The hunter got to his feet, fighting to shake the malaise that had taken hold of him.

'Yhetee!'

Darhur ignored Snikkit's yelping. He was wrong anyway. The creature was too large to be a yhetee, its hide too dark. It was a greyback, a larger and far more dangerous foe. The beast was fully a head taller than Darhur, and underneath its layer of insulating hair lay tight bunches of sinew and dextrous muscle. The greyback recovered in an instant, issuing a malevolent roar from a mouth lined with dagger teeth. It caught Golg with a backhanded blow to the head as the sabretusk pressed his attack. Scolding himself for falling asleep in the beast's lair, Darhur unhooked the hammer from his belt and attacked. The greyback blocked the hunter's opening swing, its blade snapping against his hammer. Moving in, Darhur slipped inside its reach and shot his forehead into its face. He felt teeth splinter as his stony brow smashed apart its jaw. Moist fur that reeked of stale blood and piss filled his face. Darhur fought down the urge to gag and shouldered the beast against the cave wall.

Snikkit tried to load his sling, but his fingers were too cold. At least he tried, he thought, retreating to the far end of the cave where Brija sat, holding his knees against his chest, head bobbing nervously. Snikkit envied Najkit, who was still lying on the floor, blissfully unaware of the mortal danger he was in. The mixture of the yhetee piss he'd been drinking and the thin air had rendered the snide gnoblar unconscious.

Together, Darhur and Golg pinned the greyback against the wall. They moved for the kill, but the creature avoided them. Leaping to the ceiling, it used its claws for purchase and swung over their heads. Dropping behind Darhur, it raked its talons down his back. The hunter let out a snarl of pain and spun around, lashing out with his hammer. The beast stepped back out of range, as Darhur had expected it to. Continuing his turn, the ogre threw the blade from his other hand. The knife cut through the air and sliced into the greyback's chest, burying itself up to the hilt. The beast roared, blood bubbling from its mouth, and rushed towards Darhur. Brushing aside the greyback's desperate thrashing, the hunter clamped his hand around the knife's handle. Bellowing a curse, he lifted the beast into the air and slammed it down into the ground.

Sweating, Darhur fixed the greyback in place with his foot and pulled his knife free. 'The Great Maw provides.'

The hunter began carving up his prize. The greyback was no different from the dozens of rhinox and mountain bears Darhur had slain before. Though, unlike the great mammoth whose horn adorned Darhur's gutplate, the beast would not take a week to pare. With practiced precision he cut away the pelt and sank his teeth into an artery before the blood could run cold. Piercing the larger artery on the beast's leg, Darhur bathed in the warm blood as it spat onto his face and thawed his features. With his bare hands, he ripped off chunks of muscle and fat, gorging himself on chunks of raw meat. Blood and viscera spilling from his mouth, Darhur ripped off an arm and tossed it to Golg. The sabretusk wasted no time in consuming the flesh and devouring the sweet marrow from within the beast's bones.

As the sun climbed in the sky and pushed needles of light through the dense cloud, Darhur was reinvigorated. The greyback's meat had silenced the ache in his belly and lent new strength to his limbs. He'd fashioned an extra cloak from the beast's hide, the layer of dried blood matting the pelt acting as further insulation against the cold, and used the thick tendons to bind it firmly around his shoulders. Filled with renewed purpose, the hunter continued up the mountain.

'MAW!' DARHUR ROARED in frustration and slammed his forehead into the mountain. Blood burst across his brow, freezing instantly as icy winds scraped across his face. He glared at the wall of rock and ice in front of him.

'I am Darhur Beastkiller of the Wallcrusher Tribe,' Darhur beat his chest with clenched fists, dislodging the layer of snow that had settled over his clothing. 'I am higher up your peaks than any Wallcrusher have ever been.' He tugged at the heavy pelt around his shoulders, 'I ate the greyback you sent to kill me.' He gripped his hammer as tight as his cold-sapped fingers could muster, 'I will not be beat by a pile of rock!'

Darhur attacked the rockface. Again and again he struck out, his pride rendering him proof against the shards of rock and ice that stabbed out at him as he smashed apart the snowdrift. In response, the mountain shuddered and threw a blanket of snow down upon his head. Darhur winced as the freezing shrapnel cascaded over his shoulders.

'Master Darhur, boss?' Snikkit had to shout to be heard over the winds.

'What?' Darhur spat, his gaze still locked on the wall of rock blocking his path.

'Rhinox,' Snikkit pointed a shaking finger towards a giant beast as it disappeared from view. 'See boss, they not stuck. We follow?' Snikkit nodded with such vigour that the snot-icicles that had formed around his nose snapped off.

Darhur stared at him for a moment. 'Maybe I won'ts let Golg eats you after all.' The hunter turned to the sabretusk, 'Find a path.'

At his master's command Golg took his paw off Najkit's chest and bounded after the rhinoxen.

Darhur had been surprised to see a rhinox so high in the mountains, shocked to have encountered entire herds of them. Most were thin and weak from exposure, suffering from a climb they weren't bred for. There had been others too, packs of skeletal sabretusks and ice cougars, clinging to life as they headed north. The crags were beset with the corpses of creatures that hadn't the constitution to complete the climb. Darhur patted his gut. Even his burly frame was fading under the strenuous ascent. Without an answer to why the cavalcade of beasts weren't attacking one another, the hunter had been careful to keep his distance, unwilling to count on it continuing.

The tide of beasts led Darhur up the mountain to the bottom of a sloping plateau. The storm had grown worse as he climbed. The hail was constant, punishing him for every step forward. Fierce crosswinds sped across the open plateau to topple him. Lightning stabbed from a fell sky and lit up the ground in arcing flashes that boiled the snow. On three sides the mountain had all but disappeared. To the front it continued to rise like a titanic monolith with no end, but to the sides it vanished, dropping away into the mist below. If he had believed his eyes and not the dizzying pain in his head, it would have been easy for Darhur to forget that he stood higher than the clouds his tribe followed to war. He watched as the beasts marched to the base of the mountain upon a mountain and stopped. They were not alone – hundreds more creatures had gathered there, heedless of the lightning that periodically reached down and cremated one of their number.

'Poof,' Brija clapped his hands together as another creature burst into flames.

The gorger appeared from nowhere barrelling into Darhur, knocking him to the ground. Caught off-guard, the hunter lost his footing. He recovered quickly, dropping to one knee for balance and raising his crossbow. But the gorger was quicker, fed by momentum; it was upon Darhur before he could fire. It batted away his weapon and thundered its malformed skull into his jaw. Dazed, the ogre staggered backwards, slipping over on the ice and tumbling downhill towards the edge of the pass. Darhur struggled in vain to arrest his fall, hands scrabbling to find purchase. The ground lacked even basic vegetation and the wind had long since filed the rocks smooth. In desperation Darhur drew his knife and stabbed it into the mountainside. He felt the muscles in his shoulder tear as they battled gravity to arrest his fall. Grimacing, he punched the rockface with his free hand. The impact broke his knuckles but rewarded him with a hand hold.

Golg bared his fangs and leapt at the gorger, intent on ripping out its throat. The beast turned, lifting its left arm in defence. The sabretusk's jaws closed around the limb, its oversized incisors puncturing the bicep. The gorger let out a snarl of hate, turning with Golg's momentum to avoid being bowled over. Golg's grip loosened as the gorger's fist connected with his ribs, splintering them. Sensing its foe weaken, the gorger threw its arm towards the edge of the ledge with enough force to wrench it from its socket. Gasping for breath, Golg was thrown free from the arm, his teeth raking its length and tearing off strips of flesh as he spun away over the edge.

Pain shot up the gorger's leg, a rusted bear trap locked around its left foot and ankle.

'Got 'im, got 'im.' Brija was still grinning when the gorger's other foot connected with his face, broke his nose and sent him skidding across the plain.

'Nuffin' big enuff for this. Ain't nuffin'.' Seized by panic, Snikkit dug around in his makeshift pockets for something to fire at the gorger. 'Wot Snikkit do? Wot boss do?' Desperate, the gnoblar raised his arms in the air, spreading them wide to make himself as big as possible, and ran screaming at the gorger.

Bemused, the gorger caught the undersized warrior by the waist and yanked him into the air.

'Don't work, don't work,' Snikkit cried out as he struggled to free himself from the gorger's clawed grip.

With the gorger distracted, and with the aid of several more handholds, Darhur pulled himself back onto the plateau. Scrabbling to his feet, he drew his knife. With a shout, the hunter charged the gorger, his heavy strides leaving deep furrows in the snow as his legs powered him towards his prey. The gorger tossed Snikkit aside, opened its mouth and roared. Every muscle on the creature's swollen torso rippled to attention, veins threatening to burst through its pallid skin. Clawing at its chest with maddened vigour, the gorger ran at the ogre. They slammed into each other, two titans of sinew and hate. The gorger howled as the tusk protruding from Darhur's gut plate impaled it, the sharpened ivory spearing through the beast's abdomen and out through its back. The gorger bit down into Darhur's neck, severing tendons and drinking deep of his blood. Darhur gritted his teeth and fought to stay conscious. He brought his arm up to grab the gorger's head, but the beast was quicker, catching his arm in an unyielding grip and snapping it at the elbow. Darhur's mouth dropped open as he cried silently in pain, his strength all but exhausted.

Najkit weighed up his options – run now or join the fight. If Darhur died, the gorger would likely eat him. There was a chance he could convince Brija to have another go at slaying the beast, which might just give him enough time to scarper. He cast his gaze at Brija, who was even now preparing to rush the gorger. No, that idiot would be dead far too soon to be of any use. Running, then, seemed like the best option. He looked around for Snikkit. The gnoblar was unconscious, his prized coat torn and smeared in blood. Najkit kicked a pile of snow in frustration – he didn't want the coat now, he'd never get rid of Snikkit's wretched stench. He turned to go and stopped. What if...?

He took a few steps and paused. What if somehow he managed to help the hunter kill the gorger? He might get a coat of his own. There were plenty of rhinoxen around, and Darhur could easily skin one for him. Resolved, Najkit took a swig of yhetee piss for luck and loaded his sling. Squinting through one eye, he tried to take aim through the blizzard. Snow washed into his face and filled his eye faster than he could blink it way. Giving up, he closed both eyes, muttered a prayer to the Great Maw that he didn't hit Darhur, and fired. The shard of metal shot through the air and struck the gorger in the mouth.

Coughing blood through splintered teeth, the gorger released Darhur's arm. Seeing his chance, the hunter shouldered the beast away, the horn from his gut plate inflicting more damage as he ripped it out of the gorger's abdomen.

Najkit punched the air in triumph. Remembering himself, he looked around to make sure no one saw and went back to looking sullen.

The gorger swayed unsteadily on its feet, its warped physiology straining against numerous grievous injuries. Allowing the beast no respite, Darhur swung his hammer into its face and finished what Najkit started, the gorger's teeth exploding through the air like a hail of bloodied ice slivers. The gorger stumbled, its claws clumsily raking the air as it blindly lashed out. Darhur sidestepped and brought his hammer up into the beast's midsection, cracking its ribs before driving his forehead into its ruined face. The gorger crashed to the ground, defeated. Tearing the bear trap from the beast's ankle, Darhur opened the trap's metal jaws and thrust it over the gorger's head. With a snap, the trap clamped shut, severing the head at the neck. The hunter watched for a moment as the headless body spasmed through its death throes, before kicking it off the slope.

'Feast well,' Darhur offered a prayer to Golg as he watched the gorger's body fall through the mist to join the sabretusks in the crags below.

SNIKKIT PICKED HIMSELF up out of the snow, frantically patting himself down in search of injury. There was a long cut on his ribs where the gorger's claws had gripped him, and numerous nicks and scrape on his exposed arms and face. Relieved to still be in one piece, the gnoblar shuffled over to Darhur. The hunter was in bad shape, one arm dangling lifelessly at his side.

'What's now boss?' Snikkit asked, careful not to stand too close to the edge.

Darhur wasn't listening, his attention fixed skyward.

Snikkit looked up. Stumbling backwards in shock, he hunched his back in an unconscious effort to be further from the sky. A fulgurant web hung in the air. Its arcing strands spat and crackled as incandescent fire erupted along their length. Converging, the sparking flames erupted, detonating the web in a thunderclap that hammered Snikkit to his knees. A string of tumultuous booming followed as the clouds wrenched apart.

'Run!' Darhur bellowed as bolts wreathed in flame tore down and struck the earth, sparking off the ice to form jets of steam.

There was no cover on the plateau. Darhur cursed his luck and headed for the nearest great mammoth, his tired legs fuelled by the desire to survive. Ducking under the beast's enormous torso as another hail of fire stung the earth, the hunter caught his breath. The mammoth didn't move, its four colossal legs set upon the ground. Darhur watched from the creature's shadow as all around, the other animals stood immobile. Even as another of their number was ignited by the fire-lightning, they remained oblivious to the destruction raining down on them.

'Boss...' Snikkit ventured.

Darhur growled. He had no idea what to do next.

The ground growled back, a tremor shivering out from the base of the mountain across the plateau.

'What now?' Darhur snarled as the mountain flung him into the air, the earth cracking apart as fissures opened up all around him, stone and ice breaking and forming at random. Landing on his broken arm, the hunter cried out as pain fought to rob him of consciousness. The tremor was followed by a teeth-jarring noise, like the grinding of an ancient, rust-strewn cog. It scraped at Darhur's ears and threatened to drive him mad. Lying on his back, deaf from the constant noise, Darhur stared in disbelief as this mountain upon a mountain shifted and reformed. Rocks bunched and unfolded, throwing off their blanket of snow in rumbling swathes. A tower of rock stepped forward, cracking the ground. Another column followed, bringing with them an immense torso, two arms unfolding from behind to fall in below hunched shoulders. Caves mouths dotted the... *thing* like a disease. The dark spots moved together, sliding to the summit of the mountain-thing to form a single dark lens. The *thing* opened its mouth, wisps of onyx fog drifting from its eye, and bellowed a heartless war cry to the world it would tear asunder.

Darhur stared up at the stony construct. 'By the Great Maw,' he murmured. Transfixed by its enormity, the hunter watched as the mountain-thing snatched up a great mammoth. The mammoth, which was large enough to carry most of Darhur's tribe to war, looked insignificant in the giant's gargantuan fist. The construct stuffed the mewling mammal into its mouth whole. The other animals gathered on the plateau seemed not to notice, remaining rooted to the spot, awaiting their turn to be eaten.

Darhur, however, was not on the menu. He swung his crossbow up and fired. Over two dozen strands of iron-sinew, wound tighter than a Marienburger's purse, snapped forwards and propelled the iron bolt with enough force to punch it through layers of the finest dwarf plate mail. Darhur grinned in grim resignation as the bolt impacted harmlessly off the giant's rock-skin. It seemed that the Great Maw had not finished testing him. Drawing his hammer, the hunter beat his fist against his chest twice and charged the stone colossus. Each step Darhur took fanned the fire in his belly. He was a raging inferno, the Great Maw's instrument of destruction. He would–

The rock-construct raised its right foot and thundered it down into the ground. The mountain trembled beneath Darhur's feet, throwing him to his back. The hunter landed hard on the rock and lay still, his shoulder and hip smashed by the impact.

Seeing Darhur cast aside like a human child, Snikkit stood immobile, gripped by fear and uncertainty. Najkit was running before Darhur hit the ground, moving as fast as his legs would take him to the far side of the plateau. For once, Snikkit agreed with his inebriated companion and sped off after him.

Brija rubbed the side of his face as he watched the two gnoblars run off. He had no idea what the big deal was. The stony giant was huge, bigger even than Tyrant Grut, but it was made of stone and probably very slow. Yes, judging by its size, it would be very slow indeed. Brija drew his knife and started towards it. All he needed to do was climb up to its head and stab it in the eye.

Najkit rounded a snow drift and stopped to catch his breath. He was about to set off again when a hand pulled on his shoulder.

'Najk-'

Snikkit. Najkit knew that sniffling excuse for a gnoblar would try to kill him one day. He spun round and drew his knife, levelling the blade at the older gnoblar's face.

'Wait, wait,' Snikkit held up his hands in protest. 'Looks.'

Najkit slashed Snikkit's cheek for good measure and then turned to see what the old-timer had been pointing at. Sighting a lone figure at the far end of the plateau, Najkit questioned his sanity and cursed the thin air. Wiping his eyes, he looked again. The man was still there. A purplish glow traced his outline, robes blowing against the direction of the wind. Curious, Najkit crouched low and shuffled forward. The figure was wearing a pelt. Najkit smiled – this was his chance, he'd slay the wandering fool and keep the pelt for himself. Whipping out his sling, Najkit unleashed a salvo of teeth and bone at his quarry. To his horror, the projectiles fell from the air a hand's width in front of the man's face. Diving for cover, Najkit narrowly avoided the hail of purple lightning his would-be prey sent lancing towards him. Maw be damned, he needed Darhur's help.

Darhur rolled over, letting the blood that was filling his mouth run to the ground. Pushing himself up, he began to clamber to his feet, shaking his head in an effort to clear his senses.

'Boss, boss. This way, this way,' Snikkit said, tugging on Darhur's pelt.

'I will not run!' Darhur pushed Snikkit away and looked around for a weapon. Finding nothing but a panting Najkit, he considered for a moment using the useless creature as a club.

'No, no. Not run. Win yes. Come,' Najkit motioned for Darhur to follow him.

'There,' Najkit pointed towards the hide-covered man.

Darhur glared at the figure, sizing him up. Judging by his puny build and weakling bone structure, he was clearly human. The hunter took a whiff of the air and snarled. The man stank of magics. Pulling a charm from under his furs and wrapping his fist around it for luck, Darhur offered a prayer to his tribe's Slaughtermasters for protection. Reaching down to his gut plate he grabbed hold of the mammoth tusk and with regret, snapped it off.

'By Maw, I will slay!' Darhur swore his oath, hefting the tusk in his hand. It was poorly weighted, but would suffice. The sorcerer kept one hand aloft, working his enchantment, as Darhur ran towards him. Lowering the other one, the human unleashed a ball of flickering fire towards the ogre. Darhur kept an even stride as the fireball struck the ground in front of him, tossing splintered ice into his path. He powered on, striding through the sorcerer's second blast as it struck him full in the chest, thankful for the warm glow of the charm against his skin as he emerged unscathed. Tendrils of dark lightning leapt from the sorcerer's outstretched fingers and enveloped him. Darhur felt their icy touch against his skin. Like devious blades they sought a way to his innards. With blood seeping from his pores, Darhur struck – wrapping the charm around the tusk and throwing it at the sorcerer. End over end it spun, covering the distance in a heartbeat and smacking the human across the shoulders. Knocked to the ground, the sorcerer was unable to defend himself as Darhur locked a meaty hand around his neck. The ogre squeezed until the man's eyes shot out from their sockets, the snap of the human's neck inaudible over the wind. Darhur dropped the sorcerer to the ground, stamping on his face to be sure.

The rock-giant shuddered and bellowed an inhuman roar, a thousand birds screeching in disharmony. Its body trembled, mini avalanches of snow and rock dropping away from its torso at an increasing rate. The construct tried to turn, to back away, but succeeded only in tearing off one of its legs. It stumbled and fell forward, catching itself on an outstretched hand. Turning its other massive palm upwards, it stared at the rocky appendage as it crumbled to pebbles and fell away. The rest of the titanic creature followed, breaking apart into rock-powder and dust.

DARHUR STARED AT the packs of sabretusks, rhinoxen and worse that blocked his path back down the mountain. The creatures were milling around, confused, but a few of the larger ones seemed to have reverted to their baser instincts, sizing the others up, circling them with intent. Soon the rest would shake off whatever spell the sorcerer had placed them under and descend into a feeding frenzy. Darhur didn't want to be there when that happened. The ogre's heart sank. He could barely stand. His arm was broken badly, his bones brittle from the cold and his insides felt like they'd been trampled by a giant. Pulling his pelts tighter around his shoulders, Darhur did the only thing he could. He turned away and started off in the opposite direction. He had a head to deliver, and it would be a long walk back to the tribe. *His* tribe.

HAMMER
AND BOLTER

ISSUE 11

THE CARRION ANTHEM

David Annandale

HE WAS THINKING bitter thoughts about glory. He couldn't help it. As he took his seat in the governor's private box overlooking the stage, Corvus Parthamen was surrounded by glory that was not his. The luxury of the box, a riot of crimson leather and velvet laced with gold and platinum thread, was a tribute, in the form of excess, to the honour of Governor Elpidius. That didn't trouble Corvus. The box represented a soft, false glory, a renown that came with the title, not the deeds or the man. Then there was the stage, to which all sight lines led. It was a prone monolith, carved from a single massive obsidian slab. It was an altar on which one could sacrifice gods, but instead it abased itself beneath the feet of the artist. It was stone magnificence, and tonight it paid tribute to Corvus's brother. That didn't trouble Corvus, either. He didn't understand what Gurges did, but he recognised that his twin, at least, did work for his laurels. Art was a form of deed, Corvus supposed.

What bothered him was the walls. Windowless, rising two hundred metres to meet in the distant vault of the ceiling, they were draped with immense tapestries. These were hand-woven tributes to Imperial victories. Kieldar. The Planus Steppes. Ichar IV. On and on and on. Warriors of legend both ancient and new towered above Corvus. They were meant to inspire. They were there to draw the eye as the spirit soared, moved by the majesty of the tribute paid by the music. The arts in this monumental space – stone, image and sound – were supposed to entwine to the further glory of the Emperor and his legions. But lately, the current of worship had reversed. Now the tapestry colossi, frozen in their moments of triumphant battle, were also bowing before the glory of Gurges, and that was wrong. That was what made Corvus dig his fingers in hard enough to mar the leather of his armrests.

The governor's wife, Lady Ahala, turned to him, her multiple necklaces rattling together. 'It's nice to see you, colonel,' she said. 'You must be so proud.'

Proud of what? he wanted to say. Proud of his home world's contributions to the Imperial crusades? That was a joke. Ligeta was a joke. Of the hundred tapestries here in the Performance Hall of the Imperial Palace of Culture, not one portrayed a Ligetan hero. Deep in the Segmentum Pacificus, far from the front lines of any contest, Ligeta was untouched by war beyond the usual tithe of citizens bequeathed to the Imperial Guard. Many of its sons had fought and fallen on distant soil, but how many had distinguished themselves to the point that they might be remembered and celebrated? None.

Proud of what? Of his own war effort? That he commanded Ligeta's defence regiment? That only made him part of the Ligetan joke. Officers who were posted back to their home worlds developed reputations, especially when those home worlds were pampered, decadent backwaters. The awful thing was that he couldn't even ask himself what he'd done wrong. He knew the answer. *Nothing.* He'd done everything right. He'd made all the right friends, served under all the right officers, bowed and scraped in all the right places at all the right times. He had done his duty on the battlefield, too. No one could say otherwise. But there had been no desperate charges, no last-man-standing defences. The Ligetan regiments were called upon to maintain supply lines, garrison captured territory, and mop up the token resistance of those who were defeated, but hadn't quite come to terms with the fact. They were not summoned when the need was urgent.

The injustice made him seethe. He knew his worth, and that of his fellows. They fought and died with the best, when given the chance. Not every mop-up had been routine. Not every territory had been easily pacified. Ligetans knew how to fight, and they had plenty to prove.

Only no one ever saw. No one thought to look, because everyone knew Ligeta's reputation. It was the planet of the dilettante and the artist. The planet of the song.

Proud of *that?*

And yes, that was exactly what Ahala meant. Proud of the music, proud of the song. Proud of Gurges. Ligeta's civilian population rejoiced in the planet's reputation. They saw no shame or weakness in it. They used the same logic as Corvus's superiors who thought they had rewarded his political loyalty by sending him home. Who wouldn't want a pleasant command, far from the filth of a Chaos-infested hive world? Who wouldn't want to be near Gurges Parthamen, maker not of song, but of The Song?

Yes, Corvus thought, Gurges had done a good thing there. Over a decade ago, now. The Song was a hymn to the glory of the Emperor. Hardly unusual. But *Regeat, Imperator* was rare. It was the product of the special alchemy that, every so often, fused formal magnificence with populist appeal. The tune was magisterial enough to be blasted from a Titan's combat horn, simple enough to be whistled by the lowliest trooper, catchy enough that, once heard, it was never forgotten. It kept up morale on a thousand besieged worlds, and fired up the valour of millions of troops charging to the rescue. Corvus had every right, every *duty* to be proud of his brother's accomplishment. It was a work of genius.

So he'd been told. He would have to be satisfied with the word of others. Corvus had amusia. He was as deaf to music as Gurges was attuned to it. His twin's work left him cold. He heard a clearer melody line in the squealing of a greenskin pinned beneath a dreadnought's feet.

To Lady Ahala, Corvus said, 'I couldn't be more proud.'

'Do you know what he's offering us tonight?' Elpidius asked. He settled his soft bulk more comfortably.

'I don't.'

'Really?' Ahala sounded surprised. 'But you're his twin.'

'We haven't seen each other for the best part of a year.'

Elpidius frowned. 'I didn't think you'd been away.'

Corvus fought back a humiliated wince. 'Gurges was the one off-planet,' he said. Searching the stars for inspiration, or some other pampered nonsense. Corvus didn't know and didn't care.

Hanging from the vault of the hall were hundreds of glow-globes patterned into a celestial map of the Imperium. Now they faded, silencing the white noise of tens of thousands of conversations. Darkness embraced the audience, and only the stage was illuminated. From the wings came the choir. The singers wore black uniforms as razor-creased as any officer's ceremonial garb. They marched in, until their hundreds filled the back half of the stage. They faced the audience. At first, Corvus thought they were wearing silver helmets, but then they reached up and pulled down the masks. Featureless, eyeless, the masks covered the top half of each man's face.

'How are they going to see him conduct?' Elpidius wondered.

Ahala giggled with excitement. 'That's nothing,' she whispered. She placed a confiding hand on Corvus's arm. 'I've heard that there haven't been any rehearsals. Not even the choir knows what is going to be performed.'

Corvus blinked. 'What?'

'Isn't it exciting?' She turned back to the stage, happy and placid before the prospect of the impossible.

The light continued to fade until there was only a narrow beam front and centre, a bare pinprick on the frozen night of stone. The silence was as thick and heavy as the stage. It was broken by the solemn, slow *clop* of bootheels. His pace steady as a ritual, as if he were awed by his own arrival, Gurges Parthamen, Emperor's bard and Ligeta's favourite son, walked into the light. He wore the same black uniform as the musicians, but no mask. Instead...

'What's wrong with his face?' Ahala asked.

Corvus leaned forward. Something cold scuttled through his gut. His twin's face was his own: the same severe planes, narrow chin and grey eyes, even the same cropped black hair. But now Corvus stared at a warped mirror. Gurges was wearing an appliance that flashed like gold but, even from this distance, displayed the unforgiving angles and rigidity of iron. It circled his head like a laurel wreath. At his face, it extended needle-thin claws that pierced his eyelids, pinning them open. Gurges gazed at his audience with a manic, implacable stare that was equal parts absolute knowledge and terminal fanaticism. His eyes were as much prisoners as those of his choir, but where the singers saw nothing, he saw too much, and revelled in the punishment. His smile was a peeling back of lips. His skin was too thin, his skull too close to the surface. When he spoke, Corvus heard the hollow sound of wind over rusted pipes. Insects rustled at the frayed corners of reality.

'Fellow Ligetans,' Gurges began. 'Before we begin, it would be positively heretical of me not to say something about the role of the patron of the arts. The life of a musician is a difficult one. Because we do not produce a tangible product, there are many who regard us as superfluous, a pointless luxury the Imperium could happily do without. This fact makes those who value us even more important. Patrons are the blessed few who know the artist really can make a difference.'

He paused for a moment. If he was expecting applause, the knowledge and ice in his rigid gaze stilled the audience. Unperturbed, he carried on. 'I have, over the course of my musical life, been privileged to have worked with more than my share of generous, committed, sensitive patrons. It is thanks to them that my music has been heard at all.' He lowered his head, as if overcome by modesty.

Corvus would have snorted at the conceit of the gesture, but he was too tense. He dreaded the words that might come from his brother's rictus face.

Gurges looked up, and now his eyes seemed to glow with a light the colour of dust and ash. 'Yes,' he said, 'the generous patron is to be cherished. But even more precious, even more miraculous, even more to be celebrated and glorified, is the patron who *inspires*. The patron who opens the door to new vistas of creation, and pushes the artist through. I stand before you as the servant of one such patron. I know that my humble tribute to the Emperor is held in high regard, but I can now see what a poor counterfeit of the truth that effort is. Tonight, so will you. I cannot tell you what my patron has unveiled for me. But I can *show* you.'

The composer's last words slithered out over the hall like a death rattle. Gurges turned to face the choir. He raised his arms. The singers remained unmoving. The last light went out. A terrible, far-too-late certainty hit Corvus: he must stop this.

And then Gurges began to sing.

For almost a minute, Corvus felt relief. No daemon burst from his brother's mouth. His pulse slowed. He had fallen for the theatrics of a first-rate showman, that was all. The song didn't sound any different to him than any other of Gurges's efforts. It was another succession of notes, each as meaningless as the next. Then he noticed that he was wrong. He wasn't hearing a simple succession. Even his thick ears could tell that Gurges was singing two notes at once. Then three. Then four. The song became impossible. Somehow still singing, Gurges drew a breath, and though Corvus heard no real change in the music, the breath seemed to mark the end of the refrain.

It also marked the end of peace, because now the choir began to sing. To a man, they joined in, melding with Gurges's voice. The song became a roar. The darkness began to withdraw as a glow spread across the stage. It seeped from the singers. It poured like radiation fog into the seating. It was a colour that made Corvus wince. It was a kind of green, if green could scream. It pulsed like taut flesh.

It grinned like Chaos.

Corvus leaped to his feet. So did the rest of the audience. For a crazy moment of hope, he thought of ordering the assembled people to fall upon the singers and silence them. But they weren't rising, like him, in alarm. They were at one with the music, and they joined their voices to its glory, and their souls to its power. The roar became a wave. The glow filled the hall, and it showed Corvus nothing he wanted to see. Beside him, the governor and his wife stood motionless, their faces contorted with ecstasy. They sang as if the song were their birthright. They sang to bring down the sky. Their heads were thrown back, their jaws as wide as a snake's, and their throats twitched and spasmed with the effort to produce inhuman chords. Corvus grabbed Elpidius by the shoulders and tried to shake him. The governor's frame was rigid and grounded to the core of the Ligeta. Corvus might have been wrestling with a pillar. But the man wasn't cold like stone. He was burning up. His eyes were glassy. Corvus checked his pulse. Its rhythm was violent, rapid, irregular. Corvus yanked his hands away. They felt slick with disease. Something that lived in the song scrabbled at his mind like fingernails on plastek, but couldn't find a purchase.

He opened the flap of his shoulder holster and pulled out his laspistol. He leaned over the railing of the box, and sighted on his brother's head. He felt no hesitation. He felt only necessity. He pulled the trigger.

Gurges fell, the top of his skull seared away. The song didn't care. It roared on, its joy unabated. Corvus fired six more times, each shot dropping a member of the choir. He stopped. The song wasn't a spell and it wasn't a mechanism. It was a plague, and killing individual vectors was worse than useless. It stole precious time from action that might make a difference.

He ran from the box. In the vestibule, the ushers were now part of the choir, and the song pursued Corvus as he clattered down the marble steps to the mezzanine and thence to the ground floor. The foyer, as cavernous as the Performance Hall, led to the Great Gallery of Art. Its vaulted length stretched a full kilometre to the exit of the palace. Floor-to-ceiling stained glass mosaics of the primarchs gazed down on heroic bronzes. Warriors beyond counting trampled the Imperium's enemies, smashing them into fragmented agony that sank into the pedestals. But the gallery was no longer a celebration of art and glory. It was a throat, and it howled the song after him. Though melody was a stranger to him, still he could feel the force of the music, intangible yet pushing him with the violence of a hurricane's breath. The light was at his heels, flooding the throat with its mocking bile.

He burst from grand doorway onto the plaza. He stumbled to a halt, horrified.

The concert had been broadcast.

Palestrina, Ligeta's capital and a city of thirty million, screamed. It convulsed.

The late-evening glow of the city was stained with the Chaos non-light. In the plaza, in the streets, in the windows of Palestrina's delicate and coruscating towers, the people stood and sang their demise. The roads had become a nightmare of twisted, flaming wreckage as drivers, possessed by art, slammed into each other. Victims of collisions, not quite dead, sang instead of screaming their last. Everywhere, the choir chanted to the sky, and the sky answered with flame and thunder. To the west, between the towers, the horizon strobed and rumbled, and fireballs bloomed. He was looking at the spaceport, Corvus realised, and seeing the destruction caused by every landing and departing ship suddenly losing all guidance.

There was a deafening roar overhead, and a cargo transport came in low and mad. Its engines burning blue, it plowed into the side of a tower a few blocks away. The ship exploded, filling the sky with the light and sound of its death. Corvus ducked as shrapnel the size of meteors arced down, gouging impact craters into street and stone and flesh. The tower collapsed with lazy majesty, falling against its neighbours and spreading a domino celebration of destruction. Dust billowed up in a choking, racing cloud. It rushed over Corvus, hiding the sight of the dying city, but the chant went on.

He coughed, gagging as grit filled his throat and lungs. He staggered, but started moving again. Though visibility was down to a few metres, and his eyes watered and stung, he felt that he could see clearly again. It was as if, by veiling the death of the city from his gaze, the dust had broken a spell. Palestrina was lost, but that didn't absolve him of his duty to the Emperor. Only his own death could do that. As long as he drew breath, his duty was to fight for Ligeta, and save what he could.

He had to find somewhere the song had not reached, find men who had not heard and been infected by the plague. Then he could mount a defence, perhaps even a counter-attack, even if that were nothing more than a scorched-earth purge. There would be glory in that. But first, a chance to regroup. First, a sanctuary. He had hopes that he knew where to go.

He felt his way around the grey limbo of the plaza, hand over his mouth, trying not to cough up his lungs. It took him the best part of an hour to reach the far side of the Palace of Culture. By that time, the worst of the dust had settled and the building's intervening bulk further screened him. He could breathe again. His movements picked up speed and purpose. He needed a vehicle, one he could manoeuvre through the tangled chaos of the streets. Half a kilometre down from the plaza, he found what he wanted. A civilian was straddling his idling bike. He had been caught by the song just before pulling away. Corvus tried to push him off, but he was as rigid and locked down as the governor had been. Corvus shot him. As he hauled the corpse away from the bike, he told himself that the man had already been dead. If Corvus hadn't granted him mercy, something else would have. A spreading fire. Falling debris. And if nothing violent happened, then...

Corvus stared at the singing pedestrians, and thought through the implications of what he was seeing. Nothing, he was sure, could free the victims once the song took hold. So they would stand where they were struck and sing, and do nothing else. They wouldn't sleep. They wouldn't eat. They wouldn't drink. Corvus saw the end result, and he also saw the first glimmer of salvation. With a renewed sense of mission, he climbed on the bike and drove off.

It was an hour from dawn by the time he left the city behind. Beyond the hills of Palestrina, he picked up even more speed as he hit the parched mud flats. Once fertile, the land here had had its water table drained by the city's thirst. At the horizon, the shadow of the Goreck Mesa blocked the stars. At the base of its bulk, he saw pinpricks of light. Those glimmers were his destination and his hope.

The ground rose again as he reached the base. He approached the main gate, and he heard no singing. Before him, the wall was an iron shield fifty metres high, a sloping, pleated curtain of strength. A giant aquila, a darker night on black, was engraved every ten metres along the wall's two kilometre length. Beyond the wall, he heard the diesel of engines, the report of firing ranges, the march of boots. The sounds of discipline. Discipline that was visible from the moment he arrived. If the sentries were surprised to see him, dusty and exhausted, arriving on a civilian vehicle instead of in his staff car, they showed no sign. They saluted, sharp as machines, and opened the gate for him. He passed through into Fort Goreck and the promise of salvation.

On the other side of the wall was a zone free of art and music. A weight lifted from Corvus's shoulders as he watched the pistoning, drumming rhythm of the military muscle. Strength perfected, and yet, by the Throne, it had been almost lost, too. A request had come the day before from Jeronim Tarrant, the base's captain. Given the momentous, planet-wide event that was a new composition by Gurges Parthamen, would the colonel authorise a break in the drills, long enough for the men to sit down and listen to the vox-cast of the concert? Corvus had not just rejected the request out of hand, he had forbidden any form of reception and transmission of the performance. He wanted soldiers, he had informed Jeronim. If he wanted dilettantes, he could find plenty in the boxes of the Palace of Culture.

On his way to the concert, he had wondered about his motives in issuing that order. Jealousy? Was he really that petty? He knew now that he wasn't, and that he'd been right. The purpose of a base such as this was to keep the Guard in a state of perpetual, instant readiness, because war might come from one second to the next.

As it had now.

He crossed the parade field, making for the squat command tower at the rear of the base, where it nestled against the basalt wall of the Mesa. He had barely dismounted the bike when Jeronim came pounding out of the tower. He was pale, borderline frantic, but remembered to salute. Discipline, Corvus thought. It had saved them so far. It would see them through to victory.

'Sir,' Jeronim said. 'Do you know what's going on? Are we under attack? We can't get through to anyone.'

'Yes, we are at war,' Corvus answered. He strode briskly to the door. 'No one in this base has been in contact with anyone outside it for the last ten hours?'

Jeronim shook his head. 'No, sir. Nothing that makes sense. Anyone transmitting is just sending what sounds like music–'

Corvus cut him off. 'You listened?'

'Only a couple of seconds. When we found the nonsense everywhere, we shut down the sound. No one was sending anything coherent. Not even the *Scythe of Judgement.*'

So the Ligetan flagship had fallen. He wasn't surprised, but Corvus discovered that he could still feel dismay. But the fact that the base had survived the transmissions told him something. The infection didn't take hold right away. He remembered that the choir and the audience hadn't responded until Gurges had completed a full refrain. The song's message had to be complete, it seemed, before it could sink in. 'What actions have you taken?' he asked Jeronim as they headed up the staircase to the command centre.

'We've been sending out requests for acknowledgement on all frequencies. I've placed the base on heightened alert. And since we haven't been hearing from anyone, I sent out a distress call.'

'Fine,' Corvus said. For whatever good that call will do, he thought. By the time the message was received and aid arrived, weeks or months could have elapsed. By that time, the battle for the soul of Ligeta would have been won or lost. The singers would have starved to death, and either there would be someone left to pick up the pieces, or there wouldn't be.

The communications officer looked up from the auspex as Corvus and Jeronim walked into the centre. 'Colonel,' he saluted. 'A capital ship has just transitioned into our system.'

'Really?' That was fast. Improbably fast.

'It's hailing us,' the master vox-operator announced.

Corvus lunged across the room and yanked the headphones from the operator's skull. 'All messages to be received as text only until further notice,' he ordered. 'No exceptions. Am I clear?'

The operator nodded.

'Acknowledge them,' Corvus went on. 'Request identification.'

The soldier did so. Corvus moved to the plastek window and looked out over the base while he waited. There were five thousand men here. The position was elevated, easily defensible. He had the tools. He just had to work out how to fight.

'Message received, colonel.'

Corvus turned to the vox-operator. His voice sounded all wrong, like that of a man who had suddenly been confronted with the futility of his existence. He was staring at the data-slate before him. His face was grey.

'Read it,' Corvus said, and braced himself.

'Greetings, Imperials. This is the *Terminus Est*.'

TYPHUS ENTERED THE strategium as the ship emerged in the realspace of the Ligetan system.

'Multiple contacts, lord,' the bridge attendant reported.

Of course there were. The Imperium would hardly leave Ligeta without a defending fleet. Typhus moved his bulk towards the main oculus. They were already close enough to see the swarm of Imperial cruisers and defence satellites. 'But how many are on attack trajectories?' Typhus asked. He knew the answer, but he wanted the satisfaction of hearing it.

The officer looked twice at his hololithic display, as if he doubted the reports he was receiving. 'None,' he said after a moment.

'And how many are targeting us?'

Another brief silence. 'None.'

Typhus rumbled and buzzed his pleasure. The insects that were his parasites and his identity fluttered and scrabbled with excitement. His armour rippled with their movement. He allowed himself a moment to revel in the experience, in the glorious and terrible paradox of his existence. Disease was an endless source of awe in its marriage of death and unrestrained life. It was his delight to spread the gospel of this paradox, the lesson of decay. Before him, the oculus showed how well the lesson was being learned. 'Bring us in close,' he commanded.

'At once, lord.' The bridge attendant was obedient, but was a slow learner himself. He was still thinking in terms of a normal combat situation, never mind that an Imperial fleet's lack of response to the appearance of a Chaos capital ship was far from normal. 'We are acquiring targets,' he reported.

'No need, no need,' Typhus said. 'See for yourselves. All of you.'

His officers looked up, and Typhus had an audience for the spectacle he had arranged. As the *Terminus Est* closed in on the glowing green-and-brown globe of Ligeta, the enemy ships gathered size and definition. Their distress became clear, too. Some were drifting, nothing more now than iron tombs. Others had their engines running, but there was no order to their movements. The ships, Typhus knew, were performing the last commands their crews had given them, and there would be no others to come.

'Hail the Imperials,' he ordered. 'Open all frequencies.'

The strategium was bathed in the music of disease. Across multiple channels came the same noise, a unified chaos of millions upon millions of throats singing in a single choir. The melody was a simple, sustained, multi-note chord of doom. It became the accompaniment to the view outside the *Terminus*, and now the movement of the fleet was the slow ballet of entropy and defeat. Typhus watched two cruisers follow their unalterable routes until they collided. One exploded, its fireball the expanding bloom of a poisonous flower. The other plunged towards Ligeta's atmosphere, bringing with it the terrible gift of its weapons payload and shattered reactor.

Typhus thought about its landfall, and his insects writhed in anticipation.

He also thought about the simplicity of the lesson, how pure it was, and how devastating its purity made it. Did the happenstance that had brought Gurges Parthamen into his grasp taint that purity, or was that flotsam of luck an essential piece of the composition's beauty? The composer on a self-indulgent voyage, getting caught in a localised warp storm, winding up in a near-collision with the *Terminus Est*; how could those elements be anything other than absolute contingency? His triumph could so easily have never even been an idea. Then again, that man, his ambition that made him so easily corruptible, the confluence of events that granted Typhus this perfect inspiration: they were so improbable, they could not possibly be chance. They had been threaded together by destiny.

Flies howled through the strategium as Typhus tasted the paradox, and found it to his liking. Chaos and fate, one and the same.

Perhaps Gurges had thought so, too. He had put up no resistance to being infected with the new plague. Typhus was particularly proud of it. The parasitic warp worm laid its eggs in the bloodstream and attacked the brain. It spread itself from mind to mind by the transmission of its idea, and the idea travelled on a sound, a special sound, a song that was an incantation that thinned the walls between reality and the immaterium and taught itself to all who had ears to hear.

'My lord, we are being hailed,' said the attendant.

Typhus laughed, delighted, and the boils on the deck quivered in sympathy. 'Send them our greeting,' he ordered.

NOW HE HAD an enemy. Now he could fight.

Corvus rejected despair. He rejected the odds. There was an enemy, and duty demanded combat. There was nothing else.

Corvus stood at the reviewing stand on the parade grounds, and, speakers turning his voice into Fort Goreck's voice, he addressed the assembled thousands. He explained the situation. He described the plague and its means of contagion. And he laid down the rules. One was paramount. 'Music,' he thundered, 'is a disease. It will destroy us if it finds the smallest chink in our armour. We must be free of it, and guard against it. Anyone who so much as whistles will be executed on the spot.' He felt enormous satisfaction as he gave that order. He didn't worry about why.

LESS THAN A day after his arrival, Typhus witnessed the apotheosis of his art. The entire planet was one voice. The anthem, the pestilence, the anthem that *was* pestilence, had become the sum total of existence on Ligeta. Its population lived for a single purpose. The purity was electrifying.

Or it would have been, but for the single flaw. There was that redoubt. He had thought it would succumb by itself, but it hadn't. It was still sending out desperate pleas to whatever Imperials might hear. And though Typhus could amuse himself with the thought that this one pustule of order confirmed the beauty of corruption, he also knew the truth. Over the course of the next few days, the song would begin a ragged diminuendo as its singers died. If he didn't act, his symphony would be incomplete, spoiled by one false note.

So it was time to act.

THE ATTACK CAME on the evening of the second day. Corvus was walking the parapet when he saw the sky darken. A deep, unending thunder began, and the clouds birthed a terrible rain. The drop-pods came first, plummeting with the finality of black judgement. They made landfall on the level ground a couple of kilometres from the base. They left streaks in the air, black, vertical contrails that didn't dissipate. Instead, they grew wider, broke up into fragments, and began to whirl. Corvus ran to the nearest guard tower, grabbed a marksman's sniper rifle and peered through its telescopic sight. He could see the movement in the writhing clouds more clearly. It looked like insects. Faintly, impossibly, weaving in and out of the thunder of the pods and the landing craft that now followed on, Corvus heard an insidious buzz.

The darkness flowed from the sky. It was the black of absence and grief, of putrefaction and despair, and of unnameable desire. Its touch infected the air of the landing zone, then rippled out towards the base. It was a different disease, one Corvus had no possible defence against. And though no tendrils of the black itself reached this far, Corvus felt something arrive over the wall. The quality of the evening light changed. It turned brittle and sour. He sensed something vital becoming too thin, and something wrong start to smile.

All around him, Fort Goreck's warning klaxons sounded the call to arms. The din was enormous, and he was surprised and disturbed that he could hear the buzzing of the Chaos swarms at all. That told him how sick the real world was becoming, and how hard he would have to fight for it.

The drop-pods opened, their venomous petals falling back to disgorge the monsters within. Corvus had never felt comfortable around Space Marines, his Ligetan inferiority complex made exponentially worse by their superhuman power and perfection. But he would have given anything to have one beside him now as he saw the nightmare versions of them mustering in the near distance. Their armour had long since ceased to be simple ceramite. It was darkness that was iron, and iron that was disease. They assembled into rows and then stood motionless, weapons at ready. Only they weren't entirely still. Their outlines writhed.

Landing craft poured out corrupted infantry in ever greater numbers. At length, the sky spat out a leviathan that looked to Corvus like a Goliath-class transport, only so distorted it seemed more like a terrible whale. Its hull was covered with symbols that tore at Corvus's eyes with obscenities. Around it coiled things that might be tendrils, or they might be tentacles. Its loading bay opened like a maw, and it vomited hordes of troops and vehicles onto the blackening soil of Ligeta.

The legions of plague gathered before Corvus, and he knew there was no hope of fighting them.

But he would. *Down to the last man.* And though there might no chance of survival, there would, he now realized with a stir of joy, be the hope of glory in the heroic last stand.

Night fell, and the forces of the *Terminus Est* grew in numbers and strength. The host was now far larger than needed to storm Fort Goreck, walls or no, commanding heights or no. But the dark soldiers didn't attack. They stood, massed and in the open. Once disembarked, they did nothing. Heavy artillery rumbled out of the transport and then stopped, barrels aimed at the sky, full of threat but silent. The rumble of arrivals stopped. A clammy quiet covered the land.

Corvus had returned to command centre. He could watch just as well from there, and the subaural buzzing was less noticeable on this side of the plastek.

'What are they waiting for?' Jeronim muttered.

The quiet was broken by the distant roar of engines. Corvus raised a pair of electro-binoculars. Three Rhinos were moving to the fore. There were rows of rectangular shapes on the top of the Rhinos. They were horned metal, moulded into the shape of screaming daemons. Loud-speakers, Corvus realized.

Dirge Casters.

If the Rhinos broadcast their song, Fort Goreck would fall without a shot being fired.

Corvus slammed a fist against the alarm trigger. The klaxons whooped over the base. 'Do not turn these off until I give the order,' he told the officers. Still not loud enough, he thought. He turned to the master vox. He shoved the operator aside and flipped the switches for the public address system. He grabbed the mic and ran over to the speaker above the doorway to the command centre. He jammed the mic into the speaker. Feedback pierced his skull, mauled his hearing and sought to obliterate all thought. He gasped from the pain, and staggered under the weight of the sound.

The men around him were covering their ears and weaving around as if drunk. Corvus struggled against the blast of the sound and shook the officers. 'Now!' he screamed. 'We attack now! Launch the Chimeras and take out those vehicles!'

He would have given his soul for a battery of battle cannons, so he could take out the Rhinos from within the safety of the noise shield he had just erected. But this would do. He didn't think about how little he might gain in destroying a few speakers. He saw the chance to fight the opponent.

He saw the chance for glory.

He took charge of the squads that followed behind the Chimeras. He saw the pain of the men's faces as the eternal feedback wore at them. He saw the effort it took them to focus on the simple task of readying their weapons. He understood, and hoped that they understood the necessity of his actions, and saw the heroism of their struggle for the Emperor. Gurges had been a fool, Corvus thought. What *he* did now was worthy of song.

The gates opened, and the Chimeras surged forward. The Rhinos had stopped halfway between their own forces and the wall, easily within the broadcast range of the Dirge Casters. The song was inaudible. Corvus felt his lips pull back in a snarl of triumph as he held his laspistol and chainsword high and led the charge. The courage of the Imperium burst from the confines of the wall. Corvus yelled as he pounded behind the clanking, roaring Chimera. The feedback whine faded as they left the base behind, but the vehicles had their own din, and Corvus still could hear no trace of the song.

Something spoke with the voice of ending. The sound was enormous, a deep, compound thunder. It was the Chaos artillery, all guns opening up simultaneously, firing a single, monumental barrage. The lower slope of Fort Goreck's rise exploded, earth geysering skyward. A giant made of noise and air picked Corvus up and threw him. The world tumbled end over end, a hurricane of dirt and rocks and fire. He slammed into the ground and writhed, a pinned insect, as his flattened lungs fought to pull in a breath. When the air came, it was claws and gravel in his chest. His head rang like a struck bell.

When his eyes and his ears cleared, he saw the wreckage of the Chimeras and the rout of his charge. The vehicles had taken the worst of the hits, and were shattered, smoking ruins of twisted metal. Pieces of men were scattered over the slope: an arm still clutching a lasgun, a torso that ended at the lower jaw, organs without bodies, bodies without organs. But there were survivors, and as the enemy's guns fell silent, the song washed over the field. Men picked themselves up, and froze as the refrain caught them. A minute after the barrage, Corvus was the only man left with a will of his own. He picked up his weapons and stumbled back up the slope towards the wall. As he ran, he thought he could hear laughter slither through the ranks of the Chaos force.

The gates opened just enough to let him back inside. The feedback blotted out the song, but wrapped itself around his brain like razor wire. He had lost his cap, and his uniform was in tatters. Still, he straightened his posture as he walked back through the stunned troops. Halfway across the grounds, a conscript confronted him. The man's eyes were watering from the hours of mind-destroying feedback and his nose was bleeding. 'Let us go,' he pleaded. 'Let us fight. We'll resist as long as we can.'

Corvus pushed him back. 'Are you mad?' he shouted over the whine. 'Do you know what would happen to you?'

The trooper nodded. 'I was on the wall. I saw.'

'Well then?'

'They look happy when they sing. At least that death isn't pointless torture.'

Corvus raised his pistol and shot the man through the eye. He turned in a full circle, glaring at his witnesses, making sure they understood the lesson. Then he stalked back to the command centre.

A NIGHT AND a day of the endless electronic wail. Then another night of watching with nerves scraped raw. Corvus plugged his ears with cloth, but the feedback stabbed its way through the pathetic barrier. His jaw worked, his cheek muscles twitched, and he saw the same strain in the taut, clenched faces of his men. The Rhinos came no closer, and there were no other enemy troop movements. Fort Goreck was besieged by absolute stillness, and that would be enough.

The third day of the siege was a hell of sleeplessness and claustrophobic rage. Five Guardsmen attempted to desert. Corvus had them flogged, then shot.

As the sun set, Corvus could see the end coming. There would be no holding out. The shield he had erected was torture, and madness would tear the base apart. The only thing left was a final, glorious charge that would deny the enemy the kind of triumph that he clearly desired. But how to make that attack if the troops would succumb to the anthem before they even reached the enemy front lines?

Corvus covered his ears with his hands, trying to block the whine, trying to dampen it just enough so he could think. Silence would have been the greatest gift the Emperor could bestow upon him.

Instead, he was granted the next greatest: inspiration.

The medicae centre was on the ground floor of the command block. Corvus found the medic, and explained what was required. The man blanched and refused. Corvus ordered him to do as he said. Still the medic protested. Corvus put his laspistol to the man's head, and that was convincing. Just.

The process took all night. At least, for the most part, the men didn't resist being rendered deaf. Some seemed almost relieved to be free of the feedback whine. Most submitted to the procedure with slack faces and dead looks. The men had become creatures of stoic despair held together and animated by the habits of discipline. Corvus watched yet another patient, blood pouring from his ears, contort on a gurney. At least, he thought, he was giving the soldiers back their pride for the endgame.

There wasn't time to inoculate the entire base contingent against the anthem, so Corvus settled on the best, most experienced squads. That would be enough. They were Imperial Guard, and they would give the traitor forces something to think about.

Morning came. Though one more enemy gunship had landed during the night, the enemy's disposition otherwise remained unchanged. His eyes rough as sand from sleeplessness, Corvus inspected his assembled force. The soldiers looked like the walking dead, unworthy of the glory they were about to find. Well, he would give it to them anyway, and they could thank him in the Emperor's light. He glanced at the rest of the troops. He would be abandoning them to their fate. He shrugged. They were doomed regardless, and at least he had enforced loyalty up to the last. He could go to his grave knowing that he had permitted no defection to Chaos.

He had done his duty.

He had earned his glory.

'Open the gates,' he roared, and wished he could hear the strength of his shout over the shriek of the feedback. The sentries couldn't hear him either, but his gesture was clear, and the wall of Fort Goreck opened for the last time.

There are songs that have been written about the final charge of Colonel Corvus Parthamen. But they are not sung in the mess halls of the Imperial Guard, and they are not stirring battle hymns. They are mocking, obscene doggerel, and they are snarled, rather than sung, with venomous humour, in the corridors of dark ships that ply the warp like sharks. A few men of the Imperium do hear it, in their terminal moments, as their positions are overrun by the hordes of Chaos. They do not appreciate it any more than Corvus would have.

The charge was a rout. The men ran into las-fire and bolter shells. They were blown to pieces by cannon barrage. They were shredded by chainswords and pulped by armoured fists. Still, they made it further down the hill then even Corvus could have hoped. A coherent force actually hit the Chaos front lines and did some damage before being annihilated. Their action might have seemed like the glorious heroism of nothing-to-lose desperation. But the fact that not a single man took cover, not one did anything but run straight ahead, weapon firing indiscriminately, revealed the truth: they were running to their deaths, and glad of the relief.

Corvus was the last. It took him a moment to notice that he was alone, what with the joy of battle and the ecstasy of being free of the whine. He was still running forward, running to his glory, but he wondered now why there didn't seem to be any shots aimed at him. Or why the squad of Chaos Space Marines ahead parted to let him pass. He faltered, and then he saw who was waiting for him.

The monster bulked huge in what had once been Terminator armour, but was now a buzzing, festering exoskeleton. Flies swarmed from the funnels above his shoulders and the lesions in the corrupted ceramite. His single-horned helmet transformed the being's final human traces into the purely daemonic. His grip on his giant scythe was relaxed.

Corvus saw just how powerful disease-made flesh could be. He charged anyway, draining his laspistol, then pulling his chainsword. He swung at the Herald of Nurgle. Typhus whipped the Manreaper around. The movement was as rapid as it was casual and contemptuous. He hit Corvus with the shaft and shattered his hip. Corvus collapsed in the dirt. He bit down on his scream. Typhus loomed over him.

'Kill me,' Corvus spat. 'But know that I fought you to the end. I have my own victory.'

Typhus made a sound that was the rumble of giant hives. Corvus realised he had just heard laughter. 'Kill you?' Typhus asked. His voice was deep. It was smooth as a deliquescent corpse. 'I haven't come to kill you. I have come to teach you my anthem.'

Through his pain, Corvus managed his own laugh. 'I will never sing it.'

'Really? But you have already. You believe you serve order and light, but, like your carrion emperor, everything you do blasts hope and rushes towards entropy. Look what you did to your men. You have served me well, my son. You and your brother, both.'

Corvus fought against the epiphany, but it burst over his consciousness with sickly green light. The truth took him, and infected him. He saw his actions, he saw their consequences, and he saw whose glory he had truly been serving. And as the pattern took shape for him, so did a sound. He heard the anthem, and he heard its music. There was melody there, and he was part of it. Surrender flooded his system, and the triumphant shape of Typhus filled his dying vision. Corvus's jaw snapped open. His throat contorted with ecstatic agony, and he became one with Ligeta's final choir.

◄ TIME OF LEGENDS ►

THE GODS DEMAND

Josh Reynolds

THE GATES BURST open with a thunderous groan and Hergig's doom was sealed. For twenty-two days the capitol of Hochland had stood firm against its besiegers, but no more. The gates fell, ripped from their dwarf-forged hinges by the mutated strength of the immense porcine nightmares that had crashed into them. Squealing and snorting, the barn-sized monsters charged into the city, their claws striking sparks from cobbled streets which shuddered beneath their heavy tread, and behind them came the warherd of Gorthor the Beastlord.

Braying and howling, the beastmen poured into the city like a living tide of filth. Of shapes and hues that only a madman could conceive of, they hefted rust-riddled weapons and slammed them against crude shields daubed in the blood and fluids of defeated foes. The heads of orcs and men hung from their savage standards and they hurled themselves forward like a force of nature, hard and wild and unstoppable. As they entered the foregate square, however, the men of Hochland were waiting for them with lowered spears.

The first rank of beasts impaled themselves on the spears, weighing the weapons down enough for the ranks behind to pounce with undiminished vigour upon the spearmen. Soldiers died as the creatures fell upon them and the survivors were slowly pushed back along the square.

'Hold! Hold position!' Mikael Ludendorf, Elector of Hochland, bellowed as he brained a beastman with his runefang, Goblin-Bane. Wrenching the strangely humming weapon loose of the pulped bovine skull, he grabbed the nearest soldier and shook the bloody sword beneath the man's nose. 'I said stay where you are, damn you!'

The spearman blanched and scrambled backwards, joining the rest of his unit as they retreated in ragged order in defiance of Ludendorf's order. Ludendorf turned even as another gor bounded towards him on swift hooves, a crude polearm clutched in its claws. Shrieking like a dying horse, it sprang at him. The elector count bent out of the path of the weapon and chopped the creature near in half, dropping it to the blood-soaked ground, where it twitched pitifully for a moment before going stiff.

'This is my city,' he said, spitting on the body. 'Mine!' Then he turned to face the rest of the horde as it closed in. He shook his sword. 'Mine!' he yelled. Fully-armoured and covered in the blood of his enemies, as well as some of his own, Ludendorf stood between his retreating troops and the invaders and pointed at the closest of the approaching beast-men with his brain-encrusted sword. Like all runefangs, it was not an elegant weapon, being instead the truest essence of a sword and in that it suited its wielder well. 'Who's first?' he roared.

The beastmen hesitated. Snarls ripped across the ten-foot space between them, and spears jabbed the oppressive air. Red eyes glared at him as hooves pawed at the ground. The closest beast shifted awkwardly, coming closer then sidling back. For a moment, just a moment, the elector held them at bay with only his own stubborn refusal to give ground.

He locked eyes with one of the larger gors. It had antlers a stag would have been proud of and teeth that were the envy of panthers everywhere. 'You, you look like a likely brute. You first,' he said eagerly.

The big beast charged towards him with a snort. It had an old sword, the tip long since sheared off, and it swung it with more enthusiasm than skill. Ludendorf's battered shield came up, deflecting the blow, and he jabbed his sword into the creature's protruding belly hard enough to pierce a kidney. It screamed and reared back, leaving itself open for his follow-through. His blow caught it in the throat and it toppled backwards, gagging.

Standing over his dying opponent, Ludendorf slammed his sword into the face of his shield, fighting to hide a wince. His arm had gone numb from the force of his opponent's blow. At the sound, the beastmen shrank back. At the rear of the crowd, he heard the snarls of the chieftains as they tried to restore the wild momentum of moments before.

'Hergig is mine!' he roared. 'This city – this province – is mine!'

'No,' a deep voice snarled. 'It is Gorthor's.' A heavy shape shoved through the ranks of beasts, sending them sprawling as it moved to face Ludendorf. The elector count took an unconscious step back as the being known as the Beastlord stepped into view.

The creature made for an impressive sight. As big as any three of the largest members of his warherd, he was a creature of slab-like muscle and bloated girth, with hands like spades and hooves like anvils. Tattoos and intricate brands covered his hairy flesh, creating a pattern that seemed to shift with every movement. In one huge hand was the daemon-weapon known as Impaler – a spear with a head of black iron wrought with screaming sigils.

'It is all Gorthor's,' the Beastlord said, eyes alight with un-beastlike intelligence. 'Every scrap of ground, every chunk of stone; it is all mine. The gods have sworn it.'

'Your gods, not mine, animal,' Ludendorf spat. He motioned with his sword. 'Come on then; dance with me, you overgrown mooncalf.'

Gorthor chuckled wetly, the sound echoing oddly from the creature's malformed throat. 'Why? You are dead, and Gorthor does not fight the dead.'

Ludendorf grimaced, his face twisting with hate. 'I'm not dead. Not by a long shot.' He cast a hot-eyed glare at the rabble behind Gorthor. 'I'll kill all of you. I'll choke with your own blood. I'll take your heads and mount them on my ramparts!' Flecks of foam gathered at the corners of his mouth as he cursed them. Some of the creatures cringed at the raw fury in the man's voice. Gorthor, however, was unimpressed.

The Beastlord struck the street with the butt of his spear. 'What ramparts, man-chief? Do you mean these ramparts here?' He swung his brawny arms out to indicate the walls behind him. 'These ramparts are Gorthor's!' As if to emphasise his point, flocks of shrieking harpies landed on the walls and more spun lazily through the smoke-filled air, drawn by the scent of blood and slaughter. 'This city belongs to the gods now, man-chief. We will raze it stone by stone and crush your skulls beneath our hooves as we dance in celebration.' Gorthor made a fist. 'Bow to the will of the gods, man-chief. Gorthor has no mercy, but they might.'

Ludendorf made an animal sound in his throat and he started forward, murder in his eyes. Gorthor bared sharp fangs and raised Impaler. Before either warrior could do much more, however, a rifle shot rang out, shattering the stillness of the square. Gorthor stumbled back, roaring in consternation as a bullet from a long-rifle kissed the skin on his snout, drawing a bead of blood to mark its wake. His warriors set up an enraged cacophony and stormed forward, swirling around Ludendorf as harpies sought out the hidden marksman and pulled him from his perch. The unfortunate man's screams turned shrill as the winged beasts tore him apart and showered the square with his blood and the broken remains of his weapon. Below, the elector count hewed about him with Goblin-Bane, and after a few tense seconds, managed to cut his way free and stumble away from the beasts that had sought to pull him down.

Blood in his eyes, ears ringing with the sounds of steel on steel and the stamping and shrieking of his enemies, Ludendorf raised his sword. Beneath his feet, the street trembled as something heavy approached. 'Rally to me! Up Hochland!' he shouted. 'Count's Own, to me!'

'Here, my count,' shouted a welcome voice. Ludendorf swiped at his eyes and saw the familiar figure of Aric Krumholtz, the Elector's Hound, and Ludendorf's cousin. He was a lean, lupine shape swathed in red and green livery and intricately engraved armour of the best manufacture. One gauntleted hand was clasped around the hilt of the Butcher's Blade, the weapon that came with the title. It was a brutal thing, a sword forged in Sigmar's time, or just before. There was no subtlety to the blade; it was meant to chop and tear flesh and little else. Behind him came the Count's Own; the heavily armoured swordsmen, clad in half-plate and perfumed clothing, with the hard eyes of veteran soldiers. Each carried a two-handed sword that was worth more than the entirety of a common militia-man's wage. The phalanx of Greatswords trotted forward and surrounded their Count even as the street began to shake beneath the hooves of the oncoming beastmen.

'You took your time,' Ludendorf said, chuckling harshly as Krumholtz stepped around him and blocked a blow that would have brought the Count to his knees. The Butcher's Blade sang out, its saw-edged length gutting the bulge-bellied beastman and hurling it back into its fellows.

'Couldn't let you have all the fun, now could I, Mikael?' Krumholtz said. 'Besides, if you hadn't decided to take them all on yourself, I wouldn't have had to come pull your fat out of the fire.'

'Rank impertinence,' Ludendorf said, using Krumholtz's half-cape to wipe the blood out of his face. 'Remind me to execute you after this is over.'

'You mean if we win?' Krumholtz said, taking off a gor's head with a looping cut. Even as it fell, more pressed forward, driven into the narrow street by their chieftains' exhortations.

'There's no if. I'll not be driven from my city by a band of animals. Not after all this,' Ludendorf growled. 'Form up, you lazy bastards!' he continued, glaring at the Greatswords, who were pressed close and finding it hard to wield their weapons in the packed confines of the melee. 'Prepare to scythe this city clean of those cloven-footed barbarians...'

'You should fall back, Mikael,' Krumholtz said. 'Get to safety. We'll handle this.'

'Fall back? You mean retreat?' Ludendorf grimaced. 'No. Ludendorfs don't retreat.'

'Then make a strategic advance to the rear,' Krumholtz said tersely. He grunted as a crude axe shaved a ribbon of merit from his cuirass. Ludendorf grabbed his cousin's sleeve and yanked him back, impaling his attacker on Goblin-Bane.

'Maybe you should be the one to go, eh?' Ludendorf said, yanking his weapon free. 'Not me though. I want that beast's head on my wall!'

he growled, gesturing towards where he'd last seen Gorthor. 'I want his horns for drinking cups and his teeth to adorn my daughter's necklace! And Sigmar curse me if I won't have them!' He started forward, but stopped dead as the street's trembling became a shudder. 'What in the name of–'

The minotaurs tore through the ranks of beastmen, scattering their smaller cousins or trampling them underfoot entirely as they hacked at friends, foes and even the city itself with their great axes. They were massive brutes; each one was a veritable ambulatory hill of muscle, hair, fangs and horns.

Ludendorf's heart went cold. 'Minotaurs,' he hissed.

'Sigmar preserve us,' Krumholtz grunted. 'And Myrmidia defend us. We need to fall back. Get to the guns!'

The Greatswords began to retreat.

'Stay where you are!' Ludendorf barked, glaring around him, holding the men in place. 'We hold them here. Form up!'

'Mikael–!' Krumholtz began, but there was no time to argue. The minotaurs drew closer and their snorts seemed to rattle the teeth in every soldier's head as the Count's Own stepped forward to meet the stampede, led by their elector.

A stone-headed maul thudded down, showering the count with chips of cobble and he stumbled aside, slicing his sword into a titan elbow. Malformed bone snapped and the minotaur bellowed as it turned. It reached for him with its good hand, leaving itself open for the swords of his men. The creature staggered and swatted at its attackers as Ludendorf swept his sword across the backs of its jointed ankles. His arms shuddered in their sockets, but more bones snapped and popped and the creature fell face down as the runefang chewed through its twisted flesh. Greatswords rose and fell and the monster's groans ceased. Ludendorf spun away and slammed his shield into the clacking beak of a bird-headed beastman, knocking it head over heels.

'That's one down,' he said to Krumholtz. The Elector's Hound, his face painted with blood, shook his head and pointed.

'And there are far too many to go, Mikael!' Krumholtz said. Two more of the minotaurs waded through the Greatswords, slapping the life out of any man who got in their path. One lowered its head and charged. Krumholtz shouldered Ludendorf aside and brought the Butcher's Blade down between the curling horns, dropping the beast in its tracks. But even as he hauled at the weapon, trying to yank it loose, the second minotaur was on him.

Ludendorf's sword interposed itself between his advisor's neck and the axe. The elector grunted as his arms shivered in their sockets and went numb. The minotaur roared and forced him down to his knees. Hot drool dripped from its maw and spilled across his face, burning him. Ludendorf whipped his sword aside and skidded between the creature's legs as it bent forwards, off-balance. Rising to his feet, he opened its back to the spine and the monster slumped with a strangled shriek. Ludendorf grabbed one of its thrashing horns and twisted, forcing the wounded beast to expose its hairy throat. Arms screaming with strain, he cut the minotaur's throat and stepped over it, shivering with fatigue. 'Aric?'

'I'm fine. Fall back,' Krumholtz snarled, lunging past the body of the monster and shoving Ludendorf back. 'Fall back now!'

'How dare you–' Ludendorf began, until he caught sight of what lay beyond his cousin. The Count's Own were down and dead to a man, and the warherd was advancing over them. Rage thrummed through him and he made to face the beasts, but Krumholtz slapped him.

'No! Move, Mikael. They died because you didn't know when to run! Go!' Hurrying him along, Krumholtz forced the elector to turn and stagger away, out of the blood-soaked court. Behind them came the hunting cries of Chaos hounds and the louder, more terrible cries of the monsters who had cracked the gate. The air above the city was filled with greasy smoke and shrieking harpies.

Stones hurtled from the rooftops as the citizens of Hergig joined the fray and more than one beast dropped to the street, skull cracked open. But not enough. A grotesque hound sprang at the elector as he stumbled and landed on his back. 'Mikael!' Krumholtz shouted, grabbing the animal's greasy fur.

'Get off me!' Ludendorf howled, shrugging the growling beast off and grabbing its throat. Face going red with effort, he strangled the Chaos hound as it kicked and thrashed, whining. More hounds closed in and Krumholtz killed two, putting the rest of the pack to flight. Ludendorf hurled the body of the dog at a wall and screamed in frustration as the scent of smoke reached him. 'They're burning my city! Damn it, Aric, let me–'

'Get yourself killed? No! Go, you bloody-minded fool!' Krumholtz snapped. 'Just up this street. Let's– look out!'

The street groaned as one of the barn-sized monsters charged towards them, its horns and spikes cutting vast trenches in the walls and buildings that rose to either side of the street. Krumholtz grabbed Ludendorf and threw him to the ground as artillery pieces – field cannon and organ guns – entrenched in the surrounding townhouses, coaching houses and stables at the other end of the street opened up. Men in Hochland's livery reached out to grab the stumbling count and pulled he and his cousin out of the line of fire. The bounding monster fell, its brains turned to sludge by a cannonball. Its massive body slid down the street, blocking it and preventing the beastmen that had followed it from reaching their prey.

Ludendorf turned and pulled himself free of his men's hands. 'Fire again! Pulverise them!' he spat. 'We can't let them remain within our walls!' He turned, wild-eyed. 'Form up! Spearmen to the van! We–'

As the Elector roared out orders, Krumholtz caught him by his fancy gorget and drove a knee up into his groin. Ludendorf sagged, wheezing. 'Stop it,' Krumholtz said. He turned. 'Bosche! Heinreich! Muller! We need to pull back towards the palace. Begin fortifying this street. We'll block the streets where they're the most narrow and form a choke point. Organise a spear-wall and bowmen to defend the builders... I want a proper Tilean hedgehog, by Myrmidia's brass bits, and I want it now! Bors! Commandeer some wagons from the palace walls! They'll work well enough to begin ferrying survivors to safety!'

'You... you hit me,' Ludendorf wheezed, getting to his feet.

Krumholtz looked at him. 'For your own good. We're falling back.'

'No, we can beat them,' Ludendorf said. 'We can drive them out!'

'They outnumber us fifteen to one, cousin,' Krumholtz said tiredly. 'They've taken the walls and they don't care about losses. Look around you,' he continued. Ludendorf did, albeit reluctantly. The battle-madness that had clouded his eyes faded and he saw the exhaustion and fear that was on every face, and the loose way that weapons were clutched. Hochland had fought hard, but his army was on its last legs. He looked down at the Runefang in his hand and felt the trembling weakness in his own limbs.

Ludendorf's mouth writhed as a single bitter word escaped his lips. 'Retreat,' he said hoarsely.

GORTHOR THE BEASTLORD stood in his chariot and watched as his warriors streamed back towards the walls and away from the inner city, battered and bloodied. He snorted in satisfaction. They had taken the outer defences of the town as well as a number of prisoners, as he'd hoped, despite a surprising amount of continued resistance. Even better, he had divested himself of his more fractious followers in the process.

In one stroke he had weakened both the enemy to the front and the enemy within. He knew that he was not alone in recognising that fact. Surly chieftains glared at him from their own chariots. He had insisted that they stay behind, not wanting to waste their lives, merely those of their warriors. He grinned, black lips peeling back from yellow fangs. The expression caused a brief spurt of pain to cross his snout where the bullet had touched him. Annoyed, he rubbed the still drizzling wound. His spear quivered in sympathy and he glanced at it.

The blade of Impaler was sunken haft-deep into a bucket of blood that sat beside him on his chariot. It was crafted out of a giant's skull and every so often it trembled like a sleeping predator, twitching in its dreams of savagery and mutilation. The blade craved blood and it was whispered by many among the herd that if that craving was not quenched, that Impaler would squirm through the dirt like a horrible serpent, seeking what prey it could find among the warherd. He drew the spear from its rest and ran a thumb along the blade. It pulsed in his grip, eager to taste the blood of the man called Ludendorf, even as was Gorthor himself.

Ludendorf. He sounded out the confusing syllables in his head, relishing their taste. A worthy enough foe, as men went. The man would have made a good beast, had he been born under different stars. Gorthor shook the thought aside. 'The city is ours,' he grunted, looking at Wormwhite, where the albino shaman was crouched with the other wonder-workers. They huddled and muttered and hissed. Wormwhite, as their spokesman, was shoved forward and he hopped towards Gorthor. Like all the rest, he was more a prisoner than an advisor, kept close at hand to interpret the dark dreams which sometimes blistered Gorthor's consciousness with painful visions of the future.

'No! Walls still stand,' Wormwhite whined. 'Gods say attack again!' He gestured towards the sloping walls that surrounded the inner keep of the city, where the elector's palace sat.

'Do they?' Gorthor rumbled, leaning on Impaler. The spear squirmed in his grip, hungry for death. 'Why do they want me to do this?' he said, fixing a baleful gaze on the shaman. Wormwhite cringed. 'What is there that is not here? Death? Gorthor has built cairns of skulls along the length of the man-track!' He leaned over the edge of his chariot, his teeth clicking together in a frustrated snap at the air. His nostrils flared at the scent of blood and fear. 'They are trapped! Why waste warriors?'

'Gods demand!' Wormwhite said, slinking back. The others murmured encouragement. So too did the chieftains. Gorthor growled in frustration.

'Gods demand,' he grunted, and shook his head. Black claws scratched at his wounded snout as he considered his options. The gods demanded much… at times, too much.

Visions wracked him suddenly, causing his body to shudder and his jaws to snap convulsively. When the warp was upon him, it was all he could do to keep his body from ripping itself apart. Every hair tingled and stood out from his body like a razor-spike as Wormwhite and the others gathered close, their nostrils quivering as they scented the strange magics spilling off him. He longed to drive them back, scavengers that they were, but he could only hunch forward and yelp in agony as the images ripped across his mind's eye. Ghost-memories of the future, where blighted trees of copper and meat burst through undulating, moaning soil and pale things danced continuously to the mad piping of chaotic minstrels. That was the future that Gorthor was charged with bringing to fruition, and though he saw no sign of his people there, he was determined to fulfil that destiny all the same.

Breathing heavily as the warp-spasm passed, he leaned on his spear. Amidst the screaming cacophony of the vision he had seen flashes of beasts wandering the ruins of Hergig drunk and careless, and of an avalanche of brass and steel horses falling upon them. Was that what the gods wanted? For his mighty herd-of-herds to be cut to pieces as it squatted drunk in the ruins?

His scouts had reported that forces were mobilising to the north and south. The Drakwald was being razed and while his army yet swelled, it was a tenuous thing holding it together. His people had no taste for prolonged conflict of this kind, and more and more of them would give in to the urge to attack the so-far so-solid walls of the elector's palace, or, even worse, they would slink away, glutted on the loot of the city.

Wolfenburg had been easy compared to this. Taken by surprise, the defenders had fallen back from the main gate and from there they'd slowly lost the town. With nowhere to run and nowhere to hide, they'd been easy prey. But this was more difficult. The battle with the humans on the forest road had blunted his momentum and given them time to fortify and make ready. The lands around Hergig had been turned into a killing ground, full of traps and obstacles. Speed had been his primary weapon, and now it was lost. He glanced to the side at his chieftains – they traded looks among each other, grumbling and gripping weapons that might, at any minute, be turned against him. Even the blessings of the Dark Gods could only protect him from so much.

Idly he stroked the tattoos and brands that criss-crossed his hairy flesh, tracing them with one blunt finger. Each mark had been earned in battle with one enemy or another… there, the memory of his battle with a Chaos giant as a youngling. Now he had a half-dozen of the beasts serving him. There, where the razor-fingers of one of the brides of the Goat with a Thousand Lovers had caressed him before she'd tried to devour him. Her sisters danced now at his beck and call. And had he not slain a mighty black orc warlord only weeks before, and set an army of the creatures to flight? In each battle, one common factor – he'd known the gods were watching over him. But now, now he wasn't so sure.

Every rudimentary strategic instinct the Beastlord possessed had screamed at him to ignore the walled city of Hergig and continue on, even as they now pleaded that he ignore the palace. But the gods he served demanded that the sack of this town be complete. Thus, it must be done… but it would be done well. Experience had taught Gorthor there was always a weak point in any defence… a crumbling wall, a fire-weakened gate, loose stones, something. Anything. Like the bared throat of a defeated enemy, the weak point could be torn out and the battle won in one swift blow. He just had to find it. 'Prisoners?' he grunted.

'Many-many,' Wormwhite said, holding up his claws. 'Not good though. Not many live long.'

'Show me,' Gorthor snarled, slamming the butt of his spear against the chariot base.

A few minutes later a captive screamed shrilly as he was dragged before Gorthor, blood staining his red and green livery. Arms stretched to the point of dislocation between the fists of a minotaur, he hung awkwardly. His legs were shredded masses of meat and malformed hounds pulled at them hard enough to cause the Minotaur to stumble. With a grunt, a goat-headed gor chieftain slapped the dogs aside with the flat of his axe and kicked the stubborn ones into submission with his hooves. Then he grabbed the dying man's chin and jerked his head up.

'Whrrr?' the gor rumbled, placing the notched edge of the axe against a hairless cheek. 'Whrrr?'

The man sucked in a breath as if to answer and then, with a shudder that wracked his ruined frame, he went limp, his eyes rolling to the white. The gor shook him, puzzled. Then, with a roar, he swept the corpse's head from its broken shoulders. The head bounced along the filth-covered ground, pursued by the snapping hounds. The gor spun and shook his axe at Gorthor's chariot.

Gorthor stroked Impaler like a beloved pet as he eyed the body with something that might have been consternation. Another captive dead was one less who could tell Gorthor what he needed to know. He made a disgusted noise and turned to Wormwhite, crouching nearby. 'Weak, Wormwhite,' he grunted.

'Men are weak,' the shaman replied, bovine lips curling back from the stumps of black, broken teeth. Wormwhite's eyes narrowed shrewdly. 'I talk, yes?'

'Dd!' the gor trumpeted, stomping a hoof onto a cobble, splintering it. He waved his axe at the shaman, spattering the latter's ratty cloak with blood. 'No tlk!'

'Talk,' the shaman said. He looked at Gorthor.

'Yes,' Gorthor snorted. 'Talk.'

Nodding, the shaman hopped towards the body. Grabbing a hound by the scruff of its neck he yanked it up and pried the gnawed skull out of its jaws and flung the beast aside. 'Make talk easy. Not dead long.'

With that, he drove two stiffened talons into the ragged neck stump and swung the head around to face the herdstone Gorthor had commanded raised two weeks previous, on their first night encamped before Hergig's walls. Muttering, the shaman raised the head and held it as a chill mist seeped from the surface of the herdstone and crept towards him. The tendrils of mist found the stump of the head and began to fill it. Wormwhite jerked his fingers free and let the head drop. Only it didn't. Instead, it hung supported by the clammy mist, and slowly it rose, turning the head around. Mist seeped from the punctured eyes and dripped from the slack lips and Wormwhite howled and capered.

'Ask it,' Gorthor grunted.

'Where is weakness?' Wormwhite shrilled, dancing around the column of mist and the bobbing head.

The mouth moved loosely, as if it were being manipulated by stiff fingers. 'N-nor-north wuh-wall… s… stones… luh-loose…' it said in a voice like a whisper of air. Wormwhite cackled and jerked his hand. The mist abruptly retreated and the head fell with a thump. The hounds leapt on it in a snarling pile as the shaman turned back to his chieftain.

'North wall,' Wormwhite said, stamping a hoof. 'Lead attack, crush the hairless,' he continued, his eyes blazing. The gathered warriors of the herd rumbled in assent, and weapons clattered.

Gorthor's lips twitched. 'Attack when I say, Wormwhite. Not before,' the Beastlord snorted with false laziness. His dark eyes fixed on the shaman and then passed across the muzzles of the half-dozen wargors who made up his inner circle. The gor who had been questioning the dead human was one of their number, a brute named Crushhoof who shook his axe at Gorthor in a vaguely threatening manner. 'Ttack now!' he snarled. 'Gds wnt t'ttack!'

'I speak for gods,' Gorthor said, shifting on his throne. 'Not you, Crushhoof.'

Crushhoof reared back and brayed loudly, foam flying from his jaws. He pawed the ground and his warriors howled and rattled their spears. 'Ttack! Ttack! Ttack!' they shrieked in unison. Other herds picked up the chant and Gorthor suddenly thrust himself up out of his seat. Silence fell.

Crushhoof glared up at him, his gaze challenging. It had been coming for a long time now, and Gorthor wasn't surprised. Crushhoof swung his axe through the air and grunted 'Defy gods?'

'Said before, gods speak through me,' Gorthor said slowly. 'Challenge, Crushhoof?'

'Chlnge!' Crushhoof cried and bounded up onto the dais, his axe swinging. Gorthor stepped aside with an ease that was surprising for one of his size. As he moved, he grabbed Impaler. Crushhoof reacted quickly, twisting around and slicing at Gorthor. The axe scratched across the surface of Gorthor's patchwork armour, leaving a trail of sparks.

Impaler slid across his palm smoothly and, almost of its own volition, the blade shot into Crushhoof's belly. He brayed in shock as Gorthor jerked him into the air. Impaler wriggled deeper into the wound and the tip exploded out through the dying gor's back.

Blood sloshed down onto Gorthor and he opened his jaws to accept the offering. Then, with a grunt, he tossed the twitching body to the ground, jerking Impaler free in the process. The butt of the spear thudded into the dais and Gorthor glared at his army. One big fist thumped his chest. 'I lord here! Gorthor! Not Crushhoof! Not Benthorn or Splaypaw or Doombite! By this spear, Gorthor rules!' he roared and hefted Impaler over his head. The gathered beasts howled in reply.

KRUMHOLTZ WATCHED AS the first volley of fire-arrows were loosed from the walls of the palace. His soul cringed at the thought of what would happen to any of the city's citizens who were left out there, crouching in cellars or attics. But he said nothing. Mikael had moved beyond wanting to save the city into wanting to deny it to his enemies in the two days since they'd fallen back to the palace. He shared looks with the other counsellors, all of whom had similar looks on their faces. Worry, mingled with apprehension.

Ludendorf had many virtues, among them a savage zeal that made even battle-hardened priests of Sigmar give way. But his flaws were just as fierce at times, and zeal could become blind stubbornness as easily as courage. It had ever been such with the Ludendorfs; Hochland's nobility were fiercer than almost any in the Empire. Such was the reason that the position of Elector's Hound had been created. A second head, one to remain level when the Elector inevitably gave vent to the rages of the blood. Of course, the position's authority rested on the holder's ability to get the Elector in question to listen.

'We'll burn them out like rats,' Ludendorf growled, glaring at the city as new smoke clouds began to billow up to join those created by the fires that the beasts had already started. Nearby, men poured water drawn from the palace's cistern onto the walls, to ward against the fire. 'I'll not let him have it. Not after all we did to make this place impregnable,' he continued gesturing to the stout walls that surrounded the inner town of Hergig. 'We can take back the city from here, Aric, after they've been driven out by the fire. We can take back the province. Drive the beasts into the Talabec, even!' He looked down at the cramped courtyard at the huddled groups of civilians and soldiers without really seeing them. Krumholtz watched him rant. None of the other counsellors met his eyes, and he knew it was up to him.

'We can't hold the city, Mikael,' he began evenly. 'The North Wall is unstable and the rest of the keep isn't much better. We have to retreat, and pull that monster and his herd after us. We can give our people – the people of Hergig – time to flee.' Seeing the look on the elector's face, he said, 'We would not be abandoning Hergig, Mikael… we are preserving Hochland.'

'Preserving yourself, you mean!' someone yelled from one of the surrounding buildings. Rotten fruit, broken bricks and the contents of bedpans flew at the men on the wall from the surrounding rooftops. At a barked command from Krumholtz, several men peeled off from a group below and hurried into the cramped buildings, kicking in doors and shattering windows along the way. Krumholtz watched as screaming people, starving and frightened, were dragged out of their homes and tossed into the street. Six in all, five of them labourers by their clothing. The sixth was a boy, thin and fragile-looking. He knew that they likely weren't the hecklers. It didn't matter. Krumholtz followed the elector down into the courtyard towards the prisoners.

'Cousin?' Ludendorf said, in the sudden silence.

Krumholtz swallowed and laid a hand on the hilt of the Butcher's Blade. 'My lord elector?'

'Do your duty,' Ludenhof said.

The Butcher's Blade sprang from its sheath with startling speed and five heads rolled into the gutter. The blade halted above the neck of the sixth, the stroke pulled inches from the boy's neck. Krumholtz stepped back, his face stony. 'Five is an adequate example, I think.'

'Do you?' Ludendorf said, teeth bared. His fingers twitched on the hilt of his runefang and for a moment, Krumholtz feared he would complete the execution himself. Then his hand flopped limply, draped over the pommel. Ludendorf looked around the courtyard, meeting the hollow stares of his people. 'Where would you go, Aric?' he said mildly.

'Talabheim,' someone said. The other counsellors murmured agreement.

Ludendorf smiled. 'Say you make it to Talabheim. And then? There's little chance of the beasts breaching those walls, no, but they can swarm the land unopposed, which is likely what they want. The Drakwald is cancerous as it stands... imagine it in a season, when the beasts have a province to feed on; it will be a bleeding tumour in the gut of our Empire, Aric. One that will take us years to burn clean, if it's even possible. Civilisation will be reduced to a few mighty cities, isolated and cut off from one another. Is that what you want?'

'No, but–'

'Only the preservation of the Empire matters. And that means breaking them here,' Ludendorf said.

'And what about preserving the people of Hochland?'

'There's an old hunter's saying... when you and a friend are being chased by a bear, don't try and outrun it; instead, trip your friend,' Ludendorf said, looking up at the smoke. The shapes of harpies soared out of it, wailing and shrieking. Bows and long-rifles spoke, knocking several of the grotesque shapes out of the air. 'While the bear is busy with us, we can gut it and render it impotent.' He looked at Krumholtz. 'There is a method to my madness, Aric. It's not just stubbornness.'

'Are you sure about that?' Krumholtz said, his voice pitched low. 'Be honest with me Mikael. Is this pride talking?'

'Don't presume too much on our kinship, Aric,' Ludendorf said, not looking at him.

'Mikael, Ostland has already fallen. Even if reinforcements were coming, it's unlikely they'll reach us in time. Especially not with you burning the city out from under us!' Krumholtz said, his voice growing louder. 'But we can save our people now. All we have to do is–'

'What? Abandon the capital? Flee into the wilderness?' Ludendorf said. 'And just how would you go about that, cousin?'

'We parley,' Krumholtz said. Ludendorf's face flushed.

'What did you say?'

Krumholtz took a breath. 'We parley. That monster out there is many things, but he is not dumb. The more time he takes on us, the greater the likelihood his army will be diminished by desertion, infighting and attack. But if we offer him the city, we could escape! We can escort the survivors out, let them scatter into hiding and then march towards Talabheim to join up with their forces!'

'Just give him the city? My city?' Ludendorf said.

'Better the city than the lives of our people!'

'Their lives are mine to spend as I see fit!' Ludendorf shouted. He gestured to the clumps of huddled survivors. 'I would spill every drop of blood in the province to destroy that animal! That beast that dares think to challenge us! And you want to surrender?'

'For Hochland–' Krumholtz began.

'I am Hochland!' Ludendorf roared. His voice echoed through the courtyard.

'No! You are a prideful lunatic!' Krumholtz shouted back, the words leaving his mouth before he realised it.

Ludendorf froze. Then, he pointed a shaking hand at Krumholtz. 'Give me your sword.'

'What?' Krumholtz blinked. He was suddenly aware of the others pulling away from him, and he felt a sinking sensation deep in his gut.

'Your sword. Give it to me. I'll not have a coward as my Hound.'

Krumholtz's face went stiff. 'I'm no coward.'

'No? Retreat this, fall back that. Always running, Aric, never holding. Never standing,' Ludendorf hissed. His hands curled into fists. 'Run then, Aric. Run right out those gates. Let's see how far you make it, eh?'

'Mikael…'

The runefang slid out of its sheath with an evil hiss and Krumholtz stumbled back, reaching unconsciously for his own blade. He stopped himself from drawing it and let his hands fall. 'Go,' Ludendorf said. 'Go and be damned.'

Krumholtz straightened and unbuckled his sword-belt. 'As you wish, my count.' Without looking at his cousin, he dropped the Butcher's Blade in the dust and turned away. As he made for the gates, he was aware of the world closing in around him, narrowing his vision to a pinpoint. Outside the gates, damnation waited and capered. At the back of his mind, a tiny voice wondered which was worse, what awaited him outside, or what he'd seen inside.

No one tried to stop him.

No one called him back.

And when he died, no one was watching.

Ludendorf sat in his palace, the Butcher's Blade resting over his knees, the Runefang sunk into the polished wood of the floor. He heard a distant roar, and knew his cousin was dead. His fury had abated, and there was a bitter taste in his mouth. 'You have to understand, Aric,' he said to the empty room. 'It's not pride keeping me here. It's not.'

He waited for a reply. When none was forthcoming, he closed his eyes. 'It's not,' he said again.

THE GIANT WAS a malformed thing, with jagged curls of bone bursting through its tortured flesh. It moaned as it uprooted another roof and tossed it aside with a crash. Four of the mammoth beasts worked steadily, pulling down buildings and slamming them into pieces even as hundreds of gors crawled across the shattered timbers, lashing them together. It had taken them three days, and the fire hadn't helped matters. But Gorthor watched, and was pleased. He had enslaved the giants personally, his crude magics binding their weak minds to his own. Their thoughts fluttered at the edge of his consciousness like moths caught in a storm.

'Waste of time, waste of time,' Wormwhite muttered.

Gorthor tossed a lazy glance at the shaman. 'No,' he said. 'We will take the town, as the gods want. But we will do it my way. Gorthor's way.'

'Stupid,' one of the chieftains said. It wasn't the first time that one of his sub-chieftains had commented on Gorthor's insistence on building siege towers and battering rams, as opposed to simply forcing the gates in the traditional fashion.

Gorthor grunted and reached out. He grabbed the scruff of the chieftain's neck and jerked the startled gor into the air. Muscles bulging, Gorthor shook the critic the way a hound shakes a rat and then tossed him into the dirt. 'One gate,' Gorthor growled. 'One!' He glared at them and gestured at the platforms being built. 'Many,' he said. 'Cannot crush with only one finger.' He made a fist. 'Must use all at once.' His lips quirked and he laughed. 'One herd cannot destroy them, but many – all at once?' He looked at them, wondering if the lesson had sunk in. He caught Wormwhite looking at him strangely, and Gorthor glared at the shaman. 'Speak, shaman.'

'This is not the way of the gods,' the albino said. He spread his talons and witch-light curled around their tips. 'We break, we do not build,' he continued. 'The gate is there! We should attack!'

'The gods want the town, Gorthor will give them the town,' Gorthor said matter-of-factly. 'But I will not waste warriors to do so!' He thumped a fist on his chariot. 'One hole no good. Need many.'

'Bld fr th' bldgd,' another chieftain growled. He slapped his brass-sheathed horn with his axe and set sparks to drifting down. Behind him, the red-stained hair of his followers bristled in eagerness.

'The blood-god wants man-blood, not beast-blood!' Gorthor countered, showing them his teeth. After Crushhoof, Brasshorn was one of the loudest grumblers. And Brasshorn's Khorngors with him. Eager for blood and skulls and souls, and not very particular about where they came from.

'Blood-god wants *all* blood,' Wormwhite said pointedly, eliciting snarls of agreement from Brasshorn and his followers. 'Gods demand our blood, Beastlord. Demand man-blood! Demand we dance on the cities of men and crush skulls beneath our hooves! Crush, not create! Burn, not build! Smash, not speak!' Wormwhite's voice grew ever shriller and Gorthor's hackles rose. The other shamans joined in, uttering warbling denunciations of his procrastination.

Gorthor had never feared the ire of the wonder-workers. As a blessed child of the gods, he had known that their magic was as nothing to his. But now, now he could feel the warp dancing along the edge of each prickled hair and he made his decision a moment later.

Wormwhite's skull made a wet sound as Impaler passed through it and nailed the slop of his brains to a wall. Silence fell, as it had earlier with Crushhoof's demise. Gorthor could feel the rage of the gods in his nerve-endings, but he ignored it and jerked Impaler free, brandishing it at his advisors. 'Gods will have blood... seas and messes of it! But Gorthor will deliver that blood! Gorthor will deliver it his way! In his time!'

He looked around, noting with satisfaction that none dared meet his gaze. He stamped a hoof and bounded aboard his chariot. 'And Gorthor says that time is now!' he roared, waving his spear over his head. A spasm threatened him, but he forced it aside. He would listen to the gods after. After! Now was only for doing what they demanded.

His chariot rumbled forward, picking up speed as the tuskagors pulling it snorted and chewed the ground with their hooves. The giants stomped past, easily outdistancing the chariots as they slammed the crude bridges down across the wall. And waiting there below were eager gors, carrying improvised scaling ladders and battering rams. They streamed like ants through the streets, some of them surrounding the gates of the inner palace even as one of the giants, peppered with hundreds of arrows, slumped against the weakened wall that Wormwhite's necromancy had indicated and sent it tottering.

Something flashed behind Gorthor's eyes as he squatted in the back of his chariot, waving Impaler. Visions of brass horsemen, cutting through his ranks. He shook it off. No. No, it wouldn't be that way! The gods were watching him. He was doing as they asked! They would protect him as they had always done! He roared and clutched Impaler in both hands, shaking it high as his chariot thundered towards the gates of the palace. A giant was already there, tearing at the door even as oil burned its skin and belching guns found its eyes. It screamed piteously as it fell, taking the great wooden doors with it and only stopped when the iron-bound wheels of Gorthor's chariot pulped its skull.

The last defenders of Hergig were waiting there for Gorthor and he roared as his chariot crashed into them. Impaler flashed out, lopping off limbs and piercing bodies, staining the stones red. Men fell beneath his wheels and were gored by his tuskagors. More chariots followed him, filling the wide avenue with a rolling wall of spiked death.

And then, in one moment, it all went terribly wrong.

When the horns sounded, Gorthor knew at once what his visions had been trying to tell him, and he felt a brittle sensation that might have been the laughter of the Dark Gods. Beneath his feet, the ground trembled. There were new smells on the wind and he looked up, peering back along the trail of destruction he had left in his wake. Over the heads of struggling combatants, he saw a gleam of something that might have been brass and he heard the blare of coronets. His visions returned, blasting over and through him and a chill coursed down his spine.

Horsemen clad in burnished plate charged towards him, their steeds grinding his warriors into the street as they rode on. Gorthor speared the first to reach him, hauling the man off of his horse. He swung the body of the brass man into the air and tossed it aside in a burst of furious strength. The fear that had seized him upon sighting the warrior faded into confusion. Was this what the gods had been trying to tell him? Was this what they had wanted? He snorted and turned away from the crumpled body. His warriors were locked in combat with the men and the city was burning. His nostrils flared and another spasm passed through him. He thought of Wormwhite's dead eyes and bit back a snarl.

No, he was blessed. Blessed! Hergig would be his, gods or no. More trumpets blared out and burnt his ears. He spun and watched in consternation as the defenders of Hergig fell upon his forces through the holes he'd made in their defences. The new arrivals crashed into the packed ranks of beastmen, carving through them with ease as the children of Chaos panicked, caught between the hammer and the anvil. Gorthor snarled in rage. He had to rally his troops. He had to reorder them, to pull them back and prepare to meet this new threat. He leapt from his chariot and clambered up a nearby statue with simian agility. Holding Impaler aloft, he issued desperate commands. The armoured shapes of his chieftains and bestigors responded, cutting a path to him, but too late.

Even as the cream of his warherd assembled, the rest of it began to melt away, caught as they were in the pincers of the two forces. He could hear laughter in his head and knew at once that an ending was here.

The gods had demanded a sacrifice. He had thought it was this town, but he had been mistaken. Or perhaps blind. Those beloved of the gods were often the ones they called home soonest, and the thought filled him with berserk rage. Frothing at the mouth, his mind filled with the mocking laughter of the Dark Gods, Gorthor lifted Impaler and looked towards the palace. His fangs ground together and he dropped from the statue. Stones buckled beneath his feet and he straightened. Impaler raised, he began to run and his herd followed suit.

The gods demanded blood. And though they had turned from him, Gorthor would deliver it nonetheless.

* * *

LUDENDORF DREW THE Butcher's Blade with one hand and Goblin-Bane with the other. Today, at the last, he would be his own Hound. He hadn't bothered to find another, and no one had volunteered.

He didn't blame them. On some level, Ludendorf wondered if he were truly ruthless, or simply mad. Had he sent his cousin to death and doom for causing dissension where none could be tolerated, or for simply speaking the truth?

'Aric,' he said softly, examining the Butcher's Blade in the weak light of day. 'Why couldn't you for once have just listened?' His gaze slid to Goblin-Bane and he sighed. The runefang of Hochland seemed to purr as he made a tentative pass through the air with it. A weapon passed down from father to son, it lusted for battle with a passion that matched his own. It craved death, and spells of murder had been beaten into its substance during its forging. It longed to split the Beastlord's skull, and he longed to let it. 'Soon enough,' he murmured.

He smiled grimly as he heard the strident ululation of the coronets of the Order of the Blazing Sun. When his men had reported that the knights had arrived, smashing into the rear of the army intent on breaching his gates, he'd scarcely credited it. Now he could hear battle being joined all around him as beast met man in the tangled streets before the palace, even as the walls crumbled beneath the onslaught of the giants.

The arrival of the knights was a sign that he'd been right. That Sigmar had wanted him to hold this place, to keep it from the claws of Chaos. His god had tasked him, and he fulfilled that task, though he'd been opposed at every turn. And now... now came the reward. He grinned and rotated his wrist, loosening up his sword-arm. He'd have the beast's head on a pike, and toast to it every year on the anniversary of Aric's death. His cousin would appreciate that, he was sure.

'Of course you would. Least you could do for betraying me,' he said, looking at the Butcher's Blade again. It felt wrong to hold it in his hand, but he was determined that it should shed some blood. He needed his cousin's sword at his side now more than ever. Aric had always been there for him in life, and it was only fitting he be there in death as well.

'Plus, you'd hate to miss out on a fight like this, eh?' he said out loud. If he noticed the looks some of his men gave him, he gave no sign. They hated him now, if they hadn't before. But they loved him too. Better a ruthless man than a weak one, in times like these. Better a madman than a coward, that's what they whispered in the ranks when they thought he wasn't listening.

Beasts bounded through the shattered North Wall, bugling cries of challenge. He'd known they'd get in one way or another, and had fortified the inner keep with whatever had been available. Spearmen and handgunners crouched behind overturned wagons and at a shouted command men rolled uncorked barrels of black powder towards the shattered walls. Trails of fire followed them. Explosions rocked the courtyard, filling the air with smoke, rock and bloody body parts. A giant howled in agony as its legs disintegrated in an explosion and it toppled into the courtyard. It squirmed, trying to push itself upright until a dozen spears pierced its skull.

Ludendorf laughed as the stink of roasting beast-flesh reached him. He would take back his city, or wipe it off the map in the attempt, no matter the cost. His laughter faded as he looked down at the Butcher's Blade. Frowning, he tightened his grip on the hilt. 'No pity. No remorse,' he grunted. He clashed his swords together. 'Kill them all!' he roared, and his men hastened to do the deed.

Handguns barked and arrows hissed, thudding into hairy flesh. Creatures howled and screamed as they slipped on their own blood in their haste to close with their foes. His remaining soldiers attacked with renewed courage, yelling out praises to the Emperor and Sigmar. And if no one shouted his name, Ludendorf didn't care. So long as they fought, he was satisfied.

Beastmen, having managed to avoid his troops, charged up the stairs of the palace towards him. The Butcher's Blade caught one on the side of the head, killing it instantly. He blocked a spear-point with Goblin-Bane and buried his cousin's sword in the beastman's belly, pinning it to one of the ornamental pillars that lined the doors to the palace. Pulling it loose, he met the next, blocking its axe with both swords.

With a grunt he swept his blades apart, cutting the head off of the axe. As the beastman reeled back in shock, Ludendorf kicked it down the stairs where several spearmen were waiting. 'Finish it off and join the others,' he said, shaking blood off of his sword. The spears rose and fell, cutting off the creature's squalls.

He stepped down the stairs and strode through the smoke after his troops, eager to get to grips with the beasts. A moment later, his eagerness was swept aside by surprise as a spear took the man nearest him, pinning the unfortunate soldier to a wall in a shower of brick dust and blood. Ludendorf turned and saw a familiar shape and his lips skinned back from his teeth in a fierce snarl.

Gorthor jerked his spear loose from the brick and swung it over his head like an axe. 'Ludendorf!' Gorthor bellowed.

'Gorthor!' Ludendorf barked, gesturing with his swords. 'We were interrupted earlier, animal! Decided to fight the dead after all?'

Gorthor shrieked like a wildcat and the Beastlord began to shake, his whole body rippling with spasms. The Butcher's Blade looped out, only to be caught with a wet slap in the Beastlord's palm. Gorthor jerked the weapon out of Ludendorf's grip and backhanded him, sending him skidding across the cobbles. Ludendorf coughed as he rolled to a stop. He knew his ribs were likely broken and he felt like a punctured water-skin.

'The gods demand your heart, man-chief!' Gorthor said, stamping forward. His warriors made to surge towards the downed count, and the

Beastlord twisted, gutting the closest. 'No! Gorthor's prey!' he snorted, glaring at his warriors. The beasts drew back, their weapons clattering against their shields in a dull rhythm. Gorthor shook himself, satisfied that none would interfere.

Ludendorf coughed and pushed himself to his feet. He was the only man in the courtyard, surrounded by a ring of beasts. There were soldiers on the walls, but they were too far away to save him, if he had even wanted such. He braced himself on his runefang and waited, grinning madly. 'Gorthor's prey, eh? Bit off more than you could chew this time, didn't you?' he spat, laughing. 'You're caught in a trap of your own making, you stupid animal. And now, like every other animal, you're wasting time fighting instead of fleeing.'

'Like you,' Gorthor rumbled, eyes blazing. Ludendorf's laughter choked off and the elector raised his sword, stung.

'Shut up,' he said. 'Shut up and fight, filth. Let the gods decide who's the fool here.'

Gorthor gave a howl and Impaler glided forward. Ludendorf spun around it, Goblin-Bane chopping through one of his opponent's horns. Gorthor turned, roaring, and Impaler shot out, nearly taking the head off of his attacker. Ludendorf dodged to the side and his blade flickered out again, eliciting another agonised shriek from Gorthor.

'This is my city! My territory! And it's your death-ground, cur,' Ludendorf said, lunging smoothly despite the ache in his chest. The tip of his blade burned like fire as it slid over Gorthor's leg and the Beastlord stepped back instinctively. He backpedalled, weaving a wall between himself and that cursed sword. It dove at him like a snake, biting and ripping faster than he could see and its every touch caused him torment. 'Hergig is mine! Hochland is mine! And I'll kill any who try and take it from me!' cried Ludendorf.

Frenziedly, Gorthor lashed out, flailing at his opponent with Impaler, battering the warrior off of his feet. The man slipped on the bloody cobbles and lost his balance completely. Desperately, he tried to haul himself away from Gorthor, who drove one wide hoof into his chest, denting his cuirass and pinning him to the ground. Impaler's blade swept to the side, cutting armour and flesh with a sizzle. Ludendorf screamed in agony as his belly split open like an overripe melon.

'Gorthor's now,' the Beastlord grunted, kicking him and sending the dying man rolling across the courtyard. The beastmen set up a cacophony of triumphant screeches and barks and Gorthor, breathing heavily, raised his weapon in triumph.

His eyes filled with blood, and his ears filled with the sound of his own heart stuttering, Ludendorf clambered to his feet. His intestines draped loose over the restraining arm he had clamped across his belly and his fingers tangled in the clasps of his armour. He barely had the strength to grip his sword as he stumbled towards the broad beast shape raising its hell-weapon over its head.

With all his remaining strength, he swept his sword out across the beastman's broad back. Bone blistered at the touch of the Runefang and Gorthor shrieked like a wounded goat. A hairy fist caught the Elector on the side of the head and the ground raced up to meet him. The beastman rose up over him, blood mingling with the foam dripping from his jaws. His body shuddered, as if gripped by fever.

'Die!' Gorthor growled. Impaler lived up to its name, nailing Ludendorf to the ground. Muscles bulging, Gorthor jerked spear and man up and raised them up towards the sky. 'Die for the gods!' Gorthor howled.

Ludendorf, his teeth stained red, grabbed the haft of the daemon-weapon even as it squirmed in his guts. 'You first,' he rasped, jerking himself down the weapon's length. Agony clouded his vision and his sword-arm felt like lead as it dropped down.

A moment later, Gorthor's head flew free of his thick neck. Ludendorf fell, his sword sliding from his grip.

The great form of the Beastlord staggered four steps and sank to its knees, neck-stump spraying blood even as it toppled. The spear clattered away, the ugly runes decorating its surface dimming. Mikael Ludendorf crawled towards the head of the Beastlord and clutched it as somewhere, triumphant notes were blown from a hundred horns. The beasts ran then, leaving the two chieftains alone in the courtyard.

Ludendorf, dying, stared into the glassy eyes of Gorthor. His lips moved, shaping one word, but no sound came out. Beneath his body, he felt the stones of Hergig tremble as the knights of the Blazing Sun drove the beasts from his city. He heard the cheers as his people celebrated.

When he died, no one was watching.

SHADOW KNIGHT

Aaron Dembski-Bowden

The sins of the father, they say.

Maybe. Maybe not. But we were always different. My brothers and I, we were never truly kin with the others – the Angels, the Wolves, the Ravens...

Perhaps our difference was our father's sin, and perhaps it was his triumph. I am not empowered by anyone to cast a critical eye over the history of the VIII Legion.

These words stick with me, though. The sins of the father. These words have shaped my life.

The sins of my father echo throughout eternity as heresy. Yet the sins of my father's father are worshipped as the first acts of godhood. I do not ask myself if this is fair. Nothing is fair. The word is a myth. I do not care what is fair, and what is right, and what's unfair and wrong. These concepts do not exist outside the skulls of those who waste their life in contemplation.

I ask myself, night after night, if I deserve vengeance.

I devote each beat of my heart to tearing down everything I once raised. Remember this, remember it always: my blade and bolter helped forge the Imperium. I and those like me – we hold greater rights than any to destroy mankind's sickened empire, for it was our blood, our bones, and our sweat that built it.

Look to your shining champions now. The Adeptus Astartes that scour the dark places of your galaxy. The hordes of fragile mortals enslaved to the Imperial Guard and shackled in service to the Throne of Lies. Not a soul among them was even born when my brothers and I built this empire..

Do I deserve vengeance? Let me tell you something about vengeance, little scion of the Imperium. My brothers and I swore to our dying father that we would atone for the great sins of the past. We would bleed the unworthy empire that we had built, and cleanse the stars of the False Emperor's taint.

This is not mere vengeance. This is redemption.

My right to destroy is greater than your right to live.

Remember that, when we come for you.

He is a child standing over a dying man.

The boy is more surprised than scared. His friend, who has not yet taken a life, pulls him away. He will not move. Not yet. He cannot escape the look in the bleeding man's eyes.

The shopkeeper dies.

The boy runs.

He is a child being cut open by machines.

Although he sleeps, his body twitches, betraying painful dreams and sleepless nerves firing as they register pain from the surgery. Two hearts, fleshy and glistening, beat in his cracked-open chest. A second new organ, smaller than the new heart, will alter the growth of his bones, encouraging his skeleton to absorb unnatural minerals over the course of his lifetime.

Untrembling hands, some human, some augmetic, work over the child's body, slicing and sealing, implanting and flesh-bonding. The boy trembles again, his eyes opening for a moment.

A god with a white mask shakes his head at the boy.

'Sleep.'

The boy tries to resist, but slumber grips him with comforting claws. He feels, just for a moment, as though he is sinking into the black seas of his home world.

Sleep, the god had said.

He obeys, because the chemicals within his blood force him to obey.

A third organ is placed within his chest, not far from the new heart. As the ossmodula warps his bones to grow on new minerals, the biscopea generates a flood of hormones to feed his muscles.

Surgeons seal the boy's medical wounds.

Already, the child is no longer human. Tonight's work has seen to that. Time will reveal just how different the boy will become.

He is a teenage boy, standing over another dead body.

This corpse is not like the first. This corpse is the same age as the boy, and in its last moments of life it had struggled with all its strength, desperate not to die.

The boy drops his weapon. The serrated knife falls to the ground.

Legion masters come to him. Their eyes are red, their dark armour immense. Skulls hang from their pauldrons and plastrons on chains of blackened bronze.

He draws breath to speak, to tell them it was an accident. They silence him.

'Well done,' they say.

And they call him *brother*.

He is a teenage boy, and the rifle is heavy in his hands.

He watches for a long, long time. He has trained for this. He knows how to slow his hearts, how to regulate his breathing and the biological beats of his body until his entire form remains as still as a statue.

Predator. Prey. His mind goes cold, his focus absolute. The mantra chanted internally becomes the only way to see the world. *Predator. Prey. Hunter. Hunted.* Nothing else matters.

He squeezes the trigger. One thousand metres away, a man dies.

'Target eliminated,' he says.

He is a young man, sleeping on the same surgery table as before.

In a slumber demanded by the chemicals flowing through his veins, he dreams once again of his first murder. In the waking world, needles and medical probes bore into the flesh of his back, injecting fluids directly into his spinal column.

His slumbering body reacts to the invasion, coughing once. Acidic spit leaves his lips, hissing on the ground where it lands, eating into the tiled floor.

When he wakes, hours later, he feels the sockets running down his spine. The scars, the metallic nodules…

In a universe where no gods exist, he knows this is the closest mortality can come to divinity.

He is a young man, staring into his own eyes.

He stands naked in a dark chamber, in a lined rank with a dozen other souls. Other initiates standing with him, also stripped of clothing, the marks of their surgeries fresh upon their pale skin. He barely notices them. Sexuality is a forgotten concept, alien to his mind, merely one of ten thousand humanities his consciousness has discarded. He no longer recalls the face of his mother and father. He only recalls his own name because his Legion masters never changed it.

He looks into the eyes that are now his. They stare back, slanted and murder-red, set in a helmet with its facial plate painted white. The blood-eyed, bone-pale skull watches him as he watches it.

This is his face now. Through these eyes, he will see the galaxy. Through this skulled helm he will cry his wrath at those who dare defy the Emperor's vision for mankind.

'You are Talos,' a Legion master says, 'of First Claw, Tenth Company.'

* * *

He is a young man, utterly inhuman, immortal and undying.

He sees the surface of this world through crimson vision, with data streaming in sharp, clear white runic language across his retinas. He sees the life forces of his brothers in the numbers displayed. He feels the temperature outside his sealed war armour. He sees targeting sights flicker as they follow the movements of his eyes, and feels his hand, the hand clutching his bolter, tense as it tries to follow each target lock. Ammunition counters display how many have died this day.

Around him, aliens die. Ten, a hundred, a thousand. His brothers butcher their way through a city of violet crystal, bolters roaring and chainswords howling. Here and there in the opera of battle-noise, a brother screams his rage through helm-amplifiers.

The sound is always the same. Bolters always roar. Chainblades always howl. Space Marines always cry their fury. When the VIII Legion wages war, the sound is that of lions and wolves slaying each other while vultures shriek above.

He cries words that he will one day never shout again – words that will soon become ash on his tongue. Already he cries the words without thinking about them, without *feeling* them.

For the Emperor.

He is a young man, awash in the blood of humans.

He shouts words without the heart to feel them, declaring concepts of Imperial justice and deserved vengeance. A man claws at his armour, begging and pleading.

'We are loyal! We have surrendered!'

The young man breaks the human's face with the butt of his bolter. Surrendering so late was a meaningless gesture. Their blood must run as an example, and the rest of the system's worlds would fall into line.

Around him, the riot continues unabated. Soon, his bolter is silenced, voiceless with no shells to fire. Soon after that, his chainsword dies, clogged with meat.

The Night Lords resort to killing the humans with their bare hands, dark gauntlets punching and strangling and crushing.

At a timeless point in the melee, the voice of an ally comes over the vox. It is an Imperial Fist. Their Legion watches from the bored security of their landing site.

'What are you doing?' the Imperial Fist demands. 'Brothers, are you insane?'

Talos does not answer. They do not deserve an answer. If the Fists had brought this world into compliance themselves, the Night Lords would never have needed to come here.

* * *

He is a young man, watching his home world burn.

He is a young man, mourning a father soon to die.

He is a traitor to everything he once held sacred.

STABBING LIGHTS LANCED through the gloom.

The salvage team moved slowly, neither patient nor impatient, but with the confident care of men with an arduous job to do and no deadline to meet. The team spread out across the chamber, overturning debris, examining the markings of weapons fire on the walls, their internal vox clicking as they spoke to one another.

With the ship open to the void, each of the salvage team wore atmosphere suits against the airless cold. They communicated as often by sign language as they did by words.

This interested the hunter that watched them, because he too was fluent in Adeptus Astartes battle sign. Curious, to see his enemies betray themselves so easily.

The hunter watched in silence as the spears of illumination cut this way and that, revealing the wreckage of the battles that had taken place on this deck of the abandoned vessel. The salvage team – who were clearly genhanced, but too small and unarmoured to be full Space Marines – were crippled by the atmosphere suits they wore. Such confinement limited their senses, while the hunter's ancient Mark IV war plate only enhanced his. They could not hear as he heard, nor see as he saw. That reduced their chances of survival from incredibly unlikely to absolutely none.

Smiling at the thought, the hunter whispered to the machine-spirit of his armour, a single word that enticed the war plate's soul with the knowledge that the hunt was beginning in earnest.

'Preysight.'

His vision blurred to the blue of the deepest oceans, decorated by supernova heat smears of moving, living beings. The hunter watched the team move on, separating into two teams, each of two men.

This was going to be entertaining.

TALOS FOLLOWED THE first team, shadowing them through the corridors, knowing the grating purr of his power armour and the snarling of its servo-joints were unheard by the sense-dimmed salvagers.

Salvagers was perhaps the wrong word, of course. Disrespectful to the foe.

While they were not full Space Marines, their gene-enhancement was obvious in the bulk of their bodies and the lethal grace of their motions. They, too, were hunters – just weaker examples of the breed.

Initiates.

Their icon, mounted on each shoulder plate, displayed a drop of ruby blood framed by proud angelic wings.

The hunter's pale lips curled into another crooked smile. This was unexpected. The Blood Angels had sent in a team of Scouts...

The Night Lord had little time for notions of coincidence. If the Angels were here, then they were here on the hunt. Perhaps the *Covenant of Blood* had been detected on the long-range sensors of a Blood Angel battlefleet. Such a discovery would certainly have been enough to bring them here.

Hunting for their precious sword, no doubt. And not for the first time.

Perhaps this was their initiation ceremony? A test of prowess? Bring back the blade and earn passage into the Chapter...

Oh, how unfortunate.

The stolen blade hung at the hunter's hip, as it had for years now. Tonight would not be the night it found its way back into the desperate reach of the Angels. But, as always, they were welcome to sell their lives in the attempt at reclamation.

Talos monitored the readout of his retinal displays. The temptation to blink-click certain runes was strong, but he resisted the urge. This hunt would be easy enough without combat narcotics flooding his blood. Purity lay in abstaining from such things until they became necessary.

The location runes of his brothers in First Claw flickered on his visor display. Taking note of their positions elsewhere in the ship, the hunter moved forward to shed the blood of those enslaved to the Throne of Lies.

A true hunter did not avoid being seen by his prey. Such stalking was the act of cowards and carrion-eaters, revealing themselves only when the prey was slain. Where was the skill in that? Where was the thrill?

A Night Lord was raised to hunt by other, truer principles.

Talos ghosted through the shadows, judging the strength of the Scouts' suits' audio-receptors. Just how much could they hear...

He followed them down a corridor, his gauntleted knuckles scraping along the metal walls.

The Blood Angels turned instantly, stabbing his face with their beam-lighting.

That almost worked, the hunter had to give it to them. These lesser hunters knew their prey – they knew they hunted Night Lords. For half a heartbeat, sunfire would have blazed across his vision, blinding him.

Talos ignored the beams completely. He tracked by preysight. Their tactics were meaningless.

He was already gone when they opened fire, melting into the shadows of a side corridor.

* * *

HE CAUGHT THEM again nine minutes later.

This time, he lay in wait after baiting a beautiful trap. The sword they came for was right in their path.

It was called *Aurum*. Words barely did its craftsmanship justice. Forged when the Emperor's Great Crusade took its first steps into the stars, the blade was forged for one of the Blood Angel Legion's first heroes. It had come into Talos's possession centuries later, when he'd murdered *Aurum's* heir.

It was almost amusing, how often the sons of Sanguinius tried to reclaim the sword from him. It was much less amusing how often he had to kill his own brothers when they sought to take the blade from his dead hands. Avarice shattered all unity, even among Legion brothers.

The Scouts saw their Chapter relic now, so long denied their grasp. The golden blade was embedded into the dark metal decking, its angel-winged crosspiece turned to ivory under the harsh glare of their stabbing lights.

An invitation to simply advance into the chamber and take it, but it was so obviously a trap. Yet... how could they resist?

They did not resist.

The initiates were alert, bolters high and panning fast, senses keen. The hunter saw their mouths moving as they voxed continuous updates to each other.

Talos let go of the ceiling.

He thudded to the deck behind one of the initiates, gauntlets snapping forward to clutch the Scout.

The other Angel turned and fired. Talos laughed at the zeal in his eyes, at the tightness of his clenched teeth, as the initiate fired three bolts into the body of his brother.

The Night Lord gripped the convulsing human shield against him, seeing the temperature gauge on his retinal display flicker as the dying initiate's blood hit sections of his war plate. In his grip, the shuddering Angel was little more than a burst sack of freezing meat. The bolt shells had detonated, coming close to killing him and opening the suit to the void.

'Good shooting, Angel,' Talos spoke through his helm's crackling vox-speakers. He threw his bleeding shield aside and leapt for the other initiate, fingers splayed like talons.

The fight was mercilessly brief. The Night Lord's full gene-enhancements coupled with the heightened strength of his armour's engineered muscle fibre-cables meant there was only one possible outcome. Talos backhanded the bolter from the Angel's grip and clawed at the initiate.

As the weaker warrior writhed, Talos stroked his gauntleted fingertips across the clear face-visor of the initiate's atmosphere suit.

'This looks fragile,' he said.

The Scout shouted something unheard. Hate burned in his eyes. Talos wasted several seconds just enjoying that expression. That passion.

He crashed his fist against the visor, smashing it to shards.

As one corpse froze and another swelled and ruptured on its way to asphyxiation, the Night Lord retrieved his blade, the sword he claimed by right of conquest, and moved back into the darkest parts of the ship.

'TALOS,' THE VOICE came over the vox in a sibilant hiss.

'Speak, Uzas.'

'They have sent initiates to hunt us, brother. I had to cancel my prey-sight to make sure my eyes were seeing clearly. *Initiates. Against us.*'

'Spare me your indignation. What do you want?'

Uzas's reply was a low growl and a crackle of dead vox. Talos put it from his mind. He had long grown bored of Uzas forever lamenting each time they met with insignificant prey.

'Cyrion,' he voxed.

'Aye. Talos?'

'Of course.'

'Forgive me. I thought it would be Uzas with another rant. I hear your decks are crawling with Angels. Epic glories to be earned in slaughtering their infants, eh?'

Talos didn't quite sigh. 'Are you almost done?'

'This hulk is as hollow as Uzas's head, brother. Negative on anything of worth. Not even a servitor to steal. I'm returning to the boarding pod now. Unless you need help shooting the Angels' children?'

Talos killed the vox-link as he stalked through the black corridor. This was fruitless. Time to leave – empty-handed and still desperately short on supplies. This… this *piracy* offended him now, as it always did, and as it always had since they'd been cut off from the Legion decades ago. A plague upon the long-dead Warmaster and his failures which still echoed today. A curse upon the night the VIII Legion was shattered and scattered across the stars.

Diminished. Reduced. Surviving as disparate warbands – broken echoes of the unity within loyalist Chapters.

Sins of the father.

This curious ambush by the Angels who had tracked them here was nothing more than a minor diversion. Talos was about to vox a general withdrawal after the last initiates were hunted down and slain, when his vox went live again.

'Brother,' said Xarl. 'I've found the Angels.'

'As have Uzas and I. Kill them quickly and let's get back to the *Covenant.*'

'No, Talos.' Xarl's voice was edged with anger. 'Not initiates. The real Angels.'

* * *

THE NIGHT LORDS of First Claw, Tenth Company, came together like wolves in the wild. Stalking through the darkened chambers of the ship, the four hunters met in the shadows, speaking over their vox-link, crouching with their weapons at the ready.

In Talos's hands, the relic blade *Aurum* caught what little light remained, glinting as he moved.

'Five of them,' Xarl spoke low, his voice edged with his suppressed eagerness. 'We can take five. They stand bright and proud in a control chamber not far from our boarding pod.' He racked his bolter. 'We can take five,' he repeated.

'They're just waiting?' Cyrion said. 'They must be expecting an honest fight.'

Uzas snorted at that.

'This is your fault, you know,' Cyrion said with a chuckle, nodding at Talos. 'You and that damn sword.'

'It keeps things interesting,' Talos replied. 'And I cherish every curse that their Chapter screams at me.'

He stopped speaking, narrowing his eyes for a moment. Cyrion's skulled helm blurred before him. As did Xarl's. The sound of distant bolter fire echoed in his ears, not distorted by the faint crackle of helm-filtered noise. Not a true sound. Not a real memory. Something akin to both.

'I… have a…' Talos blinked to clear his fading vision. Shadows of vast things darkened his sight. '…have a plan…'

'Brother?' Cyrion asked.

Talos shivered once, his servo-joints snarling at the shaking movement. Magnetically clasped to his thigh, his bolter didn't fall to the decking, but the golden blade did. It clattered to the steel floor with a clang.

'Talos?' Xarl asked.

'No,' Uzas growled, 'not *now.*'

Talos's head jerked once, as if his armour had sent an electrical pulse through his spine, and he crashed to the ground in a clash of war plate on metal.

'The god-machines of Crythe…' he murmured. 'They have killed the sun.'

A moment later, he started screaming.

THE OTHERS HAD to cut Talos out of the squad's internal vox-link. His screams drowned out all other speech.

'We can take five of them,' Xarl said. 'Three of us remain. We can take five Angels.'

'Almost certainly,' Cyrion agreed. 'And if they summon squads of their initiates?'

'Then we slaughter five of them *and* their initiates.'

Uzas cut in. 'We were slaying our way across the stars ten thousand years before they were even born.'

'Yes, while that's a wonderful parable, I don't need rousing rhetoric,' Cyrion said. 'I need a plan.'

'We hunt,' Uzas and Xarl said at once.

'We kill them,' Xarl added.

'We feast on their gene-seed,' Uzas finished.

'If this was an award ceremony for fervency and zeal, once again, you'd both be collapsing under the weight of medals. But you want to launch an assault on their position while we drag Talos with us? I think the scraping of his armour over the floor will rather kill the element of stealth, brothers.'

'Guard him, Cyrion,' Xarl said. 'Uzas and I will take the Angels.'

'Two against five.' Cyrion's red eye lenses didn't quite fix upon his brother's. 'Those are poor odds, Xarl.'

'Then we will finally be rid of each other,' Xarl grunted. 'Besides, we've had worse.'

That was true, at least.

'*Ave Dominus Nox*,' Cyrion said. 'Hunt well and hunt fast.'

'*Ave Dominus Nox*,' the other two replied.

CYRION LISTENED FOR a while to his brother's screams. It was difficult to make any sense from the stream of shouted words.

This came as no surprise. Cyrion had heard Talos suffering in the grip of this affliction many times before. As gene-gifts went, it was barely a blessing.

Sins of the father, he thought, watching Talos's inert armour, listening to the cries of death to come. *How they are reflected within the son.*

ACCORDING TO CYRION'S retinal chrono display, one hour and sixteen minutes had passed when he heard the explosion.

The decking shuddered under his boots.

'Xarl? Uzas?'

Static was the only answer.

Great.

WHEN UZAS'S VOICE finally broke over the vox after two hours, it was weak and coloured by his characteristic bitterness.

'Hnngh. Cyrion. It's done. Drag the prophet.'

'You sound like you got shot,' Cyrion resisted the urge to smile in case they heard it in his words.

'He did,' Xarl said. 'We're on our way back.'

'What was that detonation?'

'Plasma cannon.'

'You're… you're joking.'

'Not even for a second. I have no idea why they brought one of those to a fight in a ship's innards, but the coolant feeds made for a ripe target.'

Cyrion blink-clicked a rune by Xarl's identification symbol. It opened a private channel between the two of them.

'Who hit Uzas?'

'An initiate. From behind, with a sniper rifle.'

Cyrion immediately closed the link so no one would hear him laughing.

THE COVENANT OF BLOOD was a blade of cobalt darkness, bronze-edged and scarred by centuries of battle. It drifted through the void, sailing close to its prey like a shark gliding through black waters.

The *Encarmine Soul* was a Gladius-class frigate with a long and proud history of victories in the name of the Blood Angels Chapter – and before it, the IX Legion. It opened fire on the *Covenant of Blood* with an admirable array of weapons batteries.

Briefly, beautifully, the void shields around the Night Lords strike cruiser shimmered in a display reminiscent of oil on water.

The *Covenant of Blood* returned fire. Within a minute, the blade-like ship was sailing through void debris, its lances cooling from their momentary fury. The *Encarmine Soul*, what little chunks were left of it, clanked and sparked off the larger cruiser's void shields as it passed through the expanding cloud of wreckage.

Another ship, this one stricken and dead in space, soon fell under the *Covenant's* shadow. The strike cruiser obscured the sun, pulling in close, ready to receive its boarding pod once again.

First Claw had been away for seven hours investigating the hulk. Their mothership had come hunting for them.

BULKHEAD SEALS HISSED as the reinforced doors opened on loud, grinding hinges.

Xarl and Cyrion carried Talos into the *Covenant's* deployment bay. Uzas walked behind them, a staggering limp marring his gait. His spine was on fire from the sniper's solid slug that still lodged there. Worse, his genhanced healing had sealed and clotted the wound. He'd need surgery – or more likely a knife and a mirror – to tear the damn thing out.

One of the Atramentar, elite guard of the Exalted, stood in its hulking Terminator war plate. His skull-painted, tusked helm stared impassively. Trophy racks adorned his back, each one impaled with several helms from a number of loyalist Chapters: a history of bloodshed and betrayal, proudly displayed for his brothers to see.

It nodded to Talos's prone form.

'The Soul Hunter is wounded?' the Terminator asked, its voice a deep, rumbling growl.

'No,' Cyrion said. 'Inform the Exalted at once. His prophet is suffering another vision.'

HAMMER

AND

BOLTER

ISSUE 12

◄ TIME OF LEGENDS ►

AENARION

Gav Thorpe

THE WORLD HAD been torn asunder. Across the isle of Ulthuan the elves quailed in their towers as the skies burned with purple and blue fire and the fields and mountains heaved. Nightmare voices howled and bellowed while leering faces tortured the dark clouds that swirled around the mountain peaks and snarled in the waves of the Inner Sea.

The daemons came in their thousands; a horde of baying, shrieking slaughter. Against such ferocity and spite the elves had no defence. They fell to infernal blade and savage claw; elder and babe, lords and ladies, dragged screaming to their deaths by the minions of the Chaos Gods.

The world seemed fated to an eternity of torment.

Out of the madness arose Aenarion. He would not see his people destroyed and so called upon the gods to deliver the elves from destruction; but the gods were silent. Aenarion could see nothing but doom for the world and so he offered himself to Asuryan, lord of the gods. He strode into the Eternal Flame with oaths of sacrifice upon his lips. The flames burned bright and Aenarion was consumed. Yet the elven lord was spared the wrath of Asuryan and received the blessing of the gods. He emerged from the fire filled with a fey light and took up spear and bow to fight the daemons.

The elves proclaimed Aenarion the Defender, the blessed Phoenix King of Asuryan, and where he led others followed; where he fought, the daemons were thrown back. Great were his victories and many are the tales told elsewhere of the Phoenix King's battles. Mighty heroes rallied to Aenarion's banner; elves such as Caledor the Dragontamer, greatest of the elven mages, and Eoloran Anar who first raised the Phoenix King's standard; names forever entwined with the legend of the first Phoenix King.

After much war, peace settled upon Ulthuan again. Aenarion came to the court of the Everqueen, Astarielle, ruler of the elves from the time before Chaos. The two were wed and lived in happiness, bringing into the world their son Morelion and their daughter Yvraine.

Yet legends are not born in times of prosperity and contentment, but are created in ages of woe and strife. The peace for which Aenarion had fought so hard did not last forever, and so it was that the daemons returned to ravage the land. This time there was no surcease from the bloodshed. For a hundred years the daemons assailed the isle of the elves. Aenarion and his armies were ever hard-pressed, fighting many battles across Ulthuan. It was at Caethrin Gorge that the future of the elves would be changed forever.

LAUGHTER CACKLED ON the unnatural wind that swept down between the slopes of Tir Alinith and Anul Caethrin. The sky was heavy with clouds of purple and green, blazes of black and red flashing across the Chaotic storm. The stench of sulphur and decay carried along the gorge, heralding the daemonic host boiling up from the plains towards the mountains in the south of Ulthuan.

On the dark volcanic slopes stood Aenarion. Gold shone from his armour, his tapered shield and the tip of his long spear. Around him were arranged the lords of the elves, swathed in scales of silver, adorned with sapphire and emerald. No less shimmering were the scales of the dragons that circled overhead, watching for the approaching Chaotic horde; red and blue, bronze and ebon.

Aenarion gazed down the long valley, lifting a long-fingered hand to shield his dark eyes against the magical glare above. Black hair trailed from beneath the Phoenix King's gilded helm and whipped across his scarlet cloak. Behind him stood Eoloran, a golden stave in hand from which flew the banner of Aenarion; the white of death embroidered with a phoenix rising from multi-coloured flames. The lord of the Anars watched in silence as Aenarion turned to his left, where stood Caledor the Dragontamer, mage-lord of Ulthuan. It was by Caledor's hand that the Phoenix King's armour and weapons had been forged, in the temple of the Smith-God Vaul, hidden amongst the fires of the volcanoes behind the elven army.

The Phoenix King spoke calmly, showing no sign of apprehension.

'The time has come for you to unleash such enchantments as you possess, Caledor.'

The Dragontamer turned his gaze upon his king, eyes alight with mystical energy.

'Tis a dangerous path to tread; to turn the powers of the foe upon them. That power that keeps your speartip keen and your armour sure is the same that brings forth these abominations. I fear that the more we delve into that well, the greater the horrors we bring forth. This is not the gentle magic that our ancestors learned, but a dangerous sorcery that it would be wise to diminish.'

The Phoenix King replied quickly.

'It is not the time to speak again of this plan of yours. Battle is at hand and I would no more ask you to keep your incantations unsaid than I would lay down my spear. All that matters this day is that we are victorious. Should we fail, the Anvil of Vaul would fall to our foes. How then will your mages and priests arm us for this war?'

Caledor shook his head and took a deep breath. His blue robes fluttered in the wind as he stretched wide his arms. At the foot of the valley the daemons could be seen; a mass of riotous colour in many sizes and forms.

Creatures with blood-red skin advanced bearing swords of gleaming bronze, their commanders riding upon the back of brazen-horned beasts with bodies of metal and crimson flesh. Hounds the size of horses, with hides of red scales, bounded to the fore, baying and howling from mouths filled with fangs of iron. Loathsome slugs with frond-ringed faces slithered and lurched across the ground, leaving burning trails of acidic slime. Cyclopean daemons brandishing rusted blades advanced in long columns, leaking fluids from suppurating spores, innards bulging from rents in their bloated stomachs, the air seething thick with black flies. In contrast to the mournful carnival of decay, lithe daemonettes with lobster-claw hands and bird-like feet sprang sprightly across the rocks. Others of their kind rode upon sinuous bipedal mounts with long flicking tongues while six-limbed beasts raced alongside, sharp claws clattering and clicking. Buzzing with magical power, smaller creatures cavorted and cartwheeled, pink bodies constantly writhing and changing, sparks of energy flying from splayed fingers. Above them swooped and swerved menacing shapes with barbed lashes for tails, flat bodies edged with teeth and hooks, cutting the thick air with piercing screams.

Against the Chaotic mass, the elves seemed pitifully few; a knot of a few hundred warriors whose gleaming weapons were as a candle in an eternal night, pinpricks of light across the black slope. The light grew in strength, swimming around the warriors, forming in tendrils of energy that streamed from Caledor's outstretched fingertips. The light turned to a white flame that formed a flickering ring around the elven host, the fires reaching higher and higher into a column that pierced the dark clouds above.

Where the light struck, the storm clouds spun, whirling faster and faster, mixing with the swirling light to form a vortex of energy. Battle raged within the whirlwind, white clashed with colour, light with darkness, sparks and forks of power coruscating across the surface as the maelstrom drew tighter and tighter, speeding until it was a blaze of power.

With a thunderous detonation, the vortex collapsed, earthing itself through the body of Caledor. The mage trembled, light shining through skin, burning from wide eyes, coils of shimmering magic steaming through gritted teeth, his mane of white hair wild in the aetheric gale. All became still for a moment and the mage's trembling ceased, the air pregnant with expectation.

With a piercing cry, Caledor thrust forward his hands, the magic blazing from his palms. Spears of white fire screamed down the valley, turning and twisting about each other, spreading out into a sheet of blazing flame.

The spell struck the foremost daemons like a hurricane, hurling them through the air, their bodies disintegrating into shards of crystal and streamers of multicoloured particles. Plaintive wails were torn from vanishing throats and then silence fell.

For a moment the daemons halted. Aenarion and his followers glowered down at them, fists tight around their weapons, eyes narrowed.

With a howl the horde surge on again.

'To me, princes of Ulthuan!' cried Aenarion, spear aloft piercing the fume-filled air.

In silvered line, the elven lords stood resolute against the encroaching darkness of the daemon host. Smoke and mist was set awhirl by the thunderous flap of wings as the dragons descended from the thermals above. The largest, of silver and blue hide, landed in front of the Phoenix King, black claws sending splinters of rock cascading down the mountainside. The monstrous creature's long neck bent around and its azure eyes fell upon Aenarion. Indraugnir was his name, older even than the elves, the greatest creature to have ever flown the skies of Ulthuan. Its voice came as a rumble that stirred the hearts of the elves even as it shook the ground.

'As we have fought to protect your lands, now we fight to protect mine. Take up your spear, king of the elves, and test its sharpness against my claws and fangs. We shall see who claims the greater tally.'

Aenarion laughed and he raced forward to pull himself up to the throne-saddle upon the dragon's back.

'Never could I best your ferocity, Indraugnir. If I could wield a dozen spears I would not match your might!'

The two circled into the heavy skies to join other princes of the mountains riding upon the backs of dragons that dwelt in the caves beneath the volcanoes. Beneath them spread the daemonic army, stretching along the Caethrin Gorge as far as the plains, thousands-strong and advancing swiftly. Behind, the fumaroles and craters of the mountains steamed; the lands of Caledor, named after the Dragontamer who ruled here. Far below, the mage unleashed another spell, bolts of blue lightning springing from his staff, crackling through the ranks of the enemy.

Many princes brought forth bows forged beneath the mountains, and set upon their strings shafts that glittered with mystical light. They loosed their arrows upon the daemons, the missiles arcing far into the valley to descend as thunderbolts that struck down a handful of daemons with every shot.

On came the daemons still, filling the air with lewd threats and snarls of hatred.

Indraugnir circled slowly, wing dipped as he took the Phoenix King down towards the gorge. The daemons were no more than fifty paces from the thin line of elves. At the heart of the nobles of Ulthuan, Eoloran Anar stepped up, the banner of Aenarion held in both hands. With a shout of Asuryan's consecration that was lost on the wind, he planted the standard at his feet, the rock cracking under the golden haft. A dome of white light sprang forth from the flagbearer, enclosing the elven line. Where it touched the daemons, they were hurled back, their unholy flesh set afire by its touch. Like rabid animals, the creatures of the Chaos Gods launched themselves at the barrier, driving themselves and each other into the wall of magic, crumbling to ashes and dust as they did so.

Aenarion raised his spear to attract the attention of the other dragon-riders. He plunged its point towards the rear of the daemon army. The others waved lance and sword and spear in acknowledgement.

'Dive, my friend!' cried the Phoenix King. 'Into their heart like a dagger!'

Indraugnir gave a bellow and folded his wings tight, swooping down towards the rocks. Around the pair the princes of Caledor and their reptilian mounts descended with fierce battle cries and fearsome growls. The crest of Aenarion's helm whistled in the wind, his hair and cloak streaming behind him. The Phoenix King gritted his teeth and gripped his spear tight as he felt the reverberations of Indraugnir's massive heart thumping in the dragon's chest.

Down and down they dived, wind screaming, the ground racing towards them. From out of the mass the Phoenix King now spied individuals, many with faces upturned, glaring and snarling at their fast-approaching foe.

Just as it seemed that monster and rider might be dashed against the black mountainside, Indraugnir opened his wings. The two of them shot across the daemon army, Indraugnir's claws raking huge welts through their numbers, leaving dismembered and beheaded remains in his wake.

Flipping a wing, the dragon turned sharply as Aenarion dipped his spearhead towards the daemons. Trailing a blaze of white, the weapon carved a furrow across the chests of a dozen foes, slicing them in twain. Dark red fire erupted from Indraugnir's mouth, engulfing the daemons in their hundreds. Aenarion thrust and slashed without respite, every blow of his spear cutting down many foes.

Indraugnir landed, crushing more daemons beneath his bulk. Aenarion leapt from his saddle-throne, pinning another daemon beneath his speartip as he landed on the floor of the rocky valley. Dragon and king fought side-by-side; Aenarion's spear a white blur of destruction, Indraugnir's fangs and claws rending and tearing all that came within reach, tail snapping and cracking behind.

Around and about them the dragon princes struck, every pass heralded by a rush of wind from beneath a dragon's wings and completed with a clutch of bodies cast into the air. Higher up the slope, Caledor and Eoloran led the elven lords down into the melee, swords and spears flickering. As a fire burns across a piece of parchment, the line of elves surely advanced, leaving naught but the ruin of the daemons behind.

From noon 'til the sun was low in the skies the slaughter went on; slaughter, for it could not be truly called battle. Outnumbered by hundreds of foes, the elves were relentless and unstoppable, not a single one amongst their number fell to their enemies. As their numbers lessened, the daemons' power waned and the Chaotic storm above abated, the clouds driven away even as the army was driven back. As the final rays of dusk cut across the dark mountains, the last of the daemons crumbled and perished, their spirits banished back to the immaterial realm from which they had sprung.

At the centre of the gorge, surrounded by piles of daemonic corpses that bubbled and hissed and dissipated into fog, Aenarion stood proud. Eoloran came up to him bearing the white banner. He handed the standard to his lord, who waved it high overhead to signal the victory. Songs of celebration rang down the valley, the clear voices of the elves giving word to the joy and relief in their hearts.

THAT NIGHT, AENARION made his camp upon the mountainside, not far from the winding pathway that led up to the ruddily-lit cave that housed the Anvil of Vaul. The happiness of victory had passed and the camp was quiet as the elves remembered that many had been the triumphs over the daemons, and yet still the foe was not vanquished. In the still night, the ring of hammers and the chime of metal sounded as the priests of the Smith-God continued their labours; a timely reminder to all that the war was not over.

Eoloran and Caledor attended to their Phoenix King in his white pavilion. Still clad in his golden armour, Aenarion sat upon a simple throne of dark wood, his cloak tossed thoughtlessly across its back. The favoured lord of Asuryan smiled as they entered, but the Dragontamer did not share Aenarion's pleasure.

'None fell today, and for that I am grateful,' said Caledor. 'Yet it has not always been the case. The power of Asuryan's blessing protects you,

Aenarion, but it does not make our people invulnerable. Our foe is without number, and they are truly eternal. I have looked upon this devastated world and see that Ulthuan is not just an isle upon the sea, but an island of light in darkness. Our foes cannot be defeated by sword or spear.'

Aenarion gave a weary sigh.

'You would speak again of your plan to rid the world of magic,' said the Phoenix King. 'How many times must I tell you that it is folly to do away with that power which gives us the most strength to fight?'

'While the gales of magic that sweep our realm may be harnessed to our benefit, without them the daemons could not exist. You saw today what my vortex could do if writ on a larger scale. Without the sustaining properties of this magical wind, the daemons would no longer be able to venture here in numbers. It would take only a little preparation, a number of lodestones carefully arranged around the isle, to ready Ulthuan for the enchantment.'

The Phoenix King said nothing, for the two of them had spent many years arguing the case for Caledor's plan. It was Eoloran that broke the silence.

'The risks are too great, Caledor. Should you be wrong, your plan would leave us defenceless. It is only by the touch of magic that these apparitions can be destroyed. Without the magic our swords would be useless, our spears and arrows no more weapons than the branches of a tree.'

'We cannot prevail,' argued the Dragontamer. 'For a hundred turns of the world we have fought, and we are no step closer to victory now than on that first day. For every daemon we destroy, another springs up in its place. You stand in the flooding pool bailing as quickly as you can, while you should dam the spring that feeds it.'

Aenarion said nothing but his look was troubled, brow creased in thought. Eoloran addressed his king, breaking Aenarion from his contemplation.

'What concerns sit so heavily upon your shoulders, my lord?'

'I am troubled by the ease of our victory this day. Our enemies are not only great in number, there are those daemons amongst the host that can match the best of us by themselves. Yet where were these greater daemons today? Only chaff and fodder were sent against us. I have an ill feeling about this.'

Caledor pondered this for a moment, stroking his bottom lip with a slender finger.

'You think that perhaps the greatest daemon warriors are elsewhere?'

'Perhaps,' replied the Phoenix King.

Eoloran glanced between his two companions with an expression of worry.

'If this attack was a diversion, we have fallen for the ploy,' said the lord of the Anars. 'If the Anvil of Vaul was not the object of our foes' desire, then where would the real blow land?'

Aenarion growled and clasped his hands tightly in his lap.

'I do not know what our enemies seek to achieve; it is that which vexes me.'

THE NIGHT WAS bitterly chill. Frost crusted the black rocks of the mountainside, a glittering reflection of the stars in the clear skies above. Upon the slopes dragons basked in the pale moonlight, wings outstretched, bodies steaming in the cold air. The wind sighed over the stones, broken by the rasping exhalations of the beasts.

Indraugnir lifted his silver-scaled head, nostrils flaring. The other dragons responded to the movement, rising from their slumber with a scrape of claws and explosive breaths misting the air. All turned their eyes northwards, where a dark shape flitted across the starry sky. It sped closer, resolving into the silhouette of a large eagle, a young elf clasping tightly to its back. The eagle circled once, followed by the predatory stares of the dragons, and descended in a flapping of wings. The rider's black hair tossed behind him like a veil, his narrow face pinched, eyes tight against the cold

'I must speak with the Phoenix King!' declared the new arrival as he leapt from the back of the enormous bird.

Brought forth by the call, other elves came out of their tents, weary from the day's fighting. The stranger was garbed in smooth black leathers, his shoulders and back hidden beneath a long cloak of black feathers. All recognised him as a raven herald, one of the order of scouts that followed the movements of the daemons across Ulthuan.

The herald was directed to the Phoenix King's pavilion without delay, and a crowd of elves followed him into the marquee to hear what news he brought. Eoloran and Caledor were first amongst them. The Phoenix King sat brooding upon his throne and looked up at the disturbance.

'What news brings Telrianir so far south on such a bitter night?' asked Aenarion.

'"Tis a bitter night indeed, my king, and not for the weather alone,' replied the raven herald. His gaze was fixed upon the Phoenix King; his lip trembled as he spoke and a tear formed in his eye. 'The daemons have fallen upon Avelorn, my king, in a great army beyond counting.'

A disquieted whispering spread through the elves. Aenarion's fingers tightened upon the arms of his chair at the mention of the Everqueen's realm. He leaned forwards, piercing Telrianir with his stare. The raven herald continued hesitantly, his voice breaking with grief.

'The sacred groves have been despoiled and many were slain.'

The whispering became cries of dismay. Aenarion rose to his feet, fear flashing across his face.

'What of the Everqueen?' he snarled. 'What of my children?'

At this, Telrianir fell to his knees, a sob wrenched from his lips.

'Slain, my king.'

The silence was a deep as the ocean's depths, swallowing all sound so that it was not broken by the slightest clink of armour nor scuff of foot. Not even a sigh broke the stillness.

Aenarion slumped back into his throne, head bowed. The wood of the seat splintered between his fingers and the light of Asuryan that forever glowed faintly through his skin grew in brightness. The elves were forced to look away, such was the glare from their king. Then, like a lantern snuffed out, the light disappeared.

Blinking, the elves looked at Aenarion. He straightened and all save Caledor flinched from the king's gaze. A fire burned in his eyes, each a red ember fringed with darkness, drawing gasps from many that saw it.

'Slain?'

Aenarion's voice was hollow as it filled the pavilion. The elven princes, whose lives had been filled with battle and terror, clasped each other in their fright; that one word echoed with grief and rage through the core of their spirits. None dared speak.

Aenarion rose up to his full height, seeming taller than ever before. His fingers curled into fists at his side as he turned his gaze upwards, not seeing the roof of the tent but staring into the heavens beyond. When he spoke next, the Phoenix King's tone was calm in manner, but carried with it a sharp edge of anger.

'What a cruel fate it is that Morai-heg has spun for me. When our people were beset, I called upon the gods to harken to our cries of woe, but they did not listen. I called upon Asuryan, lord of the lords, greatest of the divine, and I offered myself to him for his aid. He laid his blessing upon me, and with his light I have battled the darkness that would engulf our world.'

Aenarion's eyes fell upon the elves and they cowered further, retreating across the rugs strewn over the floor of the pavilion.

'I did as I was bid. I took up my spear and my shield, and I stood against the daemons. For a hundred years we have shed our blood in defence of our homes, suffered torture of the spirit and bleak nightmares so that we might one day look upon the summer skies again. Many have been taken from us, the innocent beside the warrior, the babe beside the mother. Each was a sacrifice harder to bear than my own pain within the flames, but I bore each and every without complaint. If the gods demand that some must pay for the lives of others, it was a price we had to pay.'

Aenarion snatched up his throne and heaved it over his head. With a wordless shout, he dashed it to the ground, smashing it into pieces.

'No more!' he roared. 'This is a price too heavy for me to pay!'

Aenarion's gaze next fell upon his banner, hanging limply in its stand beside him. He snapped the pole across his armoured knee and tore the cloth from the gilded wood. Opening the flag, he looked at the emblazoned phoenix for a long time, limbs trembling, lips twisted in a sneer.

The ripping of the cloth made every elf shudder, as if each had been torn apart by their king's hands. Aenarion let the two ragged pieces of cloth flutter to the ground. He fell to his knees and tore the pieces into ribbons, casting them about himself like streamers. Tears of yellow flame rolled down his cheeks.

'Asuryan has no love for me,' he sobbed. 'He does not care for us. He cannot protect us from the evil that will swallow us whole if we do not fight. I cannot be the Defender, there is nothing left for me to defend. We are lost, destroyed.'

All of a sudden, Aenarion stopped. His eyes narrowed and he tilted his head to one side as if listening to a distant voice. His voice became a feral growl.

'There is only one course left to me that can ease this pain. I will destroy every creature of Chaos. I will annihilate every daemon, slay every mortal thing that crawls and slithers under the gaze of the Chaos Gods. I will become Death; I will become the Destroyer. The gods have denied us peace, and so I will give them a war that will end all wars or see the world itself annihilated.'

Caledor stepped out of the cowering crowd, one hand held out in appeasement.

'Be careful, my lord, my friend. Harsh oaths are not soon forgotten.'

Aenarion rounded on the mage and seized him by the shoulders, staring deep into Caledor's eyes with orbs of fire.

'Tell me, *friend*; what is it that you see?'

Caledor could not break from Aenarion's fierce grip, and could not turn aside his gaze from that unnatural stare. The mage-lord took a shuddering, involuntary breath and his eyes turned to gold, reflecting the flames of his king's stare. The two were locked together; the king dark and dangerous with his smouldering eyes and black hair; Caledor like the light of the moon, hair white and skin pale. The Dragontamer's voice came as a distant whisper, lips barely moving as he spoke.

> *'The Elven-king wrapped hard in woes,*
> *A gifted curse to break his grief,*
> *To slay unnumbered his wicked foes,*
> *A brightening flame that burns too brief.*
>
> *To Gods he turned and to Gods he fell,*
> *Save One alone of dark divine,*
> *In blackest heart rings murderous knell,*
> *In deepest shadow where no light shines.*

His slaying shall be as the flood,
Lets loose the Godslayer's ire,
Drowns the world in seas of blood,
Burns it all with waves of fire.

In the North this Doom awaits,
Luring like flame to moth,
Promising life of endless hate,
Bloodshed eternal, uncaring wrath.

And kindled in the fire of rage
Born from blood of anger's womb,
Child of slaughter cursed for an age,
Bearer of the elf-king's doom.'

Caledor gave a rattling hiss and fell from Aenarion's grip. He crumpled like an empty robe, lifelessly sprawled across the floor. Elf lords rushed forward to attend to the fallen mage, but the Phoenix King did not spare his friend a glance. A fey expression crossed his face even as they pronounced Caledor still living. Aenarion stormed towards the pavilion door, scattering those elves before him. He stood outside on the frost-gripped stone and pointed to the stars of the North.

'Yonder lies the Blighted Isle, where sits the dark altar of bloody Khaine! There I shall find his gift wrapped in that black shrine; Godslayer, Widowmaker, Doom of Worlds. No weapon forged by mortal hands, not by the greatest priests of Vaul if they laboured for a thousand years, can bring my revenge. So I will take up that blade made by Vaul Himself for the Bloody-Handed One and with it I shall destroy the daemons.'

All were too horror-struck to speak out against Aenarion, save for Eoloran Anar, he who had once born the standard now lying in tatters dared to lay a hand upon the Phoenix King's arm.

'Did you not hear the words of Caledor? No mortal may wield the Sword of Khaine. It is no gift, but a curse, sent to tempt us to the path of hate and war. No peace can come of such a thing. You doom not only yourself, but all future generations. Do nothing rash, my king, I plead of you! Temper your anger with the wise judgement you have shown before. Do not throw away our future in a moment of rage!'

Aenarion would not listen and threw off Eoloran's hold, casting his friend to the hard ground.

'And you do not listen to my words! There can be no future whilst daemons roam free. Yours is counsel of surrender. Peace must be won through war, and if peace be won, that war must be fought by those that wish to fight it. I am your king, not a tyrant, and I release you all from such oaths as you have sworn to me. When I return I shall still be your king, and whether you wish to follow me or your own path I leave to your conscience.'

At this speech, the dragons had gathered, looming over the heads of the elves. Aenarion now turned to Indraugnir.

'I ask that you bear me North; to the Blighted Isle, that I might take up the Sword of Khaine and forever free both my people and yours from the threat of the daemon. Feel no injunction that you must carry me, for if you do not wish to do so, I shall walk.'

Indraugnir wasted no time in replying.

'So you seek a fang to match my own, my friend? The Blighted Isle is a long enough journey for one with wings; I would not wish such a lonely trek upon a friend. The Dark Gods that now covet our world are not blind and I fear there will be those that will seek to bar your journey. When I resolved to be your ally, I swore to fight alongside you for good or ill, and my desire has not changed.'

All watched aghast as Aenarion drew himself into the throne-saddle of Indraugnir. Some cried out in fear, believing Aenarion would not return from his dire quest. They wept as Indraugnir soared into the sky with three mighty beats of his wings. Dragon and king circled once about the camp and then turned northwards and disappeared into the night.

FOR A NIGHT and a day and a night they flew, under star and sun, through clear and cloud. The mountains and volcanoes passed behind and the clear plains and fields of western Ulthuan spread beneath them. To the West glittered the ocean; to the East sparkled the Inner Seas, and between rose the ring of mountains that gird the central lands of the isle. Snow covered their summits and through the mists that blanketed the peaks they flew. Aenarion felt no chill, though ice crackled upon his armour. His fury warmed him from within, cold sorrow turned to ashes by the fire of his vengeful desires.

Across the mountains they soared for day after day, until to the East the clouds broke and Aenarion looked down upon the ruins of Avelorn. The foothills of the mountains were still swathed with forest, but the trees were sickly, leaves fallen to the ground in rotted heaps, their branches and trunks twisted and contorted by the passage of the daemons. The stench of death hung about that lifeless realm, and all seemed lost. Yet there remained the heart of the wildwoods, the Gaen Vale surrounded by the Inner Sea save for a sliver of land that joined it to the rest of Ulthuan. Here there still grew the lush woods, green canopy stretching from shore to shore.

The sight of life in the dead did not stir Aenarion's heart to anything save to punish those that had wrought such destruction. Astarielle, his wife, the life of the Avelorn forest, was dead; so too was Yvraine, their daughter, the future Everqueen. So had ended the long line of the elves' rulers from the birth of their kind. In peace and harmony had the strength of the Everqueen been found and that strength had faltered. Aenarion knew that where peace failed war would prevail. Sickened by what he saw, he bid Indraugnir to turn westwards and put the mountains between them, turning his back on the dismal sight of Avelorn desecrated.

WEARY WITH GRIEF, Aenarion flew on. That night a strange flame burned in the air, of green and purple and pink and silver. Birds with wings of fire circled about the Phoenix King, their voices a chorus of screeches and mournful cawing. The flock of firebirds surrounded Indraugnir, their harsh cries surrounding the Phoenix King, deafening and incessant.

'Begone!' he shouted.

Amongst the cacophony Aenarion discerned a voice, wrought from a thousand avian throats. The words were carried on the wind itself, swirling around him as the flock swooped and soared.

'Turn back!' the firebirds cried. 'We are all-seeing and you fly to your doom.'

'Begone!' Aenarion called again. 'I know you for what you are. Daemons given the form of birds, sent to dissuade me from my quest.'

'You guess right, but judge us wrong,' the bird chorus replied. 'Not elf nor daemon nor god wishes you to draw that which you seek. No mortal hand can wield this weapon, for it was made for Khaine's grip and Khaine alone controls it. No bloodshed can satiate its hunger; no war can quench its thirst. When every daemon is destroyed, and even the gods themselves have fallen to your rage, what then for you? You shall be kinslayer, the doom of your own people; for in them you will see weakness and cowardice and you will strike them down without thought.'

'Never!' said Aenarion. 'My bloodlust is for daemon and Chaos God alone, and no force in this world or the heavens would raise my hand against another elf. Begone with your lies.'

'Heed our warning, turn back!' the flock called, but Aenarion urged Indraugnir on and the two burst into the starry sky while the firebirds fell to smoke behind them.

DAWN BROKE IN full glory, the sun banishing winter chill, casting golden rays upon the land of the elves. Aenarion looked to the east and for a moment his heart was stirred by the beauty of the sunrise. But gladness could take no hold, for he knew that such sights would be forever banished if the daemons were spared. As the sun's light reflected from his armour, Aenarion could see lithe figures dancing in the glare. Insubstantial, like distant reflections, they leapt and twirled about the king and his dragon, shimmering with the dawn haze.

'Begone!' he shouted.

His command was greeted by lilting laughter that poured into his mind like a gentle waterfall.

'So harsh, so stern!' the daemonlights giggled. 'Why so grim, King of the Elves? For one who seeks to end all wars, your mood is sour. Exalt your noble quest and rejoice in the pleasure that will come from destroying your foes.'

'Save your guile for one that is not deaf and blind to your charms,' replied Aenarion. 'Your kind will fall with the others.'

'And even as you strike us down and relish your victories, you will become forever ours,' sang the sun-voices. 'The joy of slaying is still joy, and in that you will be trapped, your life no more than one moment of rapturous slaughter after the other.'

'Never!' cried Aenarion. 'There is no joy left in me; not in head nor heart nor any other part. I shall with a frown upon my brow take no pleasure from it, as the beekeeper drives wasps from the hives or the tree-herd disposes of the mites in his charges' bark. Your slaying is an unwanted evil that I bear, and I will do it without happiness.'

'Heed our warning, turn back!' the sun-daemons called, but Aenarion urged Indraugnir on and the two banked into the shadows of the mountains to leave behind the light of the sun.

AT DUSK A soupy smog smothered the Phoenix King, its tendrils slipping across Indraugnir's scales, pawing at Aenarion's face with wet, slimy fingers. A stench of eternal decay, of charnel morass and rotting swamp, burned Aenarion's throat and eyes. Through stinging tears with cracked voice, he cried out.

'Begone!' he shouted.

Lugubrious voices swallowed him up, words sliding into his ears like moist mud, seeping and slipping through his mind in most disgusting fashion.

'When all is dead, who shall you slay?' they asked. 'When the corpses are as mountain ranges and foetid blood fills oceans, what then? Think you to destroy Death itself? Think that you are eternal, never to be touched by the flies and the worms? Fodder you are, flesh and bones and blood and skin, and nothing more. When the daemons are gone, would you raise this weapon against disease, and strike down old age, and slice through hunger? Nothing is forever, save us, for in all life there is death.'

'All things follow their natural course, and I would no more fight nature than try to cut apart the sky,' snarled Aenarion. 'But your kind wantonly spread plague and famine in most unnatural cause, and you too shall feel the pain of destruction. You are not Death, nor its servants; merely vassal messengers of putridity and decomposition. Death comes to all mortals, and with the Godslayer in my hand it will come to the immortal also.'

'Heed our warning, turn back!' burbled the noxious fog, but Aenarion urged Indraugnir higher and higher, until they breached the rank cloud and flew on through the starlit sky.

* * *

THE FOLLOWING DAWN the crimson sky was filled with rain, so that it seemed as the air itself cried blood. Each drop falling upon dragon scale and link of armour rang as if blade against blade. Every sliding droplet screeched like metal torn or throat slit. As the shower became a downpour, Aenarion and Indraugnir were surrounded by the din of battle, the arrhythmic clashing and wailing overlapping to form words bellowed so fiercely that Aenarion feared for his hearing.

'Begone!' he shouted.

'Foolish mortal!' the voice roared in return. 'Think you to turn war against its makers? We will feed upon every blow you land, every drop of blood shed, every bone broken and every skull severed. In battle we were born and for battle we exist. The ringing of your sword shall be a clarion to us, and in hosts uncountable we will fight you. For each of us you fell, another shall be born, into war unending, battle without cease to the end of the world and the universe beyond.'

'The dead do not feed,' laughed Aenarion. 'When you are slain you shall feast no more upon violence and rage. Cold shall be your deaths, for I will be heartless and pitiless, though my rage shall outmatch yours.'

'The beasts of war cannot be vanquished! Great may be your fury, yet the harder you fight, the stronger we shall become. There is not a blade forged by man or god that does not belong to us. Every life you take shall be a life dedicated to us and your victories will be as hollow as your defiance.'

'Why would you discourage me from such?' asked Aenarion. 'It is fear, I contend! No might of mortal or immortal can stand against Vaul's darkest creation. No stronghold in the world or in the realms beyond can hold against its power. Bring on your unending war and I will end it. I shall throw down your brazen gates and topple your iron towers.'

'Heed our warning, turn back!' the voices growled, but the rainfall grew lighter as Indraugnir flew on, 'til the Phoenix King flew in clear skies again.

ON AND ON, northwards flew Indraugnir, the Phoenix King silent and resolute upon the dragon's back. They glided over barren lands, bounded to the East by sheer-sided peaks, bordered to the West by crashing sea. Withered heaths and wide marshes broke the rocky landscape, the foothills covered with desolate moorlands, the rivers cold and rimmed with ice.

Neither rider nor mount had known rest for many days, but Indraugnir flew on with steady beats of his wings. Aenarion dared not close his eyes lest some new obstacle assail him. The cold air became harsher still, Indraugnir's great breaths each a billowing cloud that swirled in the wake of his wings. Aenarion's bones ached and his eyes were rimed with frost, but he kept his grip firm on the saddle even as he shook icicles from his long hair.

The Phoenix King heard whispers. Faint and distant, and thought himself in a waking dream. Male and female, high and low, the voices urged him to turn back, seeking to turn him from his quest. With each new entreaty or threat his resolve hardened further, until his heart was as an icy stone. Coldness without and coldness within, the Phoenix King fixed his eyes upon the north and urged Indraugnir to stay strong.

As they neared the northern coast of Ulthuan, all ahead of them was swathed with dark rumbling clouds. From East to West the storm obscured all. Beneath the crashes and flashes the seas were stirred to tremendous violence, smashing and flailing against the rocky shore. The clouds towered upwards to the edge of the sky, and there was no path except through them. Lightning crackled, dancing brilliantly across the high waves. The air reverberated with thunder, shaking Aenarion in his armour. The wind became a fierce gale that whipped the breath from the Phoenix King's lips.

Aenarion leaned low and slapped an encouraging hand to Indraugnir's thick neck. He raised his voice above the howl of the wind.

'The elements themselves would see us fail, my friend. This is the last, I am sure of it. I have no doubts for your courage and tenacity, but have you the strength for this final obstacle?'

Indraugnir snorted with offence and backed up his wings so that the two stayed in place, barely buffeted by the strength of the wind. The dragon twisted his neck to look upon Aenarion, eyes slitted against the gale.

'You know better than to ask such questions, old ally. I would bear you to the moon and back if you wished it. It is a great storm, I grant you, but I have flown these skies for an age. Upon the fires of volcanoes I have soared, and into the icy vastness of the North I ventured when I was young. I have crossed mountains and oceans and deserts, and you ask if I have the strength to contest with a simple storm?'

'Well said, my friend, and proudly put!' replied the Phoenix King. 'I doubt not that we could fly round the world and back again if needed. Storm or no storm, the Blighted Isle is near at hand, somewhere beneath that scowling sky. When we have dared its wrath and found our prize, we shall be afforded our much-earned rest.'

'Say not!' said Indraugnir. 'If we succeed, there shall be no rest nor respite. I know of this thing that you seek. It is a shard of death, a splinter of the freezing void between stars, a fang from the world serpent. You ask if I have the strength to bear you to its resting place, but I must ask if you have the strength to bear what you will find there. I heard the words of Caledor. This wicked thing you seek was not meant for the mortal realm. Its touch is a curse, to its victims and its wielder. Its taint shall be in you forever, even past death. Is this truly what you seek?'

Aenarion did not reply for some time. He felt the thudding of his heart and the race of blood through his veins. All the whispering had gone save for one sharp voice; a quiet siren song that called to him through the tumult of the storm. He thought of what he had to leave behind and saw that there was nothing. His land, his people, all would suffer for eternity if he did not do this thing.

'My heart is hardened to it and my mind set upon this course. If this weapon is to be the doom all claim, it shall be my doom alone, for my wife and children are dead and with my passing its curse will carry on no more. Let us doubt each other no more. Whatever fate awaits me, it cannot be delayed.'

So Indraugnir stiffened his wings, set his long neck and dived down towards the boiling storm.

WIND HOWLED, LIGHTNING flared, thunder growled. All was enveloping darkness split by blinding brightness as Indraugnir and Aenarion plunged through the tempest. Despite the dragon's straining pinions they were tossed about like a leaf on a breeze. Aenarion leaned forwards and clasped his hands around Indraugnir's neck, laying his cheek against his scaly hide as the wind threatened to tear the Phoenix King from his perch. A swell of air or rasp of lightning would set the pair to tumbling, until Indraugnir righted himself with stentorian growls, his heart pounding so hard it shuddered through Aenarion's body.

As one they dived down, a silver and gold streak in the blackness. The sea beneath foamed wildly and Indraugnir's wingtips skimmed the waves as he pulled out of the stoop, battered left and right by the swirling hurricane. Fiercer and fiercer grew the storm as they flew on, 'til Aenarion's limbs shivered with the effort of his clinging. A mountainous wave surged out of the gloom, forcing Indraugnir to climb swiftly.

Lightning cracked, striking Aenarion. For a moment his whole body contorted. His fingers lost their grip and he fell, tumbling from Indraugnir's back towards the stormy seas below. With a cry of dismay, Indraugnir folded a wing and turned sharply. He plummeted after the falling Phoenix King, fighting against the torrent of the storm that threatened to sweep both away.

Aenarion plunged into the steep waves, what little breath he had exploding from his body. Surf crashed over him and his armour pulled him down. With a final effort, he splashed to the surface once more, filling his lungs with freezing air before sinking again, dragged down by the current.

Indraugnir hit the water like a meteor, wings furled, raising a great eruption of water. Eyes wide in the bubbling depths, he spied the glint of gold and turned and lunged awkwardly, a clawed foot closing around Aenarion's spinning body. Legs pumping, churning a froth behind him, the dragon burst clear of the sea's clawing grip, wings snapping out to carry them back into the clouds.

Turned around and about, the dragon knew not whether he flew north or south or east or west, but carried on as swiftly as he could, Aenarion's limp form hanging in his grasp. Feeling no movement from his friend, he cast his gaze about, looking for some rock or promontory where he could set down for a moment.

He spied an outcrop of black rock and turned towards it, skimming above the waves, every muscle and sinew in his enormous body a knot of agony. His breath coming in gasps, Indraugnir crashed against the hard shore, shielding Aenarion with his body, the sharp rocks shedding scales, tearing through the skin of his wings. Bloodied and limping, Indraugnir righted himself and gently set Aenarion down on a water dappled rock shelf.

Bending his head low, the dragon let out a breath across the elven king. Stirred by the heat, Aenarion heaved water from his lungs, body shuddering. Bleeding from dozens of wounds, Indraugnir lay down beside the motionless elf and draped a wing across him, shielding the Phoenix King against the surf that sprayed from the wild sea.

So it was that Aenarion and Indraugnir came to the Blighted Isle.

WHEN AENARION AWOKE he was sore in limb and numb in mind. Crawling from beneath the protective canopy of Indraugnir's wing, he looked up to see a dark sky. The storm had abated and the clouds gone, but not a single star could be seen. The cold waters lapped against the rock beside him; in the other direction he could see nothing but blackness. He looked to Indraugnir but the dragon did not stir. His body heaved and fell with massive breaths and his eyes were closed. The Phoenix King saw gouges in the flesh of the beast, and noted the tattered edges of Indraugnir's wings. He patted his companion gently upon the shoulder and sat down with his back to the dragon's foreleg.

Here he sat, alert for any danger, and kept watch.

As the first fingers of dawn touched upon the sea to the east, Indraugnir stirred. Blinking his eyes, the dragon yawned wide, puffs of smoke drifting from his open maw. Indraugnir turned towards Aenarion and saw that the king was awake. Aenarion stood as the dragon shifted his bulk and tentatively flexed a wing. Indraugnir's thick lips rippled with pain, exposing sword-long teeth.

'I fear my boast has come back to haunt me,' the dragon said gently. 'I am undone by the storm and can carry you no further.'

'No other could have seen me through the tempest. There is no shame in such a feat. We are here upon the Blighted Isle and I can find my way alone here. Rest up, for it will not be long ere we must go south again, and even I cannot walk on water.'

Indraugnir laughed with a deep rumble.

'With the Sword of Khaine in hand, perhaps you could carve apart the seas and cross the dry wound to Ulthuan.'

'I would rather be carried by a friend,' replied the Phoenix King. 'Fare well, and I shall return soon with my prize.'

The Blighted Isle was lifeless, a barren rock broken by stone spires; home to no plant nor animal nor bird nor the smallest insect. Aenarion set off away from the dawn, picking his way through the scattered rocks. Soon he spied higher ground to the west and set off with purpose. Pulling himself up a steep ridge, the king saw that the morning had all but passed and the sun was not far from noon. Yet the circle of light hung in a dark sky, its light weak, a pale disc that seemed more like the moon.

Crossing the ridge, Aenarion felt a pull to the south, and the sharp, luring whisper returned to his ear. Yet even as he turned in its direction, a mist rose from the naked rock, surrounding him until the sunlight was no more than a faint sheen in the air. Shadows stirred in the fog and Aenarion thought that the daemons had returned. He circled slowly on his heel as the shapes resolved into vague silhouettes, tall and slim, robed with cloud like gowns. They crowded closer, just out of reach, grey figures that stretched towards him with pleading hands, their insubstantial bodies evaporating and reforming.

Dark mouths opened and the fog swirled with hoarse whispers. 'He walks among us.'

'The Doom of the Elves hath come.'

'Spare us!'

'Mercy!'

'Not the blade!'

'Free us!'

'Give us peace!'

'Justice!'

'Show us pity!'

Aenarion swiped at the apparitions with his hand and stumbled back from their advance, only to find more behind him. There were thousands, a great mass of wraiths that grew in number with every passing heartbeat.

'Leave me be, foul spirits!' he snarled. 'The dead have no business with the living. Torment your slayers, not I!'

A quiet female voice beside Aenarion quelled all the others.

'They are the spirits of the Dead Yet To Be, Aenarion.'

The Phoenix King spun around, recognising the voice.

'Astarielle?' he cried.

It was she; a shimmering ghost of white and palest green among the melancholy grey. The Phoenix King looked upon her beauty again and wept. He stepped forwards to embrace her slender body, but his arms passed through air without substance, leaving only a cold sensation that prickled his skin. As the spirit of Astarielle reformed, he saw now that there were rents upon her flesh and silver blood spilled from a wound in her breast. Aenarion gave a wordless moan and fell to one knee.

'My beautiful wife! What horrors have been inflicted upon you? Is there to be no peace for your spirit?'

'In peace I lived, but in violence I died. To peace I will return, but not before I have spoken. Give up this quest for vengeance, Aenarion. Shun the lure of war and find it in your heart to treasure the memory of my life, not the haunting of my death.'

'Look what they have done to you, my beautiful wife. Look at the destruction they have wrought upon your realm.'

'All things die and then grow again. Even Averlorn has its seasons, though they last longer than the lifetimes of elves. What seems permanent now is but fleeting in the eyes of the world. The future cannot be born out of grief and anger, but is created anew with hope and love.'

'My love died with you, Astarielle,' said Aenarion, regaining his feet. 'This is your shade, fleetingly here, but soon it will be gone. Only in death will we join each other again, but I cannot needlessly throw aside my life and abandon our people. When the daemons are destroyed and Ulthuan is safe, I will return the Widowmaker to its black altar and let loose my grip on the world. Then we shall be united.'

'There are things that you are not to know, but you must believe that all is not as bleak as it seems. You sought sacrifice to end the woes of the elves, but there is greater sacrifice to come. Though in times to come we shall spread our gaze across the world and rule the seas, it will be but a brief respite in the dwindling of our people. You now must make that choice. Look to your heart! We must forego that power that makes us strong, that the daemons might be caged again within their terrible prison, and with their passing so too will our glory fade.'

'Never!' snarled Aenarion. 'We will rise anew from this war, greater than ever. Though your entreaty would break the heart of an ice fiend, my mind is set.'

Silver tears rolled down Astarielle's cheeks as Aenarion turned from her. The Phoenix King stalked away with a whisper.

'We will be together again, my love, but not yet. There is something yet that I must do.'

IT WAS NOT long before Aenarion came to a wide expanse near the centre of the Blighted Isle. Here, jagged black rocks marked with lines of red thrust up into the ruddy skies like a circle of columns. The ground within was as flat as glass and black as midnight. At the centre there stood a block of red-veined rock and something only partly visible shimmered above it.

Even as his thoughts touched upon the Godslayer, there came to Aenarion's ears a distant noise; a faint screaming. The ring of metal on metal, of fighting, echoed around the shrine. Aenarion heard a thunderous heart beating, and thought he saw knives carving wounds upon flesh, and limbs torn from bodies on the edge of his vision. The red veins of the altar were not rock at all, but pulsed like arteries, blood flowing from the stone in spurting rivers of gore. He realised that the beating heart was his own, and it hammered in his chest like a sword-smith working at an anvil.

Aenarion stood transfixed before that bloody shrine. The thing embedded in the rock danced and wavered before the Phoenix King's eyes, a blur of axe and sword and spear and bow and knife and strange weapons not known to the elves. Finally a single image emerged, of a long-bladed sword, cross guard curled into the rune of Khaine, its black blade etched with red symbols of death and blood.

Aenarion reached out... and stopped, his fingers a hair's-breadth from the hilt of the sword. All became silent; not a movement stirred the air as the world and the gods held their breath.

Aenarion knew this would be his doom. All of the warnings came back to him, the words of Caledor merged with dire predictions of the daemons and the pleading of his dead wife. It all mattered nothing to him, for his sprit was empty and only the Sword of Khaine could fill the void within him.

The ground shook and rock crumbled as Aenarion's fist closed upon the hilt. He pulled the sword free from its stone prison and held it aloft. Blood seeped from the runes etched into the blade and poured in thick rivulets across his hand and down his arm, trailing crimson across his armour.

Godslayer, Widowmaker, Doom of Worlds, Spear of Vengeance, Deathshard, Icefang and Heavenblight. By many names it was called, by mortal and daemons and gods. But one name alone it truly held: Sword of Khaine, the Lord of Murder.

Now it was the Sword of Aenarion.

The doom of the elves was sealed.

BITTER END

Sarah Cawkwell

FOR MANY YEARS, he had made bargains, accords and dark pacts, both with powers he could name and several more that he dared not. He could not remember the last time he had merely requested something and the Imperium had provided it. In the days of his hated and enforced servitude to the Corpse-Emperor, he had but to requisition something and it was his.

Now, whenever he wanted something, Huron Blackheart simply reached out with the might of his loyal Red Corsairs and he took it. His greedy, grasping claws closed around objects, people and entire star systems and stole them away. He looted and plundered, he stole and he murdered. Occasionally though, he would come upon a treasure that he could not simply claim.

When this happened, he would be roused from the shadows in which he now existed and he would hunt down his quarry in an entirely different manner. He would sit down with agents of the most powerful and most influential and he would talk. He would barter and negotiate, bringing his considerable charisma and cunning to the fore and he would make more deals.

His reputation preceded him wherever he went and many wisely shied away from reaching any sort of arrangement with the Tyrant of Badab, fearing for their lives. But there were many more who boldly sealed their agreements with him in blood.

Sometimes, Huron Blackheart even kept his word.

* * *

THIS HAD BEEN an agri-world once. But in the wake of an exterminatus it had become uninhabitable. Its given name was lost in history, leaving it with the identifier that had been bestowed upon it during the halcyon days of the Great Crusade. Eighty-Three Fourteen was a wasteland. Nothing grew here any more and the only things that lived were the most tenacious of bacteria. The seas had boiled away, leaving vast expanses of arid ground that was cracked and blistered. The ferocity of the bombardment had broken open the crust and disturbed something deep in the planet's core. Volcanic lava bubbled up through the wounds in the earth and spilled across its ruined surface like blood. There was a constant smouldering heat haze that loaned everything a slightly distorted, unreal appearance.

It was a prime example of an inhospitable environment but the gigantic figures making their steady way across its broken surface were not in the slightest bit bothered by the poisoned air or the excruciating heat. They walked without tiring, keeping up a pace they could sustain for many days if they so desired. They had marched to war in this way many times. But on this day, there was no war to be had. This was a deputation sent to accompany their lord and master to a summit.

Huron Blackheart walked in the midst of half a dozen of his Red Corsairs, the only one not wearing a helm. The countless implants and prosthetics that held his brain within what remained of his skull meant that wearing a tactical armour helm caused him great discomfort. Additionally, for the most part, it was such a laborious and time-consuming process to rewire sections of his cranial implants to accept a helm that it was little more than a hindrance. The complex, wheezing workings of his replacement lungs and respiratory system filtered the atmosphere in much the same way as a helmet anyway; and thus the choking, sulphuric air had no effect on him at all. Bareheaded, he stood out as unique amidst the group.

He could have made this journey alone but had elected to field a show of strength. He was wily and astute, blessed with cunning and guile like no other. But he did not trust the individual with whom he was dealing.

It had been a tedious process setting up this meeting. Dengesha had not been prepared to travel to Huron Blackheart's stronghold deep in the heart of the Maelstrom and neither did the Blood Reaver care to board a ship almost entirely populated by warp-witches. He had used sorcerers for his own ends before, of course. Indeed, it had been his own cabal who had suggested Dengesha as the best possible candidate for the task. Increasingly heated exchanges had taken place until an impasse had been reached. Neutral ground was the solution.

On a rocky outcrop overlooking the volcanic plains of a world that had once teemed with life, the shape of another giant could be made out. A baroque silhouette, picked out by the weak rays of the sickly yellow sun, stood alone. One of Huron's retinue pointed upwards with the muzzle of a bolter, indicating the other's presence.

'I see him,' Huron said, simply. 'I told you he would come.' A deep chuckle came from his ravaged throat. 'He could not help himself.'

DENGESHA TOOK NO sobriquet in order to convey his greatness. It was not in his nature to embrace an honorific that extolled his deeds to the outside world. He was no Despoiler or Betrayer. He chose instead to let his actions speak for themselves. For centuries he had stood at the head of the Heterodox, a cabal of sorcerers who, it was rumoured, had splintered centuries earlier from the Word Bearers. Dengesha was said to have studied the heart of Chaos Undivided for more than five thousand years and as such, his well of knowledge ran deep.

There was nothing about Dengesha that suggested such great age. His visage was timeless and its individual features unimpressive. He bore several scars on his face but more than this were the countless runes and brands that were seared into his skin. They writhed and twisted now under Huron's scrutiny, living things that spoke of a true disciple of the Dark Powers. He felt no discomfort in the sorcerer's presence. He was fully at ease with his own confidence.

The two Space Marines, the warrior and the psyker, had moved to meet one another within a cave in the rock face. Neither's attendant retinues were with them as per the terms of their agreement.

The cave had once been a natural wonder and the source of a wellspring that had kept the local agricultural workers provided with water. As high as a refinery tower within, the cave was studded with broken, jagged stalagmites and stalactites that glittered with seams of semi-precious rock. Inside this cave, high above the shattered plains, was the only moisture remaining anywhere on the planet.

The underground spring that had once nourished crops and quenched the thirst of thousands of Imperial workers was now a toxic sink hole, steaming and roiling gently. Periodically, air would escape from a fissure and expand with a rush, spraying boiling water in all directions. It spattered against the armour of the two giants who stood face-to-face. Neither gave ground for some time and then the psyker broke the stalemate with a bitter greeting.

'Blood Reaver.'

Huron greeted the sorcerer in kind and they considered each other in further mute, candid appreciation for a while. Their eyes locked and the sorcerer's head tipped slightly to one side. The master of the Red Corsairs felt the faintest brush on his mind as the other attempted a psychic evaluation. The resultant sharp intake of breath brought a smile.

'Difficulties, Dengesha?'

'You are no psyker and yet you are warded... what is it that shields your mind from my sight?'

'Are you so disappointed? Should you not be wary of being so free with the admission that you are invading my thoughts without my permission?' Huron's voice was grating and harsh, dragged from replacement vocal cords and a vox-unit that had been tuned and retuned until it sounded as close to human as it could. Which was not very.

'You know my nature, Lord Huron. It is, after all, why you sought me out. Now answer my question.' Dengesha's words were demanding, yet his tone remained deferential. Huron approved of the approach. 'What is it that grants you this protection?'

'Perhaps you should tell me what you have heard?' The question was thrown back at the sorcerer who folded his arms across his chest.

'I have heard,' he said, choosing his words carefully, 'in rumours whispered throughout the Eye that the four favour you. You carry a boon they granted you. I have heard that something walks at your side and grants you certain... benefits.'

'You are very well informed.' Dengesha took another sharp intake of breath and Huron continued. 'Does that surprise you, sorcerer? Do you taste envy? Are you curious as to why it is that the Dark Powers see fit to grant me such a gift? Look closely, Dengesha. Tell me what you see.'

The sorcerer considered the Red Corsair for a few moments. He looked the warrior up and down. A giant clad in desecrated red armour with so many augmetics and implants that he looked more like a blighted tech-priest or engineer than the scourge of the Imperium. The metal-plated head shook slightly and a quirk of amusement twitched the lipless mouth.

'No, Dengesha. Look *properly*. Use your witch-sight.'

The sorcerer *looked*. And he *saw*.

THE WORD HAMADRYA had never been a part of Huron Blackheart's vocabulary until the day he had been reborn. There had been many deals made in those few days when he had hovered in the grey mists that lingered between life and death. His body had been left all but useless in the wake of the Star Phantoms assault on the Palace of Thorns and without the anchor of its corporeal weight, his soul had been free to wander at will.

Nobody knew who – or what – he had consorted with in those days. But if the thought was never expressed aloud, all of the Red Corsairs knew that their lord and master had to have made *some* pact. He could not have survived otherwise, despite the ceaseless labours of his most faithful. They could repair the physical damage to their Chapter Master's body, but that was all.

But none ever asked of the events that had transpired and Huron Blackheart never volunteered the information.

The hamadrya had begun its life as a *thought*. A potentiality. A tendril of insubstantial warp-stuff that draped itself invisibly across Huron's mantle. Over weeks, months and years it had become something more tangible. In its earliest stages, it was nothing more than a wisp. A curl of smoky air that lingered around the warrior's shoulder like a mist snake wrapping itself protectively around him. Huron himself seemed either oblivious or indifferent to its presence, but over time began to notice that he was developing a sensitivity and then a resistance to psychic intrusions.

The more he realised this, the stronger the warding became until the ethereal presence at his shoulder took on a more corporeal form. Sometimes it was reptilian. Sometimes avian. Other times simian. Always animalistic and always no larger than the breadth of the warrior's shoulder span. Others could see it, but never for long. Most of the time it could only be glimpsed briefly out of the corner of the eye, leaving the viewer wondering if they had seen it at all.

It granted Huron Blackheart an extra layer of power that boosted an already overinflated sense of ego. But it had limitations. It was a creature of the warp, after all.

THE SORCERER LOOKED. And he *saw*.

'I confess, my Lord, that I did not believe the rumours to be true,' he confessed. He had considered the tale of the familiar to be nothing more than a figment of the mad Tyrant's overwrought imagination. Yet his witch-sight gave him a unique view. 'I have never seen its like before. Is this what they call the hamadrya?'

'Indeed it is. And you would do well not to concern yourself further with its origins or its purpose. Consider instead the question my agent put to you.' Always quick to the point, Huron Blackheart did not care to linger on matters past.

'Yes, Lord Huron.' Dengesha bowed from the waist. 'I consider it a great honour that you seek my assistance in this matter. I understand that your... blessing loses power; that it becomes weaker the further from the heart of the Maelstrom you travel. In conjunction with your own cabal...' There was unmistakable superiority in Dengesha's tone as he said the word, 'I have determined what you need to overcome this limitation.'

'The hamadrya is a thing of the warp,' Huron said. He drummed his fingers idly against his armour plated thigh. The noise reverberated through the cavernous chamber, the acoustics oddly distorted. 'It draws its strength from the powers therein. And the further from its source I travel...' He broke off and raised his head to study Dengesha. 'My cabal have told me what I need. A potent soul, shackled by arcane powers. The hamadrya can feed from its torment for all eternity. But my sorcerers, strong as they are... cannot do this one thing.'

Huron's red, artificial eye whirred softly as it focused. 'Give me my solution, Dengesha and we will share the spoils of war.'

'You need a potent soul.'

'I have found such a thing. Sister Brigitta of the Order of the Iron Rose.'

'I have heard of this Order and of this woman. The self-proclaimed saviour of her people. She who bears the sins of a generation on her shoulders.'

'Aye. One of the faithful. A powerful symbol.'

'You need a suitable vessel. Such a thing will not be easy to locate, my Lord. It could take many long months of searching...'

'You underestimate my resources, Dengesha.' Huron's twisted face distorted in a smile again and he twisted a loop on his belt bringing an object slowly into view.

The bottle was exquisite. Deep, emerald green in colour, it was a fusion of bottle and vial with a wide lip tapering to a long, slim neck that fed into a small oval bowl. It was encased within beautiful fretwork, wrought from copper or brass or some other burnished metal that snaked around its delicate surface.

'My cabal attached this vessel to my belt,' said Huron. 'They told me that only another sorcerer could remove it, that if I were to touch it myself, the power would be tainted.' He shifted his hip slightly so that it was facing Dengesha, who snapped open the belt loop, taking the bottle in his hands. He could feel its imbued power; a thrum of psychic energy that made his hands vibrate gently as he held it. Huron studied him.

'On the understanding that you will give me what I ask for, I make a gift of this vessel to you so that you may work whatever fell deeds necessary. Do you accept?'

'Gladly, my lord. Such an arcane item... such a *relic* must have cost you dearly. Where did you locate it?'

'My sources are many and varied. Do not bother yourself with detail. Is it adequate for its purpose?'

'More than adequate.' Dengesha studied the bottle in admiration for a while, then with a series of hand movements, caused it to disappear. It was little more than cheap theatrics and it did nothing to change the expression on Huron Blackheart's artificial face. 'This Sister Brigitta of yours will be heavily guarded, of course. I will need absolutely no distractions whilst I perform the binding.'

'Leave that side of the bargain to me, master sorcerer. My Red Corsairs will distract whatever pitiful forces guard her and you will take your coterie and perform your rituals. You will present me with what I want and in return, I give the Heterodox the world in her charge for your chapels and its people for,' he gave a creaking shrug, 'whatever you see fit.' His augmetic eye darkened briefly as though he blinked, a slow, thoughtful thing that was somehow unsettling. 'Do we have an agreement?'

'A world and its subjects? My lord, that is... very generous of you.'

Huron shrugged. 'My Corsairs will still take what spoils we desire, but it is not beyond me to show gratitude and generosity. Now tell me, Dengesha of the Heterodox, do we have an agreement?'

'We do.'

There were many who boldly sealed their agreements in blood. Dengesha of the Heterodox was one such individual.

Sometimes, Huron Blackheart even kept his word.

THE TEMPLE BURNED.

Since time immemorial, the Order of the Iron Rose had been cloistered within their monument to the Emperor of Mankind. A dizzyingly aesthetic building, the temple had stood proudly within well-guarded walls for countless generations. The sisters lived their studious lives quietly, only leaving at times of war when their fierce battle skills were most needed. Then, their comparative gentleness could easily be forgotten in the face of their roaring battle madness.

Sister Brigitta was the incumbent canoness, but had always eschewed the title, preferring to remain on the same level as her sisters. She was dearly beloved by all who knew her. Intelligent and insightful, her words of wisdom on any number of subjects were treated as precious jewels to be collected and admired.

She stood now, clad in her copper-coloured battle armour, her black and silver-flecked hair streaming in the breeze. The armour forced her to stand upright with a grace and dignity that added weight to her command. Her jaw was tightened and her face bore an implacable expression as she stared down from the highest chamber of the steeple at the slaughter taking place far below.

Tears ran down her face, but not of fear. They were tears of rage and regret that the sanctity of the temple had been violated. At either side, her two most trusted lieutenants also wept at the wanton destruction that rampaged below.

They had come without warning. They had struck fast and they had struck without mercy. The loyal Palatine Guard who protected the sacred grounds had done an admirable job of holding the enemy at bay but ultimately, they were only human. What hope could they have against the Adeptus Astartes?

Sister Brigitta surveyed the carnage. Seemingly countless forces of the giant Space Marines pitted against the pitiable wall of humanity. That delicate wall of mortal flesh was the only thing standing between the Chaos forces and the sisters.

From here, she could not see the faces of the brave guardsmen who died in their futile efforts to protect the Order, but she imagined that each shared the same look of zealous ferocity. The Order of the Iron Rose preached that fear made one weak and had no place on the battlefield.

The barking report of bolter fire filled the air and the murderous whine of chainblades was all-pervading. The screams of the dying were agony to listen to and the ground below was already running scarlet with the blood of the fallen. Some of the Chaos warriors fell upon their victims, hacking and dismembering. The sight sickened Sister Brigitta. Beside her, Sister Anastasia murmured a soft litany, commending the souls of the departed to the Emperor.

'We must meet in the central chamber,' the canoness finally said, tearing her eyes from the slaughter. 'Gather the Order, Sister Anastasia.'

'Yes, sister.' Anastasia left immediately to carry out her superior's command and the canoness stood for several moments longer, salt-tears running down her weather-tanned face.

'The Order of the Iron Rose will stand to the last, traitors,' she promised, raising her voice to be heard above the growing wind.

THE RED CORSAIRS had dealt with the pathetic human threat in short order. Even as the last guardsman died, pierced on the end of a chainblade, Huron Blackheart's warriors had turned their weapons on the temple walls and gates. They had been erected over the course of many years by master craftsmen and artisans.

What had taken humanity years to perfect and construct was levelled in minutes by four Traitor Space Marines and their multi-meltas. The irony of that equation amused Huron Blackheart enough to make him laugh out loud.

He had accompanied his forces to the surface of this world but had taken no part in the battle. He had stood to one side with Dengesha and his cabal of sorcerers, watching with displaced indifference as they butchered their way forwards.

Another direct hit on the wall finally reduced it to molten slag, a huge cloud of pale steam billowing outwards from the destruction and coating the armour of the warriors in a fine film of grit. The Red Corsairs did not wait for their master's order to proceed. They crossed the threshold of the sacred temple and met the second wave of PDF forces with renewed vigour.

Dengesha moved forwards dispassionately, his cabal moving with him like a flock of birds flittering around their mother. Fighting independently, each warrior-psyker was capable of incalculable destruction. Fighting as a unit, they were imbued with such power that no mortal man could look upon the forces of the warp flowing from them and hope to survive.

Dark lightning flickered from fingertips, fire burst from the palms of their hands and the very earth itself trembled where they trod. The sheer, raw power they exuded was tremendous and Huron Blackheart watched their performance with something akin to raw hunger on his face.

Three guardsmen were incinerated with a blast from Dengesha's fingers, their bodies catching fire as though they were nothing more than dead wood. They died in terrible agony, screaming and begging for mercy. Huron watched as their ravaged faces slowly melted, like candles burning down to the taper.

Another unfortunate soldier was caught in the mesmerising stare of one of the Heterodox and found himself unable to move. With a press of psychic power, the sorcerer burst the guardsman's brain like a ripe fruit. The man fell to his knees, blood and grey matter dribbling from his ears before he pitched over, face first into the dust.

The winds had whipped up to a frenzy now, but these were no natural weather conditions. This was the work of the Heterodox and the winds carried maddening whispers, half-heard promises and dire threats. They blew from the very heart of the warp itself and plucked at the souls of men with ethereal claws. Some who were caught in its path went mad in an instant, hacking and slashing at phantasms only they could see or hear. Others stood their ground more firmly, litanies of warding on their lips.

But each was slain. Each pitiful stalk was reaped and the more death and destruction there was, the more powerful the cabal seemed to grow until, with a feverish cry to the dark gods of Chaos Undivided, the Heterodox unleashed the true horror of their collective.

FROM WITHOUT, THE sounds of battle echoed. From within, the sisters of the Order radiated a calm composure. A small order, barely one hundred Sisters of Battle had gathered together in the central chamber. They were all clad in armour similar to Sister Brigitta's, although where hers was a burnished copper hue, theirs were a deeper colour, a reddish bronze that glinted in the light cast by the candles and sconces on the walls.

'Our time here is short, sisters,' the canoness began when she had Anastasia's assurance that all were present. 'Our enemy has breached the gate and they will soon dare to desecrate the most sacred inner sanctum of our beloved Order.' Brigitta reached up as she spoke and braided her thick hair into a plait that hung like a rope down her back. None of the Order would go into battle with their hair loose. It was an affectation, but an important one. Brigitta's visual reminder of the very physical pre-battle preparation instilled focus amongst the gathered sisters. In the ensemble, others mirrored her action.

'We will not stand and allow that to happen. We will hold out against these intruders for as long as the Emperor gives us the strength. We will stand our ground until the bitter end. We fight the gravest of traitors, my sisters. We battle against fallen angels. Traitor Space Marines. And they bring witch-kin with them.'

A palpable ripple of dismay ran through the sisters. They had stood proud against countless enemies. Aliens, cultists, even a preceptory of Battle Sisters who had lost their way, and they had always triumphed. They had fought alongside Space Marines many times. But the Order of the Iron Rose had never fought *against* them.

884 The Best of Hammer and Bolter: Volume One

Brigitta raised a hand for silence and she got it immediately. From outside the fortified walls of the temple, the muffled sounds of gunfire and terrible, bloody death could be heard, filling in the pauses in her impassioned speech.

'We are the beloved of the Emperor. We are the Sisters of the Iron Rose. We stand as a reminder that the flower of that name is protected by thorns. We will not allow these foul traitors to reach out and pluck us from existence without exacting our payment in blood first.'

She raised her bolter to her shoulder and cast her eyes around the assembled battle sisters. 'We will make our stand in the rear courtyard. If we draw the traitor filth out into the open, they may exact less damage on our temple.' It was unlikely, and most of the Order knew it, but they were words that encouraged her sisters. Brigitta was under no illusions; the battle that was coming towards them could well be the last thing any of them saw. But they would die as they had lived, defending the Emperor's legacy.

THE CLOUDS ABOVE the temple boiled, swirling together in a dark mass of intangible horror. The wind was now a gale, screaming its unnatural, elemental fury across the surface of the planet and whipping up the detritus from the fallen walls into plumed, choking columns. Lightning coruscated within the cloud and as it moved, it picked up dust and debris, including corpses of the fallen.

The Chaos-driven maelstrom moved with almost agonising slowness across the battlefield. Beneath it, the earth split and wept streams of tar and sulphur. Those who still stood were either knocked from their feet by the quaking of the ground beneath them, or they were caught up in the storm's passage and sucked, screaming, into its abyssal depths.

From what remained of the temple walls, valiant surviving forces turned the defence guns on the cabal who stood as a pack, their hands raised, palms upward, to the skies that bubbled overhead. Each of the twelve was the perfect mirror image of the others. Whilst all were wearing horned helms, their stance was arrogance itself.

The armoured turrets roared defiance and one of the sorcerers was destroyed, his torso chewed apart by the stream of high-velocity shells. The cabal did not change position but, as one, their heads turned towards the weapons mounted on the wall.

Dengesha made a slicing motion with his hand and the winds changed direction and increased speed, moving with impossible haste towards its new target.

SISTER BRIGITTA STOOD defiant amidst her battle sisters. She was a woman who had lived a life filled with devotion to the Emperor who she loved every bit as much as she cared for every woman who stood around her. Their honour and courage now, in the face of overwhelming odds, was a reward unlike any other.

From the youngest novice to Sister Anastasia, with whom she had fought in many engagements, she knew each one of them. She knew their life histories. She knew their hopes and she knew their fears. She was no psyker, but you could not live your whole life within an Order and not gain remarkable skills of perception.

She loved her sisters and though she may die here today, that love would bring her faith and the strength to stand her ground.

Her thoughts were wrenched back to the present as she heard the echo of a crashing thump in the distance. The sound of weapons being brought to bear against the gate.

'They come,' she said, her voice low and soft, yet carrying such authority that every one of the Order stood straighter. There was the sound of weapons being readied, of magazines being slammed into place, of swords being drawn from sheaths. There were overlaying, incomprehensible litanies and prayers.

Another sickening *crump* against the gate.

'We will stand defiant,' Brigitta said, raising her bolter above her head. '*Ave Imperator*!'

The battle cry was echoed, but was drowned out by the sound of an explosion that blew in the ancient, stained crystal windows as the enemy breached the gates.

'Be ready! Hold firm! Do not doubt in yourself for one moment. Trust to your sisters and trust to your blessed weapons. *A morte perpetua. Domine, libra nos!*'

Battle cries were torn from their throats and one hundred battle sisters took up arms and prepared to make their stand.

THE MAELSTROM RIPPED the guns from their mountings as though they were plants placed in dry soil. The guardsmen who had manned them were pulverised by the shrapnel from the destruction as the howling, unholy winds ripped the turrets into nothing more than shards. Mangled pieces of weaponry tore through their bodies, cutting them to ribbons and, in one young soldier's case, decapitating them. The spiralling morass of metal and ruined flesh added its mass to the storm and above the temple, the skies began to rain droplets of blood.

At the final gate, Huron Blackheart's traitors had set melta charges against the armoured portal. The blocky devices clamped to the towering hinges with a metallic *clang* and the Corsairs withdrew. The bombs detonated with a wash of heat and an earth-shattering explosion that rocked the ground.

Slowly, Dengesha's cabal ceased the link with their powers and the violent, raging winds began to subside. The first obstacle had been overcome. The second – and their objective – lay behind the devastated walls.

The Chaos sorcerer turned his helmeted head towards Huron. 'You must not kill her,' he said through the vox-bead in the Tyrant's ear. 'If she dies, her soul will be as good as useless to us. Do not let your barbarian horde rip the Order apart without first isolating the mark.'

A twitch of irritation showed on Huron's face. 'I am not completely without intellect, Dengesha.' The fingers that were wrapped around his massive battle axe tightened visibly. The sorcerer's face could not be seen, but Huron could *sense* his smirk. 'I will be taking care of dear Sister Brigitta myself.'

'My *sincerest* apologies. I did not mean to imply you were anything but knowledgeable in the ways of warp majesty, my lord.' His sarcasm was biting and Huron turned away from the sorcerer cursing the necessity of their temporary association. It would be over soon. The Order of the Iron Rose would be obliterated and he would take his prize.

He comforted himself with the thought. In due course, his familiar would feast from a soul most worthy of its hunger.

Striding across the courtyard, Huron surveyed the damage with an approving expression. What remained of the gate was barely recognisable as any sort of portal. Broken spurs of plasteel jutted in all directions and the metal composite that had been mixed into the gate for reinforcement was little more than dust. Occasionally, more dust would fall in a pathetic clump from the walls either side of the former door.

The Red Corsairs strode forwards, warriors with a clear objective and purpose. In the eyes of the Imperium, they were renegades. But they were still Space Marines and the regimental mindset came easily to them. Until the fighting started, at least.

'Listen to me, my Corsairs,' said Huron across the vox. 'When we locate the sisters, do not touch their leader. She belongs to me.' He addressed the entire group, but knew that not all of them would truly hear him. 'The toys we have despatched thus far have been an easy enemy and they will have sent out the word for aid. By the time that aid arrives, there will be nothing left but a smoking ruin.'

A few scattered roars of approval drew a nod from Huron. 'What we will come up against in there will be more challenging, but do not falter. We come to take a prize that will make us even greater than we are. The Imperium of Mankind and their pathetic Corpse-Emperor will rue the day they ever named us traitor.'

There were grunts of acknowledgement across the board, some coherent, others less so. Just as his band of renegades were drawn from a vast background of different Chapters, so their levels of sanity varied. Huron cared little for the butchers amongst his followers. They served a purpose in war but when it came to more delicate matters, they were an encumbrance.

Fortunately, he had enough sane followers to keep the borderline berserkers in check.

'Then we move with all haste to the final stage of our action here. Find the sisters. Kill those you must, but leave the canoness alive.'

Without further hesitation, the Red Corsairs streamed into the sacred Temple of the Blessed Dawn.

THEY RAMPAGED THROUGH the temple without thought for preservation. Marble floors cracked and split beneath their heavy tread. Chainblades chewed through statue and carvings alike, making firewood of huge portraits of sisters and saints. Some riches were left intact. Over the years, the Red Corsairs had all developed an eye for goods that would please their lord and master for, it was said, his collection of Imperial relics was beyond compare. They would retrace their steps before they departed and gather up such treasures, along with the weapons of the fallen. For them, that was the most valuable reward.

Their plundering steps ultimately took them through the central chamber where the sisters of the Order had recently gathered. Dengesha nodded approvingly.

'This will be a good place for the ritual,' he said.

'Then you remain here, sorcerer, and make whatever preparation is necessary. We will seek out Sister Brigitta and I will bring her to you personally.' Huron ran his tongue over his metal teeth in a parody of hunger. He swung his battle axe easily and it chewed its way through a beautifully painted rendition of some long-ago battle at which the Sisters had been victorious. Its shredded remnants dangled to the ground and the memory of the great war was lost after no more than a single stroke.

The first two Red Corsairs to throw open the heavy door that led out to the courtyard were torn apart by incoming bolter fire. The battle sisters had kept their weapons trained on the exit and the moment it opened they had pulled the triggers instantly. The explosive rounds buried themselves in the armoured hides of the traitors and burst them apart in a storm of gore and ceramite shards. The bodies disintegrated messily but their sacrifice bought those that followed enough time to bring their weapons to bear and return fire. Four sisters were thrown backwards, unbalancing several more. Before they were back on their feet, the Red Corsairs had flooded into the courtyard and the fight began in earnest.

The Sisters of Battle were greater in number than the Red Corsairs and their armour afforded them a degree of protection. But they were facing an undisciplined rabble whose tactics were unpredictable at best and unfathomable at worst. The battle sisters held their position, clustered around the canoness like a sea of bronze with a copper island at their centre. They formed a circle around where she stood on the rim of a fountain, crying out orders to her warriors.

The initial firefight did not last long. At a word from the Tyrant, the Red Corsairs pressed forwards, chainblades whining, and began to cut their way through the serried ranks of women. The ring surrounding the canoness grew tighter and smaller.

The stink of ruined flesh and spent bolter rounds was strong in the air and so much smoke rose from the detonations that it choked the courtyard with a fog of bloody vapour and fyceline.

'Courage, sisters!' Brigitta's voice was clear, like a bell sounding through the uproar. 'Remember your teachings! You tread the path of righteousness. Though it be paved with broken glass, you will walk it barefoot...'

Brigitta paused in the recital as she watched Sister Anastasia's broken body fall to the ground. A grief unlike any she had ever known before passed through her with a shudder. She summoned up every ounce of her considerable inner strength and brought her bolter to bear on the hated enemy. Her voice rose through the noise once again.

'Though it crosses rivers of fire, we will pass over them...'

Her voice was strong and did not waver, but the strength of her armed guard was failing. Not through lack of zeal or fire; if she were to take any reward from this abysmal horror before her, it was that her beloved sisters died honourably and bravely. But it was failing through sheer loss of its numbers. What had once been a ring that had been several bodies deep now presented a barrier of barely a dozen of her sisters.

A number of the traitor Red Corsairs had been felled, but their armour, better and more intricate than that of the Battle Sisters, deflected more and protected them for longer. Brigitta realised with a sinking heart that they were probably not even dead. That their enhanced physiology would aid their recovery and that they might rise to fight another day. And she *despised* them for it. She loathed their continued existence. To her mind, they represented the worst kind of faithless traitors the Imperium could have conceived.

She abhorred them for tearing apart the temple, her home, the place where she had grown from a teenage girl to womanhood.

She...

...was bleeding.

Brigitta tasted, for the first time in her life, a tremor of fear. It was seasoned with the coppery taste of her own blood as she bit her lip hard enough to put her teeth through the delicate skin. The flavour of her own mortality gave her enough strength to complete her fervent prayer.

'Though it wanders wide, the light of the Emperor guides my – our – step.' She slammed a fresh magazine into her bolter and, letting out a screaming roar of battle rage, unleashed her full fury at the encroaching enemy.

At her feet, dead and dying sisters spilled blood and viscera across the courtyard stones. The image of their defeat burned itself onto her retinas and branded hatred on her heart. Tears of anger and terrible, terrible grief blurred her vision, but she did not – she *would* not – falter. Not now.

She continued to fire her bolter into the enemy without caring any longer whether she hit them or not. It became an act of sheer venomous loathing.

After a few short moments, she became aware that outside her immediate sphere of awareness the sounds of battle had ceased. Only one weapon continued to fire and that was hers. It did not detract from her focus, however, and she poured ammunition at the enemy until the last bolter shell clattered to the floor.

One of the enemy, bareheaded and terrible, moved from the pack to stand before her.

'You are Sister Brigitta of the Order of the Iron Rose,' he stated. It was not a question. She looked up into his inhuman face and drew in a rasping breath. She had seen unhelmed Space Marines warriors before and was used to their over-exaggerated features. But this... *creature*... that stood before her was so far removed from anything even remotely human that she felt, against her will, the urge to scream in incoherent contempt. A poisonous air of evil came from him and she felt sick to her stomach.

She began to quietly recite litanies of faith to herself, never once taking her gaze from this augmetic monstrosity. She neither confirmed nor denied the accusation of her identity but instead ripped the combat blade from its sheath at her side and plunged it the traitor's throat. Blackheart sighed wearily before catching her wild lunge on the back of his claw. Then, with excruciating care, not wanting to kill her outright, he backhanded her into unconsciousness.

SHE WAS LIKE a rag doll in his arms, limp and lifeless, and as he carried Sister Brigitta into the chamber, Huron Blackheart marvelled as he always did at the papery inefficacy of the human body. He wondered how it was they had *any* resilience without the enhancements that he shared with all his gene-bred brothers. Brigitta's face where he had struck her was distorted. He had fractured her cheekbone at the very least and purple bruising was swelling up around her jaw. Her braided hair had come loose and hung freely down.

Dengesha turned to study them. He had removed his helm and Huron was struck once again by the wriggling sigils that marked the sorcerer's face. 'You did not kill her?'

'She is merely unconscious. Allow me a little credit.'

'Then lay her next to the vessel and I can begin the ritual.' Already Dengesha had made the preparations for the rite that would bind the potent soul to the cursed vial. The green bottle lay on its side, an innocuous and inanimate object. Around the chamber, Dengesha had marked out a number of unreadable symbols, each one drawn at the point of what formed the eight-pointed star of Chaos. One each of his cabal stood at seven of the points, the top-most remaining free and evidently waiting for Dengesha's leisure.

Huron moved forward and dumped Brigitta's body without any ceremony on the ground where the sorcerer indicated. He noted as he did so that the sigils drawn on the floor were marked in blood; most likely from that of the dead soldiers.

'You should step outside the borders of the mark, my lord. Once we channel the powers necessary to perform the binding, they will be potent.'

From beyond the broken walls of the temple, the distant sounds of shouting could be heard. The assistance that the temple guards had called for was finally arriving. Huron nodded to several of his warriors who moved wordlessly out of the chamber.

'They cannot be allowed to enter this place whilst I am working. The balance of this work is delicate.'

'My men will keep them away.' Huron took several steps back. 'Trust to their abilities to do that. I, however, will remain.'

'As you wish.'

Huron Blackheart had witnessed many rituals of this kind in his life, but he had never seen one driven with such determination and single-minded focus. He watched Dengesha closely as the sorcerer moved back to take his point at the tip of the star and listened intently to the words that he recited. It did him little good, as the sorcerer spoke in some arcane tongue that Huron did not understand, though the inflection was clear.

The seven other members of the Heterodox echoed his words, one at a time until the chant was being repeated with a discordant, impossible to follow rhythm. The sound grew and swelled and all the while there was the underscore of another battle taking place beyond the temple walls.

A thick black substance, like tar from a pit, began to bubble up in the space marked out by the points of the star. It rose upwards, never spilling over the edge of its limits and coated first the bottle and then the unconscious Sister Brigitta in a film of inky blackness. Dengesha's chant became almost musical, as though he were singing. His eyes were fevered and his expression one of pure ecstasy.

The thick, gelatinous substance became more and more viscous and at some point during its creeping encroachment, Brigitta stirred from her unconsciousness. Realising that she was being smothered, she opened her mouth to cry out. The fluid rushed into her mouth and she began to choke on it, writhing desperately on the floor as she struggled to breathe.

As soon as that happened, Dengesha stepped forward from his position and moved to stand above her. Huron watched, leaning forward ever so slightly. This was it. This was the moment. He had made countless pacts and agreements to reach this point and so had his followers. This was the point at which it would all pay off. Or the point at which it would fail.

Outside, the sounds of gunfire had stopped, but the Chaos sorcerer paid no heed.

Dengesha looked down at the wriggling human woman with a look of total contempt, then reached to take her arm firmly in his grip. He guided it to the glass vial and placed her hand upon it, wrapping his gauntlets around her tiny hands. He then spoke the only words that Huron could understand.

'Be forever bound.'

The oily liquid began to slowly ebb away, draining until all that remained was the faintest slick on the ground. Brigitta, who was in tremendous pain and almost frozen with terror stared at the green vial, then she stared up at the sorcerer.

Then, summoning every ounce of strength and fortitude she possessed, she spat in his face. Dengesha began to laugh, a hateful, booming sound that bounced around the walls of the chamber and resonated in everyone's vox-bead.

Then abruptly the laughter stopped and a look of utmost dread crept slowly over Dengesha's face. His fist, which had been ready to crush Brigitta's skull, suddenly opened out flat. His face slackened, his posture changed and he slouched suddenly as though wearied.

And Huron smiled at him.

'What is this treachery?' The sorcerer spun around to face the Tyrant of Badab, who stood watching him with an air of amusement. 'What have you done, Blackheart?'

'Ah, Dengesha. Your fate was sealed the moment you took the vial from me. You were quite right. I needed a potent soul. And my sorcerers found me one. *Yours*, in fact. And now, with the ritual of binding complete, your soul and the vial are united. You quite literally belong to me.'

'This is not possible! There is no way you could have... your sorcerers are nothing compared to the glory of the Heterodox!'

'Ah, arrogance has been the downfall of many a brother of the Adeptus Astartes over the millennia, brother. My sorcerers may not be as powerful as you and your former cabal, but they are far more cunning.' Seemingly bored of the conversation, Huron moved around the chamber, occasionally turning over the body of a fallen soldier with his booted foot. He picked up a boltgun, empty of ammunition and dropped it back down with a clang.

Dengesha's face was fury itself and he reached out to the powers of the warp. But none of them answered him. His black, tainted soul was no longer his to command. He looked to each of his cabal in turn and for their part, they turned from him.

'You all *knew* of this,' he stated flatly. 'You betrayed me to this *cur...*'

'Come now, Dengesha. If you seek to wound my feelings, you will have to try a lot harder than that.' Huron stooped and picked up a meltagun. 'My agents have been dealing with your cabal for months. They agree that their prospects with me and my Corsairs are more interesting than a lifetime of servitude under your leadership. It has been vexing, true – but I think you will agree that the ultimate reward is well worth it.'

On the ground, Sister Brigitta was listening to the exchange without understanding it. All she knew was that these two traitors were speaking such heresy as it was almost unbearable to be a party to.

Dengesha stared at Huron's back with a look that could have killed and perhaps once, before his soul had been plucked from his body, could have done.

'So you see, Dengesha. In a way, my promise to you is truth. Now that your Heterodox are part of my Corsairs, they will help themselves to the spoils of this world. You, however...'

The Tyrant of Badab crossed the distance between them with uncanny speed and fired the meltagun at the sorcerer. His head was vaporised and seconds later, what remained of his body crashed to the ground. Brigitta gazed up at Huron and there was a look of serene understanding on her face. Her doom was come and it was clad in the desecrated armour of the Imperium of Man.

'My faith is my shield,' she said, softly. The words rang hollow in her ears.

'No,' said Huron, equally softly as one of the claws of his hand tore through her breast and skewered her. He raised her to eye level. 'It is not. And it never was.'

She let out a sigh as she died and slid free from his claw to the floor below. Without looking at the two corpses at his feet, Huron reached up and plucked the vial from the ground, reattaching it to his belt.

Sometimes, Huron Blackheart kept his word. But this was not one of those times. He did not care who he betrayed to reach his goals. Loyal servants of the Imperium or those who served the dark gods of Chaos. It made little difference to him. The end *always* justified the means.

'Take what we need,' he said. 'And then we leave.'

'IT WORKED PERFECTLY.'

'Surely you did not doubt, my Lord?' Valthex turned the vial over in his hand before handing it back to Huron.

'The curse worked exactly as you said it would. Thanks to your efforts, my familiar now has the strength it needs to grant me the blessing of the four beyond the Maelstrom. Well done, Armenneus.'

'I live to serve, Blood Reaver.' Valthex dropped a low, respectful bow and Huron stalked away. Straightening himself up, the Alchemancer absently rubbed at a sigil branded into the skin of his hand.

It was not just the Tyrant who made pacts. The Patriarch would have to wait to see when he would be called upon to deliver his side of the bargain.

For biographies of the authors in this volume
visit *www.blacklibrary.com*

Hammer and Bolter

If you enjoyed this collection of stories from the first year of *Hammer and Bolter* and can't wait for more then visit *www.blacklibrary.com* to download your monthly fix of action.

Hammer and Bolter is Black Library's download only monthly fiction magazine. Each issue is packed with short stories, serialised novels, interviews, previews and more.